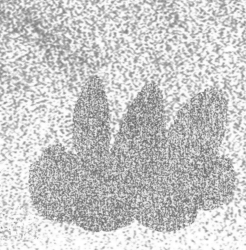

The SUPER SWOOPER DINOSAUR

For Arthur and Edith – M.W.
For Harry and Max – L.L.

ORCHARD BOOKS
338 Euston Road, London NW1 3BH
Orchard Books Australia Level 17/207 Kent Street, Sydney, NSW 2000
First published in 2012 by Orchard Books
ISBN 978 1 40830 780 9
Text © Martin Waddell 2012 Illustrations © Leonie Lord 2012
The rights of Martin Waddell to be identified as the author and
Leonie Lord to be identified as the illustrator of this work have been asserted by
them in accordance with the Copyright, Designs and Patents Act, 1988.
A CIP catalogue record for this book is available from the British Library.
2 4 6 8 10 9 7 5 3 1
Printed in China
Orchard Books is a division of Hachette Children's Books, an Hachette UK company. www.hachette.co.uk

The SUPER SWOOPER DINOSAUR

Martin Waddell & Leonie Lord

ORCHARD

One day, Hal and his little dog, Billy, were out playing when the sky darkened and . . .

A SUPER SWOOPER DINOSAUR

landed in Hal's garden.

KER-PLUMP!

"Can I play with you?" he asked Hal and Billy.
"Yes, please!" said Hal. "What games will we play?"
"Hide-and-seek!" suggested the super swooper.

So, they played hide-and-seek.
The super swooper was so excited he
got himself into a flap!

100!

99...

98...

"Here I come . . ." called Hal.

"Maybe you're a bit too big for hide-and-seek," said Hal.

"Perhaps we should try something else," Hal suggested.

"How about dino dancing?"
said the super swooper.

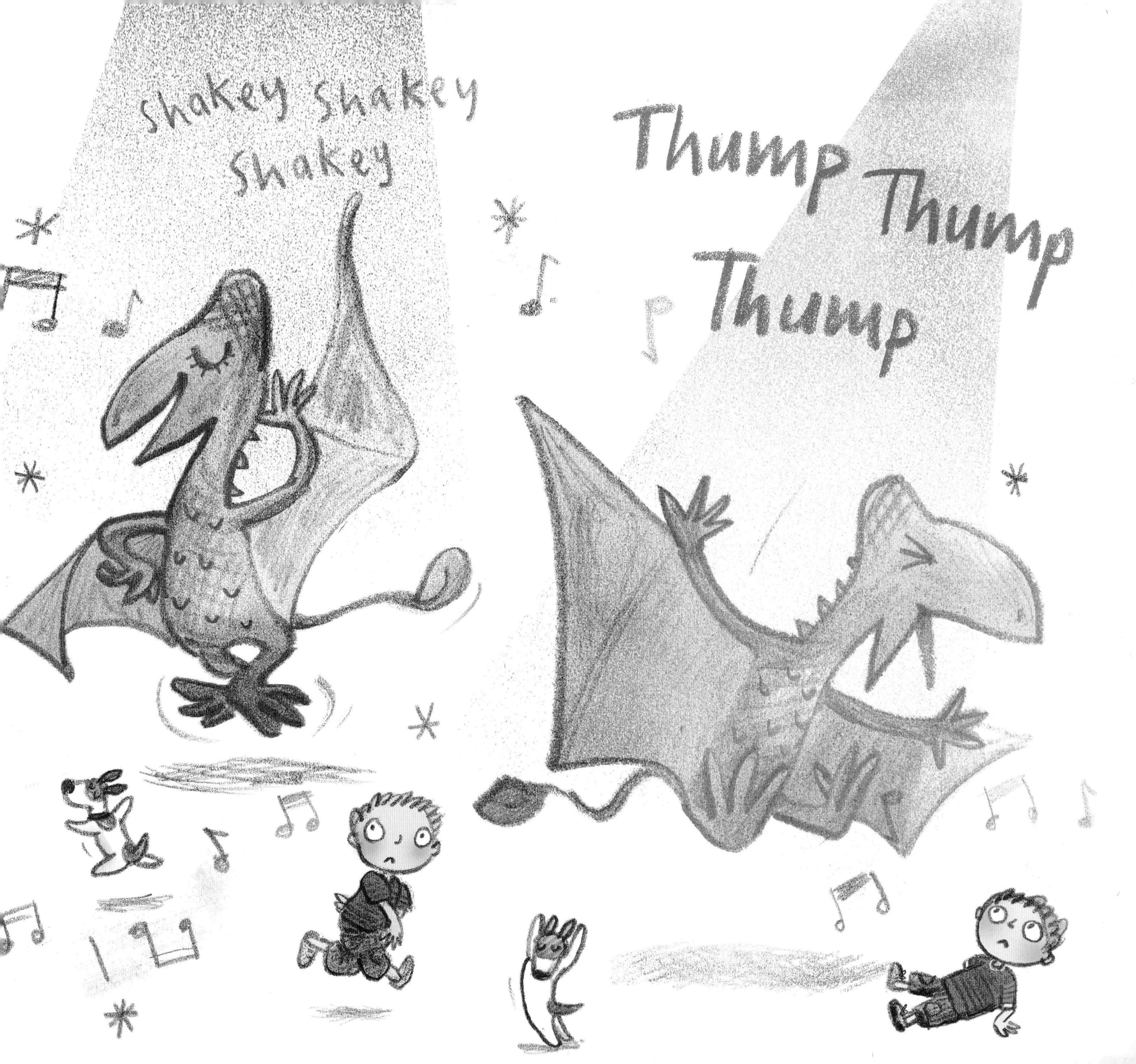
Shakey Shakey
Shakey
Thump Thump
Thump

The super swooper swooped up onto the roof of Hal's house and danced on the tiles.

"You can't dino dance on the roof!" said Hal.

Hal had to
do something,
so . . .

"Last one in the paddling pool is a BLUE BANANA!" shouted Hal.

Hal raced outside but . . .

"Look out below!"
cried the super swooper,
swooping down towards the
paddling pool.

ORION NEBULA

A sequence of close-up images of the Orion Nebula (a cloud of dust and gas within our Galaxy) revealed that the mysterious set of dark "splotches" are, in fact, dust clouds swirling around very young stars. Scientists believe that these could be embryonic solar systems.

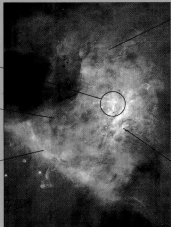

Four massive young stars known as "The Trapezium"

Molecular cloud

The "Great Wall" or "Bright Bar", made up of luminous gas

The Orion Nebula is 1,500 light years away, and spreads across 90 million million miles

Ultraviolet radiation from stars ionises gas, causing it to glow

STAR DEATH (MYCN18)

The fine detail shown in Hubble images of the star MYCN18 has helped scientists understand how a star like the sun will die. Over several thousands of years, a dying star expands, becoming cooler and redder, and gently puffs its layers of gas into space.

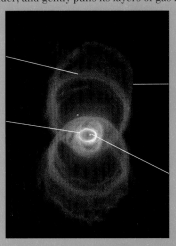

Dust clouds glowing with ultraviolet radiation

Vigorous ejection of star's internal layers

Episodic ejections of star's outer layers produces concentric shells

Hot central core cools off to become a white dwarf (a collapsed, cooling star)

INTERSTELLAR GAS AND DUST IN THE EAGLE NEBULA

Over six million million miles high and 7,000 light years away (one light year equals 6 million million miles), these columns of interstellar dust and gas are found in the Eagle Nebula. Projecting from their surfaces are small finger-like projections called EGGs (Evaporating Gas Globules). Within these extra-dense regions of gas – which are approximately the size of our solar system – young stars develop. Over millions of years, the surrounding gas globules evaporate to reveal the newly-formed stars.

Dramatic illumination is caused by nearby stars

EGGs appear as tiny bumps on the column surface

Foreground star

Smaller columns form, protected from photoevaporation by the shadow of EGGs

Molecular hydrogen gas dispersing into space

PHOTOEVAPORATION

The whitish haze surrounding each column represents the dispersal of hydrogen into space. This process of erosion, called photoevaporation, is caused by UV light from nearby stars.

Columns are formed by very dense clouds of gas and dust that will eventually erode away

An EGG that has been eroded from the main surface of column

Galileo spacecraft

PLANET JUPITER

IN DECEMBER 1995, the Galileo spacecraft finally arrived at the planet Jupiter. More than six years after it had been launched by NASA, the spacecraft's atmospheric probe, which had separated from the orbiter four months earlier, plunged through the gas giant's intense radiation belts and deep into its atmosphere. The onboard electronic systems had to be heavily shielded to protect them against the radiation and temperatures twice as hot as the Sun's surface. As the probe parachuted into Jupiter's atmosphere, pulled in by the enormous gravity, the orbiter passed close to the planet, receiving and storing information for later relay back to Earth. This was just the start of the Galileo mission – since 1995, the orbiter has been circling Jupiter and recording information about its weather and its planet-sized moons. Before arriving at Jupiter, Galileo photographed the impact of Comet P/Shoemaker-Levy 9 with Jupiter, the largest explosion ever seen in the Solar System. More recently, the spacecraft has photographed volcanic activity on the moon Io, and found evidence of water beneath the icy crust of another moon, Europa.

GALILEO'S JOURNEY

As it began its six-year flight, Galileo moved away from Earth towards Venus, then doubled back, using the gravitational fields of Venus and Earth to propel it towards Jupiter.

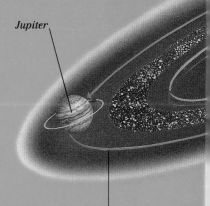

Jupiter

Jupiter's orbit

Long boom carrying magnetic sensors

Low-gain antenna

Double-dish antenna

LIFE ON MARS?

Organic molecules thought to be from Mars were recently found in a 4.5 billion-year-old rock that fell into the Antarctic 13,000 years ago. Mineral features suggesting biological activity and possible microscopic fossils of bacteria-like organisms were discovered.

Composition matches Martian rock

Water-penetrated cracks

MARTIAN METEORITE

Hydrocarbon deposits

Possible microfossil

Rock structure

Retro propulsion module

Atmospheric sampling instrument

Atmospheric descent module

Atmospheric descent probe module

Camera package

Instruments package

Radioisotope thermoelectric generator

MICROSCOPIC VIEW OF METEORITE

GALILEO

The main body of the spacecraft circling Jupiter is known as the orbiter. The probe, on the left of the diagram, descended into Jupiter's atmosphere. The probe consists of a descent module and a deceleration module; the latter protects the former from excessive heat, separating off and slowing the probe's descent.

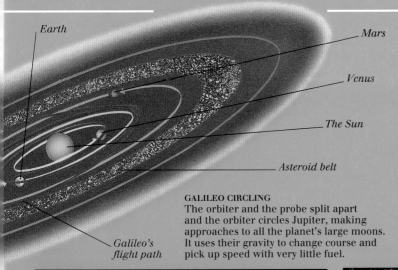

Earth

Mars

Venus

The Sun

Asteroid belt

Galileo's flight path

GALILEO CIRCLING
The orbiter and the probe split apart and the orbiter circles Jupiter, making approaches to all the planet's large moons. It uses their gravity to change course and pick up speed with very little fuel.

COMET SHOEMAKER-LEVY 9

From 16 to 22 July 1994, pieces of a comet designated P/Shoemaker-Levy 9 collided with the planet Jupiter. This was the first collision of two Solar System bodies ever to be observed. While other comets revolve around the Sun, Shoemaker-Levy 9 – named after its discoverers, Eugene and Carolyn Shoemaker and David Levy – moved around Jupiter in a very unusual elongated orbit within a period of just over two years. It became clear that the comet had recently been "captured" by the gravitational field of the planet and would soon collide with it.

Close encounter with Jupiter in 1992 broke comet apart

The gravities of Jupiter and the Sun string fragments out

Pieces consist of fragments of ice and dust

Fragment up to two kilometres in diameter

Surrounding debris cloud

Fragment a few hundred metres in diameter

TRAVELLING COMET
The comet consisted of at least 21 discernible icy fragments with diameters estimated at up to two kilometres. The fragments stretched across 1.1 million kilometres (710,000 miles) of space, almost three times the distance between Earth and the Moon.

Antenna transmits data back to Earth

Erupting volcano on the moon Io

Io, Jupiter's largest moon

Jupiter

Main parachute

Descent module

Protective shield of deceleration module

THE PROBE DESCENDING
The probe descended through Jupiter's atmosphere gathering data. The descent module split from the deceleration module and a parachute slowed its rate of descent. The module descended for 57 minutes before burning out.

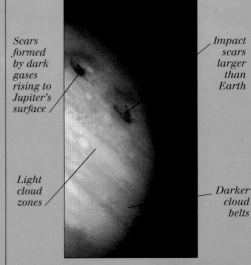

Scars formed by dark gases rising to Jupiter's surface

Impact scars larger than Earth

Light cloud zones

Darker cloud belts

POINT OF IMPACT
The impacts of the comet on Jupiter's atmosphere have been spectacular, with plumes thousands of kilometres high, hot "bubbles" of gas in the atmosphere, and large dark "scars".

Very Large Telescope

THE WORLD'S LARGEST telescope system, the Very Large Telescope (VLT), is located at Cerro Paranal in the Atacama desert, Chile. It is used to study visible light, and to collect and analyse infrared heat energy and ultraviolet radiation. During a one hour exposure, each telescope can photograph objects that are four billion times fainter than can be seen with the naked eye. The VLT consists of four telescope units, each with a mirror of 8.2 m (27 ft) in diameter. These units can be used individually or in parallel; together they simulate one large telescope with a mirror of 16 m (52 ft) in diameter. Working in parallel, a process known as interferometry, the VLT allows celestial objects to be seen in much finer detail than with the Hubble Space Telescope. On 22 May 1998, one of the telescope units took its first photograph of a celestial object, an event that astronomers call "first light". The VLT will be used principally to search for small, Earth-like planets around other stars.

SPACE PROBES

In addition to telescopes, new space probes continue to explore the Solar System. In 1997, the Mars Pathfinder successfully surveyed an ancient flood plain on Mars. In the same year, the Galileo space probe discovered strong evidence for a global ocean under the ice sheets of Europa, one of Jupiter's 16 moons. Future space probes will investigate the possible existence of alien microbes on both Mars and Europa.

Ramp from the Pathfinder

Research buggy inspects the rock, Yogi

MARS PATHFINDER MISSION

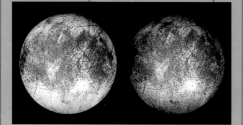

Natural colour of ice floes

Enhanced colour shows ice composition

EUROPA AS SEEN FROM GALILEO

TELESCOPE UNIT
The four telescopes of the VLT are precisely engineered structures. Each individual telescope was assembled and tested in Europe, before being taken apart and carefully transported to Chile. Final assembly took place inside the telescope enclosures on the mountain.

Small secondary mirror used to focus starlight

Tilting mechanism adjusts altitude of telescope

Primary mirror sits horizontally

Adjustable structure allows telescope to rotate

Flaw exaggerated by computer

REOSC
OPTIQUE

17/06/97
14:07:58

406.0
nm

COMPUTER MAPPING OF MIRROR DEFECT
The four mirrors of the VLT were cast in Germany and polished in France. The shape of each mirror was checked at regular intervals using laser beams, and laser data was formulated into a map of the mirror's surface. Defects (see right), perhaps only a millionth of a millimetre in diameter, were exaggerated by the computer so that they could be located and corrected.

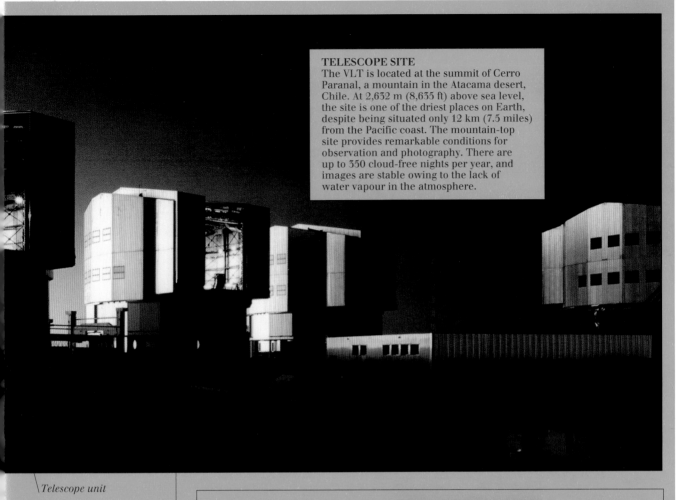

Telescope unit

Telescope enclosure

Surface of mirror

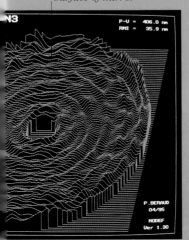

IMAGE QUALITY

The atmosphere of the Earth blurs
light from distant celestial objects.
The VLT is able to compensate for
this using a computerized system
known as adaptive optics. Every
one hundredth of a second, a
computer analyses a tiny fraction
of light from a star being observed
by the VLT. It then measures the
effect that the Earth's atmosphere
is having on the light, and
calculates how to compensate for
that effect. The computer sends
signals to a set of activators, which
support the flexible mirror. This
then refocuses the light from the
telescope. The worst effects of
the atmosphere are eliminated
and sharp images, comparable
with those taken by the Hubble
Space Telescope, are produced.
Images taken by a ground-based
telescope (above right) and the
VLT (right), show different views
of the same planetary nebula.

PLANETARY NEBULA I
This image of the
Dumbbell Nebula
shows the cloud of
gas that has drifted
away into space
from the remains
of a dead star. It was
taken by a ground-
based telescope.

*Dust and gas
of the nebula*

PLANETARY NEBULA II
Taken by the VLT,
this view of the
Dumbbell Nebula
shows the centre
of the gas cloud
in far more detail.
Complex patterns
can reveal the way
that gas is moving
within the cloud.

*Colours indicate
the types of gas*

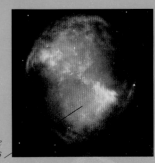

International Space Station

IN 1998, THE FIRST components of the International Space Station (ISS) were launched from Russia and the US. The ISS will provide a unique place to study the Earth, and to see how the Sun's violent eruptions affect the operation of communications satellites, and the weather on Earth. The effects of gravity inside the station will be minuscule and scientists will be able to study a myriad of subtle biological, physical, and chemical reactions, which are impossible to duplicate on Earth. Complete construction will require a total of 45 space missions and many hours of space walking by astronauts. The station is scheduled to be permanently crewed from the eighth mission onwards, due to take place in 2000. Astronauts will spend many months at a time on the station, testing equipment for future space exploration missions.

MIR SPACE STATION
Now referred to as Phase One of the International Space Station, Mir was home to American, Russian, and European astronauts as they learned to work together in space.

ARTIST'S IMPRESSION OF THE ISS
The most ambitious space project since the Apollo missions to land man on the Moon, the ISS is the next step in the human exploration of the Solar System. It is a joint venture between 16 nations, and the largest scientific co-operative programme in history. All power on the space station will be generated by the large arrays of solar panels connected to the main structure of the station. Also attached to this framework are corrugated panels, which act as radiators dispersing excess heat from the station into space. Astronauts will live and work in the cylindrical modules between the solar panel arrays, and will eventually be able to spend many years at a time in space.

SPACE HAZARDS

Dust grains travelling through space at speeds of up to 70 m (230 ft) per second can "sandblast" spacecraft and astronauts. Sub-atomic particles travel close to the speed of light, and can cause severe damage to living cells. Space stations therefore provide shields to protect astronauts from dust and particle storms, and solar flares.

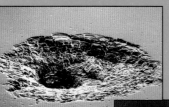

DAMAGE CRATER
This tiny crater in a window of the Space Shuttle was caused by a fleck of paint. It is 0.64mm wide and 0.63mm deep.

SOLAR FLARE
These violent eruptions from the photosphere (the visible surface of the Sun) cause major disruptions to communications satellites that orbit the Earth.

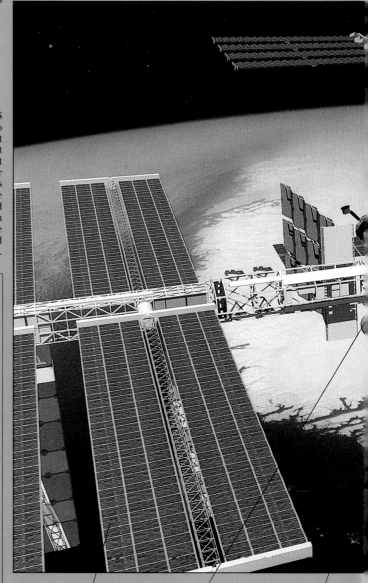

Solar panels provide energy

Zaraya control module

Russian Soyuz spacecraft

US MODULES
The US modules of the ISS were built in Alabama. Astronauts will eat and sleep in the habitat module and work in the laboratory module. A connecting unit called Node 1 will join these two modules together.

Laboratory module

Node 1 connecting unit

Habitat module

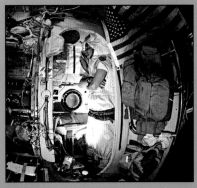

SLEEPING IN SPACE
Astronauts sleep in an upright position so that they receive a constant flow of air. If they slept horizontally, the effects of weightlessness could result in suffocation from exhaled carbon dioxide. This astronaut remains stationary by crossing his arms and using straps to anchor himself to the wall of the module.

Radiators for cooling

Exposure platform

LABORATORY MODULES
The European Columbus Orbital Facility is one of many laboratory modules that contain computer and scientific equipment for running a vast range of experiments. Some modules have access to robotic arms that will be able to conduct experiments on exposure platforms outside the station.

European Columbus Orbital Facility

Connecting module

Japanese Experiment Module

Giganotosaurus

THE BONES OF A GIANT new dinosaur, *Giganotosaurus carolinii*, were recently excavated by two scientists in Argentina. *Giganotosaurus* ("giant reptile of the south") is believed to be one of the largest carnivorous dinosaurs ever found. With a body length of 12.5 m (42 ft) and an estimated weight of between 6 and 8 tonnes, it is believed to have been even larger than the *Tyrannosaurus rex*. Like T-Rex, the *Giganotosaurus* is classified in the *Theropoda* – a suborder of the Saurischia (lizard-hipped) group of dinosaurs that were characterized by short forelimbs and an S-shaped neck. It existed an estimated 100 million years ago during the Cretaceous period, and appears to be quite closely related to a theropod that lived 50 million years previously, *Allosaurus*.

CARCHARODONTOSAURUS SAHARICUS

Another theropod rivalling the great size of T-Rex is the Moroccan-found *Carcharodontosaurus saharicus* ("shark-toothed reptile from the Sahara"). In May 1996 the discovery of a 1.65 m (5.4 ft) skull was announced by scientists from the University of Chicago. The dinosaur is estimated at being 13.7 m (45 ft) long, 3.65 m (12 ft) high, and weighing 8.3 tonnes. The skull reveals razor-sharp teeth that would have enabled this formidable dinosaur to slash and slice its prey with the greatest of ease.

RECONSTRUCTING THE SKELETON

The skeleton was actually discovered in 1993 by Ruben D. Carolini, who is credited within the full name of the dinosaur, *Giganotosaurus carolinii*. Palaeontologists Rodolfo A. Coria and Leonardo Salgado then began the work of excavating, piecing together, and studying the bones. They waited until they had completed a full examination before announcing their findings in the September 1995 issue of the journal *Nature*.

Long heavy tail

Hind limb

ARTIST'S IMPRESSION OF THE FULL SKELETON

More than 70 per cent of the skeleton has been unearthed so far and a clear idea of the full skeleton can be gained from this artist's impression.

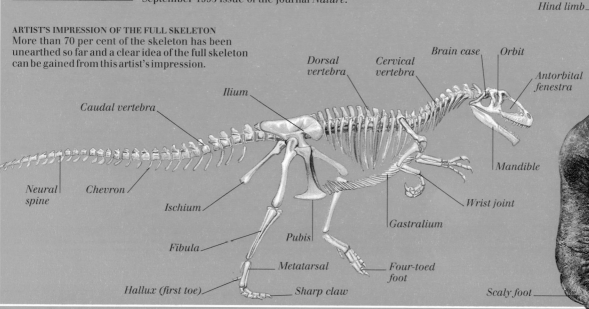

Caudal vertebra

Ilium

Dorsal vertebra

Cervical vertebra

Brain case

Orbit

Antorbital fenestra

Neural spine

Chevron

Ischium

Pubis

Gastralium

Wrist joint

Mandible

Fibula

Metatarsal

Four-toed foot

Hallux (first toe)

Sharp claw

Scaly foot

Both *Giganotosaurus* and *Tyrannosaurus* existed during the Cretaceous period, which spanned the time between 65 and 144 million years ago and saw the end of the Age of Dinosaurs. Preceding *Tyrannosaurus* by 30 million years, *Giganotosaurus* is thought to have evolved independently. The fact that both meat-eaters shared the same enormous dimensions suggests that both were equally equipped to tackle large plant-eating dinosaurs.

THEROPOD TIMELINE

MILLION YEARS AGO
248   208   144   65

TRIASSIC   JURASSIC   CRETACEOUS

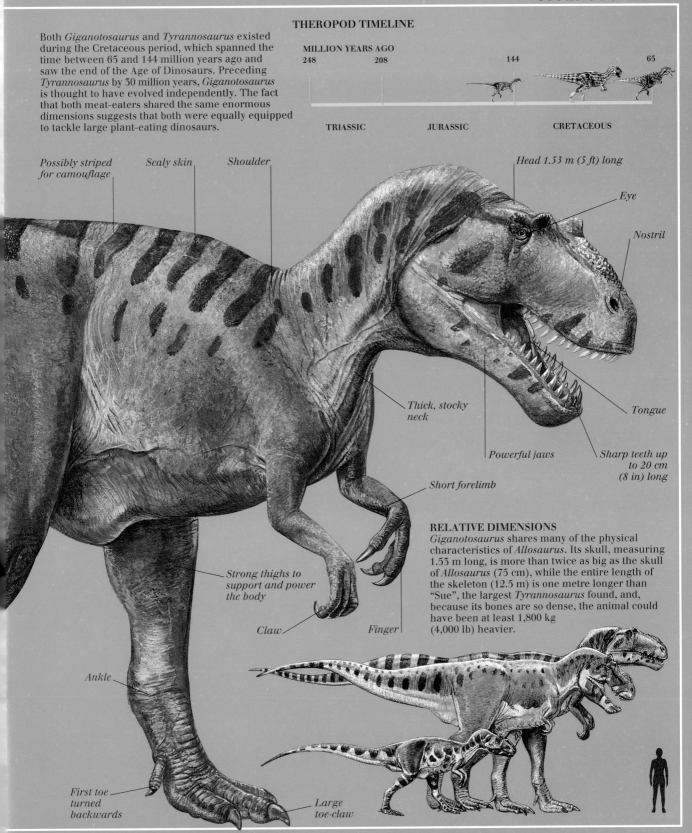

Possibly striped for camouflage

Scaly skin

Shoulder

Head 1.53 m (5 ft) long

Eye

Nostril

Thick, stocky neck

Tongue

Powerful jaws

Sharp teeth up to 20 cm (8 in) long

Short forelimb

RELATIVE DIMENSIONS

Giganotosaurus shares many of the physical characteristics of *Allosaurus*. Its skull, measuring 1.53 m long, is more than twice as big as the skull of *Allosaurus* (75 cm), while the entire length of the skeleton (12.5 m) is one metre longer than "Sue", the largest *Tyrannosaurus* found, and, because its bones are so dense, the animal could have been at least 1,800 kg (4,000 lb) heavier.

Strong thighs to support and power the body

Claw

Finger

Ankle

First toe turned backwards

Large toe-claw

From dinosaurs to birds?

WHERE THE FIRST BIRDS CAME FROM is a question that continues to baffle the experts. Although the most famous fossil bird is still *Archaeopteryx*, which dates from near the end of the Jurassic period about 155 to 150 million years ago, fossil discoveries in China from 1995 onward have started to transform the picture. In the eyes of some experts, these 'feathered' dinosaurs undoubtedly seem to strengthen the case for some form of evolutionary link between dinosaurs and birds. The recent Chinese finds also suggest that feathers could have first evolved from scales for reasons other than flying, with the actual ability to fly only developing later as a secondary role.

WHY FEATHERS?
If the Chinese dinosaurs had feathers, the as yet unanswered question is: why did the change occur? Feathers, say some of the experts, may have evolved as camouflage, to attract mates, or simply as a means of retaining body warmth (but this would imply these dinosaurs were warm-blooded, not reptilian).

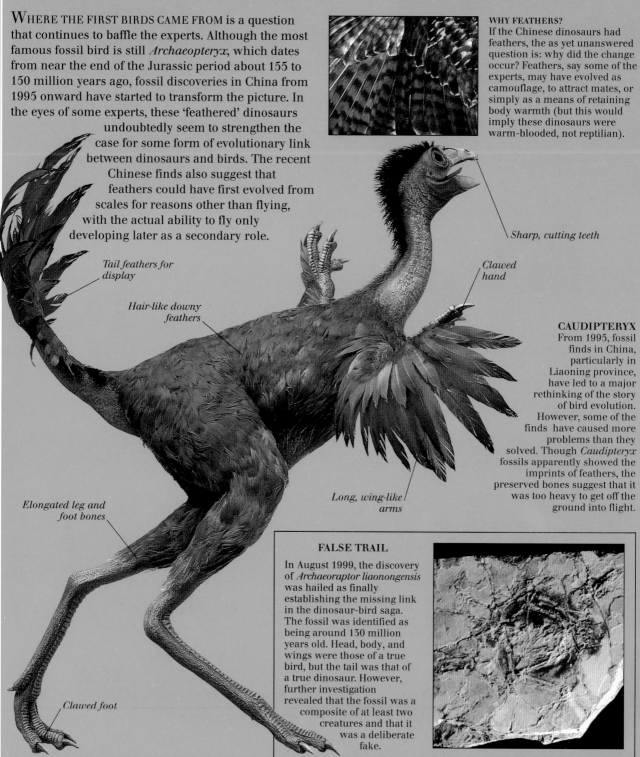

Tail feathers for display

Hair-like downy feathers

Sharp, cutting teeth

Clawed hand

CAUDIPTERYX
From 1995, fossil finds in China, particularly in Liaoning province, have led to a major rethinking of the story of bird evolution. However, some of the finds have caused more problems than they solved. Though *Caudipteryx* fossils apparently showed the imprints of feathers, the preserved bones suggest that it was too heavy to get off the ground into flight.

Elongated leg and foot bones

Long, wing-like arms

FALSE TRAIL

In August 1999, the discovery of *Archaeoraptor liaonongensis* was hailed as finally establishing the missing link in the dinosaur-bird saga. The fossil was identified as being around 130 million years old. Head, body, and wings were those of a true bird, but the tail was that of a true dinosaur. However, further investigation revealed that the fossil was a composite of at least two creatures and that it was a deliberate fake.

Clawed foot

BEFORE THE DINOSAURS

Some experts believe that the origins of birds date back to the Permian period some 250 million years ago, well before the dinosaurs themselves actually emerged. What they argue is that dinosaurs, birds, pterosaurs (the flying reptiles known as pterodactyls), and the forerunners of modern crocodiles, such as *Gracilisuchus* and *Terrestrisuchus*, may well share one common ancestor and that the most likely candidates are the ancient reptiles known as thecodonts. The most likely thecodonts to fit the bill are the ornithosuchian group, so-called because of their bird-like features, but hard factual fossil evidence to support the theory is lacking.

STARTING POINT
Four very different creatures may have had one common ancestor.

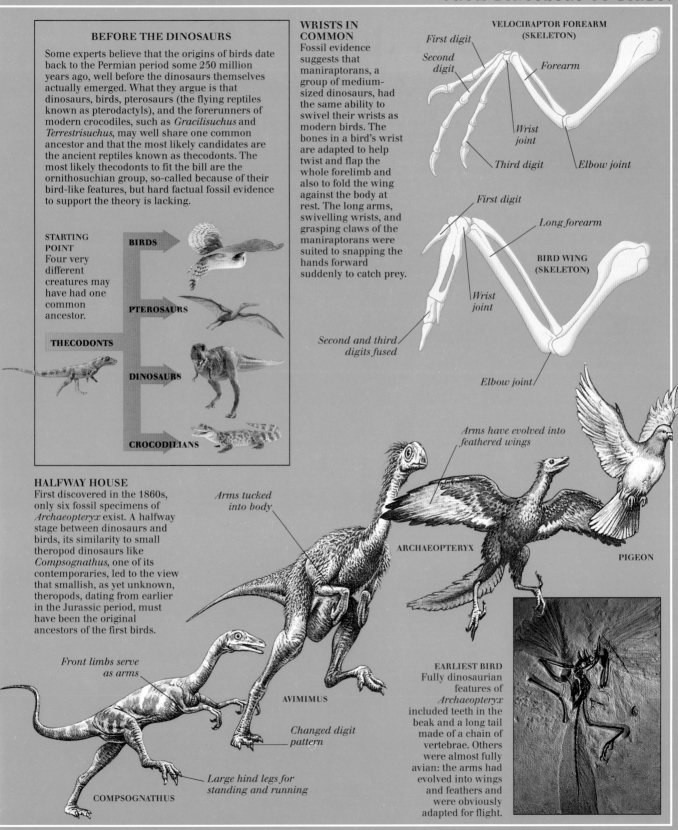

BIRDS

PTEROSAURS

THECODONTS

DINOSAURS

CROCODILIANS

WRISTS IN COMMON

Fossil evidence suggests that maniraptorans, a group of medium-sized dinosaurs, had the same ability to swivel their wrists as modern birds. The bones in a bird's wrist are adapted to help twist and flap the whole forelimb and also to fold the wing against the body at rest. The long arms, swivelling wrists, and grasping claws of the maniraptorans were suited to snapping the hands forward suddenly to catch prey.

VELOCIRAPTOR FOREARM (SKELETON)

First digit

Second digit

Forearm

Wrist joint

Third digit

Elbow joint

First digit

Long forearm

BIRD WING (SKELETON)

Wrist joint

Second and third digits fused

Elbow joint

Arms have evolved into feathered wings

ARCHAEOPTERYX

PIGEON

HALFWAY HOUSE

First discovered in the 1860s, only six fossil specimens of *Archaeopteryx* exist. A halfway stage between dinosaurs and birds, its similarity to small theropod dinosaurs like *Compsognathus*, one of its contemporaries, led to the view that smallish, as yet unknown, theropods, dating from earlier in the Jurassic period, must have been the original ancestors of the first birds.

Arms tucked into body

Front limbs serve as arms

AVIMIMUS

Changed digit pattern

Large hind legs for standing and running

COMPSOGNATHUS

EARLIEST BIRD
Fully dinosaurian features of *Archaeopteryx* included teeth in the beak and a long tail made of a chain of vertebrae. Others were almost fully avian: the arms had evolved into wings and feathers and were obviously adapted for flight.

Preserved in the ice

ONE OF THE MOST EXCITING PREHISTORIC FINDS of recent years was the discovery of a 23,000-year-old woolly mammoth mummified apparently intact in a block of ice deep in the frozen wastes of Siberia. In autumn 1999, the mammoth, still embedded in the ice that had preserved it, was airlifted by helicopter to the nearest town, where it is to be kept in a specially-built ice-laboratory, ready for scientists to study. This is the most ambitious attempt yet made to preserve such a long-dead animal so that it can be analyzed in detail.

UP AND AWAY
Buigues organized an expedition to cut into the ice around the frozen mammoth. In October 1999, the whole find was airlifted like a giant hairy ice cube to the Khatanga airstrip. Its eventual resting place will be an icy cellar-laboratory dug underground.

Small ears help to prevent heat loss

HOW BIG WERE MAMMOTHS?
Woolly mammoths, with a shoulder height of 2.3 metres (8ft), had shaggy coats to protect them against the cold. The broad ivory tusks may have been used to sweep snow away from the beast's food of grasses.

Ivory tusk

AN EXCITING DISCOVERY
The Jarkov mammoth is named after the reindeer-herding family who discovered its tusks poking from the ice in 1997. They removed the tusks to sell at a local market where the French explorer Bernard Buigues saw them. He visited the site and took samples from the head and teeth. These showed it was a male aged about 47 when it died.

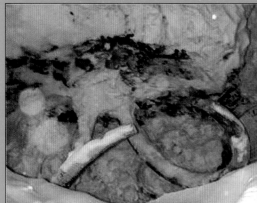

BIG PLANS FOR THE BIG BEAST
If the mammoth's sex organs are well-enough preserved, one idea is to extract frozen sperm from them, which hopefully could be used to fertilize eggs taken from an Asian elephant, the mammoth's closest living relative. If the process works, the result could be a hybrid that was half-mammoth and half-elephant. Further selective breeding among the offspring might eventually produce almost pure mammoths.

ARCTIC OCEAN

Khatanga

RUSSIA

AT KHATANGA
Work on the Jarkow mammoth may take 50 years to complete. One fear is that, if the body temperature has risen above -20°C, the DNA may be too fragmented for use. Nevertheless, the Jarkov mammoth is the best candidate yet to emerge in the quest to recreate a living creature from prehistoric times.

MAMMOTH CLONES
Cloning is another idea under active consideration once tissue samples taken from the mammoth have been analyzed. Mammoth DNA would be injected into suitable cells, such as elephant egg cells, which have had their own genetic material removed. Using the instructions in their new genes, the eggs would develop into baby mammoths.

Thick insulating coat

DEATH IN THE ANDES

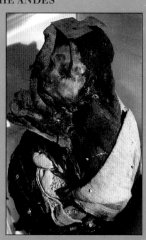

In early 1999, the frozen remains of three children – two girls and a boy – were discovered at an Inca burial site high in the Argentinian Andes. The ice had done its work well: two bodies were almost perfectly preserved, while the third seems to have been damaged by lightning. The freezing itself had taken place within hours of burial. It was clear that the children had been ritually sacrificed. Examination of the bodies and of the wealth of rich artefacts found with them will give scientists an unprecedented chance of finding out more about the Inca way of life.

DEFROSTING THE MAMMOTH
The plan is to thaw out the mammoth and the ice that encases it using nothing more complicated than domestic hairdryers. Thousands of samples will be taken as the creature is slowly defrosted in hundreds of slow stages.

Small tail

Woolly underhair

Large feet support body weight

OETZI'S SECRETS REVEALED

Oetzi (Ötzi), the Austro-Italian iceman, was another exciting discovery of the 1990s. His remains were found by accident in 1991, thawing from the ice high in an Alpine pass between Austria and Italy. Along with his clothes and tools, Oetzi's mummified body had been preserved almost intact for a staggering 5,300 years. Investigations revealed that he was around 46 years old when he died, 160 cm (5 ft 3 in) tall and weighed 60 kg (130 lb). In 1998 Oetzi was moved to a new home in a refrigerated case at the South Tyrol Museum of Archaeology in Bolzano.

AUSTRIA
Solden
ITALY
Bolzano

The valley after which Oetzi was named

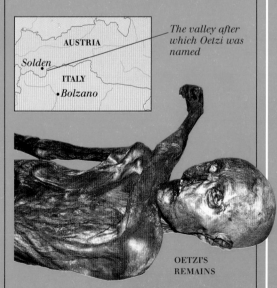

OETZI'S REMAINS

WHAT OETZI WORE
When he died, Oetzi was wearing a plaited grass waterproof cloak, a loincloth, a goat's hide tunic and leggings, a pouched belt, a bearskin hat, and deerskin boots lined with grass for extra warmth.

Medical Research

SOME SIGNIFICANT BREAKTHROUGHS have recently been made in DNA research, with enormous implications for controlling and curing diseases, reproducing identical organisms (cloning), and "decoding", or listing, the sequence of the genes that compose an organism's DNA ("genome sequencing"). In May 1996, Oxford University scientists announced that they had identified the regulatory "switch" for the gene CFTR, which, when defective, causes cystic fibrosis. The discovery will potentially enable healthy copies of the gene to be introduced into a patient's body, and activated in relevant cells. Geneticists have, for the first time, sequenced the genome of an organism larger than a bacterium, with enormous consequences for the future study into human genetics. Other areas of development include the use of highly specialized computer technology to provide long-distance medical care, and virtual reality environments for medical practice, training, and research.

THE COMPOSITION OF DNA (DEOXYRIBONUCLEIC ACID)

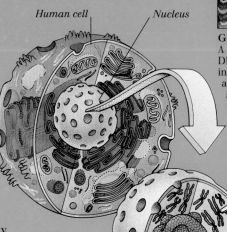

Human cell

Nucleus

Nucleolus

GENETIC CODING
A chromosome is a condensed strand of DNA. There are 23 pairs of chromosomes in the human cell and together they contain about 100,000 genes. Every gene is a tiny segment of DNA, made up of paired nucleotide bases arranged in triplets. The above computer display shows the base-pair structure of adjacent genes. The entire sequence of these bases forms the specific genetic code (genome) of an organism. A world-wide research effort, known as the Human Genome Project, has been set up to identify and code all of the genes in human DNA.

Nucleosome

Sugar phosphate backbone

Chromosome (human cells have 23 pairs)

DNA wraps around a core of binding proteins

Unravelled double helix of DNA

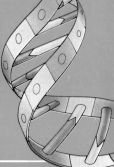

DNA GENOME SEQUENCING
Saccharomyces cerevisiae, or brewer's yeast, is the first organism more complex than a bacterium to have its entire genome sequenced. Three hundred scientists worked over a period of six years to sequence the 12,071 base pairs. Their achievement was announced at the European Commission in April 1996.

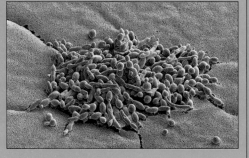

YEAST CELLS

A DNA SEGMENT
This computer representation shows the double helix (blue) of the DNA linked together by the base pairs (yellow and red).

WORM DNA
Another subject of genetic research is the *Caenorhabditis elegans*, a soil-dwelling nematode worm. Scientists have already mapped out its genes and have embarked on identifying the specific sequence of the 100 million base pairs in its genome.

NEMATODE WORM

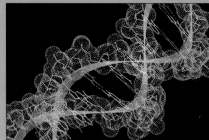

KEY TO BASES

- Adenine
- Guanine
- Thymine
- Cytosine

CLONING

A breakthrough in efforts to genetically engineer species of animals was announced in March 1996. Pictured here at nine months old, these two Welsh mountain sheep were successfully cloned by using an electric current to fuse a lab-cultured cell with an unfertilized egg (one emptied of all its chromosomes). This stimulus also fertilized the cell, which then divided, developed into an embryo, and was transferred to a surrogate mother.

CLONED SHEEP, MEGAN AND MORAG

BASE PAIRS

The four chemical compounds or bases, are paired in "rungs" and grouped in triplets, forming the double helix "ladder". The sequence of these base pairs contains the inherited coded instructions (genes) responsible for the development of an organism.

Nucleotide base

Paired nucleotide base

Gene is made up of sections of base triplets (3 successive pairs of bases)

TISSUE ENGINEERING

An artificial human ear, developed by growing human cartilage in a biodegradable polyester scaffold mould, was grafted onto the back of a mouse to see whether outer skin would form and the blood would circulate. This experiment, successfully carried out at the Massachusetts Institute of Technology by Dr. C. Vacanti, is a vital step towards using such structures in future human transplant surgery.

COMPUTER TECHNOLOGY AND MEDICINE

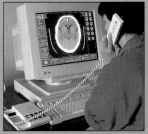

TELEMEDICAL ANALYSIS OF BRAIN SCAN

TELEMEDICINE

Telemedicine – the practice of medicine at a distance using computer networks – was pioneered by NASA to provide medical support to astronauts. Not only can it be used for consulting with patients in rural or widespread geographical areas but it can also provide emergency care in remote and disaster situations.

VIRTUAL REALITY

Virtual reality environments are being developed to provide realistic training for certain surgical procedures, much as flight simulators are used to train pilots to fly. The highly specialized techniques performed in minimally invasive "keyhole" surgery, using such instruments as the gastroscope (above), can be practised using a virtual environment that simulates tissue properties. A virtual environment developed to simulate eye surgery is shown below. The surgeon is able to experience both the visual and mechanical sensations associated with performing the operation.

Surgeon's eyepiece

Keyhole surgery instruments feed back video images

Controls

GASTROSCOPE

VIRTUAL ENVIRONMENT FOR SIMULATION OF EYE SURGERY

STRESS CONTOURS SHOWN AS INCISION IS MADE IN CORNEA

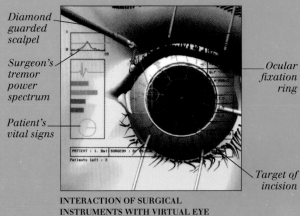

Diamond guarded scalpel

Surgeon's tremor power spectrum

Patient's vital signs

Ocular fixation ring

Target of incision

INTERACTION OF SURGICAL INSTRUMENTS WITH VIRTUAL EYE

Genetic advances

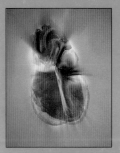

HUMAN HEART

DEVELOPMENTS IN CLONING are among the most important advances in recent genetic science. A clone is a group of genes, cells, or complete organisms in which all of the group's members have the same genetic constitution. The term is also used to refer to individual members of a clone. Clones occur in nature, especially in the case of simple organisms, such as bacteria and viruses, which reproduce merely by splitting (asexual reproduction) after their DNA has replicated itself. They also occur in humans and other animals when a single fertilized egg divides and separates to form two or more identical individuals. Artificial cloning of selected genes is one of the most significant breakthroughs ever made in biology and has powerful implications for both science and industry. Once the desired gene is obtained, the cloning can be left to organisms such as bacteria, which, under suitable conditions, reproduce almost indefinitely. In this way, enormous quantities of the particular gene may be produced. Gene cloning is most commonly done in the laboratory by means of the polymerase chain reaction (PCR), which can produce millions of copies of a single gene in a matter of hours. Far more daunting an enterprise than gene cloning is the cloning of whole animals (see below right), only recently shown to be practicable. A further key genetic advance is the creation of transgenic animals, in particular pigs, which are currently being used for the "manufacture" of human-compatible organs, such as hearts.

CREATING A TRANSGENIC ANIMAL

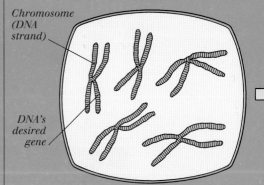

Chromosome (DNA strand)

DNA's desired gene

IDENTIFICATION
The desired gene contained within the DNA strand (chromosome) is identified.

Chromosome

Nucleus

HUMAN CELL
After cell division, perfect copies of each of its chromosomes are passed to each of the daughter cells.

BSE

Among the more worrying aspects of biological research is the discovery that the brain disease bovine spongiform encephalopathy (BSE) is identical to the fatal human condition Creutzfeldt-Jakob disease (CJD). There is general agreement that the introduction of bovine tissue from affected animals into the food chain was the cause of the recent BSE epidemic. Although the genetic modification of animals is unlikely to involve the genes active in BSE, the number of unanswered questions has caused much concern about the propriety of the procedure.

GENETICALLY MODIFIED FOODS

An increasingly controversial practice in the food industry is the genetic modification of foodstuffs in order to extend their shelf life. This means that not only foods, for example fruit and vegetables, but also food ingredients and additives that contain genes derived from animals, fish, insects, and viruses, will appear in shops unlabelled as such.

A little decay is apparent

Rotting is far more visible

GENETICALLY MODIFIED TOMATO

"NATURAL" TOMATO OF THE SAME AGE

ANIMAL CLONING

To produce a clone of an animal, a sample of its DNA must be used. Since each body cell contains a complete DNA genome, this is easily obtained. This DNA has to be introduced into an ovum (egg) of another animal of the same species after the ovum's original DNA is extracted. The egg is then inserted into a surrogate animal's womb and the pregnancy proceeds as normal. Although every body cell contains a complete genome, it will normally activate only those genes necessary for its own body part – for example kidney, brain, or bone. The other genes are not needed and are not "switched on". However, if the cell is starved of nutrients, development can be stopped at an early stage, at which point all the genes can be operative. The ovum into which the DNA is inserted will then behave as if the DNA were its own.

A donor provides the cell for cloning, e.g. mammary cell

CELL DONOR

A ewe provides an egg

EGG DONOR

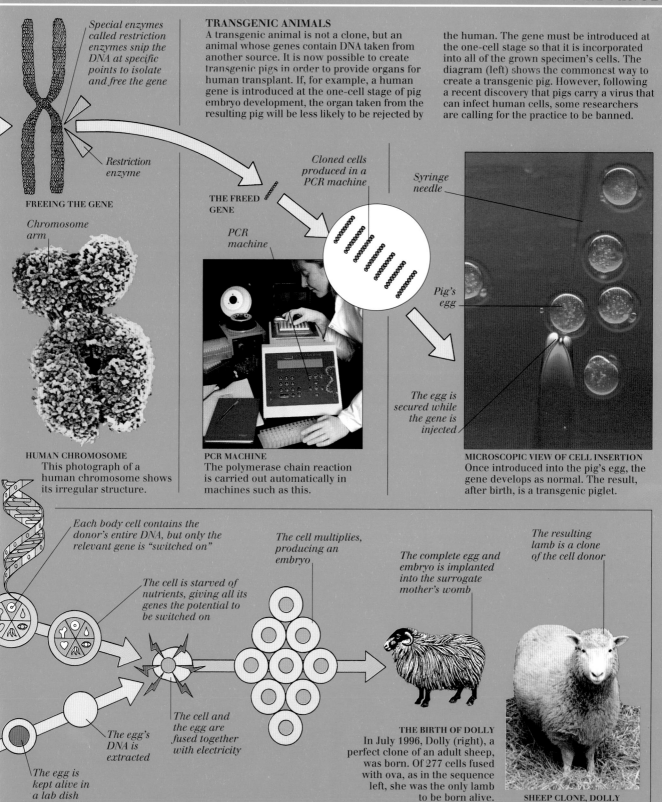

Special enzymes called restriction enzymes snip the DNA at specific points to isolate and free the gene

Restriction enzyme

FREEING THE GENE

TRANSGENIC ANIMALS

A transgenic animal is not a clone, but an animal whose genes contain DNA taken from another source. It is now possible to create transgenic pigs in order to provide organs for human transplant. If, for example, a human gene is introduced at the one-cell stage of pig embryo development, the organ taken from the resulting pig will be less likely to be rejected by the human. The gene must be introduced at the one-cell stage so that it is incorporated into all of the grown specimen's cells. The diagram (left) shows the commonest way to create a transgenic pig. However, following a recent discovery that pigs carry a virus that can infect human cells, some researchers are calling for the practice to be banned.

THE FREED GENE

Cloned cells produced in a PCR machine

Syringe needle

PCR machine

Chromosome arm

Pig's egg

The egg is secured while the gene is injected

HUMAN CHROMOSOME
This photograph of a human chromosome shows its irregular structure.

PCR MACHINE
The polymerase chain reaction is carried out automatically in machines such as this.

MICROSCOPIC VIEW OF CELL INSERTION
Once introduced into the pig's egg, the gene develops as normal. The result, after birth, is a transgenic piglet.

Each body cell contains the donor's entire DNA, but only the relevant gene is "switched on"

The cell multiplies, producing an embryo

The complete egg and embryo is implanted into the surrogate mother's womb

The resulting lamb is a clone of the cell donor

The cell is starved of nutrients, giving all its genes the potential to be switched on

The egg's DNA is extracted

The cell and the egg are fused together with electricity

The egg is kept alive in a lab dish

THE BIRTH OF DOLLY
In July 1996, Dolly (right), a perfect clone of an adult sheep, was born. Of 277 cells fused with ova, as in the sequence left, she was the only lamb to be born alive.

SHEEP CLONE, DOLLY

Modern surgery

WITH NEW DISCOVERIES AND advancing technology, medicine is constantly evolving. Developments in technical expertise have resulted in a successful hand transplant, and the repair of a congenital defect in a foetus while still in the womb. Advances in technology have also been far-reaching, providing a glimpse of what might be achieved in the future. The application of virtual reality in medicine has already enabled progress in both the teaching and practice of surgery, and may soon be used in the treatment of eating disorders and agoraphobia. Minimally invasive and robot- and computer-aided surgery allow delicate and complex surgical procedures to be carried out with the precision of a thousandth of a millimetre. This means that surgery has become safer, and patient pain and recovery time have been reduced.

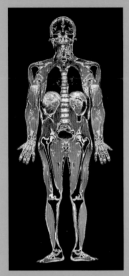

MRI SCAN OF A FEMALE BODY
This colour-enhanced Magnetic Resonance Image (MRI) is the product of a number of MRI scans made along the length of the body, which have been collated by the scanner's computer.

Headset   *Dataglove*   *Virtual leg*

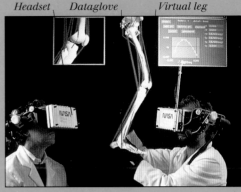

VIRTUAL SURGERY
Medical imaging such as X-ray, Computerized Tomography (CT), and Magnetic Resonance Imaging (MRI), allows visual access to the internal anatomy and functions of the human body. The precise anatomical information provided by these images can be used to create a virtual patient, on which surgeons and medical students can practise procedures. To study the anatomy of the human leg, these surgeons wear headsets equipped with a 3-D video display to view an image, and a black rubber glove (dataglove) that has woven optical fibre sensors. The glove relays details of the body part to the computer, which then generates the image.

Surgical clamp   *Muscular wall of mother's womb*

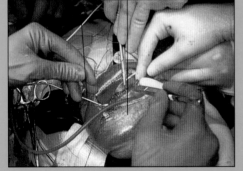

INTRA-UTERINE SURGERY
The repair of birth defects through foetal surgery has so far been mostly experimental. However, ground-breaking advances were made in 1998 with the treatment of a case of spina bifida, a developmental defect in the posterior wall of the spinal canal. With this condition, the delicate tissue of the spinal cord may be exposed to varying degrees of damage, depending on the severity of the defect. This can result in paralysis of the lower limbs and incontinence. A team of surgeons in the US corrected the defect in a 23-week-gestation foetus, after the condition had been detected during a routine ultrasound. Follow-up at the walking and toilet-training stages will be necessary to judge the success of the operation.

ROBOTS IN SURGERY

Recent advances in biomedical engineering have led to the increasing use of robots in surgery. Once a robot has been correctly programmed, it will be more accurate than a human in performing many precise but repetitive tasks. Robots may soon act as surgeons' assistants during operations, holding instruments such as an endoscope (for viewing internal parts of the body), and making incisions when required.

ROBOT-AIDED BRAIN SURGERY
A robot performs simulated brain surgery on a model head (right). The surgeon views the operation on a large screen and uses a joystick to control the robot's movements.

Robotic arm   *Model head*

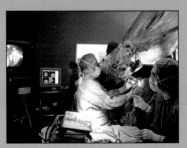

COMPUTER-AIDED BRAIN SURGERY
A surgeon uses a computer-assisted microscope to locate a brain tumour in a patient. The microscope uses MRI scans to plot the position of the tumour, and maps it in 3-D virtual reality. The surgeon can then locate and destroy the tumour using a laser integrated into the microscope.

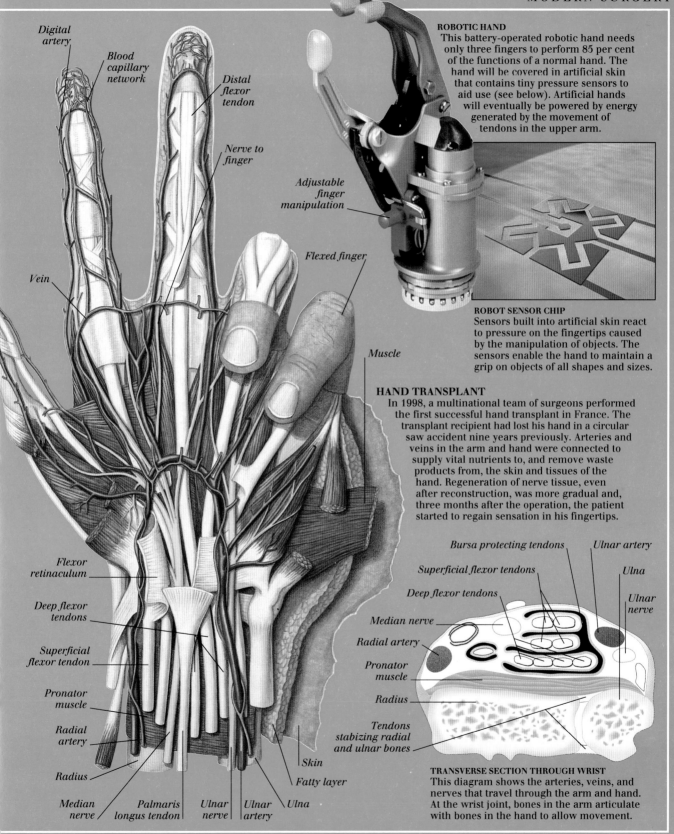

Digital
artery

Blood
capillary
network

Distal
flexor
tendon

Nerve to
finger

Vein

Flexed finger

Muscle

Flexor
retinaculum

Deep flexor
tendons

Superficial
flexor tendon

Pronator
muscle

Radial
artery

Radius

Skin

Fatty layer

Median
nerve

Palmaris
longus tendon

Ulnar
nerve

Ulnar
artery

Ulna

ROBOTIC HAND
This battery-operated robotic hand needs
only three fingers to perform 85 per cent
of the functions of a normal hand. The
hand will be covered in artificial skin
that contains tiny pressure sensors to
aid use (see below). Artificial hands
will eventually be powered by energy
generated by the movement of
tendons in the upper arm.

Adjustable
finger
manipulation

ROBOT SENSOR CHIP
Sensors built into artificial skin react
to pressure on the fingertips caused
by the manipulation of objects. The
sensors enable the hand to maintain a
grip on objects of all shapes and sizes.

HAND TRANSPLANT
In 1998, a multinational team of surgeons performed
the first successful hand transplant in France. The
transplant recipient had lost his hand in a circular
saw accident nine years previously. Arteries and
veins in the arm and hand were connected to
supply vital nutrients to, and remove waste
products from, the skin and tissues of the
hand. Regeneration of nerve tissue, even
after reconstruction, was more gradual and,
three months after the operation, the patient
started to regain sensation in his fingertips.

Bursa protecting tendons

Ulnar artery

Superficial flexor tendons

Ulna

Deep flexor tendons

Ulnar
nerve

Median nerve

Radial artery

Pronator
muscle

Radius

Tendons
stabizing radial
and ulnar bones

TRANSVERSE SECTION THROUGH WRIST
This diagram shows the arteries, veins, and
nerves that travel through the arm and hand.
At the wrist joint, bones in the arm articulate
with bones in the hand to allow movement.

Body healing

MODERN MEDICINE AND STATE-OF-THE-ART TECHNOLOGY are working hand-in-hand to transform the way in which a whole range of medical problems and conditions are treated. Microsurgery, where doctors are now able to connect blood vessels and nerves thinner than human hair, is only one area of exciting progress. Developments in tissue engineering mean that it is now possible to 'grow' replacement skin and cartilage in the laboratory, while microchips and advanced computer electronics are playing a vitally-important part in restoring full body movement and in helping people to cope with the problems of damaged hearing and sight.

Internal microcircuitry

DETECTING SOUND PATTERNS

Cochlear implants are designed to help the profoundly deaf hear. A receiver in the skull receives signals from a microphone, via a sound processor and transmitter, using them to activate electrodes implanted in the cochlear nerve. They stimulate the nerve to send electric impulses to the brain.

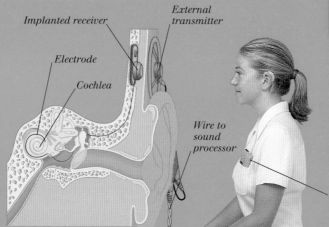

Implanted receiver

External transmitter

Electrode

Cochlea

Wire to sound processor

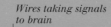

FIGHTING DEAFNESS

Modern micro-technology means that hearing aids have taken major steps forward with the development of tiny hearing aid shells called Deep Canal, MicroCanal, or CIC (completely-in-the-canal). The aids are inserted deep within the ear canal and have the ability to adjust automatically to compensate for varying noise conditions. They also need less power because of their nearness to the eardrum.

Sound processor

ARTIFICIAL SIGHT

Though 'Jerry' is blind, he can walk around chairs, through doorways, and read letters·at a distance thanks to special spectacles fitted with a small digital camera and rangefinder. These send fast-updated images as electronic signals to a computer on his waist. This processes the signals and feeds them along wires that pass through his skin and skull directly to the visual cortex of the brain, which is where nerve impulses from the eyes are normally processed. The signals pass to the brain via 68 platinum electrodes.

Wires taking signals to brain

Digital camera

Implanted electrodes

Wires from waist minicomputer

MAGIC MICROCHIPS

Microchip implants are now being used to provide artificial retinas for the eyes, mainly using CCDs (charge couple devices) of the kind fitted to video camcorders. What they do is to detect light rays, turning them into a pattern of electronic signals. These are fed through ultra-fine implanted electrodes into the retinal ganglion, or optic nerve fibres that lead to the visual centres of the brain. In another system, a retinal encoder outside the eye has the job of detecting light rays and processing them. Converted into electro-magnetic waves, these are sent to a retinal stimulator that is physically implanted in the eye, sending signals direct to the brain.

MAMMOTH OPERATION

In 2000, Edouard Herriot Hospital in Lyons saw the world's first successful double-hand transplant operation. The operation, which took 17 hours to complete, involved a 50-strong team of doctors, nurses, technicians and surgeons, led by specialists Jean-Michel Dubernard and Earl Owen. The surgical procedures themselves were extremely complicated. Each part and tissue in the region of the forearm, including bones, muscles, tendons, nerves, and blood vessels, had to be connected separately. By the time he left hospital, the patient, Denis Chatelier, could wiggle his fingertips and his fingernails had started to grow. Two years before, the team had performed the first-ever single hand transplant on Australian Clint Hallam. Though the transplant was successful, the hand has not attained full dexterity.

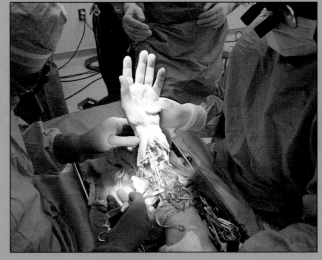

SURGICAL SUCCESS
Denis Chatelier, the world's first double hand transplant recipient, leaves hospital in Lyons in February 2000, holding his bandaged arms aloft to greet his well-wishers.

Culture of human skin

Protective clothing preserves sterility

Synthetic fibres

LOOKING TO THE FUTURE

The use of tissue-engineered skin was pioneered in the USA in 1999 to treat people suffering from certain types of burns, ulcers, and other medical problems. The notion of smart bandaging was pioneered at the University of Glasgow, in Scotland. Substitute tendon, bone and heart valve tissues are also being researched, while further down the line whole organs, such as kidneys, the liver and even the heart, may be originated. Such part living, part synthetic spare parts are known medically as neo-organs. They do not use microchips, nor should they provoke rejection once they have been implanted. Such developments could help scientists achieve their goal of ensuring that no one should have to suffer for lack of a compatible implant.

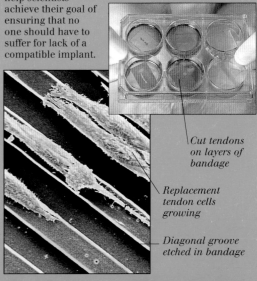

Cut tendons on layers of bandage

Replacement tendon cells growing

Diagonal groove etched in bandage

Cartilage tissue

ARTIFICIAL CARTILAGE

Growing replacement cartilage is a new medical technique, which eliminates the risk of tissue rejection. In it, artificial fibres form a template for cells that then grow and multiply to form new cartilage tissue.

LABORATORY REPLACEMENT

Tissue engineering uses a combination of artificial plastic-like fibres called bio-polymers and real human cells, which are produced by genetic engineering or obtained from human embryos. The cells are treated to make them 'think' that they are in a very early, developing embryo in the phase of growth called organogenesis, which occurs in nature during the first eight weeks after conception. What actually happens is that the cells are grown in the laboratory on to a bio-polymer 'scaffold' to give them a physical framework. Then, various chemicals, including special nutrients, can be added to stimulate and direct the course of cell development. As a result, the cells multiply and start to build their own tissue, such as skin or cartilage. This can be transplanted into the body, where the bio-polymers naturally bio-degrade, or dissolve away, leaving no traces behind. For their part, the cells continue to multiply, moving, shaping or modelling their tissue, which then integrates naturally with the recipient's own tissues.

SMART BANDAGING

When this biodegradable bandage is placed between a tendon's broken ends, the tiny diagonal grooves in it direct the growth of new tissue. When fully developed from its current experimental stage, the technology may supply templates for hip replacements and all kinds of other cell engineering projects.

El Niño and La Niña

ALSO REFERRED TO AS the El Niño-Southern Oscillation (ENSO) Cycle, El Niño and La Niña are extreme instances of the natural climate cycle of the tropical Pacific. Although scientists have been aware of the oscillation for several decades, the public has only become aware of its increasingly destructive effects in more recent years. These warm and cold seasonal variations occur due to interaction between the ocean surface, the atmosphere, and trade winds (general wind patterns). The resulting rise and fall in ocean temperature has been linked with severe weather conditions in parts of South America, Indonesia, and Australia. The cycle oscillates between warm (El Niño) to neutral or cold (La Niña) conditions every 3–7 years. Meteorologists use information provided by weather satellites in the prediction and tracking of these events, which have had a dramatic effect on climate patterns around the world since at least the last century. It is not known how the ENSO Cycle will be affected if the global climate grows warmer.

INTERPRETING INFORMATION

Weather forecasts in newspapers and on radio and television begin as observations. Thousands of surface stations on land and hundreds of weather ships at sea – many of them are fully automated – monitor visibility, air pressure, wind direction and speed, temperature, humidity, and the amount, type, and height of cloud. Together with information received from weather balloons and satellites, data is collated at weather centres to produce synoptic charts (see below). These enable meteorologists to prepare forecasts.

FORECAST PREPARATION

Centre of low pressure   *Isobar*

SYNOPTIC WEATHER CHART

NORMAL CONDITIONS

Normally, south-easterly trade winds drive water westwards across the equatorial South Pacific, causing warm surface water to form a deep pool near Indonesia. The Peru Current flows northwards along the South American coast, and cold water wells up to the surface, carrying oxygen and nutrients that sustain fish and birds.

Trade winds slacken

Cool water is suppressed

Pacific

Ocean

Sea current changes direction and flows east

Warm surface water

EL NIÑO CONDITIONS

During an El Niño episode, trade winds slacken or even reverse. Warm surface water flows from west to east, increasing the depth of warm water off the South American coast. Heavy rainfall follows the warm water, leading to flooding in Peru and drought in parts of Indonesia and Australia.

EL NIÑO SEA CURRENTS
The normal sea current reverses and warm water forms a pool near South America. This pool suppresses the nutrient-rich water of the Peru Current and, starved of nutrients, fish and sea birds move away or die.

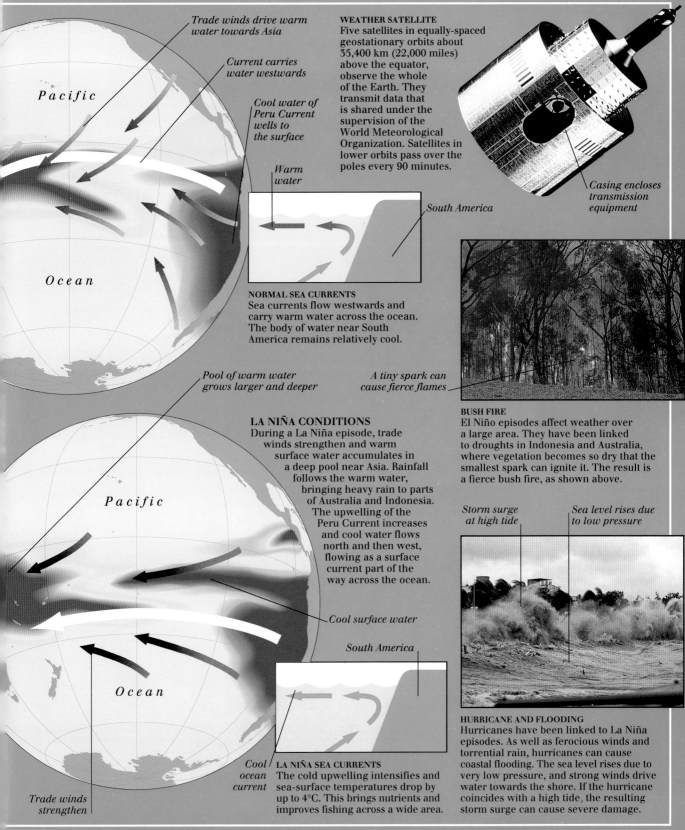

Trade winds drive warm water towards Asia

Current carries water westwards

Cool water of Peru Current wells to the surface

Warm water

South America

WEATHER SATELLITE
Five satellites in equally-spaced geostationary orbits about 35,400 km (22,000 miles) above the equator, observe the whole of the Earth. They transmit data that is shared under the supervision of the World Meteorological Organization. Satellites in lower orbits pass over the poles every 90 minutes.

Casing encloses transmission equipment

NORMAL SEA CURRENTS
Sea currents flow westwards and carry warm water across the ocean. The body of water near South America remains relatively cool.

Pool of warm water grows larger and deeper

A tiny spark can cause fierce flames

LA NIÑA CONDITIONS
During a La Niña episode, trade winds strengthen and warm surface water accumulates in a deep pool near Asia. Rainfall follows the warm water, bringing heavy rain to parts of Australia and Indonesia. The upwelling of the Peru Current increases and cool water flows north and then west, flowing as a surface current part of the way across the ocean.

Cool surface water

South America

Trade winds strengthen

Cool ocean current

LA NIÑA SEA CURRENTS
The cold upwelling intensifies and sea-surface temperatures drop by up to 4°C. This brings nutrients and improves fishing across a wide area.

BUSH FIRE
El Niño episodes affect weather over a large area. They have been linked to droughts in Indonesia and Australia, where vegetation becomes so dry that the smallest spark can ignite it. The result is a fierce bush fire, as shown above.

Storm surge at high tide

Sea level rises due to low pressure

HURRICANE AND FLOODING
Hurricanes have been linked to La Niña episodes. As well as ferocious winds and torrential rain, hurricanes can cause coastal flooding. The sea level rises due to very low pressure, and strong winds drive water towards the shore. If the hurricane coincides with a high tide, the resulting storm surge can cause severe damage.

Pacific

Ocean

House of the future

SOHO TRANSFORMABLE APARTMENT
This central-London flat can be used as one large living space, or partitioned with freestanding boxes to provide bedrooms. It was designed by architect Mark Guard.

IN THE LAST FEW decades, the environmentally friendly or sustainable house has been associated with green enthusiasts who built homes to both blend in with the natural landscape and harness renewable energy resources. As we enter the new millennium, environmental concerns will become a matter of expediency. Architects, developers, and homeowners will be pressed to take a more pragmatic approach to where they build, and the more economic use of space and energy supplies. Extreme climates currently present architects with the greatest challenge in energy conservation. In urban areas, there is a growing trend for disused buildings that can be converted into housing, and for dwellings that can be easily adapted to accommodate different types of residents.

CONVERTED WATER TOWER
This structure on the outskirts of Antwerp, Belgium, was originally built in the early 20th century. It was converted into a dramatic and unusual dwelling by architect Jo Crepain in 1998.

Platform of original tower

Drum where water originally collected

Winter garden

Columns form main structure of house

Opaque glass

MEZZANINE VIEW
A mezzanine level in the base of the tower overlooks the living room and creates a cosy space for watching television. The natural, wooded setting of the tower is emphasized by the great expanse of glass.

TOP-FLOOR WINTER GARDEN
The use of buildings that were not originally intended for domestic purposes often results in an unconventional house layout. Here, rooms inside the glass-encased water tower are stacked on top of one other. The winter garden is located below the disused water drum.

INTERIOR OF THE BASE
The architect used the original structure to divide the concrete base of the tower. The sitting area is located at the rear, and the kitchen on the street front.

OYSTER HOUSE

Nigel Coates' Oyster House was the winning entry in the Concept House competition at the 1998 Daily Mail Ideal Home Exhibition in London. It was designed to provide a new model for the speculative home on a typical suburban estate. With this design, Coates extended the popular idea of loft living to the family home. The ground floor is open plan with flexible partitions, enabling the living space to adapt as children grow up, and to incorporate friends, work, and relations. There are two staircases, which allow for separation and privacy upstairs. Each stairway leads to a bathroom, with a double bedroom on either side of the house.

EXTERIOR VIEW

INTERIOR VIEW OF GROUND FLOOR

MONOLITHIC WALLS
Among the most distinctive features of the Burnette house are its concrete walls with narrow glass slits. These walls filter the sun on the north and south walls, while the glass slits act as a giant sundial that charts the movement of the sun throughout the day.

Glass front of east elevation has low-emissivity surface

Narrow glass slit

East block contains living spaces

WENDELL BURNETTE HOUSE

This house and studio were built by the architect Wendell Burnette in 1995. The house is situated in a desert landscape on the west face of the Phoenix Mountain Preserve in Arizona. Burnette's innovative design takes a truly inspired approach to environmental concerns. It proposes imaginative solutions to both the extreme desert climate, and the existence of unsightly housing in the surrounding area.

Fully-shaded evaporative pool

Internal court divides living area and studio

Car port

Stairway to terrace

MICROCLIMATE IN THE INTERNAL COURT
Burnette's inspiration for a water-cooling system was drawn from the naturally occurring "canyon seats" or springs found in the Arizona desert. Here, his water-cooled internal court supports a lush microclimate at the entrance to the house, and divides the east and west blocks. A fully-shaded evaporative pool located below the studio floor overflows into a trough. Water runs down the natural slope of the site, cooling the internal court and improving ventilation throughout the house.

Airbus A3XX

A DOUBLE-DECKER AIRLINER with up to 1,000 seats is the response of Airbus Industrie, the European aircraft manufacturer, to the ever-growing global demand for air travel. The number of airline passengers is rising by an estimated five per cent every year, which means that the number of people travelling by air will double in 15 years and nearly treble in 20. Many existing airways, however, are already congested, while most major airports are struggling to cope with existing traffic levels. There is also environmental opposition to further expansion. The A3XX is intended to resolve the dilemma by carrying many more passengers in far fewer aircraft.

FLIGHT EFFICIENCY

The A3XX will burn up to 20 per cent less fuel per passenger than the Boeing 747-400, so reducing pollution in the upper atmosphere. The giant new engines being designed for the new super-jumbo are more fuel- and weight-efficient.

Economy seats on upper deck

Economy seats on lower deck

Electrically-controlled flaps

Business class seats on upper deck

80 m (254 ft) wing span

Fuel tanks

New engines reduce weight and lower fuel consumption

Cargo deck

First class seats on main deck

BIGGER AND BETTER

Massive development costs and uncertainty about demand deterred other major aircraft manufacturers like Boeing from going ahead with similar plans, while some airlines argued that, to make air-travel pay, what was needed were fewer passengers paying more, rather than more paying less. Nevertheless, Airbus expects to sell at least 650 aircraft by 2020.

AIRLINER EVOLUTION

Passenger air-travel started to take off in the mid-1930s with the introduction of aircraft like the Douglas DC-3, with its revolutionary retractable undercarriage. Long-haul flight began with flying boats, and entered the jet age with the De Havilland Comet.

CHINA CLIPPER
1936

STRATOCRUISER
1947

 1930   **1940**   **1950**

JUNKER JU52
1933

DOUGLAS DC-3
1936

COMET 1
1949

FLYING IN STYLE
Carrying more passengers does not necessarily mean reducing leg room, as this mock-up of the A3XX's upper deck Business Class cabin demonstrates. Other amenities, such as beds and exercise machines, are planned for the main deck.

COCKPIT TECHNOLOGY
The A3XX's cockpit, located between the two passenger decks, features eight large interactive screens. Along with other data, they will show pictures from external cameras, so the pilots can monitor what is going on during taxiing.

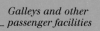

Galleys and other passenger facilities

Wide stairs make deck access easy

FASTER AND FURTHER

For decades, aircraft manufacturers and aerospace researchers have been working on plans to produce a bigger successor to the supersonic Concorde that would be commercially viable and, at the same time, environmentally acceptable. To be cost-effective, such an aircraft has to carry 300 passengers more than 10,000 km (6215 miles) at twice the speed of sound with halved per-passenger fuel consumption. To satisfy environmentalists, it would also be essential to eliminate the sonic boom that restricts Concorde's maximum-speed operation to over the ocean. Assuming the design gets the final go-ahead, Airbus estimates that the aircraft could be in world-wide passenger service by the 2020s.

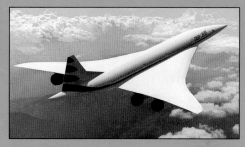

JOINT EFFORT
French, British, and German aerospace companies pooled research to produce plans for the new supersonic airliner. It could carry up to 300 passengers across the Pacific in a few hours.

TOO FAR, TOO FAST
Boeing abandoned work on its variable-geometry 2707 as a result of technical problems and consequent cost overruns. These led to a withdrawal of official support for the project.

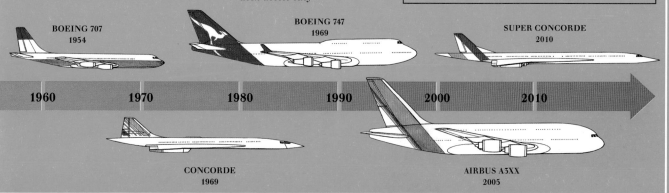

BOEING 707
1954

BOEING 747
1969

SUPER CONCORDE
2010

1960   1970   1980   1990   2000   2010

CONCORDE
1969

AIRBUS A3XX
2005

Tilting trains

SWEDISH TILTING
TRAIN (1990)

ALTHOUGH TILTING TRAINS have
been in use since the 1960s, it is only
recent technological developments
that have been able to prevent much
of the passenger discomfort caused by
cornering at high speeds. As a train goes
into a curve, it produces substantial
centrifugal force towards the outside
of the curve. By tilting the train (the
equivalent of leaning into a curve on a
bicycle), this centrifugal force is balanced by a force into
the inner curve and passenger discomfort is reduced.
Current computer-controlled active tilting systems
operate from self-steering bogies (the wheeled
undercarriage of the train). Improvements in bogie
design enhance the operation of the train by reducing
track forces, and radial self-steering bogies with "soft"
suspension have been introduced. Modern tilting trains
allow operators to achieve higher speeds on existing
curved routes without costly track improvements or the
need to consider completely new high-speed lines.

NORMAL TRAIN CARRIAGE

Centrifugal
force pushes
the carriage
contents
towards the
outside of the
curve

CENTRIFUGAL
FORCE

As the train enters
the curve, a strong
centrifugal force is
produced

Banking is
limited to 6°

NORMAL TRAIN ON CURVE
The normal train is "banked" slightly
and slows as it goes into the bend, but
the carriage body does not tilt.

Track

Train
approaches
at an angle

Strong
sideways
force
outwards

Fiat's Pendolino –
"Little Pendulum" –
tilting train

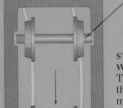

PENDOLINO
Fiat's Pendolino is the
prototype for most recent
European tilting trains.
The French tilting
train shown in the
main diagram
(opposite) will be
based on similar
technology.

STIFF-
WHEEL AXLES
The inability of
the axles to move
means that high
forces are taken
by the axles
themselves and
then by the track.

Axle

HIGH-SPEED TRAINS

The Japanese pioneered modern high-
speed rail travel with their *Shinkansen*
(High-Speed Line) trains, which entered
service in 1964. On a special new
line between Tokyo and Osaka, they
achieved speeds of up to 210 km/h (130
mph). The line was reserved for high-
speed trains, so there was no slower
moving, conflicting traffic to interfere
with operations. The latest Bullet Train,
Nozomi, pictured here, has also broken
speed records. Since the early 1980s,
similar trains have been developed in
France, intitially running between Paris
and Lyon and, like the Japanese train,
running on priority "dedicated" tracks.
German Railways have also developed
high-speed links since 1991.

Pantograph
to collect
electric
current

Single-level
passenger
cabin

Driver's cab has streamlined
profile

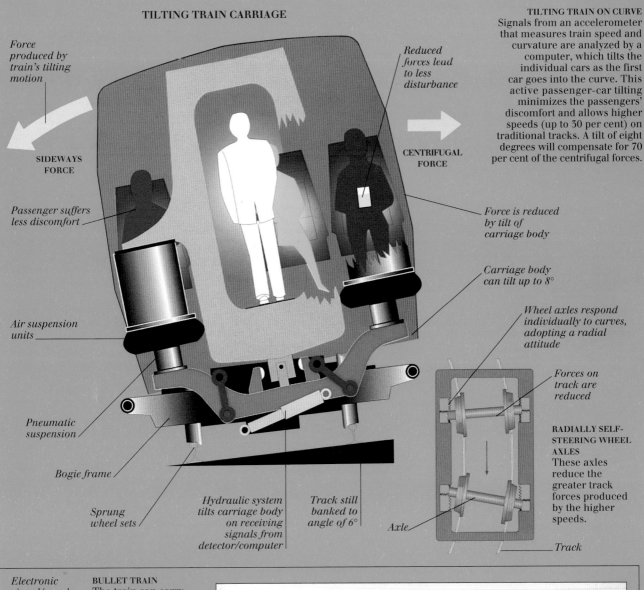

TILTING TRAIN CARRIAGE

Force produced by train's tilting motion

SIDEWAYS FORCE

Reduced forces lead to less disturbance

CENTRIFUGAL FORCE

Passenger suffers less discomfort

Air suspension units

Pneumatic suspension

Bogie frame

Sprung wheel sets

Hydraulic system tilts carriage body on receiving signals from detector/computer

Track still banked to angle of 6°

Force is reduced by tilt of carriage body

Carriage body can tilt up to 8°

Wheel axles respond individually to curves, adopting a radial attitude

Forces on track are reduced

RADIALLY SELF-STEERING WHEEL AXLES
These axles reduce the greater track forces produced by the higher speeds.

Axle

Track

TILTING TRAIN ON CURVE
Signals from an accelerometer that measures train speed and curvature are analyzed by a computer, which tilts the individual cars as the first car goes into the curve. This active passenger-car tilting minimizes the passengers' discomfort and allows higher speeds (up to 30 per cent) on traditional tracks. A tilt of eight degrees will compensate for 70 per cent of the centrifugal forces.

Electronic signal/speed detection equipment in train nose

BULLET TRAIN
The train can carry 1,324 passengers and features 64 separate traction motors, each producing 285kw of power. The body shells are made of aluminium alloy.

RECORD BREAKER
The latest prototype Bullet Train has reached speeds of 345 km/h (214 mph), but the French TGV holds the world railspeed record of 515 km/h (320 mph).

Electric Car / Le Shuttle

IN 1995, PEUGEOT LAUNCHED their first electrically powered vehicle designed for the private motorist – the Peugeot 106 Electric. Unlike conventional petrol-driven cars, the electric car has the advantage of being a "zero emission" vehicle that does not pollute or damage the environment. Other advantages include an engine that is durable, quiet, and mechanically almost trouble-free. With a top speed of 90 km/h (56 mph) and a capacity of 80 km (50 miles) per battery, the 106 Electric goes a long way towards overcoming the customary disadvantages of the electric car (low speeds and short range of distance), which had limited its use to specific commercial applications. This new vehicle represents a significant step towards the development of an alternative to petrol-driven cars. Other "zero-emission" vehicles, such as solar-powered cars (top right), are still in the experimental stages of development.

THE PEUGEOT 106 ELECTRIC
After a series of trials held throughout France, the Peugeot 106 Electric went on sale to the public. Using the body of an existing Peugeot model, it looks no different to other cars and is suited to motorists who use their vehicles for short urban journeys.

THE BATTERY
The 20-battery pack has a combined acceleration rate of 0–50 km/h (30 mph) in 8.3 seconds, a top speed of 90 km/h (56 mph) and a maximum mileage of 80 km (50 miles).

RECHARGING
The battery can be recharged from any 220v/16 amp socket. It takes up to 6 hours to fully recharge the battery, at a rate of 1 hour for every 20 km (12.5 miles).

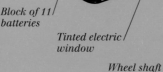

Block of 11 batteries

Tinted electric window

Wheel shaft

Fibreglass body

Connects to 220v/16 amp socket

Plugs into connector on side of car

Connector for charge plug

THE CHARGING PLUG

SOLAR-POWERED CARS

Solar power is an even better solution to the problem of air pollution than is the electric car. It represents a renewable source of energy and, unlike fossil fuels, can be generated without seriously depleting the world's finite resources. Solar-powered vehicles have external solar cell panels that can absorb sunlight and convert its energy into electricity. This prototype of a solar-powered racing car, the "Swatchmobile", was recently developed in Switzerland by the Biel Engineering School .

THE "SWATCHMOBILE"

THE SHUTTLE

SHUTTLE SERVICE
Since Spring 1995, cars and heavy goods vehicles have been able to travel between England and France through the Channel Tunnel. The train that transports them, at speeds of up to 160 km/h (100 mph), is "Le Shuttle".

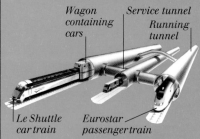

Wagon containing cars   *Service tunnel*   *Running tunnel*

Le Shuttle car train   *Eurostar passenger train*

LOADING THE CARS
Cars are loaded onto enclosed wagons at terminals in Folkestone and Coquelles. Once inside, the drivers and the passengers stay with their vehicles for the duration of the 35-minute journey under the Channel.

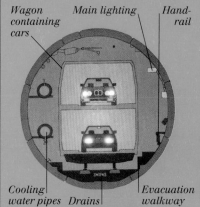

CROSS-SECTION OF THE TUNNEL
Construction of the 51.8 km- (32 mile-) long tunnels housing the rail-link was completed in 1994. They are lined with reinforced concrete rings and equipped with complex draining, cooling, and ventilation systems.

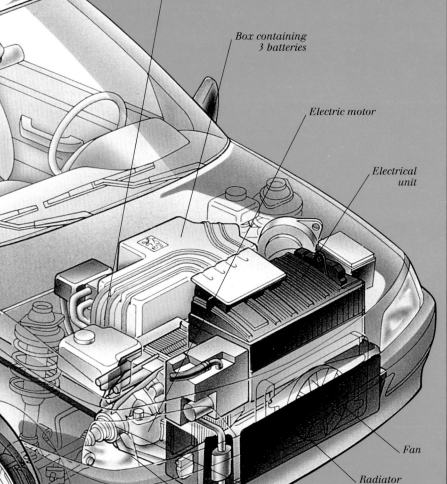

Cooling system

Box containing 3 batteries

Electric motor

Electrical unit

Fan

Radiator

Drive shaft

Batteries stored below

Wagon containing cars   *Main lighting*   *Hand-rail*

Cooling water pipes   *Drains*   *Evacuation walkway*

Record breakers

Just after dawn on 21 March 1999, after an epic flight lasting 19 days, 21 hours, and 47 minutes, a silvery balloon as tall as an 18-storey skyscraper floated down to make its landing in the Sahara. It had won the race to become the first balloon to fly around the world. Piloting Breitling Orbiter 3 were Bertrand Piccard from Switzerland and Brian Jones from England. Lifting off from the Swiss Alps, they had flown south to the Sahara to pick up the powerful jet streams they needed for their onward journey. This required a measure of luck as well as piloting skills – Piccard and Jones had to avoid no-fly zones and locate new jet streams – but fortune was with them. Precisely at 9.54 GMT on 20 March, the two fliers crossed the longitude that ran through their starting point; the next day, with their last tank of Propane – the gas that powered the balloon's burners – nearly empty, they touched down at the landing site that had been prepared for them just outside the Egyptian town of Mut.

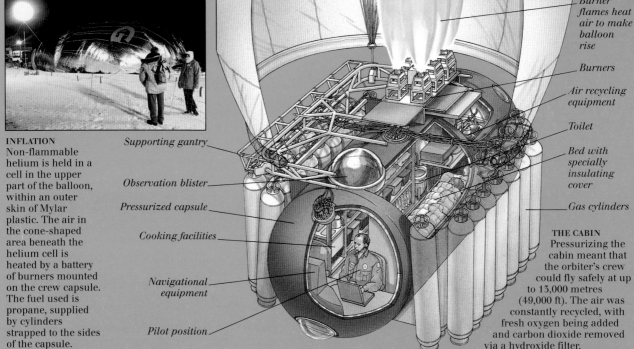

INFLATION
Non-flammable helium is held in a cell in the upper part of the balloon, within an outer skin of Mylar plastic. The air in the cone-shaped area beneath the helium cell is heated by a battery of burners mounted on the crew capsule. The fuel used is propane, supplied by cylinders strapped to the sides of the capsule.

Supporting gantry

Observation blister

Pressurized capsule

Cooking facilities

Navigational equipment

Pilot position

Burner flames heat air to make balloon rise

Burners

Air recycling equipment

Toilet

Bed with specially insulating cover

Gas cylinders

THE CABIN
Pressurizing the cabin meant that the orbiter's crew could fly safely at up to 13,000 metres (49,000 ft). The air was constantly recycled, with fresh oxygen being added and carbon dioxide removed via a hydroxide filter.

THRUST SSC

On 15 October 1997, Royal Air Force pilot Andy Green smashed the existing world land speed record in the aptly-named Thrust SSC (SuperSonic Car) on the broad expanse of the Black Rock Desert in Nevada. His average speed over the two runs was 1227.985 km/h (763 mph). The car's power came from two Rolls-Royce Spey jet engines, which developed a thrust equal to the power of 140 Formula 1 Grand Prix racers.

OVER THE ALPS
Even high over the Alps, the cabin temperature was kept at about 15° C (53° F). Power for vital instruments was provided by batteries re-charged by solar power. The crew's link to ground control was through Inmarsat satellites, while Global Positioning Satellites (GPS) helped to pinpoint their position to within metres.

UNDERSEA ADVENTURE
US oceanographer Robert Ballard holds the record for the number of explorations he has led to probe the ocean's depths. Using state-of-the-art submersibles, he discovered the wreck of the legendary liner *Titanic* (*right*). In 2000, he embarked on a quest to discover the real location of Noah's ark.

Helium balloon in upper 'tent'

Vent

Decompression valves

Helium cell

Insulating outer skin

ORBITER ESSENTIALS
The 55-metre (180-ft) high Oribiter is as tall as the Leaning Tower of Pisa when fully inflated, but, with an all-up weight of 8 tonnes, it weighs only as much as a modern jet fighter. From take off to landing during its circumnavigation, the balloon travelled a total of 45,720 km (28,415 miles) at an average cruising altitude of 7,000 metres (22,274 ft).

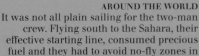

55 m
180 ft

Rip panel

Rising hot air cone

Burners

Gas cylinders

THE BALLOON
The Orbiter's design is known as a Roziere, after the first human ever to fly in a balloon. This was the Frenchman Jean Pilatre de Rozier, in 1783. It was he who first conceived the notion of combining the advantages of gas and hot-air balloons – the one offering greater buoyancy, the other greater flexibility.

TOUCH DOWN
With only four fuel tanks left out of 32, it was touch and go whether Piccard and Jones would cross the Atlantic safely. Luckily, they picked up a steady jet stream, and in the early hours of 20 March, crossed the African coast. Soon, they crossed the line of longitude that marked the official end of their circumnavigation, flying on for a few more hours to reach their final landing site.

AROUND THE WORLD
It was not all plain sailing for the two-man crew. Flying south to the Sahara, their effective starting line, consumed precious fuel and they had to avoid no-fly zones in Yemen, Egypt, and China. They sometimes lost the jet streams as well, relying on computer modelling of weather patterns at ground control in Geneva to predict where and when other jet streams might occur.

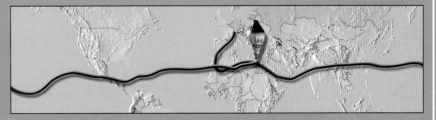

Raising Alexandria

MAP OF ALEXANDRIA HARBOUR
(ANCIENT CITY IN RED)

IN NOVEMBER 1996, the stunning revelation was made that marine archaeologists had discovered remains of the vanished royal quarter of the ancient city of Alexandria. Founded by Alexander the Great in 331BC, Alexandria was a celebrated centre of culture and learning in ancient times, as well as the scene of legendary events between Cleopatra, Mark Antony, and the Caesars. The discovery was made just 6–8 m (20–26 ft) under the Mediterranean Sea on the eastern side of modern Alexandria's harbour. A team of 16 divers made 3,500 dives over a period of four months and discovered some 9,000 blocks and pieces, including material from pavements, quays, columns, and statues. Using a satellite-based global positioning system (GPS), the team mapped out a two-acre area. Selected finds were then hoisted to the surface using air-filled balloons and cables lowered by cranes. Among the pieces raised were portions of the mighty Pharos lighthouse, once the tallest building on earth and one of the Seven Wonders of the ancient world.

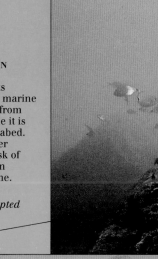

MARINE ENCRUSTATION
Underwater archaeologists often remove marine encrustation from material while it is still on the seabed. Here, the diver begins the task of uncovering an engraved stone.

Specially adapted underwater scraping tool

A huge concave mirror reflected light up to 50 km (31 miles) out to sea

Airlift hose

AIRLIFT HOSE
Among the specialist equipment used in the project was this airlift hose. Here, the sand is sucked away to unearth a magnificent sphinx statue.

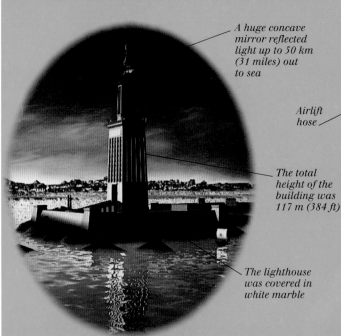

The total height of the building was 117 m (384 ft)

The lighthouse was covered in white marble

RECONSTRUCTION OF PHAROS LIGHTHOUSE
Although the lighthouse was toppled by an earthquake in the 14th century, it is possible to combine historical information with the results of the search campaign to render three-dimensional computer images of its structure.

MEASURING IN SITU
The puzzle of the sunken city was pieced together without the excavation of every find. The team precisely drew and measured material in situ, before transferring the information to computer.

The diver records the exact dimensions of the find

Scale bar

Two-tonne
sphinx

Block
inscribed with
hieroglyphics

Underwater
breathing
apparatus

Rose granite
statue head

POSITIONING THE HARNESS
Using harness equipment, the
diver prepares this statue head
for removal to the surface.

This 1.5-tonne head
completes the statue
of the Ptolemy king

THE STATUE OF THE PTOLEMY KING
The colossal bust of the Ptolemy king is
one of the great discoveries of sunken
Alexandria. The dynasty ruled Egypt
from the death of Alexander the Great
(323BC) until the death of Cleopatra (30BC).

FROM WATER TO DRY LAND
The mighty granite bust is hoisted clear
of the water and transported to the dock
using cables lowered from a crane.

SECURING THE STATUE
Even when stationary on the dock, the
priceless statue must be kept carefully
secured with sturdy ropes and cables.

EXAMINING THE STONE
Before the process of desalinization
takes place, archaeologists make an
initial examination of the stone's surface.

Rebuilding Berlin

THE WALL THAT DIVIDED EAST AND WEST BERLIN

SINCE THE BERLIN WALL'S FALL in November 1989, the capital of newly-reunified Germany has been architecturally transformed, with particular concentration on East Berlin where Communist restrictions had left large areas dilapidated. In the city centre, many of the world's great architects have been at work: outstanding buildings there include Nicholas Grimshaw's Stock Exchange, Jean Nouvell's Gallerie Lafayette store complex, Daniel Libeskind's Jewish Museum, Zaha Hadid's apartments, and, above all, Sir Norman Foster's Reichstag, with its huge glass dome.

THE BRANDENBURG TOR

Built in 1791 as a triumphal arch to celebrate Prussia's military prowess, the Brandenburg Tor saw many national celebrations up to the Second World War, including the march-past of the *Das Reich* division to celebrate its victorious return from France in 1940. Following the war, however, particularly after the building of the Wall, which left it standing in the no-man's land between west and east, the Brandenburg Tor became the symbol of a divided city. Now, Berliners again see it as a token of German unity.

THE BRANDENBURG TOR AT NIGHT

THE REICHSTAG REBORN

Sir Norman Foster's plans, which won the international competition held to find an architect for the new building, were based on his respect for Paul Wallot's original 1894 design. The focal point is the huge circular debating chamber, which sits under the building's dome.

REBUILDING THE REICHSTAG

During the years that Berlin was sliced in half by the Wall, the ruined Reichstag found itself stranded. Although physically just inside the Western sector, it was virtually isolated from the rest of the city by the River Spree, the Wall, and the vast central parkland of the Tiergarten. Once the wall came down, however, the crumbling building regained its symbolic importance, especially after Berlin's confirmation as Germany's new capital.

Reichstag

The Brandenburg Tor

Potsdamer Platz

CITY CENTRE

The Reichstag stands in the heart of Berlin, close to the Brandenburg Tor with Potsdamer Platz a little further away. The original Reichstag was the German parliament's meeting place until 1933, when the interior was destroyed in an arson attack, leaving just the shell behind.

UNDER THE DOME
The new Reichstag's 1990s refurbishment and rebuilding is truly awesome and inspired in scale. Its crowning glory, the huge glass dome, which Sir Norman Foster intended as a symbol of the open nature of German democracy, gives native Berliners and visitors to the city alike the chance to watch politicians at work. Construction started in summer 1995 and was completed in 1999.

Ventilation chimney

Angled mirrors reflect light

Seating for members of the parliament

Shiny reflective fabric

POTSDAMER PLATZ

A glittering centre for fashionable Berliners during the 1920s, Potsdamer Platz became a virtual wasteland as a result of devastating Allied bombing raids in the Second World War and the area's neglect during the decades of division that followed. Once the Berlin Wall that ran through the square finally toppled, however, Potsdamer Platz was soon well on the way to regaining much of its former glory. Working to an overall masterplan conceived by the Italian architect Renzo Piano, the area became Europe's greatest construction site. Its eye-catching, stylish buildings included imposing corporate headquarters for a string of leading multinational companies, such as Daimler-Benz and Sony. Embedded at the roots of these great towers is a sparkling new subway station delivering visitors to a vast shopping mall, which itself has proved to be a huge public attraction. The complex also houses a massive Imax cinema, 30 restaurants, a casino, and a music theatre.

SONY BUILDING
Work on the headquarters building for Sony Europe was finished in 1999. As well as 26 floors of office space, it contains entertainment centres and a multiplex cinema. Designed by architect Helmut Jahn, it is just one of the many elements that are transforming the Berlin skyline.

WRAPPING THE REICHSTAG
In June 1995, after two decades of planning and lobbying, the conceptual artists Christo and his wife Jeanne-Claude 'wrapped' the old Reichstag building in fabric. By 8 July, when the process of dismantling started, an estimated 2 million people had visited the site. The wrapping, according to the artists, got rid of the dark ghosts of the past, while the unwrapping symbolised people's hopes for a new, brighter future.

EUROPE'S BIGGEST BUILDING SITE
Construction work gets into full swing in the heart of Potsdamer Platz, as a new city quarter of 19 massive buildings starts to take shape. Planning the building programme for the area began in the early 1990s, shortly after the fall of the Berlin Wall, which, since 1961, had been a mini Iron Curtain, separating East Berlin from the west.

Kansai Airport

AERIAL VIEW OF KANSAI

OPEN FOR BUSINESS since 4 September 1994, Kansai International Airport (KIX) is one of only two artificial structures visible from space – the other is the Great Wall of China. The purpose of this project was to build Japan's first 24-hour international airport, in order to respond to the increased demand for air transport not only in Kansai but in the whole of the country. Three mountains in the southeastern part of Japan's Osaka Bay had to be levelled to provide the landmass, and transport bridges from the harbour 5 km (3 miles) away also had to be built. The cost and constructional difficulties of this ambitious undertaking were outweighed by the ideal of an isolated flight-site with future expansion possibilities and without the need for noise restrictions. Although the island is fully operational, this is only the end of Phase 1. Plans for Phase 2 include increasing the size of the island and adding a further two runways.

Each year, the runway handles 160,000 take-offs and landings

Taxiing area

Passenger boarding bridge

Check-in points

The roof comprises 90,000 stainless-steel panels – all identical in size

CROSS-SECTION OF THE TERMINAL
In the cross-section above, the aerodynamic shape of the terminal building's roof is clearly defined. Italian architect Renzo Piano developed this design to combat the local hazard – hurricanes. The central terminal uses a tiered system, which allows passengers quick and easy transfers between flights.

The island measures 1.25 x 4.37 km (³/₄ x 2³/₄ miles)

The transport bridge from the mainland has a six-lane motorway and a two-way railway

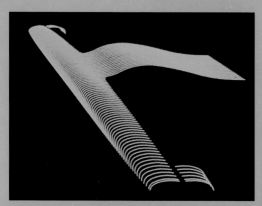

AIR CIRCULATION
This computer-rendered image illustrates the gentle, aerodynamic curve of the building's roof. This design is echoed on the ceiling inside the building, allowing the fresh air, introduced through vents, to move around freely.

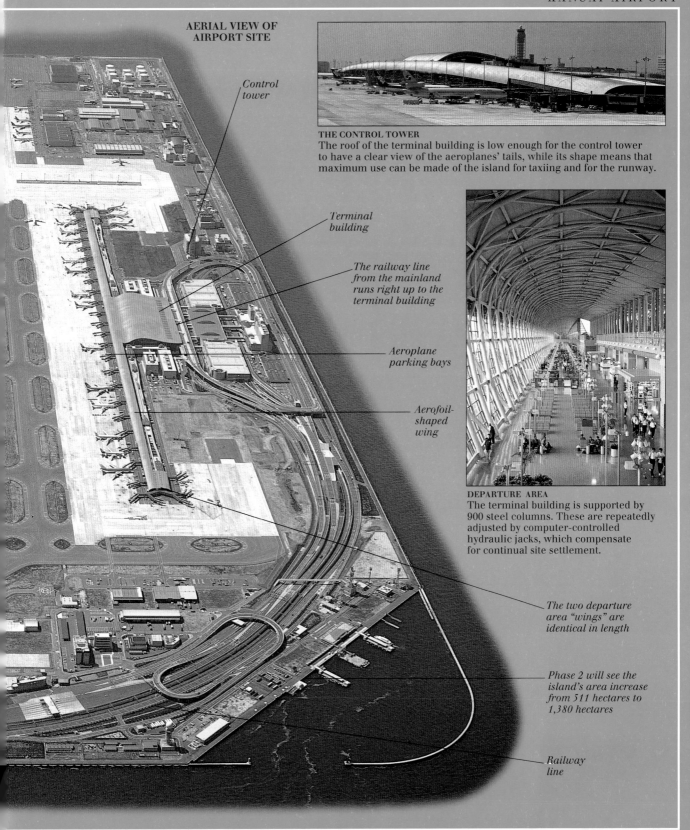

AERIAL VIEW OF
AIRPORT SITE

Control
tower

THE CONTROL TOWER
The roof of the terminal building is low enough for the control tower
to have a clear view of the aeroplanes' tails, while its shape means that
maximum use can be made of the island for taxiing and for the runway.

Terminal
building

The railway line
from the mainland
runs right up to the
terminal building

Aeroplane
parking bays

Aerofoil-
shaped
wing

DEPARTURE AREA
The terminal building is supported by
900 steel columns. These are repeatedly
adjusted by computer-controlled
hydraulic jacks, which compensate
for continual site settlement.

The two departure
area "wings" are
identical in length

Phase 2 will see the
island's area increase
from 511 hectares to
1,380 hectares

Railway
line

Pont de Normandie

THE PONT DE NORMANDIE, which spans the estuary of the River Seine, was officially opened in January 1995. Built using state-of-the-art engineering, this stunning cable-stayed bridge is the longest of its kind in the world. Its central span, measuring 856 m (2,808 ft), crosses the estuary at 52 m (170.6 ft) above water level to enable shipping traffic to pass beneath it. The team of engineers, led by Michel Virlogeux of the French road administration, SETRA, designed every aspect of the bridge to withstand fierce coastal winds, which can reach 180 km/h (112 mph). Carrying an average of 6,000 vehicles a day, the bridge cuts 50 km (31 miles) from the journey between Le Havre and Honfleur, and forms part of "The Road of the Estuaries" motorway project, designed to link Belgium with Spain.

THE FOUNDATION

At the foundation of each tower are 28 piles, bored to a depth of between 50–60 m (164–197 ft). Layers of clay and large boulders caused major problems during construction.

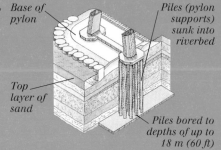

Base of pylon

Top layer of sand

Piles (pylon supports) sunk into riverbed

Piles bored to depths of up to 18 m (60 ft)

CABLE-STAYED BRIDGE DESIGN

The deck of cable-stayed bridges is supported by straight cables attached to both sides of one or more towers (pylons). The side spans may have additional suport from piers. One of the reasons why this design was chosen is because the marshy banks of the Seine estuary could not support the huge anchorage needed for a suspension bridge.

Inverted 'Y' shape of pylons increases structural capacity to reduce wind forces

23 pairs of cables attached to either side of each pylon

Cables anchored to pylon crest

Artificial island created to support northern shore pylon

4 lanes of traffic

Piers support side spans

DESIGN OF THE VEHICLE DECK

The deck is aerodynamic in design, tapering at either edge. It is made of reinforced concrete, covering the outer sectional steel box-girders of the central span. This stream-lined design reduced the weight and increased the stability of the Pont de Normandie, enabling it to exceed other cable-stayed bridges by 40 per cent.

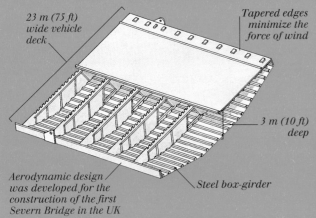

23 m (75 ft) wide vehicle deck

Tapered edges minimize the force of wind

3 m (10 ft) deep

Aerodynamic design was developed for the construction of the first Severn Bridge in the UK

Steel box-girder

BASIC PRINCIPLES OF BRIDGE ENGINEERING

BEAM (OR GIRDER) BRIDGE
The most basic bridge type has compression (pushing together) and tension (pulling apart) balanced within a single rigid beam, or girder, supported at each end.

ARCH BRIDGE
As heavy loads put all the material of an arch into compression, the forces have to be channelled downwards and outwards into the supporting abutments.

CANTILEVER BRIDGE
This develops the principle of the beam bridge by using balanced supports that extend and rise from both sides of the piers, attached to the central span.

SUSPENSION BRIDGE
This type of bridge principally exploits tension. The deck is hung from hanger cables or chains that are draped over the towers and anchored at each end.

BRIDGE DIMENSIONS

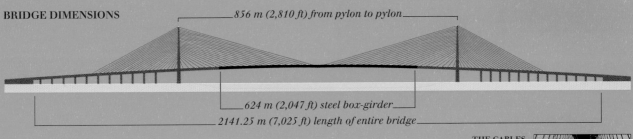

856 m (2,810 ft) from pylon to pylon

624 m (2,047 ft) steel box-girder

2141.25 m (7,025 ft) length of entire bridge

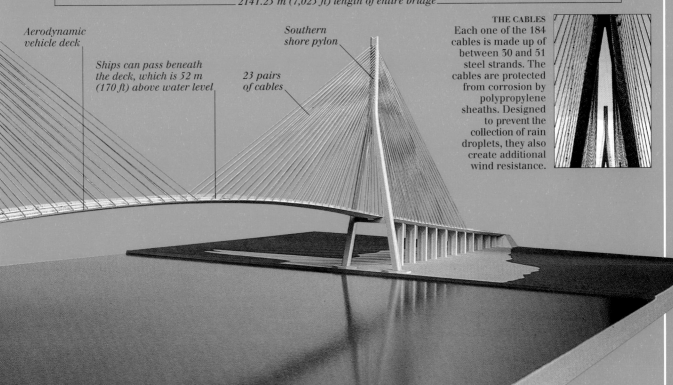

Aerodynamic vehicle deck

Ships can pass beneath the deck, which is 52 m (170 ft) above water level

Southern shore pylon

23 pairs of cables

THE CABLES
Each one of the 184 cables is made up of between 30 and 51 steel strands. The cables are protected from corrosion by polypropylene sheaths. Designed to prevent the collection of rain droplets, they also create additional wind resistance.

Guggenheim, Bilbao

AT THE BEGINNING OF the 20th century, modern architects hailed the coming of a new "age of the machine" when buildings would become as innovative as the most technically advanced cars, ships, and planes. As we enter the new millennium, computer technology, rather than engineering, is having the most impact on the form of buildings and the way that they are used. The fantastic curves and fractured planes of Frank Gehry's Guggenheim Museum in Bilbao, Spain (1997) would have been impossible to realize without the aid of computers in the design and construction processes. Technology has allowed the architect to realize what is, effectively, an enormous sculpture. Like an artist, Gehry made models out of sheets of paper and tape, which were then translated on screen into working drawings for the building's construction. Not all futuristic architectural designs have a sculptural look. Sir Norman Foster's proposal for the Millennium Tower in Tokyo, Japan (1989) brings together all the features of a city in one megastructure that was to be the highest in the world.

MILLENNIUM TOWER
In contrast to the sculptural curves of the Guggenheim, the complex structure of Sir Norman Foster's proposal for the Millennium Tower resembles a rocket.

"Sky centres" were to house public areas

GUGGENHEIM MUSEUM
Los Angeles architect Frank Gehry is well known for his striking and inventive creations. For Bilbao, he has designed a truly iconic building that now represents the city on postcards and in photographs around the world. The decision to locate the Guggenheim Foundation's modern art collection in Bilbao was part of a conscious attempt by the authorities to revitalize the city.

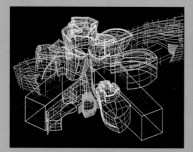

GUGGENHEIM ANIMATED MODEL
Gehry's office used a computer program called CATIA to construct on-screen models that could be worked on in an animated form.

COMPUTER RENDERING
Geometric mathematical formulae were used to define each of the building's surfaces and elements.

MONUMENTAL FISH SCULPTURE

The monumental fish sculpture was designed by Gehry's practice for a hotel in Barcelona, Spain. It was the first structure the office completed using the CATIA program, a specialized computer application developed by the French aeronautical industry. Like the Guggenheim Museum, the fish sculpture was developed directly on screen from a model. It also has a curvilinear surface with metal cladding. The CATIA computer model was the principal reference for its development, and there was little need for traditional architectural or technical drawings. The program enabled the 55 m- (180 ft-) long and 35 m- (115 ft-) high sculpture to be designed and built in just over eight months.

Curvilinear surface

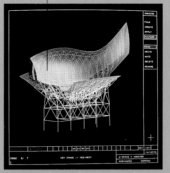

CATIA COMPUTER MODEL

Exposed structure   *Metal cladding*

WATERFRONT MONUMENT
For many years, Frank Gehry has explored movement in architecture, often using fish-like shapes. Located on the waterfront, this sculpture may also be a reference to Barcelona as a port city.

The structure crowning the museum resembles an artichoke heart

The titanium sheets were milled on site

A slight pillow effect softens the appearance of the building

INTERIOR VESTIBULE
The large central atrium connects the main entrance with three floors of galleries via a system of curvilinear bridges, glass elevators, and stair towers. A soaring space over 50 m (164 ft) high, it has a sculptural roof with forms that have been likened to the billowing shapes of Marilyn Monroe's skirt.

Olympics 2000

TO PROVIDE A FITTINGLY MODERN setting for the XXVII Olympiad – the first Olympic Games of the new millennium – Sydney created a feast of inspired architecture in a lavish building programme that took the city firmly into the 21st century. More than a dozen dazzling new stadiums and sporting venues formed the core of Australia's largest-ever urban renewal project, which, by the time it was completed, had rescued Homebush Bay and the area around it from near dereliction. The catalyst for the development was the city's successful 1993 bid to host the Olympics and the identification of Homebush Bay as the ideal setting for many of the events. It was within easy reach of the city centre, had good water as well as road access, and was large enough to accommodate all the varied facilities that a successful modern Olympic staging demands. It also gave Australians the opportunity to develop world-class expertise in the reclamation of decaying industrial sites in an ambitious drive to stage what were claimed to be the first 'green' Olympic Games.

Main Arena (Baseball)
Sydney Showground
Sydney International Aquatic Centre
Sydney International Athletic Centre
Sydney SuperDome
Stadium Australia

KEEPING IT GREEN
Stadium Australia was designed by Bligh Lobb Sports Architecture to conform to the Sydney Olympics brief of being as ecologically sensitive as possible. All the building materials were selected for their green qualities. Much use was made of natural light, while all back-up lighting conformed to energy-efficient green standards.

STADIUM AUSTRALIA
Designed to accommodate 110,000 spectators, Stadium Australia is the largest outdoor venue in Olympic history. It is distinguished by its pair of lightweight flanking 'wings' arching up over the long sides of the auditorium. Suspended from these, the roof is covered in translucent polycarbonate to shield spectators from the harsh sun, while still allowing natural light to filter through into the stadium below.

FROM WEST AND EAST

Two new sports - Triathlon and Taekwondo - made their official Olympic debuts at Sydney 2000. Triathlon is an exciting multi-sport, involving swimming, cycling and running; it is a continuous race against the clock and fellow competitor. The origins of the sport date back to around 1973 in southern California, when a group of runners, swimmers and cyclists began to train together. Taekwondo, a martial art from Korea, can trace its origins back more than 2000 years. It is one of the world's fastest-growing participation sports.

TRIATHLON

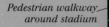

TAEKWONDO

Floodlight tower
Permanent grandstand
Temporary open Olympic grandstand
Supporting wing
Bars, restaurants, and other facilities
Access to enclosed concourses for each seating tier
Pedestrian walkway around stadium

DUNC GRAY VELODROME
Another simple, but stunning, design was produced to house the Olympic cycling events, which took place in the west Sydney suburb of Bankstown. The metal roof of the velodrome has glazed central skylights equipped with light-control slats to allow in optimum natural light, while stormwater from the roof is fed into a pond alongside. Inside, surrounding the Baltic pine banked cycling track, is permanent seating for 6,000 spectators. The stadium is named after the famous cyclist who won the country's first gold medal in cycling at the Los Angeles Olympics of 1932.

INSIDE THE STADIUM
One of the features of the design of Stadium Australia is the ability to alter the seating configuration easily to suit specific requirements. Following the Olympics, the removal of the open grandstands cut the seating capacity to 80,000.

Translucent roof reducing glare and shadow

Lower seating bowl

Temporary open Olympic grandstand

Roof-mounted solar cells generate power

ARCHERY CENTRE
Although one of the smallest stadiums at the 2000 Olympics, the Archery Centre in Homebush Bay is one of the most delightful. A simple rectangular building was offset by a large 'fly roof' – a tilted wing held at an angle on inclined column supports. The beautiful sweep of the roof is a modern interpretation of Australian vernacular shelters and provided welcome shade for the building and spectators. The centre was designed by architecture practice Stutchbury & Pape.

OLYMPIC VILLAGE
Sydney's Olympic Village is the first urban community in the world to be totally solar-powered. Its roof-mounted solar cells have the capacity to generate more than 1 million kilowatt hours of electric power a year. With accommodation for 15,300 athletes and officials, this is the first time that all the participants in the Olympics have been housed on one site.

Global telecommunications

CONSTELLATIONS OF LOW-ORBITING satellites hold the key to today's flexible global telephone networks. These systems integrate satellite communications with existing land-line and cellular networks to provide truly global coverage from a mobile phone. This enables people in remote areas, even those on tiny Pacific islands or high in the Himalayas, to keep in touch with the rest of the world. Satellite systems are the next logical step in the mobile-phone revolution that swept the world in the late 1990s. Iridium® was the first system to offer a commercial service. It was conceived and developed by the US electronics company Motorola, and began operation on 1 November 1998. The system was named after the 77th chemical element in the Periodic Table, as there were originally to be 77 satellites in the network. Other networks offering a similar service include Globalstar, which operates with a constellation of 48 satellites.

Communication aerial receieves and transmits signals

IRIDIUM HANDSET

Early satellite phones required briefcase-sized units to receive and process signals from communication satellites. The Iridium handset has similar features to a conventional mobile phone but is slightly larger in size. It is also more expensive to purchase and operate but, unlike an ordinary mobile phone, can be used in any location on Earth.

by KYOCERA

IRIDIUM

MEMO C→

1 2ABC 3DEF
4GHI 5JKL 6MNO
7PQRS 8TUV 9WXYZ
*< 0+ #>

LCD display panel

Lightweight main body

Processing unit

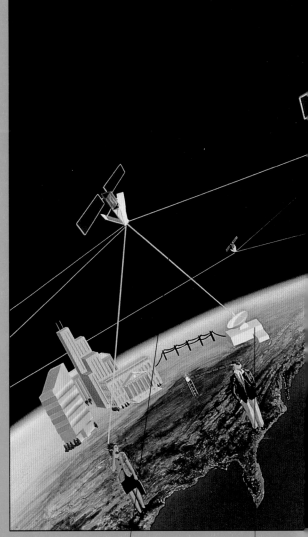

Satellite sends signal to ground-based gateway

Gateway connects with land-line system

IRIDIUM SATELLITE ORBITAL NETWORK

The Iridium network consists of 66 satellites, each providing a coverage of 16 million square km (6 million square miles). It offers a constant service, as there will always be one or more satellites over the horizon. The network operates as a constellation, which means that a failed or malfunctioning satellite will not impede the system's ability to provide global coverage. When a call is made it is routed to the nearest satellite, and then relayed around the world to its destination. If the destination is a land-based telephone, the last satellite in the chain feeds the signal to a "gateway" ground station. This gateway then connects with the existing land-line telephone system.

Connection is achieved in remote location

Message is relayed between satellites

Call is routed to nearest satellite

MICROWAVE RELAY TOWER
The Iridium communications system can route calls through an ordinary mobile telephone network, if available, and also interconnect with conventional telephone networks. Land links, such as this microwave relay tower, are often needed to route calls to their final destination.

ENVIRONMENTAL CONCERNS

Mobile phones operate using radio signals. They have a transmitter that sends a signal to an aerial, which is part of a nationwide communications network. These radios work at low power, so mobile phone users need to be within a few kilometres of an aerial for their signal to be received. The mobile-phone revolution of the late 1990s has resulted in hundreds of millions of users worldwide, and thousands of aerials have been built, both in town and country, to receive the ever-increasing number of signals. In environmentally sensitive areas, unsightly aerial masts are sometimes disguised as trees (right) or flagpoles. They have also been sited on buildings and church towers, and then camouflaged.

Satellites pass over the Poles

Satellite orbits the Earth

ORBITAL PLANES
The 66 satellites of the Iridium network circle the Earth in six different orbital planes. They pass over the North and South Poles at a height of 780 km (485 miles), circling the Earth once every 100 minutes.

APS and Digital Photography

THE ADVANCED PHOTO SYSTEM was announced in 1995 as a breakthrough in photographic technology. Developed over five years by a consortium of film and camera manufacturers (Kodak, Nikon, Fuji, Canon, Minolta), the APS was designed to maximize the quality of images taken by amateur photographers, and to overcome some of the most common problems encountered. The key to this new system is the "smart" film with its drop-in and automatic-load cassette. The film contains a magnetic strip, which records information specific to each shot, such as lighting conditions, magnification, date and time, and communicates this data to the processing equipment in the minilab. Once processed, the photographer receives a set of index prints, the photographs in any one of three different print sizes, and the developed film stored within the original cassette. APS film can be directly scanned and digitized, allowing the new system to bridge the gap between conventional 35mm film and digital photography.

PRINT FORMATS

A great advantage of APS is the variety it allows in the format of the print. When taking a picture there are three different formats which can be selected: C (Classic) gives a normal 35mm print, H (HDTV) is for a wider view and P (Panorama) provides the extra-wide landscape shot.

H and P

C

P

H and C

PRINT FORMATS

INFORMATION EXCHANGE ("IX")

Information about each frame – such as lighting conditions, selected print format, and exposure speed – is recorded on magnetic data strips. In a process called "information exchange" this data is read by processing equipment, which adjusts itself to produce the best results for each individual picture.

IX DATA TRACKS

Photofinishing magnetic data

Manufacturer's optical leader data

Camera optical data

Camera magnetic data

Manufacturer's optical frame data

APS FILM AND CARTRIDGE

To avoid misfeeding, the cassette loads, advances, and retracts the film automatically, and is also used to store processed film. A data disc tells the camera the film speed, type, and exposure length.

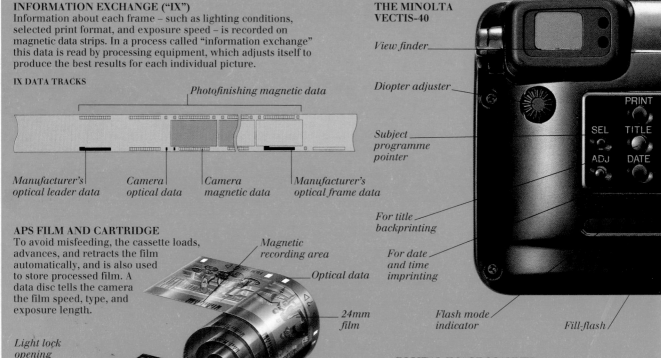

Magnetic recording area

Optical data

24mm film

Light lock opening mechanism

Data disc located at this side of cassette

○ *Unexposed*

◐ *Partially exposed*

✚ *Fully exposed but unprocessed*

□ *Processed*

Cassette spool

Film status indicator

FUJICOLOR A200
FUJIFILM

THE MINOLTA VECTIS-40

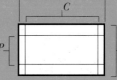

View finder

Diopter adjuster

Subject programme pointer

PRINT
SEL TITLE
ADJ DATE

For title backprinting

For date and time imprinting

Flash mode indicator

Fill-flash

DIGITAL IMAGE SCANNER

The digital image scanner allows users to input developed APS film cartridges into their personal computer. The Index view instantly displays thumbnail versions of all the images stored on the roll.

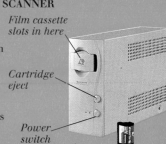

Film cassette slots in here

Cartridge eject

Power switch

INFORMATIVE DATA AND INDEX PRINTS

IX allows a variety of information to be imprinted on the back of each photo. Not only is the date and time given, but a title for each shot can be chosen. At-a-glance index prints are also provided showing the C, H, or P format of each frame plus the print number.

INDEX PRINT

Individual index print

Frame type

Frame number

Barcode

Frame number

Subject programme selection

Date/time

Cartridge ID

Automatic flash

LCD panel

Frame counter

Drop-in loading and film chamber

Film chamber door below

Self-timer

Close-ups

Film cartridge loaded

DIGITAL IMAGE WORKSTATION

Photographs are digitized and placed on templates for printing out on a colour printer. The workstation can also store the images on floppy discs or send them on-line to other locations.

Monitor

Floppy disc drive

2 Gigabyte hard disc drive

Cartridge slots in here

100 Megabyte zip™ disc drive

DIGITAL CAMERA

NO FILM OR PROCESSING REQUIRED

KODAK DC50

Filmless digital cameras are a technological advancement in the professional photography world. Within minutes a picture can be taken and transmitted anywhere in the world, either via telephone or E-mail. Digital cameras are also ideal for desktop publishing, business presentations and a variety of scientific or industrial applications.

CANON EOS-1 WITH KODAK DCS 5C

Accessory shoe for flash

Shutter release button

Lens release button

Zoom lens

PCM-CIA card slots in back

TRANSMITTING LIGHT INTO DIGITAL DATA

Electronic sensors inside the camera transmit the different levels of light, which enter through the red, green, and blue filters (seen in this order below), onto a CCD (photo-sensitive semiconductor). The CCD digitally records the image and stores it onto a PCM-CIA card – a tiny hard disc drive.

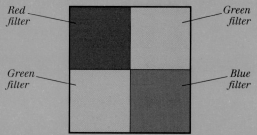

Red filter

Green filter

Green filter

Blue filter

FROM DATA TO ON-SCREEN IMAGE

Digital cameras can be plugged into a computer's serial port and the pictures can be instantly transferred from the camera's hard disc into popular applications such as Word Perfect and Pagemaker.

Interactive television

THE FUTURE OF TELEVISION is undoubtedly digital. Television or video signals can be converted from their normal analogue form (continuously varying) into a digital form, which consists of a series of definite pulses rather like Morse code. Digital signals can be transmitted, compressed, and manipulated by computers without any unwanted "noise" affecting the data. One of the advantages of digital technology is that video data can be manipulated to make interactive television possible. Interactive "video-on-demand" (VOD) services allow users to watch the material of their choice from a large central video vault. A digital server enables many users to watch the same film, starting at different times, by sending the video data in small "packets" to them. Other services include news programmes, games, music, and electronic shopping. With the latter, the user "strolls" through a virtual shop and uses a credit card to buy items, which are then delivered to the home within days.

VIDEO-ON-DEMAND

Allowing viewers to choose a film or television programme from a vast selection whenever desired, video-on-demand comes complete with all the flexibility of a video recorder (including fast-forward, rewind, and pause facilities). A typical VOD system consists of video vaults containing compressed digital video data, a sophisticated digital server that sends the requested material to the correct destination, and decoder and remote control units in the home.

REMOTE CONTROL
As well as offering the standard features, the remote control enables the user to operate the VOD, play games, and buy goods from home-shopping services.

The Fin button returns the viewer to normal cable television service

Video-on-demand button

Select button

Remote controls for interactive television are simple and user-friendly in format

Direction buttons for navigating on-screen menus

These keys allow quick selection of colour-coded, on-screen choices

SET-TOP BOX
The set-top box sends the user's choices to the digital server and decodes video data entering the home system. Depending on the system used, the digital video data from the server is converted to an analogue signal for the television either by a junction box outside the home or by the set-top box.

On-screen menus

Many new set-top boxes have considerable computing power

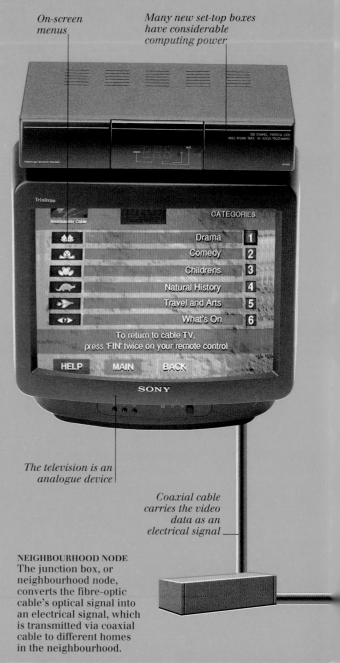

The television is an analogue device

Coaxial cable carries the video data as an electrical signal

NEIGHBOURHOOD NODE
The junction box, or neighbourhood node, converts the fibre-optic cable's optical signal into an electrical signal, which is transmitted via coaxial cable to different homes in the neighbourhood.

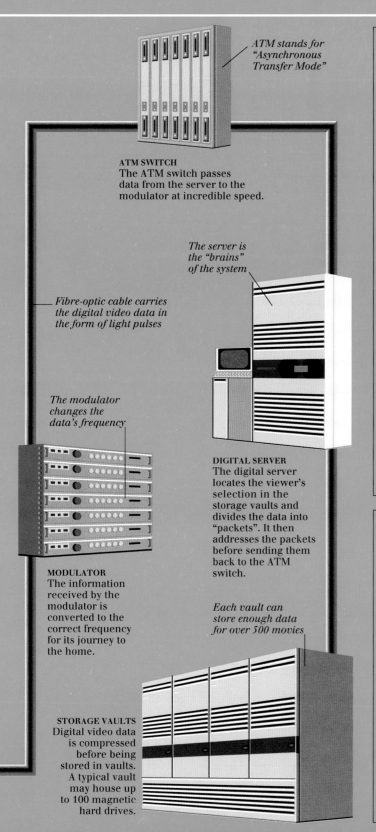

ATM stands for "Asynchronous Transfer Mode"

ATM SWITCH
The ATM switch passes data from the server to the modulator at incredible speed.

The server is the "brains" of the system

Fibre-optic cable carries the digital video data in the form of light pulses

The modulator changes the data's frequency

DIGITAL SERVER
The digital server locates the viewer's selection in the storage vaults and divides the data into "packets". It then addresses the packets before sending them back to the ATM switch.

MODULATOR
The information received by the modulator is converted to the correct frequency for its journey to the home.

Each vault can store enough data for over 500 movies

STORAGE VAULTS
Digital video data is compressed before being stored in vaults. A typical vault may house up to 100 magnetic hard drives.

DIGITAL VIDEO DISC

The video format set to replace tapes and laserdiscs in the home looks exactly like an audio compact disc (CD) – a silver platter 12 cm (4¾ in) in diameter. (To avoid a repetition of the 1980s' VHS/Beta video-cassette war, electronics companies involved have agreed on one format.) However, the digital video disc can hold up to 9 hours of data on its 2 sides, with each side containing 133 minutes of programme time. This is compared with the 74 minutes held by a CD. In addition, DVD's interactivity means that certain programmes can be viewed from a variety of camera angles.

COMPACT DISC

DIGITAL VIDEO DISC

CD "tracks"

DVD tracks are packed more tightly

CD CROSS-SECTION

DVD CROSS-SECTION

CD has one layer of data

DVD has two layers of data on each side

CINEMA BY COMPUTER

Disney Productions' *Toy Story* (1995) was the world's first feature film to be generated entirely on computer. A team of 27 animators worked on the film, producing an average of 3½ minutes of footage per week. Some of the characters and scenes were created solely on computer, whereas others were set up with models and props before being scanned into the computer for digitization.

BUZZ LIGHTYEAR AND WOODY IN *TOY STORY*

Measuring time

ALL TIMEKEEPING DEVICES depend on counting a regularly-repeated phenomenon. The earliest timekeeping devices were based on daily, monthly, or yearly cycles of the sun or moon. Most modern clocks are based on repeated mechanical or electronic oscillations (vibrations). The more frequent the vibrations, the greater the potential accuracy of the clock. The crystal in a quartz watch typically vibrates at 32,768 hertz (32,768 times a second), so it keeps better time than a pendulum clock, whose pendulum typically swings twice a second. The most accurate timekeeping devices are atomic fountains, which are based on oscillations of caesium atoms. Global communication technologies, such as computer networks and broadcasting, rely on the world using one accurate time standard. This is called UCT (Universal Coordinated Time), and is based on the average time signal received from over 200 atomic clocks worldwide. The more we rely on high technology for precise timekeeping, the more vulnerable we become to problems with that technology, for example the bug that threatens to strike at the beginning of the new millennium.

Microwave cavity

E

Trapping coils help keep the ball of atoms together

C

Mechanism advances the hands

Pendulum swings back and forth

PENDULUM CLOCK
In the 16th century, the Italian scientist Galileo Galilei used the regular swing of a pendulum to measure periods of time. He suggested that a pendulum could be connected to the hands of a clock to turn them in regular steps.

THE ATOMIC FOUNTAIN
At present, the most accurate time-keeping device is the atomic fountain. It was developed by Nobel prize-winning scientists in the early 1990s and is far more accurate than a standard atomic clock, such as NIST-7 (see below, left). The atomic fountain enables us to measure time with greater accuracy, mainly because it uses cooler, slower-moving atoms than an atomic clock. Atomic fountain devices are accurate to within one ten-billionth of a second per day.

Goggles protect eyes from radiation

Laser components held in place by an optical bench

Detector laser source

Detector laser

NIST-7 ATOMIC CLOCK
This laser forms part of an early-1990s atomic clock, developed by the US National Institute of Standards and Technology. At that time, the clock was the most accurate timekeeping device in the world, precise to within one billionth of a second per day (one second in three million years). Above, a scientist observes the laser as it "excites" caesium atoms. The atoms oscillate between two energy states, and the clock counts the oscillations.

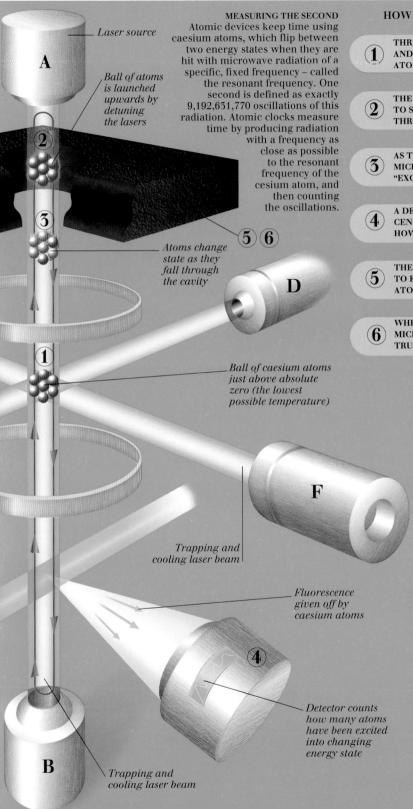

Laser source

A

Ball of atoms
is launched
upwards by
detuning
the lasers

②

③

Atoms change
state as they
fall through
the cavity

⑤ ⑥

D

①

Ball of caesium atoms
just above absolute
zero (the lowest
possible temperature)

Trapping and
cooling laser beam

F

Fluorescence
given off by
caesium atoms

④

B

Trapping and
cooling laser beam

Detector counts
how many atoms
have been excited
into changing
energy state

MEASURING THE SECOND
Atomic devices keep time using
caesium atoms, which flip between
two energy states when they are
hit with microwave radiation of a
specific, fixed frequency – called
the resonant frequency. One
second is defined as exactly
9,192,631,770 oscillations of this
radiation. Atomic clocks measure
time by producing radiation
with a frequency as
close as possible
to the resonant
frequency of the
cesium atom, and
then counting
the oscillations.

HOW THE ATOMIC FOUNTAIN WORKS

① THREE PAIRS OF LASER BEAMS (AB, CD, EF) TRAP AND COOL A BALL OF SEVERAL MILLION CAESIUM ATOMS, ALL IN ONE OF TWO ENERGY STATES

② THE LASERS ARE DETUNED SLIGHTLY TO SLOWLY LAUNCH THE BALL UPWARDS THROUGH A FIELD OF MICROWAVE RADIATION

③ AS THE ATOMS FALL THROUGH THE MICROWAVE CAVITY, MANY OF THEM ARE "EXCITED" AND CHANGE ENERGY STATE

④ A DETECTOR UNIT MEASURES THE FLUORESCENCE OF THE ATOMS AND CALCULATES HOW MANY HAVE CHANGED STATE

⑤ THE MICROWAVE FREQUENCY IS FINE-TUNED TO EXCITE A GREATER PROPORTION OF THE ATOMS TO CHANGE ENERGY STATE

⑥ WHEN THIS PROPORTION IS GREATEST, THE MICROWAVE FREQUENCY IS CLOSEST TO THE TRUE RESONANT FREQUENCY OF THE ATOM

THE MILLENNIUM BUG

The millennium or Y2K (Year 2000) bug
was a threat to computer systems that store
dates using just two digits. Thus, the year
after 1999 would be represented as 00, which
could be interpreted as 99 years earlier
rather than one year later. Systems that store
dates in this way were considered in danger
of crashing on 1 January 2000. Although
it was thought that the millennium bug could
affect personal computers, the greatest threat
it posed was to embedded systems – custom-
built computers that are used in vital service
industries such as banking, utilities,
transport, telecommunications, and air traffic
control. Severe problems were predicted if
equipment that could be affected by the bug
was not modified. The efforts made to tackle
the problem proved successful and 1 January
2000 passed without incident.

AIR TRAFFIC CONTROL ROOM

Network computers

THE INTERNET LINKS MILLIONS of computers worldwide, and anybody with a personal computer (PC) and basic communication tools can become a part of it. The ever-expanding "Net" is becoming a vital resource for business, education, and entertainment. The huge multimedia database of the World Wide Web, which is one aspect of the Net, is so sophisticated that users can "meet" in "virtual worlds". As the Net evolves, so new ways of computing are made possible. Network computing is one possible development which promises greater compatibility and efficiency than personal computing. At present, the Net consists mainly of PCs with large amounts of processing power and disk space (called "fat client computers") connected to servers (other computers that distribute data). The idea behind network computing is to replace the PC, or fat client, with a network computer (NC), or "thin client". A thin client computer has a processor, like a PC, but less memory and no disk storage, and so is much cheaper. Instead of storing application programs and data on a local hard disk (as a PC does), an NC simply downloads programs and data from a server into its RAM as needed. Network computing promises economies of scale and centralization, since all the data is stored on a few servers, and any software developments that need to be made apply to these servers only.

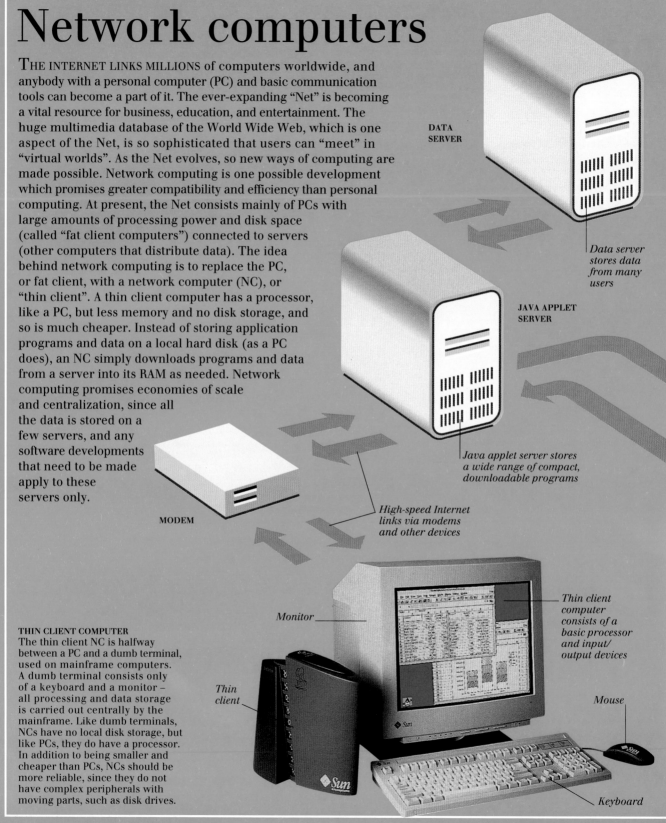

DATA SERVER

Data server stores data from many users

JAVA APPLET SERVER

Java applet server stores a wide range of compact, downloadable programs

MODEM

High-speed Internet links via modems and other devices

Monitor

Thin client computer consists of a basic processor and input/output devices

Thin client

Mouse

Keyboard

THIN CLIENT COMPUTER
The thin client NC is halfway between a PC and a dumb terminal, used on mainframe computers. A dumb terminal consists only of a keyboard and a monitor – all processing and data storage is carried out centrally by the mainframe. Like dumb terminals, NCs have no local disk storage, but like PCs, they do have a processor. In addition to being smaller and cheaper than PCs, NCs should be more reliable, since they do not have complex peripherals with moving parts, such as disk drives.

Monitor

Applet
developers
write software
for the servers

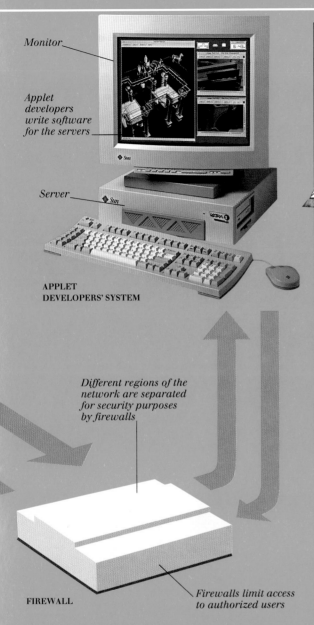

Server

**APPLET
DEVELOPERS' SYSTEM**

Different regions of the
network are separated
for security purposes
by firewalls

FIREWALL

Firewalls limit access
to authorized users

DISTRIBUTED COMPUTING

Network computing has been made possible because
the computer industry has agreed hardware and software
standards, including a new language, Java. When a thin
client – or a fat client acting as a Java station – is switched
on, its basic boot-up software connects to a network and
downloads the full Java operating system. The user can
then download Java application programs (called applets)
and data required, paying any fee with a smart card.
High-speed links between client and server mean that
processing tasks can be distributed between computers,
so the applets can be relatively small. In network
computing, the main burden falls not on the client
machines but on the network. Whether the present
Internet infrastructure (phone lines, cables, etc.) has
the required capacity, speed, and reliability to support
network computing remains to be seen.

VIRTUAL WORLDS ON THE NET

The World Wide Web has brought multimedia –
graphics, animations, sound, and hyperlinking – to
the Internet. The Virtual World Wide Web (VWWW),
with virtual environments, is a further development
where users can interact graphically with each other.
Typical VWWW environments are spread across
sites on the Net and on a CD-ROM. The basic
program runs from the CD, but "interactions"
between users occur at VWWW sites.

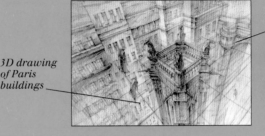

VIRTUAL PARIS

3D ENVIRONMENTS
All three-dimensional virtual worlds
must first be rendered in ink, as shown
below, after which the illustrations are
digitized by a computer.

3D drawing
of Paris
buildings

The CD-
ROM is
based on
a series of
detailed
sketches

CITIZENS OF A VIRTUAL WORLD
When a user logs on to a virtual world, he or she chooses a graphical
identity; this is how they will appear on other users' screens around
the world. These virtual people stroll around and meet in virtual
streets – although the real users might be thousands of miles apart.

Style and
measure-
ment
categories

Users can
choose their
appearance
and their
personality

REAL SERVICES IN A VIRTUAL SOCIETY
Some features of a virtual world are purely fictional, like a user's
graphical identity, while the streets or environment may be based
on a real place. But, as in the real Paris, you can "walk" into a store,
shop using your real credit card, and have the real goods delivered.

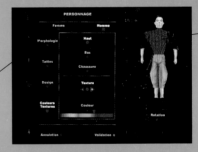

Virtual
transport
takes the
user to
other
worlds

Home
shopping
services are
located
around the
virtual city

World Wide Web

SINCE 1993, THE WORLD WIDE WEB (WWW) has become one of the fastest growing communication systems in history. Consisting of an expanding pool of "pages" created by companies, associations, and individuals, it is accessible to anyone connected to the Internet. Two features of the Web make it appealing. The first is the non-linear method of presenting information known as "hypertext". This enables users to jump between documents of subject-related material at the click of the mouse. The second is the multimedia format of Web pages, which can be designed using sophisticated graphics, sound, and animation, and displayed on-screen by a program called a "graphical browser". Since the development of the browser, the Web has become more sophisticated and easier to use and interest in the WWW has exploded.

THE INTERNET AND THE WEB

Tim Berners-Lee, the physics researcher who first conceived the Web in 1989, compared the Internet and the Web to the difference between the brain and the mind; where the Internet is the physical method of communication and the Web is the information itself.

1. Web page broken down into packets of binary data for transmission

5. Web page is downloaded onto user's screen

4. Packets of binary data are translated into a readable message

3. Analog audio signal received and converted into binary data via modem

Web site

Original Web page

2. Data is sent to destination via the Internet

WEB SITES

A web site is a collection of linked documents stored on a single computer, anywhere in the world. Sites can be linked up to each other using "hyperlinks".

NAVIGATING THE WEB

WELCOME PAGE

There are millions of pages available on the Web and graphical browsers, such as Netscape Navigator, provide a window in the computer screen on which these pages are displayed in fine detail. Keyword searches can be performed using a facility called a "search engine"; particular topics can be explored using directories called "subject trees"; and specific pages can be accessed by typing the exact address, or URL (Universal Resource Locator). Other browser tools include "history lists", "hot lists", and "bookmarks".

UNIVERSAL RESOURCE LOCATOR (URL)

Prefix "http://" (hypertext transfer protocol) indicates a Web site or page is being accessed

Locates particular folder and file

http:// | www.astro.uva.nl | / | michielb/sun | / | kaft.htm.

Commands browser to look for Web pages stored at this computer

Indicates name of document to be retrieved

CHOICE AND VARIETY ON THE INTERNET

CHILDREN'S WEB SITES
From finding a pen-pal to linking up to educational resources, the Web provides information, education, and enjoyment for children.

COMMERCE ON THE WEB
Placing sites on the World Wide Web is becoming an increasingly popular marketing strategy for many companies around the world.

MUSIC PAGES
Musicians are able to present themselves and their music to the public, and fans can find more information on their favourite bands.

NEWS AND INFORMATION
Many newspapers and magazines now have regularly updated on-line editions, such as the UK's Daily Telegraph.

HYPERTEXT AND HYPERMEDIA

Using a format called hypertext or hypermedia, Web documents contain links to other pages of text, pictures, sound recordings, or videos, which can be activated by clicking on highlighted or underlined text and picture icons, known as "hyper links" or "hot spots". These links are created by the programming language HTML (HyperText Mark-up Language), which also defines how the text and graphics will appear on the page.

URL or Web page address

Netscape browser menu contains navigation buttons

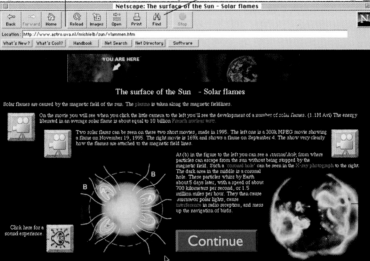

The welcome page (the first screen) usually contains an introduction or a contents list

Web pages can contain clips of film, animation, and sound (which is why hypertext is now often referred to as hypermedia)

Sound node

Browser icon

Embedded beneath hyper links or hotspots lies a command to get the relevant document or "node"

The contents of many Web sites are illustrated with colourful graphics

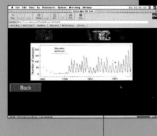

This Web site, called "Virtual Sun", was authored by a graduate student in Astronomy at the University of Amsterdam

Non-linear organization of information allows user to pursue areas of particular interest

A page can contain direct links to several other pages of related information, as well as other Web sites

Index

ACKNOWLEDGMENTS

2001 EDITION
Designer Hugh Schermuly
Editor Jeremy Harwood
Deputy Art Director Bryn Walls
Category Publisher Jonathan Metcalf

Picture researcher Franziska Marking, Anna Grapes
Picture Librarians Sally Hamilton, Diane LeGrande
Production Michelle Thomas
Indexer Jill Ford

ALL EDITIONS
Project Editors Kirstie Hills, Julie Oughton, Nichola Thomasson
Art Editors Paul Greenleaf, Sasha Howard, Joanne Mitchell, Dawn Terrey
Editors Caroline Hunt, David Tombesi-Walton
DTP Designers Mark Bracey, Rob Campbell

Consultants Michael Allaby (El Niño and La Niña), Anita Bardhan-Roy (World Wide Web), David Brown (Pont de Normandie), Helen Castle (Guggenheim, Bilbao; House of the future), Stuart Clarke (International Space Station; Very Large Telescope), John Coiley (Tilting trains), Heather Couper (Hubble Space Telescope), Bernie Fitzsimons (Airbus A5XX), Robin Kerrod (Probing the universe; Record breakers; Global telecommunications), David Lambert (Giganotosaurus), Michael Langford (APS and Digital Photography), Colin Lewis (Electric Car/Le Shuttle), Angela Marlow (Medical research), Dr. Gabrielle Murphy (Modern surgery), Steve Parker (From dinosaurs to birds; Preserved in the ice; Body healing), Mukul Patel (Interactive television; Measuring time; Network computers), Dr. Tony Smith (Medical research), Giles Sparrow (Galileo spacecraft), Fay Sweet (Rebuilding Berlin; Olympics 2000), Dr. Robert Youngsten (Genetic advances)

Senior Editors Louise Candlish, Peter Jones
Senior Art Editors Tracy Hambleton-Miles, Heather McCarry
Managing Editors Gwen Edmonds, Christine Winters
Senior Managing Editor Anna Kruger
Senior Managing Art Editor Steve Knowlden
Deputy Art Director Tina Vaughan
Category Publisher Sean Moore

Illustrations Andy Burton, Rob Campbell, Geoff Denney, Mick Gillah, Tony Graham, Nicholas H. T. Hall, Steve Kirk, Chris D. Orr, Jim Robins, Richard Tibbits, Matthew Wallis, John Woodcock
Model making Jonathan Hateley
Photography Andy Crawford, Bob Gathany, Gary Ombler, Kim Taylor, Frank Greenaway, Dave King, Tim Ridley, Philip Dowell, Mike Dunning
Picture Research Angela Anderson, Katherine Mesquita, Sam Ruston, Mariana Sonnenberg

Production Sarah Coltman, David Proffit, Meryl Silbert

Copyright © 2000 Dorling Kindersley Limited, London

Dorling Kindersley would like to thank: Christine Baker, Jonathan Biggington, Laura Buller, Brian Cooper, Nicola Erdpresser, Mike Flynn, Alan Greenwood, Steve Howard, Neil Lockley, Tim Mann, Simon Murrell, Eric Pierrat (Gallimard), Nicola Powling, Clare Ryder, Richard Shellabear, Richard Sinclair, Nigel Spencer (British Library/Holborn Reading Room), Sylvia Tombesi

The publisher would like to thank the following for their kind permission to reproduce photographs and artworks:

(a=above, b=bottom, c=centre, l=left, r=right, t=top)

Adtranz: 24A tl; *Amateur Photographer*: 59A bl; **Agence France Presse:** 27A tr; **Airbus Industrie:** 3A crb, 32A tr, 32-33A, 33A cra, 35A c. **Allsport:** Scott Barbour 51A c, Shaun Botterill 50A bl, Mark Dadswell 50A clb, Nick Wilson 1A bl, 3A clb, 50A tr, 50-51A, 51A br; 1996 **American Association for the Advancement of Science:** Excerpt from Science reprinted with permission: 12A cl; **Arcaid:** Paul Raffery, Architect: Stutchbury and Pape 51A cr. **Associated Press:** JPL/NASA 5A cr; Keystone 38A cl; NASA 4A tr; National Geographic Society 16A tc; RTRS 39A cr; **Austin Brown/Aviation Picture Library:** 35A crb; **BBC Tomorrow's World:** 15A bc; **Michiel Berger (Astronomical Institute, University of Amsterdam):** 45A br, 47A c, cla, bl, bc, br; **Boeing/Genesis Space Photo Library:** 4A bl; **Breitling SA:** 3A tr, 59A c; **Wendell Burnette Architects:** 25A cr, 25A tr, 25A bc; **Canal Plus:** 45A tr, tcr, bcr, br; **Canon (UK) Limited:** 59A cra; **Branson Coates Architecture:** Branson Coates 25A cla, Philip Vile 25A cl; **Corbis UK Ltd:** AFP 3A cra, 27A tc, 42A cl, 45A t; Bettmann 42A tl; Dave G. Houser 45A br; Gregor Schmidt 2A; Ralph White 39A t; Reuters Newmedia Inc 1A br, 18A tr, 19A tr, 26A tr, 26A bc, 53A tl; **EPA/DPA:** 42-45A; **Eumestat (European Organisation for the Exploitation of Meteorological Satellites):** 21A tr, 21A bl; **Fuji Photo Film:** 58A cl, bl, br, 59A l, bc; **Galaxy Picture Library:** 6A tl, 7A br; **Galaxy Picture Library:** 9A crb, 9A br; Victor Gedris / Ken Adams: 47A tc; **Genesis Space Photo Library:** 12-13A ca; **Mark Guard Associates:** 22A tl; **Guggenheim Museum, Bilbao:** Erika Barahona Ede 34-35a, 35A br; **K. Hiwatashi:** 30A tl; **Institut Amatller D'Art Hispanic:** 35A tr; Shunji Ishiba 30-31A cr; **Kansai International Airport Co. Ltd:** 50-51A c, 51A tr; **KeyMed (Medical & Industrial Equipment) Ltd:** 15A cra; 1996 **Knowledge Adventure Inc.** all rights reserved. JumpStart, Knowledge Land and Knowledge Adventure are trademarks of Knowledge Adventure, Inc: 47A tl; **The Kodak Library:** 39A tr; **Brigitte Lafaille:** F. Latrielle 19A c; 19A tl; **Magnum Photos:** Jean Gaumy 52A tl, 53A br; **Michelin:** 27A tl, tr; **Minolta (UK) Ltd:** 38A tl, 58-59A c; **NASA:** 41A tl, 6A bl, 6-7A tc, cr, bc, bcl, bl; 8A bl, 10A bc, tl, 10-11a, 11A tl, tr; **The Natural History Museum, London:** J. Sibbick 17A bl-cr; **Netscape Communications Corporation:** Netscape and Netscape Navigator are trademarks of Netscape Communications, all rights reserved 46A bl; **Panasonic UK Ltd:** 41A tr; **Peugeot:** 26A tl, cl, bl, 26-27a; **Popperfoto:** Reuters 1A tr, 5A cla, 18A bl, 19A br, 58-59A, 58A b, 59A br, 39A clb2; **Press Association:** 17A br; **Profile Public Relations:** 36A l; **QA Photos Ltd:** 27A tr, crb, Channel Tunnel Group Ltd. 27A cra, br; **Renzo Piano Building Workshop:** 30A l; **Rex Features:** Paul Felix 37A br; SNCF: 24A tr, 25A tl; **Mark Sagar:** 15A c, crb, br; **Science Museum:** 5A crb; **Science Photo Library:** 16-17A cr, cl, crb, 5A cl; Jim Amos 17A br, David Bewsey, Ethicon Ltd and University of Glasgow 27A crb, David Ducros 1A tl, 45A, Simon Fraser 27A cr, David Mooney 3A tl, 27A clb, David Parker 3A bl, 5A br, J.C. Revy 27A cl, Dr Seth Schostak 5A cb,; NASA 44A cr, Volker Steger, Peter Arnold Inc 26A crb, c, 8-9A, David Ducros 11A br, Simon Fraser 15A tr, Carlos Goldin 12A tl, tr, Patrice Loiez 2A c, Will & Deni McIntyre 14A br, Peter Menzel 45A br, Motorola 36-37a, 37A bl, Carlos Munoz-Yague 20A bl, N.A.S.A: 8A clb, 10A clb, David Parker 20A clb, 37A tr, J.C Revy 14A tr, David Scharf 14A bl, tc, Space Telescope Science Institute 4A cr, 5A b, tl, tr, cl, r, Sinclair Stammers 14A bl, Alexander Tsiaras 42A bl; **National Museums of Scotland:** 17A cl; **Frank Spooner Pictures / Gamma:** Clare Aaron 15A cla, 21A cr, 40A br; **Sporting Pictures (uk) Ltd:** 51A t; **Tony Stone Images:** 16A tl; **Sun Microsystems:** 44A bl, 44/45A tc; **Sygma:** 21A br, 28-29A (all except Stephanie Compoint 28A bl © Gedeon-Exmachina) Warren Winter 16A bl; © **The Telegraph plc. London 1996:** 47A t; **Topham Picturepoint:** 42A tl, 45A cr, 45A cb; **Verne Fotografie:** 22A clb, br, c, cra; **West Japan Railways:** 24A bl, 25A br, 24-25A clb; **Westminster Cable:** 40A bl, 40-41A cl.

D O R L I N G   K I N D E R S L E Y

ULTIMATE
VISUAL
DICTIONARY

EXTERNAL FEATURES OF A BUTTERFLY

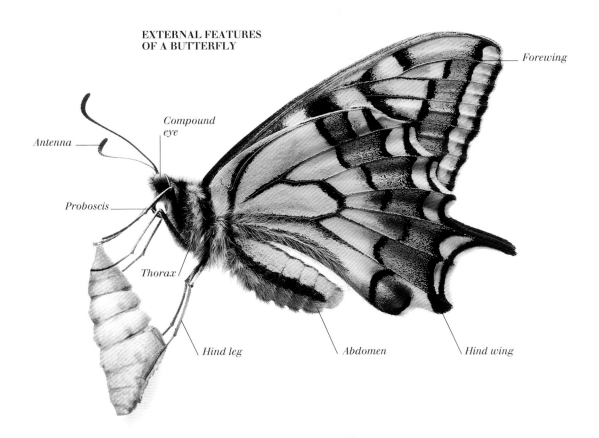

Forewing

Compound eye

Antenna

Proboscis

Thorax

Hind leg

Abdomen

Hind wing

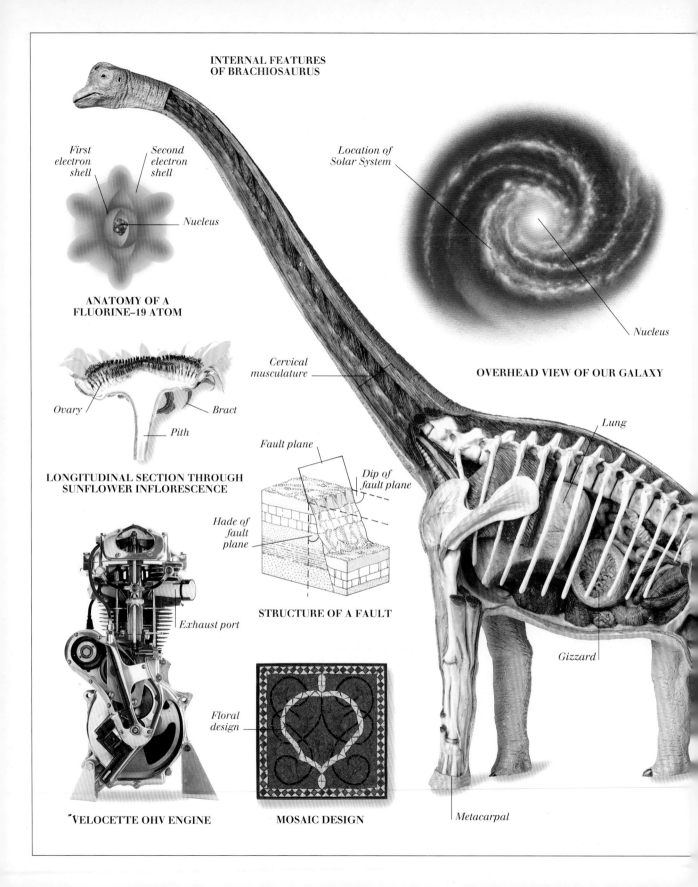

INTERNAL FEATURES OF BRACHIOSAURUS

First electron shell

Second electron shell

Nucleus

ANATOMY OF A FLUORINE–19 ATOM

Location of Solar System

Nucleus

OVERHEAD VIEW OF OUR GALAXY

Ovary

Bract

Pith

Cervical musculature

LONGITUDINAL SECTION THROUGH SUNFLOWER INFLORESCENCE

Lung

Fault plane

Dip of fault plane

Hade of fault plane

STRUCTURE OF A FAULT

Gizzard

Exhaust port

Floral design

VELOCETTE OHV ENGINE

MOSAIC DESIGN

Metacarpal

DORLING KINDERSLEY
ULTIMATE
VISUAL
DICTIONARY

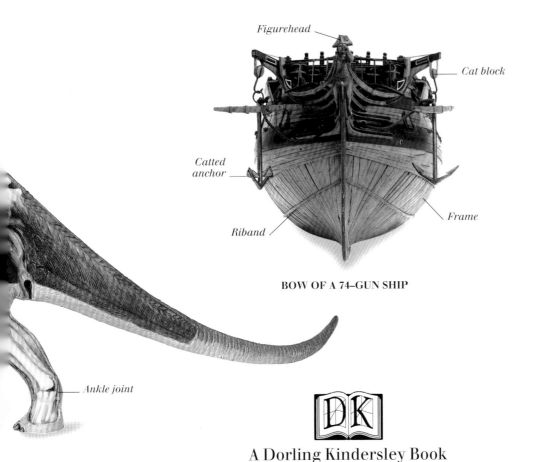

Figurehead

Cat block

Catted anchor

Frame

Riband

BOW OF A 74–GUN SHIP

Ankle joint

A Dorling Kindersley Book

Dorling Kindersley

LONDON, NEW YORK, SYDNEY, DELHI, PARIS
MUNICH, AND JOHANNESBURG

PROJECT ART EDITORS HEATHER MCCARRY, JOHNNY PAU, CHRIS WALKER, KEVIN WILLIAMS
DESIGNER SIMON MURRELL
PROJECT EDITORS LUISA CARUSO, PETER JONES, JANE MASON, GEOFFREY STALKER
EDITOR JO EVANS
US EDITOR JULEE BINDER

DTP DESIGNER ZIRRINIA AUSTIN
PICTURE RESEARCHER CHARLOTTE BUSH

MANAGING ART EDITOR TONI KAY
SENIOR EDITOR ROGER TRITTON
MANAGING EDITOR SEAN MOORE

PRODUCTION MANAGER HILARY STEPHENS

ANATOMICAL AND BOTANICAL MODELS SUPPLIED BY SOMSO MODELLE, COBURG, GERMANY

Sound hole

Hollow body

Bridge

Headstock

ACOUSTIC GUITAR

PUBLISHED IN GREAT BRITAIN IN 1994
DORLING KINDERSLEY LIMITED,
9 HENRIETTA STREET, LONDON WC2E 8PS

REVISED EDITION © 2000
COPYRIGHT © 1994 DORLING KINDERSLEY LIMITED, LONDON

A CIP CATALOGUE RECORD FOR THIS BOOK IS AVAILABLE FROM THE BRITISH LIBRARY

ISBN 0 7513 0988 5

REPRODUCED BY COLOURSCAN, SINGAPORE
PRINTED AND BOUND IN MONDADORI, ITALY

SEE OUR COMPLETE
CATALOGUE AT
www.dk.com

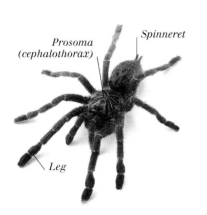

Prosoma (cephalothorax)

Spinneret

Leg

EXTERNAL FEATURES OF A SPIDER

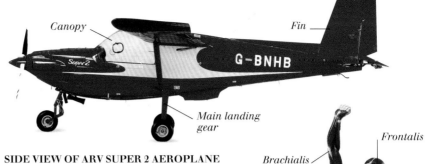

Canopy

Fin

G-BNHB

Main landing gear

SIDE VIEW OF ARV SUPER 2 AEROPLANE

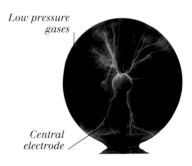

Frontalis

Brachialis

Deltoid

Rectus femoris

SUPERFICIAL SKELETAL MUSCLES

CONTENTS

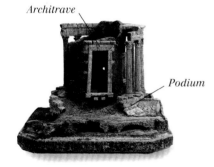

Barrel

Permanent black ink

FOUNTAIN PEN AND INK

Architrave

Podium

TEMPLE OF VESTA, TIVOLI, ITALY, C.80 BC

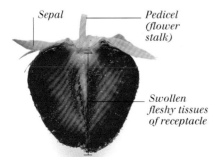

Sepal

Pedicel (flower stalk)

Swollen fleshy tissues of receptacle

LONGITUDINAL SECTION THROUGH A STRAWBERRY

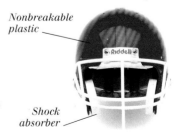

Low pressure gases

Central electrode

BALL CONTAINING HIGH TEMPERATURE GAS (PLASMA)

Nonbreakable plastic

Shock absorber

AMERICAN FOOTBALL HELMET

Introduction

THE ULTIMATE VISUAL DICTIONARY provides a link between pictures and words in a way that no ordinary encyclopedia ever has. Most encyclopedias simply tell you what a word means, but the *Ultimate Visual Dictionary* shows you, through a combination of concise introductions, informative captions, detailed annotations, and explicit photographs and illustrations. In the *Ultimate Visual Dictionary*, pictures define the annotations around them. You do not read definitions of the annotated words, you see them. The highly accessible format of the *Ultimate Visual Dictionary*, the thoroughness of its annotations, and the range of its subject matter make it a unique and helpful reference tool.

How to use the ULTIMATE VISUAL DICTIONARY

You will find the *Ultimate Visual Dictionary* simple to use. Instead of being organized alphabetically, it is divided by subject into 14 sections – THE UNIVERSE, PREHISTORIC EARTH, PLANTS, ANIMALS, THE HUMAN BODY, etc. Each section begins with a table of contents listing the major entries within that section. For example, THE VISUAL ARTS section has entries on *Drawing, Tempera, Fresco, Oils, Watercolour, Pastels, Acrylics, Calligraphy, Printmaking, Mosaic,* and *Sculpture.* Every entry has a short introduction explaining the purpose of the photographs and illustrations, and the significance of the annotations.

If you know what something looks like, but don't know its name, turn to the annotations surrounding the pictures; if you know a word, but don't know what it refers to, use the comprehensive index to direct you to the appropriate page.

Suppose that you want to know what the bone at the end of your little finger is called. With a standard encyclopedia, you wouldn't know where to begin. But with the *Ultimate Visual Dictionary* you simply turn to the entry called *Hands* – within THE HUMAN BODY section – where you will find four fully annotated, colour photographs showing the skin, muscles, and bones of the human hand. In this entry you will quickly find that the bone you are searching for is called the distal phalanx, and for good measure you will discover that it is attached to the middle phalanx by the distal interphalangeal joint.

Perhaps you want to know what a catalytic converter looks like. If you look up "catalytic converter" in an ordinary encyclopedia, you will be told what it is and possibly what it does – but you will not be able to tell what shape it is or what it is made of. However, if you look up "catalytic converter" in the index of the *Ultimate Visual Dictionary*, you will be directed to the *Modern engines* entry on page 344 – where the introduction gives you basic information about what a catalytic converter is – and to page 350 – where there is a spectacular exploded-view photograph of the mechanics of a Renault Clio. From these pages you will find out not only what a catalytic converter looks like, but also that it is attached at one end to an exhaust downpipe and at the other to a silencer.

Whatever it is that you want to find a name for, or whatever name you want to find a picture for, you will find it quickly and easily in the *Ultimate Visual Dictionary*. Perhaps you need to know where the vamp on a shoe is; or how to tell obovate and lanceolate leaves apart; or what a spiral galaxy looks like; or whether birds have nostrils. With the *Ultimate Visual Dictionary* at hand, the answers to each of these questions, and thousands more, are readily available.

The *Ultimate Visual Dictionary* does not just tell you what the names of the different parts of an object are. The photographs, illustrations, and annotations are all specially arranged to help you understand which parts relate to one another and how objects function.

With the *Ultimate Visual Dictionary* you can find in seconds the words or pictures that you are looking for; or you can simply browse through the pages of the book for your own pleasure. The *Ultimate Visual Dictionary* is not intended to replace a standard dictionary or encyclopedia, but is instead a stimulating and valuable companion to ordinary reference volumes. Giving you access to the language that is used by astronomers and architects, musicians and mechanics, scientists and sportspeople, it is the ideal reference book for specialists and generalists of all ages.

***Sections of the* ULTIMATE VISUAL DICTIONARY**
The 14 sections of the *ULTIMATE VISUAL DICTIONARY*
contain a total of more than 30,000 terms,
encompassing a wide range of topics:

●In the first section, THE UNIVERSE, spectacular
photographs and illustrations are used to show
the names of the stars and planets and to explain
the structure of solar systems, galaxies, nebulae,
comets, and black holes.

●PREHISTORIC EARTH tells the story in annotations
of how our own planet has evolved since its
formation. It includes examples of prehistoric
flora and fauna, and fascinating dinosaur
models – some with parts of the body stripped
away to show anatomical sections.

●PLANTS covers a huge range of species –
from the familiar to the exotic. In addition to
the colour photographs of plants included in
this section, there is a series of micrographic
photographs illustrating plant details – such
as pollen grains, spores, and cross-sections
of stems and roots – in close-up.

● In the ANIMALS section, skeletons, anatomical
diagrams, and different parts of animals' bodies
have been meticulously annotated. This section
provides a comprehensive guide to the vocabulary
of zoological classification and animal physiology.

●The structure of the human body, its parts,
and its systems are presented in THE HUMAN BODY.
The section includes lifelike, three-dimensional
models and the latest false-colour images.
Clear and authoritative annotations indicate
the correct anatomical terms.

●GEOLOGY, GEOGRAPHY, AND METEOROLOGY
describes the structure of the Earth – from the
inner core to the exosphere – and the physical
phenomena – such as volcanoes, rivers, glaciers,
and climate – that shape its surface.

●PHYSICS AND CHEMISTRY is a visual journey
through the fundamental principles underlying
the physical universe and provides the essential
vocabulary of these sciences.

●In RAIL AND ROAD, a wide range of trains, trams
and buses, cars, bicycles, and motorcycles are
described. Exploded-view photographs show
mechanical details with striking clarity.

●SEA AND AIR gives the names for hundreds
of parts of ships and aeroplanes. The section
includes civil and fighting craft, both
historical and modern.

●THE VISUAL ARTS shows the equipment and
materials used by painters, sculptors, printers,
and other artists. Well-known compositions
have been chosen to illustrate specific
artistic techniques and effects.

●ARCHITECTURE includes photographs
of exemplary architectural models and
illustrates dozens of additional features
such as columns, domes, and arches.

●MUSIC provides a visual introduction to
the special language of music and musical
instruments. It includes clearly annotated
photographs of each of the major groups of
traditional instruments – brass, woodwind,
strings, and percussion – together with
modern electronic instruments.

●The SPORTS section is a guide to the playing
areas, formations, equipment, and techniques
needed for many of today's most popular sports.

●In EVERYDAY THINGS, familiar objects, such
as shoes, clocks, and toasters, are taken apart
– down to the very last screw or length of thread
– to show their inner workings and to give a
special insight into the language that is used
by their manufacturers.

THE UNIVERSE

Anatomy of the Universe

THE UNIVERSE CONTAINS EVERYTHING that exists, from the tiniest subatomic particles to galactic superclusters (the largest structures known). Nobody knows how big the Universe is, but astronomers estimate that it contains about 100 billion galaxies, each comprising an average of 100 billion stars. The most widely accepted theory about the origin of the Universe is the Big Bang theory, which states that the Universe came into being in a huge explosion – the Big Bang – that took place between 10 and 20 billion years ago. The Universe initially consisted of a very hot, dense fireball of expanding, cooling gas. After about one million years, the gas probably began to condense into localized clumps called protogalaxies. During the next five billion years, the protogalaxies continued condensing, forming galaxies in which stars were being born. Today, billions of years later, the Universe as a whole is still expanding, although there are localized areas in which objects are held together by gravity; for example, many galaxies are found in clusters. The Big Bang theory is supported by the discovery of faint, cool background radiation coming evenly from all directions. This radiation is believed to be the remnant of the radiation produced by the Big Bang. Small "ripples" in the temperature of the cosmic background radiation are thought to be evidence of slight fluctuations in the density of the early Universe, which resulted in the formation of galaxies. Astronomers do not yet know if the Universe is "closed", which means it will eventually stop expanding and begin to contract, or if it is "open", which means it will continue expanding forever.

Fireball of rapidly expanding, extremely hot gas lasting about one million years

FALSE-COLOUR MICROWAVE MAP OF COSMIC BACKGROUND RADIATION

Pink indicates "warm ripples" in background radiation

Pale blue indicates "cool ripples" in background radiation

Low-energy microwave radiation corresponding to about -270°C

Deep blue indicates background radiation corresponding to -270.3°C (remnant of the Big Bang)

Red and pink band indicates radiation from our galaxy

High-energy gamma radiation corresponding to about 3,000°C

ORIGIN AND EXPANSION OF THE UNIVERSE

Quasar (probably the centre
of a galaxy containing a
massive black hole)

Universe one to five
billion years after
Big Bang

Protogalaxy
(condensing gas cloud)

Galaxy spinning and
flattening to become
spiral shaped

Dark cloud
(dust and gas
condensing
to form a
protogalaxy)

Elliptical
galaxy in
which stars
form rapidly

Universe today
(10–20 billion years
after Big Bang)

Cluster of
galaxies held
together by gravity

Elliptical galaxy
containing old stars
and little gas and dust

Irregular galaxy

Spiral galaxy
containing gas,
dust, and young stars

OBJECTS IN THE UNIVERSE

CLUSTER OF
GALAXIES IN VIRGO

FALSE-COLOUR IMAGE
OF 3C273 (QUASAR)

NGC 4406
(ELLIPTICAL GALAXY)

NGC 5236
(SPIRAL GALAXY)

NGC 6822
(IRREGULAR GALAXY)

THE ROSETTE NEBULA
(EMISSION NEBULA)

THE JEWEL BOX
(STAR CLUSTER)

THE SUN
(MAIN SEQUENCE STAR)

EARTH

THE MOON

Galaxies

SOMBRERO,
A SPIRAL GALAXY

A GALAXY IS A HUGE MASS OF STARS, nebulae, and interstellar material. The smallest galaxies contain about 100,000 stars, while the largest contain up to 3,000 billion stars. There are three main types of galaxy, classified according to their shape: elliptical, which are oval shaped; spiral, which have arms spiralling outwards from a central bulge; and irregular, which have no obvious shape. Sometimes, the shape of a galaxy is distorted by a collision with another galaxy. Quasars (quasi-stellar objects) are thought to be galactic nuclei but are so far away that their exact nature is still uncertain. They are compact, highly luminous objects in the outer reaches of the known Universe: while the furthest known "ordinary" galaxies are about 10 billion light years away, the furthest known quasar is about 15 billion light years away. Active galaxies, such as Seyfert galaxies and radio galaxies, emit intense radiation. In a Seyfert galaxy, this radiation comes from the galactic nucleus; in a radio galaxy, it also comes from huge lobes on either side of the galaxy. The radiation from active galaxies and quasars is thought to be caused by black holes (see pp. 28-29).

OPTICAL IMAGE OF NGC 4486 (ELLIPTICAL GALAXY)

Globular cluster containing very old red giants

Central region containing old red giants

Less densely populated region

Neighbouring galaxy

OPTICAL IMAGE OF LARGE MAGELLANIC CLOUD (IRREGULAR GALAXY)

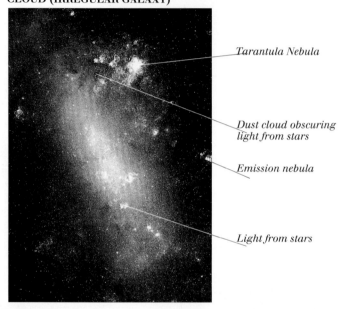

Tarantula Nebula

Dust cloud obscuring light from stars

Emission nebula

Light from stars

OPTICAL IMAGE OF NGC 2997 (SPIRAL GALAXY)

Glowing nebula in spiral arm

Spiral arm containing young stars

Galactic nucleus containing old stars

Dust in spiral arm reflecting blue light from hot young stars

Hot, ionized hydrogen gas emitting red light

Dust lane

**OPTICAL IMAGE OF CENTAURUS A
(RADIO GALAXY)**

**FALSE-COLOUR RADIO
IMAGE OF CENTAURUS A**

FALSE-COLOUR RADIO IMAGE OF 3C273 (QUASAR)

**OPTICAL IMAGE OF NGC 1566
(SEYFERT GALAXY)**

**FALSE-COLOUR OPTICAL IMAGE OF NGC 5754
(TWO COLLIDING GALAXIES)**

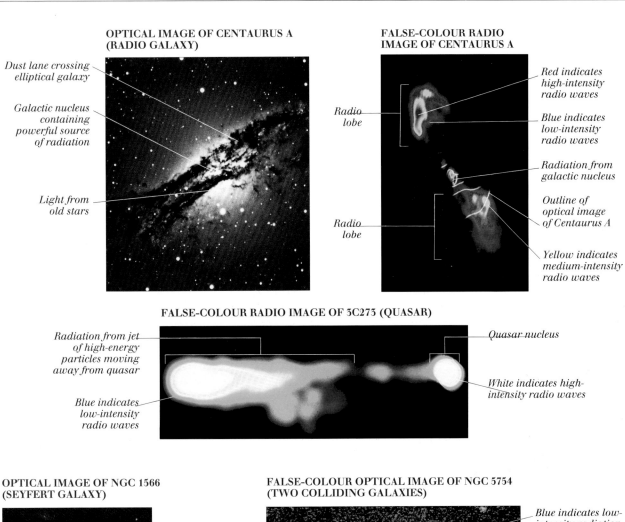

*Dust lane crossing
elliptical galaxy*

*Galactic nucleus
containing
powerful source
of radiation*

*Light from
old stars*

*Radio
lobe*

*Radio
lobe*

*Red indicates
high-intensity
radio waves*

*Blue indicates
low-intensity
radio waves*

*Radiation from
galactic nucleus*

*Outline of
optical image
of Centaurus A*

*Yellow indicates
medium-intensity
radio waves*

*Radiation from jet
of high-energy
particles moving
away from quasar*

*Blue indicates
low-intensity
radio waves*

Quasar nucleus

*White indicates high-
intensity radio waves*

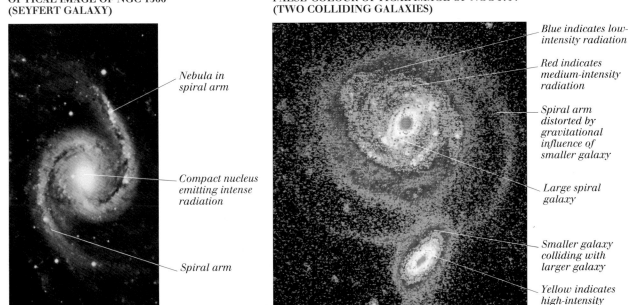

*Nebula in
spiral arm*

*Compact nucleus
emitting intense
radiation*

Spiral arm

*Blue indicates low-
intensity radiation*

*Red indicates
medium-intensity
radiation*

*Spiral arm
distorted by
gravitational
influence of
smaller galaxy*

*Large spiral
galaxy*

*Smaller galaxy
colliding with
larger galaxy*

*Yellow indicates
high-intensity
radiation*

13

The Milky Way

VIEW TOWARDS GALACTIC CENTRE

THE MILKY WAY IS THE NAME GIVEN TO THE FAINT BAND OF LIGHT that stretches across the night sky. This light comes from stars and nebulae in our galaxy, known as the Milky Way Galaxy or simply as "the Galaxy". The Galaxy is shaped like a spiral, with a dense central bulge that is encircled by four arms spiralling outwards and surrounded by a less dense halo. We cannot see the spiral shape because the Solar System is in one of the spiral arms, the Orion Arm (also called the Local Arm). From our position, the centre of the Galaxy is completely obscured by dust clouds; as a result, optical maps give only a limited view of the Galaxy. However, a more complete picture can be obtained by studying radio, infra-red, and other radiation. The central bulge of the Galaxy is a relatively small, dense sphere that contains mainly older red and yellow stars. The halo is a less dense region in which the oldest stars are situated; some of these stars may be as old as the Galaxy itself (possibly 15 billion years). The spiral arms contain mainly hot, young, blue stars, as well as nebulae (clouds of dust and gas inside which stars are born). The Galaxy is vast, about 100,000 light years across (a light year is about 9,460 billion kilometres); in comparison, the Solar System seems small, at about 12 light hours across (about 13 billion kilometres). The entire Galaxy is rotating in space, although the inner stars travel faster than those further out. The Sun, which is about two-thirds out from the centre, completes one lap of the Galaxy about every 220 million years.

SIDE VIEW OF OUR GALAXY

Disc of spiral arms containing mainly young stars

Central bulge containing mainly older stars

Halo containing oldest stars

Nucleus

100,000 light years

OVERHEAD VIEW OF OUR GALAXY

Central bulge

Nucleus

Perseus Arm

Crux-Centaurus Arm

Dust in spiral arm reflecting blue light from hot young stars

Location of Solar System

Patch of dust clouds

Orion Arm (Local Arm)

Emission nebula

Sagittarius Arm

PANORAMIC OPTICAL MAP OF OUR GALAXY AND NEARBY GALAXIES

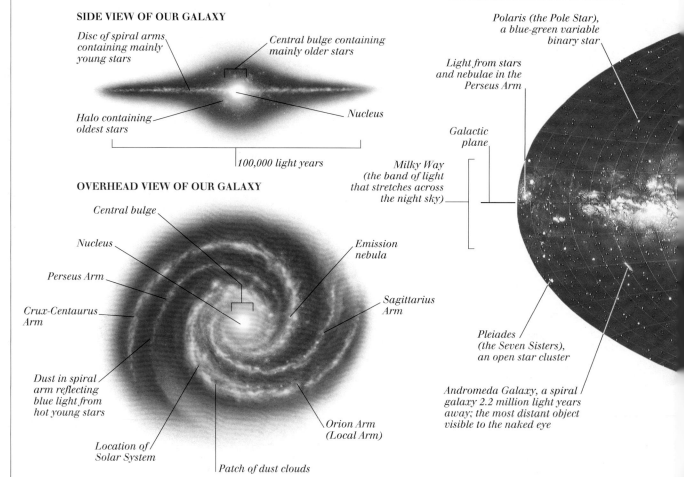

Polaris (the Pole Star), a blue-green variable binary star

Light from stars and nebulae in the Perseus Arm

Galactic plane

Milky Way (the band of light that stretches across the night sky)

Pleiades (the Seven Sisters), an open star cluster

Andromeda Galaxy, a spiral galaxy 2.2 million light years away; the most distant object visible to the naked eye

PANORAMIC RADIO MAP OF OUR GALAXY

North Galactic spur
(possibly radio emission
from a supernova remnant)

North Galactic
Pole

Red indicates
high-intensity
radio-wave emission

Galactic
plane

Blue indicates
low-intensity
radio-wave emission

South
Galactic Pole

Yellow and green
indicate medium-intensity
radio-wave emission

PANORAMIC INFRA-RED MAP OF OUR GALAXY

North Galactic
Pole

Low-intensity infra-red
radiation from interstellar
gas and dust

Galactic
plane

Galactic
plane

South Galactic Pole

High-intensity infra-red
radiation from interstellar
gas and dust

High-intensity
infra-red
radiation
from region
of starbirth

Vega, a white main
sequence star; the fifth
brightest star in the sky

North Galactic Pole

Dark clouds of dust and gas
obscuring light from part of the
Sagittarius Arm

Light from stars and nebulae in the
part of the Sagittarius Arm between
the Sun and Galactic centre

Light from stars
and nebulae in the
Perseus Arm

Galactic
plane

Orion's belt,
a row of
three bright
stars

Orion Nebula

Sirius, a white main
sequence star; the
brightest star in the sky

Canopus, a white supergiant;
the second brightest star in the sky

Dust clouds
obscuring
Galactic centre

South Galactic Pole

Small Magellanic Cloud, an irregular
galaxy 190,000 light years away; the
second nearest object to our galaxy

Large Magellanic Cloud, an
irregular galaxy 170,000 light years
away; the nearest object to our galaxy

Nebulae and star clusters

**HODGE 11, A
GLOBULAR CLUSTER**

A NEBULA IS A CLOUD OF DUST AND GAS inside a galaxy. Nebulae become visible if the gas glows, or if the cloud reflects starlight or obscures light from more distant objects. Emission nebulae shine because their gas emits light when it is stimulated by radiation from hot young stars. Reflection nebulae shine because their dust reflects light from stars in or around the nebula. Dark nebulae appear as silhouettes because they block out light from shining nebulae or stars behind them. Two types of nebula are associated with dying stars: planetary nebulae and supernova remnants. Both consist of expanding shells of gas that were once the outer layers of a star. A planetary nebula is a gas shell drifting away from a dying stellar core. A supernova remnant is a gas shell moving away from a stellar core at great speed following a violent explosion called a supernova (see pp. 26-27). Stars are often found in groups known as clusters. Open clusters are loose groups of a few thousand young stars that were born in the same cloud and are drifting apart. Globular clusters are densely packed, roughly spherical groups of hundreds of thousands of older stars.

TRIFID NEBULA (EMISSION NEBULA)

Reflection nebula

Emission nebula

Dust lane

Starbirth region (area in which dust and gas clump together to form stars)

**PLEIADES (OPEN STAR CLUSTER)
WITH A REFLECTION NEBULA**

Wisps of dust and hydrogen gas remaining from cloud in which stars formed

Young star in an open cluster of 300–500 stars

Reflection nebula

HORSEHEAD NEBULA (DARK NEBULA)

Glowing filament of hot, ionized hydrogen gas

Alnitak (star in Orion's belt)

Dust lane

Emission nebula

Star near southern end of Orion's belt

Emission nebula

Horsehead Nebula

Reflection nebula

Dark nebula obscuring light from distant stars

ORION NEBULA (DIFFUSE EMISSION NEBULA)

Glowing cloud of dust and hydrogen gas forming part of Orion Nebula

Dust cloud

Trapezium (group of four young stars)

Red light from hot, ionized hydrogen gas

Gas cloud emitting light due to ultraviolet radiation from the four young Trapezium stars

Green light from hot, ionized oxygen gas

Glowing filament of hot, ionized hydrogen gas

VELA SUPERNOVA REMNANT

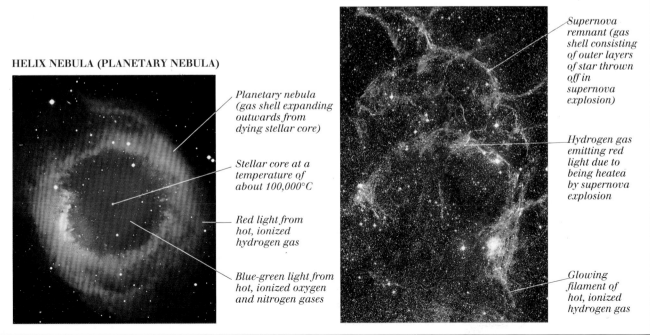

Supernova remnant (gas shell consisting of outer layers of star thrown off in supernova explosion)

Hydrogen gas emitting red light due to being heated by supernova explosion

Glowing filament of hot, ionized hydrogen gas

HELIX NEBULA (PLANETARY NEBULA)

Planetary nebula (gas shell expanding outwards from dying stellar core)

Stellar core at a temperature of about 100,000°C

Red light from hot, ionized hydrogen gas

Blue-green light from hot, ionized oxygen and nitrogen gases

Stars of northern skies

WHEN YOU LOOK AT THE NORTHERN SKY, you look away from the densely populated Galactic centre, so the northern sky generally appears less bright than the southern sky (see pp. 20-21). Among the best-known sights in the northern sky are the constellations Ursa Major (the Great Bear) and Orion. Some ancient civilizations believed that the stars were fixed to a celestial sphere surrounding the Earth, and modern maps of the sky are based on a similar idea. The North and South Poles of this imaginary celestial sphere are directly above the North and South Poles of the Earth, at the points where the Earth's axis of rotation intersects the sphere. The celestial North Pole is at the centre of the map shown here, and Polaris (the Pole Star) lies very close to it. The celestial equator marks a projection of the Earth's equator on the sphere. The ecliptic marks the path of the Sun across the sky as the Earth orbits the Sun. The Moon and planets move against the background of the stars because the stars are much more distant; the nearest star outside the Solar System (Proxima Centauri) is more than 50,000 times further away than the planet Jupiter.

ORION

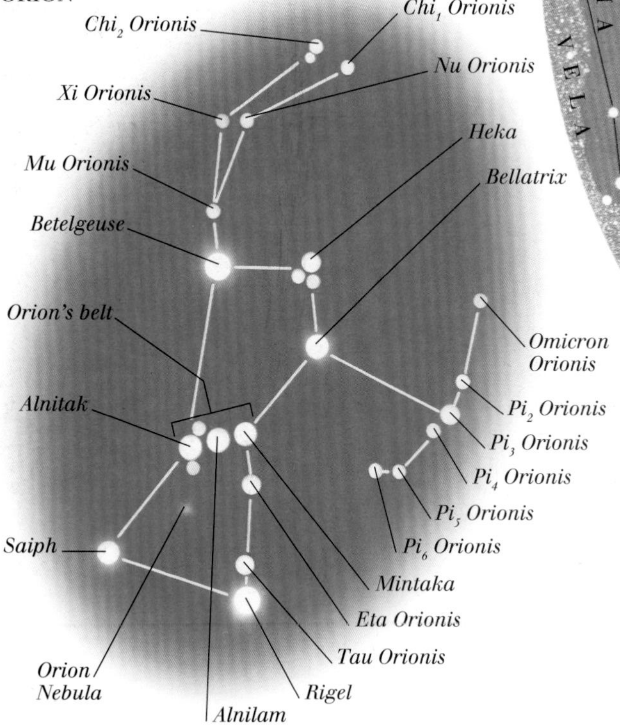

Chi$_2$ Orionis
Chi$_1$ Orionis
Nu Orionis
Xi Orionis
Heka
Mu Orionis
Bellatrix
Betelgeuse
Orion's belt
Omicron Orionis
Alnitak
Pi$_2$ Orionis
Pi$_3$ Orionis
Pi$_4$ Orionis
Pi$_5$ Orionis
Saiph
Pi$_6$ Orionis
Mintaka
Eta Orionis
Tau Orionis
Orion Nebula
Rigel
Alnilam

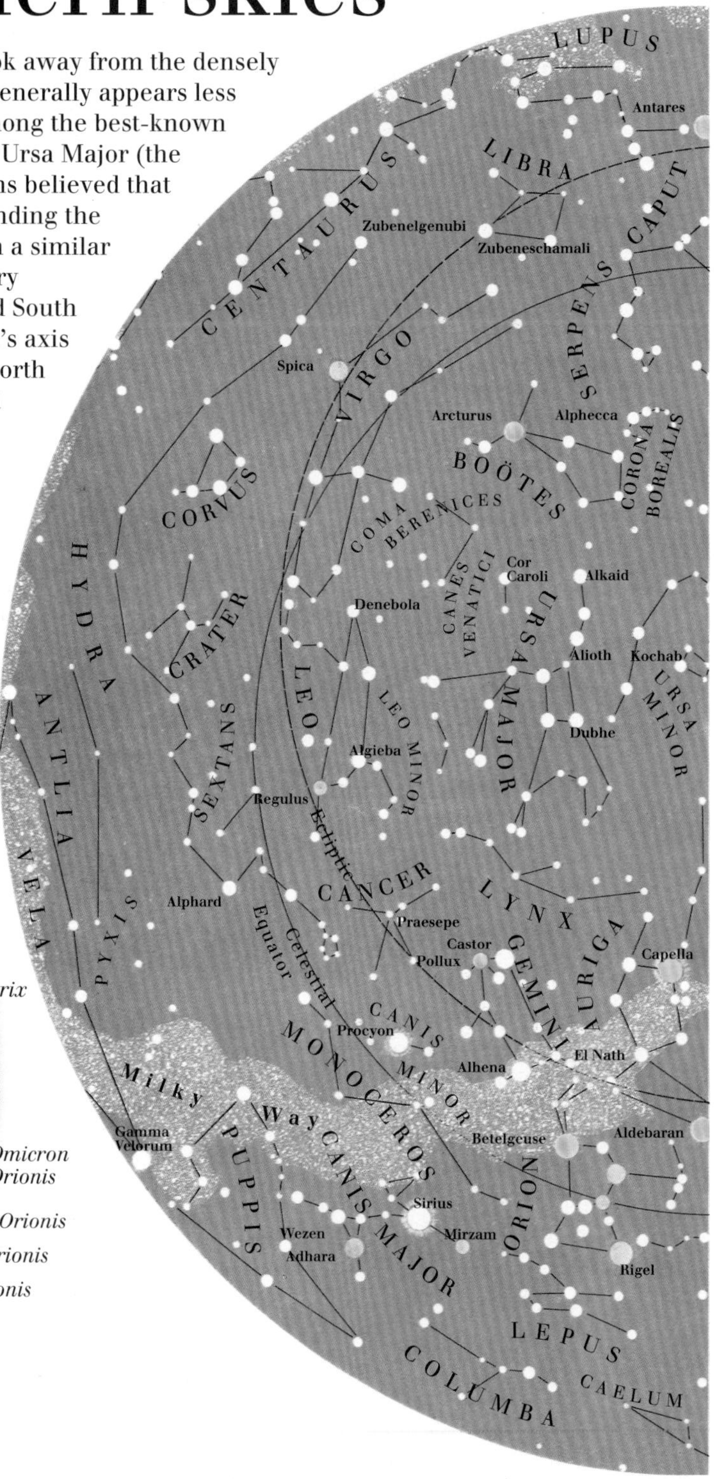

LUPUS
CENTAURUS
LIBRA
Antares
Zubenelgenubi
Zubeneschamali
SERPENS CAPUT
VIRGO
Spica
Arcturus
Alphecca
CORONA BOREALIS
BOÖTES
CORVUS
COMA BERENICES
CANES VENATICI
Cor Caroli
Alkaid
URSA MAJOR
Alioth
Kochab
Denebola
HYDRA
CRATER
LEO
LEO MINOR
Dubhe
URSA MINOR
ANTLIA
SEXTANS
Algieba
Regulus
Ecliptic
LYNX
VELA
Alphard
CANCER
Praesepe
Castor
Pollux
GEMINI
AURIGA
Capella
PYXIS
Celestial Equator
CANIS MINOR
Procyon
Alhena
El Nath
Milky Way
MONOCEROS
Betelgeuse
Aldebaran
Gamma Velorum
PUPPIS
CANIS MAJOR
Sirius
Mirzam
ORION
Wezen
Adhara
Rigel
LEPUS
COLUMBA
CAELUM

VISIBLE STARS IN THE NORTHERN SKY

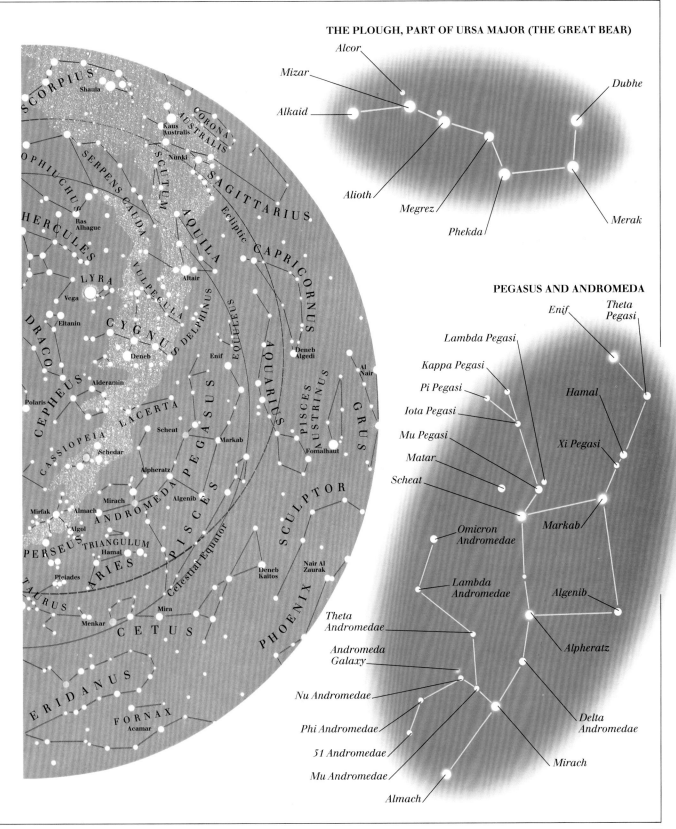

THE PLOUGH, PART OF URSA MAJOR (THE GREAT BEAR)

Alcor

Mizar

Alkaid

Dubhe

Alioth

Megrez

Merak

Phekda

PEGASUS AND ANDROMEDA

Enif

Theta Pegasi

Lambda Pegasi

Kappa Pegasi

Hamal

Pi Pegasi

Iota Pegasi

Mu Pegasi

Xi Pegasi

Matar

Scheat

Markab

Omicron Andromedae

Algenib

Lambda Andromedae

Alpheratz

Theta Andromedae

Andromeda Galaxy

Nu Andromedae

Delta Andromedae

Phi Andromedae

51 Andromedae

Mirach

Mu Andromedae

Almach

SCORPIUS

Shaula

CORONA AUSTRALIS

Kaus Australis

OPHIUCHUS

SERPENS CAUDA

SCUTUM

SAGITTARIUS

Nunki

Ras Alhague

HERCULES

AQUILA

Ecliptic

CAPRICORNUS

LYRA

VULPECULA

Altair

Vega

DELPHINUS

Eltanin

CYGNUS

EQUULEUS

AQUARIUS

Deneb Algedi

DRACO

Deneb

Enif

Al Nair

Alderamin

PEGASUS

PISCES AUSTRINUS

GRUS

Polaris

CEPHEUS

LACERTA

Scheat

Fomalhaut

CASSIOPEIA

Schedar

Markab

Alpheratz

ANDROMEDA

Algenib

Mirach

PISCES

SCULPTOR

Mirfak

Almach

TRIANGULUM

Nair Al Zaurak

Algol

Hamal

Deneb Kaitos

PERSEUS

ARIES

Celestial Equator

Pleiades

Mira

PHOENIX

TAURUS

Menkar

CETUS

ERIDANUS

FORNAX

Acamar

19

Stars of southern skies

WHEN YOU LOOK AT THE SOUTHERN SKY, you look towards the Galactic centre, which has a huge population of stars. As a result, the Milky Way appears brighter in the southern sky than in the northern sky (see pp. 18-19). The southern sky is rich in nebulae and star clusters. It contains the Large and Small Magellanic Clouds, which are the two nearest galaxies to our own. Stars make fixed patterns in the sky called constellations. However, the constellations are only apparent groupings of stars, since the distances to the stars in a constellation may vary enormously. The shapes of constellations may change over many thousands of years due to the relative motions of stars. The movement of the constellations across the sky is due to the Earth's motion in space. The daily rotation of the Earth causes the constellations to move across the sky from east to west, and the orbit of the Earth around the Sun causes different areas of sky to be visible in different seasons. The visibility of areas of sky also depends on the location of the observer. For instance, stars near the celestial equator may be seen from either hemisphere at some time during the year, whereas stars close to the celestial poles (the celestial South Pole is at the centre of the map shown here) can never be seen from the opposite hemisphere.

HYDRUS (THE WATER SNAKE) AND MENSA (THE TABLE)

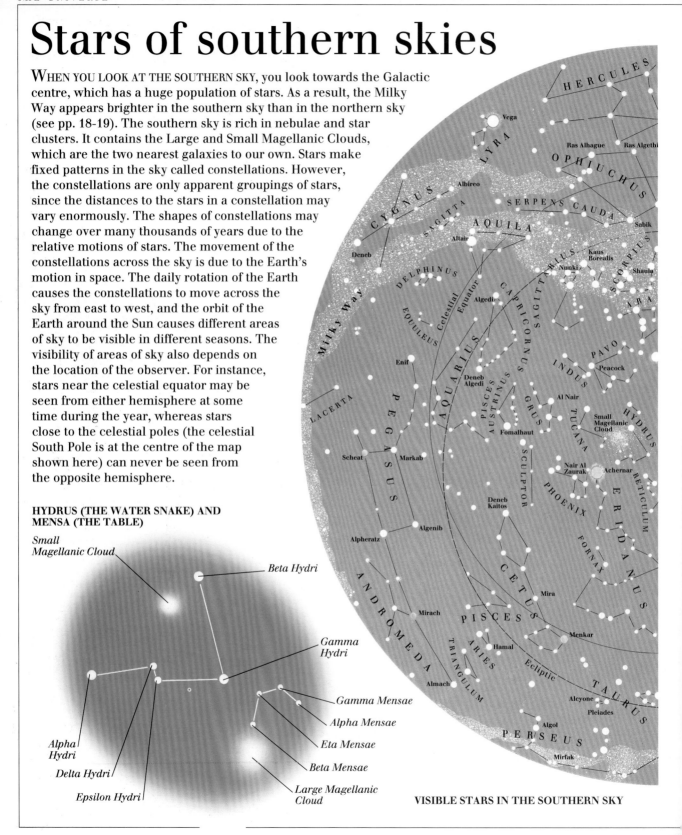

Small Magellanic Cloud

Beta Hydri

Gamma Hydri

Alpha Hydri

Delta Hydri

Epsilon Hydri

Gamma Mensae

Alpha Mensae

Eta Mensae

Beta Mensae

Large Magellanic Cloud

VISIBLE STARS IN THE SOUTHERN SKY

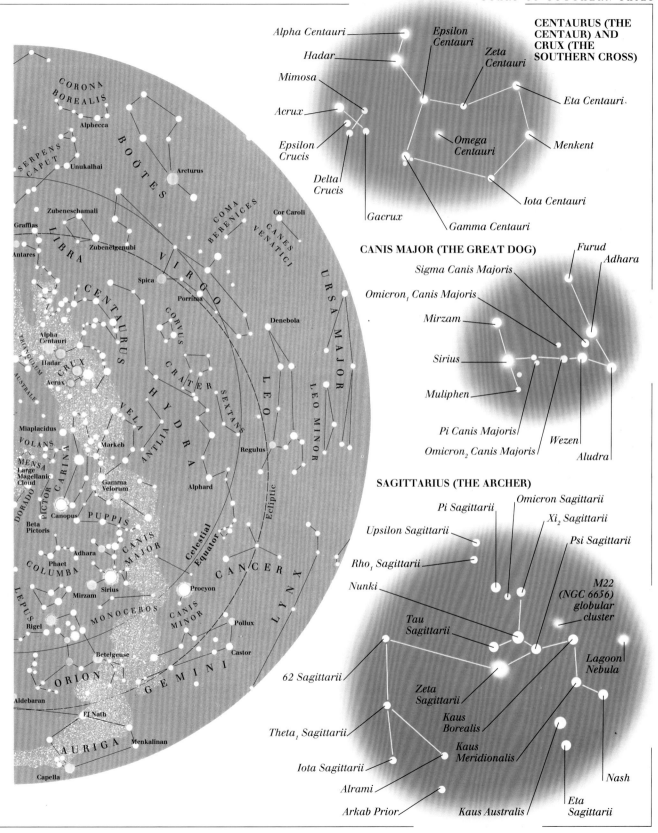

CENTAURUS (THE CENTAUR) AND CRUX (THE SOUTHERN CROSS)

Alpha Centauri
Epsilon Centauri
Hadar
Zeta Centauri
Mimosa
Eta Centauri
Acrux
Omega Centauri
Epsilon Crucis
Menkent
Delta Crucis
Iota Centauri
Gacrux
Gamma Centauri

CANIS MAJOR (THE GREAT DOG)

Furud
Adhara
Sigma Canis Majoris
Omicron$_1$ Canis Majoris
Mirzam
Sirius
Muliphen
Pi Canis Majoris
Wezen
Omicron$_2$ Canis Majoris
Aludra

SAGITTARIUS (THE ARCHER)

Pi Sagittarii
Omicron Sagittarii
Upsilon Sagittarii
Xi$_2$ Sagittarii
Rho$_1$ Sagittarii
Psi Sagittarii
Nunki
M22 (NGC 6656) globular cluster
Tau Sagittarii
Lagoon Nebula
62 Sagittarii
Zeta Sagittarii
Theta$_1$ Sagittarii
Kaus Borealis
Iota Sagittarii
Kaus Meridionalis
Alrami
Arkab Prior
Kaus Australis
Eta Sagittarii
Nash

CORONA BOREALIS
Alphecca
BOÖTES
SERPENS CAPUT
Unukalhai
Arcturus
Zubeneschamali
COMA BERENICES
CANES VENATICI
Cor Caroli
Graffias
Zubenelgenubi
LIBRA
VIRGO
URSA MAJOR
Antares
Spica
Porrima
Denebola
CENTAURUS
CORVUS
LEO
Alpha Centauri
CRATER
SEXTANS
LEO MINOR
TRIANGULUM AUSTRALE
Hadar
HYDRA
Acrux
VELA
ANTLIA
Regulus
Miaplacidus
VOLANS
Markeb
Alphard
MENSA
Large Magellanic Cloud
Gamma Velorum
Ecliptic
DORADO
PICTOR
CARINA
PUPPIS
Canopus
Celestial Equator
CANCER
Beta Pictoris
CANIS MAJOR
LYNX
Phaet
Adhara
COLUMBA
Mirzam
Sirius
Procyon
LEPUS
MONOCEROS
CANIS MINOR
Pollux
Rigel
Castor
Betelgeuse
GEMINI
ORION
Aldebaran
El Nath
Menkalinan
AURIGA
Capella

Stars

OPEN STAR CLUSTER AND DUST CLOUD

STARS ARE BODIES of hot, glowing gas that are born in nebulae (see pp. 24-27). They vary enormously in size, mass, and temperature: diameters range from about 450 times smaller to over 1,000 times bigger than that of the Sun; masses range from about a twentieth to over 50 solar masses; and surface temperatures range from about 3,000°C to over 50,000°C. The colour of a star is determined by its temperature: the hottest stars are blue and the coolest are red. The Sun, with a surface temperature of 5,500°C, is between these extremes and appears yellow. The energy emitted by a shining star is produced by nuclear fusion in the star's core. The brightness of a star is measured in magnitudes – the brighter the star, the lower its magnitude. There are two types of magnitude: apparent magnitude, which is the brightness seen from Earth, and absolute magnitude, which is the brightness that would be seen from a standard distance of 10 parsecs (32.6 light years). The light emitted by a star may be split to form a spectrum containing a series of dark lines (absorption lines). The patterns of lines indicate the presence of particular chemical elements, enabling astronomers to deduce the composition of the star's atmosphere. The magnitude and spectral type (colour) of stars may be plotted on a graph called a Hertzsprung-Russell diagram, which shows that stars tend to fall into several well-defined groups. The principal groups are main sequence stars (those which are fusing hydrogen to form helium), giants, supergiants, and white dwarfs.

STAR SIZES

Red giant (diameters between about 15 million and 150 million km)

The Sun (main sequence star with diameter about 1.4 million km)

White dwarf (diameters between about 3,000 and 50,000 km)

ENERGY EMISSION FROM THE SUN

Nuclear fusion in core produces gamma rays and neutrinos

Neutrinos travel to Earth directly from Sun's core in about 8 minutes

Lower-energy radiation travels to Earth in about 8 minutes

Earth

Sun

Lower-energy radiation (mainly ultraviolet, infra-red, and light rays) leaves surface

High-energy radiation (gamma rays) loses energy while travelling to surface over 2 million years

STAR MAGNITUDES

APPARENT MAGNITUDE

Brighter stars

-9

0

+9

Fainter stars

Sirius: apparent magnitude of -1.46

Rigel: apparent magnitude of +0.12

Objects of magnitude higher than about +5.5 cannot be seen by the naked eye

ABSOLUTE MAGNITUDE

Rigel: absolute magnitude of -7.1

Sirius: absolute magnitude of +1.4

NUCLEAR FUSION IN MAIN SEQUENCE STARS LIKE THE SUN

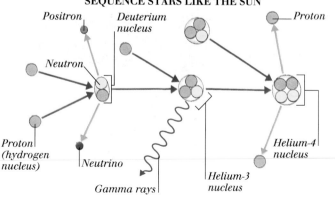

Positron

Deuterium nucleus

Proton

Neutron

Proton (hydrogen nucleus)

Neutrino

Gamma rays

Helium-3 nucleus

Helium-4 nucleus

HERTZSPRUNG-RUSSELL DIAGRAM

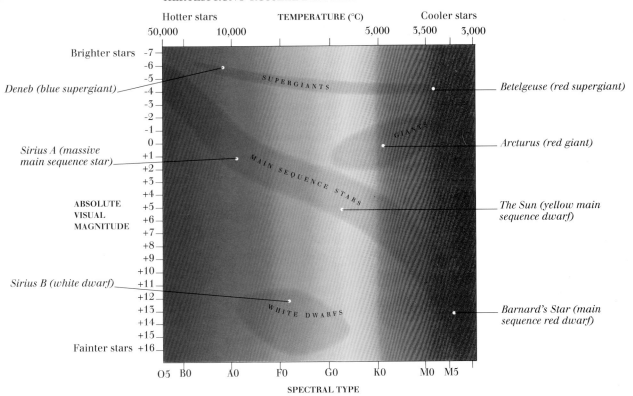

Hotter stars   TEMPERATURE (°C)   Cooler stars

50,000   10,000   5,000   3,500   3,000

Brighter stars   −7 −6 −5 −4 −3 −2 −1 0 +1 +2 +3 +4 +5 +6 +7 +8 +9 +10 +11 +12 +13 +14 +15 +16   Fainter stars

ABSOLUTE VISUAL MAGNITUDE

SUPERGIANTS

GIANTS

MAIN SEQUENCE STARS

WHITE DWARFS

Deneb (blue supergiant)

Sirius A (massive main sequence star)

Sirius B (white dwarf)

Betelgeuse (red supergiant)

Arcturus (red giant)

The Sun (yellow main sequence dwarf)

Barnard's Star (main sequence red dwarf)

O5   B0   A0   F0   G0   K0   M0 M5

SPECTRAL TYPE

STELLAR SPECTRAL ABSORPTION LINES

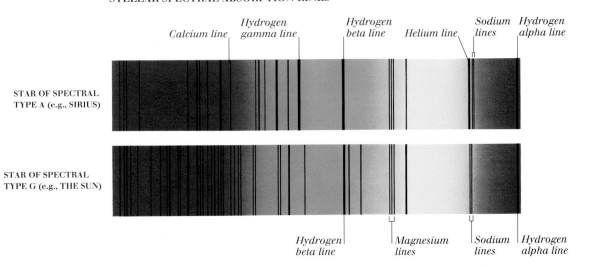

Calcium line   Hydrogen gamma line   Hydrogen beta line   Helium line   Sodium lines   Hydrogen alpha line

STAR OF SPECTRAL TYPE A (e.g., SIRIUS)

STAR OF SPECTRAL TYPE G (e.g., THE SUN)

Hydrogen beta line   Magnesium lines   Sodium lines   Hydrogen alpha line

Small stars

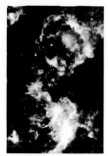

REGION OF STAR FORMATION IN ORION

SMALL STARS HAVE A MASS of up to about one and a half times that of the Sun. They begin to form when a region of higher density in a nebula condenses into a huge globule of gas and dust that contracts under its own gravity. Within a globule, regions of condensing matter heat up and begin to glow, forming protostars. If a protostar contains enough matter, the central temperature reaches about 15 million °C. At this temperature, nuclear reactions in which hydrogen fuses to form helium can start. This process releases energy, which prevents the star from contracting further and also causes it to shine; it is now a main sequence star. A star of about one solar mass remains in the main sequence for about 10 billion years, until the hydrogen in the star's core has been converted into helium. The helium core then contracts again, and nuclear reactions continue in a shell around the core. The core becomes hot enough for helium to fuse to form carbon, while the outer layers of the star expand, cool, and shine less brightly. The expanding star is known as a red giant. When the helium in the core runs out, the outer layers of the star may drift off as an expanding gas shell called a planetary nebula. The remaining core (about 80 per cent of the original star) is now in its final stages. It becomes a white dwarf star that gradually cools and dims. When it finally stops shining altogether, the dead star will become a black dwarf.

STRUCTURE OF A MAIN SEQUENCE STAR

Core containing hydrogen fusing to form helium

Radiative zone

Convective zone

Surface temperature about 5,500°C

Core temperature about 15 million °C

STRUCTURE OF A NEBULA

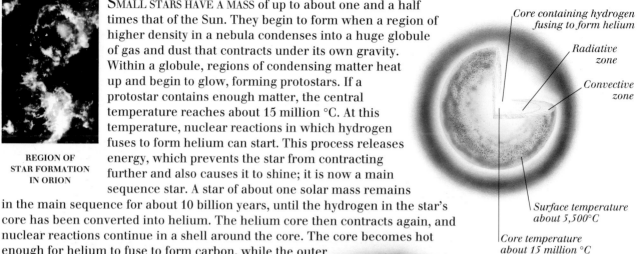

Young main sequence star

Dense region of dust and gas (mainly hydrogen) condensing under gravity to form globules

Hot, ionized hydrogen gas emitting red light due to being stimulated by radiation from hot young stars

Dark globule of dust and gas (mainly hydrogen) contracting to form protostars

LIFE OF A SMALL STAR OF ABOUT ONE SOLAR MASS

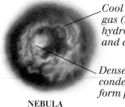

Cool cloud of gas (mainly hydrogen) and dust

Dense globule condensing to form protostars

NEBULA

Glowing ball of gas (mainly hydrogen)

Natal cocoon (shell of dust blown away by radiation from protostar)

PROTOSTAR
Duration: 50 million years

About 1.4 million km

Star producing energy by nuclear fusion in core

MAIN SEQUENCE STAR
Duration: 10 billion years

STRUCTURE OF A RED GIANT

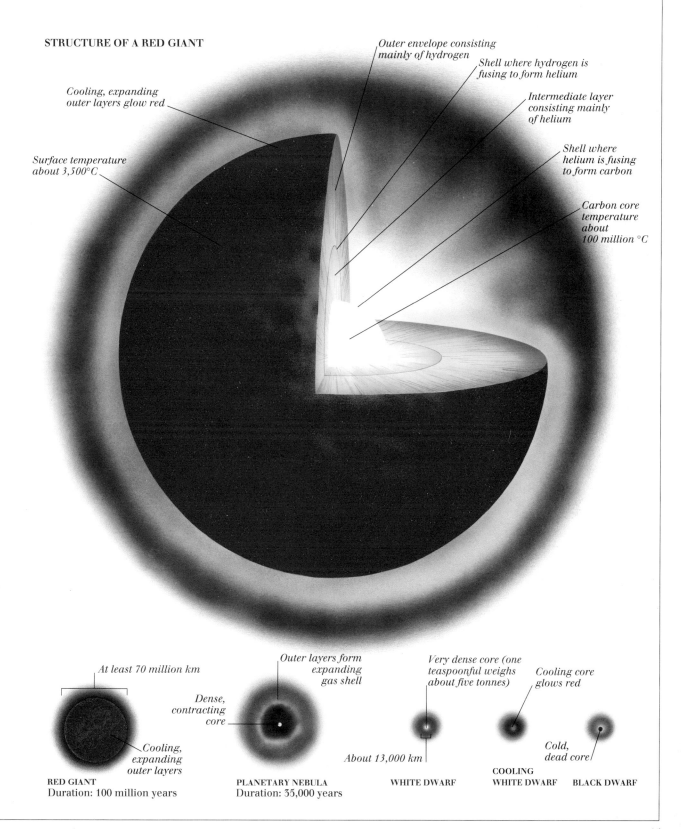

Cooling, expanding outer layers glow red

Surface temperature about 3,500°C

Outer envelope consisting mainly of hydrogen

Shell where hydrogen is fusing to form helium

Intermediate layer consisting mainly of helium

Shell where helium is fusing to form carbon

Carbon core temperature about 100 million °C

At least 70 million km

Cooling, expanding outer layers

RED GIANT
Duration: 100 million years

Outer layers form expanding gas shell

Dense, contracting core

PLANETARY NEBULA
Duration: 35,000 years

Very dense core (one teaspoonful weighs about five tonnes)

About 13,000 km

WHITE DWARF

Cooling core glows red

COOLING WHITE DWARF

Cold, dead core

BLACK DWARF

Massive stars

MASSIVE STARS HAVE A MASS AT LEAST THREE TIMES that of the Sun, and some stars are as massive as about 50 Suns. A massive star evolves in a similar way to a small star until it reaches the main sequence stage (see pp. 24-25). During the main sequence, a star shines steadily until the hydrogen in its core has fused to form helium. This process takes billions of years in a small star, but only millions of years in a massive star. A massive star then becomes a red supergiant, which initially consists of a helium core surrounded by outer layers of cooling, expanding gas. Over the next few million years, a series of nuclear reactions form different elements in shells around an iron core. The core eventually collapses in less than a second, causing a massive explosion called a supernova, in which a shock wave blows away the outer layers of the star. Supernovae shine brighter than an entire galaxy for a short time. Sometimes, the core survives the supernova explosion. If the surviving core is between about one and a half and three solar masses, it contracts to become a tiny, dense neutron star. If the core is considerably greater than three solar masses, it contracts to become a black hole (see pp. 28-29).

SUPERNOVA

TARANTULA NEBULA BEFORE
SUPERNOVA

**STRUCTURE
OF A RED SUPERGIANT**

Outer envelope consisting
mainly of hydrogen

Layer consisting
mainly of helium

Layer consisting
mainly of carbon

Layer consisting
mainly of oxygen

Layer consisting
mainly of silicon

Shell of hydrogen
fusing to form
helium

Shell of helium
fusing to form
carbon

Shell of carbon
fusing to form
oxygen

Shell of oxygen fusing
to form silicon

Shell of silicon fusing
to form iron core

Surface temperature
about 3,000°C

Cooling, expanding
outer layers glow red

Core of mainly iron at a
temperature of 3–5 billion °C

**LIFE OF A MASSIVE STAR OF
ABOUT 10 SOLAR MASSES**

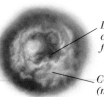

Dense globule
condensing to
form protostars

Cool cloud of gas
(mainly hydrogen)
and dust

NEBULA

Glowing
ball of gas
(mainly hydrogen)

Natal cocoon (shell
of dust blown away
by radiation from
protostar)

PROTOSTAR
Duration: a few hundred
thousand years

About 3 million km

Star producing
energy by nuclear
fusion in
core

MAIN SEQUENCE STAR
Duration: 10 million years

FEATURES OF A SUPERNOVA

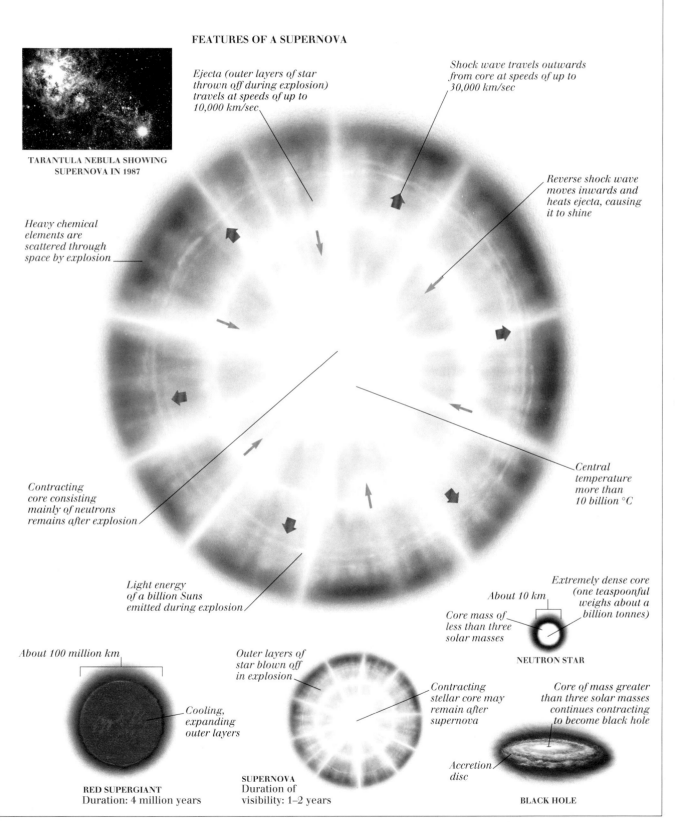

TARANTULA NEBULA SHOWING
SUPERNOVA IN 1987

*Ejecta (outer layers of star
thrown off during explosion)
travels at speeds of up to
10,000 km/sec*

*Shock wave travels outwards
from core at speeds of up to
30,000 km/sec*

*Reverse shock wave
moves inwards and
heats ejecta, causing
it to shine*

*Heavy chemical
elements are
scattered through
space by explosion*

*Contracting
core consisting
mainly of neutrons
remains after explosion*

*Central
temperature
more than
10 billion °C*

*Light energy
of a billion Suns
emitted during explosion*

*Extremely dense core
(one teaspoonful
weighs about a
billion tonnes)*

About 10 km

*Core mass of
less than three
solar masses*

NEUTRON STAR

About 100 million km

*Outer layers of
star blown off
in explosion*

*Contracting
stellar core may
remain after
supernova*

*Core of mass greater
than three solar masses
continues contracting
to become black hole*

*Cooling,
expanding
outer layers*

*Accretion
disc*

RED SUPERGIANT
Duration: 4 million years

SUPERNOVA
Duration of
visibility: 1–2 years

BLACK HOLE

Neutron stars and black holes

NEUTRON STARS AND BLACK HOLES form from the stellar cores that remain after stars have exploded as supernovae (see pp. 26-27). If the remaining core is between about one and a half and three solar masses, it contracts to form a neutron star. If the remaining core is greater than about three solar masses, it contracts to form a black hole. Neutron stars are typically only about 10 kilometres in diameter and consist almost entirely of subatomic particles called neutrons. Such stars are so dense that a teaspoonful would weigh about a billion tonnes. Neutron stars are observed as pulsars, so-called because they rotate rapidly and emit two beams of radio waves, which sweep across the sky and are detected as short pulses. Black holes are characterized by their extremely strong gravity, which is so powerful that not even light can escape; as a result, black holes are invisible. However, they may be detected if they have a close companion star. The gravity of the black hole pulls gas from the other star, forming an accretion disc that spirals around the black hole at high speed, heating up and emitting radiation. Eventually, the matter spirals in to cross the event horizon (the boundary of the black hole), thereby disappearing from the visible Universe.

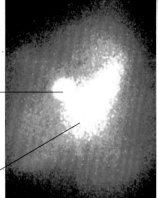

X-ray emission from pulsar (neutron star rotating 30 times each second)

X-ray emission from centre of nebula

X-RAY IMAGE OF THE CRAB NEBULA (SUPERNOVA REMNANT)

PULSAR (ROTATING NEUTRON STAR)

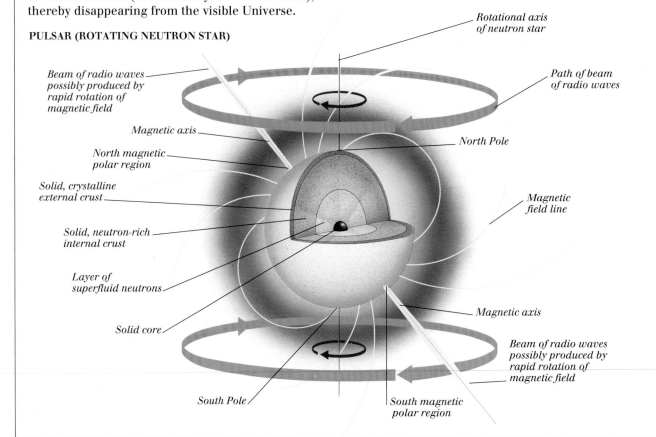

Rotational axis of neutron star

Beam of radio waves possibly produced by rapid rotation of magnetic field

Path of beam of radio waves

Magnetic axis

North magnetic polar region

North Pole

Solid, crystalline external crust

Magnetic field line

Solid, neutron-rich internal crust

Layer of superfluid neutrons

Solid core

Magnetic axis

Beam of radio waves possibly produced by rapid rotation of magnetic field

South Pole

South magnetic polar region

STELLAR BLACK HOLE

Blue supergiant star

Gas current (outer layers of nearby blue supergiant pulled towards black hole by gravity)

Singularity (theoretical region of infinite density, pressure, and temperature)

Hot spot (region of intense friction where gas current joins accretion disc)

Gas in outer part of accretion disc emitting low-energy radiation

Event horizon (boundary of black hole)

Accretion disc (matter spiralling around black hole)

Black hole

Hot gas in inner part of accretion disc emitting high-energy X-rays

Gas at temperatures of millions °C spiralling at close to the speed of light

FORMATION OF A BLACK HOLE

Stellar core remains after supernova explosion

Light rays increasingly bent by gravity as core collapses

Core shrinks beyond its event horizon to become a black hole

Light rays cannot escape because gravity is so strong

Outer layers of massive star thrown off in explosion

Core greater than three solar masses collapses under its own gravity

Density, pressure, and temperature of core increase as core collapses

Event horizon

Singularity (theoretical region of infinite density, pressure, and temperature)

SUPERNOVA

COLLAPSING STELLAR CORE

BLACK HOLE

The Solar System

THE SUN

THE SOLAR SYSTEM consists of a central star (the Sun) and the bodies that orbit it. These bodies include nine planets and their 61 known moons; asteroids; comets; and meteoroids. The Solar System also contains interplanetary gas and dust. Most of the planets fall into two groups: four small rocky planets near the Sun (Mercury, Venus, Earth, and Mars); and four planets further out, the gas giants (Jupiter, Saturn, Uranus, and Neptune). Pluto belongs to neither group but is very small, solid, and icy. Pluto is the outermost planet, except when it passes briefly inside Neptune's orbit. Between the rocky planets and gas giants is the asteroid belt, which contains thousands of chunks of rock orbiting the Sun. Most of the bodies in the Solar System move around the Sun in elliptical orbits located in a thin disc around the Sun's equator. All the planets orbit the Sun in the same direction (anticlockwise when viewed from above) and all but Venus, Uranus, and Pluto also spin about their axes in this direction. Moons also spin as they, in turn, orbit their planets. The entire Solar System orbits the centre of our galaxy, the Milky Way (see pp. 14-15).

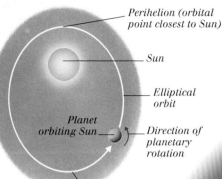

Perihelion (orbital point closest to Sun)

Sun

Elliptical orbit

Planet orbiting Sun

Direction of planetary rotation

Aphelion (orbital point furthest from Sun)

Aphelion of Neptune: 4,537 million km

ORBITS OF INNER PLANETS

Average orbital speed of Venus: 35.03 km/sec
Average orbital speed of Mercury: 47.89 km/sec
Average orbital speed of Earth: 29.79 km/sec
Average orbital speed of Mars: 24.13 km/sec

Mercury

Perihelion of Mercury: 45.9 million km
Perihelion of Venus: 107.4 million km
Perihelion of Earth: 147 million km

Mars

Perihelion of Mars: 206.7 million km

Earth

Venus

Sun

Aphelion of Mercury: 69.7 million km

Asteroid belt

Aphelion of Venus: 109 million km

Aphelion of Earth: 152 million km

Aphelion of Mars: 249 million km

Aphelion of Pluto: 7,375 million km

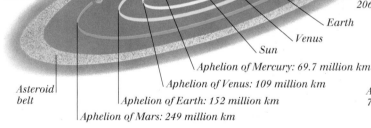

MERCURY
Year: 87.97 Earth days
Mass: 0.06 Earth masses
Diameter: 4,878 km

VENUS
Year: 224.7 Earth days
Mass: 0.81 Earth masses
Diameter: 12,103 km

EARTH
Year: 365.26 days
Mass: 1 Earth mass
Diameter: 12,756 km

MARS
Year: 1.88 Earth years
Mass: 0.11 Earth masses
Diameter: 6,786 km

JUPITER
Year: 11.86 Earth years
Mass: 317.94 Earth masses
Diameter: 142,984 km

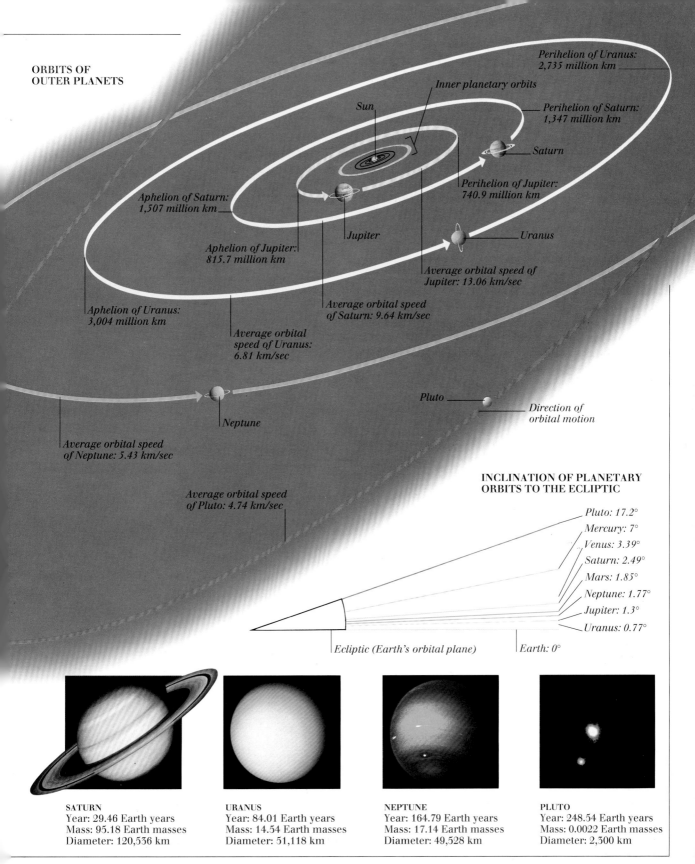

ORBITS OF
OUTER PLANETS

Perihelion of Uranus:
2,735 million km

Inner planetary orbits

Perihelion of Saturn:
1,347 million km

Sun

Saturn

Perihelion of Jupiter:
740.9 million km

Aphelion of Saturn:
1,507 million km

Aphelion of Jupiter:
815.7 million km

Jupiter

Uranus

Average orbital speed of
Jupiter: 13.06 km/sec

Aphelion of Uranus:
3,004 million km

Average orbital
speed of Uranus:
6.81 km/sec

Average orbital speed
of Saturn: 9.64 km/sec

Pluto

Direction of
orbital motion

Neptune

Average orbital speed
of Neptune: 5.43 km/sec

INCLINATION OF PLANETARY
ORBITS TO THE ECLIPTIC

Average orbital speed
of Pluto: 4.74 km/sec

Pluto: 17.2°
Mercury: 7°
Venus: 3.39°
Saturn: 2.49°
Mars: 1.85°
Neptune: 1.77°
Jupiter: 1.3°
Uranus: 0.77°

Ecliptic (Earth's orbital plane)   *Earth: 0°*

SATURN
Year: 29.46 Earth years
Mass: 95.18 Earth masses
Diameter: 120,536 km

URANUS
Year: 84.01 Earth years
Mass: 14.54 Earth masses
Diameter: 51,118 km

NEPTUNE
Year: 164.79 Earth years
Mass: 17.14 Earth masses
Diameter: 49,528 km

PLUTO
Year: 248.54 Earth years
Mass: 0.0022 Earth masses
Diameter: 2,300 km

The Sun

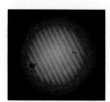

SOLAR PHOTOSPHERE

THE SUN IS THE STAR AT THE CENTRE of the Solar System. It is about five billion years old and will continue to shine as it does now for about another five billion years. The Sun is a yellow main sequence star (see pp. 22-23) about 1.4 million kilometres in diameter. It consists almost entirely of hydrogen and helium. In the Sun's core, hydrogen is converted to helium by nuclear fusion, releasing energy in the process. The energy travels from the core, through the radiative and convective zones, to the photosphere (visible surface), where it leaves the Sun in the form of heat and light. On the photosphere there are often dark, relatively cool areas called sunspots, which usually appear in pairs or groups and are thought to be caused by magnetic fields. Other types of solar activity are flares, which are usually associated with sunspots, and prominences. Flares are sudden discharges of high-energy radiation and atomic particles. Prominences are huge loops or filaments of gas extending into the solar atmosphere; some last for hours, others for months. Beyond the photosphere is the chromosphere (inner atmosphere) and the extremely rarified corona (outer atmosphere), which extends millions of kilometres into space. Tiny particles that escape from the corona give rise to the solar wind, which streams through space at hundreds of kilometres per second. The chromosphere and corona can be seen from Earth when the Sun is totally eclipsed by the Moon.

HOW A SOLAR ECLIPSE OCCURS

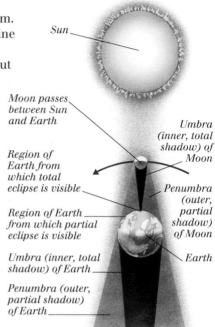

Sun

Moon passes between Sun and Earth

Region of Earth from which total eclipse is visible

Region of Earth from which partial eclipse is visible

Umbra (inner, total shadow) of Moon

Penumbra (outer, partial shadow) of Moon

Earth

Umbra (inner, total shadow) of Earth

Penumbra (outer, partial shadow) of Earth

TOTAL SOLAR ECLIPSE

Corona (outer atmosphere of extremely hot, diffuse gas)

Moon covers Sun's disc

SURFACE FEATURES

Gas loop (looped prominence)

Prominence (jet of gas at edge of Sun's disc up to hundreds of thousands of kilometres high)

Spicule (vertical jet of gas)

Photosphere (visible surface)

Chromosphere (inner atmosphere)

SUNSPOTS

Granulated surface of Sun

Penumbra (lighter, outer region) containing radial fibrils

Umbra (darker, inner region) temperature about 4,000°C

Photosphere temperature about 5,500°C

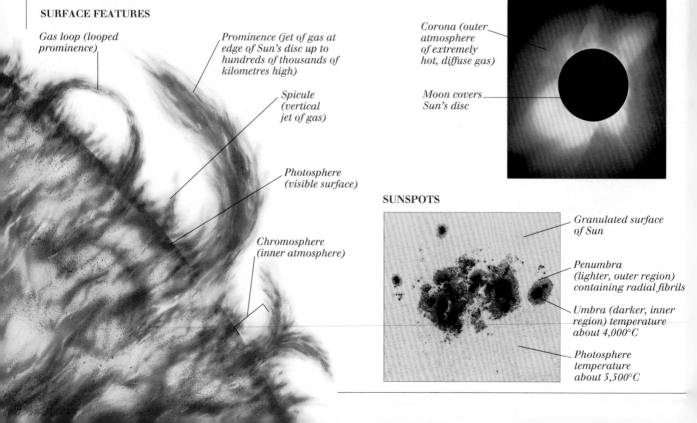

EXTERNAL FEATURES AND
INTERNAL STRUCTURE OF THE SUN

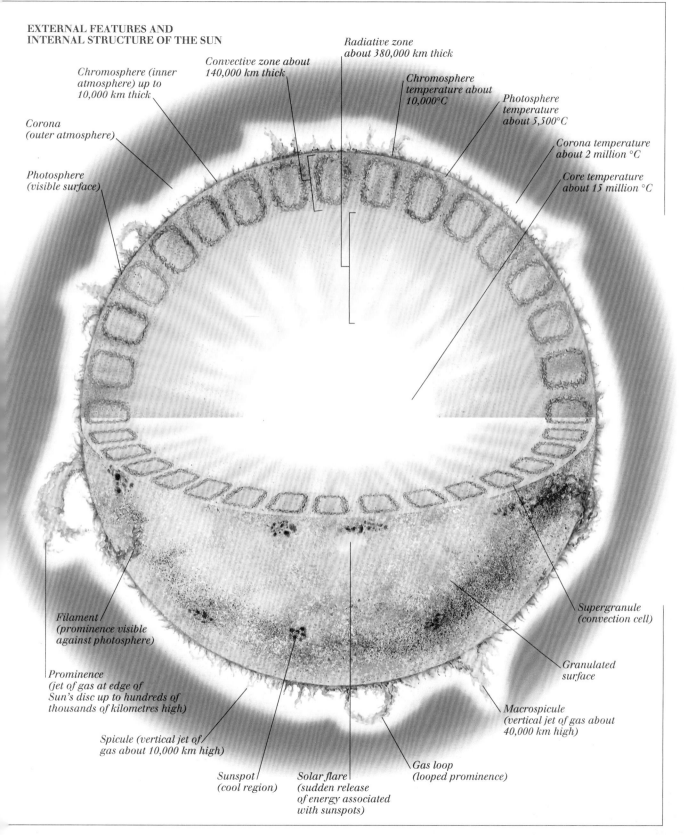

Chromosphere (inner atmosphere) up to 10,000 km thick

Convective zone about 140,000 km thick

Radiative zone about 380,000 km thick

Chromosphere temperature about 10,000°C

Corona (outer atmosphere)

Photosphere temperature about 5,500°C

Photosphere (visible surface)

Corona temperature about 2 million °C

Core temperature about 15 million °C

Supergranule (convection cell)

Filament (prominence visible against photosphere)

Granulated surface

Prominence (jet of gas at edge of Sun's disc up to hundreds of thousands of kilometres high)

Macrospicule (vertical jet of gas about 40,000 km high)

Spicule (vertical jet of gas about 10,000 km high)

Sunspot (cool region)

Solar flare (sudden release of energy associated with sunspots)

Gas loop (looped prominence)

Mercury

MERCURY

MERCURY IS THE NEAREST PLANET to the Sun, orbiting at an average distance of about 58 million kilometres. Because Mercury is the closest planet to the Sun, it moves faster than any other planet, travelling at an average speed of nearly 48 kilometres per second and completing an orbit in just under 88 days. Mercury is very small (only Pluto is smaller) and rocky. Most of the surface has been heavily cratered by the impact of meteorites, although there are also smooth, sparsely cratered plains. The Caloris Basin is the largest crater, measuring about 1,300 kilometres across. It is thought to have been formed when a rock the size of an asteroid hit the planet, and is surrounded by concentric rings of mountains thrown up by the impact. The surface also has many ridges (called rupes) that are thought to have been formed when the hot core of the young planet cooled and shrank about four billion years ago, buckling the planet's surface in the process. The planet rotates about its axis very slowly, taking nearly 59 Earth days to complete one rotation. As a result, a solar day (sunrise to sunrise) on Mercury is about 176 Earth days – twice as long as the 88-day Mercurian year. Mercury has extreme surface temperatures, ranging from a maximum of 430°C on the sunlit side to -170°C on the dark side. At nightfall, the temperature drops very quickly because the planet's atmosphere is almost non-existent. It consists only of minute amounts of helium and hydrogen captured from the solar wind, plus traces of other gases.

TILT AND ROTATION OF MERCURY

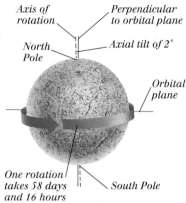

Axis of rotation

Perpendicular to orbital plane

North Pole

Axial tilt of 2°

Orbital plane

One rotation takes 58 days and 16 hours

South Pole

DEGAS AND BRONTË (RAY CRATERS)

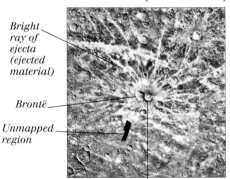

Bright ray of ejecta (ejected material)

Brontë

Unmapped region

Degas with central peak

FORMATION OF A RAY CRATER

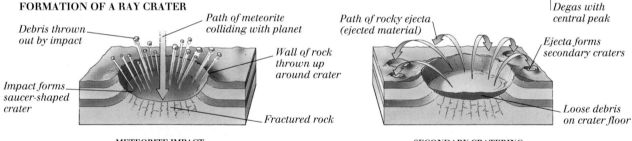

Debris thrown out by impact

Path of meteorite colliding with planet

Wall of rock thrown up around crater

Impact forms saucer-shaped crater

Fractured rock

METEORITE IMPACT

Path of rocky ejecta (ejected material)

Ejecta forms secondary craters

Loose debris on crater floor

SECONDARY CRATERING

Wall of rock forms ring of mountains

Ray of ejecta (ejected material)

Small secondary crater

Loose ejected rock

Central mountain rings form if floor of large crater recoils from meteorite impact

Falling debris forms ridges on side of wall

RAY CRATER

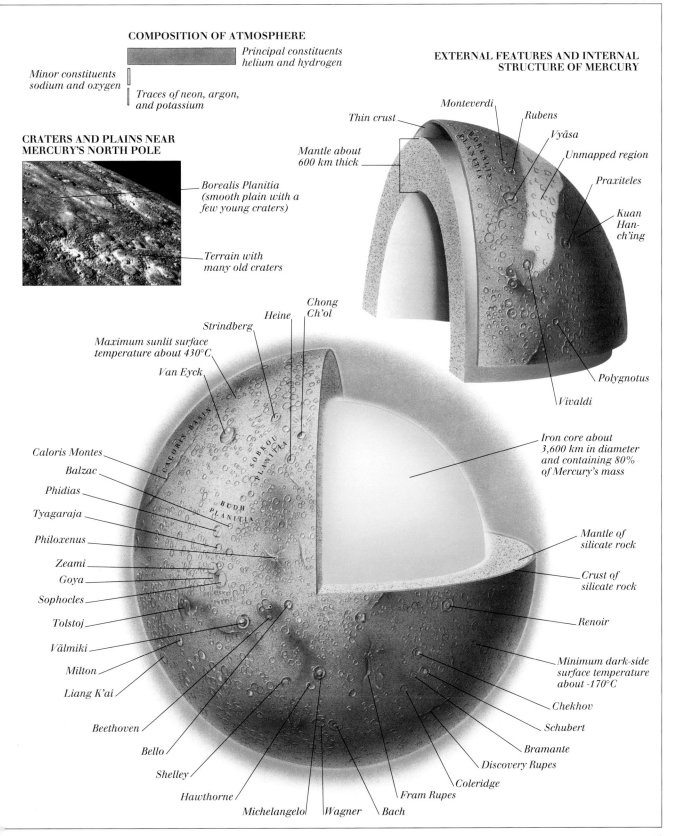

COMPOSITION OF ATMOSPHERE

Principal constituents helium and hydrogen

Minor constituents sodium and oxygen

Traces of neon, argon, and potassium

EXTERNAL FEATURES AND INTERNAL STRUCTURE OF MERCURY

Monteverdi
Rubens
Vyāsa
Thin crust
Unmapped region
Mantle about 600 km thick
Praxiteles
Kuan Han-ch'ing
BOREALIS PLANITIA
Polygnotus
Vivaldi

CRATERS AND PLAINS NEAR MERCURY'S NORTH POLE

Borealis Planitia (smooth plain with a few young craters)

Terrain with many old craters

Heine
Chong Ch'ol
Strindberg
Maximum sunlit surface temperature about 430°C
Van Eyck
Caloris Montes
Balzac
Phidias
Tyagaraja
Philoxenus
Zeami
Goya
Sophocles
Tolstoj
Vālmiki
Milton
Liang K'ai
Beethoven
Bello
Shelley
Hawthorne
Michelangelo
Wagner
Bach

CALORIS BASIN
SOBKOU PLANITIA
BUDH PLANITIA

Iron core about 3,600 km in diameter and containing 80% of Mercury's mass

Mantle of silicate rock

Crust of silicate rock

Renoir

Minimum dark-side surface temperature about -170°C

Chekhov
Schubert
Bramante
Discovery Rupes
Coleridge
Fram Rupes

Venus

RADAR IMAGE OF VENUS

VENUS IS A ROCKY PLANET and the second planet from the Sun. Venus spins slowly backwards as it orbits the Sun, causing its rotational period to be the longest in the Solar System, at about 243 Earth days. It is slightly smaller than Earth and probably has a similar internal structure, consisting of a semi-solid metal core, surrounded by a rocky mantle and crust. Venus is the brightest object in the sky after the Sun and Moon because its atmosphere reflects sunlight strongly. The main component of the atmosphere is carbon dioxide, which traps heat in a greenhouse effect far stronger than that on Earth. As a result, Venus is the hottest planet, with a maximum surface temperature of about 480°C. The thick cloud layers contain droplets of sulphuric acid and are driven around the planet by winds at speeds of up to 360 kilometres per hour. Although the planet takes 243 Earth days to rotate once, the high-speed winds cause the clouds to circle the planet in only four Earth days. The high temperature, acidic clouds, and enormous atmospheric pressure (about 90 times greater at the surface than that on Earth) make the environment extremely hostile. However, space probes have managed to land on Venus and photograph its dry, dusty surface. The Venusian surface has also been mapped by probes with radar equipment that can "see" through the cloud layers. Such radar maps reveal a terrain with craters, mountains, volcanoes, and areas where craters have been covered by plains of solidified volcanic lava. There are two large highland regions called Aphrodite Terra and Ishtar Terra.

TILT AND ROTATION OF VENUS

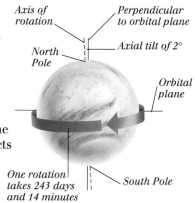

Axis of rotation
Perpendicular to orbital plane
North Pole
Axial tilt of 2°
Orbital plane
One rotation takes 243 days and 14 minutes
South Pole

CLOUD FEATURES

Polar hood
Dark, mid-latitude band
Cloud features swept around planet by winds of up to 360 km/h
Dirty yellow hue due to sulphuric acid in atmosphere
Bright polar band

VENUSIAN CRATERS

Danilova
Ejecta (ejected material)
Central peak
Howe

FALSE-COLOUR RADAR MAP OF THE SURFACE OF VENUS

Metis Regio
Maxwell Montes
Bell Regio
Tethus Regio
Atalanta Planitia
Sedna Planitia
Leda Planitia
Eisila Regio
Tellus Regio
Guinevere Planitia
Niobe Planitia
Phoebe Regio
Alpha Regio
Ovda Regio
Themis Regio
Thetis Regio
Lavinia Planitia
Aino Planitia
Helen Planitia
Lada Terra

ISHTAR TERRA

APHRODITE TERRA

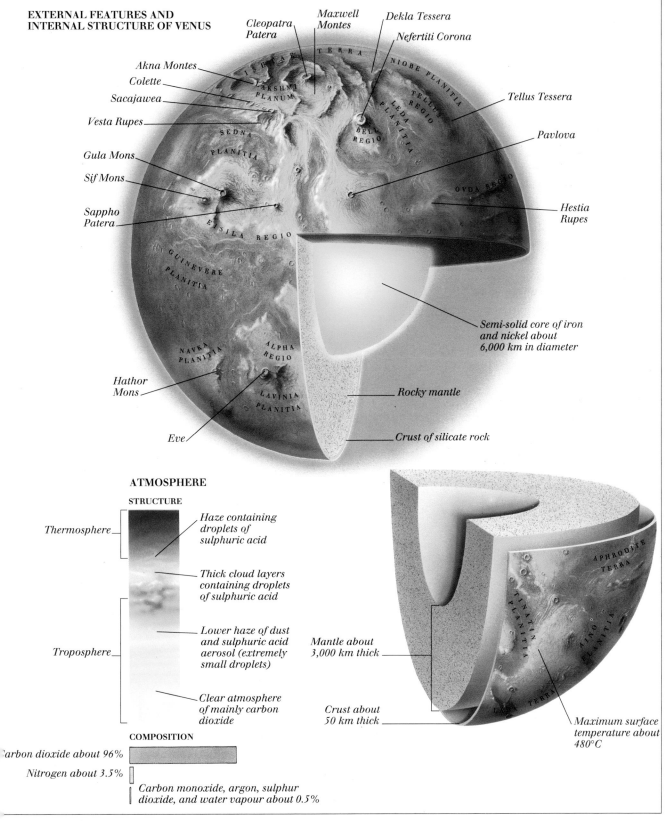

**EXTERNAL FEATURES AND
INTERNAL STRUCTURE OF VENUS**

Cleopatra
Patera

Maxwell
Montes

Dekla Tessera

Nefertiti Corona

Akna Montes

Colette

Sacajawea

Vesta Rupes

Gula Mons

Sif Mons

Sappho
Patera

ISHTAR TERRA

NIOBE PLANITIA

LAKSHMI
PLANUM

TELLUS
REGIO

LEDA
PLANITIA

SEDNA

PLANITIA

BELL
REGIO

GUINEVERE

PLANITIA

FSILA REGIO

OVDA REGIO

Tellus Tessera

Pavlova

Hestia
Rupes

Semi-solid core of iron
and nickel about
6,000 km in diameter

Rocky mantle

Crust of silicate rock

NAVKA
PLANITIA

ALPHA
REGIO

Hathor
Mons

LAVINIA
PLANITIA

Eve

ATMOSPHERE

STRUCTURE

Thermosphere

Troposphere

Haze containing
droplets of
sulphuric acid

Thick cloud layers
containing droplets
of sulphuric acid

Lower haze of dust
and sulphuric acid
aerosol (extremely
small droplets)

Clear atmosphere
of mainly carbon
dioxide

Mantle about
3,000 km thick

Crust about
50 km thick

APHRODITE
TERRA

TINATIN
PLANITIA

AINO
TERRA

Maximum surface
temperature about
480°C

COMPOSITION

Carbon dioxide about 96%

Nitrogen about 3.5%

Carbon monoxide, argon, sulphur
dioxide, and water vapour about 0.5%

The Earth

THE EARTH

THE EARTH IS THE THIRD of the nine planets that orbit the Sun. It is the largest and densest rocky planet, and the only one known to support life. About 70 per cent of the Earth's surface is covered by water, which is not found in liquid form on the surface of any other planet. There are four main layers: the inner core, the outer core, the mantle, and the crust. At the heart of the planet the solid inner core has a temperature of about 4,000°C. The heat from this inner core causes material in the molten outer core and mantle to circulate in convection currents. It is thought that these convection currents generate the Earth's magnetic field, which extends into space as the magnetosphere. The Earth's atmosphere helps screen out some of the harmful radiation from the Sun, stops meteorites from reaching the planet's surface, and traps enough heat to prevent extremes of cold. The Earth has one natural satellite, the Moon, which is large enough for both bodies to be considered a double-planet system.

TILT AND ROTATION OF THE EARTH

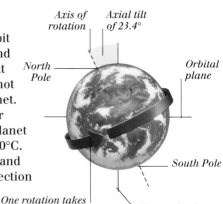

Axis of rotation

Axial tilt of 23.4°

North Pole

Orbital plane

South Pole

One rotation takes 23 hours and 56 minutes

Perpendicular to orbital plane

THE FORMATION OF THE EARTH

The heat of the collisions caused the planet to glow red

The cloud broke up into particles of ice and rock, which stuck together to form planets

Micro-organisms began to photosynthesize, creating a build up of oxygen

4,600 MILLION YEARS AGO, THE SOLAR SYSTEM FORMED FROM A CLOUD OF GAS AND DUST

THE EARTH WAS FORMED FROM COLLIDING ROCKS

4,500 MILLION YEARS AGO THE SURFACE COOLED TO FORM THE CRUST

THE CONTINENTS BROKE UP AND REFORMED, GRADUALLY TAKING THEIR PRESENT POSITIONS

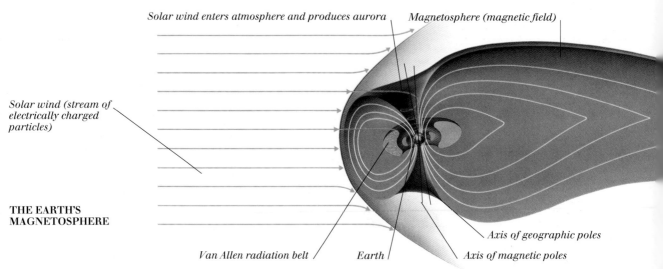

Solar wind enters atmosphere and produces aurora

Magnetosphere (magnetic field)

Solar wind (stream of electrically charged particles)

THE EARTH'S MAGNETOSPHERE

Van Allen radiation belt

Earth

Axis of geographic poles

Axis of magnetic poles

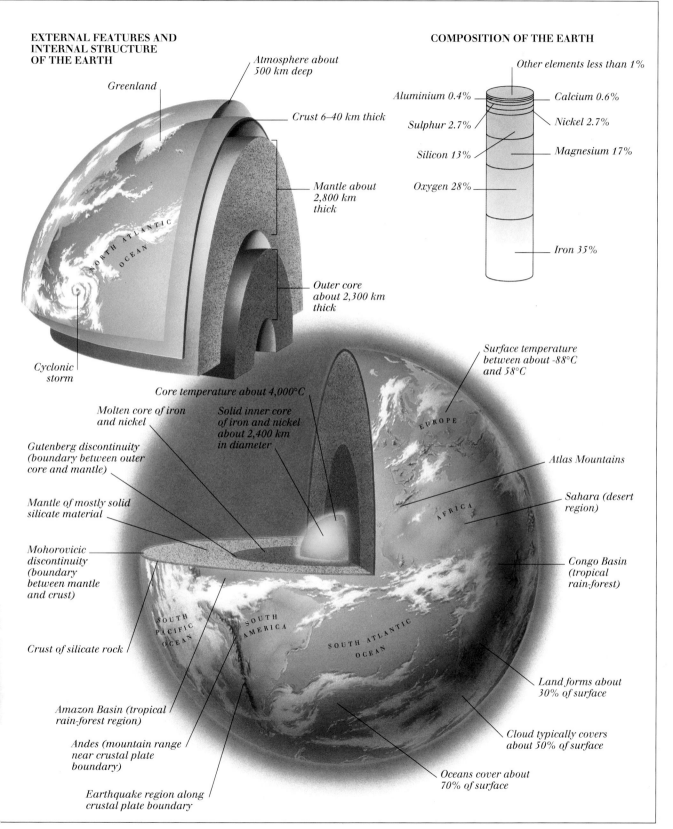

EXTERNAL FEATURES AND INTERNAL STRUCTURE OF THE EARTH

Greenland

Atmosphere about 500 km deep

Crust 6–40 km thick

Mantle about 2,800 km thick

Outer core about 2,300 km thick

NORTH ATLANTIC OCEAN

Cyclonic storm

COMPOSITION OF THE EARTH

Other elements less than 1%

Aluminium 0.4%

Calcium 0.6%

Sulphur 2.7%

Nickel 2.7%

Silicon 13%

Magnesium 17%

Oxygen 28%

Iron 35%

Core temperature about 4,000°C

Molten core of iron and nickel

Solid inner core of iron and nickel about 2,400 km in diameter

Gutenberg discontinuity (boundary between outer core and mantle)

Mantle of mostly solid silicate material

Mohorovicic discontinuity (boundary between mantle and crust)

Crust of silicate rock

Amazon Basin (tropical rain-forest region)

Andes (mountain range near crustal plate boundary)

Earthquake region along crustal plate boundary

Surface temperature between about -88°C and 58°C

EUROPE

Atlas Mountains

Sahara (desert region)

AFRICA

Congo Basin (tropical rain-forest)

SOUTH PACIFIC OCEAN

SOUTH AMERICA

SOUTH ATLANTIC OCEAN

Land forms about 30% of surface

Cloud typically covers about 50% of surface

Oceans cover about 70% of surface

The Moon

THE MOON FROM EARTH

THE MOON IS THE EARTH'S only natural satellite. It is relatively large for a moon, with a diameter of about 3,470 kilometres – just over a quarter that of the Earth. The Moon takes the same time to rotate on its axis as it takes to orbit the Earth (27.3 days), and so the same side (the near side) always faces us. However, the amount of the surface we can see – the phase of the Moon – depends on how much of the near side is in sunlight. The Moon is dry and barren, with no atmosphere or water. It consists mainly of solid rock, although its core may contain molten rock or iron. The surface is dusty, with highlands covered in craters caused by meteorite impacts, and lowlands in which large craters have been filled by solidified lava to form dark areas called maria or "seas". Maria occur mainly on the near side, which has a thinner crust than the far side. Many of the craters are rimmed by mountain ranges that form the crater walls and can be thousands of metres high.

TILT AND ROTATION OF THE MOON

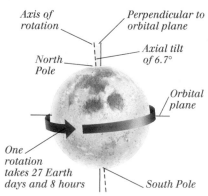

Axis of rotation

Perpendicular to orbital plane

Axial tilt of 6.7°

North Pole

Orbital plane

One rotation takes 27 Earth days and 8 hours

South Pole

CRATERS ON OCEANUS PROCELLARUM

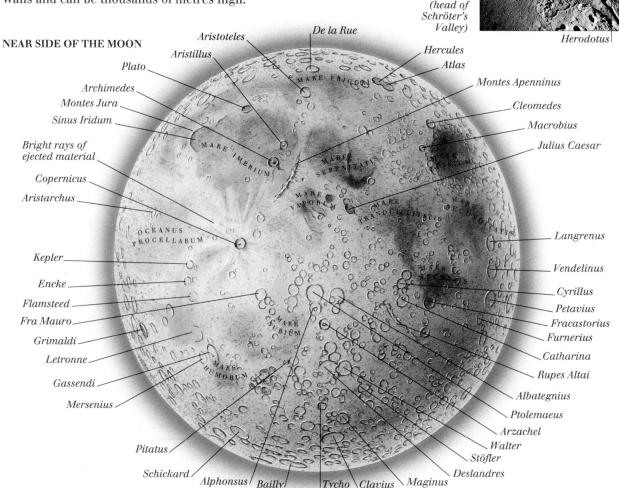

Aristarchus

Cobra Head (head of Schröter's Valley)

Herodotus

NEAR SIDE OF THE MOON

Aristoteles
De la Rue
Aristillus
Plato
Archimedes
Montes Jura
Sinus Iridum
Bright rays of ejected material
Copernicus
Aristarchus
Kepler
Encke
Flamsteed
Fra Mauro
Grimaldi
Letronne
Gassendi
Mersenius
Pitatus
Schickard
Alphonsus
Bailly
Tycho
Clavius
Maginus
Hercules
Atlas
Montes Apenninus
Cleomedes
Macrobius
Julius Caesar
Langrenus
Vendelinus
Cyrillus
Petavius
Fracastorius
Furnerius
Catharina
Rupes Altai
Albategnius
Ptolemaeus
Arzachel
Walter
Stöfler
Deslandres

MARE FRIGORIS
MARE IMBRIUM
MARE SERENITATIS
MARE VAPORUM
MARE TRANQUILLITATIS
OCEANUS PROCELLARUM
MARE NUBIUM
MARE HUMORUM

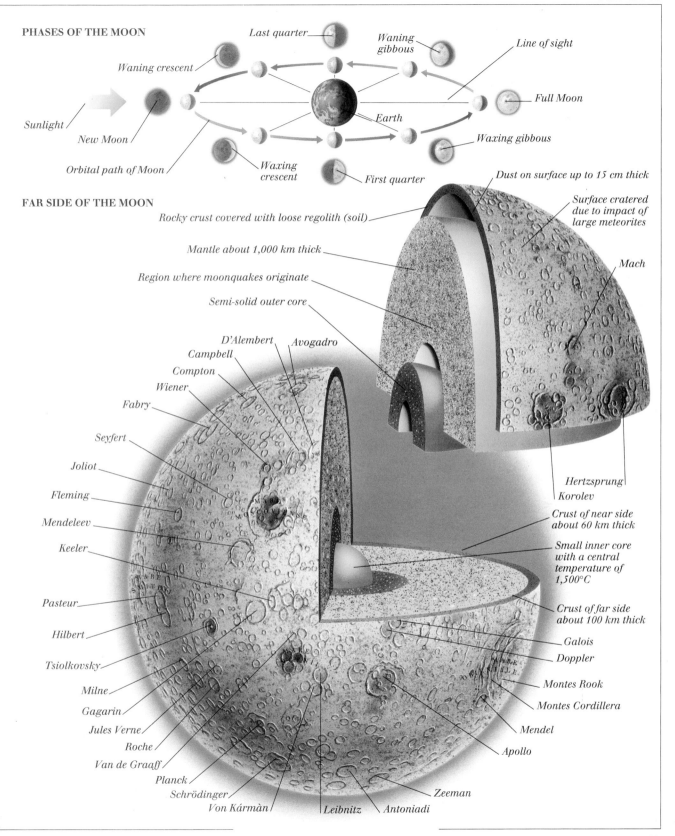

PHASES OF THE MOON

Last quarter

Waning gibbous

Waning crescent

Line of sight

Sunlight

Full Moon

New Moon

Earth

Orbital path of Moon

Waxing crescent

First quarter

Waxing gibbous

FAR SIDE OF THE MOON

Dust on surface up to 15 cm thick

Surface cratered due to impact of large meteorites

Rocky crust covered with loose regolith (soil)

Mantle about 1,000 km thick

Mach

Region where moonquakes originate

Semi-solid outer core

D'Alembert *Avogadro*

Campbell

Compton

Wiener

Fabry

Seyfert

Joliot

Fleming

Mendeleev

Keeler

Hertzsprung

Korolev

Crust of near side about 60 km thick

Small inner core with a central temperature of 1,500°C

Pasteur

Hilbert

Tsiolkovsky

Crust of far side about 100 km thick

Galois

Doppler

Milne

Montes Rook

Gagarin

Montes Cordillera

Jules Verne

Roche

Mendel

Van de Graaff

Apollo

Planck

Schrödinger

Zeeman

Von Kármàn

Leibnitz *Antoniadi*

Mars

MARS

MARS, KNOWN AS THE RED PLANET, is the fourth planet from the Sun and the outermost rocky planet. In the 19th century, astronomers first observed what were thought to be signs of life on Mars. These signs included apparent canal-like markings on the surface, and dark patches that were thought to be vegetation. It is now known that the "canals" are an optical illusion, and the dark patches are areas where the red dust that covers most of the planet has been blown away. The fine dust particles are often whipped up by winds into dust storms that occasionally obscure almost all the surface. Residual dust in the atmosphere gives the Martian sky a pinkish hue. The northern hemisphere of Mars has many large plains formed of solidified volcanic lava, whereas the southern hemisphere has many craters and large impact basins. There are also several huge, extinct volcanoes, including Olympus Mons, which, at 600 kilometres across and 25 kilometres high, is the largest known volcano in the Solar System. The surface also has many canyons and branching channels. The canyons were formed by movements of the surface crust, but the channels are thought to have been formed by flowing water that has now dried up. The Martian atmosphere is much thinner than Earth's, with only a few clouds and morning mists. Mars has two tiny, irregularly shaped moons called Phobos and Deimos. Their small size indicates that they may be asteroids that have been captured by the gravity of Mars.

TILT AND ROTATION OF MARS

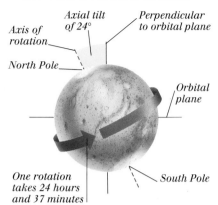

Axial tilt of 24°

Perpendicular to orbital plane

Axis of rotation

North Pole

Orbital plane

One rotation takes 24 hours and 37 minutes

South Pole

SURFACE FEATURES OF MARS

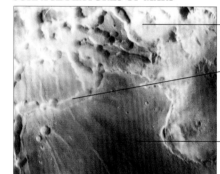

Bright water-ice fog

Fog in canyon about 20 km wide at end of Valles Marineris

Syria Planum

NOCTIS LABYRINTHUS (CANYON SYSTEM)

Summit caldera consisting of overlapping collapsed volcanic craters

Crater

Gentle slope produced by lava flow

Cloud formation

OLYMPUS MONS (EXTINCT SHIELD VOLCANO)

THE SURFACE OF MARS

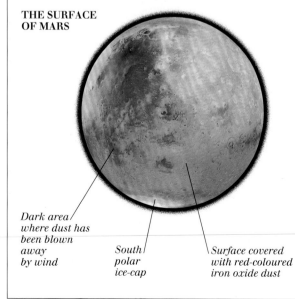

Dark area where dust has been blown away by wind

South polar ice-cap

Surface covered with red-coloured iron oxide dust

MOONS OF MARS

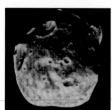

PHOBOS
Average diameter: 22 km
Average distance from planet: 9,400 km

DEIMOS
Average diameter: 13 km
Average distance from planet: 23,500 km

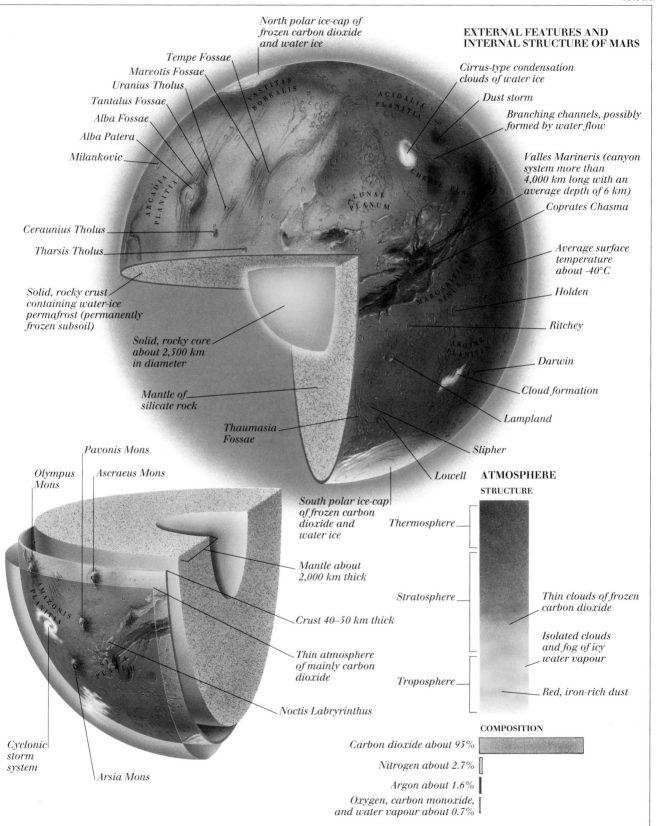

EXTERNAL FEATURES AND INTERNAL STRUCTURE OF MARS

North polar ice-cap of frozen carbon dioxide and water ice

Tempe Fossae

Mareotis Fossae

Uranius Tholus

Tantalus Fossae

Alba Fossae

Alba Patera

Milankovic

Ceraunius Tholus

Tharsis Tholus

Solid, rocky crust containing water-ice permafrost (permanently frozen subsoil)

Solid, rocky core about 2,500 km in diameter

Mantle of silicate rock

Thaumasia Fossae

Cirrus-type condensation clouds of water ice

Dust storm

Branching channels, possibly formed by water flow

Valles Marineris (canyon system more than 4,000 km long with an average depth of 6 km)

Coprates Chasma

Average surface temperature about -40°C

Holden

Ritchey

Darwin

Cloud formation

Lampland

Slipher

Lowell

South polar ice-cap of frozen carbon dioxide and water ice

ATMOSPHERE

STRUCTURE

Thermosphere

Stratosphere

Troposphere

Thin clouds of frozen carbon dioxide

Isolated clouds and fog of icy water vapour

Red, iron-rich dust

Olympus Mons

Pavonis Mons

Ascraeus Mons

Mantle about 2,000 km thick

Crust 40–50 km thick

Thin atmosphere of mainly carbon dioxide

Noctis Labryrinthus

Cyclonic storm system

Arsia Mons

COMPOSITION

Carbon dioxide about 95%

Nitrogen about 2.7%

Argon about 1.6%

Oxygen, carbon monoxide, and water vapour about 0.7%

Jupiter

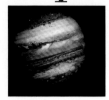

JUPITER

JUPITER IS THE FIFTH PLANET from the Sun and the first of the four gas giants. It is the largest and the most massive planet, with a diameter about 11 times that of the Earth and a mass about 2.5 times the combined mass of the eight other planets. Jupiter is thought to have a small rocky core surrounded by an inner mantle of metallic hydrogen (liquid hydrogen that acts like a metal). Outside the inner mantle is an outer mantle of liquid hydrogen and helium that merges into the gaseous atmosphere. Jupiter's rapid rate of rotation causes the clouds in its atmosphere to form belts and zones that encircle the planet parallel to the equator. Belts are dark, low-lying, relatively warm cloud layers, and zones are bright, high-altitude, cooler cloud layers. Within the belts and zones, turbulence causes the formation of cloud features such as white ovals and red spots, both of which are huge storm systems. The most prominent cloud feature is a storm called the Great Red Spot, which consists of a spiralling column of clouds three times wider than the Earth that rises about eight kilometres above the upper cloud layer. Jupiter has one thin, faint, main ring, inside which is a tenuous halo ring of tiny particles extending towards the planet. There are 16 known Jovian moons. The four largest moons (called the Galileans) are Ganymede, Callisto, Io, and Europa. Ganymede and Callisto are cratered and probably icy. Europa is smooth and icy and may contain water. Io is covered in bright red, orange, and yellow splotches. This colouring is caused by sulphurous material from active volcanoes that shoot plumes of lava hundreds of kilometres above the surface.

TILT AND ROTATION OF JUPITER

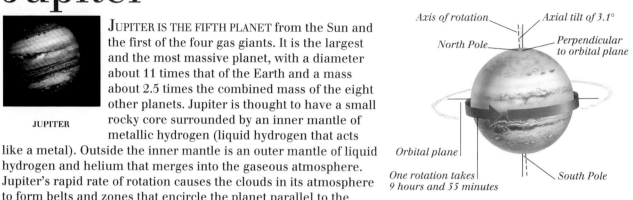

Axis of rotation

Axial tilt of 3.1°

North Pole

Perpendicular to orbital plane

Orbital plane

One rotation takes 9 hours and 55 minutes

South Pole

GREAT RED SPOT AND WHITE OVAL

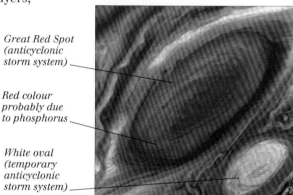

Great Red Spot (anticyclonic storm system)

Red colour probably due to phosphorus

White oval (temporary anticyclonic storm system)

GALILEAN MOONS OF JUPITER

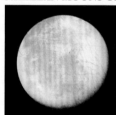

EUROPA
Diameter: 3,138 km
Average distance from planet: 670,900 km

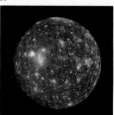

CALLISTO
Diameter: 4,800 km
Average distance from planet: 1,880,000 km

GANYMEDE
Diameter: 5,262 km
Average distance from planet: 1,070,000 km

IO
Diameter: 3,642 km
Average distance from planet: 421,800 km

RINGS OF JUPITER

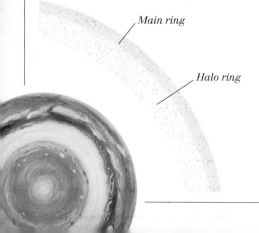

Main ring

Halo ring

ATMOSPHERE

EXTERNAL FEATURES AND INTERNAL STRUCTURE OF JUPITER

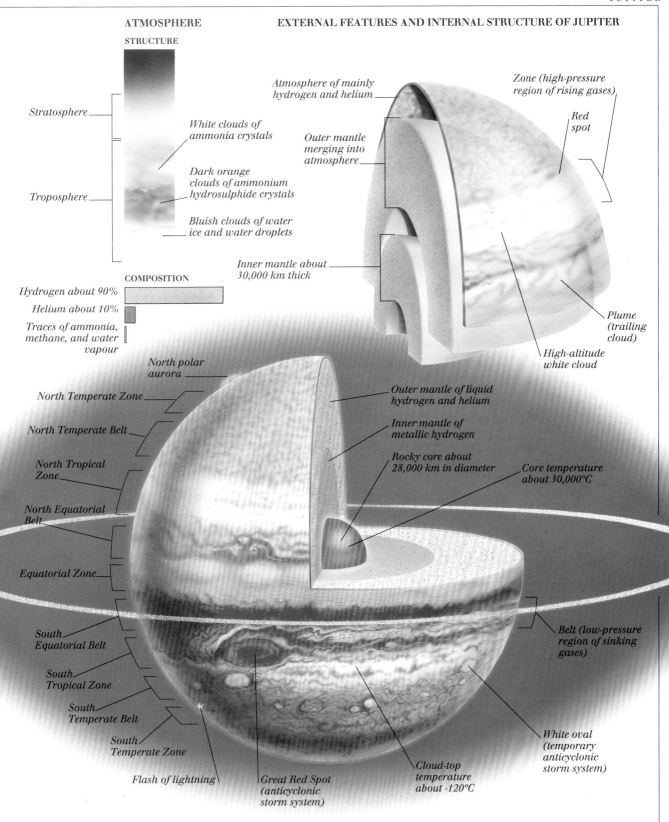

STRUCTURE

Stratosphere

Troposphere

White clouds of
ammonia crystals

Dark orange
clouds of ammonium
hydrosulphide crystals

Bluish clouds of water
ice and water droplets

COMPOSITION

Hydrogen about 90%

Helium about 10%

Traces of ammonia,
methane, and water
vapour

Atmosphere of mainly
hydrogen and helium

Outer mantle
merging into
atmosphere

Inner mantle about
30,000 km thick

Zone (high-pressure
region of rising gases)

Red
spot

Plume
(trailing
cloud)

High-altitude
white cloud

North polar
aurora

North Temperate Zone

North Temperate Belt

North Tropical
Zone

North Equatorial
Belt

Equatorial Zone

South
Equatorial Belt

South
Tropical Zone

South
Temperate Belt

South
Temperate Zone

Flash of lightning

Great Red Spot
(anticyclonic
storm system)

Outer mantle of liquid
hydrogen and helium

Inner mantle of
metallic hydrogen

Rocky core about
28,000 km in diameter

Core temperature
about 30,000°C

Belt (low-pressure
region of sinking
gases)

White oval
(temporary
anticyclonic
storm system)

Cloud-top
temperature
about -120°C

Saturn

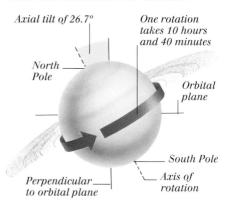

Axial tilt of 26.7°

One rotation takes 10 hours and 40 minutes

North Pole

Orbital plane

South Pole

Axis of rotation

Perpendicular to orbital plane

FALSE-COLOUR IMAGE OF SATURN

SATURN IS THE SIXTH PLANET from the Sun. It is a gas giant almost as big as Jupiter, with an equatorial diameter of about 120,500 kilometres. Saturn is thought to consist of a small core of rock and ice surrounded by an inner mantle of metallic hydrogen (liquid hydrogen that acts like a metal). Outside the inner mantle is an outer mantle of liquid hydrogen that merges into a gaseous atmosphere. Saturn's clouds form belts and zones similar to those on Jupiter, but obscured by overlying haze. Storms and eddies, seen as red or white ovals, occur in the clouds. Saturn has an extremely thin but wide system of rings that is less than one kilometre thick but extends outwards to about 420,000 kilometres from the planet's surface. The main rings comprise thousands of narrow ringlets, each made of icy lumps that range in size from tiny particles to chunks several metres across. The D, E, and G rings are very faint, the F ring is brighter, and the A, B, and C rings are bright enough to be seen from Earth with binoculars. Saturn has 18 known moons, some of which orbit inside the rings and are thought to exert a gravitational influence on the shapes of the rings. Unusually, seven of the moons are co-orbital – they share an orbit with another moon. Astronomers believe that such co-orbital moons may have originated from a single satellite that broke up.

FALSE-COLOUR IMAGE OF SATURN'S CLOUD FEATURES

Ribbon-shaped striation caused by winds of up to 540 km/h

Oval (rotating storm system)

INNER RINGS OF SATURN

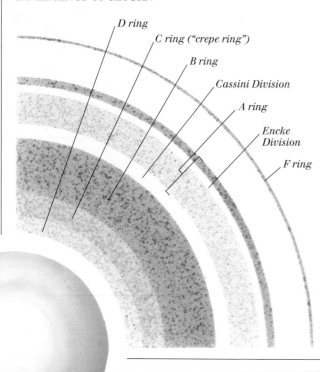

D ring

C ring ("crepe ring")

B ring

Cassini Division

A ring

Encke Division

F ring

MOONS OF SATURN

ENCELADUS
Diameter: 498 km
Average distance from planet: 238,000 km

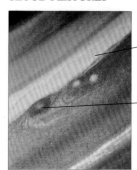

TETHYS
Diameter: 1,050 km
Average distance from planet: 295,000 km

DIONE
Diameter: 1,118 km
Average distance from planet: 377,000 km

MIMAS
Diameter: 397 km
Average distance from planet: 186,000 km

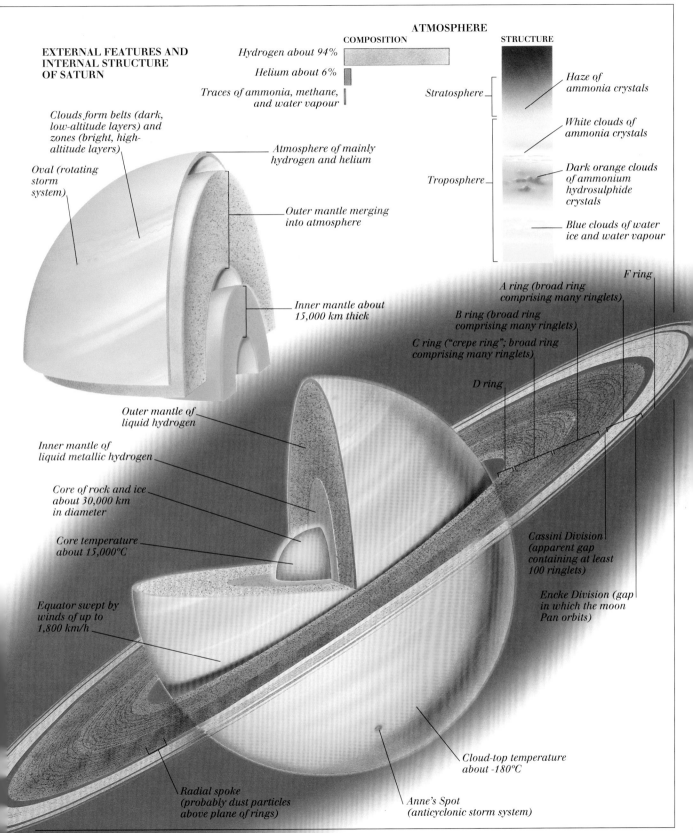

ATMOSPHERE

EXTERNAL FEATURES AND
INTERNAL STRUCTURE
OF SATURN

COMPOSITION

Hydrogen about 94%

Helium about 6%

Traces of ammonia, methane,
and water vapour

STRUCTURE

Stratosphere

Haze of
ammonia crystals

Troposphere

White clouds of
ammonia crystals

Dark orange clouds
of ammonium
hydrosulphide
crystals

Blue clouds of water
ice and water vapour

Clouds form belts (dark,
low-altitude layers) and
zones (bright, high-
altitude layers)

Oval (rotating
storm
system)

Atmosphere of mainly
hydrogen and helium

Outer mantle merging
into atmosphere

Inner mantle about
15,000 km thick

F ring

A ring (broad ring
comprising many ringlets)

B ring (broad ring
comprising many ringlets)

C ring ("crepe ring"; broad ring
comprising many ringlets)

D ring

Outer mantle of
liquid hydrogen

Inner mantle of
liquid metallic hydrogen

Core of rock and ice
about 30,000 km
in diameter

Core temperature
about 15,000°C

Cassini Division
(apparent gap
containing at least
100 ringlets)

Encke Division (gap
in which the moon
Pan orbits)

Equator swept by
winds of up to
1,800 km/h

Radial spoke
(probably dust particles
above plane of rings)

Anne's Spot
(anticyclonic storm system)

Cloud-top temperature
about -180°C

Uranus

FALSE-COLOUR IMAGE OF URANUS

URANUS IS THE SEVENTH PLANET from the Sun and the third largest, with a diameter of about 51,000 kilometres. It is thought to consist of a dense mixture of different types of ice and gas around a solid core. Its atmosphere contains traces of methane, giving the planet a blue-green hue, and the temperature at the cloud tops is about -210°C. Uranus is the most featureless planet to have been closely observed: only a few icy clouds of methane have been seen so far. Uranus is unique among the planets in that its axis of rotation lies close to its orbital plane. As a result of its strongly tilted rotational axis, Uranus rolls on its side along its orbital path around the Sun, whereas other planets spin more or less upright. Uranus is encircled by 11 rings that consist of rocks interspersed with dust lanes. The rings contain some of the darkest matter in the Solar System and are extremely narrow, making them difficult to detect: nine of them are less than 10 kilometres wide, whereas most of Saturn's rings are thousands of kilometres in width. There are 15 known Uranian moons, all of which are icy and most of which are further out than the rings. The 10 inner moons are small and dark, with diameters of less than 160 kilometres, and the five outer moons are between about 470 and 1,600 kilometres in diameter. The outer moons have a wide variety of surface features. Miranda has the most varied surface, with cratered areas broken up by huge ridges and cliffs 20 kilometres high.

TILT AND ROTATION OF URANUS

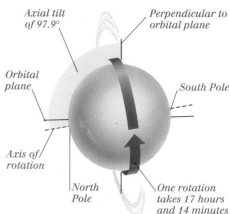

Axial tilt of 97.9°

Perpendicular to orbital plane

Orbital plane

South Pole

Axis of rotation

North Pole

One rotation takes 17 hours and 14 minutes

OUTER MOONS

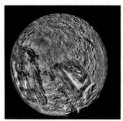

MIRANDA
Diameter: 472 km
Average distance from planet: 129,800 km

RINGS OF URANUS

Epsilon ring

Ring 1986 U1R

Delta ring

Gamma ring

Eta ring

Beta ring

Alpha ring

Rings 4 and 5

Ring 6

Ring 1986 U2R

RINGS AND DUST LANES

ARIEL
Diameter: 1,158 km
Average distance from planet: 191,200 km

UMBRIEL
Diameter: 1,169 km
Average distance from planet: 266,000 km

TITANIA
Diameter: 1,578 km
Average distance from planet: 435,900 km

OBERON
Diameter: 1,523 km
Average distance from planet: 582,600 km

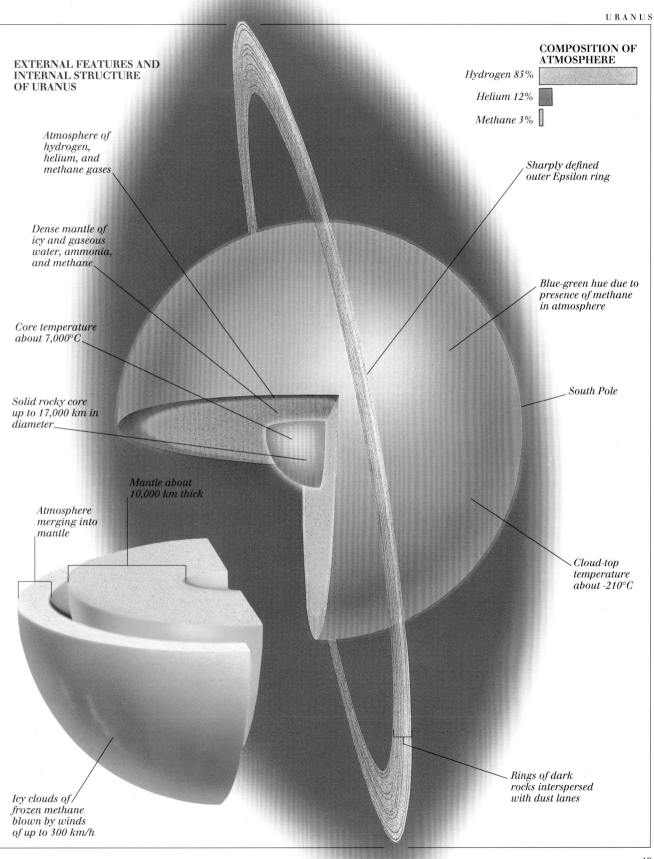

EXTERNAL FEATURES AND
INTERNAL STRUCTURE
OF URANUS

**COMPOSITION OF
ATMOSPHERE**

Hydrogen 85%

Helium 12%

Methane 3%

Atmosphere of
hydrogen,
helium, and
methane gases

Dense mantle of
icy and gaseous
water, ammonia,
and methane

Core temperature
about 7,000°C

Solid rocky core
up to 17,000 km in
diameter

Mantle about
10,000 km thick

Atmosphere
merging into
mantle

Icy clouds of
frozen methane
blown by winds
of up to 300 km/h

Sharply defined
outer Epsilon ring

Blue-green hue due to
presence of methane
in atmosphere

South Pole

Cloud-top
temperature
about -210°C

Rings of dark
rocks interspersed
with dust lanes

Neptune and Pluto

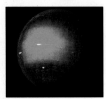

**FALSE-COLOUR
IMAGE OF NEPTUNE**

NEPTUNE AND PLUTO are the two furthest planets from the Sun, at an average distance of about 4,500 million kilometres and 5,900 million kilometres respectively. Neptune is a gas giant and is thought to consist of a small rocky core surrounded by a mixture of liquids and gases. The atmosphere contains several prominent cloud features. The largest of these are the Great Dark Spot, which is as wide as the Earth, the Small Dark Spot, and the Scooter. The Great and Small Dark Spots are huge storms that are swept around the planet by winds of about 2,000 kilometres per hour. The Scooter is a large area of cirrus cloud. Neptune has four tenuous rings and eight known moons. Triton is the largest Neptunian moon and the coldest object in the Solar System, with a temperature of -235°C. Unlike most moons in the Solar System, Triton orbits its mother planet in the opposite direction to the planet's rotation. Pluto is usually the outermost planet but its elliptical orbit causes it to pass inside the orbit of Neptune for 20 years of its 248-year orbit. Pluto is so small and far away that little is known about it. It is a rocky planet, probably covered with ice and frozen methane. Pluto's only known moon, Charon, is large for a moon, at half the size of its parent planet. Because of the small difference in their sizes, Pluto and Charon are sometimes considered to be a double-planet system.

TILT AND ROTATION OF NEPTUNE

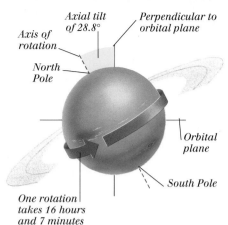

Axis of rotation

Axial tilt of 28.8°

Perpendicular to orbital plane

North Pole

Orbital plane

South Pole

One rotation takes 16 hours and 7 minutes

CLOUD FEATURES OF NEPTUNE

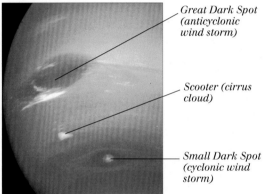

Great Dark Spot (anticyclonic wind storm)

Scooter (cirrus cloud)

Small Dark Spot (cyclonic wind storm)

HIGH-ALTITUDE CLOUDS

Methane cirrus clouds 40 km above main cloud deck

Cloud shadow

Main cloud deck blown by winds at speeds of about 2,000 km/h

RINGS OF NEPTUNE

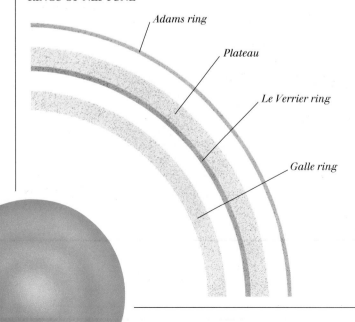

Adams ring

Plateau

Le Verrier ring

Galle ring

MOONS OF NEPTUNE

TRITON
Diameter: 2,705 km
Average distance from planet: 354,800 km

PROTEUS
Diameter: 416 km
Average distance from planet: 117,600 km

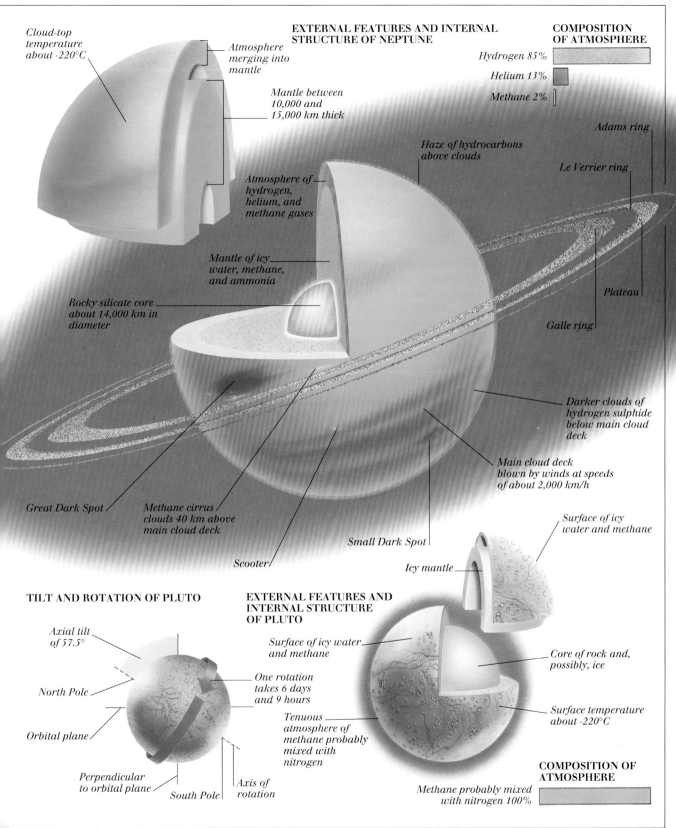

EXTERNAL FEATURES AND INTERNAL STRUCTURE OF NEPTUNE

Cloud-top temperature about -220°C

Atmosphere merging into mantle

Mantle between 10,000 and 15,000 km thick

Haze of hydrocarbons above clouds

Atmosphere of hydrogen, helium, and methane gases

Mantle of icy water, methane, and ammonia

Rocky silicate core about 14,000 km in diameter

COMPOSITION OF ATMOSPHERE

Hydrogen 85%

Helium 13%

Methane 2%

Adams ring

Le Verrier ring

Plateau

Galle ring

Darker clouds of hydrogen sulphide below main cloud deck

Main cloud deck blown by winds at speeds of about 2,000 km/h

Great Dark Spot

Methane cirrus clouds 40 km above main cloud deck

Scooter

Small Dark Spot

TILT AND ROTATION OF PLUTO

Axial tilt of 57.5°

North Pole

Orbital plane

Perpendicular to orbital plane

South Pole

Axis of rotation

One rotation takes 6 days and 9 hours

EXTERNAL FEATURES AND INTERNAL STRUCTURE OF PLUTO

Surface of icy water and methane

Tenuous atmosphere of methane probably mixed with nitrogen

Icy mantle

Surface of icy water and methane

Core of rock and, possibly, ice

Surface temperature about -220°C

COMPOSITION OF ATMOSPHERE

Methane probably mixed with nitrogen 100%

Asteroids, comets, and meteoroids

ASTEROID 951 GASPRA

ASTEROIDS, COMETS, AND METEOROIDS are all debris remaining from the nebula in which the Solar System formed 4.6 billion years ago. Asteroids are rocky bodies up to about 1,000 kilometres in diameter, although most are much smaller. Most of them orbit the Sun in the asteroid belt, which lies between the orbits of Mars and Jupiter. Comets may originate in a huge cloud (called the Oort Cloud) that is thought to surround the Solar System. They are made of frozen gases and dust, and are a few kilometres in diameter. Occasionally, a comet is deflected from the Oort Cloud to orbit the Sun in a long, elliptical path. As the comet approaches the Sun, the comet's surface starts to vaporize in the heat, producing a brightly shining coma (a huge sphere of gas and dust around the nucleus), a gas tail, and a dust tail. Meteoroids are small chunks of stone or stone and iron, some of which are fragments of asteroids or comets. Meteoroids range in size from tiny dust particles to objects tens of metres across. If a meteoroid enters the Earth's atmosphere, it is heated by friction and appears as a glowing streak of light called a meteor (also known as a shooting star). Meteor showers occur when the Earth passes through the trail of dust particles left by a comet. Most meteors burn up in the atmosphere. The few that are large enough to reach the Earth's surface are termed meteorites.

OPTICAL IMAGE OF HALLEY'S COMET

FALSE-COLOUR IMAGE OF HALLEY'S COMET

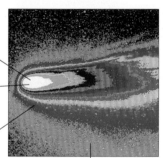

High-intensity light emission

Nucleus

Medium-intensity light emission

Low-intensity light emission

FALSE-COLOUR IMAGE OF A LEONID METEOR SHOWER

METEORITES

DEVELOPMENT OF COMET TAILS

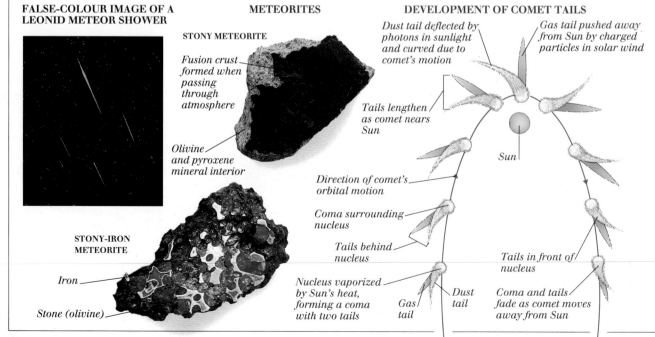

STONY METEORITE

Fusion crust formed when passing through atmosphere

Olivine and pyroxene mineral interior

STONY-IRON METEORITE

Iron

Stone (olivine)

Dust tail deflected by photons in sunlight and curved due to comet's motion

Gas tail pushed away from Sun by charged particles in solar wind

Tails lengthen as comet nears Sun

Direction of comet's orbital motion

Coma surrounding nucleus

Tails behind nucleus

Sun

Nucleus vaporized by Sun's heat, forming a coma with two tails

Gas tail

Dust tail

Tails in front of nucleus

Coma and tails fade as comet moves away from Sun

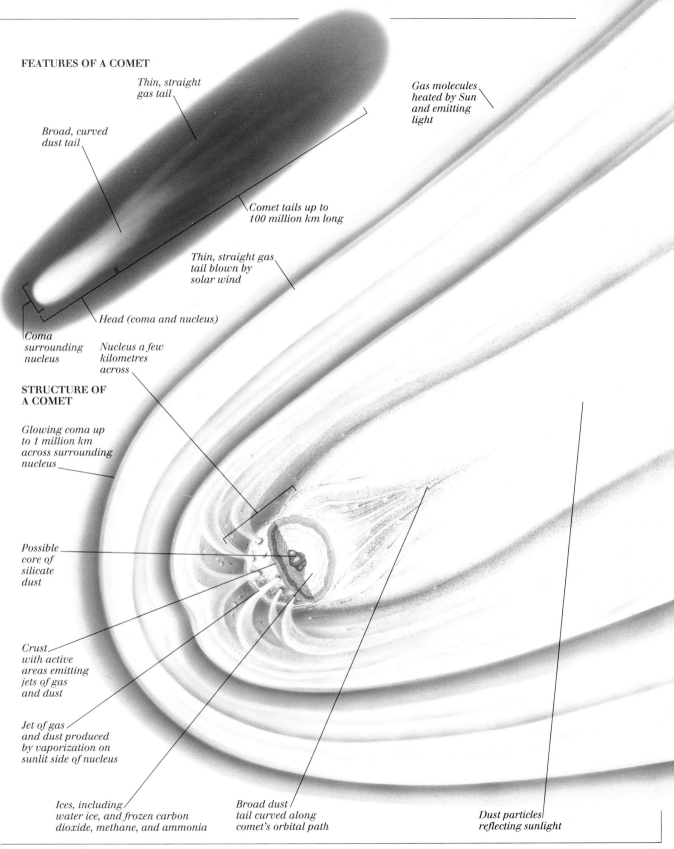

FEATURES OF A COMET

Thin, straight
gas tail

Broad, curved
dust tail

Gas molecules
heated by Sun
and emitting
light

Comet tails up to
100 million km long

Thin, straight gas
tail blown by
solar wind

Head (coma and nucleus)

Coma
surrounding
nucleus

Nucleus a few
kilometres
across

STRUCTURE OF
A COMET

Glowing coma up
to 1 million km
across surrounding
nucleus

Possible
core of
silicate
dust

Crust
with active
areas emitting
jets of gas
and dust

Jet of gas
and dust produced
by vaporization on
sunlit side of nucleus

Ices, including
water ice, and frozen carbon
dioxide, methane, and ammonia

Broad dust
tail curved along
comet's orbital path

Dust particles
reflecting sunlight

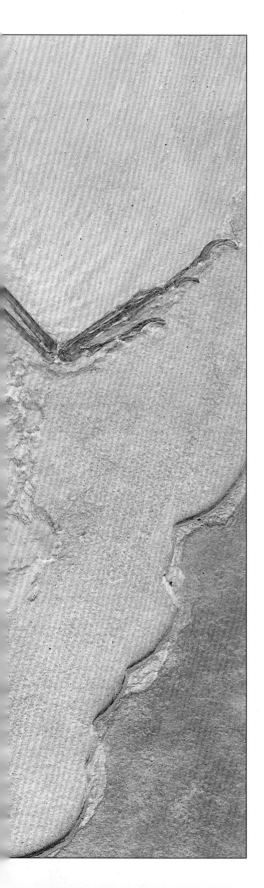

PREHISTORIC EARTH

The changing Earth

THE EARTH FORMED FROM A CLOUD OF DUST and gas drifting
through space about 4,600 million years ago. Dense minerals sank to
the centre while lighter ones formed a thin rocky crust. However,
the first known life-forms – bacteria and blue-green algae – did not
appear until about 3,400 million years ago, and it was only about
700 million years ago that more complex plants and animals
began to develop. Since then, thousands of animal and
plant species have evolved; some, such as the dinosaurs,
survived for many millions of years, while others died
out quickly. The Earth itself is continually changing.
Although continents neared their present locations
about 50 million years ago, they are still drifting
slowly over the planet's surface, and mountain
ranges such as the Himalayas – which began to
form 40 million years ago – are continually
being built up and worn away. Climate is also
subject to change: the Earth has undergone
a series of ice ages interspersed with
warmer periods (the most recent
glacial period was at its height
about 20,000 years ago).

Small mammals
appeared (e.g.,
Crusafontia)

Dinosaurs
became
extinct

Global
mountain
building
occurred

Multicellular soft-
bodied animals
appeared (e.g.,
worms and
jellyfish)

Shelled
invertebrates
appeared (e.g.,
trilobites)

Marine plants
flourished

Land plants
appeared
(e.g., Cooksonia)

Unicellular
organisms appeared
(e.g., blue-green
algae)

Earth
formed

Coral reefs
appeared

Vertebrates
appeared (e.g.,
Hemicyclaspis)

More complex
types of algae
appeared

Amphibians
appeared (e.g.,
Ichthyostega)

CRETACEO

PRECAMBRIAN TIME

CAMBRIAN

ORDOVICIAN

SILURIAN

DEVONIAN

GEOLOGICAL TIMESCALE

MILLIONS OF
YEARS AGO (MYA)

4,600	570	510	439	409	363	323	290

						MISSISSIPPIAN (NORTH AMERICA)	PENNSYLVANIAN (NORTH AMERICA)
	CAMBRIAN	ORDOVICIAN	SILURIAN	DEVONIAN	CARBONIFEROUS		
PRECAMBRIAN TIME	PALAEOZOIC						

EVOLUTION OF THE EARTH

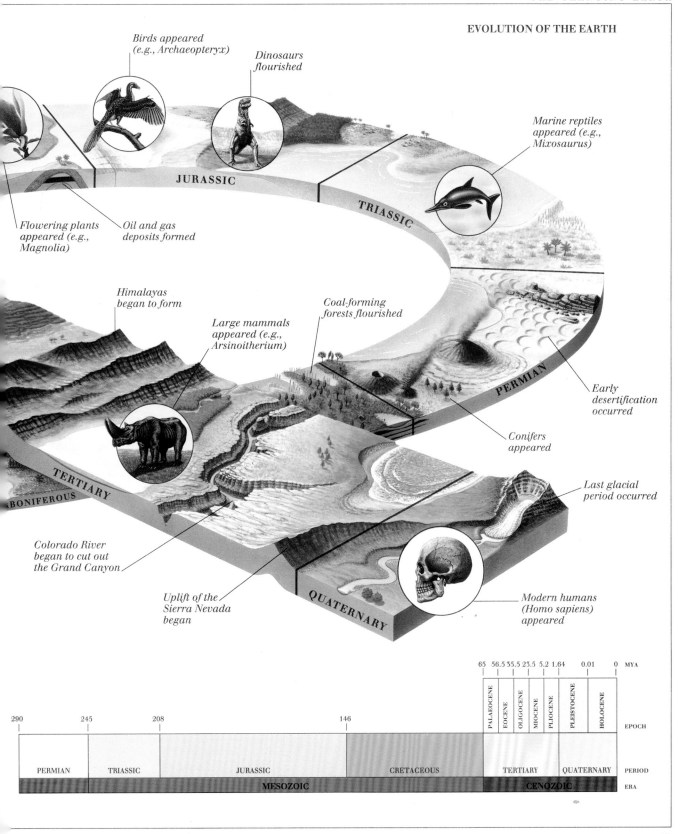

Birds appeared
(e.g., Archaeopteryx)

Dinosaurs
flourished

Marine reptiles
appeared (e.g.,
Mixosaurus)

JURASSIC

TRIASSIC

Flowering plants
appeared (e.g.,
Magnolia)

Oil and gas
deposits formed

Himalayas
began to form

Large mammals
appeared (e.g.,
Arsinoitherium)

Coal-forming
forests flourished

Early
desertification
occurred

PERMIAN

Conifers
appeared

Last glacial
period occurred

TERTIARY

BONIFEROUS

Colorado River
began to cut out
the Grand Canyon

Uplift of the
Sierra Nevada
began

QUATERNARY

Modern humans
(Homo sapiens)
appeared

			65	56.5	35.5	23.5	5.2	1.64		0.01	0 MYA	
			PALAEOCENE	EOCENE	OLIGOCENE	MIOCENE	PLIOCENE		PLEISTOCENE	HOLOCENE		EPOCH
290	245	208					146					
PERMIAN	TRIASSIC	JURASSIC			CRETACEOUS				TERTIARY		QUATERNARY	PERIOD
			MESOZOIC						CENOZOIC			ERA

The Earth's crust

THE EARTH'S CRUST IS THE SOLID outer shell of the Earth. It includes
continental crust (about 40 kilometres thick) and oceanic crust (about
six kilometres thick). The crust and the topmost layer of the mantle
form the lithosphere. The lithosphere consists of semi-rigid plates
that move relative to each other on the underlying asthenosphere
(a partly molten layer of the mantle). This process is known as plate
tectonics and helps explain continental drift. Where two plates move
apart, there are rifts in the crust. In mid-ocean, this movement results
in sea-floor spreading and the formation of ocean ridges; on continents,
crustal spreading can form rift valleys. When plates move towards each other,
one may be subducted beneath (forced under) the other. In mid-ocean, this causes
ocean trenches, seismic activity, and arcs of volcanic islands. Where oceanic crust
is subducted beneath continental crust or where continents collide, land may be
uplifted and mountains formed (see pp. 62–63). Plates may also slide past each
other – along the San Andreas fault, for example. Crustal movement on continents
may result in earthquakes, while movement under the seabed can lead to tidal waves.

ELEMENTS IN THE EARTH'S CRUST

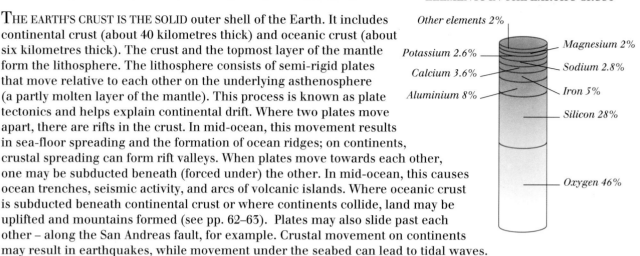

Other elements 2%

Potassium 2.6%

Magnesium 2%

Calcium 3.6%

Sodium 2.8%

Aluminium 8%

Iron 5%

Silicon 28%

Oxygen 46%

FEATURES OF PLATE MOVEMENTS

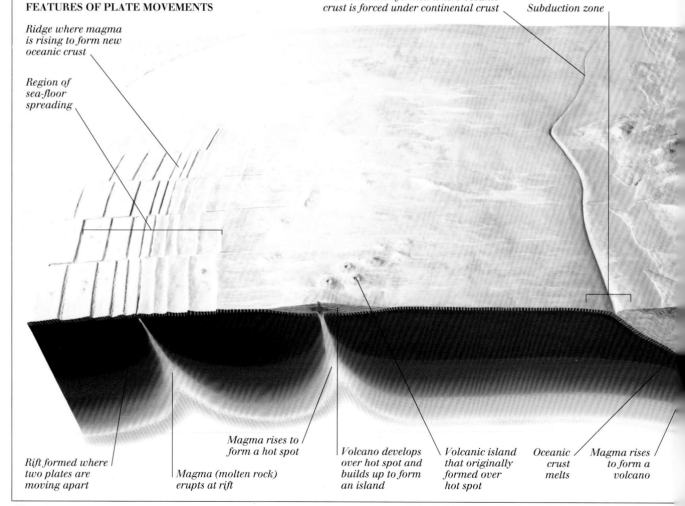

Ridge where magma
is rising to form new
oceanic crust

Region of
sea-floor
spreading

Ocean trench formed where oceanic
crust is forced under continental crust

Subduction zone

Rift formed where
two plates are
moving apart

Magma (molten rock)
erupts at rift

Magma rises to
form a hot spot

Volcano develops
over hot spot and
builds up to form
an island

Volcanic island
that originally
formed over
hot spot

Oceanic
crust
melts

Magma rises
to form a
volcano

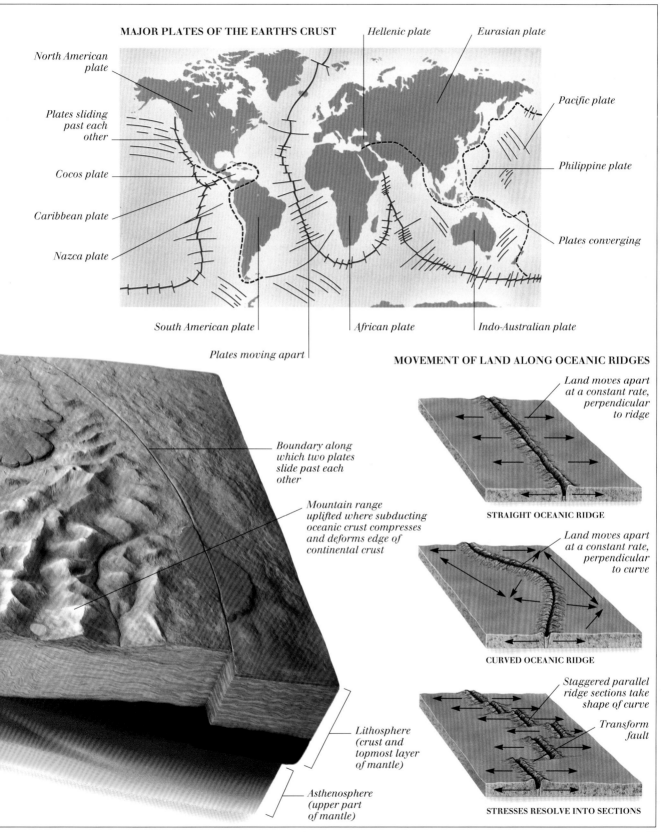

MAJOR PLATES OF THE EARTH'S CRUST

Hellenic plate

Eurasian plate

North American plate

Plates sliding past each other

Cocos plate

Caribbean plate

Nazca plate

Pacific plate

Philippine plate

Plates converging

South American plate

African plate

Indo-Australian plate

Plates moving apart

Boundary along which two plates slide past each other

Mountain range uplifted where subducting oceanic crust compresses and deforms edge of continental crust

Lithosphere (crust and topmost layer of mantle)

Asthenosphere (upper part of mantle)

MOVEMENT OF LAND ALONG OCEANIC RIDGES

Land moves apart at a constant rate, perpendicular to ridge

STRAIGHT OCEANIC RIDGE

Land moves apart at a constant rate, perpendicular to curve

CURVED OCEANIC RIDGE

Staggered parallel ridge sections take shape of curve

Transform fault

STRESSES RESOLVE INTO SECTIONS

Faults and folds

THE CONTINUOUS MOVEMENT of the Earth's crustal plates (see pp. 58–59) can squeeze, stretch, or break rock strata, deforming them and producing faults and folds. A fault is a fracture in a rock along which there is movement of one side relative to the other. The movement can be vertical, horizontal, or oblique (vertical and horizontal). Faults develop when rocks are subjected to compression or tension. They tend to occur in hard, rigid rocks, which are more likely to break than bend. The smallest faults occur in single mineral crystals and are microscopically small, whereas the largest – the Great Rift Valley in Africa, which formed between 5 million and 100,000 years ago – is more than 9,000 kilometres long. A fold is a bend in a rock layer caused by compression. Folds occur in elastic rocks, which tend to bend rather than break. The two main types of fold are anticlines (upfolds) and synclines (downfolds). Folds vary in size from a few millimetres long to folded mountain ranges hundreds of kilometres long, such as the Himalayas (see pp. 62–63) and the Alps, which are repeatedly folding. In addition to faults and folds, other features associated with rock deformations include boudins, mullions, and *en échelon* fractures.

STRUCTURE OF A FOLD

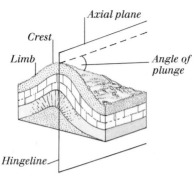

Axial plane
Crest
Limb
Angle of plunge
Hingeline

STRUCTURE OF A FAULT

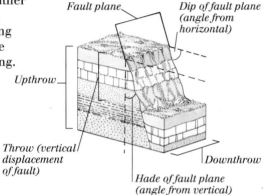

Fault plane
Dip of fault plane (angle from horizontal)
Upthrow
Throw (vertical displacement of fault)
Downthrow
Hade of fault plane (angle from vertical)

STRUCTURE OF A SLOPE

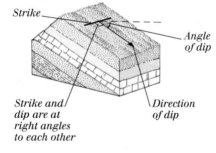

Strike
Angle of dip
Strike and dip are at right angles to each other
Direction of dip

FOLDED ROCK

Steeply dipping limbs
Crest of anticline
Plunge

SECTION THROUGH FOLDED ROCK STRATA THAT HAVE BEEN ERODED

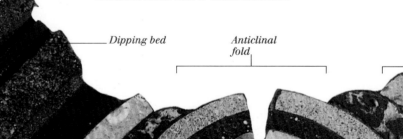

Dipping bed
Anticlinal fold
Monoclinal fold
Mineral-filled fault

Upper Carboniferous Millstone Grit

Lower Carboniferous Limestone

EXAMPLES OF FOLDS

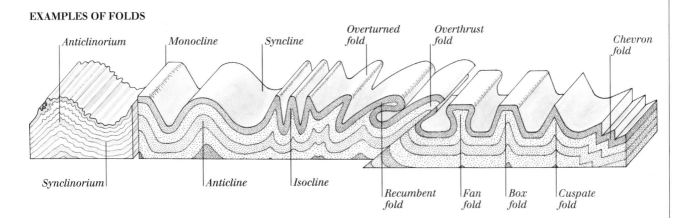

Anticlinorium

Monocline

Syncline

Overturned fold

Overthrust fold

Chevron fold

Synclinorium

Anticline

Isocline

Recumbent fold

Fan fold

Box fold

Cuspate fold

EXAMPLES OF FAULTS

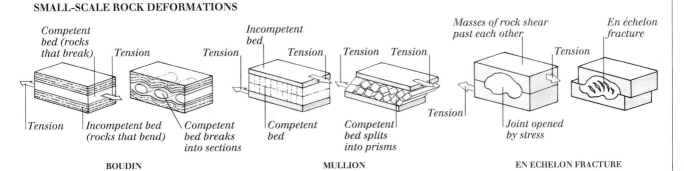

Sinistral strike-slip (lateral) fault

Dextral strike-slip (lateral) fault

Horst

Tear fault

Normal dip-slip fault

Reverse dip-slip fault

Thrust fault

Oblique-slip fault

Graben

Cylindrical fault

SMALL-SCALE ROCK DEFORMATIONS

Competent bed (rocks that break)

Tension

Incompetent bed

Tension

Tension

Tension

Masses of rock shear past each other

Tension

En échelon fracture

Tension

Incompetent bed (rocks that bend)

Competent bed breaks into sections

Competent bed

Competent bed splits into prisms

Joint opened by stress

BOUDIN

MULLION

EN ECHELON FRACTURE

Mineral-filled fault

Dipping bed

Gently folded bed

Horizontal bed

Mineral-filled fault

Dipping bed

Upper Carboniferous Millstone Grit

Upper Carboniferous Coal Measures

Mountain building

THE PROCESSES INVOLVED in mountain building – termed orogenesis – occur as a result of the movement of the Earth's crustal plates (see pp. 58–59). There are three main types of mountains: volcanic mountains, fold mountains, and block mountains. Most volcanic mountains have been formed along plate boundaries where plates have come together or moved apart and lava and other debris have been ejected onto the Earth's surface. The lava and debris may have built up to form a dome around the vent of a volcano. Fold mountains are formed where plates push together and cause the rock to buckle upwards. Where oceanic crust meets less dense continental crust, the oceanic crust is forced under the continental crust. The continental crust is buckled by the impact. This is how folded mountain ranges, such as the Appalachian Mountains in North America, were formed. Fold mountains are also formed where two areas of continental crust meet. The Himalayas, for example, began to form when India collided with Asia, buckling the sediments and parts of the oceanic crust between them. Block mountains are formed when a block of land is uplifted between two faults as a result of compression or tension in the Earth's crust (see pp. 60–61). Often, the movement along faults has taken place gradually over millions of years. However, two plates may cause an earthquake by suddenly sliding past each other along a faultline.

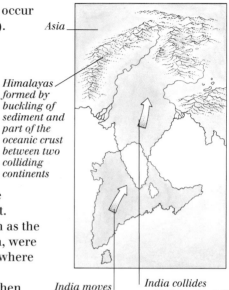

Asia

Himalayas formed by buckling of sediment and part of the oceanic crust between two colliding continents

India moves north

India collides with Asia about 40 million years ago

**BHAGIRATHI PARBAT,
HIMALAYAS**

EXAMPLES OF MOUNTAINS

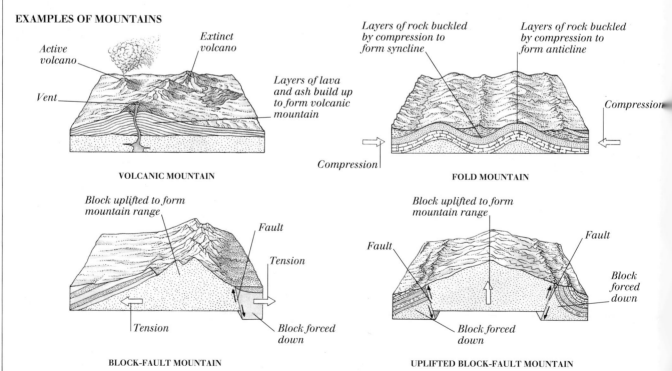

Active volcano

Extinct volcano

Vent

Layers of lava and ash build up to form volcanic mountain

VOLCANIC MOUNTAIN

Layers of rock buckled by compression to form syncline

Layers of rock buckled by compression to form anticline

Compression

Compression

FOLD MOUNTAIN

Block uplifted to form mountain range

Fault

Tension

Tension

Block forced down

BLOCK-FAULT MOUNTAIN

Block uplifted to form mountain range

Fault

Fault

Block forced down

Block forced down

UPLIFTED BLOCK-FAULT MOUNTAIN

STAGES IN THE FORMATION OF THE HIMALAYAS

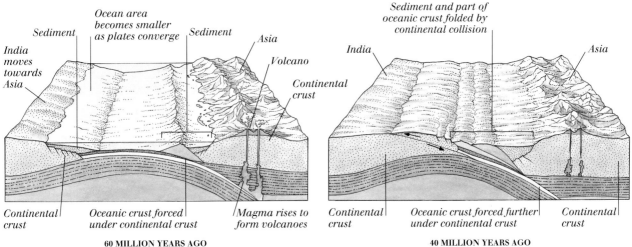

Ocean area becomes smaller as plates converge

Sediment

Sediment

Asia

India moves towards Asia

Volcano

Continental crust

Continental crust

Oceanic crust forced under continental crust

Magma rises to form volcanoes

60 MILLION YEARS AGO

Sediment and part of oceanic crust folded by continental collision

India

Asia

Continental crust

Oceanic crust forced further under continental crust

Continental crust

40 MILLION YEARS AGO

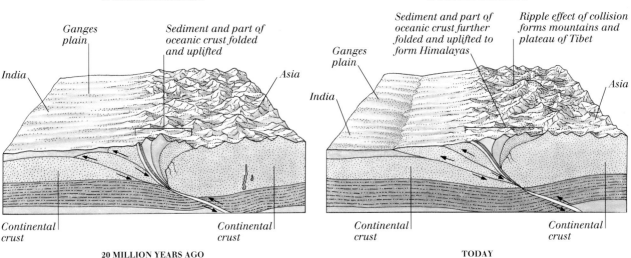

Ganges plain

Sediment and part of oceanic crust folded and uplifted

India

Asia

Continental crust

Continental crust

20 MILLION YEARS AGO

Sediment and part of oceanic crust further folded and uplifted to form Himalayas

Ripple effect of collision forms mountains and plateau of Tibet

Ganges plain

India

Asia

Continental crust

Continental crust

TODAY

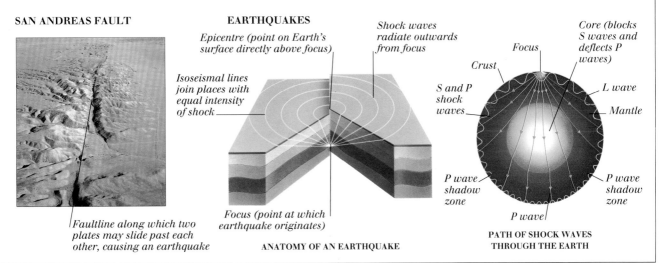

SAN ANDREAS FAULT

Faultline along which two plates may slide past each other, causing an earthquake

EARTHQUAKES

Epicentre (point on Earth's surface directly above focus)

Shock waves radiate outwards from focus

Isoseismal lines join places with equal intensity of shock

Focus (point at which earthquake originates)

ANATOMY OF AN EARTHQUAKE

Core (blocks S waves and deflects P waves)

Focus

Crust

S and P shock waves

L wave

Mantle

P wave shadow zone

P wave shadow zone

P wave

PATH OF SHOCK WAVES THROUGH THE EARTH

Precambrian to Devonian periods

MIDDLE ORDOVICIAN POSITIONS
OF PRESENT-DAY LAND-MASSES

WHEN THE EARTH FORMED about 4,600 million years ago, its atmosphere consisted of volcanic gases with little oxygen, making it hostile to most forms of life. One large supercontinent, Gondwanaland, was situated over the southern polar region, while other smaller continents were spread over the rest of the world. Constant movement of the earth's crustal plates carried continents across the earth's surface. The first primitive life-forms emerged around 3,400 million years ago in shallow, warm seas. The build up of oxygen began to form a shield of ozone around the earth, protecting living organisms from the sun's harmful rays and helping to establish an atmosphere in which life could sustain itself. The first vertebrates appeared about 470 million years ago, during the Ordovician period (510–439 million years ago), the first land plants appeared around 400 million years ago during the Devonian period (409–363 million years ago), and the first land animals about 30 million years later.

EXAMPLES OF PRECAMBRIAN TO DEVONIAN PLANT GROUPS

A PRESENT-DAY CLUBMOSS
(*Lycopodium sp.*)

A PRESENT-DAY
LAND PLANT
(*Asparagus setaceous*)

FOSSIL OF AN EXTINCT LAND PLANT
(*Cooksonia hemisphaerica*)

FOSSIL OF AN EXTINCT SWAMP PLANT
(*Zosterophyllum llanoveranum*)

EXAMPLES OF PRECAMBRIAN TO DEVONIAN TRILOBITES

ACADAGNOSTUS
Family: Agnostidae
Length: 8 mm (⅓ in)

PHACOPS
Family: Phacopidae
Length: 4.5 cm (1¾ in)

OLENELLUS
Family: Olenellidae
Length: 6 cm (2½ in)

ELRATHIA
Family: Ptychopariidae
Length: 2 cm (¾ in)

THE EARTH DURING THE MIDDLE ORDOVICIAN PERIOD

EXAMPLES OF EARLY MARINE INVERTEBRATES

Siberia

Laurentia

China

Kazakstania

Gondwanaland

Baltica

FOSSIL NAUTILOID
(Estonioceras perforatum)

FOSSIL BRACHIOPOD
(Dicoelosia bilobata)

TRACE FOSSIL
(Mawsonites spriggi)

FOSSIL GRAPTOLITE
(Monograptus convolutus)

EXAMPLES OF DEVONIAN FISH

RHAMPHODOPSIS
Family: Ptyctodontidae
Length: 15 cm (6 in)

PTERASPIS
Family: Pteraspidae
Length: 25 cm (10 in)

COCCOSTEUS
Family: Coccosteidae
Length: 35 cm (14 in)

BOTHRIOLEPIS
Family: Bothriolepidae
Length: 40 cm (16 in)

CHEIRACANTHUS
Family: Acanthodidae
Length: 30 cm (12 in)

PTERICHTHYODES
Family: Asterolepidae
Length: 15 cm (6 in)

CHEIROLEPIS
Family: Cheirolepidae
Length: 17 cm (6¾ in)

CEPHALASPIS
Family: Cephalaspidae
Length: 22 cm (8¾ in)

Carboniferous to Permian periods

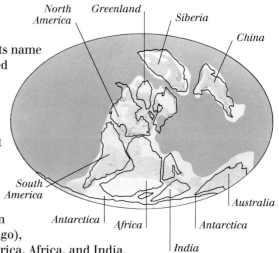

North America
Greenland
Siberia
China
South America
Antarctica
Africa
Australia
Antarctica
India

THE CARBONIFEROUS PERIOD (363–290 million years ago) takes its name from the thick, carbon-rich layers – now coal – that were produced during this period as swampy tropical forests were repeatedly drowned by shallow seas. The humid climate across northern and equatorial continents throughout Carboniferous times produced the first dense plant cover on Earth. During the early part of this period, the first reptiles appeared. Their development of a waterproof egg with a protective internal structure ended animal life's dependence on an aquatic environment. Towards the end of Carboniferous times, the earth's continents Laurasia and Gondwanaland collided, resulting in the huge land-mass of Pangaea. Glaciers smothered much of the southern hemisphere during the Permian period (290–245 million years ago), covering Antarctica, parts of Australia, and much of South America, Africa, and India. Ice locked up much of the world's water and large areas of the northern hemisphere experienced a drop in sea-level. Away from the poles, deserts and a hot dry climate predominated. As a result of these conditions, the Permian period ended with the greatest mass extinction of life on earth ever.

EXAMPLES OF CARBONIFEROUS AND PERMIAN PLANT GROUPS

A PRESENT-DAY FIR
(Abies concolor)

FOSSIL OF AN EXTINCT FERN
(Zeilleria frenzlii)

**FOSSIL OF AN
EXTINCT HORSETAIL**
(Equisetites sp.)

**FOSSIL OF AN
EXTINCT CLUBMOSS**
(Lepidodendron sp.)

EXAMPLES OF CARBONIFEROUS AND PERMIAN TREES

PECOPTERIS
Family: Marattiaceae
Height: 4 m (13 ft)

PARIPTERIS
Family: Medullosaceae
Height: 5 m (16 ft 6 in)

MARIOPTERIS
Family: Unclassified
Height: 5 m (16 ft 6 in)

MEDULLOSA
Family: Medullosaceae
Height: 5 m (16 ft 6 in)

THE EARTH DURING THE LATE CARBONIFEROUS PERIOD

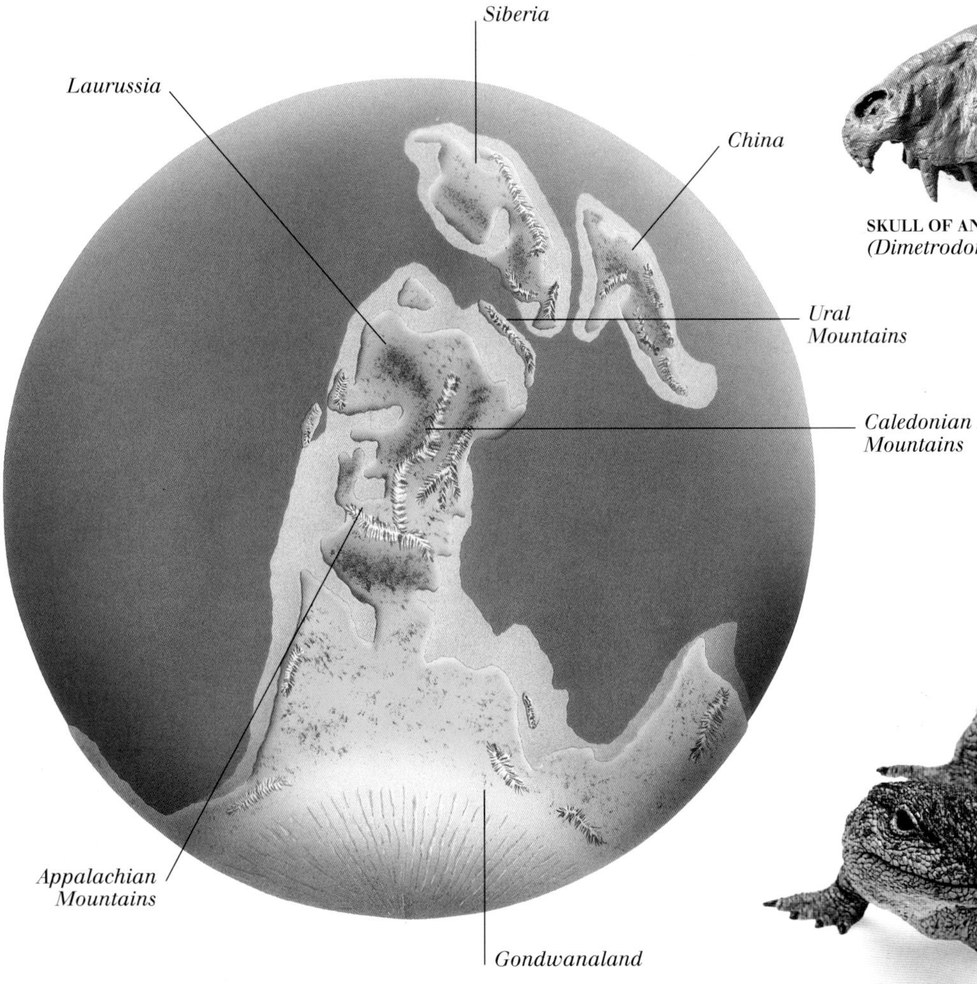

Siberia

Laurussia

China

Ural
Mountains

Caledonian
Mountains

Appalachian
Mountains

Gondwanaland

EXAMPLES OF CARBONIFEROUS
AND PERMIAN ANIMALS

SKULL OF AN EXTINCT SYNAPSID REPTILE
(Dimetrodon loomisi)

FOSSIL TEETH OF
AN EXTINCT SHARK
(Helicoprion bessonowi)

MODEL OF AN EXTINCT
CARBONIFEROUS REPTILE
(Westlothiana lizziae)

LEPIDODENDRON
Family: Lepidodendraceae
Height: 30 m (100 ft)

CORDAITES
Family: Cordaitacea
Height: 10 m (33 ft)

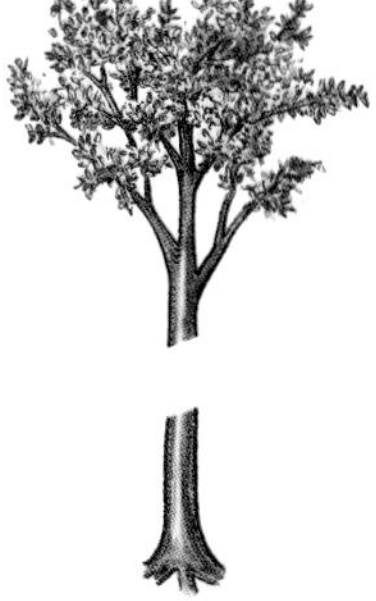

GLOSSOPTERIS
Family: Glossopteridaceae
Height: 8 m (26 ft)

ALETHOPTERIS
Family: Medullosaceae
Height: 5 m (16 ft 6 in)

Triassic period

THE TRIASSIC PERIOD (245–208 million years ago) marked the beginning of what is known as the Age of the Dinosaurs (the Mesozoic era). During this period, the present-day continents were massed together, forming one huge continent known as Pangaea. This land-mass experienced extremes of climate, with lush green areas around the coast or by lakes and rivers, and arid deserts in the interior. The only forms of plant life were non-flowering plants, such as conifers, ferns, cycads, and ginkgos; flowering plants had not yet evolved. The principal forms of animal life included primitive amphibians, rhynchosaurs ("beaked lizards"), and primitive crocodilians. Dinosaurs first appeared about 230 million years ago, at the beginning of the Late Triassic period. The earliest known dinosaurs were the carnivorous (flesh-eating) herrerasaurids and staurikosaurids, such as *Herrerasaurus* and *Staurikosaurus*. Early herbivorous (plant-eating) dinosaurs first appeared in Late Triassic times and included *Plateosaurus* and *Technosaurus*. By the end of the Triassic period, dinosaurs dominated Pangaea, possibly contributing to the extinction of many other reptiles.

TRIASSIC POSITIONS OF PRESENT-DAY LAND-MASSES

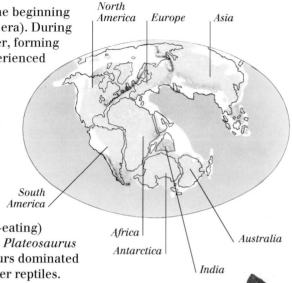

North America
Europe
Asia
South America
Africa
Antarctica
India
Australia

EXAMPLES OF TRIASSIC PLANT GROUPS

A PRESENT-DAY CYCAD
(Cycas revoluta)

A PRESENT-DAY GINKGO
(Ginkgo biloba)

A PRESENT-DAY CONIFER
(Araucaria araucana)

FOSSIL OF AN EXTINCT FERN
(Pachypteris sp.)

FOSSIL LEAF OF AN EXTINCT CYCAD
(Cycas sp.)

EXAMPLES OF TRIASSIC DINOSAURS

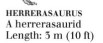

MELANOROSAURUS
A melanorosaurid
Length: 12.2 m (40 ft)

MUSSAURUS
A plateosaurid
Length: 2–3 m (6 ft 6 in–10 ft)

HERRERASAURUS
A herrerasaurid
Length: 3 m (10 ft)

PISANOSAURUS
A primitive ornithischian
Length: 90 cm (3 ft)

THE EARTH DURING THE TRIASSIC PERIOD

EXAMPLES OF TRIASSIC ANIMALS

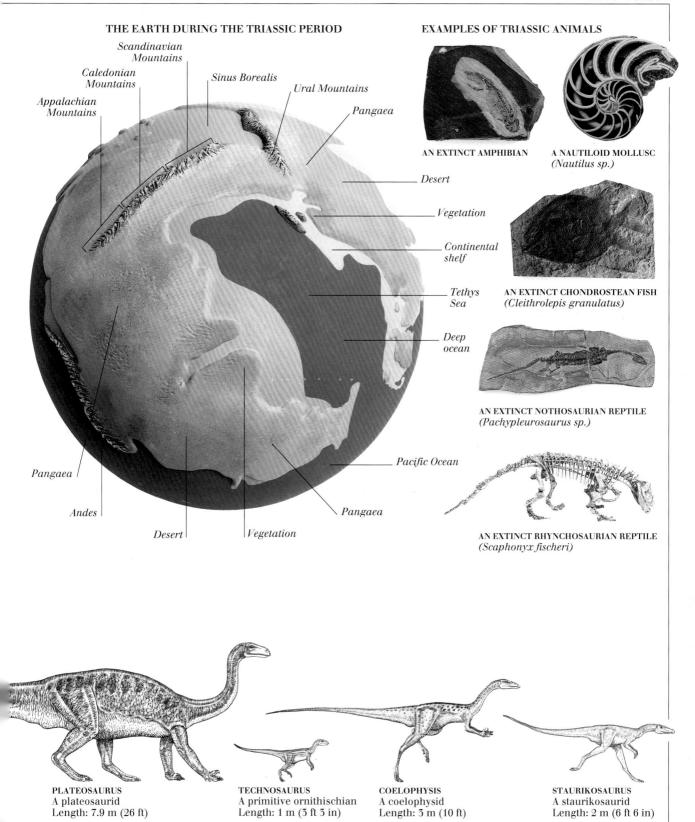

Scandinavian
Mountains

Caledonian
Mountains

Appalachian
Mountains

Sinus Borealis

Ural Mountains

Pangaea

Desert

Vegetation

Continental
shelf

Tethys
Sea

Deep
ocean

Pacific Ocean

Pangaea

Andes

Desert

Vegetation

Pangaea

AN EXTINCT AMPHIBIAN

A NAUTILOID MOLLUSC
(Nautilus sp.)

AN EXTINCT CHONDROSTEAN FISH
(Cleithrolepis granulatus)

AN EXTINCT NOTHOSAURIAN REPTILE
(Pachypleurosaurus sp.)

AN EXTINCT RHYNCHOSAURIAN REPTILE
(Scaphonyx fischeri)

PLATEOSAURUS
A plateosaurid
Length: 7.9 m (26 ft)

TECHNOSAURUS
A primitive ornithischian
Length: 1 m (3 ft 3 in)

COELOPHYSIS
A coelophysid
Length: 3 m (10 ft)

STAURIKOSAURUS
A staurikosaurid
Length: 2 m (6 ft 6 in)

Jurassic period

THE JURASSIC PERIOD, the middle part of the Mesozoic era, lasted from 208 to 146 million years ago. During Jurassic times, the land-mass of Pangaea broke up into the continents of Gondwanaland and Laurasia, and sea-levels rose, flooding areas of lower land. The Jurassic climate was warm and moist. Plants such as ginkgos, horsetails, and conifers thrived, and giant redwood trees appeared, as did the first flowering plants. The abundance of plant food coincided with the proliferation of herbivorous (plant-eating) dinosaurs, such as the large sauropods (e.g., *Diplodocus*) and stegosaurs (e.g., *Stegosaurus*). Carnivorous (flesh-eating) dinosaurs, such as *Compsognathus* and *Allosaurus*, also flourished by hunting the many animals that existed – among them other dinosaurs. Further Jurassic animals included shrew-like mammals, and pterosaurs (flying reptiles), as well as plesiosaurs and ichthyosaurs (both marine reptiles).

JURASSIC POSITIONS OF PRESENT-DAY LAND-MASSES

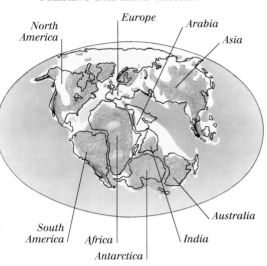

North America

Europe

Arabia

Asia

Australia

South America

Africa

India

Antarctica

EXAMPLES OF JURASSIC PLANT GROUPS

A PRESENT-DAY FERN
(*Dicksonia antarctica*)

A PRESENT-DAY HORSETAIL
(*Equisetum arvense*)

A PRESENT-DAY CONIFER
(*Taxus baccata*)

FOSSIL LEAF OF AN EXTINCT CONIFER
(*Taxus sp.*)

FOSSIL LEAF OF AN EXTINCT REDWOOD
(*Sequoiadendron affinis*)

EXAMPLES OF JURASSIC DINOSAURS

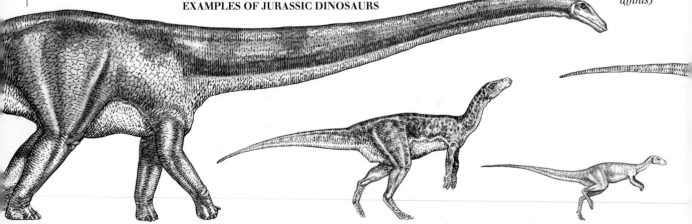

DIPLODOCUS
A diplodocid
Length: 26.8 m (88 ft)

CAMPTOSAURUS
A camptosaurid
Length: 4.9–7 m (16–23 ft)

DRYOSAURUS
A dryosaurid
Length: 3–4 m (10–13 ft)

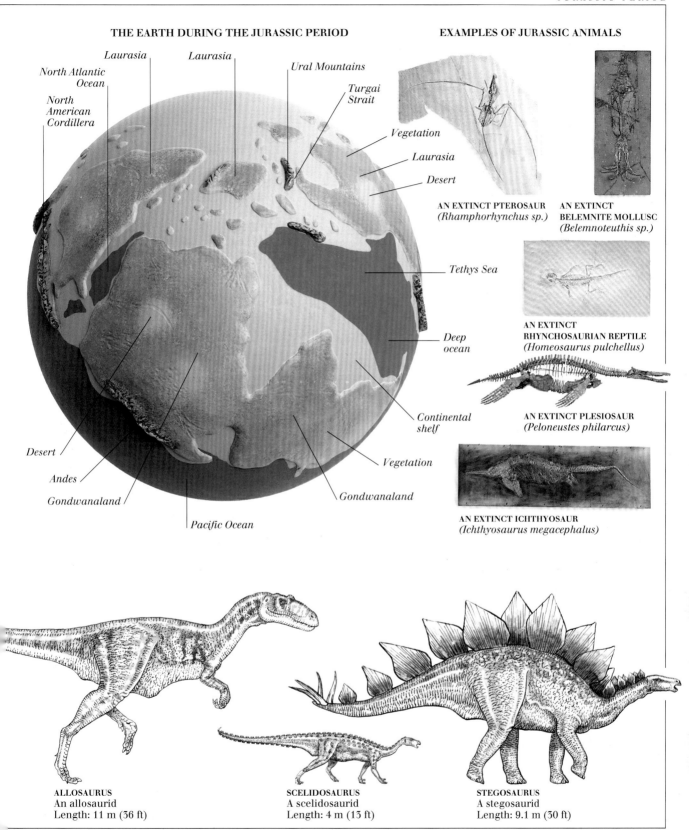

THE EARTH DURING THE JURASSIC PERIOD

Laurasia

Laurasia

North Atlantic Ocean

Ural Mountains

North American Cordillera

Turgai Strait

Vegetation

Laurasia

Desert

Tethys Sea

Deep ocean

Continental shelf

Desert

Andes

Vegetation

Gondwanaland

Gondwanaland

Pacific Ocean

EXAMPLES OF JURASSIC ANIMALS

AN EXTINCT PTEROSAUR
(*Rhamphorhynchus sp.*)

AN EXTINCT BELEMNITE MOLLUSC
(*Belemnoteuthis sp.*)

AN EXTINCT RHYNCHOSAURIAN REPTILE
(*Homeosaurus pulchellus*)

AN EXTINCT PLESIOSAUR
(*Peloneustes philarcus*)

AN EXTINCT ICHTHYOSAUR
(*Ichthyosaurus megacephalus*)

ALLOSAURUS
An allosaurid
Length: 11 m (36 ft)

SCELIDOSAURUS
A scelidosaurid
Length: 4 m (13 ft)

STEGOSAURUS
A stegosaurid
Length: 9.1 m (30 ft)

Cretaceous period

THE MESOZOIC ERA ENDED WITH the Cretaceous period, which lasted from 146 to 65 million years ago. During this period, Gondwanaland and Laurasia were breaking up into smaller land-masses that more closely resembled those of the modern continents. The climate remained mild and moist but the seasons became more marked. Flowering plants, including deciduous trees, replaced many cycads, seed ferns, and conifers. Animal species became more varied, with the evolution of new mammals, insects, fish, crustaceans, and turtles. Dinosaurs evolved into a wide variety of species during Cretaceous times; more than half of all known dinosaurs – including *Iguanodon*, *Deinonychus*, *Tyrannosaurus*, and *Hypsilophodon* – lived during this period. At the end of the Cretaceous period, however, dinosaurs became extinct. The reason for this mass extinction is unknown but it is thought to have been caused by climatic changes due to either a catastrophic meteor impact with the Earth or extensive volcanic eruptions.

CRETACEOUS POSITIONS OF PRESENT-DAY LAND-MASSES

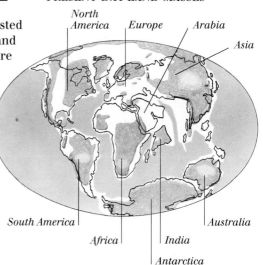

North America | Europe | Arabia | Asia
South America | Africa | India | Antarctica | Australia

EXAMPLES OF CRETACEOUS PLANT GROUPS

A PRESENT-DAY CONIFER
(*Pinus muricata*)

A PRESENT-DAY DECIDUOUS TREE
(*Magnolia sp.*)

FOSSIL OF AN EXTINCT FERN
(*Sphenopteris latiloba*)

FOSSIL OF AN EXTINCT GINKGO
(*Ginkgo pluripartita*)

FOSSIL LEAVES OF AN EXTINCT DECIDUOUS TREE
(*Cercidyphyllum sp.*)

EXAMPLES OF CRETACEOUS DINOSAURS

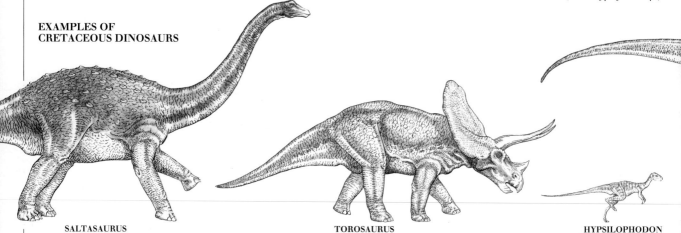

SALTASAURUS
A titanosaurid
Length: 12.2 m (40 ft)

TOROSAURUS
A ceratopsid
Length: 7.6 m (25 ft)

HYPSILOPHODON
A hypsilophodontid
Length: 1.4–2.3 m (4 ft 6 in–7 ft 6 in)

THE EARTH DURING THE CRETACEOUS PERIOD

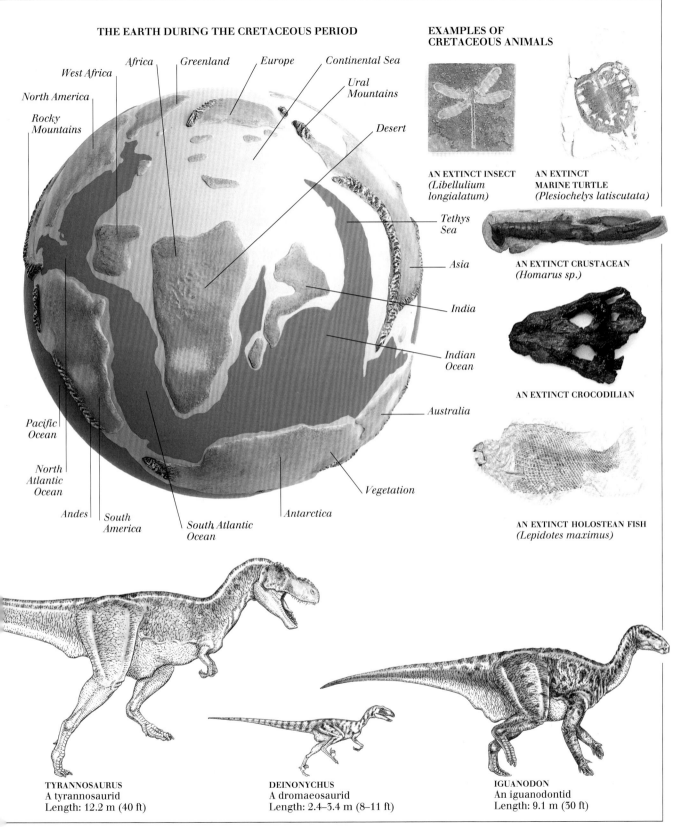

West Africa

Africa

Greenland

Europe

Continental Sea

Ural Mountains

North America

Rocky Mountains

Desert

Tethys Sea

Asia

India

Indian Ocean

Australia

Pacific Ocean

North Atlantic Ocean

Andes

South America

South Atlantic Ocean

Antarctica

Vegetation

AN EXTINCT INSECT
(Libellulium longialatum)

AN EXTINCT MARINE TURTLE
(Plesiochelys latiscutata)

AN EXTINCT CRUSTACEAN
(Homarus sp.)

AN EXTINCT CROCODILIAN

AN EXTINCT HOLOSTEAN FISH
(Lepidotes maximus)

TYRANNOSAURUS
A tyrannosaurid
Length: 12.2 m (40 ft)

DEINONYCHUS
A dromaeosaurid
Length: 2.4–3.4 m (8–11 ft)

IGUANODON
An iguanodontid
Length: 9.1 m (30 ft)

Tertiary period

FOLLOWING THE DEMISE OF THE DINOSAURS at the end of the Cretaceous period, the Tertiary period (65–1.6 million years ago), which formed the first part of the Cenozoic era (65 million years ago–present), was characterized by a huge expansion of mammal life. Placental mammals nourish and maintain the young in the mother's uterus; only three orders of placental mammals existed during Cretaceous times, compared with 25 orders during the Tertiary period. One of these 25 included the first hominid (see pp.108–109), *Australopithecus*, which appeared in Africa. By the beginning of the Tertiary period, the continents had almost reached their present position. The Tethys Sea, which had separated the northern continents from Africa and India, began to close up, forming the Mediterranean Sea and allowing the migration of terrestrial animals between Africa and western Europe. India's collision with Asia led to the formation of the Himalayas. During the middle part of the Tertiary period, the forest-dwelling and browsing mammals were replaced by mammals such as the horse, better suited to grazing the open savannahs that began to dominate. Repeated cool periods throughout the Tertiary period established the Antarctic as an icy island continent.

TERTIARY POSITIONS OF PRESENT-DAY LAND-MASSES

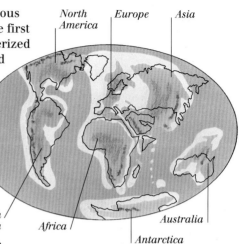

North America

Europe

Asia

South America

Africa

Australia

Antarctica

EXAMPLES OF TERTIARY PLANT GROUPS

A PRESENT-DAY OAK
(*Quercus palustris*)

A PRESENT-DAY BIRCH
(*Betula grossa*)

FOSSIL LEAF OF AN EXTINCT BIRCH
(*Betulites sp.*)

FOSSILIZED STEM OF AN EXTINCT PALM
(*Palmoxylon sp.*)

EXAMPLES OF TERTIARY ANIMAL GROUPS

HYAENODON
An hyaenodontid
Length: 2 m (6 ft 6 in)

TITANOHYRAX
A pliohyracid
Length: 2 m (6 ft 6 in)

PHORUSRHACUS
A phorusrhacid
Length: 1.5 m (5 ft)

SAMOTHERIUM
A giraffid
Length: 3 m (10 ft)

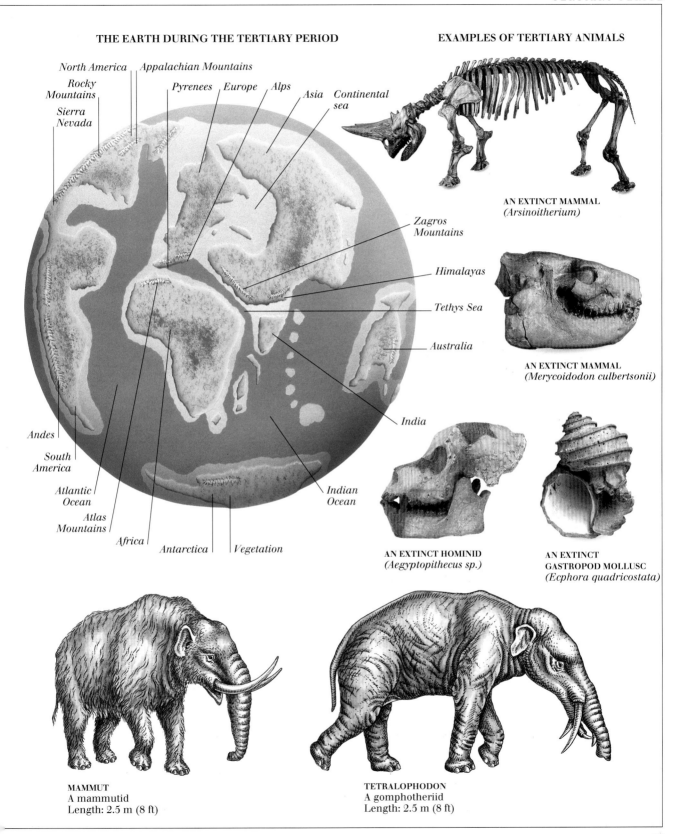

THE EARTH DURING THE TERTIARY PERIOD

North America
Appalachian Mountains
Rocky Mountains
Pyrenees
Europe
Alps
Asia
Continental sea
Sierra Nevada
Zagros Mountains
Himalayas
Tethys Sea
Australia
India
Andes
South America
Atlantic Ocean
Atlas Mountains
Indian Ocean
Africa
Antarctica
Vegetation

EXAMPLES OF TERTIARY ANIMALS

AN EXTINCT MAMMAL
(*Arsinoitherium*)

AN EXTINCT MAMMAL
(*Merycoidodon culbertsonii*)

AN EXTINCT HOMINID
(*Aegyptopithecus sp.*)

AN EXTINCT
GASTROPOD MOLLUSC
(*Ecphora quadricostata*)

MAMMUT
A mammutid
Length: 2.5 m (8 ft)

TETRALOPHODON
A gomphotheriid
Length: 2.5 m (8 ft)

Quaternary period

QUATERNARY POSITIONS OF PRESENT-DAY LAND-MASSES

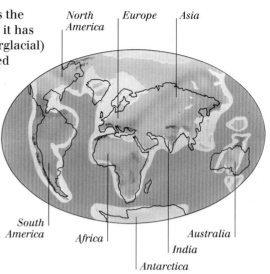

North America
Europe
Asia
South America
Africa
India
Antarctica
Australia

THE QUATERNARY PERIOD (1.6 million years ago–present) forms the second part of the Cenozoic era (65 million years ago–present): it has been characterized by alternating cold (glacial) and warm (interglacial) periods. During cold periods, ice sheets and glaciers have formed repeatedly on northern and southern continents. The cold environments in North America and Eurasia, and to a lesser extent in southern South America and parts of Australia, have caused the migration of many life forms towards the Equator. Only the specialized ice age mammals such as *Mammuthus* and *Coelodonta*, with their thick wool and fat insulation, were suited to life in very cold climates. Humans developed throughout the Pleistocene period (1.6 million–10,000 years ago) in Africa and migrated northward into Europe and Asia. Modern humans, *Homo sapiens*, lived on the cold European continent 30,000 years ago and hunted mammals. The end of the last ice age and the climatic changes that occurred about 10,000 years ago brought extinction to many Pleistocene mammals, but enabled humans to flourish.

EXAMPLES OF QUATERNARY PLANT GROUPS

A PRESENT-DAY BIRCH
(*Betula lenta*)

A PRESENT-DAY SWEETGUM
(*Liquidambar styraciflua*)

FOSSIL LEAF OF A SWEETGUM
(*Liquidambar europeanum*)

FOSSIL LEAF OF A BIRCH
(*Betula sp.*)

EXAMPLES OF QUATERNARY ANIMAL GROUPS

PROCOPTODON
A macropodid
Length: 3 m (10 ft)

DIPROTODON
A diprotodontid
Length: 3 m (10 ft)

TOXODON
A toxodontid
Length: 3 m (10 ft)

MAMMUTHUS
An elephantid
Length: 3 m (10 ft)

THE EARTH DURING THE QUATERNARY PERIOD

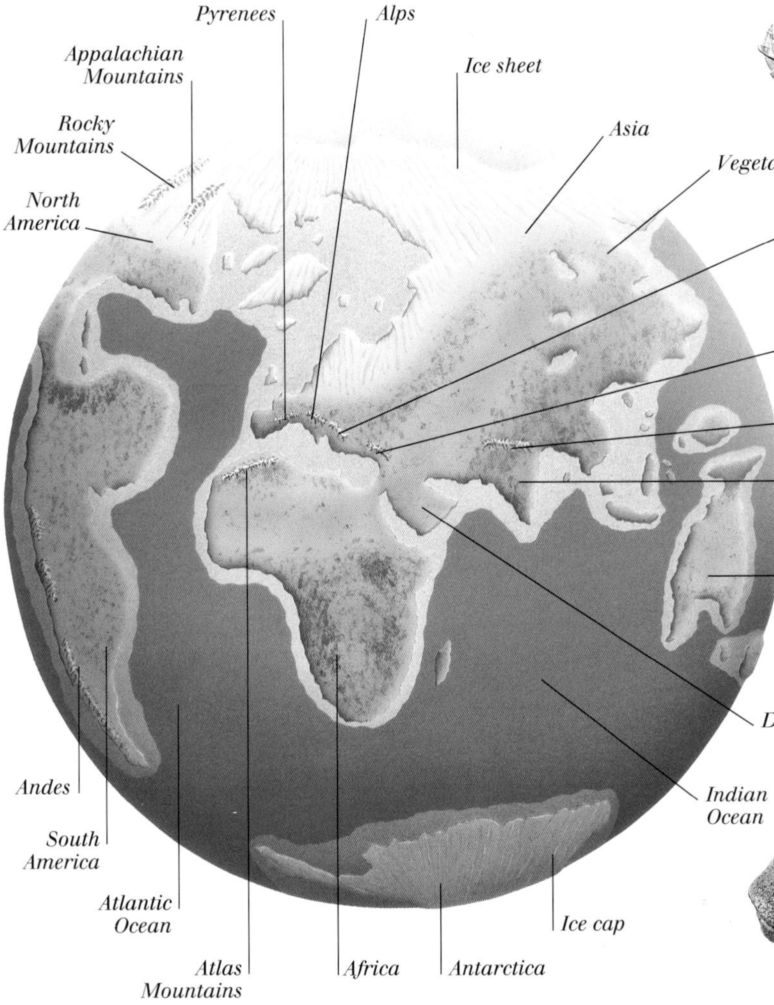

Pyrenees

Alps

Appalachian
Mountains

Ice sheet

Rocky
Mountains

Asia

North
America

Vegetation

Carpathian
Mountains

Taurus
Mountains

Himalayas

India

Australia

Desert

Andes

South
America

Indian
Ocean

Atlantic
Ocean

Ice cap

Atlas
Mountains

Africa

Antarctica

EXAMPLES OF QUATERNARY ANIMALS

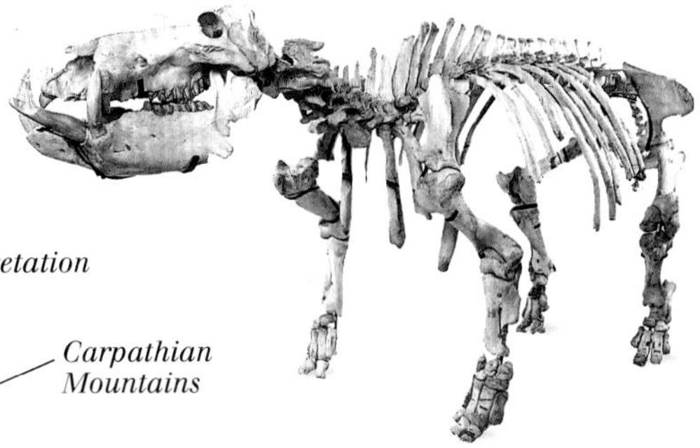

A MAMMAL SKELETON
(*Hippopotamus amphibius*)

SKULL OF AN EXTINCT CAVE BEAR
(*Ursus spelaeus*)

SKULL OF AN EXTINCT TORTOISE
(*Meiolania platyceps*)

A MAMMOTH TOOTH
(*Mammuthus primigenius*)

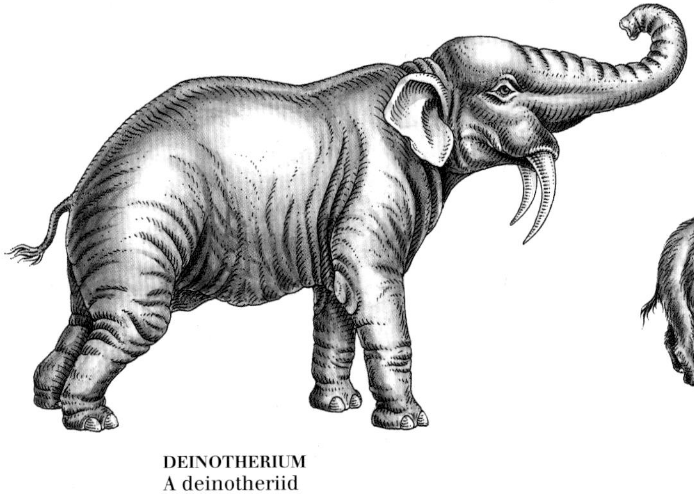

DEINOTHERIUM
A deinotheriid
Length: 4 m (13 ft)

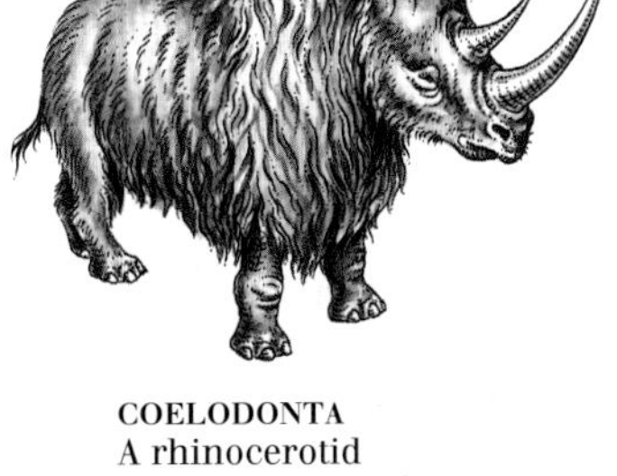

COELODONTA
A rhinocerotid
Length: 4 m (13 ft)

AUSTRALOPITHECUS
A hominid
Length: 1.2 m (4 ft)

77

Early signs of life

FOR ALMOST A THOUSAND MILLION YEARS after its formation, there was no known life on Earth. The first simple, sea-dwelling organic structures appeared about 3,400 years ago; they may have formed when certain chemical molecules joined together. Prokaryotes, single-celled micro-organisms such as blue-green algae, were able to photosynthesize (see pp. 138–139), and thus produce oxygen. A thousand million years later, sufficient oxygen had built up in the earth's atmosphere to allow multicellular organisms to proliferate in the Precambrian seas (before 570 million years ago). Soft-bodied jellyfish, corals, and seaworms flourished about 700 million years ago. Trilobites, the first animals with hard body frames, developed during the Cambrian period (570–510 million years ago). However, it was not until the beginning of the Devonian period (409–363 million years ago) that early land plants, such as *Asteroxylon*, formed a water-retaining cuticle, which ended their dependence on an aquatic environment. About 363 million years ago, the first amphibians (see pp. 80–81) crawled onto the land, although they still returned to the water to lay their soft eggs. Not until the emergence of the first reptiles would animals appear that were independent of water in this way.

STROMATOLITIC LIMESTONE

Alternate layers of mud and sand

Layers bound by algae

Layered structure

Limestone

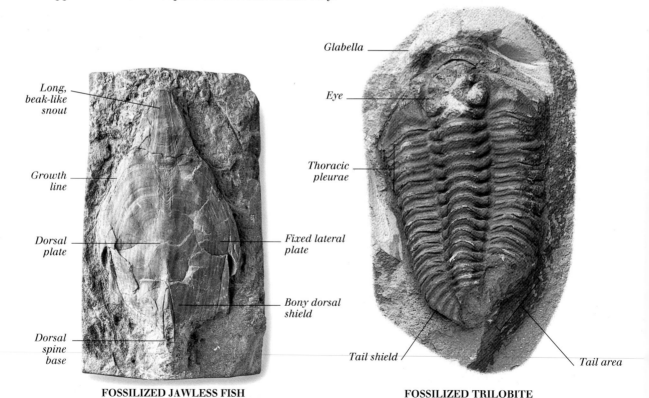

Glabella

Eye

Long, beak-like snout

Growth line

Dorsal plate

Dorsal spine base

Thoracic pleurae

Fixed lateral plate

Bony dorsal shield

Tail shield

Tail area

FOSSILIZED JAWLESS FISH

FOSSILIZED TRILOBITE

Ambulacral groove

Small ossicles of upper surface

Disc

Iron pyrites

FOSSILIZED STARFISH

Row of ossicles

Broad disc

UPPER SURFACE OF FOSSILIZED STARFISH

Row of ossicles

Short arm

LOWER SURFACE OF FOSSILIZED STARFISH

Jointed leg

Chelicera (jointed pincer)

Jointed leg with oar-shaped paddle

Segmented abdomen

UNDERSIDE OF FOSSILIZED EURYPTERID

Telson (tail spine)

Abdominal segments

Shell contains eight somites (thoracic segments)

Hingeless, bivalved shell

FOSSIL OF AN EXTINCT SHRIMP

Growing tip

Disc-shaped sporangium (spore-case)

Leaf-like scale

Stem

RECONSTRUCTION OF ASTEROXYLON

Amphibians and reptiles

THE EARLIEST KNOWN AMPHIBIANS, such as *Acanthostega* and *Ichthyostega*, lived about 363 million years ago at the end of the Devonian period (409–363 million years ago). Their limbs may have evolved from the muscular fins of lungfish. These fish can use their fins to push themselves along the bottom of lakes and some can breathe at the water's surface. While amphibians (see pp. 182–183) can exist on land, they are dependent on a wet environment because their skin does not retain moisture and they must return to the water to lay their eggs. Evolving from amphibians, reptiles (see pp. 184–187) first appeared during the Carboniferous period (363–290 million years ago): *Westlothiana*, the earliest known reptile, lived on land 338 million years ago. The development of the amniotic egg, with an embryo enclosed in its own wet environment (the amnion) and protected by a waterproof shell, freed reptiles from the amphibian's dependence on a wet habitat. A scaly skin protected the reptile from desiccation on land and enabled it to exploit ways of life closed to its amphibian ancestors. Reptiles include the dinosaurs, which came to dominate life on land during the Mesozoic era (245–65 million years ago).

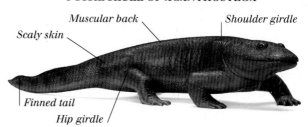

FOSSIL SKULL OF ACANTHOSTEGA

Orbit
Pocket enclosing nostril
Sculpted or pitted bone surface
Spiracle to draw in water
Mandible
Small tooth

Muscular back
Shoulder girdle
Scaly skin
Finned tail
Hip girdle

MODEL OF ICHTHYOSTEGA

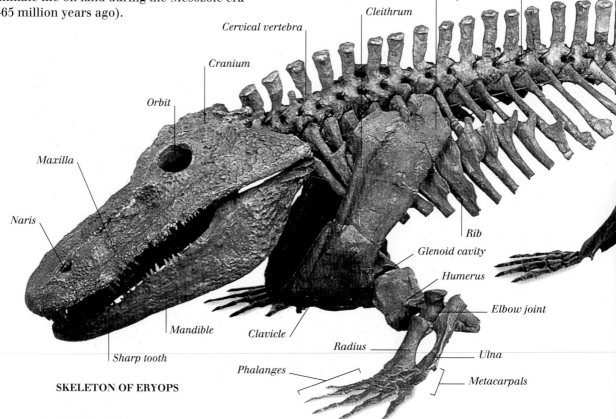

Dorsal vertebra
Scapula
Cleithrum
Cervical vertebra
Cranium
Orbit
Maxilla
Naris
Rib
Glenoid cavity
Humerus
Elbow joint
Mandible
Clavicle
Radius
Ulna
Sharp tooth
Phalanges
Metacarpals

SKELETON OF ERYOPS

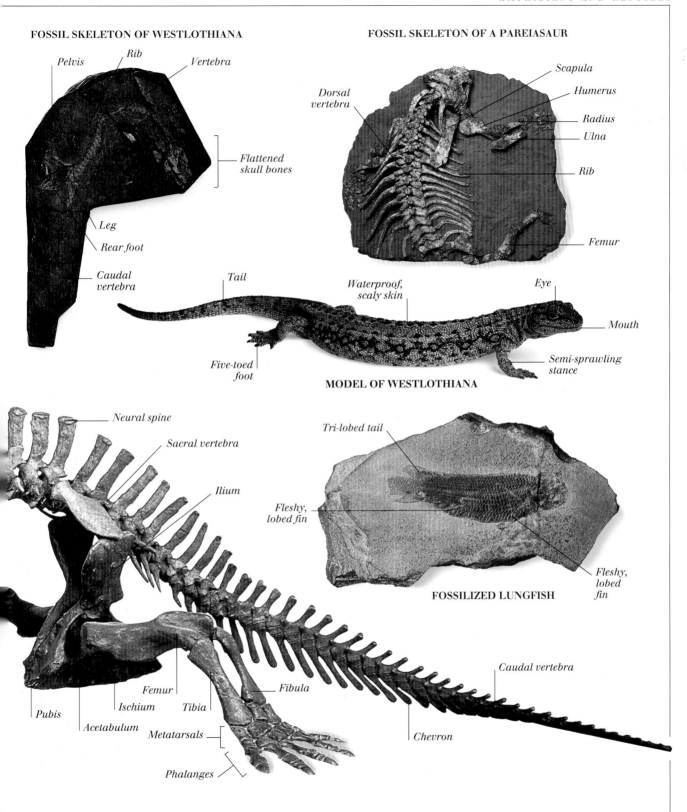

FOSSIL SKELETON OF WESTLOTHIANA

Pelvis
Rib
Vertebra
Flattened skull bones
Leg
Rear foot
Caudal vertebra

FOSSIL SKELETON OF A PAREIASAUR

Dorsal vertebra
Scapula
Humerus
Radius
Ulna
Rib
Femur

Tail
Waterproof, scaly skin
Eye
Mouth
Five-toed foot
Semi-sprawling stance

MODEL OF WESTLOTHIANA

Neural spine
Sacral vertebra
Ilium
Pubis
Acetabulum
Ischium
Femur
Metatarsals
Tibia
Fibula
Phalanges
Chevron
Caudal vertebra

Tri-lobed tail
Fleshy, lobed fin
Fleshy, lobed fin

FOSSILIZED LUNGFISH

The dinosaurs

THE DINOSAURS WERE A LARGE GROUP of reptiles that were the dominant land vertebrates (animals with backbones) for most of the Mesozoic era (245–65 million years ago). They appeared some 230 million years ago and were distinguished from other scaly, egg-laying reptiles by an important feature: dinosaurs had an erect limb stance. This enabled them to keep their bodies well above the ground, unlike the sprawling and semi-sprawling stance of other reptiles. The head of the dinosaur's femur (thigh-bone) fitted into a socket in its pelvis (hip-bone), producing efficient and mobile locomotion. Dinosaurs are categorized into two groups according to the structure of their pelvis: saurischian (lizard-hipped) and ornithischian (bird-hipped) dinosaurs. In the case of most saurischians, the pubis (part of the pelvis) jutted forward, while in ornithischians it slanted back, parallel to the ischium (another part of the pelvis). The enormous variety of dinosaur species equals that of mammals. The Dinosauria were the most successful land vertebrates ever, and survived for 165 million years, until their extinction 65 million years ago.

STRUCTURE OF SAURISCHIAN PELVIS

Ilium

Hook of preacetabular process

Postacetabular process

Ilio-pubic joint

Acetabulum

Pubis

Ilio-ischial joint

Ischium

Pubic foot

GALLIMIMUS
A saurischian dinosaur

POSITION OF PELVIS IN A SAURISCHIAN DINOSAUR

STRUCTURE OF ORNTHISCHIAN PELVIS

Ilium

Preacetabular process

Postacetabular process

Ilio-pubic joint

Ilio-ischial joint

Prepubis

Acetabulum

Pubis

Ischium

HYPSILOPHODON
An ornithischian dinosaur

POSITION OF PELVIS IN AN ORNITHISCHIAN DINOSAUR

BAROSAURUS
A saurischian dinosaur

COMPARISON OF ANIMAL STANCES

SPRAWLING STANCE
The thighs and upper arms project straight out from the body so that the knees and elbows are bent at right angles.

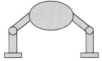

COMMON IGUANA
(*Iguana iguana*)
A present-day reptile

ERECT STANCE
The thighs and upper arms project straight down from the body so that the knees and elbows are straight.

SEMI-SPRAWLING STANCE
The thighs and upper arms project downwards and outwards so that the knees and elbows are slightly bent.

DWARF CROCODILE
(*Osteolaemus tetraspis*)
A present-day reptile

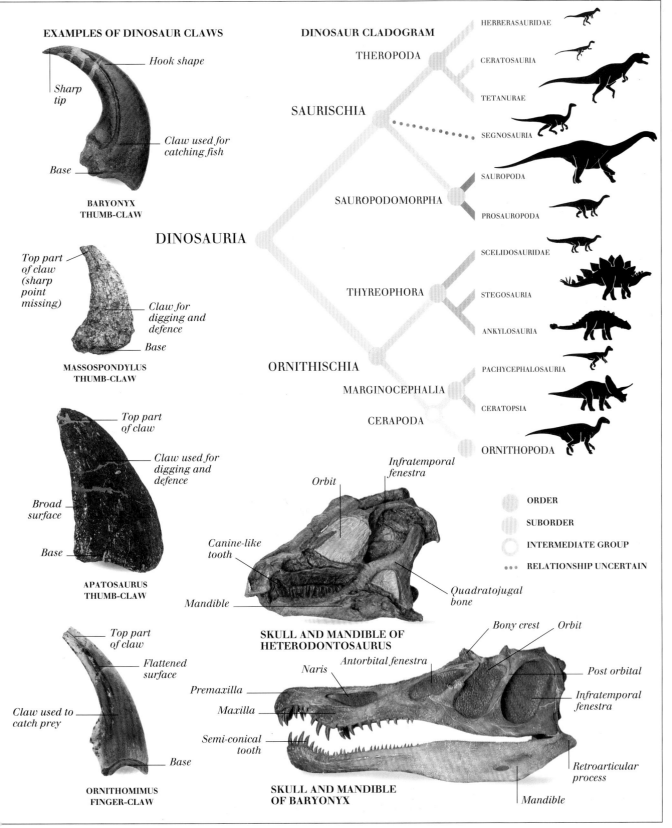

EXAMPLES OF DINOSAUR CLAWS

Hook shape

Sharp tip

Claw used for catching fish

Base

BARYONYX THUMB-CLAW

Top part of claw (sharp point missing)

Claw for digging and defence

Base

MASSOSPONDYLUS THUMB-CLAW

Top part of claw

Claw used for digging and defence

Broad surface

Base

APATOSAURUS THUMB-CLAW

Top part of claw

Flattened surface

Claw used to catch prey

Base

ORNITHOMIMUS FINGER-CLAW

DINOSAUR CLADOGRAM

HERRERASAURIDAE

THEROPODA

CERATOSAURIA

SAURISCHIA

TETANURAE

SEGNOSAURIA

SAUROPODA

SAUROPODOMORPHA

PROSAUROPODA

DINOSAURIA

SCELIDOSAURIDAE

THYREOPHORA

STEGOSAURIA

ANKYLOSAURIA

PACHYCEPHALOSAURIA

ORNITHISCHIA

MARGINOCEPHALIA

CERATOPSIA

CERAPODA

ORNITHOPODA

⬤ ORDER

▮ SUBORDER

◯ INTERMEDIATE GROUP

••• RELATIONSHIP UNCERTAIN

Infratemporal fenestra

Orbit

Canine-like tooth

Quadratojugal bone

Mandible

SKULL AND MANDIBLE OF HETERODONTOSAURUS

Bony crest   *Orbit*

Antorbital fenestra

Naris

Post orbital

Premaxilla

Infratemporal fenestra

Maxilla

Semi-conical tooth

Retroarticular process

Mandible

SKULL AND MANDIBLE OF BARYONYX

83

Theropods 1

AN ENORMOUSLY SUCCESSFUL SUBORDER of the Saurischia, the bipedal (two-footed) theropods ("beast feet") emerged 230 million years ago in Late Triassic times; the oldest known example comes from South America. Theropods spanned the whole of the Age of the Dinosaurs (230–65 million years ago) and included most of the known predatory dinosaurs. The typical theropod had small arms with sharp, clawed fingers; powerful jaws lined with sharp teeth; an S-shaped neck; long, muscular hind limbs; and clawed, usually four-toed feet. Many theropods may have been warm-blooded; most were exclusively carnivorous. Theropods ranged from animals no larger than a chicken to huge creatures, such as *Tyrannosaurus* and *Baryonyx*. The group also included ostrich-like omnivores and herbivores with toothless beaks, such as *Struthiomimus* and *Gallimimus*. Many scientists believe that birds are the closest living relatives to the dinosaurs, and share a common ancestor with the theropods. *Archaeopteryx*, small and feathered, was the first known bird and lived alongside its dinosaur relatives.

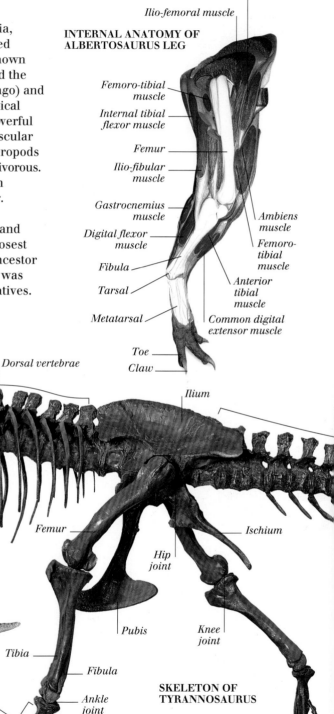

INTERNAL ANATOMY OF ALBERTOSAURUS LEG

Ilio-tibial muscle
Ilio-femoral muscle
Femoro-tibial muscle
Internal tibial flexor muscle
Femur
Ilio-fibular muscle
Gastrocnemius muscle
Digital flexor muscle
Fibula
Tarsal
Metatarsal
Ambiens muscle
Femoro-tibial muscle
Anterior tibial muscle
Common digital extensor muscle
Toe
Claw

Cranium
Orbit
Naris
Supraoccipital crest
Cervical vertebrae
Dorsal vertebrae
Ilium
Cervical rib
Scapula
Shoulder joint
Ulna
Phalanges
Metacarpals
Wrist joint
Elbow joint
Coracoid
Rib
Humerus
Mandible
Serrated tooth
Femur
Ischium
Hip joint
Pubis
Knee joint

Naris
Eye
Thigh
Scaly skin
Tail
Hand
Forelimb
Knee
Hind limb
Toe
Claw
Ankle
Foot
Tibia
Fibula
Metatarsals
Phalanges
Ankle joint
Hallux (first toe)

SKELETON OF TYRANNOSAURUS

EXTERNAL FEATURES OF TYRANNOSAURUS

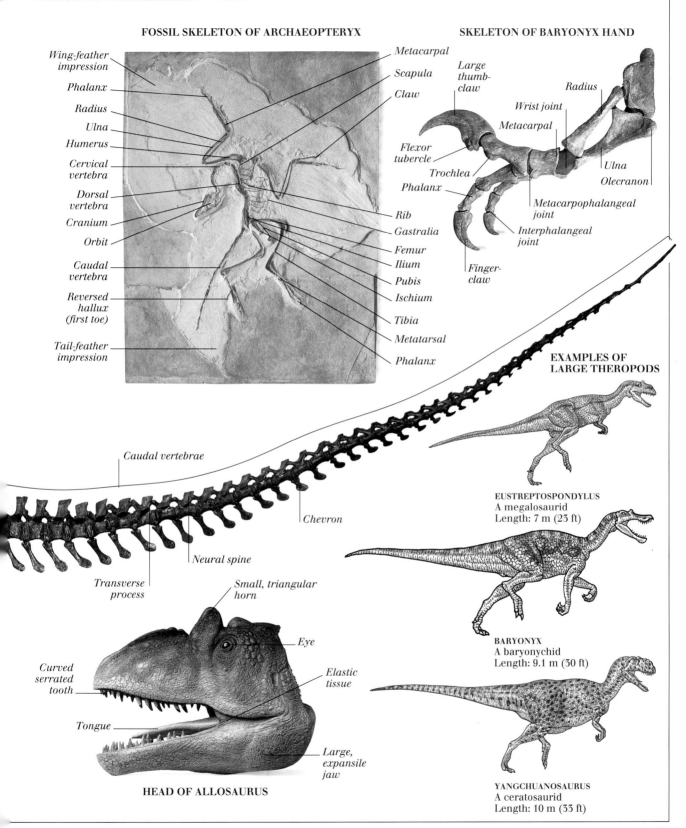

FOSSIL SKELETON OF ARCHAEOPTERYX

Wing-feather impression

Phalanx

Radius

Ulna

Humerus

Cervical vertebra

Dorsal vertebra

Cranium

Orbit

Caudal vertebra

Reversed hallux (first toe)

Tail-feather impression

Metacarpal

Scapula

Claw

Rib

Gastralia

Femur

Ilium

Pubis

Ischium

Tibia

Metatarsal

Phalanx

SKELETON OF BARYONYX HAND

Large thumb-claw

Radius

Wrist joint

Metacarpal

Flexor tubercle

Trochlea

Phalanx

Ulna

Olecranon

Metacarpophalangeal joint

Interphalangeal joint

Finger-claw

Caudal vertebrae

Chevron

Neural spine

Transverse process

Small, triangular horn

Eye

Elastic tissue

Curved serrated tooth

Tongue

Large, expansile jaw

HEAD OF ALLOSAURUS

EXAMPLES OF LARGE THEROPODS

EUSTREPTOSPONDYLUS
A megalosaurid
Length: 7 m (23 ft)

BARYONYX
A baryonychid
Length: 9.1 m (30 ft)

YANGCHUANOSAURUS
A ceratosaurid
Length: 10 m (33 ft)

Theropods 2

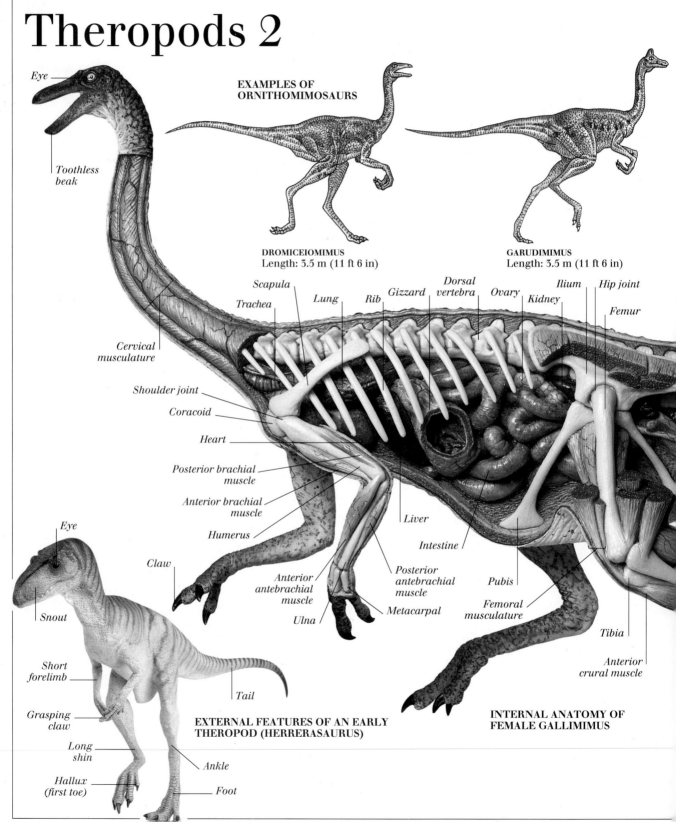

Eye

Toothless beak

EXAMPLES OF ORNITHOMIMOSAURS

DROMICEIOMIMUS
Length: 3.5 m (11 ft 6 in)

GARUDIMIMUS
Length: 3.5 m (11 ft 6 in)

Cervical musculature

Scapula

Trachea

Lung

Rib

Gizzard

Dorsal vertebra

Ovary

Kidney

Ilium

Hip joint

Femur

Shoulder joint

Coracoid

Heart

Posterior brachial muscle

Anterior brachial muscle

Humerus

Liver

Intestine

Pubis

Femoral musculature

Eye

Snout

Claw

Short forelimb

Anterior antebrachial muscle

Ulna

Posterior antebrachial muscle

Metacarpal

Tibia

Anterior crural muscle

Grasping claw

Long shin

Hallux (first toe)

Ankle

Foot

Tail

EXTERNAL FEATURES OF AN EARLY THEROPOD (HERRERASAURUS)

INTERNAL ANATOMY OF FEMALE GALLIMIMUS

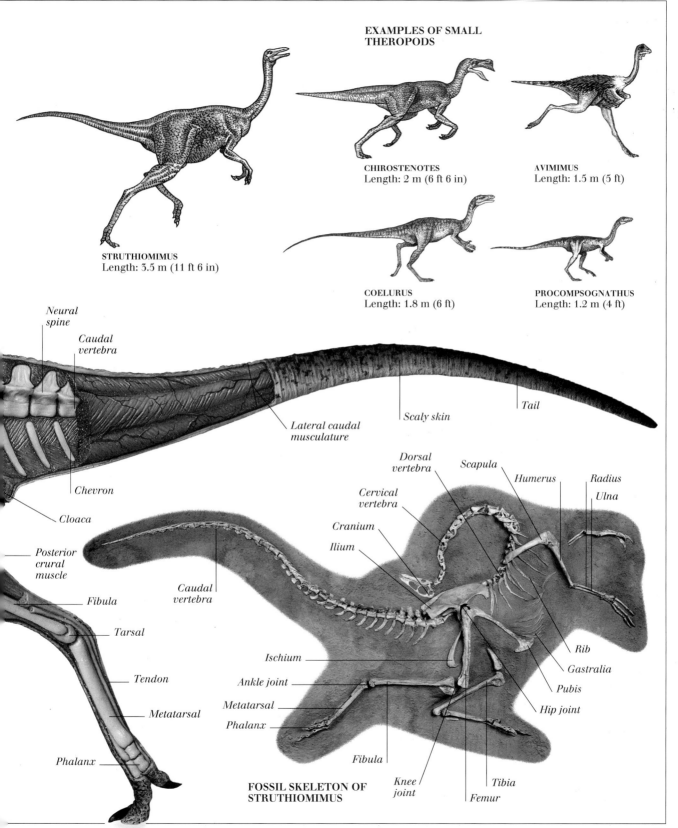

EXAMPLES OF SMALL THEROPODS

CHIROSTENOTES
Length: 2 m (6 ft 6 in)

AVIMIMUS
Length: 1.5 m (5 ft)

STRUTHIOMIMUS
Length: 3.5 m (11 ft 6 in)

COELURUS
Length: 1.8 m (6 ft)

PROCOMPSOGNATHUS
Length: 1.2 m (4 ft)

Neural spine

Caudal vertebra

Lateral caudal musculature

Scaly skin

Tail

Chevron

Cloaca

Dorsal vertebra

Scapula

Humerus

Radius

Cervical vertebra

Ulna

Cranium

Ilium

Posterior crural muscle

Caudal vertebra

Fibula

Tarsal

Rib

Gastralia

Tendon

Ischium

Pubis

Metatarsal

Ankle joint

Hip joint

Metatarsal

Phalanx

Phalanx

Fibula

Knee joint

Tibia

Femur

FOSSIL SKELETON OF STRUTHIOMIMUS

Sauropodomorphs 1

THE SAUROPODOMORPHA ("lizard-feet forms") were herbivorous, usually quadrupedal (four-footed) dinosaurs. A suborder of the Saurischia, they were characterized by small heads, bulky bodies, and long necks and tails. There were two infraorders: prosauropods and sauropods. Prosauropods lived from Late Triassic to Early Jurassic times (225–180 million years ago) and included beasts such as the small *Anchisaurus* and one of the first very large dinosaurs, *Melanosaurus*. By Middle Jurassic times (about 165 million years ago), sauropods had replaced prosauropods and spread worldwide. They included the heaviest and longest land animals ever, such as *Diplodocus* and *Brachiosaurus*. Sauropods persisted to the end of the Cretaceous period (65 million years ago). Many of these dinosaurs moved in herds, protected from predatory theropods by their huge bulk and powerful tails, which they could use to lash out at attackers. Sauropodomorphs were the most common large herbivores until Late Jurassic times (about 145 million years ago), and appear to have survived in southern continents long after they had disappeared from the north.

THECODONTOSAURUS

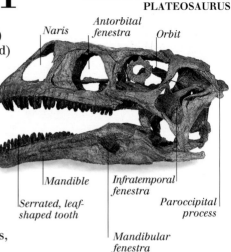

Naris

Antorbital fenestra

Orbit

Mandible

Infratemporal fenestra

Serrated, leaf-shaped tooth

Paroccipital process

Mandibular fenestra

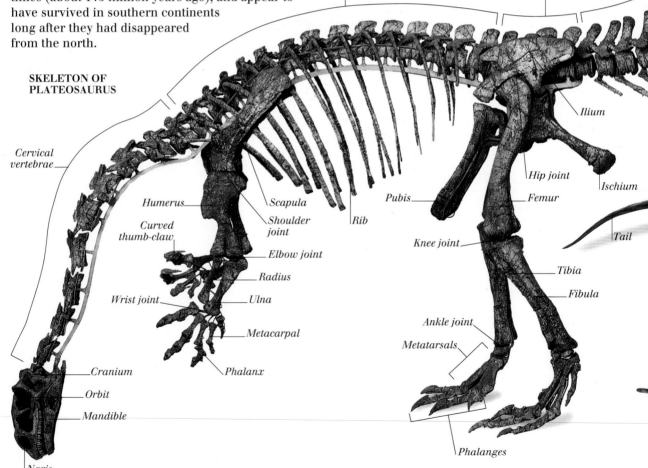

Dorsal vertebrae

Sacral vertebrae

SKELETON OF
PLATEOSAURUS

Ilium

Cervical vertebrae

Humerus

Scapula

Shoulder joint

Rib

Pubis

Femur

Hip joint

Ischium

Curved thumb-claw

Elbow joint

Knee joint

Tail

Radius

Wrist joint

Ulna

Metacarpal

Tibia

Fibula

Ankle joint

Metatarsals

Cranium

Phalanx

Orbit

Mandible

Naris

Phalanges

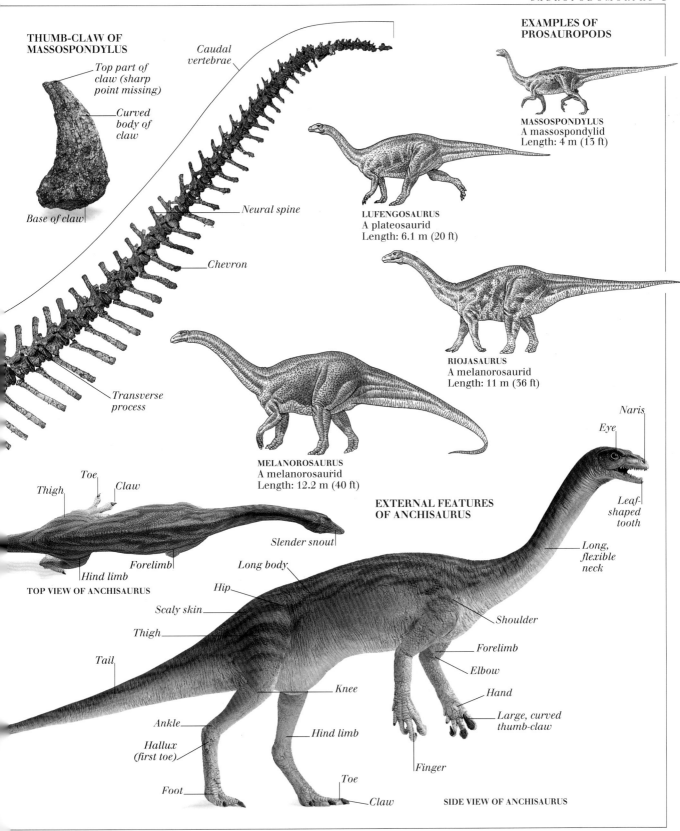

THUMB-CLAW OF MASSOSPONDYLUS

Top part of claw (sharp point missing)

Curved body of claw

Base of claw

Caudal vertebrae

Neural spine

Chevron

Transverse process

EXAMPLES OF PROSAUROPODS

MASSOSPONDYLUS
A massospondylid
Length: 4 m (13 ft)

LUFENGOSAURUS
A plateosaurid
Length: 6.1 m (20 ft)

RIOJASAURUS
A melanorosaurid
Length: 11 m (36 ft)

MELANOROSAURUS
A melanorosaurid
Length: 12.2 m (40 ft)

EXTERNAL FEATURES OF ANCHISAURUS

Thigh

Toe

Claw

Slender snout

Forelimb

Hind limb

TOP VIEW OF ANCHISAURUS

Naris

Eye

Leaf-shaped tooth

Long, flexible neck

Long body

Hip

Scaly skin

Thigh

Shoulder

Forelimb

Elbow

Hand

Large, curved thumb-claw

Tail

Knee

Ankle

Hind limb

Hallux (first toe)

Finger

Toe

Foot

Claw

SIDE VIEW OF ANCHISAURUS

Sauropodomorphs 2

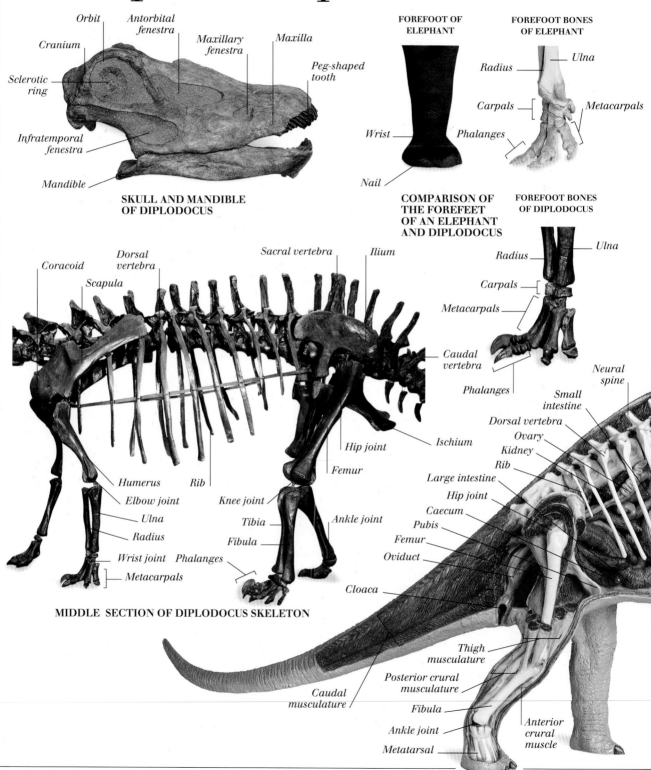

Orbit

Antorbital
fenestra

Cranium

Maxillary
fenestra

Maxilla

Sclerotic
ring

Peg-shaped
tooth

Infratemporal
fenestra

Mandible

**SKULL AND MANDIBLE
OF DIPLODOCUS**

**FOREFOOT OF
ELEPHANT**

**FOREFOOT BONES
OF ELEPHANT**

Radius

Ulna

Carpals

Metacarpals

Wrist

Phalanges

Nail

**COMPARISON OF
THE FOREFEET
OF AN ELEPHANT
AND DIPLODOCUS**

**FOREFOOT BONES
OF DIPLODOCUS**

Radius

Ulna

Carpals

Metacarpals

Phalanges

Coracoid

Dorsal
vertebra

Sacral vertebra

Ilium

Scapula

Caudal
vertebra

Neural
spine

Small
intestine

Dorsal vertebra

Ovary

Kidney

Rib

Ischium

Large intestine

Hip joint

Hip joint

Caecum

Femur

Pubis

Humerus

Rib

Knee joint

Femur

Oviduct

Elbow joint

Tibia

Ankle joint

Ulna

Fibula

Radius

Cloaca

Wrist joint

Phalanges

Metacarpals

Thigh
musculature

MIDDLE SECTION OF DIPLODOCUS SKELETON

Posterior crural
musculature

Caudal
musculature

Fibula

Anterior
crural
muscle

Ankle joint

Metatarsal

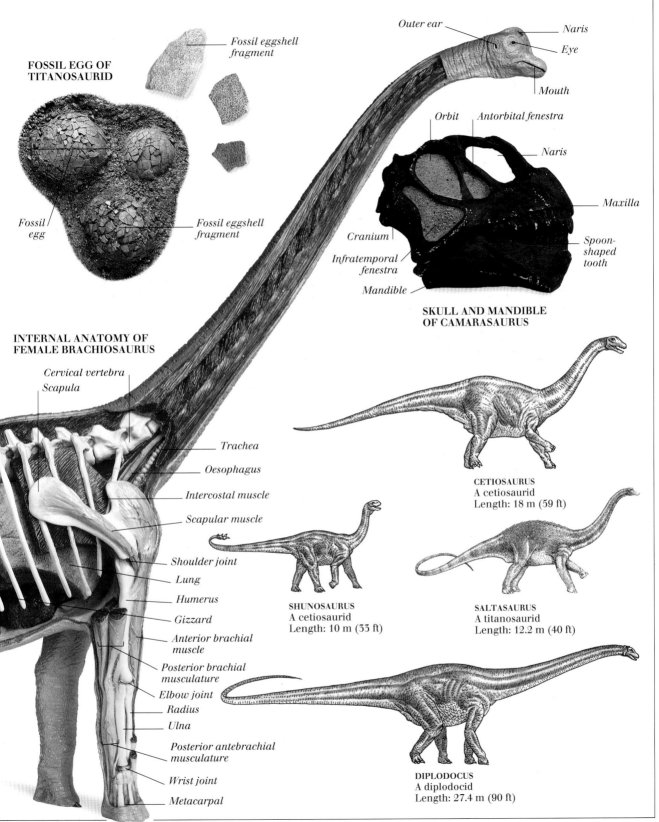

FOSSIL EGG OF TITANOSAURID

Fossil eggshell fragment

Fossil egg

Fossil eggshell fragment

Outer ear

Naris

Eye

Mouth

Orbit

Antorbital fenestra

Naris

Maxilla

Cranium

Infratemporal fenestra

Spoon-shaped tooth

Mandible

SKULL AND MANDIBLE OF CAMARASAURUS

INTERNAL ANATOMY OF FEMALE BRACHIOSAURUS

Cervical vertebra

Scapula

Trachea

Oesophagus

Intercostal muscle

Scapular muscle

Shoulder joint

Lung

Humerus

Gizzard

Anterior brachial muscle

Posterior brachial musculature

Elbow joint

Radius

Ulna

Posterior antebrachial musculature

Wrist joint

Metacarpal

CETIOSAURUS
A cetiosaurid
Length: 18 m (59 ft)

SHUNOSAURUS
A cetiosaurid
Length: 10 m (33 ft)

SALTASAURUS
A titanosaurid
Length: 12.2 m (40 ft)

DIPLODOCUS
A diplodocid
Length: 27.4 m (90 ft)

Thyreophorans 1

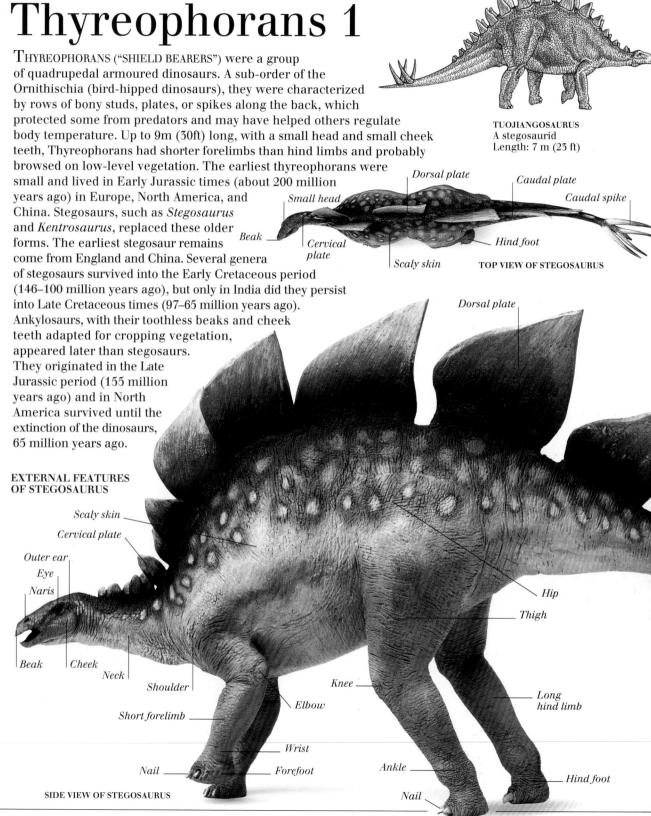

THYREOPHORANS ("SHIELD BEARERS") were a group
of quadrupedal armoured dinosaurs. A sub-order of the
Ornithischia (bird-hipped dinosaurs), they were characterized
by rows of bony studs, plates, or spikes along the back, which
protected some from predators and may have helped others regulate
body temperature. Up to 9m (30ft) long, with a small head and small cheek
teeth, Thyreophorans had shorter forelimbs than hind limbs and probably
browsed on low-level vegetation. The earliest thyreophorans were
small and lived in Early Jurassic times (about 200 million
years ago) in Europe, North America, and
China. Stegosaurs, such as *Stegosaurus*
and *Kentrosaurus*, replaced these older
forms. The earliest stegosaur remains
come from England and China. Several genera
of stegosaurs survived into the Early Cretaceous period
(146–100 million years ago), but only in India did they persist
into Late Cretaceous times (97–65 million years ago).
Ankylosaurs, with their toothless beaks and cheek
teeth adapted for cropping vegetation,
appeared later than stegosaurs.
They originated in the Late
Jurassic period (155 million
years ago) and in North
America survived until the
extinction of the dinosaurs,
65 million years ago.

TUOJIANGOSAURUS
A stegosaurid
Length: 7 m (23 ft)

Dorsal plate

Caudal plate

Caudal spike

Small head

Beak

Cervical
plate

Hind foot

Scaly skin

TOP VIEW OF STEGOSAURUS

Dorsal plate

**EXTERNAL FEATURES
OF STEGOSAURUS**

Scaly skin

Cervical plate

Outer ear

Eye

Naris

Hip

Thigh

Beak

Cheek

Neck

Shoulder

Knee

Long
hind limb

Elbow

Short forelimb

Wrist

Nail

Forefoot

Ankle

Hind foot

SIDE VIEW OF STEGOSAURUS

Nail

EXAMPLES OF STEGOSAURS

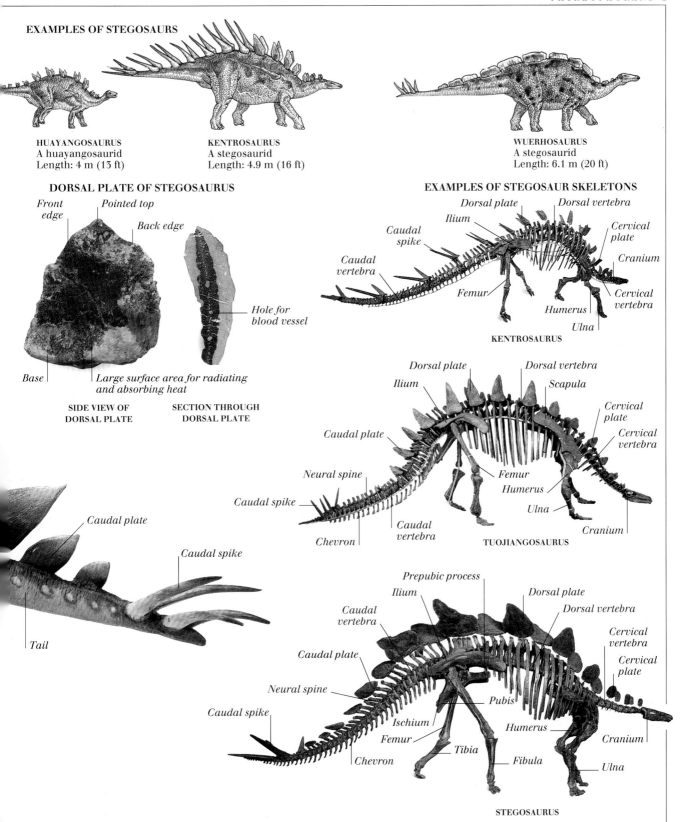

HUAYANGOSAURUS
A huayangosaurid
Length: 4 m (13 ft)

KENTROSAURUS
A stegosaurid
Length: 4.9 m (16 ft)

WUERHOSAURUS
A stegosaurid
Length: 6.1 m (20 ft)

DORSAL PLATE OF STEGOSAURUS

Front edge

Pointed top

Back edge

Hole for blood vessel

Base

Large surface area for radiating and absorbing heat

SIDE VIEW OF DORSAL PLATE

SECTION THROUGH DORSAL PLATE

EXAMPLES OF STEGOSAUR SKELETONS

Dorsal plate

Dorsal vertebra

Ilium

Cervical plate

Caudal spike

Caudal vertebra

Cranium

Femur

Cervical vertebra

Humerus

Ulna

KENTROSAURUS

Dorsal plate

Dorsal vertebra

Ilium

Scapula

Caudal plate

Cervical plate

Cervical vertebra

Neural spine

Femur

Humerus

Caudal spike

Ulna

Caudal vertebra

Cranium

Chevron

TUOJIANGOSAURUS

Caudal plate

Caudal spike

Tail

Prepubic process

Ilium

Dorsal plate

Caudal vertebra

Dorsal vertebra

Caudal plate

Cervical vertebra

Cervical plate

Neural spine

Pubis

Ischium

Humerus

Caudal spike

Femur

Cranium

Tibia

Fibula

Ulna

Chevron

STEGOSAURUS

Thyreophorans 2

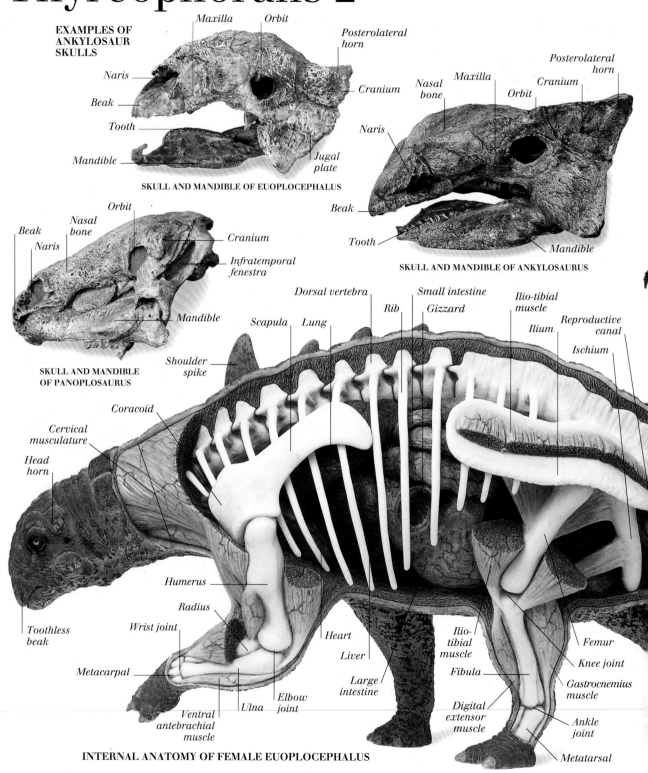

EXAMPLES OF ANKYLOSAUR SKULLS

Maxilla
Orbit
Posterolateral horn
Naris
Cranium
Beak
Tooth
Mandible
Jugal plate

SKULL AND MANDIBLE OF EUOPLOCEPHALUS

Posterolateral horn
Nasal bone
Maxilla
Cranium
Orbit
Naris
Beak
Tooth
Mandible

SKULL AND MANDIBLE OF ANKYLOSAURUS

Orbit
Nasal bone
Beak
Naris
Cranium
Infratemporal fenestra
Mandible

SKULL AND MANDIBLE OF PANOPLOSAURUS

Dorsal vertebra
Small intestine
Ilio-tibial muscle
Rib
Gizzard
Ilium
Reproductive canal
Scapula
Lung
Ischium
Shoulder spike
Coracoid
Cervical musculature
Head horn
Humerus
Radius
Toothless beak
Wrist joint
Heart
Ilio-tibial muscle
Femur
Liver
Metacarpal
Knee joint
Fibula
Gastrocnemius muscle
Elbow joint
Large intestine
Ulna
Ventral antebrachial muscle
Digital extensor muscle
Ankle joint
Metatarsal

INTERNAL ANATOMY OF FEMALE EUOPLOCEPHALUS

EXTERNAL FEATURES OF EDMONTONIA

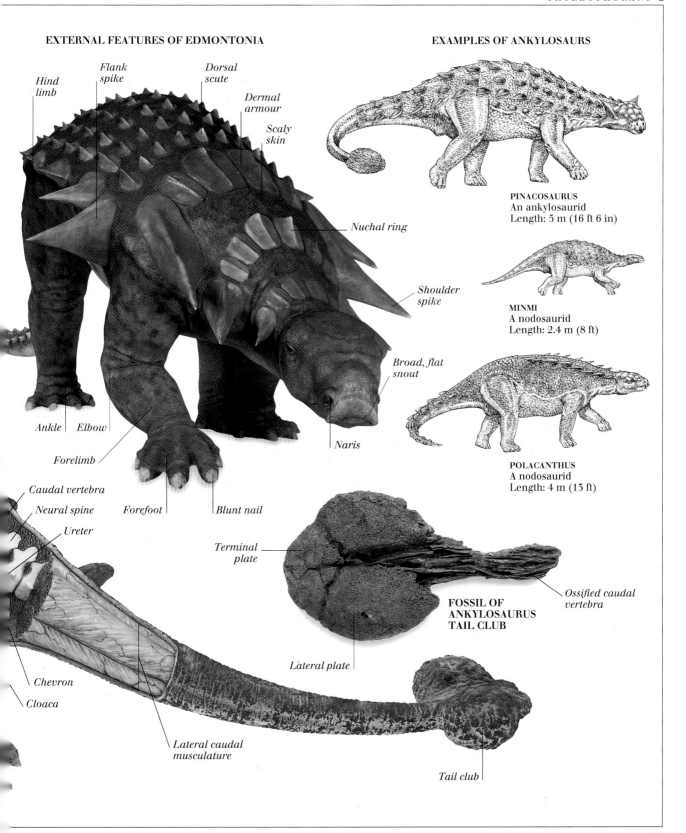

Hind limb

Flank spike

Dorsal scute

Dermal armour

Scaly skin

Nuchal ring

Shoulder spike

Broad, flat snout

Naris

Ankle

Elbow

Forelimb

Forefoot

Blunt nail

Caudal vertebra

Neural spine

Ureter

Terminal plate

Chevron

Cloaca

Lateral plate

Lateral caudal musculature

Tail club

Ossified caudal vertebra

EXAMPLES OF ANKYLOSAURS

PINACOSAURUS
An ankylosaurid
Length: 5 m (16 ft 6 in)

MINMI
A nodosaurid
Length: 2.4 m (8 ft)

POLACANTHUS
A nodosaurid
Length: 4 m (13 ft)

FOSSIL OF ANKYLOSAURUS TAIL CLUB

Ornithopods 1

IGUANODON TOOTH

ORNITHOPODS ("BIRD FEET") were a group of ornithischian ("bird-hipped") dinosaurs. These bipedal and quadrupedal herbivores had a horny beak, plant-cutting or grinding cheek teeth, and a pelvic and tail region stiffened by bony tendons. They evolved teeth and jaws adapted to pulping vegetation and flourished from the Middle Jurassic to the Late Cretaceous period (165–65 million years ago) in North America, Europe, Africa, China, Australia, and Antarctica. Some ornithopods were no larger than a dog, while others were immense creatures up to 15 m (49 ft) long. Iguanodonts, an ornithopod group, had a broad, toothless beak at the end of a long snout, large jaws with long rows of ridged, closely packed teeth for grinding vegetation, a bulky body, and a heavy tail. *Iguanodon* and some other iguanodonts had large thumb-spikes that were strong enough to stab attackers. Another group, the hadrosaurs, such as *Gryposaurus* and *Hadrosaurus,* lived in Late Cretaceous times (97–65 million years ago) and with their broad beaks are sometimes known as "duckbills". They were characterized by their deep skulls and closely packed rows of teeth, while some, such as *Corythosaurus* and *Lambeosaurus,* had tall, hollow, bony head crests.

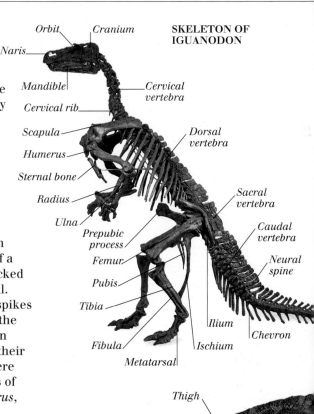

SKELETON OF IGUANODON

Orbit
Cranium
Naris
Mandible
Cervical rib
Cervical vertebra
Scapula
Dorsal vertebra
Humerus
Sternal bone
Radius
Sacral vertebra
Ulna
Prepubic process
Caudal vertebra
Femur
Neural spine
Pubis
Tibia
Fibula
Ilium
Chevron
Metatarsal
Ischium

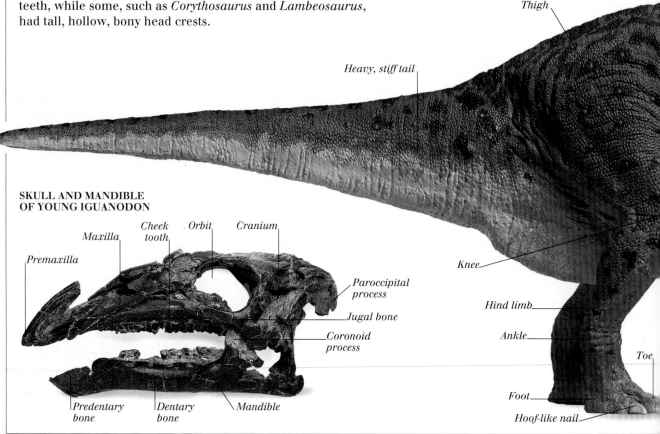

Thigh
Heavy, stiff tail
Knee
Hind limb
Ankle
Toe
Foot
Hoof-like nail

SKULL AND MANDIBLE OF YOUNG IGUANODON

Cheek tooth
Maxilla
Orbit
Cranium
Premaxilla
Paroccipital process
Jugal bone
Coronoid process
Predentary bone
Dentary bone
Mandible

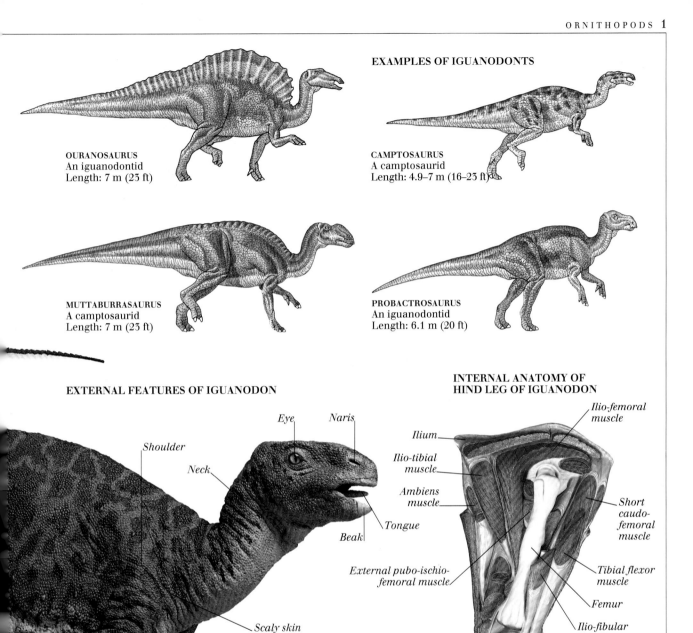

EXAMPLES OF IGUANODONTS

OURANOSAURUS
An iguanodontid
Length: 7 m (23 ft)

CAMPTOSAURUS
A camptosaurid
Length: 4.9–7 m (16–23 ft)

MUTTABURRASAURUS
A camptosaurid
Length: 7 m (23 ft)

PROBACTROSAURUS
An iguanodontid
Length: 6.1 m (20 ft)

EXTERNAL FEATURES OF IGUANODON

Eye

Naris

Shoulder

Neck

Tongue

Beak

Scaly skin

Forelimb

Elbow

Wrist

Hand

Finger

Thumb-spike

Hoof-like nail

**INTERNAL ANATOMY OF
HIND LEG OF IGUANODON**

Ilio-femoral
muscle

Ilium

Ilio-tibial
muscle

Ambiens
muscle

Short
caudo-
femoral
muscle

External pubo-ischio-
femoral muscle

Tibial flexor
muscle

Femur

Ilio-fibular
muscle

Gastrocnemius
muscle

Common digital
extensor muscle

Anterior tibial
muscle

Tibia

Fibula

Tarsal

Metatarsal

Toe

Hoof-like nail

Ornithopods 2

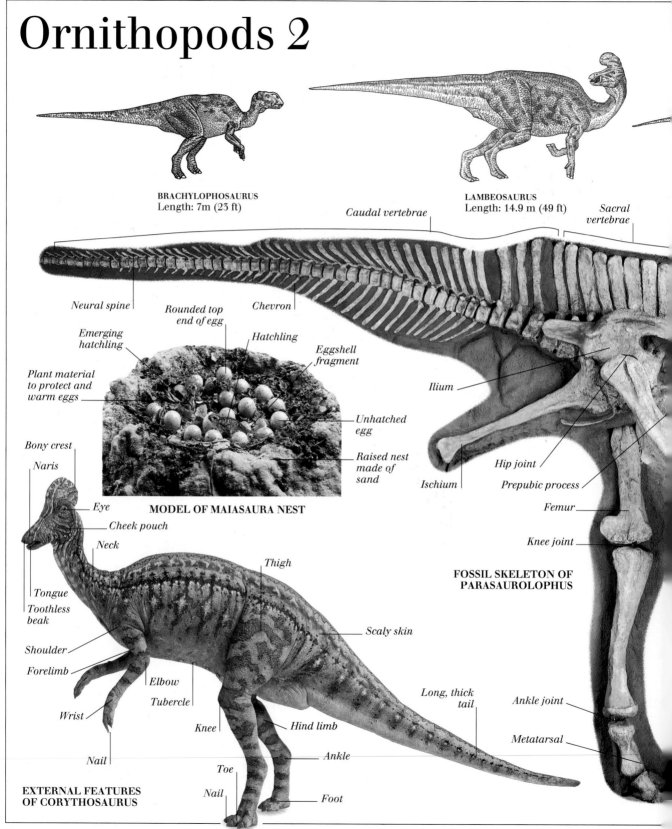

BRACHYLOPHOSAURUS
Length: 7m (23 ft)

LAMBEOSAURUS
Length: 14.9 m (49 ft)

Caudal vertebrae

Sacral vertebrae

Neural spine

Chevron

Rounded top end of egg

Hatchling

Eggshell fragment

Emerging hatchling

Plant material to protect and warm eggs

Ilium

Unhatched egg

Raised nest made of sand

Hip joint

Ischium

Prepubic process

MODEL OF MAIASAURA NEST

Bony crest

Naris

Eye

Femur

Cheek pouch

Neck

Thigh

Knee joint

Tongue

Toothless beak

FOSSIL SKELETON OF PARASAUROLOPHUS

Scaly skin

Shoulder

Forelimb

Elbow

Tubercle

Wrist

Knee

Hind limb

Long, thick tail

Ankle joint

Nail

Ankle

Metatarsal

Toe

EXTERNAL FEATURES OF CORYTHOSAURUS

Nail

Foot

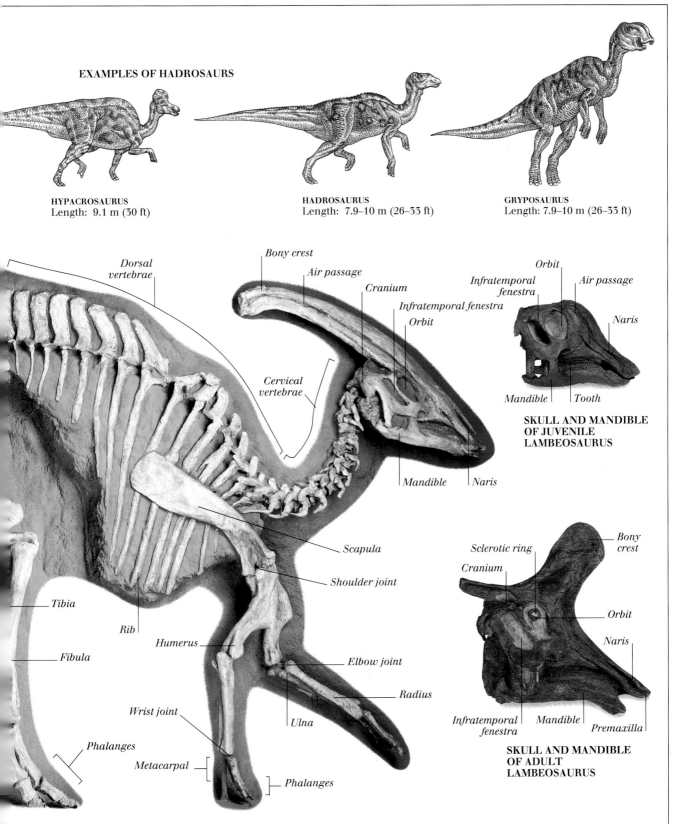

EXAMPLES OF HADROSAURS

HYPACROSAURUS
Length: 9.1 m (30 ft)

HADROSAURUS
Length: 7.9–10 m (26–33 ft)

GRYPOSAURUS
Length: 7.9–10 m (26–33 ft)

Dorsal vertebrae

Bony crest

Air passage

Cranium

Infratemporal fenestra

Orbit

Cervical vertebrae

Mandible

Naris

Scapula

Shoulder joint

Tibia

Rib

Humerus

Elbow joint

Fibula

Radius

Ulna

Wrist joint

Phalanges

Metacarpal

Phalanges

Orbit

Infratemporal fenestra

Air passage

Naris

Mandible

Tooth

**SKULL AND MANDIBLE
OF JUVENILE
LAMBEOSAURUS**

Sclerotic ring

Bony crest

Cranium

Orbit

Naris

Infratemporal fenestra

Mandible

Premaxilla

**SKULL AND MANDIBLE
OF ADULT
LAMBEOSAURUS**

Marginocephalians 1

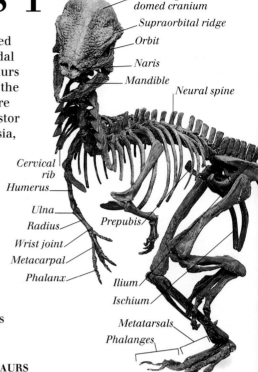

MARGINOCEPHALIA ("margined heads") were a group of bipedal and quadrupedal ornithischian dinosaurs with a narrow shelf or deep, bony frill at the back of the skull. Marginocephalians were probably descended from the same ancestor as the ornithopods and lived in what are now North America, Africa, Asia, and Europe during the Cretaceous period (146–65 million years ago). They were divided into two infraorders: Pachycephalosauria ("thick-headed lizards"), such as *Pachycephalosaurus* and *Stegoceras*, and Ceratopsia ("horned faces"), such as *Triceratops* and *Psittacosaurus*. The thick skulls of Pachycephalosauria protected their brains during head-butting contests fought to win territory and mates; their hips and spines were also strengthened to withstand the shock. The bony frill of Ceratopsia would have added to their frightening appearance when charging; the neck was strengthened for impact and to support the huge head, with its snipping beak and powerful slicing toothed jaws. A charging ceratops would have been a formidable opponent for even the largest predators. Ceratopsia were among the most abundant herbivorous dinosaurs of the Late Cretaceous period (97–65 million years ago).

HEAD-BUTTING PRENOCEPHALES

Thick, high-domed cranium
Supraorbital ridge
Orbit
Naris
Mandible
Neural spine
Cervical rib
Humerus
Ulna
Radius
Prepubis
Wrist joint
Metacarpal
Phalanx
Ilium
Ischium
Metatarsals
Phalanges

EXAMPLES OF SKULLS OF PACHYCEPHALOSAURS

Orbit
Thickened dome of cranium
Maxilla
Bony ridge
Tooth
Mandible

SKULL AND MANDIBLE OF STEGOCERAS

Orbit
Thickened dome of cranium
Maxilla
Bony nodule

SKULL OF PRENOCEPHALE

Thickened dome of cranium
Bony spike
Maxilla
Orbit
Bony nodule

SKULL OF PACHYCEPHALOSAURUS

EXTERNAL FEATURES OF PACHYCEPHALOSAURUS

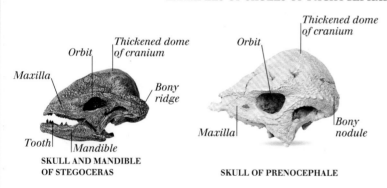

Scaly skin
Bony nodule
Domed head
Eye
Bony spike
Neck
Snout
Tail
Knee
Forelimb
Hind limb
Finger
Ankle
Hand
Foot
Claw
Toe

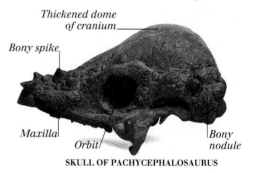

Bony nodule
Thickened dome of cranium
Buccal cavity
Brain cavity

SECTION THROUGH SKULL OF PACHYCEPHALOSAURUS

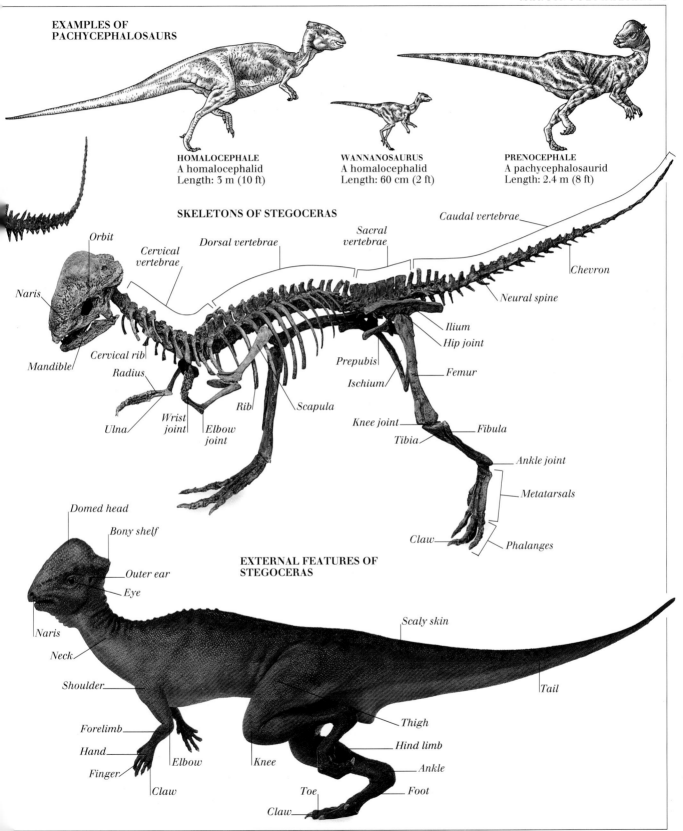

EXAMPLES OF PACHYCEPHALOSAURS

HOMALOCEPHALE
A homalocephalid
Length: 3 m (10 ft)

WANNANOSAURUS
A homalocephalid
Length: 60 cm (2 ft)

PRENOCEPHALE
A pachycephalosaurid
Length: 2.4 m (8 ft)

SKELETONS OF STEGOCERAS

Caudal vertebrae

Sacral
vertebrae

Dorsal vertebrae

Orbit

Cervical
vertebrae

Chevron

Naris

Neural spine

Ilium

Hip joint

Cervical rib

Prepubis

Mandible

Femur

Radius

Ischium

Rib

Scapula

Knee joint

Fibula

Ulna

Tibia

Wrist
joint

Elbow
joint

Ankle joint

Metatarsals

Claw

Phalanges

Domed head

Bony shelf

**EXTERNAL FEATURES OF
STEGOCERAS**

Outer ear

Eye

Scaly skin

Naris

Neck

Tail

Shoulder

Forelimb

Thigh

Hand

Hind limb

Elbow

Finger

Ankle

Knee

Claw

Toe

Foot

Claw

101

Marginocephalians 2

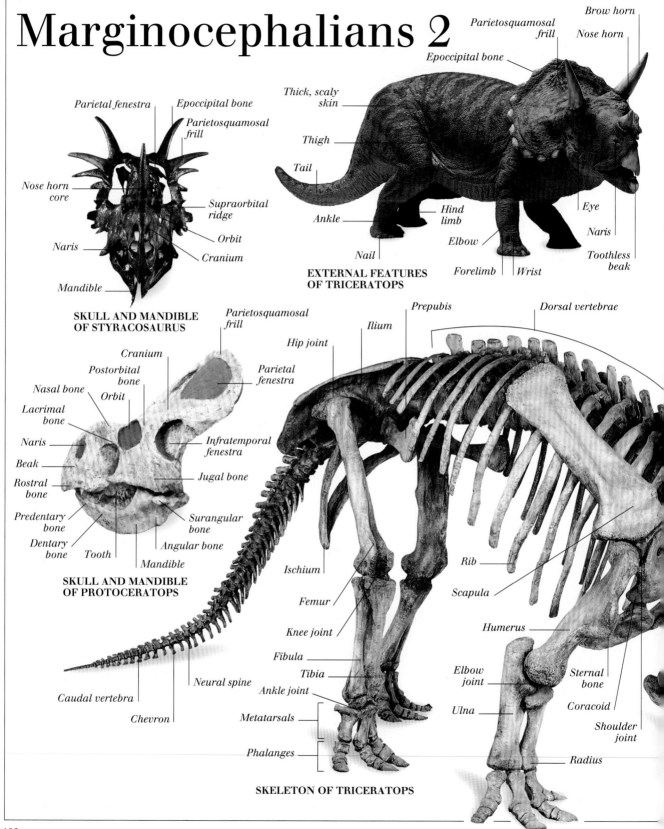

SKULL AND MANDIBLE OF STYRACOSAURUS

Parietal fenestra
Epoccipital bone
Parietosquamosal frill
Nose horn core
Supraorbital ridge
Orbit
Cranium
Naris
Mandible

EXTERNAL FEATURES OF TRICERATOPS

Parietosquamosal frill
Epoccipital bone
Brow horn
Nose horn
Thick, scaly skin
Thigh
Tail
Ankle
Hind limb
Eye
Naris
Nail
Elbow
Forelimb
Wrist
Toothless beak

SKULL AND MANDIBLE OF PROTOCERATOPS

Parietosquamosal frill
Cranium
Postorbital bone
Nasal bone
Orbit
Lacrimal bone
Parietal fenestra
Naris
Beak
Infratemporal fenestra
Rostral bone
Jugal bone
Predentary bone
Surangular bone
Dentary bone
Tooth
Angular bone
Mandible

SKELETON OF TRICERATOPS

Prepubis
Dorsal vertebrae
Ilium
Hip joint
Rib
Scapula
Ischium
Femur
Knee joint
Humerus
Fibula
Tibia
Elbow joint
Sternal bone
Ankle joint
Coracoid
Metatarsals
Ulna
Shoulder joint
Phalanges
Radius
Caudal vertebra
Neural spine
Chevron

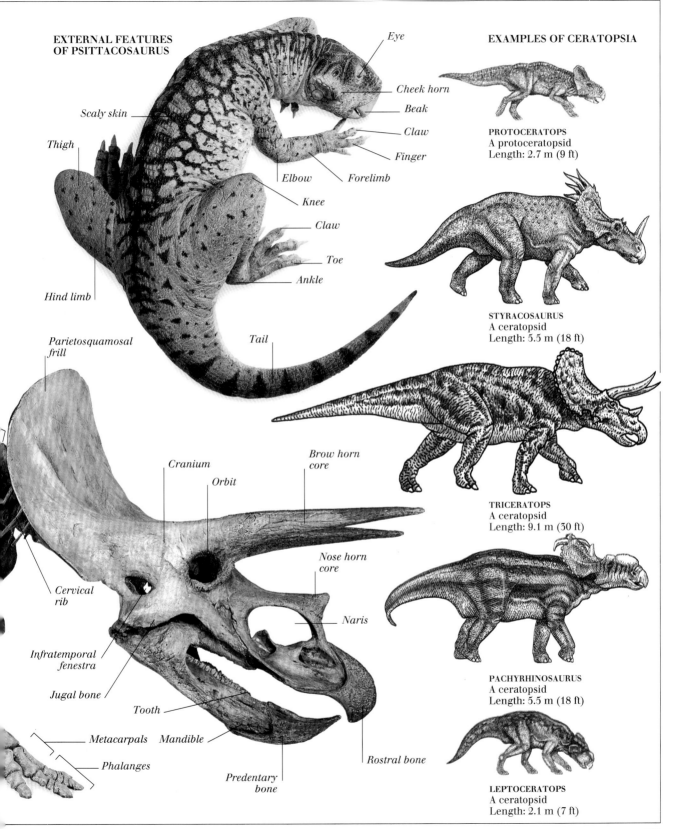

**EXTERNAL FEATURES
OF PSITTACOSAURUS**

Eye

Cheek horn

Beak

Claw

Finger

Scaly skin

Thigh

Forelimb

Elbow

Knee

Claw

Toe

Ankle

Hind limb

Parietosquamosal
frill

Tail

Cranium

Orbit

Brow horn
core

Nose horn
core

Naris

Cervical
rib

Infratemporal
fenestra

Jugal bone

Tooth

Metacarpals

Mandible

Phalanges

Predentary
bone

Rostral bone

EXAMPLES OF CERATOPSIA

PROTOCERATOPS
A protoceratopsid
Length: 2.7 m (9 ft)

STYRACOSAURUS
A ceratopsid
Length: 5.5 m (18 ft)

TRICERATOPS
A ceratopsid
Length: 9.1 m (30 ft)

PACHYRHINOSAURUS
A ceratopsid
Length: 5.5 m (18 ft)

LEPTOCERATOPS
A ceratopsid
Length: 2.1 m (7 ft)

Mammals 1

TETRALOPHODON CHEEK TEETH

SINCE THE EXTINCTION of the dinosaurs 65 million years ago, mammals have been the dominant vertebrates on Earth and include terrestrial, aerial, and aquatic forms. Having developed from the reptilian Therapsids, the first true mammals – small, nocturnal, rodent-like creatures, such as *Megazostrodon* – appeared over 200 million years ago during the Triassic period (245–208 million years ago). Mammals had several features that improved on those of their reptilian ancestors: an efficient four-chambered heart allowed these warm-blooded animals to sustain high levels of activity; a covering of hair helped them maintain a constant body temperature; an improved limb structure gave them more efficient locomotion; and the birth of live young and the immediate supply of food from the mother's milk aided their rapid growth. Since the end of the Mesozoic era (65 million years ago), the number of different mammal orders and the abundance of species in each order have varied dramatically. For example, the Perissodactyla (the order that includes *Coelodonta* and modern horses) was the most common group during the Early Tertiary period (about 54 million years ago). Today, the mammalian orders with the most populous species are the Rodentia (rats and mice), the Carnivora (bears, cats, and dogs), and the Artiodactyla (cattle, deer, and pigs), while the Proboscidea order, which included many genera, such as *Phiomia, Moeritherium, Tetralophodon,* and *Mammuthus,* now has only one member: the modern elephant. In Australia and South America, millions of years of continental isolation led to the development of the marsupials, a group of mammals distinct from the placentals (see p. 74) that existed elsewhere.

MODEL OF A MEGAZOSTRODON

Long tail aids balance

Insulating hair

Neural spine

Scapula

Cervical vertebra

Humerus

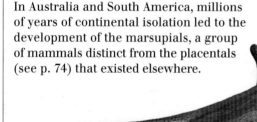

Nasal horn

Naris

Predentary bone

Orbit

Mandible

Chisel-edged molar

Radius

Ulna

Metacarpal

Phalanx

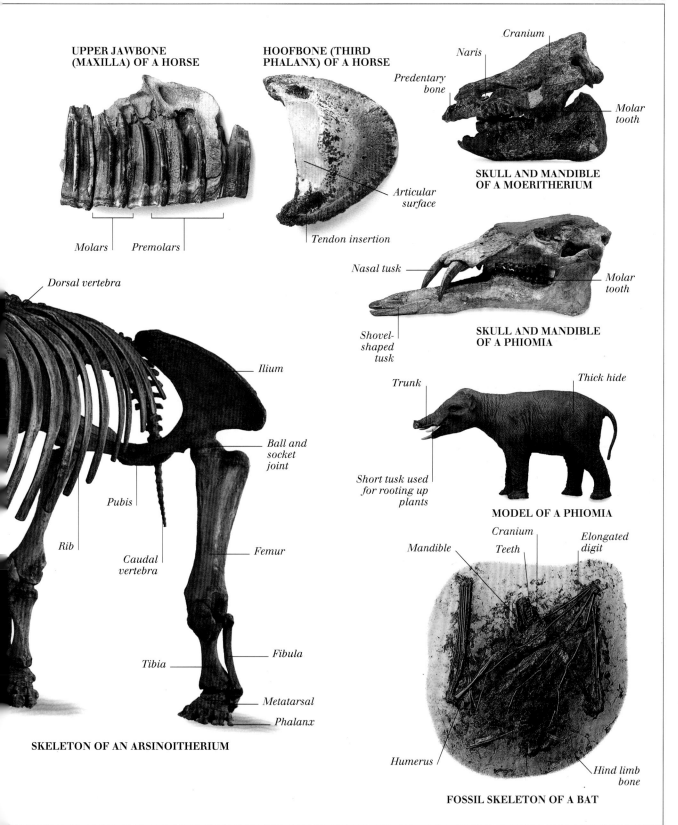

UPPER JAWBONE (MAXILLA) OF A HORSE

Molars

Premolars

HOOFBONE (THIRD PHALANX) OF A HORSE

Articular surface

Tendon insertion

SKULL AND MANDIBLE OF A MOERITHERIUM

Cranium

Naris

Predentary bone

Molar tooth

SKULL AND MANDIBLE OF A PHIOMIA

Nasal tusk

Shovel-shaped tusk

Molar tooth

MODEL OF A PHIOMIA

Trunk

Thick hide

Short tusk used for rooting up plants

SKELETON OF AN ARSINOITHERIUM

Dorsal vertebra

Ilium

Ball and socket joint

Pubis

Rib

Caudal vertebra

Femur

Tibia

Fibula

Metatarsal

Phalanx

FOSSIL SKELETON OF A BAT

Mandible

Cranium

Teeth

Elongated digit

Humerus

Hind limb bone

Mammals 2

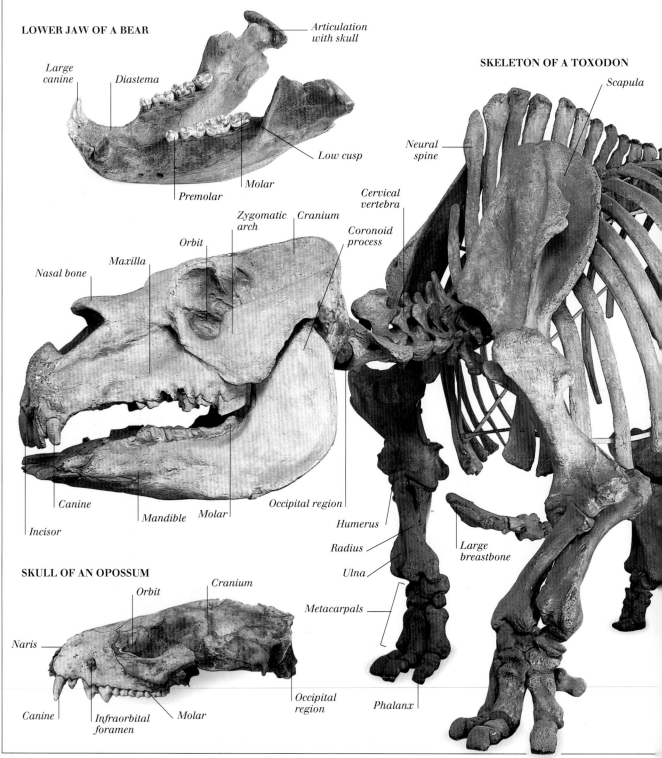

LOWER JAW OF A BEAR

Articulation with skull

Large canine

Diastema

Low cusp

Molar

Premolar

SKELETON OF A TOXODON

Scapula

Neural spine

Cervical vertebra

Coronoid process

Zygomatic arch

Cranium

Orbit

Maxilla

Nasal bone

Canine

Mandible

Molar

Occipital region

Incisor

Humerus

Radius

Ulna

Large breastbone

Metacarpals

SKULL OF AN OPOSSUM

Orbit

Cranium

Naris

Occipital region

Phalanx

Canine

Infraorbital foramen

Molar

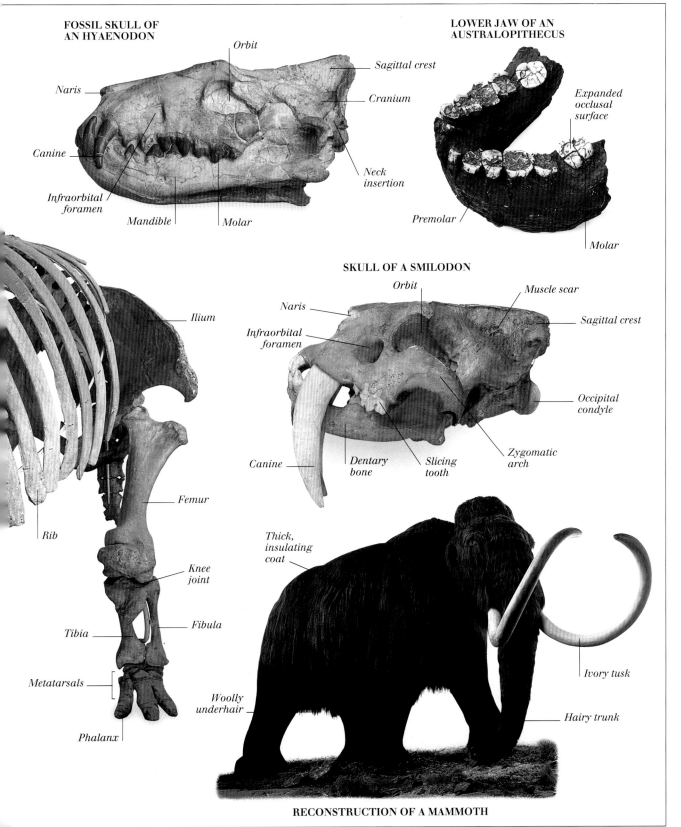

FOSSIL SKULL OF AN HYAENODON

Orbit

Naris

Canine

Infraorbital foramen

Mandible

Molar

Sagittal crest

Cranium

Neck insertion

LOWER JAW OF AN AUSTRALOPITHECUS

Expanded occlusal surface

Premolar

Molar

SKULL OF A SMILODON

Orbit

Naris

Infraorbital foramen

Canine

Dentary bone

Slicing tooth

Muscle scar

Sagittal crest

Occipital condyle

Zygomatic arch

Ilium

Femur

Rib

Knee joint

Tibia

Fibula

Metatarsals

Phalanx

Thick, insulating coat

Woolly underhair

Ivory tusk

Hairy trunk

RECONSTRUCTION OF A MAMMOTH

The first hominids

MODERN HUMANS BELONG TO THE MAMMALIAN order of primates (see pp. 202–203), which originated about 55 million years ago; they comprise the only extant hominid species. The earliest hominid was *Australopithecus* ("southern ape"), a small-brained intermediate between apes and humans that was capable of standing and walking upright. *Homo habilis*, the first known human appeared at least 2 million years ago. This larger-brained "handy man" began making tools for hunting. *Homo erectus* first appeared in Africa about 1.8 million years ago and spread into Asia about 800,000 years later. Smaller-toothed than *Homo habilis*, it developed fire as a tool, which enabled it to cook food. Neanderthals, a near relative of modern humans, originated about 200,000 years ago, and *Homo sapiens* (modern humans) appeared in Africa about 100,000 years later. The two co-existed for thousands of years, but by 30,000 years ago, *Homo sapiens* had become dominant and the Neanderthals had died out. Classification of *Homo sapiens* in relation to its ancestors is enormously problematic: modern humans must be classified not only by bone structure, but also by specific behaviour – the ability to plan future action; to follow traditions; and to use symbolic communication, including complex language and the ability to use and recognize symbols.

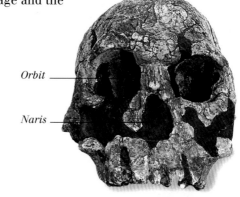

JAWBONE OF AUSTRALOPITHECUS (SOUTHERN APE)

Larger jawbone than modern human

Large back tooth

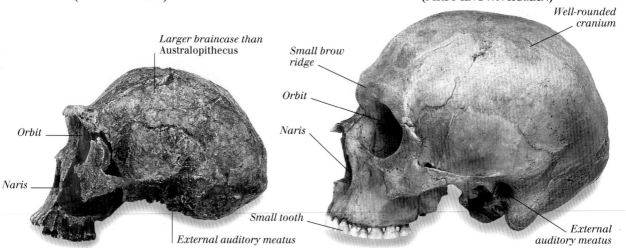

Jutting brow ridge

Cranium

Orbit

Naris

Jutting jawbone

SKULL OF AUSTRALOPITHECUS (SOUTHERN APE)

Orbit

Naris

SKULL OF HOMO HABILIS (FIRST KNOWN HUMAN)

Larger braincase than Australopithecus

Orbit

Naris

External auditory meatus

SKULL OF HOMO ERECTUS (UPRIGHT MAN)

Well-rounded cranium

Small brow ridge

Orbit

Naris

Small tooth

External auditory meatus

SKULL OF HOMO SAPIENS (MODERN HUMAN)

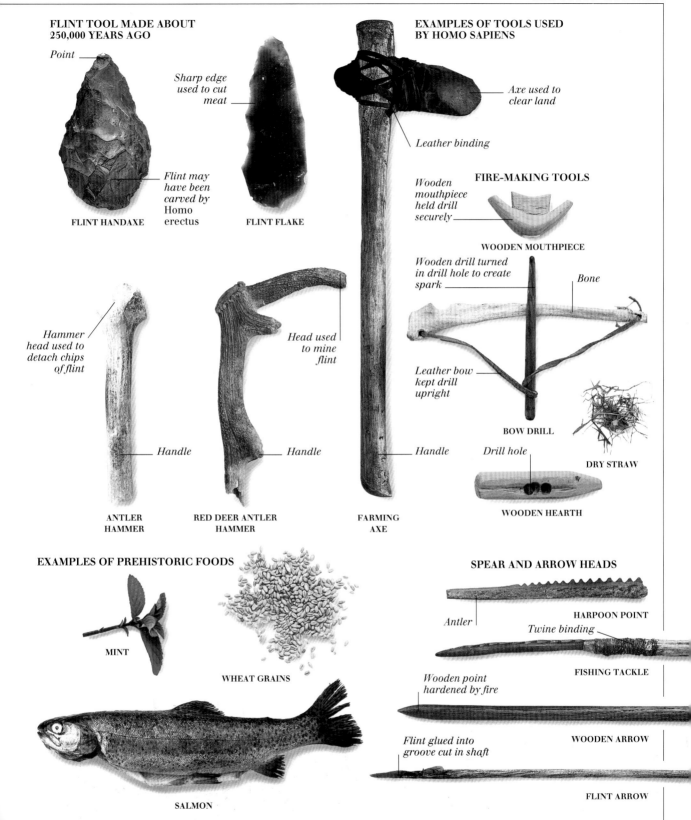

FLINT TOOL MADE ABOUT 250,000 YEARS AGO

Point

Sharp edge used to cut meat

Flint may have been carved by Homo erectus

FLINT HANDAXE

FLINT FLAKE

Hammer head used to detach chips of flint

Head used to mine flint

Handle

Handle

Handle

ANTLER HAMMER

RED DEER ANTLER HAMMER

FARMING AXE

EXAMPLES OF TOOLS USED BY HOMO SAPIENS

Axe used to clear land

Leather binding

FIRE-MAKING TOOLS

Wooden mouthpiece held drill securely

WOODEN MOUTHPIECE

Wooden drill turned in drill hole to create spark

Bone

Leather bow kept drill upright

BOW DRILL

DRY STRAW

Drill hole

WOODEN HEARTH

EXAMPLES OF PREHISTORIC FOODS

MINT

WHEAT GRAINS

SALMON

SPEAR AND ARROW HEADS

Antler

HARPOON POINT

Twine binding

FISHING TACKLE

Wooden point hardened by fire

WOODEN ARROW

Flint glued into groove cut in shaft

FLINT ARROW

PLANTS

Plant variety

FLOWERING PLANT
Bromeliad
(*Acanthostachys strobilacea*)

Leaf

THERE ARE MORE THAN 300,000 SPECIES of plants. They
show a wide diversity of forms and life-styles, ranging, for example, from delicate
liverworts, adapted for life in a damp habitat, to cacti, capable of surviving in the desert, and
from herbaceous plants, such as corn, which completes its life-cycle in one year, to the giant redwood tree,
which can live for thousands of years. This diversity reflects the adaptations of plants to survive in a wide
range of habitats. This is seen most clearly in the flowering plants (phylum Angiospermophyta), which are
the most numerous, with over 250,000 species, and the most widespread, being found from the tropics to the
poles. Despite their diversity, plants share certain characteristics: typically, plants are green, and make their
food by photosynthesis; and most plants live in or on a substrate, such as soil, and do not actively move. Algae
(kingdom Protista) and fungi (kingdom Fungi) have some plant-like characteristics and are
often studied alongside plants, although they are not true plants.

GREEN ALGA
Micrograph of desmid
(*Micrasterias sp.*)

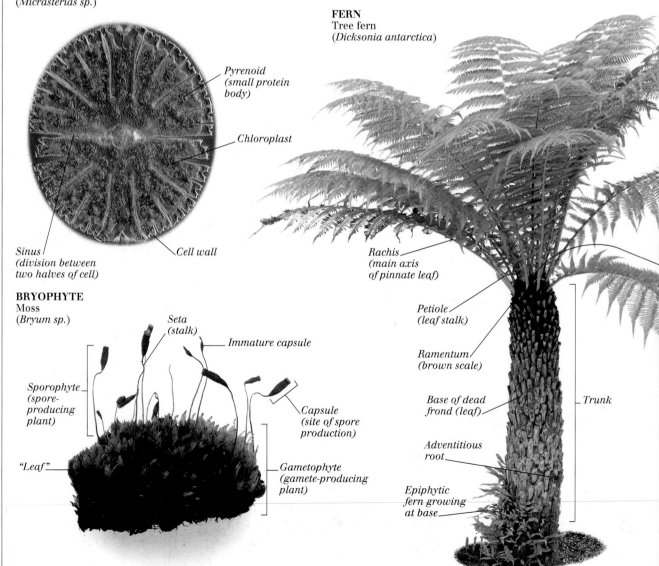

*Pyrenoid
(small protein
body)*

Chloroplast

*Sinus
(division between
two halves of cell)*

Cell wall

FERN
Tree fern
(*Dicksonia antarctica*)

*Rachis
(main axis
of pinnate leaf)*

*Petiole
(leaf stalk)*

*Ramentum
(brown scale)*

*Base of dead
frond (leaf)*

Trunk

*Adventitious
root*

*Epiphytic
fern growing
at base*

BRYOPHYTE
Moss
(*Bryum sp.*)

*Seta
(stalk)*

Immature capsule

*Sporophyte
(spore-
producing
plant)*

*Capsule
(site of spore
production)*

"Leaf"

*Gametophyte
(gamete-producing
plant)*

FLOWERING PLANT
Succulent
(*Kedrostis africana*)

Petiole
(leaf stalk)

Leaf

Stem

Caudex
(swollen
stem
base)

Root

Spine *Flower*

Bract
(leaf-like structure)

Inflorescence

Stem

FLOWERING PLANT
Micrograph of cross-section
through leaf of marram grass
(*Ammophila arenaria*)

Cuticle
(waterproof
covering)

Sclerenchyma
(strengthening
tissue)

Stiff trichome
(hair)

Xylem

Phloem

Vascular
tissue

Interlocked
trichomes (hairs)

Epidermis
(outer layer
of cells)

Hinge cells
(cause curling of leaf to
reduce water loss)

Mesophyll
(photosynthetic
tissue)

Pinna
(leaflet)

FLOWERING PLANT
Couch grass
(*Agropyron repens*)

Rachis
(main axis of
grass inflorescence)

Caryopsis
(type of
dry fruit)

Node

Frond (leaf)

Midrib of
pinna (leaflet)

Lamina
(blade)

Round, hollow
stem

Sheathing
leaf base

Adventitious
root

FLOWERING PLANT
Pitcher plant
(*Sarracenia purpurea*)

Sepal

Fruit
surrounded
by floral parts

Umbrella
of style

Pitcher (leaf
modified to trap
insects)

Pedicel
(flower
stalk)

Hood

Downward-pointing
hair (encourages
insect prey into
pitcher)

Wing

Immature
pitcher

Fungi and lichens

FUNGI WERE ONCE THOUGHT OF AS PLANTS but are now classified as a separate kingdom. This kingdom includes not only the familiar mushrooms, puffballs, stinkhorns, and moulds, but also yeasts, smuts, rusts, and lichens. Most fungi are multicellular, consisting of a mass of thread-like hyphae that together form a mycelium. However, the simpler fungi (e.g., yeasts) are microscopic, single-celled organisms. Typically, fungi reproduce by means of spores. Most fungi feed on dead or decaying matter, or on living organisms. A few fungi obtain their food from plants or algae, with which they have a symbiotic (mutually advantageous) relationship. Lichens are a symbiotic partnership between algae and fungi. Of the six types of lichens the three most common are crustose (flat and crusty), foliose (leafy), and fruticose (shrub-like). Some lichens (e.g., *Cladonia floerkeana*) are a combination of types. Lichens reproduce by means of spores or soredia (powdery vegetative fragments).

Emerging sporophore (spore-bearing structure)

Pileus (cap) continuous with stipe (stalk)

Bark of dead beech tree

Inrolled margin of pileus (cap)

Gill (site of spore production)

Sporophore (spore-bearing structure)

Stipe (stalk)

Hyphae (fungal filaments)

OYSTER FUNGUS
(*Pleurotus pulmonarius*)

EXAMPLES OF LICHENS

Secondary fruticose thallus

Branched, hollow stem

Apothecium (spore-producing body)

FRUTICOSE
Cladonia portentosa

Soredia (powdery vegetative fragments) produced at end of lobe

Tree bark

Foliose thallus

FOLIOSE
Hypogymnia physodes

Gleba (spore-producing tissue found in this type of fungus)

Sporophore (spore-bearing structure)

Porous stipe (stalk)

Volva (remains of universal veil)

STINKHORN
(*Phallus impudicus*)

Toothed branchlet

Branch

Sporophore (spore-bearing structure)

Stipe (stalk)

RAMARIA FORMOSA

Soredia (powdery vegetative fragments) released onto surface of squamulose thallus

Apothecium (spore-producing body)

Basal scale of primary squamulose thallus

Podetium (granular stalk) of secondary fruticose thallus

Moss

SQUAMULOSE (SCALY) AND FRUTICOSE THALLUS
Cladonia floerkeana

SECTION THROUGH FOLIOSE LICHEN SHOWING REPRODUCTION BY SOREDIA

Algal cell

Fungal hypha

Upper cortex

Algal layer

Medulla of fungal hyphae (mycelium)

Lower cortex

Rhizine (bundle of absorptive hyphae)

Soredium (powdery vegetative fragment involved in propagation) released from lichen

Soralium (pore in upper surface of thallus)

Upper surface of thallus

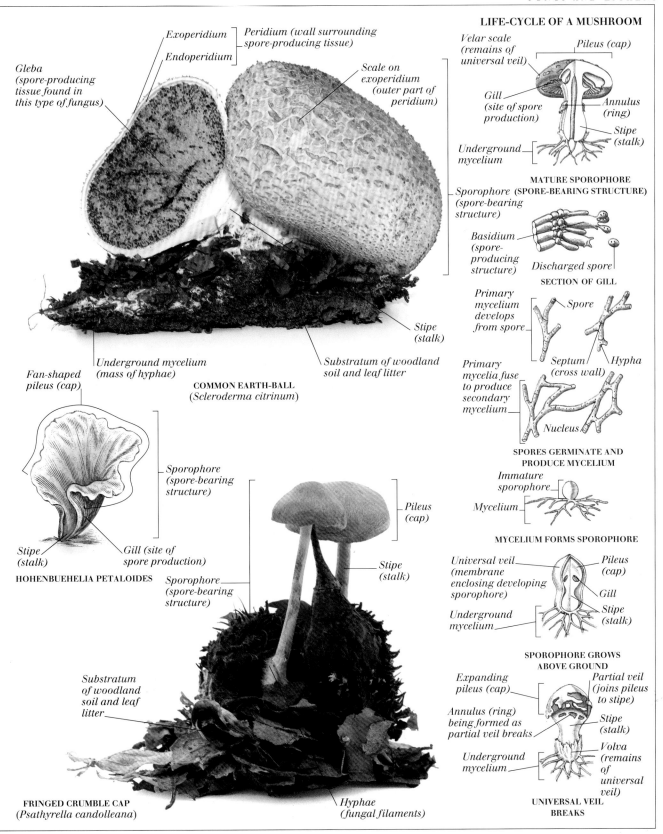

LIFE-CYCLE OF A MUSHROOM

Exoperidium

Endoperidium

Peridium (wall surrounding spore-producing tissue)

Gleba (spore-producing tissue found in this type of fungus)

Scale on exoperidium (outer part of peridium)

Velar scale (remains of universal veil)

Pileus (cap)

Gill (site of spore production)

Annulus (ring)

Stipe (stalk)

Underground mycelium

MATURE SPOROPHORE (SPORE-BEARING STRUCTURE)

Sporophore (spore-bearing structure)

Basidium (spore-producing structure)

Discharged spore

SECTION OF GILL

Underground mycelium (mass of hyphae)

Substratum of woodland soil and leaf litter

Stipe (stalk)

COMMON EARTH-BALL (Scleroderma citrinum)

Primary mycelium develops from spore

Spore

Septum (cross wall)

Hypha

Primary mycelia fuse to produce secondary mycelium

Nucleus

SPORES GERMINATE AND PRODUCE MYCELIUM

Fan-shaped pileus (cap)

Sporophore (spore-bearing structure)

Immature sporophore

Mycelium

MYCELIUM FORMS SPOROPHORE

Stipe (stalk)

Gill (site of spore production)

HOHENBUEHELIA PETALOIDES

Sporophore (spore-bearing structure)

Pileus (cap)

Stipe (stalk)

Universal veil (membrane enclosing developing sporophore)

Pileus (cap)

Gill

Underground mycelium

Stipe (stalk)

SPOROPHORE GROWS ABOVE GROUND

Substratum of woodland soil and leaf litter

Expanding pileus (cap)

Annulus (ring) being formed as partial veil breaks

Partial veil (joins pileus to stipe)

Stipe (stalk)

Underground mycelium

Volva (remains of universal veil)

FRINGED CRUMBLE CAP (Psathyrella candolleana)

Hyphae (fungal filaments)

UNIVERSAL VEIL BREAKS

Algae and seaweeds

ALGAE ARE NOT TRUE PLANTS. They form a diverse group of plant-like organisms that belong to the kingdom Protista. Like plants, algae possess the green pigment chlorophyll and make their own food by photosynthesis (see pp. 138-139). Many algae also possess other pigments by which they can be classified; for example, the brown pigment fucoxanthin is found in the brown algae. Some of the ten phyla of algae are exclusively unicellular (single-celled); others also contain aggregates of cells in filaments or colonies. Three phyla – the Chlorophyta (green algae), Rhodophyta (red algae), and Phaeophyta (brown algae) – contain larger, multicellular, thalloid (flat), marine organisms commonly known as seaweeds.

Most algae can reproduce sexually. For example, in the brown seaweed *Fucus vesiculosus*, gametes (sex cells) are produced in conceptacles (chambers) in the receptacles (fertile tips of fronds); after their release into the sea, antherozoids (male gametes) and oospheres (female gametes) fuse; the resulting zygote settles on a rock and develops into a new seaweed.

BROWN SEAWEED
Channelled wrack
(*Pelvetia canaliculata*)

Receptacle
(fertile tip
of frond)

Thallus
(plant
body)

Apical
notch

Margin of
lamina (blade)
rolled inwards
to form channel

Hapteron (holdfast)

BROWN SEAWEED
Spiral wrack
(*Fucus spiralis*)

Apical notch

Conceptacle
(chamber)

Receptacle
(fertile tip
of frond)

Lamina
(blade)

Smooth margin

Midrib

Hapteron (holdfast)

Thallus
(plant
body)

EXAMPLES OF ALGAE

Reproductive
chamber

Cap

Sterile whorl

Cell wall

Stalk

Rhizoid

GREEN ALGA
Acetabularia sp.

Flagellum

Eyespot

Contractile
vacuole

Cytoplasm

Cell
wall

Nucleus

Chloroplast

Pyrenoid
(small protein
body)

Starch
grain

GREEN ALGA
Chlamydomonas sp.

Coenobium
(colony of cells)

Daughter
coenobium

Girdle

Gelatinous
sheath

Biflagellate cell

GREEN ALGA
Volvox sp.

Spine

Cytoplasm

Vacuole

Plastid
(photosynthetic
organelle)

Nucleus

DIATOM
Thalassiosira sp.

Apical notch

Receptacle
(fertile tip
of frond)

Conceptacle
(chamber)
containing
reproductive
structures)

Lamina
(blade)

Midrib

RECEPTACLE
Spiral wrack
(*Fucus spiralis*)

BROWN SEAWEED
Oarweed
(*Laminaria digitata*)

Thallus (plant body)

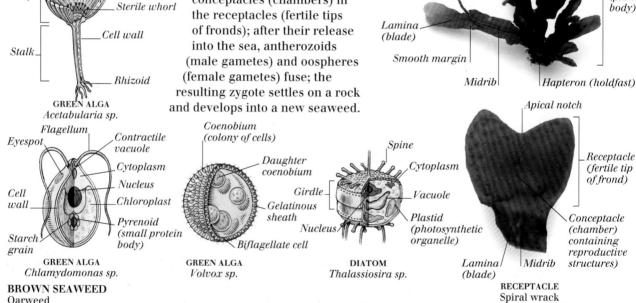

Lamina (blade)
palmately
divided

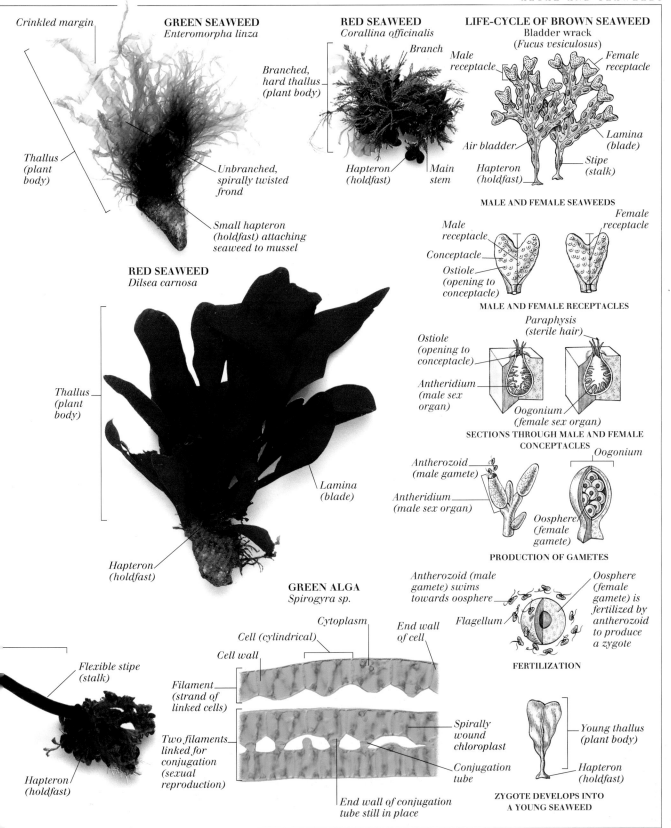

GREEN SEAWEED
Enteromorpha linza

Crinkled margin

Thallus
(plant
body)

Unbranched,
spirally twisted
frond

Small hapteron
(holdfast) attaching
seaweed to mussel

RED SEAWEED
Corallina officinalis

Branch

Branched,
hard thallus
(plant body)

Hapteron
(holdfast)

Main
stem

LIFE-CYCLE OF BROWN SEAWEED
Bladder wrack
(*Fucus vesiculosus*)

Male
receptacle

Female
receptacle

Air bladder

Lamina
(blade)

Hapteron
(holdfast)

Stipe
(stalk)

MALE AND FEMALE SEAWEEDS

Male
receptacle

Female
receptacle

Conceptacle

Ostiole
(opening to
conceptacle)

MALE AND FEMALE RECEPTACLES

Paraphysis
(sterile hair)

Ostiole
(opening to
conceptacle)

Antheridium
(male sex
organ)

Oogonium
(female sex
organ)

**SECTIONS THROUGH MALE AND FEMALE
CONCEPTACLES**

Antherozoid
(male gamete)

Oogonium

Antheridium
(male sex
organ)

Oosphere
(female
gamete)

PRODUCTION OF GAMETES

RED SEAWEED
Dilsea carnosa

Thallus
(plant
body)

Lamina
(blade)

Hapteron
(holdfast)

GREEN ALGA
Spirogyra sp.

Antherozoid (male
gamete) swims
towards oosphere

Flagellum

Oosphere
(female
gamete) is
fertilized by
antherozoid
to produce
a zygote

FERTILIZATION

Cytoplasm

Cell (cylindrical)

End wall
of cell

Cell wall

Filament
(strand of
linked cells)

Two filaments
linked for
conjugation
(sexual
reproduction)

Spirally
wound
chloroplast

Conjugation
tube

End wall of conjugation
tube still in place

Young thallus
(plant body)

Hapteron
(holdfast)

**ZYGOTE DEVELOPS INTO
A YOUNG SEAWEED**

Flexible stipe
(stalk)

Hapteron
(holdfast)

Liverworts and mosses

LIVERWORTS AND MOSSES ARE SMALL, LOW-GROWING PLANTS that belong to the phylum Bryophyta. Bryophytes do not have true stems, leaves, or roots (they are anchored to the ground by rhizoids), nor do they have the vascular tissues (xylem and phloem) that transport water and nutrients in higher plants. With no outer, waterproof cuticle, bryophytes are susceptible to drying out, and most grow in moist habitats. The bryophyte life-cycle has two stages. In stage one, the green plant (gametophyte) produces male and female gametes (sex cells), which fuse to form a zygote. In stage two, the zygote develops into a sporophyte that remains attached to the gametophyte. The sporophyte produces spores, which are released and germinate into new green plants. Liverworts (class Hepaticae) grow horizontally and may be thalloid (flat and ribbon-like) or "leafy". Mosses (class Musci) typically have an upright "stem" with spirally arranged "leaves".

A LEAFY LIVERWORT
Scapania undulata

"Stem"

"Leaf"

Rhizoid

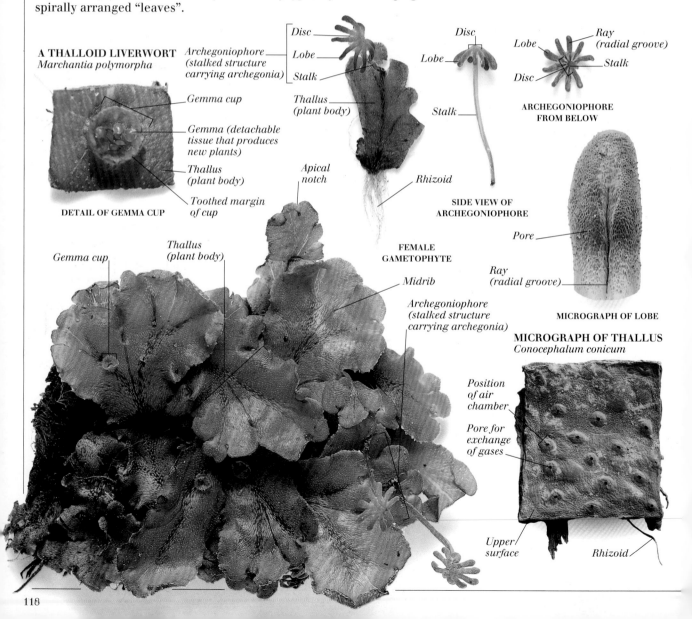

A THALLOID LIVERWORT
Marchantia polymorpha

Gemma cup

Gemma (detachable tissue that produces new plants)

Thallus (plant body)

Toothed margin of cup

DETAIL OF GEMMA CUP

Archegoniophore (stalked structure carrying archegonia)

Disc

Lobe

Stalk

Thallus (plant body)

Rhizoid

FEMALE GAMETOPHYTE

Disc

Lobe

Stalk

SIDE VIEW OF ARCHEGONIOPHORE

Lobe

Disc

Ray (radial groove)

Stalk

ARCHEGONIOPHORE FROM BELOW

Pore

Ray (radial groove)

MICROGRAPH OF LOBE

Gemma cup

Thallus (plant body)

Apical notch

Midrib

Archegoniophore (stalked structure carrying archegonia)

MICROGRAPH OF THALLUS
Conocephalum conicum

Position of air chamber

Pore for exchange of gases

Upper surface

Rhizoid

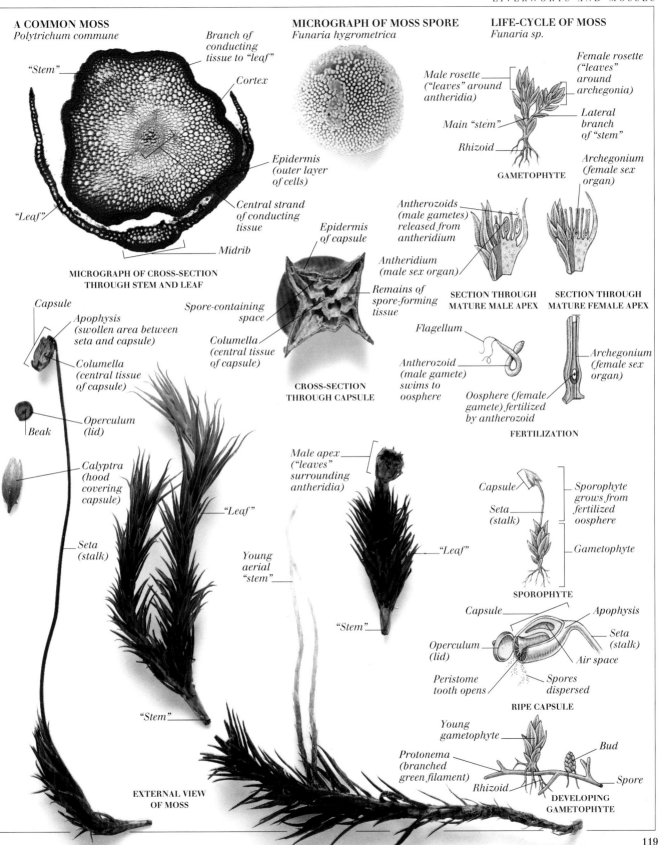

A COMMON MOSS
Polytrichum commune

Branch of conducting tissue to "leaf"

"Stem"

Cortex

Epidermis (outer layer of cells)

"Leaf"

Central strand of conducting tissue

Midrib

MICROGRAPH OF CROSS-SECTION THROUGH STEM AND LEAF

MICROGRAPH OF MOSS SPORE
Funaria hygrometrica

Epidermis of capsule

Spore-containing space

Remains of spore-forming tissue

Columella (central tissue of capsule)

CROSS-SECTION THROUGH CAPSULE

LIFE-CYCLE OF MOSS
Funaria sp.

Female rosette ("leaves" around archegonia)

Male rosette ("leaves" around antheridia)

Lateral branch of "stem"

Main "stem"

Rhizoid

Archegonium (female sex organ)

GAMETOPHYTE

Antherozoids (male gametes) released from antheridium

Antheridium (male sex organ)

Archegonium (female sex organ)

SECTION THROUGH MATURE MALE APEX

SECTION THROUGH MATURE FEMALE APEX

Flagellum

Antherozoid (male gamete) swims to oosphere

Oosphere (female gamete) fertilized by antherozoid

FERTILIZATION

Capsule

Apophysis (swollen area between seta and capsule)

Columella (central tissue of capsule)

Operculum (lid)

Beak

Calyptra (hood covering capsule)

Seta (stalk)

"Leaf"

Male apex ("leaves" surrounding antheridia)

Young aerial "stem"

"Leaf"

"Stem"

"Stem"

EXTERNAL VIEW OF MOSS

Capsule

Seta (stalk)

Sporophyte grows from fertilized oosphere

Gametophyte

SPOROPHYTE

Capsule

Apophysis

Seta (stalk)

Air space

Operculum (lid)

Peristome tooth opens

Spores dispersed

RIPE CAPSULE

Young gametophyte

Protonema (branched green filament)

Bud

Spore

Rhizoid

DEVELOPING GAMETOPHYTE

Horsetails, clubmosses, and ferns

CLUBMOSS
Lycopodium sp.

Stem with
spirally
arranged
leaves

Branch

HORSETAILS, CLUBMOSSES, AND FERNS are primitive land plants, which, like higher plants, have stems, roots, and leaves, and vascular systems that transport water, minerals, and food. However, unlike higher plants, they do not produce seeds when reproducing. Their life-cycles involve two stages. In stage one, the sporophyte (green plant) produces spores in sporangia. In stage two, the spores germinate, developing into small, short-lived gametophyte plants that produce male and female gametes (sex cells); the gametes fuse to form a zygote from which a new sporophyte plant develops. Horsetails (phylum Sphenophyta) have erect, green stems with branches arranged in whorls; some stems are fertile and have a single spore-producing strobilus (group of sporangia) at the tip. Clubmosses (phylum Lycopodophyta) typically have small leaves arranged spirally around the stem, with spore-producing strobili at the tip of some stems. Ferns (phylum Filicinophyta) typically have large, pinnate fronds (leaves); sporangia, grouped together in sori, develop on the underside of fertile fronds.

FROND
Male fern
(*Dryopteris filix-mas*)

Strobilus
(group of sporangia)

CLUBMOSS
Selaginella sp.

Epidermis
(outer layer
of cells)

Cortex (layer
between epidermis
and vascular tissue)

Vascular
tissue
Phloem
Xylem

Lacuna
(air space)

Branch

Rhizophore
(leafless
branch)

Root

Shoot
apex

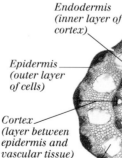

Creeping stem with
spirally arranged
leaves

**MICROGRAPH OF CROSS-SECTION
THROUGH CLUBMOSS STEM**

HORSETAIL
Common horsetail
(*Equisetum arvense*)

Apex of
sterile shoot

Sporangiophore
(structure
carrying
sporangia)

Strobilus
(group of
sporangia)

Non-photosynthetic
fertile stem

Collar of small
brown leaves

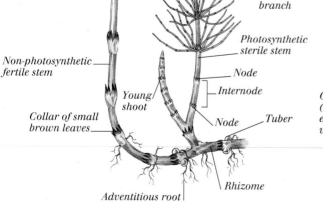

Young
shoot

Lateral
branch

Photosynthetic
sterile stem

Node
Internode

Node

Tuber

Rhizome

Adventitious root

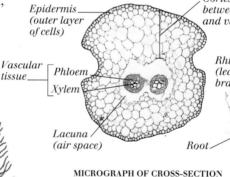

Endodermis
(inner layer of
cortex)

Vascular tissue

Sclerenchyma
(strengthening tissue)

Epidermis
(outer layer
of cells)

Chlorenchyma
(photosynthetic
tissue)

Cortex
(layer between
epidermis and
vascular tissue)

Parenchyma
(packing
tissue)

Hollow pith
cavity

Vallecular canal
(longitudinal channel)

Carinal canal
(longitudinal
channel)

**MICROGRAPH OF CROSS-SECTION
THROUGH HORSETAIL STEM**

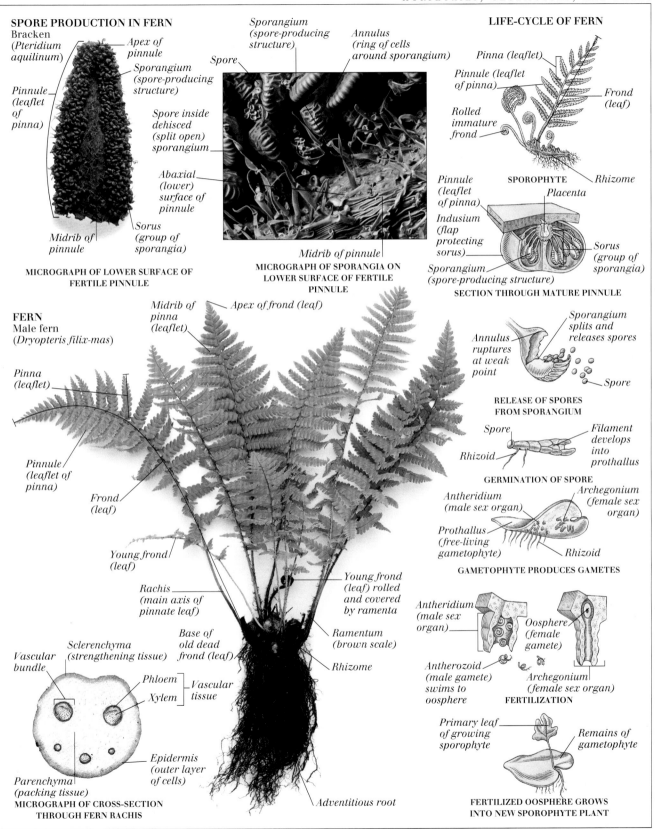

SPORE PRODUCTION IN FERN

Bracken
(*Pteridium aquilinum*)

Apex of pinnule

Sporangium (spore-producing structure)

Pinnule (leaflet of pinna)

Spore inside dehisced (split open) sporangium

Abaxial (lower) surface of pinnule

Midrib of pinnule

Sorus (group of sporangia)

MICROGRAPH OF LOWER SURFACE OF FERTILE PINNULE

Spore

Sporangium (spore-producing structure)

Annulus (ring of cells around sporangium)

Midrib of pinnule

MICROGRAPH OF SPORANGIA ON LOWER SURFACE OF FERTILE PINNULE

LIFE-CYCLE OF FERN

Pinna (leaflet)

Pinnule (leaflet of pinna)

Rolled immature frond

Frond (leaf)

SPOROPHYTE

Rhizome

Pinnule (leaflet of pinna)

Indusium (flap protecting sorus)

Sporangium (spore-producing structure)

Placenta

Sorus (group of sporangia)

SECTION THROUGH MATURE PINNULE

Sporangium splits and releases spores

Annulus ruptures at weak point

Spore

RELEASE OF SPORES FROM SPORANGIUM

Spore

Rhizoid

Filament develops into prothallus

GERMINATION OF SPORE

Antheridium (male sex organ)

Archegonium (female sex organ)

Prothallus (free-living gametophyte)

Rhizoid

GAMETOPHYTE PRODUCES GAMETES

Antheridium (male sex organ)

Antherozoid (male gamete) swims to oosphere

Oosphere (female gamete)

Archegonium (female sex organ)

FERTILIZATION

Primary leaf of growing sporophyte

Remains of gametophyte

FERTILIZED OOSPHERE GROWS INTO NEW SPOROPHYTE PLANT

FERN

Male fern
(*Dryopteris filix-mas*)

Pinna (leaflet)

Pinnule (leaflet of pinna)

Frond (leaf)

Young frond (leaf)

Midrib of pinna (leaflet)

Apex of frond (leaf)

Rachis (main axis of pinnate leaf)

Base of old dead frond (leaf)

Young frond (leaf) rolled and covered by ramenta

Ramentum (brown scale)

Rhizome

Vascular bundle

Sclerenchyma (strengthening tissue)

Phloem

Xylem

Vascular tissue

Epidermis (outer layer of cells)

Parenchyma (packing tissue)

MICROGRAPH OF CROSS-SECTION THROUGH FERN RACHIS

Adventitious root

Gymnosperms 1

THE GYMNOSPERMS ARE FOUR RELATED PHYLA of seed-producing plants; their seeds, however, lack the protective, outer covering which surrounds the seeds of flowering plants. Typically, gymnosperms are woody, perennial shrubs or trees, with stems, leaves, and roots, and a well-developed vascular (transport) system. The reproductive structures in most gymnosperms are cones: male cones produce microspores in which male gametes (sex cells) develop; female cones produce megaspores in which female gametes develop. Microspores are blown by the wind to female cones, male and female gametes fuse during fertilization, and a seed develops. The four gymnosperm phyla are the conifers (phylum Coniferophyta), mostly tall trees; cycads (phylum Cycadophyta), small palm-like trees; the ginkgo or maidenhair tree (phylum Ginkgophyta), a tall tree with bilobed leaves; and gnetophytes (phylum Gnetophyta), a diverse group of plants, mainly shrubs, but also including the horizontally growing welwitschia.

LIFE-CYCLE OF SCOTS PINE
(*Pinus sylvestris*)

Needle (foliage leaf)

Cone

Ovuliferous scale (ovule- then seed-bearing structure)

MALE CONES

YOUNG FEMALE CONE

Pollen grain in micropyle (entrance to ovule)

Ovuliferous scale

Pollen grain

Nucleus

Air sac

Ovule (contains female gamete)

POLLINATION

Integument (outer part of ovule)

Pollen tube (carries male gamete from pollen grain to ovum)

Archegonium (containing female gamete)

FERTILIZATION

Seed

Seed

Wing

MATURE FEMALE CONE AND WINGED SEED

SCALE AND SEEDS
Pine
(*Pinus sp.*)

Ovuliferous scale (ovule- then seed-bearing structure)

Wing of seed derived from ovuliferous scale

Wing scar

Seed

Seed

Seed scar

Point of attachment to axis of cone

OVULIFEROUS SCALE FROM THIRD-YEAR FEMALE CONE

Microsporangium (structure in which pollen grains are formed)

Microsporophyll (modified leaf carrying microsporangia)

Axis of cone

Scale leaf

Ovuliferous scale (ovule- then seed-bearing structure)

MICROGRAPH OF LONGITUDINAL SECTION THROUGH YOUNG MALE CONE

Ovule (contains female gametes)

Bract scale

Axis of cone

MICROGRAPH OF LONGITUDINAL SECTION THROUGH SECOND-YEAR FEMALE CONE

Plumule (embryonic shoot)

Cotyledon (seed leaf)

Root

GERMINATION OF PINE SEEDLING

WELWITSCHIA
(*Welwitschia mirabilis*)

Frayed end of leaf

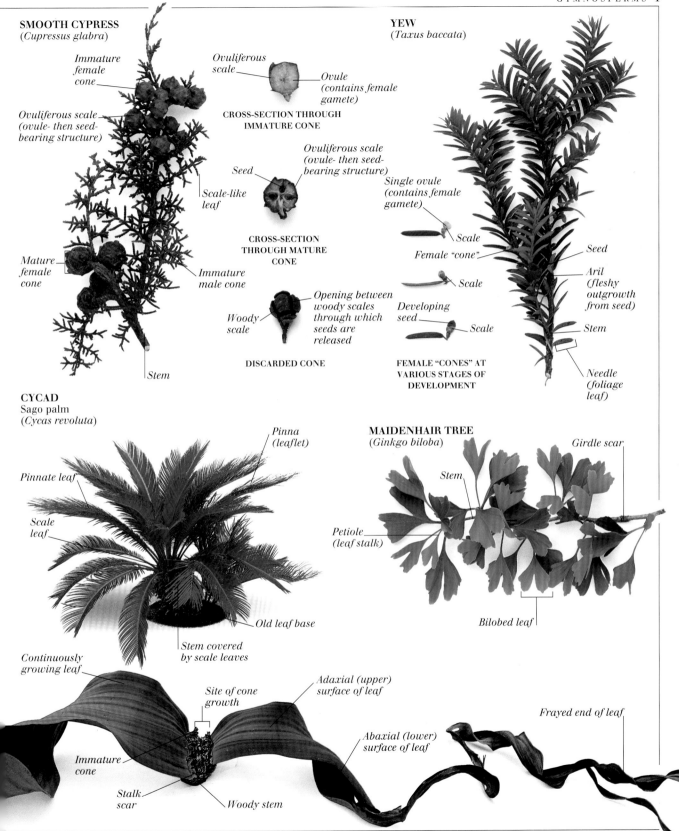

SMOOTH CYPRESS
(*Cupressus glabra*)

Immature female cone

Ovuliferous scale (ovule- then seed-bearing structure)

Scale-like leaf

Mature female cone

Immature male cone

Stem

Ovuliferous scale

Ovule (contains female gamete)

CROSS-SECTION THROUGH IMMATURE CONE

Ovuliferous scale (ovule- then seed-bearing structure)

Seed

CROSS-SECTION THROUGH MATURE CONE

Woody scale

Opening between woody scales through which seeds are released

DISCARDED CONE

YEW
(*Taxus baccata*)

Single ovule (contains female gamete)

Scale

Female "cone"

Scale

Developing seed

Scale

Seed

Aril (fleshy outgrowth from seed)

Stem

Needle (foliage leaf)

FEMALE "CONES" AT VARIOUS STAGES OF DEVELOPMENT

CYCAD
Sago palm
(*Cycas revoluta*)

Pinna (leaflet)

Pinnate leaf

Scale leaf

Old leaf base

Stem covered by scale leaves

MAIDENHAIR TREE
(*Ginkgo biloba*)

Girdle scar

Stem

Petiole (leaf stalk)

Bilobed leaf

Continuously growing leaf

Site of cone growth

Immature cone

Stalk scar

Woody stem

Adaxial (upper) surface of leaf

Abaxial (lower) surface of leaf

Frayed end of leaf

Gymnosperms 2

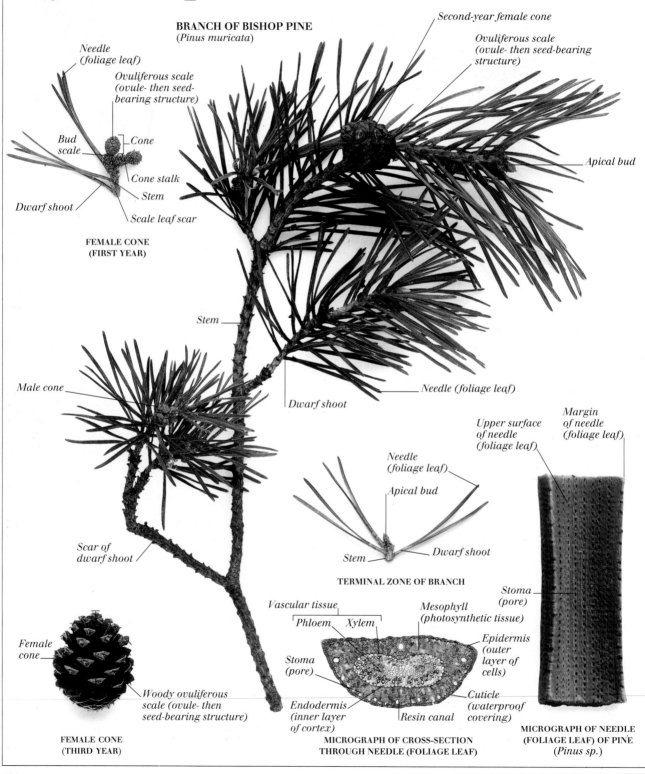

BRANCH OF BISHOP PINE
(*Pinus muricata*)

Second-year female cone

*Ovuliferous scale
(ovule- then seed-bearing
structure)*

*Needle
(foliage leaf)*

*Ovuliferous scale
(ovule- then seed-
bearing structure)*

*Bud
scale*

Cone

Cone stalk

Stem

Dwarf shoot

Scale leaf scar

**FEMALE CONE
(FIRST YEAR)**

Apical bud

Stem

Male cone

Needle (foliage leaf)

Dwarf shoot

*Scar of
dwarf shoot*

*Upper surface
of needle
(foliage leaf)*

*Margin
of needle
(foliage leaf)*

*Needle
(foliage leaf)*

Apical bud

Stem

Dwarf shoot

TERMINAL ZONE OF BRANCH

*Stoma
(pore)*

Vascular tissue

Phloem   *Xylem*

*Mesophyll
(photosynthetic tissue)*

*Stoma
(pore)*

*Epidermis
(outer
layer of
cells)*

*Female
cone*

*Endodermis
(inner layer
of cortex)*

Resin canal

*Cuticle
(waterproof
covering)*

*Woody ovuliferous
scale (ovule- then
seed-bearing structure)*

**FEMALE CONE
(THIRD YEAR)**

**MICROGRAPH OF CROSS-SECTION
THROUGH NEEDLE (FOLIAGE LEAF)**

**MICROGRAPH OF NEEDLE
(FOLIAGE LEAF) OF PINE
(*Pinus sp.*)**

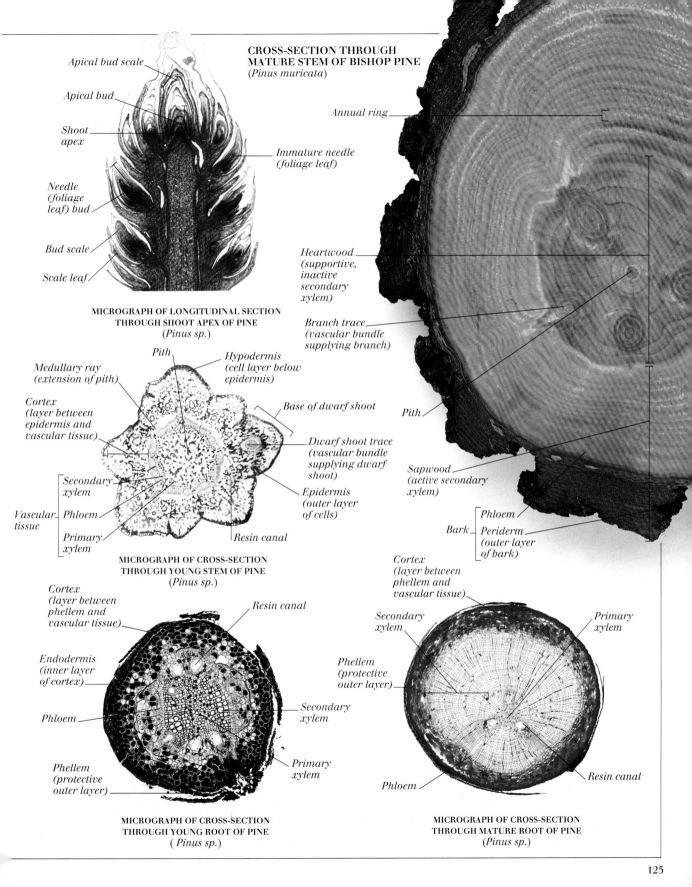

**CROSS-SECTION THROUGH
MATURE STEM OF BISHOP PINE**
(Pinus muricata)

Apical bud scale

Apical bud

Shoot apex

*Immature needle
(foliage leaf)*

*Needle
(foliage
leaf) bud*

Bud scale

Scale leaf

**MICROGRAPH OF LONGITUDINAL SECTION
THROUGH SHOOT APEX OF PINE**
(Pinus sp.)

Annual ring

*Heartwood
(supportive,
inactive
secondary
xylem)*

*Branch trace
(vascular bundle
supplying branch)*

Pith

*Sapwood
(active secondary
xylem)*

Phloem

Bark *Periderm
(outer layer
of bark)*

Pith

*Medullary ray
(extension of pith)*

*Hypodermis
(cell layer below
epidermis)*

*Cortex
(layer between
epidermis and
vascular tissue)*

Base of dwarf shoot

*Dwarf shoot trace
(vascular bundle
supplying dwarf
shoot)*

*Secondary
xylem*

*Epidermis
(outer layer
of cells)*

*Vascular
tissue*

Phloem

*Primary
xylem*

Resin canal

**MICROGRAPH OF CROSS-SECTION
THROUGH YOUNG STEM OF PINE**
(Pinus sp.)

*Cortex
(layer between
phellem and
vascular tissue)*

Resin canal

*Endodermis
(inner layer
of cortex)*

Phloem

*Secondary
xylem*

*Phellem
(protective
outer layer)*

*Primary
xylem*

**MICROGRAPH OF CROSS-SECTION
THROUGH YOUNG ROOT OF PINE**
(Pinus sp.)

*Cortex
(layer between
phellem and
vascular tissue)*

*Secondary
xylem*

*Primary
xylem*

*Phellem
(protective
outer layer)*

Phloem

Resin canal

**MICROGRAPH OF CROSS-SECTION
THROUGH MATURE ROOT OF PINE**
(Pinus sp.)

Monocotyledons and dicotyledons

FLOWERING PLANTS (PHYLUM ANGIOSPERMOPHYTA) are divided into two classes: monocotyledons (class Monocotyledoneae) and dicotyledons (class Dicotyledoneae). Typically, monocotyledons have seeds with one cotyledon (seed leaf); their foliage leaves are narrow with parallel veins; the flower components occur in multiples of three; sepals and petals are indistinguishable and are known as tepals; vascular (transport) tissues are scattered in random bundles throughout the stem; and, since they lack stem cambium (actively dividing cells that produce wood), most monocotyledons are herbaceous (see pp. 128-129). Dicotyledons have seeds with two cotyledons; leaves are broad with a central midrib and branched veins; flower parts occur in multiples of four or five; sepals are generally small and green; petals are large and colourful; vascular bundles are arranged in a ring around the edge of the stem; and, because many dicotyledons possess wood-producing stem cambium, there are woody forms (see pp. 130-131) as well as herbaceous ones.

CROSS-SECTION
THROUGH
MONOCOTYLEDONOUS
LEAF BASES

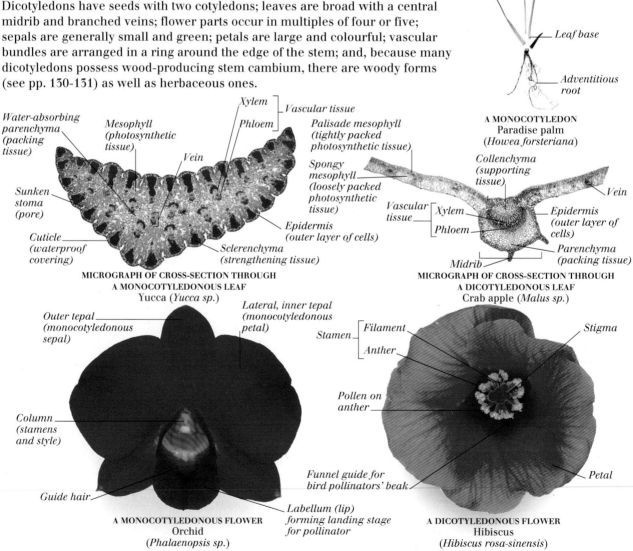

Vein (parallel venation)

Leaflet

Petiole (leaf stalk)

Emerging leaf

Leaf base

Adventitious root

A MONOCOTYLEDON
Paradise palm
(*Howea forsteriana*)

Water-absorbing parenchyma (packing tissue)

Mesophyll (photosynthetic tissue)

Xylem

Phloem

Vascular tissue

Vein

Sunken stoma (pore)

Cuticle (waterproof covering)

Epidermis (outer layer of cells)

Sclerenchyma (strengthening tissue)

MICROGRAPH OF CROSS-SECTION THROUGH A MONOCOTYLEDONOUS LEAF
Yucca (*Yucca sp.*)

Palisade mesophyll (tightly packed photosynthetic tissue)

Spongy mesophyll (loosely packed photosynthetic tissue)

Collenchyma (supporting tissue)

Vein

Vascular tissue

Xylem

Phloem

Epidermis (outer layer of cells)

Parenchyma (packing tissue)

Midrib

MICROGRAPH OF CROSS-SECTION THROUGH A DICOTYLEDONOUS LEAF
Crab apple (*Malus sp.*)

Outer tepal (monocotyledonous sepal)

Lateral, inner tepal (monocotyledonous petal)

Stamen

Filament

Anther

Stigma

Pollen on anther

Column (stamens and style)

Funnel guide for bird pollinators' beak

Petal

Guide hair

Labellum (lip) forming landing stage for pollinator

A MONOCOTYLEDONOUS FLOWER
Orchid
(*Phalaenopsis sp.*)

A DICOTYLEDONOUS FLOWER
Hibiscus
(*Hibiscus rosa-sinensis*)

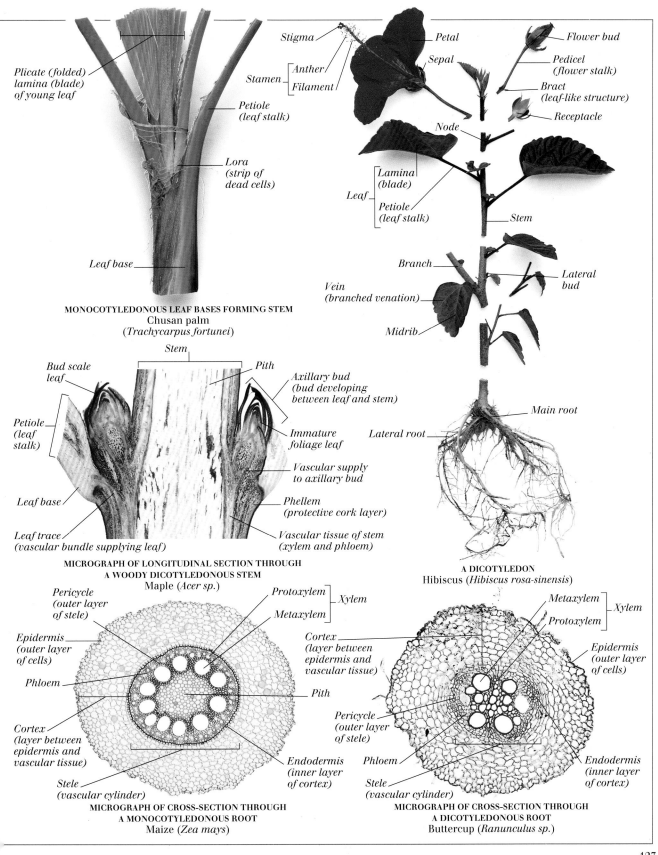

Plicate (folded)
lamina (blade)
of young leaf

Petiole
(leaf stalk)

Lora
(strip of
dead cells)

Leaf base

MONOCOTYLEDONOUS LEAF BASES FORMING STEM
Chusan palm
(*Trachycarpus fortunei*)

Stigma

Stamen { Anther
Filament

Petal

Sepal

Flower bud

Pedicel
(flower stalk)

Bract
(leaf-like structure)

Receptacle

Node

Leaf { Lamina
(blade)

Petiole
(leaf stalk)

Stem

Branch

Vein
(branched venation)

Midrib

Lateral
bud

Bud scale
leaf

Stem

Pith

Petiole
(leaf
stalk)

Leaf base

Leaf trace
(vascular bundle supplying leaf)

Axillary bud
(bud developing
between leaf and stem)

Immature
foliage leaf

Vascular supply
to axillary bud

Phellem
(protective cork layer)

Vascular tissue of stem
(xylem and phloem)

**MICROGRAPH OF LONGITUDINAL SECTION THROUGH
A WOODY DICOTYLEDONOUS STEM**
Maple (*Acer sp.*)

Main root

Lateral root

A DICOTYLEDON
Hibiscus (*Hibiscus rosa-sinensis*)

Pericycle
(outer layer
of stele)

Epidermis
(outer layer
of cells)

Phloem

Cortex
(layer between
epidermis and
vascular tissue)

Stele
(vascular cylinder)

Protoxylem } Xylem
Metaxylem

Pith

Endodermis
(inner layer
of cortex)

**MICROGRAPH OF CROSS-SECTION THROUGH
A MONOCOTYLEDONOUS ROOT**
Maize (*Zea mays*)

Cortex
(layer between
epidermis and
vascular tissue)

Metaxylem } Xylem
Protoxylem

Epidermis
(outer layer
of cells)

Pericycle
(outer layer
of stele)

Phloem

Stele
(vascular cylinder)

Endodermis
(inner layer
of cortex)

**MICROGRAPH OF CROSS-SECTION THROUGH
A DICOTYLEDONOUS ROOT**
Buttercup (*Ranunculus sp.*)

Herbaceous flowering plants

HERBACEOUS FLOWERING PLANTS TYPICALLY HAVE GREEN, NON-WOODY STEMS, and tend to be relatively short-lived. Many herbaceous plants live for only one or two years. Annuals (e.g., sweet peas) grow from seed, produce flowers and then seeds, and die within a single year. Biennials (e.g., carrots) have a two-year life cycle. In the first year, seeds grow into plants, which produce leaves and store food in underground storage organs; the stems and foliage then die back in winter. In the second year, new stems grow from the storage organs, produce leaves, flowers, and seeds, and then die. Some herbaceous plants (e.g., potatoes) are perennial. They grow back year after year, producing shoots and flowers in spring, storing food in underground tubers or rhizomes during summer, dying back in autumn, and surviving underground during winter.

Young plant forming

Petiole (stalk) of young leaf

Lateral root

Stipule (structure at base of leaf)

Trifoliate leaf

Node

Simple ovate leaflet

Root nodule

Main root

SWEET PEA
(*Lathyrus odoratus*)

STRAWBERRY
(*Fragaria* x *ananassa*)

Runner (creeping stem)

Remains of leaves

Lateral root scar

Stem

Leaf scar

Rib

Leaf base

Leaf scar

Petiole (leaf stalk)

Spine (modified leaf)

Lateral root

Tap root

CARROT
(*Daucus carota*)

Slender rhizome

Adventitious root

Stem tuber

Stem

Narrow, succulent leaf

Simple deltoid leaf

ROCK STONECROP
(*Sedum rupestre*)

POTATO
(*Solanum tuberosum*)

Adventitious root

PARTS OF HERBACEOUS FLOWERING PLANTS

Bract (leaf-like structure)

Bracteole (small bract)

Midrib

Cyme (type of inflorescence)

Succulent, simple ovate leaf

Inner, tubular disc floret

Outer, ligulate ray floret

Node

Flower bud

Dentate margin

Peduncle (inflorescence stalk)

Internode

LIVE-FOR-EVER OR ICE PLANT
(*Sedum spectabile*)

Capitulum (type of inflorescence)

Leaf

Simple lobed leaf

Peduncle (inflorescence stalk)

Flower bud

Petiole (leaf stalk)

Petiole (leaf stalk)

Leaf base

Stem

Linear leaf

Succulent stem

Leaf scar

Lateral bud

Prickle

FLORISTS' CHRYSANTHEMUM
(*Chrysanthemum morifolium*)

CEREOID CACTUS

BEGONIA
(*Begonia* x *tuberhybrida*)

Bract (leaf-like structure)

Capitulum (type of inflorescence)

Hollow stem

Sheath formed from leaf base

TOADFLAX
(*Linaria sp.*)

Spinose-dentate margin

Dentate margin

Unwinged rachis (main axis of pinnate leaf)

Rachis (main axis of pinnate leaf)

SLENDER THISTLE
(*Carduus tenuiflorus*)

Winged stem

Stipule (structure at base of leaf)

Tendril

Stem segment

Winged rachis (main axis of pinnate leaf)

Peduncle (inflorescence stalk)

HOGWEED
(*Heracleum sphondylium*)

Flower bud

Pinna (leaflet)

Margin of cladode

Toothed notch

Bract (leaf-like structure)

Tepal

Petiole (leaf stalk)

Cladode (flattened stem)

Stem branch

PERUVIAN LILY
(*Alstroemeria aurea*)

Peduncle (inflorescence stalk)

Raceme (type of inflorescence)

Petal

Sepal

EVERLASTING PEA
(*Lathyrus latifolius*)

CRAB CACTUS
(*Schlumbergera truncata*)

Woody flowering plants

WOODY FLOWERING PLANTS ARE PERENNIAL, that is, they continue to grow and reproduce for many years. They have one or more permanent stems above ground, and numerous smaller branches. The stems and branches have a strong woody core that supports the plant and contains vascular tissue for transporting water and nutrients. Outside the woody core is a layer of tough, protective bark, which has lenticels (tiny pores) in it to enable gases to pass through. Woody flowering plants may be shrubs, which have several stems arising from the soil; bushes, which are shrubs with dense branching and foliage; or trees, which typically have a single upright stem (the trunk) that bears branches. Deciduous woody plants (e.g., roses) shed all their leaves once a year and remain leafless during winter. Evergreen woody plants (e.g., ivy) shed their leaves gradually, so retaining full leaf cover throughout the year.

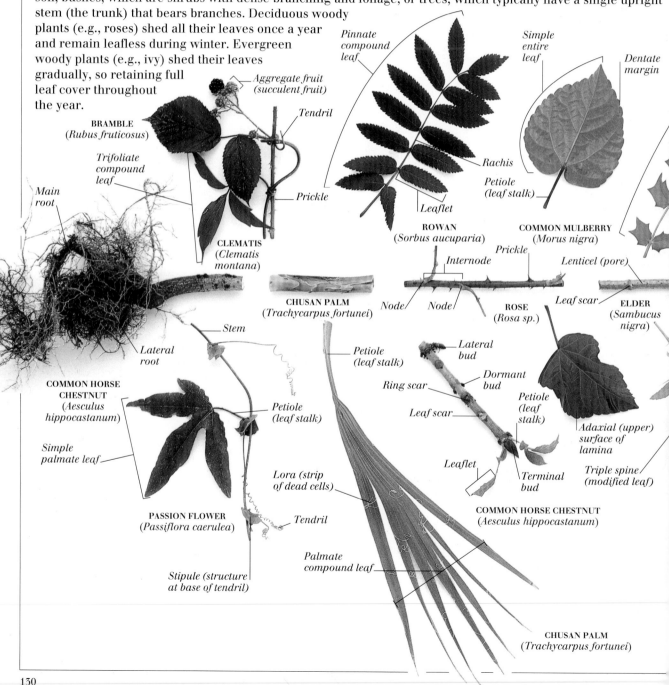

Aggregate fruit (succulent fruit)

Tendril

Pinnate compound leaf

Simple entire leaf

Dentate margin

BRAMBLE (Rubus fruticosus)

Trifoliate compound leaf

Prickle

Rachis

Petiole (leaf stalk)

Leaflet

Main root

ROWAN (Sorbus aucuparia)

COMMON MULBERRY (Morus nigra)

CLEMATIS (Clematis montana)

Internode

Prickle

Lenticel (pore)

CHUSAN PALM (Trachycarpus fortunei)

Node

Node

ROSE (Rosa sp.)

Leaf scar

ELDER (Sambucus nigra)

Stem

Petiole (leaf stalk)

Lateral bud

Lateral root

COMMON HORSE CHESTNUT (Aesculus hippocastanum)

Dormant bud

Ring scar

Petiole (leaf stalk)

Petiole (leaf stalk)

Leaf scar

Simple palmate leaf

Lora (strip of dead cells)

Leaflet

Adaxial (upper) surface of lamina

Terminal bud

Triple spine (modified leaf)

PASSION FLOWER (Passiflora caerulea)

Tendril

COMMON HORSE CHESTNUT (Aesculus hippocastanum)

Palmate compound leaf

Stipule (structure at base of tendril)

CHUSAN PALM (Trachycarpus fortunei)

PARTS OF WOODY FLOWERING PLANTS

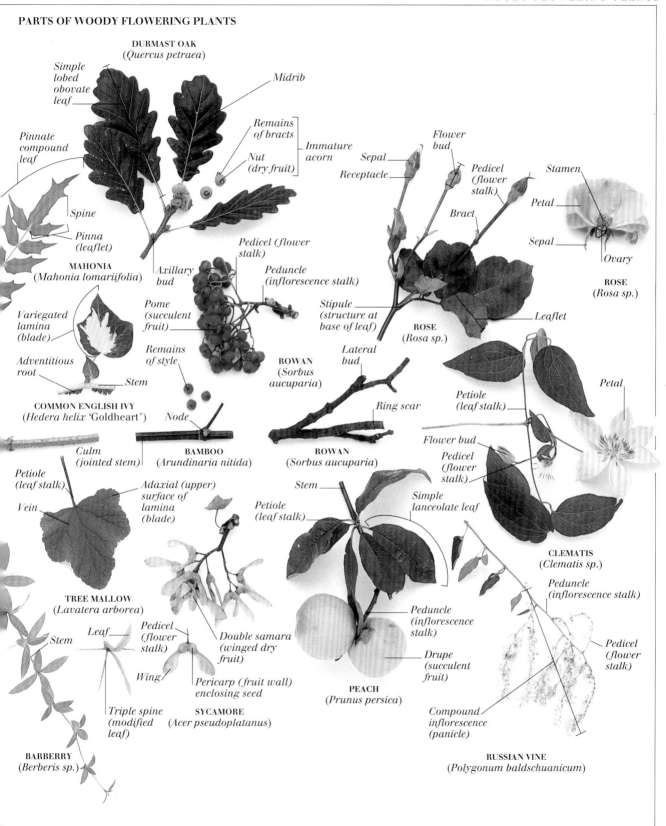

DURMAST OAK
(*Quercus petraea*)

Simple lobed obovate leaf

Midrib

Remains of bracts

Nut (dry fruit)

Immature acorn

Pinnate compound leaf

Spine

Pinna (leaflet)

Flower bud

Sepal

Receptacle

Pedicel (flower stalk)

Bract

Stamen

Petal

Sepal

Ovary

ROSE
(*Rosa sp.*)

MAHONIA
(*Mahonia lomariifolia*)

Axillary bud

Pedicel (flower stalk)

Peduncle (inflorescence stalk)

Variegated lamina (blade)

Pome (succulent fruit)

Stipule (structure at base of leaf)

Leaflet

ROSE
(*Rosa sp.*)

Adventitious root

Remains of style

Stem

COMMON ENGLISH IVY
(*Hedera helix* 'Goldheart')

Node

ROWAN
(*Sorbus aucuparia*)

Lateral bud

Ring scar

Petiole (leaf stalk)

Petal

BAMBOO
(*Arundinaria nitida*)

Culm (jointed stem)

ROWAN
(*Sorbus aucuparia*)

Flower bud

Pedicel (flower stalk)

CLEMATIS
(*Clematis sp.*)

Petiole (leaf stalk)

Vein

Adaxial (upper) surface of lamina (blade)

Stem

Petiole (leaf stalk)

Simple lanceolate leaf

Peduncle (inflorescence stalk)

TREE MALLOW
(*Lavatera arborea*)

Pedicel (flower stalk)

Double samara (winged dry fruit)

Peduncle (inflorescence stalk)

Pedicel (flower stalk)

Stem

Leaf

Wing

Pericarp (fruit wall) enclosing seed

Drupe (succulent fruit)

Triple spine (modified leaf)

SYCAMORE
(*Acer pseudoplatanus*)

PEACH
(*Prunus persica*)

Compound inflorescence (panicle)

BARBERRY
(*Berberis sp.*)

RUSSIAN VINE
(*Polygonum baldschuanicum*)

Roots

ROOTS ARE THE UNDERGROUND PARTS OF PLANTS. They have three main functions. First, they anchor the plant in the soil. Second, they absorb water and minerals from the spaces between soil particles; the roots' absorptive properties are increased by root hairs, which grow behind the root tip, allowing maximum uptake of vital substances. Third, the root is part of the plant's transport system: xylem carries water and minerals from the roots to the stem and leaves, and phloem carries nutrients from the leaves to all parts of the root system. In addition, some roots (e.g., carrots) are food stores. Roots have an outer epidermis covering a cortex of parenchyma (packing tissue), and a central cylinder of vascular tissue. This arrangement helps the roots resist the forces of compression as they grow through the soil.

CARROT
(*Daucus carota*)

MICROGRAPH OF PRIMARY ROOT DEVELOPMENT
Cabbage (*Brassica sp.*)

Split in testa
as seed
germinates

Cotyledon
(seed leaf)

Primary root

Testa
(seed coat)

Root hair

Root tip
(region of
cell division)

FEATURES OF A TYPICAL ROOT
Buttercup
(*Ranunculus sp.*)

Stele
(vascular cylinder)

Phloem sieve tube
(through which
nutrients are
transported)

Pericycle
(outer layer
of stele)

Root hair

Air space
(allowing gas
diffusion in
the root)

Companion cell
(cell associated
with phloem
sieve tube)

Cortex
(layer between
epidermis and
vascular tissue)

Root hair

Epidermis
(outer layer
of cells)

Xylem vessel
(through which water
and minerals are transported)

Endodermis
(inner layer
of cortex)

Cell wall

Nucleus

Cytoplasm

Parenchyma
(packing) cell

PRIMARY ROOT AND MICROGRAPHS OF SECTIONS THROUGH ROOTS

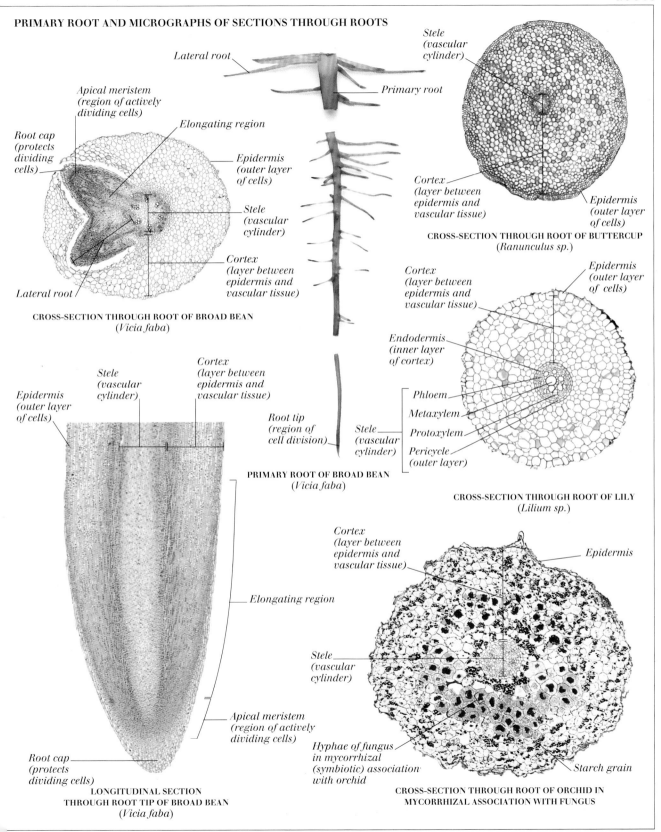

Lateral root

Primary root

Stele
(vascular
cylinder)

Apical meristem
(region of actively
dividing cells)

Elongating region

Root cap
(protects
dividing
cells)

Epidermis
(outer layer
of cells)

Stele
(vascular
cylinder)

Cortex
(layer between
epidermis and
vascular tissue)

Lateral root

CROSS-SECTION THROUGH ROOT OF BROAD BEAN
(*Vicia faba*)

Cortex
(layer between
epidermis and
vascular tissue)

Epidermis
(outer layer
of cells)

CROSS-SECTION THROUGH ROOT OF BUTTERCUP
(*Ranunculus sp.*)

Cortex
(layer between
epidermis and
vascular tissue)

Epidermis
(outer layer
of cells)

Endodermis
(inner layer
of cortex)

Phloem

Metaxylem

Protoxylem

Pericycle
(outer layer)

Stele
(vascular
cylinder)

CROSS-SECTION THROUGH ROOT OF LILY
(*Lilium sp.*)

Stele
(vascular
cylinder)

Cortex
(layer between
epidermis and
vascular tissue)

Epidermis
(outer layer
of cells)

Root tip
(region of
cell division)

Stele
(vascular
cylinder)

PRIMARY ROOT OF BROAD BEAN
(*Vicia faba*)

Elongating region

Apical meristem
(region of actively
dividing cells)

Root cap
(protects
dividing cells)

**LONGITUDINAL SECTION
THROUGH ROOT TIP OF BROAD BEAN**
(*Vicia faba*)

Cortex
(layer between
epidermis and
vascular tissue)

Epidermis

Stele
(vascular
cylinder)

Hyphae of fungus
in mycorrhizal
(symbiotic) association
with orchid

Starch grain

**CROSS-SECTION THROUGH ROOT OF ORCHID IN
MYCORRHIZAL ASSOCIATION WITH FUNGUS**

Stems

THE STEM IS THE MAIN SUPPORTIVE PART OF A PLANT that grows above ground. Stems bear leaves (organs of photosynthesis), which grow at nodes; buds (shoots covered by protective scales), which grow at the stem tip (apical or terminal buds) and in the angle between a leaf and the stem (axillary or lateral buds); and flowers (reproductive structures). The stem forms part of the plant's transport system: xylem tissue in the stem transports water and minerals from the roots to the aerial parts of the plant, and phloem tissue transports nutrients manufactured in the leaves to other parts of the plant. Stem tissues are also used for storing water and food. Herbaceous (non-woody) stems have an outer protective epidermis covering a cortex that consists mainly of parenchyma (packing tissue) but also has some collenchyma (supporting tissue). The vascular tissue of such stems is arranged in bundles, each of which consists of xylem, phloem, and sclerenchyma (strengthening tissue). Woody stems have an outer protective layer of tough bark, which is perforated with lenticels (pores) to allow gas exchange. Inside the bark is a ring of secondary phloem, which surrounds an inner core of secondary xylem.

MICROGRAPH OF LONGITUDINAL SECTION THROUGH APEX OF STEM
Coleus sp.

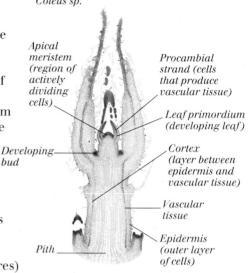

Apical meristem (region of actively dividing cells)

Procambial strand (cells that produce vascular tissue)

Leaf primordium (developing leaf)

Developing bud

Cortex (layer between epidermis and vascular tissue)

Vascular tissue

Epidermis (outer layer of cells)

Pith

YOUNG WOODY STEM
Lime
(Tilia sp.)

EMERGENT BUDS
London plane
(Platanus x acerifolia)

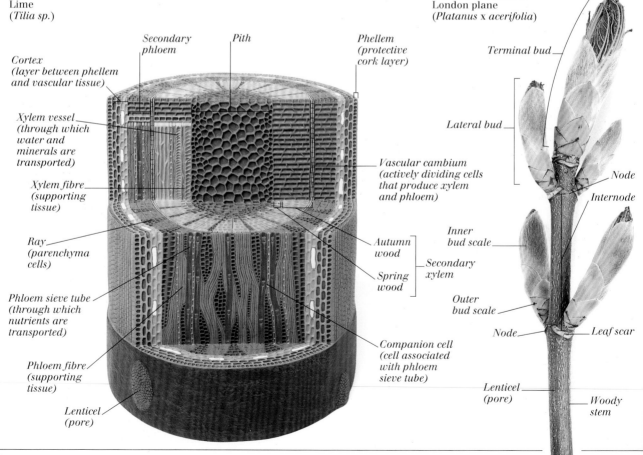

Cortex (layer between phellem and vascular tissue)

Secondary phloem

Pith

Phellem (protective cork layer)

Xylem vessel (through which water and minerals are transported)

Vascular cambium (actively dividing cells that produce xylem and phloem)

Xylem fibre (supporting tissue)

Ray (parenchyma cells)

Autumn wood

Secondary xylem

Spring wood

Phloem sieve tube (through which nutrients are transported)

Phloem fibre (supporting tissue)

Companion cell (cell associated with phloem sieve tube)

Lenticel (pore)

Young leaves emerging

Terminal bud

Lateral bud

Node

Internode

Inner bud scale

Secondary xylem

Outer bud scale

Node

Leaf scar

Lenticel (pore)

Woody stem

MICROGRAPHS OF CROSS-SECTIONS THROUGH VARIOUS STEMS

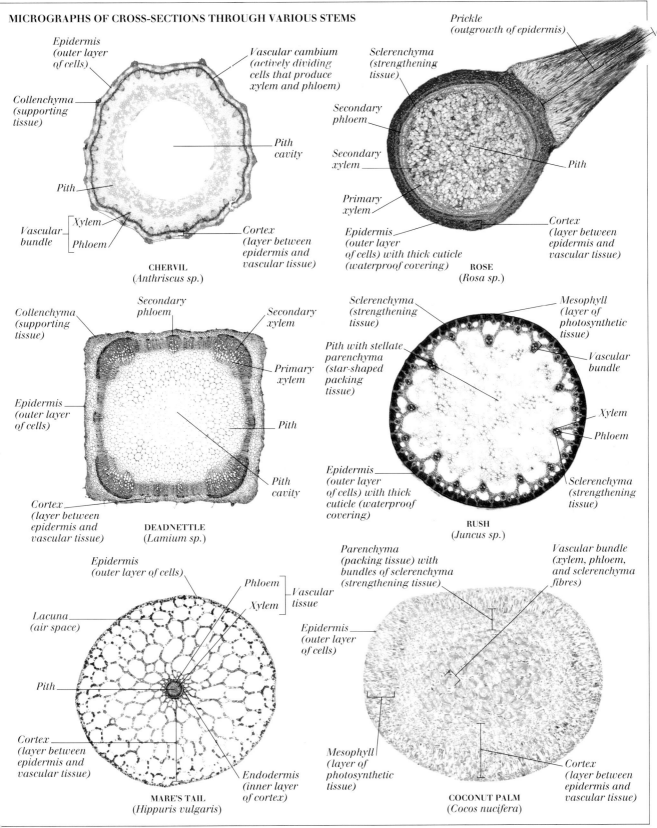

Epidermis (outer layer of cells)

Collenchyma (supporting tissue)

Pith

Vascular bundle [Xylem / Phloem]

Vascular cambium (actively dividing cells that produce xylem and phloem)

Pith cavity

Cortex (layer between epidermis and vascular tissue)

CHERVIL (Anthriscus sp.)

Prickle (outgrowth of epidermis)

Sclerenchyma (strengthening tissue)

Secondary phloem

Secondary xylem

Primary xylem

Epidermis (outer layer of cells) with thick cuticle (waterproof covering)

Pith

Cortex (layer between epidermis and vascular tissue)

ROSE (Rosa sp.)

Collenchyma (supporting tissue)

Epidermis (outer layer of cells)

Cortex (layer between epidermis and vascular tissue)

Secondary phloem

Secondary xylem

Primary xylem

Pith

Pith cavity

DEADNETTLE (Lamium sp.)

Sclerenchyma (strengthening tissue)

Pith with stellate parenchyma (star-shaped packing tissue)

Epidermis (outer layer of cells) with thick cuticle (waterproof covering)

Mesophyll (layer of photosynthetic tissue)

Vascular bundle

Xylem

Phloem

Sclerenchyma (strengthening tissue)

RUSH (Juncus sp.)

Epidermis (outer layer of cells)

Lacuna (air space)

Pith

Cortex (layer between epidermis and vascular tissue)

Phloem / Xylem] Vascular tissue

Endodermis (inner layer of cortex)

MARE'S TAIL (Hippuris vulgaris)

Parenchyma (packing tissue) with bundles of sclerenchyma (strengthening tissue)

Epidermis (outer layer of cells)

Vascular bundle (xylem, phloem, and sclerenchyma fibres)

Mesophyll (layer of photosynthetic tissue)

Cortex (layer between epidermis and vascular tissue)

COCONUT PALM (Cocos nucifera)

135

Leaves

LEAVES ARE THE MAIN SITES OF PHOTOSYNTHESIS (see pp. 138-139) and transpiration (water loss by evaporation) in plants. A typical leaf consists of a thin, flat lamina (blade) supported by a network of veins; a petiole (leaf stalk); and a leaf base, where the petiole joins the stem. Leaves can be classified as simple, in which the lamina is a single unit, or compound, in which the lamina is divided into separate leaflets. Compound leaves may be pinnate, with pinnae (leaflets) on both sides of a rachis (main axis), or palmate, with leaflets arising from a single point at the tip of the petiole. Leaves can be classified further by the overall shape of the lamina, and by the shape of the lamina's apex, margin, and base.

CHECKERBLOOM
(*Sidalcea malviflora*)

SIMPLE LEAF SHAPES

Subacute apex

Acuminate apex

Entire margin

Entire margin

Cuneate base

Cordate base

PANDURIFORM
Croton
(*Codiaeum variegatum*)

LANCEOLATE
Sea buckthorn
(*Hippophae rhamnoides*)

GENERAL LEAF FEATURES

Apex

Midrib

Margin

Lamina (blade)

Lateral vein

Lamina base

Petiole (leaf stalk)

Leaf base

Sweet chestnut
(*Castanea sativa*)

COMPOUND LEAF SHAPES

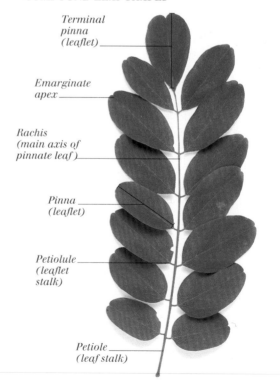

Terminal pinna (leaflet)

Emarginate apex

Rachis (main axis of pinnate leaf)

Pinna (leaflet)

Petiolule (leaflet stalk)

Petiole (leaf stalk)

ODD PINNATE
False acacia
(*Robinia pseudoacacia*)

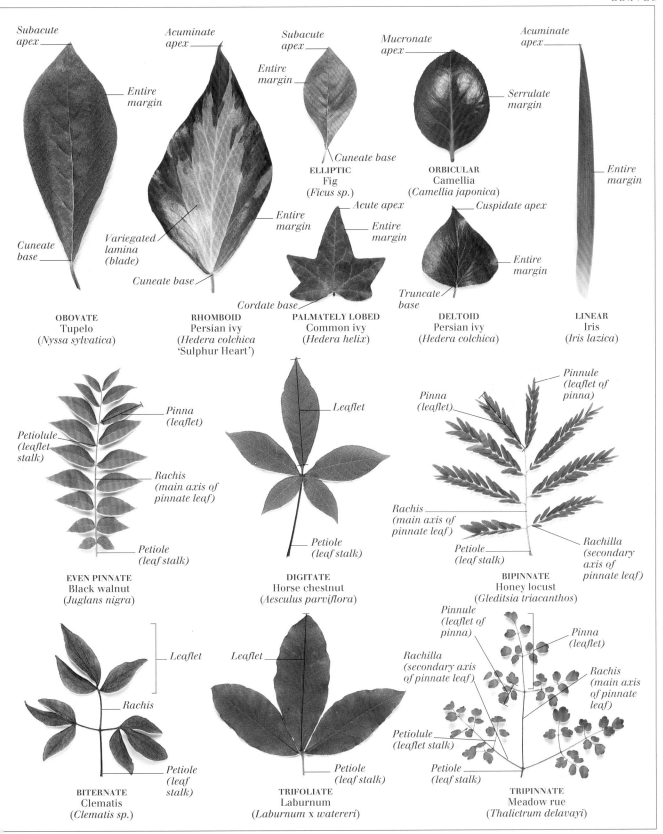

Subacute apex

Entire margin

Acuminate apex

Subacute apex

Entire margin

Mucronate apex

Acuminate apex

Serrulate margin

Entire margin

Cuneate base

Cuneate base

Variegated lamina (blade)

ELLIPTIC
Fig
(*Ficus sp.*)

Cuneate base

Entire margin

ORBICULAR
Camellia
(*Camellia japonica*)

Entire margin

Acute apex

Entire margin

Cuspidate apex

Entire margin

Cordate base

Truncate base

OBOVATE
Tupelo
(*Nyssa sylvatica*)

RHOMBOID
Persian ivy
(*Hedera colchica*
'Sulphur Heart')

PALMATELY LOBED
Common ivy
(*Hedera helix*)

DELTOID
Persian ivy
(*Hedera colchica*)

LINEAR
Iris
(*Iris lazica*)

Pinna (leaflet)

Petiolule (leaflet stalk)

Rachis (main axis of pinnate leaf)

Petiole (leaf stalk)

Leaflet

Petiole (leaf stalk)

Pinnule (leaflet of pinna)

Pinna (leaflet)

Rachis (main axis of pinnate leaf)

Petiole (leaf stalk)

Rachilla (secondary axis of pinnate leaf)

EVEN PINNATE
Black walnut
(*Juglans nigra*)

DIGITATE
Horse chestnut
(*Aesculus parviflora*)

BIPINNATE
Honey locust
(*Gleditsia triacanthos*)

Leaflet

Rachis

Petiole (leaf stalk)

Leaflet

Petiole (leaf stalk)

Pinnule (leaflet of pinna)

Pinna (leaflet)

Rachilla (secondary axis of pinnate leaf)

Rachis (main axis of pinnate leaf)

Petiolule (leaflet stalk)

Petiole (leaf stalk)

BITERNATE
Clematis
(*Clematis sp.*)

TRIFOLIATE
Laburnum
(*Laburnum x watereri*)

TRIPINNATE
Meadow rue
(*Thalictrum delavayi*)

Photosynthesis

PHOTOSYNTHESIS IS THE PROCESS by which plants make their food using sunlight, water, and carbon dioxide. It takes place inside special structures in leaf cells called chloroplasts. The chloroplasts contain chlorophyll, a green pigment that absorbs energy from sunlight. During photosynthesis, the absorbed energy is used to join together carbon dioxide and water to form the sugar glucose, which is the energy source for the whole plant; oxygen, a waste product, is released into the air. Leaves are the main sites of photosynthesis, and have various adaptations for that purpose: flat laminae (blades) provide a large surface for absorbing sunlight; stomata (pores) in the lower surface of the laminae allow gases (carbon dioxide and oxygen) to pass into and out of the leaves; and an extensive network of veins brings water into the leaves and transports the glucose produced by photosynthesis to the rest of the plant.

MICROGRAPH OF LEAF
Lily (*Lilium sp.*)

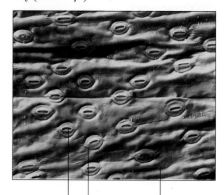

Stoma (pore)

Guard cell (controls opening and closing of stoma)

Lower surface of lamina (blade)

THE PROCESS OF PHOTOSYNTHESIS

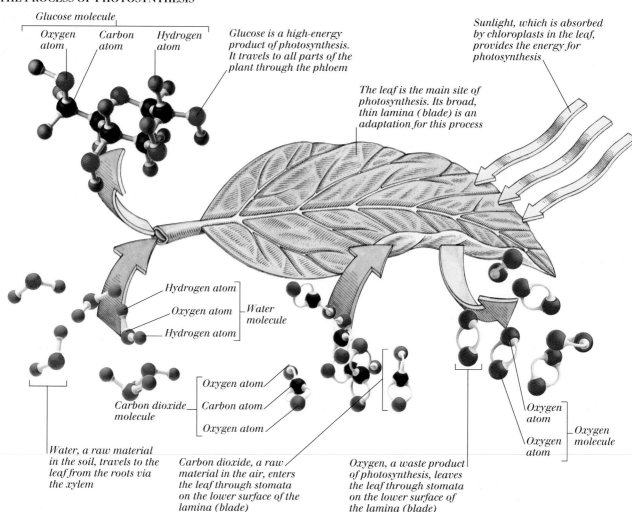

Glucose molecule

Oxygen atom

Carbon atom

Hydrogen atom

Glucose is a high-energy product of photosynthesis. It travels to all parts of the plant through the phloem

Sunlight, which is absorbed by chloroplasts in the leaf, provides the energy for photosynthesis

The leaf is the main site of photosynthesis. Its broad, thin lamina (blade) is an adaptation for this process

Hydrogen atom

Oxygen atom — Water molecule

Hydrogen atom

Carbon dioxide molecule

Oxygen atom

Carbon atom

Oxygen atom

Oxygen atom

Oxygen atom — Oxygen molecule

Water, a raw material in the soil, travels to the leaf from the roots via the xylem

Carbon dioxide, a raw material in the air, enters the leaf through stomata on the lower surface of the lamina (blade)

Oxygen, a waste product of photosynthesis, leaves the leaf through stomata on the lower surface of the lamina (blade)

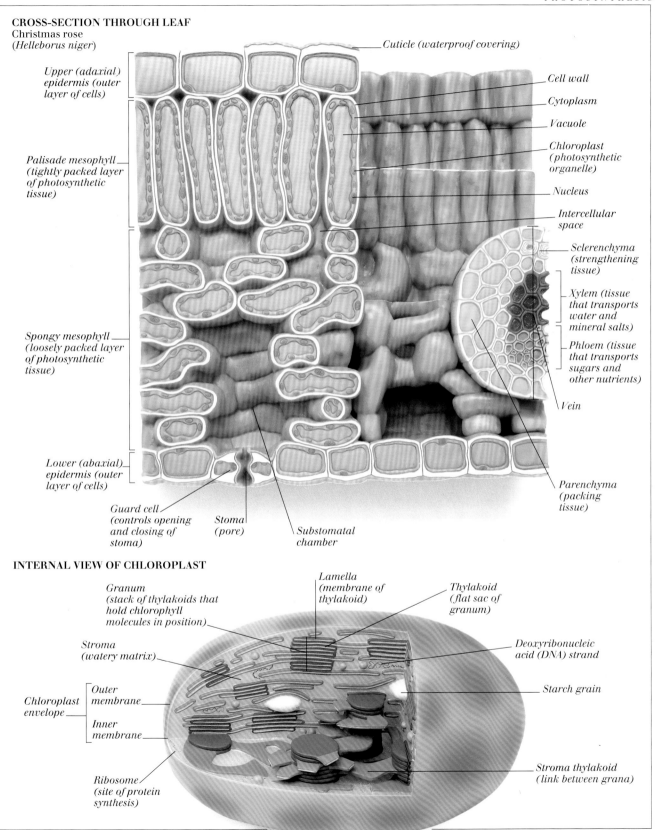

CROSS-SECTION THROUGH LEAF
Christmas rose
(*Helleborus niger*)

Cuticle (waterproof covering)

Upper (adaxial) epidermis (outer layer of cells)

Cell wall

Cytoplasm

Vacuole

Chloroplast (photosynthetic organelle)

Palisade mesophyll (tightly packed layer of photosynthetic tissue)

Nucleus

Intercellular space

Sclerenchyma (strengthening tissue)

Xylem (tissue that transports water and mineral salts)

Phloem (tissue that transports sugars and other nutrients)

Spongy mesophyll (loosely packed layer of photosynthetic tissue)

Vein

Lower (abaxial) epidermis (outer layer of cells)

Parenchyma (packing tissue)

Guard cell (controls opening and closing of stoma)

Stoma (pore)

Substomatal chamber

INTERNAL VIEW OF CHLOROPLAST

Granum (stack of thylakoids that hold chlorophyll molecules in position)

Lamella (membrane of thylakoid)

Thylakoid (flat sac of granum)

Stroma (watery matrix)

Deoxyribonucleic acid (DNA) strand

Chloroplast envelope

Outer membrane

Inner membrane

Starch grain

Ribosome (site of protein synthesis)

Stroma thylakoid (link between grana)

139

Flowers 1

Flowers are the sites of sexual reproduction in flowering plants. Their component parts are arranged in whorls around the receptacle (tip of the flower stalk). The sepals (collectively called the calyx) are outermost; typically small and green, they protect the developing flower. The petals (collectively called the corolla) are typically large and brightly coloured; they are found inside the sepals. In monocotyledonous flowers (see pp. 126-127), sepals and petals are indistinguishable; individually they are called tepals (collectively called the perianth). The petals surround the male and female reproductive structures (androecium and gynoecium). The androecium consists of stamens (male organs); each stamen is made up of a filament (stalk) and anther. The gynoecium has one or more carpels (female organs); each carpel consists of an ovary, style, and stigma. Some flowers (e.g., lily) occur singly on a pedicel (flower stalk); others (e.g., elder, sunflower) are arranged in a group (inflorescence) on a peduncle (inflorescence stalk).

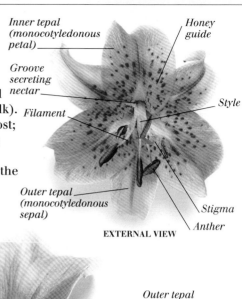

EXTERNAL VIEW

Inner tepal (monocotyledonous petal)
Honey guide
Groove secreting nectar
Filament
Style
Outer tepal (monocotyledonous sepal)
Stigma
Anther

A MONOCOTYLEDONOUS FLOWER
Lily
(*Lilium sp.*)

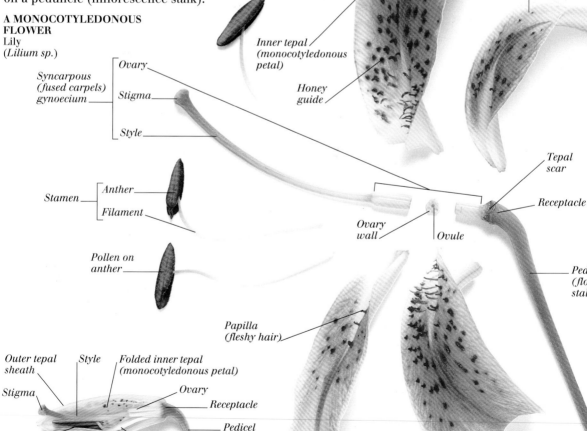

Syncarpous (fused carpels) gynoecium
Ovary
Stigma
Style

Inner tepal (monocotyledonous petal)
Honey guide

Outer tepal (monocotyledonous sepal)

Stamen
Anther
Filament

Pollen on anther

Tepal scar
Receptacle

Ovary wall
Ovule

Papilla (fleshy hair)

Pedicel (flower stalk)

Outer tepal sheath
Style
Folded inner tepal (monocotyledonous petal)
Stigma
Ovary
Receptacle
Anther
Pedicel (flower stalk)
Filament

LONGITUDINAL SECTION THROUGH FLOWER BUD

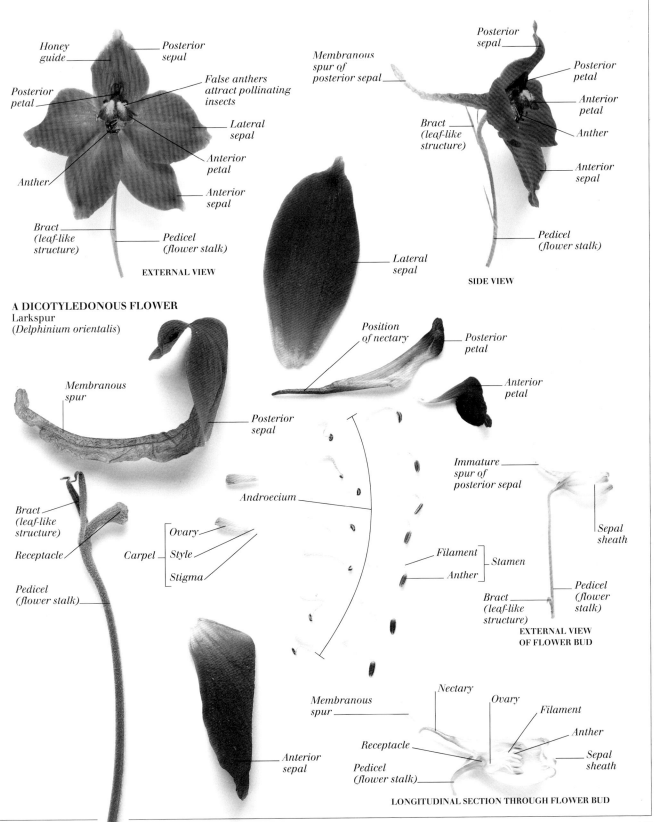

Honey guide

Posterior sepal

Posterior petal

False anthers attract pollinating insects

Lateral sepal

Anterior petal

Anterior sepal

Anther

Bract (leaf-like structure)

Pedicel (flower stalk)

EXTERNAL VIEW

Posterior sepal

Membranous spur of posterior sepal

Posterior petal

Anterior petal

Anther

Bract (leaf-like structure)

Anterior sepal

Pedicel (flower stalk)

SIDE VIEW

Lateral sepal

A DICOTYLEDONOUS FLOWER
Larkspur
(*Delphinium orientalis*)

Membranous spur

Posterior sepal

Position of nectary

Posterior petal

Anterior petal

Immature spur of posterior sepal

Sepal sheath

Bract (leaf-like structure)

Receptacle

Carpel { Ovary, Style, Stigma }

Androecium

Filament

Anther

Stamen

Pedicel (flower stalk)

Bract (leaf-like structure)

Pedicel (flower stalk)

EXTERNAL VIEW OF FLOWER BUD

Membranous spur

Anterior sepal

Nectary

Ovary

Filament

Anther

Receptacle

Pedicel (flower stalk)

Sepal sheath

LONGITUDINAL SECTION THROUGH FLOWER BUD

Flowers 2

COMPOUND INFLORESCENCE (CAPITULUM)
Sunflower
(*Helianthus annulus*)

Disc florets

Ray floret

Florets (small flowers) are grouped together to resemble a single large flower

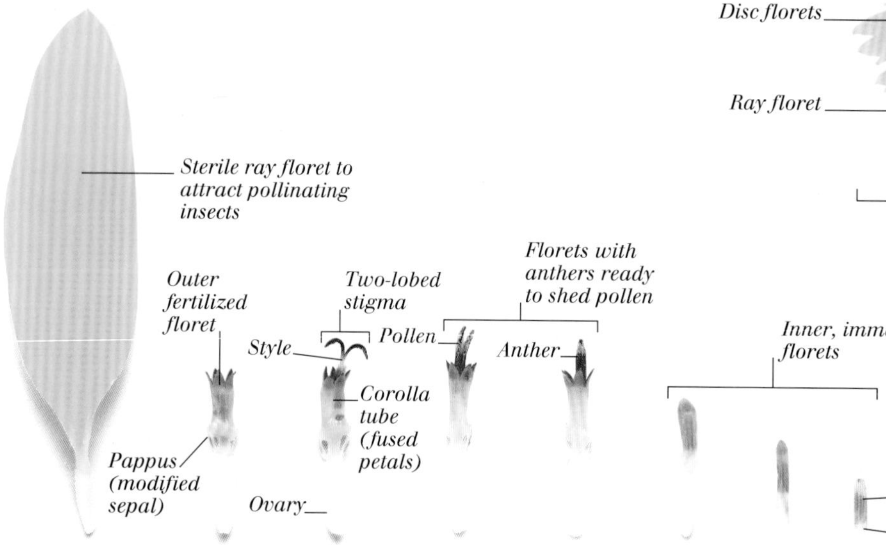

Sterile ray floret to attract pollinating insects

Outer fertilized floret

Two-lobed stigma

Florets with anthers ready to shed pollen

Style

Pollen

Anther

Inner, immature florets

Corolla tube (fused petals)

Pappus (modified sepal)

Ovary

Corolla tube (fused petals)

Ovary

FLORETS FROM SUNFLOWER

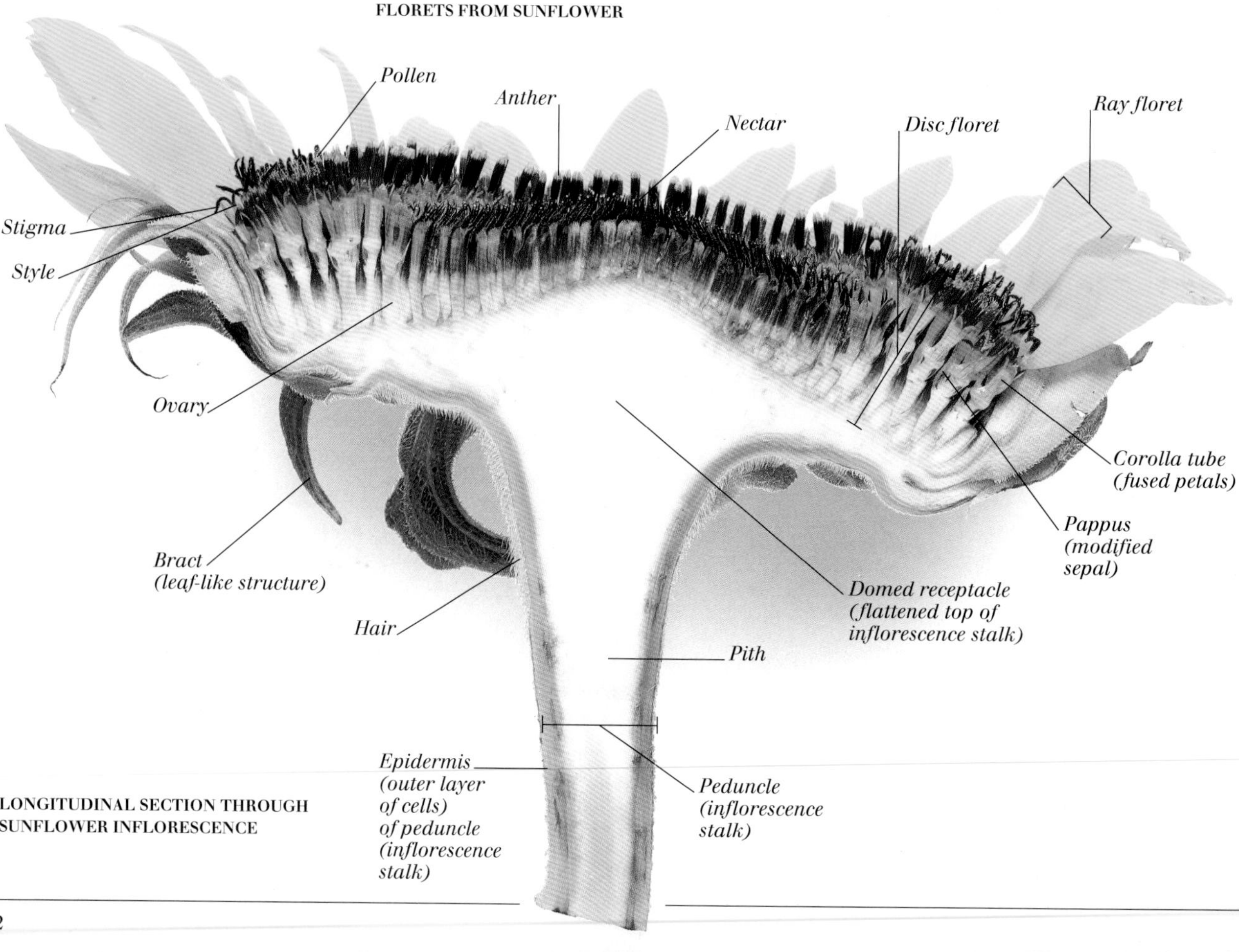

Pollen

Anther

Nectar

Disc floret

Ray floret

Stigma

Style

Ovary

Corolla tube (fused petals)

Pappus (modified sepal)

Bract (leaf-like structure)

Hair

Domed receptacle (flattened top of inflorescence stalk)

Pith

Epidermis (outer layer of cells) of peduncle (inflorescence stalk)

Peduncle (inflorescence stalk)

LONGITUDINAL SECTION THROUGH SUNFLOWER INFLORESCENCE

ARRANGEMENT OF FLOWERS ON STEM

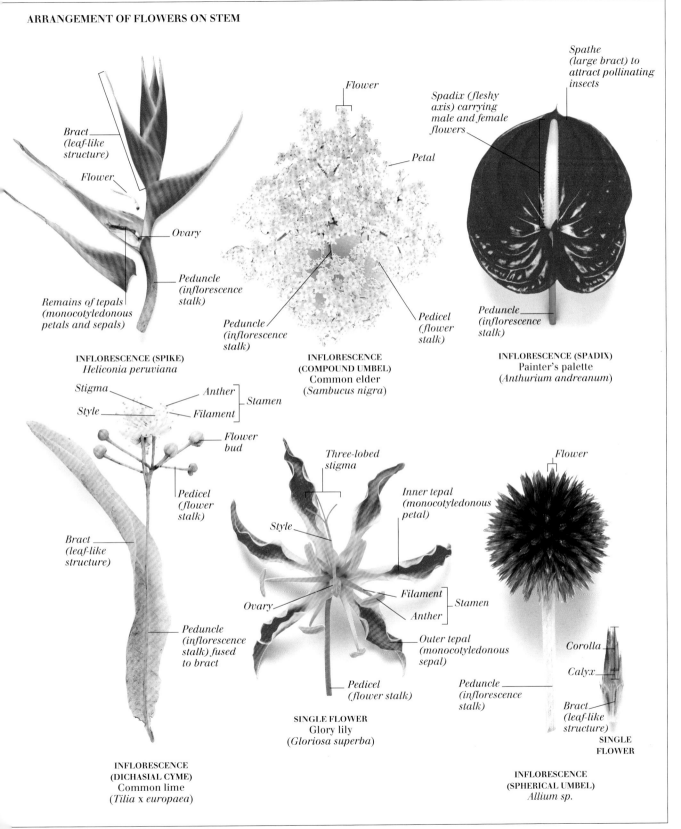

Bract
(leaf-like
structure)

Flower

Ovary

Remains of tepals
(monocotyledonous
petals and sepals)

Peduncle
(inflorescence
stalk)

INFLORESCENCE (SPIKE)
Heliconia peruviana

Flower

Petal

Peduncle
(inflorescence
stalk)

Pedicel
(flower
stalk)

**INFLORESCENCE
(COMPOUND UMBEL)**
Common elder
(*Sambucus nigra*)

Spathe
(large bract) to
attract pollinating
insects

Spadix (fleshy
axis) carrying
male and female
flowers

Peduncle
(inflorescence
stalk)

INFLORESCENCE (SPADIX)
Painter's palette
(*Anthurium andreanum*)

Stigma

Anther

Stamen

Style

Filament

Flower
bud

Pedicel
(flower
stalk)

Bract
(leaf-like
structure)

Peduncle
(inflorescence
stalk) fused
to bract

**INFLORESCENCE
(DICHASIAL CYME)**
Common lime
(*Tilia* x *europaea*)

Three-lobed
stigma

Inner tepal
(monocotyledonous
petal)

Style

Ovary

Filament

Anther

Stamen

Outer tepal
(monocotyledonous
sepal)

Pedicel
(flower stalk)

SINGLE FLOWER
Glory lily
(*Gloriosa superba*)

Flower

Peduncle
(inflorescence
stalk)

Corolla

Calyx

Bract
(leaf-like
structure)

**SINGLE
FLOWER**

**INFLORESCENCE
(SPHERICAL UMBEL)**
Allium sp.

Pollination

POLLINATION IS THE TRANSFER OF POLLEN (which contains the male sex cells) from an anther (part of the male reproductive organ) to a stigma (part of the female reproductive organ). This process precedes fertilization (see pp. 146-147). Pollination may occur within the same flower (self-pollination), or between flowers on separate plants of the same species (cross-pollination). In most plants, pollination is carried out either by insects (entomophilous pollination) or by the wind (anemophilous pollination). Less commonly, birds, bats, or water are the agents of pollination. Insect-pollinated flowers are typically brightly coloured, scented, and produce nectar, on which insects feed. Such flowers also tend to have patterns that are visible only in ultraviolet light, which many insects can see but which humans cannot. These features attract insects, which become covered with the sticky or hooked pollen grains when they visit one flower, and then transfer the pollen to the next flower they visit. Wind-pollinated flowers are generally small, relatively inconspicuous, and unscented. They produce large quantities of light pollen grains that are easily blown by the wind to other flowers.

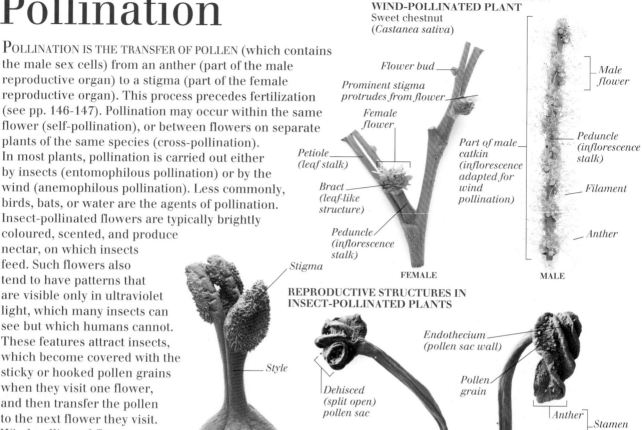

REPRODUCTIVE STRUCTURES IN WIND-POLLINATED PLANT
Sweet chestnut
(*Castanea sativa*)

Flower bud

Prominent stigma protrudes from flower

Female flower

Petiole (leaf stalk)

Bract (leaf-like structure)

Peduncle (inflorescence stalk)

FEMALE

Male flower

Part of male catkin (inflorescence adapted for wind pollination)

Peduncle (inflorescence stalk)

Filament

Anther

MALE

Stigma

Style

REPRODUCTIVE STRUCTURES IN INSECT-POLLINATED PLANTS

Endothecium (pollen sac wall)

Pollen grain

Dehisced (split open) pollen sac

Anther

Filament

Stamen

Boundary between two fused carpels (each carpel consists of a stigma, style, and ovary)

Ovary

Calyx (whorl of sepals)

MICROGRAPHS OF POLLEN GRAINS

Exine (outer coat of pollen grain)

Pore

EUROPEAN FIELD ELM
(*Ulmus minor*)

MICROGRAPH OF CARPELS (FEMALE ORGANS)
Yellow-wort
(*Blackstonia perfoliata*)

Colpus (furrow-shaped aperture)

Exine (outer coat of pollen grain)

JUSTICIA AUREA

MICROGRAPH OF STAMENS (MALE ORGANS)
Common centaury
(*Centaurium erythraea*)

Exine (outer coat of pollen grain)

Pore

Baculum (rod-shaped structure)

MEADOW CRANESBILL
(*Geranium pratense*)

Colpus (furrow-shaped aperture)

Exine (outer coat of pollen grain)

Equatorial furrow

BOX-LEAVED MILKWORT
(*Polygala chamaebuxus*)

INSECT POLLINATION OF MEADOW SAGE

Immature, unreceptive stigma

Sepal

Anther pushed on to bee's hairy abdomen

Labellum (lip) forming landing stage for bee

Pollen grains from anther stick to bee's abdomen

1. BEE VISITS FLOWER WITH MATURE ANTHERS BUT IMMATURE STIGMA

Pollen grains attached to hairy abdomen

2. BEE FLIES TO OTHER FLOWERS

Long style curves downwards when bee enters flower

Sepal

Mature, receptive stigma touches bee's abdomen, picking up pollen

Labellum (lip) forming landing stage for bee

3. BEE VISITS FLOWER WHERE THE ANTHERS HAVE WITHERED AND THE STIGMA IS MATURE

SUNFLOWER UNDER NORMAL AND ULTRAVIOLET LIGHT

Central area of disc florets

Ray floret

NORMAL LIGHT

Petal

Ovary

Stigma

Stamen { Filament / Anther }

NORMAL LIGHT

ST JOHN'S WORT UNDER NORMAL AND ULTRAVIOLET LIGHT

Honey guide directs insects to dark, central part of flower

Paler, outer part of ray floret

Darker, inner part of ray floret

Insects attracted to darkest, central part of flower, which contains nectaries, anthers, and stigmas

Dark central area containing nectaries, anthers, and stigmas

ULTRAVIOLET LIGHT

ULTRAVIOLET LIGHT

Colpus (furrow-shaped aperture)

Exine (outer coat of pollen grain)

Pore

Exine (outer coat of pollen grain)

Trilete mark (development scar)

Columella (small column-shaped structure)

Exine (outer coat of pollen grain)

Exine (outer coat of pollen grain)

Tricolpate (three colpae) pollen grain

MIMULOPSIS SOLMSH

THESIUM ALPINIUM

RUELLIA GRANDIFLORA

CROSSANDRA NILOTICA

Fertilization

FERTILIZATION IS THE FUSION of male and female gametes (sex cells) to produce a zygote (embryo). Following pollination (see pp. 144-145), the pollen grains that contain the male gametes are on the stigma, some distance from the female gamete (ovum) inside the ovule. To enable the gametes to meet, the pollen grain germinates and produces a pollen tube, which grows down and enters the embryo sac (the inner part of the ovule that contains the ovum). Two male gametes, travelling at the tip of the pollen tube, enter the embryo sac. One gamete fuses with the ovum to produce a zygote that will develop into an embryo plant. The other male gamete fuses with two polar nuclei to produce the endosperm, which acts as a food store for the developing embryo. Fertilization also initiates other changes: the integument (outer part of ovule) forms a testa (seed coat) around the embryo and endosperm; the petals fall off; the stigma and style wither; and the ovary wall forms a layer (called the pericarp) around the seed. Together, the pericarp and seed form the fruit, which may be succulent (see pp. 148-149) or dry (see pp. 150-151). In some species (e.g., blackberry), apomixis can occur: the seed develops without fertilization of the ovum by a male gamete but endosperm formation and fruit development take place as in other species.

BANANA
(*Musa 'lacatan'*)

DEVELOPMENT OF A SUCCULENT FRUIT
Blackberry
(*Rubus fruticosus*)

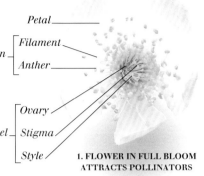

Petal
Stamen — Filament
Anther
Carpel — Ovary
Stigma
Style

**1. FLOWER IN FULL BLOOM
ATTRACTS POLLINATORS**

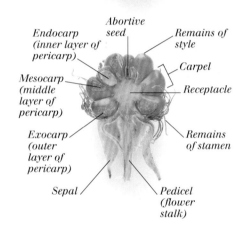

Endocarp (inner layer of pericarp)
Abortive seed
Remains of style
Carpel
Mesocarp (middle layer of pericarp)
Receptacle
Exocarp (outer layer of pericarp)
Remains of stamen
Sepal
Pedicel (flower stalk)

**4. PERICARP FORMS
FLESH, SKIN, AND A HARD INNER
LAYER (SHOWN IN CROSS-SECTION)**

Exocarp (outer layer of pericarp)
Carpel
Remains of style
Remains of stamen
Remains of sepal
Pedicel (flower stalk)

**7. MESOCARP (FLESHY PART OF PERICARP)
OF EACH CARPEL STARTS TO
CHANGE COLOUR**

Exocarp (outer layer of pericarp)
Drupelet
Remains of style
Remains of stamen
Remains of sepal
Pedicel (flower stalk)

**8. CARPELS MATURE INTO DRUPELETS
(SMALL FLESHY FRUITS WITH SINGLE SEEDS
SURROUNDED BY HARD ENDOCARP)**

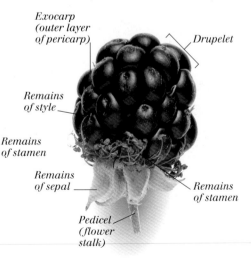

Exocarp (outer layer of pericarp)
Drupelet
Remains of style
Remains of sepal
Remains of stamen
Pedicel (flower stalk)

**9. MESOCARP OF DRUPELET BECOMES
DARKER AND SWEETER**

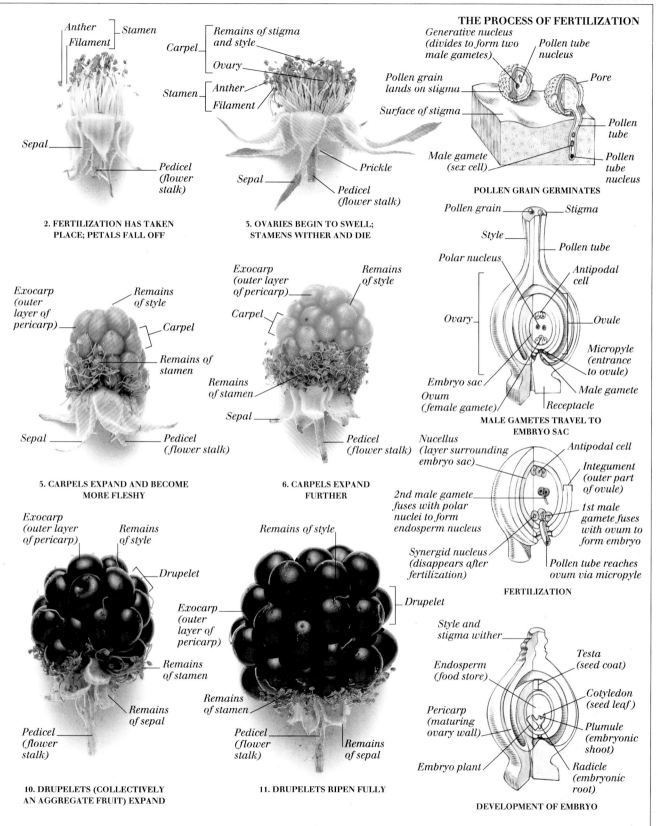

THE PROCESS OF FERTILIZATION

Anther
Filament — Stamen
Sepal
Pedicel (flower stalk)

2. FERTILIZATION HAS TAKEN PLACE; PETALS FALL OFF

Remains of stigma and style
Carpel
Ovary
Stamen
Anther
Filament
Sepal
Prickle
Pedicel (flower stalk)

3. OVARIES BEGIN TO SWELL; STAMENS WITHER AND DIE

Generative nucleus (divides to form two male gametes)
Pollen tube nucleus
Pollen grain lands on stigma
Pore
Surface of stigma
Pollen tube
Male gamete (sex cell)
Pollen tube nucleus

POLLEN GRAIN GERMINATES

Exocarp (outer layer of pericarp)
Remains of style
Carpel
Remains of stamen
Sepal
Pedicel (flower stalk)

5. CARPELS EXPAND AND BECOME MORE FLESHY

Exocarp (outer layer of pericarp)
Remains of style
Carpel
Remains of stamen
Sepal
Pedicel (flower stalk)

6. CARPELS EXPAND FURTHER

Pollen grain
Stigma
Style
Pollen tube
Polar nucleus
Antipodal cell
Ovary
Ovule
Micropyle (entrance to ovule)
Embryo sac
Male gamete
Ovum (female gamete)
Receptacle

MALE GAMETES TRAVEL TO EMBRYO SAC

Nucellus (layer surrounding embryo sac)
Antipodal cell
Integument (outer part of ovule)
2nd male gamete fuses with polar nuclei to form endosperm nucleus
1st male gamete fuses with ovum to form embryo
Synergid nucleus (disappears after fertilization)
Pollen tube reaches ovum via micropyle

FERTILIZATION

Exocarp (outer layer of pericarp)
Remains of style
Drupelet
Exocarp (outer layer of pericarp)
Remains of stamen
Remains of sepal
Pedicel (flower stalk)

10. DRUPELETS (COLLECTIVELY AN AGGREGATE FRUIT) EXPAND

Remains of style
Drupelet
Exocarp (outer layer of pericarp)
Remains of stamen
Pedicel (flower stalk)
Remains of sepal

11. DRUPELETS RIPEN FULLY

Style and stigma wither
Testa (seed coat)
Endosperm (food store)
Cotyledon (seed leaf)
Pericarp (maturing ovary wall)
Plumule (embryonic shoot)
Embryo plant
Radicle (embryonic root)

DEVELOPMENT OF EMBRYO

Succulent fruits

A FRUIT IS A FULLY DEVELOPED and ripened ovary (seed-producing part of a plant's female reproductive organs). Fruits may be succulent or dry (see pp. 150-151). Succulent fruits are fleshy and brightly coloured, making them attractive to animals, which eat them and so disperse the seeds away from the parent plant. The wall (pericarp) of a succulent fruit has three layers: an outer exocarp, a middle mesocarp, and an inner endocarp. These three layers vary in thickness and texture in different types of fruits and may blend into each other. Succulent fruits can be classed as simple (derived from one ovary) or compound (derived from several ovaries). Simple succulent fruits include berries, which typically have many seeds, and drupes, which typically have a single stone or pip (e.g., cherry and peach). Compound succulent fruits include aggregate fruits, which are formed from many ovaries in one flower, and multiple fruits, which develop from the ovaries of many flowers. Some fruits, known as false fruits or pseudocarps, develop from parts of the flower in addition to the ovaries. For example, the flesh of the apple is formed from the receptacle (the upper end of the flower stalk).

BERRY
Cocoa
(*Theobroma cacao*)

HESPERIDIUM (A TYPE OF BERRY)
Lemon
(*Citrus limon*)

Pedicel (flower stalk)
Endocarp
Mesocarp
Pedicel (flower stalk)
Exocarp
Leathery exocarp
Seed
Vesicle (juice sac)
Oil gland
Remains of style
Remains of style
Placenta

EXTERNAL VIEW OF FRUIT

LONGITUDINAL SECTION THROUGH FRUIT

Hilum (point of attachment to ovary)
Embryo
Seed
Carpel wall
Carpel
Testa (seed coat)
Cotyledon (seed leaf)
Placenta

EXTERNAL VIEW AND SECTION THROUGH SEED

CROSS-SECTION THROUGH FRUIT

SYCONIUM (A TYPE OF FALSE FRUIT)
Fig
(*Ficus carica*)

Peduncle (inflorescence stalk)
Remains of female flowers
Fleshy infolded receptacle
Remains of male flowers
Pip (seed surrounded by endocarp)
Skin
Pore closed by scales

EXTERNAL VIEW OF FRUIT

LONGITUDINAL SECTION THROUGH FRUIT

FRUIT WITH FLESHY ARIL
Lychee
(*Litchi chinensis*)

Pedicel (flower stalk)
Pedicel (flower stalk)
Seed
Aril (fleshy outgrowth from seed stalk)
Pericarp (fruit wall)
Pericarp (fruit wall)

Remains of style
Drupelet
Endocarp
Pip
Pedicel (flower stalk)
Endocarp
Embryo
Cotyledon (seed leaf)
Testa (seed coat)

EXTERNAL VIEW AND SECTION THROUGH PIP

EXTERNAL VIEW OF FRUIT

LONGITUDINAL SECTION THROUGH FRUIT

REMAINS OF A SINGLE FEMALE FLOWER

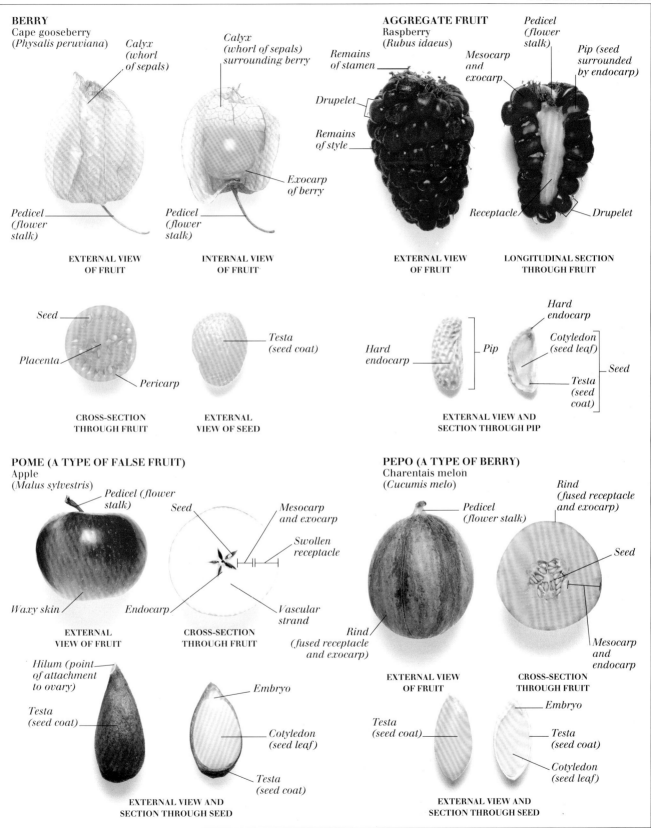

BERRY
Cape gooseberry
(*Physalis peruviana*)

Calyx (whorl of sepals)

Calyx (whorl of sepals) surrounding berry

Pedicel (flower stalk)

Exocarp of berry

Pedicel (flower stalk)

EXTERNAL VIEW OF FRUIT

INTERNAL VIEW OF FRUIT

Seed

Placenta

Pericarp

Testa (seed coat)

CROSS-SECTION THROUGH FRUIT

EXTERNAL VIEW OF SEED

AGGREGATE FRUIT
Raspberry
(*Rubus idaeus*)

Remains of stamen

Mesocarp and exocarp

Pedicel (flower stalk)

Pip (seed surrounded by endocarp)

Drupelet

Remains of style

Receptacle

Drupelet

EXTERNAL VIEW OF FRUIT

LONGITUDINAL SECTION THROUGH FRUIT

Hard endocarp

Pip

Hard endocarp

Cotyledon (seed leaf)

Testa (seed coat)

Seed

EXTERNAL VIEW AND SECTION THROUGH PIP

POME (A TYPE OF FALSE FRUIT)
Apple
(*Malus sylvestris*)

Pedicel (flower stalk)

Seed

Mesocarp and exocarp

Swollen receptacle

Waxy skin

Endocarp

Vascular strand

EXTERNAL VIEW OF FRUIT

CROSS-SECTION THROUGH FRUIT

Hilum (point of attachment to ovary)

Testa (seed coat)

Embryo

Cotyledon (seed leaf)

Testa (seed coat)

EXTERNAL VIEW AND SECTION THROUGH SEED

PEPO (A TYPE OF BERRY)
Charentais melon
(*Cucumis melo*)

Rind (fused receptacle and exocarp)

Pedicel (flower stalk)

Seed

Rind (fused receptacle and exocarp)

Mesocarp and endocarp

EXTERNAL VIEW OF FRUIT

CROSS-SECTION THROUGH FRUIT

Testa (seed coat)

Embryo

Testa (seed coat)

Cotyledon (seed leaf)

EXTERNAL VIEW AND SECTION THROUGH SEED

Dry fruits

DRY FRUITS HAVE A HARD, DRY PERICARP (fruit wall) around their seeds unlike succulent fruits, which have fleshy pericarps (see pp. 148-149). Dry fruits are divided into three types: dehiscent, in which the pericarp splits open to release the seeds; indehiscent, which do not split open; and schizocarpic, in which the fruit splits but the seeds are not exposed. Dehiscent dry fruits include capsules (e.g., love-in-a-mist), follicles (e.g., delphinium), legumes (e.g., pea), and siliquas (e.g., honesty). Typically, the seeds of dehiscent fruits are dispersed by the wind. Indehiscent dry fruits include nuts (e.g., sweet chestnut), nutlets (e.g., goosegrass), achenes (e.g., strawberry), caryopses (e.g., wheat), samaras (e.g., elm), and cypselas (e.g., dandelion). Some indehiscent dry fruits are dispersed by the wind, assisted by "wings" (e.g., elm) or "parachutes" (e.g., dandelion); others (e.g., goosegrass) have hooked pericarps to aid dispersal on animals' fur. Schizocarpic dry fruits include cremocarps (e.g., hogweed), and double samaras (e.g., sycamore); these are dispersed by the wind.

NUTLET
Goosegrass
(*Galium aparine*)

LEGUME
Pea
(*Pisum sativum*)

Pedicel (flower stalk) · Receptacle · Remains of sepal · Remains of stamen · Placenta · Pericarp (fruit wall) · Remains of style and stigma

Pedicel (flower stalk) · Receptacle · Remains of sepal · Funicle (stalk attaching seed to placenta) · Pericarp (fruit wall) · Seed · Remains of style and stigma

EXTERNAL VIEW OF FRUIT — **INTERNAL VIEW OF FRUIT**

NUT
Sweet chestnut
(*Castanea sativa*)

Line of splitting between valves of cupule · Peduncle (inflorescence stalk) · Remains of male inflorescence · Nut (indehiscent fruit) · Spiky cupule (husk around fruit formed from bracts)

EXTERNAL VIEW OF FRUIT WITH SURROUNDING CUPULE

Funicle (stalk attaching seed to placenta) · Micropyle (pore for water absorption) · Testa (seed coat) · Cotyledon (seed leaf) · Radicle (embryonic root) · Testa (seed coat) · Plumule (embryonic shoot)

EXTERIOR VIEW AND SECTION THROUGH SEED

ACHENE
Strawberry
(*Fragaria* x *ananassa*)

Sepal · Pedicel (flower stalk) · Swollen receptacle · Remains of stigma and style · Achene (one-seeded dry fruit)

EXTERNAL VIEW OF FRUIT

Sepal · Pedicel (flower stalk) · Swollen fleshy tissues of receptacle

LONGITUDINAL SECTION THROUGH FRUIT

Remains of stigma · Remains of style · Remains of stigma · Remains of style · Nut (indehiscent fruit) · Embryo · Cotyledon (seed leaf) · Testa (seed coat) · Woody pericarp (fruit wall) · Woody pericarp (fruit wall)

EXTERNAL VIEW AND SECTION THROUGH FRUIT

Pericarp (fruit wall) · Pericarp (fruit wall) · Cotyledon (seed leaf) · Testa (seed coat)

EXTERNAL VIEW AND SECTION THROUGH SEED

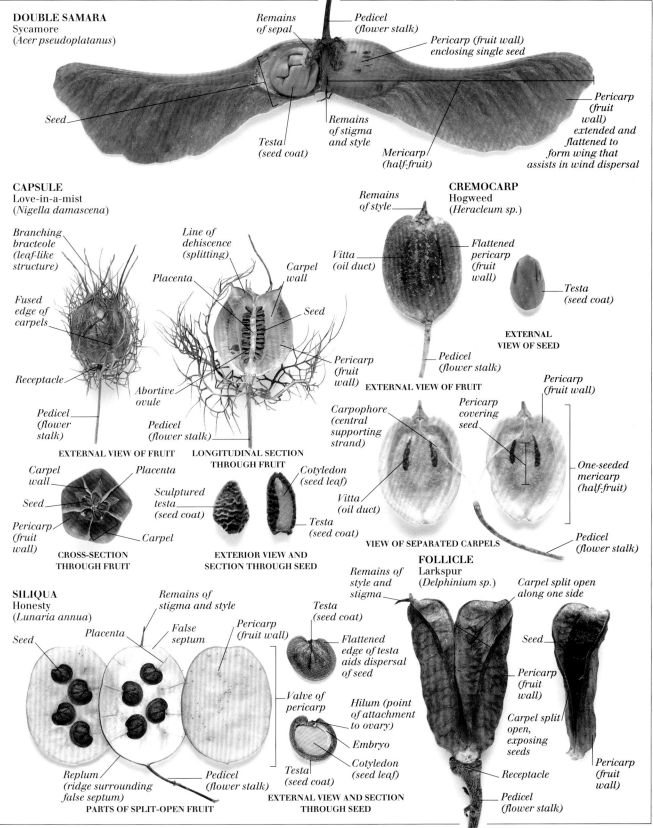

DOUBLE SAMARA
Sycamore
(*Acer pseudoplatanus*)

Remains of sepal

Pedicel (flower stalk)

Pericarp (fruit wall) enclosing single seed

Seed

Testa (seed coat)

Remains of stigma and style

Mericarp (half-fruit)

Pericarp (fruit wall) extended and flattened to form wing that assists in wind dispersal

CAPSULE
Love-in-a-mist
(*Nigella damascena*)

Branching bracteole (leaf-like structure)

Line of dehiscence (splitting)

Placenta

Carpel wall

Fused edge of carpels

Seed

Receptacle

Pericarp (fruit wall)

Pedicel (flower stalk)

Abortive ovule

Pedicel (flower stalk)

EXTERNAL VIEW OF FRUIT

LONGITUDINAL SECTION THROUGH FRUIT

Carpel wall

Placenta

Seed

Pericarp (fruit wall)

Carpel

CROSS-SECTION THROUGH FRUIT

Sculptured testa (seed coat)

Cotyledon (seed leaf)

Testa (seed coat)

EXTERIOR VIEW AND SECTION THROUGH SEED

CREMOCARP
Hogweed
(*Heracleum sp.*)

Remains of style

Vitta (oil duct)

Flattened pericarp (fruit wall)

Testa (seed coat)

EXTERNAL VIEW OF SEED

Pedicel (flower stalk)

EXTERNAL VIEW OF FRUIT

Carpophore (central supporting strand)

Pericarp covering seed

Pericarp (fruit wall)

Vitta (oil duct)

One-seeded mericarp (half-fruit)

Pedicel (flower stalk)

VIEW OF SEPARATED CARPELS

SILIQUA
Honesty
(*Lunaria annua*)

Remains of stigma and style

False septum

Placenta

Pericarp (fruit wall)

Seed

FOLLICLE
Larkspur
(*Delphinium sp.*)

Remains of style and stigma

Testa (seed coat)

Flattened edge of testa aids dispersal of seed

Carpel split open along one side

Seed

Pericarp (fruit wall)

Carpel split open, exposing seeds

Valve of pericarp

Hilum (point of attachment to ovary)

Embryo

Testa (seed coat)

Cotyledon (seed leaf)

Receptacle

Pericarp (fruit wall)

Replum (ridge surrounding false septum)

Pedicel (flower stalk)

PARTS OF SPLIT-OPEN FRUIT

EXTERNAL VIEW AND SECTION THROUGH SEED

Pedicel (flower stalk)

Germination

GERMINATION IS THE GROWTH OF SEEDS INTO SEEDLINGS. It starts when seeds become active below ground, and ends when the first foliage leaves appear above ground. A seed consists of an embryo and its food store, surrounded by a testa (seed coat). The embryo is made up of one or two cotyledons (seed leaves) attached to a central axis. The upper part of the axis consists of an epicotyl, which has a plumule (embryonic shoot) at its tip. The lower part of the axis consists of a hypocotyl and a radicle (embryonic root). After dispersal from the parent plant, the seeds dehydrate and enter a period of dormancy. Following this dormant period, germination begins, provided that the seeds have enough water, oxygen, warmth, and, in some cases, light. In the first stages of germination, the seed takes in water; the embryo starts to use its food store; and the radicle swells, breaks through the testa, and grows downwards. Germination then proceeds in one of two ways, depending on the type of seed. In epigeal germination, the hypocotyl lengthens, pulling the plumule and its protective cotyledons out of the soil. In hypogeal germination, the cotyledons remain below ground and the epicotyl lengthens, pushing the plumule upwards.

HYPOGEAL GERMINATION
Broad bean
(*Vicia faba*)

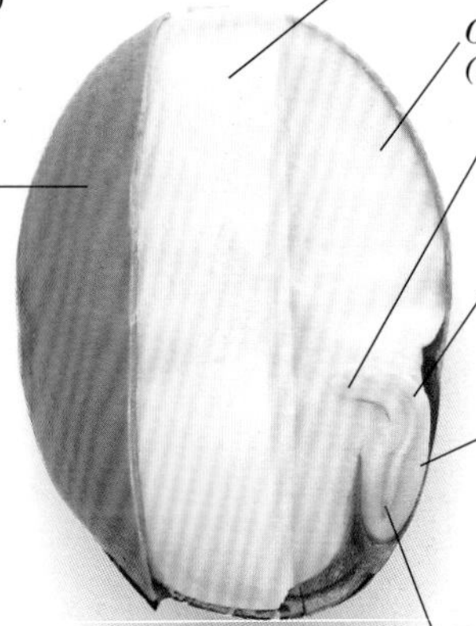

Cotyledon (seed leaf)

Cotyledon (seed leaf)

Plumule (embryonic shoot)

Testa (seed coat)

Epicotyl (upper part of axis)

Hypocotyl (region between epicotyl and radicle)

Radicle (embryonic root)

SEED AT START OF GERMINATION

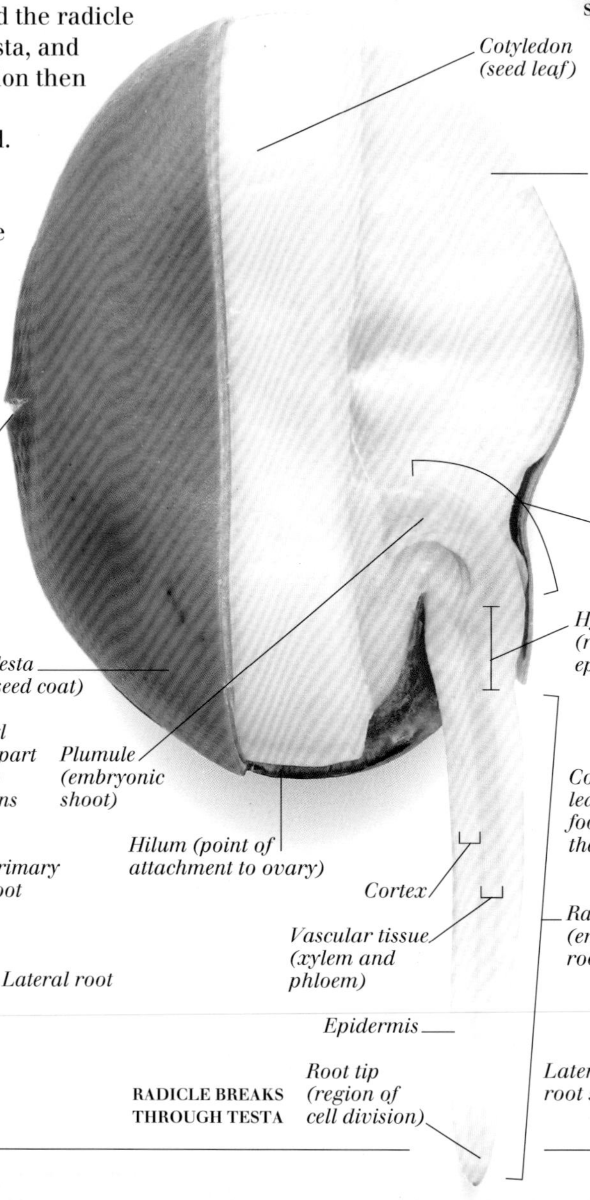

Cotyledon (seed leaf)

Foliage leaf

Cotyledon (seed leaf)

Stipule (structure at base of leaf)

Epicotyl increases in length and turns green

Cataphyll (scale leaf of plumule)

Epicotyl (upper part of axis)

Hypocotyl (region between epicotyl and radicle)

FOLIAGE LEAVES APPEAR

Cotyledons (seed leaves) remain food source for the seedling

Primary root

Radicle (embryonic root)

Split in testa (seed coat) due to expanding cotyledons

Young shoot

Cataphyll (scale leaf of plumule)

Testa (seed coat)

Epicotyl (upper part of axis) lengthens

Plumule (embryonic shoot)

Cotyledons (seed leaves) remain within testa (seed coat) below soil's surface

Primary root

Hilum (point of attachment to ovary)

Lateral root

Cortex

Vascular tissue (xylem and phloem)

Epidermis

Lateral root system

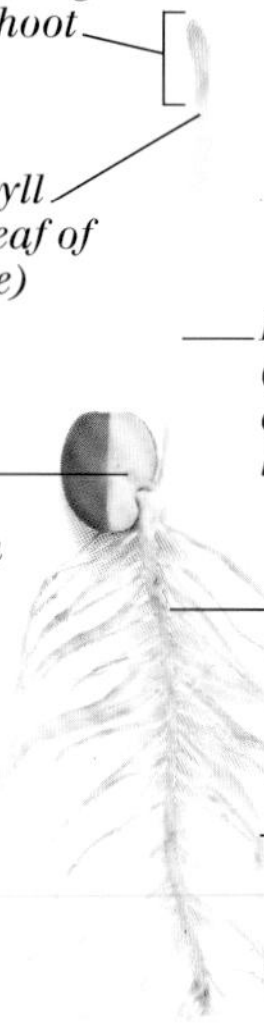

SHOOT APPEARS ABOVE SOIL

RADICLE BREAKS THROUGH TESTA

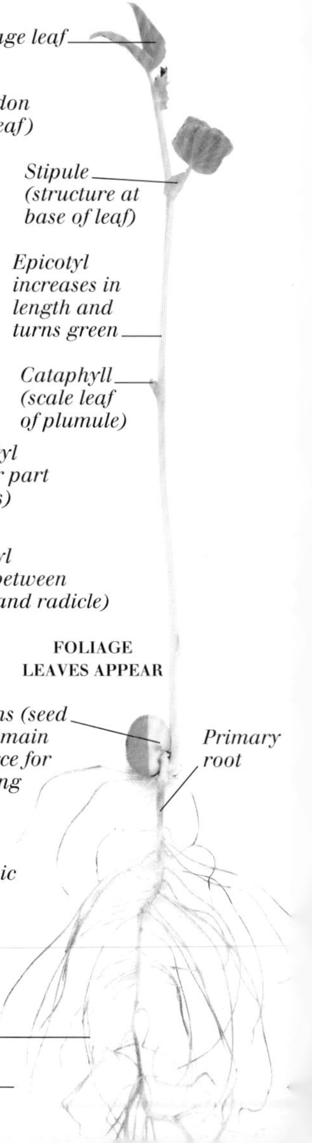

Root tip (region of cell division)

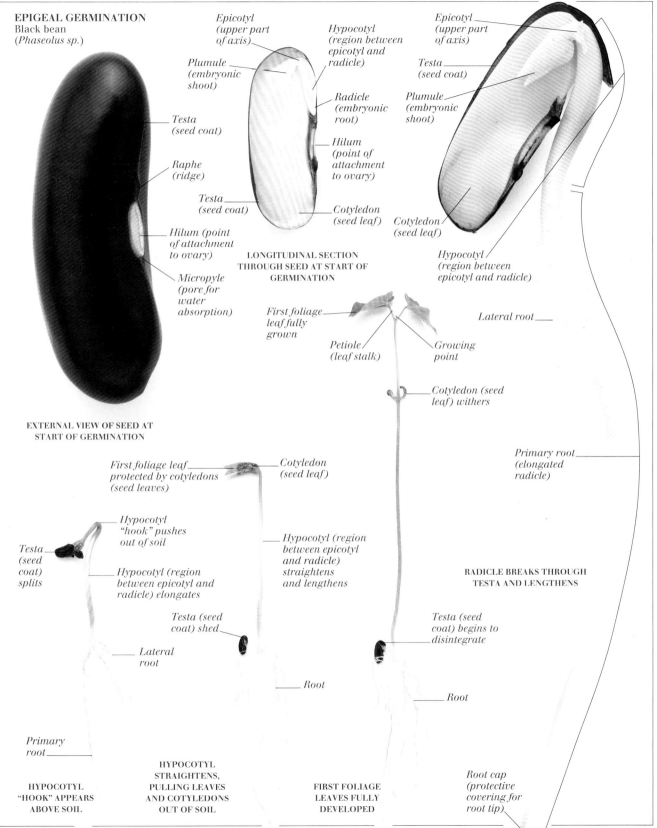

EPIGEAL GERMINATION
Black bean
(*Phaseolus sp.*)

Testa (seed coat)

Raphe (ridge)

Hilum (point of attachment to ovary)

Micropyle (pore for water absorption)

EXTERNAL VIEW OF SEED AT START OF GERMINATION

Epicotyl (upper part of axis)

Plumule (embryonic shoot)

Hypocotyl (region between epicotyl and radicle)

Radicle (embryonic root)

Hilum (point of attachment to ovary)

Testa (seed coat)

Cotyledon (seed leaf)

LONGITUDINAL SECTION THROUGH SEED AT START OF GERMINATION

Epicotyl (upper part of axis)

Testa (seed coat)

Plumule (embryonic shoot)

Cotyledon (seed leaf)

Hypocotyl (region between epicotyl and radicle)

Lateral root

Primary root (elongated radicle)

RADICLE BREAKS THROUGH TESTA AND LENGTHENS

First foliage leaf fully grown

Petiole (leaf stalk)

Growing point

Cotyledon (seed leaf) withers

First foliage leaf protected by cotyledons (seed leaves)

Cotyledon (seed leaf)

Hypocotyl (region between epicotyl and radicle) straightens and lengthens

Testa (seed coat) splits

Hypocotyl "hook" pushes out of soil

Hypocotyl (region between epicotyl and radicle) elongates

Testa (seed coat) shed

Lateral root

Testa (seed coat) begins to disintegrate

Root

Root

Primary root

HYPOCOTYL "HOOK" APPEARS ABOVE SOIL

HYPOCOTYL STRAIGHTENS, PULLING LEAVES AND COTYLEDONS OUT OF SOIL

FIRST FOLIAGE LEAVES FULLY DEVELOPED

Root cap (protective covering for root tip)

Vegetative reproduction

ADVENTITIOUS BUD
Mexican hat plant
(*Kalanchoe
daigremontiana*)

MANY PLANTS CAN PROPAGATE THEMSELVES by vegetative reproduction. In this process, part of a plant separates off, takes root, and grows into a new plant. Vegetative reproduction is a type of asexual reproduction; that is, it involves only one parent, and there is no fusion of gametes (sex cells). Plants use various structures to reproduce vegetatively. Some plants use underground storage organs. Such organs include rhizomes (horizontal, underground stems), the branches of which produce new plants; bulbs (swollen leaf bases) and corms (swollen stems), which produce daughter bulbs or corms that separate off from the parent; and stem tubers (thickened underground stems) and root tubers (swollen adventitious roots), which also separate off from the parent. Other propagative structures include runners and stolons, creeping horizontal stems that take root and produce new plants; bulbils, small bulbs that develop on the stem or in the place of flowers, and then drop off and grow into new plants; and adventitious buds, miniature plants that form on leaf margins before dropping to the ground and growing into mature plants.

CORM
Gladiolus
(*Gladiolus sp.*)

*Apex of
leaf*

*Lamina
(blade) of
leaf*

*Leaf
margin*

*Notch in leaf
margin containing
meristematic
(actively dividing)
cells*

*Adventitious bud
(detachable bud
with adventitious
roots) drops
from leaf*

*Petiole
(leaf stalk)*

BULBIL IN PLACE OF FLOWER
Orange lily
(*Lilium bulbiferum*)

*Scar left
by flower*

Leaf

*Pedicel
(flower stalk)*

STOLON
Ground ivy
(*Glechoma hederacea*)

*Terminal
bud*

Internode

*Parent
plant*

Node

*Stolon
(creeping stem)*

*Detachable
bulbil formed
in place of
flower*

Node

*Peduncle
(inflorescence
stalk)*

*Adventitious root
of daughter plant*

*Daughter plant
developed from
lateral bud*

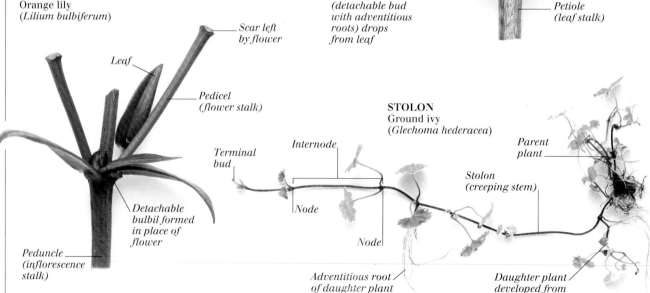

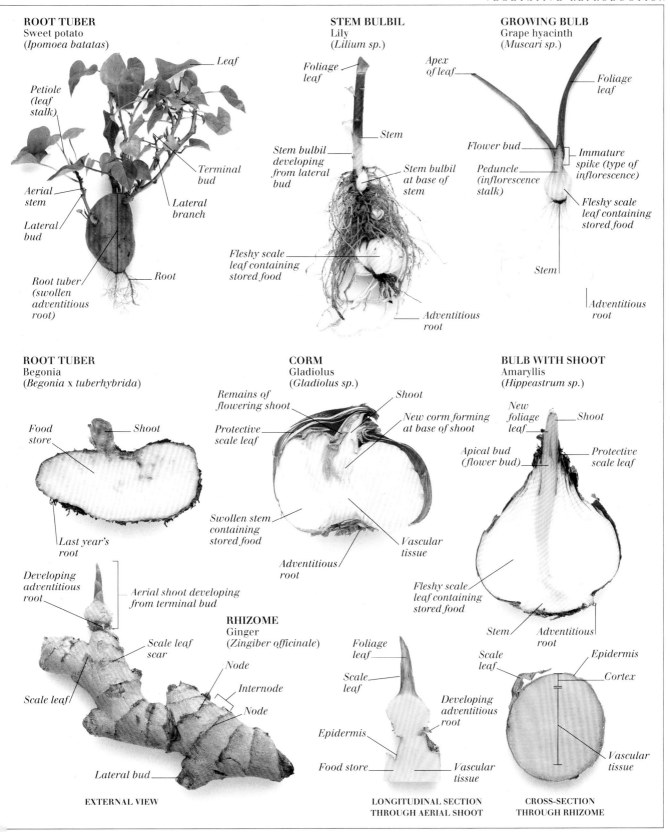

ROOT TUBER
Sweet potato
(*Ipomoea batatas*)

Leaf

Petiole
(leaf
stalk)

Terminal
bud

Aerial
stem

Lateral
branch

Lateral
bud

Root

Root tuber
(swollen
adventitious
root)

STEM BULBIL
Lily
(*Lilium sp.*)

Foliage
leaf

Stem

Stem bulbil
developing
from lateral
bud

Stem bulbil
at base of
stem

Fleshy scale
leaf containing
stored food

Adventitious
root

GROWING BULB
Grape hyacinth
(*Muscari sp.*)

Apex
of leaf

Foliage
leaf

Flower bud

Immature
spike (type of
inflorescence)

Peduncle
(inflorescence
stalk)

Fleshy scale
leaf containing
stored food

Stem

Adventitious
root

ROOT TUBER
Begonia
(*Begonia* x *tuberhybrida*)

Food
store

Shoot

Last year's
root

Developing
adventitious
root

Aerial shoot developing
from terminal bud

Scale leaf
scar

Node

Internode

Node

Scale leaf

Lateral bud

EXTERNAL VIEW

CORM
Gladiolus
(*Gladiolus sp.*)

Remains of
flowering shoot

Shoot

New corm forming
at base of shoot

Protective
scale leaf

Swollen stem
containing
stored food

Adventitious
root

Vascular
tissue

RHIZOME
Ginger
(*Zingiber officinale*)

Foliage
leaf

Scale
leaf

Developing
adventitious
root

Epidermis

Food store

Vascular
tissue

**LONGITUDINAL SECTION
THROUGH AERIAL SHOOT**

BULB WITH SHOOT
Amaryllis
(*Hippeastrum sp.*)

New
foliage
leaf

Shoot

Apical bud
(flower bud)

Protective
scale leaf

Fleshy scale
leaf containing
stored food

Stem

Adventitious
root

Scale
leaf

Epidermis

Cortex

Vascular
tissue

**CROSS-SECTION
THROUGH RHIZOME**

Dryland plants

DRYLAND PLANTS (XEROPHYTES) are able to survive in unfavourable habitats. All are found in places where little water is available; some live in high temperatures that cause excessive loss of water from the leaves. Xerophytes show a number of adaptations to dry conditions; these include reduced leaf area, rolled leaves, sunken stomata, hairs, spines, and thick cuticles. One group, succulent plants, stores water in specially enlarged spongy tissues found in leaves, roots, or stems. Leaf succulents have enlarged, fleshy, water-storing leaves. Root succulents have a large, underground water-storage organ with short-lived stems and leaves above ground. Stem succulents are represented by the cacti (family Cactaceae). Cacti stems are fleshy, green, and photosynthetic; they are typically ribbed or covered by tubercles in rows, with leaves being reduced to spines or entirely absent.

LEAF SUCCULENT
Lithops sp.

STEM SUCCULENT
Golden barrel cactus
(*Echinocactus grusonii*)

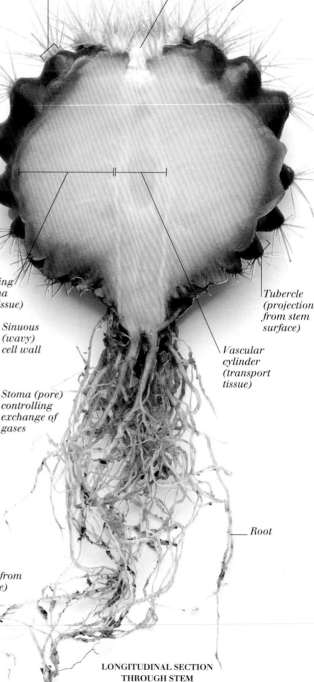

Areole (modified lateral shoot)

Trichome (hair)

Spine (modified leaf)

Tubercle (projection from stem surface)

Vascular cylinder (transport tissue)

Root

LONGITUDINAL SECTION THROUGH STEM

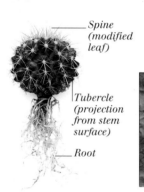

Spine (modified leaf)

Tubercle (projection from stem surface)

Root

EXTERNAL VIEW

Waxy cuticle (waterproof covering)

Water-storing parenchyma (packing tissue)

Sinuous (wavy) cell wall

Stoma (pore) controlling exchange of gases

MICROGRAPH OF STEM SURFACE

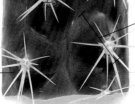

Spine (modified leaf)

Areole (modified lateral shoot)

Tubercle (projection from stem surface)

Waxy cuticle (waterproof covering)

DETAIL OF STEM SURFACE

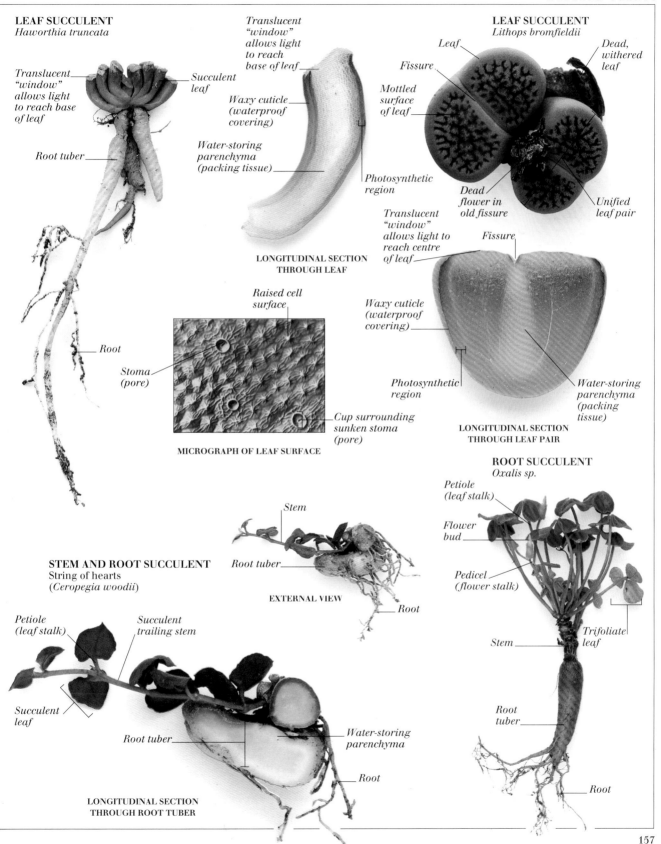

LEAF SUCCULENT
Haworthia truncata

Translucent "window" allows light to reach base of leaf

Succulent leaf

Root tuber

Root

Translucent "window" allows light to reach base of leaf

Waxy cuticle (waterproof covering)

Water-storing parenchyma (packing tissue)

Photosynthetic region

LONGITUDINAL SECTION THROUGH LEAF

Raised cell surface

Stoma (pore)

Cup surrounding sunken stoma (pore)

MICROGRAPH OF LEAF SURFACE

LEAF SUCCULENT
Lithops bromfieldii

Leaf

Fissure

Mottled surface of leaf

Dead, withered leaf

Dead flower in old fissure

Unified leaf pair

Translucent "window" allows light to reach centre of leaf

Fissure

Waxy cuticle (waterproof covering)

Photosynthetic region

Water-storing parenchyma (packing tissue)

LONGITUDINAL SECTION THROUGH LEAF PAIR

ROOT SUCCULENT
Oxalis sp.

Petiole (leaf stalk)

Flower bud

Pedicel (flower stalk)

Stem

Trifoliate leaf

Root tuber

Root

STEM AND ROOT SUCCULENT
String of hearts
(*Ceropegia woodii*)

Stem

Root tuber

Root

EXTERNAL VIEW

Petiole (leaf stalk)

Succulent trailing stem

Succulent leaf

Root tuber

Water-storing parenchyma

Root

LONGITUDINAL SECTION THROUGH ROOT TUBER

157

Wetland plants

WETLAND PLANTS GROW SUBMERGED IN WATER, either partially (e.g., water hyacinth) or completely (e.g., pond weeds), and show various adaptations to this habitat. Typically, there are numerous air spaces inside the stems, leaves, and roots; these aid gas exchange and buoyancy. Submerged parts generally have no cuticle (waterproof covering), enabling the plants to absorb minerals and gases directly from the water; in addition, being supported by the water, they need little of the supportive tissue found in land plants. Stomata, the gas exchange pores, are absent from plants that are completely submerged; in partially submerged plants with floating leaves (e.g., water lilies), stomata are found on the upper leaf surfaces, where they cannot be flooded.

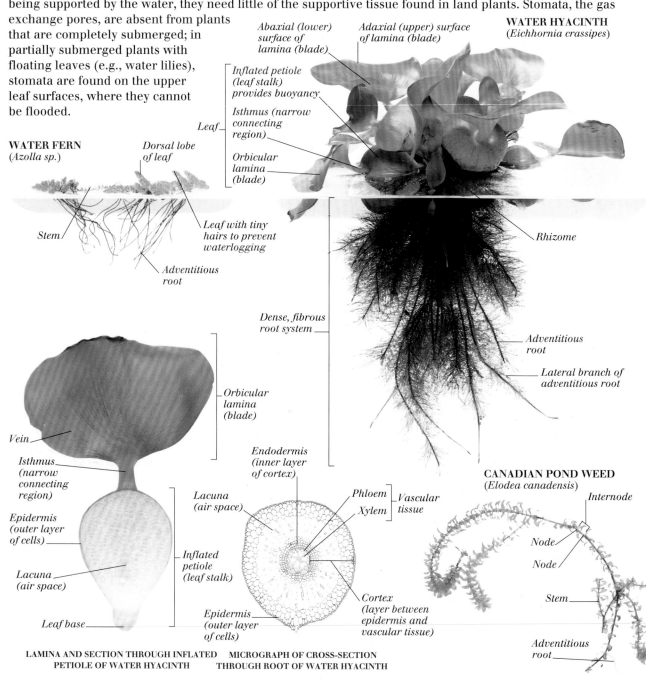

WATER FERN
(*Azolla sp.*)

Dorsal lobe of leaf

Stem

Adventitious root

Leaf with tiny hairs to prevent waterlogging

Abaxial (lower) surface of lamina (blade)

Adaxial (upper) surface of lamina (blade)

WATER HYACINTH
(*Eichhornia crassipes*)

Inflated petiole (leaf stalk) provides buoyancy

Isthmus (narrow connecting region)

Leaf

Orbicular lamina (blade)

Rhizome

Dense, fibrous root system

Adventitious root

Lateral branch of adventitious root

Orbicular lamina (blade)

Vein

Isthmus (narrow connecting region)

Epidermis (outer layer of cells)

Lacuna (air space)

Leaf base

Endodermis (inner layer of cortex)

Lacuna (air space)

Phloem

Xylem

Vascular tissue

Inflated petiole (leaf stalk)

Epidermis (outer layer of cells)

Cortex (layer between epidermis and vascular tissue)

CANADIAN POND WEED
(*Elodea canadensis*)

Internode

Node

Node

Stem

Adventitious root

LAMINA AND SECTION THROUGH INFLATED PETIOLE OF WATER HYACINTH

MICROGRAPH OF CROSS-SECTION THROUGH ROOT OF WATER HYACINTH

WATER LILY
(Nymphaea sp.)

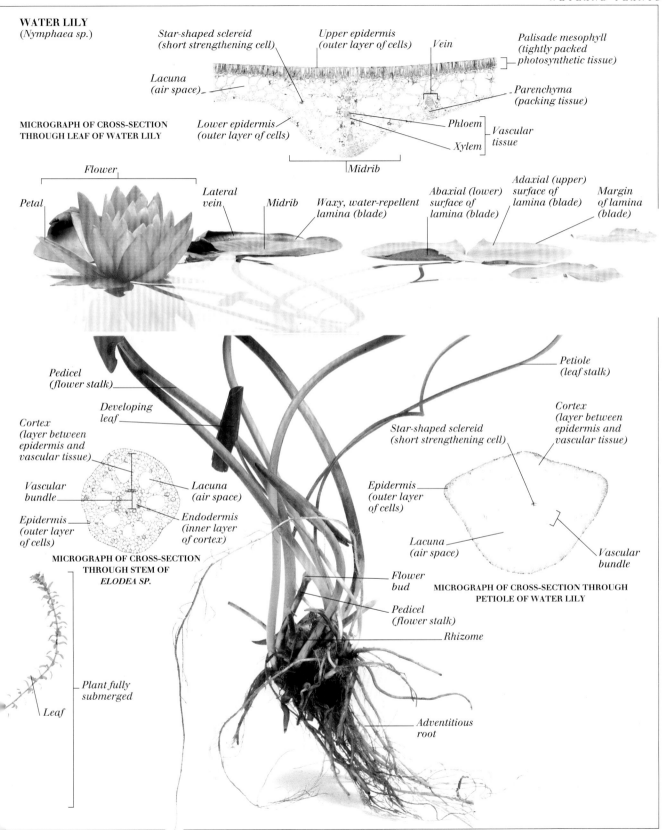

*Star-shaped sclereid
(short strengthening cell)*

*Upper epidermis
(outer layer of cells)*

Vein

*Palisade mesophyll
(tightly packed
photosynthetic tissue)*

*Lacuna
(air space)*

*Parenchyma
(packing tissue)*

MICROGRAPH OF CROSS-SECTION
THROUGH LEAF OF WATER LILY

*Lower epidermis
(outer layer of cells)*

Phloem
Xylem

*Vascular
tissue*

Midrib

Flower

*Lateral
vein*

Midrib

*Waxy, water-repellent
lamina (blade)*

*Abaxial (lower)
surface of
lamina (blade)*

*Adaxial (upper)
surface of
lamina (blade)*

*Margin
of lamina
(blade)*

Petal

*Pedicel
(flower stalk)*

*Petiole
(leaf stalk)*

*Developing
leaf*

*Cortex
(layer between
epidermis and
vascular tissue)*

*Star-shaped sclereid
(short strengthening cell)*

*Cortex
(layer between
epidermis and
vascular tissue)*

*Vascular
bundle*

*Lacuna
(air space)*

*Epidermis
(outer layer
of cells)*

*Epidermis
(outer layer
of cells)*

*Endodermis
(inner layer
of cortex)*

*Lacuna
(air space)*

*Vascular
bundle*

MICROGRAPH OF CROSS-SECTION
THROUGH STEM OF
ELODEA SP.

MICROGRAPH OF CROSS-SECTION THROUGH
PETIOLE OF WATER LILY

*Flower
bud*

*Pedicel
(flower stalk)*

Rhizome

*Plant fully
submerged*

Leaf

*Adventitious
root*

Carnivorous plants

CARNIVOROUS (INSECTIVOROUS) PLANTS FEED ON INSECTS and other small animals, in addition to producing food in their leaves by photosynthesis. The nutrients absorbed from trapped insects enable carnivorous plants to thrive in acid, boggy soils that lack essential minerals, especially nitrates, where most other plants could not survive. All carnivorous plants have some leaves modified as traps; many use bright colours and scented nectar to attract prey; and most use enzymes to digest the prey. There are three types of traps. Pitcher plants, such as the monkey cup and cobra lily, have leaves modified as pitcher-shaped pitfall traps, half-filled with water; once lured inside the mouth of the trap, insects lose their footing on the slippery surface, fall into the liquid, and either decompose or are digested. Venus fly traps use a spring-trap mechanism; when an insect touches trigger hairs on the inner surfaces of the leaves, the two lobes of the trap snap shut. Butterworts and sundews entangle prey by sticky droplets on the leaf surface, while the edges of the leaves slowly curl over to envelop and digest the prey.

PITCHER PLANT
Cobra lily (*Darlingtonia californica*)

Areola ("window" of transparent tissue)

Fishtail nectary

Wing

Hood

Pitcher

Tubular petiole (leaf stalk)

Areola ("window" of transparent tissue)

Smooth surface

Nectar roll

Dome-shaped hood develops

Fishtail nectary appears

Immature pitcher

Wing

Mouth

Downward pointing hair

DEVELOPMENT OF MODIFIED LEAF IN COBRA LILY

Immature trap

Interlocked teeth

Closed trap

Red colour of trap attracts insects

Trigger hair

Sensory hinge

Inner surface of trap

VENUS FLY TRAP
(*Dionaea muscipula*)

Phyllode (flattened petiole)

Summer petiole (leaf stalk)

Nectary zone (glands secrete nectar)

Digestive zone (glands secrete digestive enzymes)

Lobe of trap

Midrib (hinge of trap)

Trap (twin-lobed leaf blade)

Spring petiole (leaf stalk)

Digestive gland

Tooth

Trigger hair

MICROGRAPH OF LOBE OF VENUS FLY TRAP

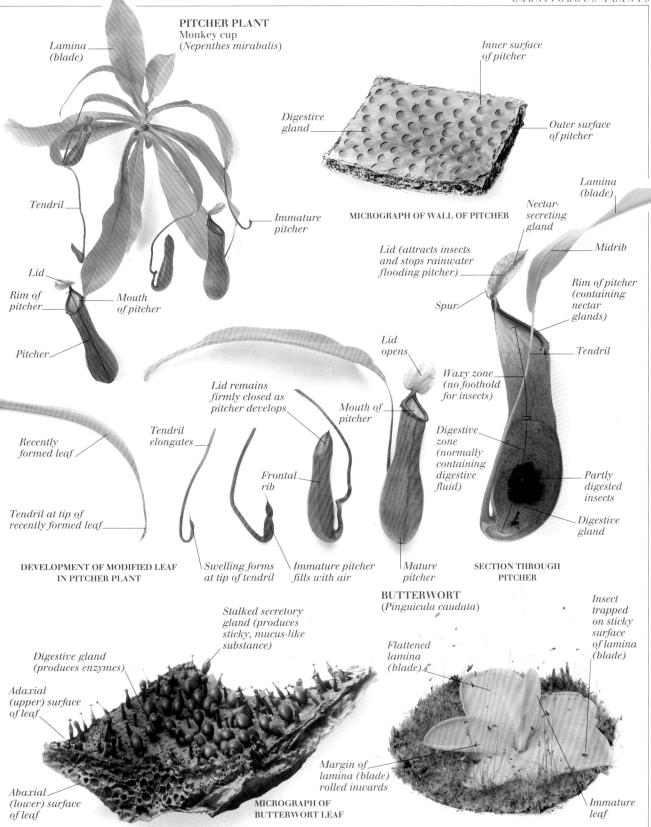

PITCHER PLANT
Monkey cup
(*Nepenthes mirabalis*)

Lamina
(blade)

Tendril

Immature
pitcher

Lid

Rim of
pitcher

Mouth
of pitcher

Pitcher

Digestive
gland

Inner surface
of pitcher

Outer surface
of pitcher

MICROGRAPH OF WALL OF PITCHER

Nectar-
secreting
gland

Lid (attracts insects
and stops rainwater
flooding pitcher)

Spur

Lid
opens

Mouth of
pitcher

Lamina
(blade)

Midrib

Rim of pitcher
(containing
nectar
glands)

Tendril

Waxy zone
(no foothold
for insects)

Digestive
zone
(normally
containing
digestive
fluid)

Partly
digested
insects

Digestive
gland

Recently
formed leaf

Tendril at tip of
recently formed leaf

Tendril
elongates

Lid remains
firmly closed as
pitcher develops

Frontal
rib

Swelling forms
at tip of tendril

Immature pitcher
fills with air

Mature
pitcher

**DEVELOPMENT OF MODIFIED LEAF
IN PITCHER PLANT**

**SECTION THROUGH
PITCHER**

BUTTERWORT
(*Pinguicula caudata*)

Stalked secretory
gland (produces
sticky, mucus-like
substance)

Digestive gland
(produces enzymes)

Adaxial
(upper) surface
of leaf

Flattened
lamina
(blade)

Insect
trapped
on sticky
surface
of lamina
(blade)

Margin of
lamina (blade)
rolled inwards

Abaxial
(lower) surface
of leaf

**MICROGRAPH OF
BUTTERWORT LEAF**

Immature
leaf

Epiphytic and parasitic plants

EPIPHYTIC AND PARASITIC PLANTS GROW ON OTHER LIVING PLANTS. Typically, epiphytic plants are not rooted in the soil; instead, they live above ground level on the stems and branches of other plants. Epiphytes obtain water from trapped rainwater and from moisture in the air, and minerals from organic matter that has accumulated on the surface of the plant on which they are growing. Like other green plants, epiphytes produce their food by photosynthesis. Epiphytes include tropical orchids and bromeliads (air plants), and some mosses that live in temperate regions. Parasitic plants obtain all their nutrient requirements from the host plants on which they grow. The parasites produce haustoria, root-like organs that penetrate the stem or roots of the host and grow inwards to merge with the host's vascular tissue, from which the parasite extracts water, minerals, and manufactured nutrients. As they have no need to produce their own food, parasitic plants lack chlorophyll, the green photosynthetic pigment, and they have no foliage leaves. Partial parasitic plants (e.g., mistletoe) obtain water and minerals from the host plant but have green leaves and stems and are therefore able to produce their own food by photosynthesis.

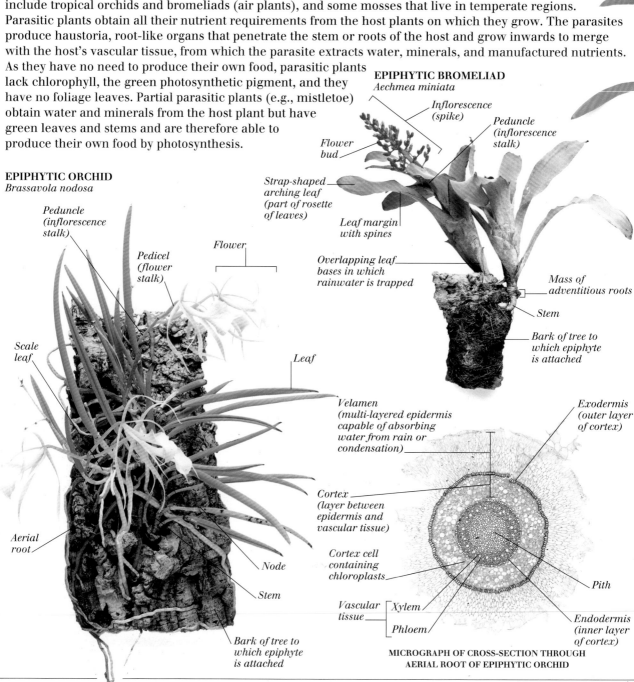

EPIPHYTIC BROMELIAD
Aechmea miniata

Inflorescence (spike)

Peduncle (inflorescence stalk)

Flower bud

Strap-shaped arching leaf (part of rosette of leaves)

Leaf margin with spines

Overlapping leaf bases in which rainwater is trapped

Mass of adventitious roots

Stem

Bark of tree to which epiphyte is attached

EPIPHYTIC ORCHID
Brassavola nodosa

Peduncle (inflorescence stalk)

Pedicel (flower stalk)

Flower

Scale leaf

Leaf

Velamen (multi-layered epidermis capable of absorbing water from rain or condensation)

Aerial root

Node

Stem

Cortex (layer between epidermis and vascular tissue)

Cortex cell containing chloroplasts

Vascular tissue

Xylem

Phloem

Exodermis (outer layer of cortex)

Pith

Endodermis (inner layer of cortex)

Bark of tree to which epiphyte is attached

MICROGRAPH OF CROSS-SECTION THROUGH AERIAL ROOT OF EPIPHYTIC ORCHID

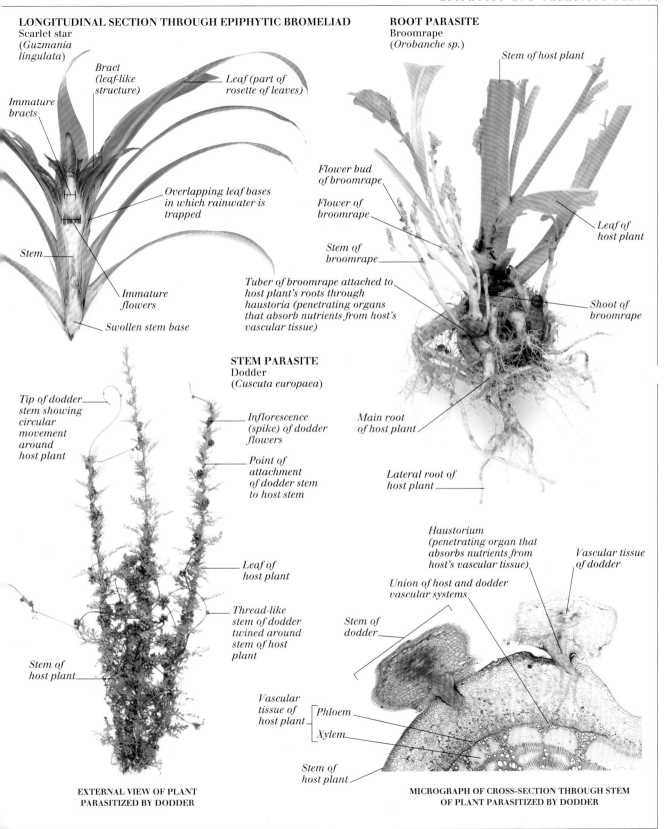

LONGITUDINAL SECTION THROUGH EPIPHYTIC BROMELIAD
Scarlet star
(*Guzmania lingulata*)

Immature bracts

Bract (leaf-like structure)

Leaf (part of rosette of leaves)

Overlapping leaf bases in which rainwater is trapped

Stem

Immature flowers

Swollen stem base

ROOT PARASITE
Broomrape
(*Orobanche sp.*)

Stem of host plant

Flower bud of broomrape

Flower of broomrape

Stem of broomrape

Tuber of broomrape attached to host plant's roots through haustoria (penetrating organs that absorb nutrients from host's vascular tissue)

Leaf of host plant

Shoot of broomrape

Main root of host plant

Lateral root of host plant

STEM PARASITE
Dodder
(*Cuscuta europaea*)

Tip of dodder stem showing circular movement around host plant

Inflorescence (spike) of dodder flowers

Point of attachment of dodder stem to host stem

Leaf of host plant

Thread-like stem of dodder twined around stem of host plant

Stem of host plant

EXTERNAL VIEW OF PLANT PARASITIZED BY DODDER

Haustorium (penetrating organ that absorbs nutrients from host's vascular tissue)

Vascular tissue of dodder

Union of host and dodder vascular systems

Stem of dodder

Vascular tissue of host plant

Phloem

Xylem

Stem of host plant

MICROGRAPH OF CROSS-SECTION THROUGH STEM OF PLANT PARASITIZED BY DODDER

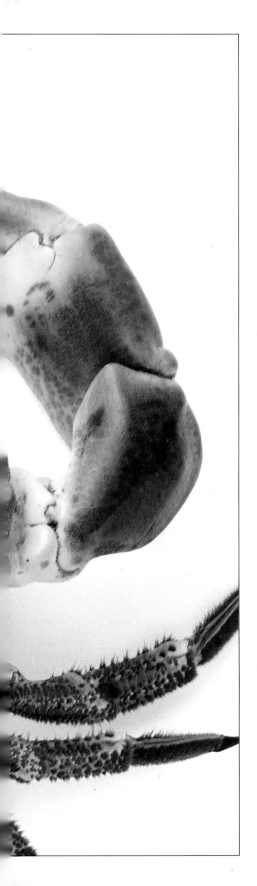

ANIMALS

Sponges, jellyfish, and sea anemones

SPONGES ARE MAINLY MARINE animals that make up the phylum Porifera. They are among the simplest of all animals, having no tissues or organs. Their bodies consist of two layers of cells separated by a jelly-like layer (mesohyal) that is strengthened by mineral spicules or protein fibres. The body is perforated by a system of pores and water channels called the aquiferous system. Special cells (choanocytes) with whip-like structures (flagella) draw water through the aquiferous system, thereby bringing tiny food particles to the sponge's cells. Jellyfish (class Scyphozoa), sea anemones (class Anthozoa), and corals (also class Anthozoa) belong to the phylum Cnidaria, also known as Coelenterata. More complex than sponges, coelenterates have simple tissues, such as nervous tissue; a radially symmetrical body; and a mouth surrounded by tentacles with unique stinging cells (cnidocytes).

INTERNAL ANATOMY OF A SPONGE

Amoebocyte

Osculum (excurrent pore)

Choanocyte (collar cell)

Ostium (incurrent pore)

Porocyte (pore cell)

Mesohyal

Spongocoel (atrium; paragaster)

Spicule

Pinacocyte (epidermal cell)

Ostium (incurrent pore)

SKELETON OF A SPONGE

Protein matrix

Pore

EXTERNAL FEATURES OF A SEA ANEMONE

Tentacle

EXAMPLES OF SEA ANEMONES

JEWEL ANEMONE
(*Corynactis viridis*)

PARASITIC ANEMONE
(*Calliactis parasitica*)

PLUMOSE ANEMONE
(*Metridium senile*)

MEDITERRANEAN SEA ANEMONE
(*Condylactis sp.*)

GREEN SNAKELOCK ANEMONE
(*Anemonia viridis*)

BEADLET ANEMONE
(*Actinia equina*)

GHOST ANEMONE
(*Actinothoe sphyrodeta*)

Sagartia elegans

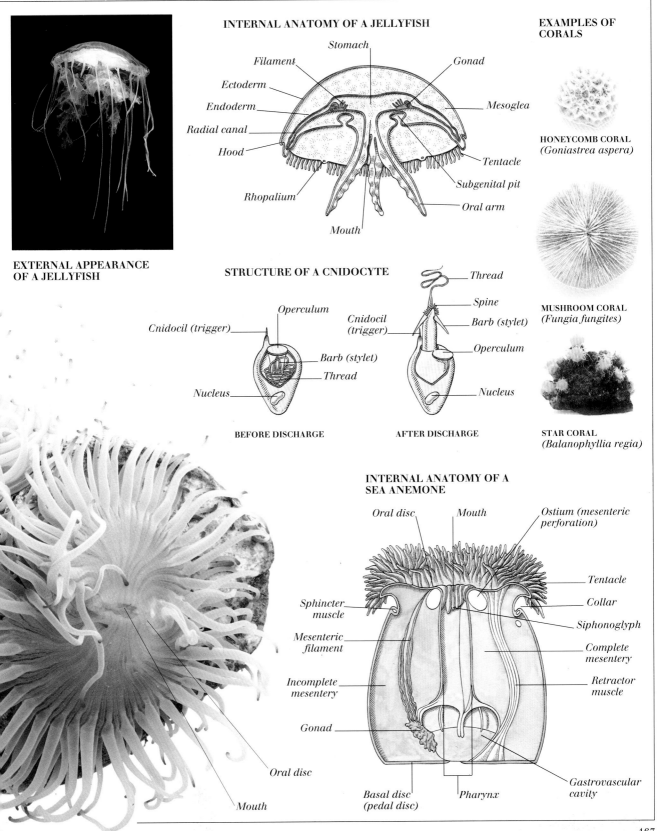

EXTERNAL APPEARANCE OF A JELLYFISH

INTERNAL ANATOMY OF A JELLYFISH

Stomach
Filament
Gonad
Ectoderm
Mesoglea
Endoderm
Radial canal
Hood
Tentacle
Rhopalium
Subgenital pit
Oral arm
Mouth

EXAMPLES OF CORALS

HONEYCOMB CORAL
(*Goniastrea aspera*)

MUSHROOM CORAL
(*Fungia fungites*)

STAR CORAL
(*Balanophyllia regia*)

STRUCTURE OF A CNIDOCYTE

Operculum
Cnidocil (trigger)
Barb (stylet)
Thread
Nucleus

BEFORE DISCHARGE

Thread
Spine
Cnidocil (trigger)
Barb (stylet)
Operculum
Nucleus

AFTER DISCHARGE

INTERNAL ANATOMY OF A SEA ANEMONE

Oral disc
Mouth
Ostium (mesenteric perforation)
Sphincter muscle
Tentacle
Collar
Siphonoglyph
Mesenteric filament
Complete mesentery
Incomplete mesentery
Retractor muscle
Gonad
Basal disc (pedal disc)
Pharynx
Gastrovascular cavity

Oral disc
Mouth

Insects

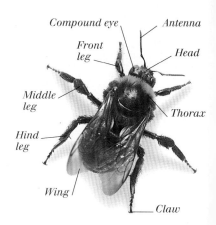

PUPA
(CHRYSALIS)

THE WORD INSECT REFERS to small invertebrate creatures, especially those with bodies divided into sections. Insects, including beetles, ants, bees, butterflies, and moths, belong to various orders in the class Insecta, which is a division of the phylum Arthropoda. Features common to all insects are an exoskeleton (external skeleton); three pairs of jointed legs; three body sections (head, thorax, and abdomen); and one pair of sensory antennae. Beetles (order Coleoptera) are the biggest group of insects, with about 300,000 species (about 30 per cent of all known insects). They have a pair of hard elytra (wing cases), which are modified front wings. The principal function of the elytra is to protect the hind wings, which are used for flying. Ants, together with bees and wasps, form the order Hymenoptera, which contains about 200,000 species. This group is characterized by a marked narrowing between the thorax and abdomen. Butterflies and moths form the order Lepidoptera, which has about 150,000 species. They have wings covered with tiny scales, hence the name of their order (Lepidoptera means "scale wings"). The separation of lepidopterans into butterflies and moths is largely artificial as there are no features that categorically distinguish one group from the other. In general, however, most butterflies fly by day, whereas most moths are night-flyers. Some insects, including butterflies and moths, undergo complete metamorphosis (transformation) during their life-cycle. A butterfly metamorphoses from an egg to a larva (caterpillar), then to a pupa (chrysalis), and finally to an imago (adult).

EXAMPLES OF INSECTS

Compound eye • Antenna
Front leg • Head
Middle leg
Thorax
Hind leg
Wing
Claw

BUMBLEBEE

Compound eye
Stigma (spot)
Vein
Abdomen

DAMSELFLY

EXTERNAL FEATURES OF A BEETLE

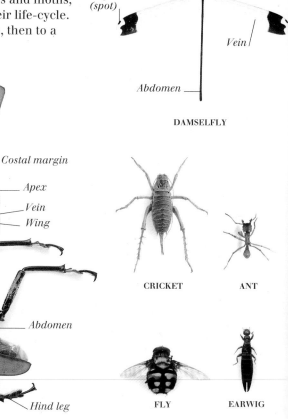

Elytron
Tarsus
Claw
Tibia
Costal margin
Pedicel
Apex
Flagellum
Femur
Vein
Trochanter
Wing
Mandible
Scape
Coxa
Labrum
Labial palp
Abdomen
Compound eye
Head
Prothorax
Mesothorax
Front leg
Scutellum
Hind leg
Metathorax
Middle leg

CRICKET

ANT

FLY

EARWIG

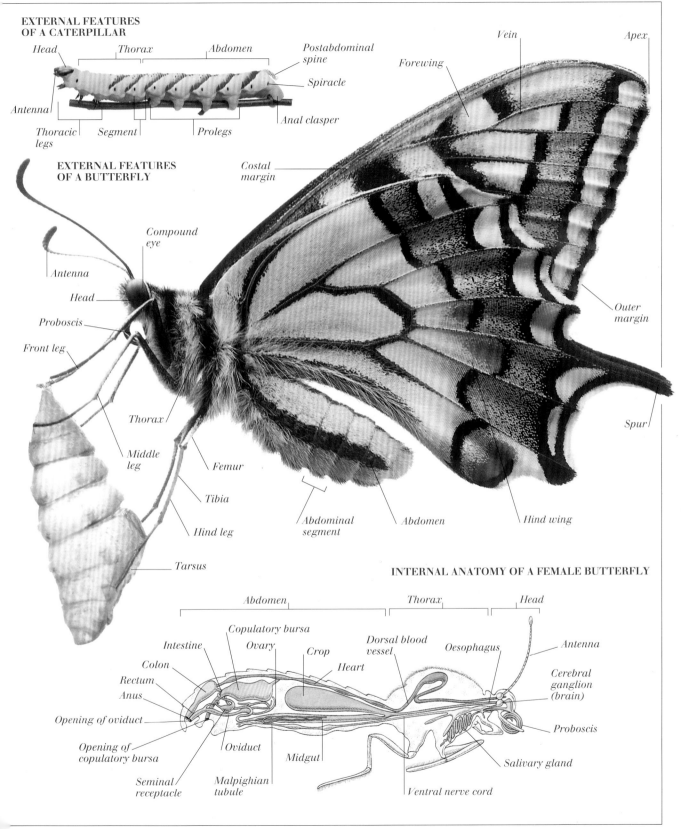

**EXTERNAL FEATURES
OF A CATERPILLAR**

Head
Thorax
Abdomen
Postabdominal
spine
Spiracle
Antenna
Thoracic
legs
Segment
Prolegs
Anal clasper

**EXTERNAL FEATURES
OF A BUTTERFLY**

Vein
Forewing
Apex

Costal
margin

Compound
eye

Antenna

Head

Proboscis

Front leg

Outer
margin

Thorax

Middle
leg

Femur

Tibia

Hind leg

Tarsus

Abdominal
segment

Abdomen

Hind wing

Spur

INTERNAL ANATOMY OF A FEMALE BUTTERFLY

Abdomen
Thorax
Head

Intestine
Copulatory bursa
Ovary
Crop
Dorsal blood
vessel
Oesophagus
Antenna

Colon
Heart
Cerebral
ganglion
(brain)

Rectum

Anus

Opening of oviduct
Proboscis

Opening of
copulatory bursa
Oviduct
Midgut
Salivary gland

Seminal
receptacle
Malpighian
tubule
Ventral nerve cord

Arachnids

THE CLASS ARACHNIDA INCLUDES SPIDERS (order Araneae) and scorpions (order Scorpiones). The class is part of the phylum Arthropoda, which also includes insects and crustaceans.

Spiders and scorpions are characterized by having four pairs of walking legs; a pair of pincer-like mouthparts called chelicerae; another pair of frontal appendages called pedipalps, which are sensory in spiders but used for grasping in scorpions; and a body divided into two sections (a combined head and thorax called a cephalothorax or prosoma, and an abdomen or opisthosoma). Unlike other arthropods, spiders and scorpions lack antennae. Spiders and scorpions are carnivorous. Spiders poison prey by biting with the fanged chelicerae, scorpions by stinging with the end of the metasoma (tail).

MEXICAN TRUE RED-LEGGED TARANTULA
(Euathlus emilia)

INTERNAL ANATOMY OF A FEMALE SPIDER

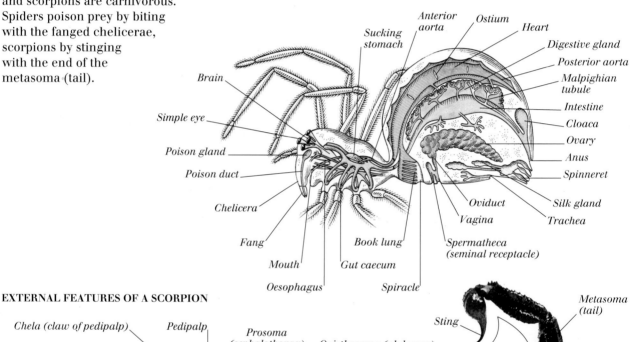

Anterior aorta
Ostium
Heart
Sucking stomach
Digestive gland
Posterior aorta
Malpighian tubule
Intestine
Cloaca
Ovary
Anus
Spinneret
Silk gland
Trachea
Oviduct
Vagina
Spermatheca (seminal receptacle)
Book lung
Gut caecum
Spiracle
Oesophagus
Mouth
Fang
Chelicera
Poison duct
Poison gland
Simple eye
Brain

EXTERNAL FEATURES OF A SCORPION

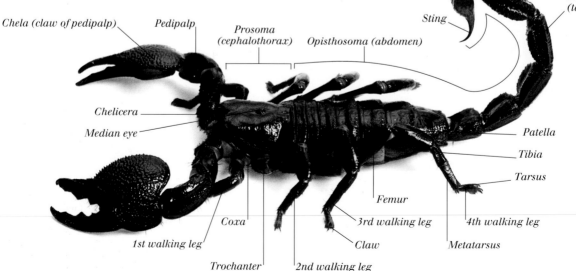

Chela (claw of pedipalp)
Pedipalp
Prosoma (cephalothorax)
Opisthosoma (abdomen)
Sting
Metasoma (tail)
Chelicera
Median eye
Patella
Tibia
Tarsus
Femur
Coxa
3rd walking leg
4th walking leg
1st walking leg
Claw
Metatarsus
Trochanter
2nd walking leg

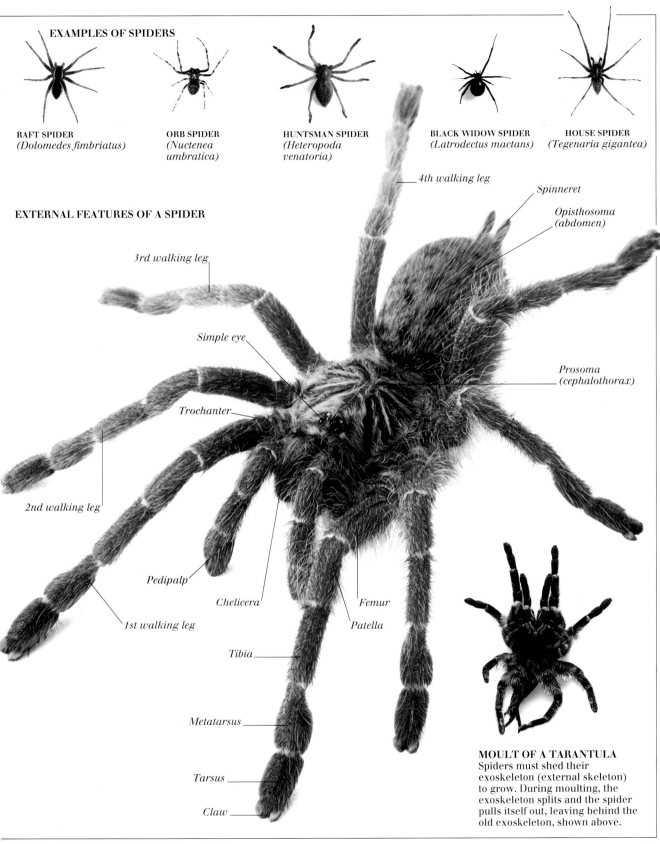

EXAMPLES OF SPIDERS

RAFT SPIDER
(*Dolomedes fimbriatus*)

ORB SPIDER
(*Nuctenea umbratica*)

HUNTSMAN SPIDER
(*Heteropoda venatoria*)

BLACK WIDOW SPIDER
(*Latrodectus mactans*)

HOUSE SPIDER
(*Tegenaria gigantea*)

EXTERNAL FEATURES OF A SPIDER

4th walking leg

Spinneret

Opisthosoma (abdomen)

3rd walking leg

Prosoma (cephalothorax)

Simple eye

Trochanter

2nd walking leg

Pedipalp

Chelicera

Femur

Patella

1st walking leg

Tibia

Metatarsus

Tarsus

Claw

MOULT OF A TARANTULA
Spiders must shed their exoskeleton (external skeleton) to grow. During moulting, the exoskeleton splits and the spider pulls itself out, leaving behind the old exoskeleton, shown above.

Crustaceans

THE SUBPHYLUM CRUSTACEA is one of the largest groups in the phylum Arthropoda. The subphylum is divided into several classes, the most important of which are Malacostraca and Cirripedia. The class Malacostraca includes crayfish, crabs, lobsters, and shrimps. Typical features of malacostracans include a body divided into two sections (a combined head and thorax called a cephalothorax, and an abdomen); an exoskeleton (external skeleton) with a large plate (carapace) covering the cephalothorax; stalked, compound eyes; and two pairs of antennae. The class Cirripedia includes barnacles, which, unlike other crustaceans, spend their adult lives attached to a surface, such as a rock. Other characteristics of cirripedes include an exoskeleton of overlapping calcareous plates; a body consisting almost entirely of thorax (the abdomen and head are minute); and six pairs of thoracic appendages (cirri) used for filter feeding.

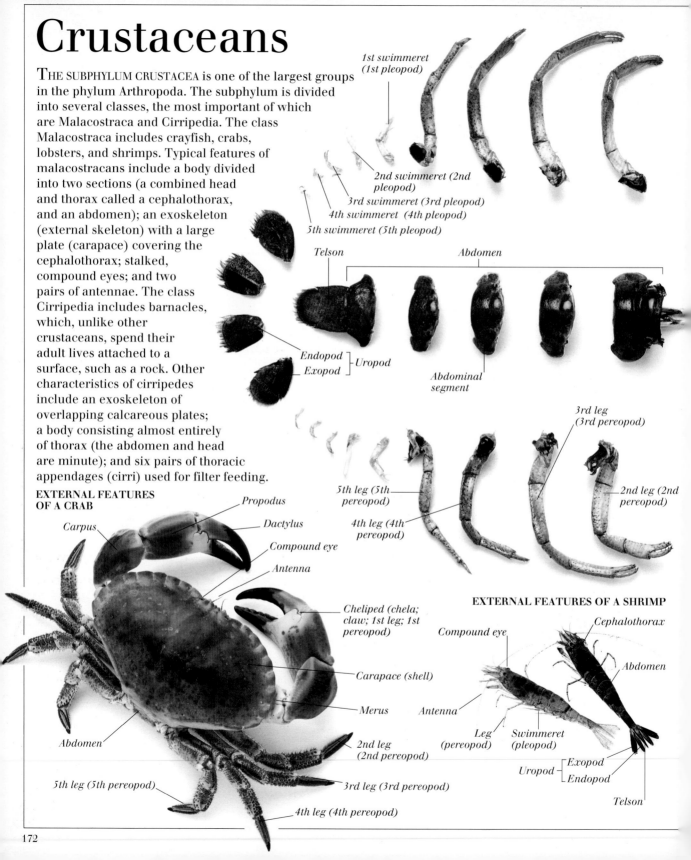

1st swimmeret (1st pleopod)

2nd swimmeret (2nd pleopod)

3rd swimmeret (3rd pleopod)

4th swimmeret (4th pleopod)

5th swimmeret (5th pleopod)

Telson

Abdomen

Endopod
Exopod — Uropod

Abdominal segment

3rd leg (3rd pereopod)

2nd leg (2nd pereopod)

5th leg (5th pereopod)

4th leg (4th pereopod)

EXTERNAL FEATURES OF A CRAB

Propodus

Carpus

Dactylus

Compound eye

Antenna

Cheliped (chela; claw; 1st leg; 1st pereopod)

Carapace (shell)

Merus

Abdomen

2nd leg (2nd pereopod)

5th leg (5th pereopod)

3rd leg (3rd pereopod)

4th leg (4th pereopod)

EXTERNAL FEATURES OF A SHRIMP

Compound eye

Cephalothorax

Abdomen

Antenna

Leg (pereopod)

Swimmeret (pleopod)

Uropod — Exopod
— Endopod

Telson

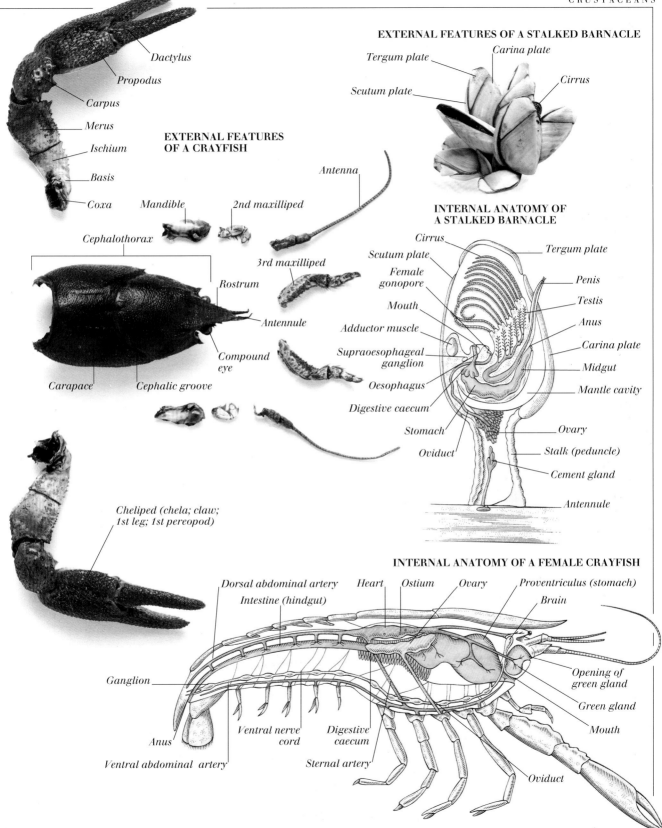

EXTERNAL FEATURES OF A STALKED BARNACLE

Tergum plate
Carina plate
Scutum plate
Cirrus

Dactylus
Propodus
Carpus
Merus
Ischium
Basis
Coxa

**EXTERNAL FEATURES
OF A CRAYFISH**

Mandible
2nd maxilliped
Antenna

Cephalothorax
Rostrum
3rd maxilliped
Antennule
Compound eye
Carapace
Cephalic groove

**INTERNAL ANATOMY OF
A STALKED BARNACLE**

Cirrus
Scutum plate
Female gonopore
Mouth
Adductor muscle
Supraoesophageal ganglion
Oesophagus
Digestive caecum
Stomach
Oviduct

Tergum plate
Penis
Testis
Anus
Carina plate
Midgut
Mantle cavity
Ovary
Stalk (peduncle)
Cement gland
Antennule

*Cheliped (chela; claw;
1st leg; 1st pereopod)*

INTERNAL ANATOMY OF A FEMALE CRAYFISH

Dorsal abdominal artery
Heart
Ostium
Ovary
Proventriculus (stomach)
Intestine (hindgut)
Brain
Ganglion
Opening of green gland
Green gland
Anus
Ventral nerve cord
Digestive caecum
Mouth
Ventral abdominal artery
Sternal artery
Oviduct

173

Starfish and sea urchins

STARFISH, SEA URCHINS, AND THEIR relatives (including feather stars, brittle stars, basket stars, sea daisies, sea lilies, and sea cucumbers) make up the phylum Echinodermata. A unique feature of echinoderms is the water vascular system, which consists of a series of water-filled canals from which protrude thousands of tiny tube feet. The tube feet may be used for movement, feeding, or respiration. Other features include pentaradiate symmetry (that is, the body can be divided into five parts radiating from the centre); no head; a diffuse, decentralized nervous system that lacks a brain; and no excretory organs. Typically, echinoderms also have an endoskeleton (internal skeleton) consisting of hard calcite ossicles embedded in the body wall and often bearing protruding spines or tubercles. The ossicles may fit together to form a test (as in sea urchins) or remain separate (as in sea cucumbers).

EXTERNAL FEATURES OF A STARFISH (UPPER, OR ABORAL, SURFACE)

Disc

Madreporite

Spine

Arm

INTERNAL ANATOMY OF A STARFISH

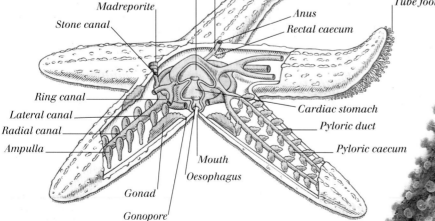

Rectum

Pyloric stomach

Madreporite

Stone canal

Anus

Rectal caecum

Tube foot

Ring canal

Lateral canal

Radial canal

Ampulla

Cardiac stomach

Pyloric duct

Pyloric caecum

Mouth

Oesophagus

Gonad

Gonopore

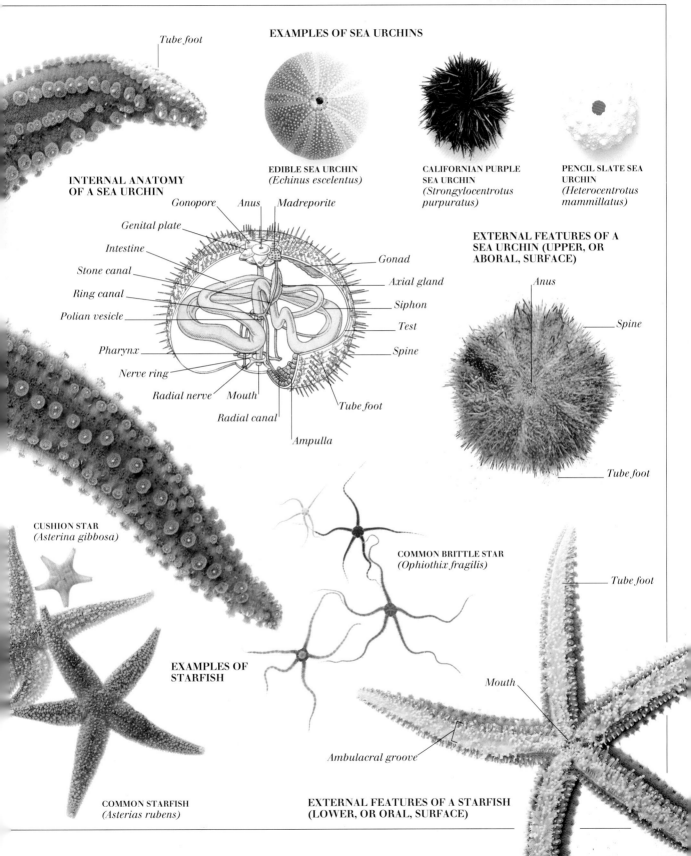

Tube foot

EXAMPLES OF SEA URCHINS

EDIBLE SEA URCHIN
(*Echinus escelentus*)

CALIFORNIAN PURPLE SEA URCHIN
(*Strongylocentrotus purpuratus*)

PENCIL SLATE SEA URCHIN
(*Heterocentrotus mammillatus*)

INTERNAL ANATOMY OF A SEA URCHIN

Gonopore
Anus
Madreporite
Genital plate
Intestine
Stone canal
Ring canal
Polian vesicle
Pharynx
Nerve ring
Radial nerve
Mouth
Radial canal
Ampulla
Gonad
Axial gland
Siphon
Test
Spine
Tube foot

EXTERNAL FEATURES OF A SEA URCHIN (UPPER, OR ABORAL, SURFACE)

Anus
Spine
Tube foot

CUSHION STAR
(*Asterina gibbosa*)

COMMON BRITTLE STAR
(*Ophiothix fragilis*)

EXAMPLES OF STARFISH

Tube foot

Mouth

Ambulacral groove

COMMON STARFISH
(*Asterias rubens*)

EXTERNAL FEATURES OF A STARFISH (LOWER, OR ORAL, SURFACE)

Molluscs

THE PHYLUM MOLLUSCA (MOLLUSCS) is a large group of animals that includes octopuses, snails, and scallops. Octopuses and their relatives —including squid and cuttlefish—form the class Cephalopoda. Cephalopods typically have a head with a radula (a file-like feeding organ) and beak; a well-developed nervous system; sucker-bearing tentacles; a muscular mantle (part of the body wall) that can expel water through the siphon, enabling movement by jet propulsion; and a small shell or no shell. Snails and their relatives—including slugs, limpets, and abalones—make up the class Gastropoda. Gastropods typically have a coiled external shell, although some, such as slugs, have a small internal shell or no shell; a flat foot; and a head with tentacles and a radula. Scallops and their relatives—including clams, mussels, and oysters—make up the class Bivalvia (also called Pelecypoda). Features of bivalves include a shell with two halves (valves); large gills that are used for breathing and filter feeding; and no radula.

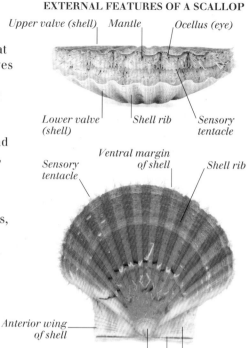

EXTERNAL FEATURES OF A SCALLOP

Upper valve (shell) Mantle Ocellus (eye)

Lower valve (shell) Shell rib Sensory tentacle

Sensory tentacle Ventral margin of shell Shell rib

Anterior wing of shell Umbo Posterior wing of shell

Dorsal margin of shell

INTERNAL ANATOMY OF AN OCTOPUS

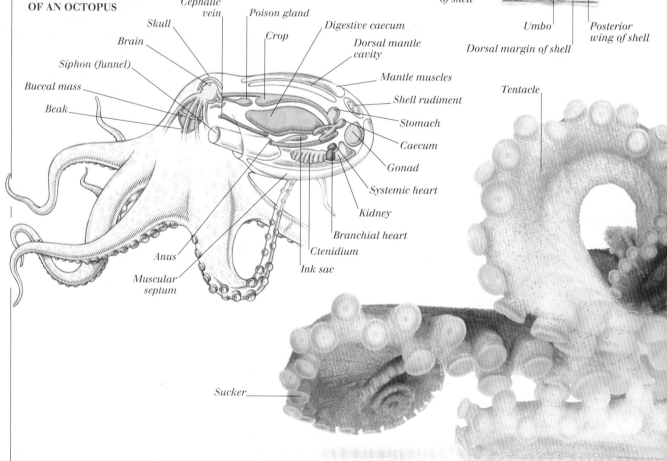

Cephalic vein
Skull
Poison gland
Crop
Digestive caecum
Brain
Dorsal mantle cavity
Siphon (funnel)
Mantle muscles
Buccal mass
Shell rudiment
Beak
Stomach
Caecum
Gonad
Systemic heart
Kidney
Branchial heart
Anus
Ctenidium
Muscular septum
Ink sac
Sucker
Tentacle

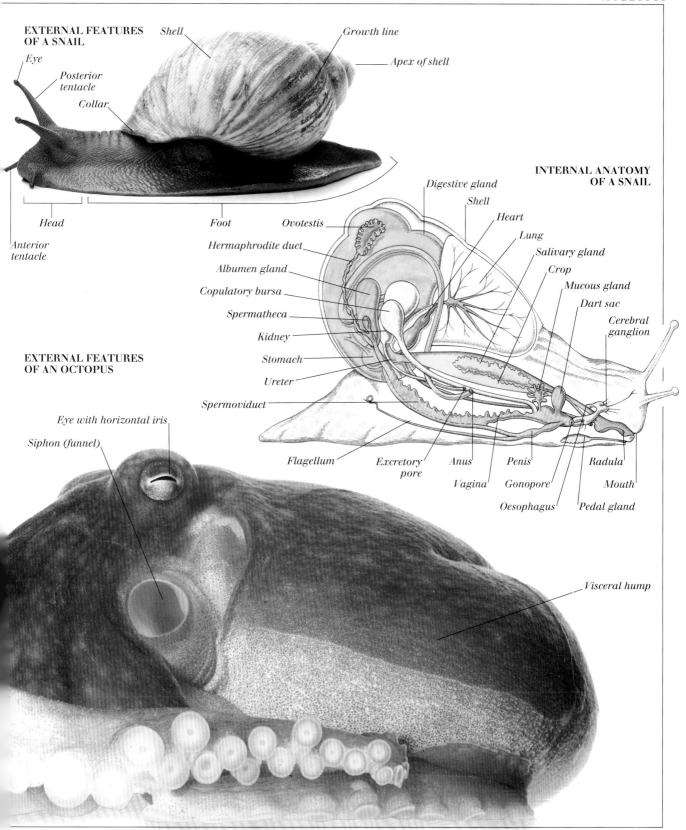

**EXTERNAL FEATURES
OF A SNAIL**

Eye

Posterior
tentacle

Collar

Shell

Growth line

Apex of shell

Head

Foot

Anterior
tentacle

**INTERNAL ANATOMY
OF A SNAIL**

Digestive gland

Shell

Heart

Lung

Salivary gland

Crop

Mucous gland

Dart sac

Cerebral
ganglion

Ovotestis

Hermaphrodite duct

Albumen gland

Copulatory bursa

Spermatheca

Kidney

Stomach

Ureter

Spermoviduct

Flagellum

Excretory
pore

Anus

Vagina

Penis

Gonopore

Oesophagus

Radula

Mouth

Pedal gland

**EXTERNAL FEATURES
OF AN OCTOPUS**

Eye with horizontal iris

Siphon (funnel)

Visceral hump

177

Sharks and jawless fish

SHARKS, DOGFISH (WHICH ARE actually small sharks), skates, and rays belong to a class of fishes called Chondrichthyes, which is a division of the superclass Gnathostomata (meaning "jawed mouths"). Also sometimes known as elasmobranchs, sharks and their relatives have a skeleton made of cartilage (hence their common name, cartilaginous fish), a characteristic that distinguishes them from bony fish (see pp. 180-181). Other important features of cartilaginous fish are extremely tough, tooth-like scales, and lack of a swim bladder. Jawless fish—lampreys and hagfish—are primitive, eel-like fish that make up the order Cyclostomata (meaning "round mouths"), a division of the superclass Agnatha (meaning "without jaws"). In addition to their characteristic round, sucker-like mouths and lack of jaws, cyclostomes also have smooth, slimy skin without scales, and unpaired fins.

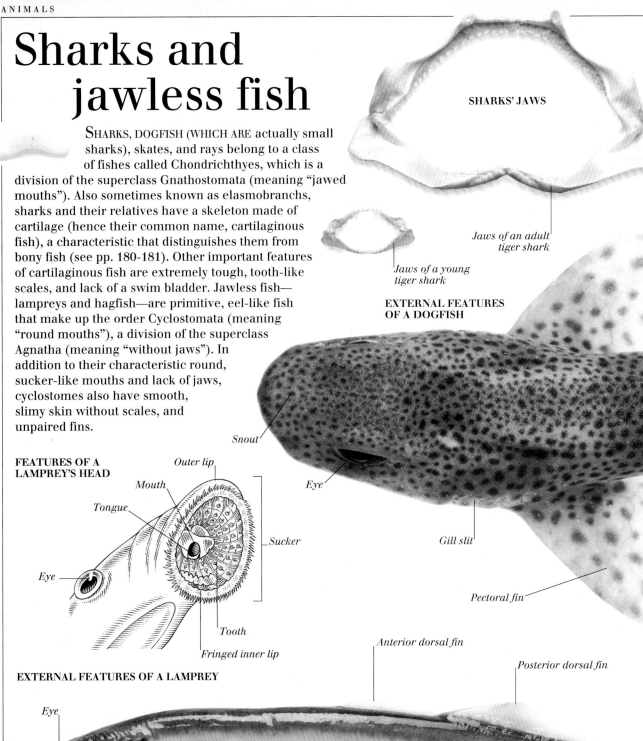

SHARKS' JAWS

Jaws of an adult tiger shark

Jaws of a young tiger shark

EXTERNAL FEATURES OF A DOGFISH

Snout

Eye

Gill slit

Pectoral fin

Anterior dorsal fin

Posterior dorsal fin

FEATURES OF A LAMPREY'S HEAD

Outer lip

Mouth

Tongue

Sucker

Eye

Tooth

Fringed inner lip

EXTERNAL FEATURES OF A LAMPREY

Eye

Gill opening

Anal fin

Caudal fin

Sucker

EXAMPLES OF CARTILAGINOUS FISH

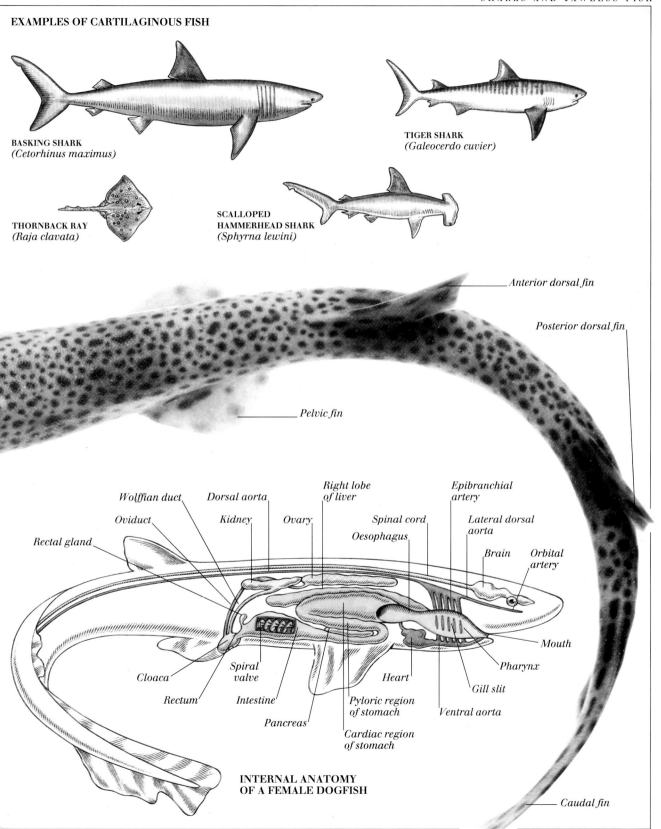

BASKING SHARK
(*Cetorhinus maximus*)

TIGER SHARK
(*Galeocerdo cuvier*)

THORNBACK RAY
(*Raja clavata*)

**SCALLOPED
HAMMERHEAD SHARK**
(*Sphyrna lewini*)

Anterior dorsal fin

Posterior dorsal fin

Pelvic fin

Wolffian duct

Dorsal aorta

Right lobe
of liver

Epibranchial
artery

Oviduct

Kidney

Ovary

Spinal cord

Lateral dorsal
aorta

Rectal gland

Oesophagus

Brain

Orbital
artery

Mouth

Cloaca

Spiral
valve

Pharynx

Rectum

Intestine

Heart

Gill slit

Pancreas

Pyloric region
of stomach

Ventral aorta

Cardiac region
of stomach

**INTERNAL ANATOMY
OF A FEMALE DOGFISH**

Caudal fin

Bony fish

BONY FISH, SUCH AS CARP, TROUT, SALMON, perch, and cod, are by far the best known and largest group of fish, with more than 20,000 species (over 95 per cent of all known fish). As their name suggests, bony fish have skeletons made of bone, in contrast to the cartilaginous skeletons of sharks, jawless fish, and their relatives (see pp. 178-179). Other typical features of bony fish include a swim bladder, which functions as a variable-buoyancy organ, enabling a fish to remain effortlessly at whatever depth it is swimming; relatively thin, bone-like scales; a flap (called an operculum) covering the gills; and paired pelvic and pectoral fins. Scientifically, bony fish belong to the class Osteichthyes, which is a division of the superclass Gnathostomata (meaning "jawed mouths").

HOW FISH BREATHE

Fish "breathe" by extracting oxygen from water through their gills. Water is sucked in through the mouth; simultaneously, the opercula close to prevent the water from escaping. The mouth is then closed, and muscles in the walls of the mouth, pharynx, and opercular cavity contract to pump the water inside over the gills and out through the opercula. Some fish rely on swimming with their mouths open to keep water flowing over the gills.

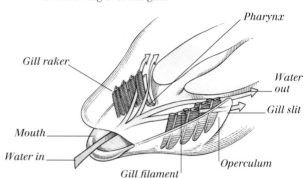

Gill raker
Pharynx
Water out
Gill slit
Mouth
Water in
Gill filament
Operculum

EXAMPLES OF BONY FISH

MANDARINFISH
(Synchiropus splendidus)

ANGLERFISH
(Caulophryne jordani)

LIONFISH
(Pterois volitans)

OCEANIC SEAHORSE
(Hippocampus kuda)

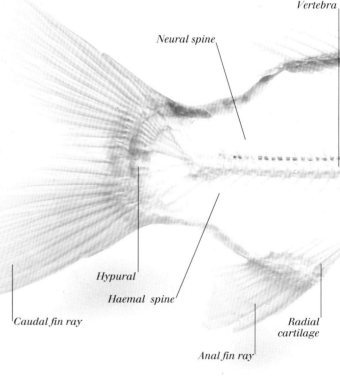

Vertebra
Neural spine
Hypural
Haemal spine
Caudal fin ray
Anal fin ray
Radial cartilage

STURGEON
(Acipenser sturio)

SNOWFLAKE MORAY EEL
(Echidna nebulosa)

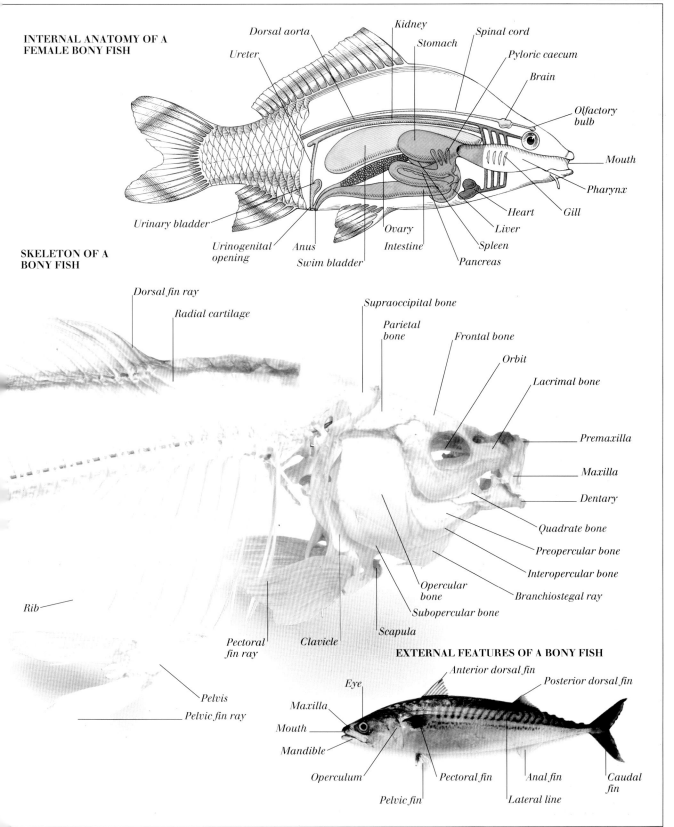

INTERNAL ANATOMY OF A FEMALE BONY FISH

Dorsal aorta

Ureter

Kidney

Stomach

Spinal cord

Pyloric caecum

Brain

Olfactory bulb

Mouth

Pharynx

Gill

Heart

Liver

Spleen

Pancreas

Intestine

Swim bladder

Ovary

Anus

Urinogenital opening

Urinary bladder

SKELETON OF A BONY FISH

Dorsal fin ray

Radial cartilage

Supraoccipital bone

Parietal bone

Frontal bone

Orbit

Lacrimal bone

Premaxilla

Maxilla

Dentary

Quadrate bone

Preopercular bone

Interopercular bone

Branchiostegal ray

Opercular bone

Subopercular bone

Scapula

Clavicle

Pectoral fin ray

Rib

Pelvis

Pelvic fin ray

EXTERNAL FEATURES OF A BONY FISH

Anterior dorsal fin

Posterior dorsal fin

Eye

Maxilla

Mouth

Mandible

Operculum

Pelvic fin

Pectoral fin

Anal fin

Lateral line

Caudal fin

181

Amphibians

THE CLASS AMPHIBIA INCLUDES FROGS and toads (which make up the order Anura), and newts and salamanders (which make up the order Urodela). Amphibians typically have moist, scaleless, hairless skin; lungs; and are cold-blooded. They also undergo complete metamorphosis, from eggs laid in water through various water-living larval stages (such as tadpoles) to land-living adults. Typical features of adult frogs and toads include a squat body with no tail; long, powerful hind legs; and large, often bulging, eyes. Adult newts and salamanders typically have a long body with a well-developed tail; and relatively short, equal-sized legs. However, newts and salamanders show considerable variation; for example, in some species the adults have minute legs, external gills rather than lungs, and spend their entire lives in water.

INTERNAL ANATOMY OF A FEMALE FROG

Larynx
Right bronchus
Stomach
Pulmonary artery
Right lung
Left lung
Heart
Pancreas
Liver
Duodenum
Posterior vena cava
Spleen
Right kidney
Left kidney
Dorsal aorta
Mesentery
Cloaca
Small intestine (ileum)
Rectum
Left ureter

EXTERNAL FEATURES OF A FROG

Hind limb
Trunk
Head
Forelimb
External nostril
5 digits
Mouth
Tympanum (eardrum)
Eye
Web
4 digits

EXTERNAL FEATURES OF A SALAMANDER

Eye
Tail
Forelimb
Hind limb
Digit

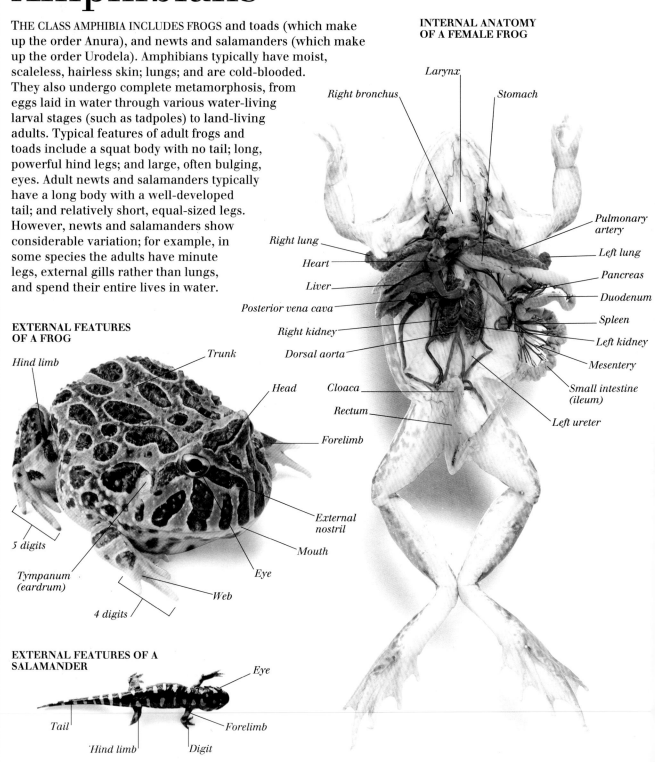

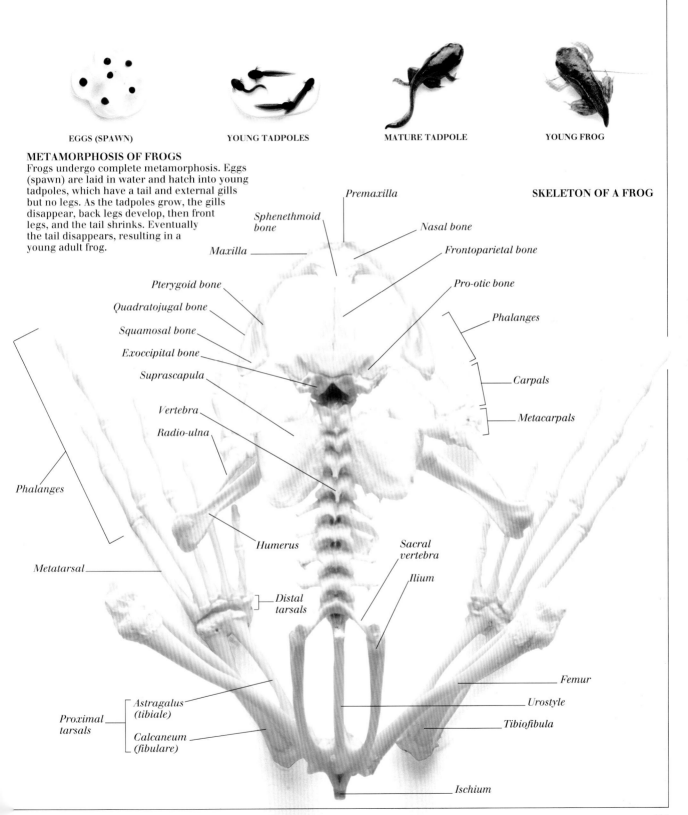

EGGS (SPAWN) YOUNG TADPOLES MATURE TADPOLE YOUNG FROG

METAMORPHOSIS OF FROGS
Frogs undergo complete metamorphosis. Eggs (spawn) are laid in water and hatch into young tadpoles, which have a tail and external gills but no legs. As the tadpoles grow, the gills disappear, back legs develop, then front legs, and the tail shrinks. Eventually the tail disappears, resulting in a young adult frog.

SKELETON OF A FROG

Premaxilla

Sphenethmoid bone

Nasal bone

Maxilla

Frontoparietal bone

Pterygoid bone

Pro-otic bone

Quadratojugal bone

Phalanges

Squamosal bone

Exoccipital bone

Suprascapula

Carpals

Vertebra

Metacarpals

Radio-ulna

Phalanges

Humerus

Metatarsal

Sacral vertebra

Ilium

Distal tarsals

Proximal tarsals

Astragalus (tibiale)

Calcaneum (fibulare)

Femur

Urostyle

Tibiofibula

Ischium

Lizards and snakes

LIZARDS AND SNAKES BELONG to the order Squamata, a division of the class Reptilia. Characteristic reptilian features include scaly skin, lungs, and cold-bloodedness. Most reptiles lay leathery-shelled eggs, although some hatch the eggs inside their bodies and give birth to live young. Lizards belong to the suborder Lacertilia. Typically, they have long tails, and shed their skin in several pieces. Many lizards can regenerate a tail if it is lost; some can change colour; and some are limbless. Snakes make up the suborder Ophidia (also called Serpentes). All snakes have long, limbless bodies; can dislocate their lower jaw to swallow large prey; and have eyelids that are joined together to form a single transparent covering over the front of the eye. Most snakes shed their skin in a single piece. Constrictor snakes kill their prey by squeezing; venomous snakes poison their prey.

EXAMPLES OF SNAKES

MEXICAN MOUNTAIN KING SNAKE *(Lampropeltis triangulum annulata)*

EXTERNAL FEATURES OF A LIZARD

Eye

Mouth

BANDED MILK SNAKE *(Lampropeltis ruthveni)*

Crest

Eardrum

Masseteric scale

Dorsal scale

External nostril

Dewlap

Foreleg

Belly

Ventral scale

SKELETON OF A LIZARD

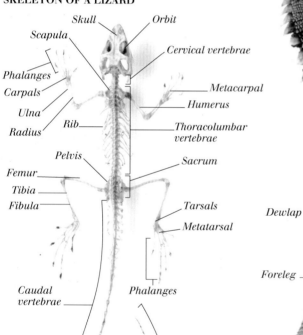

Skull

Orbit

Scapula

Cervical vertebrae

Phalanges

Carpals

Metacarpal

Ulna

Humerus

Radius

Rib

Thoracolumbar vertebrae

Pelvis

Femur

Sacrum

Tibia

Fibula

Tarsals

Metatarsal

Caudal vertebrae

Phalanges

Toe

Claw

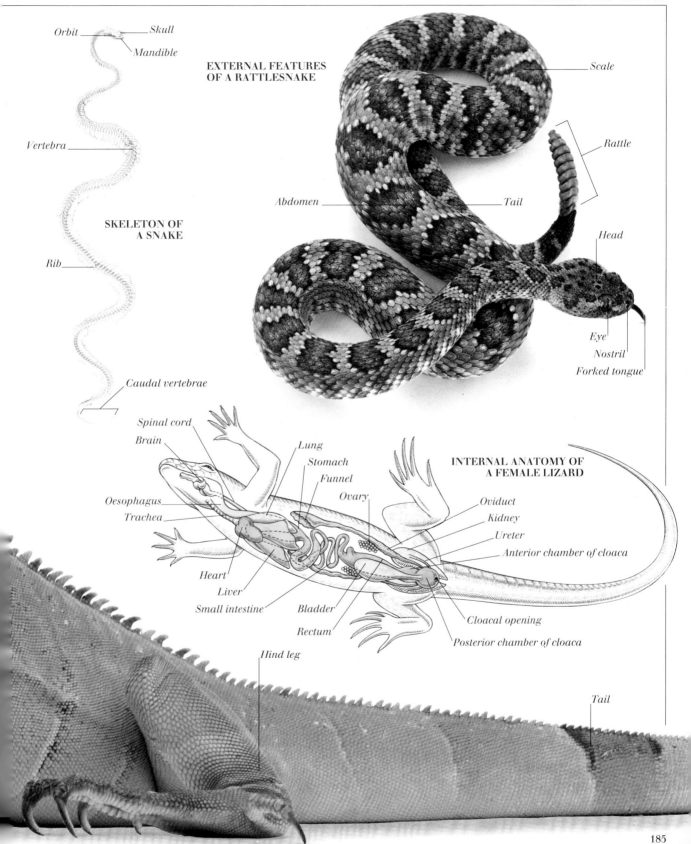

Orbit

Skull

Mandible

**EXTERNAL FEATURES
OF A RATTLESNAKE**

Scale

Vertebra

Rattle

**SKELETON OF
A SNAKE**

Abdomen

Tail

Rib

Head

Eye

Nostril

Forked tongue

Caudal vertebrae

Spinal cord

Brain

Lung

Stomach

Funnel

**INTERNAL ANATOMY OF
A FEMALE LIZARD**

Ovary

Oesophagus

Trachea

Oviduct

Kidney

Ureter

Anterior chamber of cloaca

Heart

Liver

Small intestine

Bladder

Rectum

Cloacal opening

Posterior chamber of cloaca

Hind leg

Tail

185

Crocodilians and turtles

GHARIAL
(Gavialis gangeticus)

NILE CROCODILE
(Crocodylus niloticus)

AMERICAN ALLIGATOR
(Alligator mississippiensis)

CROCODILIANS AND TURTLES BELONG to different orders in the class Reptilia. The order Crocodilia includes crocodiles, alligators, caimans, and gharials. Typically, crocodilians are carnivores (flesh-eaters), and have a long snout, sharp teeth for gripping prey, and hard, square scales. All crocodilians are adapted to living on land and in water: they have four strong legs for moving on land; a powerful tail for swimming; and their eyes and nostrils are high on the head so that they stay above water while the rest of the body is submerged. The order Chelonia includes marine turtles, terrapins (freshwater turtles), and tortoises (land turtles). Characteristically, chelonians have a short, broad body encased in a bony shell with an outer horny covering, into which the head and limbs can be withdrawn; and a horny beak instead of teeth.

SKELETON OF A CROCODILE

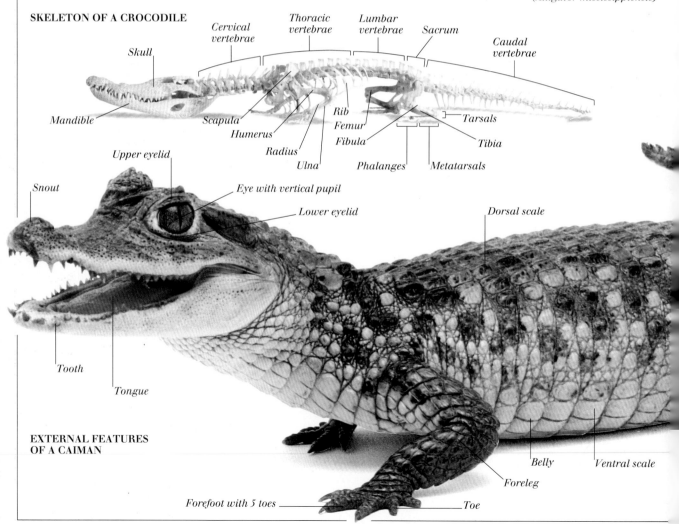

EXTERNAL FEATURES OF A CAIMAN

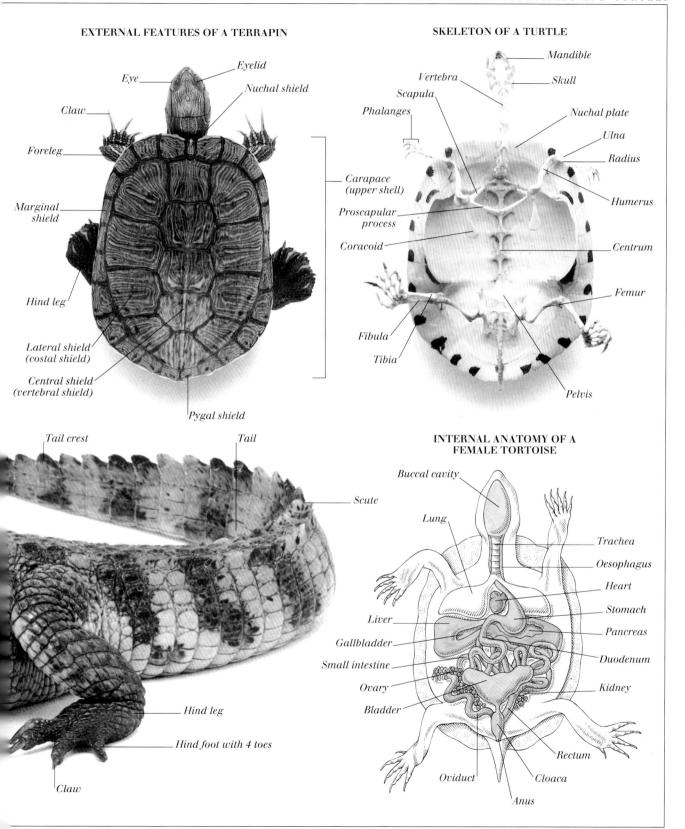

EXTERNAL FEATURES OF A TERRAPIN

Eye

Eyelid

Nuchal shield

Claw

Foreleg

Carapace
(upper shell)

Marginal
shield

Hind leg

Lateral shield
(costal shield)

Central shield
(vertebral shield)

Pygal shield

Tail crest

Tail

Scute

Hind leg

Hind foot with 4 toes

Claw

SKELETON OF A TURTLE

Mandible

Vertebra

Skull

Scapula

Phalanges

Nuchal plate

Ulna

Radius

Humerus

Proscapular
process

Coracoid

Centrum

Femur

Fibula

Tibia

Pelvis

**INTERNAL ANATOMY OF A
FEMALE TORTOISE**

Buccal cavity

Lung

Trachea

Oesophagus

Heart

Stomach

Pancreas

Liver

Duodenum

Gallbladder

Small intestine

Kidney

Ovary

Bladder

Rectum

Oviduct

Cloaca

Anus

Birds 1

Birds make up the class Aves. There are more than 9,000 species, almost all of which can fly (the only flightless birds are penguins, ostriches, rheas, cassowaries, and kiwis). The ability to fly is reflected in the typical bird features: forelimbs modified as wings; a streamlined body; and hollow bones to reduce weight. All birds lay hard-shelled eggs, which the parents incubate. Birds' beaks and feet vary according to diet and way of life. Beaks range from general-purpose types suitable for a mixed diet (those of thrushes, for example), to types specialized for particular foods (such as the large, curved, sieving beaks of flamingos). Feet range from the webbed "paddles" of ducks, to the talons of birds of prey. Plumage also varies widely, and in many species the male is brightly coloured for courtship display whereas the female is drab.

EXTERNAL FEATURES OF A BIRD

Forehead

Eye

Crown

Nostril

Nape

Upper mandible

Beak

Lower mandible

Chin

Throat

Breast

EXAMPLES OF BIRDS

Minor coverts

Lesser wing coverts

Median wing coverts

MALE TUFTED DUCK
(*Aythya fuligula*)

Greater wing coverts
(major coverts)

Secondary flight feathers
(secondary remiges)

Belly

Flank

Primary flight feathers
(primaryremiges)

Thigh

WHITE STORK
(*Ciconia ciconia*)

Under tail
coverts

Claw

Tarsus

Toe

Tail feathers (retrices)

MALE OSTRICH
(*Struthio camelus*)

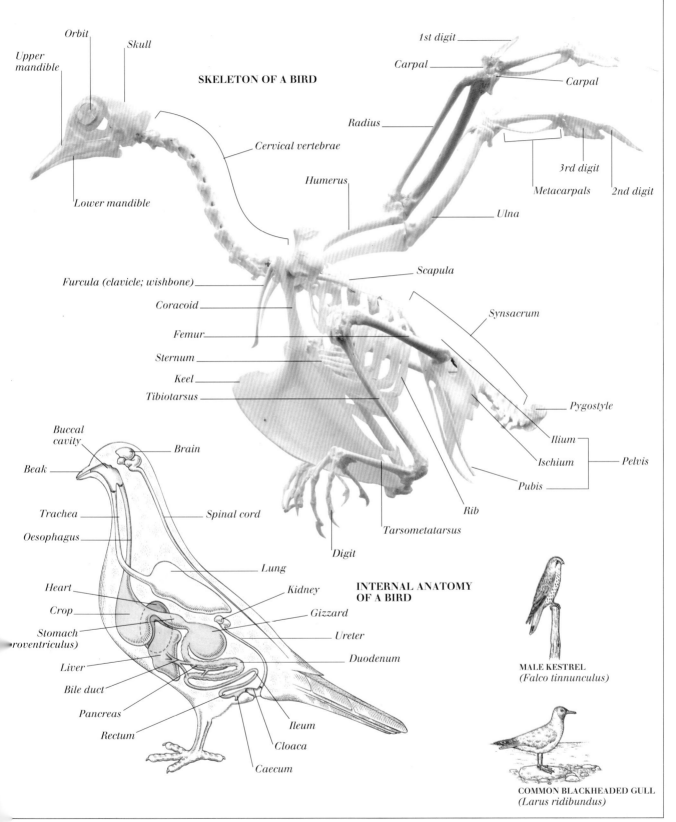

Orbit

Upper mandible

Skull

1st digit

Carpal

Carpal

SKELETON OF A BIRD

Radius

Cervical vertebrae

3rd digit

Humerus

Metacarpals

2nd digit

Lower mandible

Ulna

Furcula (clavicle; wishbone)

Scapula

Coracoid

Synsacrum

Femur

Sternum

Keel

Tibiotarsus

Pygostyle

Ilium

Ischium

Pelvis

Pubis

Buccal cavity

Brain

Beak

Trachea

Spinal cord

Oesophagus

Heart

Kidney

Rib

Crop

Gizzard

Tarsometatarsus

Stomach (proventriculus)

Ureter

Digit

Liver

Duodenum

Lung

Bile duct

INTERNAL ANATOMY OF A BIRD

Pancreas

Rectum

Ileum

Cloaca

Caecum

MALE KESTREL
(*Falco tinnunculus*)

COMMON BLACKHEADED GULL
(*Larus ridibundus*)

Birds 2

EXAMPLES OF BIRDS' FEET

KITTIWAKE
(Rissa tridactyla)
The webbed feet are
adapted for paddling
through water.

LITTLE GREBE
(Tachybaptus ruficollis)
The lobed, flattened feet
are adapted for swimming
underwater.

TAWNY OWL
(Strix aluco)
The clawed feet are adapted
for gripping prey.

EXAMPLES OF BIRDS' BEAKS

KING VULTURE
(Sarcorhamphus papa)
The hooked beak is adapted
for pulling apart flesh.

GREATER FLAMINGO
(Phoenicopterus ruber)
In the living bird, the large,
curved beak contains a
cartilaginous "sieve" for
filtering food particles
from water.

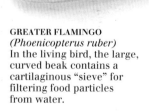

MISTLE THRUSH
(Turdus viscivorus)
The general-purpose beak is
suitable for a wide range of animal
and plant foods.

BLUE-AND-YELLOW MACAW
(Ara ararauna)
The broad, powerful, hooked beak
is adapted for crushing seeds and
eating fruit.

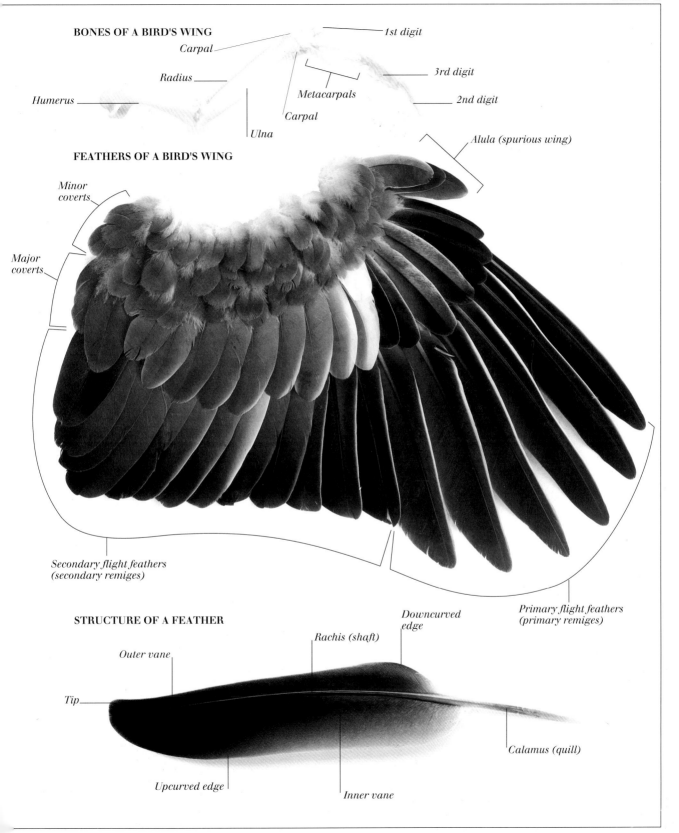

BONES OF A BIRD'S WING

1st digit

Carpal

Radius

3rd digit

Humerus

Metacarpals

2nd digit

Carpal

Ulna

Alula (spurious wing)

FEATHERS OF A BIRD'S WING

Minor coverts

Major coverts

Secondary flight feathers
(secondary remiges)

Downcurved edge

Primary flight feathers
(primary remiges)

STRUCTURE OF A FEATHER

Rachis (shaft)

Outer vane

Tip

Calamus (quill)

Upcurved edge

Inner vane

Eggs

AN EGG IS A SINGLE CELL, produced by the female, with the capacity to develop into a new individual. Development may take place inside the mother's body (as in most mammals) or outside, in which case the egg has a protective covering such as a shell. Egg yolk nourishes the growing young. Eggs developing inside the mother generally have little yolk, because the young are nourished from her body. Eggs developing outside may also have little yolk if they are produced by animals whose young go through a larval stage (such as a caterpillar) that feeds itself while developing into the adult form. The shelled eggs of birds and reptiles contain enough yolk to sustain the young until it hatches into a juvenile version of the adult.

SECTION THROUGH A CHICKEN'S EGG

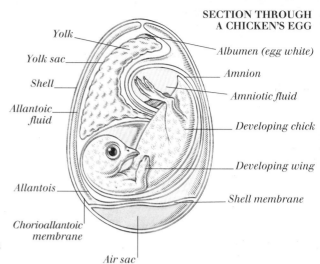

Yolk

Yolk sac

Shell

Allantoic fluid

Allantois

Chorioallantoic membrane

Air sac

Albumen (egg white)

Amnion

Amniotic fluid

Developing chick

Developing wing

Shell membrane

VARIETY OF EGGS

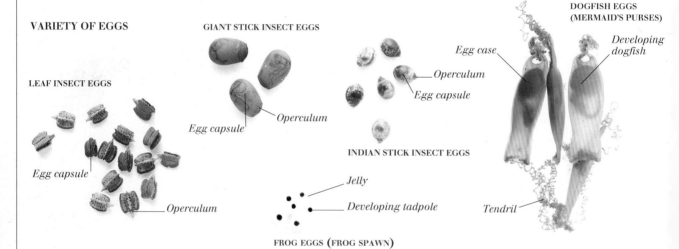

LEAF INSECT EGGS

Egg capsule

Operculum

GIANT STICK INSECT EGGS

Egg capsule

Operculum

INDIAN STICK INSECT EGGS

Operculum

Egg capsule

FROG EGGS (FROG SPAWN)

Jelly

Developing tadpole

DOGFISH EGGS (MERMAID'S PURSES)

Egg case

Developing dogfish

Tendril

HATCHING OF A QUAIL'S EGG

EGG AT THE POINT OF HATCHING

Rounded end of egg

Shell

Pointed end of egg

Shell membrane

Camouflage coloration

Crack caused by chick pecking through the shell

CUTTING THROUGH THE EGG

Chick

Shell

Crack extended by further pecking by the chick

BREAKING OUT OF THE EGG

Chick pushes off the top of the shell

Shell membrane

Shell

Eye

Beak

Egg-tooth

Crack runs completely around the shell

EXAMPLES OF BIRDS' EGGS

BEE HUMMINGBIRD
(Calypte helenae)

GREATER BLACKBACKED GULL
(Larus marinus)

BALTIMORE ORIOLE
(Icterus galbula)

WILLOW GROUSE
(Lagopus lagopus)

COMMON TERN
(Sterna hirundo)

CARRION CROW
(Corvus corone)

CHAFFINCH
(Fringilla coelebs)

OSTRICH
(Struthio camelus)

EMERGING FROM THE EGG

Eye

Beak

Egg-tooth

Chick heaves itself out of the egg

Tympanum (eardrum)

Shell

Wet down

Remains of egg membranes (amnion and allantois)

THE NEWLY HATCHED CHICK

Eye

Beak

Egg-tooth

Nostril

Tympanum (eardrum)

Chick is dry about an hour after hatching

Dry down

Toe

Claw

Leg

Eggshell

Carnivores

THE MAMMALIAN ORDER CARNIVORA includes cats, dogs, bears, raccoons, pandas, weasels, badgers, skunks, otters, civets, mongooses, and hyenas. The order's name is derived from the fact that most of its members are carnivores (flesh-eaters). Typical carnivore features therefore reflect a hunting life-style: speed and agility; sharp claws and well-developed canine teeth for holding and killing prey; carnassial teeth (cheek teeth) for cutting flesh; and forward-facing eyes for good distance judgment. However, some members of the order—bears, badgers, and foxes, for example—have a more mixed diet, and a few are entirely herbivorous (plant-eating), notably pandas. Such animals have no carnassial teeth and tend to be slower-moving than pure flesh-eaters.

EXTERNAL FEATURES OF A MALE LION

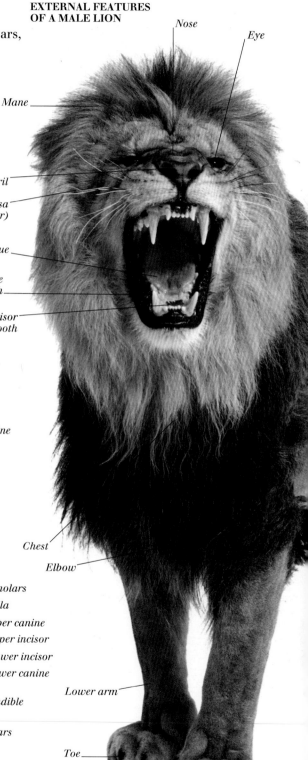

Nose
Eye
Mane
Nostril
Vibrissa (whisker)
Tongue
Canine tooth
Incisor tooth
Chest
Elbow
Lower arm
Toe

SKULL OF A LION

Zygomatic arch
Coronoid process
Sagittal crest
Orbit
Nasal bone
Maxilla
Upper premolars
Upper canine
Lower canine
Mandible
Lower premolars
Occipital condyle
Tympanic bulla
Condyle
Angular process
Upper carnassial tooth (4th upper premolar)

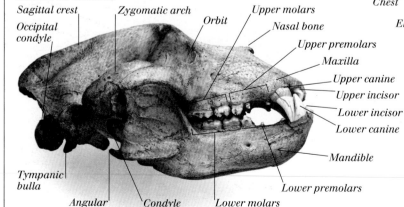

SKULL OF A BEAR

Sagittal crest
Occipital condyle
Zygomatic arch
Orbit
Upper molars
Nasal bone
Upper premolars
Maxilla
Upper canine
Upper incisor
Lower incisor
Lower canine
Mandible
Lower arm
Tympanic bulla
Angular process
Condyle
Lower molars
Lower premolars

EXAMPLES OF CARNIVORES

ALSATIAN DOG
(Canis familiaris)

MANED WOLF
(Chrysocyon brachyurus)

RACCOON
(Procyon lotor)

AMERICAN BLACK BEAR
(Ursus americanus)

SKELETON OF A DOMESTIC CAT

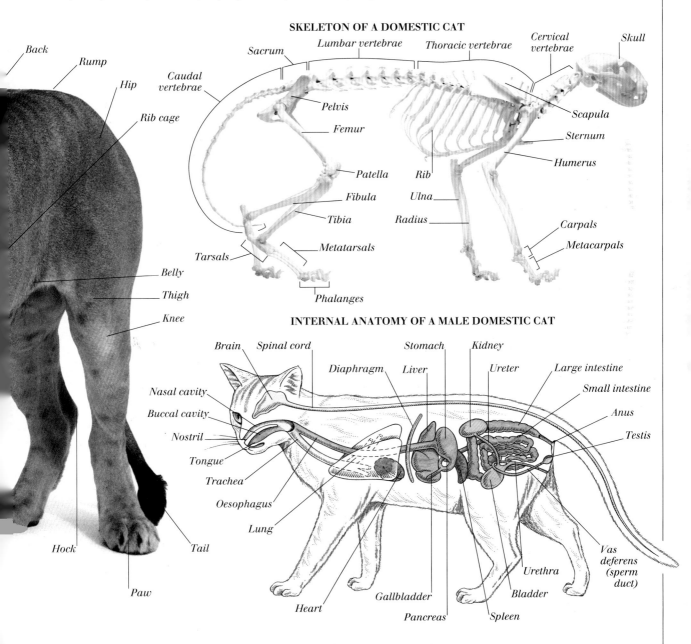

Back

Rump

Hip

Rib cage

Sacrum

Lumbar vertebrae

Thoracic vertebrae

Cervical vertebrae

Skull

Caudal vertebrae

Pelvis

Scapula

Femur

Sternum

Humerus

Patella

Rib

Fibula

Ulna

Tibia

Radius

Carpals

Metacarpals

Tarsals

Metatarsals

Belly

Thigh

Knee

Phalanges

INTERNAL ANATOMY OF A MALE DOMESTIC CAT

Brain

Spinal cord

Stomach

Kidney

Diaphragm

Liver

Ureter

Large intestine

Nasal cavity

Small intestine

Buccal cavity

Anus

Nostril

Testis

Tongue

Trachea

Oesophagus

Lung

Vas deferens (sperm duct)

Hock

Tail

Urethra

Bladder

Paw

Heart

Gallbladder

Spleen

Pancreas

Rabbits and rodents

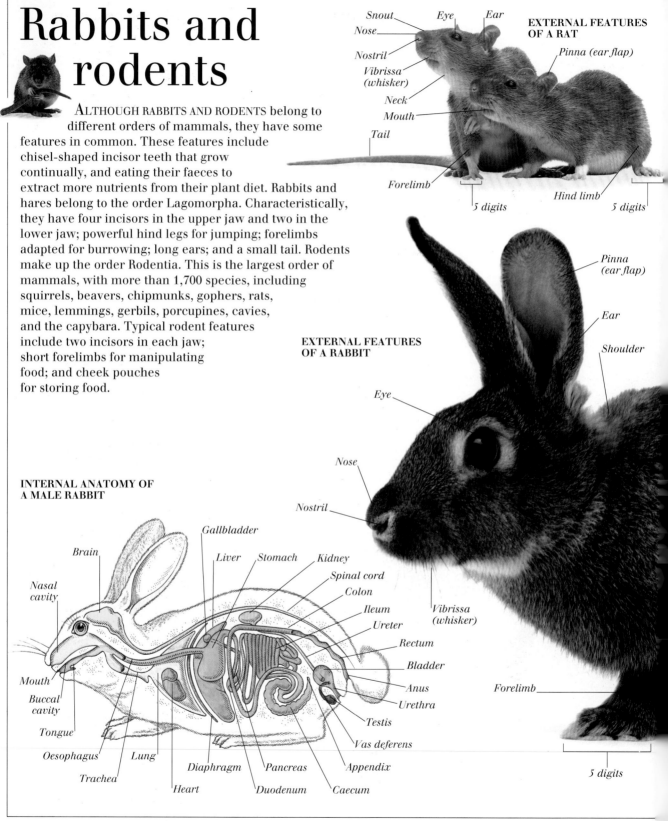

ALTHOUGH RABBITS AND RODENTS belong to different orders of mammals, they have some features in common. These features include chisel-shaped incisor teeth that grow continually, and eating their faeces to extract more nutrients from their plant diet. Rabbits and hares belong to the order Lagomorpha. Characteristically, they have four incisors in the upper jaw and two in the lower jaw; powerful hind legs for jumping; forelimbs adapted for burrowing; long ears; and a small tail. Rodents make up the order Rodentia. This is the largest order of mammals, with more than 1,700 species, including squirrels, beavers, chipmunks, gophers, rats, mice, lemmings, gerbils, porcupines, cavies, and the capybara. Typical rodent features include two incisors in each jaw; short forelimbs for manipulating food; and cheek pouches for storing food.

EXTERNAL FEATURES OF A RAT

Snout
Eye
Ear
Nose
Nostril
Pinna (ear flap)
Vibrissa (whisker)
Neck
Mouth
Tail
Forelimb
Hind limb
5 digits
5 digits

EXTERNAL FEATURES OF A RABBIT

Pinna (ear flap)
Ear
Shoulder
Eye
Nose
Nostril
Vibrissa (whisker)
Forelimb
5 digits

INTERNAL ANATOMY OF A MALE RABBIT

Brain
Nasal cavity
Gallbladder
Liver
Stomach
Kidney
Spinal cord
Colon
Ileum
Ureter
Rectum
Bladder
Anus
Urethra
Testis
Vas deferens
Appendix
Caecum
Duodenum
Heart
Pancreas
Diaphragm
Lung
Trachea
Oesophagus
Tongue
Buccal cavity
Mouth

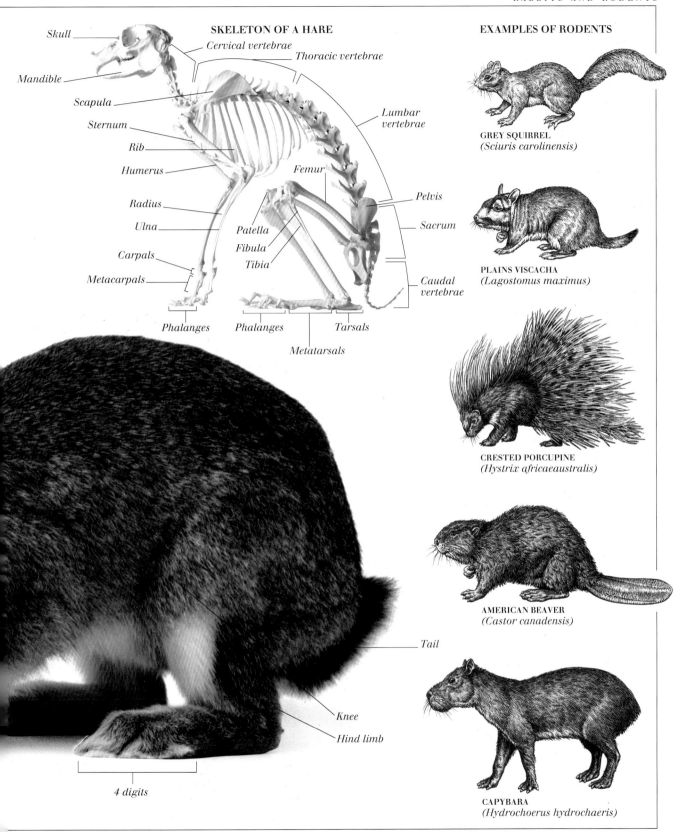

SKELETON OF A HARE

Skull

Mandible

Cervical vertebrae

Thoracic vertebrae

Scapula

Sternum

Rib

Humerus

Radius

Ulna

Carpals

Metacarpals

Lumbar vertebrae

Femur

Pelvis

Sacrum

Patella

Fibula

Tibia

Caudal vertebrae

Phalanges

Phalanges

Tarsals

Metatarsals

Tail

Knee

Hind limb

4 digits

EXAMPLES OF RODENTS

GREY SQUIRREL
(Sciuris carolinensis)

PLAINS VISCACHA
(Lagostomus maximus)

CRESTED PORCUPINE
(Hystrix africaeaustralis)

AMERICAN BEAVER
(Castor canadensis)

CAPYBARA
(Hydrochoerus hydrochaeris)

Ungulates

UNGULATES IS A GENERAL TERM FOR a large, varied group of mammals that includes horses, cattle, and their relatives. The ungulates are divided into two orders on the basis of the number of toes. Members of the order Perissodactyla (odd-toed ungulates) have one or three toes. Perissodactyls include horses, asses, and zebras (all of which are one-toed), and rhinoceroses and tapirs (which are three-toed). Members of the order Artiodactyla (even-toed ungulates) have two or four toes. Most artiodactyls have two toes, which are typically encased in hooves to give the so-called cloven hoof. Two-toed, cloven-hoofed artiodactyls include cows and other cattle, sheep, goats, antelopes, deer, and giraffes. The other main two-toed artiodactyls are camels and llamas. Most two-toed artiodactyls are ruminants; that is, they have a four-chambered stomach and chew the cud. The principal four-toed artiodactyls are pigs, peccaries, and hippopotamuses.

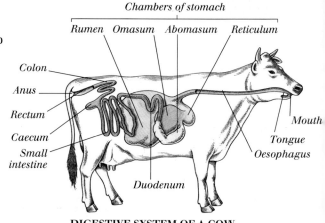

DIGESTIVE SYSTEM OF A COW

**COMPARISON OF THE FRONT FEET
OF A HORSE AND A COW**

SKELETON OF THE LEFT
FRONT FOOT OF A HORSE

SKELETON OF THE RIGHT
FRONT FOOT OF A COW

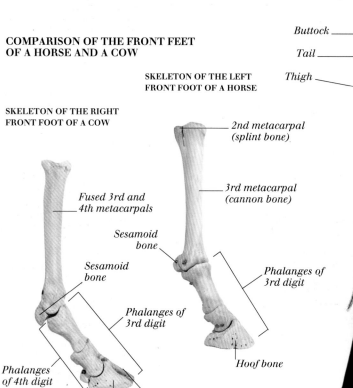

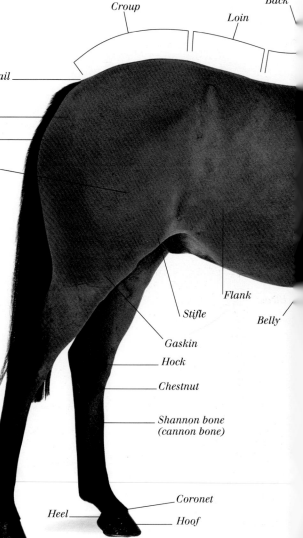

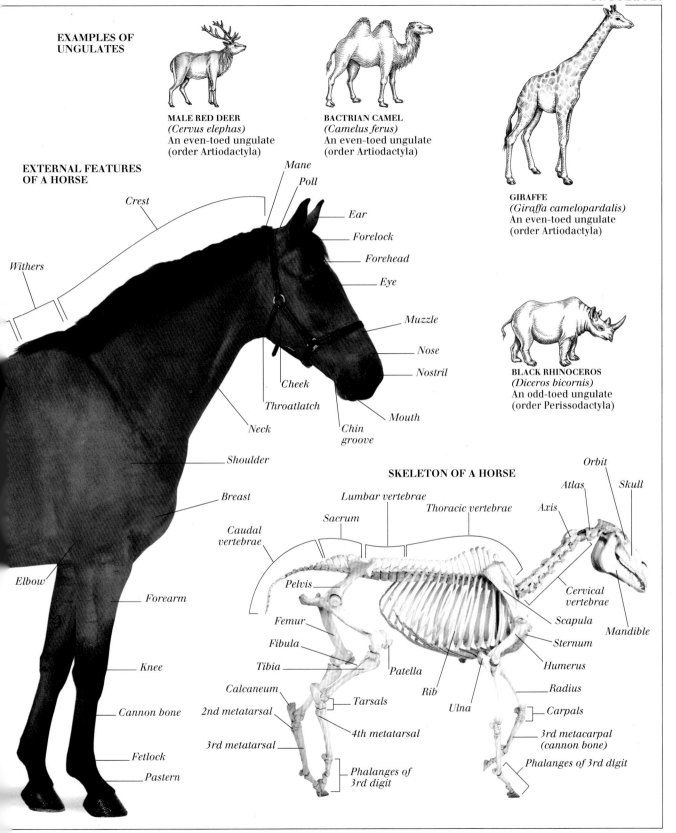

**EXAMPLES OF
UNGULATES**

MALE RED DEER
(Cervus elephas)
An even-toed ungulate
(order Artiodactyla)

BACTRIAN CAMEL
(Camelus ferus)
An even-toed ungulate
(order Artiodactyla)

GIRAFFE
(Giraffa camelopardalis)
An even-toed ungulate
(order Artiodactyla)

BLACK RHINOCEROS
(Diceros bicornis)
An odd-toed ungulate
(order Perissodactyla)

**EXTERNAL FEATURES
OF A HORSE**

Mane
Poll
Crest
Ear
Forelock
Forehead
Eye
Withers
Muzzle
Nose
Nostril
Cheek
Throatlatch
Mouth
Neck
*Chin
groove*
Shoulder
Breast
Elbow
Forearm
Knee
Cannon bone
Fetlock
Pastern

SKELETON OF A HORSE

Orbit
Atlas
Skull
Axis
Lumbar vertebrae
Thoracic vertebrae
Sacrum
*Caudal
vertebrae*
*Cervical
vertebrae*
Pelvis
Scapula
Femur
Mandible
Fibula
Sternum
Tibia
Humerus
Patella
Calcaneum
Rib
Radius
2nd metatarsal
Tarsals
Ulna
Carpals
4th metatarsal
3rd metatarsal
*3rd metacarpal
(cannon bone)*
*Phalanges of
3rd digit*
Phalanges of 3rd digit

Elephants

THE TWO SPECIES OF elephants—African and Asian—are the only members of the mammalian order Proboscidea. The bigger African elephant is the largest land animal: a fully grown male may be up to 4 m (13 ft) tall and weigh as much as 7 tonnes (6.9 tons). A fully grown male Asian elephant may be 3.3 m (11 ft) tall and weigh 5.4 tonnes (5.3 tons). The trunk—an extension of the nose and upper lip—is the elephant's other most obvious feature. It is used for manipulating and lifting, feeding, drinking and spraying water, smelling, touching, and producing trumpeting sounds. Other characteristic features include a pair of tusks, used for defence and for crushing vegetation; thick, pillar-like legs and broad feet to support the massive body; and large ear flaps that act as radiators to keep the elephant cool.

DIFFERENCES BETWEEN AFRICAN AND ASIAN ELEPHANTS

Flat forehead
Very large ears
2 "lips" at the end of the trunk
Concave back
4 toenails
3 toenails

AFRICAN ELEPHANT
(Loxodonta africana)

Twin-domed forehead
Smaller ears
1 "lip" at the end of the trunk
Arched back
5 toenails
4 toenails

ASIAN ELEPHANT
(Elephas maximus)

INTERNAL ANATOMY OF A FEMALE ELEPHANT

Spinal cord
Heart
Stomach
Duodenum
Kidney
Ureter
Uterus
Rectum
Bladder
Anal flap
Anus
Vagina
Rump
Brain
Nasal cavity
Buccal cavity
Mouth
Tongue
Tusk
Epiglottis
Oesophagus
Trachea
Lung
Diaphragm
Nasal passage
Nostril
Spleen
Vulva
Small intestine
Hind leg
Toenail

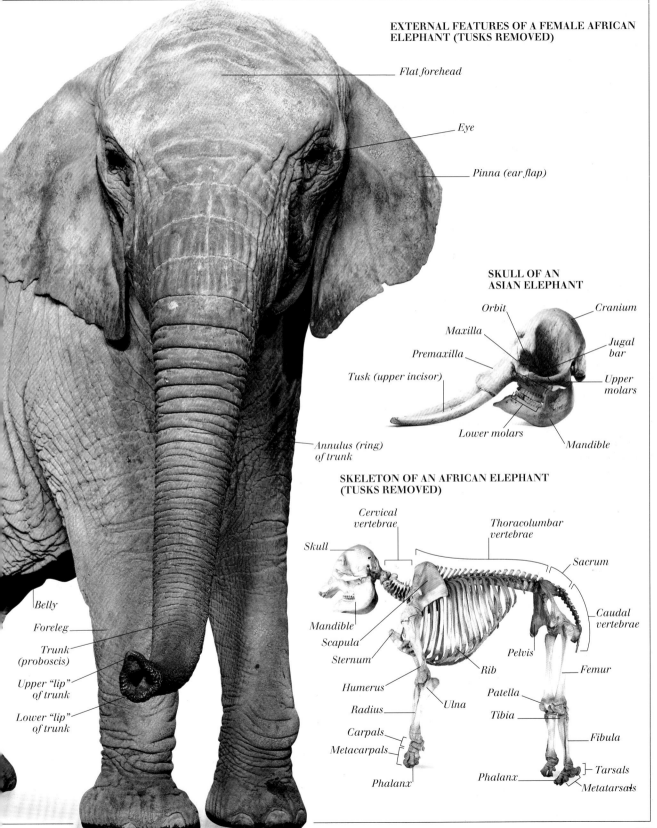

EXTERNAL FEATURES OF A FEMALE AFRICAN ELEPHANT (TUSKS REMOVED)

Flat forehead

Eye

Pinna (ear flap)

Belly

Foreleg

Trunk (proboscis)

Upper "lip" of trunk

Lower "lip" of trunk

Annulus (ring) of trunk

SKULL OF AN ASIAN ELEPHANT

Orbit

Maxilla

Premaxilla

Tusk (upper incisor)

Cranium

Jugal bar

Upper molars

Lower molars

Mandible

SKELETON OF AN AFRICAN ELEPHANT (TUSKS REMOVED)

Cervical vertebrae

Thoracolumbar vertebrae

Skull

Sacrum

Mandible

Scapula

Sternum

Humerus

Radius

Carpals

Metacarpals

Phalanx

Rib

Ulna

Pelvis

Patella

Tibia

Caudal vertebrae

Femur

Fibula

Tarsals

Phalanx

Metatarsals

Primates

THE MAMMALIAN ORDER PRIMATES consists of monkeys, apes, and their relatives (including humans). There are two suborders of primates: Prosimii, the primitive primates, which include lemurs, tarsiers, and lorises; and Anthropoidea, the advanced primates, which include monkeys, apes, and humans. The anthropoids are divided into New World monkeys, Old World monkeys, and hominids. New World monkeys typically have wide-apart nostrils that open to the side; and long tails, which are prehensile (grasping) in some species. This group of monkeys lives in South America, and includes marmosets, tamarins, and howler monkeys. Old World monkeys typically have close-set nostrils that open forwards or downwards; and non-prehensile tails. This group of monkeys lives in Africa and Asia, and includes langurs, mandrills, macaques, and baboons. Hominids typically have large brains, and no tail. This group includes the apes—chimpanzees, gibbons, gorillas, and orangutans—and humans.

INTERNAL ANATOMY OF A FEMALE CHIMPANZEE

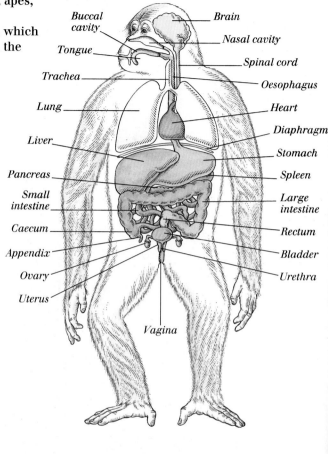

Buccal cavity
Tongue
Trachea
Lung
Liver
Pancreas
Small intestine
Caecum
Appendix
Ovary
Uterus
Vagina
Brain
Nasal cavity
Spinal cord
Oesophagus
Heart
Diaphragm
Stomach
Spleen
Large intestine
Rectum
Bladder
Urethra

SKELETON OF A RHESUS MONKEY

Skull
Orbit
Cervical vertebrae
Mandible
Thoracic vertebrae
Clavicle
Scapula
Rib
Humerus
Lumbar vertebrae
Radius
Ulna
Sacrum
Femur
Patella
Tibia
Fibula
Carpals
Metacarpals
Pelvis
Phalanges
Caudal vertebrae
Tarsals
Metatarsals
Phalanges

SKULL OF A CHIMPANZEE

Temporal bone
Suture
Frontal bone
Parietal bone
Supraorbital ridge
Orbit
Occipital bone
Maxilla
Premaxilla
Auditory meatus
Zygomatic arch
Incisor tooth
Mandible
Molar tooth
Premolar tooth
Canine tooth

EXAMPLES OF PRIMATES

RING-TAILED LEMUR
(Lemur catta)
A prosimian

MALE RED HOWLER MONKEY
(Alouatta seniculus)
A New World monkey

MALE MANDRILL
(Mandrillus sphinx)
An Old World monkey

CHIMPANZEE
(Pan troglodytes)
An ape

EXTERNAL FEATURES OF
A YOUNG GORILLA

GOLDEN LION TAMARIN
(Leontopithecus rosalia)
A New World monkey

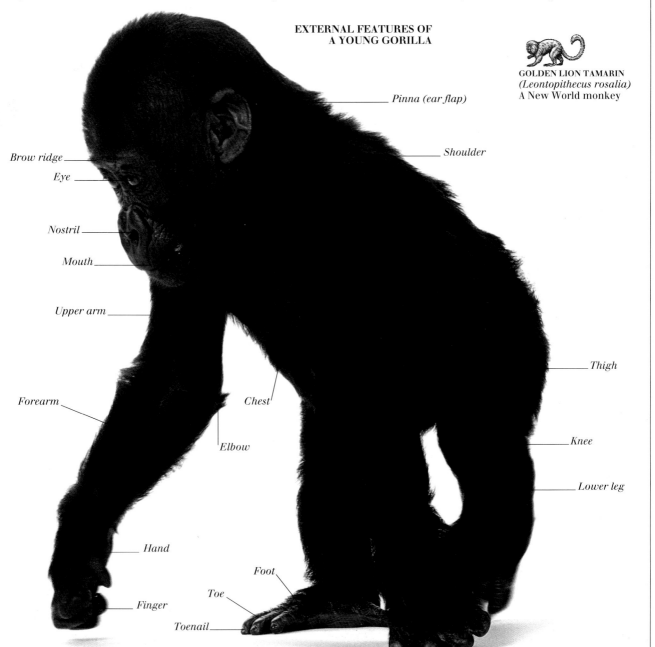

Pinna (ear flap)

Shoulder

Brow ridge

Eye

Nostril

Mouth

Upper arm

Thigh

Forearm

Chest

Knee

Elbow

Lower leg

Hand

Foot

Toe

Finger

Toenail

Dolphins, whales, and seals

DOLPHINS, WHALES, AND SEALS belong to
two orders of mammals adapted to living
in water. Dolphins and whales make up the
order Cetacea. Typical cetacean features include
a streamlined, fish-like shape; forelimbs in the form
of flippers; no visible hind limbs; a horizontally flattened
tail; and thick blubber under the skin. There are two groups
of cetaceans: toothed whales, including sperm whales, white whales,
beaked whales, dolphins, and porpoises; and the larger whalebone (baleen)
whales, including rorquals, grey whales, and right whales. The blue whale—a
rorqual—is the largest living animal: an adult may be up to 30 m (100 ft) long
and weigh 130 tonnes (128 tons). Seals and their relatives—sea lions and
walruses—make up the order Pinnipedia. Characteristically, they have a
streamlined, torpedo-shaped body; forelimbs and hind limbs modified as
flippers; thick blubber; and no external ears.

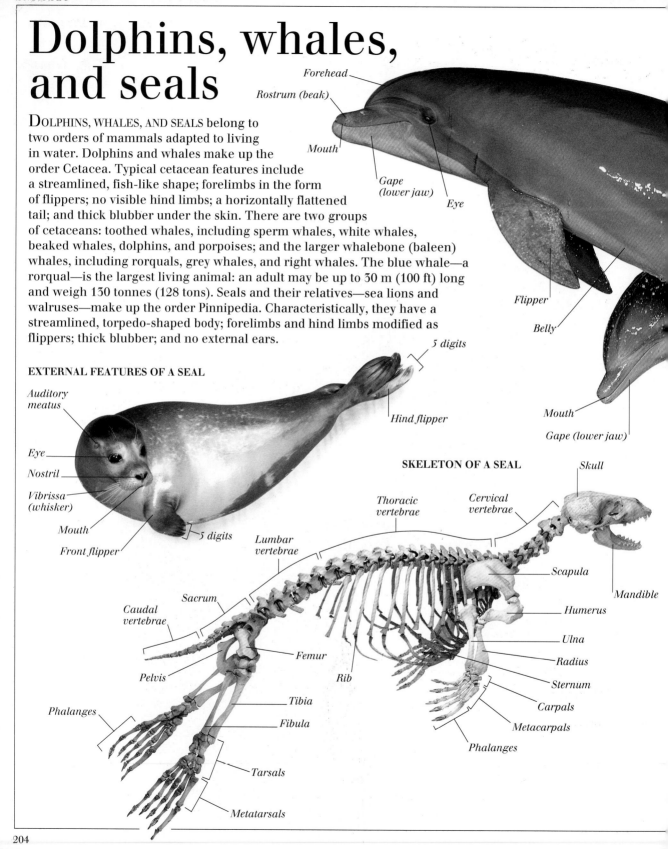

Forehead

Rostrum (beak)

Mouth

Gape
(lower jaw)

Eye

Flipper

Belly

Mouth

Gape (lower jaw)

EXTERNAL FEATURES OF A SEAL

Auditory
meatus

5 digits

Hind flipper

Eye

Nostril

Vibrissa
(whisker)

Mouth

Front flipper

5 digits

SKELETON OF A SEAL

Skull

Thoracic
vertebrae

Cervical
vertebrae

Lumbar
vertebrae

Scapula

Mandible

Sacrum

Caudal
vertebrae

Humerus

Ulna

Radius

Femur

Sternum

Pelvis

Rib

Carpals

Metacarpals

Phalanges

Tibia

Fibula

Phalanges

Tarsals

Metatarsals

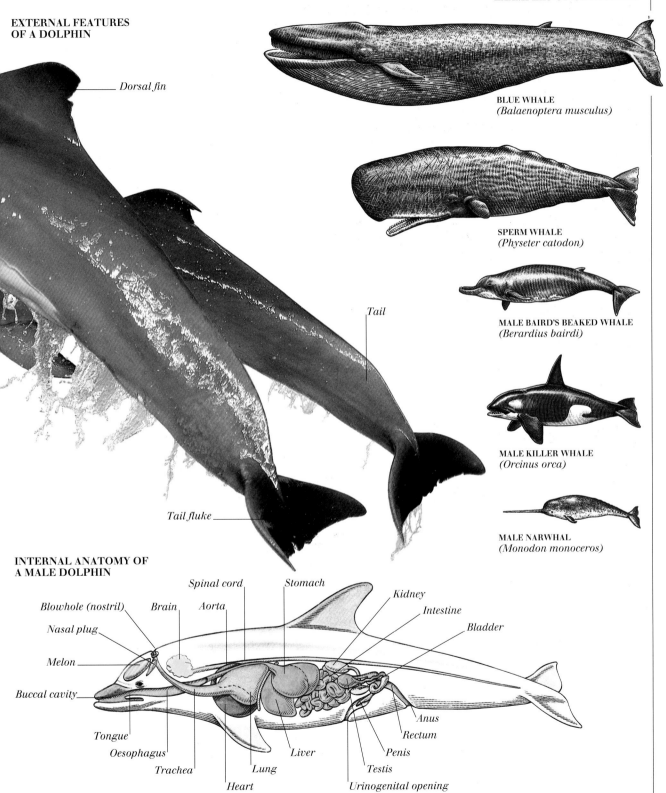

EXAMPLES OF CETACEANS

**EXTERNAL FEATURES
OF A DOLPHIN**

Dorsal fin

Tail

Tail fluke

BLUE WHALE
(Balaenoptera musculus)

SPERM WHALE
(Physeter catodon)

MALE BAIRD'S BEAKED WHALE
(Berardius bairdi)

MALE KILLER WHALE
(Orcinus orca)

MALE NARWHAL
(Monodon monoceros)

**INTERNAL ANATOMY OF
A MALE DOLPHIN**

Spinal cord

Stomach

Kidney

Blowhole (nostril)

Brain

Aorta

Intestine

Nasal plug

Bladder

Melon

Buccal cavity

Anus

Rectum

Tongue

Penis

Oesophagus

Testis

Liver

Trachea

Lung

Urinogenital opening

Heart

205

Marsupials and Monotremes

MARSUPIALS AND MONOTREMES are two orders of mammals that differ from other mammalian groups in the ways that their young develop. The order Marsupalia, the pouched mammals, is made up of kangaroos and their relatives. Typically, marsupials give birth to their young at a very early stage of development. The young then crawls to the mother's pouch (which is on the outside of her abdomen), where it attaches itself to a nipple and remains until fully developed. Most marsupials live in Australia, although the opossums—which are classified as marsupials despite not having a pouch—live in the Americas. The order Monotremata is made up of the platypus and its relatives (the echidnas, or spiny anteaters). The monotremes are primitive mammals that lay eggs, which the mother incubates. The monotremes are found only in Australia and New Guinea.

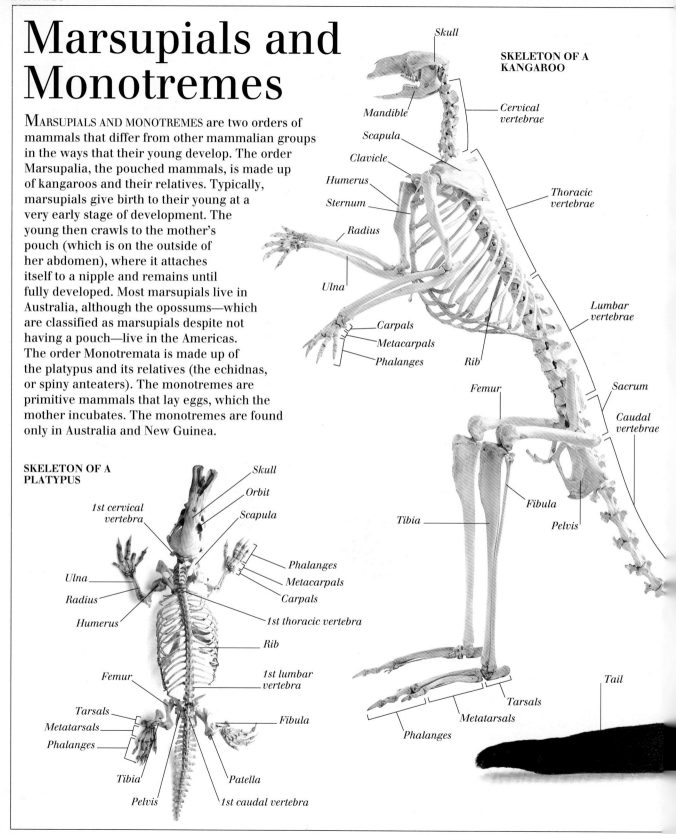

SKELETON OF A KANGAROO

Skull
Mandible
Scapula
Clavicle
Humerus
Sternum
Radius
Ulna
Cervical vertebrae
Thoracic vertebrae
Lumbar vertebrae
Carpals
Metacarpals
Phalanges
Rib
Femur
Sacrum
Caudal vertebrae
Fibula
Pelvis
Tibia
Tail
Tarsals
Metatarsals
Phalanges

SKELETON OF A PLATYPUS

Skull
Orbit
Scapula
1st cervical vertebra
Phalanges
Metacarpals
Carpals
1st thoracic vertebra
Ulna
Radius
Humerus
Rib
Femur
1st lumbar vertebra
Tarsals
Metatarsals
Phalanges
Fibula
Tibia
Patella
Pelvis
1st caudal vertebra

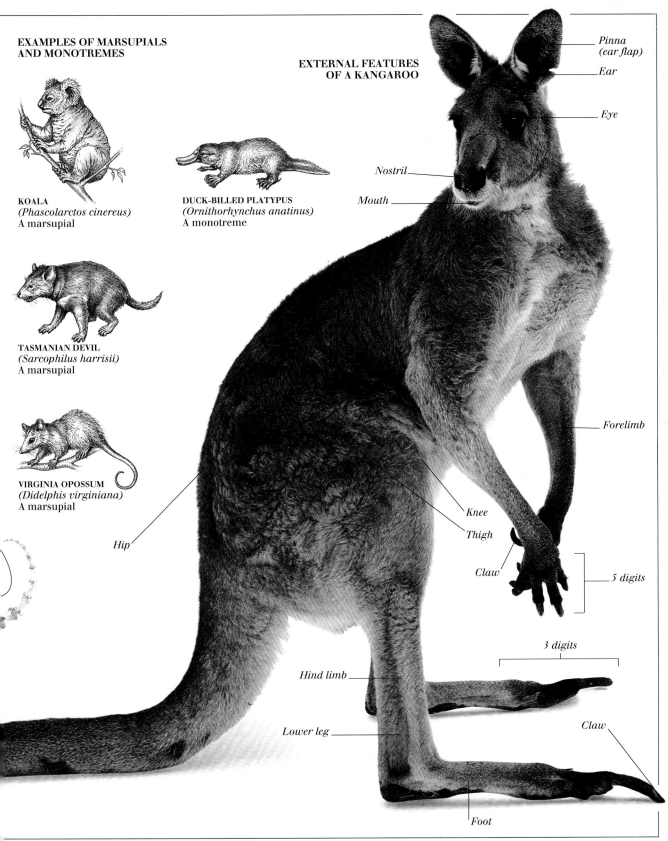

**EXAMPLES OF MARSUPIALS
AND MONOTREMES**

**EXTERNAL FEATURES
OF A KANGAROO**

KOALA
(Phascolarctos cinereus)
A marsupial

DUCK-BILLED PLATYPUS
(Ornithorhynchus anatinus)
A monotreme

TASMANIAN DEVIL
(Sarcophilus harrisii)
A marsupial

VIRGINIA OPOSSUM
(Didelphis virginiana)
A marsupial

*Pinna
(ear flap)*

Ear

Eye

Nostril

Mouth

Forelimb

Knee

Thigh

Claw

5 digits

Hip

3 digits

Hind limb

Lower leg

Claw

Foot

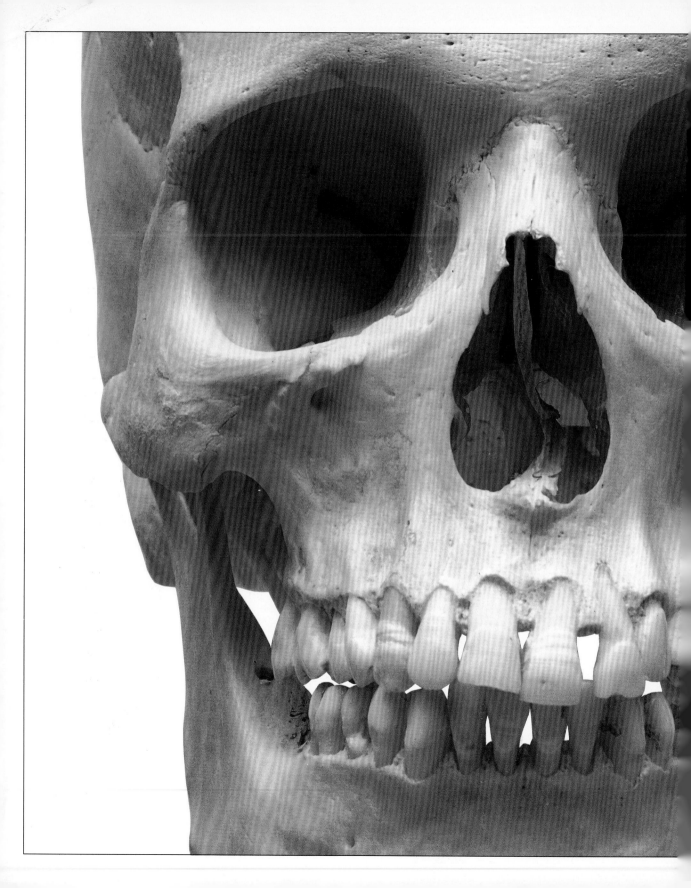

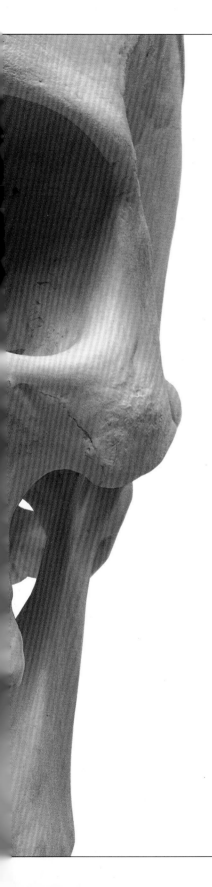

The Human Body

Body features

ALTHOUGH THERE IS enormous variation between the external appearances of humans, all bodies contain the same basic features. The outward form of the human body depends on the size of the skeleton, the shape of the muscles, the thickness of the fat layer beneath the skin, the elasticity or sagginess of the skin, and the person's age and sex. Males tend to be taller than females, with broader shoulders, more body hair, and a different pattern of fat deposits under the skin; the female body tends to be less muscular and has a shallower and wider pelvis to allow for childbirth.

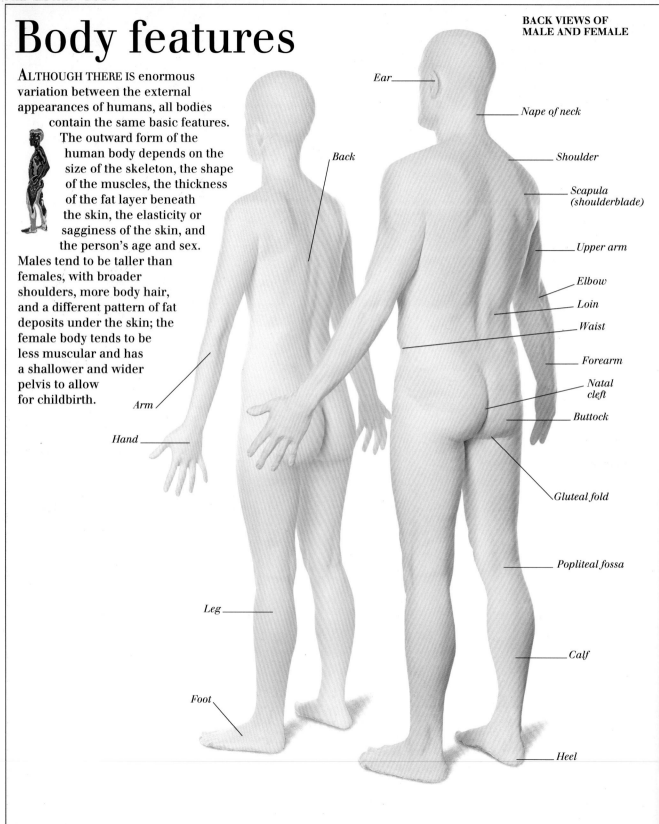

Ear

Nape of neck

Shoulder

Scapula
(shoulderblade)

Upper arm

Elbow

Loin

Waist

Forearm

Natal
cleft

Buttock

Gluteal fold

Popliteal fossa

Calf

Heel

Back

Arm

Hand

Leg

Foot

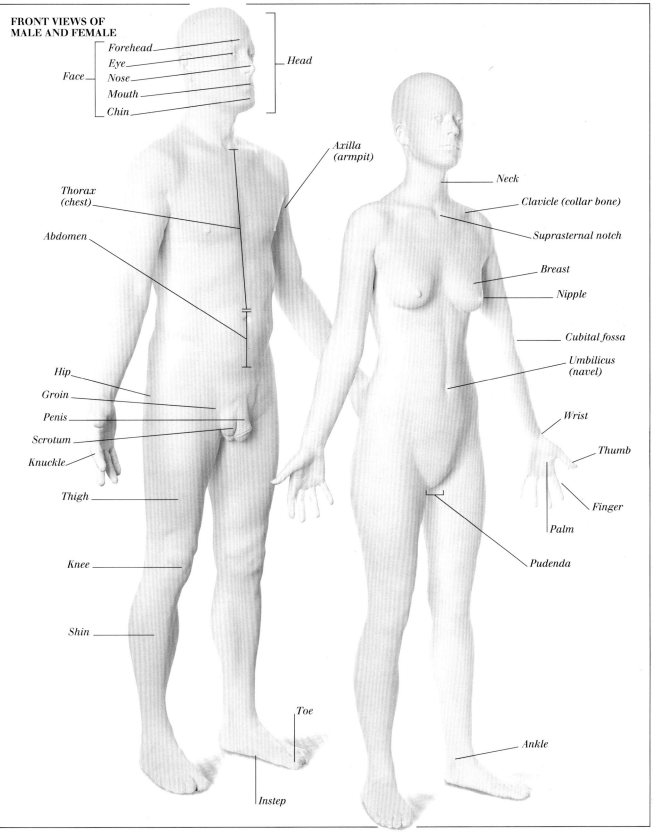

**FRONT VIEWS OF
MALE AND FEMALE**

Forehead

Eye

Face — Nose

Mouth

Chin

Head

Axilla
(armpit)

Neck

Clavicle (collar bone)

Suprasternal notch

Thorax
(chest)

Breast

Nipple

Abdomen

Cubital fossa

Umbilicus
(navel)

Hip

Groin

Penis

Scrotum

Wrist

Thumb

Knuckle

Finger

Thigh

Palm

Knee

Pudenda

Shin

Toe

Ankle

Instep

Head

IN A NEWBORN BABY, the head accounts for one-quarter of the total body length; by adulthood, the proportion has reduced to one-eighth. Contained in the head are the body's main sense organs: eyes, ears, olfactory nerves that detect smells, and the taste buds of the tongue. Signals from these organs pass to the body's great coordination centre: the brain, housed in the protective, bony dome of the skull. Hair on the head insulates against heat loss, and adult males also grow thick facial hair. The face has three important openings: two nostrils through which air passes, and the mouth, which takes in nourishment and helps form speech. Although all heads are basically similar, differences in the size, shape, and colour of features produce an infinite variety of appearances.

SIDE VIEW OF EXTERNAL FEATURES OF HEAD

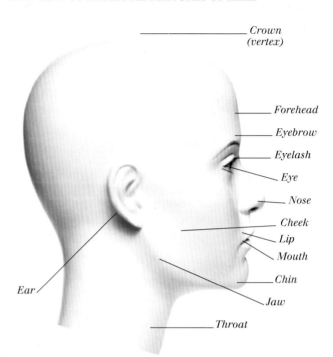

Crown (vertex)

Forehead

Eyebrow

Eyelash

Eye

Nose

Cheek

Lip

Mouth

Chin

Jaw

Throat

Ear

SECTION THROUGH HEAD

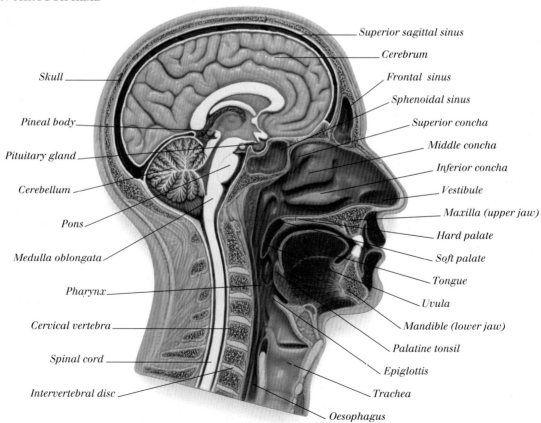

Skull

Pineal body

Pituitary gland

Cerebellum

Pons

Medulla oblongata

Pharynx

Cervical vertebra

Spinal cord

Intervertebral disc

Superior sagittal sinus

Cerebrum

Frontal sinus

Sphenoidal sinus

Superior concha

Middle concha

Inferior concha

Vestibule

Maxilla (upper jaw)

Hard palate

Soft palate

Tongue

Uvula

Mandible (lower jaw)

Palatine tonsil

Epiglottis

Trachea

Oesophagus

**FRONT VIEW OF EXTERNAL
FEATURES OF HEAD**

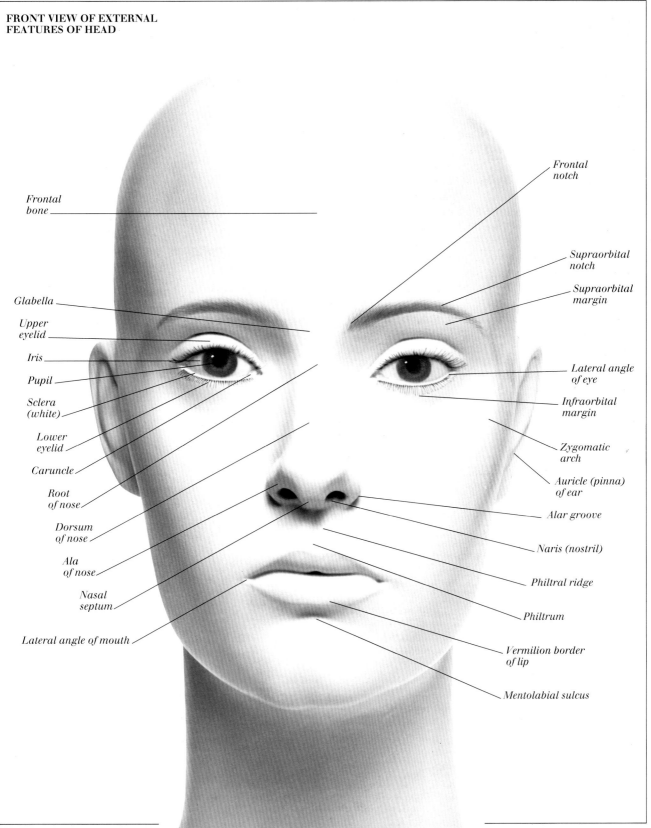

*Frontal
notch*

*Supraorbital
notch*

*Supraorbital
margin*

*Frontal
bone*

*Lateral angle
of eye*

Glabella

*Upper
eyelid*

*Infraorbital
margin*

Iris

Pupil

*Zygomatic
arch*

*Sclera
(white)*

*Auricle (pinna)
of ear*

*Lower
eyelid*

Caruncle

Alar groove

*Root
of nose*

Naris (nostril)

*Dorsum
of nose*

Philtral ridge

*Ala
of nose*

Philtrum

*Nasal
septum*

Lateral angle of mouth

*Vermilion border
of lip*

Mentolabial sulcus

Body organs

ALL THE VITAL BODY ORGANS except for the brain are enclosed within the trunk or torso (the body apart from the head and limbs). The trunk contains two large cavities separated by a muscular sheet called the diaphragm. The upper cavity, known as the thorax or chest cavity, contains the heart and lungs. The lower cavity, called the abdominal cavity, contains the stomach, intestines, liver, and pancreas, which all play a role in digesting food. Also within the trunk are the kidneys and bladder, which are part of the urinary system, and the reproductive organs, which hold the seeds of new human life. Modern imaging techniques, such as contrast X-rays and different types of scans, make it possible to see and study body organs without the need to cut through their protective coverings of skin, fat, muscle, and bone.

MAJOR INTERNAL STRUCTURES

Thyroid gland

Larynx

Heart

Right lung

Left lung

Diaphragm

Liver

Large intestine

Stomach

Small intestine

Greater omentum

IMAGING THE BODY

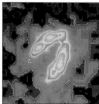

SCINTIGRAM OF HEART CHAMBERS

ANGIOGRAM OF RIGHT LUNG

CONTRAST X-RAY OF GALLBLADDER

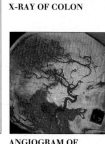

SCINTIGRAM OF NERVOUS SYSTEM

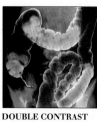

DOUBLE CONTRAST X-RAY OF COLON

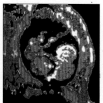

ULTRASOUND SCAN OF TWINS IN UTERUS

ANGIOGRAM OF KIDNEYS

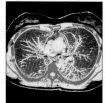

ANGIOGRAM OF ARTERIES OF HEAD

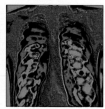

CT SCAN THROUGH FEMALE CHEST

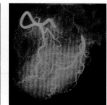

THERMOGRAM OF CHEST REGION

ANGIOGRAM OF ARTERIES OF HEART

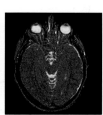

MRI SCAN THROUGH HEAD AT EYE LEVEL

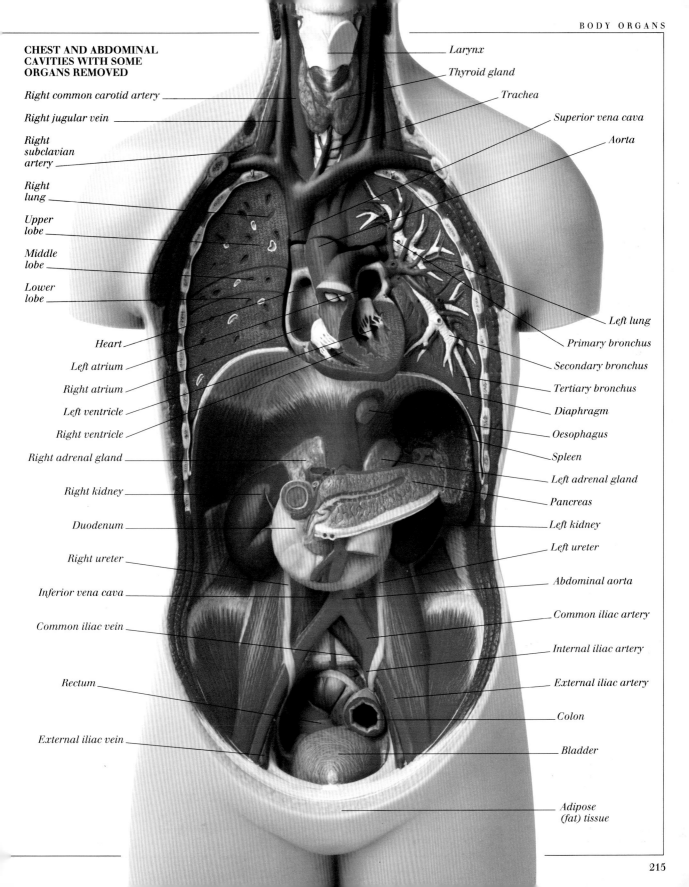

**CHEST AND ABDOMINAL
CAVITIES WITH SOME
ORGANS REMOVED**

Right common carotid artery

Right jugular vein

Right
subclavian
artery

Right
lung

Upper
lobe

Middle
lobe

Lower
lobe

Heart

Left atrium

Right atrium

Left ventricle

Right ventricle

Right adrenal gland

Right kidney

Duodenum

Right ureter

Inferior vena cava

Common iliac vein

Rectum

External iliac vein

Larynx

Thyroid gland

Trachea

Superior vena cava

Aorta

Left lung

Primary bronchus

Secondary bronchus

Tertiary bronchus

Diaphragm

Oesophagus

Spleen

Left adrenal gland

Pancreas

Left kidney

Left ureter

Abdominal aorta

Common iliac artery

Internal iliac artery

External iliac artery

Colon

Bladder

Adipose
(fat) tissue

Body cells

EVERYONE IS MADE UP OF BILLIONS OF CELLS, which are the basic structural units of the body. Bones, muscles, nerves, skin, blood, and all other body tissues are formed from different types of cells. Each cell has a specific function but works with other types of cells to perform the enormous number of tasks needed to sustain life. Most body cells have a similar basic structure. Each cell has an outer layer (called the cell membrane) and contains a fluid material (cytoplasm). Within the cytoplasm are many specialized structures (organelles). The most important organelle is the nucleus, which contains vital genetic material and acts as the cell's control centre.

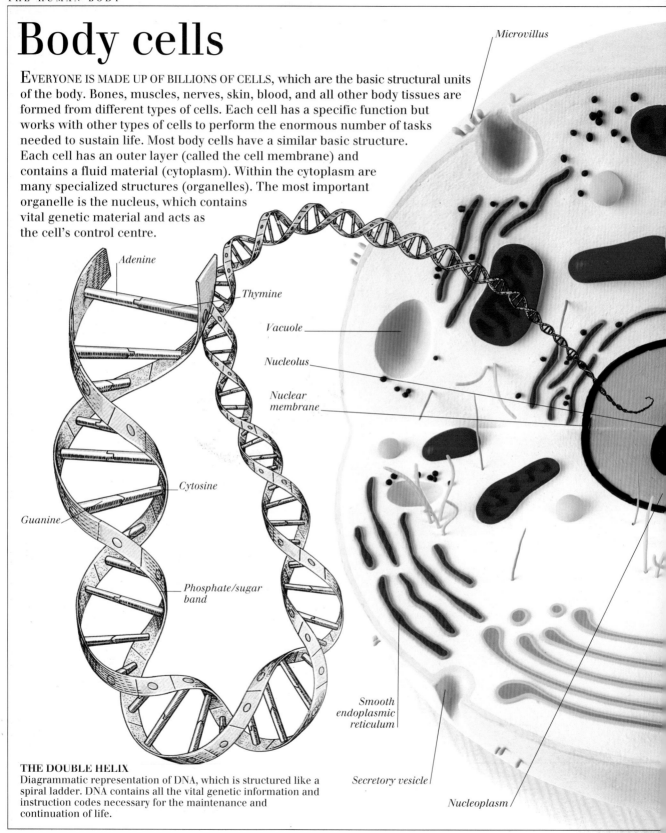

Microvillus

Adenine

Thymine

Vacuole

Nucleolus

Nuclear membrane

Cytosine

Guanine

Phosphate/sugar band

Smooth endoplasmic reticulum

Secretory vesicle

Nucleoplasm

THE DOUBLE HELIX
Diagrammatic representation of DNA, which is structured like a spiral ladder. DNA contains all the vital genetic information and instruction codes necessary for the maintenance and continuation of life.

GENERALIZED HUMAN CELL

Cytoplasm

Lysosome

Cell membrane

Mitochondrial crista

Nucleus

Rough endoplasmic reticulum

Microfilament

Pore of nuclear membrane

Ribosome

Centriole

Mitochondrion

Microtubule

Peroxisome

Pinocytotic vesicle

Golgi complex (Golgi apparatus; Golgi body)

TYPES OF CELLS

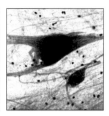

BONE-FORMING CELL

NERVE CELLS IN SPINAL CORD

SPERM CELLS IN SEMEN

SECRETORY THYROID GLAND CELLS

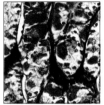

ACID-SECRETING STOMACH CELLS

CONNECTIVE TISSUE CELLS

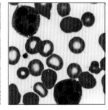

MUCUS-SECRETING DUODENAL CELLS

RED AND TWO WHITE BLOOD CELLS

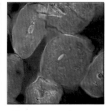

FAT CELLS IN ADIPOSE TISSUE

EPITHELIAL CELLS IN CHEEK

217

Skeleton

THE SKELETON IS A MOBILE FRAMEWORK made up of 206 bones, approximately half of which are in the hands and feet. Although individual bones are rigid, the skeleton as a whole is remarkably flexible and allows the human body a huge range of movement. The skeleton serves as an anchorage for the skeletal muscles, and as a protective cage for the body's internal organs. Female bones are usually smaller and lighter than male bones, and the female pelvis is shallower and has a wider cavity.

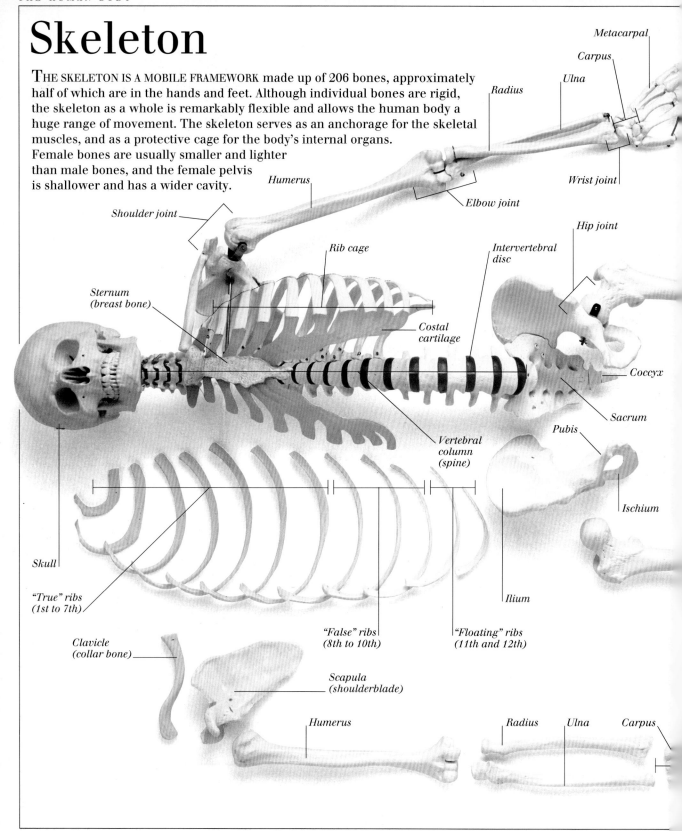

Metacarpal

Carpus

Ulna

Radius

Humerus

Shoulder joint

Rib cage

Intervertebral disc

Hip joint

Elbow joint

Wrist joint

Sternum
(breast bone)

Costal
cartilage

Coccyx

Sacrum

Pubis

Vertebral
column
(spine)

Ischium

Skull

Ilium

"True" ribs
(1st to 7th)

"False" ribs
(8th to 10th)

"Floating" ribs
(11th and 12th)

Clavicle
(collar bone)

Scapula
(shoulderblade)

Humerus

Radius   Ulna   Carpus

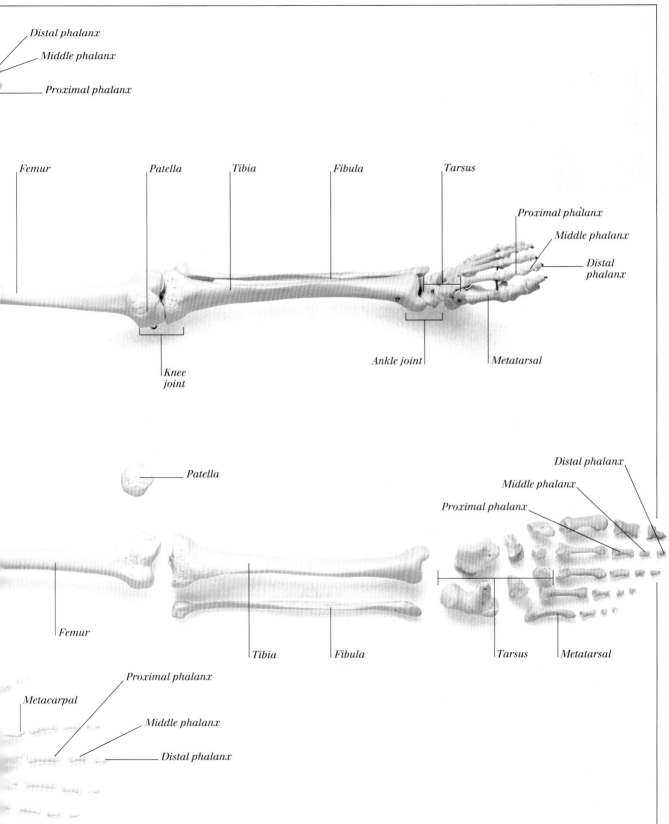

Distal phalanx

Middle phalanx

Proximal phalanx

Femur

Patella

Tibia

Fibula

Tarsus

Proximal phàlanx

Middle phalanx

Distal phalanx

Knee joint

Ankle joint

Metatarsal

Patella

Distal phalanx

Middle phalanx

Proximal phalanx

Femur

Tibia

Fibula

Tarsus

Metatarsal

Metacarpal

Proximal phalanx

Middle phalanx

Distal phalanx

219

Skull

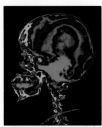

THE SKULL is the most complicated bony structure of the body but every feature serves a purpose. Internally, the main hollow chamber of the skull has three levels that support the brain, with every bump and hollow corresponding to the shape of the brain. Underneath and towards the back of the skull is a large round hole, the foramen magnum, through which the spinal cord passes. To the front of this are many smaller openings through which nerves, arteries, and veins pass to and from the brain. The roof of the skull is formed from four thin, curved bones that are firmly fixed together from the age of about two years. At the front of the skull are the two orbits, which contain the eyeballs, and a central hole for the airway of the nose. The jaw bone hinges on either side at ear level.

RIGHT SIDE VIEW OF A FETAL SKULL

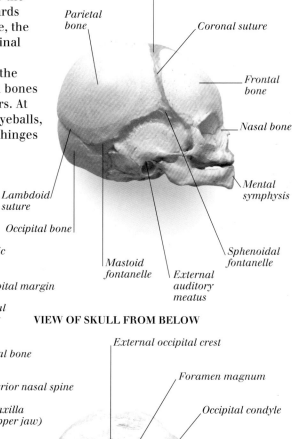

Anterior fontanelle

Parietal bone

Coronal suture

Frontal bone

Nasal bone

Mental symphysis

Lambdoid suture

Occipital bone

Mastoid fontanelle

External auditory meatus

Sphenoidal fontanelle

RIGHT SIDE VIEW OF SKULL

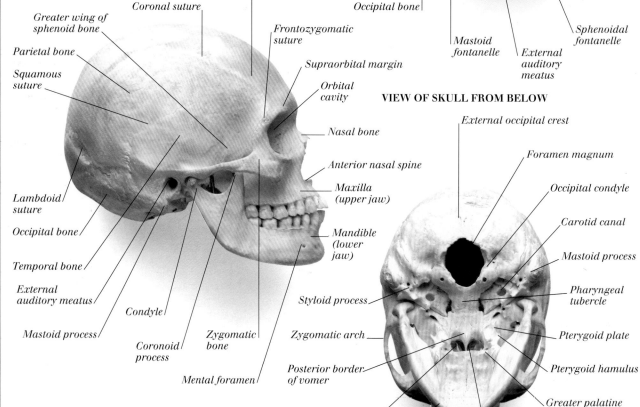

Greater wing of sphenoid bone

Coronal suture

Frontal bone

Frontozygomatic suture

Parietal bone

Squamous suture

Supraorbital margin

Orbital cavity

Nasal bone

Anterior nasal spine

Maxilla (upper jaw)

Lambdoid suture

Occipital bone

Temporal bone

External auditory meatus

Mastoid process

Condyle

Coronoid process

Zygomatic bone

Mental foramen

Mandible (lower jaw)

Styloid process

Zygomatic arch

Posterior border of vomer

Concha

Mandible (lower jaw)

VIEW OF SKULL FROM BELOW

External occipital crest

Foramen magnum

Occipital condyle

Carotid canal

Mastoid process

Pharyngeal tubercle

Pterygoid plate

Pterygoid hamulus

Greater palatine foramen

Posterior nasal aperture

FRONT VIEW OF SKULL

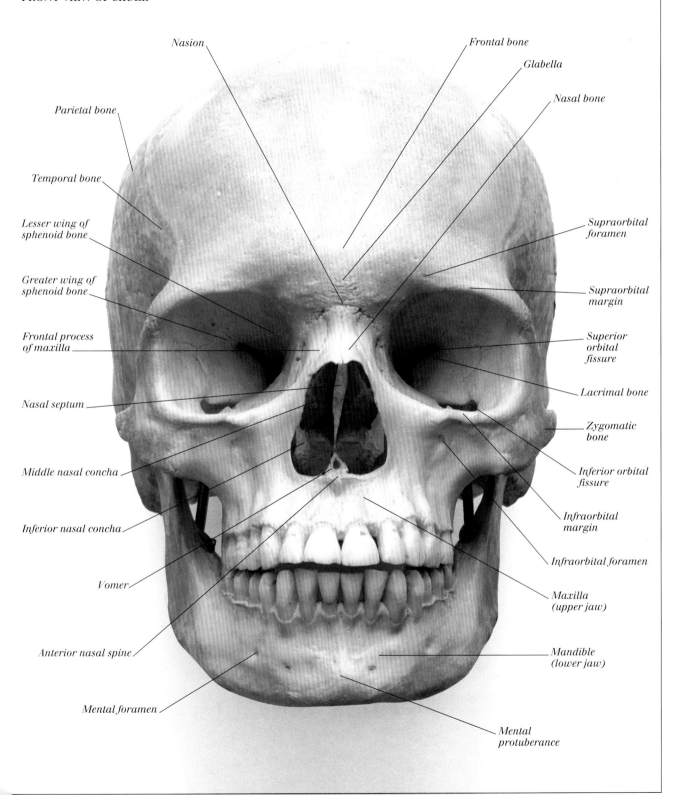

Nasion

Frontal bone

Glabella

Nasal bone

Parietal bone

Temporal bone

Lesser wing of
sphenoid bone

Greater wing of
sphenoid bone

Frontal process
of maxilla

Nasal septum

Middle nasal concha

Inferior nasal concha

Vomer

Anterior nasal spine

Mental foramen

Supraorbital
foramen

Supraorbital
margin

Superior
orbital
fissure

Lacrimal bone

Zygomatic
bone

Inferior orbital
fissure

Infraorbital
margin

Infraorbital foramen

Maxilla
(upper jaw)

Mandible
(lower jaw)

Mental
protuberance

Spine

THE SPINE (OR VERTEBRAL COLUMN) has two main functions: it serves as a protective surrounding for the delicate spinal cord and forms the supporting back bone of the skeleton. The spine consists of 24 separate differently shaped bones (vertebrae) with a curved, triangular bone (the sacrum) at the bottom. The sacrum is made up of fused vertebrae; at its lower end is a small tail-like structure made up of tiny bones collectively called the coccyx. Between each pair of vertebrae is a disc of cartilage that cushions the bones during movement. The top two vertebrae differ in appearance from the others and work as a pair: the first, called the atlas, rotates around a stout vertical peg on the second, the axis. This arrangement allows the skull to move freely up and down, and from side to side.

SPINE DIVIDED INTO VERTEBRAL SECTIONS

FRONT

- Cervical vertebrae
- Thoracic vertebrae
- Lumbar vertebrae
- Sacral vertebrae
- Coccygeal vertebrae

TYPES OF VERTEBRAE (VIEWED FROM ABOVE)

ATLAS

- Anterior arch
- Anterior tubercle
- Vertebral foramen
- Transverse process
- Lateral mass with superior articular facet
- Posterior arch
- Posterior tubercle
- Transverse foramen

AXIS

- Facet
- Dens
- Vertebral foramen
- Spinous process
- Lamina
- Transverse process and foramen

CERVICAL VERTEBRA

- Body
- Anterior tubercle
- Posterior tubercle
- Superior articular process
- Spinous process
- Vertebral foramen
- Transverse foramen

SKULL AND SPINE

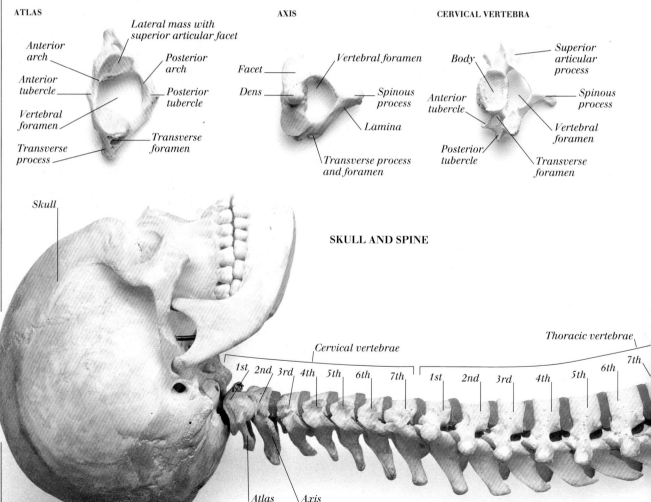

- Skull
- Cervical vertebrae: 1st, 2nd, 3rd, 4th, 5th, 6th, 7th
- Thoracic vertebrae: 1st, 2nd, 3rd, 4th, 5th, 6th, 7th
- Atlas
- Axis

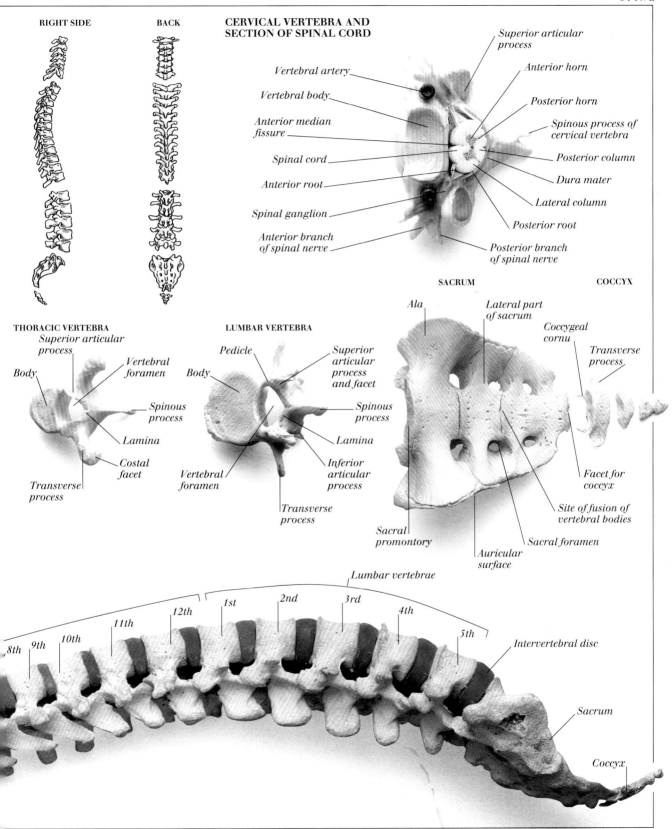

RIGHT SIDE

BACK

CERVICAL VERTEBRA AND SECTION OF SPINAL CORD

Vertebral artery

Vertebral body

Anterior median fissure

Spinal cord

Anterior root

Spinal ganglion

Anterior branch of spinal nerve

Superior articular process

Anterior horn

Posterior horn

Spinous process of cervical vertebra

Posterior column

Dura mater

Lateral column

Posterior root

Posterior branch of spinal nerve

THORACIC VERTEBRA

Superior articular process

Body

Vertebral foramen

Spinous process

Lamina

Costal facet

Transverse process

LUMBAR VERTEBRA

Pedicle

Body

Superior articular process and facet

Spinous process

Lamina

Inferior articular process

Vertebral foramen

Transverse process

SACRUM

Ala

Lateral part of sacrum

Sacral promontory

Auricular surface

Site of fusion of vertebral bodies

Sacral foramen

COCCYX

Coccygeal cornu

Transverse process

Facet for coccyx

Lumbar vertebrae

1st   2nd   3rd   4th   5th

8th 9th 10th 11th 12th

Intervertebral disc

Sacrum

Coccyx

Bones and joints

BONES FORM the body's hard, strong skeletal framework. Each bone has a hard, compact exterior surrounding a spongy, lighter interior. The long bones of the arms and legs, such as the femur (thigh bone), have a central cavity containing bone marrow. Bones are composed chiefly of calcium, phosphorus, and a fibrous substance known as collagen. Bones meet at joints, which are of several different types. For example, the hip is a ball-and-socket joint that allows the femur a wide range of movement, whereas finger joints are simple hinge joints that allow only bending and straightening. Joints are held in place by bands of tissue called ligaments. Movement of joints is facilitated by the smooth hyaline cartilage that covers the bone ends and by the synovial membrane that lines and lubricates the joint.

LIGAMENTS SURROUNDING HIP JOINT

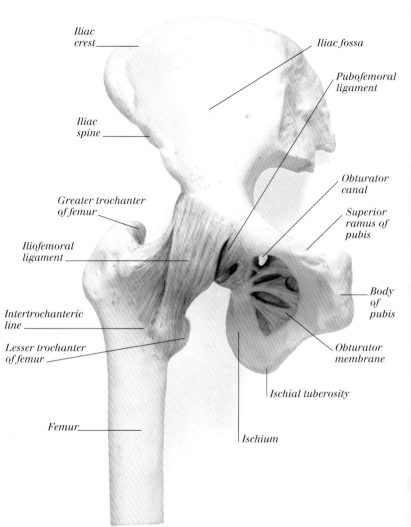

Iliac crest

Iliac spine

Greater trochanter of femur

Iliofemoral ligament

Intertrochanteric line

Lesser trochanter of femur

Femur

Iliac fossa

Pubofemoral ligament

Obturator canal

Superior ramus of pubis

Body of pubis

Obturator membrane

Ischial tuberosity

Ischium

SECTION THROUGH LEFT FEMUR

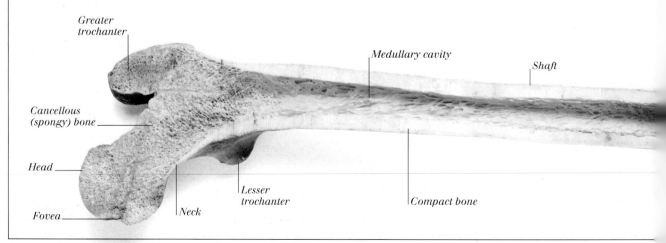

Greater trochanter

Medullary cavity

Shaft

Cancellous (spongy) bone

Head

Lesser trochanter

Compact bone

Fovea

Neck

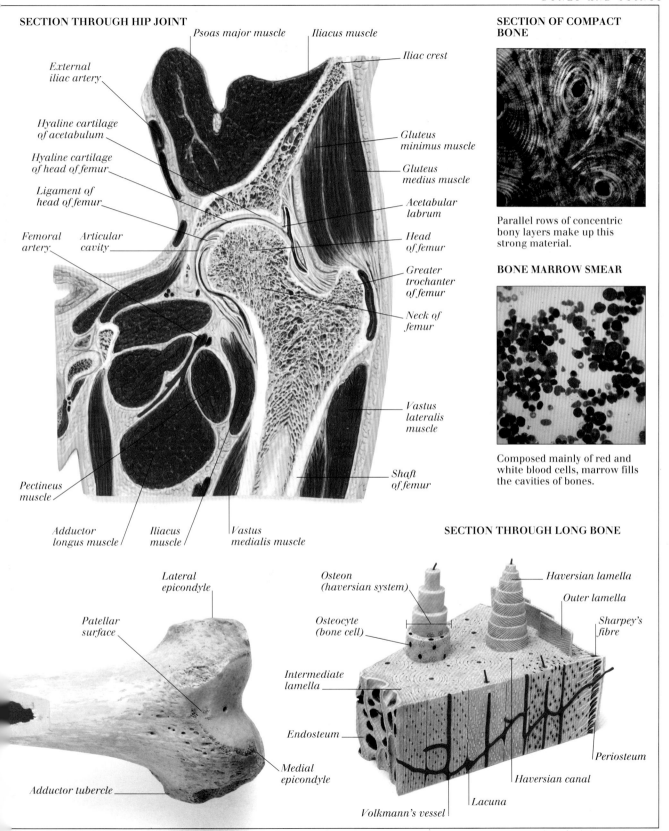

SECTION THROUGH HIP JOINT

Psoas major muscle

Iliacus muscle

Iliac crest

External
iliac artery

Hyaline cartilage
of acetabulum

Hyaline cartilage
of head of femur

Ligament of
head of femur

Femoral
artery

Articular
cavity

Pectineus
muscle

Adductor
longus muscle

Iliacus
muscle

Vastus
medialis muscle

Gluteus
minimus muscle

Gluteus
medius muscle

Acetabular
labrum

Head
of femur

Greater
trochanter
of femur

Neck of
femur

Vastus
lateralis
muscle

Shaft
of femur

**SECTION OF COMPACT
BONE**

Parallel rows of concentric
bony layers make up this
strong material.

BONE MARROW SMEAR

Composed mainly of red and
white blood cells, marrow fills
the cavities of bones.

Lateral
epicondyle

Patellar
surface

Adductor tubercle

Medial
epicondyle

SECTION THROUGH LONG BONE

Osteon
(haversian system)

Osteocyte
(bone cell)

Intermediate
lamella

Endosteum

Volkmann's vessel

Lacuna

Haversian lamella

Outer lamella

Sharpey's
fibre

Periosteum

Haversian canal

Muscles 1

THERE ARE THREE MAIN TYPES OF MUSCLE: skeletal muscle (also called voluntary muscle because it can be consciously controlled); smooth muscle (also called involuntary muscle because it is not under voluntary control); and the specialized muscle tissue of the heart. Humans have more than 600 skeletal muscles, which differ in size and shape according to the jobs they do. Skeletal muscles are attached either directly or indirectly (via tendons) to bones, and work in opposing pairs (one muscle in the pair contracts while the other relaxes) to produce body movements as diverse as walking, threading a needle, and an array of facial expressions. Smooth muscles occur in the walls of internal body organs and perform actions such as forcing food through the intestines, contracting the uterus (womb) in childbirth, and pumping blood through the blood vessels.

SOME OTHER MUSCLES IN THE BODY

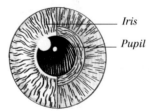

Iris

Pupil

IRIS
The muscle fibres contract and dilate (expand) to alter pupil size.

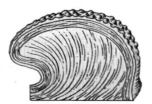

TONGUE
Interlacing layers of muscle allow great mobility.

ILEUM
Opposing muscle layers transport semi-digested food.

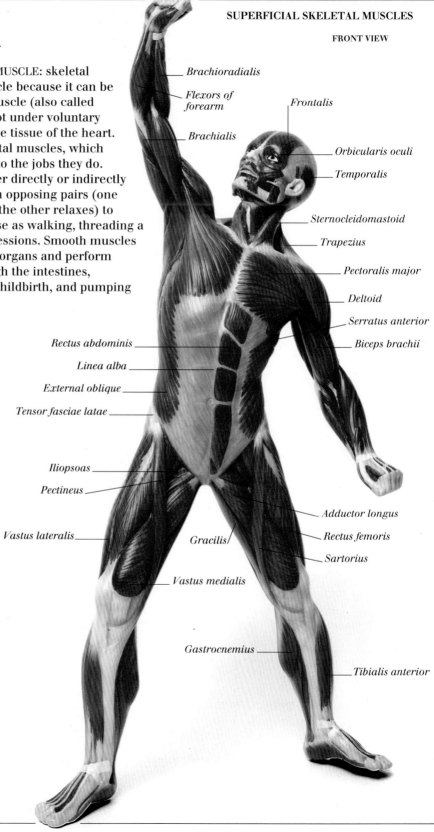

SUPERFICIAL SKELETAL MUSCLES

FRONT VIEW

Brachioradialis

Flexors of forearm

Brachialis

Frontalis

Orbicularis oculi

Temporalis

Sternocleidomastoid

Trapezius

Pectoralis major

Deltoid

Serratus anterior

Biceps brachii

Rectus abdominis

Linea alba

External oblique

Tensor fasciae latae

Iliopsoas

Pectineus

Adductor longus

Rectus femoris

Sartorius

Vastus lateralis

Gracilis

Vastus medialis

Gastrocnemius

Tibialis anterior

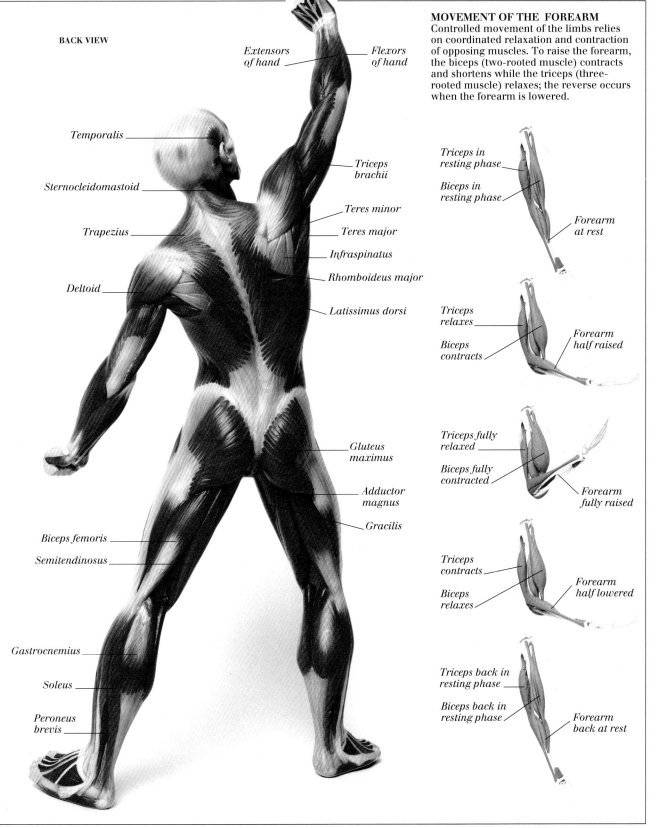

BACK VIEW

Extensors
of hand

Flexors
of hand

Temporalis

Sternocleidomastoid

Trapezius

Deltoid

Triceps
brachii

Teres minor

Teres major

Infraspinatus

Rhomboideus major

Latissimus dorsi

Gluteus
maximus

Adductor
magnus

Gracilis

Biceps femoris

Semitendinosus

Gastrocnemius

Soleus

Peroneus
brevis

MOVEMENT OF THE FOREARM
Controlled movement of the limbs relies
on coordinated relaxation and contraction
of opposing muscles. To raise the forearm,
the biceps (two-rooted muscle) contracts
and shortens while the triceps (three-
rooted muscle) relaxes; the reverse occurs
when the forearm is lowered.

Triceps in
resting phase

Biceps in
resting phase

Forearm
at rest

Triceps
relaxes

Biceps
contracts

Forearm
half raised

Triceps fully
relaxed

Biceps fully
contracted

Forearm
fully raised

Triceps
contracts

Biceps
relaxes

Forearm
half lowered

Triceps back in
resting phase

Biceps back in
resting phase

Forearm
back at rest

Muscles 2

SKELETAL MUSCLE FIBRE

Myofibril

Sarcomere

Motor end plate

Nucleus

Synaptic knob

Sarcoplasmic reticulum

Sarcolemma

Schwann cell

Endomysium

Motor neuron

Node of Ranvier

MUSCLES OF FACIAL EXPRESSION
A single expression is the result of movement of many muscles; the main muscles of expression are shown in action below.

FRONTALIS

CORRUGATOR SUPERCILII

ORBICULARIS ORIS

ZYGOMATICUS MAJOR

DEPRESSOR ANGULI ORIS

TYPES OF MUSCLE

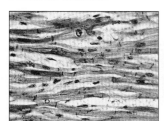

CARDIAC MUSCLE

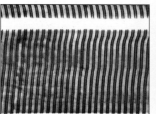

SKELETAL MUSCLE

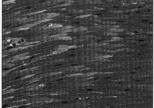

SMOOTH MUSCLE

CONTRACTION OF SKELETAL MUSCLE

RELAXED STATE

CONTRACTED STATE

**MUSCLES OF
HEAD AND NECK**

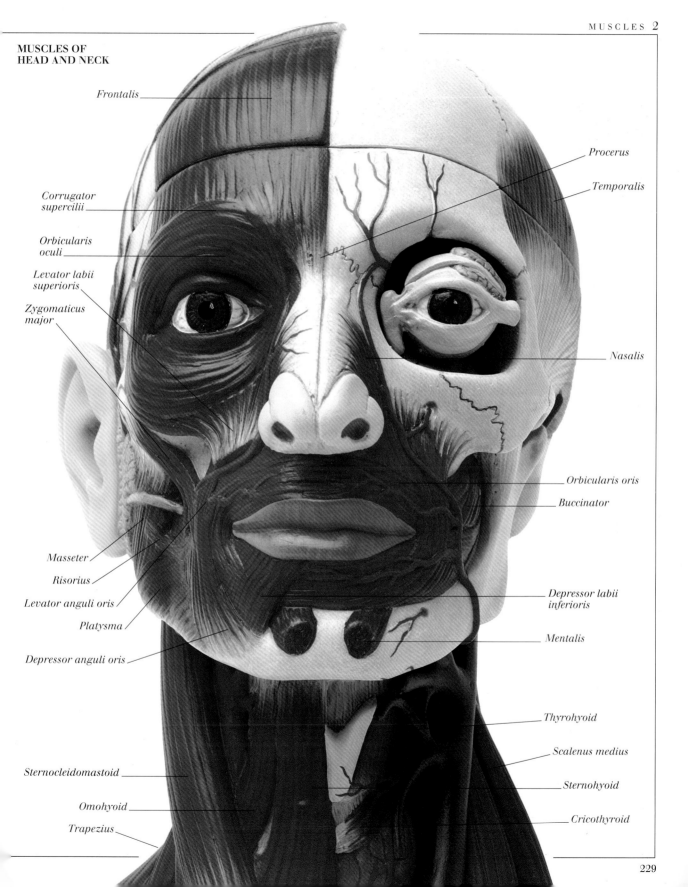

Frontalis

Procerus

Temporalis

Corrugator
supercilii

Orbicularis
oculi

Levator labii
superioris

Zygomaticus
major

Nasalis

Orbicularis oris

Buccinator

Masseter

Risorius

Levator anguli oris

Platysma

Depressor labii
inferioris

Mentalis

Depressor anguli oris

Thyrohyoid

Scalenus medius

Sternocleidomastoid

Sternohyoid

Omohyoid

Cricothyroid

Trapezius

Hands

THE HUMAN HAND is an extremely versatile tool, capable of delicate manipulation as well as powerful gripping actions. The arrangement of its 27 small bones, moved by 37 skeletal muscles that are connected to the bones by tendons, allows a wide range of movements. Our ability to bring the tips of our thumbs and fingers together, combined with the extraordinary sensitivity of our fingertips due to their rich supply of nerve endings, makes our hands uniquely dextrous.

X-RAY OF LEFT HAND OF A YOUNG CHILD

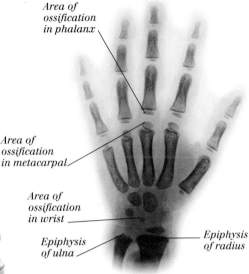

Area of ossification in phalanx

Area of ossification in metacarpal

Area of ossification in wrist

Epiphysis of ulna

Epiphysis of radius

Areas of cartilage in the wrist and at the ends of the finger bones are the sites of growth and have still to ossify.

BONES OF HAND

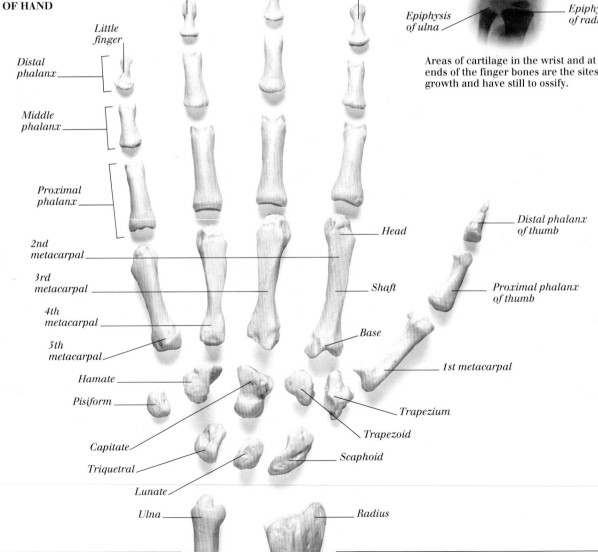

Ring finger

Middle finger

Index finger

Little finger

Distal phalanx

Middle phalanx

Proximal phalanx

2nd metacarpal

3rd metacarpal

4th metacarpal

5th metacarpal

Hamate

Pisiform

Capitate

Triquetral

Lunate

Ulna

Head

Shaft

Base

Distal phalanx of thumb

Proximal phalanx of thumb

1st metacarpal

Trapezium

Trapezoid

Scaphoid

Radius

**STRUCTURES UNDERLYING SKIN
OF PALM OF HAND**

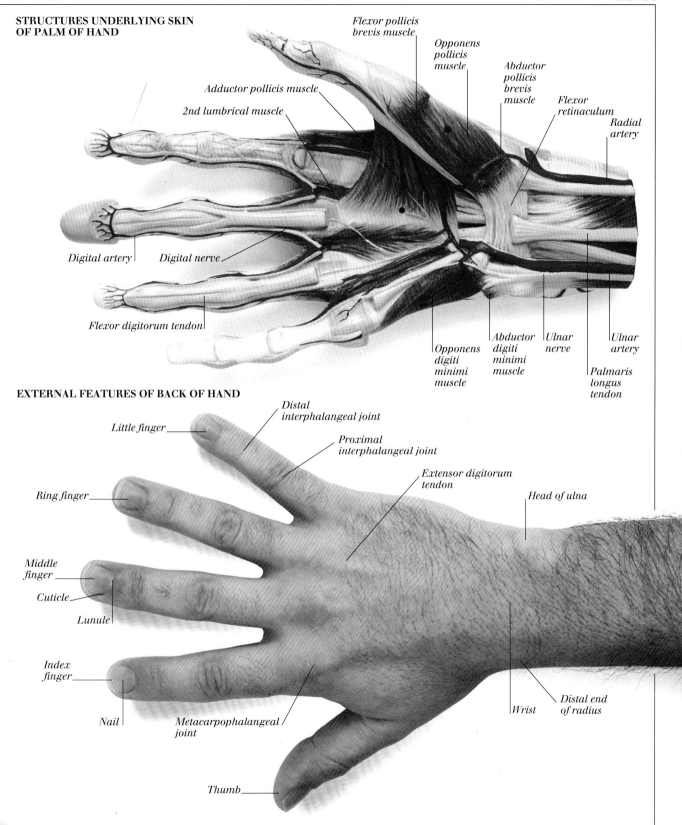

*Flexor pollicis
brevis muscle*

*Opponens
pollicis
muscle*

*Abductor
pollicis
brevis
muscle*

*Flexor
retinaculum*

*Radial
artery*

Adductor pollicis muscle

2nd lumbrical muscle

Digital artery

Digital nerve

Flexor digitorum tendon

*Opponens
digiti
minimi
muscle*

*Abductor
digiti
minimi
muscle*

*Ulnar
nerve*

*Ulnar
artery*

*Palmaris
longus
tendon*

EXTERNAL FEATURES OF BACK OF HAND

*Distal
interphalangeal joint*

Little finger

*Proximal
interphalangeal joint*

Ring finger

*Extensor digitorum
tendon*

Head of ulna

*Middle
finger*

Cuticle

Lunule

*Index
finger*

Nail

*Metacarpophalangeal
joint*

Wrist

*Distal end
of radius*

Thumb

Feet

THE FEET AND TOES are essential elements in body movement. They bear and propel the weight of the body during walking and running, and also help to maintain balance during changes of body position. Each foot has 26 bones, more than 100 ligaments, and 33 muscles, some of which are attached to the lower leg. The heel pad and the arch of the foot act as shock absorbers, providing a cushion against the jolts that occur with every step.

BONES OF FOOT

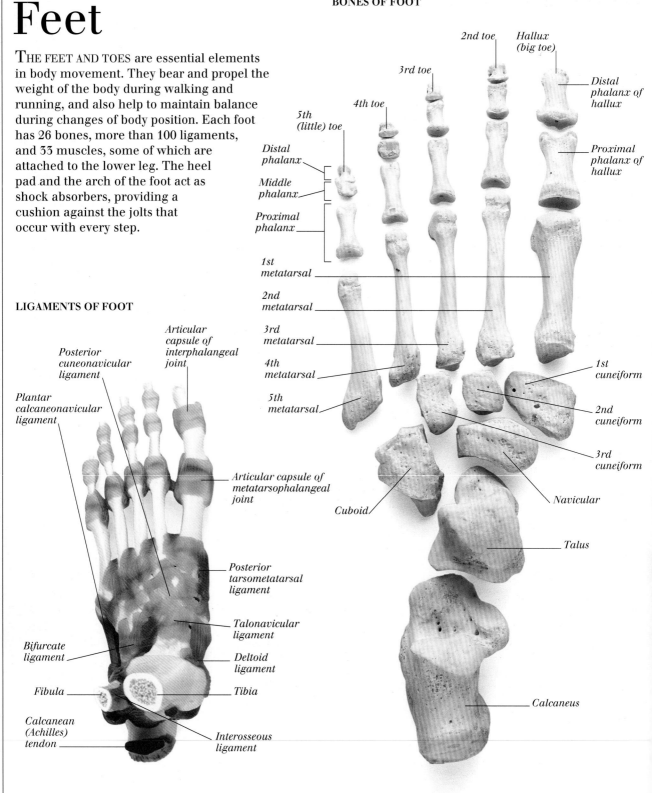

2nd toe

Hallux (big toe)

3rd toe

Distal phalanx of hallux

4th toe

Proximal phalanx of hallux

5th (little) toe

Distal phalanx

Middle phalanx

Proximal phalanx

1st metatarsal

2nd metatarsal

3rd metatarsal

4th metatarsal

5th metatarsal

1st cuneiform

2nd cuneiform

3rd cuneiform

Navicular

Cuboid

Talus

Calcaneus

LIGAMENTS OF FOOT

Articular capsule of interphalangeal joint

Posterior cuneonavicular ligament

Plantar calcaneonavicular ligament

Articular capsule of metatarsophalangeal joint

Posterior tarsometatarsal ligament

Talonavicular ligament

Bifurcate ligament

Deltoid ligament

Fibula

Tibia

Calcanean (Achilles) tendon

Interosseous ligament

STRUCTURES UNDERLYING SKIN OF FOOT

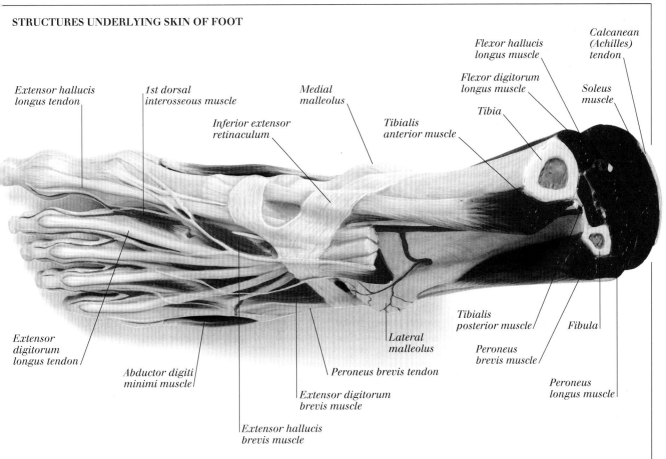

Extensor hallucis longus tendon

1st dorsal interosseous muscle

Medial malleolus

Flexor hallucis longus muscle

Calcanean (Achilles) tendon

Inferior extensor retinaculum

Flexor digitorum longus muscle

Soleus muscle

Tibialis anterior muscle

Tibia

Extensor digitorum longus tendon

Abductor digiti minimi muscle

Extensor digitorum brevis muscle

Lateral malleolus

Peroneus brevis tendon

Tibialis posterior muscle

Fibula

Peroneus brevis muscle

Peroneus longus muscle

Extensor hallucis brevis muscle

EXTERNAL FEATURES OF FOOT

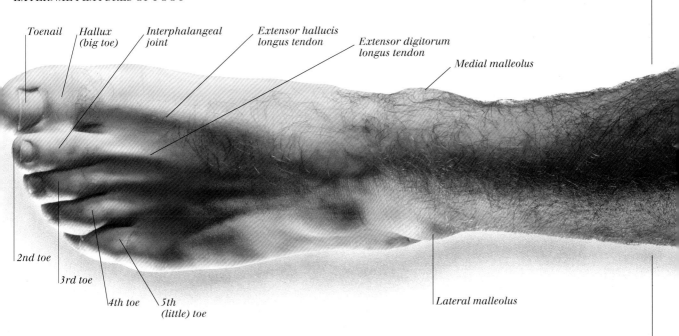

Toenail

Hallux (big toe)

Interphalangeal joint

Extensor hallucis longus tendon

Extensor digitorum longus tendon

Medial malleolus

2nd toe

3rd toe

4th toe

5th (little) toe

Lateral malleolus

Skin and hair

SKIN IS THE BODY'S LARGEST ORGAN, a waterproof barrier that protects the internal organs against infection, injury, and harmful sun rays. The skin is also an important sensory organ and helps to control body temperature. The outer layer of the skin, known as the epidermis, is coated with keratin, a tough, horny protein that is also the chief constituent of hair and nails. Dead cells are shed from the skin's surface and are replaced by new cells from the base of the epidermis, the region that also produces the skin pigment, melanin. The dermis contains most of the skin's living structures, and includes nerve endings, blood vessels, elastic fibres, sweat glands that cool the skin, and sebaceous glands that produce oil to keep the skin supple. Beneath the dermis lies the subcutaneous tissue (hypodermis), which is rich in fat and blood vessels. Hair shafts grow from hair follicles situated in the dermis and subcutaneous tissue. Hair grows on every part of the skin apart from the palms of the hands and soles of the feet.

SECTION OF HAIR

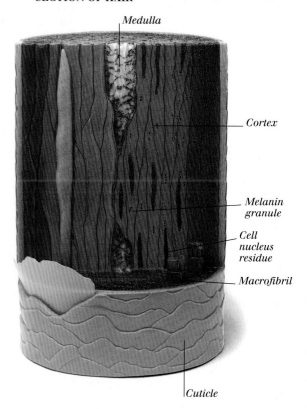

Medulla

Cortex

Melanin granule

Cell nucleus residue

Macrofibril

Cuticle

SECTIONS OF DIFFERENT TYPES OF SKIN

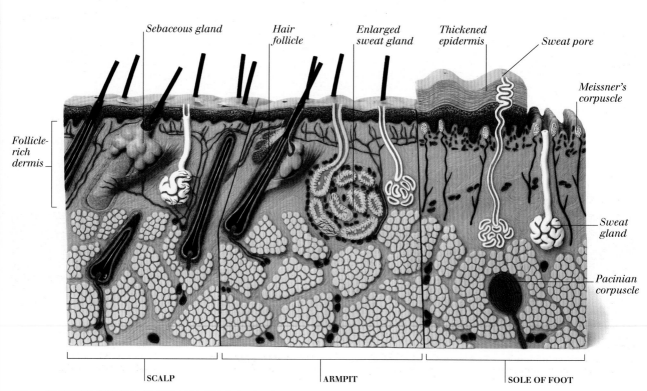

Sebaceous gland

Hair follicle

Enlarged sweat gland

Thickened epidermis

Sweat pore

Meissner's corpuscle

Follicle-rich dermis

Sweat gland

Pacinian corpuscle

SCALP

ARMPIT

SOLE OF FOOT

SECTION OF SKIN

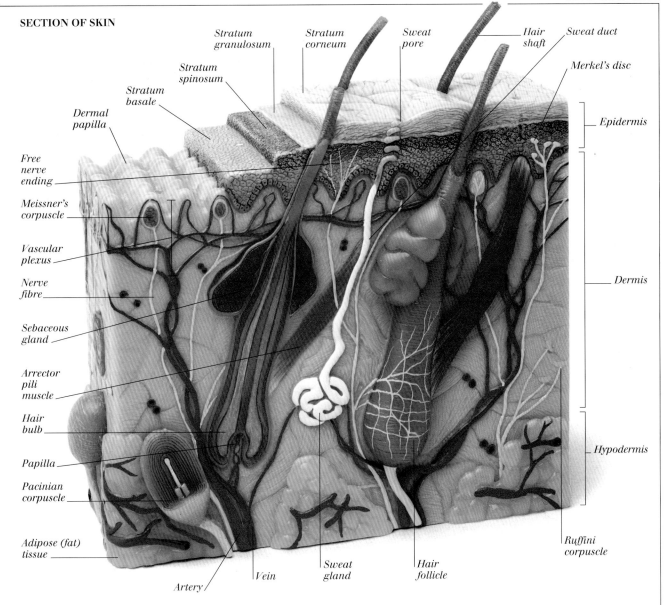

Stratum granulosum

Stratum corneum

Sweat pore

Hair shaft

Sweat duct

Merkel's disc

Stratum spinosum

Stratum basale

Dermal papilla

Free nerve ending

Meissner's corpuscle

Vascular plexus

Nerve fibre

Sebaceous gland

Arrector pili muscle

Hair bulb

Papilla

Pacinian corpuscle

Adipose (fat) tissue

Artery

Vein

Sweat gland

Hair follicle

Ruffini corpuscle

Epidermis

Dermis

Hypodermis

PHOTOMICROGRAPHS OF SKIN AND HAIR

SECTION OF SKIN
The flaky cells at the skin's surface are shed continuously.

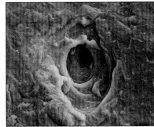

SWEAT PORE
This allows loss of fluid as part of temperature control.

SKIN HAIR
Two hairs pushing through the outer layer of skin.

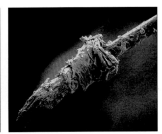

HEAD HAIR
The root and part of the shaft of a hair from the scalp.

Brain

THE BRAIN IS THE MAJOR ORGAN of the central nervous system and the control centre for all the body's voluntary and involuntary activities. It is also responsible for the complexities of thought, memory, emotion, and language. In adults, this complex organ is a mere 1.4 kg (3 lb) in weight, containing over 10 thousand million nerve cells. Three distinct regions can easily be seen – the brainstem, the cerebellum, and the large cerebrum. The brainstem controls vital body functions, such as breathing and digestion. The cerebellum's main functions are the maintenance of posture and the coordination of body movements. The cerebrum, which consists of the right and left cerebral hemispheres joined by the corpus callosum, is the site of most conscious and intelligent activities.

MRI SCAN OF TRANSVERSE SECTION THROUGH BRAIN

White matter
Grey matter
Skull
Scalp
Longitudinal fissure
Lateral ventricle
Coronal section
Sagittal section
Cerebrum

SAGITTAL SECTION THROUGH BRAIN

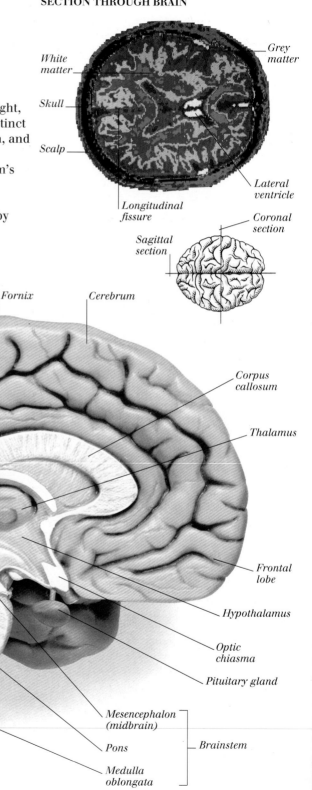

Central sulcus
Fornix
Cerebrum
Parietal lobe
Corpus callosum
Parieto-occipital sulcus
Thalamus
Pineal body
Occipital lobe
Frontal lobe
Aqueduct
Hypothalamus
Cerebellum
Optic chiasma
4th ventricle
Pituitary gland
Mesencephalon (midbrain)
Spinal cord
Pons
Brainstem
Medulla oblongata

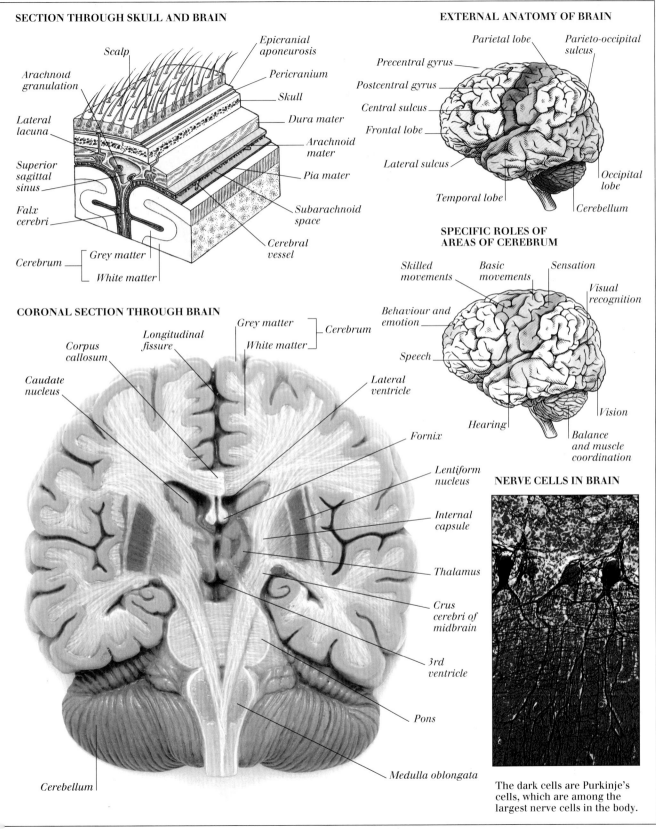

SECTION THROUGH SKULL AND BRAIN

Scalp
Epicranial aponeurosis
Arachnoid granulation
Pericranium
Skull
Lateral lacuna
Dura mater
Arachnoid mater
Superior sagittal sinus
Pia mater
Falx cerebri
Subarachnoid space
Cerebrum
Grey matter
White matter
Cerebral vessel

EXTERNAL ANATOMY OF BRAIN

Parietal lobe
Parieto-occipital sulcus
Precentral gyrus
Postcentral gyrus
Central sulcus
Frontal lobe
Lateral sulcus
Occipital lobe
Temporal lobe
Cerebellum

SPECIFIC ROLES OF AREAS OF CEREBRUM

Skilled movements
Basic movements
Sensation
Visual recognition
Behaviour and emotion
Speech
Hearing
Vision
Balance and muscle coordination

CORONAL SECTION THROUGH BRAIN

Corpus callosum
Longitudinal fissure
Grey matter
White matter
Cerebrum
Caudate nucleus
Lateral ventricle
Fornix
Lentiform nucleus
Internal capsule
Thalamus
Crus cerebri of midbrain
3rd ventricle
Pons
Medulla oblongata
Cerebellum

NERVE CELLS IN BRAIN

The dark cells are Purkinje's cells, which are among the largest nerve cells in the body.

Nervous system

THE NERVOUS SYSTEM IS THE BODY'S internal, electrochemical, communications network. Its main parts are the brain, spinal cord, and nerves. The brain and spinal cord form the central nervous system (CNS), the body's chief controlling and coordinating centres. Billions of long neurons, many grouped as nerves, make up the peripheral nervous system, transmitting nerve impulses between the CNS and other regions of the body. Each neuron has three parts: a cell body, branching dendrites that receive chemical signals from other neurons, and a tube-like axon that conveys these signals as electrical impulses.

CENTRAL AND PERIPHERAL NERVOUS SYSTEMS

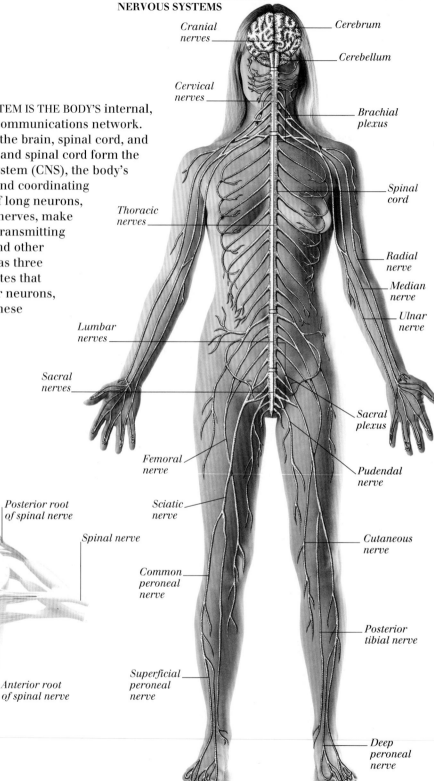

Cranial nerves

Cerebrum

Cerebellum

Cervical nerves

Brachial plexus

Thoracic nerves

Spinal cord

Radial nerve

Median nerve

Ulnar nerve

Lumbar nerves

Sacral nerves

Sacral plexus

Femoral nerve

Pudendal nerve

Sciatic nerve

Cutaneous nerve

Common peroneal nerve

Posterior tibial nerve

Superficial peroneal nerve

Deep peroneal nerve

SECTION THROUGH SPINAL CORD

Spinal ganglion

Grey matter

Central canal

Posterior root of spinal nerve

Spinal nerve

White matter

Anterior median fissure

Anterior root of spinal nerve

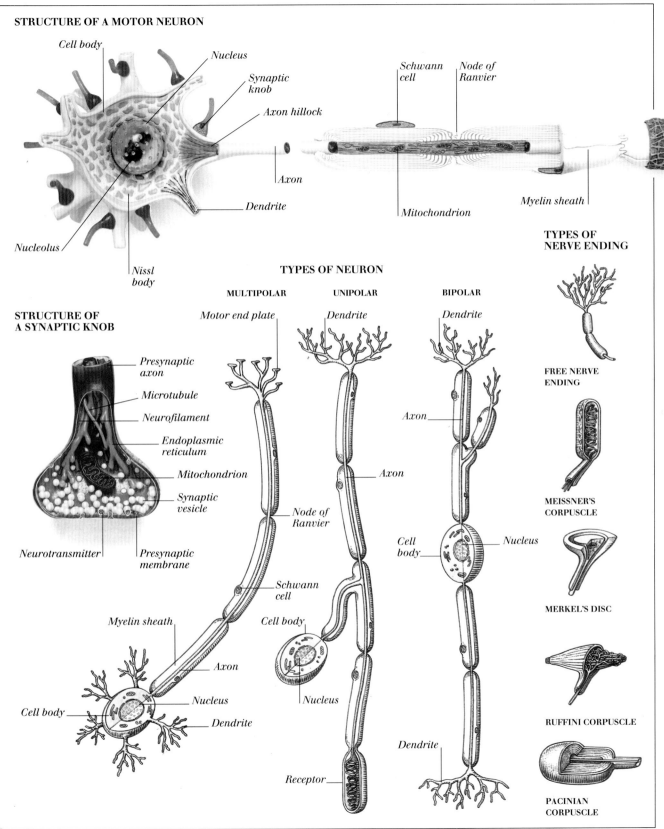

STRUCTURE OF A MOTOR NEURON

Cell body

Nucleus

Synaptic knob

Axon hillock

Axon

Dendrite

Nucleolus

Nissl body

Schwann cell

Node of Ranvier

Mitochondrion

Myelin sheath

TYPES OF NERVE ENDING

FREE NERVE ENDING

MEISSNER'S CORPUSCLE

MERKEL'S DISC

RUFFINI CORPUSCLE

PACINIAN CORPUSCLE

STRUCTURE OF A SYNAPTIC KNOB

Presynaptic axon

Microtubule

Neurofilament

Endoplasmic reticulum

Mitochondrion

Synaptic vesicle

Neurotransmitter

Presynaptic membrane

TYPES OF NEURON

MULTIPOLAR

Motor end plate

Node of Ranvier

Schwann cell

Myelin sheath

Axon

Nucleus

Cell body

Dendrite

UNIPOLAR

Dendrite

Axon

Cell body

Nucleus

Receptor

BIPOLAR

Dendrite

Axon

Cell body

Nucleus

Dendrite

Eye

THE EYE IS THE ORGAN OF SIGHT. The two eyeballs, protected within bony sockets called orbits and on the outside by the eyelids, eyebrows, and tear film, are directly connected to the brain by the optic nerves. Each eye is moved by six muscles, which are attached around the eyeball. Light rays entering the eye through the pupil are focused by the cornea and lens to form an image on the retina. The retina contains millions of light-sensitive cells, called rods and cones, which convert the image into a pattern of nerve impulses. These impulses are transmitted along the optic nerve to the brain. Information from the two optic nerves is processed in the brain to produce a single coordinated image.

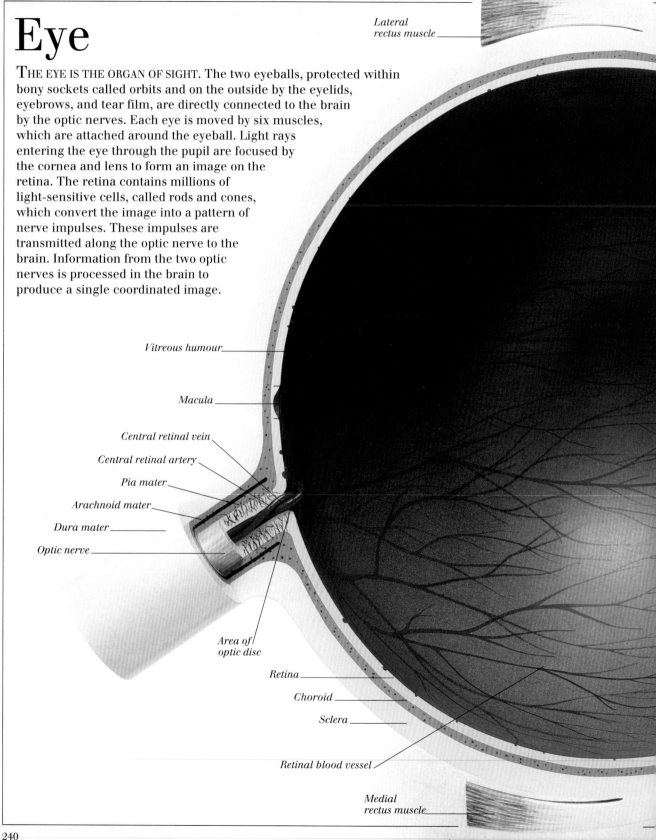

Lateral rectus muscle

Vitreous humour

Macula

Central retinal vein

Central retinal artery

Pia mater

Arachnoid mater

Dura mater

Optic nerve

Area of optic disc

Retina

Choroid

Sclera

Retinal blood vessel

Medial rectus muscle

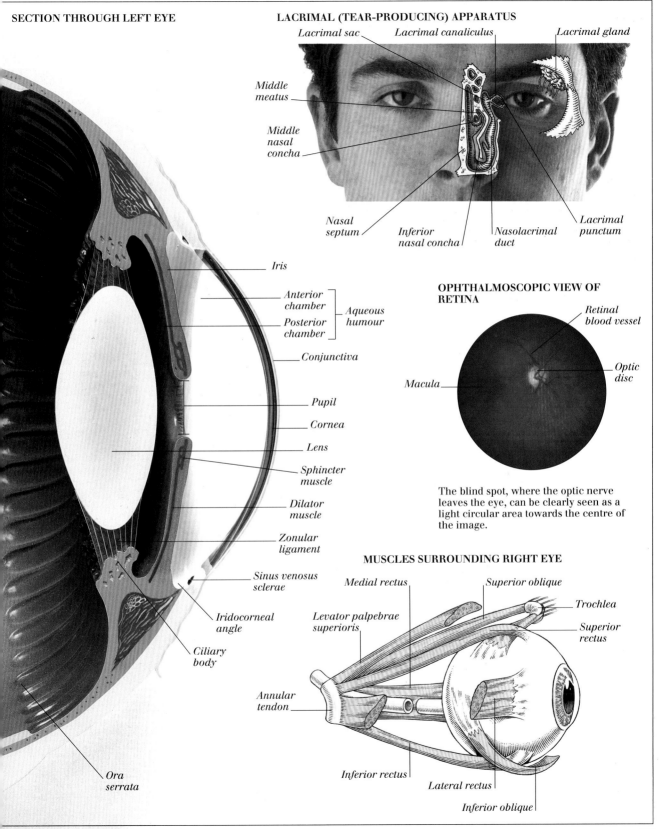

SECTION THROUGH LEFT EYE

LACRIMAL (TEAR-PRODUCING) APPARATUS

Lacrimal sac
Lacrimal canaliculus
Lacrimal gland

Middle meatus

Middle nasal concha

Nasal septum

Inferior nasal concha

Nasolacrimal duct

Lacrimal punctum

Iris

Anterior chamber

Posterior chamber

Aqueous humour

Conjunctiva

Pupil

Cornea

Lens

Sphincter muscle

Dilator muscle

Zonular ligament

Sinus venosus sclerae

Iridocorneal angle

Ciliary body

Ora serrata

OPHTHALMOSCOPIC VIEW OF RETINA

Retinal blood vessel

Optic disc

Macula

The blind spot, where the optic nerve leaves the eye, can be clearly seen as a light circular area towards the centre of the image.

MUSCLES SURROUNDING RIGHT EYE

Medial rectus
Superior oblique
Trochlea
Superior rectus

Levator palpebrae superioris

Annular tendon

Inferior rectus
Lateral rectus
Inferior oblique

Ear

THE EAR IS THE ORGAN OF HEARING AND BALANCE. The outer ear consists of a flap called the auricle or pinna and the auditory canal. The main functional parts – the middle and inner ears – are enclosed within the skull. The middle ear consists of three tiny bones, known as auditory ossicles, and the eustachian tube, which links the ear to the back of the nose. The inner ear consists of the spiral-shaped cochlea, and also the semicircular canals and the vestibule, which are the organs of balance. Sound waves entering the ear travel through the auditory canal to the tympanic membrane (eardrum), where they are converted to vibrations that are transmitted via the ossicles to the cochlea. Here, the vibrations are converted by millions of microscopic hairs into electrical nerve signals to be interpreted by the brain.

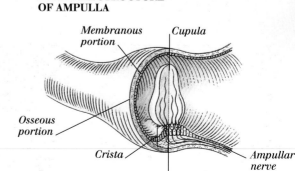

Temporal bone

Cartilage
of auricle

Auricle
(pinna)

Auditory canal

Mastoid
process

Lobule

Cartilaginous
part of meatus

RIGHT AURICLE (PINNA)

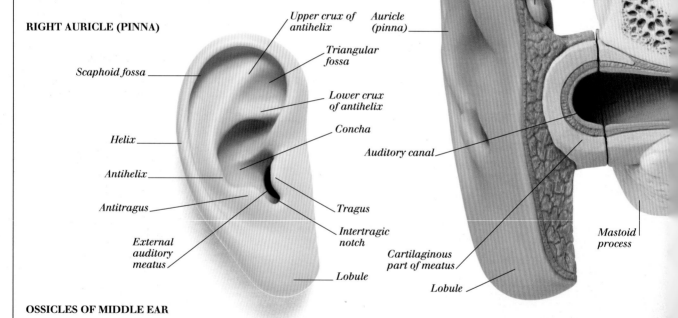

Upper crux of
antihelix

Triangular
fossa

Lower crux
of antihelix

Concha

Scaphoid fossa

Helix

Antihelix

Antitragus

External
auditory
meatus

Tragus

Intertragic
notch

Lobule

OSSICLES OF MIDDLE EAR

INTERNAL STRUCTURE
OF AMPULLA

Membranous
portion

Cupula

Osseous
portion

Crista

Hair cell
of crista

Ampullar
nerve

MALLEUS (HAMMER)   **INCUS (ANVIL)**   **STAPES (STIRRUP)**

These three tiny bones connect to form a bridge between the tympanic membrane and the oval window. With a system of membranes they convey sound vibrations to the inner ear.

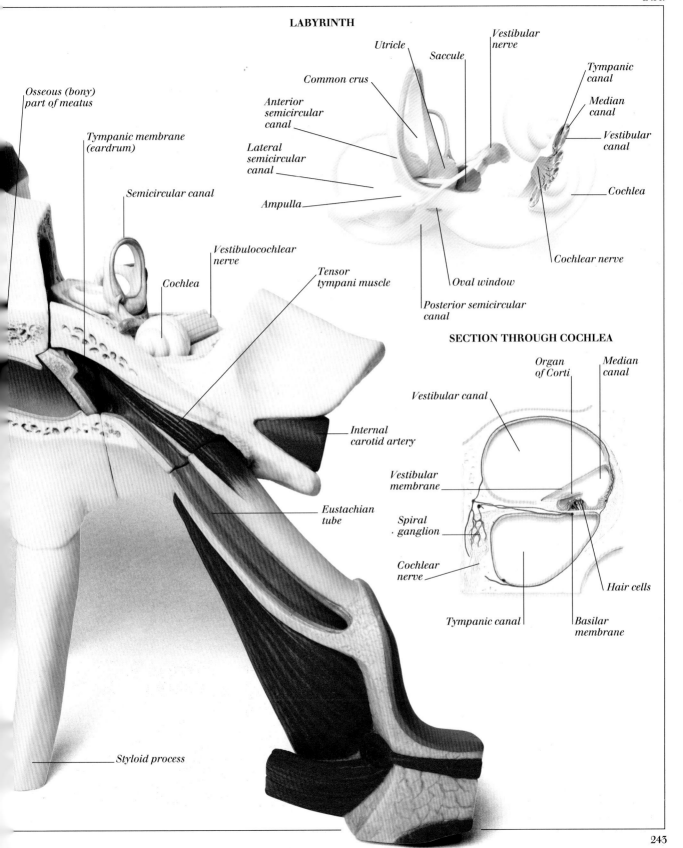

LABYRINTH

Utricle

Saccule

Vestibular nerve

Common crus

Tympanic canal

Anterior semicircular canal

Median canal

Osseous (bony) part of meatus

Vestibular canal

Tympanic membrane (eardrum)

Lateral semicircular canal

Cochlea

Semicircular canal

Ampulla

Vestibulocochlear nerve

Cochlear nerve

Cochlea

Tensor tympani muscle

Oval window

Posterior semicircular canal

Internal carotid artery

SECTION THROUGH COCHLEA

Organ of Corti

Median canal

Vestibular canal

Eustachian tube

Vestibular membrane

Spiral ganglion

Cochlear nerve

Hair cells

Styloid process

Tympanic canal

Basilar membrane

Nose, mouth, and throat

WITH EVERY BREATH, air passes through the nasal cavity down the pharynx (throat), larynx ("voice box"), and trachea (windpipe) to the lungs. The nasal cavity warms and moistens air, and the tiny layers in its lining protect the airway against damage by foreign bodies. During swallowing, the tongue moves up and back, the larynx rises, the epiglottis closes off the entrance to the trachea, and the soft palate separates the nasal cavity from the pharynx. Saliva, secreted from three pairs of salivary glands, lubricates food to make swallowing easier; it also begins the chemical breakdown of food, and helps to produce taste. The senses of taste and smell are closely linked. Both depend on the detection of dissolved molecules by sensory receptors in the olfactory nerve endings of the nose and in the taste buds of the tongue.

STRUCTURE OF TONGUE

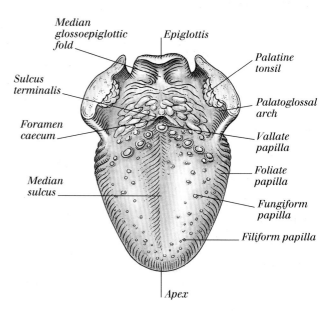

- Median glossoepiglottic fold
- Epiglottis
- Palatine tonsil
- Sulcus terminalis
- Palatoglossal arch
- Foramen caecum
- Vallate papilla
- Foliate papilla
- Median sulcus
- Fungiform papilla
- Filiform papilla
- Apex

TASTE AREAS ON TONGUE

- Bitter
- Sour
- Salt
- Sweet

STRUCTURES SURROUNDING PHARYNX

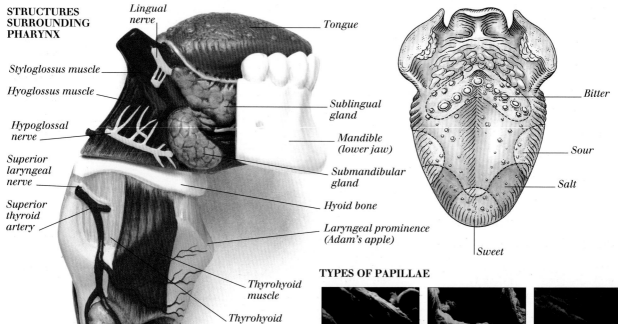

- Lingual nerve
- Tongue
- Styloglossus muscle
- Hyoglossus muscle
- Sublingual gland
- Hypoglossal nerve
- Mandible (lower jaw)
- Superior laryngeal nerve
- Submandibular gland
- Superior thyroid artery
- Hyoid bone
- Laryngeal prominence (Adam's apple)
- Thyrohyoid muscle
- Thyrohyoid membrane
- Cricothyroid muscle
- Cricothyroid ligament
- Thyroid gland
- Trachea

TYPES OF PAPILLAE

FILIFORM PAPILLAE   FUNGIFORM PAPILLAE   VALLATE PAPILLAE

SECTION THROUGH NOSE, MOUTH, AND THROAT

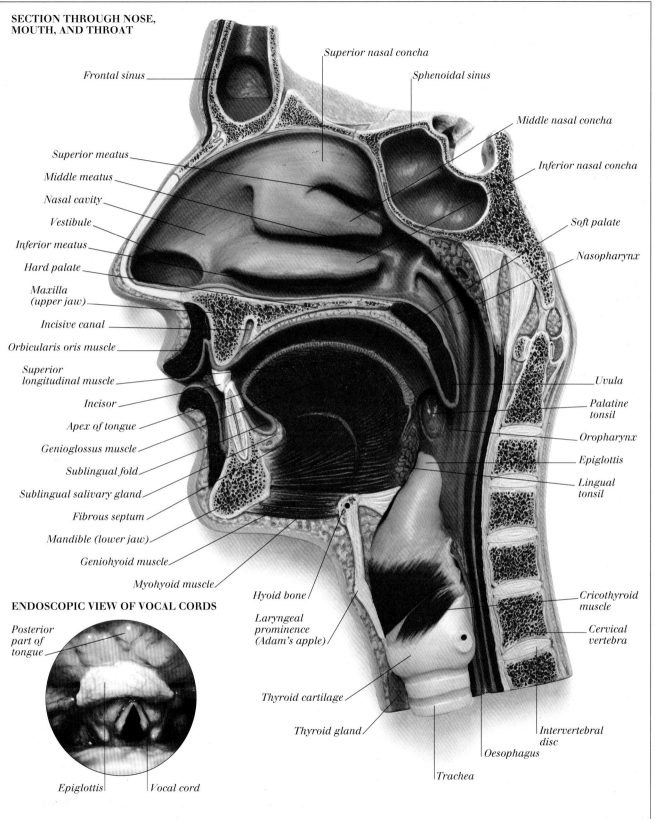

Frontal sinus

Superior nasal concha

Sphenoidal sinus

Middle nasal concha

Inferior nasal concha

Superior meatus

Middle meatus

Nasal cavity

Vestibule

Inferior meatus

Hard palate

Soft palate

Nasopharynx

Maxilla (upper jaw)

Incisive canal

Orbicularis oris muscle

Superior longitudinal muscle

Incisor

Apex of tongue

Genioglossus muscle

Sublingual fold

Sublingual salivary gland

Fibrous septum

Mandible (lower jaw)

Geniohyoid muscle

Myohyoid muscle

Uvula

Palatine tonsil

Oropharynx

Epiglottis

Lingual tonsil

Cricothyroid muscle

Cervical vertebra

Intervertebral disc

Oesophagus

Trachea

Hyoid bone

Laryngeal prominence (Adam's apple)

Thyroid cartilage

Thyroid gland

ENDOSCOPIC VIEW OF VOCAL CORDS

Posterior part of tongue

Epiglottis

Vocal cord

Teeth

THE 20 PRIMARY TEETH (also called deciduous or milk teeth) usually begin to erupt when a baby is about six months old. They start to be replaced by the permanent teeth when the child is about six years old. By the age of 20, most adults have a full set of 32 teeth although the third molars (commonly called wisdom teeth) may never erupt. While teeth help people to speak clearly and give shape to the face, their main function is the chewing of food. Incisors and canines shear and tear the food into pieces; premolars and molars crush and grind it further. Although tooth enamel is the hardest substance in the body, it tends to be eroded and destroyed by acid produced in the mouth during the breakdown of food.

DEVELOPMENT OF TEETH IN A FETUS

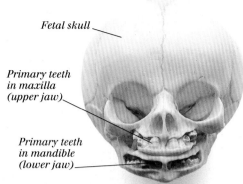

Fetal skull

*Primary teeth
in maxilla
(upper jaw)*

*Primary teeth
in mandible
(lower jaw)*

FETAL JAWS
By the sixth week of embryonic development areas of thickening occur in each jaw; these areas give rise to tooth buds. By the time the fetus is six months old, enamel has formed on the tooth buds.

DEVELOPMENT OF JAW AND TEETH

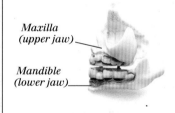

*Maxilla
(upper jaw)*

*Mandible
(lower jaw)*

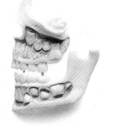

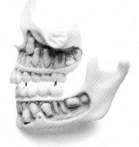

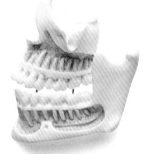

A NEWBORN BABY'S JAWS
The primary teeth can be seen developing in the jaw bones; they begin to erupt around the age of six months.

A FIVE-YEAR-OLD CHILD'S TEETH
There is a full set of 20 erupted primary teeth; the permanent teeth can be seen developing in the upper and lower jaws.

A NINE-YEAR-OLD CHILD'S TEETH
Most of the teeth are primary teeth but the permanent incisors and first molars have now emerged.

AN ADULT'S TEETH
By the age of 20, the full set of 32 permanent teeth (including the wisdom teeth) should be in position.

THE PERMANENT TEETH

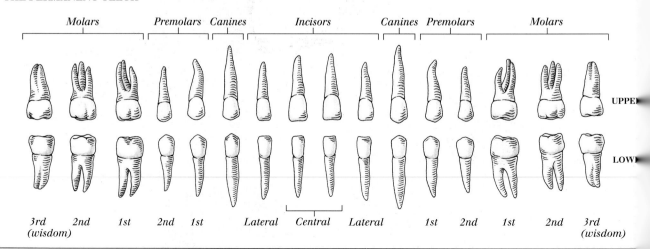

| Molars | | | Premolars | | Canines | Incisors | | | Canines | Premolars | | Molars | | |

| 3rd (wisdom) | 2nd | 1st | 2nd | 1st | | Lateral | Central | Lateral | | 1st | 2nd | 1st | 2nd | 3rd (wisdom) |

UPPER

LOWER

STRUCTURE OF A TOOTH

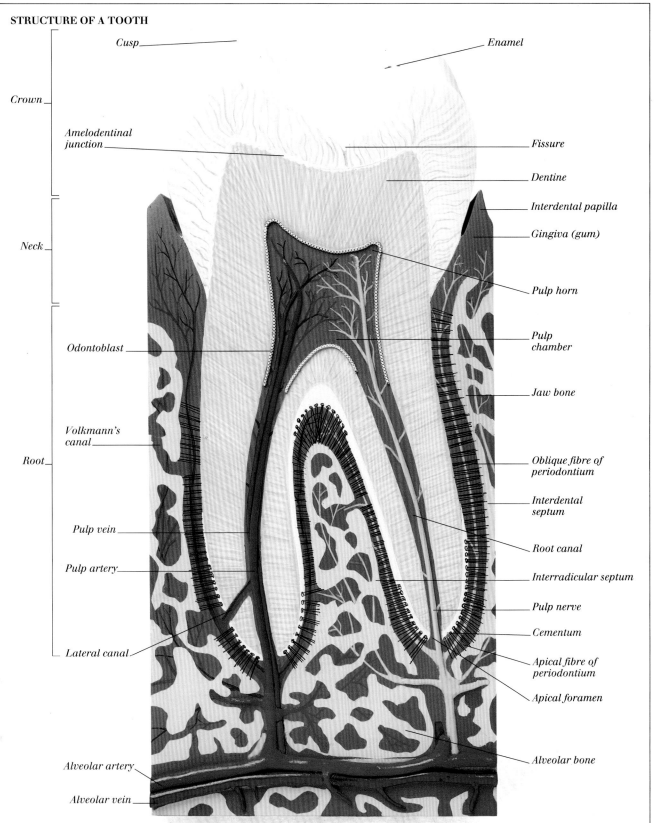

Cusp

Enamel

Crown

Amelodentinal junction

Fissure

Dentine

Neck

Interdental papilla

Gingiva (gum)

Pulp horn

Odontoblast

Pulp chamber

Jaw bone

Volkmann's canal

Root

Oblique fibre of periodontium

Interdental septum

Pulp vein

Root canal

Pulp artery

Interradicular septum

Pulp nerve

Cementum

Lateral canal

Apical fibre of periodontium

Apical foramen

Alveolar artery

Alveolar bone

Alveolar vein

Digestive system

THE DIGESTIVE SYSTEM BREAKS DOWN FOOD into particles so tiny that blood can take nourishment to all parts of the body. The system's main part is a 9 m (30 ft) tube from mouth to rectum; muscles in this alimentary canal force food along. Chewed food first travels through the oesophagus to the stomach, which churns and liquidizes food before it passes through the duodenum, jejunum, and ileum – the three parts of the long, convoluted small intestine. Here, digestive juices from the gallbladder and pancreas break down food particles; many filter out into the blood through tiny fingerlike villi that line the small intestine's inner wall. Undigested food in the colon forms faeces that leave the body through the anus.

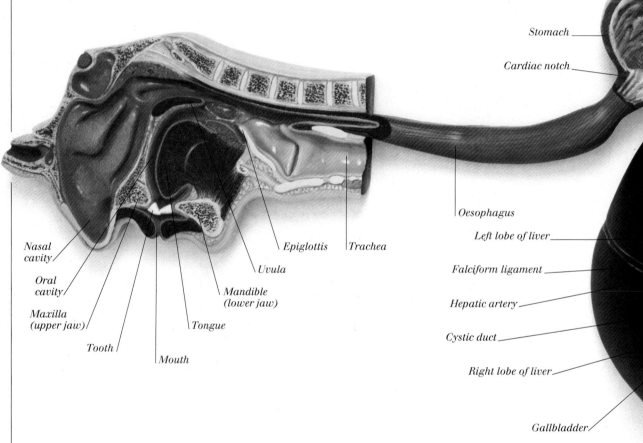

Stomach

Cardiac notch

Oesophagus

Left lobe of liver

Falciform ligament

Hepatic artery

Cystic duct

Right lobe of liver

Gallbladder

Nasal cavity

Oral cavity

Maxilla (upper jaw)

Tooth

Mouth

Tongue

Mandible (lower jaw)

Uvula

Epiglottis

Trachea

ENDOSCOPIC VIEWS INSIDE ALIMENTARY CANAL

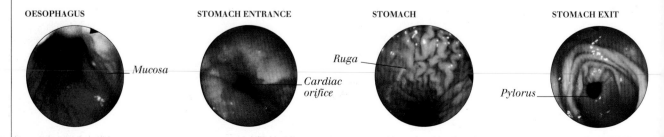

OESOPHAGUS

Mucosa

STOMACH ENTRANCE

Cardiac orifice

STOMACH

Ruga

STOMACH EXIT

Pylorus

ALIMENTARY CANAL

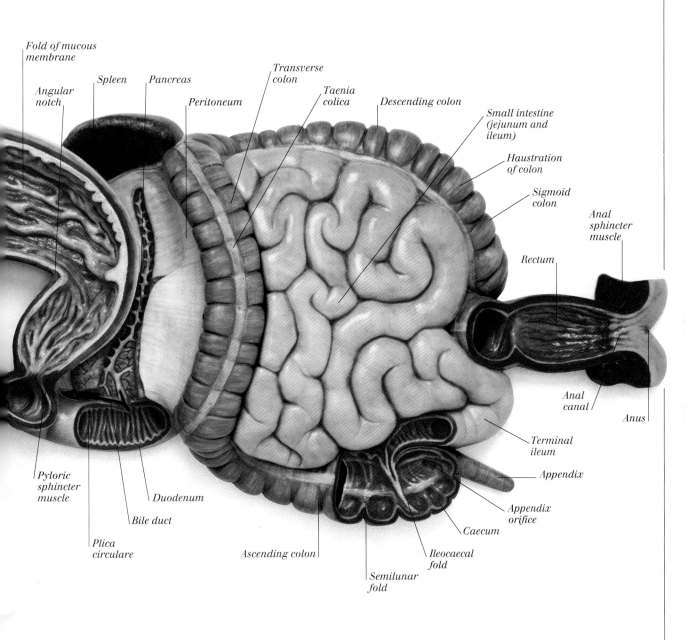

Fold of mucous membrane

Angular notch

Spleen

Pancreas

Peritoneum

Transverse colon

Taenia colica

Descending colon

Small intestine (jejunum and ileum)

Haustration of colon

Sigmoid colon

Anal sphincter muscle

Rectum

Anal canal

Anus

Terminal ileum

Appendix

Appendix orifice

Caecum

Ileocaecal fold

Semilunar fold

Ascending colon

Pyloric sphincter muscle

Duodenum

Bile duct

Plica circulare

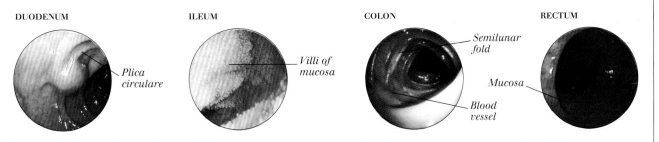

DUODENUM

Plica circulare

ILEUM

Villi of mucosa

COLON

Semilunar fold

Blood vessel

RECTUM

Mucosa

Heart

THE HEART IS A HOLLOW MUSCLE in the middle of the chest that pumps blood around the body, supplying cells with oxygen and nutrients. A muscular wall, called the septum, divides the heart lengthways into left and right sides. A valve divides each side into two chambers: an upper atrium and a lower ventricle. When the heart muscle contracts, it squeezes blood through the atria and then through the ventricles. Oxygenated blood from the lungs flows from the pulmonary veins into the left atrium, through the left ventricle, and then out via the aorta to all parts of the body. Deoxygenated blood returning from the body flows from the vena cava into the right atrium, through the right ventricle, and then out via the pulmonary artery to the lungs for reoxygenation. At rest the heart beats between 60 and 80 times a minute; during exercise or at times of stress or excitement the rate may increase to 200 beats a minute.

ARTERIES AND VEINS SURROUNDING HEART

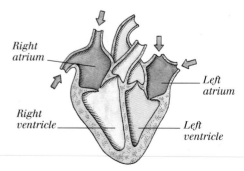

Aorta

Left coronary artery

Cardiac vein

Right coronary artery

Coronary sinus

Main branch of left coronary artery

SECTION THROUGH HEART WALL

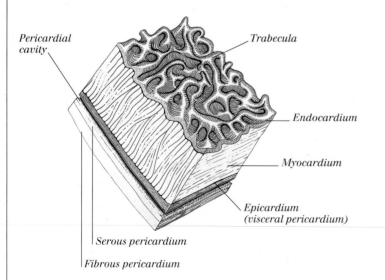

Pericardial cavity

Trabecula

Endocardium

Myocardium

Epicardium (visceral pericardium)

Serous pericardium

Fibrous pericardium

HEARTBEAT SEQUENCE

ATRIAL DIASTOLE

Right atrium

Left atrium

Right ventricle

Left ventricle

Deoxygenated blood enters the right atrium while the left atrium receives oxygenated blood.

STRUCTURE OF HEART

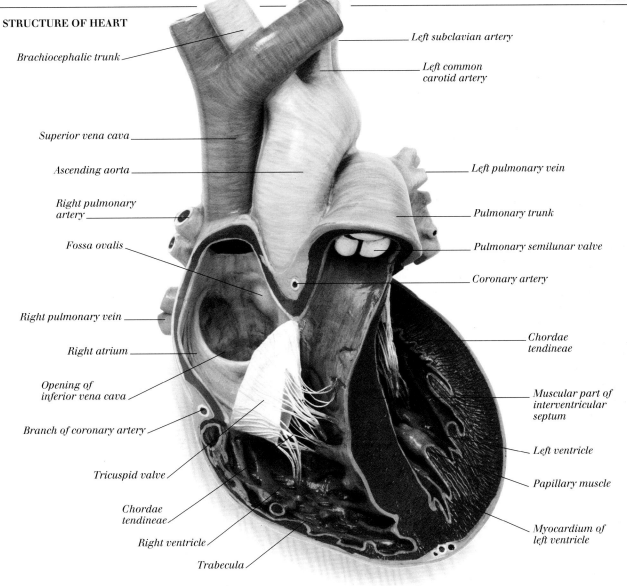

Brachiocephalic trunk

Superior vena cava

Ascending aorta

Right pulmonary artery

Fossa ovalis

Right pulmonary vein

Right atrium

Opening of inferior vena cava

Branch of coronary artery

Tricuspid valve

Chordae tendineae

Right ventricle

Trabecula

Left subclavian artery

Left common carotid artery

Left pulmonary vein

Pulmonary trunk

Pulmonary semilunar valve

Coronary artery

Chordae tendineae

Muscular part of interventricular septum

Left ventricle

Papillary muscle

Myocardium of left ventricle

ATRIAL SYSTOLE (VENTRICULAR DIASTOLE)

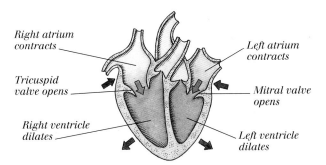

Right atrium contracts

Tricuspid valve opens

Right ventricle dilates

Left atrium contracts

Mitral valve opens

Left ventricle dilates

Left and right atria contract, forcing blood into the relaxed ventricles.

VENTRICULAR SYSTOLE

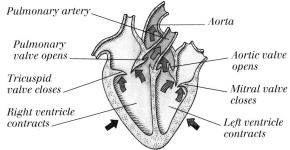

Pulmonary artery

Pulmonary valve opens

Tricuspid valve closes

Right ventricle contracts

Aorta

Aortic valve opens

Mitral valve closes

Left ventricle contracts

Ventricles contract and force blood to the lungs for oxygenation and via the aorta to the rest of the body.

251

Circulatory system

THE CIRCULATORY SYSTEM consists of the heart and blood vessels, which together maintain a continuous flow of blood around the body. The heart pumps oxygen-rich blood from the lungs to all parts of the body through a network of tubes called arteries, and smaller branches called arterioles. Blood returns to the heart via small vessels called venules, which lead in turn into larger tubes called veins. Arterioles and venules are linked by a network of tiny vessels called capillaries, where the exchange of oxygen and carbon dioxide between blood and body cells takes place. Blood has four main components: red blood cells, white blood cells, platelets, and liquid plasma.

ARTERIAL SYSTEM OF BRAIN

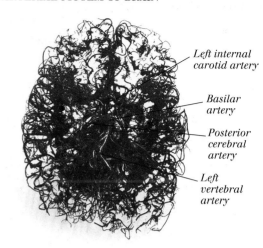

Left internal carotid artery

Basilar artery

Posterior cerebral artery

Left vertebral artery

CIRCULATORY SYSTEM OF HEART AND LUNGS

Superior vena cava

Aorta

Right ventricle

Left ventricle

CIRCULATORY SYSTEM OF LIVER

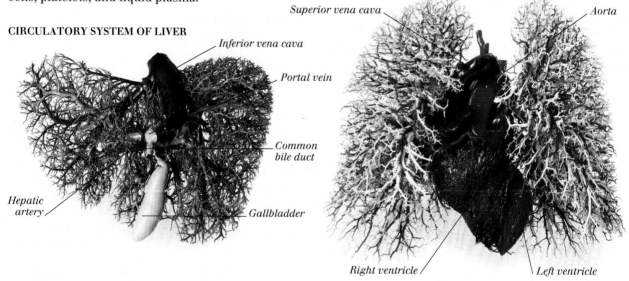

Inferior vena cava

Portal vein

Common bile duct

Hepatic artery

Gallbladder

SECTION OF MAIN ARTERY

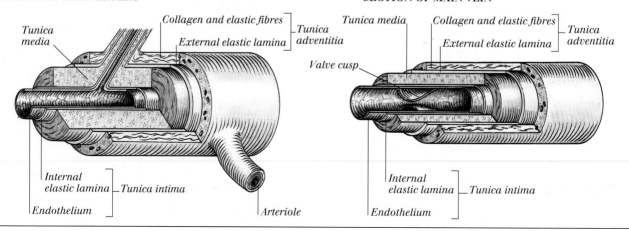

Tunica media

Collagen and elastic fibres

External elastic lamina

Tunica adventitia

Internal elastic lamina

Tunica intima

Endothelium

Arteriole

SECTION OF MAIN VEIN

Tunica media

Collagen and elastic fibres

External elastic lamina

Tunica adventitia

Valve cusp

Internal elastic lamina

Tunica intima

Endothelium

PRINCIPAL ARTERIES AND VEINS OF CIRCULATORY SYSTEM

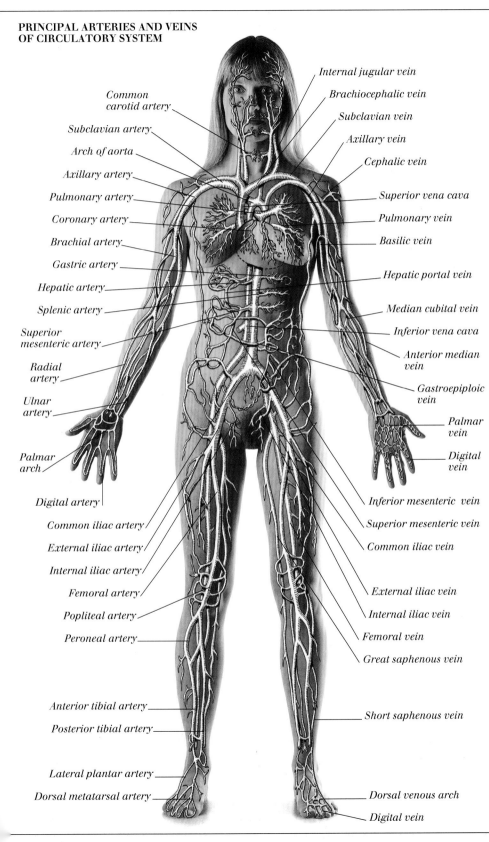

Common carotid artery

Subclavian artery

Arch of aorta

Axillary artery

Pulmonary artery

Coronary artery

Brachial artery

Gastric artery

Hepatic artery

Splenic artery

Superior mesenteric artery

Radial artery

Ulnar artery

Palmar arch

Digital artery

Common iliac artery

External iliac artery

Internal iliac artery

Femoral artery

Popliteal artery

Peroneal artery

Anterior tibial artery

Posterior tibial artery

Lateral plantar artery

Dorsal metatarsal artery

Internal jugular vein

Brachiocephalic vein

Subclavian vein

Axillary vein

Cephalic vein

Superior vena cava

Pulmonary vein

Basilic vein

Hepatic portal vein

Median cubital vein

Inferior vena cava

Anterior median vein

Gastroepiploic vein

Palmar vein

Digital vein

Inferior mesenteric vein

Superior mesenteric vein

Common iliac vein

External iliac vein

Internal iliac vein

Femoral vein

Great saphenous vein

Short saphenous vein

Dorsal venous arch

Digital vein

TYPES OF BLOOD CELLS

RED BLOOD CELLS
These cells are biconcave in shape to maximize their oxygen-carrying capacity.

WHITE BLOOD CELLS
Lymphocytes are the smallest white blood cells; they form antibodies against disease.

PLATELETS
Tiny cells that are activated whenever blood clotting or repair to vessels is necessary.

BLOOD CLOTTING

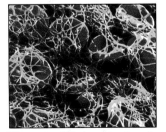

Filaments of fibrin enmesh red blood cells as part of the process of blood clotting.

Respiratory system

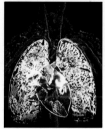

THE RESPIRATORY SYSTEM supplies the oxygen needed by body cells and carries off their carbon dioxide waste. Inhaled air passes via the trachea (windpipe) through two narrower tubes, the bronchi, to the lungs. Each lung comprises many fine, branching tubes called bronchioles that end in tiny clustered chambers called alveoli. Gases cross the thin alveolar walls to and from a network of tiny blood vessels. Intercostal (rib) muscles and the muscular diaphragm below the lungs operate the lungs like bellows, drawing air in and forcing it out at regular intervals.

BRONCHIOLE AND ALVEOLI

Bronchial nerve

Visceral cartilage

Branch of pulmonary vein

Mucosal gland

Terminal bronchiole

Bronchial vein

Branch of pulmonary artery

Elastic fibres

Interalveolar septum

Alveolus

Connective tissue

Capillary network

Epithelium

SEGMENTS OF BRONCHIAL TREE

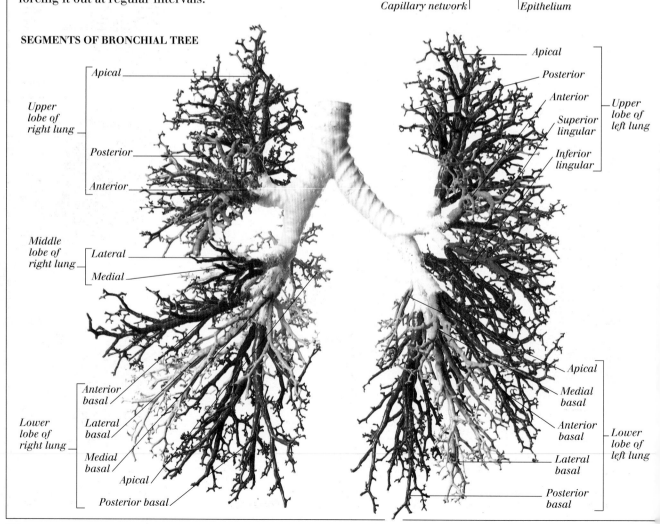

Apical

Upper lobe of right lung

Posterior

Anterior

Middle lobe of right lung

Lateral

Medial

Lower lobe of right lung

Anterior basal

Lateral basal

Medial basal

Apical

Posterior basal

Apical

Posterior

Anterior

Superior lingular

Inferior lingular

Upper lobe of left lung

Apical

Medial basal

Anterior basal

Lateral basal

Posterior basal

Lower lobe of left lung

STRUCTURES OF THORACIC CAVITY

Epiglottis

Hyoid bone

Thyroid cartilage

Thyroid gland

Cricoid cartilage

Apex of lung

Trachea

Superior vena cava

Aorta

Upper lobe of right lung

Upper lobe of left lung

Horizontal fissure

Pulmonary trunk

Oblique fissure

Left pulmonary artery

Heart

Lower lobe of left lung

Secondary bronchus

Tertiary bronchus

Lower lobe of right lung

Middle lobe of right lung

Right crus of diaphragm

Abdominal aorta

Left crus of diaphragm

Oesophagus

Muscular wall of diaphragm

GASEOUS EXCHANGE IN ALVEOLUS

Oxygen diffuses into blood

Oxygenated blood

Alveolus

Deoxygenated blood rich in carbon dioxide

Carbon dioxide diffuses from blood into alveolus

MECHANISM OF RESPIRATION

INSPIRATION

Lung expands

Air drawn into lungs

Diaphragm contracts and flattens

Intercostal muscles contract

EXPIRATION

Lung contracts

Air forced out of lungs

Diaphragm relaxes and moves up

Intercostal muscles relax

255

Urinary system

THE URINARY SYSTEM FILTERS WASTE PRODUCTS from the blood and removes them from the body via a system of tubes. Blood is filtered in the two kidneys, which are fist-sized, bean-shaped organs. The renal arteries carry blood to the kidneys; the renal veins remove blood after filtering. Each kidney contains about one million tiny units called nephrons. Each nephron is made up of a tubule and a filtering unit called a glomerulus, which consists of a collection of tiny blood vessels surrounded by the hollow Bowman's capsule. The filtering process produces a watery fluid that leaves the kidney as urine. The urine is carried via two tubes called ureters to the bladder, where it is stored until its release from the body through another tube called the urethra.

ARTERIAL SYSTEM OF KIDNEYS

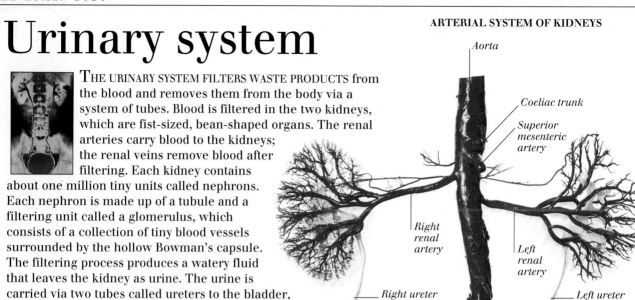

Aorta

Coeliac trunk

Superior mesenteric artery

Right renal artery

Left renal artery

Right ureter

Left ureter

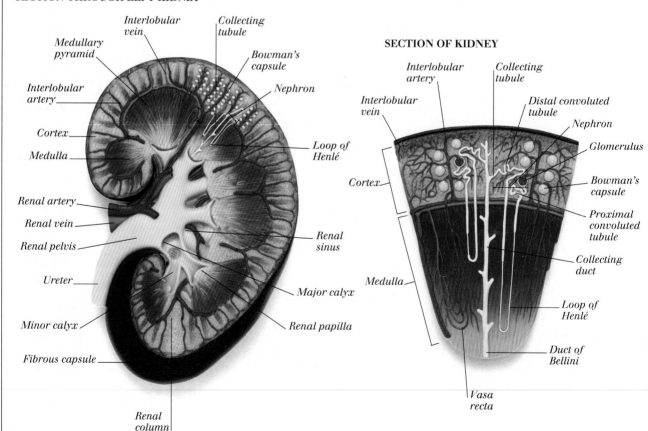

SECTION THROUGH LEFT KIDNEY

Interlobular vein

Collecting tubule

Medullary pyramid

Bowman's capsule

Interlobular artery

Nephron

Cortex

Medulla

Loop of Henlé

Renal artery

Renal vein

Renal pelvis

Renal sinus

Ureter

Major calyx

Minor calyx

Renal papilla

Fibrous capsule

Renal column

SECTION OF KIDNEY

Interlobular artery

Collecting tubule

Interlobular vein

Distal convoluted tubule

Nephron

Glomerulus

Cortex

Bowman's capsule

Proximal convoluted tubule

Medulla

Collecting duct

Loop of Henlé

Duct of Bellini

Vasa recta

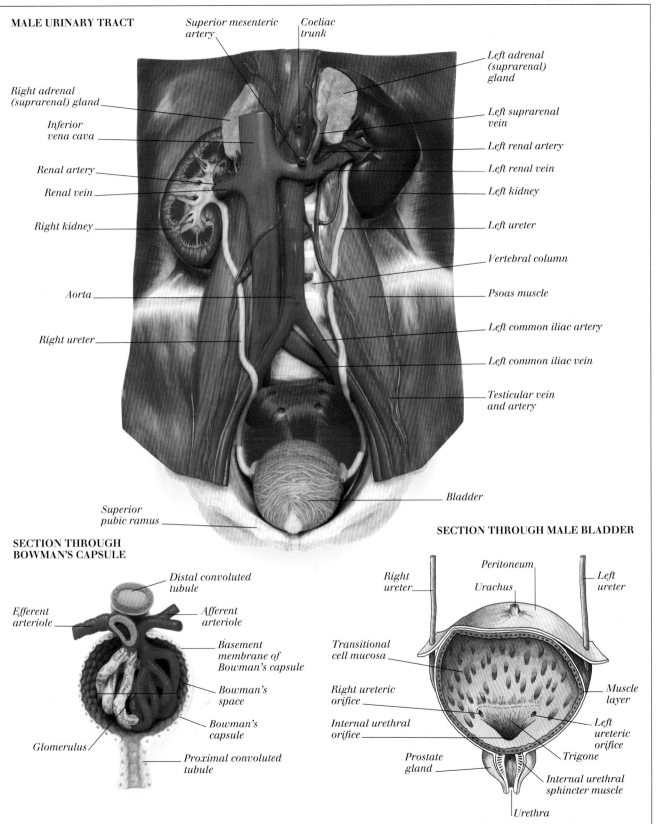

MALE URINARY TRACT

Superior mesenteric artery

Coeliac trunk

Left adrenal (suprarenal) gland

Right adrenal (suprarenal) gland

Left suprarenal vein

Inferior vena cava

Left renal artery

Renal artery

Left renal vein

Renal vein

Left kidney

Right kidney

Left ureter

Vertebral column

Aorta

Psoas muscle

Left common iliac artery

Right ureter

Left common iliac vein

Testicular vein and artery

Bladder

Superior pubic ramus

SECTION THROUGH BOWMAN'S CAPSULE

Distal convoluted tubule

Efferent arteriole

Afferent arteriole

Basement membrane of Bowman's capsule

Bowman's space

Bowman's capsule

Glomerulus

Proximal convoluted tubule

SECTION THROUGH MALE BLADDER

Right ureter

Peritoneum

Urachus

Left ureter

Transitional cell mucosa

Right ureteric orifice

Muscle layer

Internal urethral orifice

Left ureteric orifice

Prostate gland

Trigone

Internal urethral sphincter muscle

Urethra

257

Reproductive system

SEX ORGANS LOCATED IN THE PELVIS create new human lives. Each month a ripe egg is released from one of the female's ovaries into a fallopian tube leading to the uterus (womb), a muscular pear-sized organ. A male produces minute tadpole-like sperm in two oval glands called testes. When the male is ready to release sperm into the female's vagina, many millions pass into his urethra and leave his body through the fleshy penis. The sperm travel up through the vagina into the uterus and one sperm may enter and fertilize an egg. The fertilized egg becomes embedded in the uterus wall and starts to grow into a new human being.

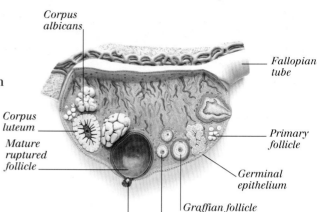

SECTION THROUGH OVARY

Corpus albicans

Fallopian tube

Corpus luteum

Mature ruptured follicle

Oocyte (egg)

Primary follicle

Germinal epithelium

Graffian follicle

Secondary follicle

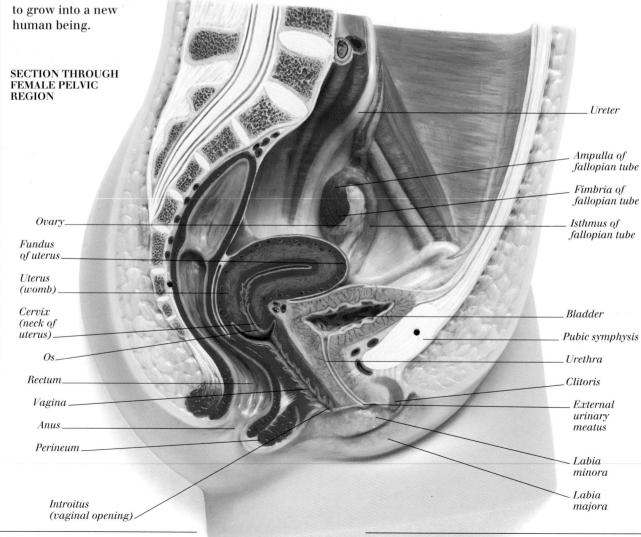

SECTION THROUGH FEMALE PELVIC REGION

Ovary

Fundus of uterus

Uterus (womb)

Cervix (neck of uterus)

Os

Rectum

Vagina

Anus

Perineum

Introitus (vaginal opening)

Ureter

Ampulla of fallopian tube

Fimbria of fallopian tube

Isthmus of fallopian tube

Bladder

Pubic symphysis

Urethra

Clitoris

External urinary meatus

Labia minora

Labia majora

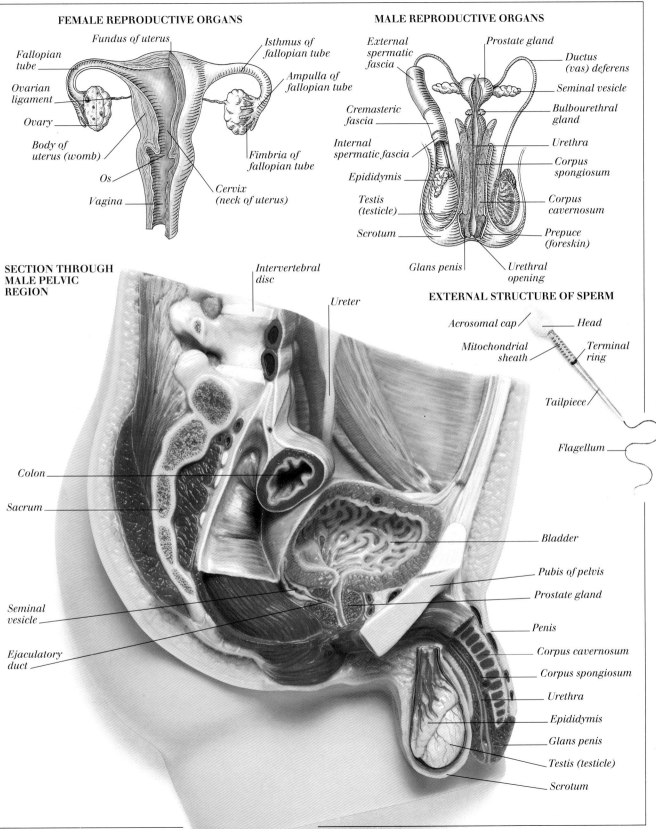

FEMALE REPRODUCTIVE ORGANS

Fundus of uterus
Fallopian tube
Isthmus of fallopian tube
Ovarian ligament
Ampulla of fallopian tube
Ovary
Body of uterus (womb)
Fimbria of fallopian tube
Os
Cervix (neck of uterus)
Vagina

MALE REPRODUCTIVE ORGANS

External spermatic fascia
Prostate gland
Ductus (vas) deferens
Cremasteric fascia
Seminal vesicle
Bulbourethral gland
Internal spermatic fascia
Urethra
Epididymis
Corpus spongiosum
Testis (testicle)
Corpus cavernosum
Scrotum
Prepuce (foreskin)
Glans penis
Urethral opening

SECTION THROUGH MALE PELVIC REGION

Intervertebral disc
Ureter

EXTERNAL STRUCTURE OF SPERM

Acrosomal cap
Head
Mitochondrial sheath
Terminal ring
Tailpiece
Flagellum

Colon
Sacrum
Bladder
Pubis of pelvis
Prostate gland
Penis
Corpus cavernosum
Seminal vesicle
Corpus spongiosum
Ejaculatory duct
Urethra
Epididymis
Glans penis
Testis (testicle)
Scrotum

Development of a baby

A FERTILIZED EGG IS NOURISHED AND PROTECTED as it develops into an embryo and then a fetus during the 40 weeks of pregnancy. The placenta, a mass of blood vessels implanted in the uterus lining, delivers nourishment and oxygen, and removes waste through the umbilical cord. Meanwhile, the fetus lies snugly in its amniotic sac, a bag of fluid that protects it against any sudden jolts. In the last weeks of the pregnancy, the rapidly growing fetus turns head-down: a baby ready to be born.

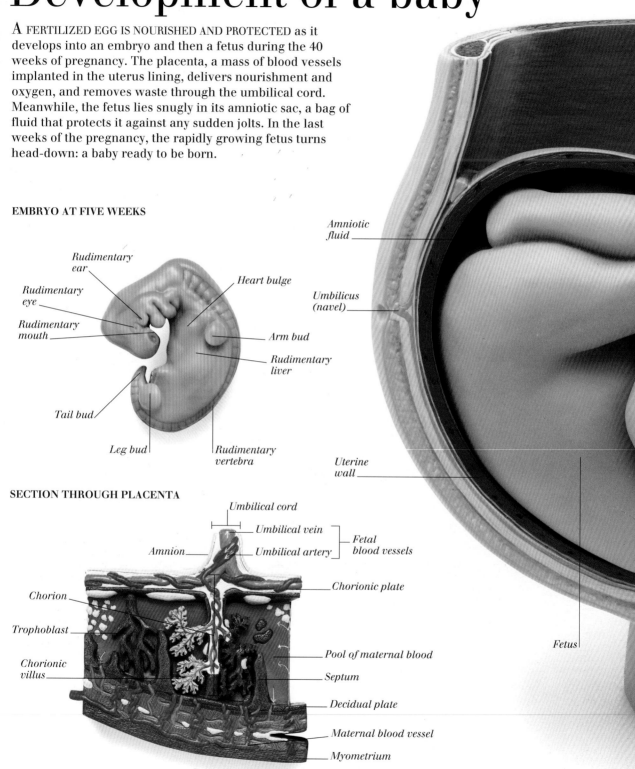

EMBRYO AT FIVE WEEKS

Rudimentary ear

Rudimentary eye

Rudimentary mouth

Heart bulge

Arm bud

Rudimentary liver

Tail bud

Leg bud

Rudimentary vertebra

Amniotic fluid

Umbilicus (navel)

Uterine wall

Fetus

SECTION THROUGH PLACENTA

Umbilical cord

Umbilical vein

Umbilical artery

Fetal blood vessels

Amnion

Chorionic plate

Chorion

Trophoblast

Pool of maternal blood

Septum

Chorionic villus

Decidual plate

Maternal blood vessel

Myometrium

**SECTION THROUGH PELVIS IN
NINTH MONTH OF PREGNANCY**

THE DEVELOPING FETUS

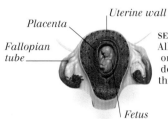

Uterine wall

Placenta

*Fallopian
tube*

Fetus

SECOND MONTH
All the internal
organs have
developed by
this stage.

*Umbilical
cord*

THIRD MONTH
The fetus is
fully formed
and now
begins a
period of rapid
growth.

*Intervertebral
disc*

Vertebra

Spinal cord

FIFTH MONTH
Although the fetus
is here in breech
(bottom down)
position, it
will probably
turn by 180°
before birth. By
the fifth month
the baby is moving
actively and responds
to sound.

Cervix

SEVENTH MONTH
The internal organs
are maturing in
preparation for life
outside the uterus.
The baby has grown
to such a size that
there is less room
for movement
within the uterus.

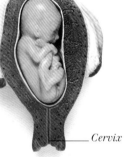

Bladder

Cervix

Rectum

Anus

*Pubic
bone*

Vagina

Urethra

Placenta

GEOLOGY, GEOGRAPHY, AND METEOROLGY

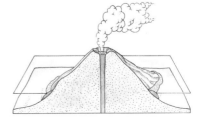

Earth's physical features

MOST OF THE EARTH'S SURFACE (about 70 per cent) is covered with water. The largest single body of water, the Pacific Ocean, alone covers about 30 per cent of the surface. Most of the land is distributed as seven continents; these are (from largest to smallest) Asia, Africa, North America, South America, Antarctica, Europe, and Australasia. The physical features of the land are remarkably varied. Among the most notable are mountain ranges, rivers, and deserts. The largest mountain ranges – the Himalayas in Asia and the Andes in South America – extend for thousands of kilometres. The Himalayas include the world's highest mountain, Mount Everest (8,848 metres). The longest rivers are the River Nile in Africa (6,695 kilometres) and the Amazon River in South America (6,437 kilometres). Deserts cover about 20 per cent of the total land area. The largest is the Sahara, which covers nearly a third of Africa. The Earth's surface features can be represented in various ways. Only a globe can correctly represent areas, shapes, sizes, and directions, because there is always distortion when a spherical surface – the Earth's, for example – is projected on to the flat surface of a map. Each map projection is therefore a compromise: it shows some features accurately but distorts others. Even satellite mapping does not produce completely accurate maps, although they can show physical features with great clarity.

EXAMPLES OF MAP PROJECTIONS

CYLINDRICAL PROJECTION

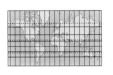

CYLINDRICAL-PROJECTION MAP

SATELLITE MAPPING OF THE EARTH

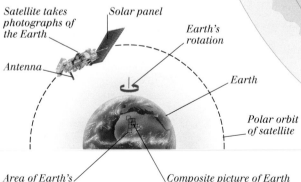

Satellite takes photographs of the Earth

Solar panel

Earth's rotation

Antenna

Earth

Polar orbit of satellite

Area of Earth's surface on each photograph

Composite picture of Earth created from thousands of separate images

CONICAL PROJECTION

CONICAL-PROJECTION MAP

AZIMUTHAL PROJECTION

AZIMUTHAL-PROJECTION MAP

MODIFIED AZIMUTHAL-PROJECTION MAP

SATELLITE MAP OF THE EARTH

160° 180°

120°

80°

40°

0°

ARCTIC OCEAN

Ural Mountains

Kara Kum

River Ob-Irtysh

River Lena

ARCTIC CIRCLE (66° 52'N)

Aral Sea

Caucasus

Carpathians

Alps

River Amur

Pyrenees

E U R O P E

A S I A

Black Sea

Lake Baikal

Sea of Japan

Honshu

Mediterranean Sea

ains

TROPIC OF CANCER (23° 30'N)

Gobi Desert

PACIFIC OCEAN

Red Sea

A F R I C A

Pamirs

Yellow River (Huang He)

Caspian Sea

Thar Desert

Himalayas

South China Sea

Yangtze River (Chang Jiang)

Arabian Desert

Takla Makan Desert

River Mekong

River Nile

Borneo

New Guinea

EQUATOR (0°)

River Congo (Zaire)

Lake Victoria

Sumatra

Lake Tanganyika

Australian Desert

INDIAN OCEAN

A U S T R A L A S I A

Namib Desert

Madagascar

TROPIC OF CAPRICORN (23° 30'S)

Lake Nyasa

Kalahari Desert

Drakensberg

New Zealand

ANTARCTIC CIRCLE (66° 52'S)

A N T A R C T I C A

0°

40°

80°

120°

160° 180°

GREENWICH MERIDIAN

EAST OF GREENWICH MERIDIAN

265

The rock cycle

THE ROCK CYCLE IS A CONTINUOUS PROCESS through which old rocks are transformed into new ones. Rocks can be divided into three main groups: igneous, sedimentary, and metamorphic. Igneous rocks are formed when magma (molten rock) from the Earth's interior cools and solidifies (see pp. 274-275). Sedimentary rocks are formed when sediment (rock particles, for example) becomes compressed and cemented together in a process known as lithification (see pp. 276-277). Metamorphic rocks are formed when igneous, sedimentary, or other metamorphic rocks are changed by heat or pressure (see pp. 274-275). Rocks are added to the Earth's surface by crustal movements and volcanic activity. Once exposed on the surface, the rocks are broken down into rock particles by weathering (see pp. 282-283). The particles are then transported by glaciers, rivers, and wind, and deposited as sediment in lakes, deltas, deserts, and on the ocean floor. Some of this sediment undergoes lithification and forms sedimentary rock. This rock may be thrust back to the surface by crustal movements or forced deeper into the Earth's interior, where heat and pressure transform it into metamorphic rock. The metamorphic rock in turn may be pushed up to the surface or may be melted to form magma. Eventually, the magma cools and solidifies – below or on the surface – forming igneous rock. When the sedimentary, igneous, and metamorphic rocks are exposed once more on the Earth's surface, the cycle begins again.

**HEXAGONAL BASALT
COLUMNS, ICELAND**

STAGES IN THE ROCK CYCLE

*Magma extruded as lava,
which solidifies to form
igneous rock*

*Lava
flow*

Vent

*Main
conduit*

*Secondary
conduit*

Lava

Ash

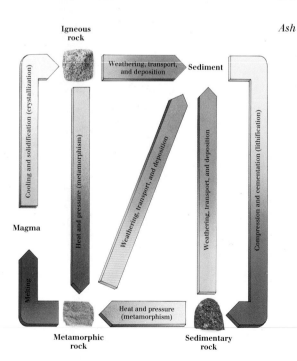

*Rock surrounding
magma changed
by heat to form
metamorphic rock*

*Sedimentary rock
crushed and folded to
form metamorphic rock*

*Intense heat of rising
magma melts some of
the surrounding rock*

THE ROCK CYCLE

Igneous
rock

Cooling and solidification (crystallization)

Weathering, transport, and deposition

Sediment

Heat and pressure (metamorphism)

Weathering, transport, and deposition

Weathering, transport, and deposition

Compression and cementation (lithification)

Magma

Melting

Heat and pressure
(metamorphism)

Metamorphic
rock

Sedimentary
rock

IGNEOUS ROCK

Pyroxene crystal

Olivine crystal

Plagioclase feldspar

Coarse-grained texture

Dark pyroxene crystal

PHOTOMICROGRAPH OF GABBRO

PIECE OF GABBRO

SEDIMENTARY ROCK

Mud groundmass (matrix)

Ammonite shell

Brown colouring from iron oxides

Fine-grained texture

Ammonite shell embedded in rock

PHOTOMICROGRAPH OF SHELLY LIMESTONE

PIECE OF SHELLY LIMESTONE

METAMORPHIC ROCK

Garnet crystal (pink)

Quartz and feldspar crystals (grey)

Red garnet crystal

Wavy foliation

PHOTOMICROGRAPH OF GARNET-MICA SCHIST

PIECE OF GARNET-MICA SCHIST

Mountain

Glacier erodes rocks and carries rock particles to river

Waterfall erodes rock

River erodes valley floor and carries rock particles downstream

Rock particles deposited as sediment in lake

Rock particles deposited by wind to form sand dunes

Rock particles deposited in delta

Heavier rock particles deposited on continental shelf

Continental shelf

Continental slope

Lighter rock particles collect on ocean floor to form layers of sediment

Layers of sediment compressed and cemented to form sedimentary rock

Minerals

A MINERAL IS A NATURALLY OCCURRING SUBSTANCE that has a characteristic chemical composition and specific physical properties, such as habit and streak (see pp. 270-271). A rock, by comparison, is an aggregate of minerals and need not have a specific chemical composition. Minerals are made up of elements (substances that cannot be broken down chemically into simpler substances), each of which can be represented by a chemical symbol. Minerals can be divided into two main groups: native elements and compounds. Native elements are made up of a pure element. Examples include gold (chemical symbol Au), silver (Ag), copper (Cu), and carbon (C); carbon occurs as a native element in two forms, diamond and graphite. Compounds are combinations of two or more elements. For example, sulphides are compounds of sulphur (S) and one or more other elements, such as lead (Pb) in the mineral galena, or antimony (Sb) in the mineral stibnite.

NATIVE ELEMENTS

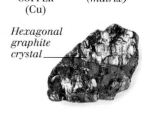

Dendritic (branching) copper

Limonite groundmass (matrix)

COPPER (Cu)

SULPHIDES

Cubic galena crystal

GALENA (PbS)

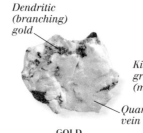

Dendritic (branching) gold

Kimberlite groundmass (matrix)

Quartz vein

GOLD (Au)

White diamond

DIAMOND (C)

Hexagonal graphite crystal

GRAPHITE (C)

OXIDES/HYDROXIDES

Milky quartz groundmass (matrix)

Smoky quartz crystal

SMOKY QUARTZ (SiO$_2$)

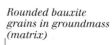

Rounded bauxite grains in groundmass (matrix)

Mass of specular haematite crystals

SPECULAR HAEMATITE (Fe$_2$O$_3$)

BAUXITE (FeO(OH) and Al$_2$O$_3$.2H$_2$O)

Prismatic stibnite crystal

Quartz groundmass (matrix)

STIBNITE (Sb$_2$S$_3$)

Perfect octahedral pyrites crystal

Quartz crystal

Parallel bands of onyx

PYRITES (FeS$_2$)

ONYX (SiO$_2$)

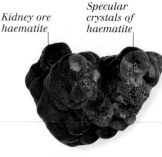

Kidney ore haematite

Specular crystals of haematite

KIDNEY ORE HAEMATITE (Fe$_2$O$_3$)

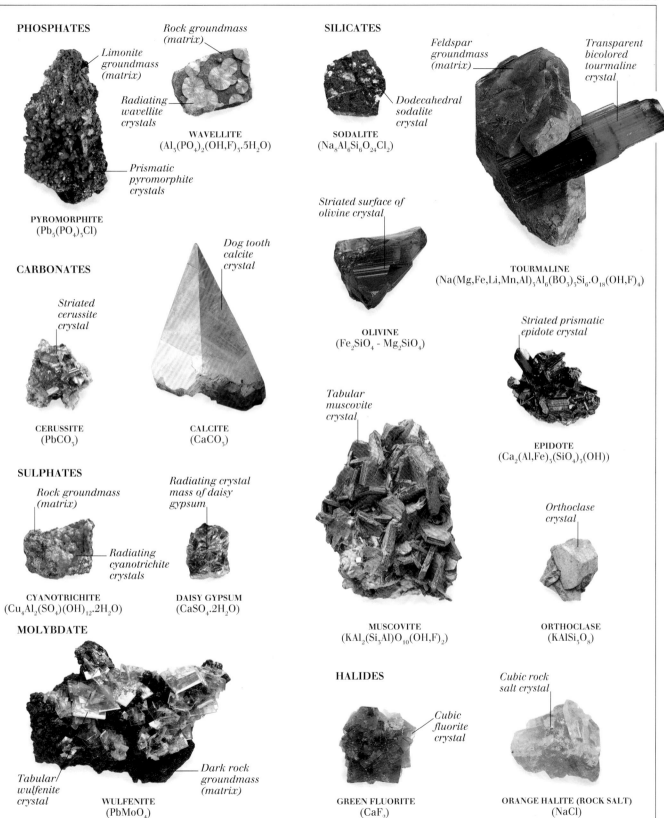

PHOSPHATES

Limonite groundmass (matrix)

Rock groundmass (matrix)

Radiating wavellite crystals

WAVELLITE
$(Al_5(PO_4)_2(OH,F)_5.5H_2O)$

Prismatic pyromorphite crystals

PYROMORPHITE
$(Pb_5(PO_4)_5Cl)$

CARBONATES

Striated cerussite crystal

Dog tooth calcite crystal

CERUSSITE
$(PbCO_5)$

CALCITE
$(CaCO_5)$

SULPHATES

Rock groundmass (matrix)

Radiating crystal mass of daisy gypsum

Radiating cyanotrichite crystals

CYANOTRICHITE
$(Cu_4Al_2(SO_4)(OH)_{12}.2H_2O)$

DAISY GYPSUM
$(CaSO_4.2H_2O)$

MOLYBDATE

Tabular wulfenite crystal

Dark rock groundmass (matrix)

WULFENITE
$(PbMoO_4)$

SILICATES

Feldspar groundmass (matrix)

Transparent bicolored tourmaline crystal

Dodecahedral sodalite crystal

SODALITE
$(Na_8Al_6Si_6O_{24}Cl_2)$

Striated surface of olivine crystal

TOURMALINE
$(Na(Mg,Fe,Li,Mn,Al)_3Al_6(BO_5)_5Si_6.O_{18}(OH,F)_4)$

OLIVINE
$(Fe_2SiO_4 - Mg_2SiO_4)$

Striated prismatic epidote crystal

Tabular muscovite crystal

EPIDOTE
$(Ca_2(Al,Fe)_5(SiO_4)_5(OH))$

Orthoclase crystal

MUSCOVITE
$(KAl_2(Si_5Al)O_{10}(OH,F)_2)$

ORTHOCLASE
$(KAlSi_5O_8)$

HALIDES

Cubic rock salt crystal

Cubic fluorite crystal

GREEN FLUORITE
(CaF_2)

ORANGE HALITE (ROCK SALT)
$(NaCl)$

Mineral features

MINERALS CAN BE IDENTIFIED BY STUDYING features such as fracture, cleavage, crystal system, habit, hardness, colour, and streak. Minerals can break in different ways. If a mineral breaks in an irregular way, leaving rough surfaces, it possesses fracture. If a mineral breaks along well-defined planes of weakness, it possesses cleavage. Specific minerals have distinctive patterns of cleavage; for example, mica cleaves along one plane. Most minerals form crystals, which can be categorized into crystal systems according to their symmetry and number of faces. Within each system, several different but related forms of crystal are possible; for example, a cubic crystal can have six, eight, or twelve sides. A mineral's habit is the typical form taken by an aggregate of its crystals. Examples of habit include botryoidal (like a bunch of grapes) and massive (no definite form). The relative hardness of a mineral may be assessed by testing its resistance to scratching. This property is usually measured using Mohs scale, which increases in hardness from 1 (talc) to 10 (diamond). The colour of a mineral is not a dependable guide to its identity as some minerals have a range of colours. Streak (the colour the powdered mineral makes when rubbed across an unglazed tile) is a more reliable indicator.

CLEAVAGE

Cleavage in one direction

CLEAVAGE ALONG ONE PLANE

Cleavage in three directions, forming a block cube

CLEAVAGE ALONG THREE PLANES

Horizontal cleavage

Vertical cleavage

CLEAVAGE ALONG TWO PLANES

Cleavage in four directions, forming a double-pyramid crystal

CLEAVAGE ALONG FOUR PLANES

CRYSTAL SYSTEMS

Cubic iron pyrites crystal

Tetragonal idocrase crystal

Representation of tetragonal system

TETRAGONAL SYSTEM

CUBIC SYSTEM

Representation of cubic system

Hexagonal beryl crystal

Representation of hexagonal/ trigonal system

HEXAGONAL/TRIGONAL SYSTEM

Orthorhombic barytes crystal

Representation of orthorhombic system

ORTHORHOMBIC SYSTEM

FRACTURE

Fire opal with conchoidal (shell-like) fracture

CONCHOIDAL FRACTURE

Nickel-iron with hackly (jagged) fracture

HACKLY FRACTURE

Orpiment with uneven fracture

UNEVEN FRACTURE

Garnierite with splintery fracture

SPLINTERY FRACTURE

Monoclinic selenite crystal

Representation of monoclinic system

MONOCLINIC SYSTEM

Representation of triclinic system

Triclinic axinite crystal

TRICLINIC SYSTEM

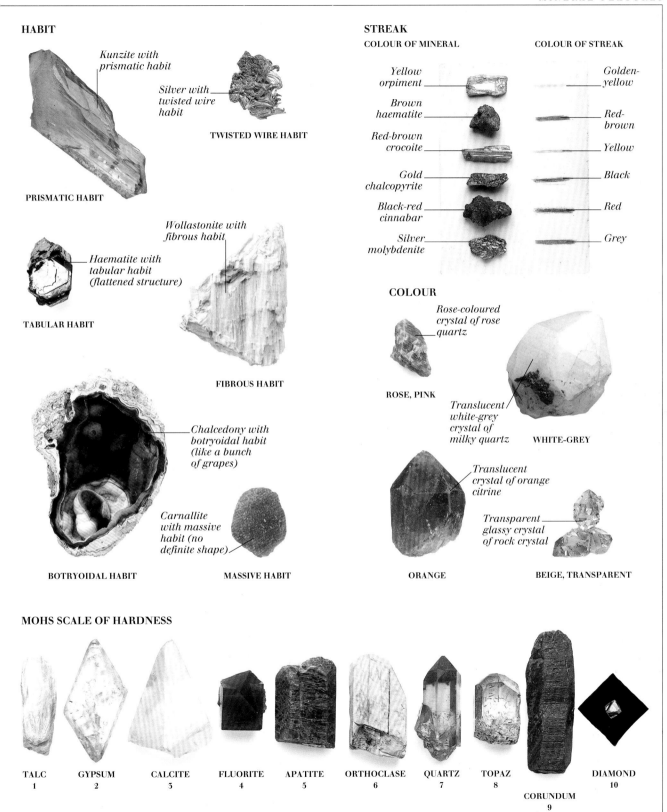

HABIT

Kunzite with prismatic habit

Silver with twisted wire habit

TWISTED WIRE HABIT

PRISMATIC HABIT

Wollastonite with fibrous habit

Haematite with tabular habit (flattened structure)

TABULAR HABIT

FIBROUS HABIT

Chalcedony with botryoidal habit (like a bunch of grapes)

Carnallite with massive habit (no definite shape)

BOTRYOIDAL HABIT

MASSIVE HABIT

STREAK

COLOUR OF MINERAL

Yellow orpiment

Brown haematite

Red-brown crocoite

Gold chalcopyrite

Black-red cinnabar

Silver molybdenite

COLOUR OF STREAK

Golden-yellow

Red-brown

Yellow

Black

Red

Grey

COLOUR

Rose-coloured crystal of rose quartz

ROSE, PINK

Translucent white-grey crystal of milky quartz

WHITE-GREY

Translucent crystal of orange citrine

Transparent glassy crystal of rock crystal

ORANGE

BEIGE, TRANSPARENT

MOHS SCALE OF HARDNESS

TALC	GYPSUM	CALCITE	FLUORITE	APATITE	ORTHOCLASE	QUARTZ	TOPAZ	CORUNDUM	DIAMOND
1	2	3	4	5	6	7	8	9	10

Volcanoes

VOLCANOES ARE VENTS OR FISSURES in the Earth's crust through which magma (molten rock that originates from deep beneath the crust) is forced on to the surface as lava. They occur most commonly along the boundaries of crustal plates; most volcanoes lie in a belt called the "Ring of Fire", which runs along the edge of the Pacific Ocean. Volcanoes can be classified according to the violence and frequency of their eruptions. Non-explosive volcanic eruptions generally occur where crustal plates pull apart. These eruptions produce runny basaltic lava that spreads quickly over a wide area to form relatively flat cones. The most violent eruptions take place where plates collide. Such eruptions produce thick rhyolitic lava and may also blast out clouds of dust and pyroclasts (lava fragments). The lava does not flow far before cooling and therefore builds up steep-sided, conical volcanoes. Some volcanoes produce lava and ash eruptions, which build up composite volcanic cones. Volcanoes that erupt frequently are described as active; those that erupt rarely are termed dormant; and those that have stopped erupting altogether are termed extinct. As well as the volcanoes themselves, other features associated with volcanic regions include geysers, hot mineral springs, solfataras, fumaroles, and bubbling mud pools.

Folded, rope-like surface

PAHOEHOE
(ROPY LAVA)

HORU GEYSER,
NEW ZEALAND

VOLCANO TYPES

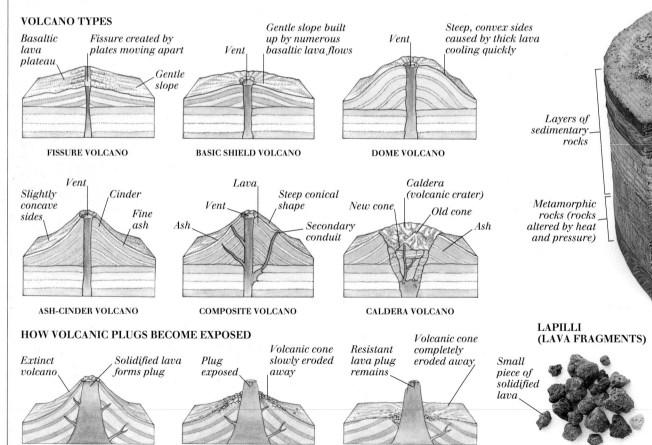

Basaltic lava plateau

Fissure created by plates moving apart

Gentle slope

FISSURE VOLCANO

Gentle slope built up by numerous basaltic lava flows

Vent

BASIC SHIELD VOLCANO

Steep, convex sides caused by thick lava cooling quickly

Vent

DOME VOLCANO

Slightly concave sides

Vent

Cinder

Fine ash

ASH-CINDER VOLCANO

Lava

Vent

Ash

Steep conical shape

Secondary conduit

COMPOSITE VOLCANO

Caldera (volcanic crater)

New cone

Old cone

Ash

CALDERA VOLCANO

Layers of sedimentary rocks

Metamorphic rocks (rocks altered by heat and pressure)

HOW VOLCANIC PLUGS BECOME EXPOSED

Extinct volcano

Solidified lava forms plug

PLUG FORMATION

Plug exposed

Volcanic cone slowly eroded away

INITIAL EROSION AROUND PLUG

Resistant lava plug remains

Volcanic cone completely eroded away

COMPLETE DENUDATION OF PLUG

LAPILLI
(LAVA FRAGMENTS)

Small piece of solidified lava

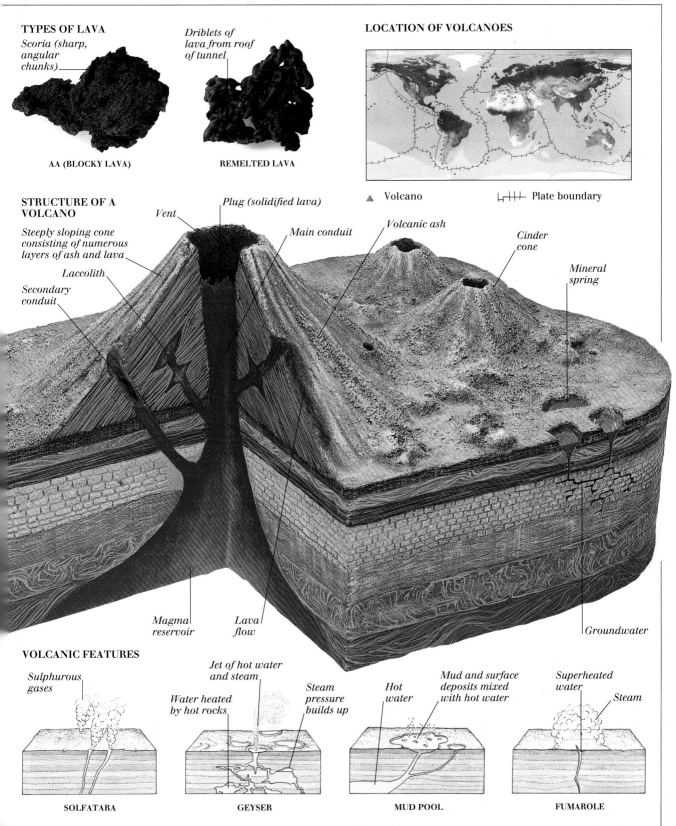

TYPES OF LAVA

Scoria (sharp, angular chunks)

Driblets of lava from roof of tunnel

AA (BLOCKY LAVA)

REMELTED LAVA

LOCATION OF VOLCANOES

▲ Volcano   ⊢┼┼┼ Plate boundary

STRUCTURE OF A VOLCANO

Steeply sloping cone consisting of numerous layers of ash and lava

Laccolith

Secondary conduit

Vent

Plug (solidified lava)

Main conduit

Volcanic ash

Cinder cone

Mineral spring

Magma reservoir

Lava flow

Groundwater

VOLCANIC FEATURES

Sulphurous gases

Jet of hot water and steam

Water heated by hot rocks

Steam pressure builds up

Hot water

Mud and surface deposits mixed with hot water

Superheated water

Steam

SOLFATARA

GEYSER

MUD POOL

FUMAROLE

Igneous and metamorphic rocks

BASALT COLUMNS

IGNEOUS ROCKS ARE FORMED WHEN MAGMA (molten rock that originates from deep beneath the Earth's crust) cools and solidifies. There are two main types of igneous rock: intrusive and extrusive. Intrusive rocks are formed deep underground where magma is forced into cracks or between rock layers to form structures such as sills, dykes, and batholiths. The magma cools slowly to form coarse-grained rocks such as gabbro and pegmatite. Extrusive rocks are formed above the Earth's surface from lava (magma that has been ejected in a volcanic eruption). The molten lava cools quickly, producing fine-grained rocks such as rhyolite and basalt. Metamorphic rocks are those that have been altered by intense heat (contact metamorphism) or extreme pressure (regional metamorphism). Contact metamorphism occurs when rocks are changed by heat from, for example, an igneous intrusion or lava flow. Regional metamorphism occurs when rock is crushed in the middle of a folding mountain range. Metamorphic rocks can be formed from igneous rocks, sedimentary rocks, or even from other metamorphic rocks.

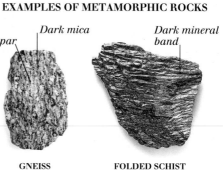

Cinder cone

Large eroded lava flow

Cedar-tree laccolith

Butte

Plug

Cone sheet

Ring dyke

Batholith

Dyke

Sill

Dyke swarm

Lopolith

IGNEOUS ROCK STRUCTURES

CONTACT METAMORPHISM

Metamorphic aureole (region where contact metamorphism occurs)

Hot igneous intrusion

Limestone

Shale

Marble (metamorphosed limestone)

Slate (metamorphosed shale)

REGIONAL METAMORPHISM

Mountain range

Slate, formed under low pressure and temperature

Compression

Compression

Schist, formed under medium pressure and temperature

Gneiss, formed under high pressure and temperature

Crust

Mantle

Magma

EXAMPLES OF METAMORPHIC ROCKS

Pale feldspar

Dark mica

Dark mineral band

Pale calcite

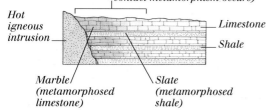

GNEISS

FOLDED SCHIST

SKARN

EXAMPLES OF EXTRUSIVE IGNEOUS ROCKS

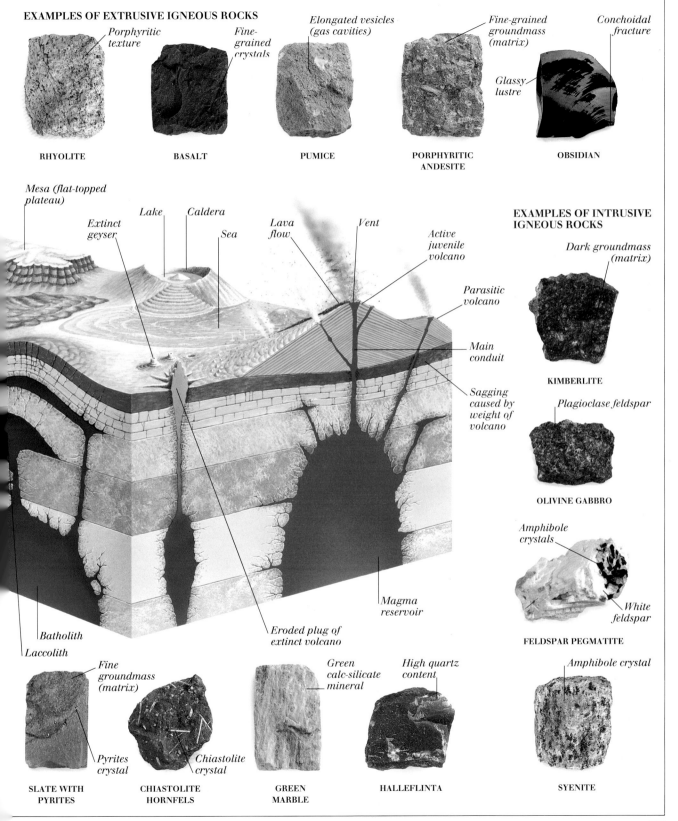

Porphyritic texture

Fine-grained crystals

Elongated vesicles (gas cavities)

Fine-grained groundmass (matrix)

Conchoidal fracture

Glassy lustre

RHYOLITE

BASALT

PUMICE

PORPHYRITIC ANDESITE

OBSIDIAN

Mesa (flat-topped plateau)

Extinct geyser

Lake

Caldera

Sea

Lava flow

Vent

Active juvenile volcano

Parasitic volcano

Main conduit

Sagging caused by weight of volcano

Magma reservoir

Eroded plug of extinct volcano

Batholith

Laccolith

EXAMPLES OF INTRUSIVE IGNEOUS ROCKS

Dark groundmass (matrix)

KIMBERLITE

Plagioclase feldspar

OLIVINE GABBRO

Amphibole crystals

White feldspar

FELDSPAR PEGMATITE

Amphibole crystal

SYENITE

Fine groundmass (matrix)

Pyrites crystal

SLATE WITH PYRITES

Chiastolite crystal

CHIASTOLITE HORNFELS

Green calc-silicate mineral

GREEN MARBLE

High quartz content

HALLEFLINTA

Sedimentary rocks

SEDIMENTARY ROCKS ARE FORMED BY THE ACCUMULATION and consolidation of sediments (see pp. 266-267). There are three main types of sedimentary rock. Clastic sedimentary rocks, such as breccia or sandstone, are formed from other rocks that have been broken down into fragments by weathering (see pp. 282-283), which have then been transported and deposited elsewhere. Organic sedimentary rocks – for example, coal (see pp. 280-281) – are derived from plant and animal remains. Chemical sedimentary rocks are formed by chemical processes. For example, rock salt is formed when salt dissolved in water is deposited as the water evaporates. Sedimentary rocks are laid down in layers, called beds or strata. Each new layer is laid down horizontally over older ones. There are usually some gaps in the sequence, called unconformities. These represent periods in which no new sediments were being laid down, or when earlier sedimentary layers were raised above sea level and eroded away.

THE GRAND CANYON, USA

EXAMPLES OF UNCONFORMITIES

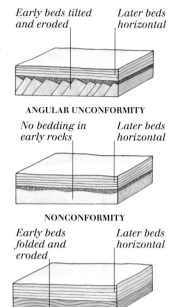

Early beds tilted and eroded

Later beds horizontal

ANGULAR UNCONFORMITY

No bedding in early rocks

Later beds horizontal

NONCONFORMITY

Early beds folded and eroded

Later beds horizontal

DISCONFORMITY

SEDIMENTARY LAYERS OF THE GRAND CANYON REGION

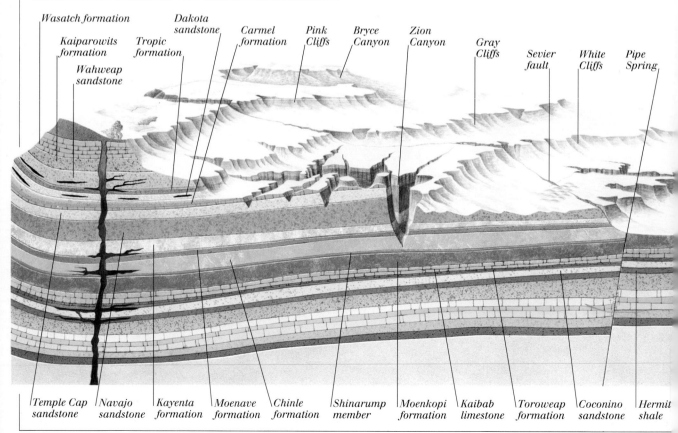

Wasatch formation
Kaiparowits formation
Wahweap sandstone
Tropic formation
Dakota sandstone
Carmel formation
Pink Cliffs
Bryce Canyon
Zion Canyon
Gray Cliffs
Sevier fault
White Cliffs
Pipe Spring

Temple Cap sandstone
Navajo sandstone
Kayenta formation
Moenave formation
Chinle formation
Shinarump member
Moenkopi formation
Kaibab limestone
Toroweap formation
Coconino sandstone
Hermit shale

EXAMPLES OF SEDIMENTARY ROCKS

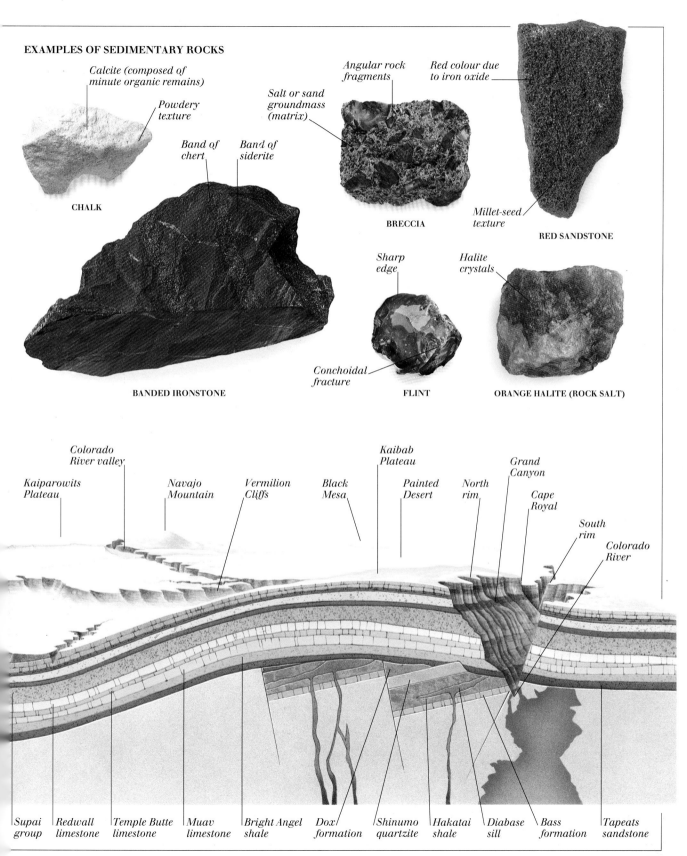

Calcite (composed of
minute organic remains)

Powdery
texture

CHALK

Band of
chert

Band of
siderite

BANDED IRONSTONE

Angular rock
fragments

Salt or sand
groundmass
(matrix)

BRECCIA

Red colour due
to iron oxide

Millet-seed
texture

RED SANDSTONE

Sharp
edge

Conchoidal
fracture

FLINT

Halite
crystals

ORANGE HALITE (ROCK SALT)

Kaiparowits
Plateau

Colorado
River valley

Navajo
Mountain

Vermilion
Cliffs

Black
Mesa

Kaibab
Plateau

Painted
Desert

North
rim

Grand
Canyon

Cape
Royal

South
rim

Colorado
River

Supai
group

Redwall
limestone

Temple Butte
limestone

Muav
limestone

Bright Angel
shale

Dox
formation

Shinumo
quartzite

Hakatai
shale

Diabase
sill

Bass
formation

Tapeats
sandstone

277

Fossils

FOSSILS ARE THE REMAINS of plants and animals that have been preserved in rock. A fossil may be the preserved remains of an organism itself, an impression of it in rock, or preserved traces (known as trace fossils) left by an organism while it was alive, such as organic carbon outlines, fossilized footprints, or droppings. Most dead organisms soon rot away or are eaten by scavengers. For fossilization to occur, rapid burial by sediment is necessary. The organism decays, but the harder parts – bones, teeth, and shells, for example – may be preserved and hardened by minerals from the surrounding sediment. Fossilization may also occur even when the hard parts of an organism are dissolved away to leave an impression called a mould. The mould is filled by minerals, thereby creating a cast of the organism. The study of fossils (palaeontology) can not only show how living things have evolved, but can also help to reveal the Earth's geological history – for example, by aiding in the dating of rock strata.

PROCESS OF FOSSILIZATION

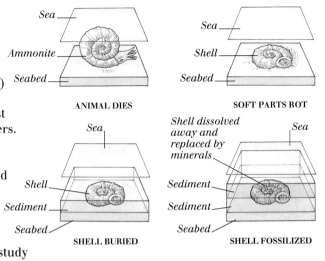

Sea

Ammonite

Seabed

ANIMAL DIES

Sea

Shell

Seabed

SOFT PARTS ROT

Sea

Shell

Sediment

Seabed

SHELL BURIED

Shell dissolved away and replaced by minerals

Sea

Sediment

Sediment

Seabed

SHELL FOSSILIZED

EXAMPLES OF FOSSILS

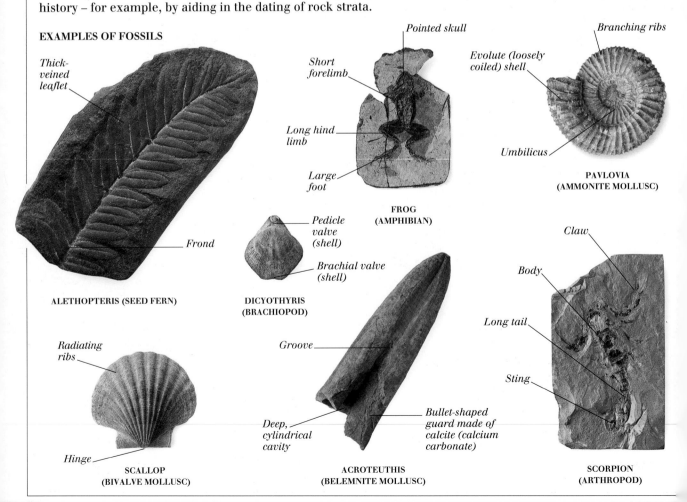

Thick-veined leaflet

Frond

ALETHOPTERIS (SEED FERN)

Radiating ribs

Hinge

SCALLOP (BIVALVE MOLLUSC)

Pointed skull

Short forelimb

Long hind limb

Large foot

FROG (AMPHIBIAN)

Pedicle valve (shell)

Brachial valve (shell)

DICYOTHYRIS (BRACHIOPOD)

Groove

Deep, cylindrical cavity

Bullet-shaped guard made of calcite (calcium carbonate)

ACROTEUTHIS (BELEMNITE MOLLUSC)

Branching ribs

Evolute (loosely coiled) shell

Umbilicus

PAVLOVIA (AMMONITE MOLLUSC)

Claw

Body

Long tail

Sting

SCORPION (ARTHROPOD)

THE FOSSIL RECORD

Precambrian time

Proterozoic eon

Palaeozoic era

Phanerozoic eon

Mesozoic era

Cenozoic era

570 — *Cambrian period*
570
510 — *Ordovician period*
439 — *Silurian period*
409 — *Devonian period*
363
— *Carboniferous period*
290
245 — *Permian period*
245
208 — *Triassic period*
146 — *Jurassic period*
65 — *Cretaceous period*

Trilobites

Dinosaurs

Ammonites and Belemnites

Seed fern

Fish
Amphibians
Birds
Reptiles
Mammals
Primates

Echinoderms
Brachiopods
Chelicerates
Insects
Crustaceans
Bivalves
Gastropods
Cephalopods
Worms
Corals and jellyfish
Bryozoans
Sponges
Foraminiferans

Algae
Vascular plants
Sphenopsids
Ferns
Cycads
Angiosperms
Ginkgos
Conifers

VERTEBRATES
INVERTEBRATES
PLANTS

65
56.5 — *Palaeocene epoch*
35.5 — *Eocene epoch*
25.5 — *Oligocene epoch*
5.2 — *Miocene epoch*
1.64 — *Pliocene epoch*
0.01 — *Pleistocene epoch*
0 — *Holocene epoch*

Tertiary period
Quaternary period

MILLIONS OF YEARS AGO (MYA)

Ambulacral area

Tiny tubercle

Genital pore

Turreted spire

Ribs

Large body whorl

Aperture

**STRUTHIOLARIA
(GASTROPOD MOLLUSC)**

Large, elevated eye

Spiny, segmented body

Wide head

Spiny tail

**LEONASPIS
(TRILOBITE)**

Claw

Carapace

**MUD CRAB
(CRUSTACEAN)**

**CLYPEASTER
(ECHINODERM)**

Mineral resources

MINERAL RESOURCES CAN BE DEFINED AS naturally occurring substances that can be extracted from the Earth and are useful as fuels and raw materials. Coal, oil, and gas – collectively called fossil fuels – are commonly included in this group, but are not strictly minerals, because they are of organic origin. Coal formation begins when vegetation is buried and partly decomposed to form peat. Overlying sediments compress the peat and transform it into lignite (soft brown coal). As the overlying sediments accumulate, increasing pressure and temperature eventually transform the lignite into bituminous and hard anthracite coals. Oil and gas are usually formed from organic matter that was deposited in marine sediments. Under the effects of heat and pressure, the compressed organic matter undergoes complex chemical changes to form oil and gas. The oil and gas percolate upwards through water-saturated, permeable rocks and they may rise to the Earth's surface or accumulate below an impermeable layer of rock that has been folded or faulted to form a trap – an anticline (upfold) trap, for example. Minerals are inorganic substances that may consist of a single chemical element, such as gold, silver, or copper, or combinations of elements (see pp. 268-269). Some minerals are concentrated in mineralization zones in rock associated with crustal movements or volcanic activity. Others may be found in sediments as placer deposits – accumulations of high-density minerals that have been weathered out of rocks, transported, and deposited (on river-beds, for example).

OIL RIG, NORTH SEA

STAGES IN THE FORMATION OF COAL

Stalk
Leaf

PLANT MATTER

Decayed plant matter

About 60% carbon
PEAT

About 70% carbon

Crumbly texture
LIGNITE (BROWN COAL)

Powdery texture

About 80% carbon

Shiny surface
BITUMINOUS COAL
About 95% carbon

HOW COAL IS FORMED

Vegetation

Increasing pressure and temperature

Increasing layers of overlying sediment

Increasing pressure and temperature

Increasing layers of overlying sediment

Increasing pressure and temperature

Peat (about 60% carbon)

Lignite (about 70% carbon)

Bituminous coal (about 80% carbon)

PEAT

LIGNITE (BROWN COAL)

BITUMINOUS COAL

ANTHRACITE COAL

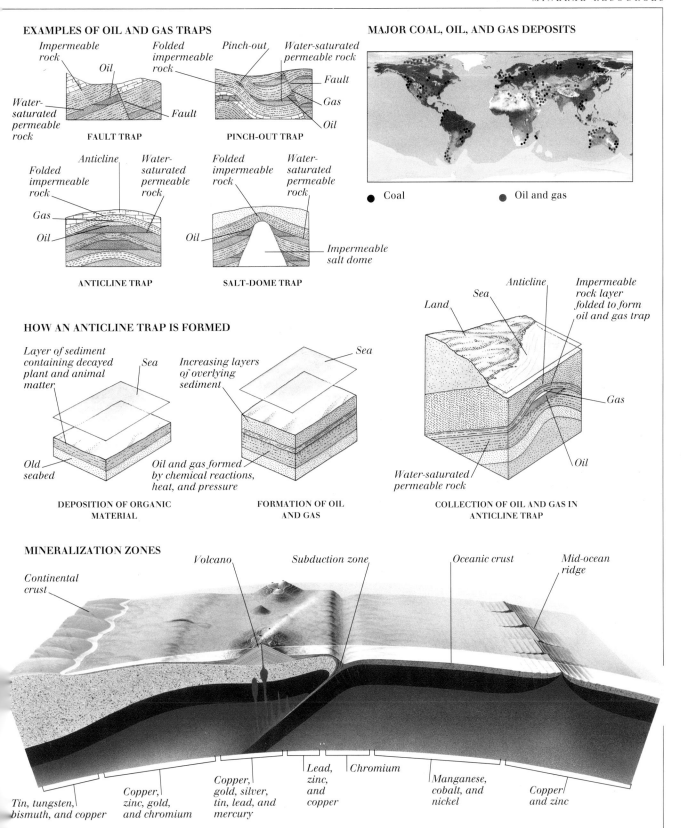

EXAMPLES OF OIL AND GAS TRAPS

Impermeable rock
Oil
Water-saturated permeable rock
Fault
FAULT TRAP

Pinch-out
Folded impermeable rock
Water-saturated permeable rock
Fault
Gas
Oil
PINCH-OUT TRAP

Anticline
Folded impermeable rock
Water-saturated permeable rock
Gas
Oil
ANTICLINE TRAP

Folded impermeable rock
Water-saturated permeable rock
Oil
Impermeable salt dome
SALT-DOME TRAP

MAJOR COAL, OIL, AND GAS DEPOSITS

● Coal   ● Oil and gas

HOW AN ANTICLINE TRAP IS FORMED

Layer of sediment containing decayed plant and animal matter
Sea
Old seabed
DEPOSITION OF ORGANIC MATERIAL

Increasing layers of overlying sediment
Sea
Oil and gas formed by chemical reactions, heat, and pressure
FORMATION OF OIL AND GAS

Land
Sea
Anticline
Impermeable rock layer folded to form oil and gas trap
Gas
Oil
Water-saturated permeable rock
COLLECTION OF OIL AND GAS IN ANTICLINE TRAP

MINERALIZATION ZONES

Continental crust
Volcano
Subduction zone
Oceanic crust
Mid-ocean ridge

Tin, tungsten, bismuth, and copper
Copper, zinc, gold, and chromium
Copper, gold, silver, tin, lead, and mercury
Lead, zinc, and copper
Chromium
Manganese, cobalt, and nickel
Copper and zinc

Weathering and erosion

WEATHERING IS THE BREAKING DOWN of rocks on the Earth's surface. There are two main types: physical (or mechanical) and chemical. Physical weathering may be caused by temperature changes, such as freezing and thawing, or by abrasion from material carried by winds, rivers, or glaciers. Rocks may also be broken down by the actions of animals and plants, such as the burrowing of animals and the growth of roots. Chemical weathering causes rocks to decompose by changing their chemical composition – for example, rainwater may dissolve certain minerals in a rock. Erosion is the wearing away and removal of land surfaces by water, wind, or ice. It is greatest in areas of little or no surface vegetation, such as deserts, where sand dunes may form.

FORMATION OF A HAMADA (ROCK PAVEMENT)

Wind blows away small particles

Larger particles aggregate

Hamada forms

FIRST STAGE

SECOND STAGE

FINAL STAGE

FEATURES OF WEATHERING AND EROSION

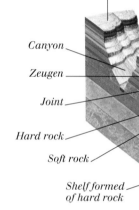

Mesa (flat-topped plateau)

Canyon

Zeugen

Joint

Hard rock

Soft rock

Shelf formed of hard rock

Talus (scree)

Alluvial fan (alluvial cone)

Bahada (gentle slope covered with loose rock)

Bolson (alluvium-filled basin)

FEATURES PRODUCED BY WIND ACTION

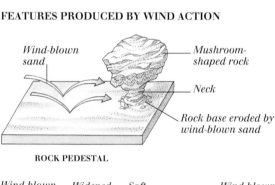

Wind-blown sand

Mushroom-shaped rock

Neck

Rock base eroded by wind-blown sand

ROCK PEDESTAL

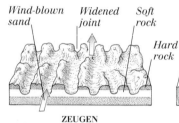

Wind-blown sand

Widened joint

Soft rock

Hard rock

ZEUGEN

Wind-blown sand

Furrow

Hard rock

Soft rock eroded by wind-blown sand

YARDANG

EXAMPLES OF PHYSICAL WEATHERING PROCESSES

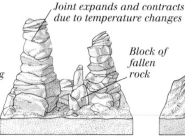

Heated rock surface expands

Exfoliation dome

Flaking rock

Fallen debris

EXFOLIATION (ONION-SKIN WEATHERING)

Joint expands and contracts due to temperature changes

Block of fallen rock

BLOCK DISINTEGRATION

Talus (scree)

Joint widened by frozen water

FROST WEDGING

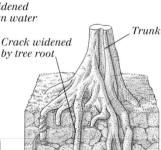

Trunk

Crack widened by tree root

TREE ROOT ACTION

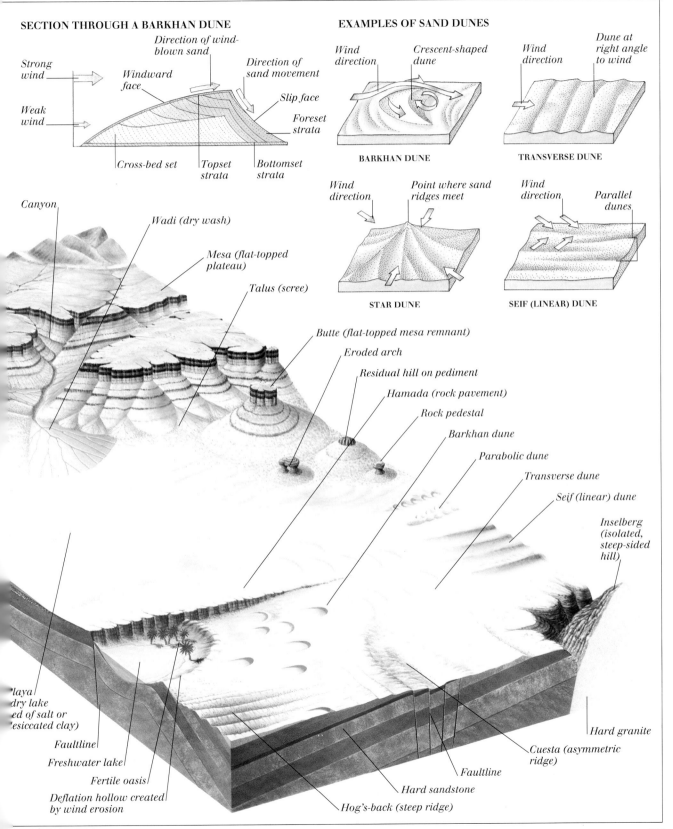

SECTION THROUGH A BARKHAN DUNE

Strong wind

Weak wind

Windward face

Direction of wind-blown sand

Direction of sand movement

Slip face

Foreset strata

Cross-bed set

Topset strata

Bottomset strata

EXAMPLES OF SAND DUNES

Wind direction

Crescent-shaped dune

BARKHAN DUNE

Wind direction

Dune at right angle to wind

TRANSVERSE DUNE

Wind direction

Point where sand ridges meet

STAR DUNE

Wind direction

Parallel dunes

SEIF (LINEAR) DUNE

Canyon

Wadi (dry wash)

Mesa (flat-topped plateau)

Talus (scree)

Butte (flat-topped mesa remnant)

Eroded arch

Residual hill on pediment

Hamada (rock pavement)

Rock pedestal

Barkhan dune

Parabolic dune

Transverse dune

Seif (linear) dune

Inselberg (isolated, steep-sided hill)

Playa (dry lake bed of salt or desiccated clay)

Faultline

Freshwater lake

Fertile oasis

Deflation hollow created by wind erosion

Hog's-back (steep ridge)

Hard sandstone

Faultline

Cuesta (asymmetric ridge)

Hard granite

Caves

CAVES COMMONLY FORM in areas of limestone, although on coastlines they also occur in other rocks. Limestone is made of calcite (calcium carbonate), which dissolves in the carbonic acid naturally present in rainwater, and in humic acids from the decay of vegetation. The acidic water trickles down through cracks and joints in the limestone and between rock layers, breaking up the surface terrain into clints (blocks of rock), separated by grikes (deep cracks), and punctuated by sink-holes (also called swallow-holes or potholes) into which surface streams may disappear. Underground, the acidic water dissolves the rock around crevices, opening up a network of passages and caves, which can become large caverns if the roofs collapse. Various features are formed when the dissolved calcite is redeposited; for example, it may be redeposited along an underground stream to form a gour (series of calcite ridges), or in caves and passages to form stalactites and stalagmites. Stalactites develop where calcite is left behind as water drips from the roof; where the drops land, stalagmites build up.

STALACTITE WITH RING MARKS

Ring mark

MERGED STALACTITES

SURFACE TOPOGRAPHY OF A CAVE SYSTEM

Doline (depression caused by collapse of cave roof)

Sink-hole

Porous limestone

Gorge where cave roof has fallen in

Resurgence

Limestone terrain with clints and grikes

Impermeable rock

Scar of bare rock

STALAGMITE FORMATIONS

Calcite (calcium carbonate) crystallized under water

Thin encrustations of calcite (calcium carbonate)

CALCAREOUS TUFA

CRYSTALLINE STALAGMITIC FLOOR

Former water table

Permeable limestone

Encrustations on dead stems of small plants

Calcite (calcium carbonate)

Calcite (calcium carbonate)

STALAGMITIC FLOOR

Resurgence

Encrustations with fungoid structure

STALAGMITIC BOSS

Layer of impermeable rock

Present water table

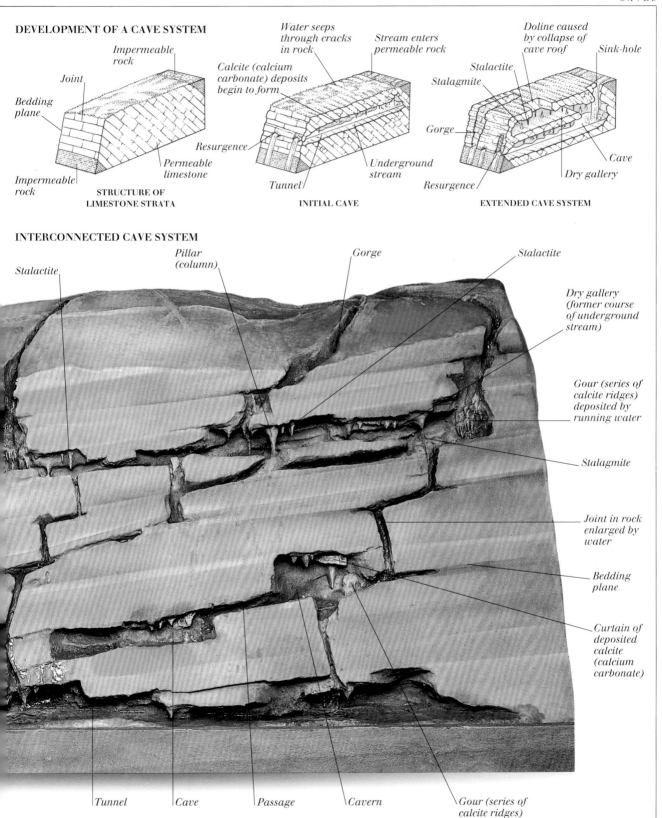

DEVELOPMENT OF A CAVE SYSTEM

Impermeable rock
Joint
Bedding plane
Impermeable rock
Permeable limestone

STRUCTURE OF LIMESTONE STRATA

Water seeps through cracks in rock
Stream enters permeable rock
Calcite (calcium carbonate) deposits begin to form
Resurgence
Tunnel
Underground stream

INITIAL CAVE

Doline caused by collapse of cave roof
Sink-hole
Stalactite
Stalagmite
Gorge
Resurgence
Cave
Dry gallery

EXTENDED CAVE SYSTEM

INTERCONNECTED CAVE SYSTEM

Stalactite
Pillar (column)
Gorge
Stalactite
Dry gallery (former course of underground stream)
Gour (series of calcite ridges) deposited by running water
Stalagmite
Joint in rock enlarged by water
Bedding plane
Curtain of deposited calcite (calcium carbonate)
Tunnel
Cave
Passage
Cavern
Gour (series of calcite ridges)

Glaciers

GLACIER BAY, ALASKA

A VALLEY GLACIER IS A LARGE MASS OF ICE that forms on land and moves slowly downhill under its own weight. It is formed from snow that collects in cirques (mountain hollows also known as corries) and compresses into ice as more and more snow accumulates. The cirque is deepened by frost wedging and abrasion (see pp. 282-283), and arêtes (sharp ridges) develop between adjacent cirques. Eventually, so much ice builds up that the glacier begins to move downhill. As the glacier moves it collects moraine (debris), which may range in size from particles of dust to large boulders. The rocks at the base of the glacier erode the glacial valley, giving it a U-shaped cross-section. Under the glacier, *roches moutonnées* (eroded outcrops of hard rock) and drumlins (rounded mounds of rock and clay) are left behind on the valley floor. The glacier ends at a terminus (the snout), where the ice melts as fast as it arrives. If the temperature increases, the ice melts faster than it arrives, and the glacier retreats. The retreating glacier leaves behind its moraine and also erratics (isolated single boulders). Glacial streams from the melting glacier deposit eskers and kames (ridges and mounds of sand and gravel), but carry away the finer sediment to form a stratified outwash plain. Lumps of ice carried on to this plain melt, creating holes called kettles.

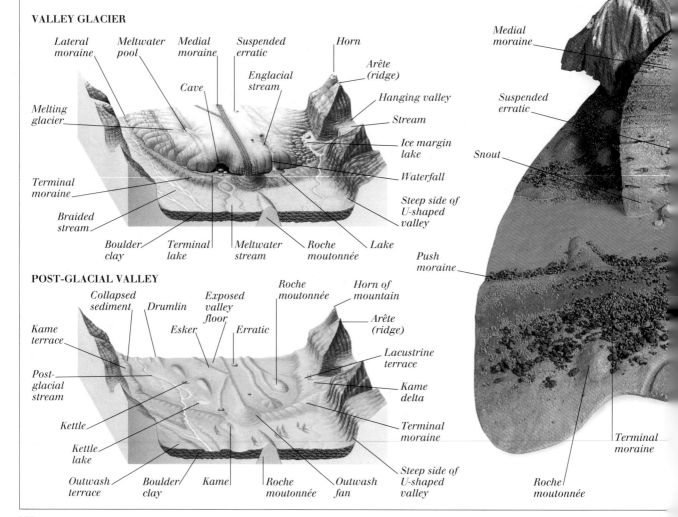

VALLEY GLACIER

Lateral moraine
Meltwater pool
Medial moraine
Suspended erratic
Horn
Arête (ridge)
Englacial stream
Cave
Hanging valley
Melting glacier
Stream
Ice margin lake
Terminal moraine
Waterfall
Braided stream
Steep side of U-shaped valley
Boulder clay
Terminal lake
Meltwater stream
Roche moutonnée
Lake
Medial moraine
Suspended erratic
Snout
Push moraine

POST-GLACIAL VALLEY

Collapsed sediment
Drumlin
Exposed valley floor
Erratic
Roche moutonnée
Horn of mountain
Arête (ridge)
Kame terrace
Esker
Lacustrine terrace
Post-glacial stream
Kame delta
Kettle
Terminal moraine
Kettle lake
Steep side of U-shaped valley
Outwash terrace
Boulder clay
Kame
Roche moutonnée
Outwash fan
Terminal moraine
Roche moutonnée

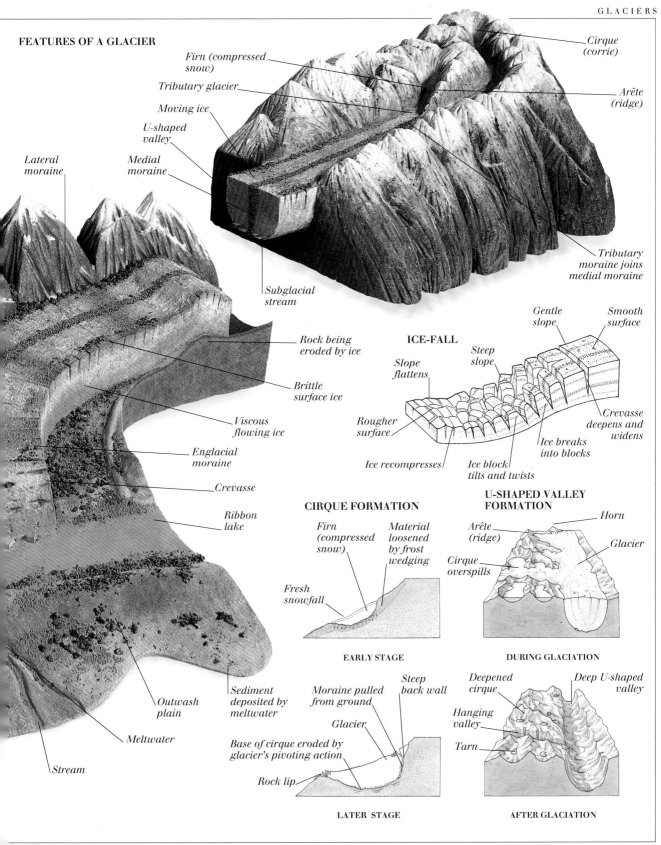

FEATURES OF A GLACIER

Cirque (corrie)

Firn (compressed snow)

Tributary glacier

Arête (ridge)

Moving ice

U-shaped valley

Medial moraine

Lateral moraine

Tributary moraine joins medial moraine

Subglacial stream

Rock being eroded by ice

Brittle surface ice

Viscous flowing ice

Englacial moraine

Crevasse

Ribbon lake

Sediment deposited by meltwater

Outwash plain

Meltwater

Stream

ICE-FALL

Gentle slope

Smooth surface

Steep slope

Slope flattens

Rougher surface

Crevasse deepens and widens

Ice recompresses

Ice block tilts and twists

Ice breaks into blocks

CIRQUE FORMATION

Firn (compressed snow)

Material loosened by frost wedging

Fresh snowfall

EARLY STAGE

Moraine pulled from ground

Steep back wall

Glacier

Base of cirque eroded by glacier's pivoting action

Rock lip

LATER STAGE

U-SHAPED VALLEY FORMATION

Horn

Arête (ridge)

Glacier

Cirque overspills

DURING GLACIATION

Deepened cirque

Deep U-shaped valley

Hanging valley

Tarn

AFTER GLACIATION

287

Rivers

RIVERS FORM PART of the water cycle – the continuous circulation of water between the land, sea, and atmosphere. The source of a river may be a mountain spring or lake, or a melting glacier. The course that the river subsequently takes depends on the slope of the terrain and on the rock types and formations over which it flows. In its early, upland stages, a river tumbles steeply over rocks and boulders and cuts a steep-sided V-shaped valley. Farther downstream, it flows smoothly over sediments and forms winding meanders, eroding sideways to create broad valleys and plains. On reaching the coast, the river may deposit sediment to form an estuary or delta (see pp. 290-291).

RIVER CAPTURE

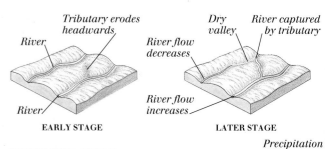

Tributary erodes headwards
River
River

EARLY STAGE

Dry valley
River captured by tributary
River flow decreases
River flow increases

LATER STAGE

THE WATER CYCLE

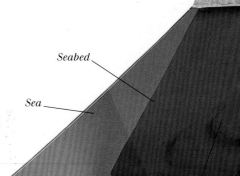

Precipitation falls on high ground
Wind
Water carried downstream by river
Water vapour released into atmosphere by trees and other plants
Wind
Water vapour forms clouds
Water evaporates from sea
Water stored in sea
River flows into sea
Water seeps underground and flows to sea
Water evaporates from lake
Water seeps underground and flows to sea
Seabed
Sea
Sediment layers

SATELLITE IMAGE OF GANGES RIVER DELTA, BANGLADESH

River Ganges
Ganges delta
Infertile swampland
Distributary
Large volume of sediment

RIVER DRAINAGE PATTERNS

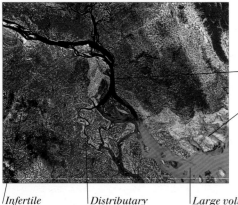

RADIAL   **CENTRIPETAL**   **PARALLEL**   **DENDRITIC**

DERANGED   **TRELLISED**   **ANNULAR**   **RECTANGULAR**

STAGES IN A RIVER'S DEVELOPMENT

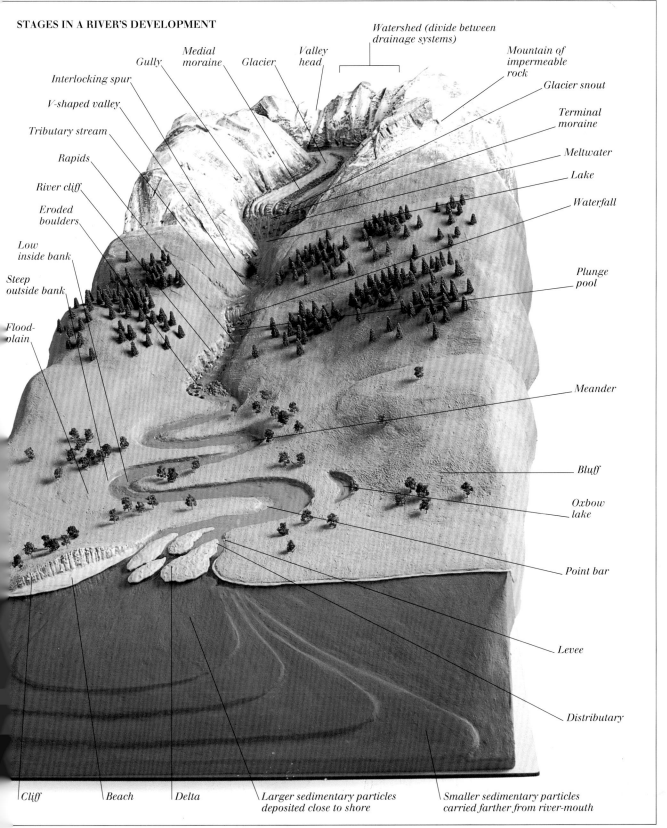

Watershed (divide between drainage systems)

Medial moraine

Gully

Interlocking spur

V-shaped valley

Tributary stream

Rapids

River cliff

Eroded boulders

Low inside bank

Steep outside bank

Flood-plain

Glacier

Valley head

Mountain of impermeable rock

Glacier snout

Terminal moraine

Meltwater

Lake

Waterfall

Plunge pool

Meander

Bluff

Oxbow lake

Point bar

Levee

Distributary

Cliff

Beach

Delta

Larger sedimentary particles deposited close to shore

Smaller sedimentary particles carried farther from river-mouth

River features

RIVERS ARE ONE OF THE MAJOR FORCES that shape the landscape. Near its source, a river is steep (see pp. 288-289). It erodes downwards, carving out V-shaped valleys and deep gorges. Waterfalls and rapids are formed where the river flows from hard rock to softer, more easily eroded rock. Farther downstream, meanders may form and there is greater sideways erosion, resulting in a broad river valley. The river sometimes erodes through the neck of a meander to form an oxbow lake. Sediment deposited on the valley floor by meandering rivers and during floods helps to create a flood-plain. Floods may also deposit sediment on the banks of the river to form levees. As a river spills into the sea or a lake, it deposits large amounts of sediment, and may form a delta. A delta is an area of sand-bars, swamps, and lagoons through which the river flows in several channels called distributaries – the Mississippi delta, for example. Often, a rise in sea level may have flooded the river-mouth to form a broad estuary, a tidal section where seawater mixes with fresh water.

HOW WATERFALLS AND RAPIDS ARE FORMED

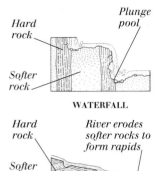

WATERFALL

RAPIDS

A RIVER VALLEY DRAINAGE SYSTEM

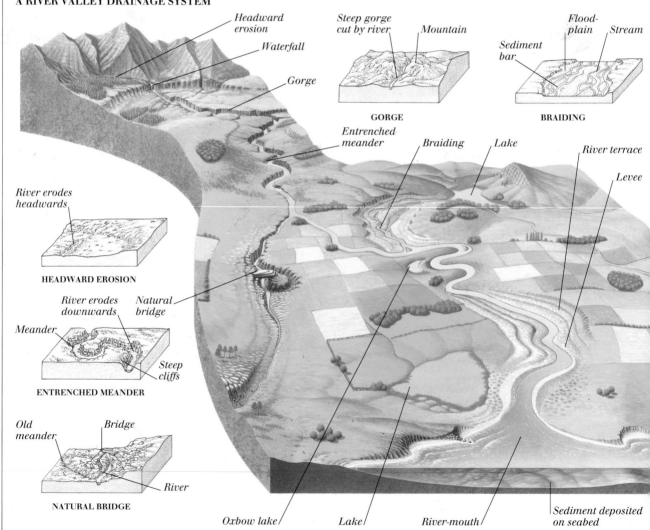

GORGE

BRAIDING

HEADWARD EROSION

ENTRENCHED MEANDER

NATURAL BRIDGE

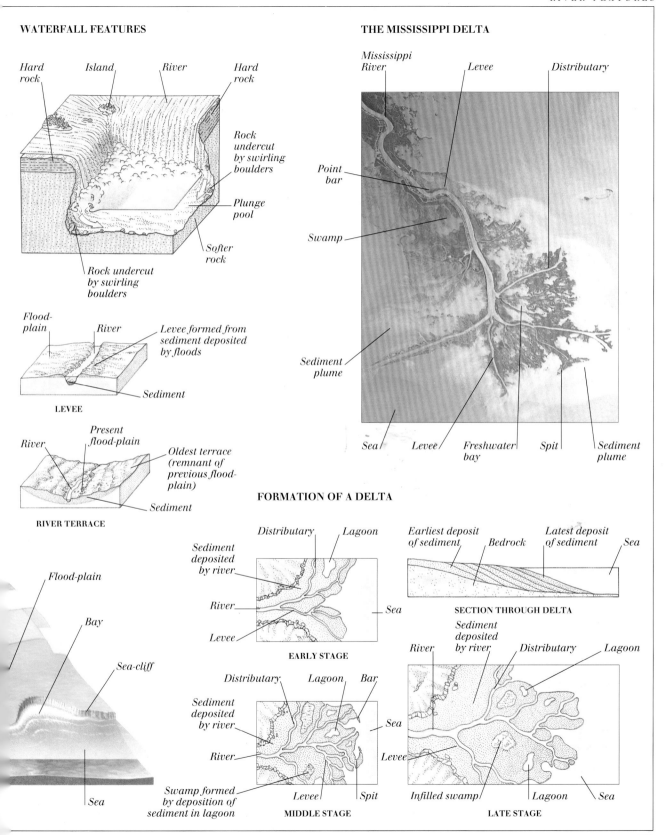

WATERFALL FEATURES

Hard rock · Island · River · Hard rock

Rock undercut by swirling boulders

Plunge pool

Softer rock

Rock undercut by swirling boulders

Flood-plain · River · Levee formed from sediment deposited by floods

Sediment

LEVEE

River · Present flood-plain · Oldest terrace (remnant of previous flood-plain)

Sediment

RIVER TERRACE

Flood-plain

Bay

Sea-cliff

Sea

THE MISSISSIPPI DELTA

Mississippi River · Levee · Distributary

Point bar

Swamp

Sediment plume

Sea · Levee · Freshwater bay · Spit · Sediment plume

FORMATION OF A DELTA

Distributary · Lagoon

Sediment deposited by river

River

Levee

Sea

EARLY STAGE

Earliest deposit of sediment · Bedrock · Latest deposit of sediment · Sea

SECTION THROUGH DELTA

Distributary · Lagoon · Bar

Sediment deposited by river

River

Levee · Spit

Sea

MIDDLE STAGE

Swamp formed by deposition of sediment in lagoon

River · Sediment deposited by river · Distributary · Lagoon

Levee

Infilled swamp · Lagoon · Sea

LATE STAGE

Lakes and groundwater

NATURAL LAKES OCCUR WHERE a large quantity of water collects in a hollow in impermeable rock, or is prevented from draining away by a barrier, such as moraine (glacial deposits) or solidified lava. Lakes are often relatively short-lived landscape features, as they tend to become silted up by sediment from the streams and rivers that feed them. Some of the more long-lasting

LAKE BAIKAL, RUSSIA

lakes are found in deep rift valleys formed by vertical movements of the Earth's crust (see pp. 58-59) – for example, Lake Baikal in Russia, the world's largest freshwater lake, and the Dead Sea in the Middle East, one of the world's saltiest lakes. Where water is able to drain away, it sinks into the ground until it reaches a layer of impermeable rock, then accumulates in the permeable rock above it; this water-saturated permeable rock is called an aquifer. The saturated zone varies in depth according to seasonal and climatic changes. In wet conditions, the water stored underground builds up, while in dry periods it becomes depleted.

Where the upper edge of the saturated zone – the water table – meets the ground surface, water emerges as springs. In an artesian basin, where the aquifer is below an aquiclude (layer of impermeable rock), the water table throughout the basin is determined by its height at the rim. In the centre of such a basin, the water table is above ground level. The water in the basin is thus trapped below the water table and can rise under its own pressure along faultlines or well shafts.

EXAMPLES OF SPRINGS

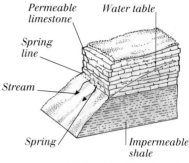

LIMESTONE SPRING

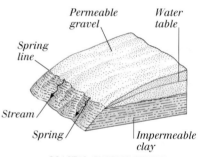

COASTAL (VALLEY) SPRING

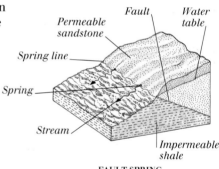

FAULT SPRING

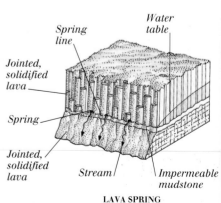

LAVA SPRING

STRUCTURE OF AN ARTESIAN BASIN

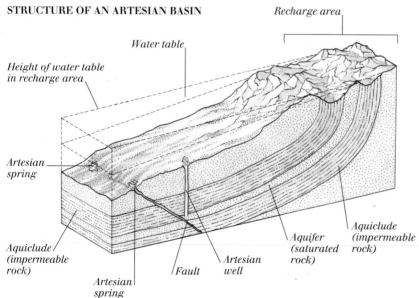

FEATURES OF A GROUNDWATER SYSTEM

Marsh

Lake

Stream

Zone of aeration

Layer of soil moisture

Zone of aeration

Capillary fringe

Water table

Saturated zone

CLOSE-UP OF SURFACE LAYER

Dry-season water table

Present water table (wet season)

Temporarily saturated zone (saturated only in wet season)

Permanently saturated zone (saturated in wet and dry seasons)

EXAMPLES OF LAKES

Glacial deposits

Lake in kettle (former site of ice block)

KETTLE LAKE

Oxbow lake (cut-off river meander)

River

OXBOW LAKE

Caldera (collapsed crater)

Volcanic lake

VOLCANIC LAKE

Movement along strike-slip (lateral) fault

Strike-slip (lateral) fault

Lake in elongated hollow

STRIKE-SLIP (LATERAL) FAULT LAKE

Rift valley

High valley walls

Sinking graben (block fault)

GRABEN (BLOCK-FAULT) LAKE

Steep back wall eroded by frost and ice

Moraine or rock lip damming lake

Tarn (circular mountain lake)

TARN

THE DEAD SEA, ISRAEL/JORDAN

River Jordan

Dead Sea

Steep rift-valley walls

Salt left by evaporation

Israel

Shallow flats

Jordan

Coastlines

COASTLINES ARE AMONG THE MOST RAPIDLY changing landscape features. Some are eroded by waves, wind, and rain, causing cliffs to be undercut and caves to be hollowed out of solid rock. Others are built up by waves transporting sand and small rocks in a process known as longshore drift, and by rivers depositing sediment in deltas. Additional influences include the activities of living organisms such as coral, crustal movements, and sea-level variations due to climatic changes. Rising land or a drop in sea level creates an emergent coastline, with cliffs and beaches stranded above the new shoreline. Sinking land or a rise in sea level produces a drowned coastline, typified by fjords (submerged glacial valleys) or submerged river valleys.

FEATURES OF A SEA-CLIFF

Cliff-top
Cliff-face
High tide level
Low tide level
Offshore deposits
Wave-cut platform
Undercut area of cliff

Mature river

FEATURES OF WAVES

Wave height
Crest
Wavelength
Trough
Shorter wavelength near beach
Circular orbit of water and suspended particles
Orbit deformed into ellipse as water gets shallower

Headland
Bedding plane
Sea-cliff
Remnants of former headland
Estuary

LONGSHORE DRIFT

Pebble
Backwash
Movement of material along beach
Build-up of material against groyne
Beach
Groyne
Swash zone
Swash
Waves approaching shore at an oblique angle

DEPOSITIONAL FEATURES OF COASTLINES

Bay-head beach
Wave direction
Headland

Wave direction
Tombolo
Island

Wave direction
Cuspate foreland

Wave direction
Barrier beach
Lagoon

BAY-HEAD BEACH

TOMBOLO

CUSPATE FORELAND

BARRIER BEACH

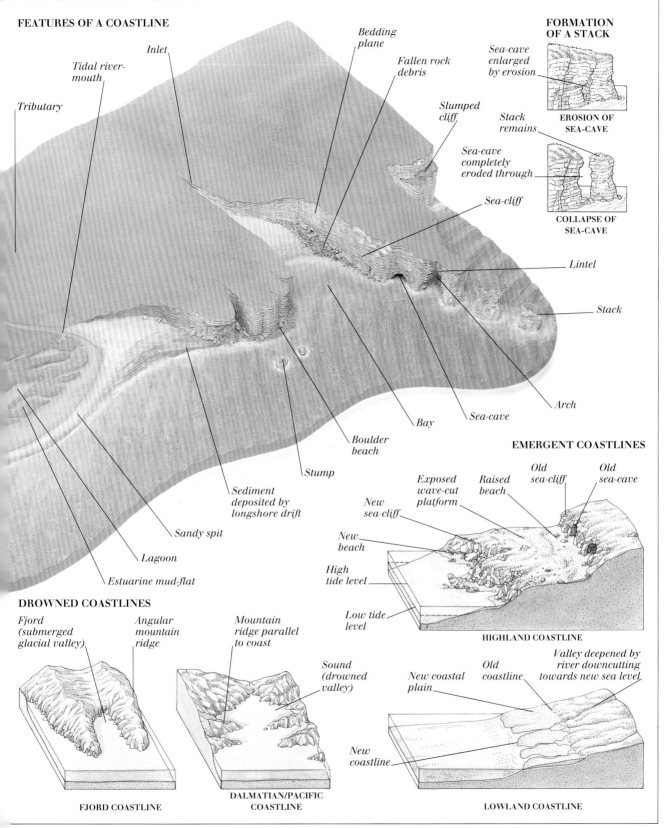

FEATURES OF A COASTLINE

Tributary

Tidal river-mouth

Inlet

Bedding plane

Fallen rock debris

Slumped cliff

Sea-cliff

Lintel

Stack

Arch

Sea-cave

Bay

Boulder beach

Stump

Sediment deposited by longshore drift

Sandy spit

Lagoon

Estuarine mud-flat

FORMATION OF A STACK

Sea-cave enlarged by erosion

EROSION OF SEA-CAVE

Stack remains

Sea-cave completely eroded through

COLLAPSE OF SEA-CAVE

EMERGENT COASTLINES

Exposed wave-cut platform

Raised beach

Old sea-cliff

Old sea-cave

New sea-cliff

New beach

High tide level

Low tide level

HIGHLAND COASTLINE

Old coastline

New coastal plain

Valley deepened by river downcutting towards new sea level

New coastline

LOWLAND COASTLINE

DROWNED COASTLINES

Fjord (submerged glacial valley)

Angular mountain ridge

Mountain ridge parallel to coast

Sound (drowned valley)

FJORD COASTLINE

DALMATIAN/PACIFIC COASTLINE

Oceans and seas

OCEANS AND SEAS COVER ABOUT 70 PER CENT of the Earth's
surface and account for about 97 per cent of its total
water. These oceans and seas play a crucial role
in regulating temperature variations and
determining climate. Their waters absorb
heat from the Sun, especially in tropical
regions, and the surface currents distribute
it around the Earth, warming overlying
air masses and neighbouring land in
winter and cooling them in summer.
The oceans are never still. Differences
in temperature and salinity drive
deep current systems, while surface
currents are generated by winds
blowing over the oceans. All currents
are deflected – to the right in the
Northern Hemisphere, to the left in
the Southern Hemisphere – as a result
of the Earth's rotation. This deflective
factor is known as the Coriolis force.
A current that begins on the surface is
immediately deflected. This current in
turn generates a current in the layer of water
beneath, which is also deflected. As the movement
is transmitted downwards, the deflections form an
Ekman spiral. The waters of the oceans and seas are
also moved by the constant ebb and flow of tides. These
are caused by the gravitational pull of the Moon and Sun.
The highest tides (Spring tides) occur at full and new Moon;
the lowest tides (neap tides) occur at first and last quarter.

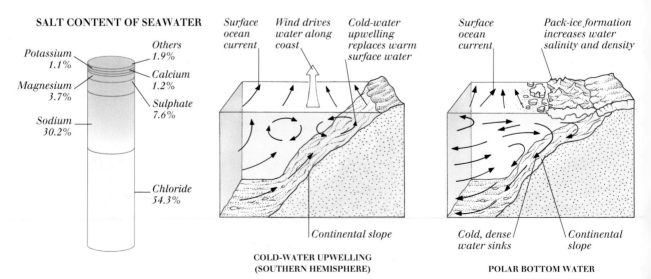

SALT CONTENT OF SEAWATER

Potassium
1.1%

Others
1.9%

Magnesium
3.7%

Calcium
1.2%

Sulphate
7.6%

Sodium
30.2%

Chloride
54.3%

Surface ocean current

Wind drives water along coast

Cold-water upwelling replaces warm surface water

Surface ocean current

Pack-ice formation increases water salinity and density

Continental slope

Cold, dense water sinks

Continental slope

**COLD-WATER UPWELLING
(SOUTHERN HEMISPHERE)**

POLAR BOTTOM WATER

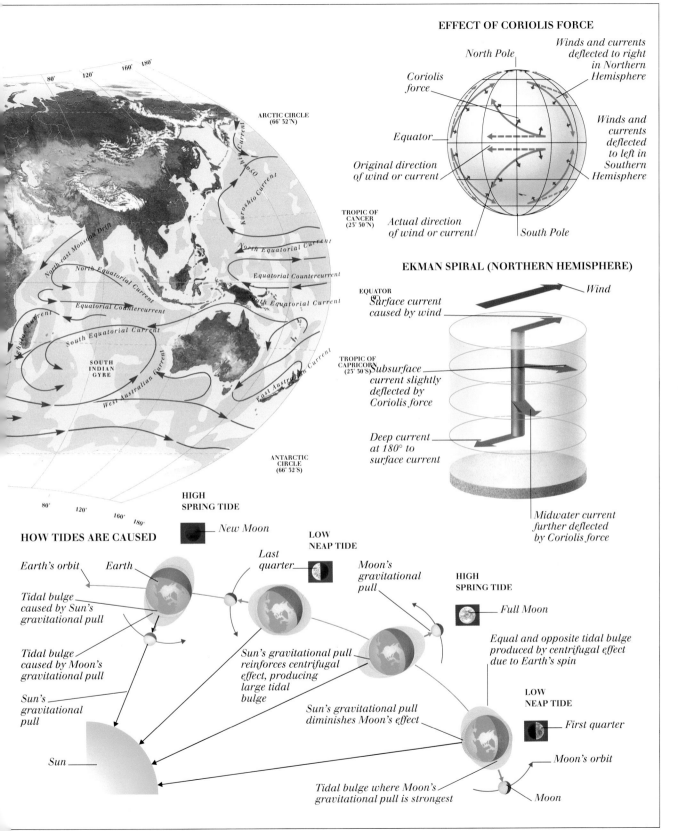

EFFECT OF CORIOLIS FORCE

North Pole

Coriolis force

Winds and currents deflected to right in Northern Hemisphere

Equator

Winds and currents deflected to left in Southern Hemisphere

Original direction of wind or current

Actual direction of wind or current

South Pole

EKMAN SPIRAL (NORTHERN HEMISPHERE)

EQUATOR

Wind

Surface current caused by wind

TROPIC OF CAPRICORN (25° 50'S)

Subsurface current slightly deflected by Coriolis force

Deep current at 180° to surface current

Midwater current further deflected by Coriolis force

ARCTIC CIRCLE (66° 52'N)

TROPIC OF CANCER (25° 50'N)

Oyo

Kuroshio Current

North-east Monsoon Drift

North Equatorial Current

North Equatorial Current

Equatorial Countercurrent

Equatorial Countercurrent

South Equatorial Current

South Equatorial Current

SOUTH INDIAN GYRE

West Australian Current

East Australian Current

ANTARCTIC CIRCLE (66° 52'S)

HOW TIDES ARE CAUSED

HIGH SPRING TIDE

New Moon

LOW NEAP TIDE

Last quarter

Moon's gravitational pull

HIGH SPRING TIDE

Full Moon

Earth's orbit

Earth

Tidal bulge caused by Sun's gravitational pull

Tidal bulge caused by Moon's gravitational pull

Sun's gravitational pull

Sun's gravitational pull reinforces centrifugal effect, producing large tidal bulge

Sun's gravitational pull diminishes Moon's effect

Equal and opposite tidal bulge produced by centrifugal effect due to Earth's spin

LOW NEAP TIDE

First quarter

Moon's orbit

Sun

Tidal bulge where Moon's gravitational pull is strongest

Moon

The ocean floor

THE OCEAN FLOOR COMPRISES TWO SECTIONS: the continental shelf and slope, and the deep-ocean floor. The continental shelf and slope are part of the continental crust, but may extend far into the ocean. Sloping quite gently to a depth of about 140 metres, the continental shelf is covered in sandy deposits shaped by waves and tidal currents. At the edge of the continental shelf, the seabed slopes down to the abyssal plain, which lies at an average depth of about 3,800 metres. On this deep-ocean floor is a layer of sediment made up of clays, fine oozes formed from the remains of tiny sea creatures, and occasional mineral-rich deposits. Echo-sounding and remote sensing from satellites has revealed that the abyssal plain is divided by a system of mountain ranges, far bigger than any on land – the mid-ocean ridge. Here, magma (molten rock) wells up from the Earth's interior and solidifies, widening the ocean floor (see pp. 58-59). As the ocean floor spreads, volcanoes that have formed over hot spots in the crust move away from their magma source; they become extinct and are increasingly submerged and eroded. Volcanoes eroded below sea level remain as seamounts (underwater mountains). In warm waters, a volcano that projects above the ocean surface often acquires a fringing coral reef, which may develop into an atoll as the volcano becomes submerged.

CONTINENTAL-SHELF FLOOR

Bedrock exposed by tidal scour

Shoreline

Parallel strips of coarse material left by strong tidal currents

Sand deposited in wavy pattern by weaker currents

Irregular patches of fine sand deposited by weakest currents

FEATURES OF THE OCEAN FLOOR

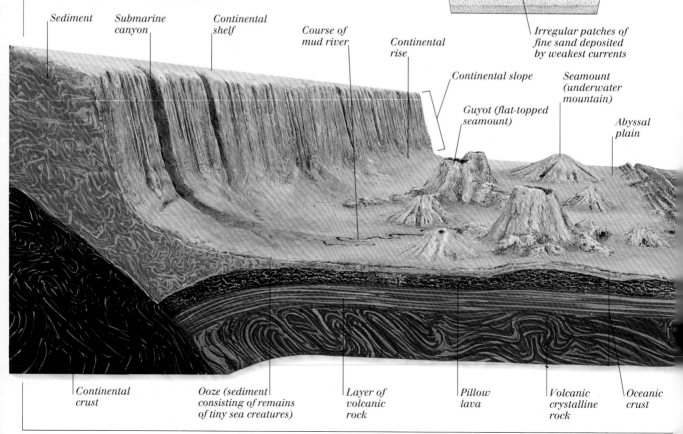

Sediment

Submarine canyon

Continental shelf

Course of mud river

Continental rise

Continental slope

Guyot (flat-topped seamount)

Seamount (underwater mountain)

Abyssal plain

Continental crust

Ooze (sediment consisting of remains of tiny sea creatures)

Layer of volcanic rock

Pillow lava

Volcanic crystalline rock

Oceanic crust

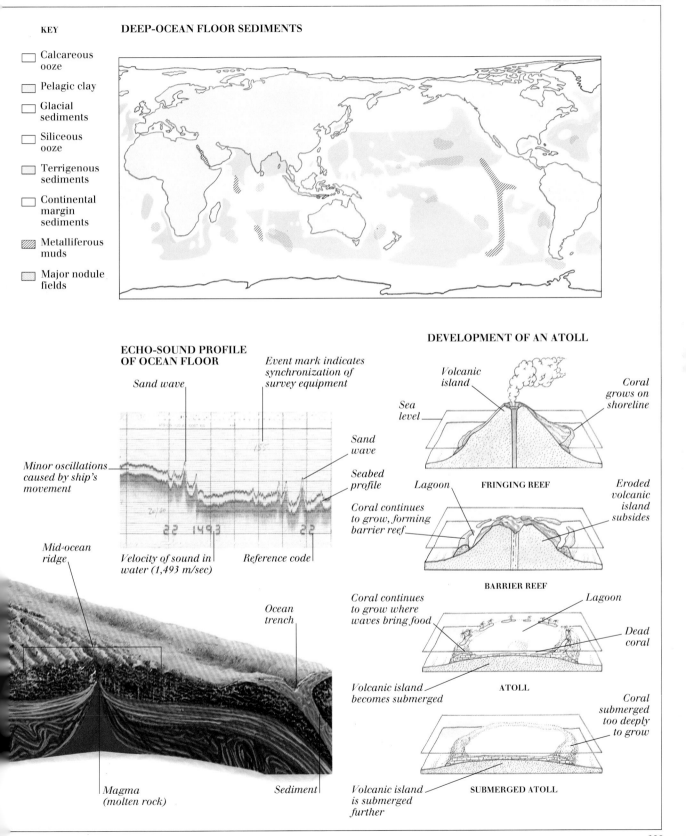

KEY

☐ Calcareous ooze

☐ Pelagic clay

☐ Glacial sediments

☐ Siliceous ooze

☐ Terrigenous sediments

☐ Continental margin sediments

▨ Metalliferous muds

☐ Major nodule fields

DEEP-OCEAN FLOOR SEDIMENTS

ECHO-SOUND PROFILE OF OCEAN FLOOR

Sand wave

Event mark indicates synchronization of survey equipment

Sand wave

Seabed profile

Minor oscillations caused by ship's movement

Velocity of sound in water (1,493 m/sec)

Reference code

Mid-ocean ridge

Ocean trench

Magma (molten rock)

Sediment

DEVELOPMENT OF AN ATOLL

Volcanic island

Sea level

Coral grows on shoreline

FRINGING REEF

Lagoon

Coral continues to grow, forming barrier reef

Eroded volcanic island subsides

BARRIER REEF

Coral continues to grow where waves bring food

Lagoon

Dead coral

Volcanic island becomes submerged

ATOLL

Coral submerged too deeply to grow

Volcanic island is submerged further

SUBMERGED ATOLL

The atmosphere

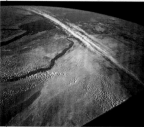

JET STREAM

THE EARTH IS SURROUNDED BY ITS ATMOSPHERE, a blanket of gases that enables life to exist on the planet. This layer has no definite outer edge, gradually becoming thinner until it merges into space, but over 80 per cent of atmospheric gases are held by gravity within about 20 kilometres of the Earth's surface. The atmosphere blocks out much harmful ultraviolet solar radiation, and insulates the Earth against extremes of temperature by limiting both incoming solar radiation and the escape of re-radiated heat into space. This natural balance may be distorted by the greenhouse effect, as gases such as carbon dioxide have built up in the atmosphere, trapping more heat. Close to the Earth's surface, differences in air temperature and pressure cause air to circulate between the equator and poles. This circulation, together with the Coriolis force, gives rise to the prevailing surface winds and the high-level jet streams.

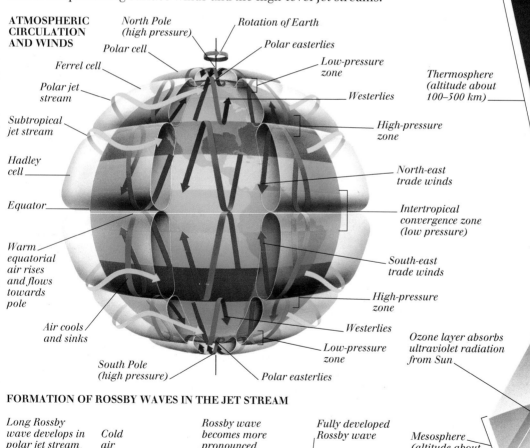

ATMOSPHERIC CIRCULATION AND WINDS

- North Pole (high pressure)
- Rotation of Earth
- Polar cell
- Polar easterlies
- Ferrel cell
- Low-pressure zone
- Polar jet stream
- Westerlies
- Subtropical jet stream
- High-pressure zone
- Hadley cell
- North-east trade winds
- Equator
- Intertropical convergence zone (low pressure)
- Warm equatorial air rises and flows towards pole
- South-east trade winds
- High-pressure zone
- Air cools and sinks
- Westerlies
- Low-pressure zone
- South Pole (high pressure)
- Polar easterlies

Exosphere (altitude above about 500 km)

Corona

Thermosphere (altitude about 100–500 km)

Ozone layer absorbs ultraviolet radiation from Sun

Mesosphere (altitude about 50–100 km)

Stratosphere (altitude about 10–50 km)

Troposphere (altitude up to about 10 km)

FORMATION OF ROSSBY WAVES IN THE JET STREAM

Long Rossby wave develops in polar jet stream

Cold air

Rossby wave becomes more pronounced

Fully developed Rossby wave

Warm air

INITIAL UNDULATION

DEEPENING WAVE

DEVELOPED WAVE

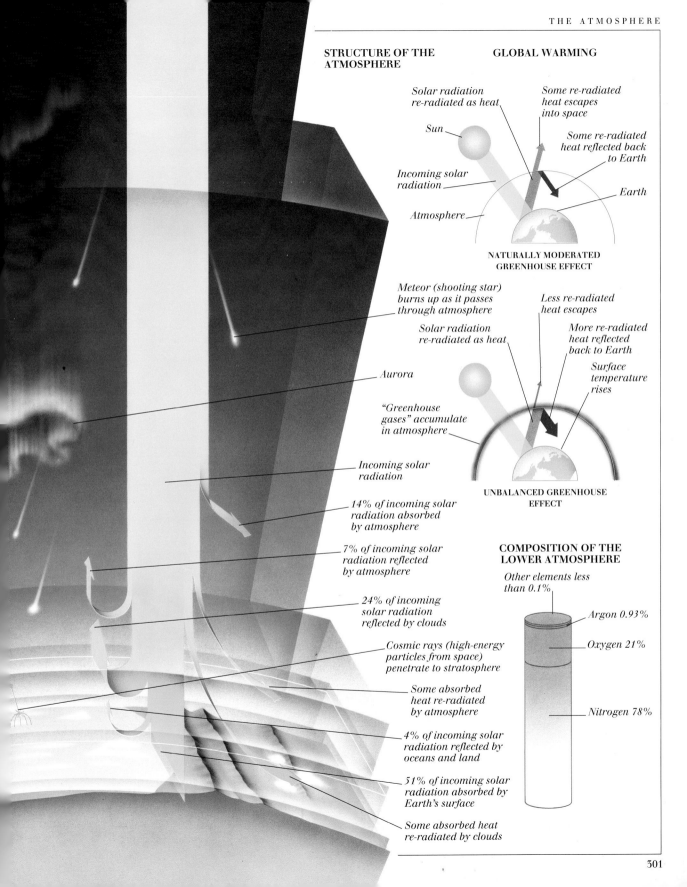

**STRUCTURE OF THE
ATMOSPHERE**

GLOBAL WARMING

Solar radiation
re-radiated as heat

Sun

Incoming solar
radiation

Atmosphere

Some re-radiated
heat escapes
into space

Some re-radiated
heat reflected back
to Earth

Earth

**NATURALLY MODERATED
GREENHOUSE EFFECT**

Meteor (shooting star)
burns up as it passes
through atmosphere

Solar radiation
re-radiated as heat

Aurora

"Greenhouse
gases" accumulate
in atmosphere

Incoming solar
radiation

14% of incoming solar
radiation absorbed
by atmosphere

7% of incoming solar
radiation reflected
by atmosphere

24% of incoming
solar radiation
reflected by clouds

Cosmic rays (high-energy
particles from space)
penetrate to stratosphere

Some absorbed
heat re-radiated
by atmosphere

4% of incoming solar
radiation reflected by
oceans and land

51% of incoming solar
radiation absorbed by
Earth's surface

Some absorbed heat
re-radiated by clouds

Less re-radiated
heat escapes

More re-radiated
heat reflected
back to Earth

Surface
temperature
rises

**UNBALANCED GREENHOUSE
EFFECT**

**COMPOSITION OF THE
LOWER ATMOSPHERE**

Other elements less
than 0.1%

Argon 0.93%

Oxygen 21%

Nitrogen 78%

301

Weather

WEATHER IS DEFINED AS THE ATMOSPHERIC CONDITIONS at a particular time and place; climate is the average weather conditions for a given region over time. Weather is assessed in terms of temperature, wind, cloud cover, and precipitation, such as rain or snow. Fine weather is associated with high-pressure areas, where air is sinking. Cloudy, wet, changeable weather is common in low-pressure zones with rising, unstable air. Such conditions occur at temperate latitudes, where warm air meets cool air along the polar fronts. Here, spiralling low-pressure cells known as depressions (mid-latitude cyclones) often form. A depression usually contains a sector of warmer air, beginning at a warm front and ending at a cold front. If the two fronts merge, forming an occluded front, the warm air is pushed upwards. An extreme form of low-pressure cell is a hurricane (also called a typhoon or tropical cyclone), which brings torrential rain and exceptionally strong winds.

TYPES OF OCCLUDED FRONT

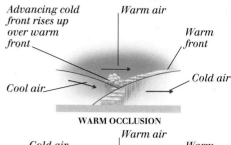

WARM OCCLUSION

Advancing cold front rises up over warm front

Warm air

Warm front

Cool air

Cold air

COLD OCCLUSION

Cold air

Warm air

Cold front undercuts warm front

Warm front

Cool air

FORMS OF PRECIPITATION

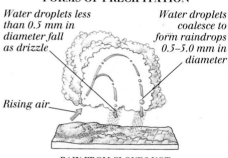

Water droplets less than 0.5 mm in diameter fall as drizzle

Water droplets coalesce to form raindrops 0.5–5.0 mm in diameter

Rising air

RAIN FROM CLOUDS NOT REACHING FREEZING LEVEL

Coalesced water droplets fall as rain

Ice crystal

Snowflakes grown from ice crystals fall as snow

Snowflakes melt to fall as rain

Rising air

RAIN AND SNOW FROM CLOUDS REACHING FREEZING LEVEL

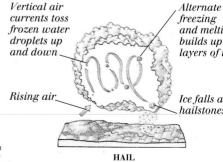

Vertical air currents toss frozen water droplets up and down

Alternate freezing and melting builds up layers of ice

Rising air

Ice falls as hailstones

HAIL

TYPES OF CLOUD

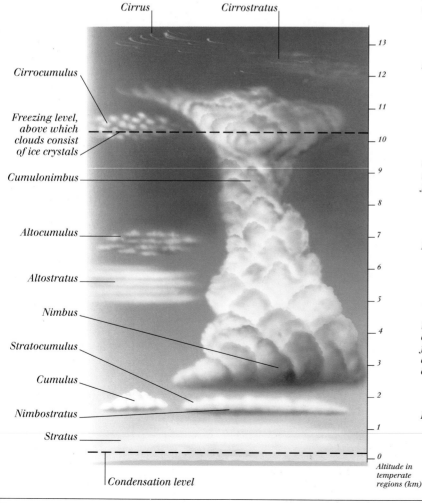

Cirrus

Cirrostratus

Cirrocumulus

Freezing level, above which clouds consist of ice crystals

Cumulonimbus

Altocumulus

Altostratus

Nimbus

Stratocumulus

Cumulus

Nimbostratus

Stratus

Condensation level

Altitude in temperate regions (km)

13
12
11
10
9
8
7
6
5
4
3
2
1
0

STRUCTURE OF A HURRICANE

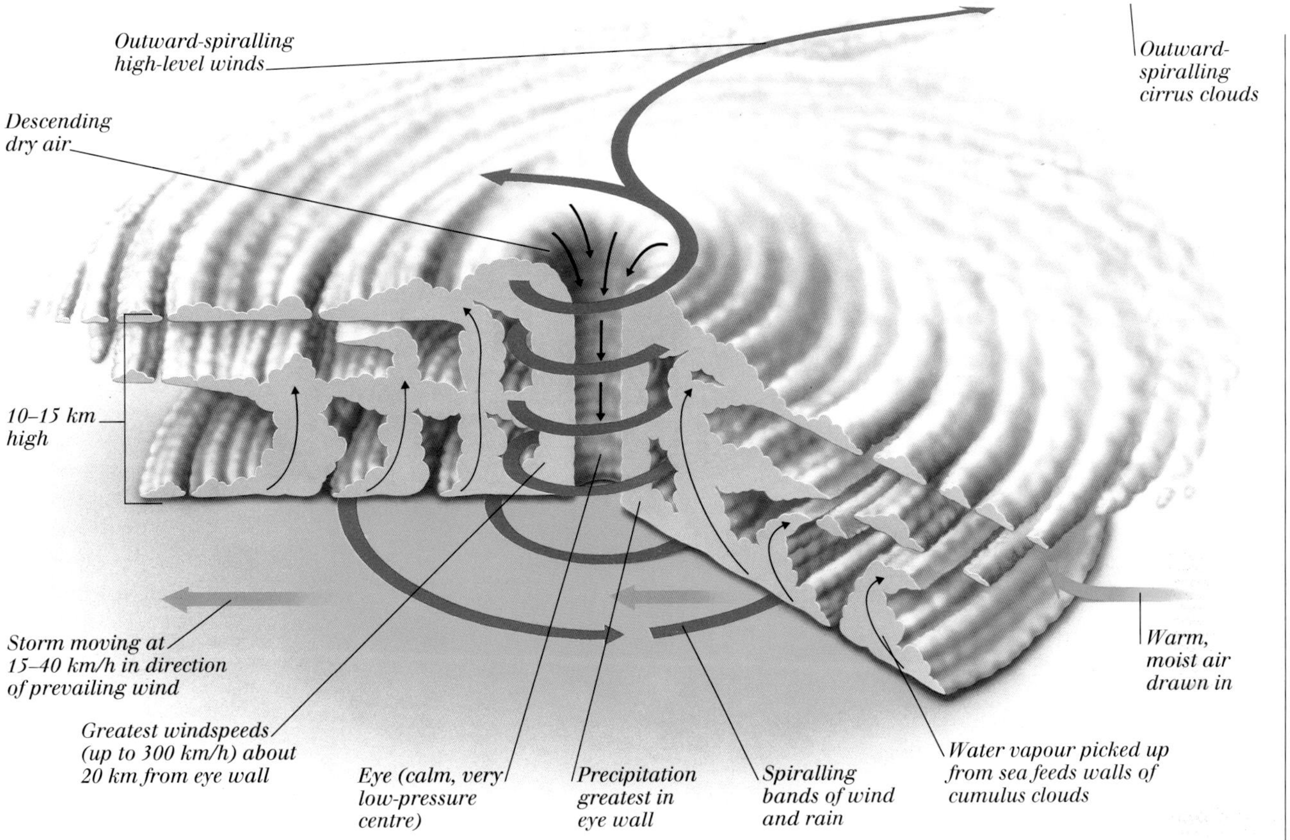

Outward-spiralling high-level winds
Outward-spiralling cirrus clouds
Descending dry air
10–15 km high
Storm moving at 15–40 km/h in direction of prevailing wind
Warm, moist air drawn in
Greatest windspeeds (up to 300 km/h) about 20 km from eye wall
Eye (calm, very low-pressure centre)
Precipitation greatest in eye wall
Spiralling bands of wind and rain
Water vapour picked up from sea feeds walls of cumulus clouds

WEATHER MAP

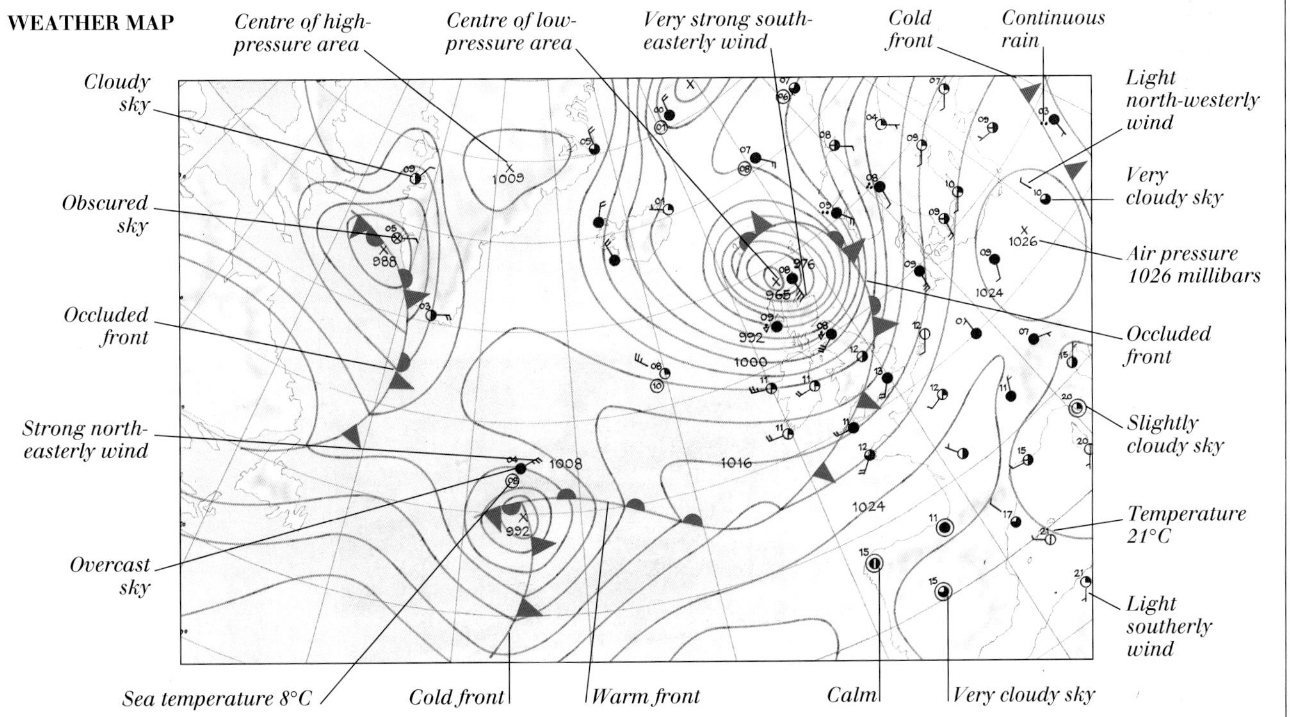

Centre of high-pressure area
Centre of low-pressure area
Very strong south-easterly wind
Cold front
Continuous rain
Cloudy sky
Light north-westerly wind
Obscured sky
Very cloudy sky
Air pressure 1026 millibars
Occluded front
Occluded front
Strong north-easterly wind
Slightly cloudy sky
Temperature 21°C
Overcast sky
Light southerly wind
Sea temperature 8°C
Cold front
Warm front
Calm
Very cloudy sky
1009
988
968
976
992
1000
1008
1016
1024
1026
992

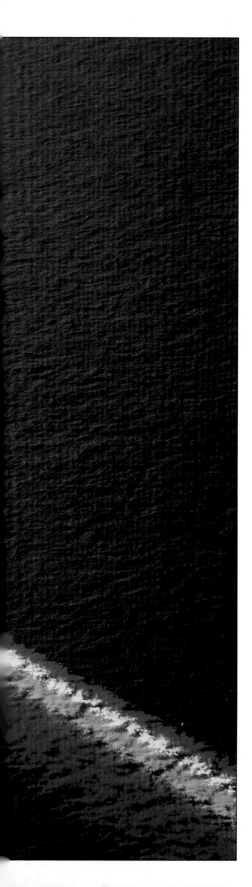

Physics and Chemistry

The variety of matter

**PLANT AND INSECT
(LIVING MATTER)**

MATTER IS ANYTHING THAT OCCUPIES SPACE. It includes everything from natural substances, such as minerals or living organisms, to synthetic materials. Matter can exist in three distinct states – solid, liquid, and gas. A solid is rigid and retains its shape. A liquid is fluid, has a definite volume, and will take the shape of its container. A gas (also fluid) fills a space, so its volume will be the same as the volume of its container. Most substances can exist as a solid, a liquid, or a gas: the state is determined by temperature. At very high temperatures, matter becomes plasma, often considered to be a fourth state of matter. All matter is composed of microscopic particles, such as atoms and molecules (see pp. 308-309). The arrangement and interactions of these particles give a substance its physical and chemical properties, by which matter can be identified. There is a huge variety of matter because particles can arrange themselves in countless ways, in one substance or by mixing with others. Natural glass, for example, seems to be a solid but is, in fact, a supercool liquid: the atoms are not locked into a pattern and can flow. Pure substances known as elements (see p. 310) combine to form compounds or mixtures. Mixtures called colloids are made up of larger particles of matter suspended in a solid, liquid, or gas, while a solution is one substance dissolved in another.

TYPES OF COLLOID

HAIR GEL (SOLID IN LIQUID)

**SHAVING FOAM
(AIR IN LIQUID)**

**MIST
(LIQUID IN GAS)**

EXAMPLES OF MATTER

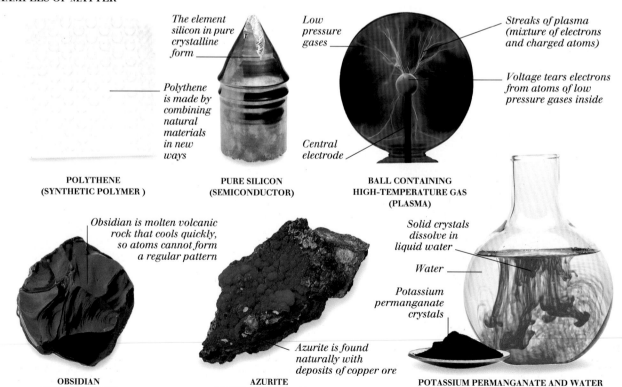

The element silicon in pure crystalline form

Polythene is made by combining natural materials in new ways

Low pressure gases

Streaks of plasma (mixture of electrons and charged atoms)

Voltage tears electrons from atoms of low pressure gases inside

Central electrode

**POLYTHENE
(SYNTHETIC POLYMER)**

**PURE SILICON
(SEMICONDUCTOR)**

**BALL CONTAINING
HIGH-TEMPERATURE GAS
(PLASMA)**

Obsidian is molten volcanic rock that cools quickly, so atoms cannot form a regular pattern

Solid crystals dissolve in liquid water

Water

Potassium permanganate crystals

Azurite is found naturally with deposits of copper ore

**OBSIDIAN
(NATURAL GLASS)**

**AZURITE
(CRYSTALLINE MINERAL)**

**POTASSIUM PERMANGANATE AND WATER
(SOLUTION)**

STATES OF MATTER

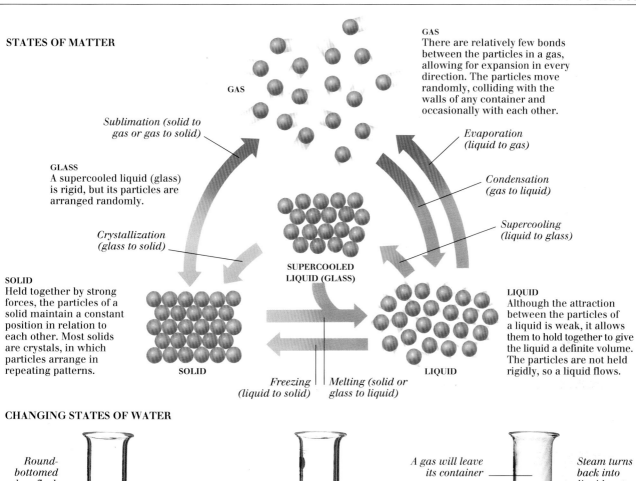

GAS

Sublimation (solid to gas or gas to solid)

GLASS
A supercooled liquid (glass) is rigid, but its particles are arranged randomly.

GAS
There are relatively few bonds between the particles in a gas, allowing for expansion in every direction. The particles move randomly, colliding with the walls of any container and occasionally with each other.

Evaporation (liquid to gas)

Condensation (gas to liquid)

Crystallization (glass to solid)

Supercooling (liquid to glass)

SUPERCOOLED LIQUID (GLASS)

SOLID
Held together by strong forces, the particles of a solid maintain a constant position in relation to each other. Most solids are crystals, in which particles arrange in repeating patterns.

SOLID

LIQUID
Although the attraction between the particles of a liquid is weak, it allows them to hold together to give the liquid a definite volume. The particles are not held rigidly, so a liquid flows.

LIQUID

Freezing (liquid to solid) *Melting (solid or glass to liquid)*

CHANGING STATES OF WATER

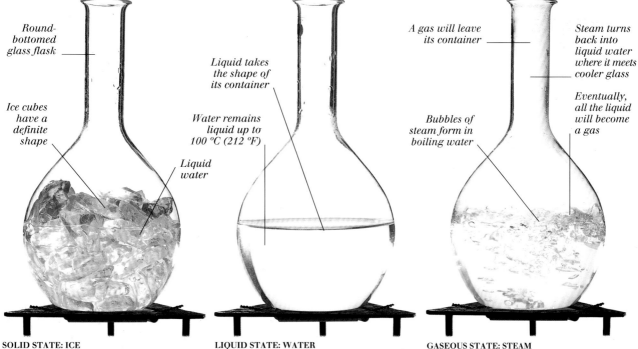

Round-bottomed glass flask

Ice cubes have a definite shape

Liquid water

Liquid takes the shape of its container

Water remains liquid up to 100 ºC (212 ºF)

A gas will leave its container

Bubbles of steam form in boiling water

Steam turns back into liquid water where it meets cooler glass

Eventually, all the liquid will become a gas

SOLID STATE: ICE
The solid state of water, ice, forms when liquid water is cooled sufficiently. Ice cubes are rigid, with a definite shape and volume.

LIQUID STATE: WATER
When the temperature of a substance rises above its freezing point, it melts to become a liquid. Ice changes to water.

GASEOUS STATE: STEAM
Above its boiling point, a substance will become a gas. When heated sufficiently, liquid water turns to steam, a colourless gas.

Atoms and molecules

FALSE-COLOUR
IMAGE OF ACTUAL
GOLD ATOMS

ATOMS ARE THE smallest individual parts of an element (see pp. 310-311). They are tiny, with diameters in the order of one ten-thousand-millionth of a metre (10^{-10} m). Two or more atoms join together (bond) to form a molecule of a substance known as a compound. For example, when atoms of the elements hydrogen and fluorine join together, they form a molecule of the compound hydrogen fluoride. So molecules are the smallest individual parts of a compound. Atoms themselves are not indivisible – they possess an internal structure. At their centre is a dense nucleus, consisting of protons, which have a positive electric charge (see p. 316), and neutrons, which are uncharged. Around the nucleus are the negatively charged electrons. It is the electrons that give a substance most of its physical and chemical properties. They do not follow definite paths around the nucleus. Instead, electrons are said to be found within certain regions, called orbitals. These are arranged around the nucleus in "shells", each containing electrons of a particular energy. For example, the first shell (1) can hold up to two electrons, in a so-called s-orbital (1s). The second shell (2) can hold up to eight electrons, in s-orbitals (2s) and p-orbitals (2p). If an atom loses an electron, it becomes a positive ion (cation). If an electron is gained, an atom becomes a negative ion (anion). Ions of opposite charges will attract and join together, in a type of bonding known as ionic bonding. In covalent bonding, the atoms bond by sharing their electrons in what become molecular orbitals.

ATOMIC ORBITALS

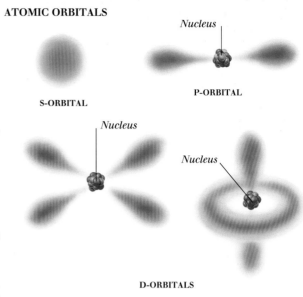

S-ORBITAL

P-ORBITAL

D-ORBITALS

MOLECULAR ORBITALS

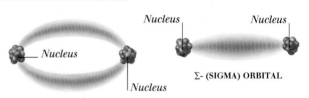

π- (PI) ORBITAL

Σ- (SIGMA) ORBITAL

SP³-HYBRID ORBITAL

EXAMPLE OF IONIC BONDING

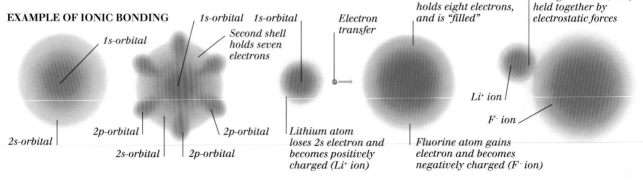

1s-orbital

1s-orbital   1s-orbital
Second shell
holds seven
electrons

2s-orbital

2p-orbital   2p-orbital

2s-orbital   2p-orbital

**1. NEUTRAL LITHIUM
ATOM (Li)**

**NEUTRAL FLUORINE
ATOM (F)**

Electron
transfer

Lithium atom
loses 2s electron and
becomes positively
charged (Li⁺ ion)

2. ELECTRON TRANSFER

Second shell now
holds eight electrons,
and is "filled"

Charged atoms (ions)
held together by
electrostatic forces

Li⁺ ion

F⁻ ion

Fluorine atom gains
electron and becomes
negatively charged (F⁻ ion)

**5. IONIC BONDING:
LITHIUM FLUORIDE MOLECULE (LiF)**

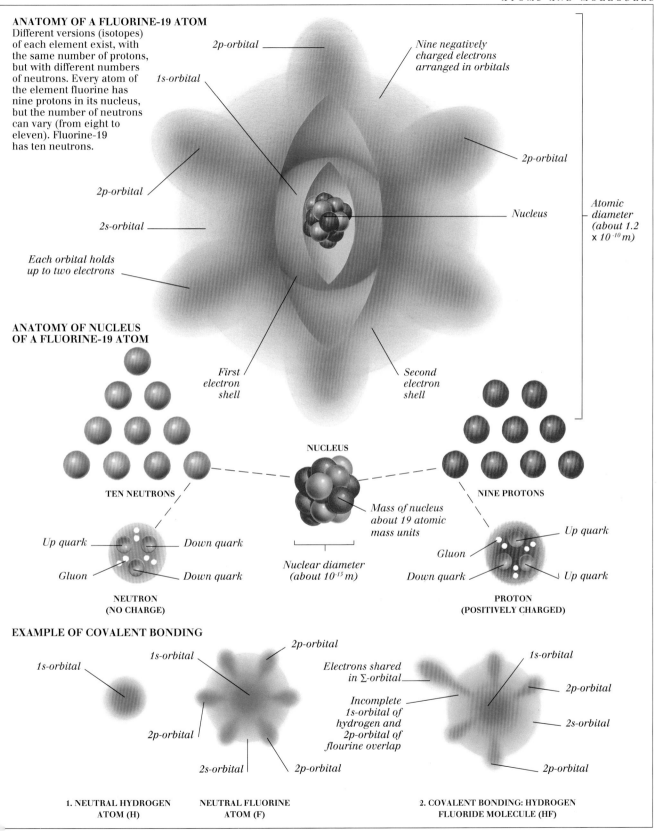

ANATOMY OF A FLUORINE-19 ATOM
Different versions (isotopes) of each element exist, with the same number of protons, but with different numbers of neutrons. Every atom of the element fluorine has nine protons in its nucleus, but the number of neutrons can vary (from eight to eleven). Fluorine-19 has ten neutrons.

2p-orbital

1s-orbital

Nine negatively charged electrons arranged in orbitals

2p-orbital

2p-orbital

2s-orbital

Nucleus

Atomic diameter (about 1.2 x 10⁻¹⁰ m)

Each orbital holds up to two electrons

ANATOMY OF NUCLEUS OF A FLUORINE-19 ATOM

First electron shell

Second electron shell

NUCLEUS

TEN NEUTRONS

NINE PROTONS

Mass of nucleus about 19 atomic mass units

Up quark   *Down quark*

Up quark

Gluon   *Down quark*

Gluon

Down quark   *Up quark*

Nuclear diameter (about 10⁻¹⁵ m)

NEUTRON (NO CHARGE)

PROTON (POSITIVELY CHARGED)

EXAMPLE OF COVALENT BONDING

1s-orbital

1s-orbital   *2p-orbital*

Electrons shared in Σ-orbital

1s-orbital

2p-orbital

Incomplete 1s-orbital of hydrogen and 2p-orbital of flourine overlap

2p-orbital

2s-orbital

2s-orbital   *2p-orbital*

2p-orbital

1. NEUTRAL HYDROGEN ATOM (H)

NEUTRAL FLUORINE ATOM (F)

2. COVALENT BONDING: HYDROGEN FLUORIDE MOLECULE (HF)

The periodic table

AN ELEMENT is a substance that consists of atoms of one type only. The 92 elements that occur naturally, and the 17 elements created artificially, are often arranged into a chart called the periodic table. Each element is defined by its atomic number – the number of protons in the nucleus of each of its atoms (it is also the number of electrons present). Atomic number increases along each row (period) and down each column (group). The shape of the table is determined by the way in which electrons arrange themselves around the nucleus: the positioning of elements in order of increasing atomic number brings together atoms with a similar pattern of orbiting electrons (orbitals). These appear in blocks. Electrons occupy shells of a certain energy (see pp. 308-309). Periods are ordered according to the filling of successive shells with electrons, while groups reflect the number of electrons in the outer shell (valency electrons). These outer electrons are important – they decide the chemical properties of the atom. Elements that appear in the same group have similar properties because they have the same number of electrons in their outer shell. Elements in Group 0 have "filled shells", where the outer shell holds its maximum number of electrons, and are stable. Atoms of Group I elements have just one electron in their outer shell. This makes them unstable – and ready to react with other substances.

Atomic number — 1
Chemical symbol — H
Chemical name — Hydrogen
Relative atomic mass — 1.0

RELATIVE ATOMIC MASS
Atomic mass (formerly atomic weight) is the mass of each atom of an element. It is equal to the number of protons plus the number of neutrons (electrons have negligible mass). The figures given are the averages for all the different versions (isotopes) of each element, measured relative to the mass of carbon-12.

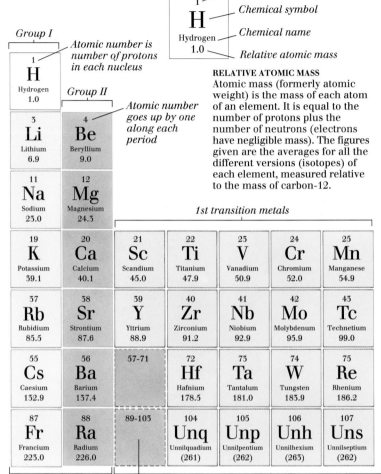

Group I — 1 **H** Hydrogen 1.0 / *Atomic number is number of protons in each nucleus*

Group II / *Atomic number goes up by one along each period*

Group I	Group II	1st transition metals				
1 **H** Hydrogen 1.0						
3 **Li** Lithium 6.9	4 **Be** Beryllium 9.0					
11 **Na** Sodium 23.0	12 **Mg** Magnesium 24.3					
19 **K** Potassium 39.1	20 **Ca** Calcium 40.1	21 **Sc** Scandium 45.0	22 **Ti** Titanium 47.9	23 **V** Vanadium 50.9	24 **Cr** Chromium 52.0	25 **Mn** Manganese 54.9
37 **Rb** Rubidium 85.5	38 **Sr** Strontium 87.6	39 **Y** Yttrium 88.9	40 **Zr** Zirconium 91.2	41 **Nb** Niobium 92.9	42 **Mo** Molybdenum 95.9	43 **Tc** Technetium 99.0
55 **Cs** Caesium 132.9	56 **Ba** Barium 137.4	57-71	72 **Hf** Hafnium 178.5	73 **Ta** Tantalum 181.0	74 **W** Tungsten 183.9	75 **Re** Rhenium 186.2
87 **Fr** Francium 223.0	88 **Ra** Radium 226.0	89-103	104 **Unq** Unnilquadium (261)	105 **Unp** Unnilpentium (262)	106 **Unh** Unnilhexium (263)	107 **Uns** Unnilseptium (262)

s-block / *Two series always separated out from the table to give it a coherent shape* / *d-block*

METALS AND NON-METALS
Elements at the left-hand side of each period are metals. Metals easily lose electrons and form positive ions. Non-metals, on the right of a period, tend to become negative ions. Semi-metals, which have properties of both metals and non-metals, are between the two.

Soft, silvery, and highly reactive metal

SODIUM: GROUP 1 METAL

Silvery, reactive metal

MAGNESIUM: GROUP 2 METAL

Hard, silvery metal

CHROMIUM: 1ST TRANSITION METAL

TYPES OF ELEMENT KEY:

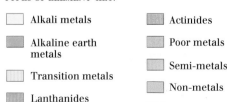

- Alkali metals
- Alkaline earth metals
- Transition metals
- Lanthanides (rare earths)
- Actinides
- Poor metals
- Semi-metals
- Non-metals
- Noble gases

Radioactive metal

PLUTONIUM: ACTINIDE SERIES METAL

57 **La** Lanthanum 138.9	58 **Ce** Cerium 140.1	59 **Pr** Praseodymium 140.9	60 **Nd** Neodymium 144.2
89 **Ac** Actinium 227.0	90 **Th** Thorium 232.0	91 **Pa** Protactinium 231.0	92 **U** Uranium 238.0

Bright yellow crystal

**IODINE:
GROUP 7
SOLID NON-
METAL**

Purple-black solid turns to gas easily

Group 0

DIAMOND

ALLOTROPES OF CARBON
Some elements exist in more than one form – these are known as allotropes. Carbon powder, graphite, and diamond are allotropes of carbon. They all consist of carbon atoms, but have very different physical properties.

Boron and carbon groups

Nitrogen and oxygen groups

Halogens

**SULPHUR:
GROUP 6 SOLID NON-METAL**

Group III	Group IV	Group V	Group VI	Group VII	
					2 **He** Helium 4.0
5 **B** Boron 10.8	6 **C** Carbon 12.0	7 **N** Nitrogen 14.0	8 **O** Oxygen 16.0	9 **F** Fluorine 19.0	10 **Ne** Neon 20.2
13 **Al** Aluminium 27.0	14 **Si** Silicon 28.1	15 **P** Phosphorus 31.0	16 **S** Sulphur 32.1	17 **Cl** Chlorine 35.5	18 **Ar** Argon 40.0

Period

Short period

Long period

GRAPHITE

CARBON POWDER

2nd transition metals *3rd transition metals*

26 **Fe** Iron 55.9	27 **Co** Cobalt 58.9	28 **Ni** Nickel 58.7	29 **Cu** Copper 63.5	30 **Zn** Zinc 65.4	31 **Ga** Gallium 69.7	32 **Ge** Germanium 72.6	33 **As** Arsenic 74.9	34 **Se** Selenium 79.0	35 **Br** Bromine 79.9	36 **Kr** Krypton 83.8
44 **Ru** Ruthenium 101.0	45 **Rh** Rhodium 102.9	46 **Pd** Palladium 106.4	47 **Ag** Silver 107.9	48 **Cd** Cadmium 112.4	49 **In** Indium 114.8	50 **Sn** Tin 118.7	51 **Sb** Antimony 121.8	52 **Te** Tellurium 127.6	53 **I** Iodine 126.9	54 **Xe** Xenon 151.3
76 **Os** Osmium 190.2	77 **Ir** Iridium 192.2	78 **Pt** Platinum 195.1	79 **Au** Gold 197.0	80 **Hg** Mercury 200.6	81 **Tl** Thallium 204.4	82 **Pb** Lead 207.2	83 **Bi** Bismuth 209.0	84 **Po** Polonium 210.0	85 **At** Astatine 210.0	86 **Rn** Radon 222.0

| 108 **Uno** Unniloctium (265) | 109 **Une** Unnilennium (266) |

d-block *p-block*

Atomic mass is estimated, as element exists fleetingly

Shiny semi-metal

Unreactive, colourless gas glows red in discharge tube

NOBLE GASES
Group 0 contains elements that have a filled (complete) outer shell of electrons, which means the atoms do not need to lose or gain electrons by bonding with other atoms. This makes them stable and they do not easily form ions or react with other elements. Noble gases are also called rare or inert gases.

Yellow, unreactive precious metal

Soft, shiny, reactive metal

**NEON:
GROUP 0
COLOURLESS GAS**

**GOLD:
3RD TRANSITION METAL**

**TIN:
GROUP 4 POOR METAL**

**ANTIMONY:
GROUP 5 SEMI-METAL**

| 61 **Pm** Promethium 147.0 | 62 **Sm** Samarium 150.4 | 63 **Eu** Europium 152.0 | 64 **Gd** Gadolinium 157.3 | 65 **Tb** Terbium 158.9 | 66 **Dy** Dysprosium 162.5 | 67 **Ho** Holmium 164.9 | 68 **Er** Erbium 167.3 | 69 **Tm** Thulium 168.9 | 70 **Yb** Ytterbium 173.0 | 71 **Lu** Lutetium 175.0 |
| 93 **Np** Neptunium 237.0 | 94 **Pu** Plutonium 242.0 | 95 **Am** Americium 243.0 | 96 **Cm** Curium 247.0 | 97 **Bk** Berkelium 247.0 | 98 **Cf** Californium 251.0 | 99 **Es** Einsteinium 254.0 | 100 **Fm** Fermium 253.0 | 101 **Md** Mendelevium 256.0 | 102 **No** Nobelium 254.0 | 103 **Lr** Lawrencium 257.0 |

f-block

Chemical reactions

A CHEMICAL REACTION TAKES PLACE whenever bonds between atoms are broken or made. In each case, atoms or groups of atoms rearrange, making new substances (products) from the original ones (reactants). Reactions happen naturally, or can be made to happen; they may take years, or only an instant. Some of the main types are shown here. A reaction usually involves a change in energy (see pp. 314-315). In a burning reaction, for example, the making of new bonds between atoms releases energy as heat and light. This type of reaction, in which heat is given off, is an exothermic reaction. Many reactions, like burning, are irreversible, but some can take place in either direction, and are said to be reversible. Reactions can be used to form solids from solutions: in a double decomposition reaction, two compounds in solution break down and re-form into two new substances, often creating a precipitate (insoluble solid); in displacement, an element (eg. copper) displaces another element (eg. silver) from a solution. The rate (speed) of a reaction is determined by many different factors, such as temperature, and the size and shape of the reactants. To describe and keep track of reactions, internationally recognized chemical symbols and equations are used. Reactions are also used in the laboratory to identify matter. An experiment with candle wax, for example, demonstrates that it contains carbon and hydrogen.

SALT FORMATION (ACID ON METAL)

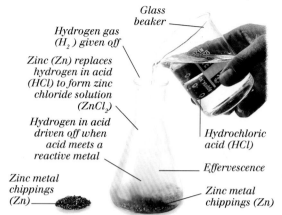

Glass beaker

Hydrogen gas (H_2) given off

Zinc (Zn) replaces hydrogen in acid (HCl) to form zinc chloride solution ($ZnCl_2$)

Hydrogen in acid driven off when acid meets a reactive metal

Zinc metal chippings (Zn)

Hydrochloric acid (HCl)

Effervescence

Zinc metal chippings (Zn)

THE REACTION
Hydrochloric acid added to zinc produces zinc chloride and hydrogen.
$$Zn + 2HCl \rightarrow ZnCl_2 + H_2$$

DISPLACEMENT

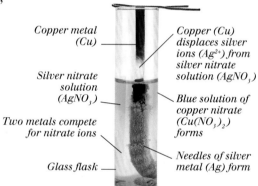

Copper metal (Cu)

Silver nitrate solution ($AgNO_3$)

Two metals compete for nitrate ions

Glass flask

Copper (Cu) displaces silver ions (Ag^{2+}) from silver nitrate solution ($AgNO_3$)

Blue solution of copper nitrate ($Cu(NO_3)_2$) forms

Needles of silver metal (Ag) form

THE REACTION
Copper metal added to silver nitrate solution produces copper nitrate and silver metal.
$$Cu + 2AgNO_3 \rightarrow Cu(NO_3)_2 + 2Ag$$

BURNING MATTER

Ammonium dichromate (($NH_4)_2Cr_2O_7$)

Flame

In this burning reaction, atoms form simpler substances and give off heat and light

Ammonium dichromate (($NH_4)_2Cr_2O_7$) converts to chromium oxide (Cr_2O_3)

Nitrogen monoxide (NO) and water vapour (H_2O) given off as colourless gases

THE REACTION
When lit, ammonium dichromate combines with oxygen from air.
$$(NH_4)_2Cr_2O_7 + O_2 \rightarrow Cr_2O_3 + 4H_2O + 2NO$$

A REVERSIBLE REACTION

Flat-bottomed glass flask

Potassium chromate solution (K_2CrO_4)

Bright yellow solution contains potassium and chromate ions

1. THE REACTANT
Potassium chromate dissolves in water to form potassium ions and chromate ions.
$$K_2CrO_4 \rightarrow 2K^+ + CrO_4^{2-}$$

Pipette

Hydrochloric acid (HCl) added in drops

Acid causes reaction to take place

Chromate ions converted to orange dichromate ions

Potassium dichromate (KCr_2O_7) forms

2. THE REACTION
Addition of hydrochloric acid changes chromate ions into dichromate ions.
$$2CrO_4^{2-} \rightarrow Cr_2O_7^{2-}$$

Pipette

Sodium hydroxide (NaOH) added in drops

Sodium hydroxide (NaOH) neutralizes the acid

Solution turns to bright orange of potassium dichromate

Potassium dichromate (KCr_2O_7) re-forms to potassium chromate (K_2CrO_4)

Solution returns to original bright yellow colour

3. REVERSING
Addition of sodium hydroxide changes dichromate ions back into chromate ions.
$$Cr_2O_7^{2-} \rightarrow 2CrO_4^{2-}$$

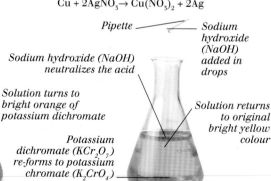

FERMENTATION

Yeast converts sugar into alcohol (C_2H_5OH) and carbon dioxide gas (CO_2)

Airtight stopper

Flat-bottomed glass flask

Yeast mixed with warm water and sugar $(C_6H_{12}O_6)$

Carbon dioxide bubbles (CO_2)

THE REACTION
Yeast converts sugar and warm water into alcohol and carbon dioxide.
$C_6H_{12}O_6 \rightarrow 2C_2H_5OH + 2CO_2$

DOUBLE DECOMPOSITION

Potassium iodide solution (KI)

Lead nitrate solution $(Pb(NO_3)_2)$

Two solutions swap partners

Potassium iodide solution added to lead nitrate solution

Lead iodide (PbI_2), a yellow solid, forms

Potassium nitrate solution (KNO_3) forms

1. THE REACTANTS
Potassium iodide in water (KI) and lead nitrate in water $(Pb(NO_5)_2)$ each form colourless solutions.

2. THE REACTION
When the solutions are mixed, lead iodide, a precipitate, and potassium nitrate solution are formed.
$2KI + Pb(NO_5)_2 \rightarrow PbI_2 + 2KNO_5$

TESTING CANDLE WAX, AN ORGANIC COMPOUND

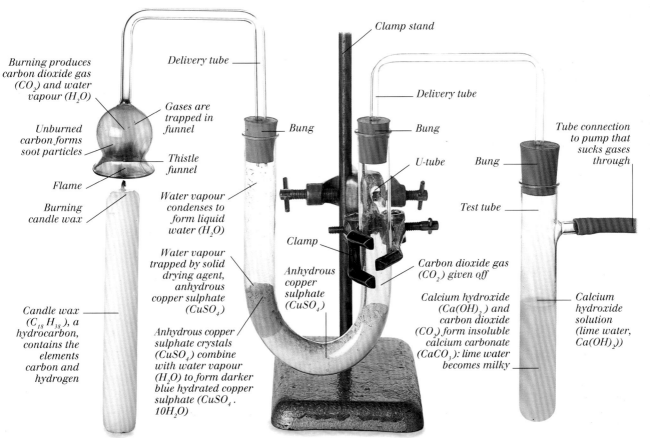

Burning produces carbon dioxide gas (CO_2) and water vapour (H_2O)

Delivery tube

Clamp stand

Delivery tube

Bung

Bung

Tube connection to pump that sucks gases through

Unburned carbon forms soot particles

Gases are trapped in funnel

U-tube

Bung

Flame

Thistle funnel

Burning candle wax

Water vapour condenses to form liquid water (H_2O)

Test tube

Water vapour trapped by solid drying agent, anhydrous copper sulphate $(CuSO_4)$

Clamp

Anhydrous copper sulphate $(CuSO_4)$

Carbon dioxide gas (CO_2) given off

Calcium hydroxide $(Ca(OH)_2)$ and carbon dioxide (CO_2) form insoluble calcium carbonate $(CaCO_3)$: lime water becomes milky

Calcium hydroxide solution (lime water, $Ca(OH)_2)$)

Candle wax $(C_{18}H_{38})$, a hydrocarbon, contains the elements carbon and hydrogen

Anhydrous copper sulphate crystals $(CuSO_4)$ combine with water vapour (H_2O) to form darker blue hydrated copper sulphate $(CuSO_4 . 10H_2O)$

1. THE BURNING REACTION
Burning wax produces carbon dioxide gas and water vapour.
$2C_{18}H_{38} + 55O_2 \rightarrow 36CO_2 + 38H_2O$

2. TESTING FOR WATER VAPOUR
A solid drying agent traps water vapour, proving the presence of hydrogen in the candle wax.
$CuSO_4 + 10H_2O \rightarrow CuSO_4 . 10H_2O$

3. TESTING FOR CARBON DIOXIDE
Calcium hydroxide in solution reacts with carbon dioxide, forming a carbonate and turning milky.
$Ca(OH)_2 + CO_2 \rightarrow CaCO_5 + H_2O$

Energy

ANYTHING THAT HAPPENS – from a pin-drop to an explosion – requires energy. Energy is the capacity for "doing work" (making something happen). Various forms of energy exist, including light, heat, sound, electrical, chemical, nuclear, kinetic, and potential energies. The Law of Conservation of Energy states that the total amount of energy in the Universe is fixed – energy cannot be created or destroyed. It means that energy can only change from one form to another (energy transfer). For example, potential energy is energy that is "stored", and can be used in the future. An object gains potential energy when it is lifted; as the object is released, potential energy changes into the energy of motion (kinetic energy). During transference, some of the energy converts into heat. A combined heat and power station can put some of the otherwise "waste" heat to useful effect in local schools and housing. Most of the Earth's energy is provided by the Sun, in the form of electromagnetic radiation (see pp. 316-317). Some of this energy transfers to plant and animal life, and ultimately to fossil fuels, where it is stored in chemical form. Our bodies obtain energy from the food we eat, while energy needed for other tasks, such as heating and transport, can be obtained by burning fossil fuels – or by harnessing natural forces like wind or moving water – to generate electricity. Another source is nuclear power, where energy is released by reactions in the nucleus of an atom. All energy is measured by the international unit, the joule (J). As a guide, one joule is about equal to the amount of energy needed to lift an apple one metre.

SANKEY DIAGRAM SHOWING ENERGY FLOW IN A COAL-FIRED COMBINED HEAT AND POWER STATION

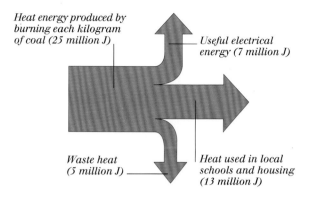

Heat energy produced by burning each kilogram of coal (25 million J)

Useful electrical energy (7 million J)

Waste heat (5 million J)

Heat used in local schools and housing (13 million J)

CROSS-SECTION OF HYDROELECTRIC POWER STATION WITH FRANCIS TURBINE

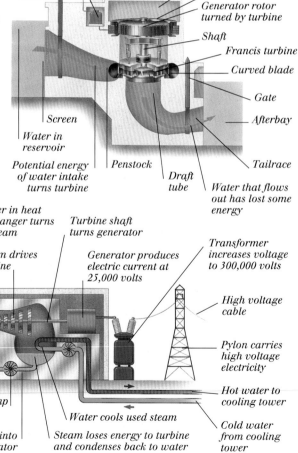

Transformer

Insulator

High voltage cable

Switch gear including circuit braker

Bushing

Rotor house

Gate

Generator unit

Generator rotor turned by turbine

Shaft

Francis turbine

Curved blade

Gate

Afterbay

Screen

Water in reservoir

Potential energy of water intake turns turbine

Penstock

Draft tube

Tailrace

Water that flows out has lost some energy

CROSS-SECTION OF NUCLEAR POWER STATION WITH PRESSURIZED WATER REACTOR

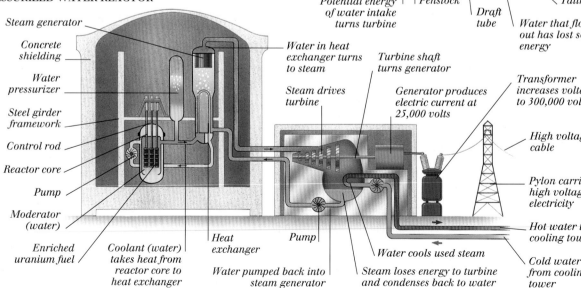

Steam generator

Concrete shielding

Water pressurizer

Steel girder framework

Control rod

Reactor core

Pump

Moderator (water)

Enriched uranium fuel

Coolant (water) takes heat from reactor core to heat exchanger

Heat exchanger

Water pumped back into steam generator

Water in heat exchanger turns to steam

Steam drives turbine

Turbine shaft turns generator

Generator produces electric current at 25,000 volts

Pump

Water cools used steam

Steam loses energy to turbine and condenses back to water

Transformer increases voltage to 300,000 volts

High voltage cable

Pylon carries high voltage electricity

Hot water to cooling tower

Cold water from cooling tower

ENERGY SYSTEMS

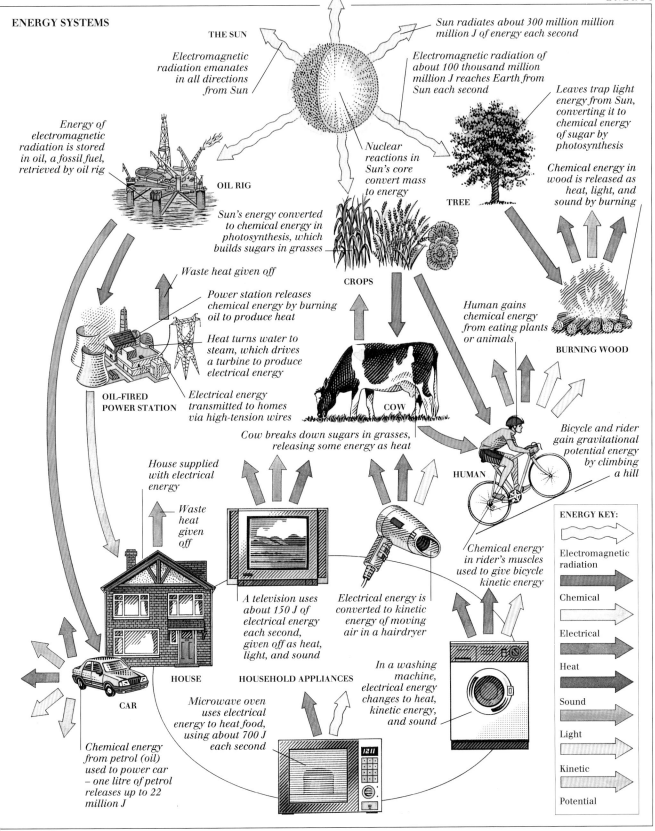

THE SUN

Electromagnetic radiation emanates in all directions from Sun

Sun radiates about 300 million million million J of energy each second

Electromagnetic radiation of about 100 thousand million million J reaches Earth from Sun each second

Leaves trap light energy from Sun, converting it to chemical energy of sugar by photosynthesis

Energy of electromagnetic radiation is stored in oil, a fossil fuel, retrieved by oil rig

OIL RIG

Nuclear reactions in Sun's core convert mass to energy

Chemical energy in wood is released as heat, light, and sound by burning

TREE

Sun's energy converted to chemical energy in photosynthesis, which builds sugars in grasses

CROPS

Waste heat given off

Power station releases chemical energy by burning oil to produce heat

Heat turns water to steam, which drives a turbine to produce electrical energy

Electrical energy transmitted to homes via high-tension wires

OIL-FIRED POWER STATION

Human gains chemical energy from eating plants or animals

BURNING WOOD

COW

Cow breaks down sugars in grasses, releasing some energy as heat

House supplied with electrical energy

Waste heat given off

Bicycle and rider gain gravitational potential energy by climbing a hill

HUMAN

Chemical energy in rider's muscles used to give bicycle kinetic energy

A television uses about 150 J of electrical energy each second, given off as heat, light, and sound

Electrical energy is converted to kinetic energy of moving air in a hairdryer

HOUSE

HOUSEHOLD APPLIANCES

In a washing machine, electrical energy changes to heat, kinetic energy, and sound

CAR

Chemical energy from petrol (oil) used to power car – one litre of petrol releases up to 22 million J

Microwave oven uses electrical energy to heat food, using about 700 J each second

ENERGY KEY:

Electromagnetic radiation

Chemical

Electrical

Heat

Sound

Light

Kinetic

Potential

Electricity and magnetism

ELECTRICAL EFFECTS result from an imbalance of electric charge. There are two types of electric charge, named positive (carried by protons) and negative (carried by electrons). If charges are opposite (unlike), they attract one another, while like charges repel. Forces of attraction and repulsion (electrostatic forces) exist between any two charged particles. Matter is normally uncharged, but if electrons are gained, an object will gain an overall negative charge; if they are removed, it becomes positive. Objects with an overall negative or positive charge are said to have an imbalance of charge, and exert the same forces as individual negative and positive charges. On this larger scale, the forces will always act to regain the balance of charge. This causes static electricity. Lightning, for example, is produced by clouds discharging a huge excess of negative electrons. If charges are "free" – in a wire or material that allows electrons to pass through it – the forces cause a flow of charge called an electric current. Some substances exhibit the strange phenomenon of magnetism – which also produces attractive and repulsive forces. Magnetic substances consist of small regions called domains. Normally unmagnetized, they can be magnetized by being placed in a magnetic field. Magnetism and electricity are inextricably linked, a fact put to use in motors and generators.

LIGHTNING

VAN DE GRAAFF (ELECTROSTATIC) GENERATOR

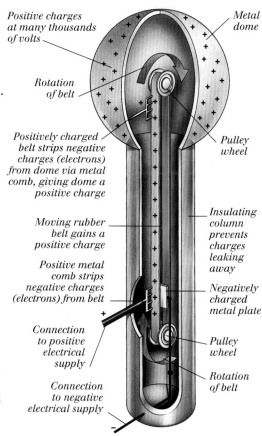

Positive charges at many thousands of volts

Metal dome

Rotation of belt

Positively charged belt strips negative charges (electrons) from dome via metal comb, giving dome a positive charge

Pulley wheel

Moving rubber belt gains a positive charge

Insulating column prevents charges leaking away

Positive metal comb strips negative charges (electrons) from belt

Negatively charged metal plate

Connection to positive electrical supply

Pulley wheel

Rotation of belt

Connection to negative electrical supply

CURRENT ELECTRICITY

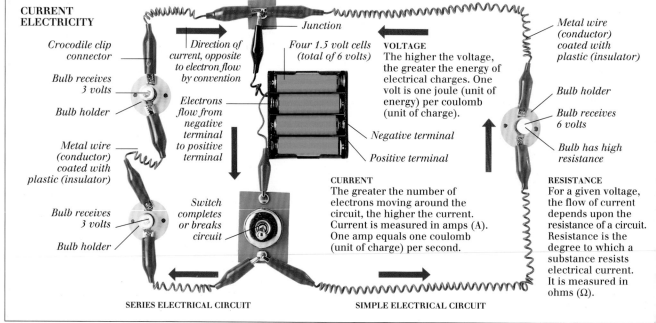

Crocodile clip connector

Junction

Direction of current, opposite to electron flow by convention

Four 1.5 volt cells (total of 6 volts)

Bulb receives 3 volts

Bulb holder

Electrons flow from negative terminal to positive terminal

Metal wire (conductor) coated with plastic (insulator)

Bulb receives 3 volts

Bulb holder

Switch completes or breaks circuit

Metal wire (conductor) coated with plastic (insulator)

Bulb holder

Bulb receives 6 volts

Bulb has high resistance

VOLTAGE
The higher the voltage, the greater the energy of electrical charges. One volt is one joule (unit of energy) per coulomb (unit of charge).

Negative terminal

Positive terminal

CURRENT
The greater the number of electrons moving around the circuit, the higher the current. Current is measured in amps (A). One amp equals one coulomb (unit of charge) per second.

RESISTANCE
For a given voltage, the flow of current depends upon the resistance of a circuit. Resistance is the degree to which a substance resists electrical current. It is measured in ohms (Ω).

SERIES ELECTRICAL CIRCUIT

SIMPLE ELECTRICAL CIRCUIT

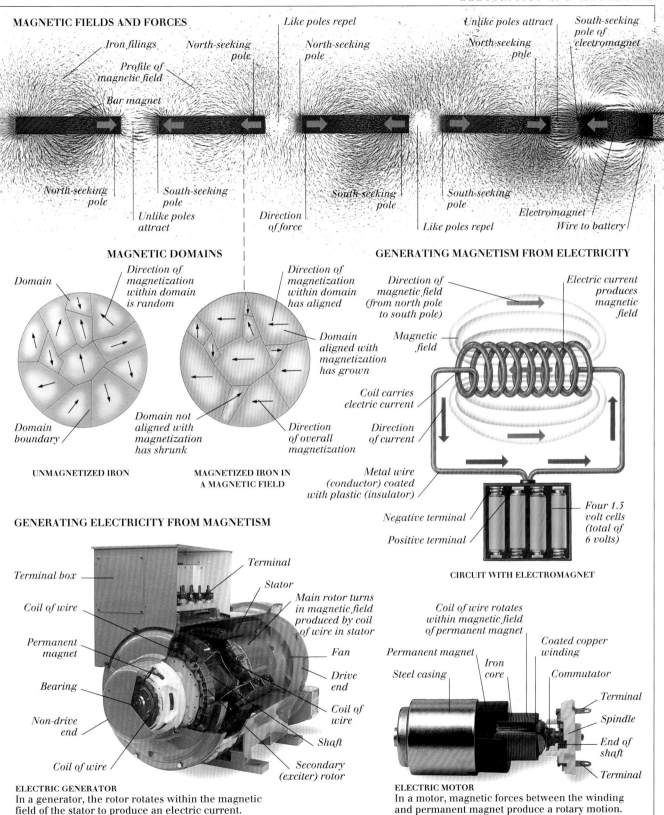

MAGNETIC FIELDS AND FORCES

Iron filings

Profile of magnetic field

North-seeking pole

Bar magnet

North-seeking pole

South-seeking pole

Unlike poles attract

Like poles repel

North-seeking pole

Direction of force

South-seeking pole

Unlike poles attract

North-seeking pole

Like poles repel

South-seeking pole

South-seeking pole of electromagnet

Electromagnet

Wire to battery

MAGNETIC DOMAINS

Domain

Direction of magnetization within domain is random

Domain

Direction of magnetization within domain has aligned

Domain aligned with magnetization has grown

Domain boundary

Domain not aligned with magnetization has shrunk

Direction of overall magnetization

UNMAGNETIZED IRON

MAGNETIZED IRON IN A MAGNETIC FIELD

GENERATING MAGNETISM FROM ELECTRICITY

Direction of magnetic field (from north pole to south pole)

Electric current produces magnetic field

Magnetic field

Coil carries electric current

Direction of current

Metal wire (conductor) coated with plastic (insulator)

Negative terminal

Positive terminal

Four 1.5 volt cells (total of 6 volts)

CIRCUIT WITH ELECTROMAGNET

GENERATING ELECTRICITY FROM MAGNETISM

Terminal box

Coil of wire

Permanent magnet

Bearing

Non-drive end

Coil of wire

Terminal

Stator

Main rotor turns in magnetic field produced by coil of wire in stator

Fan

Drive end

Coil of wire

Shaft

Secondary (exciter) rotor

ELECTRIC GENERATOR
In a generator, the rotor rotates within the magnetic field of the stator to produce an electric current.

Coil of wire rotates within magnetic field of permanent magnet

Permanent magnet

Steel casing

Iron core

Coated copper winding

Commutator

Terminal

Spindle

End of shaft

Terminal

ELECTRIC MOTOR
In a motor, magnetic forces between the winding and permanent magnet produce a rotary motion.

INFRA-RED IMAGE OF A HOUSE

Light

LIGHT IS A FORM OF ENERGY. It is a type of electromagnetic radiation, like X-rays or radio waves. All electromagnetic radiation is produced by electric charges (see pp. 316-317): it is caused by the effects of oscillating electric and magnetic fields as they travel through space. Electromagnetic radiation is considered to have both wave and particle properties. It can be thought of as a wave of electricity and magnetism. In that case, the difference between the various forms of radiation is their wavelength. Radiation can also be said to consist of particles, or packets of energy, called photons. The difference between light and X-rays, for instance, is the amount of energy that each photon carries. The complete range of radiation is referred to as the electromagnetic spectrum, extending from low energy, long wavelength radio waves to high energy, short wavelength gamma rays. Light is the only part of the electromagnetic spectrum that is visible. White light from the Sun is made up of all the visible wavelengths of radiation, which can be seen when it is separated by using a prism. Light, like all forms of electromagnetic radiation, can be reflected (bounced back) and refracted (bent). Different parts of the electromagnetic spectrum are produced in different ways. Sometimes visible light – and infra-red radiation – is generated by the vibrating particles of warm or hot objects. The emission of light in this way is called incandescence. Light can also be produced by fluorescence, a phenomenon in which electrons gain and lose energy within atoms.

MAXWELLIAN DIAGRAM OF ELECTROMAGNETIC RADIATION AS WAVES

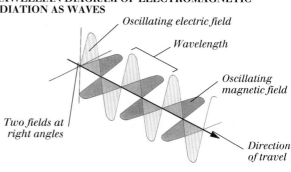

Oscillating electric field

Wavelength

Oscillating magnetic field

Two fields at right angles

Direction of travel

ELECTROMAGNETIC RADIATION AS PARTICLES

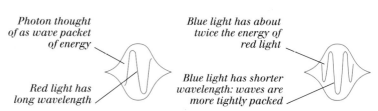

Photon thought of as wave packet of energy

Blue light has about twice the energy of red light

Red light has long wavelength

Blue light has shorter wavelength: waves are more tightly packed

PHOTON OF RED LIGHT

PHOTON OF BLUE LIGHT

SPLITTING WHITE LIGHT INTO THE SPECTRUM

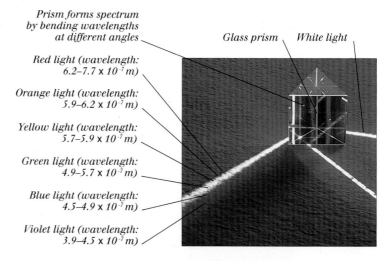

Prism forms spectrum by bending wavelengths at different angles

Glass prism

White light

Red light (wavelength: 6.2–7.7 x 10⁻⁷ m)

Orange light (wavelength: 5.9–6.2 x 10⁻⁷ m)

Yellow light (wavelength: 5.7–5.9 x 10⁻⁷ m)

Green light (wavelength: 4.9–5.7 x 10⁻⁷ m)

Blue light (wavelength: 4.5–4.9 x 10⁻⁷ m)

Violet light (wavelength: 3.9–4.5 x 10⁻⁷ m)

THE ELECTROMAGNETIC SPECTRUM

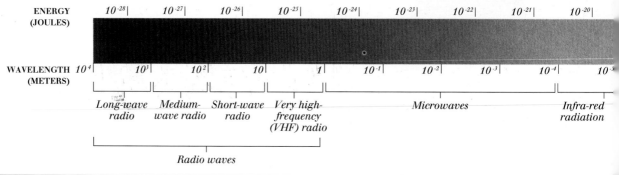

| ENERGY (JOULES) | 10^{-28} | 10^{-27} | 10^{-26} | 10^{-25} | 10^{-24} | 10^{-23} | 10^{-22} | 10^{-21} | 10^{-20} |

| WAVELENGTH (METERS) | 10^4 | 10^3 | 10^2 | 10 | 1 | 10^{-1} | 10^{-2} | 10^{-3} | 10^{-4} | 10^{-5} |

Long-wave radio *Medium-wave radio* *Short-wave radio* *Very high-frequency (VHF) radio* *Microwaves* *Infra-red radiation*

Radio waves

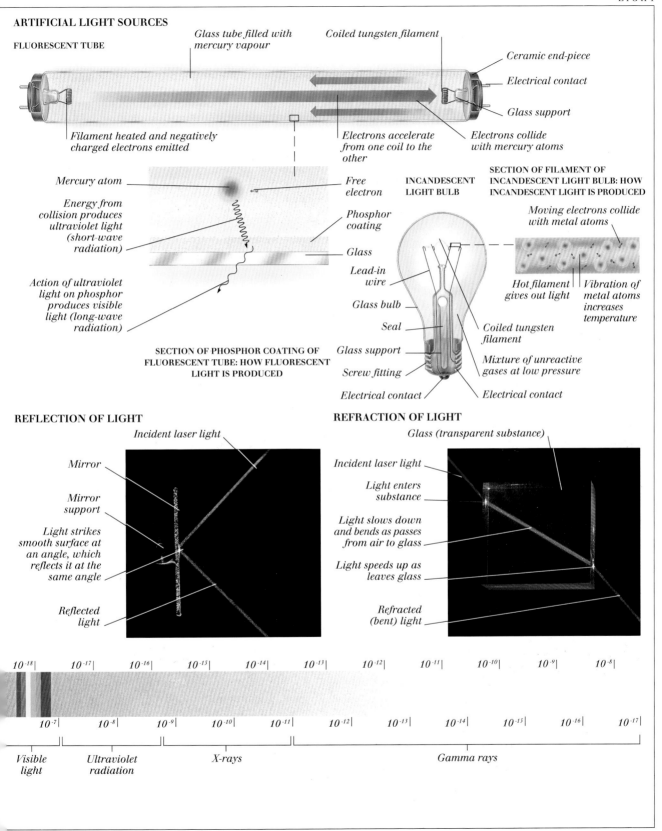

ARTIFICIAL LIGHT SOURCES

FLUORESCENT TUBE

Glass tube filled with mercury vapour

Coiled tungsten filament

Ceramic end-piece

Electrical contact

Glass support

Filament heated and negatively charged electrons emitted

Electrons accelerate from one coil to the other

Electrons collide with mercury atoms

Mercury atom

Free electron

Energy from collision produces ultraviolet light (short-wave radiation)

Action of ultraviolet light on phosphor produces visible light (long-wave radiation)

SECTION OF PHOSPHOR COATING OF FLUORESCENT TUBE: HOW FLUORESCENT LIGHT IS PRODUCED

INCANDESCENT LIGHT BULB

Phosphor coating

Glass

Lead-in wire

Glass bulb

Seal

Glass support

Screw fitting

Electrical contact

Coiled tungsten filament

Mixture of unreactive gases at low pressure

Electrical contact

SECTION OF FILAMENT OF INCANDESCENT LIGHT BULB: HOW INCANDESCENT LIGHT IS PRODUCED

Moving electrons collide with metal atoms

Hot filament gives out light

Vibration of metal atoms increases temperature

REFLECTION OF LIGHT

Incident laser light

Mirror

Mirror support

Light strikes smooth surface at an angle, which reflects it at the same angle

Reflected light

REFRACTION OF LIGHT

Glass (transparent substance)

Incident laser light

Light enters substance

Light slows down and bends as passes from air to glass

Light speeds up as leaves glass

Refracted (bent) light

10^{-18} | 10^{-17} | 10^{-16} | 10^{-15} | 10^{-14} | 10^{-13} | 10^{-12} | 10^{-11} | 10^{-10} | 10^{-9} | 10^{-8} |

10^{-7} | 10^{-8} | 10^{-9} | 10^{-10} | 10^{-11} | 10^{-12} | 10^{-13} | 10^{-14} | 10^{-15} | 10^{-16} | 10^{-17} |

Visible light

Ultraviolet radiation

X-rays

Gamma rays

Force and motion

FORCES ARE PUSHES OR PULLS that change the motion of objects. To make a stationary object move, or a moving object stop, a force is needed. A force is also required to change the speed or direction of an object. This change in speed or direction is known as acceleration. Acceleration depends on the size (magnitude) of the force, and on the mass of the object. The effects of forces were first summarized by Isaac Newton in his three laws of motion. The international unit of force, named after him, is the newton (N), which is approximately equal to the weight of one apple. Gravity – the force of attraction between any two masses – can be measured using a newton meter (spring balance). Forces are put to useful effect in machines. A simple machine, such as a wheel and axle, is a device that changes the size or direction of an applied force. It allows an applied force (the effort) to produce another force (the load). A lever uses a bar that turns on a fulcrum to exert force. In all simple machines, there is a relationship between force and distance. A small force (in a compound pulley, for instance) moves through a large distance to lift a heavy object a small distance. This is called the Law of Simple Machines.

SIMPLE MACHINES

Single-pulley system (simple pulley)

Pulley wheel

Simple pulley only changes direction of a force

Effort is the same size as the load (10 N) and is pulled the same distance

One rope attached to load

Load of 10 N

Two-pulley system (simple pulley)

Pulley wheel

Effort is half the load (5 N), but the rope must be pulled twice the distance

Two ropes share the force and distance

Pulley wheel

Load of 10 N

Four-pulley system (compound pulley)

Two pulley wheels

Effort is one quarter of the load (2.5 N), but the rope must be pulled four times the distance

Four ropes share the force and distance

SIMPLE AND COMPOUND PULLEYS

Two pulley wheels

Load of 10 N

NEWTON METERS (SPRING BALANCES)

Weight is measured using a spring

When weight pulls downwards, pointer moves along scale and measures force

Weight is 10 N

Weight is 20 N

Mass of 1 kg

Mass of 2 kg

WEIGHT AND MASS
The "mass" of an object is a measure of the quantity of matter that it possesses. Mass is usually measured in grams (g) or kilograms (kg). The "weight" of an object is the force exerted on the object's mass by gravity. Since weight is a force, its unit is the newton (N).

Wheel and axle multiplies the effort

Force is transmitted to the wheels by the chain

Pedal

Crank

A larger force, the load, is produced at the axle

Effort, provided by cyclist's muscles, is smaller than the load, but moves through a greater distance

WHEEL AND AXLE

A screw, acting like a wedge wrapped around a shaft, multiplies the effort

Effort, a turning force supplied through a screwdriver

Pitch (the angle of the screw thread)

The smaller the angle of pitch, the less force is required, but more turns are needed to move it through a greater distance

A larger force, the load, pulls the screw into wood

SCREW

Effort pushes axe into wood

Axe blade has wedge shape

Wedge multiplies effort

A larger force, the load, moves through a smaller distance to push wood apart

WEDGE

NEWTON'S THREE LAWS OF MOTION

NEWTON'S FIRST LAW
When no force acts on a body, it will
continue in a state of rest or uniform motion.

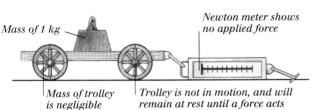

Mass of 1 kg

*Newton meter shows
no applied force*

*Mass of trolley
is negligible*

*Trolley is not in motion, and will
remain at rest until a force acts*

NO FORCE, NO ACCELERATION: STATE OF REST

*Constant
speed*

Mass of 1 kg

*Newton meter
shows no
applied force*

*Trolley is in motion, and will continue at a
constant speed in a straight line until a force acts*

NO FORCE, NO ACCELERATION: UNIFORM MOTION

NEWTON'S SECOND LAW
When a force acts on a body, the motion of the body will change. The size of the change
will depend upon the mass of the object and the magnitude of the applied force.

*Acceleration
is 2 ms^{-2}*

*Trolley and mass (1 kg) gain
2 metres per second of speed
each second (2 ms^{-2})*

*Newton meter registers
force of 2 N*

Mass of 1 kg

*Acceleration is
1 ms^{-2}*

*Trolley and mass (2 kg)
gain 1 metre per second of
speed each second (1 ms^{-2})*

*Newton meter
registers force of 2 N*

Mass of 2 kg

*With the same applied force, an object with 2 kg mass
accelerates at half the rate of object with 1 kg mass*

FORCE AND ACCELERATION: SMALL MASS, LARGE ACCELERATION   **FORCE AND ACCELERATION: LARGE MASS, SMALL ACCELERATION**

NEWTON'S THIRD LAW
If one object exerts a force on another, an equal and opposite force,
called the reaction force, is applied by the second object on the first.

*Newton meters pull on each other with
equal and opposite forces*

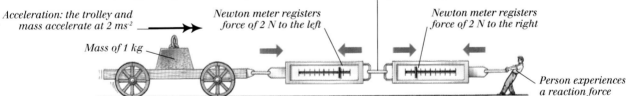

*Acceleration: the trolley and
mass accelerate at 2 ms^{-2}*

*Newton meter registers
force of 2 N to the left*

*Newton meter registers
force of 2 N to the right*

Mass of 1 kg

*Person experiences
a reaction force*

ACTION AND REACTION

THREE CLASSES OF LEVER

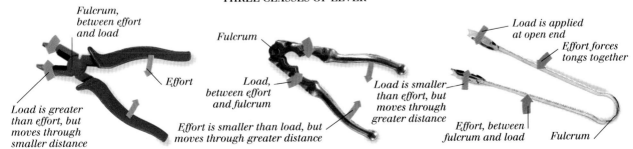

*Fulcrum,
between effort
and load*

Effort

*Load is greater
than effort, but
moves through
smaller distance*

Fulcrum

*Load,
between effort
and fulcrum*

*Effort is smaller than load, but
moves through greater distance*

*Load is applied
at open end*

*Effort forces
tongs together*

*Load is smaller
than effort, but
moves through
greater distance*

*Effort, between
fulcrum and load*

Fulcrum

CLASS 1 LEVER
Pliers consist of two class 1 levers.

CLASS 2 LEVER
Nutcrackers consist of two class 2 levers.

CLASS 3 LEVER
Tongs consist of two class 3 levers.

Rail and Road

Steam locomotives

Wagons that are pulled along tracks have been used to transport material since the 16th century, but these trains were drawn by men or horses until the invention of the steam locomotive. Steam locomotives enabled the basic railway system to realize its true potential. In 1804, Richard Trevithick built the world's first working steam locomotive in South Wales. It was not entirely successful, but it encouraged others to develop new designs. By 1829, the British engineer Robert Stephenson had built the "Rocket", considered to be the forerunner of the modern locomotive. The "Rocket" was a self-sufficient unit, carrying coal to heat the boiler and a water supply for generating steam. Steam passed from the boiler to force the pistons back and forth, and this movement turned the driving wheels, propelling the train forwards. Used steam was then expelled in characteristic "chuffs". Later steam locomotives, like "Ellerman Lines" and the "Mallard", worked in a similar way, but on a much larger scale. The simple design and reliability of steam locomotives ensured that they changed very little in 120 years of use, before being replaced from the 1950s by more efficient diesel and electric power (see pp. 326-329).

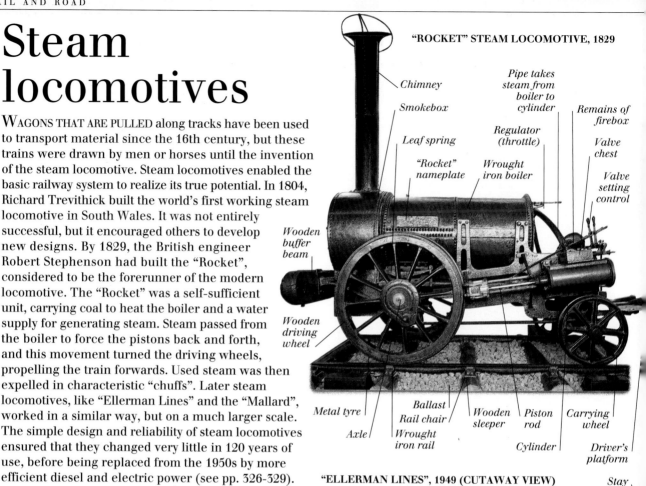

"ROCKET" STEAM LOCOMOTIVE, 1829

Chimney
Smokebox
Leaf spring
"Rocket" nameplate
Pipe takes steam from boiler to cylinder
Regulator (throttle)
Wrought iron boiler
Remains of firebox
Valve chest
Valve setting control
Wooden buffer beam
Wooden driving wheel
Metal tyre
Axle
Ballast
Rail chair
Wrought iron rail
Wooden sleeper
Piston rod
Cylinder
Carrying wheel
Driver's platform
Stay

"ELLERMAN LINES", 1949 (CUTAWAY VIEW)

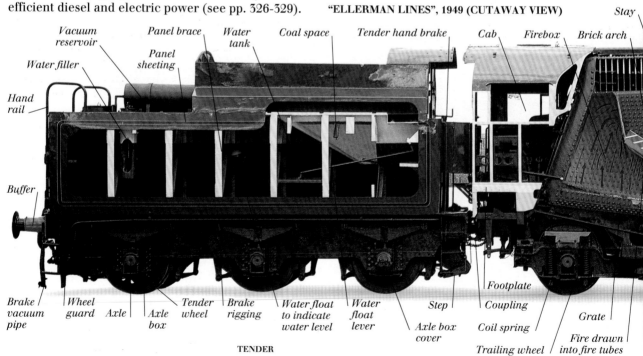

Vacuum reservoir
Panel brace
Panel sheeting
Water filler
Water tank
Coal space
Tender hand brake
Cab
Firebox
Brick arch
Hand rail
Buffer
Brake vacuum pipe
Wheel guard
Axle
Axle box
Tender wheel
Brake rigging
Water float to indicate water level
Water float lever
Step
Axle box cover
Coupling
Coil spring
Trailing wheel
Footplate
Grate
Fire drawn into fire tubes

TENDER

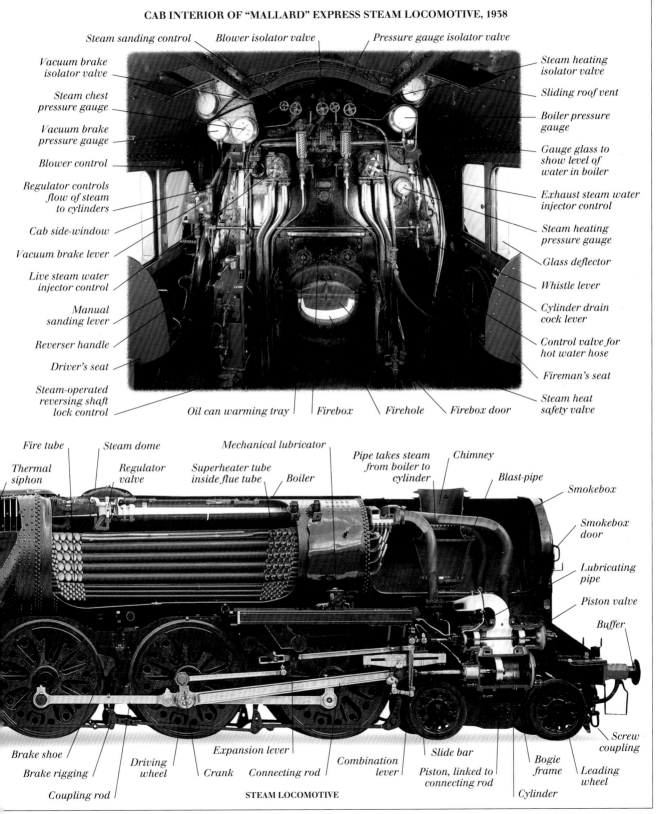

CAB INTERIOR OF "MALLARD" EXPRESS STEAM LOCOMOTIVE, 1938

Steam sanding control
Blower isolator valve
Pressure gauge isolator valve
Vacuum brake isolator valve
Steam heating isolator valve
Steam chest pressure gauge
Sliding roof vent
Vacuum brake pressure gauge
Boiler pressure gauge
Blower control
Gauge glass to show level of water in boiler
Regulator controls flow of steam to cylinders
Exhaust steam water injector control
Cab side-window
Steam heating pressure gauge
Vacuum brake lever
Glass deflector
Live steam water injector control
Whistle lever
Manual sanding lever
Cylinder drain cock lever
Reverser handle
Control valve for hot water hose
Driver's seat
Fireman's seat
Steam-operated reversing shaft lock control
Oil can warming tray
Firebox
Firehole
Firebox door
Steam heat safety valve

Fire tube
Steam dome
Mechanical lubricator
Pipe takes steam from boiler to cylinder
Chimney
Thermal siphon
Regulator valve
Superheater tube inside flue tube
Boiler
Blast-pipe
Smokebox
Smokebox door
Lubricating pipe
Piston valve
Buffer
Screw coupling
Brake shoe
Expansion lever
Slide bar
Bogie frame
Brake rigging
Driving wheel
Crank
Connecting rod
Combination lever
Piston, linked to connecting rod
Leading wheel
Coupling rod
Cylinder

STEAM LOCOMOTIVE

Diesel trains

RUDOLF DIESEL FIRST DEMONSTRATED the diesel engine in Germany in 1898, but it was not until the 1940s that diesel locomotives were successfully established on both passenger and freight services, in the US. Early diesel locomotives like the "Union Pacific" were more expensive to build than steam locomotives, but were more efficient and cheaper to operate, especially where oil was plentiful. One feature of diesel engines is that the power output cannot be coupled directly to the wheels. To convert the mechanical energy produced by diesel engines, a transmission system is needed. Almost all diesel locomotives have electric transmissions, and are known as "diesel-electric" locomotives. The diesel engine works by drawing air into the cylinders and compressing it to increase its temperature; a small quantity of diesel fuel is then injected into it. The resulting combustion drives the generator (more recently an alternator) to produce electricity, which is fed to electric motors connected to the wheels. Diesel-electric locomotives are essentially electric locomotives that carry their own power plants, and are used worldwide today. The "Deltic" diesel-electric locomotive, similar to the one shown here, replaced classic express steam locomotives, and ran at speeds up to 160 kph (100 mph).

FRONT VIEW OF "UNION PACIFIC" DIESEL-ELECTRIC LOCOMOTIVE, 1950s

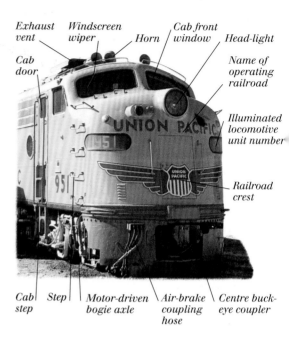

Exhaust vent
Windscreen wiper
Horn
Cab front window
Head-light
Cab door
Name of operating railroad
Illuminated locomotive unit number
Railroad crest

Cab step
Step
Motor-driven bogie axle
Air-brake coupling hose
Centre buck-eye coupler

PROTOTYPE "DELTIC" DIESEL-ELECTRIC LOCOMOTIVE, 1956

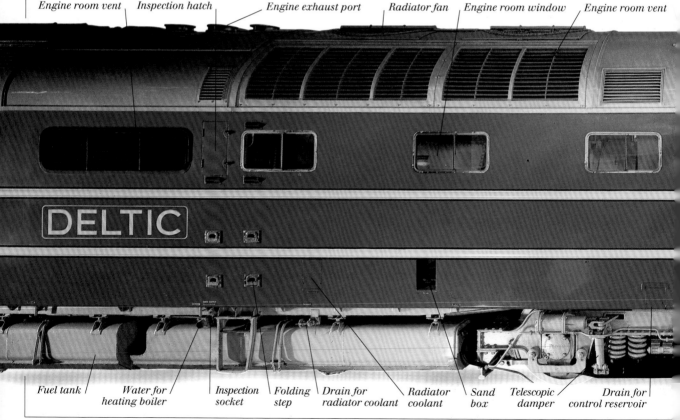

Engine room vent
Inspection hatch
Engine exhaust port
Radiator fan
Engine room window
Engine room vent

Fuel tank
Water for heating boiler
Inspection socket
Folding step
Drain for radiator coolant
Radiator coolant
Sand box
Telescopic damper
Drain for control reservoir

DIESEL ENGINE OF BRITISH RAIL CLASS 20
DIESEL-ELECTRIC LOCOMOTIVE

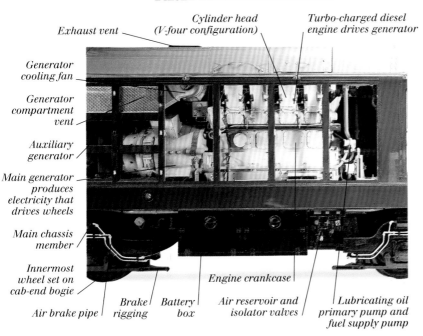

Exhaust vent

Cylinder head
(V-four configuration)

Turbo-charged diesel
engine drives generator

Generator
cooling fan

Generator
compartment
vent

Auxiliary
generator

Main generator
produces
electricity that
drives wheels

Main chassis
member

Innermost
wheel set on
cab-end bogie

Air brake pipe

Brake
rigging

Battery
box

Engine crankcase

Air reservoir and
isolator valves

Lubricating oil
primary pump and
fuel supply pump

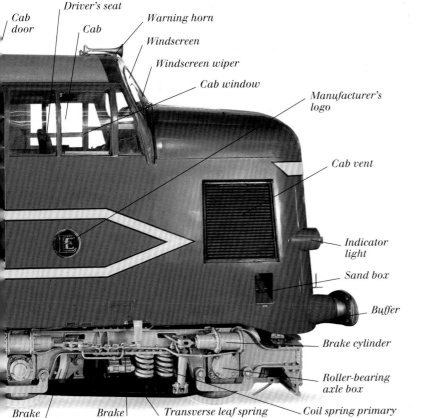

Cab
door

Driver's seat

Cab

Warning horn

Windscreen

Windscreen wiper

Cab window

Manufacturer's
logo

Cab vent

Indicator
light

Sand box

Buffer

Brake cylinder

Roller-bearing
axle box

Brake
shoe

Brake
actuating chain

Transverse leaf spring
secondary suspension

Coil spring primary
suspension

EXAMPLES OF FREIGHT CARS

BOX CAR

HOPPER CAR

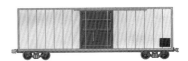

REFRIGERATOR CAR

LIVESTOCK CAR

FLAT CAR WITH BULKHEADS

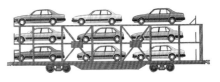

AUTOMOBILE CAR

Electric and high-speed trains

THE FIRST ELECTRIC LOCOMOTIVE ran in 1879 in Berlin, Germany. In Europe, electric trains developed as a more efficient alternative to the steam locomotive and diesel-electric power. Like diesels, electric trains employ electric motors to drive the wheels but, unlike diesels, the electricity is generated externally at a power station. Electric current is picked up either from a catenary (overhead cable) via a pantograph, or from a third rail. Since it does not carry its own power-generating equipment, an electric locomotive has a better power-to-weight ratio and greater acceleration than its diesel-electric equivalent. This makes electric trains suitable for urban routes with many stops. They are also faster, quieter, and less polluting. The latest electric French TGV (Train à Grande Vitesse) reaches 300 kph (186 mph); other trains, like the London to Paris and Brussels "Eurostar", can run at several voltages and operate between different countries. Simpler electric trains perform special duties – the "People Mover" at Gatwick Airport in Britain runs between terminals.

HOW ALTERNATING CURRENT (AC) ELECTRIC TRAINS WORK

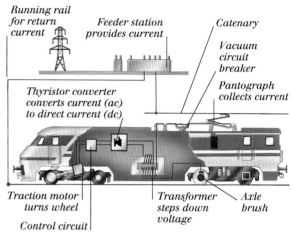

Running rail for return current

Feeder station provides current

Catenary

Vacuum circuit breaker

Pantograph collects current

Thyristor converter converts current (ac) to direct current (dc)

Traction motor turns wheel

Control circuit

Transformer steps down voltage

Axle brush

FRONT VIEW OF PARIS METRO

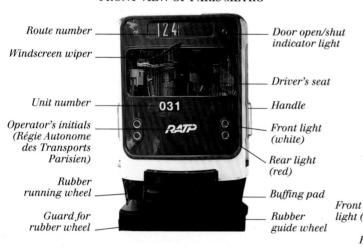

Route number

Windscreen wiper

Unit number

Operator's initials (Régie Autonome des Transports Parisien)

Rubber running wheel

Guard for rubber wheel

Door open/shut indicator light

Driver's seat

Handle

Front light (white)

Rear light (red)

Buffing pad

Rubber guide wheel

FRONT VIEW OF ITALIAN STATE RAILWAYS CLASS 402 ELECTRIC LOCOMOTIVE

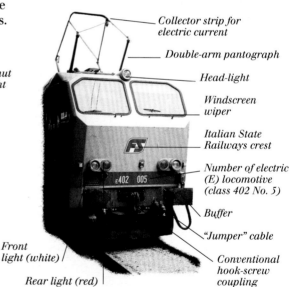

Collector strip for electric current

Double-arm pantograph

Head-light

Windscreen wiper

Italian State Railways crest

Number of electric (E) locomotive (class 402 No. 5)

Buffer

"Jumper" cable

Conventional hook-screw coupling

Front light (white)

Rear light (red)

SIDE VIEW OF GATWICK EXPRESS "PEOPLE MOVER"

Pneumatic rubber wheel

Concrete track

Automatic door

No driver (train controlled by central computer)

"EUROSTAR" MULTI-VOLTAGE ELECTRIC TRAIN

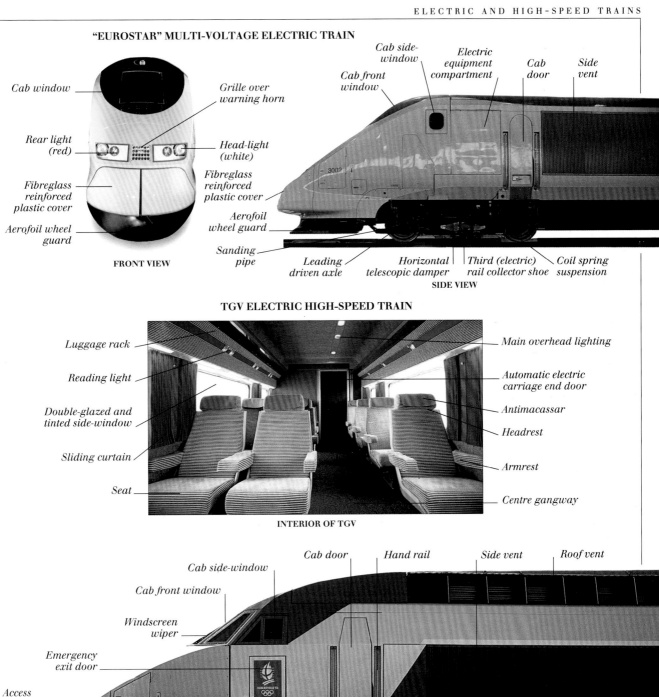

Cab window

Grille over warning horn

Rear light (red)

Head-light (white)

Fibreglass reinforced plastic cover

Fibreglass reinforced plastic cover

Aerofoil wheel guard

Aerofoil wheel guard

Sanding pipe

FRONT VIEW

Cab side-window

Electric equipment compartment

Cab door

Side vent

Cab front window

Leading driven axle

Horizontal telescopic damper

Third (electric) rail collector shoe

Coil spring suspension

SIDE VIEW

TGV ELECTRIC HIGH-SPEED TRAIN

Luggage rack

Reading light

Double-glazed and tinted side-window

Sliding curtain

Seat

Main overhead lighting

Automatic electric carriage end door

Antimacassar

Headrest

Armrest

Centre gangway

INTERIOR OF TGV

Cab door

Hand rail

Side vent

Roof vent

Cab side-window

Cab front window

Windscreen wiper

Emergency exit door

Access panel for servicing

Nose air deflector dam

Vertical damper

Horizontal damper

SIDE VIEW OF TGV

Train equipment

MODERN RAILWAY TRACK consists of two parallel steel rails clipped on to a support called a sleeper. Sleepers are usually made of reinforced concrete, although wood and steel are still used. The distance between the inside edges of the rails is the track gauge. It evolved in Britain, which uses a gauge of 1,435 mm (4 ft 8½ in), known as the standard gauge. As engineering grew more sophisticated, narrower gauges were adopted because they cost less to build. The loading gauge, which is equally important, determines the size of the largest loaded vehicle that may pass through tunnels and under bridges with adequate clearance. Safe train operation relies on following a signalling system. At first, signalling was based on a simple time interval between trains, but it now depends on maintaining a safe distance between successive trains travelling in the same direction. Most modern signals are colour lights, but older mechanical semaphore signals are still used. On the latest high-speed lines, train drivers receive control instructions by electronic means. Signalling depends on reliable control of the train by effective braking. For fast, modern trains, which have considerable momentum, it is essential that each vehicle in the train can be braked by the driver or by a train control system, such as Automatic Train Protection (ATP). Braking is achieved by the brake shoe acting on the wheel rim (rim brakes), by disc brakes, or, increasingly, by electrical braking.

MECHANICAL SEMAPHORE SIGNAL

Red, square-ended arm in raised position means "all clear"

Red glass

Green glass

Actuating lever system

Motor operating "home" stop signal

Green glass

Yellow glass

Yellow, "distant" warning arm in horizontal position means "caution"

Tubular steel post

Ladder

Electrical relay box

FOUR-ASPECT COLOUR LIGHT SIGNAL

Glass (yellow)

Glass (green)

Yellow glass (lit)

Glass (red)

Lifting lug

Lamp shield

Clip

Base

FRONT VIEW

SIDE VIEW

HOW A MODERN MAIN-LINE SIGNALLING SYSTEM WORKS

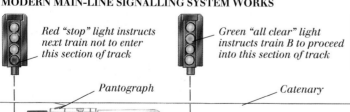
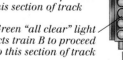

Red "stop" light instructs next train not to enter this section of track

Green "all clear" light instructs train B to proceed into this section of track

Green "all clear" light instructs train B to proceed into this section of track

Green "all clear" light instructs train B to proceed into this section of track

Pantograph

Catenary

Train B

Track

EXAMPLES OF INTERNATIONAL TRACK GAUGES

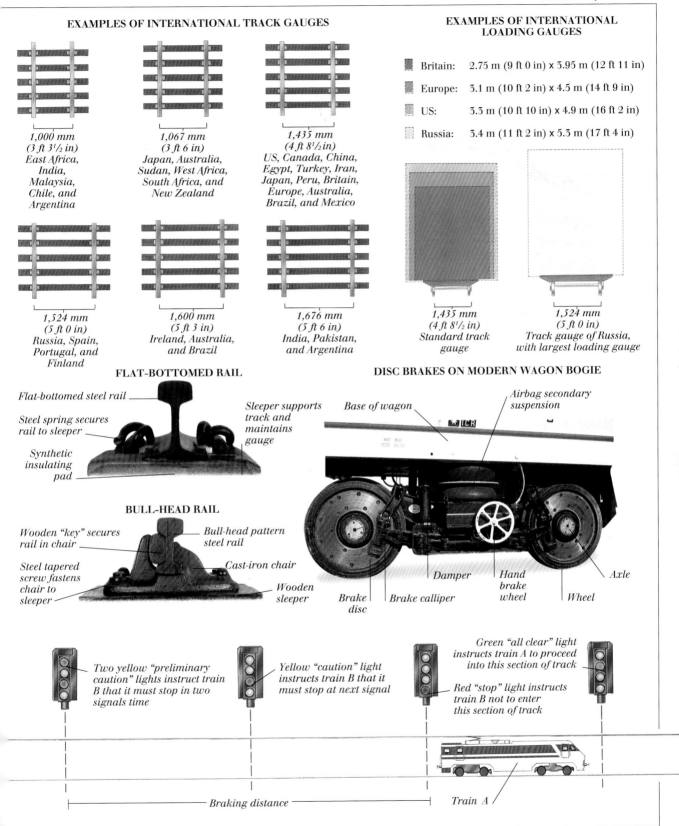

1,000 mm
(3 ft 3¹/₂ in)
East Africa, India, Malaysia, Chile, and Argentina

1,067 mm
(3 ft 6 in)
Japan, Australia, Sudan, West Africa, South Africa, and New Zealand

1,435 mm
(4 ft 8¹/₂ in)
US, Canada, China, Egypt, Turkey, Iran, Japan, Peru, Britain, Europe, Australia, Brazil, and Mexico

1,524 mm
(5 ft 0 in)
Russia, Spain, Portugal, and Finland

1,600 mm
(5 ft 3 in)
Ireland, Australia, and Brazil

1,676 mm
(5 ft 6 in)
India, Pakistan, and Argentina

EXAMPLES OF INTERNATIONAL LOADING GAUGES

Britain: 2.75 m (9 ft 0 in) x 3.95 m (12 ft 11 in)

Europe: 3.1 m (10 ft 2 in) x 4.5 m (14 ft 9 in)

US: 3.3 m (10 ft 10 in) x 4.9 m (16 ft 2 in)

Russia: 3.4 m (11 ft 2 in) x 5.3 m (17 ft 4 in)

1,435 mm
(4 ft 8¹/₂ in)
Standard track gauge

1,524 mm
(5 ft 0 in)
Track gauge of Russia, with largest loading gauge

FLAT-BOTTOMED RAIL

Flat-bottomed steel rail

Steel spring secures rail to sleeper

Synthetic insulating pad

Sleeper supports track and maintains gauge

BULL-HEAD RAIL

Wooden "key" secures rail in chair

Steel tapered screw fastens chair to sleeper

Bull-head pattern steel rail

Cast-iron chair

Wooden sleeper

DISC BRAKES ON MODERN WAGON BOGIE

Base of wagon

Airbag secondary suspension

Brake disc

Brake calliper

Damper

Hand brake wheel

Axle

Wheel

Two yellow "preliminary caution" lights instruct train B that it must stop in two signals time

Yellow "caution" light instructs train B that it must stop at next signal

Green "all clear" light instructs train A to proceed into this section of track

Red "stop" light instructs train B not to enter this section of track

— Braking distance —

Train A

Trams and buses

METROLINK TRAM, MANCHESTER, BRITAIN

AS CITY POPULATIONS exploded in the 1800s, there was an urgent need for mass transportation. Trams were an early solution. The first trams, like buses, were horse-drawn, but in 1881, electric street tramways appeared in Berlin, Germany. Electric trams soon became widespread throughout Europe and North America. Trams run on rails along a fixed route, using electric motors that receive power from overhead cables. As road networks developed, motorized buses offered a flexible alternative to trams. By the 1930s, they had replaced tram systems in many cities. City buses typically have doors at both front and rear to make loading and unloading easier. Double-decker designs are popular, occupying the same amount of street space as single-decker buses but able to transport twice the number of people. Buses are also commonly used for inter-city travel and touring. Tour buses have reclining seats, large windows, luggage space, and toilets. Recently, as city traffic has become increasingly congested, many city planners have designed new tram routes to run alongside bus routes as part of an integrated transport system.

EARLY TRAM, c.1900

Trolley boom

Trolley head

Trolley base

Drop window

Upper deck

Quarter light

Brake

Stair

Lower deck

Underframe

Platform

Controller

Truck

Lifeguard

MCW METROBUS, LONDON, BRITAIN

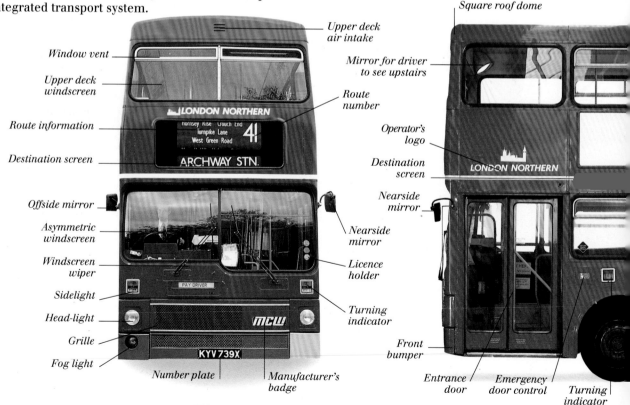

Square roof dome

Upper deck air intake

Window vent

Upper deck windscreen

Mirror for driver to see upstairs

Route number

Route information

Operator's logo

Destination screen

Destination screen

LONDON NORTHERN

Offside mirror

Nearside mirror

Asymmetric windscreen

Windscreen wiper

Nearside mirror

Sidelight

Licence holder

Head-light

Grille

Turning indicator

Fog light

Front bumper

Number plate

Manufacturer's badge

Entrance door

Emergency door control

Turning indicator

FRONT VIEW

SINGLE-DECKER BUS, NEW YORK, US

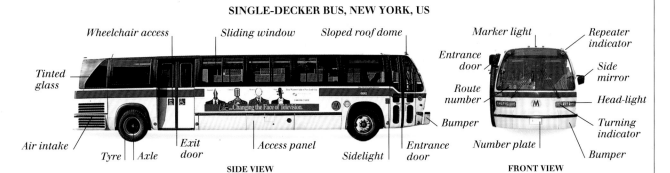

Wheelchair access
Sliding window
Sloped roof dome
Tinted glass
Air intake
Tyre
Axle
Exit door
Access panel
Sidelight
Entrance door

SIDE VIEW

Marker light
Repeater indicator
Entrance door
Side mirror
Route number
Head-light
Turning indicator
Bumper
Number plate
Bumper

FRONT VIEW

DOUBLE-DECKER TOUR BUS, PARIS, FRANCE

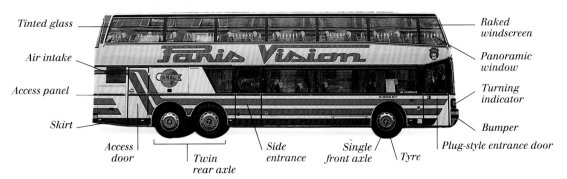

Tinted glass
Air intake
Access panel
Skirt
Access door
Twin rear axle
Side entrance
Single front axle
Tyre
Raked windscreen
Panoramic window
Turning indicator
Bumper
Plug-style entrance door

Paris Vision

CARLUX

Sliding window vent
Upper saloon window
Advertising panel
Air intake
Lower saloon window
Fleet number
Engine access panel
Rear bumper
Emergency door control
Two-leaf style exit door
Legal lettering
London Buses logo
Tyre
Skirt
Axle

HT
M1041
LONDON BUSES

SIDE VIEW

The first cars

THE EARLIEST ROAD VEHICLE powered by an engine, the Cugnot steam traction engine, was built in 1770. More practical steam carriages, such as the Bordino, were available in the early 19th century, but they were heavy and cumbersome. Restrictive laws and the introduction of railways, faster and able to carry more passengers, saw the decline of "cars" powered by steam. It was not until 1860 that the first practical power unit for road vehicles was developed, with the invention of the internal combustion engine by the Belgian Etienne Lenoir. By around 1890, Karl Benz and Gottlieb Daimler in Germany, and Albert de Dion and Armand Peugeot in France were building cars for sale to the public. These early cars, despite being primitive, expensive, and produced in limited numbers, heralded the age of the motor car.

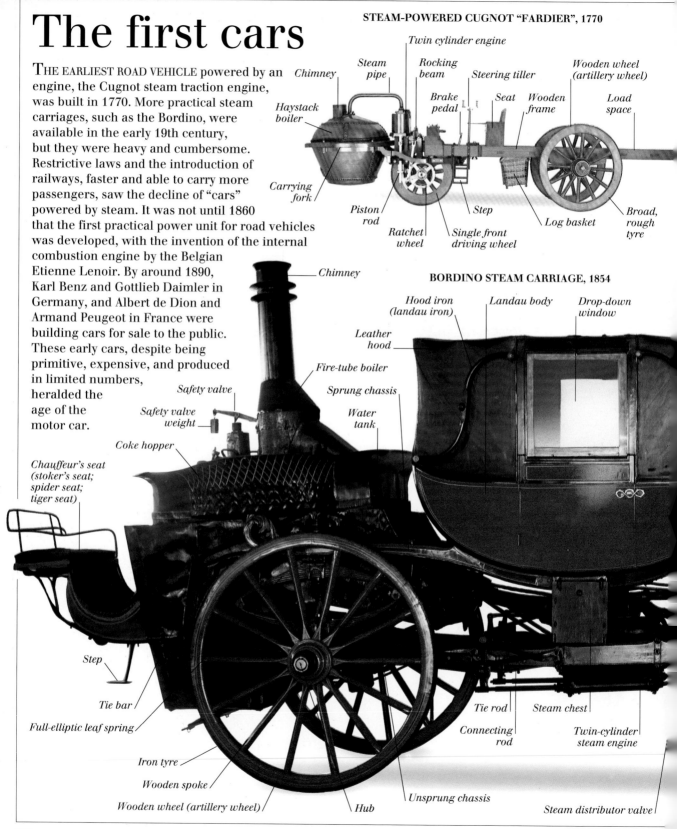

STEAM-POWERED CUGNOT "FARDIER", 1770

Chimney

Steam pipe

Twin cylinder engine

Rocking beam

Steering tiller

Wooden wheel (artillery wheel)

Brake pedal

Seat

Wooden frame

Load space

Haystack boiler

Carrying fork

Piston rod

Ratchet wheel

Single front driving wheel

Step

Log basket

Broad, rough tyre

BORDINO STEAM CARRIAGE, 1854

Chimney

Hood iron (landau iron)

Landau body

Drop-down window

Leather hood

Fire-tube boiler

Sprung chassis

Water tank

Safety valve

Safety valve weight

Coke hopper

Chauffeur's seat (stoker's seat; spider seat; tiger seat)

Step

Tie bar

Full-elliptic leaf spring

Iron tyre

Wooden spoke

Wooden wheel (artillery wheel)

Hub

Unsprung chassis

Tie rod

Steam chest

Connecting rod

Twin-cylinder steam engine

Steam distributor valve

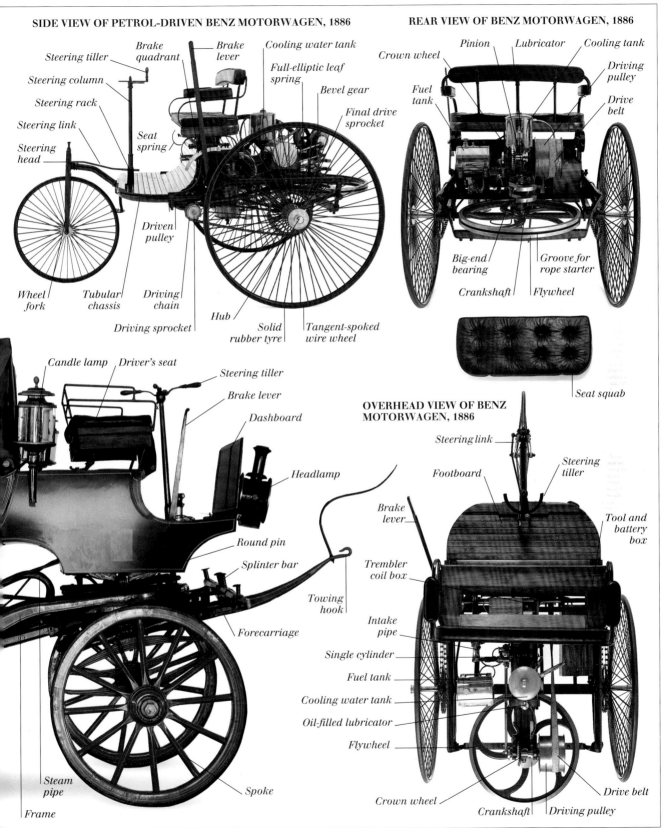

SIDE VIEW OF PETROL-DRIVEN BENZ MOTORWAGEN, 1886

Steering tiller

Steering column

Steering rack

Steering link

Steering head

Brake quadrant

Brake lever

Cooling water tank

Full-elliptic leaf spring

Bevel gear

Final drive sprocket

Seat spring

Driven pulley

Wheel fork

Tubular chassis

Driving chain

Driving sprocket

Hub

Solid rubber tyre

Tangent-spoked wire wheel

REAR VIEW OF BENZ MOTORWAGEN, 1886

Pinion

Lubricator

Cooling tank

Crown wheel

Driving pulley

Drive belt

Fuel tank

Big-end bearing

Groove for rope starter

Crankshaft

Flywheel

Seat squab

OVERHEAD VIEW OF BENZ MOTORWAGEN, 1886

Steering link

Footboard

Steering tiller

Brake lever

Tool and battery box

Trembler coil box

Intake pipe

Single cylinder

Fuel tank

Cooling water tank

Oil-filled lubricator

Flywheel

Crown wheel

Crankshaft

Drive belt

Driving pulley

Candle lamp

Driver's seat

Steering tiller

Brake lever

Dashboard

Headlamp

Round pin

Splinter bar

Towing hook

Forecarriage

Steam pipe

Spoke

Frame

Elegance and utility

DURING THE FIRST DECADE OF THIS CENTURY, the motorist who could afford it had a choice of some of the finest cars ever made. These handbuilt cars were powerful and luxurious, using the finest woods, leathers, and cloths, and bodywork made to the customer's individual requirements; some had six-cylinder engines as big as 15 litres. The price of such cars was several times that of an average house, and their yearly running costs were also very high. As a result, basic, utilitarian cars became popular. Costing perhaps one-tenth of the price of a luxury car, these cars had very little trim and often had only single-cylinder engines.

1904 OLDSMOBILE SINGLE-CYLINDER ENGINE

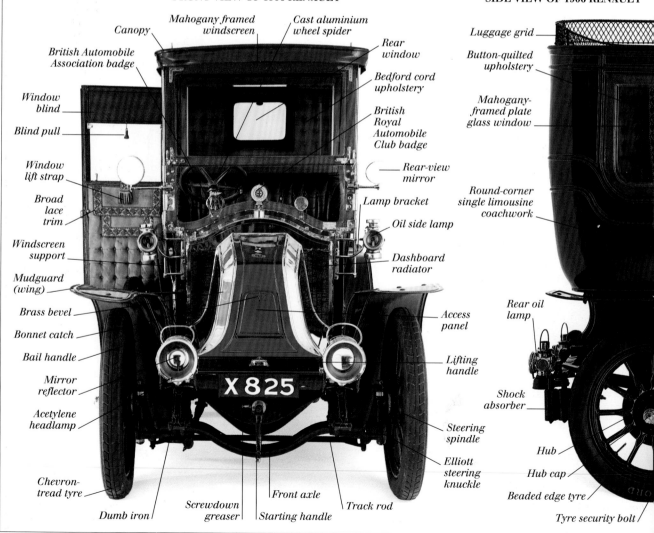

Oil bottle dripfeed
Crankcase
Starting handle bracket
Exhaust pipe
Cylinder head
Cylinder
Starter cog
Carburettor
Engine timing gear
Crankshaft
Flywheel
Gear band

FRONT VIEW OF 1906 RENAULT

Canopy
Mahogany framed windscreen
Cast aluminium wheel spider
Rear window
British Automobile Association badge
Bedford cord upholstery
British Royal Automobile Club badge
Window blind
Blind pull
Rear-view mirror
Window lift strap
Lamp bracket
Broad lace trim
Oil side lamp
Windscreen support
Dashboard radiator
Mudguard (wing)
Brass bevel
Access panel
Bonnet catch
Bail handle
Lifting handle
Mirror reflector
Acetylene headlamp
X 825
Chevron-tread tyre
Steering spindle
Elliott steering knuckle
Dumb iron
Screwdown greaser
Front axle
Starting handle
Track rod

SIDE VIEW OF 1906 RENAULT

Luggage grid
Button-quilted upholstery
Mahogany-framed plate glass window
Round-corner single limousine coachwork
Rear oil lamp
Shock absorber
Hub
Hub cap
Beaded edge tyre
Tyre security bolt

1904 OLDSMOBILE TRIM AND BODYWORK

Reflector

Rear lamp

Engine cover handle

Engine cover

Mudguard

Mudguard stay

Seat back rest frame

Ignition switch

Seat squab

Dashboard

Tiller

Brake pedal

Throttle pedal

Mirror

1904 OLDSMOBILE CHASSIS

Front steering track-rod

Brake rod

Steering wiffletree

Rear spring

Starting handle bracket

Combined spring and chassis unit

Front spring

Full-elliptic steering spring

Front axle

Non-skid tyre

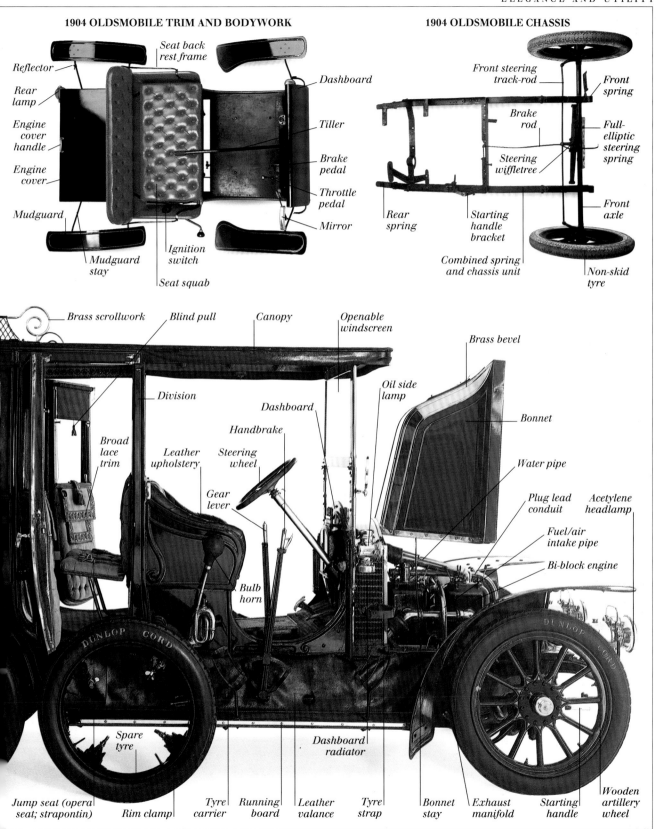

Brass scrollwork

Blind pull

Canopy

Openable windscreen

Division

Broad lace trim

Leather upholstery

Steering wheel

Gear lever

Handbrake

Dashboard

Bulb horn

Oil side lamp

Brass bevel

Bonnet

Water pipe

Plug lead conduit

Fuel/air intake pipe

Bi-block engine

Acetylene headlamp

Jump seat (opera seat; strapontin)

Rim clamp

Tyre carrier

Running board

Leather valance

Spare tyre

Tyre strap

Dashboard radiator

Bonnet stay

Exhaust manifold

Starting handle

Wooden artillery wheel

Mass-production

THE FIRST CARS WERE HAND-ASSEMBLED from individually built parts, a time-consuming procedure that required skilled mechanics and made cars very expensive. This problem was solved, in America, by a Detroit car manufacturer named Henry Ford; he introduced mass-production by using standardized parts, and later combined these with a moving production line. The work was brought to the workers, each of whom performed one simple task in the construction process as the chassis moved along the line. The first mass-produced car, the Ford Model T, was launched in 1908 and was available in a limited range of body styles and colours. However, when the production line was introduced in 1914, the colour range was cut back; the Model T became available, as Henry Ford said, in "any colour you like, so long as it's black". Ford cut the production time for a car from several days to about 12 hours, and eventually to minutes, making cars much cheaper than before. As a result, by 1920 half the cars in the world were Model T Fords.

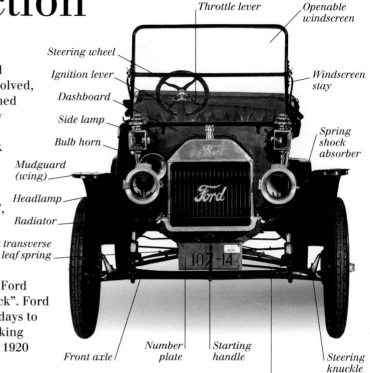

Throttle lever
Openable windscreen
Steering wheel
Ignition lever
Windscreen stay
Dashboard
Side lamp
Spring shock absorber
Bulb horn
Mudguard (wing)
Headlamp
Radiator
Ford
Front transverse leaf spring
10?-14
Number plate
Starting handle
Steering knuckle
Front axle
Steering spindle connecting-rod

STAGES OF FORD MODEL T PRODUCTION

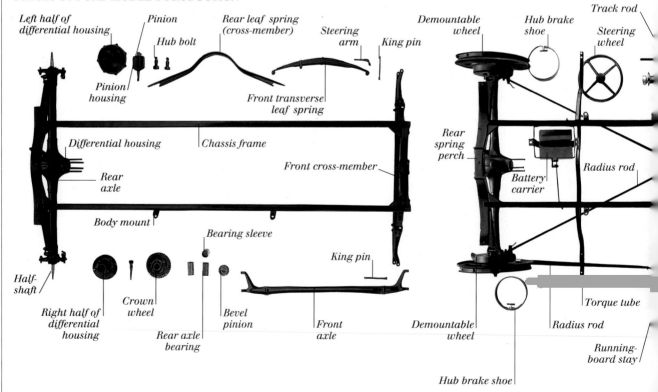

Left half of differential housing
Pinion
Rear leaf spring (cross-member)
Steering arm
King pin
Demountable wheel
Hub brake shoe
Track rod
Steering wheel
Hub bolt
Pinion housing
Front transverse leaf spring
Differential housing
Chassis frame
Rear spring perch
Radius rod
Rear axle
Front cross-member
Battery carrier
Body mount
Bearing sleeve
King pin
Half-shaft
Crown wheel
Bevel pinion
Front axle
Demountable wheel
Torque tube
Right half of differential housing
Rear axle bearing
Radius rod
Running-board stay
Hub brake shoe

SIDE VIEW OF 1913 FORD MODEL T

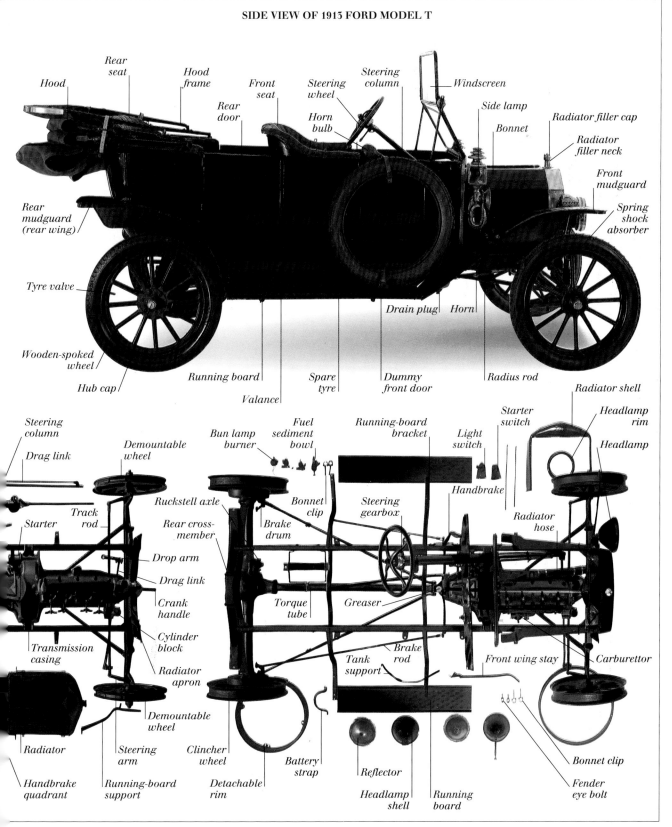

Hood

Rear seat

Hood frame

Front seat

Rear door

Steering wheel

Steering column

Horn bulb

Windscreen

Side lamp

Bonnet

Radiator filler cap

Radiator filler neck

Front mudguard

Spring shock absorber

Rear mudguard (rear wing)

Tyre valve

Wooden-spoked wheel

Hub cap

Running board

Valance

Spare tyre

Drain plug

Horn

Dummy front door

Radius rod

Radiator shell

Starter switch

Light switch

Handbrake

Running-board bracket

Fuel sediment bowl

Bun lamp burner

Steering column

Drag link

Demountable wheel

Ruckstell axle

Brake drum

Bonnet clip

Steering gearbox

Headlamp rim

Headlamp

Radiator hose

Starter

Track rod

Rear cross-member

Drop arm

Drag link

Crank handle

Cylinder block

Radiator apron

Transmission casing

Torque tube

Greaser

Brake rod

Tank support

Front wing stay

Carburettor

Demountable wheel

Radiator

Steering arm

Running-board support

Clincher wheel

Detachable rim

Battery strap

Reflector

Headlamp shell

Running board

Bonnet clip

Fender eye bolt

Handbrake quadrant

The "people's car"

WORKING PARTS OF
VOLKSWAGEN BEETLE

THE MOST POPULAR CAR in the history of car manufacture is the Volkswagen Beetle, originally called the KdF Wagen. The car was developed in Germany in the 1930s by Dr. Ferdinand Porsche. At that time, Germany had only half the number of cars of Britain or France, and Adolf Hitler took a personal interest in the development of the Volkswagen ("people's car"). The intention was to provide a new industry, new jobs, and a car so cheap that anyone in work could afford it. Dr. Porsche designed a car that was cheap to build and run; its rear-mounted, air-cooled engine cut down the number of parts needed and also reduced weight. However, few civilians managed to obtain the Beetle before the outbreak of the Second World War in 1939. After the war, the Beetle proved so popular that eventually more than 20 million were sold.

**CUSTOMIZED
VOLKSWAGEN
BEETLE**

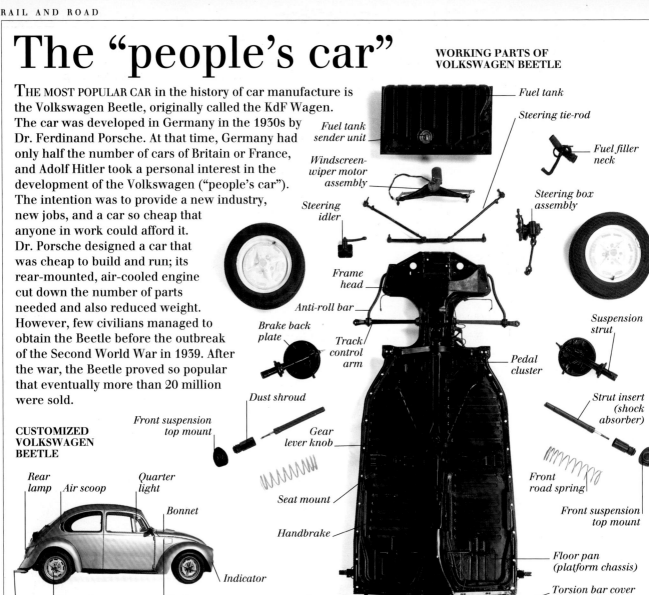

Fuel tank
Fuel tank sender unit
Steering tie-rod
Fuel filler neck
Windscreen-wiper motor assembly
Steering idler
Steering box assembly
Frame head
Anti-roll bar
Suspension strut
Brake back plate
Track control arm
Pedal cluster
Dust shroud
Strut insert (shock absorber)
Front suspension top mount
Gear lever knob
Seat mount
Front road spring
Handbrake
Front suspension top mount
Floor pan (platform chassis)
Torsion bar cover
Rear brake drum
Trailing arm
Tyre
Sports wheel
Rear shock absorber
Drive shaft
Transaxle (gearbox and final drive)
Heat exchanger
Clutch and flywheel
Starter motor
Flat-four engine
Air filter
Tail pipe

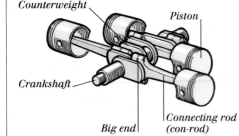

Rear lamp
Air scoop
Quarter light
Bonnet
Indicator
Tail pipe
Pressed steel wheel
Fuel filler cap

**FLAT-FOUR
CYLINDER
ARRANGEMENT**

Counterweight
Piston
Crankshaft
Big end
Connecting rod (con-rod)

BODY SHELL OF VOLKSWAGEN BEETLE

Front bumper

Bonnet release handle

Nearside headlamp unit

Offside headlamp unit

Nearside front indicator lens

Chrome trim strip

Bonnet

Offside front indicator lens

Nearside front mudguard (front wing)

Offside front mudguard (front wing)

Front wing piping

Spare-wheel well

Bonnet hinge

Front wing piping

Blade

Offside running board

Quarter light

Arm

Mirror

Windscreen wiper

Nearside running board

Door catch

Steering column

Wind deflector (baffle)

Sun roof

Quarter light

Door handle

Window winder handle

Passenger door

Body shell

Window winder regulator

Drop glass

Rear wing piping

Air intake vents

Rear wing piping

Nearside rear mudguard (rear wing)

Engine lid (engine cover)

Offside rear mudguard (rear wing)

Rear valance

Air intake vents

Number plate light

Number plate

Offside rear lamp cluster (rear lamp unit)

Nearside rear lamp cluster (rear lamp unit)

WRV 408L

Rear bumper

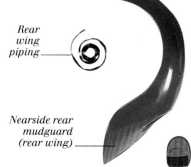

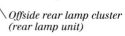

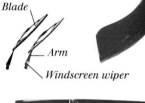

Early engines

STEAM AND ELECTRICITY were used to power cars until early this century, but neither power source was ideal. Electric cars had to stop frequently to recharge their heavy batteries, and steam cars gave smooth power delivery but were too complicated for the average motorist to use. A rival power source, the internal combustion engine, was invented in 1860 by Etienne Lenoir (see pp. 334-335). This engine converted the force of an explosion into rotary motion, to turn the wheels of a vehicle. Early variations on this basic model included sleeve valves, separately cast cylinders, and the two-stroke combustion cycle. Today, all combustion engines, including the Wankel rotary and diesels (see pp. 346-347), use the four-stroke cycle, first demonstrated by Nikolaus Otto in 1876. The Otto cycle, often described as "suck, squeeze, bang, blow", has proved the best method of ensuring that the engine turns over smoothly and that exhaust emissions are controllable.

TROJAN TWO-STROKE ENGINE, 1927

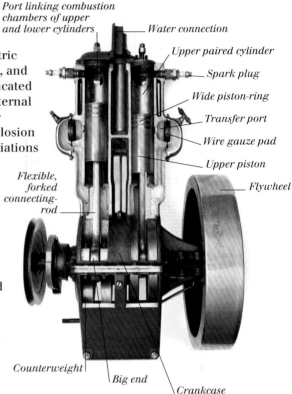

Port linking combustion chambers of upper and lower cylinders

Water connection

Upper paired cylinder

Spark plug

Wide piston-ring

Transfer port

Wire gauze pad

Upper piston

Flywheel

Flexible, forked connecting-rod

Counterweight

Big end

Crankcase

BERSEY ELECTRIC CAB, 1896

Mounting for tray of 40 batteries

Housing for electric motors

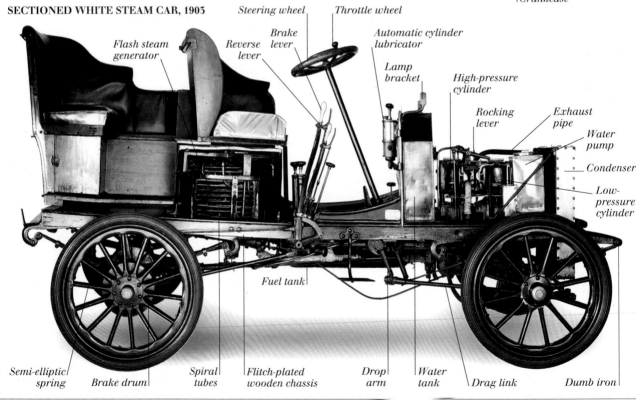

SECTIONED WHITE STEAM CAR, 1903

Steering wheel

Throttle wheel

Brake lever

Reverse lever

Automatic cylinder lubricator

Flash steam generator

Lamp bracket

High-pressure cylinder

Rocking lever

Exhaust pipe

Water pump

Condenser

Low-pressure cylinder

Fuel tank

Semi-elliptic spring

Brake drum

Spiral tubes

Flitch-plated wooden chassis

Drop arm

Water tank

Drag link

Dumb iron

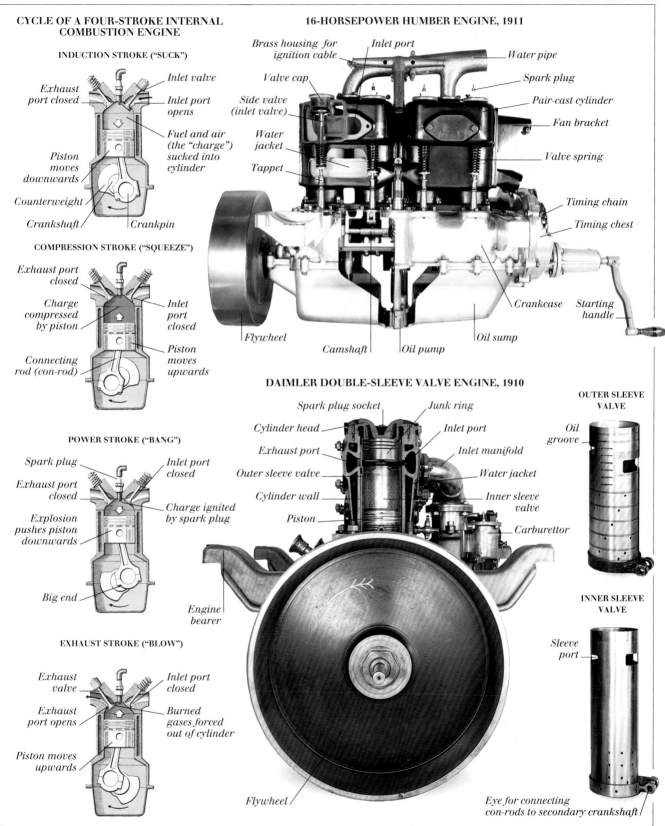

CYCLE OF A FOUR-STROKE INTERNAL COMBUSTION ENGINE

INDUCTION STROKE ("SUCK")

Exhaust port closed
Inlet valve
Inlet port opens
Fuel and air (the "charge") sucked into cylinder
Piston moves downwards
Counterweight
Crankshaft
Crankpin

COMPRESSION STROKE ("SQUEEZE")

Exhaust port closed
Charge compressed by piston
Inlet port closed
Connecting rod (con-rod)
Piston moves upwards

POWER STROKE ("BANG")

Spark plug
Inlet port closed
Exhaust port closed
Charge ignited by spark plug
Explosion pushes piston downwards
Big end

EXHAUST STROKE ("BLOW")

Exhaust valve
Inlet port closed
Exhaust port opens
Burned gases forced out of cylinder
Piston moves upwards

16-HORSEPOWER HUMBER ENGINE, 1911

Brass housing for ignition cable
Inlet port
Water pipe
Valve cap
Spark plug
Side valve (inlet valve)
Pair-cast cylinder
Fan bracket
Water jacket
Valve spring
Tappet
Timing chain
Timing chest
Flywheel
Camshaft
Oil pump
Oil sump
Crankcase
Starting handle

DAIMLER DOUBLE-SLEEVE VALVE ENGINE, 1910

Spark plug socket
Junk ring
Cylinder head
Inlet port
Exhaust port
Inlet manifold
Outer sleeve valve
Water jacket
Cylinder wall
Inner sleeve valve
Piston
Carburettor
Engine bearer
Flywheel

OUTER SLEEVE VALVE

Oil groove

INNER SLEEVE VALVE

Sleeve port
Eye for connecting con-rods to secondary crankshaft

543

Modern engines

TODAY'S PETROL ENGINE WORKS on the same basic principles as the first car engines of a century ago, although it has been greatly refined. Modern engines, often made from special metal alloys, are much lighter than earlier engines. Computerized ignition systems, fuel injectors, and multi-valve cylinder heads achieve a more efficient combustion of the fuel/air mixture (the charge) so that less fuel is wasted. As a result of this greater efficiency, the power and performance of a modern engine are increased, and the level of pollution in the exhaust gases is reduced. Exhaust pollution levels today are also lowered by the increasing use of special filters called catalytic converters, which absorb many exhaust pollutants. The need to produce ever more efficient engines means that it can take up to seven years to develop a new engine for a family car, at a cost of many millions of pounds.

FRONT VIEW OF A FORD COSWORTH V6 12-VALVE

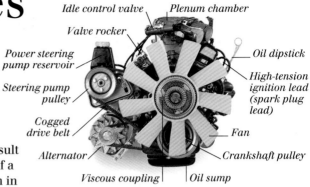

Idle control valve
Valve rocker
Power steering pump reservoir
Steering pump pulley
Cogged drive belt
Alternator
Viscous coupling
Plenum chamber
Oil dipstick
High-tension ignition lead (spark plug lead)
Fan
Crankshaft pulley
Oil sump

FRONT VIEW OF A FORD COSWORTH V6 24-VALVE

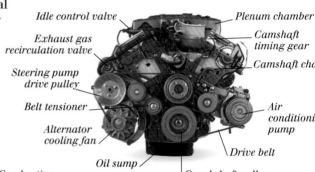

Idle control valve
Exhaust gas recirculation valve
Steering pump drive pulley
Belt tensioner
Alternator cooling fan
Oil sump
Plenum chamber
Camshaft timing gear
Camshaft chain
Air conditioning pump
Drive belt
Crankshaft pulley

SECTIONED VIEW OF A JAGUAR STRAIGHT 6

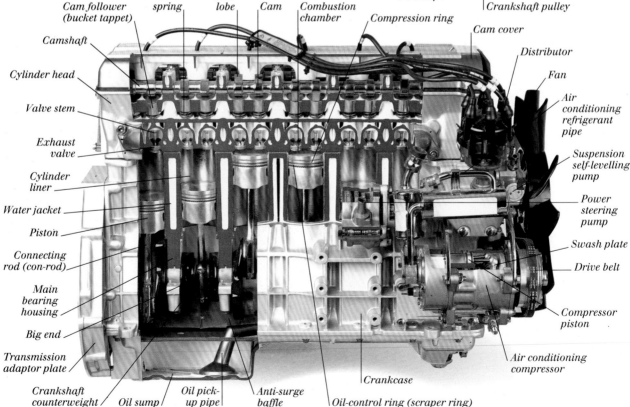

Cam follower (bucket tappet)
Valve spring
Cam lobe
Cam
Combustion chamber
Compression ring
Camshaft
Cam cover
Cylinder head
Distributor
Valve stem
Fan
Exhaust valve
Air conditioning refrigerant pipe
Cylinder liner
Water jacket
Suspension self-levelling pump
Piston
Power steering pump
Connecting rod (con-rod)
Swash plate
Main bearing housing
Drive belt
Big end
Compressor piston
Transmission adaptor plate
Air conditioning compressor
Crankshaft counterweight
Oil sump
Oil pick-up pipe
Anti-surge baffle
Crankcase
Oil-control ring (scraper ring)

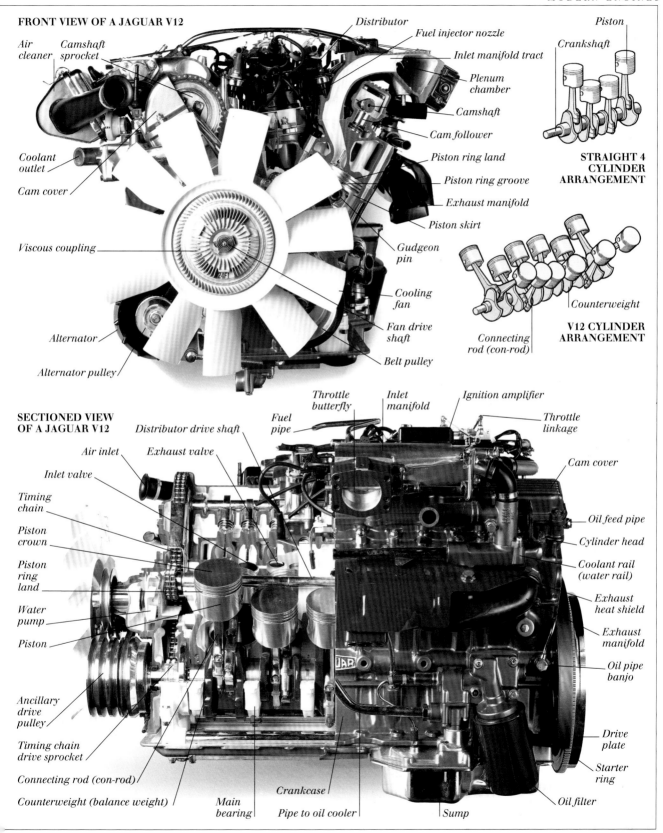

FRONT VIEW OF A JAGUAR V12

Air cleaner

Camshaft sprocket

Distributor

Fuel injector nozzle

Piston

Crankshaft

Inlet manifold tract

Plenum chamber

Camshaft

Cam follower

STRAIGHT 4 CYLINDER ARRANGEMENT

Coolant outlet

Cam cover

Piston ring land

Piston ring groove

Exhaust manifold

Piston skirt

Viscous coupling

Gudgeon pin

Cooling fan

Connecting rod (con-rod)

Counterweight

V12 CYLINDER ARRANGEMENT

Alternator

Fan drive shaft

Alternator pulley

Belt pulley

SECTIONED VIEW OF A JAGUAR V12

Distributor drive shaft

Fuel pipe

Throttle butterfly

Inlet manifold

Ignition amplifier

Throttle linkage

Air inlet

Exhaust valve

Inlet valve

Cam cover

Timing chain

Piston crown

Oil feed pipe

Cylinder head

Piston ring land

Coolant rail (water rail)

Water pump

Exhaust heat shield

Piston

Exhaust manifold

Oil pipe banjo

Ancillary drive pulley

Timing chain drive sprocket

Drive plate

Connecting rod (con-rod)

Starter ring

Counterweight (balance weight)

Main bearing

Crankcase

Pipe to oil cooler

Sump

Oil filter

Alternative engines

THE MOST COMMON TYPE OF ALTERNATIVE ENGINE is the diesel engine, which, instead of igniting the compressed fuel/air mixture with a spark, uses compression alone, heating the mixture to the point where it explodes. A diesel engine's fuel consumption is low in comparison with similarly sized piston engines, despite its heavier, reinforced moving parts and cylinder block. Another type of engine is the rotary-combustion, first successfully developed by Felix Wankel in the 1950s. Its two trilobate (three-sided) rotors revolve in housings shaped in a fat figure-of-eight. The four sequences of the four-stroke cycle, which occur consecutively in a piston engine, occur simultaneously in a rotary engine, producing power in a continuous stream.

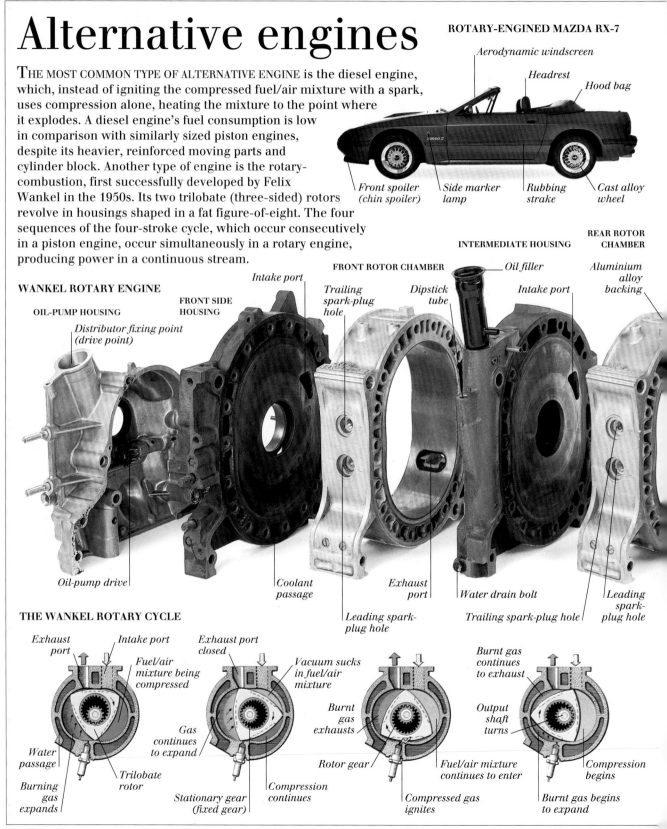

ROTARY-ENGINED MAZDA RX-7

Aerodynamic windscreen

Headrest

Hood bag

Front spoiler (chin spoiler)

Side marker lamp

Rubbing strake

Cast alloy wheel

WANKEL ROTARY ENGINE

OIL-PUMP HOUSING

FRONT SIDE HOUSING

Distributor fixing point (drive point)

Intake port

FRONT ROTOR CHAMBER

Trailing spark-plug hole

Dipstick tube

INTERMEDIATE HOUSING

Oil filler

Intake port

REAR ROTOR CHAMBER

Aluminium alloy backing

Oil-pump drive

Coolant passage

Exhaust port

Leading spark-plug hole

Water drain bolt

Trailing spark-plug hole

Leading spark-plug hole

THE WANKEL ROTARY CYCLE

Exhaust port

Intake port

Fuel/air mixture being compressed

Water passage

Burning gas expands

Trilobate rotor

Gas continues to expand

Stationary gear (fixed gear)

Exhaust port closed

Vacuum sucks in fuel/air mixture

Compression continues

Burnt gas exhausts

Rotor gear

Compressed gas ignites

Burnt gas continues to exhaust

Output shaft turns

Fuel/air mixture continues to enter

Burnt gas begins to expand

Compression begins

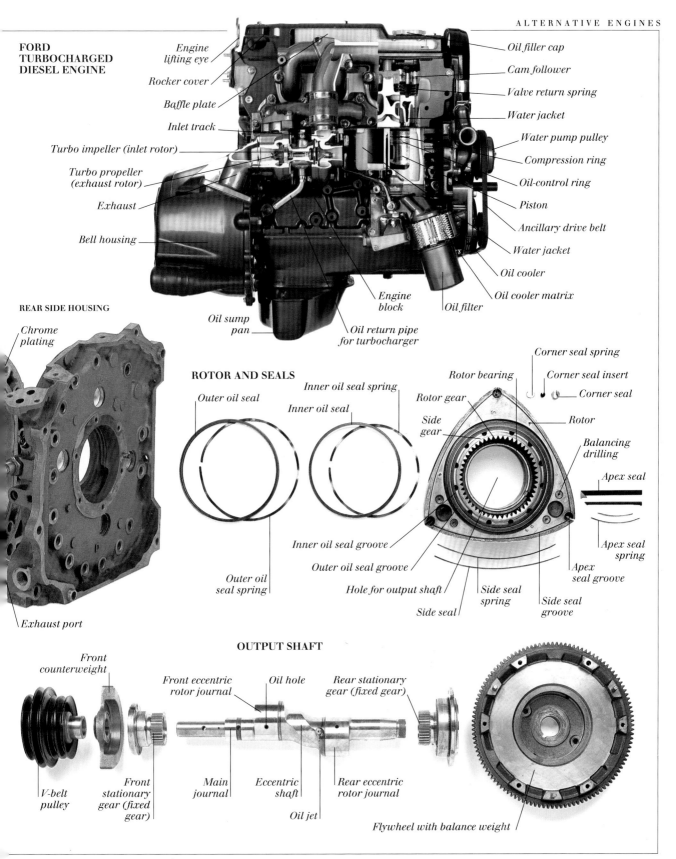

FORD TURBOCHARGED DIESEL ENGINE

Engine lifting eye

Rocker cover

Baffle plate

Inlet track

Turbo impeller (inlet rotor)

Turbo propeller (exhaust rotor)

Exhaust

Bell housing

Oil filler cap

Cam follower

Valve return spring

Water jacket

Water pump pulley

Compression ring

Oil-control ring

Piston

Ancillary drive belt

Water jacket

Oil cooler

Oil cooler matrix

Oil filter

Engine block

Oil sump pan

Oil return pipe for turbocharger

REAR SIDE HOUSING

Chrome plating

Exhaust port

ROTOR AND SEALS

Outer oil seal

Inner oil seal spring

Inner oil seal

Rotor bearing

Corner seal spring

Corner seal insert

Corner seal

Rotor gear

Side gear

Rotor

Balancing drilling

Apex seal

Apex seal spring

Inner oil seal groove

Outer oil seal groove

Outer oil seal spring

Hole for output shaft

Side seal spring

Side seal

Side seal groove

Apex seal groove

OUTPUT SHAFT

Front counterweight

Front eccentric rotor journal

Oil hole

Rear stationary gear (fixed gear)

V-belt pulley

Front stationary gear (fixed gear)

Main journal

Eccentric shaft

Oil jet

Rear eccentric rotor journal

Flywheel with balance weight

Modern bodywork

THE BODY OF A MODERN MASS-PRODUCED CAR is built on the monocoque (single-shell) principle, in which the roof, side panels, and floor are welded into a single integral unit. This bodyshell protects and supports the car's internal parts. Steel and glass are used to construct the bodyshell, creating a unit that is both light and strong. Its lightness helps to conserve energy, while its strength protects the occupants. Modern bodywork is designed with the aid of computers, which are used to predict factors such as aerodynamic efficiency and impact-resistance. High-technology is also employed on the production line, where robots are used to assemble, weld, and paint the body.

RENAULT LOGO

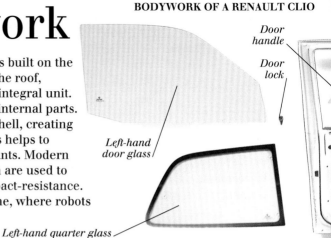

Door handle

Door lock

Left-hand door glass

Left-hand quarter glass

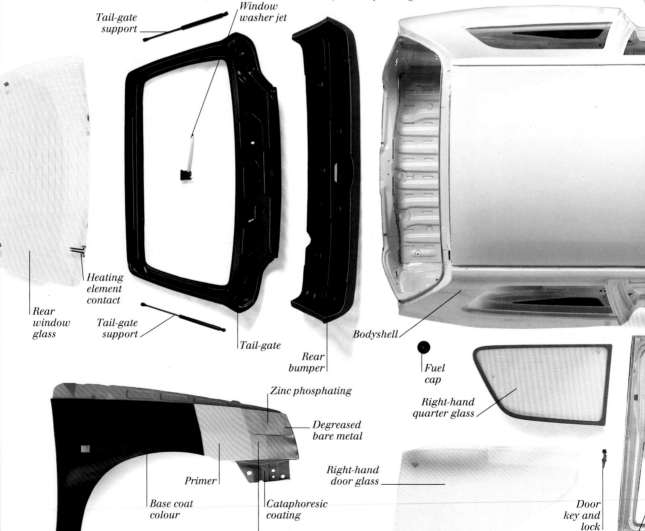

Tail-gate support

Window washer jet

Heating element contact

Rear window glass

Tail-gate support

Tail-gate

Rear bumper

Bodyshell

Fuel cap

Right-hand quarter glass

Zinc phosphating

Degreased bare metal

Primer

Base coat colour

Cataphoresic coating

Chrome passivation

Varnish

Right-hand door glass

Door key and lock

Door handle

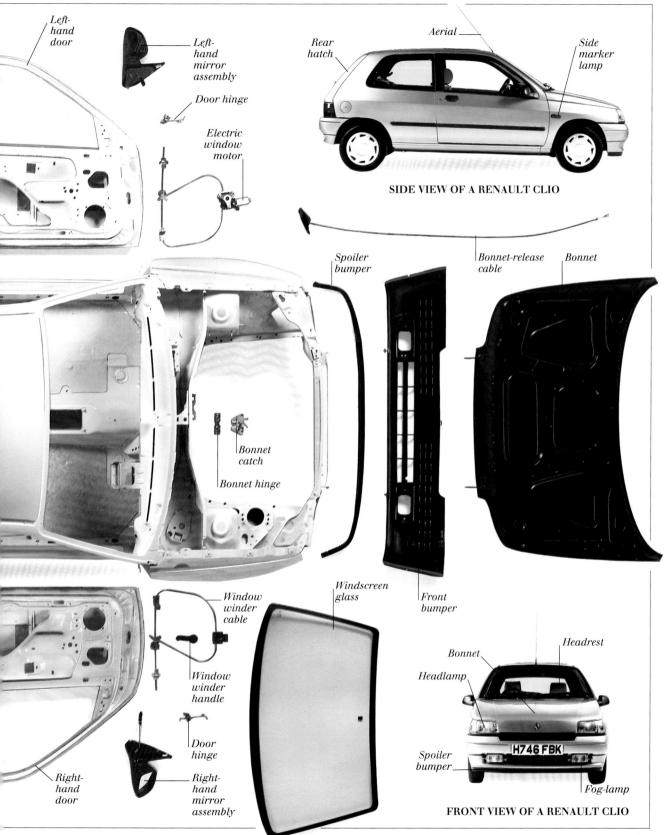

Left-hand door

Left-hand mirror assembly

Door hinge

Electric window motor

Aerial

Rear hatch

Side marker lamp

SIDE VIEW OF A RENAULT CLIO

Spoiler bumper

Bonnet-release cable

Bonnet

Bonnet catch

Bonnet hinge

Window winder cable

Windscreen glass

Front bumper

Window winder handle

Door hinge

Right-hand door

Right-hand mirror assembly

Headrest

Bonnet

Headlamp

H746 FBK

Spoiler bumper

Fog-lamp

FRONT VIEW OF A RENAULT CLIO

Modern mechanics

A TYPICAL MODERN CAR has several thousand individual mechanical components. These are assembled to form the car's various mechanical systems: engine and exhaust, transmission, steering, suspension, and brakes. To ensure that each system functions properly, components are manufactured to extremely fine tolerances – to within a five-hundredth of a millimetre (about one ten-thousandth of an inch) in some cases.

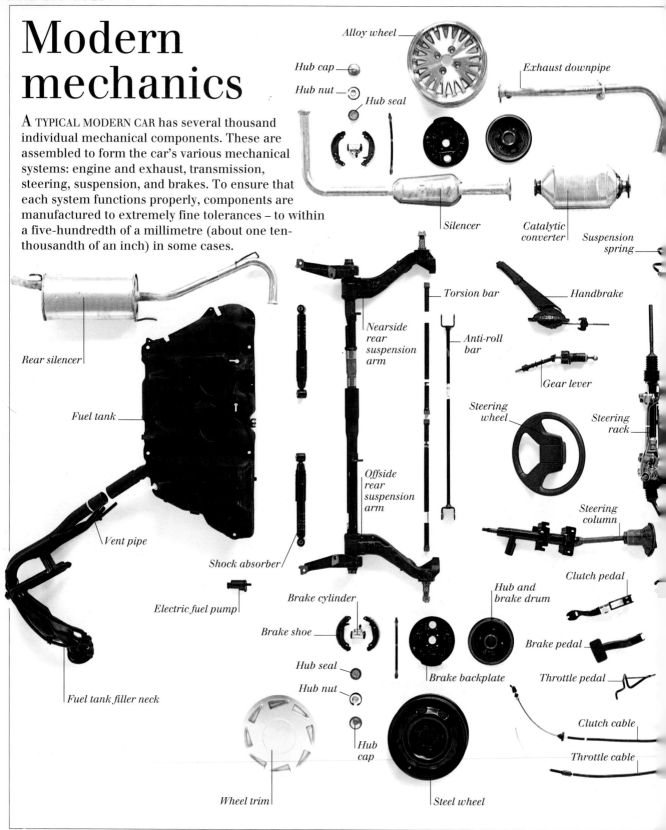

Alloy wheel

Hub cap

Hub nut

Hub seal

Exhaust downpipe

Silencer

Catalytic converter

Suspension spring

Rear silencer

Fuel tank

Vent pipe

Shock absorber

Electric fuel pump

Brake cylinder

Brake shoe

Hub seal

Hub nut

Hub cap

Fuel tank filler neck

Wheel trim

Nearside rear suspension arm

Offside rear suspension arm

Torsion bar

Anti-roll bar

Gear lever

Steering wheel

Handbrake

Steering rack

Steering column

Clutch pedal

Hub and brake drum

Brake pedal

Brake backplate

Throttle pedal

Clutch cable

Throttle cable

Steel wheel

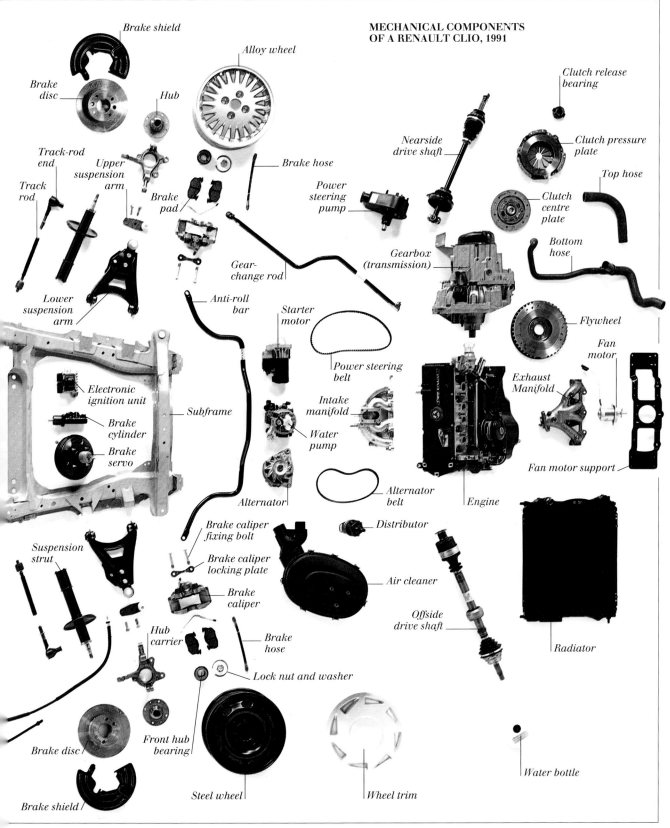

MECHANICAL COMPONENTS OF A RENAULT CLIO, 1991

Brake shield

Alloy wheel

Clutch release bearing

Brake disc

Hub

Nearside drive shaft

Clutch pressure plate

Track-rod end

Upper suspension arm

Brake hose

Top hose

Track rod

Brake pad

Power steering pump

Clutch centre plate

Bottom hose

Lower suspension arm

Gear-change rod

Gearbox (transmission)

Anti-roll bar

Starter motor

Flywheel

Fan motor

Power steering belt

Exhaust Manifold

Electronic ignition unit

Subframe

Intake manifold

Brake cylinder

Water pump

Fan motor support

Brake servo

Alternator

Alternator belt

Engine

Brake caliper fixing bolt

Distributor

Suspension strut

Brake caliper locking plate

Air cleaner

Brake caliper

Hub carrier

Brake hose

Offside drive shaft

Radiator

Lock nut and washer

Brake disc

Front hub bearing

Water bottle

Brake shield

Steel wheel

Wheel trim

Modern trim

A MODERN CAR HAS TWO TYPES OF TRIM, according to the materials used: hard (chrome and plastics) and soft (upholstery materials). Safety and comfort are priorities in the trim's design: seats help the occupants to maintain a comfortable posture, rubber seals keep out dirt and moisture, and headlamps light the way. Older cars had interior or leather panelling cut and fitted by craftsmen; modern cars use precisely moulded plastics and seat fabrics cut by robot-controlled lasers to reduce costs and production time. Doors are now trimmed off the production line so that complex wiring can be built in.

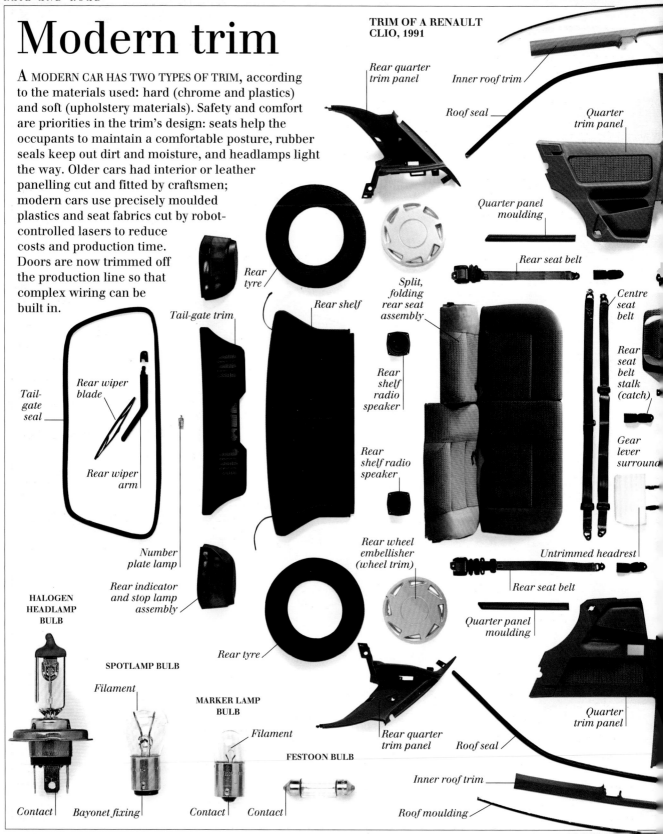

TRIM OF A RENAULT CLIO, 1991

Rear quarter trim panel

Inner roof trim

Roof seal

Quarter trim panel

Quarter panel moulding

Rear seat belt

Centre seat belt

Rear seat belt stalk (catch)

Rear tyre

Rear shelf

Split, folding rear seat assembly

Gear lever surround

Tail-gate trim

Rear shelf radio speaker

Rear wiper blade

Tail-gate seal

Rear shelf radio speaker

Rear wiper arm

Number plate lamp

Rear indicator and stop lamp assembly

Rear wheel embellisher (wheel trim)

Untrimmed headrest

Rear seat belt

Quarter panel moulding

HALOGEN HEADLAMP BULB

Rear tyre

SPOTLAMP BULB

Filament

MARKER LAMP BULB

Filament

FESTOON BULB

Rear quarter trim panel

Roof seal

Quarter trim panel

Inner roof trim

Contact

Bayonet fixing

Contact

Contact

Roof moulding

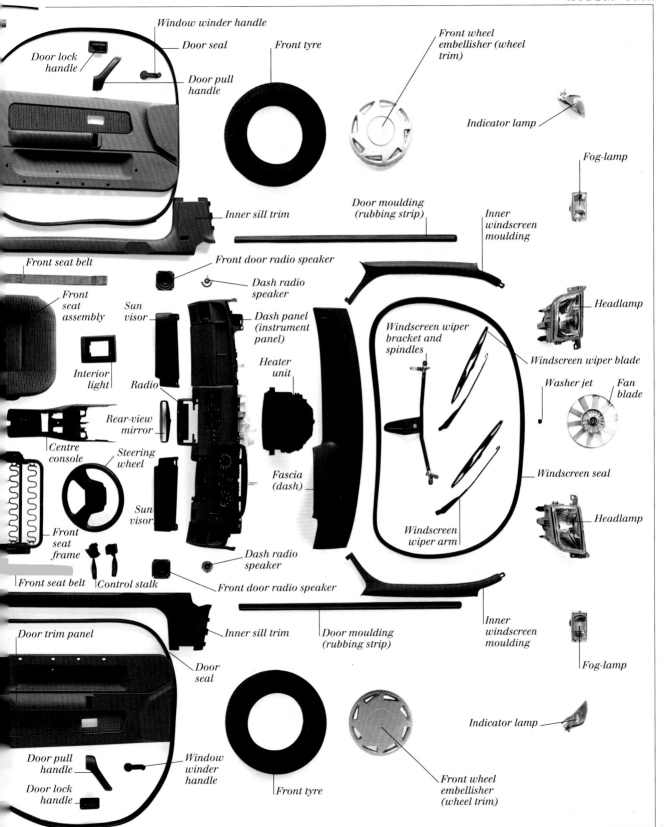

Window winder handle

Door seal

Front tyre

Front wheel embellisher (wheel trim)

Door lock handle

Door pull handle

Indicator lamp

Fog-lamp

Inner sill trim

Door moulding (rubbing strip)

Inner windscreen moulding

Front seat belt

Front door radio speaker

Front seat assembly

Dash radio speaker

Sun visor

Dash panel (instrument panel)

Headlamp

Heater unit

Windscreen wiper bracket and spindles

Windscreen wiper blade

Interior light

Washer jet

Fan blade

Radio

Rear-view mirror

Centre console

Steering wheel

Windscreen seal

Sun visor

Fascia (dash)

Windscreen wiper arm

Headlamp

Front seat frame

Dash radio speaker

Front seat belt

Control stalk

Front door radio speaker

Inner windscreen moulding

Door trim panel

Inner sill trim

Door moulding (rubbing strip)

Fog-lamp

Door seal

Door pull handle

Window winder handle

Door lock handle

Front tyre

Front wheel embellisher (wheel trim)

Indicator lamp

All-terrain vehicles

THE MODERN ALL-TERRAIN VEHICLE has its origins in the US military Jeep of the 1940s and the British Land Rover. Such vehicles have been used for a wide range of purposes, from safari travel to fire-fighting. The principal special features of such cars – including four- or six-wheel drive, high ground clearance, and toughened braking, suspension, and transmission systems – are designed to enable driving under the most difficult off-road conditions. The vehicle shown here is equipped for safari travel and carries a comprehensive range of survival apparatus.

COOKING EQUIPMENT

TWO-BURNER ALCOHOL STOVE

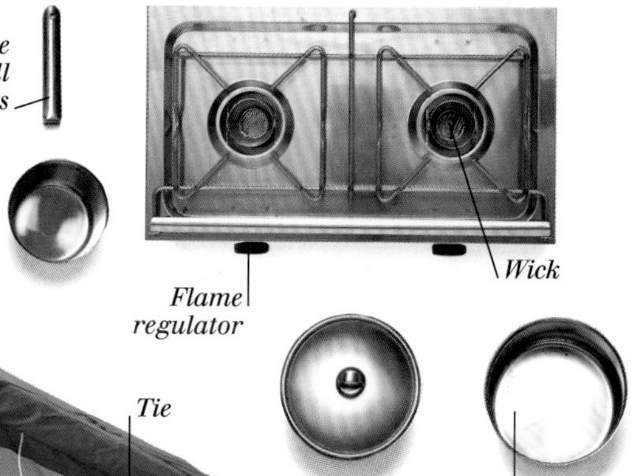

Handle for all pans

Flame regulator

Wick

Cooking pot

HAND WINCH

SIDE VIEW OF PINZGAUER TURBO D

Mosquito netting

Zip

Tie

Ventilation flap

Locking fuel filler cap

Raised air intake

Dust trap

Guard

Folding rooftop tent

Galvanized roof-rack

Steel body

Jerrycan

Spare wheel and tyre

Rubbing strip (rubbing strake)

TYRE PUMP

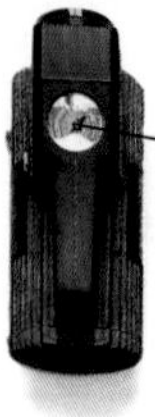

Pressure gauge

TYRE LEVER

Heavy-duty shovel

Tubular backbone chassis

Fuel tank

Metal jerrycan for fuel

Plastic jerrycan for water

LEFT-HAND TREAD PLATE

RIGHT-HAND TREAD PLATE

TOW STRAP

HEAVY-DUTY SHACKLE

SAFETY WINDSCREEN CLAMPS

WASHING BUCKET

Radio aerial

Observation roof hatch

Grab handle

Rear-view mirror

Windscreen washer bottle

Wrap-around bumper

Access step

SECURITY CHAIN

FRONT VIEW OF PINZGAUER TURBO D

Observation roof hatch

Radio aerial

Galvanized roof-rack

Laminated windscreen

Rear-view mirror

Air vent

Radiator grille

Indicator

Headlamp

Lamp guard

External step

Independent portal swing axle

Locking differential

Towing pintle

Off-road tyre

REAR VIEW OF PINZGAUER TURBO D

Roof-rack

Observation platform

External step for roof

Jerrycan

Jerrycan carrier

Spare wheel

Offset door hinge

Rubbing strip (rubbing strake)

Rear bumper

Rear lamp cluster

Door and wheel support frame

Mudflap

Off-road tyre

Locking differential

Independent portal swing axle

Racing cars

SINCE MOTORING BEGAN, racing cars have been a major focus of innovation in car design. Features that are now commonplace, such as disc brakes, turbochargers, and even safety belts, were used first on competition cars. Research into racing cars has contributed to a new understanding of engine performance, aerodynamics, and tyre adhesion, and has led to the development of ultra-light materials such as carbon-fibre for car bodies. Like the 1937 Bugatti Type 57S below, a modern Williams Formula One car has a low, streamlined body and an open cockpit, but, unlike its forerunner, it also has a front wing that pushes the front wheels firmly on to the track, huge slick tyres for extra grip, and electrical sensors that continually relay information to the pits about the car's performance.

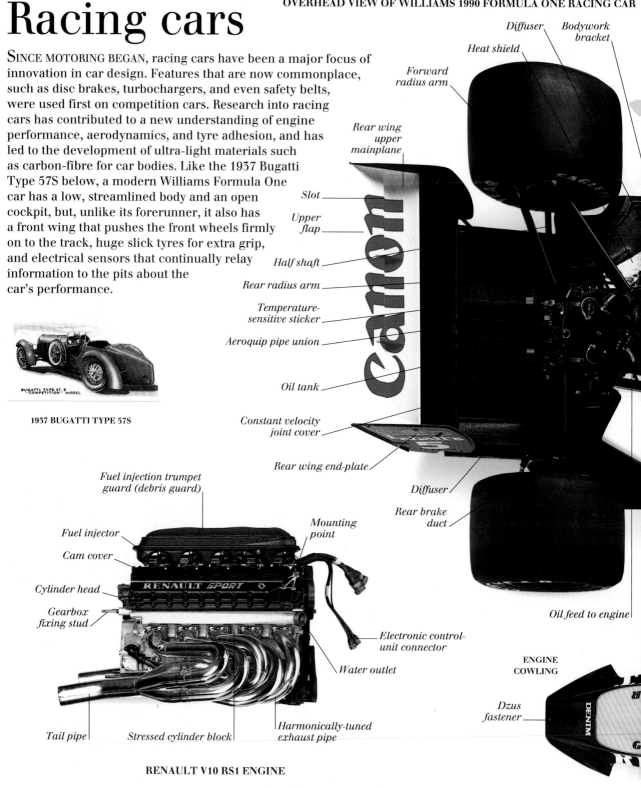

1937 BUGATTI TYPE 57S

Diffuser

Bodywork bracket

Heat shield

Forward radius arm

Rear wing upper mainplane

Slot

Upper flap

Half shaft

Rear radius arm

Temperature-sensitive sticker

Aeroquip pipe union

Oil tank

Constant velocity joint cover

Rear wing end-plate

Diffuser

Rear brake duct

Oil feed to engine

Fuel injection trumpet guard (debris guard)

Fuel injector

Cam cover

Cylinder head

Gearbox fixing stud

Mounting point

Electronic control-unit connector

Water outlet

Tail pipe

Stressed cylinder block

Harmonically-tuned exhaust pipe

ENGINE COWLING

Dzus fastener

RENAULT V10 RS1 ENGINE

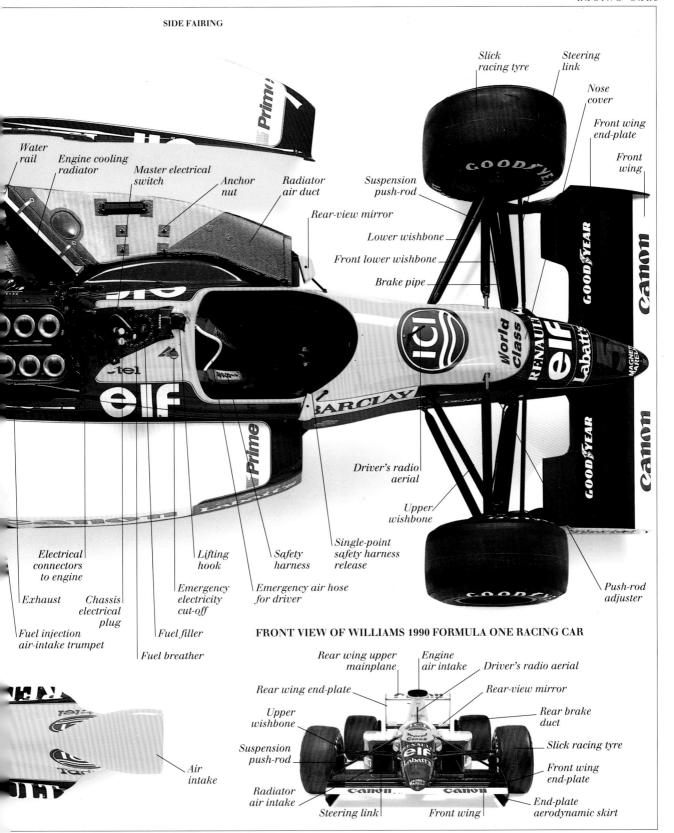

SIDE FAIRING

Water rail

Engine cooling radiator

Master electrical switch

Anchor nut

Radiator air duct

Rear-view mirror

Slick racing tyre

Steering link

Nose cover

Front wing end-plate

Front wing

Suspension push-rod

Lower wishbone

Front lower wishbone

Brake pipe

Driver's radio aerial

Upper wishbone

Push-rod adjuster

Electrical connectors to engine

Exhaust

Chassis electrical plug

Fuel injection air-intake trumpet

Lifting hook

Emergency electricity cut-off

Fuel filler

Fuel breather

Safety harness

Emergency air hose for driver

Single-point safety harness release

FRONT VIEW OF WILLIAMS 1990 FORMULA ONE RACING CAR

Air intake

Rear wing upper mainplane

Engine air intake

Driver's radio aerial

Rear wing end-plate

Rear-view mirror

Upper wishbone

Rear brake duct

Suspension push-rod

Slick racing tyre

Front wing end-plate

Radiator air intake

Steering link

Front wing

End-plate aerodynamic skirt

Bicycle anatomy

THE BICYCLE IS A TWO-WHEELED, light-weight machine, which is propelled by human power. It is efficient, cheap, easily manufactured, and one of the world's most popular forms of transport. The first pedal-driven bicycle was built in Scotland in 1839. Since then the basic design – of a frame, wheels, brakes, handlebars, and saddle – has been gradually improved, with the addition of a chain, gear system, and pneumatic tyres (tyres inflated with air). The recent invention of the mountain bike (all-terrain bike) has been an important development. With its strong, rugged frame, wide tyres, and 21 gears, a mountain bike enables riders to reach rough and hilly areas that were previously inaccessible to cyclists.

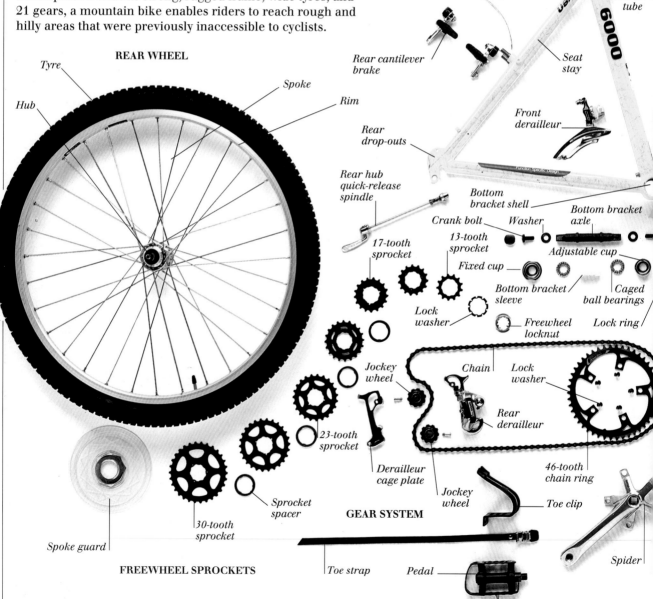

REAR WHEEL

Tyre

Hub

Spoke

Rim

Saddle

Seat post

Seat post quick-release bolt

Cable guide

Straddle wire

Seat tube

6000

Rear cantilever brake

Seat stay

Front derailleur

Rear drop-outs

Rear hub quick-release spindle

Bottom bracket shell

Crank bolt

Washer

Bottom bracket axle

17-tooth sprocket

13-tooth sprocket

Adjustable cup

Fixed cup

Bottom bracket sleeve

Caged ball bearings

Lock washer

Freewheel locknut

Lock ring

Jockey wheel

Chain

Lock washer

Rear derailleur

23-tooth sprocket

Derailleur cage plate

Jockey wheel

46-tooth chain ring

Toe clip

30-tooth sprocket

Sprocket spacer

GEAR SYSTEM

Spoke guard

FREEWHEEL SPROCKETS

Toe strap

Pedal

Spider

438

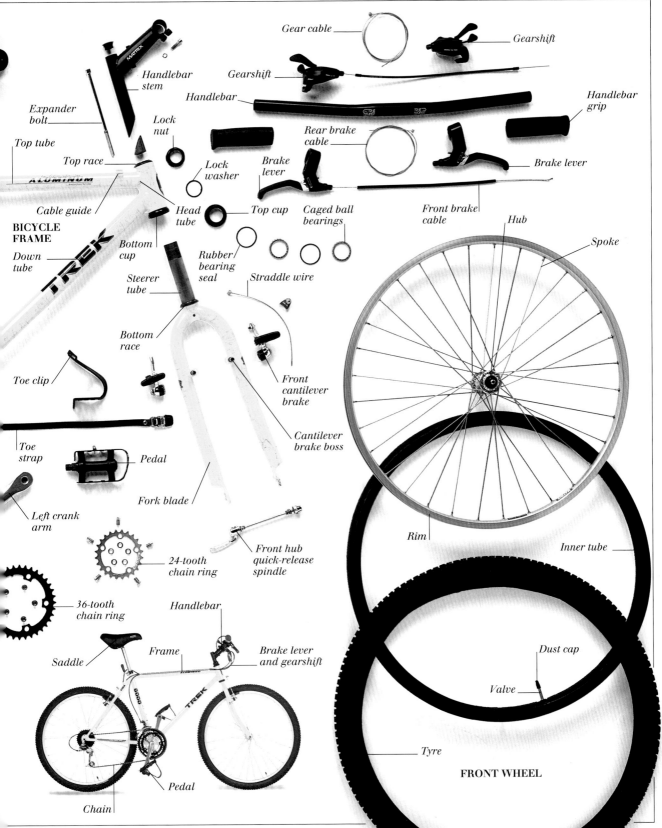

Gear cable

Gearshift

Handlebar
stem

Gearshift

Handlebar

Handlebar
grip

Expander
bolt

Lock
nut

Rear brake
cable

Top tube

Top race

Lock
washer

Brake
lever

Brake lever

Cable guide

Head
tube

Top cup

Caged ball
bearings

Front brake
cable

Hub

**BICYCLE
FRAME**

Spoke

Bottom
cup

Down
tube

Rubber
bearing
seal

Straddle wire

Steerer
tube

Bottom
race

Toe clip

Front
cantilever
brake

Cantilever
brake boss

Rim

Toe
strap

Inner tube

Pedal

Left crank
arm

Fork blade

24-tooth
chain ring

Front hub
quick-release
spindle

36-tooth
chain ring

Handlebar

Dust cap

Saddle

Frame

Brake lever
and gearshift

Valve

Tyre

Pedal

FRONT WHEEL

Chain

Bicycles

ALTHOUGH ALL BICYCLES are made up of the same
basic components, they can vary greatly in design. A
racing bike, such as the Eddy Merckx model, with its
light frame and steep head- and seat-angles, is built for
speed. Its design forces the rider to adopt the "aerotuck",
a crouched, aerodynamic position. While a touring bike
resembles the racing bike in many respects, it is designed
for comfort and stability on long-distance journeys.
Touring bikes are characterized by more relaxed frame
angles, heavy chain stays that support the rear panniers,
and a long wheelbase (the distance between the wheel
axles) for reliable handling. All-round bicycles, known
as "hybrids", combine the light weight and speed of sports
bikes with the rugged durability of mountain bikes (see
pp. 358-359). Bicycles that are not designed for conventional
road use include time-trial bikes, which have a short
head tube, sloping top tube, "aero" handlebars, and
aerodynamic tubing. Most Human Powered Vehicles
(HPVs) are recumbents – the rider has a recumbent
position – which maximize power output and minimize
drag (resistance). Essential to the safety of all
riders are helmets, and both front and rear
lights; locks protect against theft.

FRONT AND REAR LIGHTS

HELMET

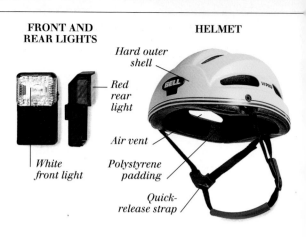

White front light

Red rear light

Hard outer shell

Air vent

Polystyrene padding

Quick-release strap

EDDY MERCKX RACING BICYCLE

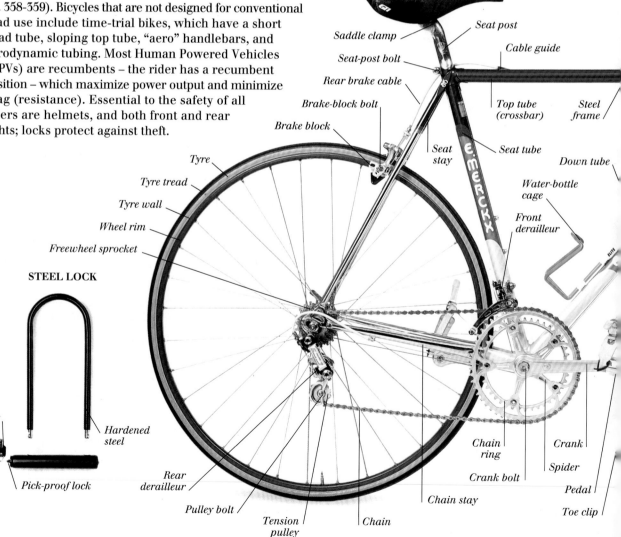

Saddle

Seat post

Cable guide

Saddle clamp

Seat-post bolt

Rear brake cable

Brake-block bolt

Brake block

Top tube (crossbar)

Steel frame

Seat stay

Seat tube

Down tube

Tyre

Tyre tread

Tyre wall

Wheel rim

Freewheel sprocket

Water-bottle cage

Front derailleur

STEEL LOCK

Key

Hardened steel

Pick-proof lock

Rear derailleur

Pulley bolt

Tension pulley

Chain

Chain stay

Chain ring

Crank bolt

Crank

Spider

Pedal

Toe clip

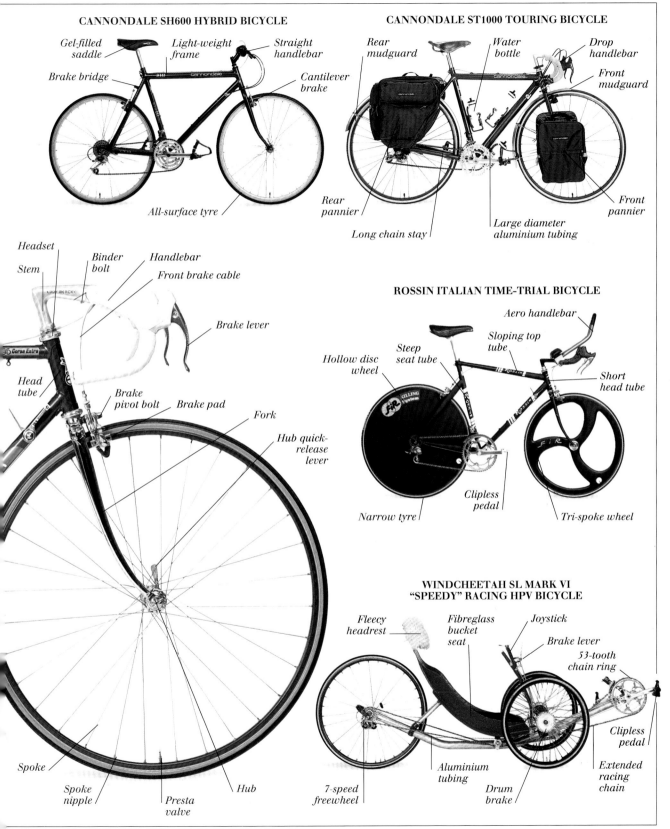

CANNONDALE SH600 HYBRID BICYCLE

Gel-filled saddle

Light-weight frame

Straight handlebar

Brake bridge

Cantilever brake

All-surface tyre

CANNONDALE ST1000 TOURING BICYCLE

Rear mudguard

Water bottle

Drop handlebar

Front mudguard

Rear pannier

Front pannier

Long chain stay

Large diameter aluminium tubing

Headset

Stem

Binder bolt

Handlebar

Front brake cable

Brake lever

Head tube

Brake pivot bolt

Brake pad

Fork

Hub quick-release lever

Spoke

Spoke nipple

Presta valve

Hub

ROSSIN ITALIAN TIME-TRIAL BICYCLE

Aero handlebar

Sloping top tube

Steep seat tube

Hollow disc wheel

Short head tube

Clipless pedal

Narrow tyre

Tri-spoke wheel

WINDCHEETAH SL MARK VI "SPEEDY" RACING HPV BICYCLE

Fleecy headrest

Fibreglass bucket seat

Joystick

Brake lever

53-tooth chain ring

Clipless pedal

7-speed freewheel

Aluminium tubing

Drum brake

Extended racing chain

The motorcycle

THE MOTORCYCLE HAS EVOLVED from a motorized cycle – a basic bicycle with an engine – into a sophisticated, high-performance machine. In 1901, the Werner brothers established the most viable location for the engine by positioning it low in the centre of the chassis (see pp. 364-365): the new Werner became the basis for the modern motorcycle. Motorcycles are used for many purposes – for commuting, delivering messages, touring, and racing – and different machines have been developed according to the demands of different types of riders. The Vespa scooter, for instance, which is small-wheeled, economical, and easy-to-ride, was designed to meet the needs of the commuter. Sidecars provided transport for the family until the arrival of cheap cars caused their popularity to decline. Enthusiast riders generally favour larger capacity machines that are capable of greater performance and offer more comfort. Four-cylinder machines have been common since the Honda CB750 appeared in 1969. Despite advances in motorcycle technology, many riders are attracted to the traditional looks of motorcycles like the twin-cylinder Harley-Davidson. The Harley-Davidson Glides exploit the style of the classic American V-twin engine, where the cylinders are placed in a V-formation.

1901 WERNER MOTORCYCLE

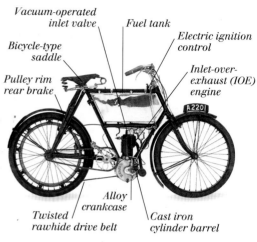

Vacuum-operated inlet valve
Fuel tank
Bicycle-type saddle
Electric ignition control
Pulley rim rear brake
Inlet-over-exhaust (IOE) engine
Alloy crankcase
Cast iron cylinder barrel
Twisted rawhide drive belt

1988 HARLEY-DAVIDSON FLHS ELECTRA GLIDE

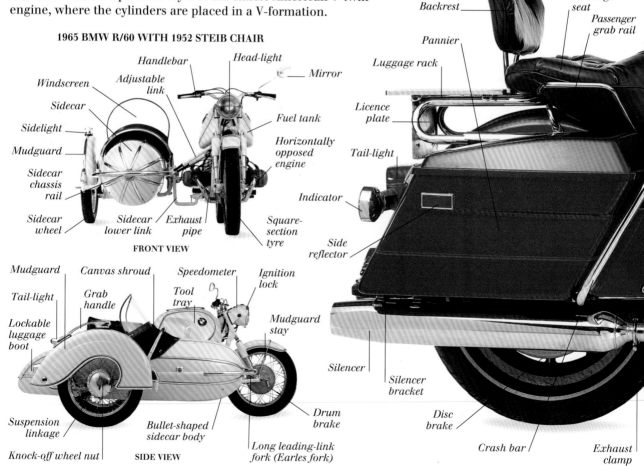

1965 BMW R/60 WITH 1952 STEIB CHAIR

Handlebar
Head-light
Windscreen
Adjustable link
Mirror
Sidecar
Sidelight
Fuel tank
Mudguard
Horizontally opposed engine
Sidecar chassis rail
Sidecar wheel
Sidecar lower link
Exhaust pipe
Square-section tyre
FRONT VIEW

Backrest
Passenger seat
Passenger grab rail
Pannier
Luggage rack
Licence plate
Tail-light
Indicator
Side reflector

Mudguard
Canvas shroud
Speedometer
Ignition lock
Tail-light
Grab handle
Tool tray
Lockable luggage boot
Mudguard stay
Silencer
Silencer bracket
Suspension linkage
Bullet-shaped sidecar body
Drum brake
Disc brake
Knock-off wheel nut
SIDE VIEW
Long leading-link fork (Earles fork)
Crash bar
Exhaust clamp

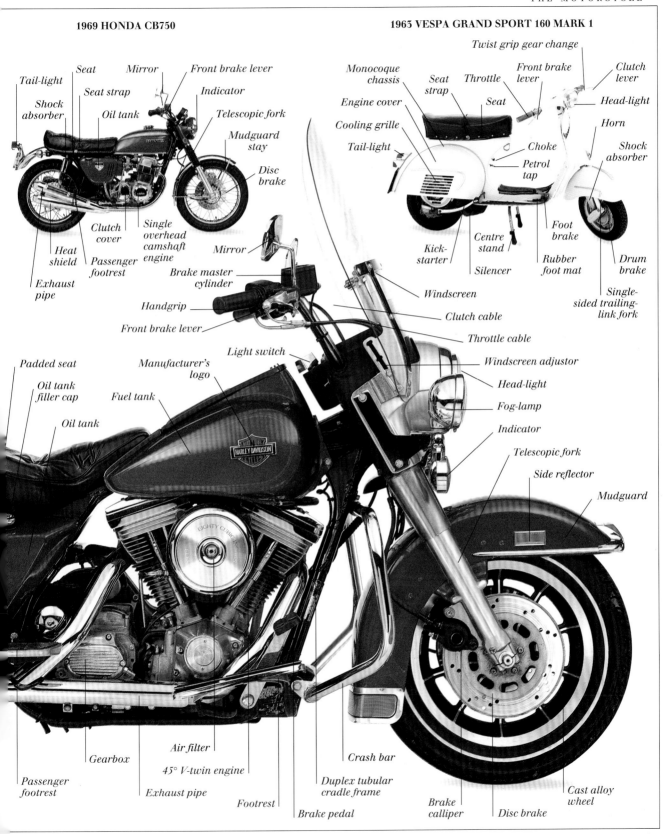

1969 HONDA CB750

1963 VESPA GRAND SPORT 160 MARK 1

Tail-light

Seat

Mirror

Front brake lever

Shock absorber

Seat strap

Indicator

Oil tank

Telescopic fork

Mudguard stay

Disc brake

Clutch cover

Single overhead camshaft engine

Heat shield

Passenger footrest

Exhaust pipe

Monocoque chassis

Twist grip gear change

Engine cover

Seat strap

Throttle

Front brake lever

Clutch lever

Cooling grille

Seat

Head-light

Tail-light

Horn

Choke

Shock absorber

Petrol tap

Kick-starter

Centre stand

Foot brake

Silencer

Rubber foot mat

Drum brake

Single-sided trailing-link fork

Mirror

Brake master cylinder

Handgrip

Front brake lever

Windscreen

Clutch cable

Throttle cable

Light switch

Windscreen adjustor

Head-light

Fog-lamp

Indicator

Padded seat

Manufacturer's logo

Oil tank filler cap

Fuel tank

Oil tank

Telescopic fork

Side reflector

Mudguard

HARLEY-DAVIDSON

EIGHTY CUBIC

Passenger footrest

Gearbox

Air filter

45° V-twin engine

Exhaust pipe

Footrest

Crash bar

Duplex tubular cradle frame

Brake pedal

Brake calliper

Disc brake

Cast alloy wheel

The motorcycle chassis

THE MOTORCYCLE CHASSIS is the main "body" of the motorcycle, to which the engine is attached. Consisting of the frame, wheels, suspension, and brakes, the chassis performs various functions. The frame, which is built from steel or alloy, keeps the wheels in line to maintain the handling of the motorcycle, and serves as a structure for mounting other components. The engine and gearbox unit is bolted into place, while items such as the seat, the mudguards, and the fairing are more easily removable. Suspension cushions the rider from irregularities in the road surface. In most suspension systems, coil springs controlled by an oil damper separate the main mass of the motorcycle from the wheels. At the front, the spring and damper are usually incorporated in a telescopic fork; the rear employs a pivoted swingarm. The suspension also helps to retain maximum contact between the tyres and the road, necessary to effective braking and steering. Drum brakes were common until the 1970s, but modern motorcycles use disc brakes, which are more powerful.

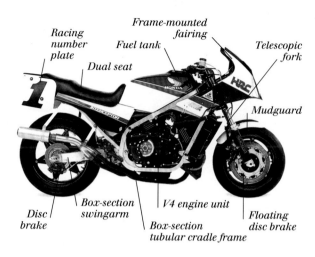

1985 HONDA VF750 WITH BODYWORK

Racing number plate · Dual seat · Fuel tank · Frame-mounted fairing · Telescopic fork · Mudguard · Disc brake · Box-section swingarm · V4 engine unit · Box-section tubular cradle frame · Floating disc brake

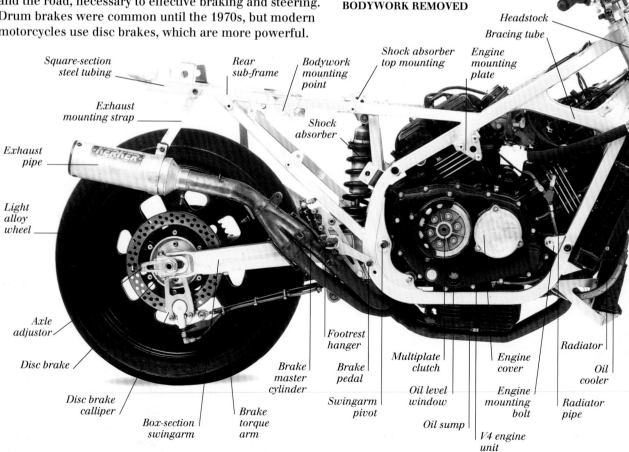

1985 HONDA VF750 WITH BODYWORK REMOVED

Brake master cylinder · Headstock · Bracing tube · Square-section steel tubing · Rear sub-frame · Bodywork mounting point · Shock absorber top mounting · Engine mounting plate · Exhaust mounting strap · Shock absorber · Exhaust pipe · Light alloy wheel · Axle adjustor · Disc brake · Disc brake calliper · Box-section swingarm · Brake torque arm · Brake master cylinder · Brake pedal · Footrest hanger · Swingarm pivot · Multiplate clutch · Oil level window · Oil sump · Engine cover · Engine mounting bolt · V4 engine unit · Radiator · Oil cooler · Radiator pipe

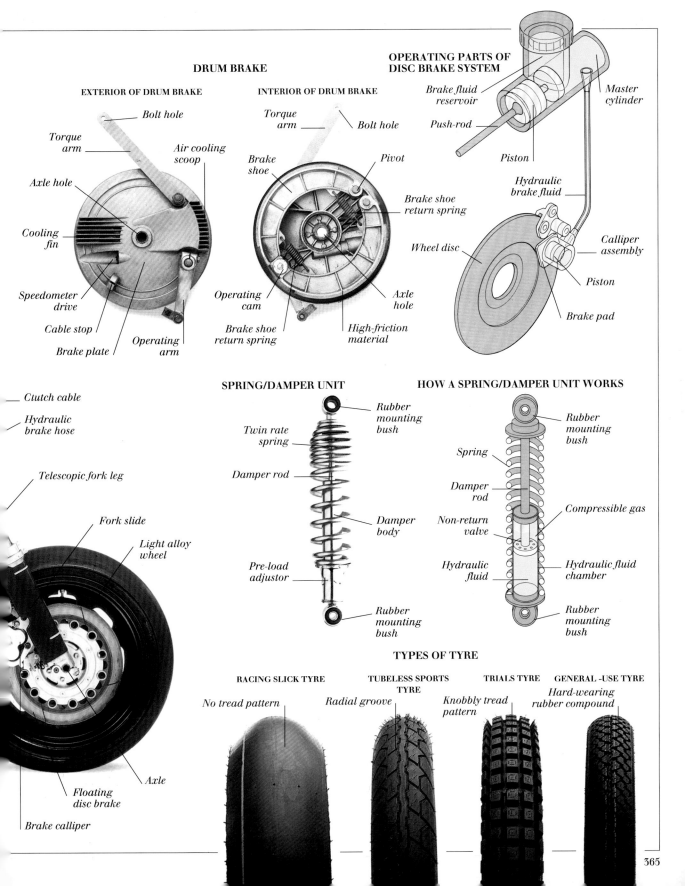

DRUM BRAKE

OPERATING PARTS OF DISC BRAKE SYSTEM

EXTERIOR OF DRUM BRAKE

Bolt hole

Torque arm

Air cooling scoop

Axle hole

Cooling fin

Speedometer drive

Cable stop

Brake plate

Operating arm

INTERIOR OF DRUM BRAKE

Torque arm

Bolt hole

Brake shoe

Pivot

Brake shoe return spring

Operating cam

Axle hole

Brake shoe return spring

High-friction material

Brake fluid reservoir

Master cylinder

Push-rod

Piston

Hydraulic brake fluid

Wheel disc

Calliper assembly

Piston

Brake pad

Clutch cable

Hydraulic brake hose

Telescopic fork leg

Fork slide

Light alloy wheel

Axle

Floating disc brake

Brake calliper

SPRING/DAMPER UNIT

Rubber mounting bush

Twin rate spring

Damper rod

Damper body

Pre-load adjustor

Rubber mounting bush

HOW A SPRING/DAMPER UNIT WORKS

Rubber mounting bush

Spring

Damper rod

Non-return valve

Hydraulic fluid

Compressible gas

Hydraulic fluid chamber

Rubber mounting bush

TYPES OF TYRE

RACING SLICK TYRE

No tread pattern

TUBELESS SPORTS TYRE

Radial groove

TRIALS TYRE

Knobbly tread pattern

GENERAL -USE TYRE

Hard-wearing rubber compound

Motorcycle engines

MOTORCYCLE ENGINES must be light-weight and compact, and have a good power output. They have between one and six cylinders, can be cooled by air or water, and the capacity of the combustion chamber varies from 49cc (cubic centimetres) to 1500cc. Two types of internal combustion engine are common: the four-stroke, which is used in cars (see pp. 342-343), and the two-stroke. A basic two-stroke engine has only three moving parts – the crankshaft, the connecting rod, and the piston – but the power output is high. The engine fires every two strokes (rather than every four), giving a "power stroke" every revolution (see p. 343). Power is conveyed from the engine to the rear wheel by the transmission system. This usually consists of a clutch, a gearbox, and a final drive system. Clutches are multiplate devices, which run in oil. Gearboxes have five or six speeds and are operated by foot pedal. Shaft and belt drive systems are used in some cases, but chain drive to the rear wheel is most common.

EXTERIOR OF STANDARD TWO-STROKE ENGINE

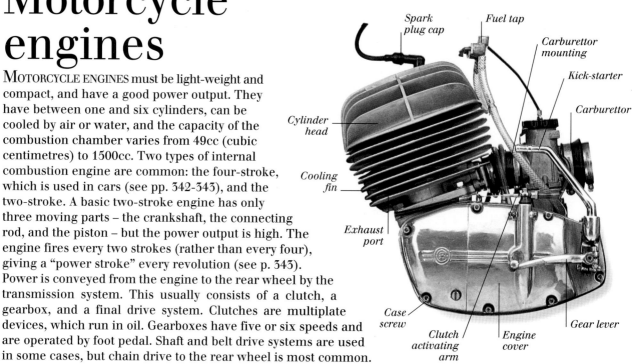

Spark plug cap
Fuel tap
Carburettor mounting
Kick-starter
Carburettor
Cylinder head
Cooling fin
Exhaust port
Case screw
Clutch activating arm
Engine cover
Gear lever

TRANSMISSION SYSTEM

GEARBOX

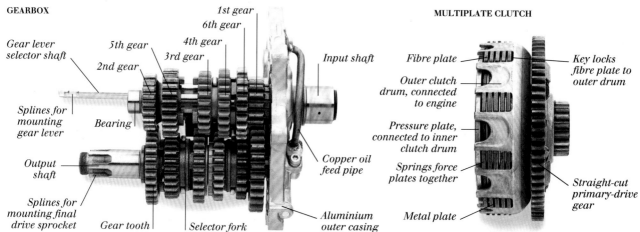

Gear lever selector shaft
5th gear
2nd gear
1st gear
6th gear
4th gear
3rd gear
Input shaft
Splines for mounting gear lever
Bearing
Output shaft
Splines for mounting final drive sprocket
Gear tooth
Selector fork
Copper oil feed pipe
Aluminium outer casing

MULTIPLATE CLUTCH

Fibre plate
Outer clutch drum, connected to engine
Pressure plate, connected to inner clutch drum
Springs force plates together
Metal plate
Key locks fibre plate to outer drum
Straight-cut primary-drive gear

MODERN "O RING" DRIVE CHAIN

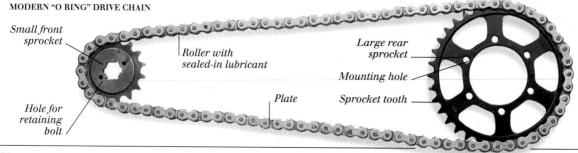

Small front sprocket
Roller with sealed-in lubricant
Large rear sprocket
Mounting hole
Hole for retaining bolt
Plate
Sprocket tooth

**VELOCETTE OVERHEAD
VALVE (OHV) ENGINE**

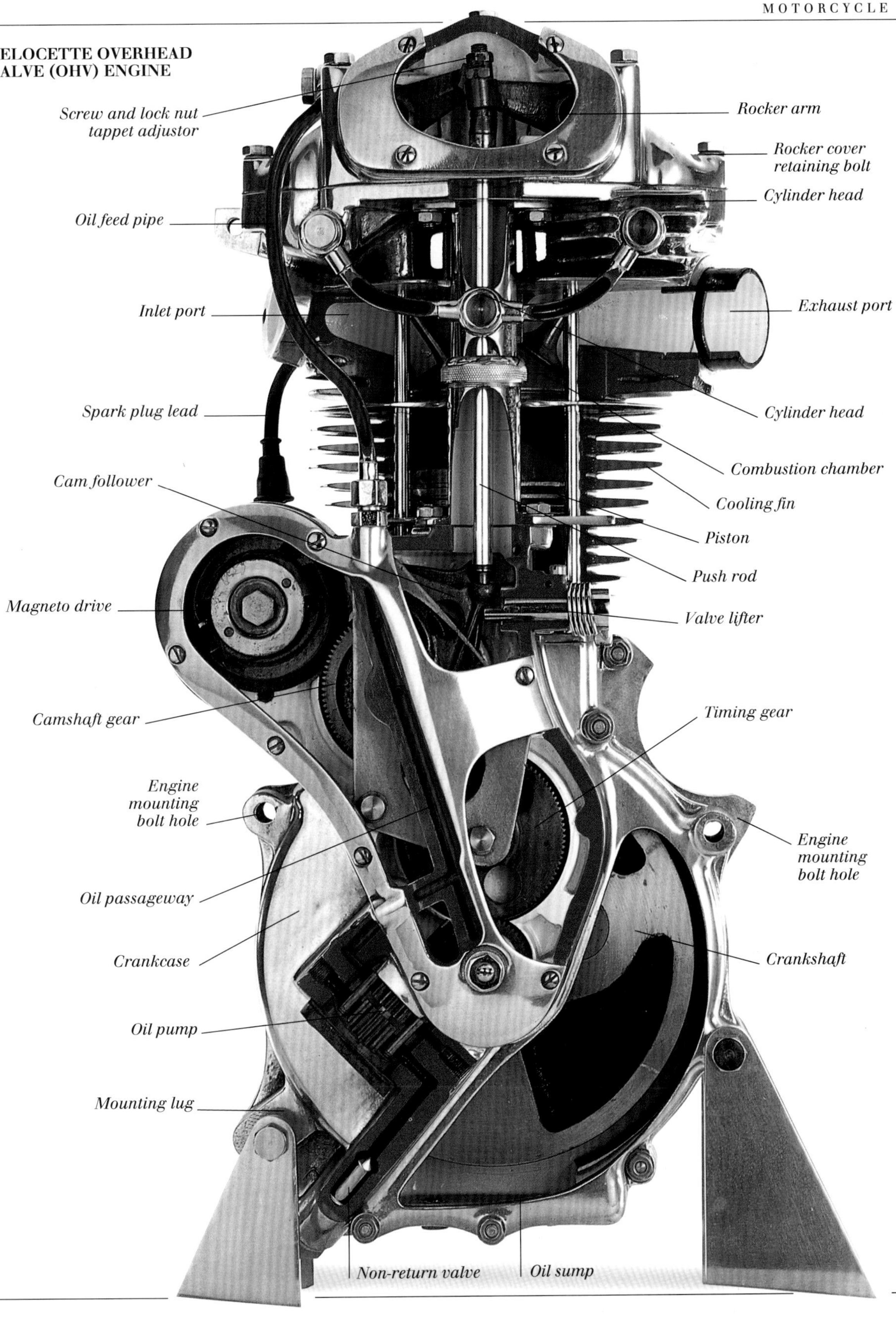

Screw and lock nut
tappet adjustor

Oil feed pipe

Inlet port

Spark plug lead

Cam follower

Magneto drive

Camshaft gear

Engine
mounting
bolt hole

Oil passageway

Crankcase

Oil pump

Mounting lug

Rocker arm

Rocker cover
retaining bolt

Cylinder head

Exhaust port

Cylinder head

Combustion chamber

Cooling fin

Piston

Push rod

Valve lifter

Timing gear

Engine
mounting
bolt hole

Crankshaft

Non-return valve

Oil sump

Competition motorcycles

THERE ARE MANY TYPES of motorcycle sport and in each, a specialist machine has evolved to perform to specific requirements. Races take place on roads or tracks or "off-road", in fields, dirt tracks, and even the desert. "Grand Prix" world championships in road-racing exist for 125cc, 250cc, and 500cc classes, as well as for sidecars. The latest racing sidecars have more in common with racing cars than motorcycles. The rider and passenger operate within an all-enclosing, aerodynamic fairing. The Suzuki RGV500 shown here, like other Grand Prix machines, carries advertising, which promotes the manufacturer and helps to cover the cost of developing motorcycle technology. In Speedway, which originated in the US in 1902, motorcycles operate without brakes or a gearbox. Off-road competition motorcycles have less emphasis on high power output. In Motocross, for example, which is held on rough terrain, they must have high ground clearance, flexible long-travel suspension, and tyres with a chunky tread pattern, to allow them to grip in sand or mud.

1992 HUSQVARNA MOTOCROSS TC610

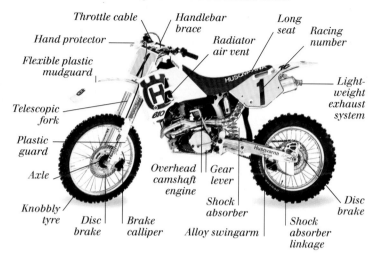

Throttle cable
Handlebar brace
Long seat
Racing number
Hand protector
Radiator air vent
Flexible plastic mudguard
Light-weight exhaust system
Telescopic fork
Plastic guard
Axle
Overhead camshaft engine
Gear lever
Disc brake
Knobbly tyre
Disc brake
Brake calliper
Shock absorber
Alloy swingarm
Shock absorber linkage

1992 SUZUKI RGV500
SIDE VIEW

Exhaust pipe
Racing number
Air vent
One-piece seat and tail unit
Shock absorber
Minimal seat padding
Arched alloy swingarm

Exhaust pipe
Vent
Handlebar
Silencer
Footrest
Shock absorber mounting
Rear brake pedal
Three-spoke alloy wheel
Drive chain
Exhaust pipe
Wide, slick tyre
Axle adjustor

REAR VIEW

Exhaust pipe
Brake pedal
Disc brake master cylinder
Footrest
Disc brake
Drive chain
Rear brake calliper
Slick racing tyre
Light-weight alloy frame

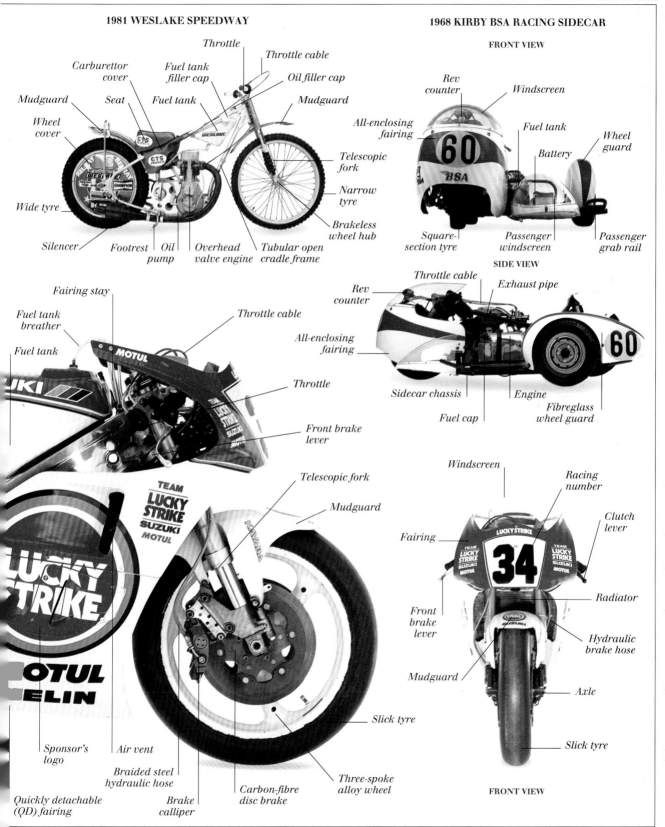

1981 WESLAKE SPEEDWAY

Throttle

Carburettor cover

Fuel tank filler cap

Throttle cable

Oil filler cap

Mudguard

Seat

Fuel tank

Mudguard

Wheel cover

Telescopic fork

Narrow tyre

Wide tyre

Brakeless wheel hub

Silencer

Footrest

Oil pump

Overhead valve engine

Tubular open cradle frame

Fairing stay

Fuel tank breather

Throttle cable

Fuel tank

Throttle

Front brake lever

Telescopic fork

Mudguard

Sponsor's logo

Air vent

Braided steel hydraulic hose

Brake calliper

Carbon-fibre disc brake

Three-spoke alloy wheel

Slick tyre

Quickly detachable (QD) fairing

1968 KIRBY BSA RACING SIDECAR

FRONT VIEW

Rev counter

Windscreen

All-enclosing fairing

Fuel tank

Battery

Wheel guard

60

BSA

Square-section tyre

Passenger windscreen

Passenger grab rail

SIDE VIEW

Throttle cable

Exhaust pipe

Rev counter

All-enclosing fairing

60

Sidecar chassis

Fuel cap

Engine

Fibreglass wheel guard

Windscreen

Racing number

Clutch lever

Fairing

34

Radiator

Front brake lever

Hydraulic brake hose

Mudguard

Axle

Slick tyre

FRONT VIEW

369

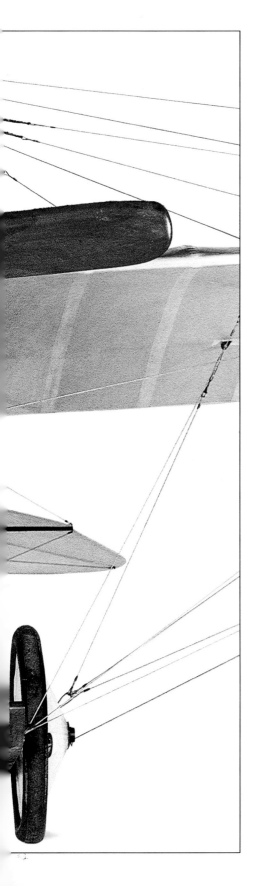

Sea and Air

Ships of Greece and Rome

ROMAN ANCHOR

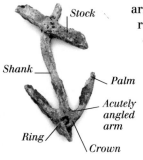

Stock

Shank

Palm

Acutely
angled
arm

Ring

Crown

IN THE EXPANSIVE EMPIRES OF GREECE AND ROME, powerful fleets were needed for battle, trade, and communication. Greek galleys were powered by a sail and many oars. A new armament, the embolos (ram), was fitted on to the galley bow. As ramming duels required fast and manoeuvrable boats, extra rows of oarsmen were added, culminating in the trireme. During the fifth and fourth centuries B.C., the trireme dominated the Mediterranean. It was powered by 170 oarsmen, rowing with one oar each. The oarsmen were ranged on three levels, as the model opposite shows. The trireme also carried archers and soldiers for boarding. Galleys were pulled out of the water when not in use, and were kept in dockyard ship-sheds. The merchant ships of the Greeks and Romans were mighty vessels too. The full-bodied Roman corbita, for example, could hold up to 400 tons and carried a cargo of spices, gems, silk, and animals. The construction of these boats was based on a stout hull with planking secured by mortice and tenon. Some of these ships embarked on long voyages, sailing even as far as India. To make them easier to steer, corbitas set a fore sail called an "artemon". It flew from a forward-leaning mast that was a forerunner of the long bowsprits carried by the great clipper ships of the 19th century.

ATTIC VASE SHOWING A GALLEY

Double halyard   **ROMAN CORBITA**

Bullseye

Antenna
(yard)

Fore mast

Buntline

Brace

Fore stay

Artemon
(fore sail)

Oculus
(eye)

Tabling

Bolt rope

Prow

Windlass

Roband
(rope band)

Ceruchi
(lift)

Heraldic device

Ring

Ruden
(brail line)

Anchor

Sheet

Bronze mast
truck

Keraia (yard)

Kalos
(brailing
rope)

Mast

Embolos
(ram;
beak)

Ophthalmos
(eye)

Kope (oar)

Kubernetes
(helmsman)

Sternpost

Pedalia
(twin rudder)

Oar port sleeve

Scala
(ladder)

Catena
(riding bitt)

Ancorale
(anchor rope;
anchor rode)

Hatch board

Deck beam

Zosteres (rubbing strake)

Cargo hold

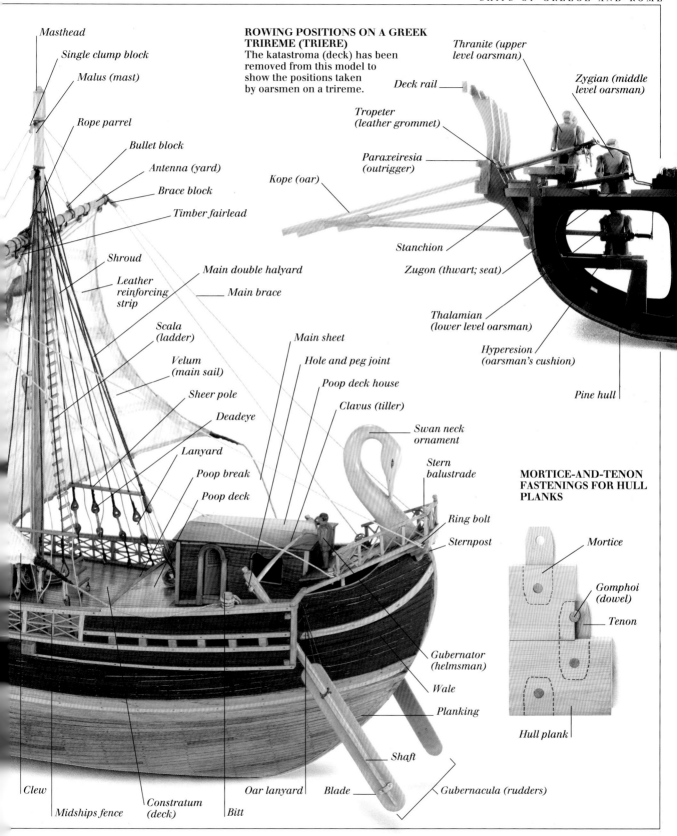

Masthead

Single clump block

Malus (mast)

Rope parrel

Bullet block

Antenna (yard)

Brace block

Timber fairlead

Shroud

Leather reinforcing strip

Scala (ladder)

Velum (main sail)

Sheer pole

Deadeye

Lanyard

Poop break

Poop deck

Clew

Midships fence

Constratum (deck)

Bitt

ROWING POSITIONS ON A GREEK TRIREME (TRIERE)
The katastroma (deck) has been removed from this model to show the positions taken by oarsmen on a trireme.

Deck rail

Thranite (upper level oarsman)

Zygian (middle level oarsman)

Tropeter (leather grommet)

Paraxeiresia (outrigger)

Kope (oar)

Stanchion

Zugon (thwart; seat)

Thalamian (lower level oarsman)

Hyperesion (oarsman's cushion)

Pine hull

Main double halyard

Main brace

Main sheet

Hole and peg joint

Poop deck house

Clavus (tiller)

Swan neck ornament

Stern balustrade

Ring bolt

Sternpost

Gubernator (helmsman)

Wale

Planking

Shaft

Blade

Oar lanyard

Gubernacula (rudders)

MORTICE-AND-TENON FASTENINGS FOR HULL PLANKS

Mortice

Gomphoi (dowel)

Tenon

Hull plank

Viking ships

IN THE DARK AGES and early medieval times, the longships of Scandinavia were one of the most feared sights for people of northern Europe. The Vikings launched raids from Scandinavia every summer in longships equipped with a single steering oar on the right, or "steerboard", side (hence "starboard"). A longship had one row of oars on each side and a single sail. The hull had clinker (overlapping) planks. Prowheads adorned fighting ships during campaigns of war. The sailing longship was also used for local coastal travel. The karv below was probably built as transport for an important family, while the smaller faering (top right) was a rowing boat only. The fleet of William of Normandy that invaded England in 1066 owed much to the Viking boatbuilding tradition, and has been depicted in the Bayeux Tapestry (above). Seals used by port towns and royal courts through the ages provide an excellent record of contemporary ship design. The seal opposite shows how ships changed from the Viking period to the end of the Middle Ages. The introduction of the fighting platform – the castle – and the addition of extra masts and sails changed the character of the medieval ship. Note also that the steering oar has been replaced by a centred rudder.

BOATBUILDERS' TOOLS

Shave

Broad axe

Breast auger

Sheer

Master shipwright

Stempost

Hood end

Keel

T-handle auger

Axe

Strake

Tree cut for planking

Roband

Leather diagonal reinforcement

Square sail of homespun yarn

Leech (leach)

Zoomorphic head

Eye

Tooth

Braiding

Serpentine neck

Lozenge-shaped recess

Rectangular cross-band

Snake-tail ornament

VIKING KARV (COASTER)

Tye halyard

Foot

Sternpost

Tiller

Boss (rudder pivot)

DRAGON PROWHEAD

Steering oar (side rudder)

Oar

Starboard (steerboard) side

Keel

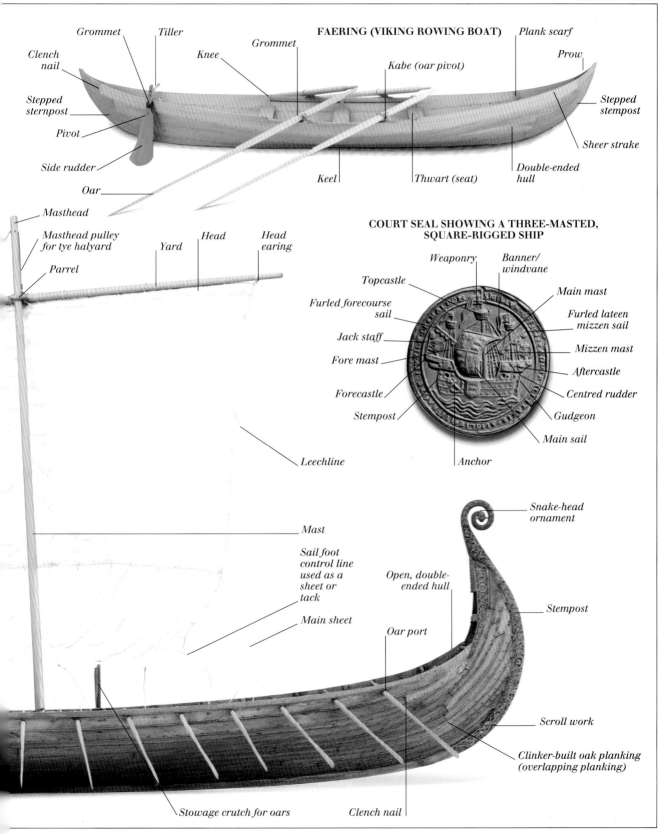

FAERING (VIKING ROWING BOAT)

Grommet

Tiller

Knee

Grommet

Kabe (oar pivot)

Plank scarf

Prow

Clench nail

Stepped sternpost

Pivot

Side rudder

Oar

Stepped stempost

Sheer strake

Double-ended hull

Keel

Thwart (seat)

Masthead

Masthead pulley for tye halyard

Yard

Head

Head earing

Parrel

COURT SEAL SHOWING A THREE-MASTED, SQUARE-RIGGED SHIP

Weaponry

Banner/ windvane

Topcastle

Main mast

Furled forecourse sail

Jack staff

Fore mast

Furled lateen mizzen sail

Mizzen mast

Aftercastle

Forecastle

Centred rudder

Stempost

Gudgeon

Main sail

Leechline

Anchor

Mast

Snake-head ornament

Sail foot control line used as a sheet or tack

Open, double-ended hull

Stempost

Main sheet

Oar port

Scroll work

Clinker-built oak planking (overlapping planking)

Stowage crutch for oars

Clench nail

Medieval warships and traders

FROM THE 16TH CENTURY, SHIPS WERE BUILT WITH A NEW FORM OF HULL, constructed from carvel (edge-to-edge) planking. Warships of the time, like King Henry VIII of England's Mary Rose, boasted awesome fire power. This ship carried both long-range cannon in bronze, and short-range, anti-personnel guns in iron. Elsewhere, ships took on a multiformity of shapes. Dhows transported slaves from East Africa to Arabia, their fore-and-aft rigged lateen sails allowing them to sail close to the wind around the lands of the Indian Ocean. The Chinese sailed to East Africa and Arabia in junks, trading goods that were carried in watertight compartments. New astronomical tools helped medieval sailors to find their way. Cross-staves and astrolabes were used to measure the altitude of the sun or stars. One of a choice of four cross-pieces was slid up or down the staff of the cross-stave – which was graduated in degrees of altitude – until its top aligned with the celestial body and its base with the horizon. The sighting rule of the astrolabe was simply lined up with a known body, and its altitude read from marks on the metal disc. With sundials, the sailor could use the shadow of the sun to show the time of day.

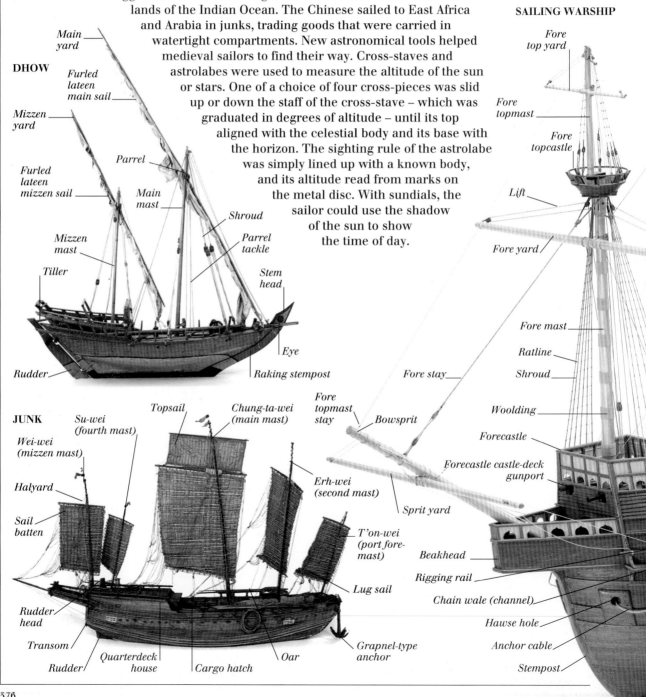

DHOW

Main yard
Furled lateen main sail
Mizzen yard
Furled lateen mizzen sail
Parrel
Main mast
Mizzen mast
Shroud
Parrel tackle
Tiller
Stem head
Rudder
Eye
Raking stempost

JUNK

Su-wei (fourth mast)
Wei-wei (mizzen mast)
Halyard
Sail batten
Topsail
Chung-ta-wei (main mast)
Erh-wei (second mast)
T'on-wei (port fore-mast)
Lug sail
Rudder head
Transom
Quarterdeck house
Rudder
Cargo hatch
Oar
Grapnel-type anchor

SAILING WARSHIP

Fore top yard
Fore topmast
Fore topcastle
Lift
Fore yard
Fore mast
Ratline
Shroud
Fore stay
Fore topmast stay
Bowsprit
Sprit yard
Woolding
Forecastle
Forecastle castle-deck gunport
Beakhead
Rigging rail
Chain wale (channel)
Hawse hole
Anchor cable
Stempost

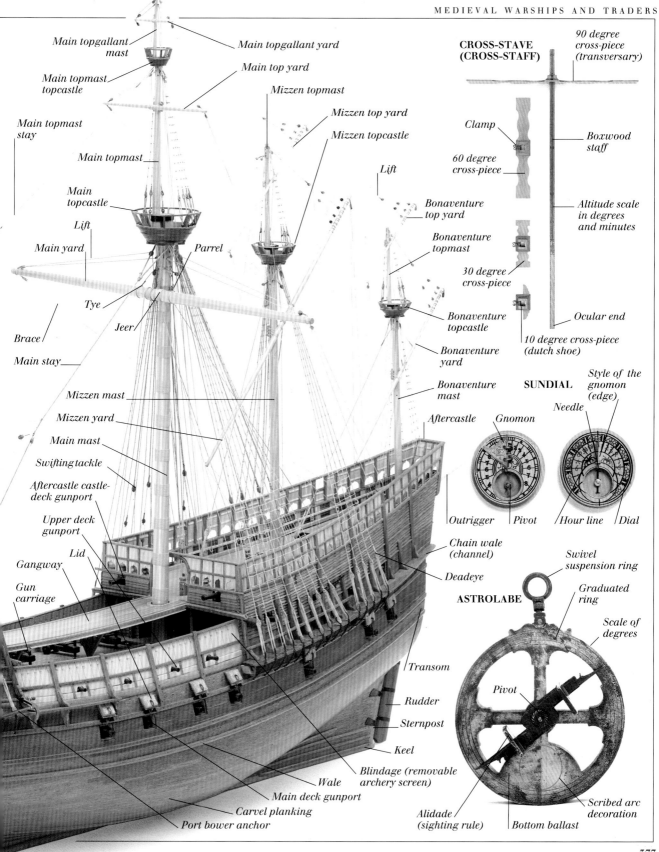

Main topgallant mast

Main topgallant yard

Main topmast topcastle

Main top yard

Mizzen topmast

Main topmast stay

Mizzen top yard

Mizzen topcastle

Main topmast

Lift

Main topcastle

Bonaventure top yard

Lift

Parrel

Bonaventure topmast

Main yard

Tye

30 degree cross-piece

Jeer

Bonaventure topcastle

Brace

Bonaventure yard

Main stay

Mizzen mast

Bonaventure mast

Mizzen yard

Aftercastle

Main mast

Swifting tackle

Aftercastle castle-deck gunport

Chain wale (channel)

Upper deck gunport

Deadeye

Lid

Gangway

Gun carriage

Transom

Rudder

Sternpost

Keel

Blindage (removable archery screen)

Wale

Main deck gunport

Carvel planking

Port bower anchor

CROSS-STAVE (CROSS-STAFF)

90 degree cross-piece (transversary)

Clamp

Boxwood staff

60 degree cross-piece

Altitude scale in degrees and minutes

30 degree cross-piece

Ocular end

10 degree cross-piece (dutch shoe)

SUNDIAL

Style of the gnomon (edge)

Gnomon

Needle

Outrigger

Pivot

Hour line

Dial

ASTROLABE

Swivel suspension ring

Graduated ring

Scale of degrees

Pivot

Alidade (sighting rule)

Bottom ballast

Scribed arc decoration

The expansion of sail

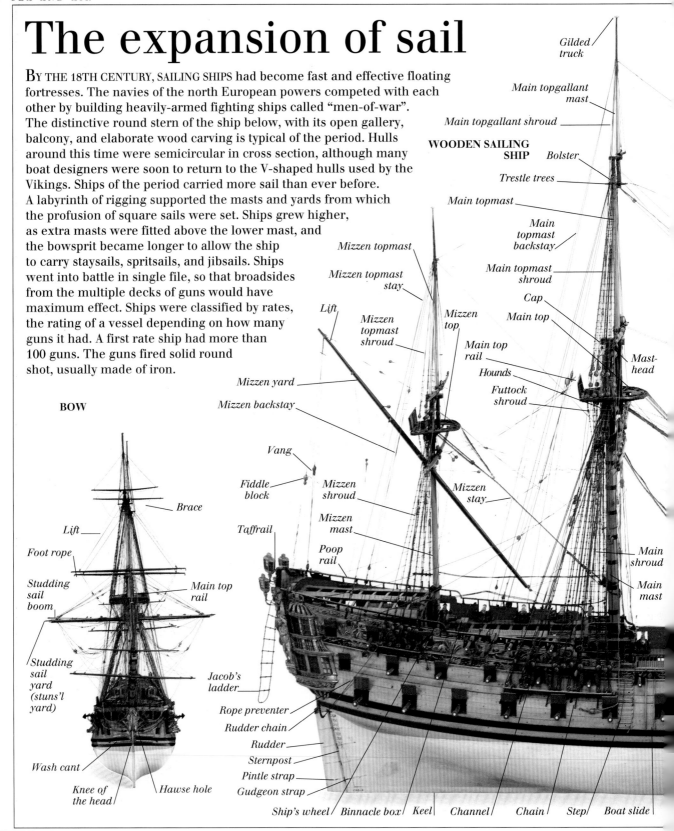

BY THE 18TH CENTURY, SAILING SHIPS had become fast and effective floating fortresses. The navies of the north European powers competed with each other by building heavily-armed fighting ships called "men-of-war". The distinctive round stern of the ship below, with its open gallery, balcony, and elaborate wood carving is typical of the period. Hulls around this time were semicircular in cross section, although many boat designers were soon to return to the V-shaped hulls used by the Vikings. Ships of the period carried more sail than ever before. A labyrinth of rigging supported the masts and yards from which the profusion of square sails were set. Ships grew higher, as extra masts were fitted above the lower mast, and the bowsprit became longer to allow the ship to carry staysails, spritsails, and jibsails. Ships went into battle in single file, so that broadsides from the multiple decks of guns would have maximum effect. Ships were classified by rates, the rating of a vessel depending on how many guns it had. A first rate ship had more than 100 guns. The guns fired solid round shot, usually made of iron.

BOW

WOODEN SAILING SHIP

Gilded truck

Main topgallant mast

Main topgallant shroud

Bolster

Trestle trees

Main topmast

Main topmast backstay

Main topmast shroud

Cap

Main top

Mast-head

Mizzen topmast

Mizzen topmast stay

Lift

Mizzen topmast shroud

Mizzen top

Main top rail

Hounds

Futtock shroud

Mizzen yard

Mizzen backstay

Vang

Fiddle block

Mizzen shroud

Mizzen mast

Mizzen stay

Poop rail

Taffrail

Brace

Lift

Foot rope

Studding sail boom

Main top rail

Studding sail yard (stuns'l yard)

Jacob's ladder

Rope preventer

Rudder chain

Rudder

Sternpost

Pintle strap

Gudgeon strap

Wash cant

Knee of the head

Hawse hole

Main shroud

Main mast

Ship's wheel   Binnacle box   Keel   Channel   Chain   Step   Boat slide

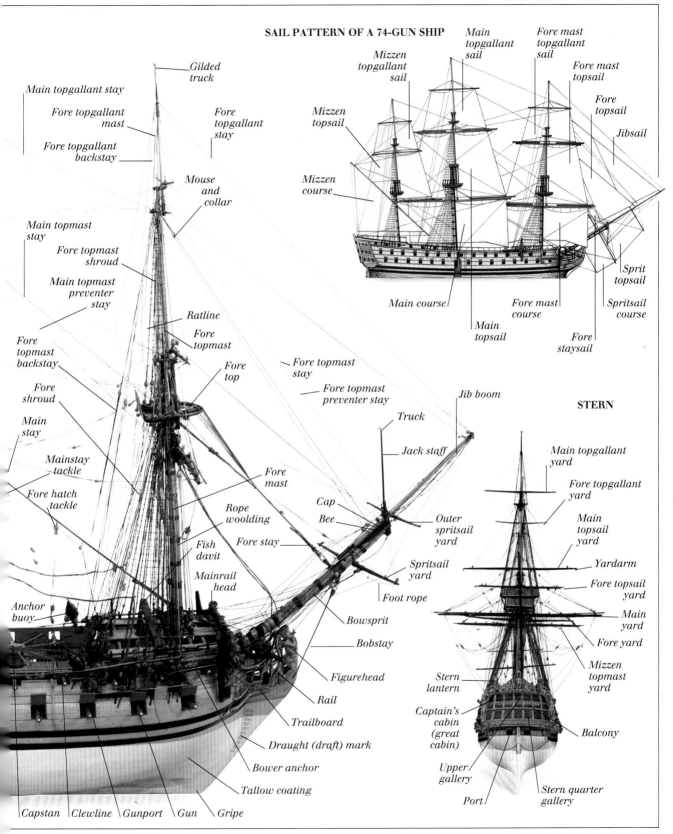

SAIL PATTERN OF A 74-GUN SHIP

Main topgallant stay

Fore topgallant mast

Fore topgallant backstay

Gilded truck

Fore topgallant stay

Mouse and collar

Main topmast stay

Fore topmast shroud

Main topmast preventer stay

Fore topmast backstay

Fore shroud

Main stay

Mainstay tackle

Fore hatch tackle

Ratline

Fore topmast

Fore top

Fore mast

Rope woolding

Fore stay

Fish davit

Mainrail head

Anchor buoy

Fore topmast stay

Fore topmast preventer stay

Truck

Jack staff

Cap

Bee

Jib boom

Outer spritsail yard

Spritsail yard

Foot rope

Bowsprit

Bobstay

Figurehead

Rail

Trailboard

Draught (draft) mark

Bower anchor

Tallow coating

Capstan   Clewline   Gunport   Gun   Gripe

Mizzen topgallant sail

Mizzen topsail

Mizzen course

Main topgallant sail

Fore mast topgallant sail

Fore mast topsail

Fore topsail

Jibsail

Main course

Fore mast course

Main topsail

Sprit topsail

Spritsail course

Fore staysail

STERN

Main topgallant yard

Fore topgallant yard

Main topsail yard

Yardarm

Fore topsail yard

Main yard

Fore yard

Mizzen topmast yard

Balcony

Stern lantern

Captain's cabin (great cabin)

Upper gallery

Port

Stern quarter gallery

A ship of the line

THE 74-GUN WOODEN SHIP WAS A MAINSTAY of British and French battlefleets in the late 18th and early 19th centuries. This "ship of the line" was heavy enough to fight with the most potent of rivals, yet nimble too. The length of such a ship was determined by the number of guns required for each deck, allowing enough room for crews to man them. The gun deck was about 52 m (170 ft) long. The decks had to be very strong to carry the weight of the guns. The deck planks have been removed on the vessel pictured below, to show just how close together the beams had to be to make the hull strong enough. Only timber with a perfect grain was used. The upper deck was open at the waist, but afore and abaft were officers' cabins. The forecastle and quarterdeck carried light guns and acted as platforms for working rigging and for reconnaissance. The ship's longboats (launches) were carried on booms between the gangways.

LONGBOAT

UPPER DECK OF A 74-GUN SHIP

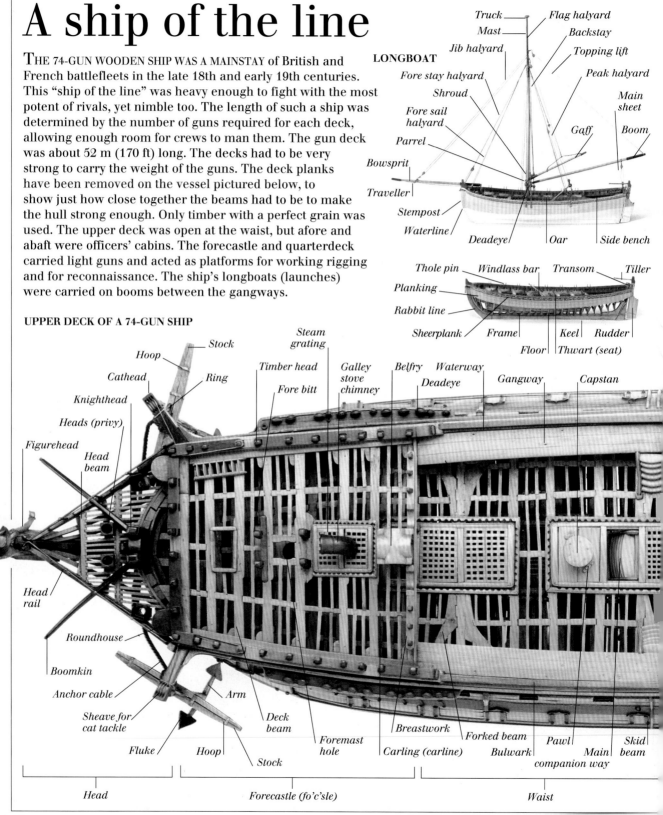

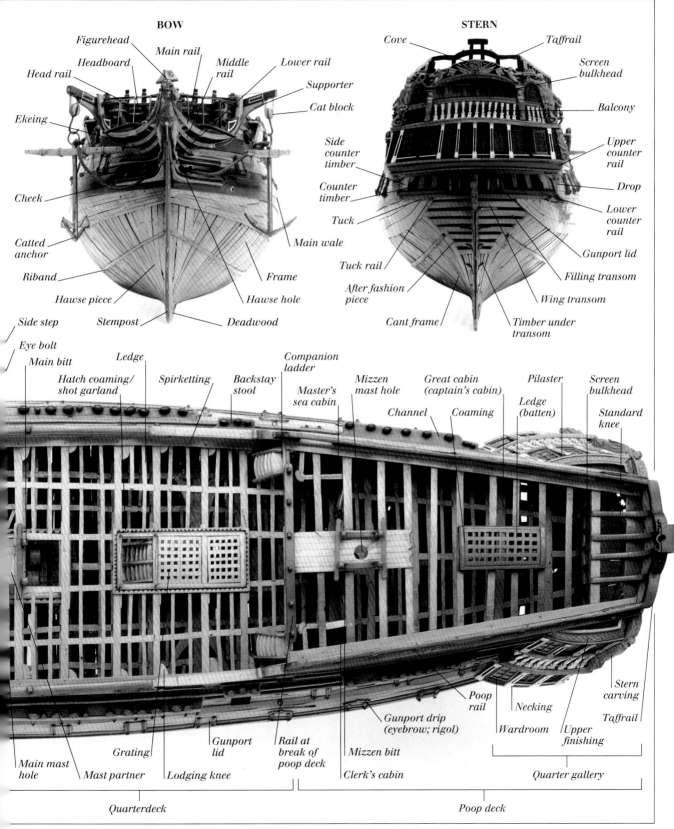

BOW

Figurehead
Main rail
Headboard
Middle rail
Head rail
Lower rail
Supporter
Cat block
Ekeing
Cheek
Catted anchor
Riband
Hawse piece
Stempost
Deadwood
Hawse hole
Frame
Main wale
Side step
Eye bolt

STERN

Cove
Taffrail
Screen bulkhead
Balcony
Side counter timber
Upper counter rail
Counter timber
Drop
Tuck
Lower counter rail
Tuck rail
Gunport lid
After fashion piece
Filling transom
Cant frame
Wing transom
Timber under transom

Main bitt
Ledge
Spirketting
Backstay stool
Companion ladder
Master's sea cabin
Mizzen mast hole
Great cabin (captain's cabin)
Channel
Coaming
Pilaster
Ledge (batten)
Screen bulkhead
Standard knee
Poop rail
Necking
Stern carving
Gunport drip (eyebrow; rigol)
Wardroom
Upper finishing
Taffrail
Main mast hole
Mast partner
Grating
Lodging knee
Gunport lid
Rail at break of poop deck
Mizzen bitt
Clerk's cabin
Quarter gallery
Quarterdeck
Poop deck

Rigging

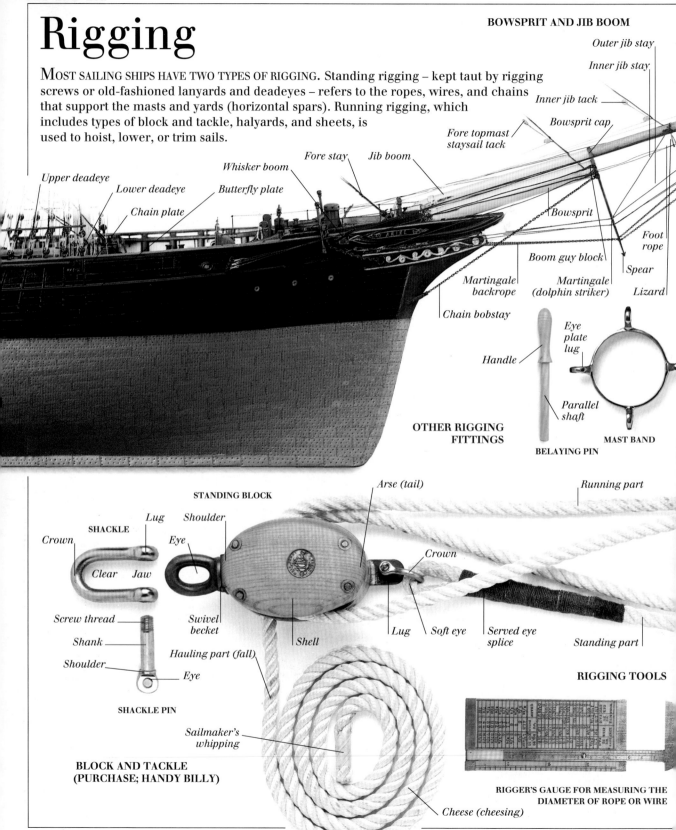

MOST SAILING SHIPS HAVE TWO TYPES OF RIGGING. Standing rigging – kept taut by rigging screws or old-fashioned lanyards and deadeyes – refers to the ropes, wires, and chains that support the masts and yards (horizontal spars). Running rigging, which includes types of block and tackle, halyards, and sheets, is used to hoist, lower, or trim sails.

BOWSPRIT AND JIB BOOM

Outer jib stay

Inner jib stay

Inner jib tack

Bowsprit cap

Fore topmast staysail tack

Fore stay

Jib boom

Whisker boom

Butterfly plate

Upper deadeye

Lower deadeye

Chain plate

Bowsprit

Foot rope

Boom guy block

Martingale backrope

Martingale (dolphin striker)

Spear

Lizard

Chain bobstay

OTHER RIGGING FITTINGS

Handle

Eye plate lug

Parallel shaft

MAST BAND

BELAYING PIN

STANDING BLOCK

Arse (tail)

Running part

Shoulder

Lug

Eye

Crown

SHACKLE

Crown

Clear   Jaw

Swivel becket

Shell

Lug

Soft eye

Served eye splice

Standing part

Screw thread

Shank

Shoulder

Eye

Hauling part (fall)

SHACKLE PIN

Sailmaker's whipping

RIGGING TOOLS

BLOCK AND TACKLE (PURCHASE; HANDY BILLY)

Cheese (cheesing)

RIGGER'S GAUGE FOR MEASURING THE DIAMETER OF ROPE OR WIRE

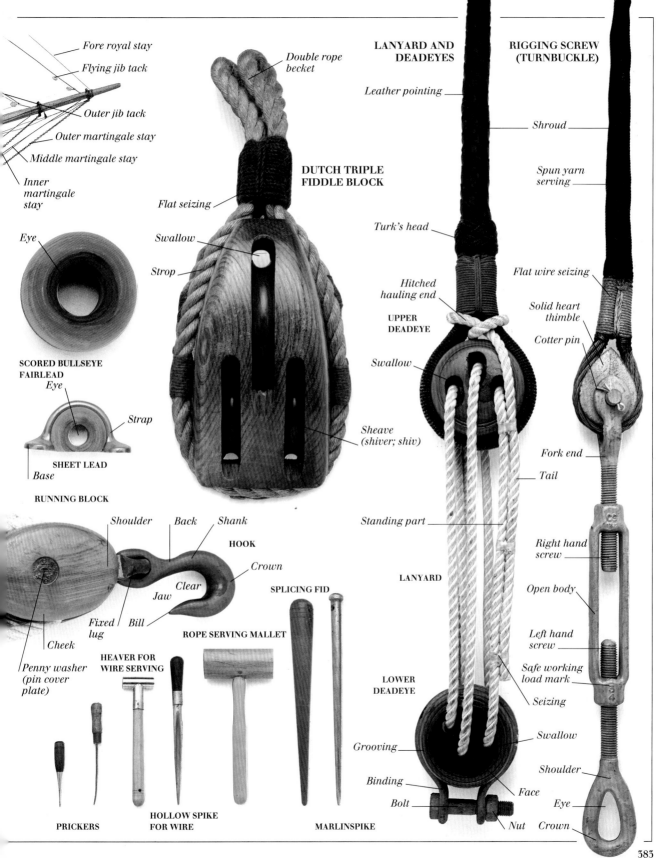

Fore royal stay

Flying jib tack

Outer jib tack

Outer martingale stay

Middle martingale stay

Inner martingale stay

Eye

SCORED BULLSEYE FAIRLEAD

Eye

Strap

SHEET LEAD

Base

RUNNING BLOCK

Shoulder

Back

Shank

HOOK

Crown

Clear

Jaw

Fixed lug

Bill

Cheek

Penny washer (pin cover plate)

HEAVER FOR WIRE SERVING

ROPE SERVING MALLET

SPLICING FID

PRICKERS

HOLLOW SPIKE FOR WIRE

MARLINSPIKE

Double rope becket

DUTCH TRIPLE FIDDLE BLOCK

Flat seizing

Swallow

Strop

Sheave (shiver; shiv)

LANYARD AND DEADEYES

Leather pointing

Turk's head

Hitched hauling end

UPPER DEADEYE

Swallow

Standing part

LANYARD

LOWER DEADEYE

Grooving

Binding

Bolt

Face

Nut

RIGGING SCREW (TURNBUCKLE)

Shroud

Spun yarn serving

Flat wire seizing

Solid heart thimble

Cotter pin

Fork end

Tail

Right hand screw

Open body

Left hand screw

Safe working load mark

Seizing

Swallow

Shoulder

Eye

Crown

Sails

THERE ARE TWO MAIN TYPES OF SAIL, often used in combination. Square sails are driving sails. They are usually attached by parrels to yards, square to the mast to catch the following wind. On fore-and-aft sails, such as lateen and lug sails, the luff (leading edge) usually abuts a mast or a stay. The head of the sail may abut a gaff, and the foot a boom. Around the world, a great range of rigs (sail patterns), such as the ketch, lugger, and schooner, have evolved to suit local needs. Sails are made from strips of cloth, cut to give the sail a belly and strong enough to resist the most violent of winds. Cotton and flax are the traditional sail materials, but synthetic fabrics are now commonly used.

SECTION OF A SAIL

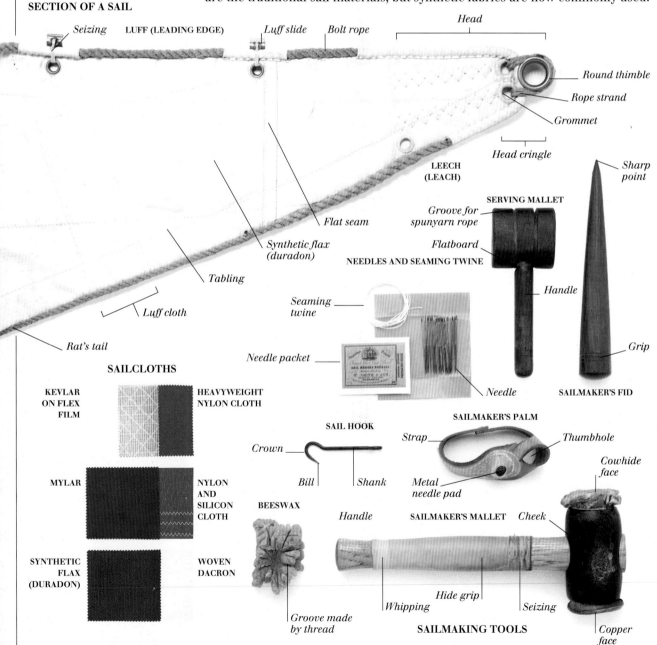

Seizing LUFF (LEADING EDGE) Luff slide Bolt rope Head

Round thimble

Rope strand

Grommet

Head cringle

LEECH (LEACH)

Flat seam

Synthetic flax (duradon)

Tabling

Luff cloth

Rat's tail

Sharp point

SERVING MALLET

Groove for spunyarn rope

Flatboard

NEEDLES AND SEAMING TWINE

Handle

Seaming twine

Needle packet

Needle

Grip

SAILMAKER'S FID

SAILCLOTHS

KEVLAR ON FLEX FILM

HEAVYWEIGHT NYLON CLOTH

SAIL HOOK

SAILMAKER'S PALM

Strap

Thumbhole

Crown

Bill   Shank

Metal needle pad

Cowhide face

MYLAR

NYLON AND SILICON CLOTH

BEESWAX

Handle

SAILMAKER'S MALLET

Cheek

SYNTHETIC FLAX (DURADON)

WOVEN DACRON

Whipping

Hide grip

Seizing

Groove made by thread

SAILMAKING TOOLS

Copper face

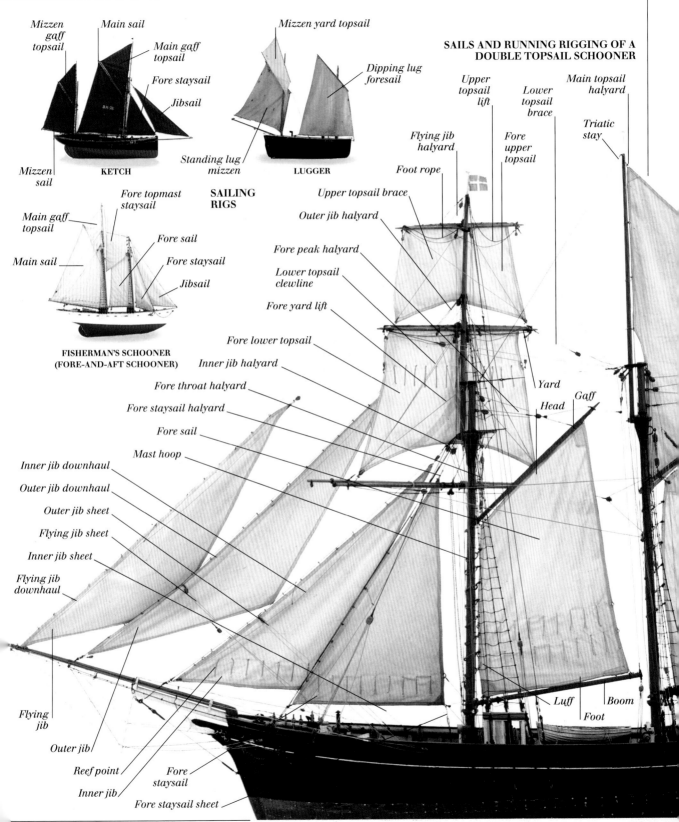

Mizzen gaff topsail

Main sail

Main gaff topsail

Fore staysail

Jibsail

Mizzen sail

KETCH

Mizzen yard topsail

Dipping lug foresail

Standing lug mizzen

LUGGER

SAILING RIGS

Main gaff topsail

Fore topmast staysail

Fore sail

Fore staysail

Jibsail

Main sail

FISHERMAN'S SCHOONER (FORE-AND-AFT SCHOONER)

SAILS AND RUNNING RIGGING OF A DOUBLE TOPSAIL SCHOONER

Upper topsail lift

Lower topsail brace

Main topsail halyard

Flying jib halyard

Fore upper topsail

Triatic stay

Foot rope

Upper topsail brace

Outer jib halyard

Fore peak halyard

Lower topsail clewline

Fore yard lift

Fore lower topsail

Inner jib halyard

Fore throat halyard

Fore staysail halyard

Fore sail

Mast hoop

Yard

Head

Gaff

Inner jib downhaul

Outer jib downhaul

Outer jib sheet

Flying jib sheet

Inner jib sheet

Flying jib downhaul

Luff

Boom

Foot

Flying jib

Outer jib

Reef point

Fore staysail

Inner jib

Fore staysail sheet

Mooring and anchoring

FOR LARGE VESSELS IN OPEN WATER, ANCHORAGE IS ESSENTIAL. By holding a ship securely to the seabed, an anchor prevents the vessel from being at the mercy of wave, tide, and current. The earliest anchors were nothing more than stones. In later years, many anchors had a standard design, much like the Admiralty pattern anchor shown on this page. The Danforth anchor is somewhat different. It has particularly deep flukes to give it great holding power. On large sailing ships, anchors were worked by teams of sailors. They turned the drum of a capstan by pushing on bars slotted into the revolving cylinder. This, in turn, lifted or lowered the anchor chain. In calm harbours and estuaries, ships can moor (make fast) without using anchors. Berthing ropes can be attached to bollards both inboard and on the quayside. Berthing ropes are joined to each other by bends, like those opposite.

STONE ANCHOR (KILLICK)

Rope hole

TYPES OF ANCHOR

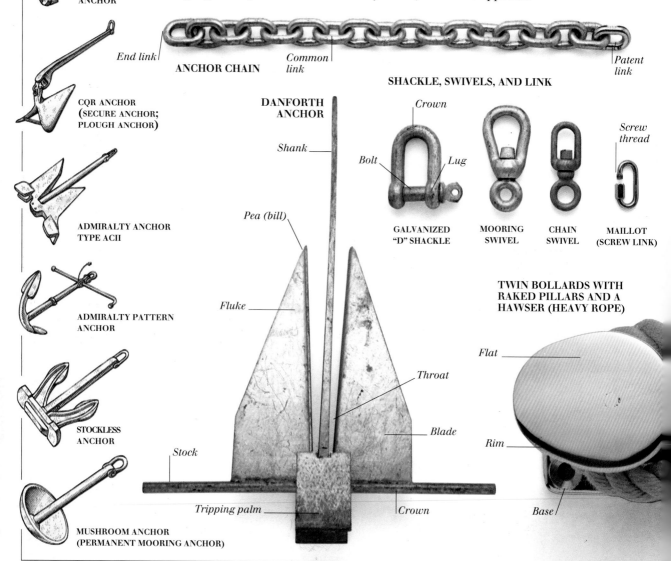

CLOSE-STOWING ANCHOR

CQR ANCHOR (SECURE ANCHOR; PLOUGH ANCHOR)

ADMIRALTY ANCHOR TYPE ACII

ADMIRALTY PATTERN ANCHOR

STOCKLESS ANCHOR

MUSHROOM ANCHOR (PERMANENT MOORING ANCHOR)

ANCHOR CHAIN

End link
Common link
Patent link

DANFORTH ANCHOR

Shank
Pea (bill)
Fluke
Stock
Tripping palm
Throat
Blade
Crown

SHACKLE, SWIVELS, AND LINK

Crown
Bolt
Lug
Screw thread

GALVANIZED "D" SHACKLE

MOORING SWIVEL

CHAIN SWIVEL

MAILLOT (SCREW LINK)

TWIN BOLLARDS WITH RAKED PILLARS AND A HAWSER (HEAVY ROPE)

Flat
Rim
Base

BERTHING ROPES (HAWSERS)

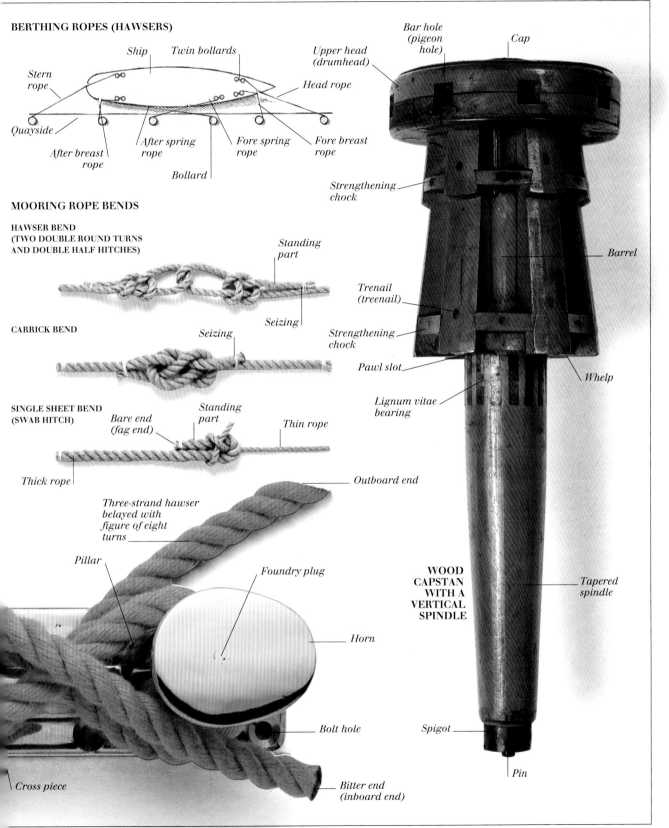

Bar hole (pigeon hole)

Cap

Ship

Twin bollards

Upper head (drumhead)

Stern rope

Head rope

Quayside

After spring rope

Fore spring rope

Fore breast rope

After breast rope

Bollard

Strengthening chock

Barrel

MOORING ROPE BENDS

HAWSER BEND (TWO DOUBLE ROUND TURNS AND DOUBLE HALF HITCHES)

Standing part

Seizing

Trenail (treenail)

Strengthening chock

CARRICK BEND

Seizing

Pawl slot

Whelp

SINGLE SHEET BEND (SWAB HITCH)

Bare end (fag end)

Standing part

Thin rope

Lignum vitae bearing

Thick rope

Outboard end

Three-strand hawser belayed with figure of eight turns

Pillar

Foundry plug

WOOD CAPSTAN WITH A VERTICAL SPINDLE

Tapered spindle

Horn

Bolt hole

Spigot

Cross piece

Bitter end (inboard end)

Pin

Ropes and knots

ALL KINDS OF ROPES ARE USED AT SEA, from thin twines and yarns to thick hawsers. Synthetic fibres have been developed specifically for use at sea. Nylon ropes stretch, and so are ideal for anchoring; polypropylene has little stretch, so is ideal for halyards and sheets. Different types of knots are used for different purposes. Knots that join two ropes are called bends; hitches join a rope to another object; and bowlines produce an eye (loop) in the end of a rope. Ropes can be joined by splicing (unravelling the ends and weaving them together) or seizing (lashing the ropes together side by side).

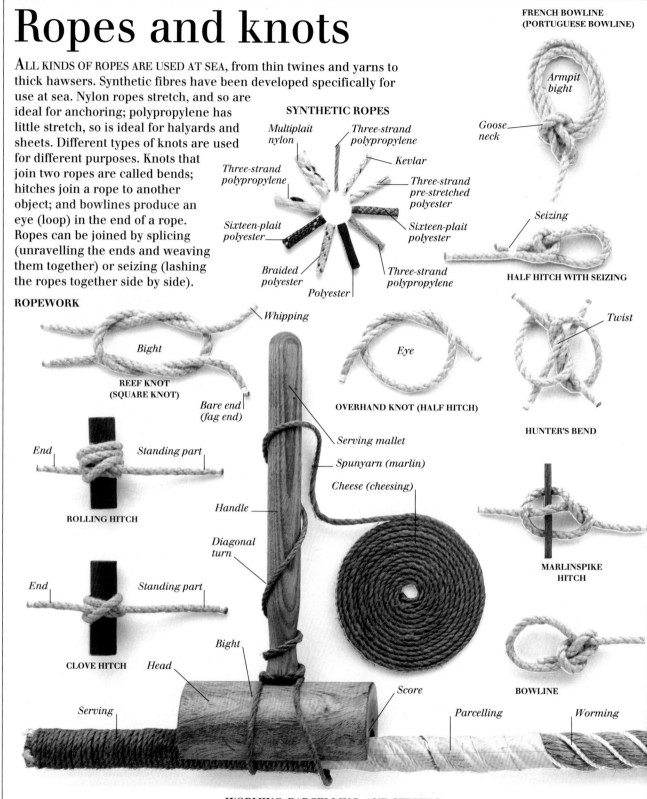

FRENCH BOWLINE (PORTUGUESE BOWLINE)

Armpit bight

Goose neck

Seizing

HALF HITCH WITH SEIZING

SYNTHETIC ROPES

Multiplait nylon

Three-strand polypropylene

Kevlar

Three-strand polypropylene

Three-strand pre-stretched polyester

Sixteen-plait polyester

Sixteen-plait polyester

Braided polyester

Three-strand polypropylene

Polyester

ROPEWORK

Whipping

Bight

REEF KNOT (SQUARE KNOT)

Bare end (fag end)

Eye

OVERHAND KNOT (HALF HITCH)

Twist

HUNTER'S BEND

End

Standing part

ROLLING HITCH

Serving mallet

Spunyarn (marlin)

Cheese (cheesing)

Handle

Diagonal turn

MARLINSPIKE HITCH

End

Standing part

CLOVE HITCH

Head

Bight

BOWLINE

Serving

Score

Parcelling

Worming

WORMING, PARCELLING, AND SERVING

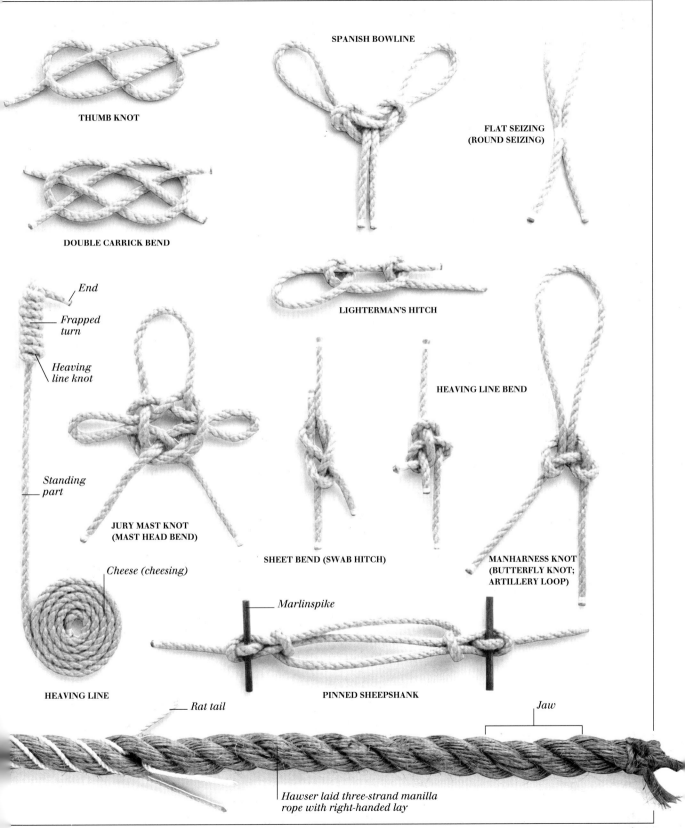

SPANISH BOWLINE

THUMB KNOT

**FLAT SEIZING
(ROUND SEIZING)**

DOUBLE CARRICK BEND

End

*Frapped
turn*

*Heaving
line knot*

LIGHTERMAN'S HITCH

HEAVING LINE BEND

*Standing
part*

**JURY MAST KNOT
(MAST HEAD BEND)**

Cheese (cheesing)

SHEET BEND (SWAB HITCH)

**MANHARNESS KNOT
(BUTTERFLY KNOT;
ARTILLERY LOOP)**

Marlinspike

HEAVING LINE

PINNED SHEEPSHANK

Rat tail

Jaw

*Hawser laid three-strand manilla
rope with right-handed lay*

Paddle wheels and propellers

THE INVENTION OF THE STEAM ENGINE IN THE 18TH CENTURY made mechanically driven ships fitted with paddle wheels or propellers a viable alternative to sails. Paddle wheels have fixed or feathered floats, and the model shown below features both types. Feathered floats give more propulsive power than fixed floats because they are almost upright at all times in the water. Paddle wheels were superseded by the propeller on ocean-going vessels in the mid-19th century. Propellers are more efficient, work better in rough water, and are less vulnerable in collisions. The first propellers were two-bladed but later three- and four-bladed versions are more powerful; the shape and pitch of blades have also been refined over the years. At the beginning of the 18th century, tillers were superseded on many larger ships by the ship's wheel as a means of steering.

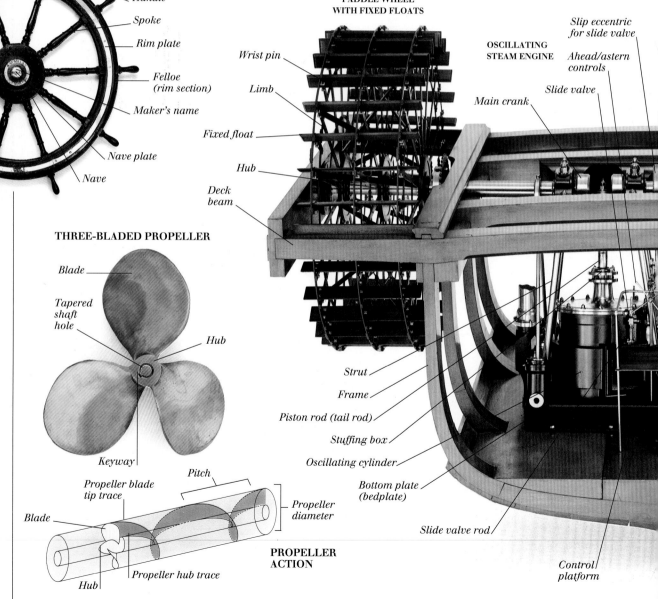

SHIP'S WHEEL

King spoke handle

Handle

Spoke

Rim plate

Felloe (rim section)

Maker's name

Nave plate

Nave

PADDLE WHEEL WITH FIXED FLOATS

Wrist pin

Limb

Fixed float

Hub

Deck beam

OSCILLATING STEAM ENGINE

Slip eccentric for slide valve

Ahead/astern controls

Slide valve

Main crank

THREE-BLADED PROPELLER

Blade

Tapered shaft hole

Hub

Keyway

Strut

Frame

Piston rod (tail rod)

Stuffing box

Oscillating cylinder

Bottom plate (bedplate)

Slide valve rod

Control platform

PROPELLER ACTION

Pitch

Propeller blade tip trace

Blade

Hub

Propeller hub trace

Propeller diameter

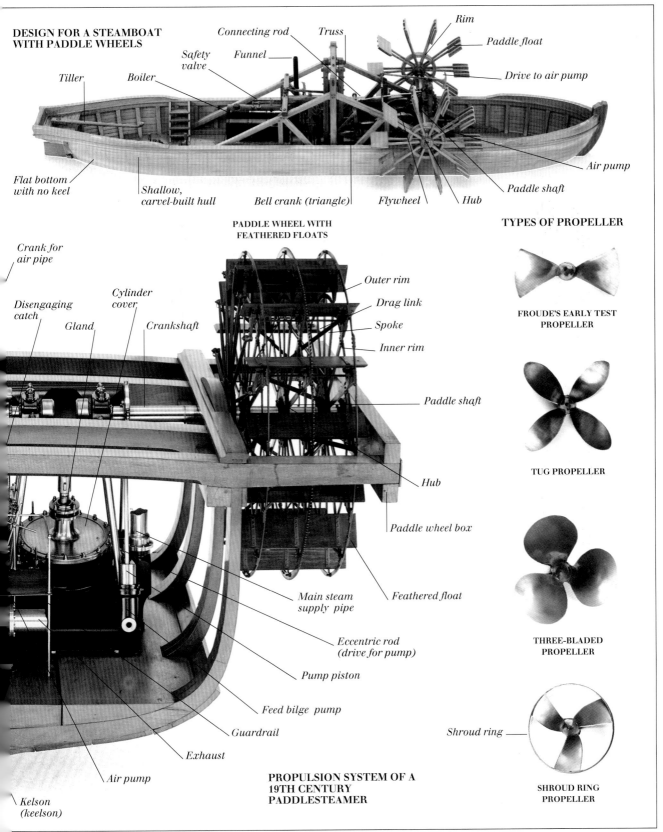

DESIGN FOR A STEAMBOAT WITH PADDLE WHEELS

Connecting rod

Truss

Rim

Paddle float

Safety valve

Funnel

Drive to air pump

Tiller

Boiler

Flat bottom with no keel

Shallow, carvel-built hull

Bell crank (triangle)

Flywheel

Hub

Paddle shaft

Air pump

PADDLE WHEEL WITH FEATHERED FLOATS

TYPES OF PROPELLER

Crank for air pipe

Outer rim

Drag link

Disengaging catch

Cylinder cover

Spoke

Gland

Crankshaft

Inner rim

Paddle shaft

Hub

FROUDE'S EARLY TEST PROPELLER

TUG PROPELLER

Paddle wheel box

Feathered float

Main steam supply pipe

Eccentric rod (drive for pump)

Pump piston

THREE-BLADED PROPELLER

Feed bilge pump

Guardrail

Exhaust

Shroud ring

Air pump

Kelson (keelson)

PROPULSION SYSTEM OF A 19TH CENTURY PADDLESTEAMER

SHROUD RING PROPELLER

Anatomy of an iron ship

IRON PARTS WERE USED IN THE HULLS OF WOODEN SHIPS AS EARLY AS 1675, often in the same form as the wooden parts that they replaced. Eventually, as on the tea clipper Cutty Sark (below), iron rigging was found to be stronger than the traditional rope. The first "ironclads" were warships whose wooden hulls were protected by iron armour plates. Later ironclads actually had iron hulls. The model opposite is based on the British warship HMS Warrior, launched in 1860, the first battleship built entirely of iron. The plan of the iron paddlesteamer (bottom), built somewhat later, shows that this vessel was a sailing ship; but it also boasted a steam propulsion plant amidships that turned two side paddlewheels. Early iron hulls were made from plates that were painstakingly rivetted together (as below), but by the 20th century vessels began to be welded together, whole sections at a time. The Second World War "liberty ship" was one of the first of these "production-line vessels".

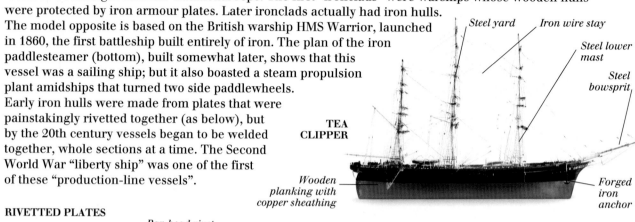

TEA CLIPPER

Steel yard

Iron wire stay

Steel lower mast

Steel bowsprit

Wooden planking with copper sheathing

Forged iron anchor

RIVETTED PLATES

Pan head rivet

Plate

Button head rivet (snap head)

Seam

LIBERTY SHIP

Gun section

Accommodation section

Cargo derrick

Weld line

Stern section

Midships section

Cargo hold

Bow section

PLAN OF AN IRON PADDLESTEAMER

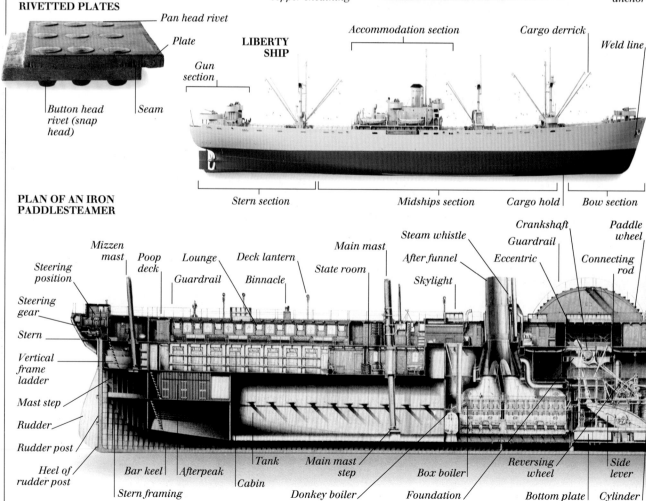

Mizzen mast

Steering position

Steering gear

Stern

Vertical frame ladder

Mast step

Rudder

Rudder post

Heel of rudder post

Poop deck

Lounge

Guardrail

Deck lantern

Binnacle

Main mast

State room

Steam whistle

After funnel

Skylight

Crankshaft

Guardrail

Eccentric

Paddle wheel

Connecting rod

Bar keel

Afterpeak

Cabin

Tank

Main mast step

Donkey boiler

Box boiler

Foundation

Reversing wheel

Bottom plate

Side lever

Cylinder

Stern framing

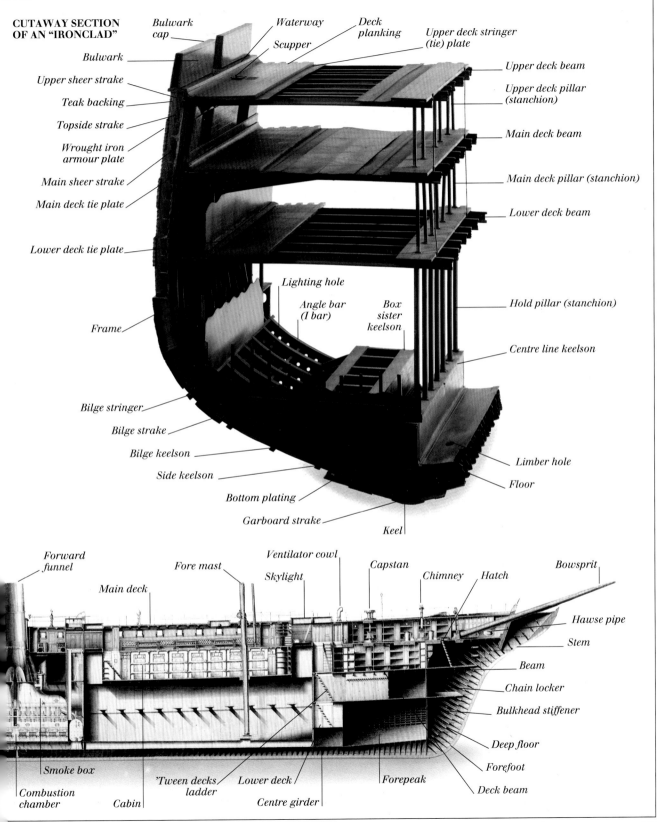

CUTAWAY SECTION OF AN "IRONCLAD"

Bulwark cap

Waterway

Deck planking

Upper deck stringer (tie) plate

Scupper

Bulwark

Upper deck beam

Upper sheer strake

Upper deck pillar (stanchion)

Teak backing

Topside strake

Main deck beam

Wrought iron armour plate

Main sheer strake

Main deck pillar (stanchion)

Main deck tie plate

Lower deck beam

Lower deck tie plate

Lighting hole

Angle bar (I bar)

Box sister keelson

Hold pillar (stanchion)

Frame

Centre line keelson

Bilge stringer

Bilge strake

Bilge keelson

Limber hole

Side keelson

Floor

Bottom plating

Garboard strake

Keel

Forward funnel

Fore mast

Ventilator cowl

Capstan

Bowsprit

Main deck

Skylight

Chimney

Hatch

Hawse pipe

Stem

Beam

Chain locker

Bulkhead stiffener

Deep floor

Smoke box

'Tween decks ladder

Lower deck

Forepeak

Forefoot

Combustion chamber

Cabin

Centre girder

Deck beam

The battleship

IN THE EARLY YEARS OF THE 20TH CENTURY, sea warfare –
attacking enemy vessels or defending a ship – was
revolutionized by the introduction of Dreadnought-type
battleships like the Brazilian vessel below. These new
ships combined the latest advances in steam
propulsion, gunnery, and armour plating. The gun
turret was designed to fire shells over huge distances.
It was protected by armour 30 cm (12 in) thick. The
measurements given for the guns of this ship refer
to the bore diameter. Where "weight" is quoted, this
is the weight of the shell that the gun fires. Torpedoes –
as portrayed on the upper cigarette card (right) – were
self-propelled underwater missiles, often steered by gyro-
control. Depth charges were designed in the First World
War for use against submerged U-boats. They are
canisters filled with explosives that are detonated
by depth-sensitive pistols. The lower cigarette
card shows depth charges being fired by
a "thrower", fired from a torpedo tube,
and rolled from the stern. Ship's shields
were fitted to warships from the late
19th century onwards. The shield
shown opposite depicts a
traditional ship's cannon.

20TH CENTURY WEAPONRY

Torpedo tube

Sight

Warhead

TORPEDOES

DEPTH
CHARGES

Side-thrown
canister

Stern-rolled
canister

Torpedo-fired
canister

Boat handling
derrick

BRAZILIAN BATTLESHIP

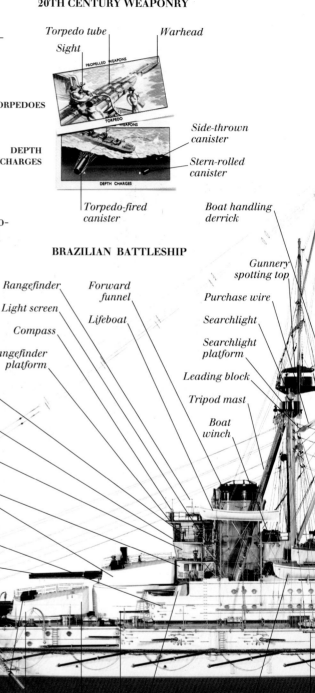

Rangefinder

Forward
funnel

Light screen

Lifeboat

Compass

Compass and rangefinder
platform

Ship's wheel

Navigating bridge

Conning tower

Captain's shelter/
chart house

Weather shutter
for gun

"F" turret

30 cm (12 in)
gun

Skylight

Arms of
Brazil

Jack staff

Gunnery
spotting top

Purchase wire

Searchlight

Searchlight
platform

Leading block

Tripod mast

Boat
winch

Stem
(false ram bow)

Porthole

Belt
armour

Forward
accommodation
ladder

Sighting
hood

"A" turret

Turret barbette

Open gun mounting

12 cm (4.7 in) gun

Steam launch

Guest boat boom

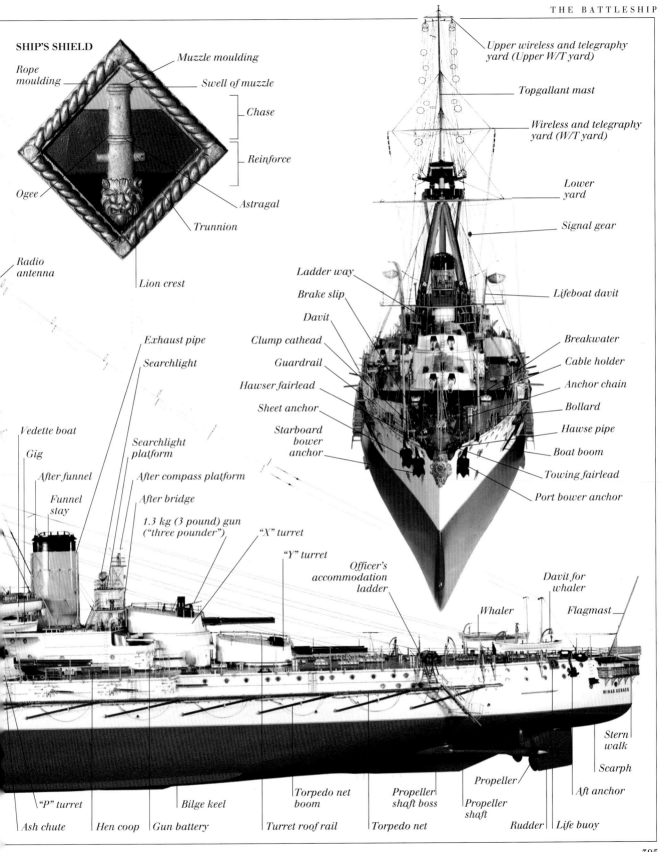

SHIP'S SHIELD

Rope moulding

Muzzle moulding

Swell of muzzle

Chase

Reinforce

Ogee

Astragal

Trunnion

Radio antenna

Lion crest

Upper wireless and telegraphy yard (Upper W/T yard)

Topgallant mast

Wireless and telegraphy yard (W/T yard)

Lower yard

Signal gear

Ladder way

Brake slip

Davit

Clump cathead

Guardrail

Hawser fairlead

Sheet anchor

Starboard bower anchor

Lifeboat davit

Breakwater

Cable holder

Anchor chain

Bollard

Hawse pipe

Boat boom

Towing fairlead

Port bower anchor

Exhaust pipe

Searchlight

Vedette boat

Gig

After funnel

Funnel stay

Searchlight platform

After compass platform

After bridge

1.3 kg (3 pound) gun ("three pounder")

"X" turret

"Y" turret

Officer's accommodation ladder

Whaler

Davit for whaler

Flagmast

"P" turret

Ash chute

Hen coop

Bilge keel

Gun battery

Torpedo net boom

Turret roof rail

Propeller shaft boss

Torpedo net

Propeller

Propeller shaft

Rudder

Stern walk

Scarph

Aft anchor

Life buoy

Frigates and submarines

FROM THE MID-19TH CENTURY, ARMOURED SHIPS provided a new challenge to enemy craft. In response, huge revolving gun turrets were developed. These could fire in any direction, could be loaded from the breech very rapidly, and, instead of cannonballs, they discharged exploding shells. Modern fighting ships, like the frigate, combine heavy ship-borne armament with light helicopter weaponry. Submarines function below the surface of the sea. Their speed and ability to fire missiles from under water are their major assets. The nuclear submarine can stay under water for several years without refuelling.

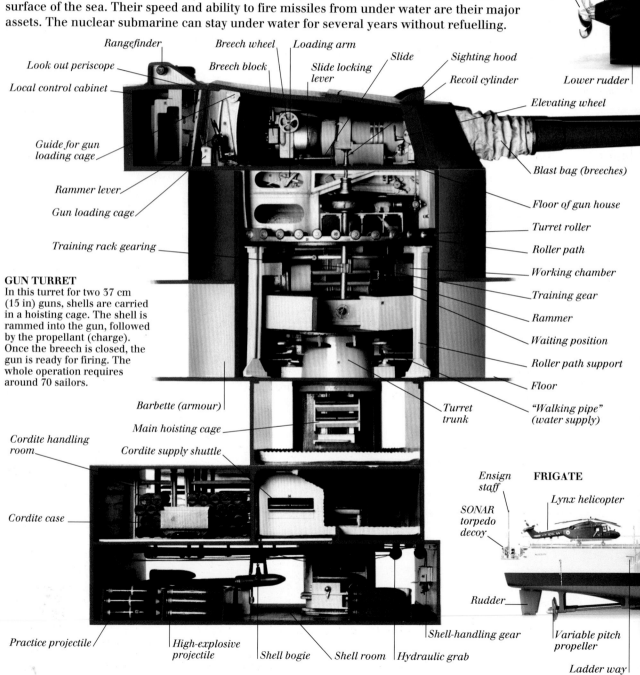

Stabilizer fin

Aft hydroplane

Propeller

Lower rudder

Rangefinder

Look out periscope

Local control cabinet

Breech wheel

Breech block

Loading arm

Slide locking lever

Slide

Sighting hood

Recoil cylinder

Elevating wheel

Guide for gun loading cage

Blast bag (breeches)

Floor of gun house

Rammer lever

Gun loading cage

Turret roller

Roller path

Training rack gearing

Working chamber

Training gear

GUN TURRET
In this turret for two 37 cm (15 in) guns, shells are carried in a hoisting cage. The shell is rammed into the gun, followed by the propellant (charge). Once the breech is closed, the gun is ready for firing. The whole operation requires around 70 sailors.

Rammer

Waiting position

Roller path support

Floor

Barbette (armour)

Main hoisting cage

Turret trunk

"Walking pipe" (water supply)

Cordite handling room

Cordite supply shuttle

Ensign staff

FRIGATE

Lynx helicopter

SONAR torpedo decoy

Cordite case

Rudder

Practice projectile

High-explosive projectile

Shell bogie

Shell room

Hydraulic grab

Shell-handling gear

Variable pitch propeller

Ladder way

Steam pipework

Machinery raft

Main turbine

Snort mast

Conning tower

Machinery control room

Switchboard room

Electronic warfare mast

Periscope

NUCLEAR "HUNTER-KILLER" SUBMARINE

Control room

Sonar room

Galley

Officers' mess

SONAR transducer array

Main engine steam condenser

Distiller

Diesel motor compartment

Reactor space

Wireless office

Junior ratings' mess

Carbon dioxide scrubber compartment

Torpedo compartment

Torpedo tube

Forward hydroplane

Junior ratings' bunk space

Senior ratings' mess

Muzzle

Barrel

15 cm (6 in) SHELL
This shell is designed to burst in the air above its target.

Bursting charge (explosive)

Flash tube

Body

Wooden packing

Transit plug

Driving band

SHELL CASE

Expelling plate

CROSS-SECTION OF THE SHELL

Bullet

Surveillance RADAR

Navigation/helicopter control RADAR antenna

RADAR for gunnery and missile control

Mast

Signalling lamp

Jack staff

Seacat missile launcher

Motor whaler

Vent

Aerial rig

Oerlikon gun position

Stern gallery

Funnel

Enclosed bridge

Exocet missile launcher

Aerial

Gun turret

11 cm (4.5 in) gun

F174

Anchor

RADAR for gunnery and missile control

Stabilizer

Liferaft cylinder

Signal flag compartment

Reel

Fairlead

SONAR bulge

Breakwater

Anti-submarine torpedo tube

Triple "chaff" rocket launcher

Bilge keel

Pennant number

Porthole

Bollard

Draught (draft) mark

397

Pioneers of flight

FLIGHT HAS FASCINATED MANKIND for centuries, and countless unsuccessful flying machines have been designed. The first successful flight was made by the French Montgolfier brothers in 1783, when they flew a balloon over Paris. The next major advance was the development of gliders, notably by the Englishman Sir George Cayley, who in 1845 designed the first glider to make a sustained flight, and by the German Otto Lilienthal, who became known as the world's first pilot because he managed to achieve controlled flights. However, powered flight did not become a practical possibility until the invention of lightweight, petrol-driven internal combustion engines at the end of the 19th century. Then, in 1903, the American brothers Orville and Wilbur Wright made the first powered flight in their Wright Flyer biplane, which used a four-cylinder, petrol-driven engine. Aircraft design advanced rapidly, and in 1909 the Frenchman Louis Blériot made his pioneering flight across the English Channel (see pp. 400-401). The American Glenn Curtiss also achieved several "firsts" in his Model-D Pusher and its variants, most notably winning the world's first competition for airspeed at Reims in 1909.

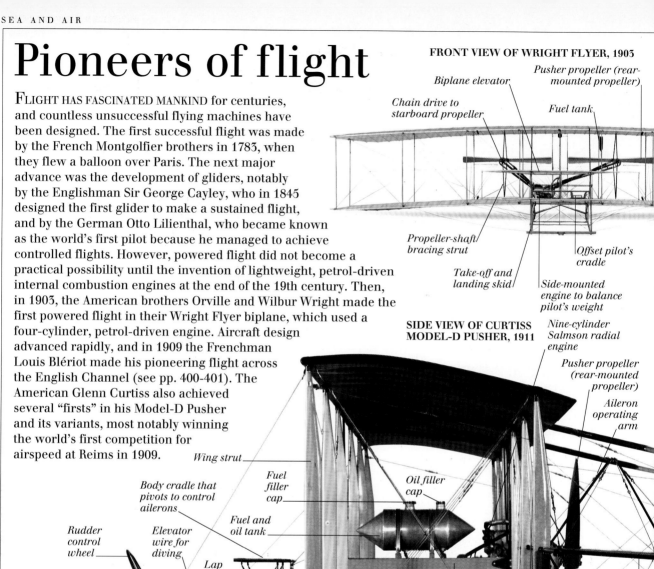

FRONT VIEW OF WRIGHT FLYER, 1903

Biplane elevator

Pusher propeller (rear-mounted propeller)

Chain drive to starboard propeller

Fuel tank

Propeller-shaft bracing strut

Offset pilot's cradle

Take-off and landing skid

Side-mounted engine to balance pilot's weight

SIDE VIEW OF CURTISS MODEL-D PUSHER, 1911

Nine-cylinder Salmson radial engine

Pusher propeller (rear-mounted propeller)

Aileron operating arm

Wing strut

Fuel filler cap

Oil filler cap

Body cradle that pivots to control ailerons

Fuel and oil tank

Rudder control wheel

Elevator wire for diving

Lap strap

Control column

Throttle

Nose-wheel brake

Footrest

Aileron

Turnbuckle

Fuel pipe

Seat support strut

Elevator wire for climbing

Thin, cambered lower wing

Pneumatic tyre

Rubber-tyred nose-wheel

Pilot's seat

Wing-protecting skid

Engine and propeller thrust frame

Starboard main landing gear

SIDE VIEW OF WRIGHT FLYER, 1903

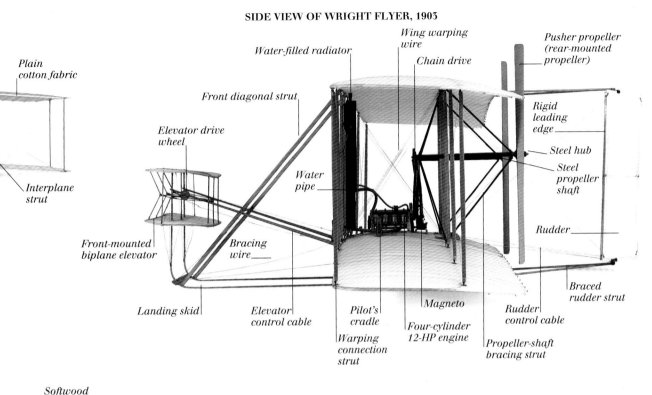

Plain cotton fabric

Interplane strut

Water-filled radiator

Front diagonal strut

Wing warping wire

Chain drive

Pusher propeller (rear-mounted propeller)

Elevator drive wheel

Rigid leading edge

Steel hub

Steel propeller shaft

Water pipe

Front-mounted biplane elevator

Bracing wire

Rudder

Landing skid

Elevator control cable

Pilot's cradle

Magneto

Rudder control cable

Braced rudder strut

Warping connection strut

Four-cylinder 12-HP engine

Propeller-shaft bracing strut

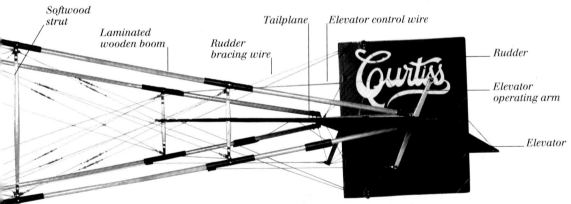

Softwood strut

Laminated wooden boom

Tailplane

Elevator control wire

Rudder

Rudder bracing wire

Elevator operating arm

Elevator

FRONT VIEW OF CURTISS MODEL-D PUSHER, 1911

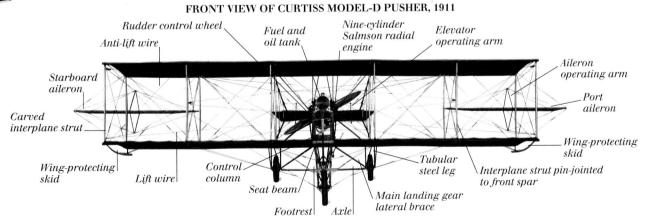

Rudder control wheel

Fuel and oil tank

Nine-cylinder Salmson radial engine

Elevator operating arm

Anti-lift wire

Aileron operating arm

Starboard aileron

Port aileron

Carved interplane strut

Wing-protecting skid

Wing-protecting skid

Lift wire

Control column

Seat beam

Footrest

Axle

Tubular steel leg

Main landing gear lateral brace

Interplane strut pin-jointed to front spar

Early monoplanes

RUMPLER MONOPLANE, 1908

MONOPLANES HAVE ONE WING on each side of the fuselage. The principal disadvantage of this arrangement in early, wooden-framed aircraft was that single wings were weak and required strong wires to brace them to king-posts above and below the fuselage. However, single wings also had advantages: they experienced less drag than multiple wings, allowing greater speed; they also made aircraft more manoeuvrable because single wings were easier to warp (twist) than double wings, and warping the wings was how pilots controlled the roll of early aircraft. By 1912, the French pilot Louis Blériot had used a monoplane to make the first flight across the English Channel, and the Briton Robert Blackburn and the Frenchman Armand Deperdussin had proved the greater speed of monoplanes. However, a spate of crashes caused by broken wings discouraged monoplane production, except in Germany, where all-metal monoplanes were developed in 1917. The wings of all-metal monoplanes did not need strengthening by struts or bracing wires, but despite this, such planes were not widely adopted until the 1930s.

FRONT VIEW OF BLACKBURN MONOPLANE, 1912

Taut fabric

Carved wooden propeller

King-post

Nose-ring

Hub bolted to propeller

Pilot's viewing aperture

Gnome seven-cylinder rotary engine

Exhaust valve push-rod

Elevator hinge

Elevator

Landing gear rear cross-member

Wheel fairing

Rubber-sprung wheel

Landing gear front strut

Tailskid

Axle

Landing skid

Landing gear rear strut

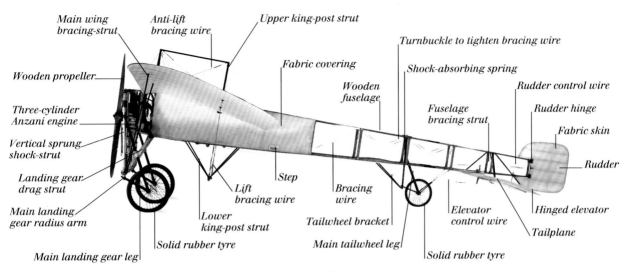

Main wing bracing-strut

Anti-lift bracing wire

Upper king-post strut

Wooden propeller

Fabric covering

Turnbuckle to tighten bracing wire

Wooden fuselage

Shock-absorbing spring

Three-cylinder Anzani engine

Fuselage bracing strut

Rudder control wire

Rudder hinge

Vertical sprung shock-strut

Fabric skin

Landing gear drag strut

Rudder

Main landing gear radius arm

Step

Lift bracing wire

Bracing wire

Hinged elevator

Main landing gear leg

Lower king-post strut

Tailwheel bracket

Elevator control wire

Tailplane

Solid rubber tyre

Main tailwheel leg

Solid rubber tyre

SIDE VIEW OF BLÉRIOT XI, 1909

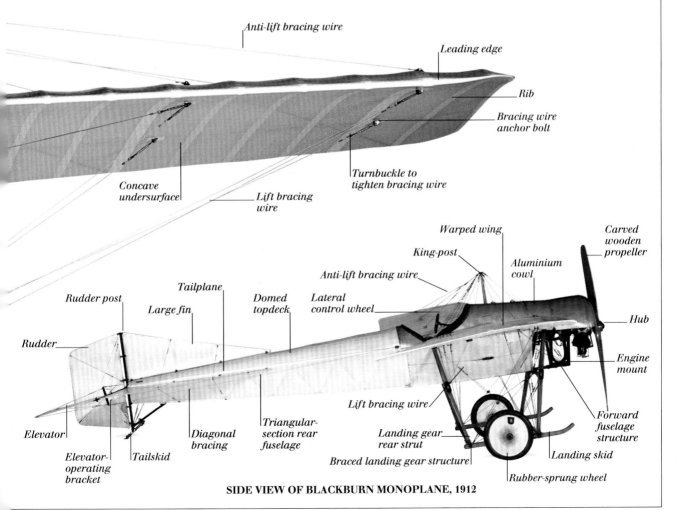

Anti-lift bracing wire

Leading edge

Rib

Bracing wire anchor bolt

Concave undersurface

Turnbuckle to tighten bracing wire

Lift bracing wire

Warped wing

Carved wooden propeller

King-post

Aluminium cowl

Anti-lift bracing wire

Tailplane

Domed topdeck

Lateral control wheel

Rudder post

Large fin

Hub

Rudder

Engine mount

Lift bracing wire

Forward fuselage structure

Elevator

Diagonal bracing

Triangular-section rear fuselage

Landing gear rear strut

Landing skid

Elevator-operating bracket

Tailskid

Braced landing gear structure

Rubber-sprung wheel

SIDE VIEW OF BLACKBURN MONOPLANE, 1912

Biplanes and triplanes

BIPLANES DOMINATED AIRCRAFT DESIGN until the 1930s, largely because some early monoplanes (see pp. 400-401) were too fragile to withstand the stresses of flight. The struts between biplanes' wings made the wings strong compared with those of early monoplanes, although the greater surface area of biplanes' wings increased drag and reduced speed. Many aircraft designers also developed triplanes, which had a particular advantage over biplanes: more wings meant a shorter wingspan to achieve the same lifting power, and a shorter wingspan gave greater manoeuvrability. Triplanes were most successful as fighters during World War I, the German Fokker triplane being a notable example. However, the greater manoeuvrability of triplanes was no advantage for normal flying and so most manufacturers continued to make biplanes. Many other aircraft designs were attempted. Some were quadruplanes, with four pairs of wings. Some had tandem wings (two pairs of monoplane wings, one behind the other). One of the most bizarre designs was by the Englishman Horatio Phillips: it had 20 sets of narrow wings and looked rather like a Venetian blind.

LAMINATED PROPELLER

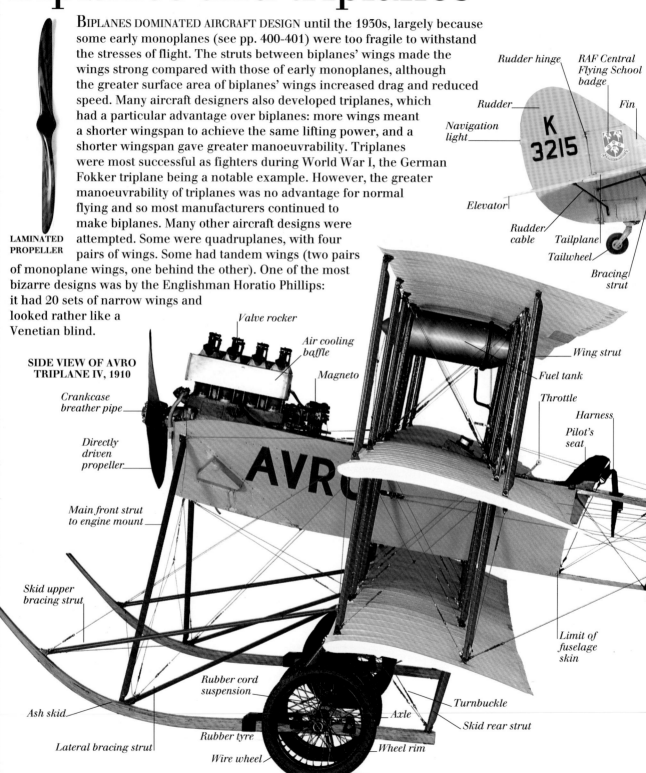

Rudder hinge
RAF Central Flying School badge
Rudder
Fin
Navigation light
K 3215
Elevator
Rudder cable
Tailplane
Tailwheel
Bracing strut

SIDE VIEW OF AVRO TRIPLANE IV, 1910

Valve rocker
Air cooling baffle
Magneto
Wing strut
Fuel tank
Throttle
Harness
Pilot's seat
Crankcase breather pipe
Directly driven propeller
Main front strut to engine mount
Limit of fuselage skin
Skid upper bracing strut
Rubber cord suspension
Turnbuckle
Ash skid
Axle
Skid rear strut
Lateral bracing strut
Rubber tyre
Wheel rim
Wire wheel

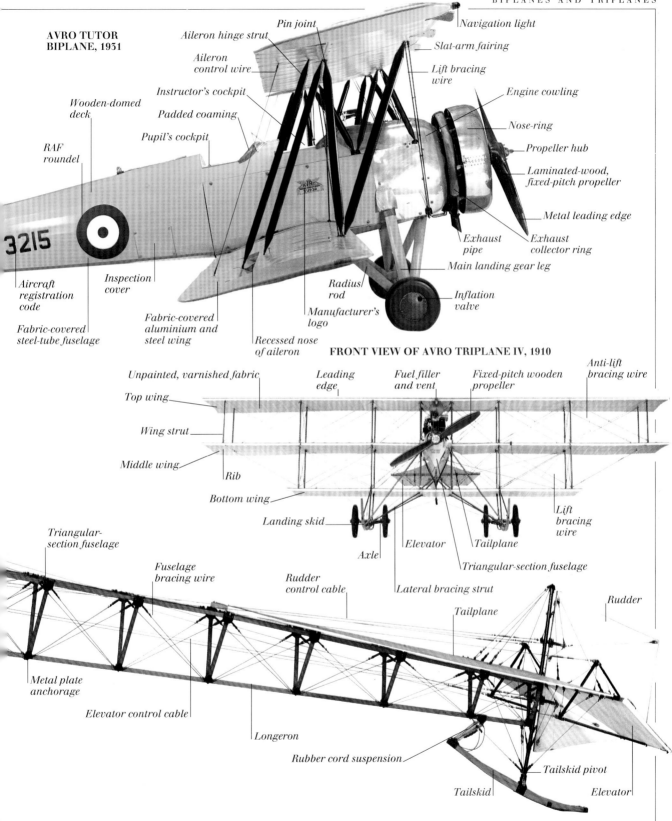

AVRO TUTOR BIPLANE, 1931

Navigation light

Pin joint

Aileron hinge strut

Slat-arm fairing

Aileron control wire

Lift bracing wire

Instructor's cockpit

Engine cowling

Padded coaming

Wooden-domed deck

Nose-ring

Pupil's cockpit

Propeller hub

RAF roundel

Laminated-wood, fixed-pitch propeller

Metal leading edge

3215

Exhaust collector ring

Exhaust pipe

Main landing gear leg

Aircraft registration code

Inspection cover

Radius rod

Inflation valve

Manufacturer's logo

Fabric-covered steel-tube fuselage

Fabric-covered aluminium and steel wing

Recessed nose of aileron

FRONT VIEW OF AVRO TRIPLANE IV, 1910

Unpainted, varnished fabric

Leading edge

Fuel filler and vent

Fixed-pitch wooden propeller

Anti-lift bracing wire

Top wing

Wing strut

Middle wing

Rib

Bottom wing

Lift bracing wire

Landing skid

Elevator

Tailplane

Axle

Triangular-section fuselage

Lateral bracing strut

Triangular-section fuselage

Fuselage bracing wire

Rudder control cable

Tailplane

Rudder

Metal plate anchorage

Elevator control cable

Longeron

Rubber cord suspension

Tailskid pivot

Tailskid

Elevator

World War I aircraft

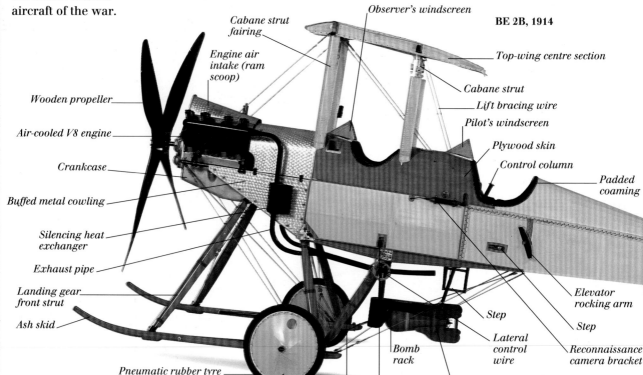

FLYING HELMET

WHEN WORLD WAR I STARTED in 1914, the main purpose of military aircraft was reconnaissance. The British-built BE 2, of which the BE 2B was a variant, was well-suited to this duty; it was very stable in flight, allowing the occupants to study the terrain, take photographs, and make notes. The BE 2 was also one of the first aircraft to drop bombs. One of the biggest problems for aircraft designers during the war was mounting machine-guns. On aircraft that had front-mounted propellers, the field of fire was restricted by the propeller and other parts of the aircraft. The problem was solved in 1915 by the Dutchman Anthony Fokker, who designed an interrupter gear that prevented a machine-gun from firing when a propeller blade passed in front of the barrel. The German LVG CVI had a forward-firing gun to the right of the engine, as well as a rear-cockpit gun, and a bombing capability. It was one of the most versatile aircraft of the war.

PORT WINGS FROM A BE 2B

Interplane-strut attachment
Intermediate leading-edge rib
Airspeed-indicator tube
Leading edge
Wingtip

Airspeed-indicator tube
Main rib
Root
Airspeed pitot tube
Interplane strut
Trailing edge
Interplane-strut attachment

Upper side of lower wing
Attachment lug

BE 2B, 1914

Cabane strut fairing
Observer's windscreen
Engine air intake (ram scoop)
Top-wing centre section
Cabane strut
Wooden propeller
Lift bracing wire
Air-cooled V8 engine
Pilot's windscreen
Plywood skin
Crankcase
Control column
Buffed metal cowling
Padded coaming
Silencing heat exchanger
Exhaust pipe
Landing gear front strut
Elevator rocking arm
Ash skid
Step
Step
Lateral control wire
Reconnaissance camera bracket
Pneumatic rubber tyre
Bomb rack
Wheel cover
V-strut
Lower-wing attachment
112 lb (51 kg) bomb

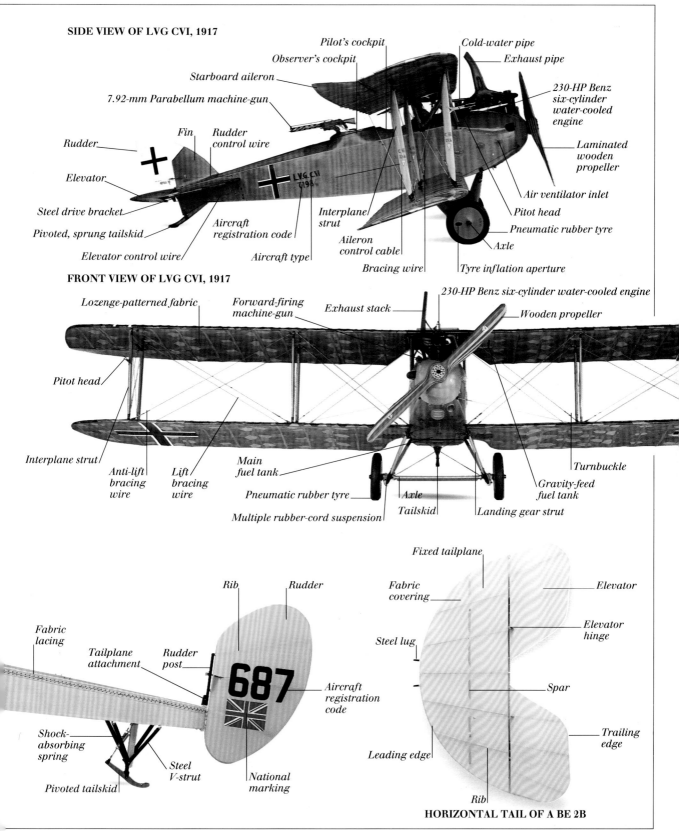

SIDE VIEW OF LVG CVI, 1917

Pilot's cockpit
Observer's cockpit
Cold-water pipe
Exhaust pipe
Starboard aileron
230-HP Benz six-cylinder water-cooled engine
7.92-mm Parabellum machine-gun
Fin
Rudder control wire
Rudder
Elevator
Laminated wooden propeller
Steel drive bracket
Air ventilator inlet
Pivoted, sprung tailskid
Pitot head
Aircraft registration code
Interplane strut
Pneumatic rubber tyre
Elevator control wire
Aileron control cable
Axle
Aircraft type
Bracing wire
Tyre inflation aperture

FRONT VIEW OF LVG CVI, 1917

Lozenge-patterned fabric
Forward-firing machine-gun
Exhaust stack
230-HP Benz six-cylinder water-cooled engine
Wooden propeller
Pitot head
Interplane strut
Anti-lift bracing wire
Lift bracing wire
Main fuel tank
Pneumatic rubber tyre
Axle
Tailskid
Landing gear strut
Multiple rubber-cord suspension
Turnbuckle
Gravity-feed fuel tank

Fabric lacing
Rib
Rudder
Fixed tailplane
Fabric covering
Elevator
Steel lug
Elevator hinge
Tailplane attachment
Rudder post
687
Aircraft registration code
Spar
Shock-absorbing spring
Steel V-strut
National marking
Leading edge
Trailing edge
Pivoted tailskid
Rib

HORIZONTAL TAIL OF A BE 2B

Early passenger aircraft

UNTIL THE 1930s, most passenger aircraft were biplanes, with two pairs of wings and a wooden or metal framework covered with fabric or, sometimes, plywood. Such aircraft were restricted to low speeds and low altitudes because of the drag on their wings. Many had an open cockpit, situated behind or in front of an enclosed – but unpressurized – cabin that carried a maximum of ten people. The passengers usually sat in wicker chairs that were not bolted to the floor, and the journey could be bumpy when flying through turbulence. Warm clothing, and ear plugs to reduce the effects of prolonged noise, were often required. During the 1930s, powerful, streamlined, all-metal monoplanes, such as the Lockheed Electra shown here, became widespread. By 1939, the advent of pressurized cabins allowed fast flights at high altitudes, where there is less turbulence. Flying boats were still necessary on many routes until 1945 because of inadequate runways and the frequency of emergency sea-landings. World War II, however, resulted in enough good runways being built for land-planes to become standard on all major airline routes.

Green starboard navigation light

Flush-riveted metal-skinned wing

Leading edge

Fuel-jettison valve

Static discharge wick

Split flap in landing position

Roof trim panel

PASSENGER CABIN TRIM PANELS

Passenger service-panel aperture

Forward bulkhead upper panel

Ash-tray

Starboard wall forward panel

Cockpit door panel

Forward bulkhead lower panel

Starboard wall mid-forward panel

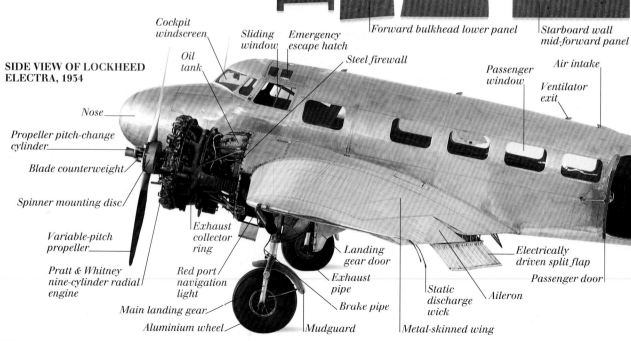

SIDE VIEW OF LOCKHEED ELECTRA, 1934

Cockpit windscreen

Sliding window

Emergency escape hatch

Oil tank

Steel firewall

Passenger window

Air intake

Ventilator exit

Nose

Propeller pitch-change cylinder

Blade counterweight

Spinner mounting disc

Variable-pitch propeller

Exhaust collector ring

Landing gear door

Electrically driven split flap

Passenger door

Pratt & Whitney nine-cylinder radial engine

Red port navigation light

Exhaust pipe

Static discharge wick

Aileron

Main landing gear

Brake pipe

Aluminium wheel

Mudguard

Metal-skinned wing

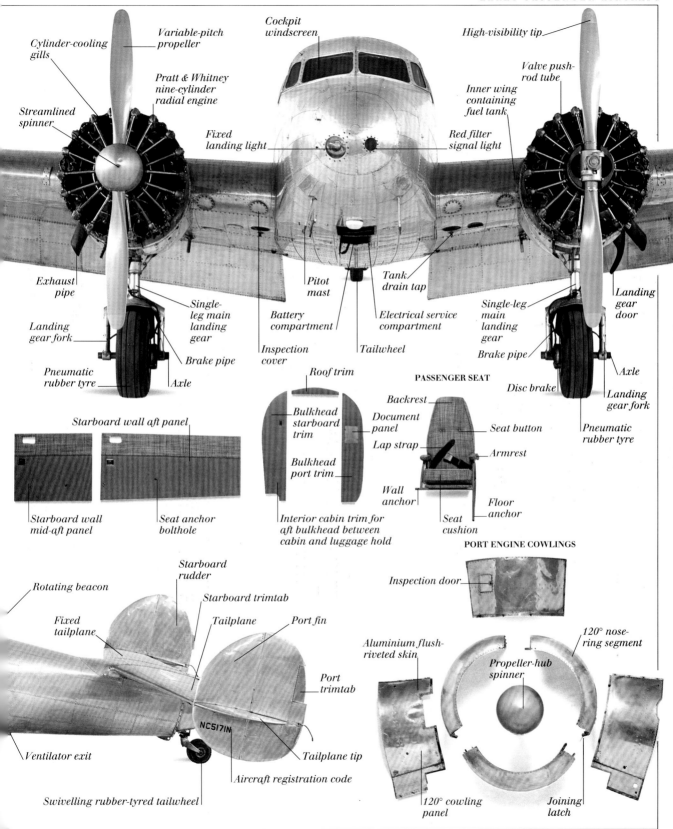

Cylinder-cooling gills

Variable-pitch propeller

Cockpit windscreen

High-visibility tip

Pratt & Whitney nine-cylinder radial engine

Valve push-rod tube

Streamlined spinner

Inner wing containing fuel tank

Fixed landing light

Red filter signal light

Exhaust pipe

Single-leg main landing gear

Landing gear fork

Pitot mast

Tank drain tap

Landing gear door

Single-leg main landing gear

Battery compartment

Electrical service compartment

Brake pipe

Pneumatic rubber tyre

Axle

Inspection cover

Tailwheel

Disc brake

Axle

Landing gear fork

Pneumatic rubber tyre

Roof trim

PASSENGER SEAT

Starboard wall aft panel

Bulkhead starboard trim

Backrest

Document panel

Seat button

Bulkhead port trim

Lap strap

Armrest

Starboard wall mid-aft panel

Seat anchor bolthole

Interior cabin trim for aft bulkhead between cabin and luggage hold

Wall anchor

Floor anchor

Seat cushion

PORT ENGINE COWLINGS

Rotating beacon

Starboard rudder

Inspection door

Starboard trimtab

Fixed tailplane

Tailplane

Port fin

120° nose-ring segment

Aluminium flush-riveted skin

Propeller-hub spinner

Port trimtab

Ventilator exit

Tailplane tip

NC5171N

Swivelling rubber-tyred tailwheel

Aircraft registration code

120° cowling panel

Joining latch

World War II aircraft

WHEN WORLD WAR II began in 1939, air forces had already replaced most of their fabric-skinned biplanes with all-metal, stressed-skin monoplanes. Aircraft played a far greater role in military operations during World War II than ever before. The wide range of aircraft duties, and the introduction of radar tracking and guidance systems, put pressure on designers to improve aircraft performance. The main areas of improvement were speed, range, and engine power. Bombers became larger and more powerful – converting from two to four engines – in order to carry a heavier bomb load; the US B-17 Flying Fortress could carry up to 6.2 tonnes (6.1 tons) of bombs over a distance of about 3,200 km (2,000 miles). Some aircraft increased their range by using drop tanks (fuel tanks that were jettisoned when empty to reduce drag). Fighters needed speed and manoeuvrability: the Hawker Tempest shown here had a maximum speed of 700 kph (435 mph), and was one of the few Allied aircraft capable of catching the German jet-powered V1 "flying bomb". By 1944, Britain had introduced its first turbojet-powered aircraft, the Gloster Meteor fighter, and Germany had introduced the fastest fighter in the world, the turbojet-powered Me 262, which had a maximum speed of 868 kph (540 mph).

PROPELLER

High-visibility yellow tip

Light-alloy propeller spinner

Variable-pitch aluminium-alloy blade

COMPONENTS OF A HAWKER TEMPEST MARK V, c.1943

Radiator-access cowling

Lower side-cowling

Upper side-cowling

STARBOARD ENGINE COWLINGS

Cowling fastener

Cartridge starter

2,400-HP Napier Sabre 24-cylinder engine

Propeller governor

Radiator header tank

Propeller drive shaft

Distributor

Ejector exhaust

Magneto

Starter motor

Engine top cowling

Upper side-cowling

Lower side-cowling

Radiator-access cowling

Cowling fastener

PORT ENGINE COWLINGS

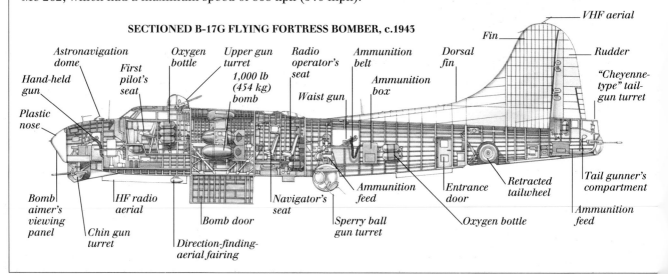

SECTIONED B-17G FLYING FORTRESS BOMBER, c.1943

Astronavigation dome

First pilot's seat

Oxygen bottle

Upper gun turret

1,000 lb (454 kg) bomb

Radio operator's seat

Ammunition belt

Ammunition box

Dorsal fin

Fin

VHF aerial

Rudder

"Cheyenne-type" tail-gun turret

Hand-held gun

Plastic nose

Waist gun

Bomb aimer's viewing panel

Chin gun turret

HF radio aerial

Bomb door

Direction-finding-aerial fairing

Navigator's seat

Sperry ball gun turret

Ammunition feed

Entrance door

Retracted tailwheel

Oxygen bottle

Tail gunner's compartment

Ammunition feed

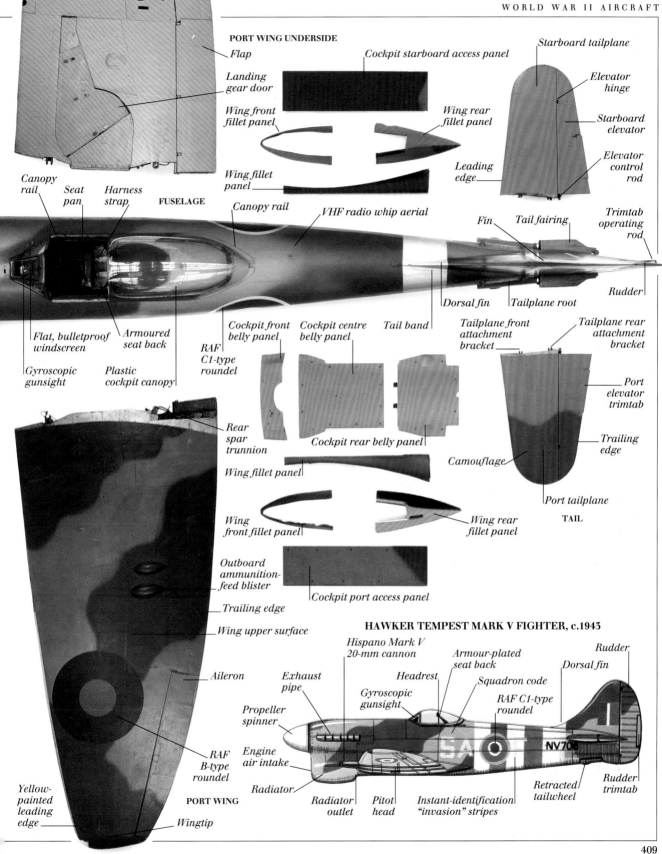

PORT WING UNDERSIDE

Flap

Cockpit starboard access panel

Starboard tailplane

Landing gear door

Elevator hinge

Wing front fillet panel

Wing rear fillet panel

Starboard elevator

Leading edge

Elevator control rod

Wing fillet panel

Canopy rail

Seat pan

Harness strap

FUSELAGE

Canopy rail

VHF radio whip aerial

Fin

Tail fairing

Trimtab operating rod

Rudder

Flat, bulletproof windscreen

Armoured seat back

Dorsal fin

Tailplane root

Tailplane front attachment bracket

Tailplane rear attachment bracket

Gyroscopic gunsight

Plastic cockpit canopy

RAF C1-type roundel

Cockpit front belly panel

Cockpit centre belly panel

Tail band

Port elevator trimtab

Rear spar trunnion

Cockpit rear belly panel

Camouflage

Trailing edge

Wing fillet panel

Port tailplane

Wing front fillet panel

Wing rear fillet panel

TAIL

Outboard ammunition-feed blister

Cockpit port access panel

Trailing edge

Wing upper surface

HAWKER TEMPEST MARK V FIGHTER, c.1943

Hispano Mark V 20-mm cannon

Rudder

Armour-plated seat back

Dorsal fin

Aileron

Exhaust pipe

Headrest

Squadron code

Propeller spinner

Gyroscopic gunsight

RAF C1-type roundel

RAF B-type roundel

Engine air intake

Radiator

Radiator outlet

Pitot head

Instant-identification "invasion" stripes

Retracted tailwheel

Rudder trimtab

Yellow-painted leading edge

PORT WING

Wingtip

NV70

Modern piston aero-engines

PISTON ENGINES today are used mainly to power the vast numbers of light aircraft and microlights, as well as crop-sprayers and crop-dusters, small helicopters, and fire-bombers (which dump water on large fires). Virtually all heavier aircraft are now powered by jet engines. Modern piston aero-engines work on the same basic principles as the engine used by the Wright brothers in the first powered flight in 1903. However, today's engines are more sophisticated than earlier engines. For example, modern aero-engines may use a two-stroke or a four-stroke combustion cycle; they may have from one to nine air- or water-cooled cylinders, which may be arranged horizontally, in-line, in V formation, or radially; and they may drive the aircraft's propeller either directly or through a reduction gearbox. One of the more unconventional types of modern aero-engine is the rotary engine shown here, which has a trilobate (three-sided) rotor spinning in a chamber shaped like a fat figure-of-eight.

MID WEST TWO-STROKE, THREE-CYLINDER ENGINE

MID WEST 75-HP TWO-STROKE, THREE-CYLINDER ENGINE

Spark plug

Coolant outlet

Cylinder head

Piston

Cylinder barrel

Exhaust manifold

Exhaust port

Cylinder liner

Upper crankcase

Reduction gearbox

Driven gear

Gearbox drive splines

Connecting rod (con-rod)

Pump drive belt

Coolant pump

Small end

Generator rotor

Propeller drive flange

Big end

Counterweight

Stator

Torsional vibration damper

Sprag clutch

Crankshaft

Ignition trigger housing

Gearbox mounting plate

Lower crankcase

Engine mounting plate

ROTOR AND HOUSINGS OF A MID WEST SINGLE-ROTOR ENGINE

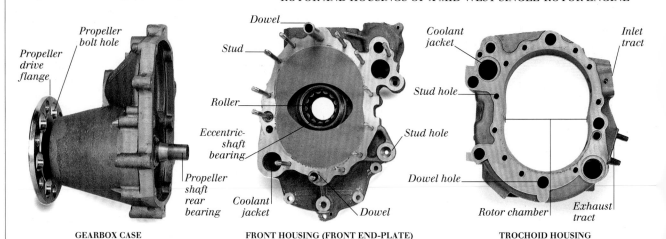

Propeller bolt hole

Dowel

Coolant jacket

Inlet tract

Propeller drive flange

Stud

Stud hole

Roller

Eccentric-shaft bearing

Stud hole

Propeller shaft rear bearing

Coolant jacket

Dowel hole

Dowel

Rotor chamber

Exhaust tract

GEARBOX CASE

FRONT HOUSING (FRONT END-PLATE)

TROCHOID HOUSING

MID WEST 90-HP TWIN-ROTOR ENGINE

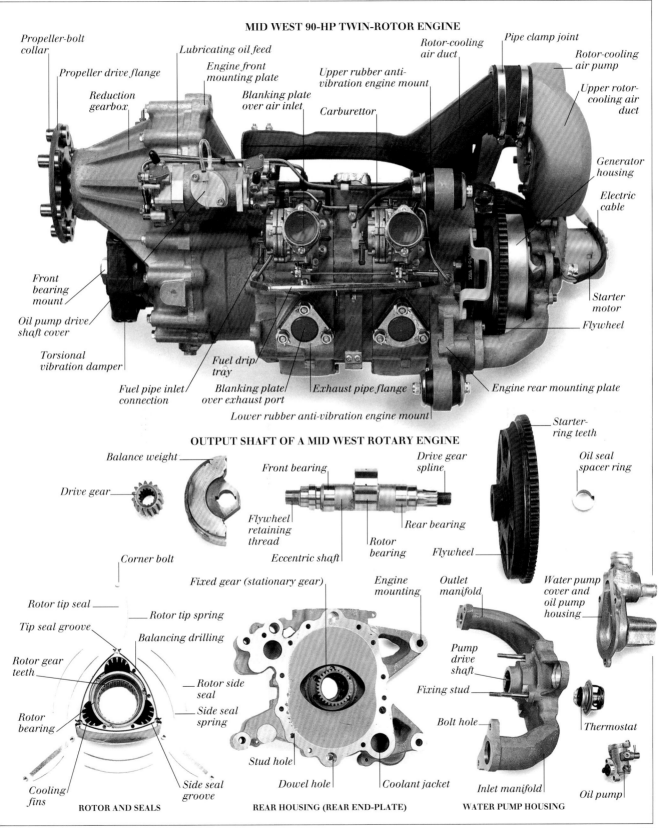

Propeller-bolt collar

Propeller drive flange

Reduction gearbox

Lubricating oil feed

Engine front mounting plate

Blanking plate over air inlet

Upper rubber anti-vibration engine mount

Carburettor

Rotor-cooling air duct

Pipe clamp joint

Rotor-cooling air pump

Upper rotor-cooling air duct

Generator housing

Electric cable

Front bearing mount

Oil pump drive shaft cover

Torsional vibration damper

Fuel pipe inlet connection

Fuel drip tray

Blanking plate over exhaust port

Exhaust pipe flange

Lower rubber anti-vibration engine mount

Starter motor

Flywheel

Engine rear mounting plate

OUTPUT SHAFT OF A MID WEST ROTARY ENGINE

Balance weight

Drive gear

Front bearing

Flywheel retaining thread

Eccentric shaft

Rotor bearing

Drive gear spline

Rear bearing

Flywheel

Starter-ring teeth

Oil seal spacer ring

Corner bolt

Rotor tip seal

Tip seal groove

Rotor gear teeth

Rotor bearing

Cooling fins

Balancing drilling

Rotor tip spring

Rotor side seal

Side seal spring

Side seal groove

ROTOR AND SEALS

Fixed gear (stationary gear)

Engine mounting

Stud hole

Dowel hole

Coolant jacket

REAR HOUSING (REAR END-PLATE)

Outlet manifold

Pump drive shaft

Fixing stud

Bolt hole

Inlet manifold

Water pump cover and oil pump housing

Thermostat

Oil pump

WATER PUMP HOUSING

411

Modern jetliners 1

BAE-146 JETLINER

MODERN JETLINERS HAVE ENABLED ordinary people to travel to places where once only the wealthy could afford to go. Compared with the first jetliners (which were introduced in the 1940s), modern ones are much quieter, burn fuel more efficiently, and produce less air pollution. These advances are largely due to the replacement of turbojet engines with turbofan engines (see pp. 418-419). The greater power of turbofan engines at low speeds enables modern jetliners to carry more fuel and passengers than turbojet aircraft; a modern Boeing 747-400 (popularly known as a "jumbo jet") can fly 400 people for 13,700 km (8,500 miles) without needing to refuel. Jetliners fly at high altitudes, typically cruising at 8,000-11,000 m (26,000-36,000 ft), where they can use fuel efficiently and usually avoid bad weather. The pilot always controls the aircraft during take-off and landing, but at other times the aircraft is usually controlled by an autopilot. Autopilots are complex on-board mechanisms that detect deviations from an aircraft's route and make appropriate adjustments to the flight controls. Flight decks are also equipped with radars that warn pilots of approaching hazards, such as mountain ranges, bad weather, and other aircraft.

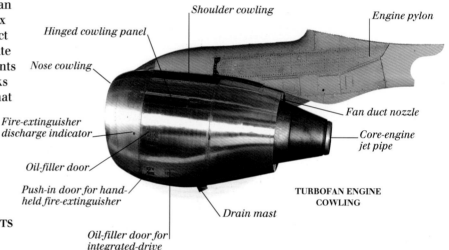

Shoulder cowling

Engine pylon

Hinged cowling panel

Nose cowling

Fire-extinguisher discharge indicator

Fan duct nozzle

Core-engine jet pipe

Oil-filler door

Push-in door for hand-held fire-extinguisher

Drain mast

TURBOFAN ENGINE COWLING

STRUCTURAL COMPONENTS OF A BAE-146 JETLINER

Oil-filler door for integrated-drive generator

FUSELAGE NOSE-SECTION

FUSELAGE MID-SECTION

Electrically heated, birdproof windscreen

Side window

Anchor for open door

Rain gutter

Hinge

Peephole

Finger recess

Static air-pressure plate

Forward main door aperture

Passenger window aperture

VHF omni-range and instrument-landing-system aerials

Light-alloy door frame

Main external operating handle

Multiple-pinned lock

Floor level

Radome

Toilet service connector

Air temperature probe

Stall warning vane

Pitot head for dynamic air pressure

FORWARD MAIN DOOR

Anchor for open door

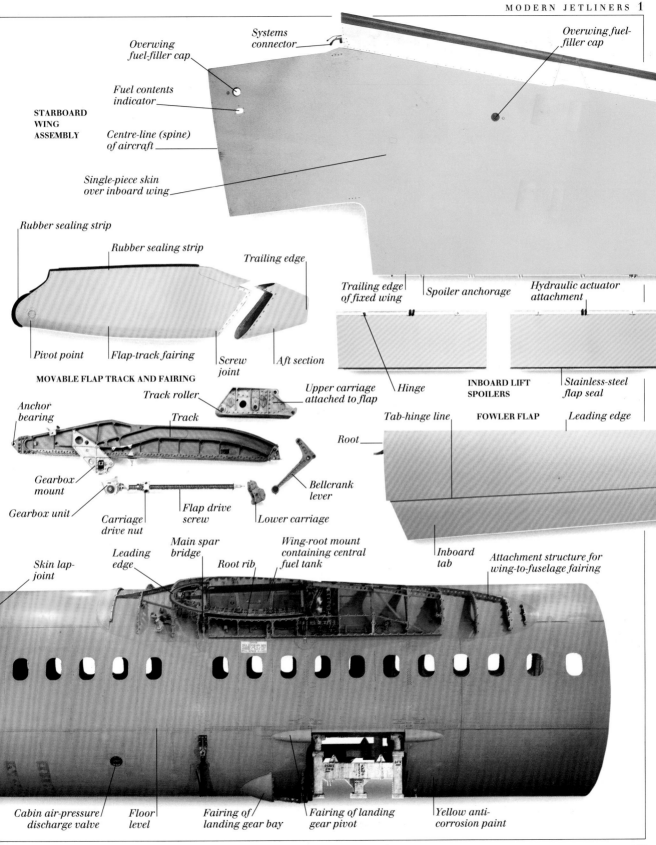

Overwing
fuel-filler cap

Systems
connector

Overwing fuel-
filler cap

**STARBOARD
WING
ASSEMBLY**

Fuel contents
indicator

Centre-line (spine)
of aircraft

Single-piece skin
over inboard wing

Rubber sealing strip

Rubber sealing strip

Trailing edge

Trailing edge
of fixed wing

Spoiler anchorage

Hydraulic actuator
attachment

Pivot point

Flap-track fairing

Screw
joint

Aft section

MOVABLE FLAP TRACK AND FAIRING

Upper carriage
attached to flap

Hinge

**INBOARD LIFT
SPOILERS**

Stainless-steel
flap seal

Track roller

Track

Anchor
bearing

Tab-hinge line

FOWLER FLAP

Leading edge

Root

Gearbox
mount

Bellcrank
lever

Gearbox unit

Carriage
drive nut

Flap drive
screw

Lower carriage

Skin lap-
joint

Leading
edge

Main spar
bridge

Root rib

Wing-root mount
containing central
fuel tank

Inboard
tab

Attachment structure for
wing-to-fuselage fairing

Cabin air-pressure
discharge valve

Floor
level

Fairing of
landing gear bay

Fairing of landing
gear pivot

Yellow anti-
corrosion paint

413

Modern jetliners 2

Landing and taxiing light

STARBOARD WING

Heated de-icing leading edge

Roll-spoiler hinge

Roll-spoiler hydraulic actuator attachment

Fixed trailing edge

Aileron hinge

Starboard navigation light

Hinge

Hydraulic actuator attachment

Spoiler arm

Aerodynamic balance

Horn balance

Hinge bracket

Recessed hinge

INTERMEDIATE LIFT SPOILER

Flap seal

OUTBOARD ROLL SPOILER

AILERON

Trimtab

Servo-tab

MAIN FOWLER FLAP

Leading edge

Static discharge wick attachment

Flap tip

FUSELAGE SPINE FAIRING

Tab-hinge line

Outboard tab

Finger recess

Peephole

Hot-air de-icing duct

Landing gear door

Hydraulic brake pipe

Main pivot

Skin lap-joint

Electrical harness

Oleo lock-jack

Passenger window aperture

Light-alloy beam

Direction bar

Main external operating handle

Shock-strut bearing

Brake pipe

Hinge

Pneumatic tyre

Outer wheel axle

Side brace and retraction jack trunnions

Lower pivot

Pivoted trailing-link arm

Hydraulic brake pipe

Wheel hub

Anchor for open door

Cabin air-discharge aperture

STARBOARD TWIN-WHEEL MAIN LANDING GEAR

AFT MAIN DOOR

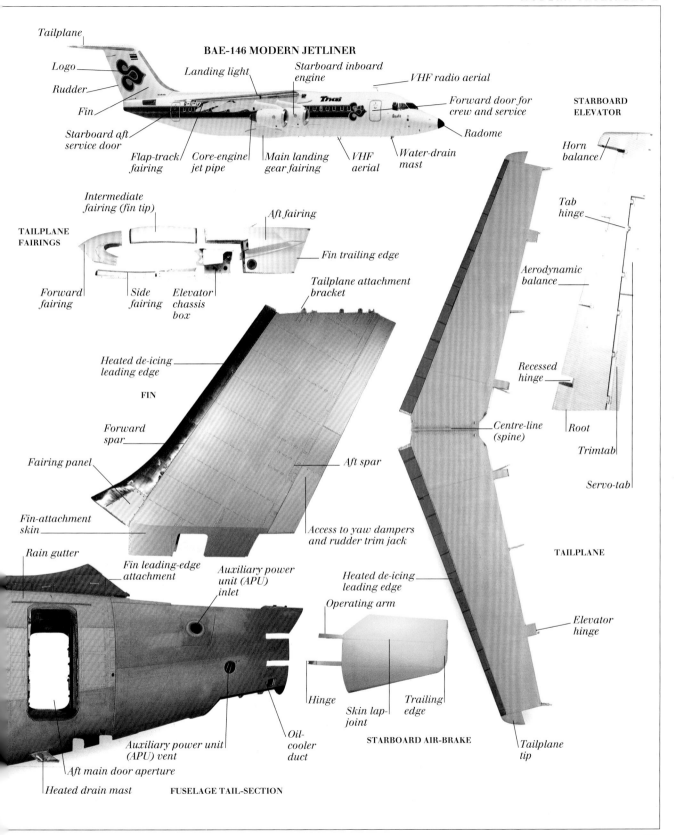

BAE-146 MODERN JETLINER

Tailplane

Logo

Rudder

Fin

Landing light

Starboard inboard engine

VHF radio aerial

STARBOARD ELEVATOR

Forward door for crew and service

Radome

Horn balance

Starboard aft service door

Flap-track fairing

Core-engine jet pipe

Main landing gear fairing

VHF aerial

Water-drain mast

Tab hinge

TAILPLANE FAIRINGS

Intermediate fairing (fin tip)

Aft fairing

Fin trailing edge

Aerodynamic balance

Forward fairing

Side fairing

Elevator chassis box

Tailplane attachment bracket

Recessed hinge

Heated de-icing leading edge

Centre-line (spine)

Root

FIN

Trimtab

Forward spar

Aft spar

Servo-tab

Fairing panel

Fin-attachment skin

Access to yaw dampers and rudder trim jack

TAILPLANE

Rain gutter

Fin leading-edge attachment

Auxiliary power unit (APU) inlet

Heated de-icing leading edge

Operating arm

Elevator hinge

Hinge

Trailing edge

Auxiliary power unit (APU) vent

Oil-cooler duct

Skin lap-joint

Aft main door aperture

STARBOARD AIR-BRAKE

Tailplane tip

Heated drain mast

FUSELAGE TAIL-SECTION

415

Supersonic jetliners

**COMPUTER-
DESIGNED SST**

SUPERSONIC AIRCRAFT FLY FASTER than the speed of sound (Mach 1). There are many supersonic military aircraft, but only two supersonic passenger-carrying aircraft (also called SSTs, or supersonic transports) have been produced: the Russian Tu-144, and Concorde, produced jointly by Britain and France. The Tu-144 had a greater maximum speed than Concorde but was withdrawn in 1978, after only seven months in service. Concorde has remained in service since 1976. It features many innovations, including a droop nose, which is lowered during take-off and landing to aid visibility from the cockpit, and the pumping of fuel between forward and aft trim tanks to help stabilize the aircraft. Concorde has a narrow fuselage and short-span wings to reduce drag during supersonic flight. Its noisy turbojet engines with afterburners enable it to carry 100 passengers at a cruising speed of Mach 2 at 15,000-18,000 m (50,000-60,000 ft). Once an aircraft is flying faster than Mach 1, it produces a continuous air-pressure wave, which is heard as a "sonic boom".

Strake

Fin

Standby
pitot head

Starboard
outboard
engine air-intake

Inboard
elevon-
jack
fairing

Nose-
gear
leg

FRONT VIEW OF CONCORDE

**OVERHEAD VIEW
OF CONCORDE**

Variable
nozzle

Leading edge

Toilets

Electrothermal
de-icing panel

Starboard
forward trim tank

Overhead hand-baggage bin

Passenger
accommodation

Underfloor air-
conditioning duct

Seat
attachment
rail

Life-raft

VHF
aerial

Wardrobe

Forward galley

Additional crew's seat

Aluminium-alloy layers
and insulation

Third pilot's
seat

Erosion-
resistant
radome

Cockpit
windscreen

Retractable
visor

Lateral bracing strut

Telescopic strut

Port
forward
trim tank

"A" frame

Nose-
gear
leg

Steering
actuator

Standby
flight-control
hydraulic jack

Plug-type
passenger
door

Nose-gear
door

Multi-ply
high-pressure
tyre

Machined
skin panel

Weather
radar

Captain's
seat

Upper
rudder

Fin

Visor jack

Dorsal fin

Droop-
nose hinge

Cockpit air-
conditioning
duct

Emergency exit

Pivoted
retractable frame

Tail cone

G-BOAG

Aft door

Elevon (combined elevator and aileron)

Hot-section steel and titanium skin

Engine cowling

Landing gear door

Bogie main landing gear

SECTIONED VIEW OF CONCORDE

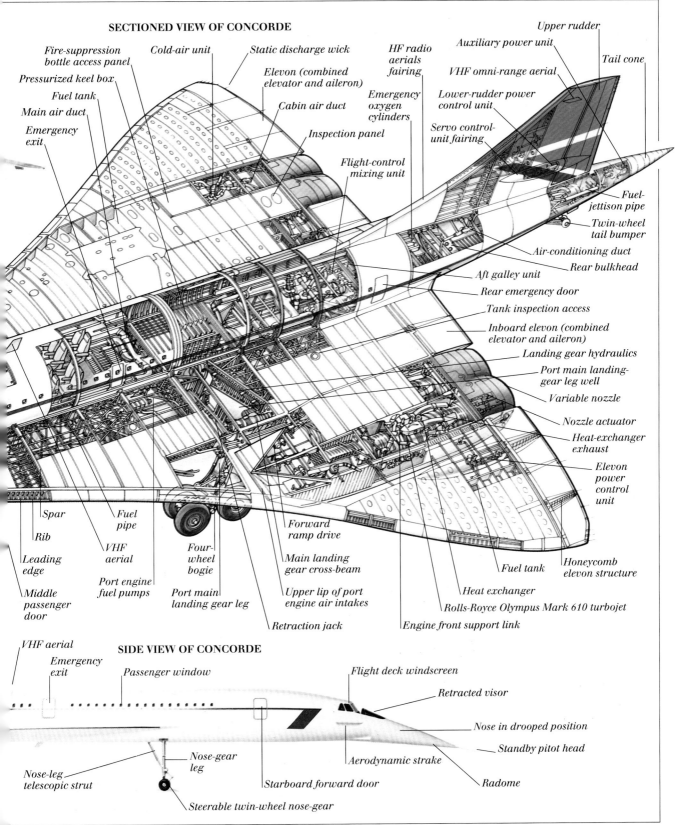

Fire-suppression bottle access panel

Cold-air unit

Static discharge wick

Elevon (combined elevator and aileron)

HF radio aerials fairing

Upper rudder

Auxiliary power unit

VHF omni-range aerial

Tail cone

Pressurized keel box

Fuel tank

Main air duct

Emergency exit

Cabin air duct

Inspection panel

Emergency oxygen cylinders

Lower-rudder power control unit

Servo control-unit fairing

Flight-control mixing unit

Fuel-jettison pipe

Twin-wheel tail bumper

Air-conditioning duct

Rear bulkhead

Aft galley unit

Rear emergency door

Tank inspection access

Inboard elevon (combined elevator and aileron)

Landing gear hydraulics

Port main landing-gear leg well

Variable nozzle

Nozzle actuator

Heat-exchanger exhaust

Elevon power control unit

Spar

Rib

Leading edge

Middle passenger door

Fuel pipe

VHF aerial

Port engine fuel pumps

Four-wheel bogie

Port main landing gear leg

Retraction jack

Forward ramp drive

Main landing gear cross-beam

Upper lip of port engine air intakes

Heat exchanger

Rolls-Royce Olympus Mark 610 turbojet

Engine front support link

Fuel tank

Honeycomb elevon structure

SIDE VIEW OF CONCORDE

VHF aerial

Emergency exit

Passenger window

Flight deck windscreen

Retracted visor

Nose in drooped position

Standby pitot head

Nose-gear leg

Aerodynamic strake

Starboard forward door

Radome

Nose-leg telescopic strut

Steerable twin-wheel nose-gear

Jet engines

JET ENGINES ARE USED BY MOST MILITARY and heavy aircraft, and by many helicopters. The simplest type of jet engine, or gas turbine, is the turbojet. It works by continuously burning a mixture of fuel and air in a combustion chamber to produce a jet of hot exhaust gas that is expelled through a nozzle to produce thrust. The hot gas also spins turbine blades, which, in turn, spin the blades of an air compressor; the compressor forces air into the combustion chamber. Many of the fastest aircraft use turbojets, with additional booster units called afterburners, but their use is restricted by their high noise emission. Most jetliners use turbofan jet engines, which are quieter. An enormous fan, driven by a low-pressure turbine, feeds some air into the compressor but feeds most of it through bypass ducts to join the exhaust jetstream in the tail cone. The bypass stream produces most of the thrust. Many smaller, propeller-driven aircraft use turboprop jet engines, in which the engine powers a propeller.

NPT 301 MODERN TURBOJET

Fuel sprayer
Reverse-flow combustion chamber
Radial diffuser
Turbine rotor
Centrifugal compressor
Exhaust diffuser
Inducer
Tail cone
Air intake
Jet pipe
Exhaust nozzle
Nose cone
Igniter
Alternator
Nozzle guide vane
Air impingement starter
Combustion chamber casing

Plenum ring for hot anti-icing air
Flow splitter
Gearbox bevel drive
Integral oil tank
High-pressure compressor
Combustion chamber
Fuel manifold
High-pressure turbine
Fuel nozzle
Centrifugal compressor
Temperature and pressure sensor
Low-pressure fan
Inlet cone (rotating spinner)
Pressure line
Fancase with special structure to contain broken fan
Electronic engine control and airframe interface connector
Fan duct
Electronic engine control (EEC) unit
Compressor front bearing
Engine front mount
Electrical wiring harness
Fuel and oil heat exchanger
Oil filter
Compressor air-bleed connection

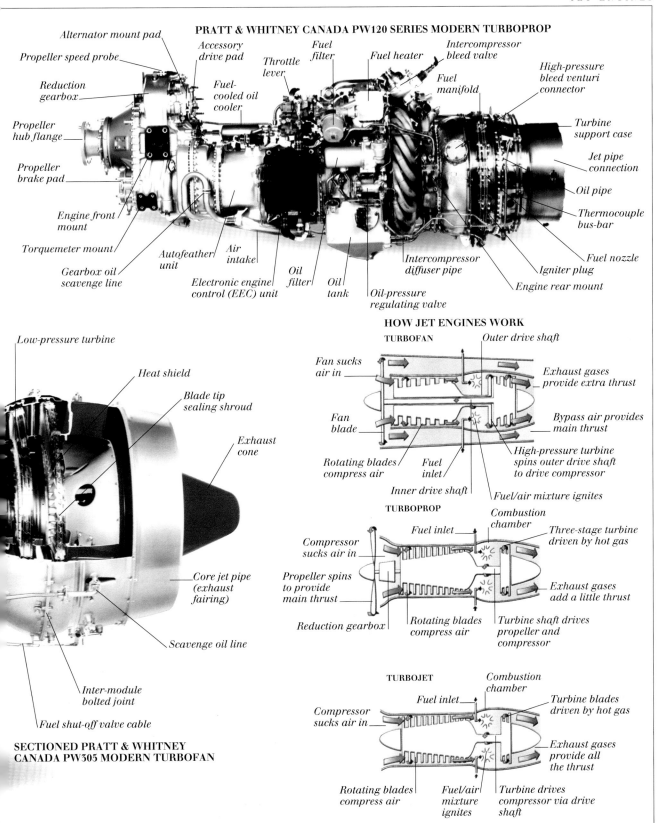

PRATT & WHITNEY CANADA PW120 SERIES MODERN TURBOPROP

Alternator mount pad
Accessory drive pad
Fuel filter
Intercompressor bleed valve
High-pressure bleed venturi connector
Propeller speed probe
Throttle lever
Fuel heater
Fuel manifold
Reduction gearbox
Fuel-cooled oil cooler
Fuel
Turbine support case
Propeller hub flange
Jet pipe connection
Oil pipe
Propeller brake pad
Thermocouple bus-bar
Engine front mount
Air intake
Fuel nozzle
Torquemeter mount
Igniter plug
Gearbox oil scavenge line
Autofeather unit
Oil filter
Intercompressor diffuser pipe
Engine rear mount
Electronic engine control (EEC) unit
Oil tank
Oil-pressure regulating valve

HOW JET ENGINES WORK

TURBOFAN

Fan sucks air in
Outer drive shaft
Exhaust gases provide extra thrust
Fan blade
Bypass air provides main thrust
Rotating blades compress air
Fuel inlet
High-pressure turbine spins outer drive shaft to drive compressor
Inner drive shaft
Fuel/air mixture ignites

TURBOPROP

Fuel inlet
Combustion chamber
Compressor sucks air in
Three-stage turbine driven by hot gas
Propeller spins to provide main thrust
Exhaust gases add a little thrust
Reduction gearbox
Rotating blades compress air
Turbine shaft drives propeller and compressor

TURBOJET

Fuel inlet
Combustion chamber
Compressor sucks air in
Turbine blades driven by hot gas
Exhaust gases provide all the thrust
Rotating blades compress air
Fuel/air mixture ignites
Turbine drives compressor via drive shaft

Low-pressure turbine
Heat shield
Blade tip sealing shroud
Exhaust cone
Core jet pipe (exhaust fairing)
Scavenge oil line
Inter-module bolted joint
Fuel shut-off valve cable

SECTIONED PRATT & WHITNEY CANADA PW305 MODERN TURBOFAN

419

Modern military aircraft

MODERN MILITARY AIRCRAFT ARE AMONG THE MOST SOPHISTICATED and expensive products of the 20th century. Fighters need computer-operated controls for manoeuvrability, powerful engines, and effective air-to-air weapons. Most modern fighters also have guided missiles, radar, and passive, infra-red sensors. These developments enable today's fighters to engage in combat with adversaries that are outside visual range. Bombers carry a large weapon load and enough fuel for long-range flights. A few military aircraft, such as the Tornado and the F-14 Tomcat, have variable-sweep ("swing") wings. During take-off and landing their wings are fully extended, but for high-speed flight and low-level attacks the wings are pivoted fully back. A recent development is the "stealth" bomber, which is designed to absorb or deflect enemy radar in order to remain undetected. Earlier bombers, such as the Tornado, use terrain-following radars to fly so close to the ground that they avoid enemy radar detection.

FRONT VIEW OF A PANAVIA TORNADO

Instrument landing system aerial

Birdproof windscreen

Air data probe

Port variable-incidence air intake

Wing-root glove fairing

Starboard inboard stores pylon

Taileron

Starboard main landing gear door

Main landing gear leg

Laser ranger and marked-target seeker

Starboard nose-gear door

Steerable twin-wheel nose-gear

Radome containing ground-mapping, attack, and terrain-following radars

Taxiing light

Wing extended for take-off and landing

Wing pivoted back for high-speed flight

SWING-WING F-14 TOMCAT FIGHTER

SIDE VIEW OF A PANAVIA TORNADO GR1A (RECONNAISSANCE VERSION), 1986

Pilot's cockpit

Navigator's instrument console

Navigator's cockpit

Single canopy over both cockpits

Engine air intake

Navigation light

Flat, birdproof windscreen

High-velocity air duct to disperse rain

Upper "request identification" aerial

Air data probe

RESCUE

Radome containing ground-mapping, attack, and terrain-following radars

UHF aerial

Angle-of-attack probe

Tacan (tactical air navigation) aerial

Emergency canopy release handle

Nose-gear door

Steerable nose-gear leg

Twin nose-wheel

Pitot head

Hinged auxiliary air intake

Cold air intake (ram scoop)

Heat exchanger exhaust duct

Window covering infra-red reconnaissance camera

NORTHROP B-2 ("STEALTH" BOMBER), 1989

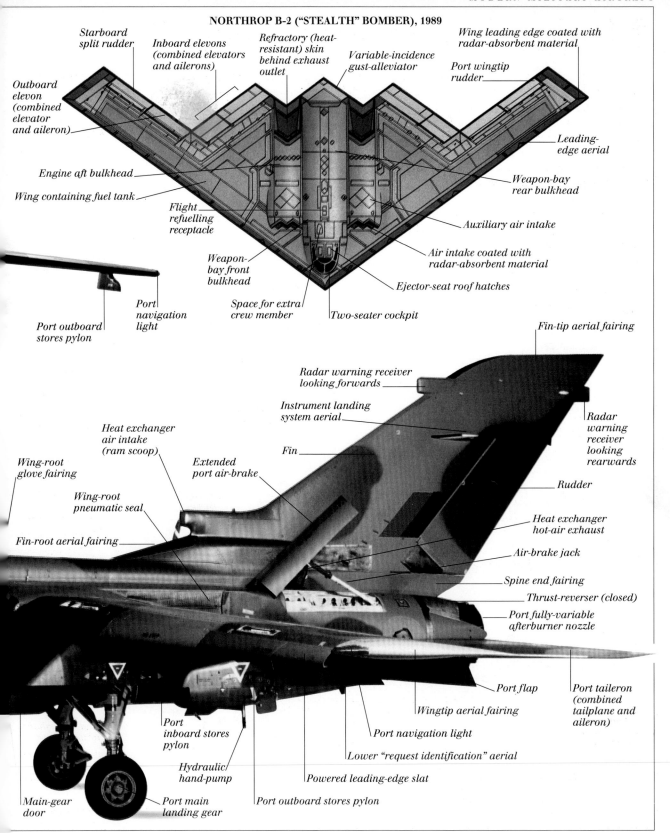

Starboard split rudder

Inboard elevons (combined elevators and ailerons)

Refractory (heat-resistant) skin behind exhaust outlet

Variable-incidence gust-alleviator

Wing leading edge coated with radar-absorbent material

Port wingtip rudder

Outboard elevon (combined elevator and aileron)

Leading-edge aerial

Engine aft bulkhead

Wing containing fuel tank

Flight refuelling receptacle

Weapon-bay rear bulkhead

Weapon-bay front bulkhead

Auxiliary air intake

Air intake coated with radar-absorbent material

Space for extra crew member

Ejector-seat roof hatches

Two-seater cockpit

Port outboard stores pylon

Port navigation light

Fin-tip aerial fairing

Radar warning receiver looking forwards

Instrument landing system aerial

Fin

Heat exchanger air intake (ram scoop)

Extended port air-brake

Radar warning receiver looking rearwards

Wing-root glove fairing

Wing-root pneumatic seal

Rudder

Fin-root aerial fairing

Heat exchanger hot-air exhaust

Air-brake jack

Spine end fairing

Thrust-reverser (closed)

Port fully-variable afterburner nozzle

Port inboard stores pylon

Hydraulic hand-pump

Port flap

Wingtip aerial fairing

Port taileron (combined tailplane and aileron)

Port navigation light

Lower "request identification" aerial

Powered leading-edge slat

Main-gear door

Port main landing gear

Port outboard stores pylon

Helicopters

HELICOPTERS USE ROTATING BLADES for lift, propulsion, and steering. The first machine to achieve sustained, controlled flight using rotating blades was the autogiro built in the 1920s by the Spaniard Juan de la Cierva. His machine had unpowered blades above the fuselage that relied on the flow of air to rotate them and provide lift as the autogiro was driven forwards by a conventional propeller. Then, in 1939, the Russian-born American Igor Sikorsky produced his VS-300, the forerunner of modern helicopters. Its engine-driven blades provided lift, propulsion, and steering. It could take off vertically, hover, and fly in any direction, and had a tail rotor to prevent the helicopter body from spinning. The introduction of gas turbine jet engines to helicopters in 1955 produced quieter, safer, and more powerful machines. Because of their versatility in flight, helicopters are today used for many purposes, including crop-spraying, traffic surveillance, and transporting crews to deep-sea oil rigs, as well as acting as gunships, air ambulances, and air taxis.

BELL 47G-3B1

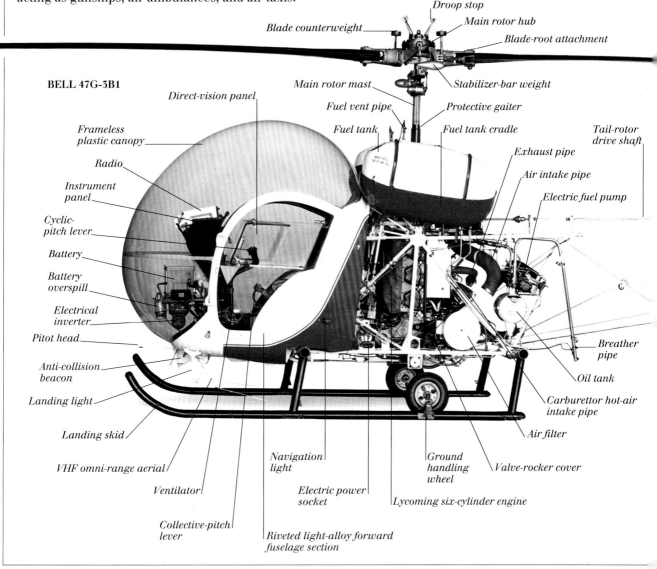

BELL 47G-3B1

Droop stop

Blade counterweight

Main rotor hub

Blade-root attachment

Main rotor mast

Stabilizer-bar weight

Direct-vision panel

Fuel vent pipe

Protective gaiter

Frameless plastic canopy

Fuel tank

Fuel tank cradle

Tail-rotor drive shaft

Radio

Exhaust pipe

Air intake pipe

Instrument panel

Electric fuel pump

Cyclic-pitch lever

Battery

Battery overspill

Electrical inverter

Pitot head

Breather pipe

Anti-collision beacon

Oil tank

Landing light

Carburettor hot-air intake pipe

Landing skid

Air filter

VHF omni-range aerial

Navigation light

Ground handling wheel

Valve-rocker cover

Ventilator

Electric power socket

Lycoming six-cylinder engine

Collective-pitch lever

Riveted light-alloy forward fuselage section

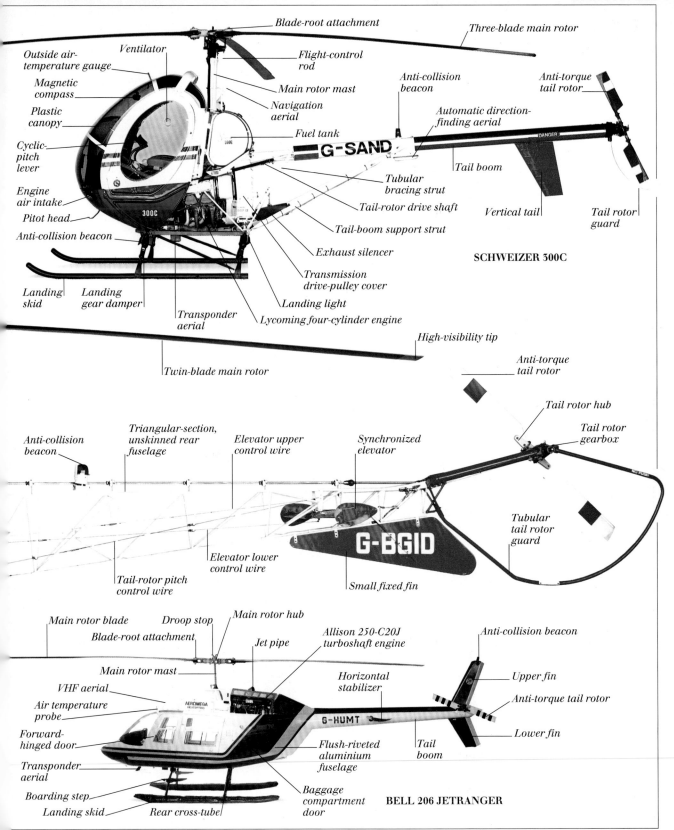

Blade-root attachment

Three-blade main rotor

Outside air-temperature gauge

Ventilator

Flight-control rod

Anti-collision beacon

Anti-torque tail rotor

Magnetic compass

Main rotor mast

Automatic direction-finding aerial

Plastic canopy

Navigation aerial

Cyclic-pitch lever

Fuel tank

G-SAND

Tail boom

Engine air intake

Tubular bracing strut

Pitot head

Tail-rotor drive shaft

Vertical tail

Tail rotor guard

Anti-collision beacon

Tail-boom support strut

Exhaust silencer

SCHWEIZER 300C

Landing skid

Landing gear damper

Transmission drive-pulley cover

Transponder aerial

Landing light

Lycoming four-cylinder engine

High-visibility tip

Twin-blade main rotor

Anti-torque tail rotor

Tail rotor hub

Anti-collision beacon

Triangular-section, unskinned rear fuselage

Elevator upper control wire

Synchronized elevator

Tail rotor gearbox

Tubular tail rotor guard

Elevator lower control wire

G-BGID

Tail-rotor pitch control wire

Small fixed fin

Main rotor blade

Droop stop

Main rotor hub

Allison 250-C20J turboshaft engine

Anti-collision beacon

Blade-root attachment

Jet pipe

Main rotor mast

Horizontal stabilizer

Upper fin

VHF aerial

Anti-torque tail rotor

Air temperature probe

G-HUMT

Lower fin

Forward-hinged door

Flush-riveted aluminium fuselage

Tail boom

Transponder aerial

Boarding step

Landing skid

Rear cross-tube

Baggage compartment door

BELL 206 JETRANGER

Light aircraft

LIGHT AIRCRAFT, SUCH AS THE ARV SUPER 2 shown here, are small, lightweight, and of simple construction. More than a million have been built since World War I, mainly for recreational use by private owners. Virtually all light aircraft have piston engines, most of which are air-cooled, although some are liquid-cooled. Open cockpits, almost universal in the 1920s, have today been replaced by enclosed cabins. The cabins of high-wing aircraft have one or two doors, whereas those of low-wing aircraft usually have a sliding or hinged canopy. Most modern light aircraft are made of aluminium alloy, although some are made of wood or of fibre-reinforced materials. Light aircraft today also usually have navigational instruments, an electrical system, cabin heating, wheel brakes, and a two-way radio.

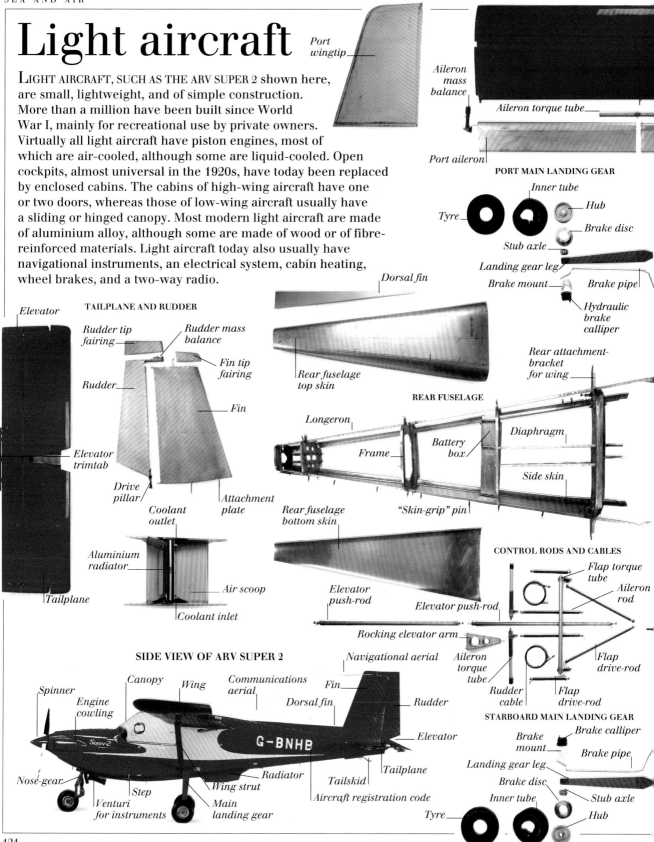

Port wingtip

Aileron mass balance

Aileron torque tube

Port aileron

PORT MAIN LANDING GEAR

Tyre

Inner tube

Hub

Brake disc

Stub axle

Landing gear leg

Brake mount

Brake pipe

Hydraulic brake calliper

Dorsal fin

TAILPLANE AND RUDDER

Elevator

Rudder tip fairing

Rudder mass balance

Fin tip fairing

Rudder

Fin

Elevator trimtab

Drive pillar

Coolant outlet

Attachment plate

Aluminium radiator

Air scoop

Coolant inlet

Tailplane

Rear fuselage top skin

Rear attachment-bracket for wing

REAR FUSELAGE

Longeron

Frame

Battery box

Diaphragm

Side skin

Rear fuselage bottom skin

"Skin-grip" pin

Elevator push-rod

Elevator push-rod

Rocking elevator arm

CONTROL RODS AND CABLES

Flap torque tube

Aileron rod

Aileron torque tube

Rudder cable

Flap drive-rod

Flap drive-rod

SIDE VIEW OF ARV SUPER 2

Spinner

Canopy

Wing

Communications aerial

Navigational aerial

Fin

Dorsal fin

Rudder

Elevator

Engine cowling

G-BNHB

Nose-gear

Step

Venturi for instruments

Wing strut

Radiator

Main landing gear

Tailskid

Tailplane

Aircraft registration code

STARBOARD MAIN LANDING GEAR

Brake mount

Brake calliper

Brake pipe

Landing gear leg

Brake disc

Inner tube

Stub axle

Hub

Tyre

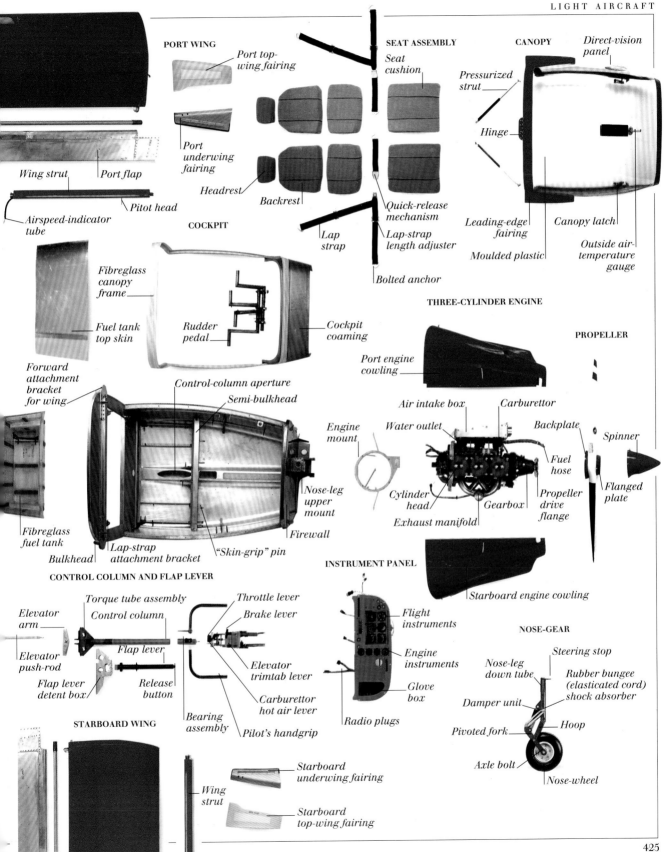

PORT WING

Port top-wing fairing

Port underwing fairing

Headrest

Wing strut

Port flap

Pitot head

Airspeed-indicator tube

SEAT ASSEMBLY

Seat cushion

Backrest

Lap strap

Quick-release mechanism

Lap-strap length adjuster

Bolted anchor

CANOPY

Direct-vision panel

Pressurized strut

Hinge

Leading-edge fairing

Moulded plastic

Canopy latch

Outside air-temperature gauge

COCKPIT

Fibreglass canopy frame

Fuel tank top skin

Rudder pedal

Cockpit coaming

THREE-CYLINDER ENGINE

Port engine cowling

Engine mount

Air intake box

Water outlet

Carburettor

Backplate

Fuel hose

Cylinder head

Exhaust manifold

Gearbox

Propeller drive flange

PROPELLER

Spinner

Flanged plate

Forward attachment bracket for wing

Control-column aperture

Semi-bulkhead

Nose-leg upper mount

Firewall

Fibreglass fuel tank

Bulkhead

Lap-strap attachment bracket

"Skin-grip" pin

Starboard engine cowling

CONTROL COLUMN AND FLAP LEVER

Elevator arm

Torque tube assembly

Control column

Throttle lever

Brake lever

Elevator trimtab lever

Carburettor hot air lever

Elevator push-rod

Flap lever

Release button

Flap lever detent box

Bearing assembly

Pilot's handgrip

INSTRUMENT PANEL

Flight instruments

Engine instruments

Glove box

Radio plugs

NOSE-GEAR

Steering stop

Nose-leg down tube

Rubber bungee (elasticated cord) shock absorber

Damper unit

Hoop

Pivoted fork

Axle bolt

Nose-wheel

STARBOARD WING

Wing strut

Starboard underwing fairing

Starboard top-wing fairing

Gliders, hang-gliders, and microlights

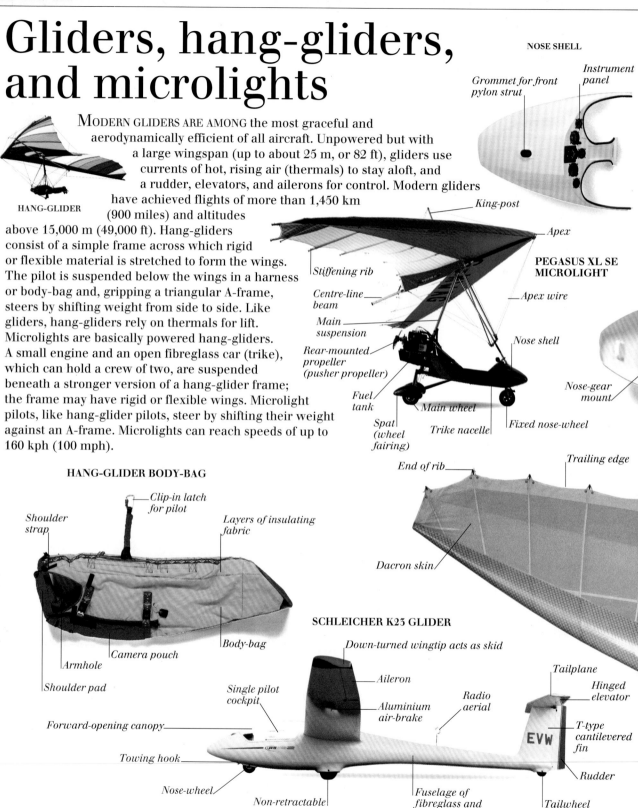

MODERN GLIDERS ARE AMONG the most graceful and aerodynamically efficient of all aircraft. Unpowered but with a large wingspan (up to about 25 m, or 82 ft), gliders use currents of hot, rising air (thermals) to stay aloft, and a rudder, elevators, and ailerons for control. Modern gliders have achieved flights of more than 1,450 km (900 miles) and altitudes above 15,000 m (49,000 ft). Hang-gliders consist of a simple frame across which rigid or flexible material is stretched to form the wings. The pilot is suspended below the wings in a harness or body-bag and, gripping a triangular A-frame, steers by shifting weight from side to side. Like gliders, hang-gliders rely on thermals for lift. Microlights are basically powered hang-gliders. A small engine and an open fibreglass car (trike), which can hold a crew of two, are suspended beneath a stronger version of a hang-glider frame; the frame may have rigid or flexible wings. Microlight pilots, like hang-glider pilots, steer by shifting their weight against an A-frame. Microlights can reach speeds of up to 160 kph (100 mph).

HANG-GLIDER

NOSE SHELL

Grommet for front pylon strut

Instrument panel

King-post

Apex

PEGASUS XL SE MICROLIGHT

Stiffening rib

Apex wire

Centre-line beam

Main suspension

Nose shell

Rear-mounted propeller (pusher propeller)

Nose-gear mount

Fuel tank

Main wheel

Spat (wheel fairing)

Trike nacelle

Fixed nose-wheel

End of rib

Trailing edge

HANG-GLIDER BODY-BAG

Clip-in latch for pilot

Shoulder strap

Layers of insulating fabric

Dacron skin

Camera pouch

Body-bag

Armhole

Shoulder pad

SCHLEICHER K23 GLIDER

Down-turned wingtip acts as skid

Single pilot cockpit

Aileron

Tailplane

Hinged elevator

Aluminium air-brake

Radio aerial

Forward-opening canopy

T-type cantilevered fin

Towing hook

EVW

Rudder

Nose-wheel

Non-retractable main wheel

Fuselage of fibreglass and foam layers

Tailwheel

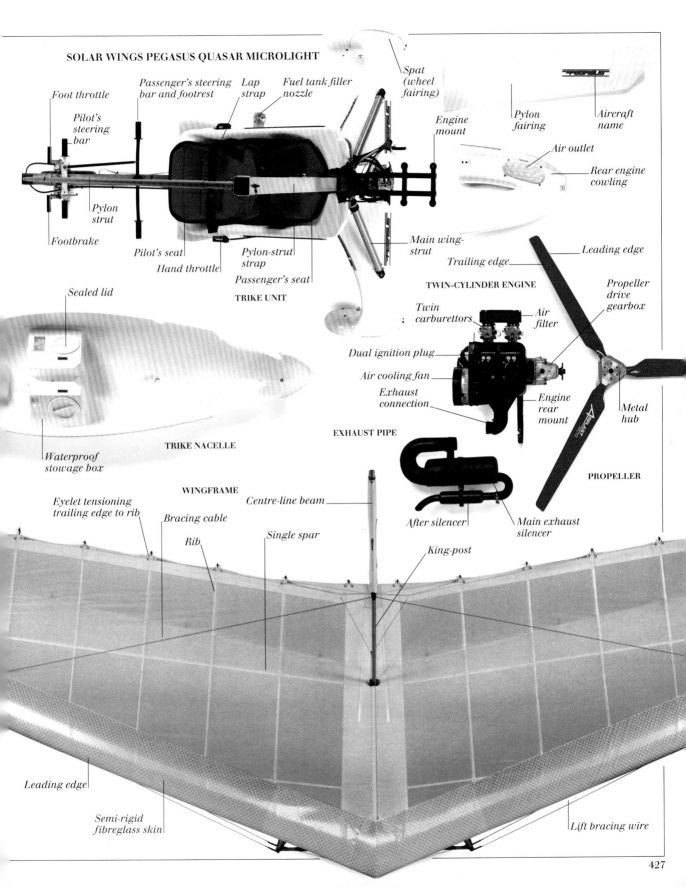

SOLAR WINGS PEGASUS QUASAR MICROLIGHT

Foot throttle

Pilot's steering bar

Passenger's steering bar and footrest

Lap strap

Fuel tank filler nozzle

Spat (wheel fairing)

Engine mount

Pylon fairing

Aircraft name

Air outlet

Rear engine cowling

Pylon strut

Footbrake

Pilot's seat

Hand throttle

Pylon-strut strap

Passenger's seat

Main wing-strut

Trailing edge

Leading edge

TRIKE UNIT

Sealed lid

Waterproof stowage box

TRIKE NACELLE

TWIN-CYLINDER ENGINE

Twin carburettors

Air filter

Dual ignition plug

Air cooling fan

Exhaust connection

Engine rear mount

Propeller drive gearbox

Metal hub

EXHAUST PIPE

PROPELLER

WINGFRAME

Eyelet tensioning trailing edge to rib

Bracing cable

Rib

Centre-line beam

Single spar

King-post

After silencer

Main exhaust silencer

Leading edge

Semi-rigid fibreglass skin

Lift bracing wire

427

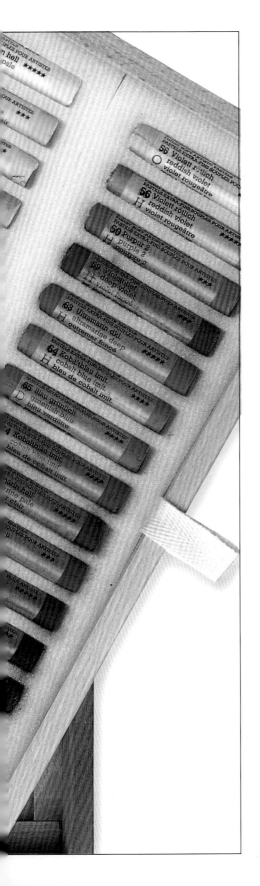

THE
VISUAL ARTS

Drawing

DRAWINGS CAN BE FINISHED WORKS OF ART, or preparatory studies for paintings and other visual arts. They can be made using a wide variety of drawing instruments such as pencils, graphite sticks, chalks, charcoal, pens and inks, and silver wires. The most common drawing instrument is the graphite pencil. A graphite pencil consists of a thin rod of graphite mixed with clay, encased in wood. Charcoal is one of the oldest drawing instruments. It is produced by firing twigs of willow, vine, or other woods at high temperatures in airtight containers. Erasers can be used to rub out marks made by drawing materials such as graphite pencils or charcoal, or to achieve a particular effect – such as smudging. Fixative is often applied – using a mouth diffuser or aerosol spray fixative – to prevent smudging once a drawing is finished. Silver lines can be produced by drawing silver wire across specially prepared paper – a technique known as silverpoint. The lines are permanent and cannot be erased. In time the silver lines oxidize and turn brown.

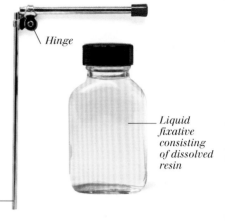

FIXATIVE AND MOUTH DIFFUSER

Hinge

Liquid fixative consisting of dissolved resin

Fixative is sucked into tube and sprayed on to drawing

DRAWING INSTRUMENTS

2B GRAPHITE PENCIL

Medium-soft, light line

8B GRAPHITE PENCIL

Very soft, dark line

SILVER WIRE IN A METAL HOLDER

ERASERS

Hard texture

PLASTIC ERASER

Soft texture

PUTTY ERASER

CHALK, CRAYON, AND CHARCOAL

Calcite (calcium carbonate) mixed with pigment

BLUE CHALK

Iron oxide mixed with chalk

SANGUINE CRAYON

Carbonized wood

WILLOW CHARCOAL

DRAWING MATERIALS

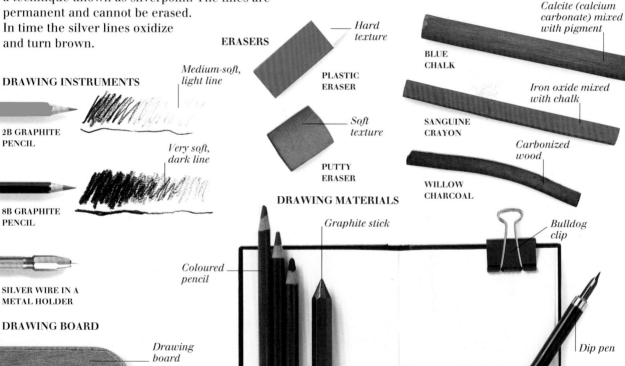

DRAWING BOARD

Drawing board

Paper

Drawing clip

Coloured pencil

Graphite stick

Bulldog clip

Dip pen

Pencil sharpener

Sketch book

Ink bottle

Silver lines
oxidize to a
light brown
colour

Vanishing
point located
on head of
man riding
rearing horse

Figures drawn
in ink on top
of lines

Lines of
squared
pavement slabs
recede toward
a single
vanishing
point

Line drawn
in silverpoint
using a rule

Complex perspective
drawing done as a
preparatory study
for a painting

Paper prepared
with size (glue)
and pigment

EXAMPLE OF A SILVERPOINT DRAWING
The Adoration of the Magi, Leonardo da Vinci, 1481
Pen and ink over silverpoint on paper
16.5 x 29.2 cm (6½ x 11½ in)

Handmade, tinted
paper

One of a series
of drawings
recording
London during
1944–1945

Charcoal lines
softened by
rubbing and
smudging

Broad charcoal
mark

Charcoal
gives strong,
expressive lines

Lines rapidly
drawn on site

EXAMPLE OF A CHARCOAL DRAWING
St. Paul's and the River, David Bomberg, 1945
Charcoal on paper
50.8 x 65.8 cm (20 x 25⅛ in)

Tempera

THE TERM TEMPERA is applied to any paint in which pigment is tempered (mixed) with a water-based binding medium – usually egg yolk. Egg tempera is applied to a smooth surface such as vellum (for illuminated manuscripts) or more commonly to hardwood panels prepared with gesso – a mixture of chalk and size (glue). Hog hair brushes are used to apply the gesso. A layer of gesso grosso (coarse gesso) is followed by successive layers of gesso sotile (fine gesso) that are sanded between coats to provide a smooth, yet absorbent ground. The paint is applied with fine sable brushes in thin layers, using light brushstrokes. Tempera dries quickly to form a tough skin with a satin sheen. The luminous white surface of the gesso combined with the overlaid paint produces the brilliant crispness and rich colours particular to this medium. Egg tempera paintings are frequently gilded with gold. Leaves of finely beaten gold are applied to a bole (reddish-brown clay) base and polished by burnishing.

MATERIALS FOR GILDING

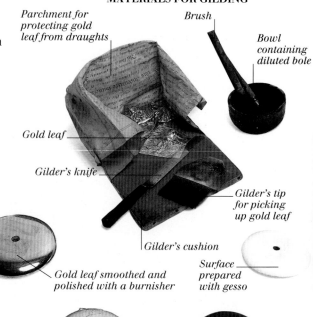

Parchment for protecting gold leaf from draughts

Brush

Bowl containing diluted bole

Gold leaf

Gilder's knife

Gilder's tip for picking up gold leaf

Gilder's cushion

Surface prepared with gesso

Gold leaf smoothed and polished with a burnisher

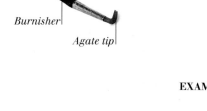

Gold leaf applied in overlapping layers

Bole brushed on to gesso

Burnisher

Agate tip

MATERIALS FOR TEMPERA PANEL PAINTING

Yolk

EGG

White

SIZE (GLUE)

GESSO

Lip

EGG YOLK BINDING MEDIUM

MORTAR AND PESTLE

Mortar

Pestle for crushing and grinding pigments

EXAMPLES OF BRUSHES

FLAT HOG HAIR BRUSH

SABLE BRUSH SIZE 6

SABLE BRUSH SIZE 1

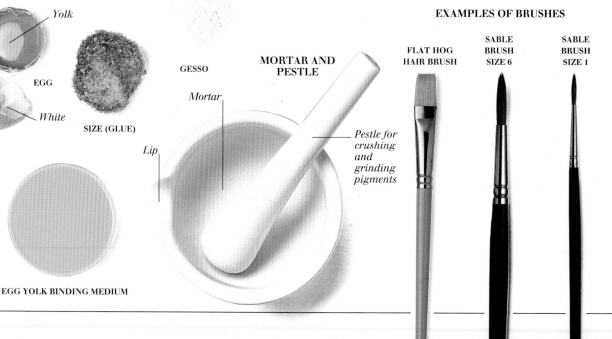

EXAMPLE OF A TEMPERA PAINTING
Presentation in the Temple, Ambrogio Lorenzetti, 1342
Tempera on wood, 257 x 168 cm (8 ft 5⅛ in x 5 ft 6⅛ in)

PIGMENTS FOR FLESH-COLOUR PAINTING

VERDACCIO

VERMILION AND LEAD WHITE

VERMILION

Altarpiece commissioned for Siena Cathedral, Italy

Textured gold ornament made by punching motifs into the gilded surface

The red tinge of the bole is just visible beneath the gold

Edge of a sheet of gold leaf

Crisp edge characteristic of tempera painting

Vine black used to create the dim cathedral interior

Highlights on the beard made by applying thin layers of white over dried paint

Red drapery painted in vermilion

Raised right hand and pointing finger is the gesture of prophecy

Receding floor tiles create the impression of depth

Patch of discoloured varnish, left from last cleaning

RED EARTH (IRON OXIDE)

EXAMPLES OF PIGMENTS

MALACHITE

ULTRAMARINE LAPIS LAZULI

VINE BLACK

LEAD TIN YELLOW

Warm flesh tones achieved by layering vermilion and white over an undercoat of verdaccio

Ultramarine lapis lazuli, as costly as gold, was reserved for significant figures such as the Virgin Mary

Patterned gold halo glitters in candlelight

Craquelure (pattern of cracks in the paint)

DETAIL FROM "PRESENTATION IN THE TEMPLE"

Fresco

FRESCO IS A METHOD OF WALL PAINTING. In buon fresco (true fresco), pigments are mixed with water and applied to an intonaco (layer of fresh, damp lime-plaster). The intonaco absorbs and binds the pigments as it dries making the picture a permanent part of the wall surface. The intonaco is applied in sections called giornate (daily sections). The size of each giornata depends on the artist's estimate of how much can be painted before the plaster sets. The junctions between giornate are sometimes visible on a finished fresco. The range of colours used in buon fresco are limited to lime-resistant pigments such as earth colours (below). Slaked lime (burnt lime mixed with water), bianco di San Giovanni (slaked lime that has been partly exposed to air), and chalk can be used to produce fresco whites. In fresco secco (dry fresco), pigments are mixed with a binding medium and applied to dry plaster. The pigments are not completely absorbed into the plaster and may flake off over time.

CROSS-SECTION SHOWING FRESCO LAYERS

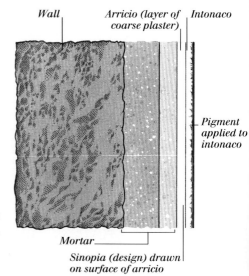

Wall

Arricio (layer of coarse plaster)

Intonaco

Pigment applied to intonaco

Mortar

Sinopia (design) drawn on surface of arricio

EXAMPLES OF EARTH COLOUR PIGMENTS

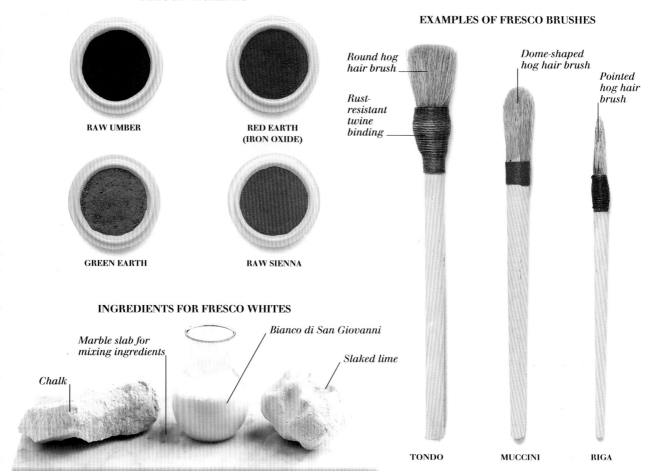

RAW UMBER

RED EARTH (IRON OXIDE)

GREEN EARTH

RAW SIENNA

EXAMPLES OF FRESCO BRUSHES

Round hog hair brush

Rust-resistant twine binding

Dome-shaped hog hair brush

Pointed hog hair brush

INGREDIENTS FOR FRESCO WHITES

Marble slab for mixing ingredients

Bianco di San Giovanni

Slaked lime

Chalk

TONDO

MUCCINI

RIGA

EXAMPLE OF A FRESCO
The Expulsion of the Merchants from the Temple, Giotto, c.1306
Fresco, 200 x 185 cm (78 x 72 in)

Temple acts as a backdrop for the action

Bianco di San Giovanni often used for fresco whites

Gold leaf applied to apostle's halo

Green earth pigment applied to robe

Child painted on top of apostle's robe

One of a series of frescoes in the Arena Chapel, Padua, Italy

Patches of azurite blue have turned green due to reaction with carbon dioxide

Hairline junction between giornate is visible

Red earth pigment applied in buon fresco has retained rich hue

Azurite blue applied in fresco secco has flaked off to reveal the plaster beneath

Dry, matt surface characteristic of buon fresco

Paint applied in buon fresco to child's face

White dove represents the Holy Ghost

Paint applied in fresco secco to child's body has flaked off

Sinopia (design) sketched in red earth

DETAIL FROM "THE EXPULSION"

Artist has to finish giornata before plaster dries

A fresco was generally worked in zones from the top down

Junction between giornate

Area with little detail can be painted quickly, allowing a larger giornata to be completed

Highly detailed area takes a longer time to paint, restricting the size of the giornata

GIORNATE (DAILY SECTIONS) IN "THE EXPULSION"

Oils

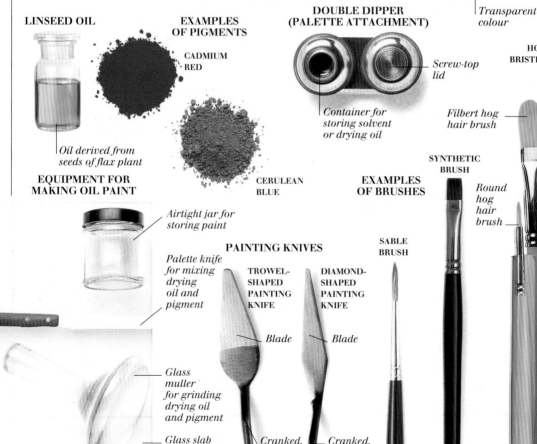

OIL PAINTS ARE MADE BY MIXING and grinding pigment with a drying vegetable oil such as linseed oil. The paint can be applied to many different surfaces and textures – the most common being canvas. Before painting, the canvas is stretched on a wooden frame and its surface is prepared with layers of size (glue) and primer. The two main types of brushes used in oil painting are stiff hog hair bristle brushes – generally used for covering large areas; and soft hair brushes made from sable or synthetic material – generally used for fine detail. Other tools, including painting knives, can also be used to achieve different effects. Oil paint can be applied thickly (a technique known as impasto), or can be thinned down using a solvent – such as turpentine or white spirit. Varnishes are sometimes applied to finished paintings to protect their surface and to give them a matt or gloss finish.

KIDNEY-SHAPED PALETTE

DAMMAR RESIN VARNISH

Crystals are dissolved and applied to painting to protect its surface

COMMERCIAL OIL PAINTS

CADMIUM RED

ULTRAMARINE

Lightfast opaque colour

Transparent colour

LINSEED OIL

Oil derived from seeds of flax plant

EQUIPMENT FOR MAKING OIL PAINT

EXAMPLES OF PIGMENTS

CADMIUM RED

CERULEAN BLUE

DOUBLE DIPPER (PALETTE ATTACHMENT)

Screw-top lid

Container for storing solvent or drying oil

EXAMPLES OF BRUSHES

HOG HAIR BRISTLE BRUSHES

Flat hog hair brush

Filbert hog hair brush

Flat hog hair brush

Filbert hog hair brush

SYNTHETIC BRUSH

Round hog hair brush

Airtight jar for storing paint

Palette knife for mixing drying oil and pigment

PAINTING KNIVES

TROWEL-SHAPED PAINTING KNIFE

DIAMOND-SHAPED PAINTING KNIFE

SABLE BRUSH

Long, wooden handle

Glass muller for grinding drying oil and pigment

Glass slab with abrasive surface

Blade

Blade

Cranked, steel shank

Cranked, steel shank

Protective, plastic case

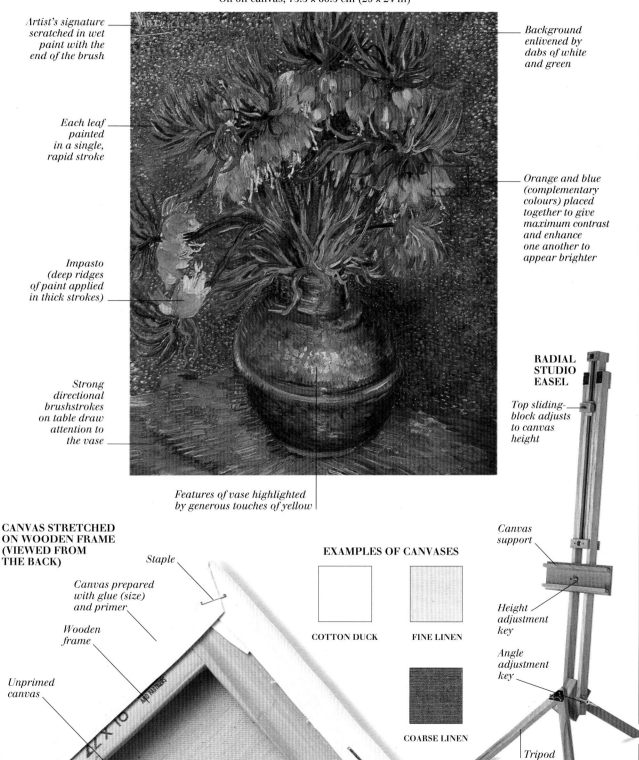

EXAMPLE OF AN OIL PAINTING
Fritillarias, Vincent van Gogh, 1886
Oil on canvas, 73.5 x 60.5 cm (29 x 24 in)

Artist's signature scratched in wet paint with the end of the brush

Each leaf painted in a single, rapid stroke

Impasto (deep ridges of paint applied in thick strokes)

Strong directional brushstrokes on table draw attention to the vase

Background enlivened by dabs of white and green

Orange and blue (complementary colours) placed together to give maximum contrast and enhance one another to appear brighter

Features of vase highlighted by generous touches of yellow

RADIAL STUDIO EASEL

Top sliding-block adjusts to canvas height

Canvas support

Height adjustment key

Angle adjustment key

Tripod

CANVAS STRETCHED ON WOODEN FRAME (VIEWED FROM THE BACK)

Staple

Canvas prepared with glue (size) and primer

Wooden frame

Unprimed canvas

EXAMPLES OF CANVASES

COTTON DUCK

FINE LINEN

COARSE LINEN

Watercolour

WATERCOLOUR PAINT IS MADE OF GROUND PIGMENT mixed with a water-soluble binding medium, usually gum arabic. It is usually applied to paper using soft hair brushes such as sable, goat hair, squirrel, and synthetic brushes. Watercolours are often diluted and applied as overlaying washes (thin, transparent layers) to build up depth of colour. Washes can be laid in a variety of ways to create a range of different effects. For example, a wet-in-wet wash can be achieved by laying a wash on top of another wet wash. The two washes blend together to give a fused effect. Sponges are used to modify washes by soaking up paint so that areas of pigment are lightened or removed from the paper. Watercolours can also be applied undiluted – a technique known as dry brush – to create a broken-colour effect. Watercolours are generally transparent and allow light to reflect from the surface of the paper through the layers of paint to give a luminous effect. They can be thickened and made opaque by adding body colour (Chinese white).

GUM ARABIC

Natural sap from acacia tree

NATURAL SPONGE

ANATOMY OF A SABLE BRUSH

Soft red sable hair

Toe (tip)

Wooden handle

SOFT HAIR BRUSHES

ROUND SABLE BRUSH (SIZE 6)

ROUND SABLE BRUSH (SIZE 1)

Hair trimmed and cemented into ferrule

Round ferrule

Hair tied with clove hitch knot

SYNTHETIC WASH BRUSH

TUBES OF WATERCOLOUR PAINT

WINSOR GREEN

SQUIRREL MOP WASH BRUSH

PORTABLE BOX OF WATERCOLOUR PAINTS

CADMIUM YELLOW

Painted colour swatch

Chinese white

Pan of watercolour paint

Lid can be used for mixing colours

LARGE GOAT HAKE WASH BRUSH

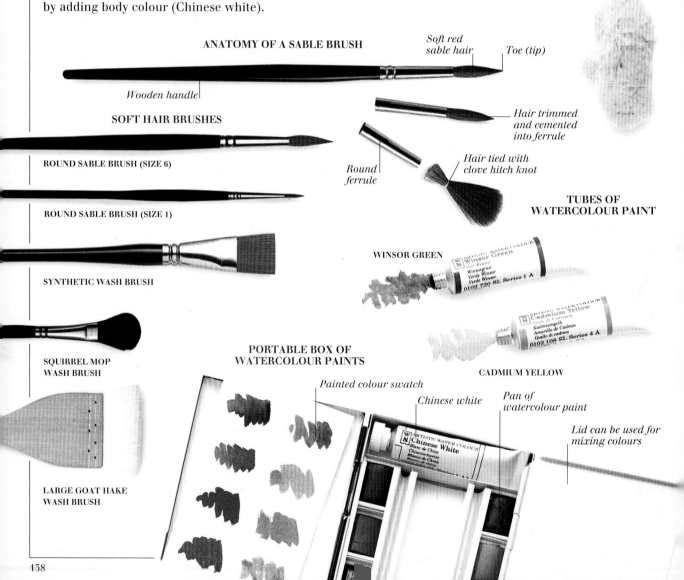

EXAMPLE OF A WATERCOLOUR
Burning of the Houses of Parliament, Turner, 1834
Watercolour on paper, 29.2 x 44.5 cm (11½ x 17½ in)

Transparent washes laid on top of each other to create tonal depth

Transparent washes allow light to reflect off the surface of the paper to give a luminous effect

Highlight scratched out with a scalpel

Paper shows through thin wash to give flames added highlight

Crowd painted with thin strokes laid over a pale wash

Undiluted paint applied, then partly washed out, to create the impression of water

EXAMPLES OF WATERCOLOUR PAPERS

SMOOTH-TEXTURED PAPER

EXAMPLES OF WASHES

WASH OVER DRY BRUSH
Wash laid over paint applied with dry brush gives two-tone effect

GRADED WASH
Strong wash applied to tilted paper gives graded effect

DRY BRUSH
Undiluted paint dragged across surface of paper gives broken effect

MEDIUM-TEXTURED PAPER

COLOUR WHEEL OF WATERCOLOUR PAINTS

ROUGH-TEXTURED PAPER

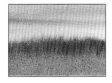

WET-IN-WET
Two diluted washes left to run together to give fused effect

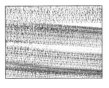

Yellow (primary colour)

Secondary colours made by mixing yellow and blue

Secondary colours made by mixing red and yellow

Blue (primary colour)

Red (primary colour)

Secondary colours made by mixing blue and red

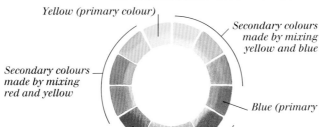

Pastels

PASTELS ARE STICKS OF PIGMENT made by mixing ground pigment with chalk and a binding medium, such as gum arabic. They vary in hardness depending on the proportion of the binding medium to the chalk. Soft pastel – the most common form of pastel – contains just enough binding medium to hold the pigment in stick form. Pastels can be applied directly to any support (surface) with sufficient tooth (texture). When a pastel is drawn over a textured surface, the pigment crumbles and lodges in the fibres of the support. Pastel marks have a particular soft, matt quality and are suitable for techniques such as blending, scumbling, and feathering. Blending is a technique of rubbing and fusing two or more colours on the support using fingers or various tools such as tortillons (paper stumps), soft hair brushes, putty erasers, and soft bread. Scumbling is a technique of building up layers of pastel colours. The side or blunted tip of a soft pastel is lightly drawn over an underpainted area so that patches of the colour beneath show through. Feathering is a technique of applying parallel strokes of colour with the point of a pastel, usually over an existing layer of pastel colour. A thin spray of fixative can be applied – using a mouth diffuser (see pp. 430-431) or aerosol spray fixative – to a finished pastel painting, or in between layers of colour, to prevent smudging.

EQUIPMENT FOR MAKING PASTELS

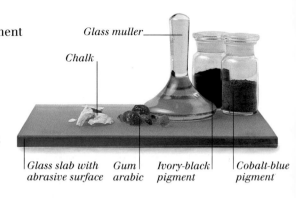

Glass muller

Chalk

Glass slab with abrasive surface

Gum arabic

Ivory-black pigment

Cobalt-blue pigment

EXAMPLES OF SOFT PASTELS

COBALT-BLUE HALF PASTEL

VERMILION HALF PASTEL

OLIVE-GREEN FULL PASTEL

MAUVE FULL PASTEL

BOXED PASTEL SET

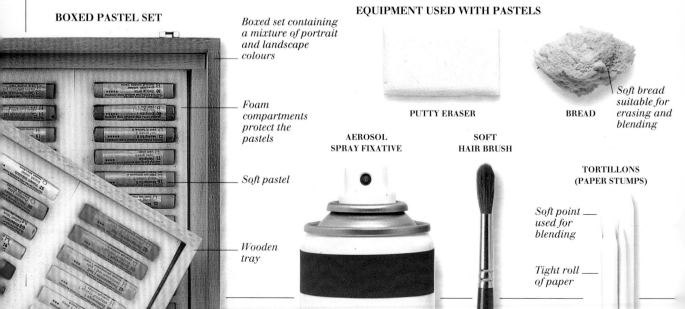

Boxed set containing a mixture of portrait and landscape colours

Foam compartments protect the pastels

Soft pastel

Wooden tray

EQUIPMENT USED WITH PASTELS

PUTTY ERASER

BREAD

Soft bread suitable for erasing and blending

AEROSOL SPRAY FIXATIVE

SOFT HAIR BRUSH

TORTILLONS (PAPER STUMPS)

Soft point used for blending

Tight roll of paper

EXAMPLE OF A PASTEL PAINTING
Woman Drying her Neck, Edgar Degas, c.1898
Pastel on cardboard, 62.5 x 65.5 cm (24½ x 25½ in)

Pastels applied directly to support

Colours are blended together using fingers or tools such as tortillons

Built up layers of pastel

Rich colour of fabric created by overlaying yellows and oranges

Broken colours, characteristic of scumbling technique

Toned colour of paper visible beneath thinly applied pastels

Pure bright colours laid side by side produce strong contrasts

DETAIL FROM "WOMAN DRYING HER NECK"

Feathering technique used to produce skin tones

EXAMPLES OF TEXTURED PAPERS AND PASTEL BOARDS

WATERCOLOUR PAPER (ROUGH TEXTURE)

GLASS PAPER

WATERCOLOUR PAPER (MEDIUM TEXTURE)

INGRES PAPER

FLOCKED PASTEL BOARD

CANSON PAPER

EXAMPLES OF COLOURED AND TINTED PAPERS

Acrylics

ACRYLIC PAINT IS MADE BY MIXING PIGMENT with a synthetic resin. It can be thinned with water but dries to become water insoluble. Acrylics are applied to many surfaces, such as paper and acrylic-primed board and canvas. A variety of brushes, painting knives, rollers, air-brushes, plastic scrapers, and other tools are used in acrylic painting. The versatility of acrylics makes them suitable for a wide range of techniques. They can be used opaquely or – by adding water – in a transparent, watercolour style. Acrylic mediums can be added to the paint to adjust its consistency for special effects such as glazing and impasto (ridges of paint applied in thick strokes) or to make it more matt or glossy. Acrylics are quick-drying, which allows layers of paint to be applied on top of each other almost immediately.

EXAMPLES OF BRUSHES

Sable brush

Hog hair sash brush

Synthetic hog hair brush

Synthetic sable brush

Hog hair brush

Goat hair brush

Synthetic wash brush

Ox hair brush

EXAMPLES OF PAINTS USED IN ACRYLICS

Azo yellow

Phthalo green

Cerulean blue

Phthalo blue

Quinacridone red

Titanium white

Pad of disposable paper palettes

Yellow ochre

Burnt umber

Burnt sienna

Credit card

Paint spread evenly

Flexible, plastic blade

PAINTING TOOLS

Stippled effect achieved using thick paint

Striated effect

PLASTIC PAINTING KNIFE

Glue spreader

PLASTIC SCRAPERS

Paint cup

Main lever

Blended tones

Nozzle

AIR-BRUSH

Plastic handle

SPONGE ROLLER

Uniform tone

Air hose

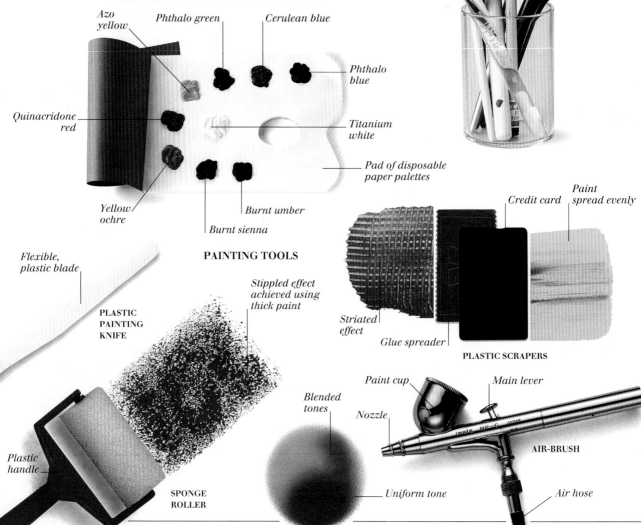

EXAMPLE OF AN ACRYLIC PAINTING
A Bigger Splash, David Hockney, 1967
Acrylic on canvas, 242.5 x 243.8 cm (95½ x 96 in)

Paint applied evenly using a roller

Cotton duck canvas support (surface)

Flatness of rollered areas enhanced by adding gel medium to the paint

Masking tape stuck on to canvas to define main shapes, and paint applied within these areas using a roller

Thin strip of pool edge left unpainted

Splash painted using thicker paint and small brush

Imprecise edge on end of spring board where paint has seeped under masking tape

EXAMPLES OF ACRYLIC PAINTS AND TECHNIQUES

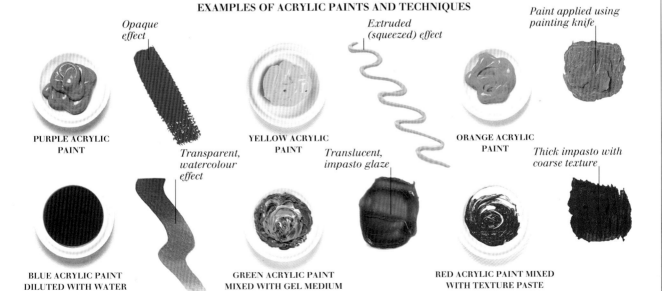

Opaque effect

Extruded (squeezed) effect

Paint applied using painting knife

PURPLE ACRYLIC PAINT

YELLOW ACRYLIC PAINT

ORANGE ACRYLIC PAINT

Transparent, watercolour effect

Translucent, impasto glaze

Thick impasto with coarse texture

BLUE ACRYLIC PAINT DILUTED WITH WATER

GREEN ACRYLIC PAINT MIXED WITH GEL MEDIUM

RED ACRYLIC PAINT MIXED WITH TEXTURE PASTE

Calligraphy

CALLIGRAPHY IS BEAUTIFULLY FORMED LETTERING. The term applies to written text and illumination (the decoration of manuscripts using gold leaf and colour). The essential materials needed to practise calligraphy are a writing tool, ink, and a writing surface. Quills are among the oldest writing tools. They are usually made from goose or turkey feathers, and are noted for their flexibility and ability to produce fine lines. A quill point, however, is not very durable and constant recutting and trimming is required. The most commonly used writing instrument in western calligraphy is a detachable, metal nib held in a penholder. The metal nib is very durable, and there are a wide range of different types. Particular types of nibs – such as copperplate, speedball, and roundhand nibs – are used for specific styles of lettering. Some nibs have integral ink reservoirs and others have reservoirs that are detachable. Brushes are also used for writing, and for filling in outlined letters and painting decoration. Other writing tools used in calligraphy are fountain pens, felt-tip pens, rotring pens, and reed pens. Calligraphy inks may come in liquid form, or as a solid ink stick. Ink sticks are ground down in distilled water to form a liquid ink. The most common writing surfaces for calligraphy are good quality, smooth-surfaced papers. To achieve the best writing position, the calligrapher places the paper on a drawing board set at an angle.

EQUIPMENT USED IN BRUSH LETTERING

Brush rest

Wolf hair brush

Goat hair brush

BRUSHES AND BRUSH REST

Liquid ink made by grinding down ink stick in distilled water

Solid carbon ink stick

Ink stone

INK STICK AND STONE

Feather

PENS, NIBS, AND BRUSHES USED IN CALLIGRAPHY

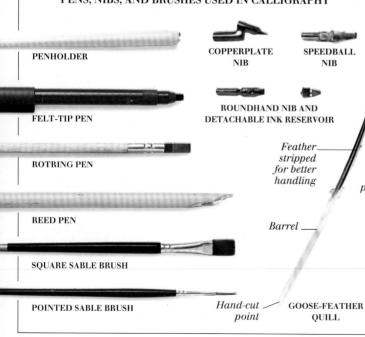

PENHOLDER

COPPERPLATE NIB

SPEEDBALL NIB

FELT-TIP PEN

ROUNDHAND NIB AND DETACHABLE INK RESERVOIR

ROTRING PEN

Feather stripped for better handling

REED PEN

Barrel

SQUARE SABLE BRUSH

POINTED SABLE BRUSH

Hand-cut point

GOOSE-FEATHER QUILL

GOAT HAIR BRUSH

WOLF HAIR BRUSH

FOUNTAIN PEN AND INK

Bottle of permanent black ink

Barrel

Clip

Nib

Outer cap

EXAMPLES OF LETTERING STYLES

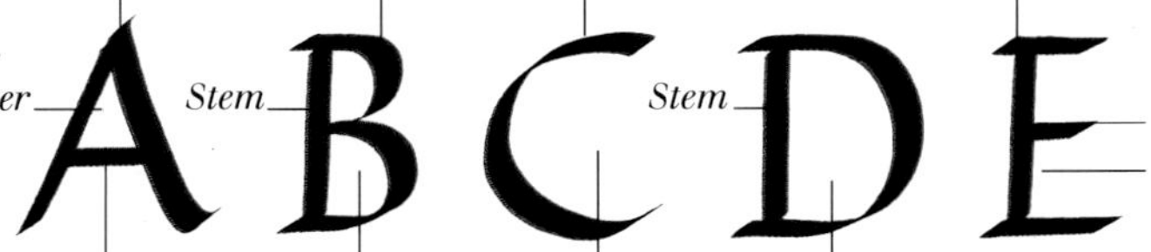

Apex

Bowl

Curved stroke

Stem

Inner counter

Stem

Stem

Arm

Counter

Crossbar

Inner counter

Counter

Inner counter

ROMAN CAPITALS

Cap line

X line

Ascender

Curved stroke

Ear

Arch

Base line

Crossbar

Descender line

Serif

Neck

Descender

Height of letter determined by ladder of nib widths

ITALIC ROMAN

Slightly pinched (curved) vertical stroke

Letter filled in using brush

Inner counter

Tail

Spine

Pointed apex

VERSAL

CHINESE LETTERING

Rice paper

Broad brush stroke

Chinese character meaning long life

Artist's stamped signature

ARTIST'S STAMP

Stamp

Stamped signature of the artist

Ink pad

DRAWING BOARD

Adjustable set square

Blade with parallel motion

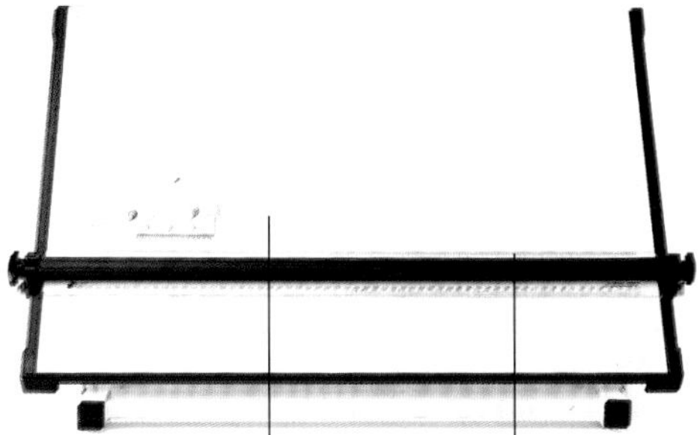

EXAMPLES OF CALLIGRAPHY PAPERS

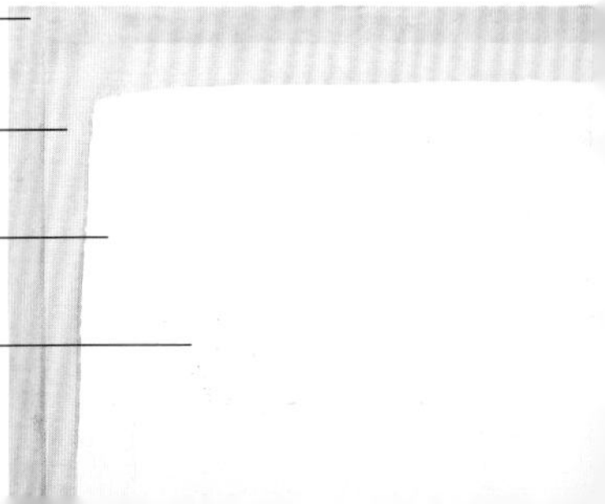

Standard European paper

Indian handmade paper

Flecked, tinted paper

Imitation parchment paper

AN ILLUMINATED MANUSCRIPT

Style of lettering called Gothic book script

Large decorative letter used to mark the opening of a chapter

Words written carefully by hand

Gold leaf

Grid lines provide guide to position of words and pictures

Printmaking 1

PRINTS ARE MADE BY FOUR BASIC printing processes – intaglio, lithographic, relief, and screen. In intaglio printing, lines are engraved or etched into the surface of a metal plate. Lines are engraved by hand using sharp metal tools. They are etched by corroding the metal plate with acid, using acid-resistant ground to protect the areas not to be etched. The plate is then inked and wiped, leaving the grooves filled with ink and the surface clean. Dampened paper is laid over the plate, and both paper and plate are passed through the rollers of an etching press. The pressure of the rollers forces the paper into the grooves, so that it takes up the ink, leaving an impression on the paper. Lithographic printing is based on the antipathy between grease and water. An image is drawn on a surface – usually a stone or metal plate – with a greasy medium, such as tusche (lihographic ink). The greasy drawing is fixed on to the plate by applying an acidic solution, such as gum arabic. The surface is then dampened and rolled with ink. The ink adheres only to the greasy areas and is repelled by the water. Paper is laid on the plate and pressure is applied by means of a press. In relief printing, the non-printing areas of a wood or linoleum block are cut away using gouges, knives, and other tools. The printing areas are left raised in relief and are rolled with ink. Paper is laid on the inked block and pressure is applied by means of a press or by burnishing (rubbing) the back of the paper. The most common forms of relief printing are woodcut, wood engraving, and linocut. In screen printing, the printing surface is a mesh stretched across a wooden frame. A stencil is applied to the mesh to seal the non-printing areas and ink is scraped through the mesh to produce an image.

THE FOUR MAIN PRINTING PROCESSES

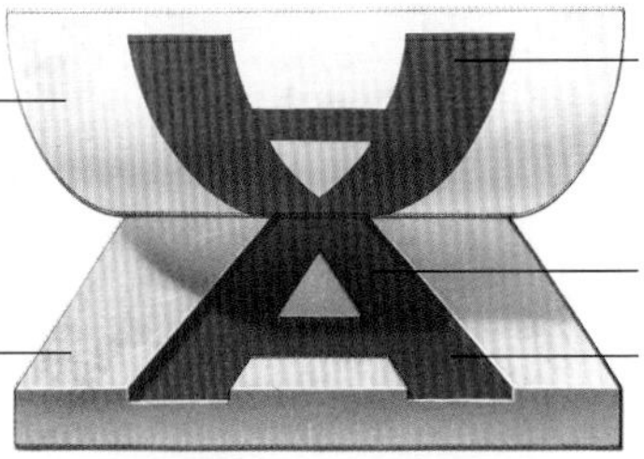
Paper
Printed image
Engraved or etched image
Metal plate
Inked area

INTAGLIO

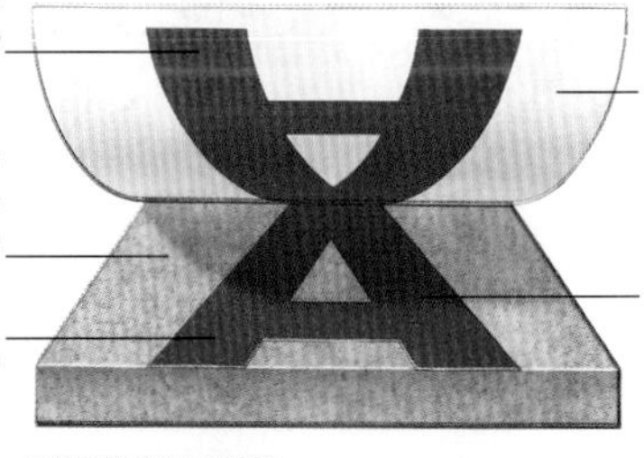
Printed image
Paper
Damp surface rejects ink
Image drawn on stone with greasy medium
Ink adheres to greasy image

LITHOGRAPHIC

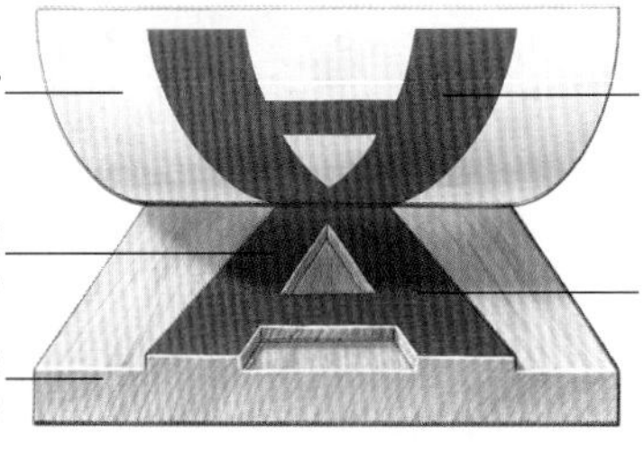
Paper
Printed image
Raised figure
Inked surface
Wood block

RELIEF

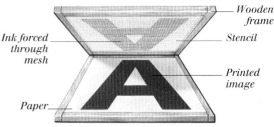

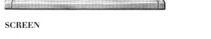

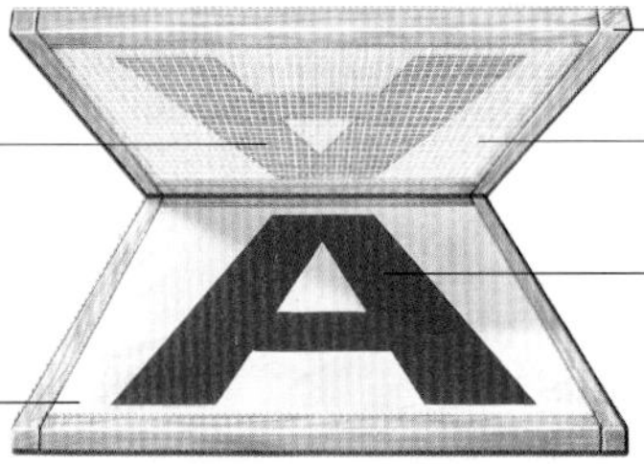
Wooden frame
Ink forced through mesh
Stencil
Printed image
Paper

SCREEN

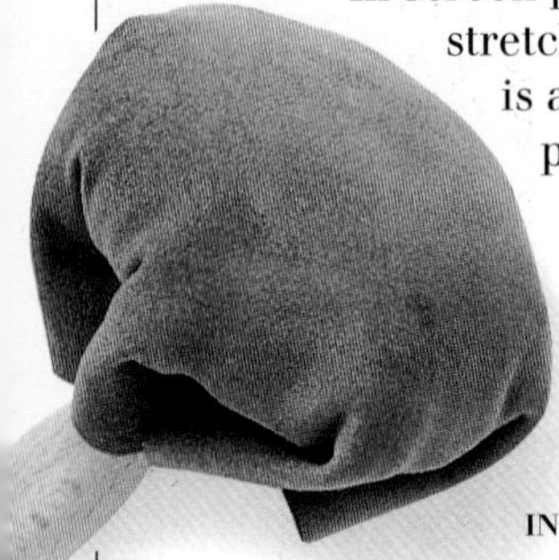

LEATHER INK DABBER

EQUIPMENT USED IN INTAGLIO PRINTING

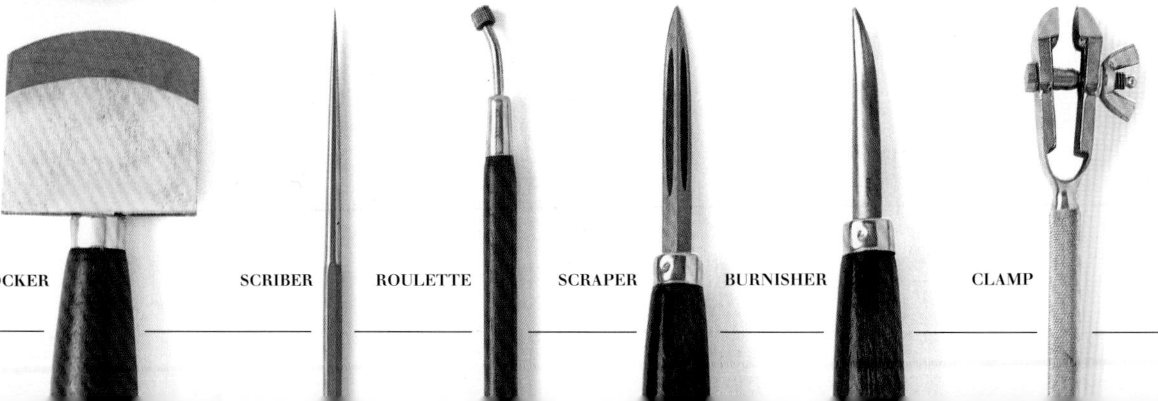

ROCKER

SCRIBER

ROULETTE

SCRAPER

BURNISHER

CLAMP

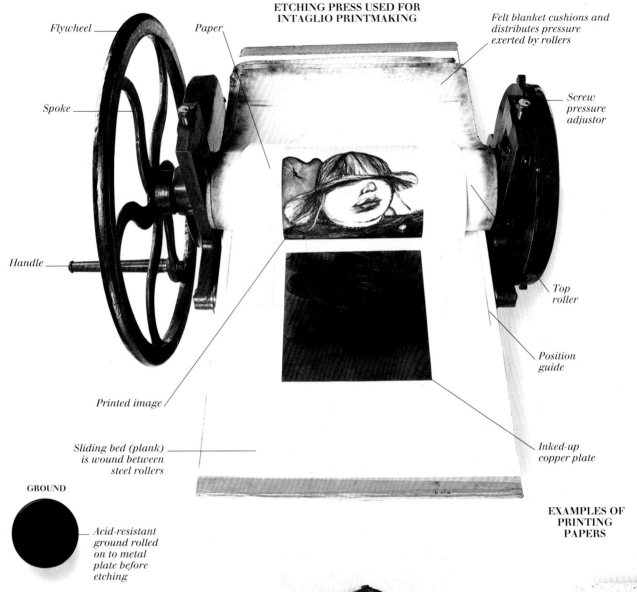

ETCHING PRESS USED FOR INTAGLIO PRINTMAKING

Flywheel

Paper

Felt blanket cushions and distributes pressure exerted by rollers

Spoke

Screw pressure adjustor

Handle

Top roller

Position guide

Printed image

Sliding bed (plank) is wound between steel rollers

Inked-up copper plate

GROUND

Acid-resistant ground rolled on to metal plate before etching

EXAMPLES OF PRINTING PAPERS

GROUND ROLLER

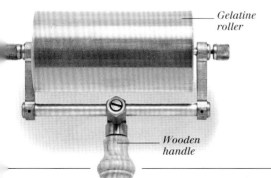

Gelatine roller

Wooden handle

EXAMPLE OF AN INTAGLIO PRINT
Annie with a Sun Hat, Jock McFadyen, 1993
Etched copper plate, 41 x 40 cm (16 x 15¾ in)

Printmaking 2

EXAMPLE OF A LITHOGRAPHIC STONE AND PRINT
Crown Gateway 2, Mandy Bonnell, 1987
Lithograph, 50 x 40 cm (19½ x 15¾ in)

IMAGE DRAWN ON STONE **LITHOGRAPIC PRINT**

EXAMPLE OF A SCREEN PRINT
Sea Change, Patrick Hughes, 1992
Screen print, 77 x 94.5 cm (30 x 37 in)

SCREEN AND SQUEEGEE

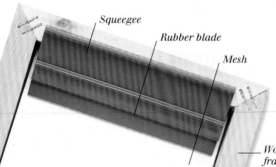

Squeegee

Rubber blade

Mesh

Wooden frame

EQUIPMENT USED IN LITHOGRAPHIC PRINTING

CRAYON AND HOLDER

LITHOGRAPHIC PENCIL

TUSCHE (LITHOGRAPHIC INK) PEN

ERASING STICK

EXPANDABLE SPONGE

TUSCHE (LITHOGRAPHIC INK) STICK

RUBBING INK

INK ROLLER

MILD ACIDIC SOLUTION **GUM ARABIC SOLUTION**

WATER-BASED SCREEN PRINTING INKS

BLUE ACRYLIC INK **RED ACRYLIC INK** **BROWN TEXTILE INK**

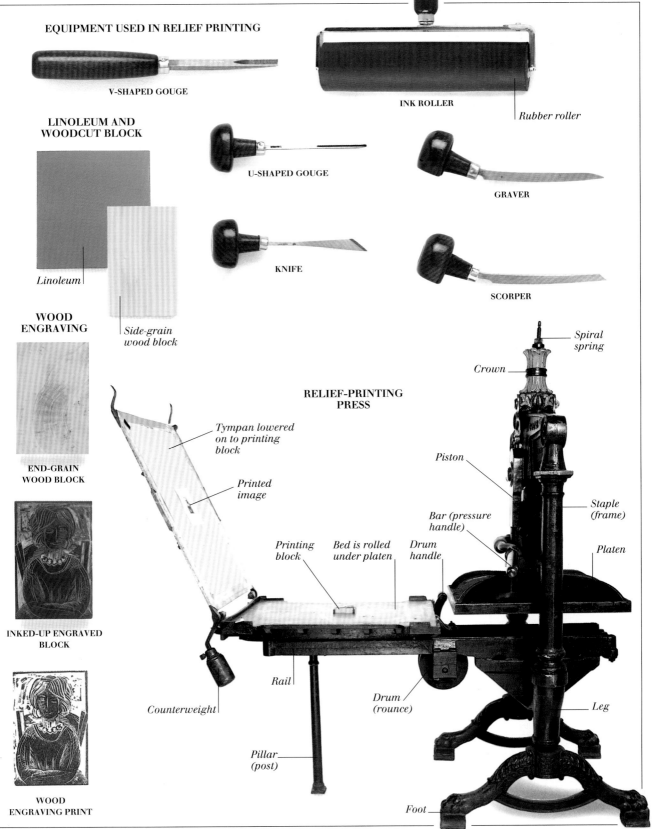

EQUIPMENT USED IN RELIEF PRINTING

V-SHAPED GOUGE

INK ROLLER

Rubber roller

LINOLEUM AND WOODCUT BLOCK

U-SHAPED GOUGE

GRAVER

Linoleum

KNIFE

SCORPER

WOOD ENGRAVING

Side-grain wood block

END-GRAIN WOOD BLOCK

INKED-UP ENGRAVED BLOCK

WOOD ENGRAVING PRINT

RELIEF-PRINTING PRESS

Spiral spring

Crown

Tympan lowered on to printing block

Piston

Printed image

Staple (frame)

Bar (pressure handle)

Printing block

Bed is rolled under platen

Drum handle

Platen

Counterweight

Rail

Drum (rounce)

Leg

Pillar (post)

Foot

Mosaic

MOSAIC IS THE ART OF MAKING patterns and pictures from tesserae (small, coloured pieces of glass, marble, and other materials). Different materials are cut into tesserae using different tools. Smalti (glass enamel) and marble are cut into pieces using a hammer and a hardy (a pointed blade) embedded in a log. Vitreous glass is cut into pieces using a pair of nippers. Mosaics can be made using a direct or indirect method. In the direct method, the tesserae are laid directly into a bed of cement–based adhesive. In the indirect method, the design is drawn in reverse on paper or cloth. The tesserae are then stuck face-down on the paper or cloth using water-soluble glue. Adhesive is spread with a trowel on to a solid surface – such as a wall – and the back of the mosaic is laid into the adhesive. Finally, the paper or cloth is soaked off to reveal the mosaic. Gaps between tesserae can be filled with grout. Grout is forced into gaps by dragging a grouting squeegee across the face of the mosaic. Mosaics are usually used to decorate walls and floors, but they can also be applied to smaller objects.

EQUIPMENT FOR BREAKING MARBLE

Sawn strip of marble, ready for breaking into cubes

Mosaic hammer

Alicante (red marble) pieces

Hardy (pointed blade) embedded in a log

NIPPERS

Hardwearing, tungsten carbide tip

Handle with rubber grip

SMALTI (GLASS ENAMEL)

RED SMALTI

EXAMPLE OF A MOSAIC (DIRECT METHOD)
Seascape, Tessa Hunkin, 1993
Smalti mosaic on board
80 cm (31½ in) diameter

MOSAIC TOOLS

CEMENT-BASED ADHESIVE

GROUT

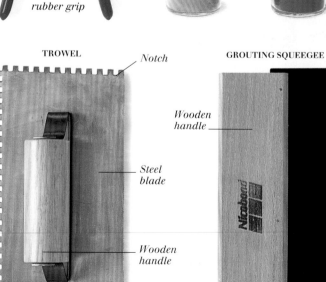

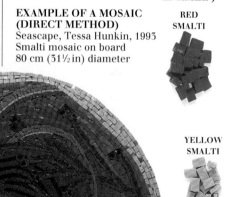

YELLOW SMALTI

BLUE SMALTI

Gold-leaf smalti

TROWEL

Notch

Steel blade

Wooden handle

GROUTING SQUEEGEE

Wooden handle

Rubber blade

Nicobond

STAGES IN THE CREATION OF A MOSAIC (INDIRECT METHOD)

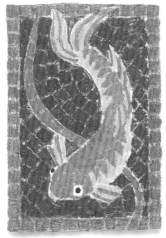

COLOUR SKETCH
A colour sketch is drawn
in oil pastel to give a clear
impression of how the finished
mosaic will look.

REVERSE IMAGE
Tesserae are glued face-down
on reverse image on paper.
Mosaic is then attached to solid
surface and paper is removed.

MOSAIC POT

Geometric design

Grout

MOSAIC MOSQUE DESIGN

Floral design

Geometric border

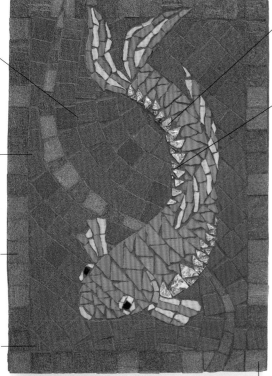

Andamenti (line along which tesserae are laid)

Grout fills the gaps between the tesserae

Mosaic mounted on board

Vitreous glass cut into triangular shape with nippers

Gold tessera with ripple finish

Gold tessera placed upside-down

Border of square vitreous glass

FINISHED MOSAIC
Goldfish, Tessa Hunkin, 1993
Vitreous glass mosaic on board
35.5 x 25.5 cm (14 x 10 in)

VITREOUS GLASS

**GREEN VITREOUS
GLASS WITH GOLD LEAF**

Plain finish

Ripple finish

**RED VITREOUS
GLASS**

**BLUE VITREOUS
GLASS**

SHEETS OF VITREOUS GLASS

Sculpture 1

THE TWO TRADITIONAL METHODS OF MAKING SCULPTURE are carving and modelling.
A carved sculpture is made by cutting away the surplus from a block of hard material
such as stone, marble, or wood. The tools used for carving vary according to the
material being carved. Heavy steel points, claws, and chisels that are struck with a
lump hammer are generally used for stone and marble. Sharp gouges and chisels
that are struck with a wooden mallet are used for wood. Sculptures formed from hard
materials are generally finished by filing with rasps, rifflers, and other abrasive
implements. Modelling is a process by which shapes are built up, using malleable
materials such as clay, plaster, and wax. The material is cut with wire-ended tools
and modelled with the fingers or a variety of hardwood and metal implements. For
large or intricate modelled sculptures an armature (frame), made from metal or
wood, is used to provide internal support. Sculptures formed in soft materials may
harden naturally or can be made more durable by firing in a kiln. Modelled
sculptures are often first designed in wax or another material to be cast later in a
metal (see pp. 454-455) such as bronze. The development of many new materials in
the 20th century has enabled sculptors to experiment with new techniques such as
construction (joining preformed pieces of material such as machine components,
mirrors, and furniture) and kinetic (mobile) sculpture.

EXAMPLES OF MARBLE CARVING TOOLS

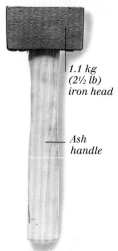

1.1 kg
(2½ lb)
iron head

Ash
handle

LUMP HAMMER

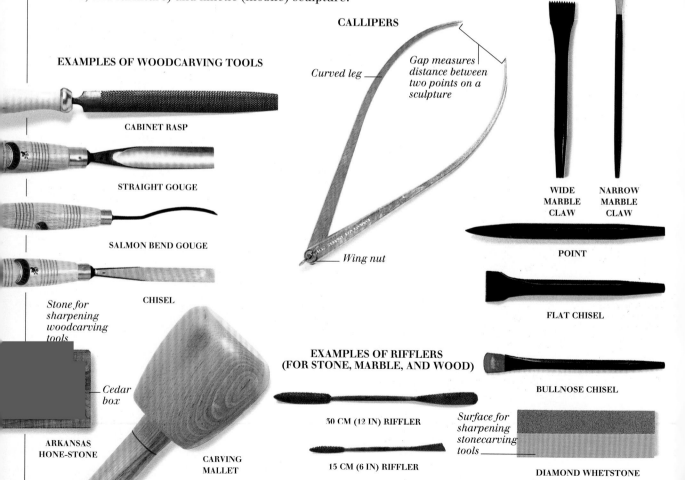

EXAMPLES OF WOODCARVING TOOLS

CABINET RASP

STRAIGHT GOUGE

SALMON BEND GOUGE

CHISEL

Stone for
sharpening
woodcarving
tools

Cedar
box

ARKANSAS
HONE-STONE

CARVING
MALLET

CALLIPERS

Curved leg

Gap measures
distance between
two points on a
sculpture

Wing nut

EXAMPLES OF RIFFLERS
(FOR STONE, MARBLE, AND WOOD)

30 CM (12 IN) RIFFLER

15 CM (6 IN) RIFFLER

WIDE
MARBLE
CLAW

NARROW
MARBLE
CLAW

POINT

FLAT CHISEL

BULLNOSE CHISEL

Surface for
sharpening
stonecarving
tools

DIAMOND WHETSTONE

Tiny holes along
the hairline made
with a point

Soft skin texture tooled
with a fine-toothed
marble claw

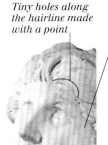

**DETAIL OF
SLAVE'S HEAD**

EXAMPLE OF A CARVED WOOD SCULPTURE
Mary Magdalene, Donatello, 1454-1455
Poplar wood, height 188 cm (6 ft 2 in)

EXAMPLE OF A CARVED MARBLE SCULPTURE
The Rebel Slave, Michelangelo, 1513-1516
Marble, height 213 cm (7ft)

Hair worked
with a narrow
claw

Delicately
modelled
hand carved
with a chisel

Hair
highlighted
with gold
leaf

Translucent white
marble, quarried at
Carrara, Italy

Figure cut
from single
length of
poplar

Deep
ridges of
hair cut
with a
gouge

Surface rubbed
smooth with
rifflers and
pumice

Strut gives added
support to long
slender limb

Wood prepared
with gesso
(chalk and glue)
and painted

Series of tiny
punch holes,
made with a
fine point,
outline the
form

Base scored with
jagged parallel
cuts made with
point and lump
hammer

Foot carved in
deep relief

Rough surface
made by driving
a point into the
marble at an
oblique angle

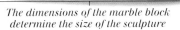

*The dimensions of the marble block
determine the size of the sculpture*

DETAIL OF SLAVE'S FOOT

Sculpture 2

EXAMPLES OF MODELLING TOOLS

WIRE-ENDED CUTTING TOOL

CURVED MOULDING TOOL

SPATULA-ENDED WAX MODELLING TOOL

ROUNDED WAX MODELLING TOOL

EXAMPLES OF BRONZE FINISHING TOOLS

HOOKED RIFFLER

POINTED RIFFLER

SPIRIT LAMP (FOR HEATING WAX MODELLING TOOLS)

Wick

Brass holder

Glass bowl

Methylated spirit

STAGES IN THE LOST-WAX METHOD OF CASTING
Based on Mars, Giambologna, c.1546

Wax-covered wire armature

ORIGINAL MODEL
An original, solid wax model is made and preserved so that numerous replicas can be cast.

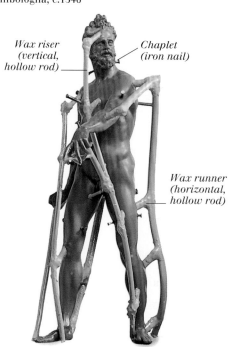

Wax riser (vertical, hollow rod)

Chaplet (iron nail)

Wax runner (horizontal, hollow rod)

HOLLOW WAX FIGURE IS CAST
A new, hollow wax model is cast from the original model. It is filled with a plaster core that is held in place with nails. Wax runners and risers are attached.

Fire-resistant clay

FIGURE IS BAKED IN CASTING MOULD
The model is encased in clay and baked. The wax melts away (through the channels made by the wax rods) and is replaced by molten bronze.

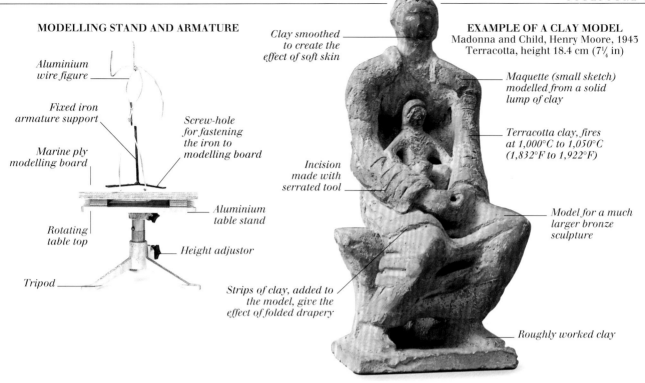

MODELLING STAND AND ARMATURE

Aluminium wire figure

Fixed iron armature support

Marine ply modelling board

Rotating table top

Tripod

Screw-hole for fastening the iron to modelling board

Aluminium table stand

Height adjustor

Clay smoothed to create the effect of soft skin

Incision made with serrated tool

Strips of clay, added to the model, give the effect of folded drapery

EXAMPLE OF A CLAY MODEL
Madonna and Child, Henry Moore, 1943
Terracotta, height 18.4 cm (7¼ in)

Maquette (small sketch) modelled from a solid lump of clay

Terracotta clay, fires at 1,000°C to 1,050°C (1,832°F to 1,922°F)

Model for a much larger bronze sculpture

Roughly worked clay

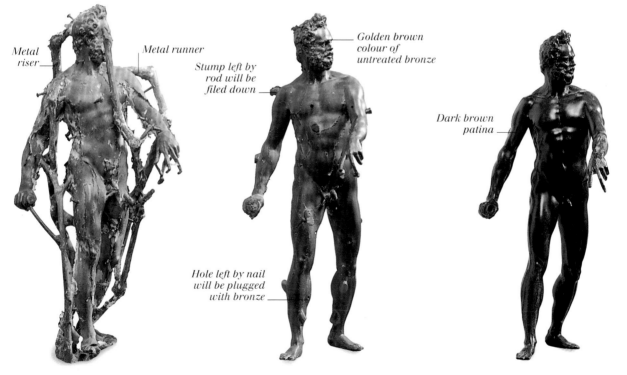

Metal riser

Metal runner

Golden brown colour of untreated bronze

Stump left by rod will be filed down

Dark brown patina

Hole left by nail will be plugged with bronze

STATUE IS STRIPPED OF CLAY
When the bronze has cooled, the clay mould is broken open to reveal the bronze statue with solid metal runners and risers.

STATUE IS FINISHED
The nails are pulled out and a large hole is made to remove the plaster core. When the metal rods have been sawn off, the sculpture is filed to refine the surface.

STATUE IS CLEANED
Finally the work is cleaned and polished. An artificial patina (colouring) is achieved by treating the surface with chemicals.

ARCHITECTURE

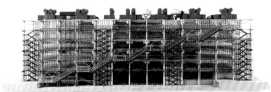

Ancient Egypt

THE CIVILIZATION OF THE ANCIENT EGYPTIANS (which lasted from about 3100 BC until it was finally absorbed into the Roman empire in 30 BC) is famous for its temples and tombs. Egyptian temples were often huge and geometric, like the Temple of Amon-Re (below and right). They were usually decorated with hieroglyphs (sacred characters used for picture-writing) and painted reliefs depicting gods, Pharaohs (kings), and queens. Tombs were particularly important to the Egyptians, who believed that the dead were resurrected in the after-life. The tombs were often decorated – as, for example, the surround of the false door opposite – in order to give comfort to the dead. The best-known ancient Egyptian tombs are the pyramids, which were designed to symbolize the rays of the sun. Many of the architectural forms used by the ancient Egyptians were later adopted by other civilizations; for example, columns and capitals were later used by the ancient Greeks (see pp. 460-461) and ancient Romans (see pp. 462-465).

SIDE VIEW OF HYPOSTYLE HALL, TEMPLE OF AMON-RE, KARNAK, EGYPT, c.1290 BC

FRONT VIEW OF HYPOSTYLE HALL, TEMPLE OF AMON-RE

Cornice decorated with cavetto moulding

Campaniform (open papyrus) capital

Architrave

Papyrus-bud capital

Socle

Side aisle

Central nave

Side aisle

Horus, the sun-god

Architrave

Stone slab forming flat roof of side aisle

Kepresh crown with disc

Chons, the moon-god

Amon-Re, king of the gods

Hathor, the sky-goddess

Papyrus motif

Cartouche (oval border) containing the titles of the Pharaoh (king)

Socle

Aisle running north-south

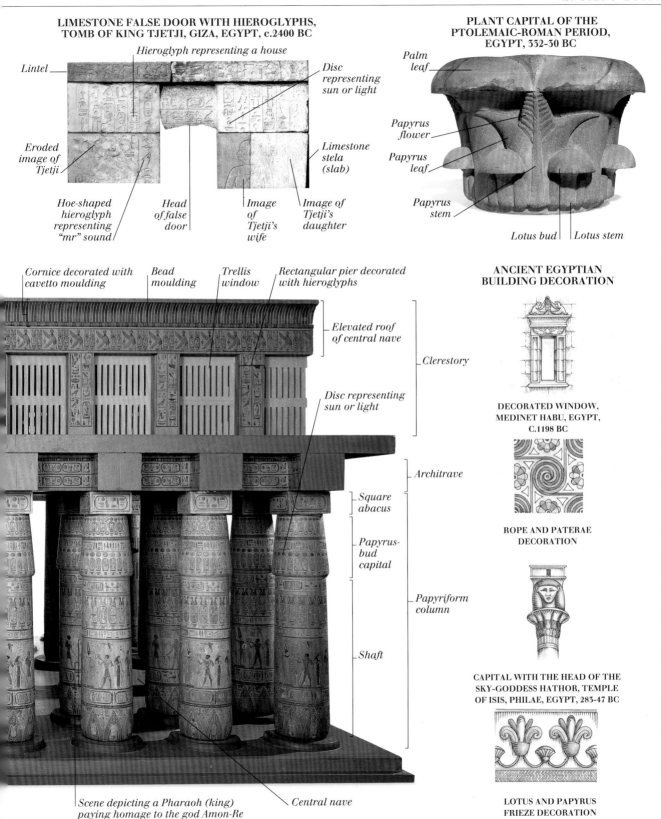

LIMESTONE FALSE DOOR WITH HIEROGLYPHS, TOMB OF KING TJETJI, GIZA, EGYPT, c.2400 BC

Hieroglyph representing a house

Lintel

Disc representing sun or light

Eroded image of Tjetji

Limestone stela (slab)

Hoe-shaped hieroglyph representing "mr" sound

Head of false door

Image of Tjetji's wife

Image of Tjetji's daughter

PLANT CAPITAL OF THE PTOLEMAIC-ROMAN PERIOD, EGYPT, 332-30 BC

Palm leaf

Papyrus flower

Papyrus leaf

Papyrus stem

Lotus bud

Lotus stem

Cornice decorated with cavetto moulding

Bead moulding

Trellis window

Rectangular pier decorated with hieroglyphs

Elevated roof of central nave

Clerestory

Disc representing sun or light

Architrave

Square abacus

Papyrus-bud capital

Papyriform column

Shaft

Scene depicting a Pharaoh (king) paying homage to the god Amon-Re

Central nave

ANCIENT EGYPTIAN BUILDING DECORATION

DECORATED WINDOW, MEDINET HABU, EGYPT, C.1198 BC

ROPE AND PATERAE DECORATION

CAPITAL WITH THE HEAD OF THE SKY-GODDESS HATHOR, TEMPLE OF ISIS, PHILAE, EGYPT, 283-47 BC

LOTUS AND PAPYRUS FRIEZE DECORATION

Ancient Greece

THE CLASSICAL TEMPLES OF ANCIENT GREECE were built according to the belief that certain forms and proportions were pleasing to the gods. There were three main ancient Greek architectural orders (styles), which can be distinguished by the decoration and proportions of their columns, capitals (column tops), and entablatures (structures resting on the capitals). The oldest is the Doric order, which dates from the seventh century BC and was used mainly on the Greek mainland and in the western colonies, such as Sicily and southern Italy. The Temple of Neptune, shown here, is a classic example of this order. It is hypaethral (roofless) and peripteral (surrounded by a single row of columns). About a century later, the more decorative Ionic order developed on the Aegean Islands. Features of this order include volutes (spiral scrolls) on capitals and acroteria (pediment ornaments). The Corinthian order was invented in Athens in the fifth century BC and is typically identified by an acanthus leaf on the capitals. This order was later widely used in ancient Roman architecture.

CAPITALS OF THE THREE ORDERS OF ANCIENT GREEK ARCHITECTURE

Abacus

Echinus

Annulet

Trachelion (neck)

DORIC CAPITAL, THE PROPYLAEUM (GATEWAY), THE ACROPOLIS, ATHENS, GREECE, 449 BC

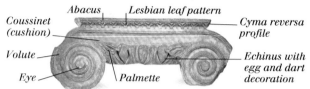

Coussinet (cushion)

Abacus

Lesbian leaf pattern

Cyma reversa profile

Volute

Echinus with egg and dart decoration

Eye

Palmette

IONIC CAPITAL, THE PROPYLAEUM (GATEWAY), TEMPLE OF ATHENA POLIAS, PRIENE, GREECE, c.334 BC

Mask

Abacus

Volute

Cauliculus

Acanthus leaf

Bell-shaped core

CORINTHIAN CAPITAL FROM A STOA (PORTICO), PROBABLY FROM ASIA MINOR

TEMPLE OF NEPTUNE, PAESTUM, ITALY, c.460 BC

Raking cornice

Pediment

Trachelion (neck)

Taenia

Triglyph

Metope

Glyph (channel)

Doric entablature

Pteron (external colonnade)

Euthynteria

Drum

Stylobate

Column of the Doric order

PLAN OF THE TEMPLE OF NEPTUNE, PAESTUM

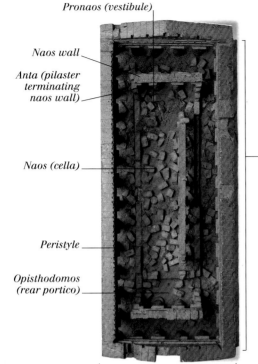

Pronaos (vestibule)

Naos wall

Anta (pilaster terminating naos wall)

Naos (cella)

Pteron (external colonnade)

Peristyle

Opisthodomos (rear portico)

Hexastyle pteron (colonnade of six columns)

ANCIENT GREEK BUILDING DECORATION

Volute

FACADE, TREASURY OF ATREUS, MYCENAE, GREECE, 1350-1250 BC

Meander

FRETWORK, PARTHENON, ATHENS, GREECE, 447-436 BC

ACROTERION, TEMPLE OF APHAIA, AEGINA, GREECE, 490 BC

Griffon (gryphon)

Raking cornice

ANTEFIXA, TEMPLE OF APHAIA, AEGINA, GREECE, 490 BC

Palmette

Volute

Regula (short fillet beneath taenia)

Eaves

Cornice

Frieze

Architrave

Capital

Shaft

Crepidoma (stepped base)

Entasis (slight curve of a column)

Intercolumniation

Fluting

461

Ancient Rome 1

IN THE EARLY PERIOD OF THE ROMAN EMPIRE extensive use was made of ancient Greek architectural ideas, particularly those of the Corinthian order (see pp. 460-461). As a result, many early Roman buildings – such as the Temple of Vesta (opposite) – closely resemble ancient Greek buildings. A distinctive Roman style began to evolve in the first century AD. This style developed the interiors of buildings (the Greeks had concentrated on the exterior) by using arches, vaults, and domes inside the buildings, and by ornamenting internal walls. Many of these features can be seen in the Pantheon. Exterior columns were often used for decorative, rather than structural, purposes, as in the Colosseum and the Porta Nigra (see pp. 464-465). Smaller buildings had timber frames with wattle-and-daub walls, as in the mill (see pp. 464-465). Roman architecture remained influential for many centuries, with some of its principles being used in the 11th century in Romanesque buildings (see pp. 468-469) and also in the 15th and 16th centuries in Renaissance buildings (see pp. 474-477).

ANCIENT ROMAN BUILDING DECORATION

FESTOON, TEMPLE OF VESTA,
TIVOLI, ITALY, C.80 BC

RICHLY DECORATED
ROMAN OVUM

INTERIOR OF THE PANTHEON, ROME, ITALY, 118-c.128

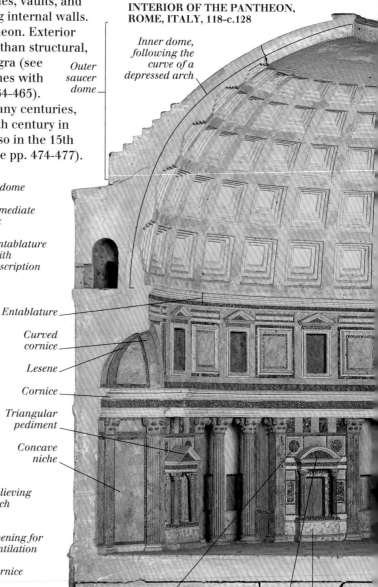

Outer saucer dome

Inner dome, following the curve of a depressed arch

Entablature

Curved cornice

Lesene

Cornice

Triangular pediment

Concave niche

Marble veneer

Segmental pediment

Pedestal

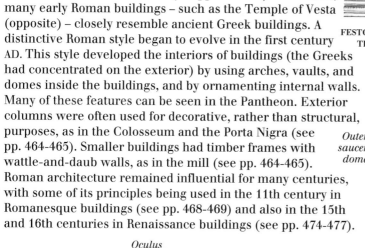

Oculus

Series of concentric, step-like rings

Dentil ornament

Engaged pediment

Raking cornice

Pediment

Rotunda

Outer saucer dome

Intermediate block

Entablature with inscription

Octastyle portico (eight-column portico)

FRONT VIEW OF THE PANTHEON

SIDE VIEW OF THE PANTHEON

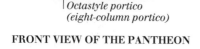

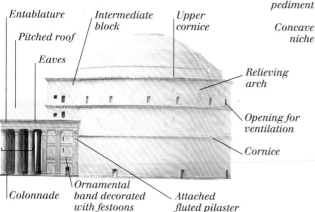

Entablature

Pitched roof

Eaves

Intermediate block

Upper cornice

Relieving arch

Opening for ventilation

Cornice

Colonnade

Ornamental band decorated with festoons

Attached fluted pilaster

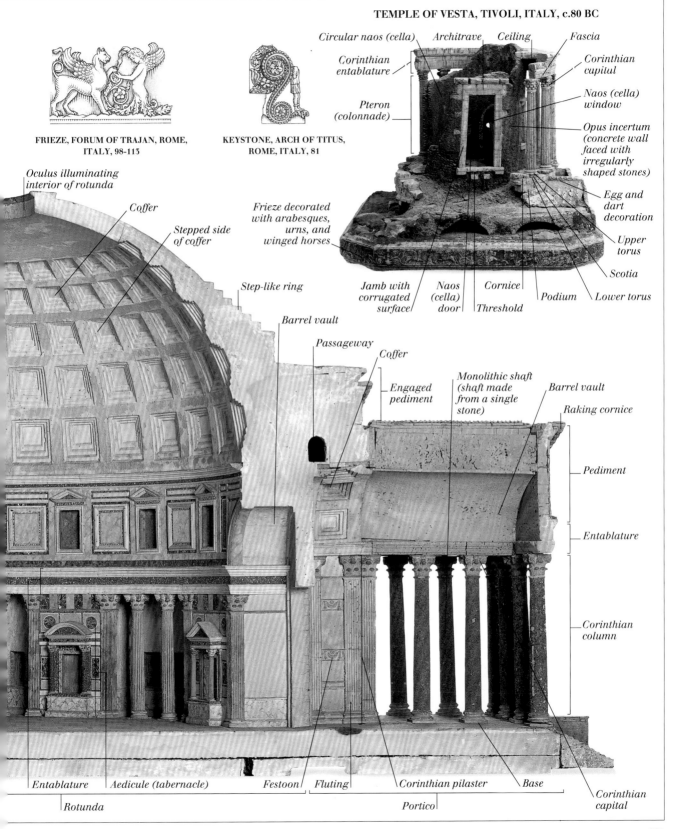

FRIEZE, FORUM OF TRAJAN, ROME,
ITALY, 98-113

KEYSTONE, ARCH OF TITUS,
ROME, ITALY, 81

TEMPLE OF VESTA, TIVOLI, ITALY, c.80 BC

Circular naos (cella)

Architrave

Ceiling

Fascia

Corinthian
entablature

Corinthian
capital

Pteron
(colonnade)

Naos (cella)
window

Opus incertum
(concrete wall
faced with
irregularly
shaped stones)

Egg and
dart
decoration

Upper
torus

Scotia

Jamb with
corrugated
surface

Naos
(cella)
door

Cornice

Podium

Lower torus

Threshold

Oculus illuminating
interior of rotunda

Coffer

Stepped side
of coffer

Frieze decorated
with arabesques,
urns, and
winged horses

Step-like ring

Barrel vault

Passageway

Coffer

Engaged
pediment

Monolithic shaft
(shaft made
from a single
stone)

Barrel vault

Raking cornice

Pediment

Entablature

Corinthian
column

Entablature

Aedicule (tabernacle)

Festoon

Fluting

Corinthian pilaster

Base

Corinthian
capital

Rotunda

Portico

Ancient Rome 2

SIDE VIEW OF A ROMAN MILL

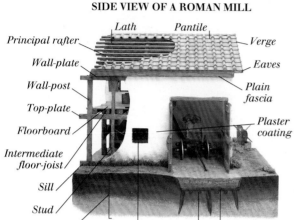

Lath
Pantile
Principal rafter
Verge
Wall-plate
Eaves
Wall-post
Plain fascia
Top-plate
Floorboard
Plaster coating
Intermediate floor-joist
Sill
Stud
Foundation
Grille
Joist
Boarding

FRONT VIEW OF A ROMAN MILL, 1ST CENTURY BC

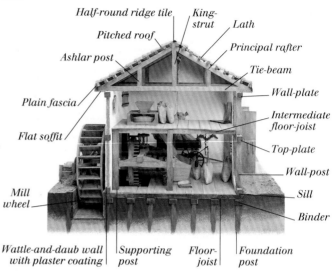

Half-round ridge tile
King-strut
Pitched roof
Lath
Ashlar post
Principal rafter
Tie-beam
Plain fascia
Wall-plate
Flat soffit
Intermediate floor-joist
Top-plate
Wall-post
Mill wheel
Sill
Binder
Wattle-and-daub wall with plaster coating
Supporting post
Floor-joist
Foundation post

THE COLOSSEUM (FLAVIAN AMPHITHEATRE), ROME, ITALY, 70-82

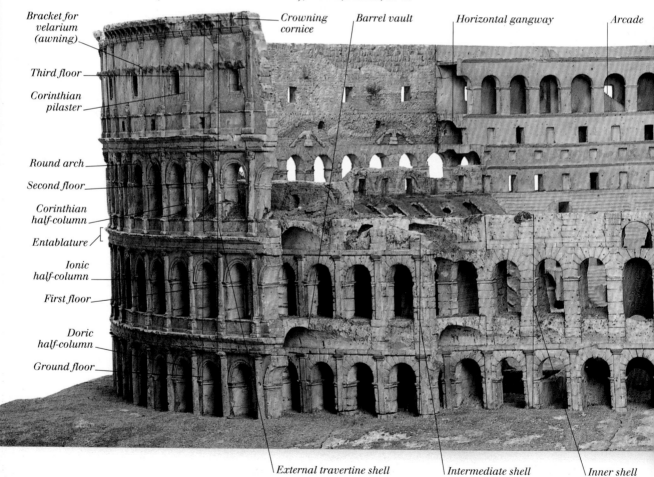

Bracket for velarium (awning)
Crowning cornice
Barrel vault
Horizontal gangway
Arcade
Third floor
Corinthian pilaster
Round arch
Second floor
Corinthian half-column
Entablature
Ionic half-column
First floor
Doric half-column
Ground floor
External travertine shell
Intermediate shell
Inner shell

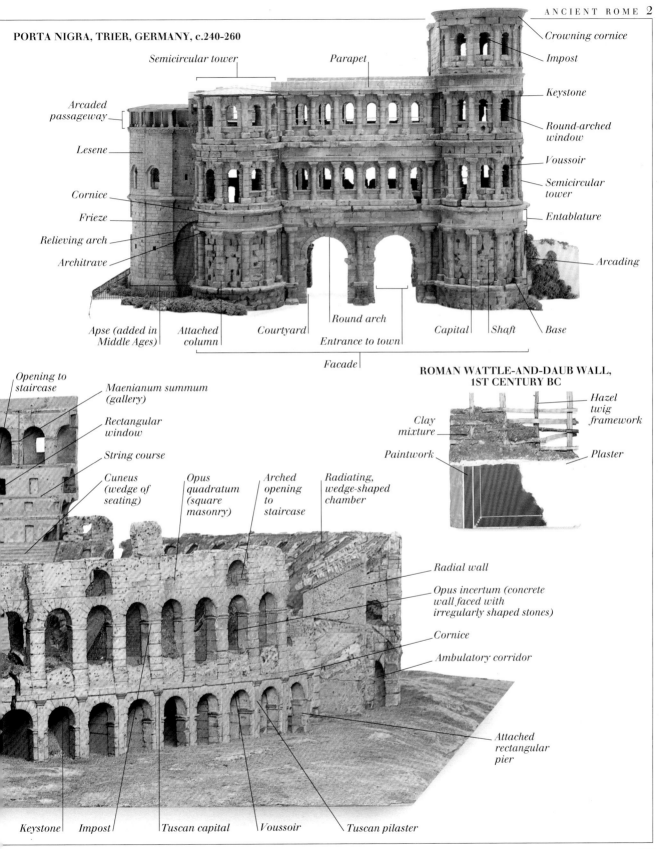

PORTA NIGRA, TRIER, GERMANY, c.240-260

Semicircular tower

Parapet

Crowning cornice

Impost

Arcaded passageway

Keystone

Round-arched window

Lesene

Voussoir

Semicircular tower

Cornice

Entablature

Frieze

Relieving arch

Arcading

Architrave

Apse (added in Middle Ages)

Attached column

Courtyard

Round arch

Entrance to town

Capital

Shaft

Base

Facade

ROMAN WATTLE-AND-DAUB WALL, 1ST CENTURY BC

Opening to staircase

Maenianum summum (gallery)

Hazel twig framework

Clay mixture

Rectangular window

String course

Paintwork

Plaster

Cuneus (wedge of seating)

Opus quadratum (square masonry)

Arched opening to staircase

Radiating, wedge-shaped chamber

Radial wall

Opus incertum (concrete wall faced with irregularly shaped stones)

Cornice

Ambulatory corridor

Attached rectangular pier

Keystone

Impost

Tuscan capital

Voussoir

Tuscan pilaster

Medieval castles and houses

WARFARE WAS COMMON IN EUROPE in the Middle Ages, and many monarchs and nobles built castles as a form of defence. Typical medieval castles have outer walls surrounding a moat. Inside the moat is a bailey (courtyard), protected by a chemise (jacket-wall). The innermost and strongest part of a medieval castle is the keep. There are two main types of keep: towers called donjons, such as the Tour de César and Coucy-le-Château, and rectangular keeps ("hall-keeps"), such as the Tower of London. Castles were often guarded by salients (projecting fortifications), like those of the Bastille. Medieval houses typically had timber cruck (tent-like) frames, wattle-and-daub walls, and pitched roofs, like those on medieval London Bridge (opposite).

DONJON, TOUR DE CESAR, PROVINS, FRANCE, 12TH CENTURY

Oculus
Loophole
Conical spire
Flying buttress
Hexahedral hall
Semicircular turret
Fireplace
Bailey
Embrasure
Battlements (crenellations)
Hemispherical cupola
Gallery
Squinch
Vaulted room
Main entrance
Staircase to chemise (jacket-wall)
Chemise (jacket-wall)
Plain impost
Depressed cupola
Vaulted staircase
Motte

Loophole

SALIENT, CAERNARVON CASTLE, BRITAIN, 1283-1323

Timber cruck frame

CRUCK-FRAMED HOUSE, BRITAIN, c.1200

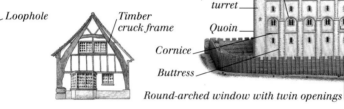

Blind, rounded relieving arch
Merlon
Battlements (crenellations)
Tetrahedral spire
Crenel
Loophole
Rectangular turret
Wooden staircase leading to entrance above ground level
Quoin
Cornice
Buttress
Timber-framed house
Round-arched window with twin openings
Cruck frame
Paling

TOWER OF LONDON, BRITAIN, FROM 1070

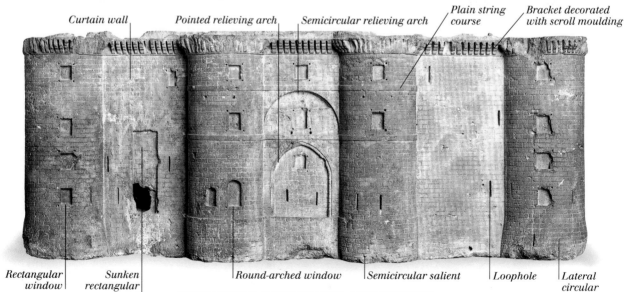

Curtain wall
Pointed relieving arch
Semicircular relieving arch
Plain string course
Bracket decorated with scroll moulding
Rectangular window
Sunken rectangular panel
Round-arched window
Semicircular salient
Loophole
Lateral circular salient

THE BASTILLE, PARIS, FRANCE, 14TH CENTURY

MEDIEVAL LONDON BRIDGE, BRITAIN, 1176 (WITH 14TH-CENTURY BATTLEMENTED BUILDING, NONESUCH HOUSE, AND TWO-TOWERED GATE)

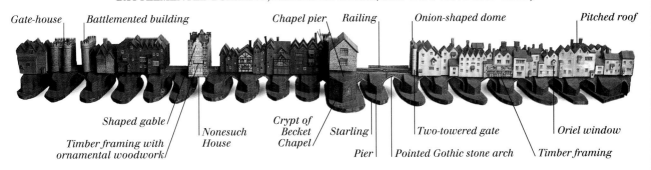

Gate-house

Battlemented building

Chapel pier

Railing

Onion-shaped dome

Pitched roof

Shaped gable

Nonesuch House

Crypt of Becket Chapel

Starling

Two-towered gate

Oriel window

Timber framing with ornamental woodwork

Pier

Pointed Gothic stone arch

Timber framing

DONJON, COUCY-LE-CHATEAU, AISNE, FRANCE, 1225-1245

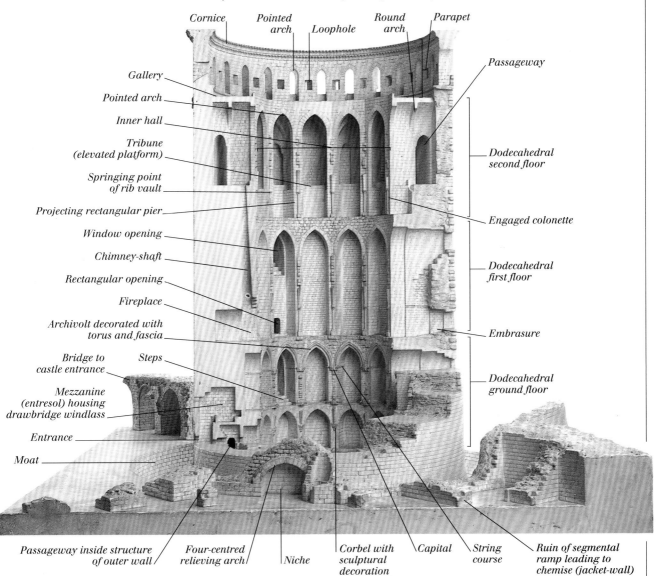

Cornice

Pointed arch

Loophole

Round arch

Parapet

Gallery

Passageway

Pointed arch

Inner hall

Tribune (elevated platform)

Dodecahedral second floor

Springing point of rib vault

Projecting rectangular pier

Engaged colonette

Window opening

Chimney-shaft

Dodecahedral first floor

Rectangular opening

Fireplace

Archivolt decorated with torus and fascia

Embrasure

Bridge to castle entrance

Steps

Mezzanine (entresol) housing drawbridge windlass

Dodecahedral ground floor

Entrance

Moat

Passageway inside structure of outer wall

Four-centred relieving arch

Niche

Corbel with sculptural decoration

Capital

String course

Ruin of segmental ramp leading to chemise (jacket-wall)

Medieval churches

DURING THE MIDDLE AGES, large numbers of churches were built in Europe. European churches of this period typically have high vaults supported by massive piers and columns. In the 10th century, the Romanesque style developed. Romanesque architects adopted many Roman or early Christian architectural ideas, such as cross-shaped ground-plans – like that of Angoulême Cathedral (opposite) – and the basilican system of a nave with a central vessel and side aisles. In the mid-12th century, flying buttresses and pointed vaults appeared. These features later became widely used in Gothic architecture (see pp. 470-471). Bagneux Church (opposite) has both styles: a Romanesque tower, and a Gothic nave and choir.

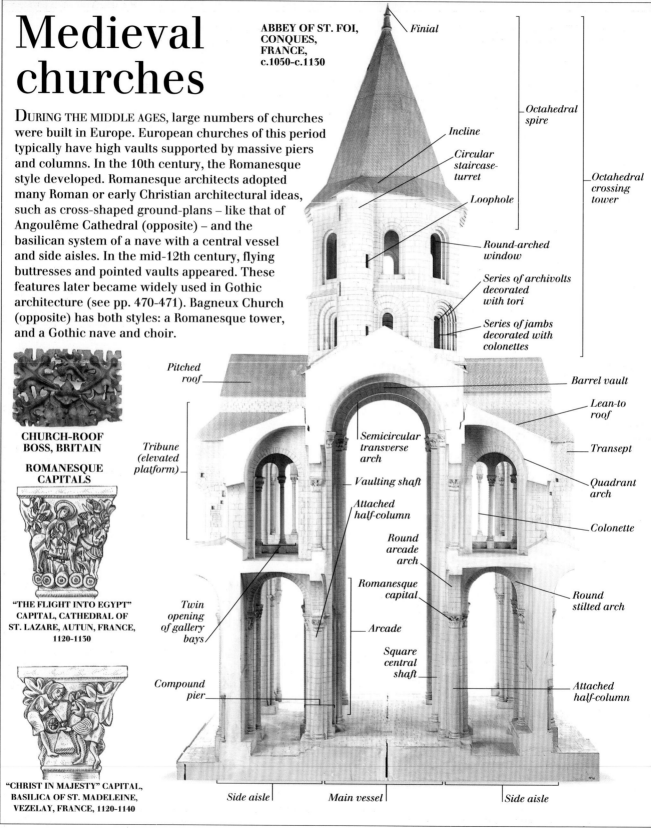

Finial

Incline

Circular staircase-turret

Loophole

Octahedral spire

Octahedral crossing tower

Round-arched window

Series of archivolts decorated with tori

Series of jambs decorated with colonettes

CHURCH-ROOF BOSS, BRITAIN

ROMANESQUE CAPITALS

"THE FLIGHT INTO EGYPT" CAPITAL, CATHEDRAL OF ST. LAZARE, AUTUN, FRANCE, 1120-1130

"CHRIST IN MAJESTY" CAPITAL, BASILICA OF ST. MADELEINE, VEZELAY, FRANCE, 1120-1140

Pitched roof

Tribune (elevated platform)

Twin opening of gallery bays

Compound pier

Semicircular transverse arch

Vaulting shaft

Attached half-column

Round arcade arch

Romanesque capital

Arcade

Square central shaft

Barrel vault

Lean-to roof

Transept

Quadrant arch

Colonette

Round stilted arch

Attached half-column

Side aisle

Main vessel

Side aisle

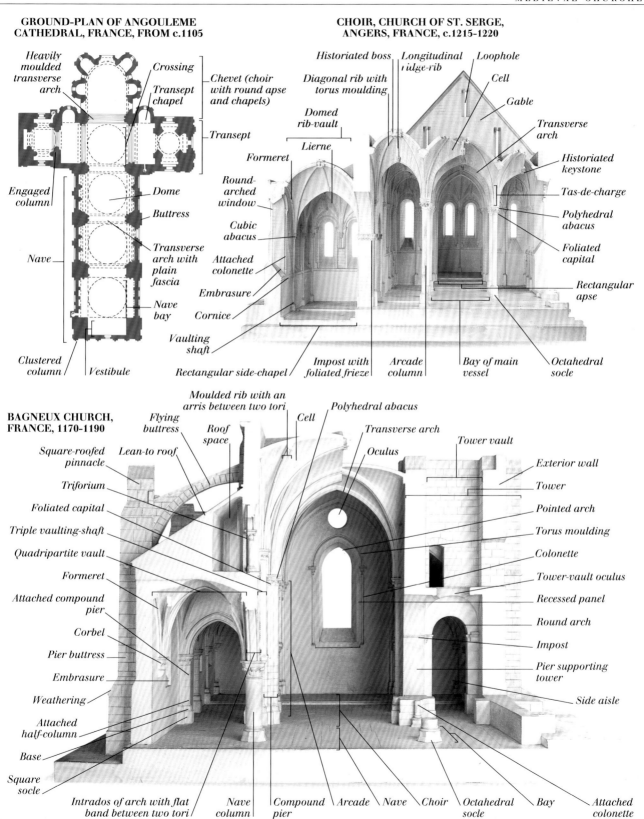

GROUND-PLAN OF ANGOULEME CATHEDRAL, FRANCE, FROM c.1105

Heavily moulded transverse arch

Crossing

Transept chapel

Chevet (choir with round apse and chapels)

Transept

Engaged column

Dome

Buttress

Transverse arch with plain fascia

Nave

Nave bay

Clustered column

Vestibule

CHOIR, CHURCH OF ST. SERGE, ANGERS, FRANCE, c.1215-1220

Historiated boss

Longitudinal ridge-rib

Loophole

Diagonal rib with torus moulding

Cell

Gable

Domed rib-vault

Transverse arch

Lierne

Formeret

Historiated keystone

Round-arched window

Tas-de-charge

Cubic abacus

Polyhedral abacus

Attached colonette

Foliated capital

Embrasure

Rectangular apse

Cornice

Vaulting shaft

Rectangular side-chapel

Impost with foliated frieze

Arcade column

Bay of main vessel

Octahedral socle

BAGNEUX CHURCH, FRANCE, 1170-1190

Moulded rib with an arris between two tori

Flying buttress

Roof space

Cell

Polyhedral abacus

Transverse arch

Tower vault

Square-roofed pinnacle

Lean-to roof

Oculus

Exterior wall

Triforium

Tower

Foliated capital

Pointed arch

Triple vaulting-shaft

Torus moulding

Quadripartite vault

Colonette

Formeret

Tower-vault oculus

Attached compound pier

Recessed panel

Corbel

Round arch

Pier buttress

Impost

Embrasure

Pier supporting tower

Weathering

Attached half-column

Side aisle

Base

Square socle

Intrados of arch with flat band between two tori

Nave column

Compound pier

Arcade

Nave

Choir

Octahedral socle

Bay

Attached colonette

469

Gothic 1

GOTHIC STAINED GLASS WITH FOLIATED SCROLL MOTIF, ON WOODEN FORM

GOTHIC BUILDINGS are characterized by rib vaults, pointed or lancet arches, flying buttresses, decorative tracery and gables, and stained-glass windows. Typical Gothic buildings include the Cathedrals of Salisbury and old St. Paul's in England, and Notre Dame de Paris in France (see pp. 472-473). The Gothic style developed out of Romanesque architecture in France (see pp. 468-469) in the mid-12th century, and then spread throughout Europe. The decorative elements of Gothic architecture became highly developed in buildings of the English Decorated style (late 13th-14th century) and the French Flamboyant style (15th-16th century). These styles are exemplified by the tower of Salisbury Cathedral and the staircase in the Church of St. Maclou (see pp. 472-473), respectively. In both of these styles, embellishments such as ballflowers and curvilinear (flowing) tracery were used liberally. The English Perpendicular style (late 14th-15th century), which followed the Decorated style, emphasized the vertical and horizontal elements of a building. A notable feature of this style is the hammer-beam roof.

GROUND-PLAN OF SALISBURY CATHEDRAL

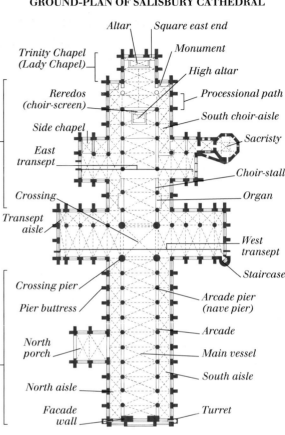

Altar
Square east end
Trinity Chapel (Lady Chapel)
Monument
High altar
Reredos (choir-screen)
Processional path
Side chapel
South choir-aisle
Choir
Sacristy
East transept
Choir-stall
Crossing
Organ
Transept aisle
West transept
Staircase
Crossing pier
Arcade pier (nave pier)
Pier buttress
Arcade
North porch
Main vessel
Nave
South aisle
North aisle
Facade wall
Turret

GOTHIC TORUS WITH BALLFLOWERS

Limestone block
Block members carved into rolls
Block members cut polygonally
Pencil guideline
Early stage of ballflower carving

BLOCK AFTER INITIAL CUTTING

BLOCK WITH MEMBERS CUT INTO ROLLS

Torus
Ballflower
Fillet
Mason's mark

FINISHED BLOCK

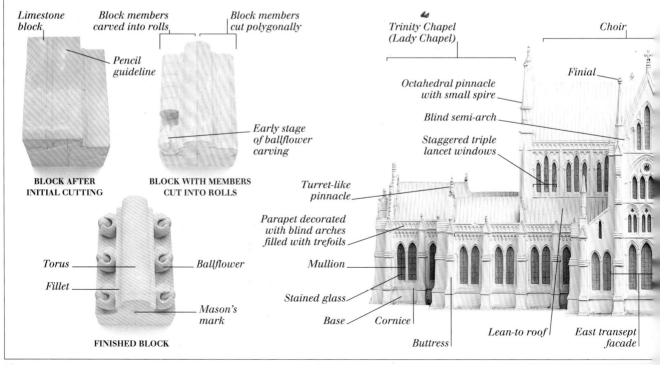

Trinity Chapel (Lady Chapel)
Choir
Finial
Octahedral pinnacle with small spire
Blind semi-arch
Staggered triple lancet windows
Turret-like pinnacle
Parapet decorated with blind arches filled with trefoils
Mullion
Stained glass
Base
Cornice
Lean-to roof
East transept facade
Buttress

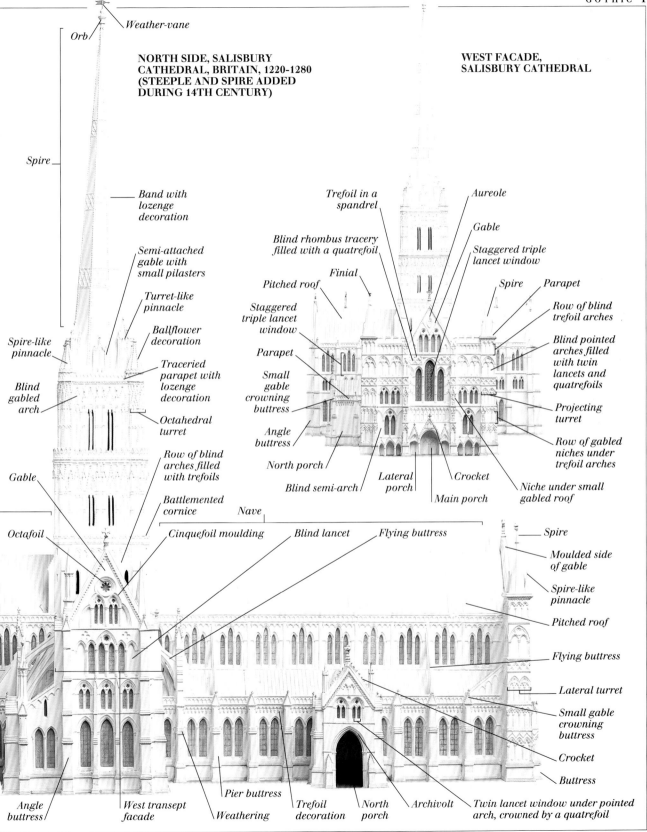

NORTH SIDE, SALISBURY CATHEDRAL, BRITAIN, 1220-1280 (STEEPLE AND SPIRE ADDED DURING 14TH CENTURY)

WEST FACADE, SALISBURY CATHEDRAL

Weather-vane

Orb

Spire

Band with lozenge decoration

Semi-attached gable with small pilasters

Turret-like pinnacle

Ballflower decoration

Traceried parapet with lozenge decoration

Octahedral turret

Spire-like pinnacle

Blind gabled arch

Row of blind arches filled with trefoils

Battlemented cornice

Gable

Octafoil

Cinquefoil moulding

Nave

Blind lancet

Flying buttress

Trefoil in a spandrel

Aureole

Blind rhombus tracery filled with a quatrefoil

Gable

Staggered triple lancet window

Finial

Pitched roof

Spire

Parapet

Staggered triple lancet window

Row of blind trefoil arches

Parapet

Blind pointed arches filled with twin lancets and quatrefoils

Small gable crowning buttress

Angle buttress

Projecting turret

North porch

Lateral porch

Crocket

Row of gabled niches under trefoil arches

Blind semi-arch

Main porch

Niche under small gabled roof

Spire

Moulded side of gable

Spire-like pinnacle

Pitched roof

Flying buttress

Lateral turret

Small gable crowning buttress

Crocket

Buttress

Angle buttress

West transept facade

Pier buttress

Weathering

Trefoil decoration

North porch

Archivolt

Twin lancet window under pointed arch, crowned by a quatrefoil

Gothic 2

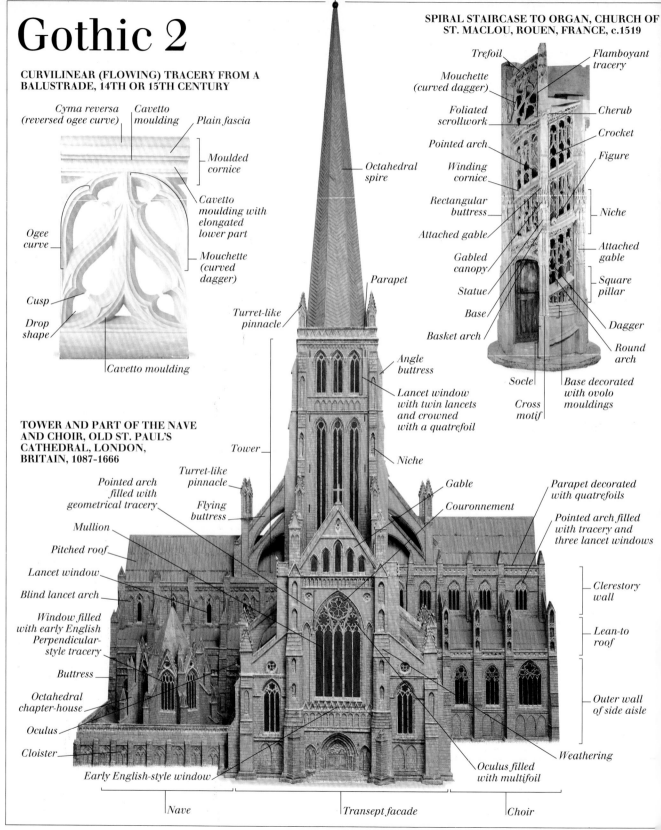

CURVILINEAR (FLOWING) TRACERY FROM A BALUSTRADE, 14TH OR 15TH CENTURY

Cyma reversa (reversed ogee curve)
Cavetto moulding
Plain fascia
Moulded cornice
Cavetto moulding with elongated lower part
Mouchette (curved dagger)
Ogee curve
Cusp
Drop shape
Cavetto moulding

SPIRAL STAIRCASE TO ORGAN, CHURCH OF ST. MACLOU, ROUEN, FRANCE, c.1519

Trefoil
Flamboyant tracery
Mouchette (curved dagger)
Foliated scrollwork
Cherub
Pointed arch
Crocket
Winding cornice
Figure
Rectangular buttress
Niche
Attached gable
Attached gable
Gabled canopy
Square pillar
Statue
Base
Dagger
Basket arch
Round arch
Socle
Base decorated with ovolo mouldings
Cross motif

TOWER AND PART OF THE NAVE AND CHOIR, OLD ST. PAUL'S CATHEDRAL, LONDON, BRITAIN, 1087-1666

Octahedral spire
Parapet
Turret-like pinnacle
Angle buttress
Lancet window with twin lancets and crowned with a quatrefoil
Tower
Niche
Turret-like pinnacle
Flying buttress
Pointed arch filled with geometrical tracery
Mullion
Pitched roof
Lancet window
Blind lancet arch
Window filled with early English Perpendicular-style tracery
Buttress
Octahedral chapter-house
Oculus
Cloister
Early English-style window
Gable
Couronnement
Parapet decorated with quatrefoils
Pointed arch filled with tracery and three lancet windows
Clerestory wall
Lean-to roof
Outer wall of side aisle
Weathering
Oculus filled with multifoil
Nave
Transept facade
Choir

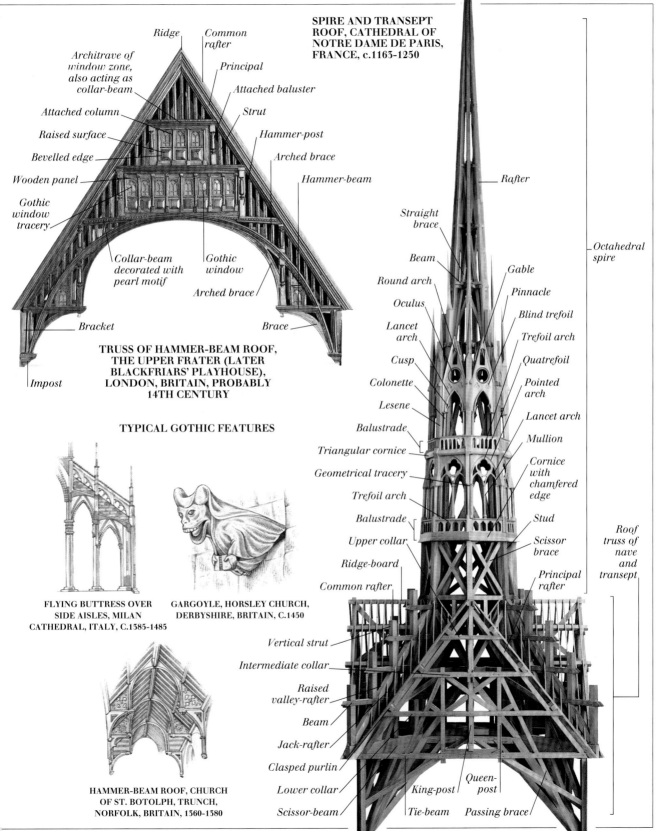

SPIRE AND TRANSEPT ROOF, CATHEDRAL OF NOTRE DAME DE PARIS, FRANCE, c.1163-1250

Ridge

Common rafter

Architrave of window zone, also acting as collar-beam

Principal

Attached baluster

Attached column

Strut

Raised surface

Hammer-post

Bevelled edge

Arched brace

Wooden panel

Hammer-beam

Gothic window tracery

Collar-beam decorated with pearl motif

Gothic window

Arched brace

Bracket

Brace

Impost

TRUSS OF HAMMER-BEAM ROOF, THE UPPER FRATER (LATER BLACKFRIARS' PLAYHOUSE), LONDON, BRITAIN, PROBABLY 14TH CENTURY

TYPICAL GOTHIC FEATURES

FLYING BUTTRESS OVER SIDE AISLES, MILAN CATHEDRAL, ITALY, C.1385-1485

GARGOYLE, HORSLEY CHURCH, DERBYSHIRE, BRITAIN, C.1450

HAMMER-BEAM ROOF, CHURCH OF ST. BOTOLPH, TRUNCH, NORFOLK, BRITAIN, 1360-1380

Rafter

Straight brace

Beam

Gable

Round arch

Pinnacle

Oculus

Blind trefoil

Lancet arch

Trefoil arch

Cusp

Quatrefoil

Colonette

Pointed arch

Lesene

Lancet arch

Balustrade

Mullion

Triangular cornice

Cornice with chamfered edge

Geometrical tracery

Trefoil arch

Stud

Balustrade

Scissor brace

Upper collar

Principal rafter

Ridge-board

Common rafter

Octahedral spire

Roof truss of nave and transept

Vertical strut

Intermediate collar

Raised valley-rafter

Beam

Jack-rafter

Clasped purlin

Lower collar

Scissor-beam

King-post

Queen-post

Tie-beam

Passing brace

Renaissance 1

THE RENAISSANCE was a European movement – lasting roughly from the 14th century to the mid-17th century – in which the arts and sciences underwent great changes. In architecture, these changes were marked by a return to the classical forms and proportions of ancient Roman buildings. The Renaissance originated in Italy, and the buildings most characteristic of its style can be found there, such as the Palazzo Strozzi shown here. Mannerism is a branch of the Renaissance style that distorts the classical forms; an example is the Laurentian Library staircase. As the Renaissance style spread to other European countries, many of its features were incorporated into the local architecture; for example, the Château de Montal in France (see pp. 476-477) incorporates aedicules (tabernacles).

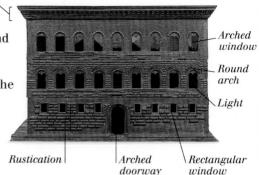

Crowning cornice

Arched window

Round arch

Light

Rustication

Arched doorway

Rectangular window

SIDE VIEW OF PALAZZO STROZZI, FLORENCE, ITALY, 1489 (BY G. DA SANGALLO, B. DA MAIANO, AND CRONACA)

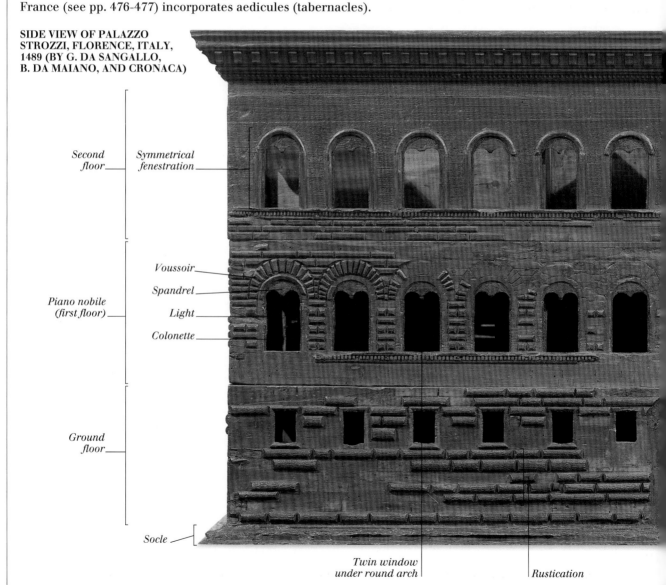

Second floor

Symmetrical fenestration

Piano nobile (first floor)

Voussoir

Spandrel

Light

Colonette

Ground floor

Socle

Twin window under round arch

Rustication

DETAILS FROM ITALIAN RENAISSANCE BUILDINGS

**PANEL FROM DRUM OF DOME,
FLORENCE CATHEDRAL, 1420-1436**

**COFFERING IN DOME,
PAZZI CHAPEL,
FLORENCE, 1429-1461**

**STAIRCASE,
LAURENTIAN LIBRARY,
FLORENCE, 1559**

**PORTICO, VILLA ROTUNDA,
VICENZA, 1567-1569**

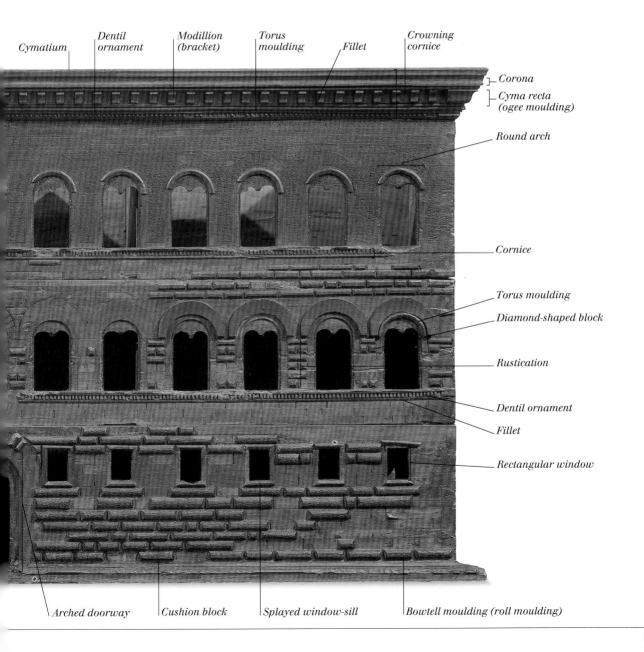

Cymatium

Dentil ornament

Modillion (bracket)

Torus moulding

Fillet

Crowning cornice

Corona

Cyma recta (ogee moulding)

Round arch

Cornice

Torus moulding

Diamond-shaped block

Rustication

Dentil ornament

Fillet

Rectangular window

Arched doorway

Cushion block

Splayed window-sill

Bowtell moulding (roll moulding)

Renaissance 2

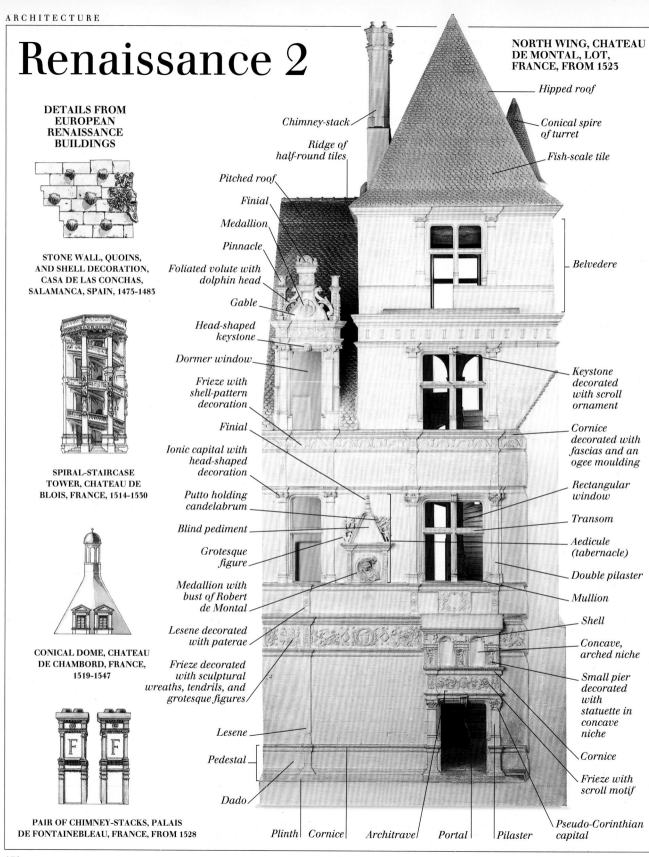

DETAILS FROM EUROPEAN RENAISSANCE BUILDINGS

STONE WALL, QUOINS, AND SHELL DECORATION, CASA DE LAS CONCHAS, SALAMANCA, SPAIN, 1475-1483

SPIRAL-STAIRCASE TOWER, CHATEAU DE BLOIS, FRANCE, 1514-1530

CONICAL DOME, CHATEAU DE CHAMBORD, FRANCE, 1519-1547

PAIR OF CHIMNEY-STACKS, PALAIS DE FONTAINEBLEAU, FRANCE, FROM 1528

NORTH WING, CHATEAU DE MONTAL, LOT, FRANCE, FROM 1523

Chimney-stack

Ridge of half-round tiles

Pitched roof

Finial

Medallion

Pinnacle

Foliated volute with dolphin head

Gable

Head-shaped keystone

Dormer window

Frieze with shell-pattern decoration

Finial

Ionic capital with head-shaped decoration

Putto holding candelabrum

Blind pediment

Grotesque figure

Medallion with bust of Robert de Montal

Lesene decorated with paterae

Frieze decorated with sculptural wreaths, tendrils, and grotesque figures

Lesene

Pedestal

Dado

Plinth   Cornice   Architrave   Portal   Pilaster

Hipped roof

Conical spire of turret

Fish-scale tile

Belvedere

Keystone decorated with scroll ornament

Cornice decorated with fascias and an ogee moulding

Rectangular window

Transom

Aedicule (tabernacle)

Double pilaster

Mullion

Shell

Concave, arched niche

Small pier decorated with statuette in concave niche

Cornice

Frieze with scroll motif

Pseudo-Corinthian capital

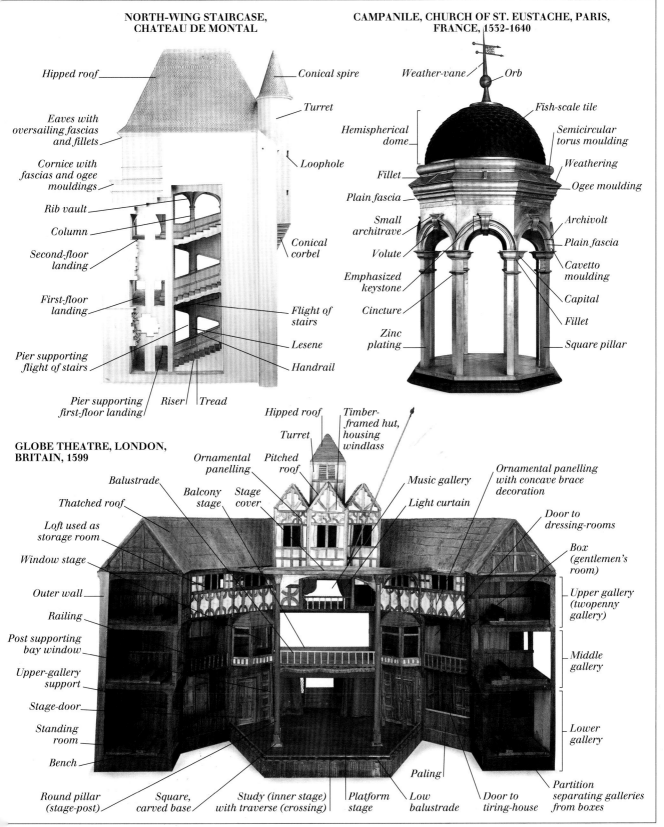

NORTH-WING STAIRCASE, CHATEAU DE MONTAL

Hipped roof

Eaves with oversailing fascias and fillets

Cornice with fascias and ogee mouldings

Rib vault

Column

Second-floor landing

First-floor landing

Pier supporting flight of stairs

Pier supporting first-floor landing

Riser

Tread

Conical spire

Turret

Loophole

Conical corbel

Flight of stairs

Lesene

Handrail

CAMPANILE, CHURCH OF ST. EUSTACHE, PARIS, FRANCE, 1532-1640

Weather-vane

Orb

Fish-scale tile

Hemispherical dome

Semicircular torus moulding

Weathering

Fillet

Ogee moulding

Plain fascia

Small architrave

Archivolt

Volute

Plain fascia

Emphasized keystone

Cavetto moulding

Cincture

Capital

Zinc plating

Fillet

Square pillar

GLOBE THEATRE, LONDON, BRITAIN, 1599

Balustrade

Thatched roof

Loft used as storage room

Window stage

Outer wall

Railing

Post supporting bay window

Upper-gallery support

Stage-door

Standing room

Bench

Round pillar (stage-post)

Square, carved base

Balcony stage

Stage cover

Ornamental panelling

Hipped roof

Turret

Pitched roof

Timber-framed hut, housing windlass

Music gallery

Light curtain

Ornamental panelling with concave brace decoration

Door to dressing-rooms

Box (gentlemen's room)

Upper gallery (twopenny gallery)

Middle gallery

Lower gallery

Study (inner stage) with traverse (crossing)

Platform stage

Paling

Low balustrade

Door to tiring-house

Partition separating galleries from boxes

Baroque and neoclassical 1

THE BAROQUE STYLE EVOLVED IN THE EARLY 17TH CENTURY in Rome. It is characterized by curved outlines and ostentatious decoration, as can be seen in the Italian church details (right). The baroque style was particularly widely favoured in Italy, Spain, and Germany. It was also adopted in Britain and France, but with adaptations. The British architects Sir Christopher Wren and Nicholas Hawksmoor, for example, used baroque features – such as the concave walls of St. Paul's Cathedral and the curved buttresses of the Church of St. George in the East (see pp. 480-481) – but they did so with restraint. Similarly, the curved buttresses and volutes of the Parisian Church of St. Paul-St. Louis are relatively plain. In the second half of the 17th century, a distinct classical style (known as neoclassicism) developed in northern Europe as a reaction to the excesses of baroque. Typical of this new style were churches such as the Madeleine (a proposed facade is shown below), as well as secular buildings such as the Cirque Napoleon (opposite) and the buildings of the British architect Sir John Soane (see pp. 482-483). In early 18th-century France, an extremely lavish form of baroque developed, known as rococo. The balcony from Nantes (see pp. 482-483) with its twisted ironwork and head-shaped corbels is typical of this style.

DETAILS FROM ITALIAN BAROQUE CHURCHES

SCROLLED BUTTRESS, CHURCH OF ST. MARIA DELLA SALUTE, VENICE, 1631-1682

STATUE OF THE ECSTASY OF ST. THERESA, CHURCH OF ST. MARIA DELLA VITTORIA, ROME, 1645-1652

Attic storey

Round-arched window

Twin pilaster

Coved dome

Triple keystone

Triangular pediment

Balustrade

Re-entrant entablature

Composite capital

Attached triangular pediment

Blind window

Composite column

Composite pilaster

Socle

Raking cornice

Frieze

Panel

Door jamb

Architrave

Attached segmental pediment

Lantern

Parapet

Cornice

Finial

Dentil ornament

Urn

Modillion (bracket)

Cornice

Entablature

Raised panel

Festoon

Intermediate cornice

Volute

Fluted shaft

Base

Blind door

PROPOSED FACADE, THE MADELEINE (NEOCLASSICAL), PARIS, FRANCE, 1764 (BY P. CONTANT D'IVRY)

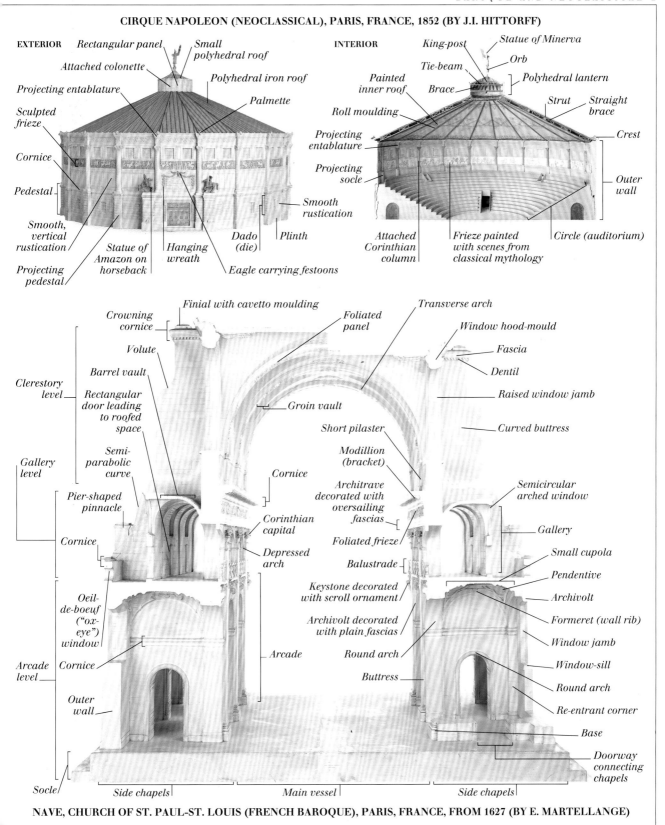

CIRQUE NAPOLEON (NEOCLASSICAL), PARIS, FRANCE, 1852 (BY J.I. HITTORFF)

EXTERIOR

Rectangular panel

Small polyhedral roof

Attached colonette

Projecting entablature

Polyhedral iron roof

Palmette

Sculpted frieze

Cornice

Pedestal

Smooth, vertical rustication

Projecting pedestal

Statue of Amazon on horseback

Hanging wreath

Dado (die)

Plinth

Smooth rustication

Eagle carrying festoons

INTERIOR

King-post

Statue of Minerva

Tie-beam

Orb

Painted inner roof

Brace

Polyhedral lantern

Roll moulding

Strut

Straight brace

Projecting entablature

Crest

Projecting socle

Outer wall

Attached Corinthian column

Frieze painted with scenes from classical mythology

Circle (auditorium)

Crowning cornice

Finial with cavetto moulding

Foliated panel

Transverse arch

Window hood-mould

Volute

Fascia

Barrel vault

Dentil

Clerestory level

Rectangular door leading to roofed space

Groin vault

Raised window jamb

Short pilaster

Curved buttress

Semi-parabolic curve

Modillion (bracket)

Gallery level

Cornice

Semicircular arched window

Pier-shaped pinnacle

Corinthian capital

Architrave decorated with oversailing fascias

Gallery

Cornice

Depressed arch

Foliated frieze

Small cupola

Oeil-de-boeuf ("ox-eye") window

Balustrade

Pendentive

Cornice

Keystone decorated with scroll ornament

Archivolt

Archivolt decorated with plain fascias

Formeret (wall rib)

Arcade

Round arch

Window jamb

Arcade level

Arcade

Buttress

Window-sill

Outer wall

Round arch

Re-entrant corner

Base

Doorway connecting chapels

Socle

Side chapels

Main vessel

Side chapels

NAVE, CHURCH OF ST. PAUL-ST. LOUIS (FRENCH BAROQUE), PARIS, FRANCE, FROM 1627 (BY E. MARTELLANGE)

Baroque and neoclassical 2

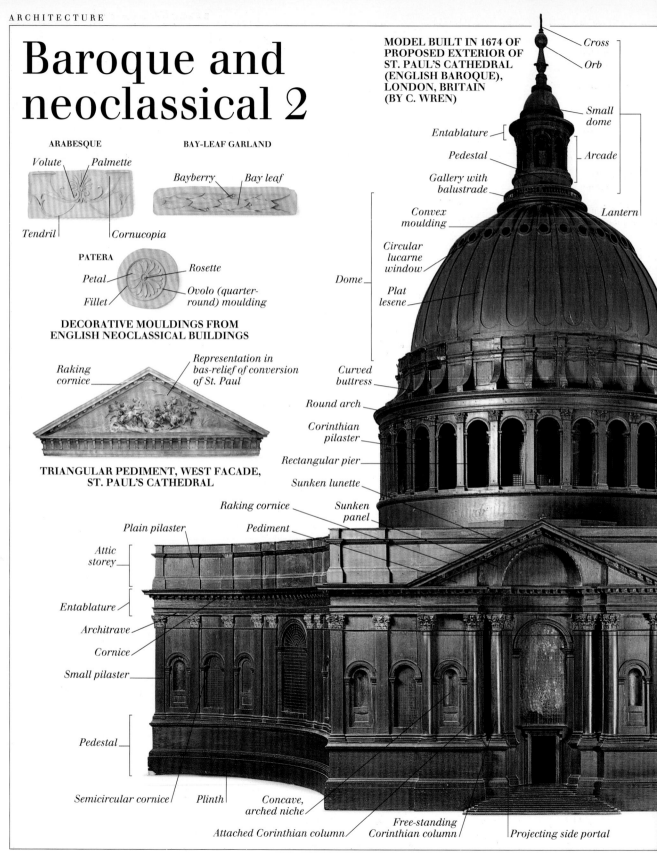

ARABESQUE

Volute
Palmette
Tendril
Cornucopia

BAY-LEAF GARLAND

Bayberry
Bay leaf

PATERA

Rosette
Petal
Ovolo (quarter-round) moulding
Fillet

DECORATIVE MOULDINGS FROM ENGLISH NEOCLASSICAL BUILDINGS

Raking cornice
Representation in bas-relief of conversion of St. Paul

TRIANGULAR PEDIMENT, WEST FACADE, ST. PAUL'S CATHEDRAL

Plain pilaster
Attic storey
Entablature
Architrave
Cornice
Small pilaster
Pedestal
Semicircular cornice
Plinth
Concave, arched niche
Attached Corinthian column
Free-standing Corinthian column
Projecting side portal
Raking cornice
Pediment
Sunken panel

MODEL BUILT IN 1674 OF PROPOSED EXTERIOR OF ST. PAUL'S CATHEDRAL (ENGLISH BAROQUE), LONDON, BRITAIN (BY C. WREN)

Cross
Orb
Small dome
Entablature
Pedestal
Arcade
Gallery with balustrade
Lantern
Convex moulding
Circular lucarne window
Dome
Plat lesene
Curved buttress
Round arch
Corinthian pilaster
Rectangular pier
Sunken lunette

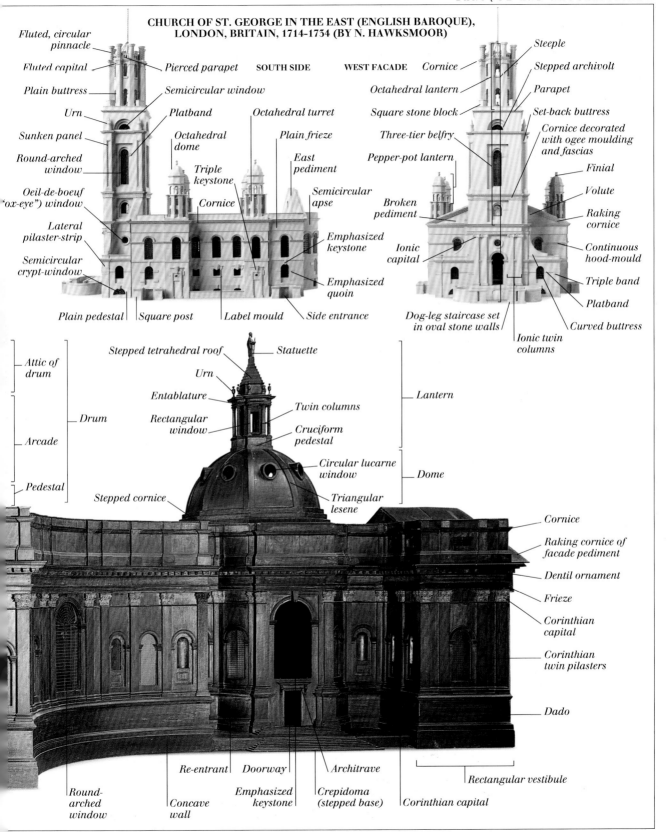

CHURCH OF ST. GEORGE IN THE EAST (ENGLISH BAROQUE), LONDON, BRITAIN, 1714-1734 (BY N. HAWKSMOOR)

SOUTH SIDE

Fluted, circular pinnacle
Fluted capital
Pierced parapet
Plain buttress
Semicircular window
Urn
Platband
Sunken panel
Octahedral turret
Round-arched window
Octahedral dome
Plain frieze
Triple keystone
East pediment
Oeil-de-boeuf ("ox-eye") window
Cornice
Semicircular apse
Lateral pilaster-strip
Emphasized keystone
Semicircular crypt-window
Emphasized quoin
Plain pedestal
Square post
Label mould
Side entrance

WEST FACADE

Steeple
Cornice
Stepped archivolt
Octahedral lantern
Parapet
Square stone block
Set-back buttress
Three-tier belfry
Cornice decorated with ogee moulding and fascias
Pepper-pot lantern
Finial
Broken pediment
Volute
Ionic capital
Raking cornice
Continuous hood-mould
Triple band
Platband
Dog-leg staircase set in oval stone walls
Curved buttress
Ionic twin columns

Attic of drum
Stepped tetrahedral roof
Statuette
Urn
Lantern
Entablature
Twin columns
Drum
Rectangular window
Cruciform pedestal
Arcade
Circular lucarne window
Dome
Pedestal
Stepped cornice
Triangular lesene
Cornice
Raking cornice of facade pediment
Dentil ornament
Frieze
Corinthian capital
Corinthian twin pilasters
Dado
Round-arched window
Re-entrant
Doorway
Architrave
Concave wall
Emphasized keystone
Crepidoma (stepped base)
Rectangular vestibule
Corinthian capital

Baroque and neoclassical 3

DETAILS FROM BAROQUE, NEOCLASSICAL, AND ROCOCO BUILDINGS

PORTICO, THE VYNE, HAMPSHIRE, BRITAIN, 1654 (NEOCLASSICAL)

GILT IRONWORK FROM SCREEN, PALAIS DE VERSAILLES, FRANCE, 1669-1674 (FRENCH BAROQUE)

WINDOW, PALAZZO STANGA, CREMONA, ITALY, EARLY 18TH CENTURY (ROCOCO)

ATLAS (MALE CARYATID), UPPER BELVEDERE, VIENNA, AUSTRIA, 1721 (GERMAN-STYLE BAROQUE)

BALCONY, NANTES, FRANCE, 1750-1740 (ROCOCO)

MASONRY OF A NICHE IN THE ROTUNDA (NEOCLASSICAL), BANK OF ENGLAND, LONDON, BRITAIN, 1794 (BY J. SOANE)

Scoop-pattern concave moulding

Keystone

Frieze

Semi-dome

Spandrel

Voussoir

Rotunda wall

Flat, rectangular niche

Rounded niche

Flat, square niche

CORNER OF THE NEW STATE PAPER OFFICE (NEOCLASSICAL), LONDON, BRITAIN, 1830-1831 (BY J. SOANE)

Classical-style entablature

Cornice

Frieze

Architrave

Pantile (S-shaped roofing tile)

Eaves

Fascia

Scroll-shaped corbel

Curved corbel

Second-floor window

Smooth rustication

Cornice

Drip-cap

Cornice

Frieze

Window architrave

Window jamb

First-floor window

Window-sill in the form of a frieze

Ground-floor window

Splayed window-sill

Vermiculated rustication

TYRINGHAM HOUSE (NEOCLASSICAL), BUCKINGHAMSHIRE, BRITAIN, 1793-1797 (BY J. SOANE)

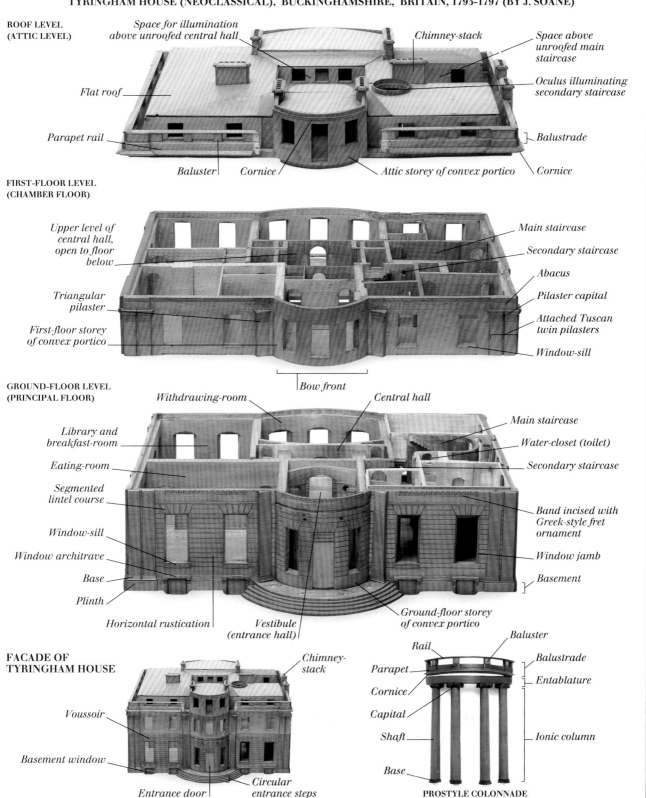

ROOF LEVEL (ATTIC LEVEL)

Space for illumination above unroofed central hall

Chimney-stack

Space above unroofed main staircase

Oculus illuminating secondary staircase

Flat roof

Parapet rail

Balustrade

Baluster

Cornice

Attic storey of convex portico

Cornice

FIRST-FLOOR LEVEL (CHAMBER FLOOR)

Upper level of central hall, open to floor below

Main staircase

Secondary staircase

Abacus

Pilaster capital

Triangular pilaster

Attached Tuscan twin pilasters

First-floor storey of convex portico

Window-sill

Bow front

GROUND-FLOOR LEVEL (PRINCIPAL FLOOR)

Withdrawing-room

Central hall

Main staircase

Library and breakfast-room

Water-closet (toilet)

Eating-room

Secondary staircase

Segmented lintel course

Band incised with Greek-style fret ornament

Window-sill

Window architrave

Window jamb

Base

Basement

Plinth

Horizontal rustication

Vestibule (entrance hall)

Ground-floor storey of convex portico

FACADE OF TYRINGHAM HOUSE

Chimney-stack

Voussoir

Basement window

Entrance door

Circular entrance steps

Rail

Baluster

Parapet

Balustrade

Cornice

Entablature

Capital

Shaft

Ionic column

Base

PROSTYLE COLONNADE

Arches and vaults

ARCHES ARE CURVED STRUCTURES used to bridge spans and to support the weight of upper parts of buildings, such as domes, as in St. Paul's Cathedral (below) and the antique temple (opposite). The voussoirs (wedge-shaped blocks) that form an arch (right) support each other and convert the downward force of the weight of the building into an outward force. This outward force is in turn transferred to buttresses, piers, or abutments. A vault is an arched roof or ceiling. There are four main types of vault (opposite). A barrel vault is a single vault, semicircular in cross-section; a groin vault consists of two barrel vaults intersecting at right-angles; a rib vault is a groin vault reinforced by ribs; and a fan vault is a rib vault in which the ribs radiate from the springing point (where the arch begins) like a fan.

PARTS OF AN ARCH

Voussoir · Keystone · Crown · Abutment

Keystone

Abutment

Extrados

Intrados (soffit)

Haunch

Impost

Abutment

Springing point

Intrados (soffit)

Span

Abutment

FRONT

SIDE

ARCHES AND BASE OF DOME, ST. PAUL'S CATHEDRAL, LONDON, BRITAIN, 1675-1710 (BY C. WREN)

Inner dome

Colonnade

Passageway

Pilaster

Cornice

Base

Pedestal of outer dome

Opening to passageway

"Whispering Gallery"

Pendentive

Triangular buttress

Upper arch (concealing difference in heights between main arch and minor arches)

Moulded bracket

Round arch

Semi-dome

Extrados

Upper barrel-vaulted passage opening on to side aisle

Intrados (soffit)

Springing point

Barrel vault

Impost

Passage leading to side aisle

Abutment

Strut built into masonry to strengthen pier (added in the 20th century)

Minor arch leading to side aisle

Main arch leading to nave

Pier

Minor arch

TYPES OF ARCH

HORSESHOE ARCH (MOORISH ARCH), GREAT MOSQUE, CORDOBA, SPAIN, 785

BASKET ARCH (SEMI-ELLIPTICAL ARCH), PALATINE CHAPEL, AIX-LA-CHAPELLE, FRANCE, 790-798

TUDOR ARCH, TOWER OF LONDON, BRITAIN, C.1086-1097

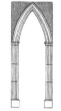

LANCET ARCH, WESTMINSTER ABBEY, LONDON, BRITAIN, 1505-1519

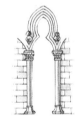

TREFOIL ARCH, BEVERLEY MINSTER, YORKSHIRE, BRITAIN, C.1500

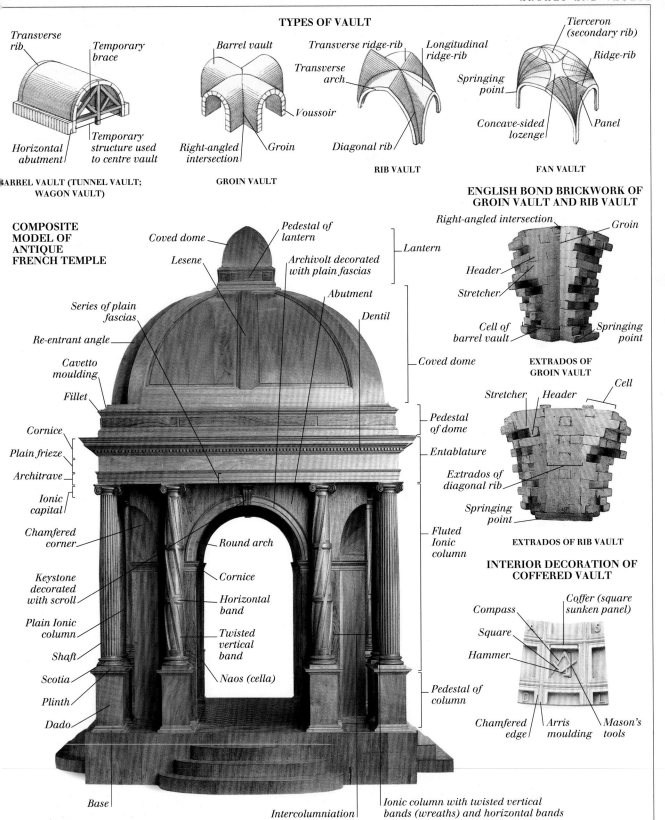

TYPES OF VAULT

Transverse rib

Temporary brace

Horizontal abutment

Temporary structure used to centre vault

BARREL VAULT (TUNNEL VAULT; WAGON VAULT)

Barrel vault

Right-angled intersection

Voussoir

Groin

GROIN VAULT

Transverse ridge-rib

Longitudinal ridge-rib

Transverse arch

Diagonal rib

RIB VAULT

Tierceron (secondary rib)

Ridge-rib

Springing point

Concave-sided lozenge

Panel

FAN VAULT

COMPOSITE MODEL OF ANTIQUE FRENCH TEMPLE

Coved dome

Lesene

Series of plain fascias

Re-entrant angle

Cavetto moulding

Fillet

Cornice

Plain frieze

Architrave

Ionic capital

Chamfered corner

Keystone decorated with scroll

Plain Ionic column

Shaft

Scotia

Plinth

Dado

Pedestal of lantern

Archivolt decorated with plain fascias

Abutment

Dentil

Coved dome

Round arch

Cornice

Horizontal band

Twisted vertical band

Naos (cella)

Lantern

Pedestal of dome

Entablature

Fluted Ionic column

Pedestal of column

Base

Intercolumniation

Ionic column with twisted vertical bands (wreaths) and horizontal bands

ENGLISH BOND BRICKWORK OF GROIN VAULT AND RIB VAULT

Right-angled intersection

Groin

Header

Stretcher

Cell of barrel vault

Springing point

EXTRADOS OF GROIN VAULT

Stretcher

Header

Cell

Extrados of diagonal rib

Springing point

EXTRADOS OF RIB VAULT

INTERIOR DECORATION OF COFFERED VAULT

Coffer (square sunken panel)

Compass

Square

Hammer

Chamfered edge

Arris moulding

Mason's tools

485

Domes

A DOME IS A CONVEX ROOF. Domes are categorized according to the shapes of both the base and the section through the centre of the dome. The base may be circular, square, or polygonal (many-sided), depending on the plan of the drum (the walls on which the dome rests). The section of a dome may be the same shape as any arch (see pp. 484-485). Various types of dome are illustrated here: a hemispherical dome, which has a circular base and a semicircular section; a saucer dome, which has a circular base and a segmental (less than a semicircle) section; a polyhedral dome, which is a dome on a polygonal base whose sides meet at the top of the dome; and an onion dome, which has a circular or polygonal base and an ogee-shaped section. Many domes have a lantern (a turret with windows) to provide light inside.

LANTERN AND UPPER DOME TIMBERING, ST. PAUL'S CATHEDRAL

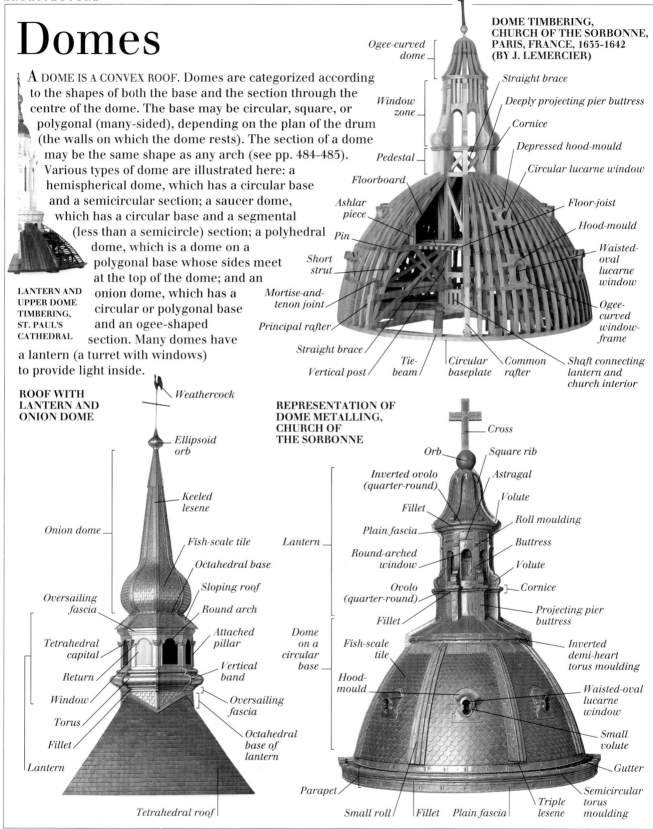

DOME TIMBERING, CHURCH OF THE SORBONNE, PARIS, FRANCE, 1635-1642 (BY J. LEMERCIER)

Ogee-curved dome
Window zone
Pedestal
Floorboard
Ashlar piece
Pin
Short strut
Mortise-and-tenon joint
Principal rafter
Straight brace
Vertical post
Tie-beam
Circular baseplate
Common rafter
Straight brace
Deeply projecting pier buttress
Cornice
Depressed hood-mould
Circular lucarne window
Floor-joist
Hood-mould
Waisted-oval lucarne window
Ogee-curved window-frame
Shaft connecting lantern and church interior

ROOF WITH LANTERN AND ONION DOME

Weathercock
Ellipsoid orb
Keeled lesene
Fish-scale tile
Octahedral base
Sloping roof
Round arch
Attached pillar
Vertical band
Oversailing fascia
Octahedral base of lantern
Onion dome
Oversailing fascia
Tetrahedral capital
Return
Window
Torus
Fillet
Lantern
Tetrahedral roof

REPRESENTATION OF DOME METALLING, CHURCH OF THE SORBONNE

Cross
Orb
Square rib
Astragal
Volute
Roll moulding
Buttress
Volute
Cornice
Projecting pier buttress
Inverted demi-heart torus moulding
Waisted-oval lucarne window
Small volute
Gutter
Semicircular torus moulding
Triple lesene
Plain fascia
Fillet
Small roll
Parapet
Hood-mould
Fish-scale tile
Dome on a circular base
Lantern
Inverted ovolo (quarter-round)
Fillet
Plain fascia
Round-arched window
Ovolo (quarter-round)
Fillet

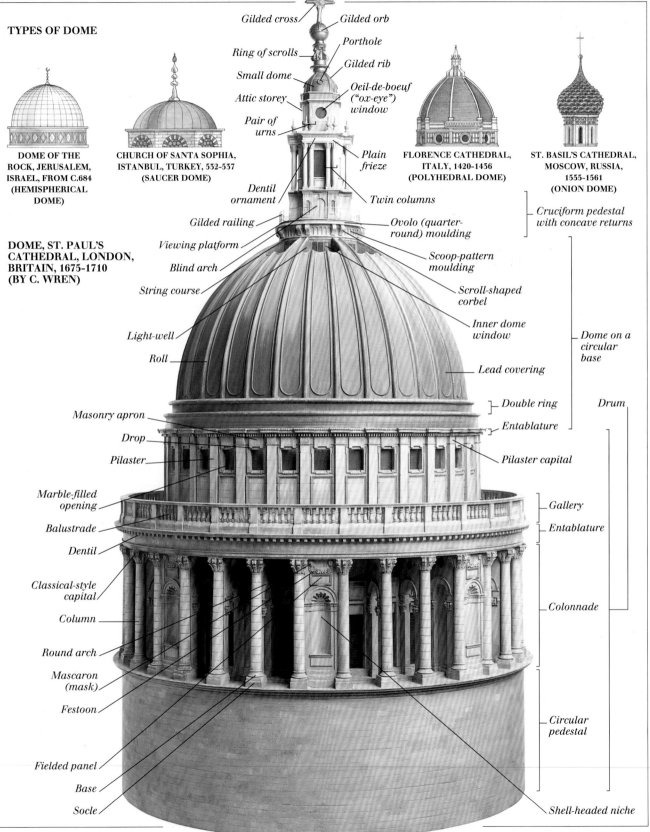

TYPES OF DOME

DOME OF THE
ROCK, JERUSALEM,
ISRAEL, FROM C.684
(HEMISPHERICAL
DOME)

CHURCH OF SANTA SOPHIA,
ISTANBUL, TURKEY, 532-537
(SAUCER DOME)

FLORENCE CATHEDRAL,
ITALY, 1420-1456
(POLYHEDRAL DOME)

ST. BASIL'S CATHEDRAL,
MOSCOW, RUSSIA,
1555-1561
(ONION DOME)

Gilded cross

Gilded orb

Porthole

Ring of scrolls

Small dome

Gilded rib

Attic storey

Oeil-de-boeuf
("ox-eye")
window

Pair of
urns

Plain
frieze

Dentil
ornament

Twin columns

Gilded railing

Ovolo (quarter-
round) moulding

DOME, ST. PAUL'S
CATHEDRAL, LONDON,
BRITAIN, 1675-1710
(BY C. WREN)

Viewing platform

Blind arch

String course

Light-well

Roll

Scoop-pattern
moulding

Scroll-shaped
corbel

Inner dome
window

Lead covering

Cruciform pedestal
with concave returns

Dome on a
circular
base

Double ring

Entablature

Drum

Masonry apron

Drop

Pilaster

Pilaster capital

Marble-filled
opening

Balustrade

Dentil

Classical-style
capital

Column

Round arch

Mascaron
(mask)

Festoon

Gallery

Entablature

Colonnade

Fielded panel

Base

Socle

Circular
pedestal

Shell-headed niche

Islamic buildings

OPUS SECTILE MOSAIC DESIGN

THE ISLAMIC RELIGION was founded by the prophet Mohammed, who was born in Mecca (in present-day Saudi Arabia) about 570 AD. In the following three centuries, Islam spread from Arabia to North Africa and Spain, as well as to India and much of the rest of Asia. The worldwide influence of Islam remains strong today. Common characteristics of Islamic buildings include ogee arches and roofs, onion domes, and walls decorated with carved stone, paintings, inlays, or mosaics. The most important type of Islamic building is the mosque – the place of worship – which generally has a minaret (tower) from which the muezzin (official crier) calls Muslims to prayer. Most mosques have a mihrab (decorative niche) that indicates the direction of Mecca. As figurative art is not allowed in Islam, buildings are ornamented with geometric and arabesque motifs, and inscriptions (frequently Koranic verses).

Bud-like onion dome
Depressed arch surrounding mihrab
Painted roof pavilion
Lotus-flower pendentive
Arabic inscription
Turkish-crescent finial
Crest
Painted minaret with censer (incense burner)
Spandrel
Series of recessed arches
Semi-dome
Arched niche within a niche
Mural resembling tomb
Polyhedral niche
Recessed colonettes

MIHRAB, JAMI MASJID (PRINCIPAL OR CONGREGATIONAL MOSQUE), BIJAPUR, INDIA, c.1636

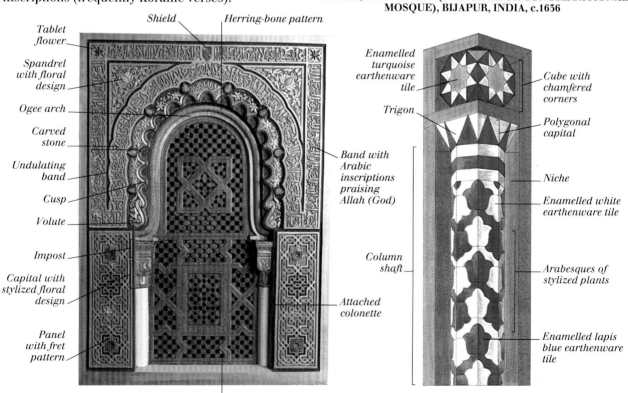

Tablet flower
Shield
Herring-bone pattern
Spandrel with floral design
Ogee arch
Carved stone
Undulating band
Cusp
Volute
Impost
Capital with stylized floral design
Panel with fret pattern
Band with Arabic inscriptions praising Allah (God)
Attached colonette
Jali (latticed screen) with geometrical patterns

ARCH, THE ALHAMBRA, GRANADA, SPAIN, 1333-1354

Enamelled turquoise earthenware tile
Trigon
Cube with chamfered corners
Polygonal capital
Niche
Enamelled white earthenware tile
Column shaft
Arabesques of stylized plants
Enamelled lapis blue earthenware tile

MIHRAB WITH COLUMN, EL-AINYI MOSQUE, CAIRO, EGYPT, 15TH CENTURY

EXAMPLES OF ISLAMIC MOSAICS, EGYPT AND SYRIA

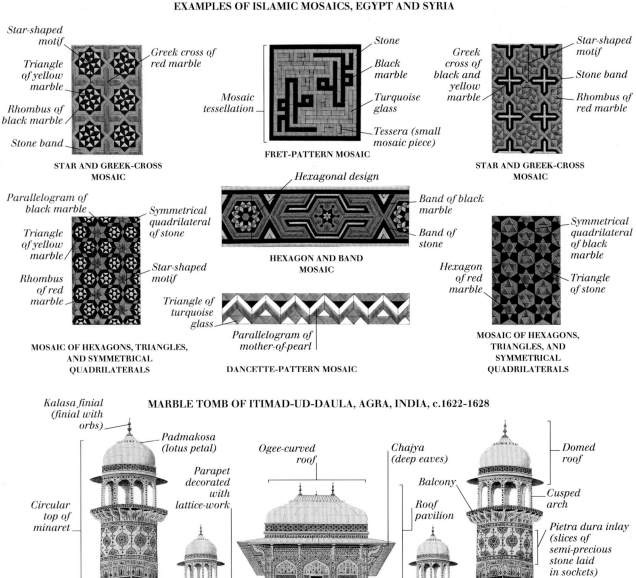

Star-shaped motif

Triangle of yellow marble

Rhombus of black marble

Stone band

Greek cross of red marble

STAR AND GREEK-CROSS MOSAIC

Stone

Black marble

Turquoise glass

Mosaic tessellation

Tessera (small mosaic piece)

FRET-PATTERN MOSAIC

Greek cross of black and yellow marble

Star-shaped motif

Stone band

Rhombus of red marble

STAR AND GREEK-CROSS MOSAIC

Parallelogram of black marble

Triangle of yellow marble

Rhombus of red marble

Symmetrical quadrilateral of stone

Star-shaped motif

MOSAIC OF HEXAGONS, TRIANGLES, AND SYMMETRICAL QUADRILATERALS

Hexagonal design

Band of black marble

Band of stone

HEXAGON AND BAND MOSAIC

Triangle of turquoise glass

Parallelogram of mother-of-pearl

DANCETTE-PATTERN MOSAIC

Symmetrical quadrilateral of black marble

Hexagon of red marble

Triangle of stone

MOSAIC OF HEXAGONS, TRIANGLES, AND SYMMETRICAL QUADRILATERALS

MARBLE TOMB OF ITIMAD-UD-DAULA, AGRA, INDIA, c.1622-1628

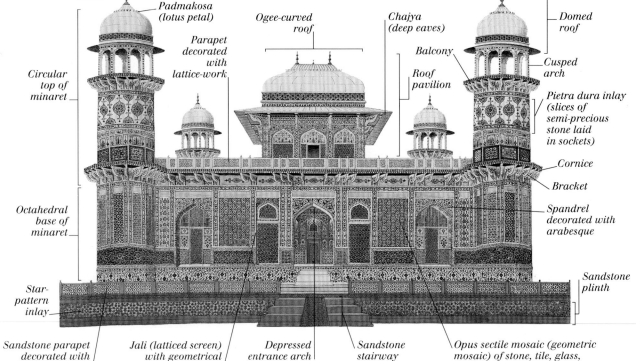

Kalasa finial (finial with orbs)

Padmakosa (lotus petal)

Ogee-curved roof

Parapet decorated with lattice-work

Chajya (deep eaves)

Balcony

Roof pavilion

Domed roof

Cusped arch

Circular top of minaret

Pietra dura inlay (slices of semi-precious stone laid in sockets)

Cornice

Bracket

Octahedral base of minaret

Spandrel decorated with arabesque

Star-pattern inlay

Sandstone plinth

Sandstone parapet decorated with lattice-work

Jali (latticed screen) with geometrical patterns

Depressed entrance arch

Sandstone stairway

Opus sectile mosaic (geometric mosaic) of stone, tile, glass, and enamel

South and east Asia

THE TRADITIONAL ARCHITECTURE of south and east Asia has been profoundly influenced by the spread from India of Buddhism and Hinduism. This influence is shown both by the abundance and by the architectural styles of temples and shrines in the region. Many early Hindu temples consist of rooms carved from solid rock-faces. However, free-standing structures began to be built in southern India from about the eighth century AD. Many were built in the Dravidian style, like the Temple of Virupaksha (opposite) with its characteristic antarala (terraced tower), perforated windows, and numerous arches, pilasters, and carvings. The earliest Buddhist religious monuments were Indian stupas, which consisted of a single hemispherical dome surmounted by a chattravali (shaft) and surrounded by railings with ornate gates. Later Indian stupas and those built elsewhere were sometimes modified; for example, in Sri Lanka, the dome became bell-shaped, and was called a dagoba. Buddhist pagodas, such as the Burmese example (right), are multistoreyed temples, each storey having a projecting roof. The form of these buildings probably derived from the yasti (pointed spire) of the stupa. Another feature of many traditional Asian buildings is their imaginative roof-forms, such as gambrel (mansard) roofs, and roofs with angle-rafters (below).

SEVEN-STOREYED PAGODA IN BURMESE STYLE, c.9TH-10TH CENTURY

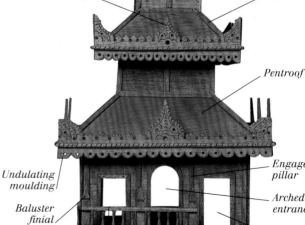

Gilded band

Gilded iron hti (crown)

Dubika (mast)

Arrow motif

Torus moulding with spiral carving

Decorative eaves board

Ogee-arched motif with decorative carvings

Ogee-arched motif forming horn

Hip-rafter

Pentroof

Undulating moulding

Baluster finial

Balustrade

Pillar

Engaged pillar

Arched entrance

Rectangular window

Baluster

Straight brace

DETAILS FROM EAST ASIAN BUILDINGS

KASUGA-STYLE ROOF WITH SUMIGI (ANGLE-RAFTERS), KASUGADO SHRINE OF ENJOJI, NARA, JAPAN, 12TH-14TH CENTURY

TERRACES, TEMPLE OF HEAVEN, BEIJING, CHINA, 15TH CENTURY

GAMBREL (MANSARD) ROOF WITH UPSWEPT EAVES AND UNDULATING GABLES, HIMEJI CASTLE, HIMEJI, JAPAN, 1608-1609

CORNER CAPITAL WITH ROOF BEAMS, POPCHU-SA TEMPLE, POPCHU-SA, SOUTH KOREA, 17TH CENTURY

PERFORATED STONE WINDOWS, TEMPLES OF VIRUPAKSHA AND MALLIKARJUNA, PATTADAKAL, INDIA, 8TH CENTURY

Tablet flower

Fret motif

Chain motif

Floral pattern

Leaf

Scroll motif

Sickle motif

Semicircle

DAGOBA STUPA, KANDY, SRI LANKA, c.2ND CENTURY BC-7TH CENTURY AD

Chattra (umbrella)

Hanging ornament

Chattravali (shaft)

Ring with indentations symbolizing chattras

Ornamental metalwork

Yasti (tee; pointed spire)

Harmika (stylized square railing)

Auda (bell-shaped dome)

Trimala (series of three circular courses)

Circular base

SIDE VIEW AND PLAN VIEW, TEMPLE OF VIRUPAKSHA, PATTADAKAL, INDIA, c.746

Stupica (small stupa) of the Dravidian order

Dravidian finial

Blind chataya arch

Perforated window

Gopuram finial (wagon-like finial)

Bracketed capital

Small gopuram (gate-head)

Parapet

Roll cornice

Antarala (terraced tower)

Niche with statue

Gate

Panel with bas-relief carving

Pillar

Plan view

Twin pilasters

Pradakshina (circumambulatory passage around shrine)

Shrine

Shrine chamber

Niche

Gate

Mandapa (pillared hall)

The 19th century

BUILDINGS OF THE 19TH CENTURY are characterized by the use of new materials and by a great diversity of architectural styles. From the end of the 18th century, iron and steel became widely used as alternatives to wood for the framework of buildings, as in the flax-spinning mill shown here. Built in Britain in 1796, this mill exemplifies an architectural style that became common throughout the industrialized world for more than a century. The Industrial Revolution also brought mass-production of building parts – a development that enabled the British architect Sir Joseph Paxton to erect London's Crystal Palace (a building made entirely of iron and glass) in only nine months, ready for the Great Exhibition of 1851. The 19th century saw a widespread revival of older architectural styles. For example, in the USA and Germany, Neo-Greek architecture was fashionable; in Britain and France, Neo-Baroque, Neo-Byzantine, and Neo-Gothic styles (as seen in the Palace of Westminster and Tower Bridge) were dominant.

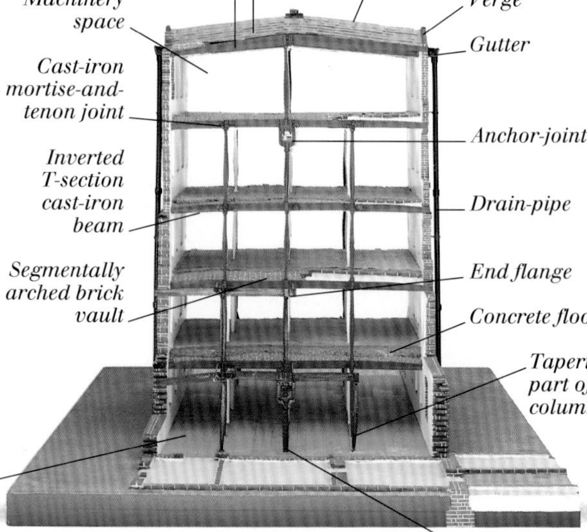

FLAX-SPINNING MILL, SHREWSBURY, BRITAIN, 1796 (BY C. BAGE)

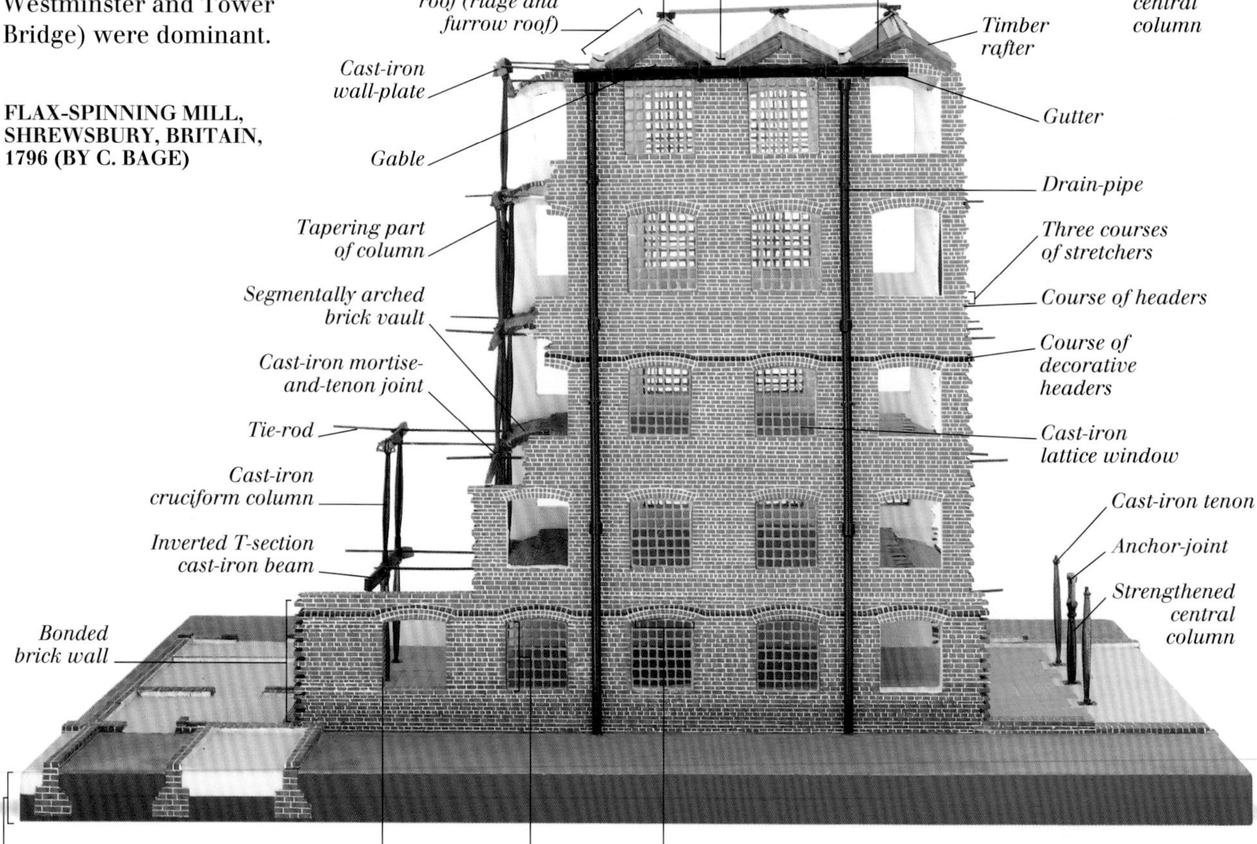

SECTION THROUGH A FLAX-SPINNING MILL

Cast-iron wall-plate

Pitched roof

Ridge

Verge

Gutter

Machinery space

Cast-iron mortise-and-tenon joint

Anchor-joint

Inverted T-section cast-iron beam

Drain-pipe

End flange

Segmentally arched brick vault

Concrete floor

Tapering part of column

Paved ground floor

Strengthened central column

Multi-gabled roof (ridge and furrow roof)

Ridge

Furrow

Verge

Timber rafter

Cast-iron wall-plate

Gutter

Gable

Drain-pipe

Tapering part of column

Three courses of stretchers

Segmentally arched brick vault

Course of headers

Cast-iron mortise-and-tenon joint

Course of decorative headers

Tie-rod

Cast-iron lattice window

Cast-iron cruciform column

Cast-iron tenon

Inverted T-section cast-iron beam

Anchor-joint

Strengthened central column

Bonded brick wall

Stone foundation

Quoin

Jamb

Gauged arch (segmental arch of tapered bricks)

492

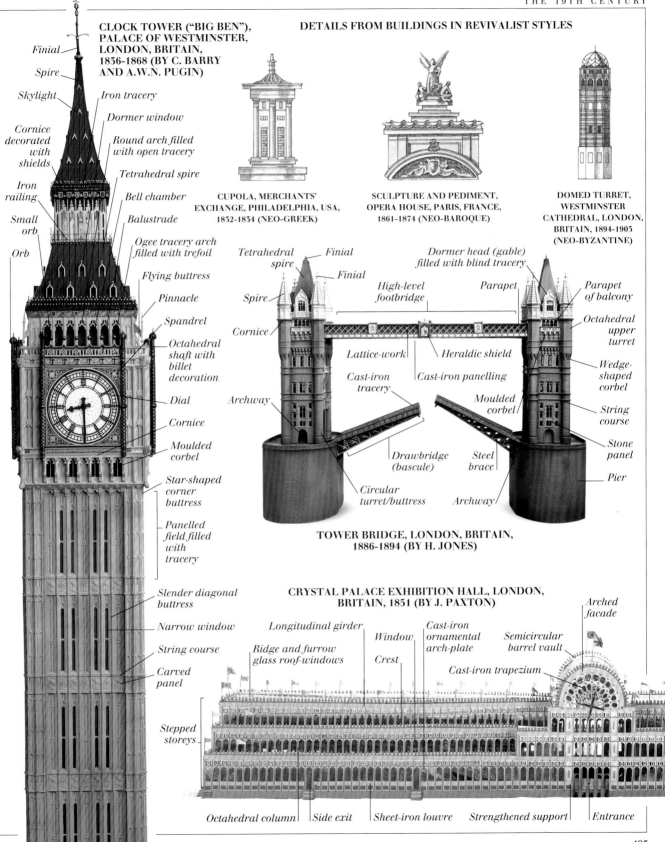

CLOCK TOWER ("BIG BEN"), PALACE OF WESTMINSTER, LONDON, BRITAIN, 1836-1868 (BY C. BARRY AND A.W.N. PUGIN)

Finial
Spire
Skylight
Iron tracery
Dormer window
Cornice decorated with shields
Round arch filled with open tracery
Tetrahedral spire
Iron railing
Bell chamber
Small orb
Balustrade
Orb
Ogee tracery arch filled with trefoil
Flying buttress
Pinnacle
Spandrel
Octahedral shaft with billet decoration
Dial
Cornice
Moulded corbel
Star-shaped corner buttress
Panelled field filled with tracery
Slender diagonal buttress
Narrow window
String course
Carved panel
Stepped storeys

DETAILS FROM BUILDINGS IN REVIVALIST STYLES

CUPOLA, MERCHANTS' EXCHANGE, PHILADELPHIA, USA, 1832-1834 (NEO-GREEK)

SCULPTURE AND PEDIMENT, OPERA HOUSE, PARIS, FRANCE, 1861-1874 (NEO-BAROQUE)

DOMED TURRET, WESTMINSTER CATHEDRAL, LONDON, BRITAIN, 1894-1903 (NEO-BYZANTINE)

Tetrahedral spire
Finial
Finial
Dormer head (gable) filled with blind tracery
Parapet
Parapet of balcony
Spire
High-level footbridge
Octahedral upper turret
Cornice
Lattice-work
Heraldic shield
Wedge-shaped corbel
Cast-iron tracery
Cast-iron panelling
String course
Archway
Moulded corbel
Drawbridge (bascule)
Steel brace
Stone panel
Circular turret/buttress
Archway
Pier

TOWER BRIDGE, LONDON, BRITAIN, 1886-1894 (BY H. JONES)

CRYSTAL PALACE EXHIBITION HALL, LONDON, BRITAIN, 1851 (BY J. PAXTON)

Arched facade
Longitudinal girder
Cast-iron ornamental arch-plate
Semicircular barrel vault
Window
Ridge and furrow glass roof-windows
Crest
Cast-iron trapezium
Octahedral column
Side exit
Sheet-iron louvre
Strengthened support
Entrance

The early 20th century

ARCHITECTURE OF THE EARLY 20TH CENTURY is notable for radical new types of steel-and-glass buildings – particularly skyscrapers – and the widespread use of steel-reinforced concrete. The steel-framed skyscraper was pioneered in Chicago in the 1880s, but did not become widespread until the first decades of the 20th century. As construction techniques were refined, skyscrapers became higher and higher; for example, the Empire State Building (right) of 1929-1931 has 102 storeys. Many buildings of this period were constructed from lightweight concrete slabs, which could be supported by cantilever beams or by pilotis (stilts), as in the Villa Savoye (below). The early 20th century also produced a great variety of architectural styles, some of which are illustrated opposite. Despite their diversity, the styles of this period generally had one thing in common: they were completely new, with few links to past architectural styles. This originality is in marked contrast to 19th-century architecture (see pp. 492-493), much of which was revivalist.

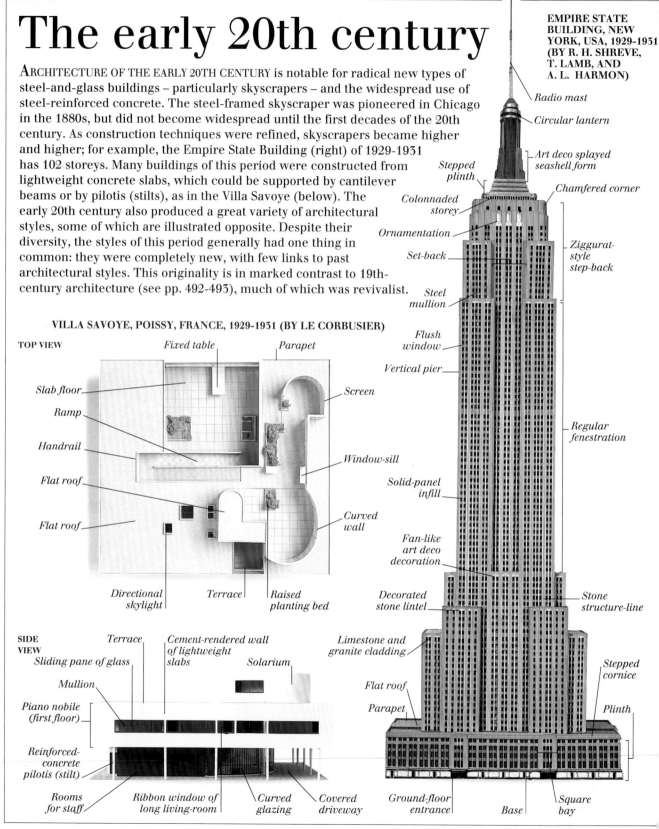

EMPIRE STATE BUILDING, NEW YORK, USA, 1929-1931 (BY R. H. SHREVE, T. LAMB, AND A. L. HARMON)

- Radio mast
- Circular lantern
- Art deco splayed seashell form
- Stepped plinth
- Chamfered corner
- Colonnaded storey
- Ziggurat-style step-back
- Ornamentation
- Set-back
- Steel mullion
- Flush window
- Vertical pier
- Regular fenestration
- Solid-panel infill
- Fan-like art deco decoration
- Decorated stone lintel
- Stone structure-line
- Limestone and granite cladding
- Flat roof
- Stepped cornice
- Parapet
- Plinth
- Ground-floor entrance
- Base
- Square bay

VILLA SAVOYE, POISSY, FRANCE, 1929-1931 (BY LE CORBUSIER)

TOP VIEW

- Fixed table
- Parapet
- Slab floor
- Screen
- Ramp
- Handrail
- Window-sill
- Flat roof
- Flat roof
- Curved wall
- Directional skylight
- Terrace
- Raised planting bed

SIDE VIEW

- Terrace
- Cement-rendered wall of lightweight slabs
- Solarium
- Sliding pane of glass
- Mullion
- Piano nobile (first floor)
- Reinforced-concrete pilotis (stilt)
- Rooms for staff
- Ribbon window of long living-room
- Curved glazing
- Covered driveway

MIDWAY GARDENS, CHICAGO, USA, 1914 (BY F. L. WRIGHT)

Flagpole

Plain coping-stone

Main floor

Decorated cement frieze

Terrace

Steps

Stage

Orchestra shell

Tiled, shallow pitched roof

Projecting balustrade

Ridge

Ornamental light

Hip

Main pavilion

Arcade

Terrace

Ornamental sculpture

Octagonal window

Stone plinth

EAST SIDE

NORTH SIDE

Tiled frieze

Flat roof

Cantilevered, latticed shade

Deep-set window

Planting bed

Brick pier

Slit window

Stepped flat-roofs

Terrace

Ornamented coping-stone

EARLY 20TH-CENTURY ARCHITECTURAL STYLES

DORMER WINDOW, STUDIO ELVIRA, MUNICH, GERMANY, 1902 (ART NOUVEAU)

AEG TURBINE HALL, BERLIN, GERMANY, 1909 (DEUTSCHER WERKBUND)

ROBIE HOUSE, CHICAGO, USA, 1909-1910 (PRAIRIE STYLE)

GRUNDTVIG CHURCH, COPENHAGEN, DENMARK, 1920 (EXPRESSIONIST)

VERTEX, CHRYSLER BUILDING, NEW YORK, USA, 1928-1930 (ART DECO)

TOWER, TOWN HALL, HILVERSUM, NETHERLANDS, 1930 (DUTCH CUBIST)

CASA DEL FASCIO, COMO, ITALY, 1932-1936 (GRUPPO SEVEN CUBIST)

MOTIF ABOVE DOORWAY, HOOVER FACTORY, LONDON, BRITAIN, 1933 (ART DECO)

Modern buildings 1

ARCHITECTURE SINCE ABOUT THE 1950s is generally known as modern architecture. One of its main influences has been functionalism – a belief that a building's function should be apparent in its design. Both the Centre Georges Pompidou (below and opposite) and the Hong Kong and Shanghai Bank (see pp. 498-499) are functionalist buildings: on each, elements of engineering and the building's services are clearly visible on the outside. In the 1980s, some architects rejected functionalism in favour of post-modernism, in which historical styles – particularly neoclassicism – were revived, using modern building materials and techniques. In many modern buildings, walls are made of glass or concrete hung from a frame, as in the Kawana House (right); this type of wall construction is known as curtain walling. Other modern construction techniques include the intricate interlocking of concrete vaults – as in the Sydney Opera House (see pp. 498-499) – and the use of high-tension beams to create complex roof shapes, such as the paraboloid roof of the Church of St. Pierre de Libreville (see pp. 498-499).

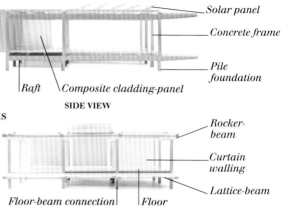

Solar panel
Concrete frame
Pile foundation
Raft
Composite cladding-panel

SIDE VIEW

Rocker-beam
Curtain walling
Lattice-beam
Floor-beam connection
Floor

FRONT VIEW

SERVICES FACADE, CENTRE GEORGES POMPIDOU, PARIS, FRANCE, 1977 (BY R. PIANO AND R. ROGERS)

Metal-faced, fire-resistant panel
Air-conditioning duct
Cooling tower
Water-pipe

Grand gallery level
Main gallery levels
Library level
Administrative level
Mezzanine gallery level
Reception level

Staircase to grand hall
Electrical plant
Water-cooled, fire-resistant column
Continuous glazing
Tinted glass
Services entrance

PRINCIPAL FACADE, CENTRE GEORGES POMPIDOU

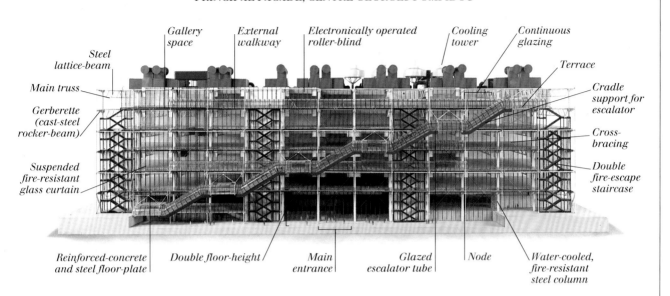

Gallery space

External walkway

Electronically operated roller-blind

Cooling tower

Continuous glazing

Steel lattice-beam

Main truss

Gerberette (cast-steel rocker-beam)

Suspended fire-resistant glass curtain

Terrace

Cradle support for escalator

Cross-bracing

Double fire-escape staircase

Reinforced-concrete and steel floor-plate

Double floor-height

Main entrance

Glazed escalator tube

Node

Water-cooled, fire-resistant steel column

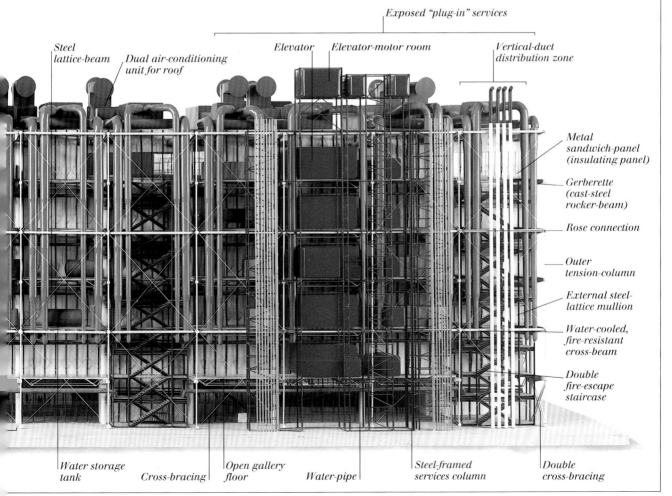

Exposed "plug-in" services

Steel lattice-beam

Dual air-conditioning unit for roof

Elevator

Elevator-motor room

Vertical-duct distribution zone

Metal sandwich-panel (insulating panel)

Gerberette (cast-steel rocker-beam)

Rose connection

Outer tension-column

External steel-lattice mullion

Water-cooled, fire-resistant cross-beam

Double fire-escape staircase

Water storage tank

Cross-bracing

Open gallery floor

Water-pipe

Steel-framed services column

Double cross-bracing

Modern buildings 2

HONG KONG AND SHANGHAI BANK, HONG KONG, 1981-1985 (BY N. FOSTER)

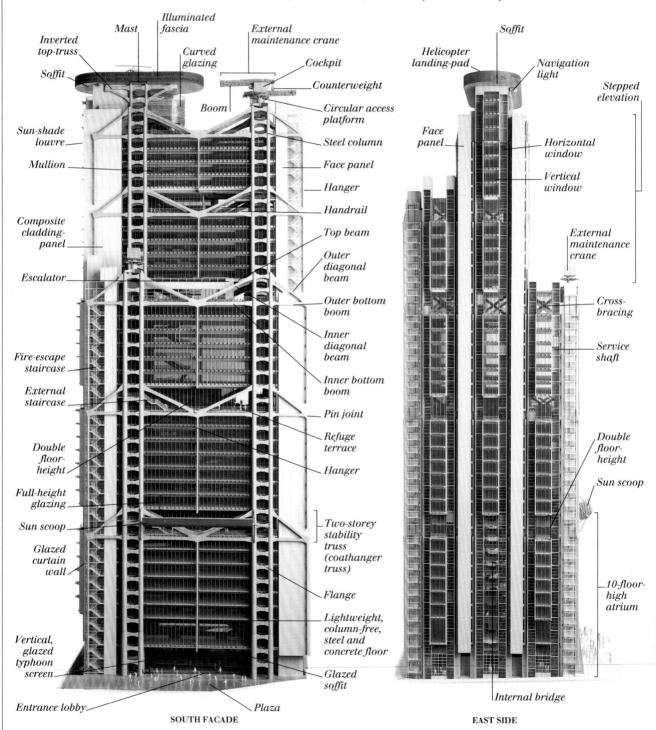

Inverted top-truss

Mast

Illuminated fascia

Curved glazing

External maintenance crane

Soffit

Cockpit

Counterweight

Boom

Circular access platform

Soffit

Helicopter landing-pad

Navigation light

Stepped elevation

Sun-shade louvre

Steel column

Face panel

Face panel

Horizontal window

Mullion

Hanger

Vertical window

Handrail

Top beam

Composite cladding-panel

Outer diagonal beam

External maintenance crane

Escalator

Outer bottom boom

Inner diagonal beam

Cross-bracing

Inner bottom boom

Service shaft

Fire-escape staircase

Pin joint

External staircase

Refuge terrace

Double floor-height

Hanger

Double floor-height

Full-height glazing

Sun scoop

Two-storey stability truss (coathanger truss)

Glazed curtain wall

Flange

Sun scoop

Lightweight, column-free, steel and concrete floor

10-floor-high atrium

Vertical, glazed typhoon screen

Glazed soffit

Entrance lobby

Plaza

Internal bridge

SOUTH FACADE

EAST SIDE

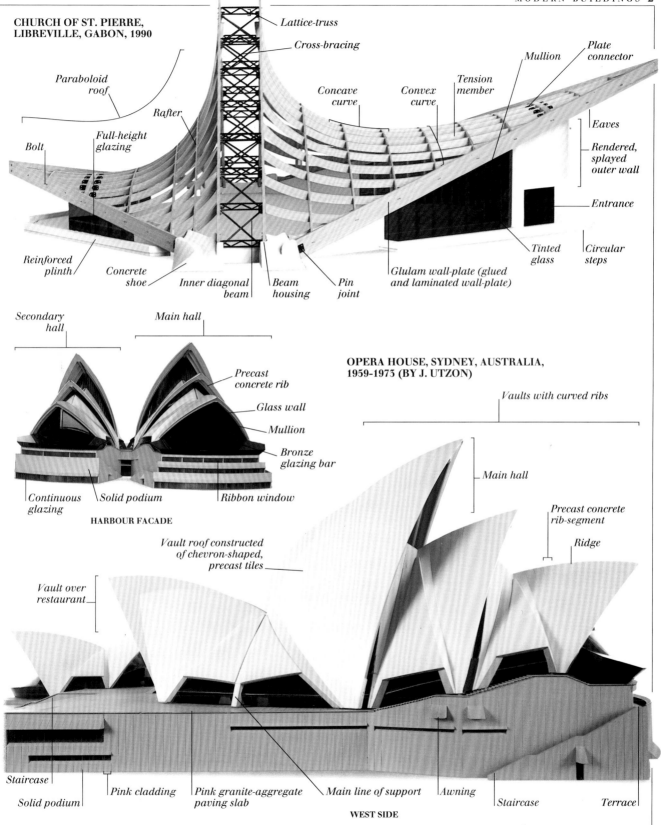

CHURCH OF ST. PIERRE, LIBREVILLE, GABON, 1990

Lattice-truss

Cross-bracing

Paraboloid roof

Rafter

Concave curve

Convex curve

Tension member

Mullion

Plate connector

Full-height glazing

Bolt

Eaves

Rendered, splayed outer wall

Entrance

Tinted glass

Circular steps

Reinforced plinth

Concrete shoe

Inner diagonal beam

Beam housing

Pin joint

Glulam wall-plate (glued and laminated wall-plate)

Secondary hall

Main hall

OPERA HOUSE, SYDNEY, AUSTRALIA, 1959-1973 (BY J. UTZON)

Precast concrete rib

Glass wall

Mullion

Bronze glazing bar

Continuous glazing

Solid podium

Ribbon window

HARBOUR FACADE

Vaults with curved ribs

Main hall

Precast concrete rib-segment

Ridge

Vault roof constructed of chevron-shaped, precast tiles

Vault over restaurant

Staircase

Solid podium

Pink cladding

Pink granite-aggregate paving slab

Main line of support

Awning

Staircase

Terrace

WEST SIDE

499

Music

Musical notation

MUSICAL NOTATION IS ANY METHOD by which sounds are written down so that they can be read and performed by others. The present-day conventional system of notation uses a five-line stave (staff) – divided by vertical lines into sections known as bars – on which notes, rests, clefs, key signatures, time signatures, accidentals, and other symbols are written. A note indicates the duration of a sound and, according to its position on the stave, its pitch. Notes can be arranged on the stave in order of pitch to form a scale. A silence in the music is indicated by a rest. The clef, which is placed at the begininng of a stave, fixes the pitch. The key signature, which is placed after the clef, indicates the key. The time signature, placed after the key signature, shows the number of beats in a bar. Accidentals are used to indicate the raising or lowering of the pitch of a note.

ELEMENTS OF MUSICAL NOTATION

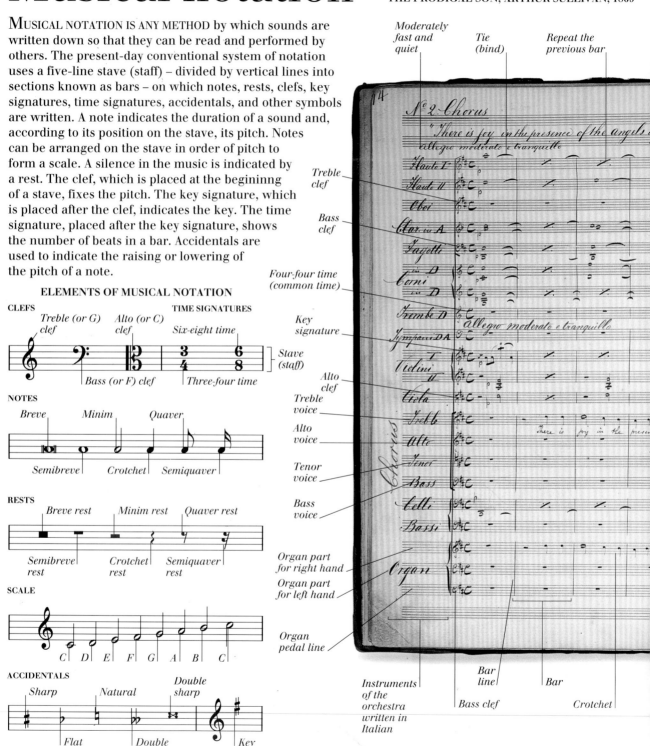

CLEFS

Treble (or G) clef

Alto (or C) clef

Bass (or F) clef

TIME SIGNATURES

Six-eight time

Three-four time

Stave (staff)

NOTES

Breve

Minim

Quaver

Semibreve

Crotchet

Semiquaver

RESTS

Breve rest

Minim rest

Quaver rest

Semibreve rest

Crotchet rest

Semiquaver rest

SCALE

C D E F G A B C

ACCIDENTALS

Sharp

Natural

Double sharp

Flat

Double flat

Key signature

Moderately fast and quiet

Tie (bind)

Repeat the previous bar

Treble clef

Bass clef

Four-four time (common time)

Key signature

Alto clef

Treble voice

Alto voice

Tenor voice

Bass voice

Organ part for right hand

Organ part for left hand

Organ pedal line

Instruments of the orchestra written in Italian

Bar line

Bar

Bass clef

Crotchet

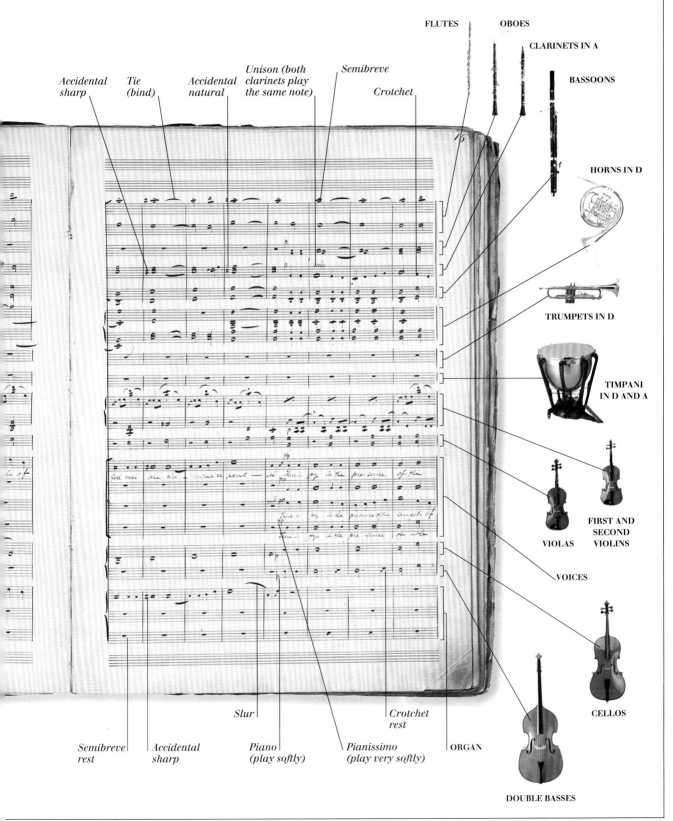

FLUTES

OBOES

CLARINETS IN A

BASSOONS

HORNS IN D

Accidental sharp

Tie (bind)

Accidental natural

Unison (both clarinets play the same note)

Semibreve

Crotchet

TRUMPETS IN D

TIMPANI IN D AND A

FIRST AND SECOND VIOLINS

VIOLAS

VOICES

CELLOS

Semibreve rest

Accidental sharp

Slur

Piano (play softly)

Pianissimo (play very softly)

Crotchet rest

ORGAN

DOUBLE BASSES

503

Orchestras

AN ORCHESTRA IS A GROUP of musicians that plays music written for a specific combination of instruments. The number and type of instruments included in the orchestra depends on the style of music being played. The modern orchestra (also known as a symphony orchestra) is made up of four sections of instruments – stringed, woodwind, brass, and percussion. The stringed section consists of violins, violas, cellos (violoncellos), double basses, and sometimes a harp (see pp. 510-511). The main instruments of the woodwind section are flutes, oboes, clarinets, and bassoons – the piccolo, cor anglais, bass clarinet, saxophone, and double bassoon (contrabassoon) can also be included if the music requires them (see pp. 508-509). The brass section usually consists of horns, trumpets, trombones, and the tuba (see pp. 506-507). The main instruments of the percussion section are the timpani (see pp. 518-519). The side drum, bass drum, cymbals, tambourine, triangle, tubular bells, xylophone, vibraphone, tam-tam (gong), castanets, and maracas can also be included in the percussion section (see pp. 516-517). The musicians are usually arranged in a semi-circle – strings spread along the front, woodwind and brass in the centre, and percussion at the back. A conductor stands in front of the musicians and controls the tempo (speed) of the music and the overall balance of the sound, ensuring that no instruments are too loud or too soft in relation to the others.

TUBULAR BELLS

TAM-TAM (GONG)

VIBRAPHONE

XYLOPHONE

CASTANETS

TAMBOURINE

TRUMPETS

MARACAS

TRIANGLE

HORNS

CLARINETS

BASS CLARINET

SAXOPHONE

PICCOLO

HARP

SECOND VIOLINS

FIRST VIOLINS

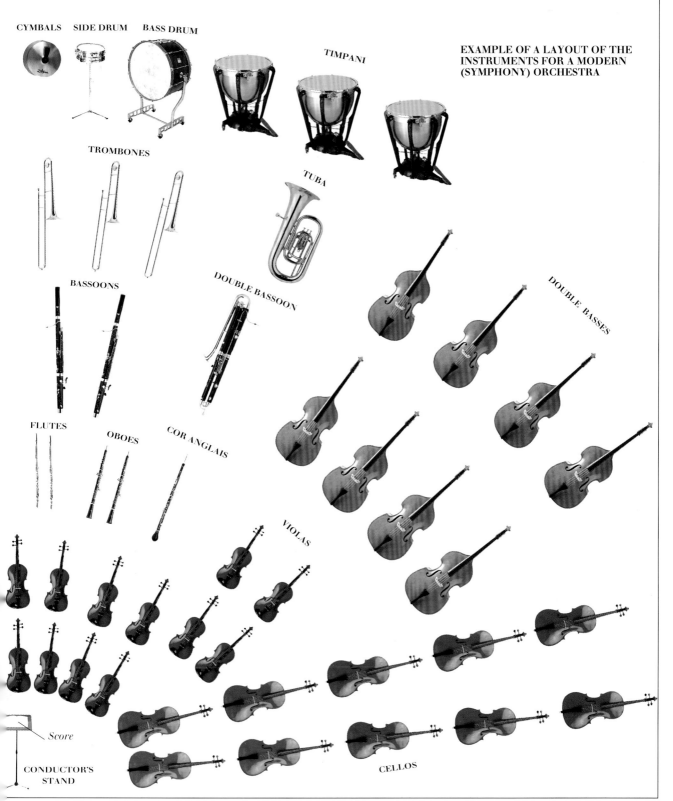

CYMBALS SIDE DRUM BASS DRUM

TIMPANI

EXAMPLE OF A LAYOUT OF THE INSTRUMENTS FOR A MODERN (SYMPHONY) ORCHESTRA

TROMBONES

TUBA

BASSOONS

DOUBLE BASSOON

DOUBLE BASSES

FLUTES

OBOES

COR ANGLAIS

VIOLAS

Score

CONDUCTOR'S STAND

CELLOS

Brass instruments

BUGLE

BRASS INSTRUMENTS ARE WIND INSTRUMENTS that are made of metal, usually brass. Although they appear in many different shapes and sizes, all brass instruments have a mouthpiece, a length of hollow tube, and a flared bell. The mouthpiece of a brass instrument may be cup-shaped, as in the cornet, or cone-shaped, as in the horn. The tube may be wide or narrow, mainly conical, as in the horn and tuba, or mainly cylindrical, as in the trumpet and trombone. The sound of a brass instrument is made by the player's lips vibrating against the mouthpiece, so that the air vibrates in the tube. By changing lip tension, the player can vary the vibrations and produce notes of different pitches. The range of notes produced by a brass instrument can be extended by means of a valve system. Most brass instruments, such as the trumpet, have piston valves that divert the air in the instrument along an extra piece of tubing (known as a valve slide) when pressed down. The total length of the tube is increased and the pitch of the note produced is lowered. Instead of valves, the trombone has a movable slide that can be pushed away from or drawn toward the player. The sound of a brass instrument can also be changed by inserting a mute into the bell of the instrument.

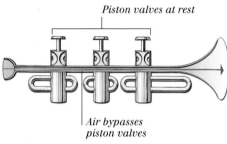

Brace

Tuning slide

Counterbalancing weight

SIMPLIFIED DIAGRAM SHOWING HOW A PISTON VALVE SYSTEM WORKS

Piston valves at rest

Air bypasses piston valves

PISTON VALVES AT REST

First piston valve pressed down

Second and third piston valves at rest

Air diverted through first valve slide

PISTON VALVE PRESSED DOWN

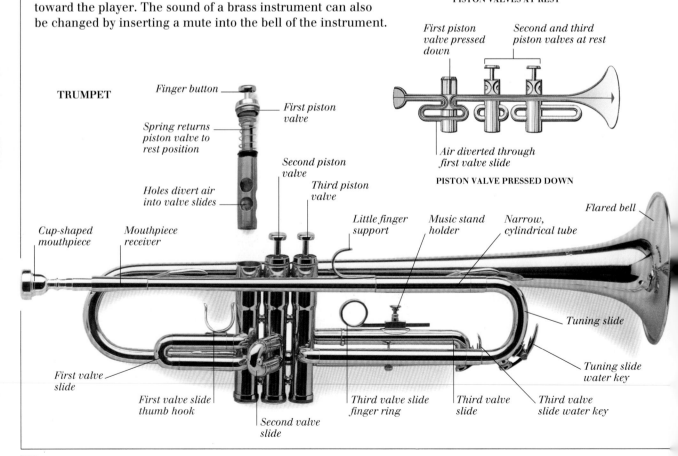

TRUMPET

Finger button

First piston valve

Spring returns piston valve to rest position

Holes divert air into valve slides

Second piston valve

Third piston valve

Little finger support

Music stand holder

Narrow, cylindrical tube

Flared bell

Cup-shaped mouthpiece

Mouthpiece receiver

First valve slide

First valve slide thumb hook

Second valve slide

Third valve slide finger ring

Third valve slide

Tuning slide

Tuning slide water key

Third valve slide water key

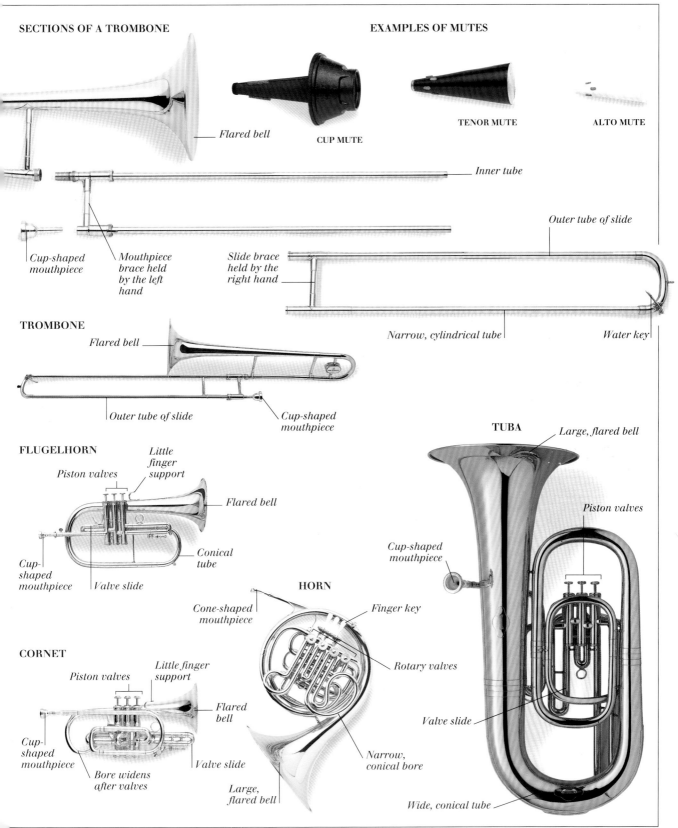

SECTIONS OF A TROMBONE

EXAMPLES OF MUTES

Flared bell

CUP MUTE

TENOR MUTE

ALTO MUTE

Inner tube

Outer tube of slide

Cup-shaped mouthpiece

Mouthpiece brace held by the left hand

Slide brace held by the right hand

Narrow, cylindrical tube

Water key

TROMBONE

Flared bell

Outer tube of slide

Cup-shaped mouthpiece

FLUGELHORN

Little finger support

Piston valves

Flared bell

Cup-shaped mouthpiece

Valve slide

Conical tube

TUBA

Large, flared bell

Piston valves

Cup-shaped mouthpiece

Valve slide

HORN

Cone-shaped mouthpiece

Finger key

Rotary valves

Narrow, conical bore

Large, flared bell

CORNET

Little finger support

Piston valves

Flared bell

Cup-shaped mouthpiece

Bore widens after valves

Valve slide

Wide, conical tube

507

Woodwind instruments

WOODWIND INSTRUMENTS ARE wind instruments that are generally made of wood, although some are made of metal or plastic. The sound of a woodwind instrument is produced by the vibration of air in a hollow tube. The air is made to vibrate by blowing across a blow hole – as in the flute and piccolo – or by blowing through a single reed – as in the clarinet and saxophone – or a double reed – as in the bassoon, cor anglais, and oboe. The pitch of a woodwind instrument can be changed by opening or closing holes cut into the tube of the instrument.

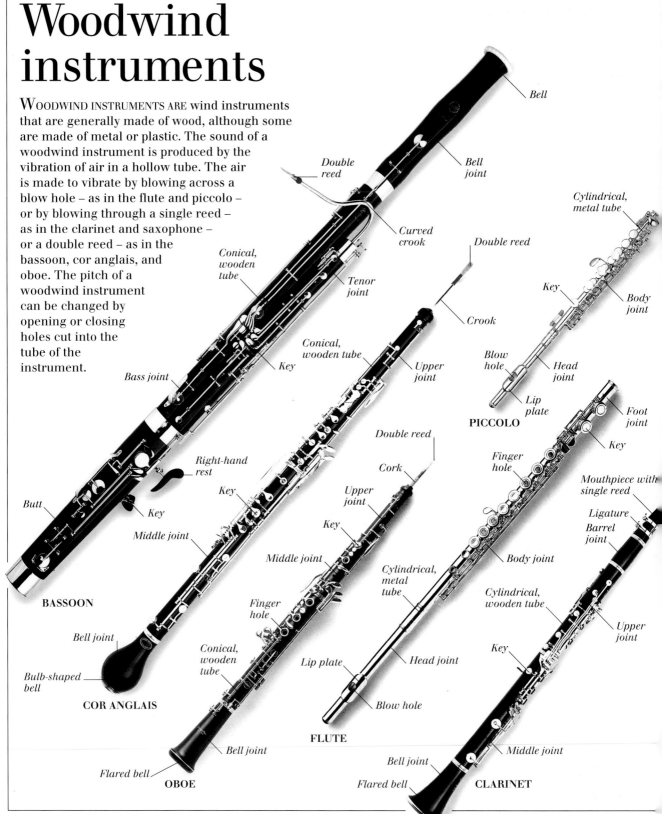

Bell

Double reed

Bell joint

Curved crook

Conical, wooden tube

Tenor joint

Double reed

Cylindrical, metal tube

Key

Body joint

Crook

Blow hole

Head joint

Lip plate

PICCOLO

Conical, wooden tube

Upper joint

Foot joint

Key

Bass joint

Key

Double reed

Finger hole

Right-hand rest

Cork

Mouthpiece with single reed

Key

Upper joint

Key

Middle joint

Key

Middle joint

Cylindrical, metal tube

Body joint

Ligature
Barrel joint

Butt

Key

Cylindrical, wooden tube

BASSOON

Finger hole

Key

Upper joint

Bell joint

Conical, wooden tube

Lip plate

Head joint

Bulb-shaped bell

COR ANGLAIS

Blow hole

FLUTE

Middle joint

Bell joint

Bell joint

Flared bell

OBOE

Flared bell

CLARINET

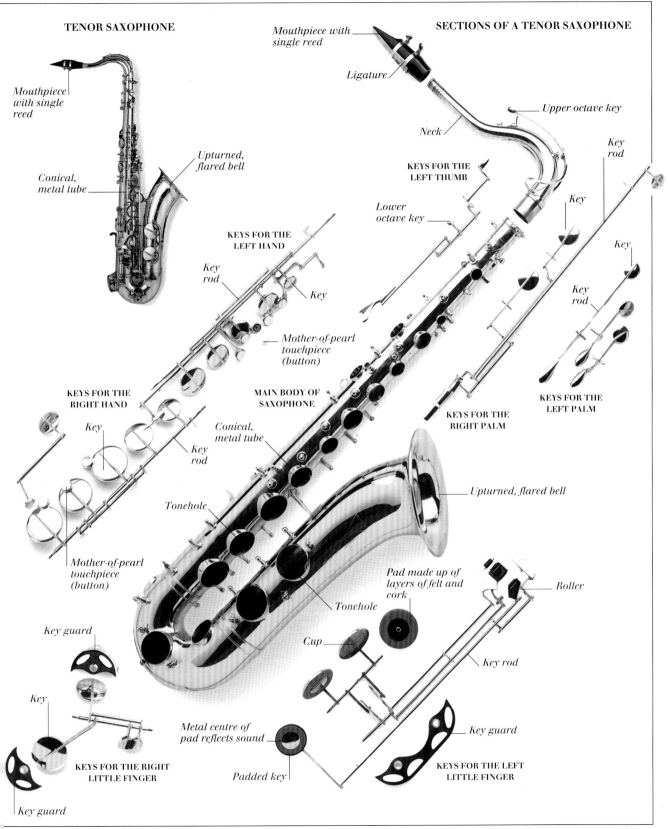

TENOR SAXOPHONE

Mouthpiece with single reed

Conical, metal tube

Upturned, flared bell

Mouthpiece with single reed

SECTIONS OF A TENOR SAXOPHONE

Ligature

Neck

Upper octave key

Key rod

KEYS FOR THE LEFT THUMB

Lower octave key

Key

KEYS FOR THE LEFT HAND

Key rod

Key

Key rod

Key

Mother-of-pearl touchpiece (button)

MAIN BODY OF SAXOPHONE

KEYS FOR THE RIGHT HAND

Key

Key rod

Conical, metal tube

KEYS FOR THE RIGHT PALM

KEYS FOR THE LEFT PALM

Mother-of-pearl touchpiece (button)

Tonehole

Upturned, flared bell

Tonehole

Pad made up of layers of felt and cork

Roller

Cup

Key guard

Key rod

Key

Metal centre of pad reflects sound

KEYS FOR THE RIGHT LITTLE FINGER

Padded key

Key guard

**KEYS FOR THE LEFT LITTLE FINGER*

Key guard

Stringed instruments

STRINGED INSTRUMENTS PRODUCE SOUND by the vibration of stretched strings. This may be done by drawing a bow across the strings, as in the violin; or by plucking the strings, as in the harp and guitar (see pp. 512-513). The four modern members of the bowed string family are the violin, viola, cello (violoncello), and double bass. Each consists of a hollow, wooden body, a long neck, and four strings. The bow is a wooden stick with horsehair stretched across its length. The vibrations made by drawing the bow across the strings are transmitted to the hollow body, and this itself vibrates, amplifying and enriching the sound produced. The harp consists of a set of strings of different lengths stretched across a wooden frame. The strings are plucked by the player's thumbs and fingers – except the little finger of each hand – which produces vibrations that are amplified by the harp's soundboard. The pitch of the note produced by any stringed instrument depends on the length, weight, and tension of the string. A shorter, lighter, or tighter string gives a higher note.

Scroll eye

Scroll

Peg-hole

Ebony tuning-pegs

Neck made of maple wood

Strings

Fingerboard

Rounded shoulder

Belly (soundboard)

Waist

Sound-hole

Rib

Purfling

Bridge

Tailpiece

Chin rest

Tailpiece loop fits around end-pin

End-pin (tail-pin)

SECTIONS OF A VIOLIN

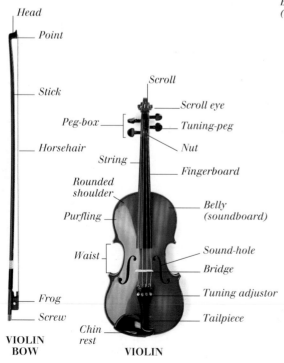

Head

Point

Stick

Scroll

Peg-box

Scroll eye

Tuning-peg

Horsehair

Nut

String

Fingerboard

Rounded shoulder

Purfling

Belly (soundboard)

Waist

Sound-hole

Bridge

Frog

Tuning adjustor

Screw

Tailpiece

Chin rest

VIOLIN BOW

VIOLIN

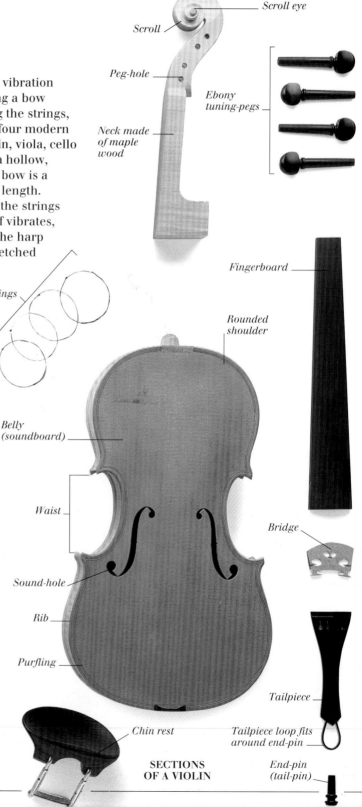

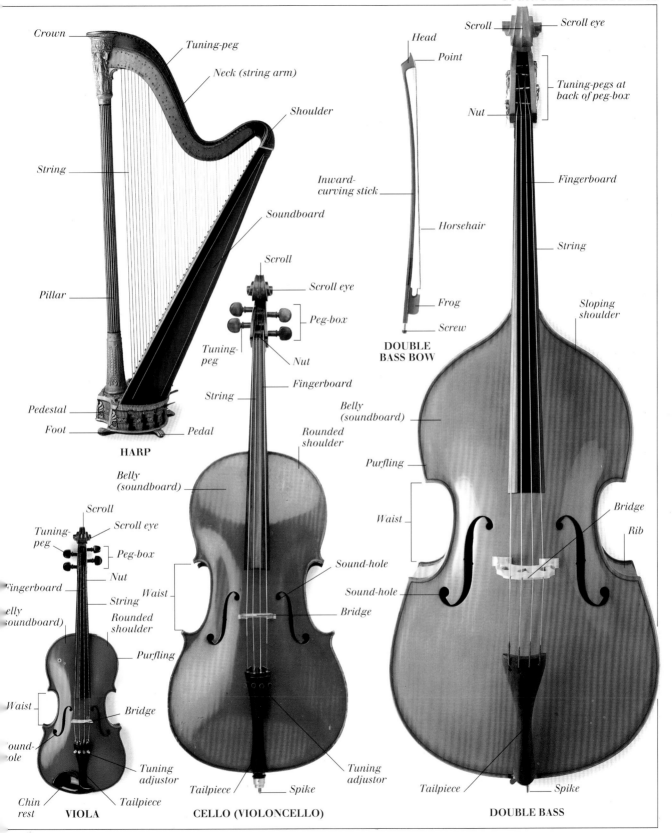

Crown

Tuning-peg

Neck (string arm)

Shoulder

String

Soundboard

Pillar

Pedestal

Foot

Pedal

HARP

Scroll

Scroll eye

Peg-box

Tuning-peg

Nut

Fingerboard

String

Rounded shoulder

Belly (soundboard)

Waist

Sound-hole

Bridge

Tuning adjustor

Tailpiece

Spike

CELLO (VIOLONCELLO)

Scroll

Tuning-peg

Scroll eye

Peg-box

Nut

Fingerboard

Belly (soundboard)

String

Rounded shoulder

Purfling

Waist

Bridge

Sound-hole

Tuning adjustor

Chin rest

Tailpiece

VIOLA

Head

Point

Inward-curving stick

Horsehair

Frog

Screw

DOUBLE BASS BOW

Scroll

Scroll eye

Tuning-pegs at back of peg-box

Nut

Fingerboard

String

Sloping shoulder

Belly (soundboard)

Purfling

Waist

Bridge

Rib

Sound-hole

Tailpiece

Spike

DOUBLE BASS

Guitars

THE GUITAR IS A PLUCKED stringed instrument
(see pp. 510-511). There are two types of guitar –
acoustic and electric. Acoustic guitars have hollow
bodies and six or twelve strings. Plucking the strings
produces vibrations that are amplified by their hollow
bodies. Electric guitars usually have solid bodies and
six strings. Pick-ups placed under the strings convert
their vibrations into electronic signals that are magnified
by an amplifier, and sent to a loudspeaker where they are
converted into sounds (see pp. 520-521). Electric bass
guitars are very similar in structure to electric guitars,
and produce sound in the same way, but have four
strings and play bass notes.

ACOUSTIC GUITAR

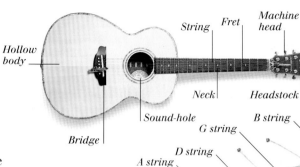

String
Fret
Machine head
Hollow body
Neck
Headstock
Sound-hole
Bridge
B string
G string
D string
A string
Low E string

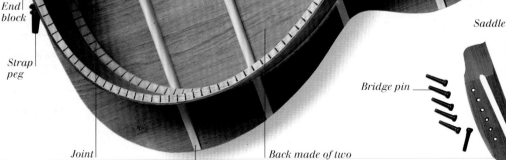

Maker's label

Lining glued along top
and bottom edge of rib

Rib

End block

Strap peg

Joint

Transverse
(crosswise) strut
strengthens back

Back made of two
pieces of cherry wood
joined together

Saddle

Bridge pin

Bridge

Binding

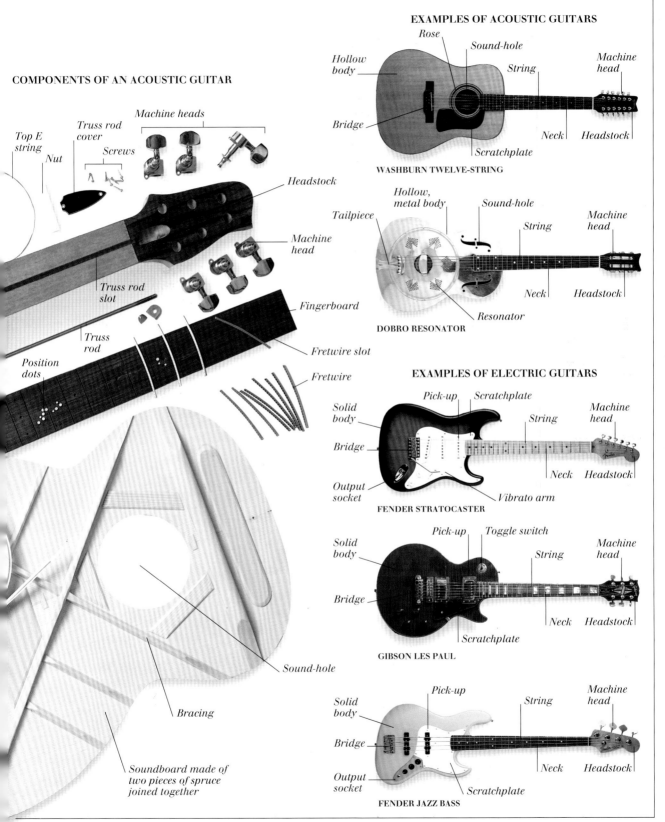

EXAMPLES OF ACOUSTIC GUITARS

Rose
Sound-hole
Hollow body
String
Machine head
Bridge
Neck
Headstock
Scratchplate

WASHBURN TWELVE-STRING

COMPONENTS OF AN ACOUSTIC GUITAR

Top E string
Nut
Truss rod cover
Screws
Machine heads
Headstock
Machine head
Truss rod slot
Fingerboard
Truss rod
Fretwire slot
Position dots
Fretwire

Sound-hole

Bracing

Soundboard made of two pieces of spruce joined together

Hollow, metal body
Tailpiece
Sound-hole
Machine head
String
Neck
Headstock
Resonator

DOBRO RESONATOR

EXAMPLES OF ELECTRIC GUITARS

Solid body
Pick-up
Scratchplate
String
Machine head
Bridge
Neck
Headstock
Output socket
Vibrato arm

FENDER STRATOCASTER

Solid body
Pick-up
Toggle switch
String
Machine head
Bridge
Neck
Headstock
Scratchplate

GIBSON LES PAUL

Solid body
Pick-up
String
Machine head
Bridge
Neck
Headstock
Output socket
Scratchplate

FENDER JAZZ BASS

Keyboard instruments

KEYBOARD INSTRUMENTS are instruments that are sounded by means of a keyboard. The organ and piano are two of the principal members of the keyboard family. The organ consists of pipes which are operated by one or more manuals (keyboards) and a pedal board. The pipes are lined up in rows (known as ranks or registers) on top of a wind chest. The sound of the organ is made when air is admitted into a pipe by pressing a key or pedal. The piano

ORGAN PIPE

consists of wire strings stretched over a metal frame, and a keyboard and pedals that operate hammers and dampers. The piano frame is either vertical – as in the upright piano – or horizontal – as in the grand piano. When a key is at rest, a damper lies against the string to stop it vibrating. When a key is pressed down, the damper moves away from the string as the hammer strikes it, causing the string to vibrate and sound a note.

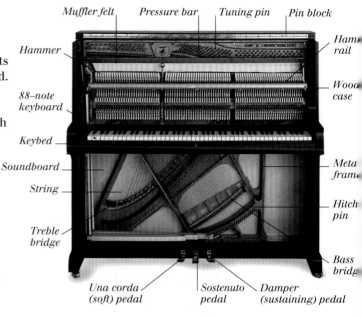

UPRIGHT PIANO

Muffler felt
Pressure bar
Tuning pin
Pin block
Hamm rail
Hammer
Wood case
88–note keyboard
Keybed
Meta fram
Soundboard
String
Hitch pin
Treble bridge
Bass bridg
Una corda (soft) pedal
Sostenuto pedal
Damper (sustaining) pedal

ORGAN CONSOLE

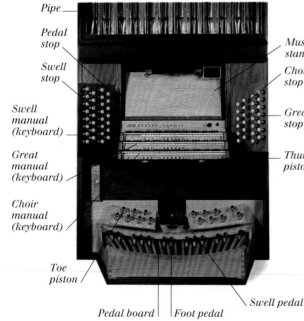

Pipe
Pedal stop
Swell stop
Swell manual (keyboard)
Great manual (keyboard)
Choir manual (keyboard)
Music stand
Choir stop
Great stop
Thumb piston
Toe piston
Pedal board
Foot pedal
Swell pedal

UPRIGHT PIANO ACTION

KEY AT REST

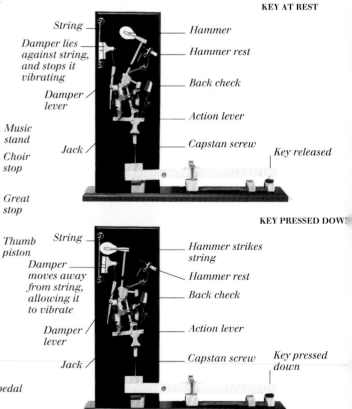

String
Damper lies against string, and stops it vibrating
Damper lever
Jack
Hammer
Hammer rest
Back check
Action lever
Capstan screw
Key released

KEY PRESSED DOW

String
Damper moves away from string, allowing it to vibrate
Damper lever
Jack
Hammer strikes string
Hammer rest
Back check
Action lever
Capstan screw
Key pressed down

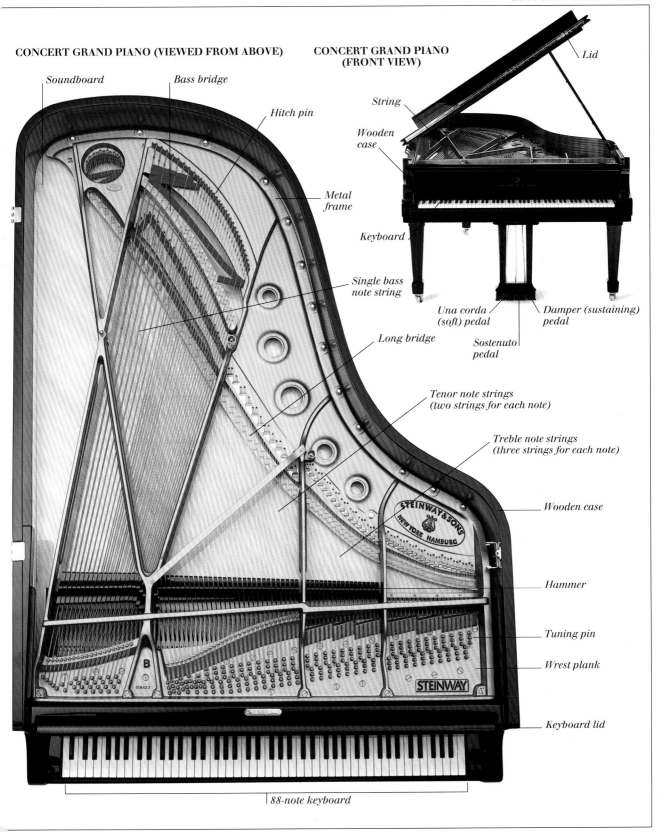

CONCERT GRAND PIANO (VIEWED FROM ABOVE)

CONCERT GRAND PIANO (FRONT VIEW)

Soundboard

Bass bridge

Hitch pin

Metal frame

Single bass note string

Long bridge

Tenor note strings (two strings for each note)

Treble note strings (three strings for each note)

Wooden case

Hammer

Tuning pin

Wrest plank

Keyboard lid

88-note keyboard

Lid

String

Wooden case

Keyboard

Una corda (soft) pedal

Sostenuto pedal

Damper (sustaining) pedal

Percussion instruments

PERCUSSION INSTRUMENTS are a large group of instruments that produce sound by being struck, shaken, scraped, or clashed together. Most percussion instruments – such as the tam-tam (gong), cymbals, and maracas – do not have a definite pitch and are used for rhythm and impact, and the distinctive timbre (colour) of their sound. Other percussion instruments – such as the xylophone, vibraphone, and tubular bells – are tuned to a definite pitch and can play melody, harmony, and rhythms. The xylophone and vibraphone each have two rows of bars that are arranged in a similar way to the black and white keys of a piano. Metal tubes are suspended below the bars to amplify the sound. The vibraphone has electrically operated fans that rotate in the tubes and produce a vibrato (wavering pitch) effect.

TEMPLE BLOCKS

TUBULAR BELLS

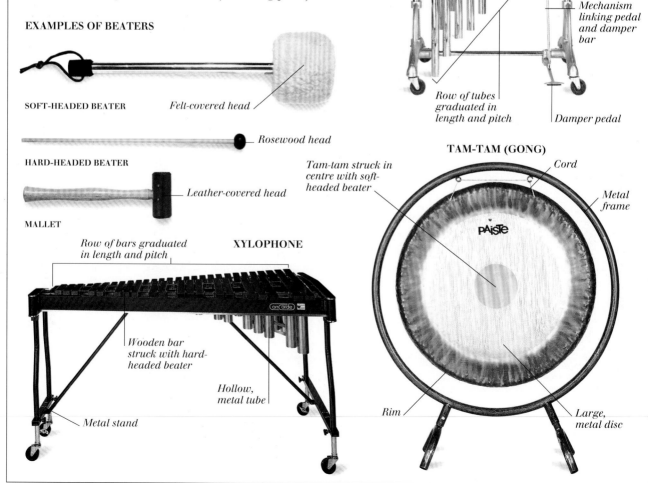

Tube struck with mallet

Hollow, metal tube

Damper bar

Metal frame

Mechanism linking pedal and damper bar

Row of tubes graduated in length and pitch

Damper pedal

EXAMPLES OF BEATERS

SOFT-HEADED BEATER   *Felt-covered head*

HARD-HEADED BEATER   *Rosewood head*

MALLET   *Leather-covered head*

Row of bars graduated in length and pitch   **XYLOPHONE**

Wooden bar struck with hard-headed beater

Hollow, metal tube

Metal stand

Tam-tam struck in centre with soft-headed beater

TAM-TAM (GONG)

Cord

Metal frame

PAiSTE

Rim

Large, metal disc

CYMBALS

Leather strap fits around player's hand

Pad protects hands from vibrations

Thin, convex disc of copper and tin alloy

SECTIONS OF A MARACA

Wooden handle

Lead shot

Hollow, wooden head

TRIANGLE

Steel rod bent into triangular shape

Steel beater

CLAVES

Hardwood sticks clashed together to give a sharp crack

CASTANETS

Cord

Hollowed wood

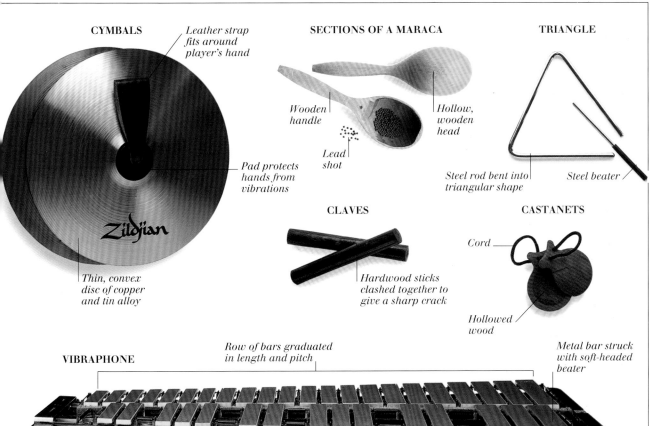

VIBRAPHONE

Row of bars graduated in length and pitch

Metal bar struck with soft-headed beater

Metal frame

Damper pedal

Metal tube containing electrically operated fan that produces vibrato (wavering pitch) effect

Electric cable

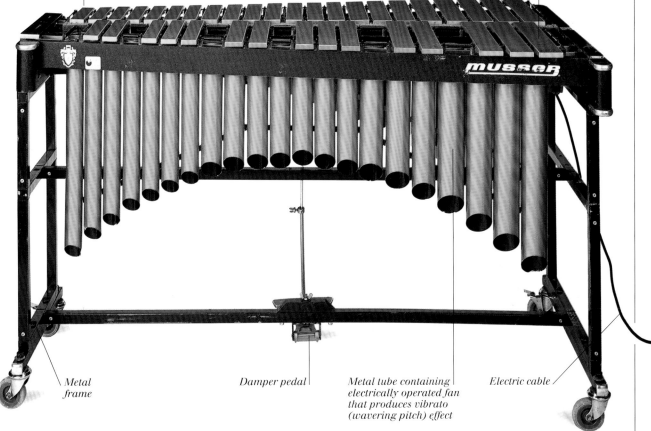

Drums

A DRUM IS A percussion instrument that consists of a drumhead, made of skin or plastic, stretched over one or both ends of a hollow vessel (the body-shell). Drums are played in most parts of the world and are made in a number of different shapes and sizes. They can be divided into three groups according to the shape of the body-shell: frame drums (e.g., tambourines), bowl-shaped drums (e.g., timpani), and tubular drums (e.g., congas). Drums are usually sounded by striking the drumhead with the hands or with beaters, such as a hard-headed stick. The drumhead vibrates, and its vibrations are amplified by the hollow body-shell. The snare drum has wires – known as snares – stretched across the lower drumhead; the snares vibrate against the lower drumhead when the drum is played. Most drums, such as congas, do not have a definite pitch and can play only rhythms (see pp. 516-517). Other drums, such as timpani, have a definite pitch and can play melody, harmony, and rhythms. They can be tuned by adjusting the tension of the drumhead. Different types of drum can be combined together with other percussion instruments to form a drum kit. The basic components of the drum kit are bass drum, tom-toms, floor tom (tenor drum), snare drum, and cymbals.

TAMBOURINE

DRUM KIT

Crash cymbal

Tension key

Tension rod

Tom-tom

Lug

Hi-hat cymbal

Snare drum

Tripod stand

Chain

Tension screw

Felt-covered beater

Pedal

Pedal

SNARE DRUM (VIEWED FROM BELOW)

Snare mounting

Adjustable damper

Lug

Transparent lower drumhead

Upper drumhead

Snare

Stick

Snare release lever

EXAMPLES OF BEATERS

Acorn

HARD-HEADED STICK

Taper

SOFT-HEADED STICK

Felt-covered head

Wire bristles

WIRE BRUSH

Ride cymbal

Tension key

Tom-tom

Height adjustment key

Tension rod

Lug

Floor tom (tenor drum)

Tension rod

Lug

Wooden body-shell

Bass drum

Height adjustment key

Leg

Rubber foot

CONGAS

Metal hoop

Drumhead

Tension rod

Wooden body-shell

Tripod stand

Leg

TIMPANUM (KETTLE DRUM)

Drumhead

Tension rod

Metal hoop

Tuning gauge

Copper body-shell

Strut

Crown

Tension rod

Tuning pedal

Castor

Electronic instruments

ELECTRONIC DRUMS

ELECTRONIC INSTRUMENTS generate electronic signals
that are magnified by an amplifier, and sent to a loudspeaker
where they are converted into sounds. Synthesizers, and other
electronic instruments, simulate the characteristic sounds of
conventional instruments, and also create entirely new sounds.
Most electronic instruments are keyboard instruments, but electronic
wind and percussion instruments are also popular. A digital sampler
records and stores sounds from musical instruments or other sources.
When the sound is played back, the pitch of the original sound can be
altered. A keyboard can be connected to the sampler so that a tune can
be played using the sampled sounds. With a MIDI (Musical Instrument
Digital Interface) system, a computer can be linked with other electronic
instruments, such as keyboards and electronic drums, to make sounds
together or in sequence. It is also possible, using music software, to
compose and play music on a home computer.

Drum pad

Height adjustment key

HOME KEYBOARD

Power button   *Volume control*   *Function display*   *Memory record button*   *Tone editor control*

Demonstration tune button

Pitch modulator   *Multi-accompaniment system control*   *Tone and rhythm pattern selector*   *Key*

Tripod

SYNTHESIZER

Memory card slot   *Joystick*   *Function display*   *Edit control*   *Data entry key pad*

Sound structure guide

Volume control

Pitch modulator   *Sound selection control*   *Key*

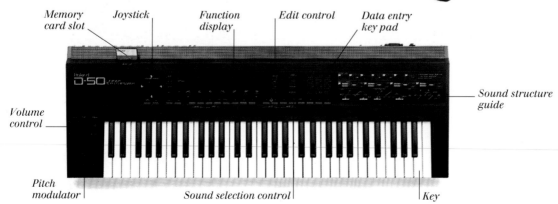

WIND SYNTHESIZER

Mouthpiece

Keys for left hand

DIGITAL SAMPLER

WIND CONTROLLER

Keys for right hand

Contrast control

Function display

Power button

Data increment control

POWER PACK

MIDI (Musical Instrument Digital Interface) cable

Connecting cable

SOUND MODULE

Floppy-disc drive

Play button

Data entry key pad

Record trigger

Microphone input

Store button

Input connector socket

Data entry key pad

Volume control

HOME COMPUTER SYSTEM

VISUAL DISPLAY UNIT

Edit control

Play button

Function display

Effect balance control

Music sequencing software

Score for harpsichord

SOUND MODULE

SPEAKER

SPEAKER

Hard-disc drive

Floppy-disc drive

Volume control

Volume and tone controls

KEYBOARD

Data entry key pad

Mouse pad

Mouse

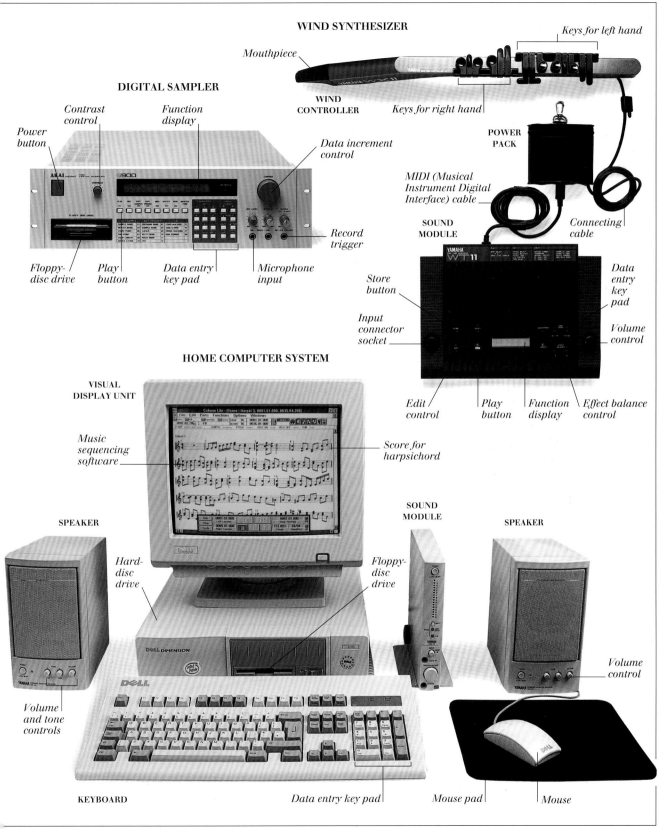

521

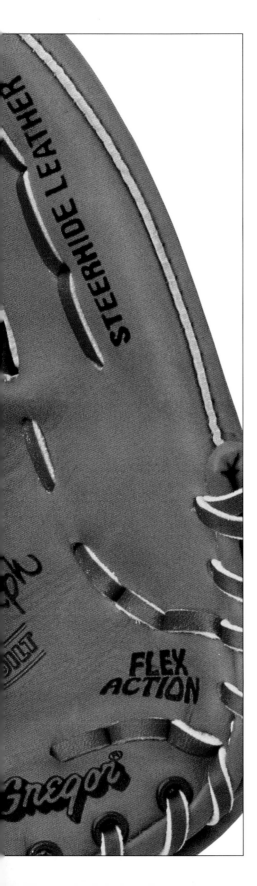

SPORTS

Soccer

GAMES INVOLVING KICKING A BALL have a long history and were recorded in China as early as 300 BC; in medieval Europe, street football was banned as a menace to the public; only in 1863 were the rules established, specifically banning carrying the ball for all players except the goalkeeper, and separating rugby from soccer. Soccer, officially termed association football, is a team sport in which players attempt to score goals by passing and dribbling the ball down the field past opposing defenders, and kicking or heading the ball into the goal net, outwitting the defending goalkeeper. Each team consists of ten outfield players (defenders, midfielders, and strikers) and a goalkeeper. Players from the opposing team may challenge the player in possession of the ball, but an illegal or foul tackle results in a penalty if a foul occurs inside the penalty area or a free kick if outside the penalty area. The round ball used in soccer is more easily controlled than the oval balls used in American, Canadian, and Australian rules football and in rugby. The result is a more "open" or flowing game which is played and watched by millions of people worldwide.

LINESMAN'S FLAG

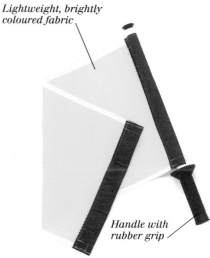

Lightweight, brightly coloured fabric

Handle with rubber grip

REFEREE'S EQUIPMENT

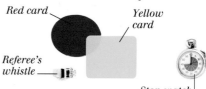

Red card

Yellow card

Referee's whistle

Stop-watch

SOCCER PITCH

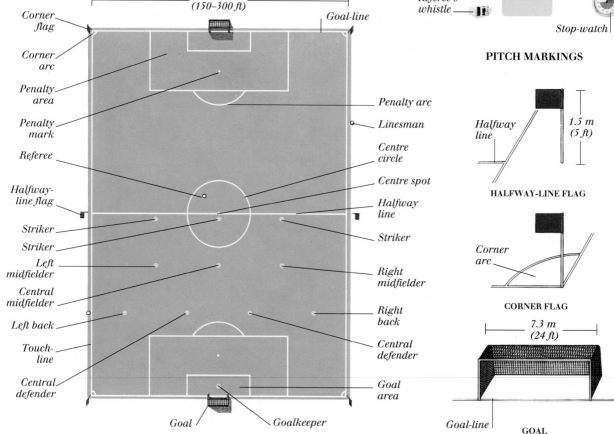

46–91 m (150–300 ft)

Corner flag

Corner arc

Penalty area

Penalty mark

Referee

Halfway-line flag

Striker

Striker

Left midfielder

Central midfielder

Left back

Touch-line

Central defender

Goal

Goalkeeper

Goal-line

Penalty arc

Linesman

Centre circle

Centre spot

Halfway line

Striker

Right midfielder

Right back

Central defender

Goal area

PITCH MARKINGS

Halfway line

1.5 m (5 ft)

HALFWAY-LINE FLAG

Corner arc

CORNER FLAG

7.3 m (24 ft)

Goal-line

GOAL

GOALKEEPER

Goalkeeper's shirt

Shorts

Glove

Shin guard

Sock

Soccer boot

SOCCER STRIP

Open-neck collar

Lightweight, man-made fabric team shirt

Team logo

Manufacturer's logo

Ribbed welt

Sponsor's logo

Ball size number

Manufacturer's name

Edge cut to fit perfectly

MAKING A SOCCER BALL

Hole punched in panel for stitching

Mitre

F.I.F.A. APPROVED

MULTIPLEX

Waxed thread

Mitre
MULTIPLEX

5

22–23 cm (8¹⁄₂–9 in)

Needle

Bladder valve

Bladder made from latex rubber

Panels sewn together with ball inside out

Laminated panel

Long cotton sock

Club crest

Team shorts

Synthetic bootlace

Interchangeable nylon stud

SOCCER BOOT

American football

IN AMERICAN AND CANADIAN FOOTBALL, the object of the game is to get the ball across the opponent's goal line, either by passing or carrying it across (a touch-down), or by kicking it between their goalposts (a field goal). An American football team has 11 players on the field at a time, although up to 40 players can appear for each side in a single game. The agile "offence" tries to score points, and the heavy hitting "defence" holds back the opposition. When in possession of the ball, a team has four chances ("downs"), to move it at least ten yards (nine metres) up the field to make a "first down". The opposition gains possession if they fail, or by tackling and intercepting the ball. Canadian football is played on a larger field, with 12 men on each side. A team has only three chances to achieve a first down. Otherwise, the game is very similar to American football. Helmets, face masks, and layers of body padding are worn by the players for protection.

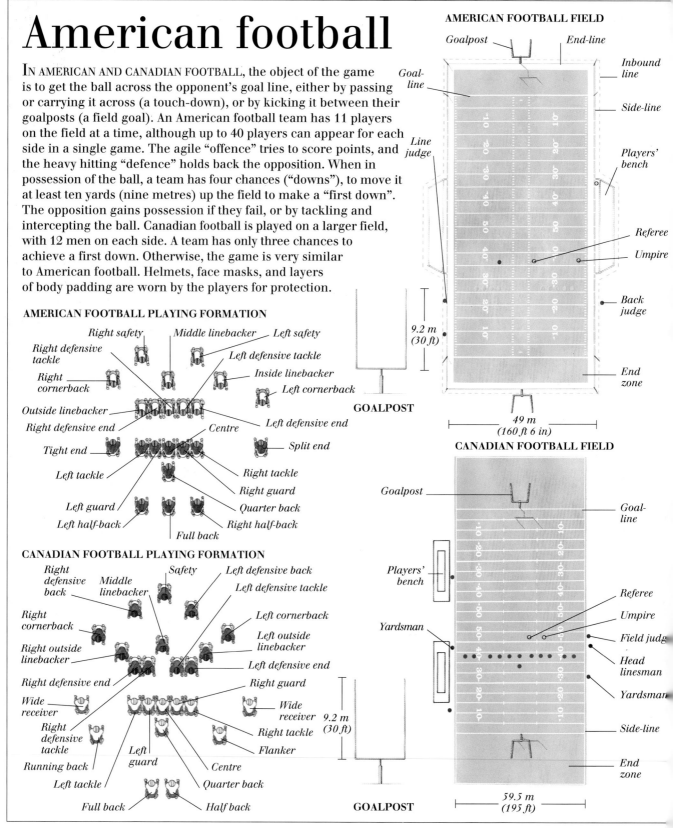

AMERICAN FOOTBALL FIELD

Goalpost · End-line · Inbound line · Goal-line · Side-line · Line judge · Players' bench · Referee · Umpire · Back judge · End zone

9.2 m (30 ft) — **GOALPOST**

49 m (160 ft 6 in)

CANADIAN FOOTBALL FIELD

Goalpost · Goal-line · Players' bench · Referee · Umpire · Field judge · Yardsman · Head linesman · Yardsman · Side-line · End zone

9.2 m (30 ft) — **GOALPOST**

59.5 m (195 ft)

AMERICAN FOOTBALL PLAYING FORMATION

Right safety · Middle linebacker · Left safety · Right defensive tackle · Left defensive tackle · Right cornerback · Inside linebacker · Left cornerback · Outside linebacker · Right defensive end · Centre · Left defensive end · Tight end · Split end · Left tackle · Right tackle · Right guard · Left guard · Quarter back · Left half-back · Right half-back · Full back

CANADIAN FOOTBALL PLAYING FORMATION

Right defensive back · Middle linebacker · Safety · Left defensive back · Left defensive tackle · Right cornerback · Left cornerback · Left outside linebacker · Right outside linebacker · Left defensive end · Right defensive end · Right guard · Wide receiver · Wide receiver · Right defensive tackle · Right tackle · Flanker · Left guard · Centre · Running back · Left tackle · Quarter back · Full back · Half back

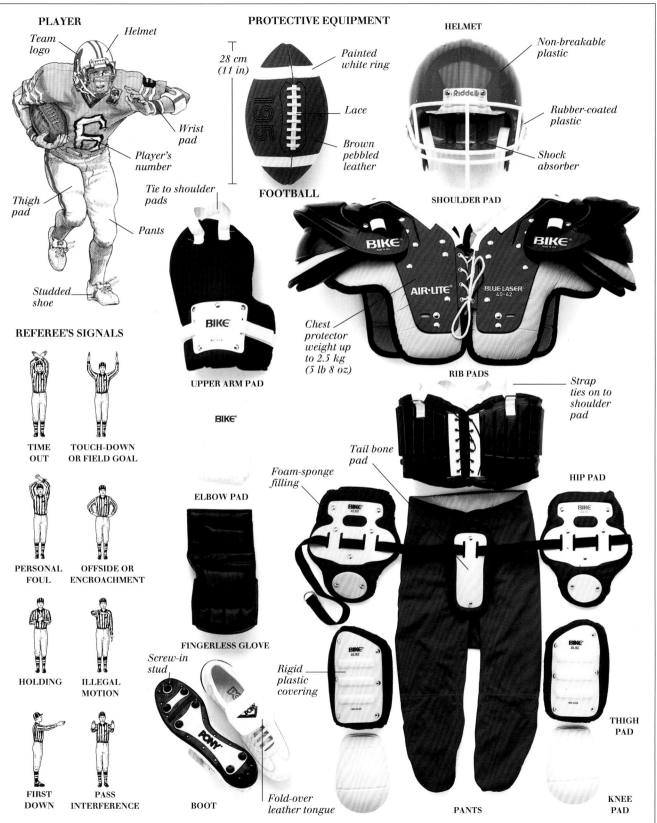

PLAYER

Team logo

Helmet

Wrist pad

Player's number

Thigh pad

Pants

Studded shoe

PROTECTIVE EQUIPMENT

28 cm (11 in)

Painted white ring

Lace

Brown pebbled leather

FOOTBALL

HELMET

Non-breakable plastic

Rubber-coated plastic

Shock absorber

Tie to shoulder pads

SHOULDER PAD

BIKE

AIR·LITE

BLUE LASER 40-42

Chest protector weight up to 2.5 kg (5 lb 8 oz)

RIB PADS

UPPER ARM PAD

BIKE

Strap ties on to shoulder pad

ELBOW PAD

HIP PAD

Tail bone pad

Foam-sponge filling

BIKE AL60

BIKE AL61

FINGERLESS GLOVE

Screw-in stud

Rigid plastic covering

BIKE AL92

BIKE AL92

THIGH PAD

PONY

BOOT

Fold-over leather tongue

PANTS

KNEE PAD

REFEREE'S SIGNALS

TIME OUT

TOUCH-DOWN OR FIELD GOAL

PERSONAL FOUL

OFFSIDE OR ENCROACHMENT

HOLDING

ILLEGAL MOTION

FIRST DOWN

PASS INTERFERENCE

527

Australian rules and Gaelic football

VARIETIES OF FOOTBALL have developed all over the world and Australian rules football is considered to be one of the roughest versions, allowing full body tackles although participants wear no protective padding. The game is played on a large, oval pitch by two sides, each of 18 players. Players can kick or punch the ball, which is shaped like a rugby ball, but cannot throw it. Running with the ball is permitted, as long as the ball touches the ground at least once every ten metres. The full backs defend two sets of posts. Teams try to score "goals" (six points) between the inner posts or "behinds" (one point) inside the outer posts. Each game has four quarters of 25 minutes, and the team with the most points at the end of the allotted time is the winner. In Gaelic football, an Irish version of soccer (see pp. 524–525), a size 5 soccer ball is used. Each team can have 15 players on the field at a time. Players are allowed to catch, fist, and kick the ball, or dribble it using their hands or feet, but cannot throw it. Teams are awarded three points for getting the ball into the net, and one point for getting it through the posts above the crossbar. Gaelic football is rarely played outside of Ireland.

START OF PLAY

Field umpire

Centre circle

SCORING

GOAL (6 POINTS)

BEHIND (1 POINT)

AUSTRALIAN RULES FOOTBALL FIELD

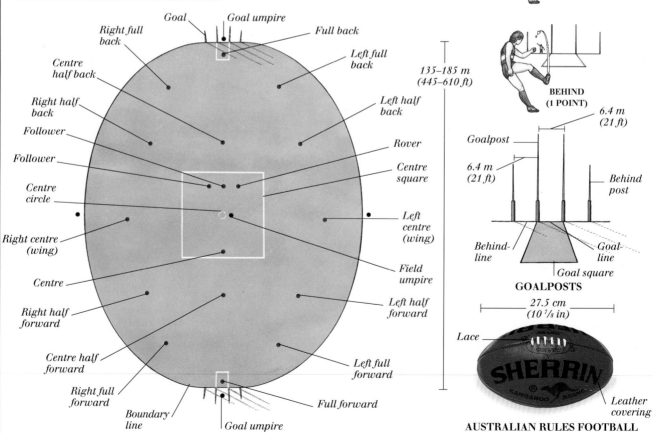

Goal

Goal umpire

Right full back

Full back

Centre half back

Left full back

Right half back

Left half back

Follower

Rover

Follower

Centre square

Centre circle

Left centre (wing)

Right centre (wing)

Field umpire

Centre

Left half forward

Right half forward

Left full forward

Centre half forward

Right full forward

Full forward

Boundary line

Goal umpire

135–185 m (445–610 ft)

6.4 m (21 ft)

Goalpost

6.4 m (21 ft)

Behind post

Behind-line

Goal-line

Goal square

GOALPOSTS

27.5 cm (10 ⁷/₈ in)

Lace

SHERRIN

Leather covering

AUSTRALIAN RULES FOOTBALL

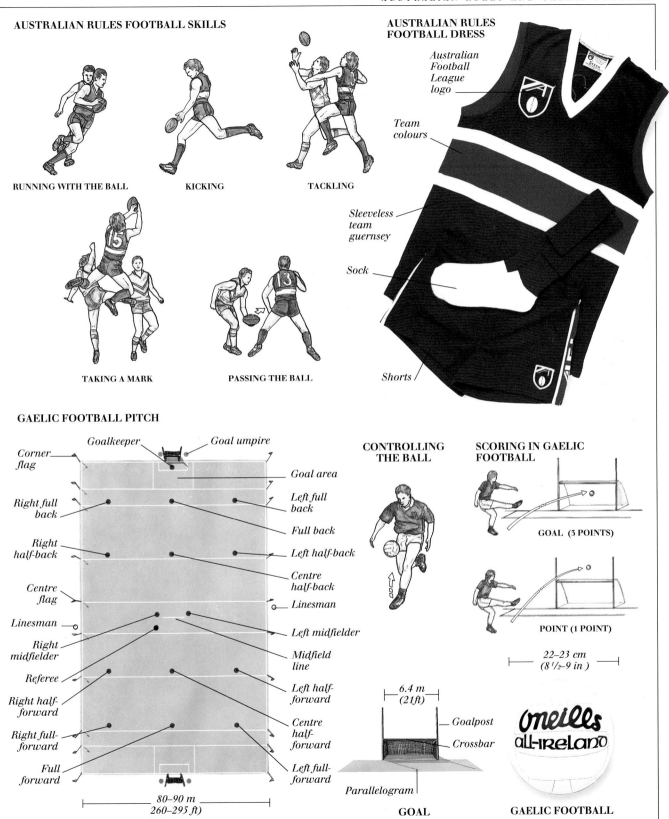

AUSTRALIAN RULES FOOTBALL SKILLS

RUNNING WITH THE BALL

KICKING

TACKLING

TAKING A MARK

PASSING THE BALL

AUSTRALIAN RULES FOOTBALL DRESS

Australian Football League logo

Team colours

Sleeveless team guernsey

Sock

Shorts

GAELIC FOOTBALL PITCH

Corner flag

Goalkeeper

Goal umpire

Goal area

Right full back

Left full back

Full back

Right half-back

Left half-back

Centre half-back

Centre flag

Linesman

Linesman

Left midfielder

Right midfielder

Midfield line

Referee

Left half-forward

Right half-forward

Centre half-forward

Right full-forward

Left full-forward

Full forward

80–90 m
260–295 ft)

CONTROLLING THE BALL

SCORING IN GAELIC FOOTBALL

GOAL (3 POINTS)

POINT (1 POINT)

22–23 cm
(8 1/2–9 in)

6.4 m
(21ft)

Goalpost

Crossbar

Parallelogram

GOAL

oneills
all-ireland

GAELIC FOOTBALL

Rugby

RUGBY IS PLAYED WITH AN OVAL BALL which may be carried, thrown, or kicked. There are two codes of rugby. Rugby Union is an amateur game played by two teams of 15 players. They can score points in two ways: by placing the ball by hand over the opponents' goal-line (a try, scoring four points) or by kicking it over the crossbar of the opponent's goal (a conversion of a try, scoring two points; a penalty kick, scoring three points; or a drop-kick, scoring three points). Rugby League developed from the Union game but is played by 13 players at amateur and professional levels. In League games, a try scores four points; a conversion of a try scores two points; a drop goal scores three points, and a penalty kick scores two points. Scrummages occur in both forms of the game when play stops following an infringement.

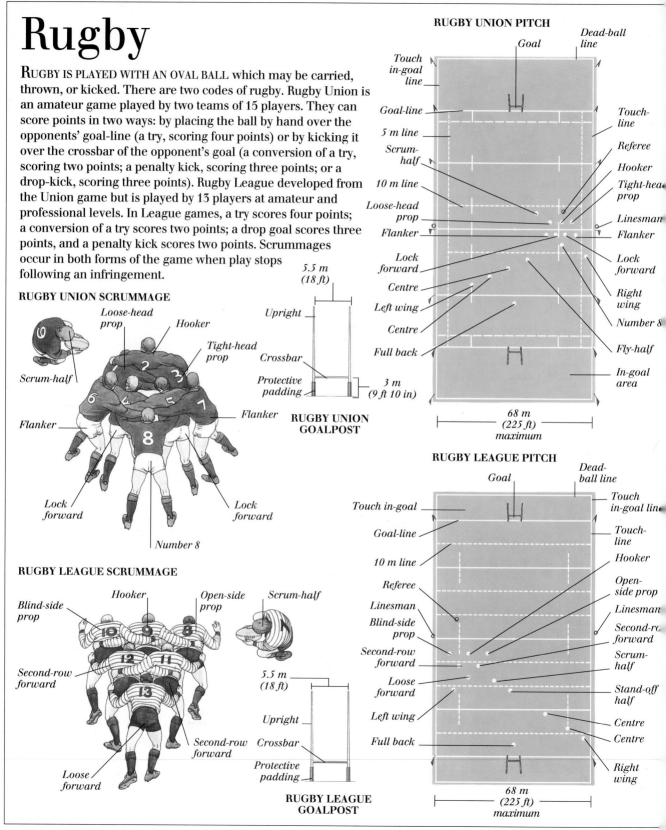

RUGBY UNION SCRUMMAGE

Loose-head prop
Hooker
Tight-head prop
Scrum-half
Flanker
Flanker
Lock forward
Lock forward
Number 8

5.5 m (18 ft)
Upright
Crossbar
Protective padding
3 m (9 ft 10 in)

RUGBY UNION GOALPOST

RUGBY LEAGUE SCRUMMAGE

Blind-side prop
Hooker
Open-side prop
Scrum-half
Second-row forward
Second-row forward
Loose forward

5.5 m (18 ft)
Upright
Crossbar
Protective padding

RUGBY LEAGUE GOALPOST

RUGBY UNION PITCH

Goal
Dead-ball line
Touch in-goal line
Goal-line
5 m line
Scrum-half
10 m line
Loose-head prop
Flanker
Lock forward
Centre
Left wing
Centre
Full back
Touch-line
Referee
Hooker
Tight-head prop
Linesman
Flanker
Lock forward
Right wing
Number 8
Fly-half
In-goal area
68 m (225 ft) maximum

RUGBY LEAGUE PITCH

Goal
Dead-ball line
Touch in-goal
Goal-line
10 m line
Referee
Linesman
Blind-side prop
Second-row forward
Loose forward
Left wing
Full back
Touch in-goal line
Touch-line
Hooker
Open-side prop
Linesman
Second-row forward
Scrum-half
Stand-off half
Centre
Centre
Right wing
68 m (225 ft) maximum

RUGBY SCORING AND SKILLS

GOAL

Goal-line

TRY

PASS

PLACE KICK

FLYING TACKLE

RUGBY UNION PLAYER

Shirt in team colour

Knee-high sock

Team shorts

Studded boot

RUGBY UNION BALL

Laminated leather panel covered with textured plastic

Four-panel construction

Mitre
MULTIPLEX

28–30 cm (11–12 in)

RUGBY LEAGUE BALL

Four-panel construction

Laminated leather panel covered with smooth plastic

Mitre
MULTIPLEX T

28 cm (11 in)

RUGBY LEAGUE SHIRT

Button-up collar

Team crest

Official logo of the British Rugby Football League

Three-quarter sleeve

UMBRO

WIDNES R.L.F.C.

Team crest

Long sleeve

RUGBY UNION SHIRT

Ankle support

Circular stud

RUGBY BOOT

Team colour

RUGBY SHIRTS

531

Basketball

BASKETBALL IS A BALL GAME for two teams of five players, originally devised in 1890 by James Naismath for the Y.M.C.A. in Springfield, Massachusetts, U.S.A. The object of the game is to take possession of the ball and score points by throwing the ball into the opposing team's basket. A player moves the ball up and down the court by bouncing it along the ground or "dribbling"; the ball may be passed between players by throwing, bouncing, or rolling. Players may not run with or kick the ball, although pivoting on one foot is allowed. The game begins with the referee throwing the ball into the air and a player from each team jumping up to try and "tip" the ball to a team-mate. The length of the game and the number of periods played varies at different levels. There are amateur, professional, and international rules. No game ends in a draw. An extra period of five minutes is played, plus as many extra periods as are necessary to break the tie. In addition to the five players on court, each team has up to seven substitutes, but players may only leave the court with the permission of the referee. Basketball is a non-contact sport and fouls on other players are penalized by a throw-in awarded against the offending team; a free throw at the basket is awarded when a player is fouled in the act of shooting. Basketball is a fast-moving game, requiring both physical and mental coordination. Skilful tactical play matters more than simple physical strength and the agility of the players makes the game an excellent spectator sport.

INTERNATIONAL BASKETBALL COURT

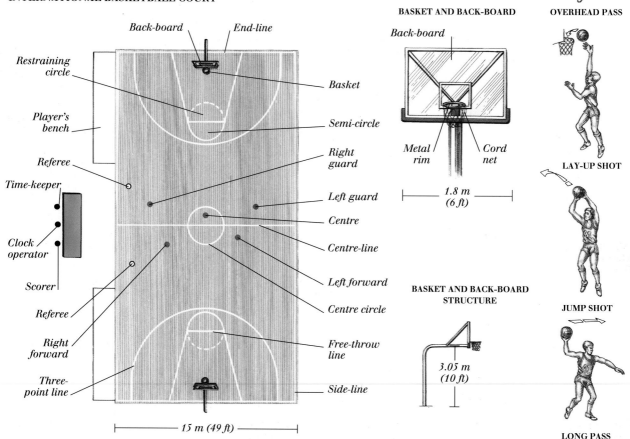

BASKETBALL SKILLS

CHEST PASS

DRIBBLE

OVERHEAD PASS

BASKET AND BACK-BOARD

Back-board

Metal rim

Cord net

1.8 m (6 ft)

LAY-UP SHOT

BASKET AND BACK-BOARD STRUCTURE

3.05 m (10 ft)

JUMP SHOT

LONG PASS

Back-board
End-line
Restraining circle
Basket
Player's bench
Semi-circle
Referee
Right guard
Time-keeper
Left guard
Centre
Clock operator
Centre-line
Scorer
Left forward
Referee
Centre circle
Right forward
Free-throw line
Three-point line
Side-line
15 m (49 ft)

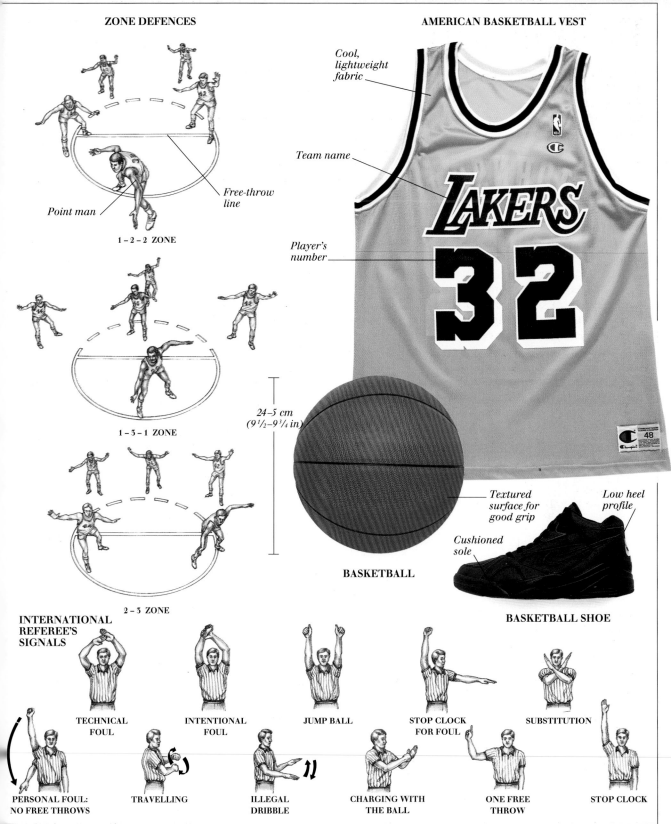

ZONE DEFENCES

Point man

Free-throw line

1 – 2 – 2 ZONE

1 – 3 – 1 ZONE

2 – 3 ZONE

AMERICAN BASKETBALL VEST

Cool, lightweight fabric

Team name

Player's number

BASKETBALL

24–5 cm
(9 1/2–9 3/4 in)

Textured surface for good grip

Low heel profile

Cushioned sole

BASKETBALL SHOE

INTERNATIONAL REFEREE'S SIGNALS

TECHNICAL FOUL

INTENTIONAL FOUL

JUMP BALL

STOP CLOCK FOR FOUL

SUBSTITUTION

PERSONAL FOUL: NO FREE THROWS

TRAVELLING

ILLEGAL DRIBBLE

CHARGING WITH THE BALL

ONE FREE THROW

STOP CLOCK

Volleyball, netball, and handball

VOLLEYBALL, NETBALL, AND HANDBALL are fast-moving team sports played with balls on courts with a hard surface. In volleyball, the object of the game is to hit the ball over a net strung across the centre of the court so that it touches the ground on the opponent's side. The team of six players can take three hits to direct the ball over the net, although the same player cannot hit the ball twice in a row. Players can hit the ball with their arms, hands or any other part of their upper body. Teams score points only while serving. The first team to score 15 points, with a two-point margin over their opponent, wins the game. Netball is one of the few sports played exclusively by women. Similar to basketball (see pp.532–533), it is played on a slightly larger court with seven players instead of five. A team moves the ball towards the goal by throwing, passing, and catching it with the aim of throwing the ball through the opponents' goal net. Players are confined by their playing position to specific areas of the court. Team handball is one of the world's fastest games. Each side has seven players. A team moves the ball by dribbling, passing, or bouncing it as they run. Players may stop, catch, throw, bounce, or strike the ball with any part of the body above the knees. Each team tries to score goals by directing the ball past the opposition's goalkeeper into the net, which is similar to a soccer net.

VOLLEYBALL SHOTS

OVERHAND SERVE SPIKE (SMASH)

UNDERHAND SERVE FOREARM PASS (DIG)

VOLLEYBALL KIT

Team colours

Ribbed cuff

Cotton-knit jersey

Leather covering

Elasticated waist

VOLLEYBALL COURT

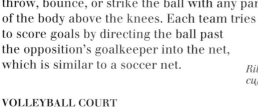

End-line Linesman

Clear space

Linesman

Side-line

Players' bench

Referee

Scorer

Net

Left forward

Back zone

Left back

Linesman

Attack zone

Attack line

Umpire

Centre forward

Right forward

Centre back

Linesman

Service area

Server

9 m (29 ft 6 in)

21 cm (8¼ in)

VOLLEYBALL

Shorts

VOLLEYBALL NET

Tape Net Antenna

Men's: 2.4 m (8 ft)
Women's: 2.2 m (7 ft 4 in)

Post

Elasticated knit fabric

Injected moulded padding

KNEE PADS

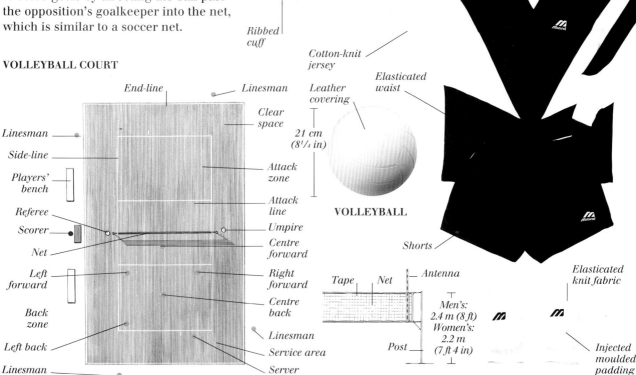

NETBALL COURT

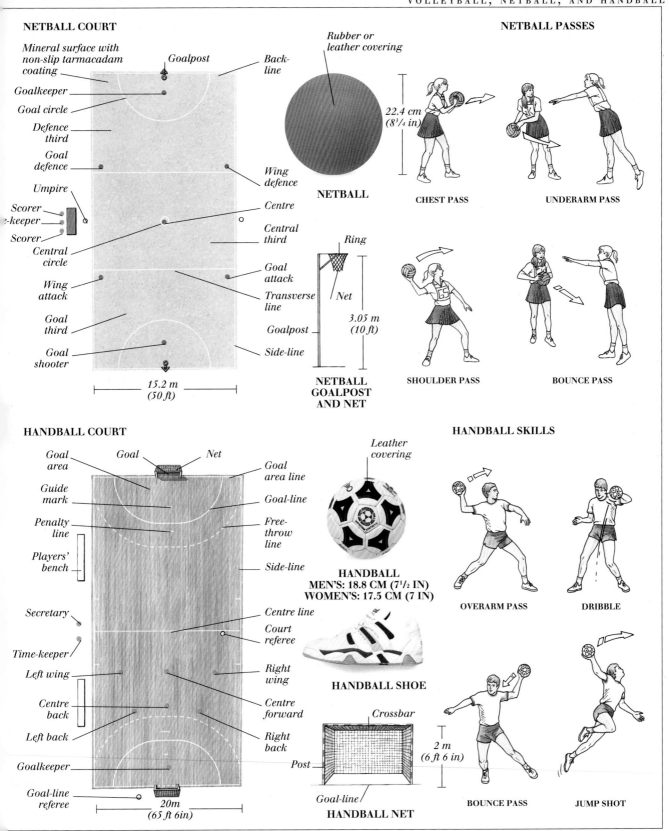

Mineral surface with non-slip tarmacadam coating

Goalpost

Back-line

Goalkeeper

Goal circle

Defence third

Goal defence

Wing defence

Umpire

Scorer

-keeper

Scorer

Central circle

Centre

Central third

Goal attack

Wing attack

Transverse line

Goal third

Goal shooter

Side-line

**15.2 m
(50 ft)**

NETBALL PASSES

Rubber or leather covering

**22.4 cm
(8¾ in)**

NETBALL

CHEST PASS

UNDERARM PASS

Ring

Net

**3.05 m
(10 ft)**

Goalpost

**NETBALL
GOALPOST
AND NET**

SHOULDER PASS

BOUNCE PASS

HANDBALL COURT

Goal area

Goal

Net

Goal area line

Guide mark

Goal-line

Penalty line

Free-throw line

Players' bench

Side-line

Secretary

Centre line

Court referee

Time-keeper

Left wing

Right wing

Centre back

Centre forward

Left back

Right back

Goalkeeper

Goal-line referee

**20m
(65 ft 6in)**

HANDBALL SKILLS

Leather covering

**HANDBALL
MEN'S: 18.8 CM (7½ IN)
WOMEN'S: 17.5 CM (7 IN)**

HANDBALL SHOE

OVERARM PASS

DRIBBLE

Crossbar

**2 m
(6 ft 6 in)**

Post

Goal-line

HANDBALL NET

BOUNCE PASS

JUMP SHOT

Baseball

BASEBALL IS A BALL GAME for two teams of nine players. The batter hits the ball thrown by the opposing team's pitcher, into the area between the foul lines. He then runs round all four fixed bases in order to score a run, touching or "tagging" each base in turn. The pitcher must throw the ball at a height between the batter's armpits and knees, a height which is called the "strike zone". A ball pitched in this area that crosses over the "home plate" is called a "strike" and the batter has three strikes in which to try and hit the ball (otherwise he is "struck out"). The fielding team tries to get the batting team out by catching the ball before it bounces, tagging a player of the batting team with the ball who is running between bases, or by tagging a base before the player has reached it. Members of the batting team may stop safely at a base as long as it is not occupied by another member of their team. When the batter runs to first base, his team-mate at first base must run on to second – this is called "force play". A game consists of nine innings and each team will bat once during an inning. When three members of the batting team are out, the teams swap roles. The team with the greatest number of runs wins the game.

BATTER'S HELMET

Plastic shell

Peak

Foam padding

Wire coated in strong nylon

Plastic-coated foam padding

CATCHER'S MASK

BASEBALL PITCH

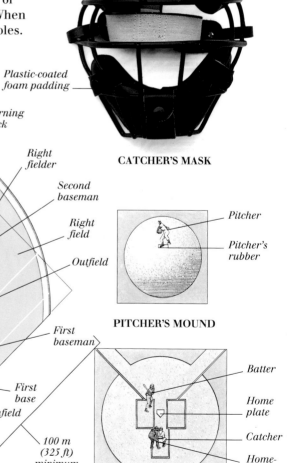

Centre fielder

Centre field

Warning track

Left fielder

Right fielder

Left field

Second baseman

Right field

Foul line

Outfield

Pitcher

Pitcher's rubber

PITCHER'S MOUND

Shortstop

First baseman

Umpire

Batter

Third baseman

First base

Home plate

Third base

Infield

Catcher

Coach's box

Home run

100 m (325 ft) minimum

Home-plate umpire

Second base

Dugout

On-deck circle

Pitcher's mound

HOME PLATE

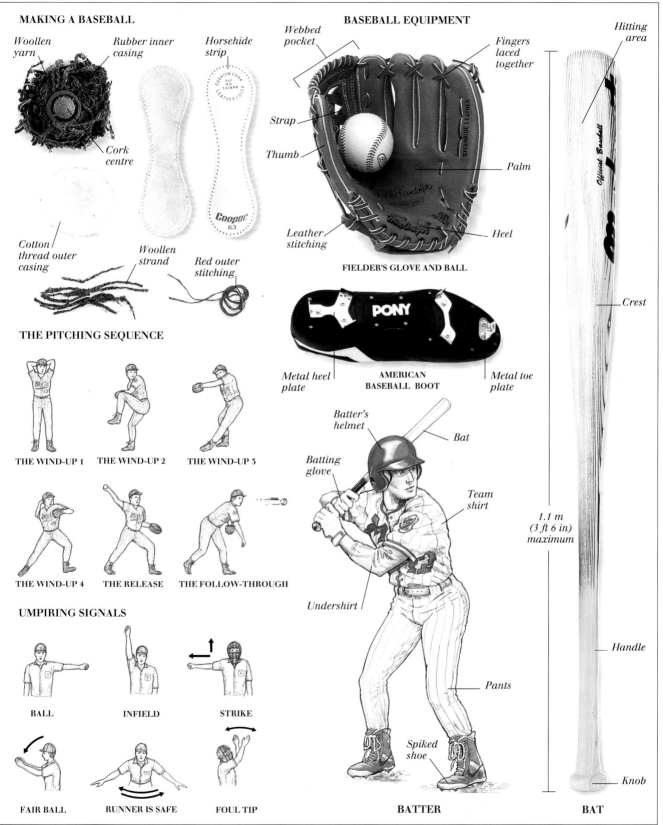

MAKING A BASEBALL

Woollen yarn

Rubber inner casing

Horsehide strip

CUSHION CORK
50% 9%
LEATHER COVER

TAIWAN ®

Cooper
63

Cork centre

Cotton thread outer casing

Woollen strand

Red outer stitching

THE PITCHING SEQUENCE

THE WIND-UP 1

THE WIND-UP 2

THE WIND-UP 3

THE WIND-UP 4

THE RELEASE

THE FOLLOW-THROUGH

UMPIRING SIGNALS

BALL

INFIELD

STRIKE

FAIR BALL

RUNNER IS SAFE

FOUL TIP

BASEBALL EQUIPMENT

Webbed pocket

Fingers laced together

Strap

STEERHIDE LEATHER

Thumb

Palm

Leather stitching

Heel

FIELDER'S GLOVE AND BALL

PONY

Metal heel plate

AMERICAN BASEBALL BOOT

Metal toe plate

Batter's helmet

Bat

Batting glove

Team shirt

Undershirt

Pants

Spiked shoe

BATTER

Hitting area

Official Baseball

Crest

1.1 m
(3 ft 6 in)
maximum

Handle

Knob

BAT

537

Cricket

CRICKET IS A BALL GAME PLAYED by two teams of eleven players on a pitch with two sets of three stumps (wickets). The bowler bowls the ball down the pitch to the batsman of the opposing team, who must defend the wicket in front of which he stands. The object of the game is to score as many runs as possible. Runs can be scored individually by running the length of the playing strip, or by hitting a ball which lands outside the boundary ("six"), or which lands inside the boundary but bounces or rolls outside ("four"); the opposing team will bowl and field, attempting to dismiss the batsmen. A batsman can be dismissed in one of several ways: by the bowler hitting the wicket with the ball ("bowled"); by a fielder catching the ball hit by the batsman before it touches the ground ("caught"); by the wicket-keeper or another fielder breaking the wicket while the batsman is attempting a run and is therefore out of his ground ("stumped" or "run out"); by the batsman breaking the wicket with his own bat or body ("hit wicket"); by a part of the batsman's body being hit by a ball that would otherwise have hit the wicket ("leg before wicket" ["lbw"]). A match consists of one or two innings and each innings ends when the tenth batsman of the batting team is out, when a certain number of overs (a series of six balls bowled) have been played, or when the captain of the batting team "declares" ending the innings voluntarily.

CRICKET STROKES

FORWARD DEFENSIVE STROKE

BACKWARD DEFENSIVE STROKE

ON-DRIVE

OFF-DRIVE

PULL

HOOK

SQUARE CUT

LEG GLANCE

CRICKET BALL AND WICKET

Leather skin

Seam

BALL

Bail

WICKET

Stump

POSSIBLE FIELD POSITIONS FOR AN AWAY SWING BOWLER TO A RIGHT-HANDED BATSMAN (IN RED) AND OTHER FIELD POSITIONS

Long on

Umpire

Long off

Boundary line

Bowler

Deep mid-wicket

Non-striking batsman

Mid-on

Extra cover

Silly mid-on

Forward short leg

Mid-off

Square leg

Silly mid-off

Deep square leg

Cover

Square-leg umpire

Point

Batsman

Gulley

Long leg

Third man

Leg slip

Second slip

Wicket-keeper

First slip

Fine leg

Sight screen

CRICKET PITCH

Wicket-keeper

Batsman

Wicket

Bowling crease

20 m (66 ft)

Bowler

Return crease

Umpire

Non-striking batsman

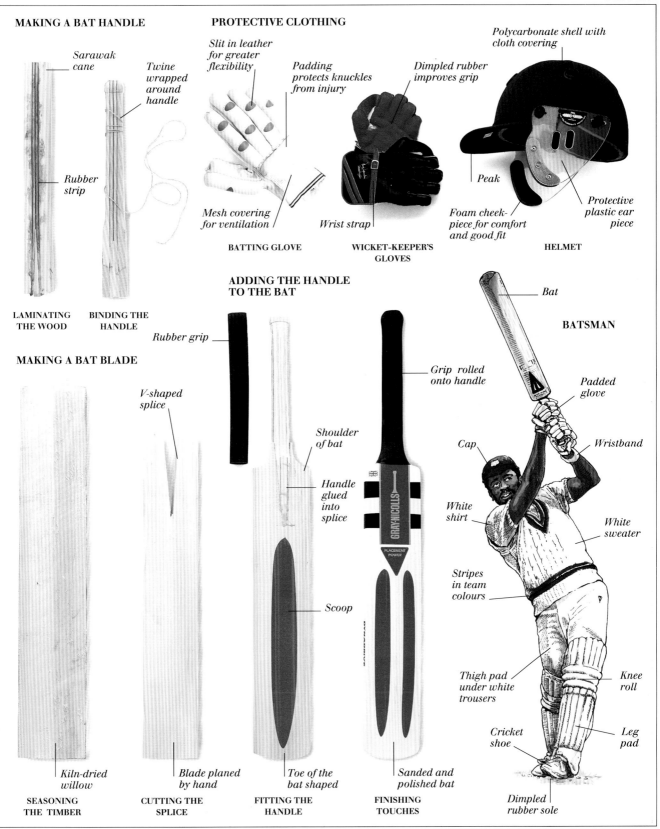

MAKING A BAT HANDLE

Sarawak cane

Twine wrapped around handle

Rubber strip

LAMINATING THE WOOD

BINDING THE HANDLE

PROTECTIVE CLOTHING

Slit in leather for greater flexibility

Padding protects knuckles from injury

Mesh covering for ventilation

Wrist strap

Dimpled rubber improves grip

BATTING GLOVE

WICKET-KEEPER'S GLOVES

Polycarbonate shell with cloth covering

Peak

Foam cheek-piece for comfort and good fit

Protective plastic ear piece

HELMET

MAKING A BAT BLADE

V-shaped splice

Kiln-dried willow

SEASONING THE TIMBER

Blade planed by hand

CUTTING THE SPLICE

ADDING THE HANDLE TO THE BAT

Rubber grip

Shoulder of bat

Handle glued into splice

Scoop

Toe of the bat shaped

FITTING THE HANDLE

Grip rolled onto handle

Sanded and polished bat

FINISHING TOUCHES

Bat

BATSMAN

Padded glove

Wristband

Cap

White shirt

White sweater

Stripes in team colours

Thigh pad under white trousers

Knee roll

Cricket shoe

Leg pad

Dimpled rubber sole

Hockey, lacrosse, and hurling

ALL OVER THE WORLD, TEAM GAMES have evolved which require that a ball be struck or carried, and tossed at the end of a stick. Early forms of these games include hurling, shinty, bandy, and pelota. Hockey is played by men and women: two teams of eleven players try to gain and keep possession of the ball and score goals by using the hockey stick to propel the ball into their opponents' goal net. Skills such as passing, pushing, or hitting the ball by slapping or lifting it in a flicking movement, and shooting at goal are crucial. Hockey is played indoors and outdoors on grass or synthetic pitches. Lacrosse is played internationally as a 12-a-side game for women and as 10-a-side game for men. The women's pitch has no absolute boundaries but the men's pitch has clearly defined side-lines and end-lines. The ball is kept in play by being carried, thrown or batted with the crosse, and rolled or kicked in any direction. In men's and women's lacrosse, play can continue behind the marked goal areas. Similar skills are required in hurling – a Gaelic field game played on the same pitch as Gaelic football (see pp. 528–529), using the same goalposts and net. In hurling, the ball may be struck with or carried on the hurley and, when off the ground, may be struck with the hand or kicked. Goals (three points) are scored when the ball passes between the posts and under the crossbar; one point is scored when it passes between the posts and over the crossbar.

GOALKEEPER'S EQUIPMENT

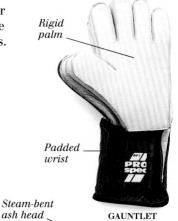

Face mask

Hard shell

Air vent

HELMET

Strap

Rigid palm

Padded wrist

GAUNTLET

HOCKEY STICK AND BALL

STICK

Handle

Tape

Steam-bent ash head

Blade

Stitched seam

7–7.5 cm (2³/₄–3 in)

Slazenger FLEXI

91 cm (3 ft)

BALL

HOCKEY FIELD

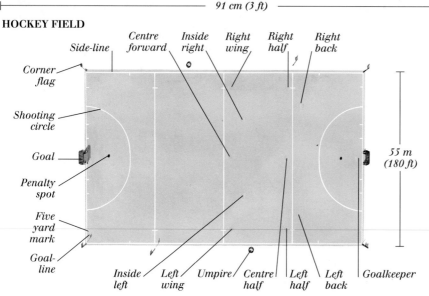

Side-line

Centre forward

Inside right

Right wing

Right half

Right back

Corner flag

Shooting circle

Goal

Penalty spot

Five yard mark

Goal-line

Inside left

Left wing

Umpire

Centre half

Left half

Left back

Goalkeeper

55 m (180 ft)

Protective overshoe

Padding protects toes against the hard ball

Strap

GOALKEEPER'S KICKER

2.1 m (7 ft)

HOCKEY GOAL

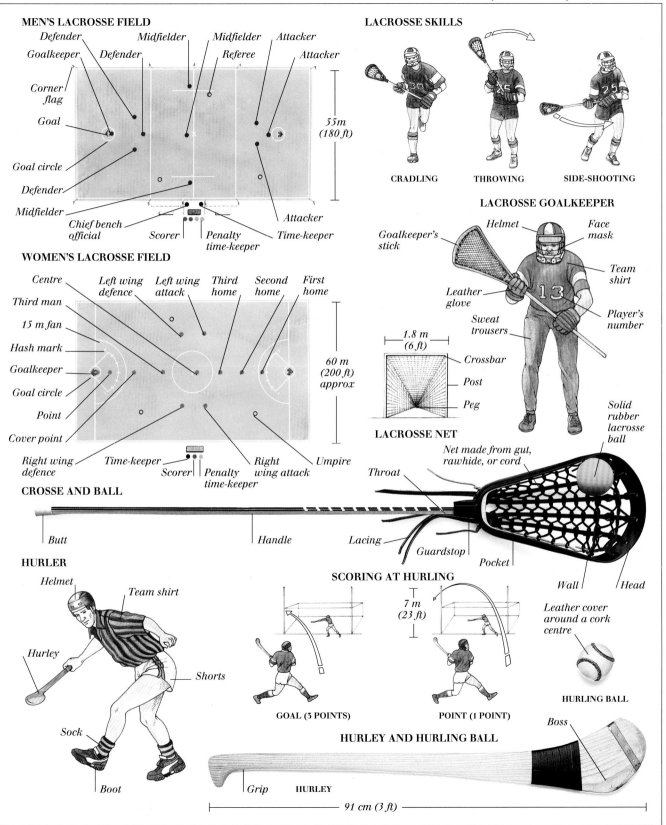

MEN'S LACROSSE FIELD

Defender
Goalkeeper
Defender
Corner flag
Goal
Goal circle
Defender
Midfielder
Chief bench official
Scorer
Midfielder
Referee
Midfielder
Attacker
Attacker
Attacker
Penalty time-keeper
Time-keeper

55m (180 ft)

WOMEN'S LACROSSE FIELD

Centre
Third man
15 m fan
Hash mark
Goalkeeper
Goal circle
Point
Cover point
Right wing defence
Time-keeper
Scorer
Left wing defence
Left wing attack
Third home
Second home
First home
Penalty time-keeper
Right wing attack
Umpire

60 m (200 ft) approx

LACROSSE SKILLS

CRADLING
THROWING
SIDE-SHOOTING

LACROSSE GOALKEEPER

Goalkeeper's stick
Leather glove
Sweat trousers
Helmet
Face mask
Team shirt
Player's number
Solid rubber lacrosse ball

1.8 m (6 ft)
Crossbar
Post
Peg

LACROSSE NET

CROSSE AND BALL

Butt
Handle
Throat
Lacing
Guardstop
Pocket
Net made from gut, rawhide, or cord
Wall
Head

HURLER

Helmet
Team shirt
Hurley
Shorts
Sock
Boot

SCORING AT HURLING

7 m (23 ft)

GOAL (3 POINTS)
POINT (1 POINT)

Leather cover around a cork centre

HURLING BALL

HURLEY AND HURLING BALL

Boss
Grip
HURLEY

91 cm (3 ft)

Athletics

THE SPORTS that make up athletics are divided into two main groups: track events – which include sprinting, middle, and long distance running, relay running, hurdling, and walking – and field events which require jumping and throwing skills. Contests designed to test the speed, strength, agility, and stamina of athletes were held by the ancient Greeks over 4,000 years ago. However, the abolition of the Olympic Games in 393 AD meant that athletics were neglected until the revival of large-scale competitions in the mid-nineteenth century. Modern stadia offer areas reserved for the long jump, triple jump, and pole vault usually situated outside the running track. The javelin, shot, hammer, and discus are thrown within the track area. Most athletes specialize in one or two events but, in the heptathlon, women compete in seven events, held over two days: 200 m and 800 m races, 100 m hurdles, javelin, shot put, high jump, and long jump. In the decathlon, men compete in ten events over two days: 100 m, 400 m, and 1,500 m races, 110 m hurdles, javelin, discus, shot put, pole vault, high jump, and long jump.

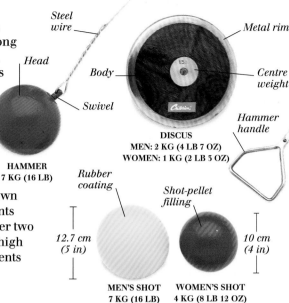

FIELD EVENT EQUIPMENT

Steel wire

Head

Swivel

HAMMER 7 KG (16 LB)

Body

Metal rim

Centre weight

**DISCUS
MEN: 2 KG (4 LB 7 OZ)
WOMEN: 1 KG (2 LB 3 OZ)**

Hammer handle

Rubber coating

Shot-pellet filling

12.7 cm (5 in)

10 cm (4 in)

MEN'S SHOT 7 KG (16 LB)

WOMEN'S SHOT 4 KG (8 LB 12 OZ)

JAVELIN   *Cord grip*   *Shaft*   *Tip*

Men: 2.6 m (8 ft 6 in)
Women: 2.3 m (7 ft 6 in)

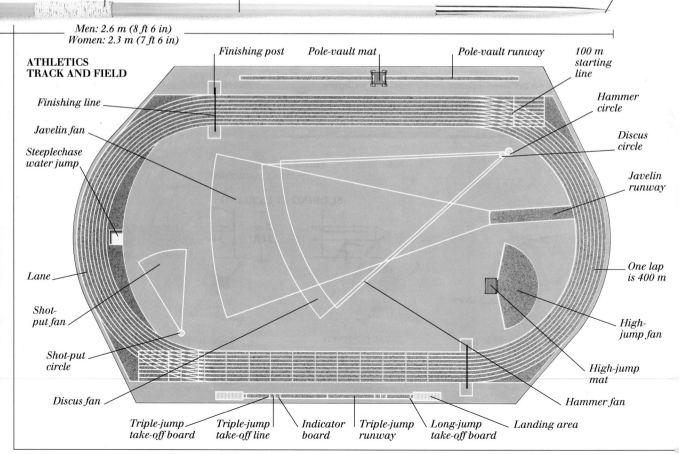

ATHLETICS TRACK AND FIELD

Finishing post   *Pole-vault mat*   *Pole-vault runway*   *100 m starting line*

Finishing line

Javelin fan

Steeplechase water jump

Hammer circle

Discus circle

Javelin runway

Lane

Shot-put fan

Shot-put circle

Discus fan

One lap is 400 m

High-jump fan

High-jump mat

Hammer fan

Triple-jump take-off board   *Triple-jump take-off line*   *Indicator board*   *Triple-jump runway*   *Long-jump take-off board*   *Landing area*

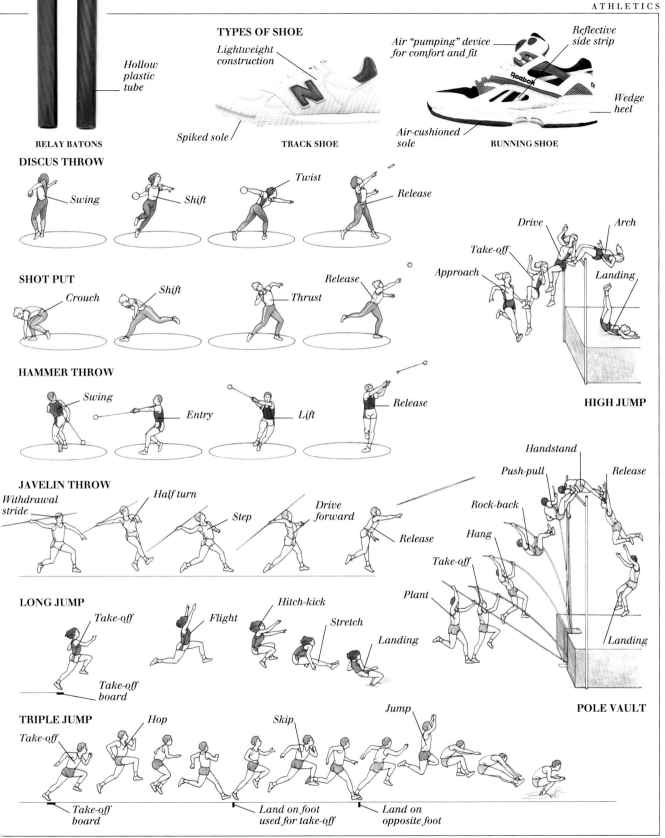

RELAY BATONS

Hollow plastic tube

TYPES OF SHOE

Lightweight construction

Spiked sole

TRACK SHOE

Air "pumping" device for comfort and fit

Reflective side strip

Wedge heel

Air-cushioned sole

RUNNING SHOE

DISCUS THROW

Swing

Shift

Twist

Release

SHOT PUT

Crouch

Shift

Thrust

Release

HAMMER THROW

Swing

Entry

Lift

Release

JAVELIN THROW

Withdrawal stride

Half turn

Step

Drive forward

Release

HIGH JUMP

Drive

Arch

Take-off

Approach

Landing

LONG JUMP

Take-off

Flight

Hitch-kick

Stretch

Landing

Take-off board

POLE VAULT

Handstand

Push-pull

Release

Rock-back

Hang

Take-off

Plant

Landing

TRIPLE JUMP

Hop

Skip

Jump

Take-off

Take-off board

Land on foot used for take-off

Land on opposite foot

Racket sports

PROTECTIVE EYEWEAR

THE OBJECT OF ALL RACKET SPORTS is to make shots the opponent cannot return. Games are played by two players (singles) or four players (doubles). Racket shape and size is tailored to each sport, but all rackets are constructed of wood, plastic, aluminium, or high-performance materials such as fibreglass and carbon graphite. Racket strings are usually synthetic, although natural gut is still used. Tennis is played on a court divided by a low net. Opposing players serve alternate games. At least six games must be won to gain a set, and two or sometimes three sets are needed to win a match. Tennis courts may be concrete, grass, clay, or synthetic, each surface requiring a different style of play. Badminton is an indoor sport that is played with light, flexible rackets and a feather shuttlecock on a court with a high net. Players can score points only on their serve. The first to reach 15 points (11 points for women's singles) wins the game. Two games are needed to win a match. Squash and racketball are both played in enclosed courts. One player hits the ball against the front wall, and the other tries to return it before it bounces on the floor more than once. Squash rackets have smaller, rounder heads and stiffer frames than badminton rackets. In America, the game is played on a narrower court than an international court using a much harder ball. Squash games are played to nine points (international) or 15 points (American). In racketball, players use a ball that is larger and bouncier than a squash ball. The racket is thick and sturdy, with a large head, short handle, and a thong that loops around the wrist. Points can be won only when serving, and the first player to reach 21 points wins.

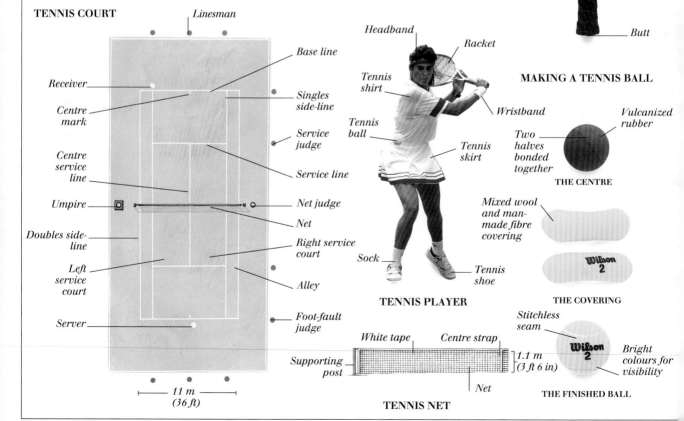

TENNIS RACKET

- Synthetic string
- Frame
- Head
- Logo
- Throat
- Grip
- Butt

TENNIS COURT

- Linesman
- Base line
- Receiver
- Singles side-line
- Centre mark
- Service judge
- Centre service line
- Service line
- Umpire
- Net judge
- Net
- Doubles side-line
- Right service court
- Left service court
- Alley
- Server
- Foot-fault judge

11 m (36 ft)

TENNIS PLAYER

- Headband
- Racket
- Tennis shirt
- Wristband
- Tennis ball
- Tennis skirt
- Sock
- Tennis shoe

TENNIS NET

- White tape
- Centre strap
- Supporting post
- Net
- 1.1 m (3 ft 6 in)

MAKING A TENNIS BALL

- Vulcanized rubber
- Two halves bonded together

THE CENTRE

- Mixed wool and man-made fibre covering

THE COVERING

- Stitchless seam
- Bright colours for visibility

THE FINISHED BALL

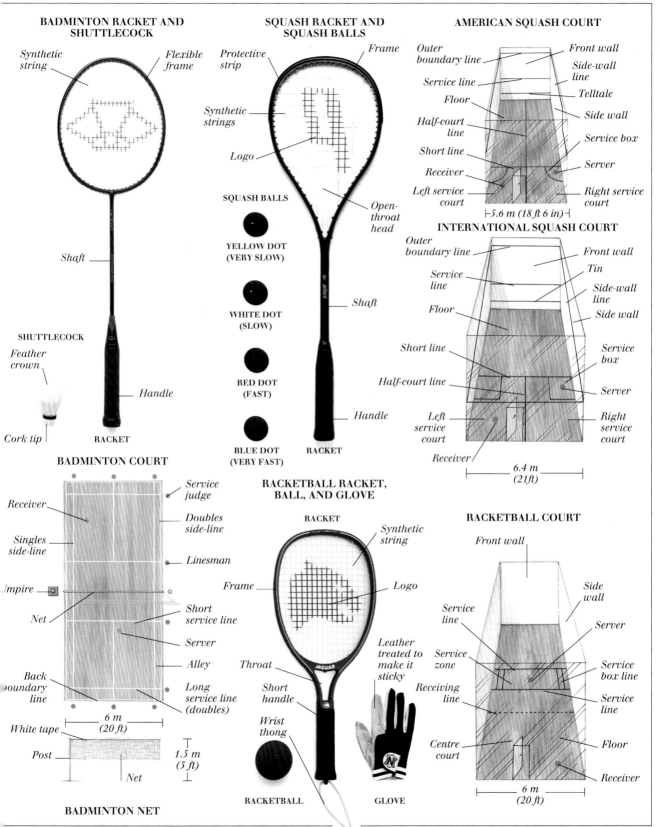

BADMINTON RACKET AND SHUTTLECOCK

Synthetic string

Flexible frame

Shaft

SHUTTLECOCK

Feather crown

Handle

Cork tip

RACKET

SQUASH RACKET AND SQUASH BALLS

Protective strip

Frame

Synthetic strings

Logo

Open-throat head

Shaft

Handle

RACKET

SQUASH BALLS

YELLOW DOT (VERY SLOW)

WHITE DOT (SLOW)

RED DOT (FAST)

BLUE DOT (VERY FAST)

AMERICAN SQUASH COURT

Outer boundary line

Front wall

Service line

Side-wall line

Floor

Telltale

Half-court line

Side wall

Short line

Service box

Receiver

Server

Left service court

Right service court

⊢5.6 m (18 ft 6 in)⊣

INTERNATIONAL SQUASH COURT

Outer boundary line

Front wall

Service line

Tin

Floor

Side-wall line

Side wall

Short line

Service box

Half-court line

Server

Left service court

Right service court

Receiver

6.4 m (21ft)

BADMINTON COURT

Receiver

Service judge

Singles side-line

Doubles side-line

Umpire

Linesman

Net

Short service line

Server

Alley

Back boundary line

Long service line (doubles)

6 m (20 ft)

White tape

1.5 m (5 ft)

Post

Net

BADMINTON NET

RACKETBALL RACKET, BALL, AND GLOVE

RACKET

Synthetic string

Frame

Logo

Leather treated to make it sticky

Throat

Short handle

Wrist thong

RACKETBALL

GLOVE

RACKETBALL COURT

Front wall

Side wall

Service line

Server

Service zone

Service box line

Receiving line

Service line

Centre court

Floor

Receiver

6 m (20 ft)

545

Golf

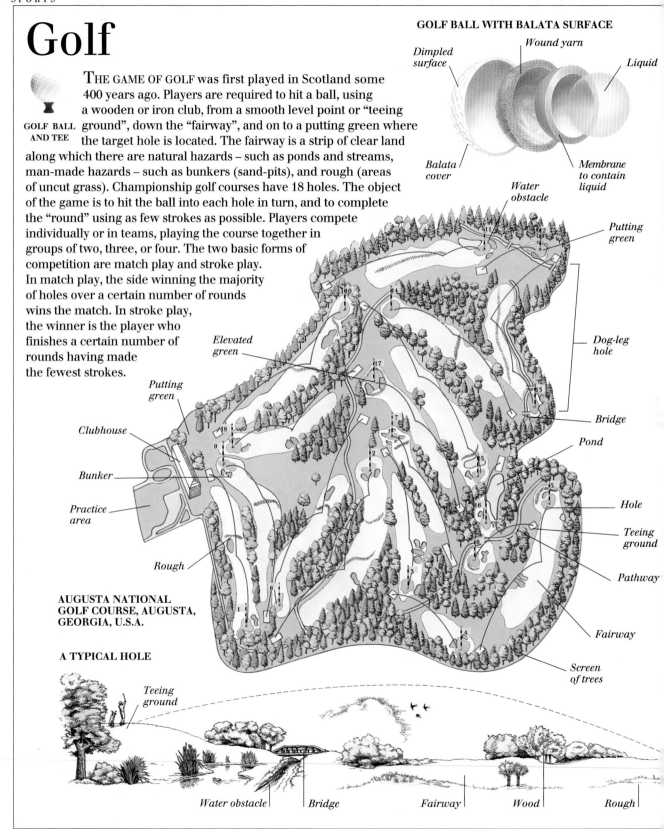

GOLF BALL AND TEE

THE GAME OF GOLF was first played in Scotland some 400 years ago. Players are required to hit a ball, using a wooden or iron club, from a smooth level point or "teeing ground", down the "fairway", and on to a putting green where the target hole is located. The fairway is a strip of clear land along which there are natural hazards – such as ponds and streams, man-made hazards – such as bunkers (sand-pits), and rough (areas of uncut grass). Championship golf courses have 18 holes. The object of the game is to hit the ball into each hole in turn, and to complete the "round" using as few strokes as possible. Players compete individually or in teams, playing the course together in groups of two, three, or four. The two basic forms of competition are match play and stroke play. In match play, the side winning the majority of holes over a certain number of rounds wins the match. In stroke play, the winner is the player who finishes a certain number of rounds having made the fewest strokes.

GOLF BALL WITH BALATA SURFACE

Dimpled surface

Wound yarn

Liquid

Balata cover

Membrane to contain liquid

Water obstacle

Putting green

Elevated green

Dog-leg hole

Putting green

Bridge

Clubhouse

Pond

Bunker

Hole

Practice area

Teeing ground

Rough

Pathway

AUGUSTA NATIONAL GOLF COURSE, AUGUSTA, GEORGIA, U.S.A.

Fairway

Screen of trees

A TYPICAL HOLE

Teeing ground

Water obstacle | Bridge | Fairway | Wood | Rough

MAKING A WOODEN CLUB

Close grain of wood

Streamlined back

Plastic insert on face

Sand, stain, and varnish finish

Persimmon wood

Slot cut for plate

Metal sole plate protects the wood

Outline of head

RAW MATERIAL

CREATING THE BASIC SHAPE

ADDING THE LEAD WEIGHT

THE FINISHED CLUB HEAD

PUTTER, WOOD, AND IRON

WOOD

Textured vulcanized rubber grip

IRON

PUTTER

Shaped pistol grip

RANGE OF WOODEN CLUBS

10 degree loft — **DRIVER**

15 degree loft — **3-WOOD**

21 degree loft — **5-WOOD**

RANGE OF IRON CLUBS

22 degree loft — **3-IRON**

26 degree loft — **4-IRON**

30 degree loft — **5-IRON**

34 degree loft — **6-IRON**

38 degree loft — **7-IRON**

42 degree loft — **8-IRON**

46 degree loft — **9-IRON**

50 degree loft — **PITCHING WEDGE**

56 degree loft — **SAND WEDGE**

GOLF ACCESSORIES

GOLF SCORE RECORD

BALL MARKERS

SCORECARD AND PENCIL

TEE PEGS

PITCHMARK REPAIRER

PRACTICE BALL

Spiked sole

LIGHTWEIGHT SHOE

Flag pole or pin

Green

Bunker (sand-pit)

Stainless steel shaft

Steel shaft

Steel shaft

84 cm (33 in)

94 cm (37 in)

109 cm (43 in)

Neck

Neck

Face

Angled neck

Heel

Heel

Toe

Toe

Blade

Toe

Groove

Sole

Heel

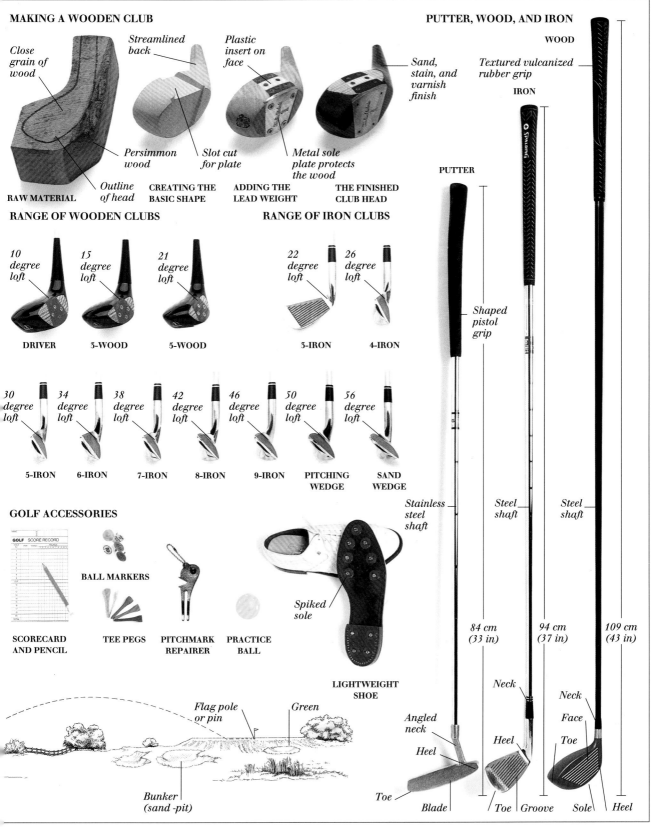

547

Archery and shooting

TARGET SHOOTING AND ARCHERY EVOLVED as practice for hunting and battle skills. Modern bows, although designed according to the principles of early hunting bows, use laminates, fibreglass, dacron, and carbon, and are equipped with sights and stabilizers. Competitors in target archery shoot over distances of 30 m (100 ft), 50 m (165 ft), 70 m (230 ft), and 90 m (300 ft) for men, and 30 m (100 ft), 50 m (165 ft), 60 m (200 ft), and 70 m (230 ft) for women. The closer the shot is to the centre of the target, the higher the score. The individual scores are added up, and the archer with the highest total wins the competition. Crossbows are used in match competitions over 10 m (33 ft), and 30 m (100 ft). Rifle shooting is divided into three categories: smallbore, bigbore, and air rifle. Contests take place over a variety of distances and further subdivisions are based on the type of shooting position used: prone, kneeling, or standing. The Olympic biathlon combines cross-country skiing and rifle shooting over a course of approximately 20 km (12½ miles). Additional magazines of ammunition are carried in the butt of the rifles. Bigbore rifles fitted with a telescopic sight can be used for hunting and running game target shooting. Pistol shooting events, using rapid-fire pistols, target pistols, and air pistols, take place over 10 m (33 ft), 25 m (82 ft), and 50 m (165 ft) distances. In rapid-fire pistol shooting, a total of 60 shots are fired from a distance of 25 m (83 ft).

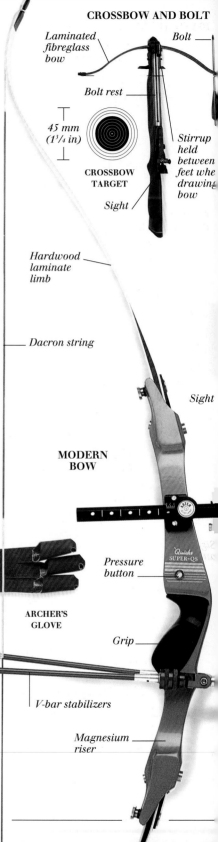

CROSSBOW AND BOLT

Laminated fibreglass bow

Bolt

Bolt rest

45 mm (1¼ in)

Stirrup held between feet whe drawing bow

CROSSBOW TARGET

Sight

Hardwood laminate limb

Dacron string

Sight

MODERN BOW

Pressure button

Grip

V-bar stabilizers

Magnesium riser

SUPER-QS

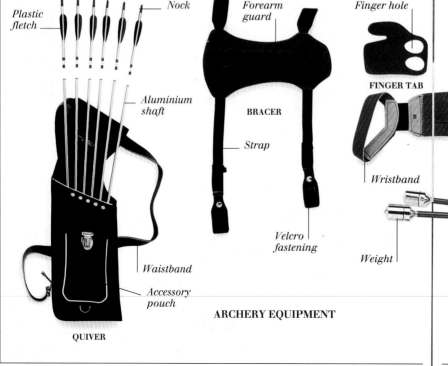

Plastic fletch

Nock

Forearm guard

Finger hole

Aluminium shaft

BRACER

Strap

FINGER TAB

ARCHER'S GLOVE

Wristband

Weight

Velcro fastening

Waistband

Accessory pouch

ARCHERY EQUIPMENT

QUIVER

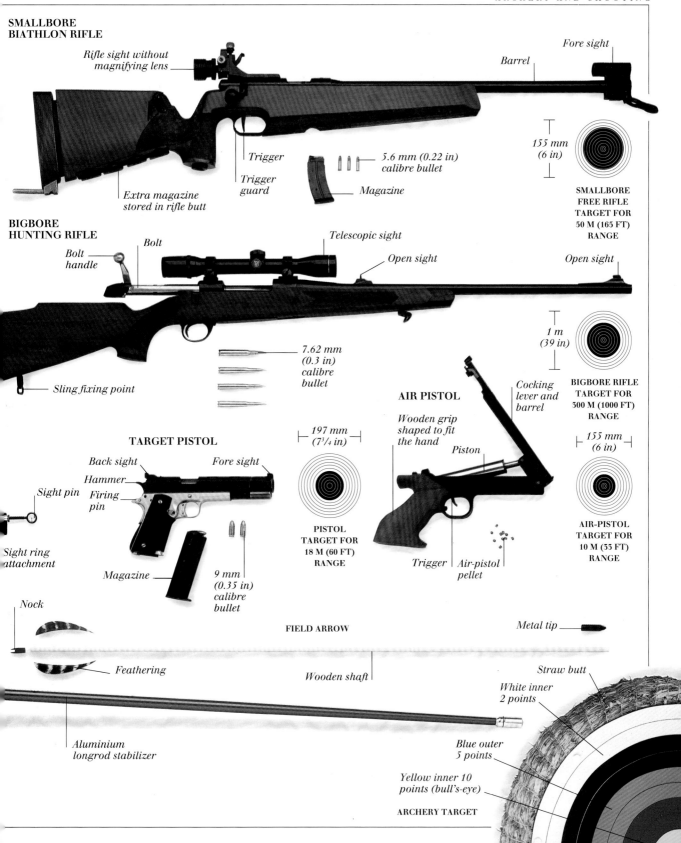

SMALLBORE BIATHLON RIFLE

Rifle sight without magnifying lens

Fore sight

Barrel

Trigger

5.6 mm (0.22 in) calibre bullet

Trigger guard

Magazine

Extra magazine stored in rifle butt

155 mm (6 in)

SMALLBORE FREE RIFLE TARGET FOR 50 M (165 FT) RANGE

BIGBORE HUNTING RIFLE

Bolt handle

Bolt

Telescopic sight

Open sight

Open sight

7.62 mm (0.3 in) calibre bullet

Sling fixing point

1 m (39 in)

BIGBORE RIFLE TARGET FOR 300 M (1000 FT) RANGE

AIR PISTOL

Wooden grip shaped to fit the hand

Cocking lever and barrel

155 mm (6 in)

TARGET PISTOL

Back sight

Fore sight

Hammer

Piston

Firing pin

Sight pin

Sight ring attachment

Magazine

9 mm (0.35 in) calibre bullet

197 mm (7¼ in)

PISTOL TARGET FOR 18 M (60 FT) RANGE

Trigger

Air-pistol pellet

AIR-PISTOL TARGET FOR 10 M (33 FT) RANGE

Nock

FIELD ARROW

Metal tip

Feathering

Wooden shaft

Straw butt

White inner 2 points

Aluminium longrod stabilizer

Blue outer 5 points

Yellow inner 10 points (bull's-eye)

ARCHERY TARGET

Ice hockey

ICE HOCKEY IS PLAYED by two teams of six players on an ice rink, with a goal net at each end. The object of this fast, and often dangerous, game is to hit a frozen rubber puck into the opposing team's net with a ice hockey stick. The game begins when the referee drops the puck between the sticks of two players from opposing teams, who "face off". The rink is divided into three areas: defending, neutral, and attacking zones. Players may move with the puck and pass the puck to one another along the ice, but may not pass it more than two zones across the rink markings. A goal is scored when the puck entirely crosses the goal-line between the posts and under the crossbar of the goal. A team may field up to 20 players although only six players are allowed on the ice at one time; substitutions occur frequently. Each game consists of three periods of 20 minutes, divided by breaks of 15 minutes.

GOALKEEPER

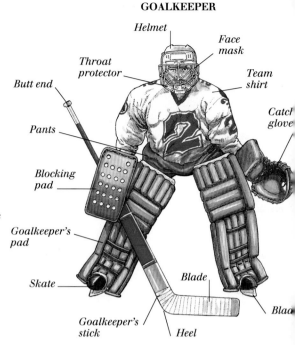

Helmet

Face mask

Throat protector

Team shirt

Butt end

Catch glove

Pants

Blocking pad

Goalkeeper's pad

Blade

Skate

Blade

Goalkeeper's stick

Heel

ICE HOCKEY RINK

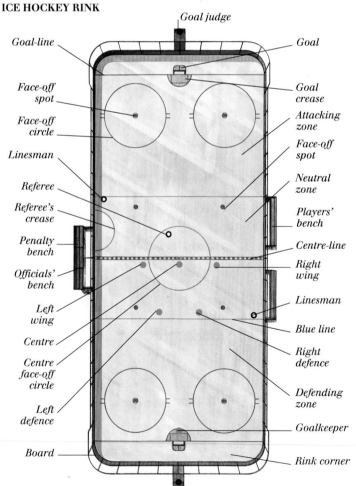

Goal judge

Goal-line

Goal

Face-off spot

Goal crease

Face-off circle

Attacking zone

Linesman

Face-off spot

Referee

Neutral zone

Referee's crease

Players' bench

Penalty bench

Centre-line

Officials' bench

Right wing

Left wing

Linesman

Centre

Blue line

Centre face-off circle

Right defence

Left defence

Defending zone

Board

Goalkeeper

Rink corner

|— 26–30 m (85–100 ft) —|

THE FACE-OFF

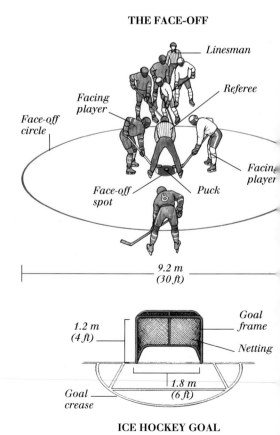

Linesman

Facing player

Referee

Face-off circle

Facing player

Face-off spot

Puck

9.2 m (30 ft)

Goal frame

1.2 m (4 ft)

Netting

1.8 m (6 ft)

Goal crease

ICE HOCKEY GOAL

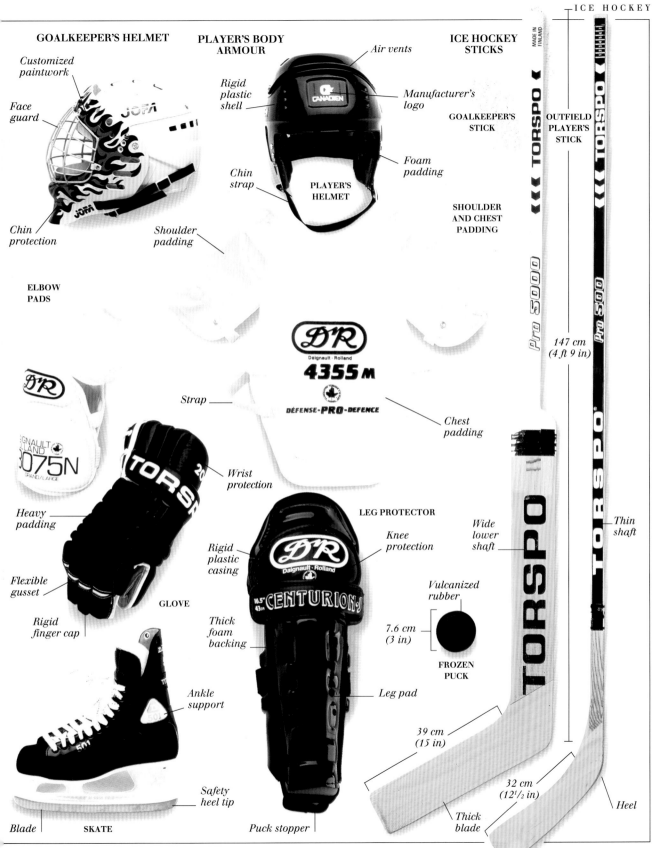

GOALKEEPER'S HELMET

Customized paintwork

Face guard

JOFA

Chin protection

JOFA

PLAYER'S BODY ARMOUR

Rigid plastic shell

Air vents

CANADIEN

Manufacturer's logo

Chin strap

Foam padding

PLAYER'S HELMET

Shoulder padding

ELBOW PADS

ICE HOCKEY STICKS

GOALKEEPER'S STICK

SHOULDER AND CHEST PADDING

MADE IN FINLAND

TORSPO

Pro 5000

OUTFIELD PLAYER'S STICK

TORSPO

Pro 500

147 cm (4 ft 9 in)

D'R Daignault · Rolland

4355 M

DÉFENSE · **PRO** · DEFENCE

Strap

Chest padding

DAIGNAULT ROLLAND

3075N

GRAND/LARGE

TORSPO 20

Wrist protection

Heavy padding

Flexible gusset

Rigid finger cap

GLOVE

LEG PROTECTOR

Rigid plastic casing

D'R Daignault · Rolland

Knee protection

16.5" 43cm **CENTURION-J**

Thick foam backing

Wide lower shaft

Vulcanized rubber

7.6 cm (3 in)

FROZEN PUCK

Thin shaft

TORSPO

TORSPO

Ankle support

502

5M1

Leg pad

39 cm (15 in)

32 cm (12½ in)

Safety heel tip

Heel

Blade **SKATE**

Puck stopper

Thick blade

Alpine skiing

COMPETITIVE ALPINE SKIING is divided into four disciplines: downhill, slalom, giant slalom, and super-giant slalom (Super-G). Each one tests different skills. In downhill skiing, competitors race down a slope marked out by control flags, known as "gates", and are timed on a single run only. Competitors wear crash helmets, one-piece Lycra suits, and long skis with flattened tips to minimize air resistance. Slalom and giant slalom skiers negotiate a twisting course requiring balance, agility, and quick reactions. Courses are defined by pairs of gates. Racers must pass through each pair of gates to complete the course successfully. Competitors are timed on two runs over different courses, and the skier who completes the courses in the shortest time wins. The equipment and protective guards used by slalom skiers are shown opposite. In Super-G races, competitors ski a single run that combines the technical challenge of slalom with the speed of downhill. The course requires skiers to complete medium-to-long radius turns at high speed, and contain up to two jumps. Clothing is the same as for downhill, but slightly shorter skis are used.

DOWNHILL SKIER

Ski goggles

Helmet

One-piece lycra ski suit

Wrist strap

Ski pole

Basket

Ski boot

Safety binding

Tail

Ski glo

ALPINE SKI SLOPE COURSES

Downhill start

Downhill racing control flag

Super-G start

Pine forest

Giant slalom start

Giant slalom gate

Slalom start

Slalom gate

Safety barrier

Finish line

Polyamide inner boot

Tongue

Upper cuff

Upper strap

Buckle

Energy-distributing bonnet

Power bar

Adjusting catch

Tension control

Sole

Lower shell of boot

Heel grip

SKI BOOT

Wing

Toe-piece

Anti-friction pad

Heel-piece

Blind release lever

Housing

Release adjustment screw

Base plate

Brake arm

SAFETY BINDING

SLALOM CLOTHING AND EQUIPMENT

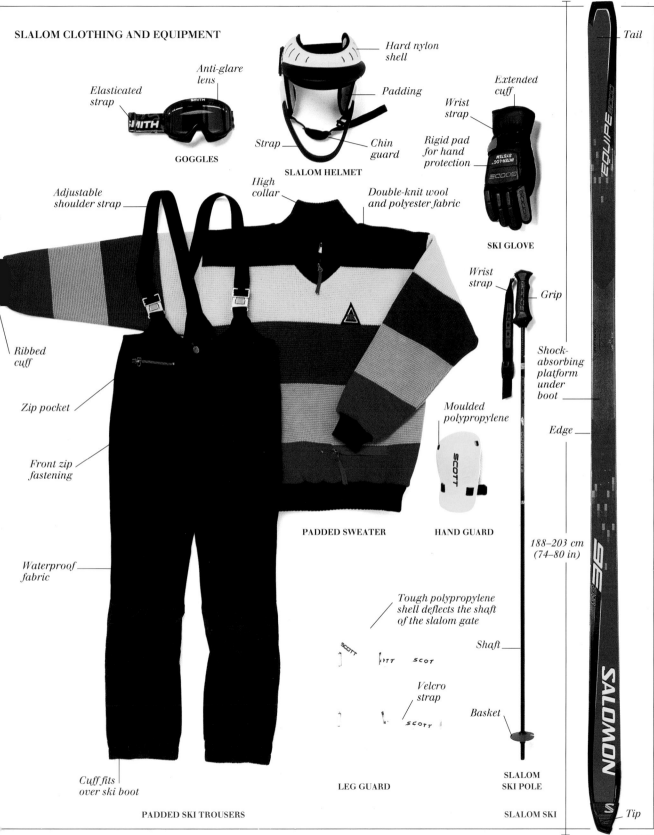

GOGGLES

Elasticated strap

Anti-glare lens

SLALOM HELMET

Hard nylon shell

Padding

Strap

Chin guard

SKI GLOVE

Extended cuff

Wrist strap

Rigid pad for hand protection

Double-knit wool and polyester fabric

High collar

Adjustable shoulder strap

Ribbed cuff

Zip pocket

Front zip fastening

Waterproof fabric

Cuff fits over ski boot

PADDED SKI TROUSERS

PADDED SWEATER

HAND GUARD

Moulded polypropylene

LEG GUARD

Tough polypropylene shell deflects the shaft of the slalom gate

Velcro strap

Wrist strap

Grip

Shock-absorbing platform under boot

Edge

188–203 cm (74–80 in)

Shaft

Basket

SLALOM SKI POLE

Tail

SLALOM SKI

Tip

553

Equestrian sports

EQUESTRIAN SPORTS HAVE TAKEN place throughout the world for centuries: events involving mounted horses were recorded in the Olympic Games of 642 BC. Showjumping, however, is a much more recent innovation, and the first competitions were held at the beginning of the 1900s. In this sport, horse and rider must negotiate a course of variable, unfixed obstacles, making as few mistakes as possible. Showjumping fences consist of wooden stands, known as standards or wings, that support planks or poles. Parts of the fence are designed to collapse on impact, preventing injury to the horse and rider. Judges penalise competitors for errors, such as knocking down obstacles, refusing jumps, or deviating from the course. Depending on the type of competition, the rider with the fewest faults, most points, or fastest time wins. There are two basic forms of horse racing – flat races and races with jumps, such as steeplechase or hurdle-races. Thoroughbred horses are used in this sport, as they have great strength and stamina and can achieve speeds of up to 65 kph (40 mph). Jockeys wear "silks" – caps and jackets designed in distinctive colours and patterns which help identify the horses. In harness racing, the horse is driven from a light, two-wheeled carriage called a sulky. Horses are trained to trot and to pace, and different races are held for each of these types of gait. In pacing races, the horses wear hobbles to prevent them from breaking into a trot or gallop. Breeds such as the Standardbred and the French Trotter have been developed especially for this sport.

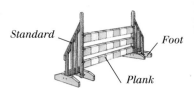

SHOWJUMPING SADDLE

High cantle

Deep seat

Pommel

Forward-cut flap

Knee roll

SHOWJUMPING FENCES

Standard

Foot

Plank

UPRIGHT PLANKS

Standard

Foot

Pole

UPRIGHT POLES

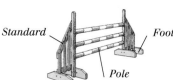

Back pole

Standard

Foot

Pole

TRIPLE BAR (STAIRCASE)

Standard

Pole

Foot

HOG'S-BACK

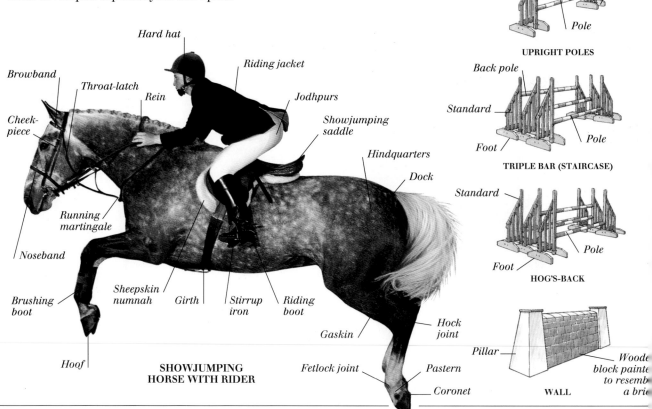

Hard hat

Riding jacket

Browband

Throat-latch

Rein

Jodhpurs

Cheek-piece

Showjumping saddle

Hindquarters

Dock

Running martingale

Noseband

Brushing boot

Sheepskin numnah

Girth

Stirrup iron

Riding boot

Hock joint

Gaskin

Hoof

SHOWJUMPING HORSE WITH RIDER

Fetlock joint

Pastern

Coronet

Pillar

Wooden block painted to resemble a brick

WALL

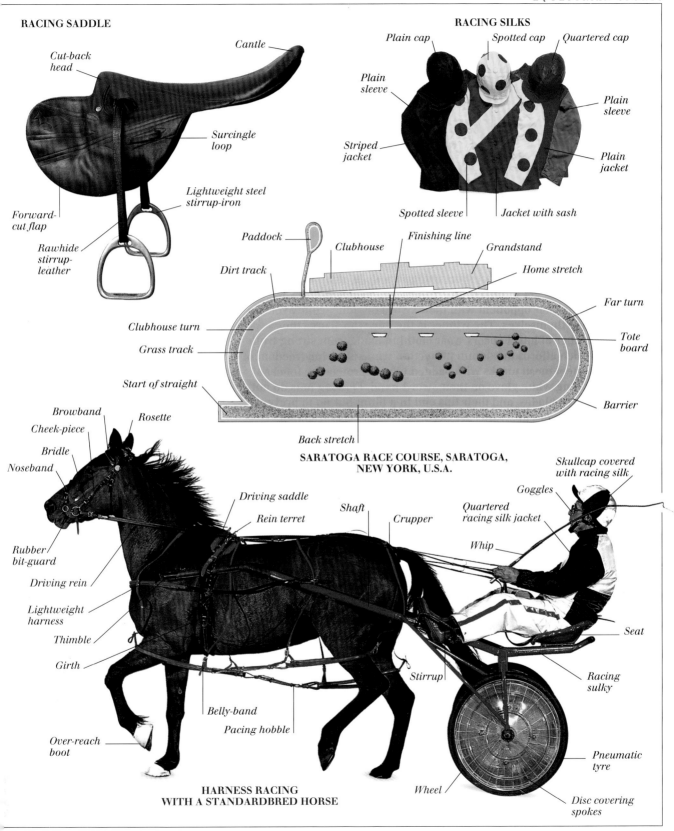

RACING SADDLE

Cut-back head

Cantle

Surcingle loop

Lightweight steel stirrup-iron

Forward-cut flap

Rawhide stirrup-leather

RACING SILKS

Plain cap

Spotted cap

Quartered cap

Plain sleeve

Plain sleeve

Striped jacket

Plain jacket

Spotted sleeve

Jacket with sash

Paddock

Clubhouse

Finishing line

Grandstand

Dirt track

Home stretch

Far turn

Clubhouse turn

Grass track

Tote board

Start of straight

Barrier

Back stretch

SARATOGA RACE COURSE, SARATOGA, NEW YORK, U.S.A.

Browband

Rosette

Cheek-piece

Bridle

Noseband

Rubber bit-guard

Driving rein

Lightweight harness

Thimble

Girth

Over-reach boot

Driving saddle

Rein terret

Shaft

Crupper

Skullcap covered with racing silk

Goggles

Quartered racing silk jacket

Whip

Seat

Stirrup

Racing sulky

Belly-band

Pacing hobble

Pneumatic tyre

Wheel

Disc covering spokes

HARNESS RACING WITH A STANDARDBRED HORSE

Judo and fencing

COMBAT SPORTS ARE BASED ON THE SKILLS used in fighting. In these sports, the competitors may be unarmed – as in judo and boxing – or armed – as in fencing and kendo. Judo is a system of unarmed combat developed in the East. Translated from the Japanese the name means "the gentle way". Students learn how to turn an opponent's force to their own advantage. The usual costume is loose white trousers and a jacket, fastened with a cloth belt. The colour of belt indicates the student's level of expertise, from white-belted novices to the expert "black belts". Competitions take place on a mat or "shiaijo", 9 or 10 m (30 or 33 ft) square in size, bounded by "danger" and "safety" areas to prevent injury. Competitors try to throw, pin, or master their opponent by applying pressure to the arm joints or neck. Judo bouts are strictly monitored, and competitors receive points for superior technique, not for injuring their opponent. Fencing is a combat sport using swords, which takes place on a narrow "piste" 14 m (46 ft) long. Competitors try to touch specific target areas on their opponent with their sword or "foil" while avoiding being touched themselves. The winner is the one who scores the greatest number of hits. Fencers wear clothing made from strong white material, which affords maximum protection while allowing freedom of movement, steel mesh masks with padded bibs to protect the fencer's neck, and a long white glove on their sword hand. Fencing foils do not have sharpened blades, and their tips end in a blunt button to prevent injuries. Three types of swords are used – foils, épées, and sabres. Official foil and épée competitions always use an electric scoring system. The sword tips are connected to lights by a long wire that passes underneath each fencer's jacket. A bulb flashes when a hit is made.

JUDO HOLDS AND THROWS

SIDE FOUR QUARTER HOLD

SINGLE WING

BODY DROP

ONE ARM SHOULDER THROW

SHOULDER WHEEL

SWEEPING LOW THROW

STOMACH THROW

KNEE WHEEL

JUDO MAT

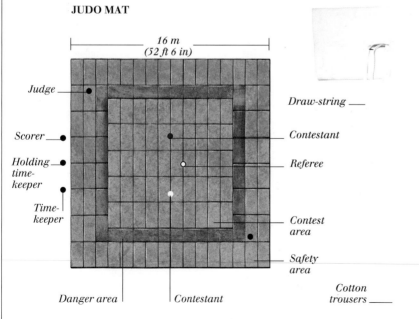

16 m
(52 ft 6 in)

Judge

Scorer

Holding time-keeper

Time-keeper

Danger area

Contestant

Draw-string

Contestant

Referee

Contest area

Safety area

JUDO KIT

Cotton trousers

Black belt

Heavy-duty cotton jacket

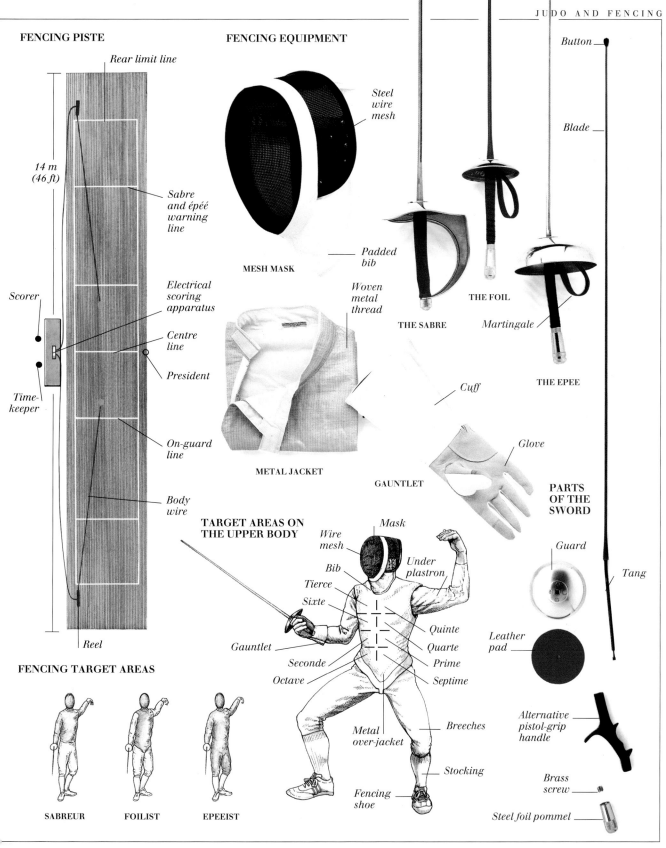

FENCING PISTE

Rear limit line

14 m
(46 ft)

Sabre
and épéé
warning
line

Scorer

Electrical
scoring
apparatus

Centre
line

President

Time-
keeper

On-guard
line

Body
wire

Reel

FENCING TARGET AREAS

SABREUR

FOILIST

EPEEIST

FENCING EQUIPMENT

Steel
wire
mesh

Padded
bib

MESH MASK

Woven
metal
thread

Cuff

METAL JACKET

GAUNTLET

Glove

**TARGET AREAS ON
THE UPPER BODY**

Mask

Wire
mesh

Bib

Tierce

Sixte

Under
plastron

Gauntlet

Seconde

Octave

Quinte

Quarte

Prime

Septime

Metal
over-jacket

Breeches

Stocking

Fencing
shoe

THE SABRE

THE FOIL

Martingale

THE EPEE

Button

Blade

Tang

Guard

**PARTS
OF THE
SWORD**

Leather
pad

Alternative
pistol-grip
handle

Brass
screw

Steel foil pommel

Swimming and diving

SWIMMING GOGGLES

SWIMMING WAS INCLUDED in the first modern Olympic Games in 1896 and diving events were added in 1904. Swimming is both an individual and a team sport and races take place over a predetermined distance in one of the four major categories of stroke – freestyle (usually front crawl), butterfly, breaststroke, and backstroke. Competition pools are clearly marked for racing and anti-turbulence lane lines are used to separate the swimmers and help keep the water calm. The first team or individual to finish the race is the winner. Competitive diving is divided into men's and women's springboard and platform (highboard) events. There are six official groups of dives: forward dives, backward dives, armstand dives, twist dives, reverse dives, and inward dives. Competitors perform a set number of dives and after each one a panel of judges awards marks according to the quality of execution and the degree of difficulty.

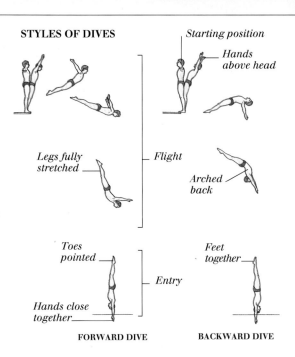

STYLES OF DIVES

Starting position

Hands above head

Legs fully stretched

Flight

Arched back

Toes pointed

Entry

Feet together

Hands close together

FORWARD DIVE

BACKWARD DIVE

SWIMWEAR

Latex rubber moulds to shape of head

CAPS

Rubber-covered wire

NOSE CLIP

Moulded rubber

EARPLUG

High neckline

Man-made stretch fabric

Drawstring

High-cut leg

Strong seam

SWIMSUIT

TRUNKS

SWIMMING POOL

Swimmer

Chief time-keeper

Lane number

Starting block

Lane time-keeper

End wall

Placing judge

Starter

Recorder

Side wall

Backstroke marker 15 m (49 ft) from end of pool

Anti-turbulence lane line

Referee

Stroke judge

Backstroke turn indicator 5 m (16 ft) from end of pool

Bottom line

Turning judge

Turning wall

Lane

23 m (75 ft 6 in)

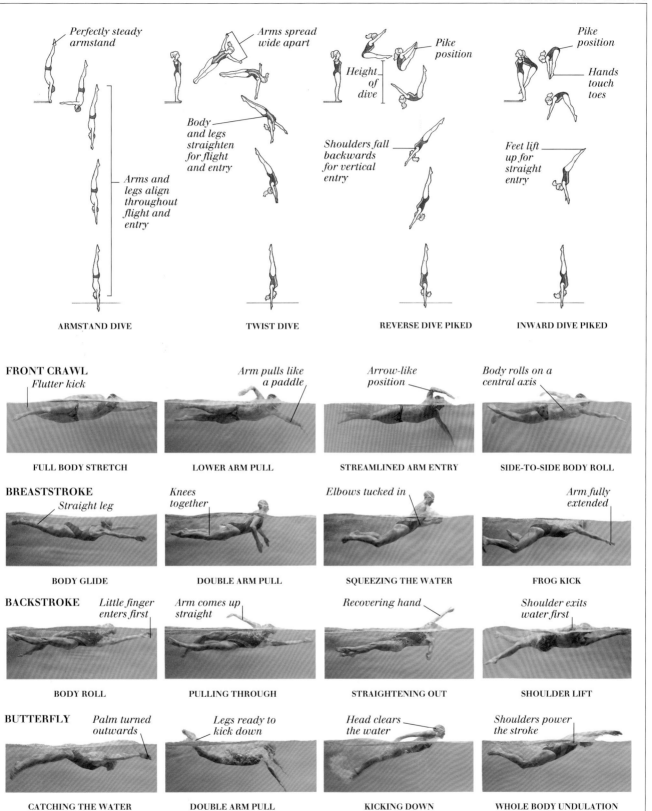

Perfectly steady armstand

Arms and legs align throughout flight and entry

ARMSTAND DIVE

Arms spread wide apart

Body and legs straighten for flight and entry

TWIST DIVE

Pike position

Height of dive

Shoulders fall backwards for vertical entry

REVERSE DIVE PIKED

Pike position

Hands touch toes

Feet lift up for straight entry

INWARD DIVE PIKED

FRONT CRAWL

Flutter kick

Arm pulls like a paddle

Arrow-like position

Body rolls on a central axis

FULL BODY STRETCH

LOWER ARM PULL

STREAMLINED ARM ENTRY

SIDE-TO-SIDE BODY ROLL

BREASTSTROKE

Straight leg

Knees together

Elbows tucked in

Arm fully extended

BODY GLIDE

DOUBLE ARM PULL

SQUEEZING THE WATER

FROG KICK

BACKSTROKE

Little finger enters first

Arm comes up straight

Recovering hand

Shoulder exits water first

BODY ROLL

PULLING THROUGH

STRAIGHTENING OUT

SHOULDER LIFT

BUTTERFLY

Palm turned outwards

Legs ready to kick down

Head clears the water

Shoulders power the stroke

CATCHING THE WATER

DOUBLE ARM PULL

KICKING DOWN

WHOLE BODY UNDULATION

Canoeing, rowing, and sailing

WATERBORNE SPORTS are as varied as the crafts used. There are two disciplines in rowing; sweep rowing, in which each rower has one oar and sculling, in which rowers use two oars. There are a number of different Olympic and competitive rowing events for both men and women. The number of rowers and weight classes vary. Some rowing events use a coxswain; a steersman who does not row but directs the crew. Kayaks and canoes are used in straight sprint and slalom races. Slalom races take place over a course consisting of 20 to 25 gates, including at least six upstream gates. In yacht racing, competitors must complete prescribed courses, organized by the race committees, in the shortest possible time, using sail power only. Olympic events include classes for keel boats, dinghies, and catamarans.

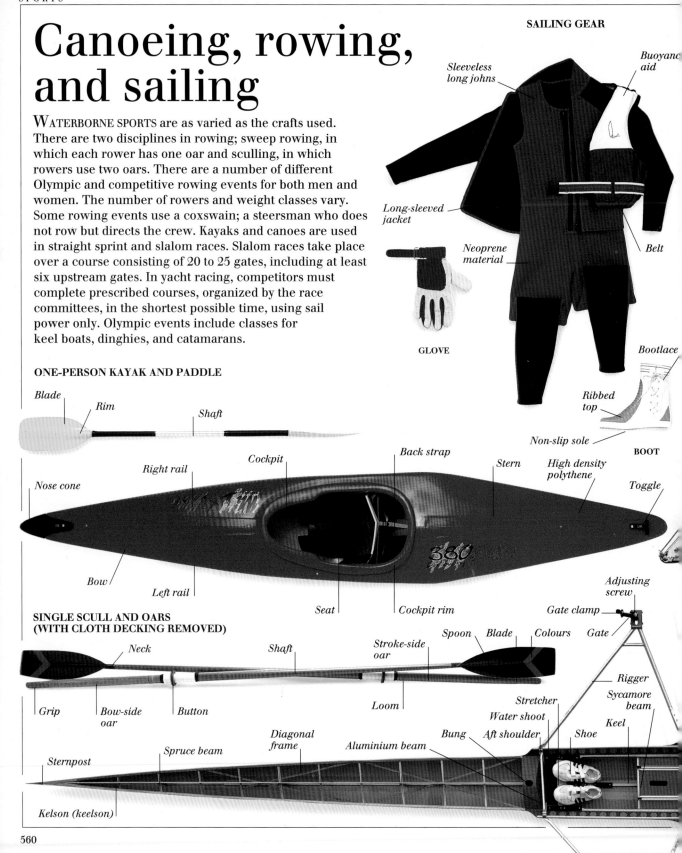

SAILING GEAR

Sleeveless long johns

Buoyancy aid

Long-sleeved jacket

Neoprene material

Belt

GLOVE

Bootlace

Ribbed top

Non-slip sole

BOOT

ONE-PERSON KAYAK AND PADDLE

Blade

Rim

Shaft

Nose cone

Right rail

Cockpit

Back strap

Stern

High density polythene

Toggle

Bow

Left rail

Seat

Cockpit rim

Adjusting screw

Gate clamp

Gate

**SINGLE SCULL AND OARS
(WITH CLOTH DECKING REMOVED)**

Neck

Shaft

Stroke-side oar

Spoon

Blade

Colours

Rigger

Grip

Bow-side oar

Button

Loom

Sycamore beam

Stretcher

Water shoot

Keel

Sternpost

Diagonal frame

Aluminium beam

Bung

Aft shoulder

Shoe

Spruce beam

Kelson (keelson)

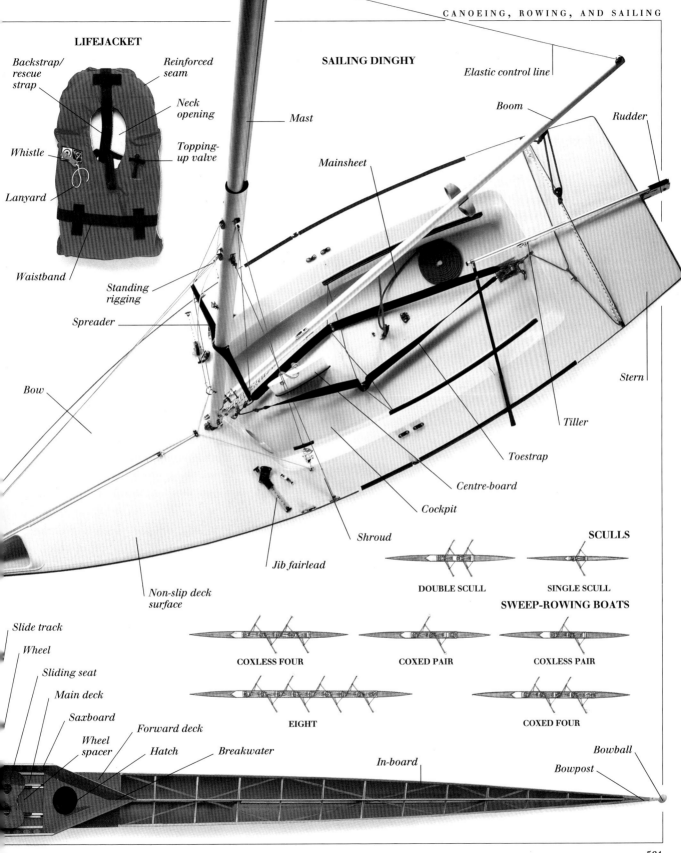

LIFEJACKET

Backstrap/
rescue
strap

Reinforced
seam

Neck
opening

Whistle

Topping-
up valve

Lanyard

Waistband

Standing
rigging

Spreader

Bow

SAILING DINGHY

Elastic control line

Boom

Rudder

Mast

Mainsheet

Tiller

Toestrap

Centre-board

Cockpit

Shroud

Jib fairlead

Non-slip deck
surface

Stern

SCULLS

DOUBLE SCULL

SINGLE SCULL

SWEEP-ROWING BOATS

COXLESS FOUR

COXED PAIR

COXLESS PAIR

EIGHT

COXED FOUR

Slide track

Wheel

Sliding seat

Main deck

Saxboard

Wheel
spacer

Forward deck

Hatch

Breakwater

In-board

Bowball

Bowpost

Angling

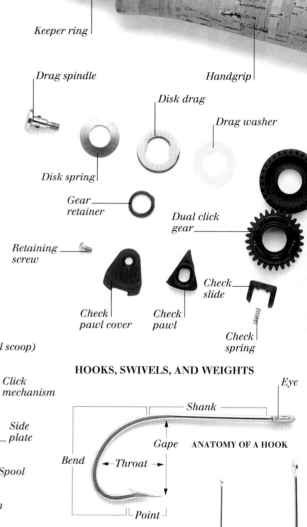

ANGLING MEANS FISHING WITH A ROD, reel, line, and lure. There are several different types of angling: freshwater coarse angling, for members of the carp family and pike; freshwater game angling, for salmon and trout; and sea angling, for sea fish such as flatfish, bass, and mackerel. Anglers use a variety of methods of catching fish. These include bait fishing, in which bait (food to allure the fish) is placed on a hook and cast into the water; fly fishing, in which a natural or artificial fly is used to lure the fish; and spinning, in which a lure that looks like a small fish revolves as it is pulled through the water. The angler uses the rod, reel, and line to cast the lure over the water. The reel controls the line as it spills off the spool and as it is wound back. Weights may be fixed to the line so that it will sink. Swivels are attached to prevent the line from twisting. When a fish bites, the hook must become embedded in its mouth and remain there while the catch is reeled in.

Keeper ring

Handgrip

Drag spindle

Disk drag

Drag washer

Disk spring

Gear retainer

Dual click gear

Retaining screw

Check slide

Check pawl cover

Check pawl

Check spring

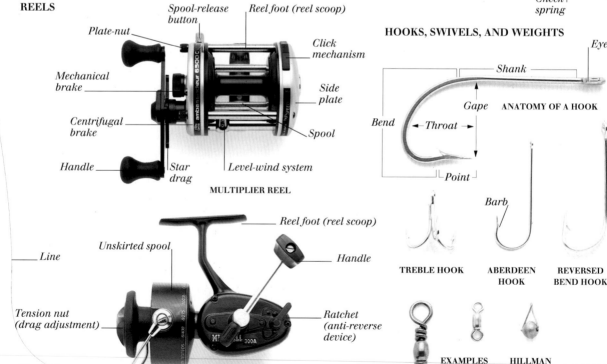

REELS

Spool-release button

Reel foot (reel scoop)

Plate-nut

Click mechanism

Mechanical brake

Side plate

Centrifugal brake

Spool

Handle

Star drag

Level-wind system

MULTIPLIER REEL

HOOKS, SWIVELS, AND WEIGHTS

Eye

Shank

Gape

ANATOMY OF A HOOK

Bend

Throat

Point

TREBLE HOOK

Barb

ABERDEEN HOOK

REVERSED BEND HOOK

Reel foot (reel scoop)

Unskirted spool

Handle

Line

Tension nut (drag adjustment)

Ratchet (anti-reverse device)

Handgrip

Reel

Bail arm

FIXED-SPOOL REEL

EXAMPLES OF BARREL SWIVELS

HILLMAN ANTI-KINK WEIGHT

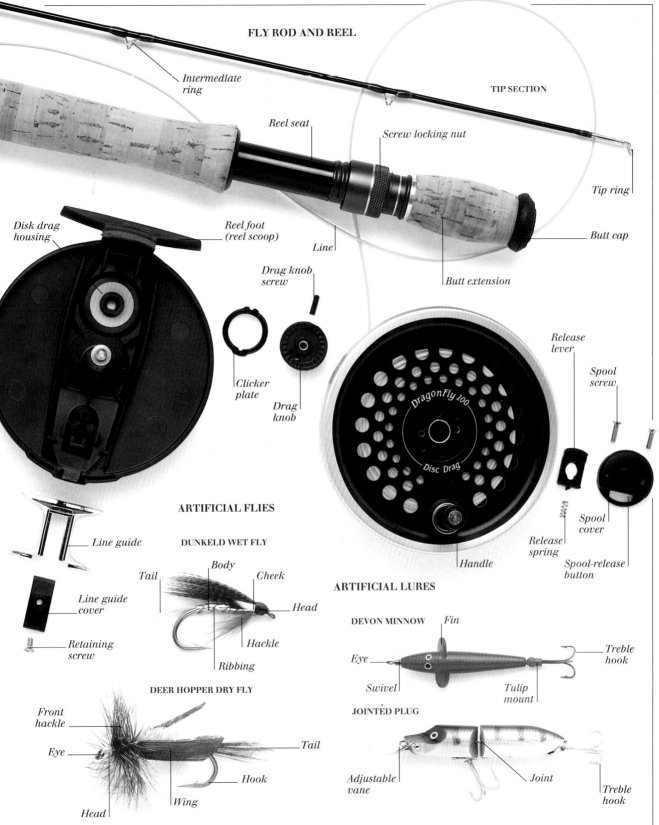

FLY ROD AND REEL

Intermedlate ring

TIP SECTION

Reel seat

Screw locking nut

Tip ring

Disk drag housing

Reel foot (reel scoop)

Butt cap

Line

Drag knob screw

Butt extension

Release lever

Spool screw

DragonFly 100

Disc Drag

Clicker plate

Drag knob

Release spring

Spool cover

Spool-release button

ARTIFICIAL FLIES

Line guide

Handle

DUNKELD WET FLY

Body

Tail

Cheek

Line guide cover

Head

ARTIFICIAL LURES

Hackle

Retaining screw

Ribbing

DEVON MINNOW

Fin

Treble hook

Eye

Swivel

Tulip mount

DEER HOPPER DRY FLY

JOINTED PLUG

Front hackle

Eye

Tail

Adjustable vane

Joint

Hook

Treble hook

Wing

Head

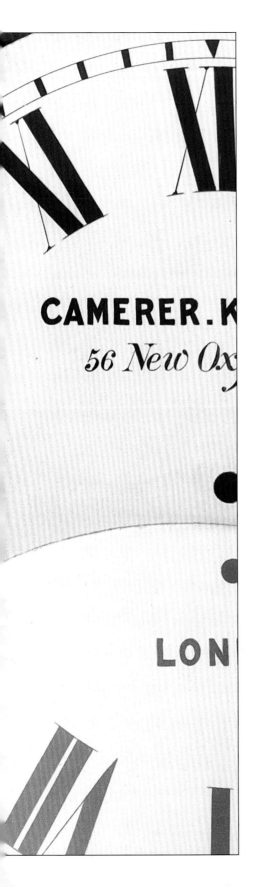

EVERYDAY THINGS

Drills

THE ELECTRICALLY POWERED MOTOR OF A POWER DRILL, cooled by a fan, turns a shaft at high speed. The shaft connects, in turn, to a system of gears that rotates a chuck even faster. Clamped by the chuck, a sharp bit cuts out the hole, and at the same time the bit's screw-shaped grooves channel the waste out of the hole. For drilling hard materials, many power drills have a hammer mechanism: when this is operated a ratchet in the gearcase causes the chuck and bit to pound in and out as they drill. A hand drill, although slower and less forceful than a power drill, is easier to control. For cutting wide holes, carpenters often prefer a brace-and-bit. This acts like a lever: the bowed handle of the brace moves a larger distance than the bit, turning the bit with extra force.

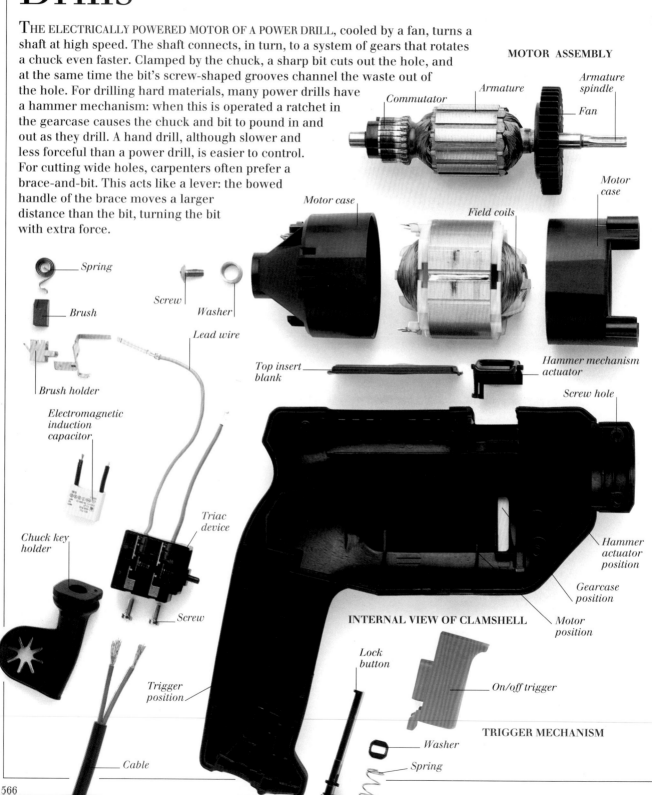

MOTOR ASSEMBLY

Commutator

Armature

Armature spindle

Fan

Motor case

Motor case

Field coils

Spring

Brush

Screw

Washer

Lead wire

Brush holder

Electromagnetic induction capacitor

Top insert blank

Hammer mechanism actuator

Screw hole

Chuck key holder

Triac device

Screw

Hammer actuator position

Gearcase position

INTERNAL VIEW OF CLAMSHELL

Motor position

Lock button

On/off trigger

Trigger position

Cable

Washer

Spring

TRIGGER MECHANISM

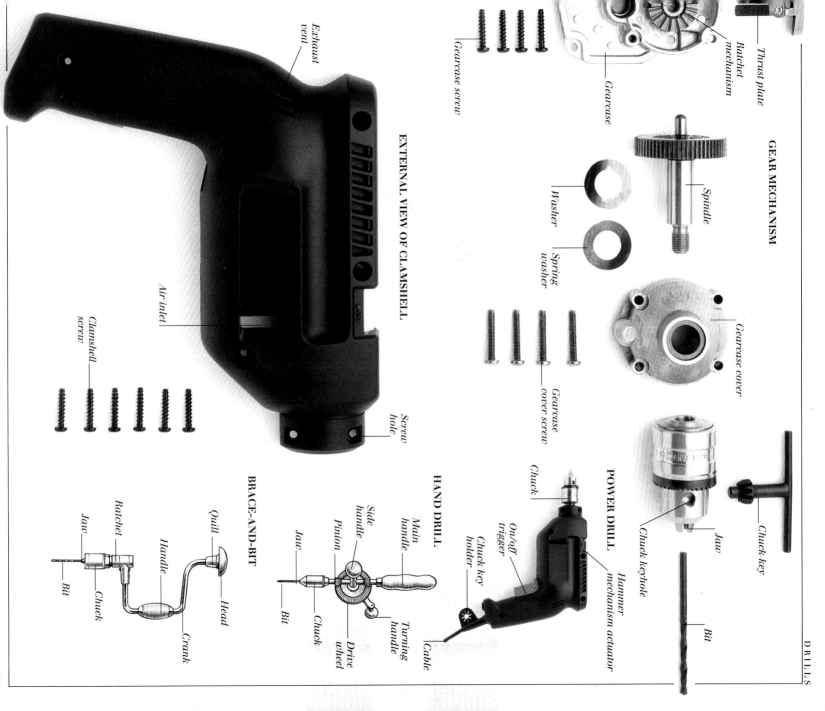

GEAR MECHANISM

Thrust plate

Ratchet mechanism

Gearcase

Gearcase screw

Spindle

Washer

Spring washer

Gearcase cover

Gearcase cover screw

Chuck

Jaw

Chuck key

Chuck keyhole

Bit

EXTERNAL VIEW OF CLAMSHELL

Exhaust vent

Air inlet

Clamshell screw

Screw hole

POWER DRILL

On/off trigger

Chuck key holder

Cable

Hammer mechanism actuator

HAND DRILL

Main handle

Side handle

Pinion

Jaw

Bit

Chuck

Drive wheel

Turning handle

BRACE-AND-BIT

Ratchet

Jaw

Bit

Chuck

Handle

Crank

Quill

Head

Shoes

WELL-MADE SHOES PROTECT THE FEET and are also comfortable and long-lasting. The best shoemakers use a wooden or plastic mould, called a last, which matches the shape of the customer's foot. The different parts of a shoe are stitched and glued together around the last; rivets and nails are used only in the heel, which is built up from layers of leather and rubber. The steel shank gives support to the arch of the foot and, with the seat lift, helps the wearer maintain posture. The layers of the sole give strength, while the soft insole cushions the foot. The leather welt sewn between the leather uppers and the sole ensures a strong join.

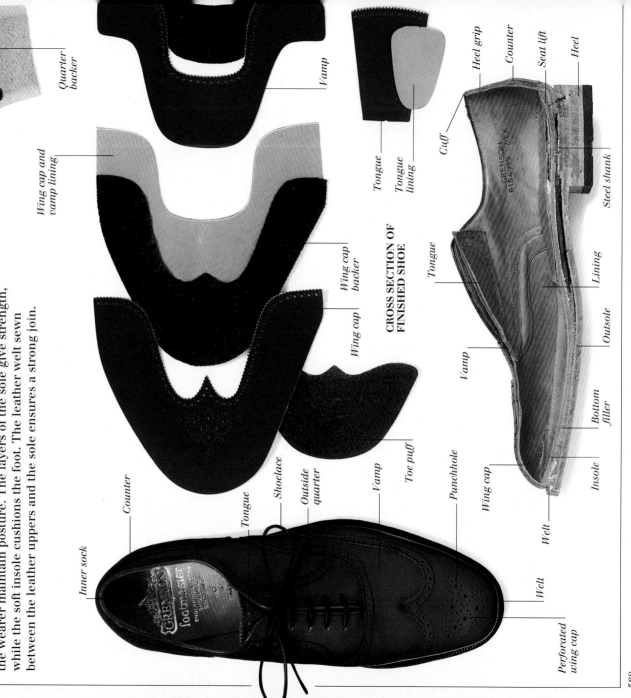

Inside quarter

Quarter lining

Quarter backer

Vamp

Wing cap and vamp lining

Wing cap backer

Wing cap

Tongue

Tongue lining

CROSS SECTION OF FINISHED SHOE

Heel grip

Counter

Seat lift

Heel

Cuff

Tongue

Steel shank

Lining

Vamp

Outsole

Bottom filler

Wing cap

Insole

Welt

Inner sock

Counter

Tongue

Shoelace

Outside quarter

Vamp

Toe puff

Punchhole

Welt

Perforated wing cap

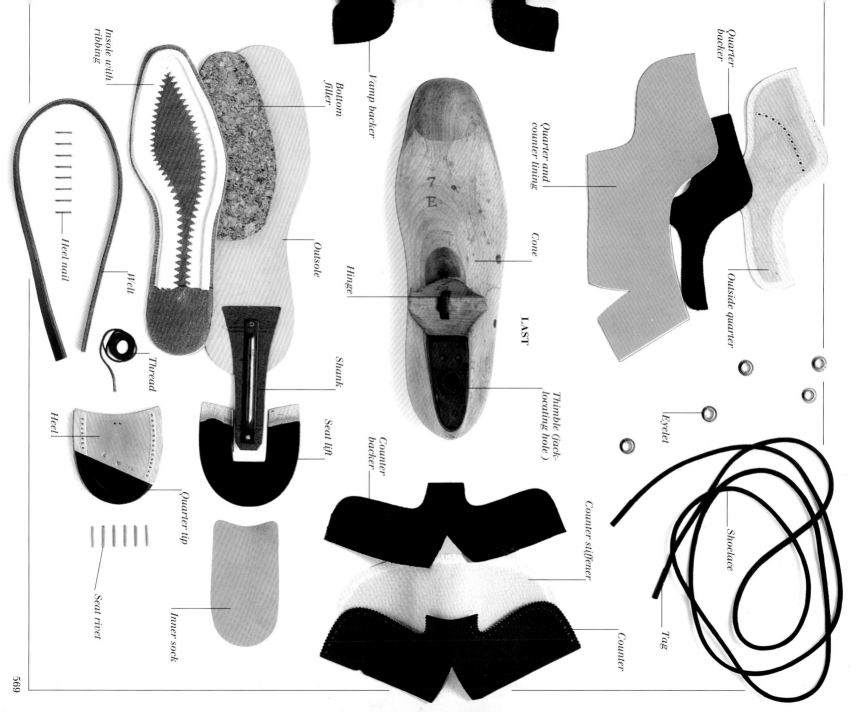

Insole with
ribbing

Bottom
filler

Vamp backer

Quarter
backer

Quarter and
counter lining

Heel nail

Well

Outside quarter

Outsole

Cone

Thread

Hinge

LAST

Heel

Shank

Thimble (Jack-
locating hole)

Seat lift

Counter
backer

Quarter tip

Seat rivet

Inner sock

Counter stiffener

Shoelace

Counter

Tag

Eyelet

569

Clock

MECHANICAL CLOCKS HAVE TWO essential elements: a mainspring and a pendulum. When the clock is wound with the key, the mainspring is tightened. As the mainspring unwinds, it turns the gears, which move the minute and hour hands at different speeds around the face of the clock. The pendulum ensures that the hands move at a regular pace. At the top of the pendulum are two hooks called pallets. As the pendulum swings, the pallets allow the escape wheel to turn slowly and evenly.

CLOCK CASE

Steady pin hole

Screw hole

Pallet arbour position

Barrel pivot hole

Wooden peg

Fusee pivot hole

Pillar

CLOCK TRAIN

Pallet screw

Pallet

Pallet cock screw

Pallet cock

Pallet arbour

Escape wheel

Crutch

Pinion

Third wheel

Pinion

Pinion

Centre wheel

Fusee

Fusee chain

FRONT PLATE

Pivot hole

Fusee stop

Tension spring

Fusee stop screw

Tension spring screw

PENDULUM ASSEMBLY

Ratchet pawl

Click wheel

Ratchet screw

Winding key

Barrel arbour hook

Mainspring barrel arbour

Crutch screw

Suspension spring

Mainspring barrel cap

Mainspring barrel

Pendulum rod

Mainspring barrel

Lenticular bob

Rating nut

Mainspring

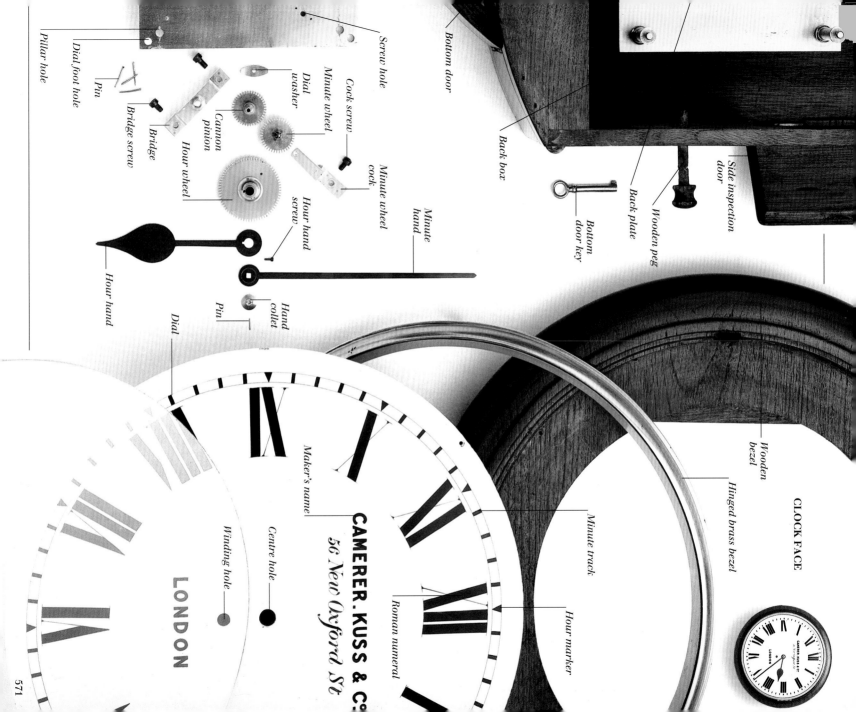

Screw hole

Bottom door

Cock screw

Dial washer

Minute wheel

Cannon pinion

Hour wheel

Minute wheel cock

Hour hand screw

Minute hand

Back box

Side inspection door

Wooden peg

Back plate

Bottom door key

Pillar hole

Dial foot hole

Pin

Bridge screw

Bridge

Hour hand

Dial

Pin

Hand collet

Wooden bezel

Hinged brass bezel

CLOCK FACE

Maker's name

CAMERER. KUSS & Cº
56 New Oxford St

LONDON

Winding hole

Centre hole

Dial

Minute track

Hour marker

Roman numeral

Lamp

THE FIRST SPRING-TENSIONED, adjustable work lamp was designed in 1934 by George Carwardine. This type of lamp imitates the human arm in the way that it can be kept in a fixed position or moved easily and precisely. In the arm, such control is achieved by coordinating the opposing action of paired muscles (e.g., when the biceps contracts, the triceps relaxes and the arm bends). In the work lamp, one muscle of a pair is represented by the springs that pull on the rigid bars of the lamp; the other muscle is represented by the nuts, bolts, screws, and washers in the lamp's joints that resist the pull of the springs. By balancing the pull of the springs against the resistance in the joints, the lamp's height and angle can be adjusted with minimal pressure.

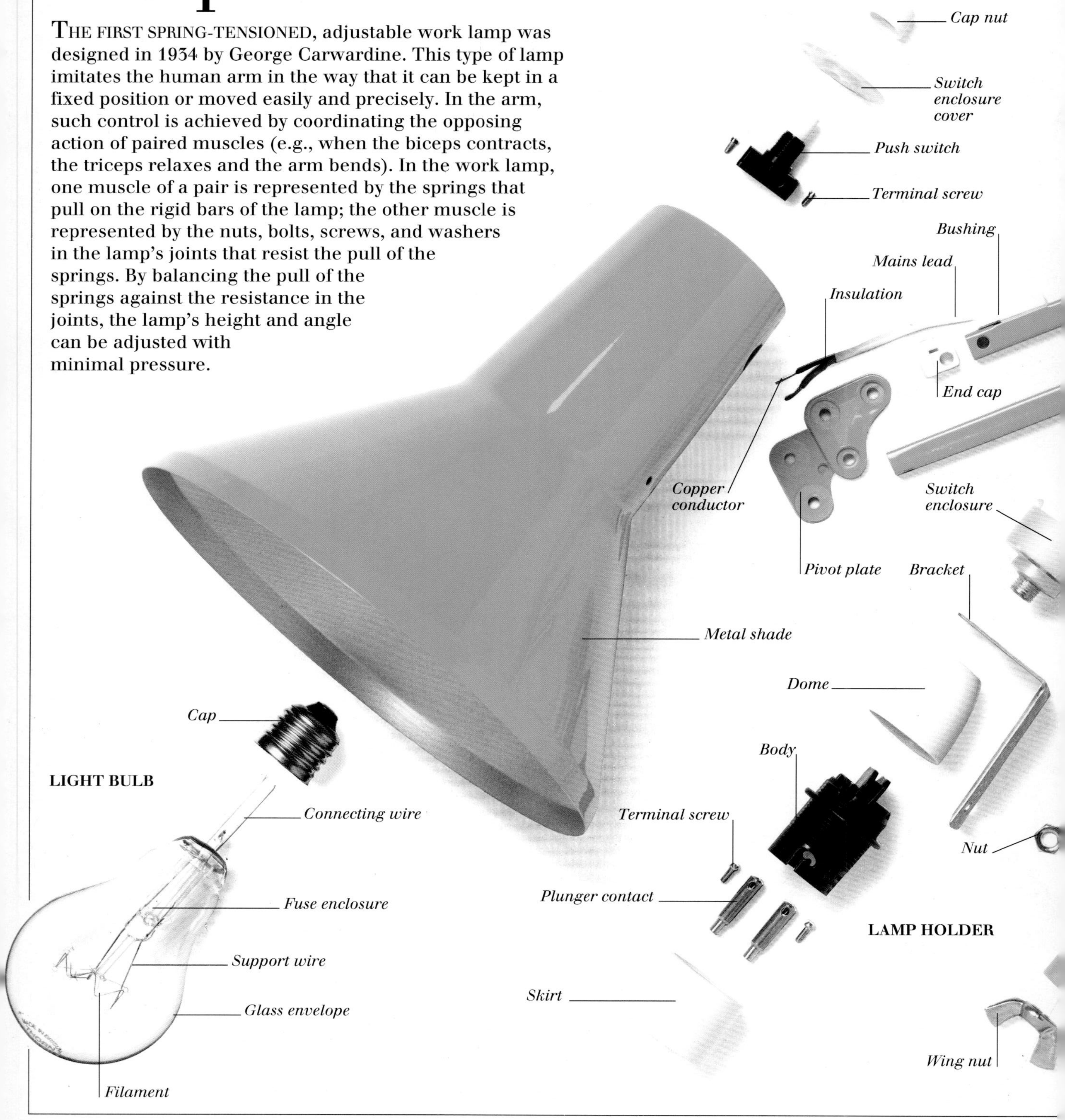

Cap nut

Switch enclosure cover

Push switch

Terminal screw

Bushing

Mains lead

Insulation

End cap

Switch enclosure

Bracket

Pivot plate

Copper conductor

Metal shade

Dome

Nut

LAMP HOLDER

Wing nut

Body

Terminal screw

Plunger contact

Skirt

Connecting wire

Fuse enclosure

Support wire

Glass envelope

Cap

LIGHT BULB

Filament

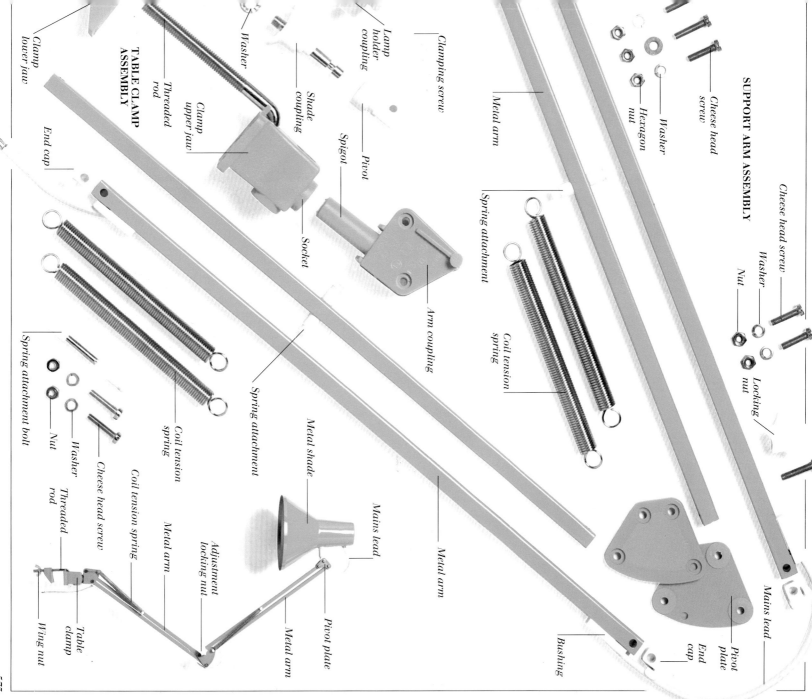

SUPPORT ARM ASSEMBLY

Cheese head screw

Washer

Hexagon nut

Cheese head screw

Washer

Nut

Locking nut

Mains lead

Metal arm

Spring attachment

Coil tension spring

Metal arm

Bushing

End cap

Pivot plate

Mains lead

Clamping screw

Washer

Lamp holder coupling

Threaded rod

Clamp upper jaw

Shade coupling

Spigot

Pivot

Socket

Arm coupling

Spring attachment

Metal shade

Mains lead

Pivot plate

TABLE CLAMP ASSEMBLY

Clamp lower jaw

End cap

Spring attachment

Metal arm

Metal arm

Adjustment locking nut

Pivot plate

Spring attachment bolt

Nut

Washer

Cheese head screw

Threaded rod

Table clamp

Wing nut

Coil tension spring

Coil tension spring

573

Mini-television

MINIATURIZED TELEVISION SETS are small enough to be held in the hand while being watched. A signal sent by a broadcast transmitter is picked up by the television aerial and passed to an electron gun at the back of the television set. In response to the signal this gun produces an electron beam that is passed through a deflection yoke. The yoke contains magnets and coils that cause the beam to scan across the screen in a series of lines. The screen is coated with phosphor, which glows when hit by the beam. As the beam scans the screen, its strength is varied so that the phosphor glows with different intensities in different parts of the screen. A continuous sequence of 25 black-and-white pictures per second appears on the screen so rapidly that the illusion of a moving picture is created.

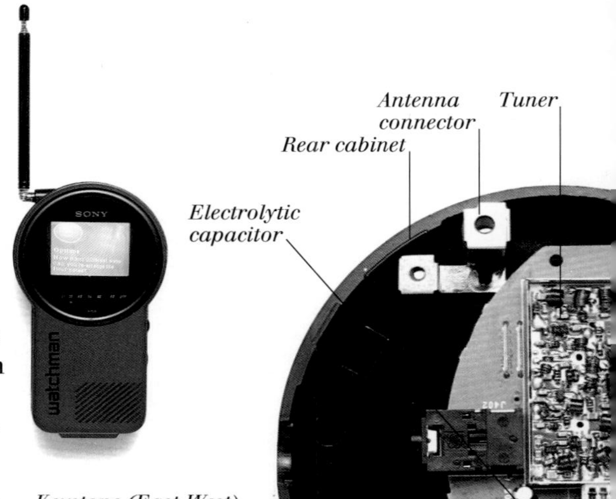

CATHODE RAY TUBE (CRT)

CRT cover

Dial pointer

Tuning drive gear

Tuning knob

Tuning printed circuit board

Deflection coil

Keystone (East-West) amplifier integrated circuit

Earphone jack

Direct current jack

Metal shield

Battery compartment

Screw

CRT bracket

Battery case lid

Positive pole

Mounting bracket

Scan coil clamp

SCAN COIL DEFLECTION YOKE

Tape

Electron gun

Connecting pin

Centring magnet

TUBE NECK

Nipple

Tuner

Antenna connector

Rear cabinet

Electrolytic capacitor

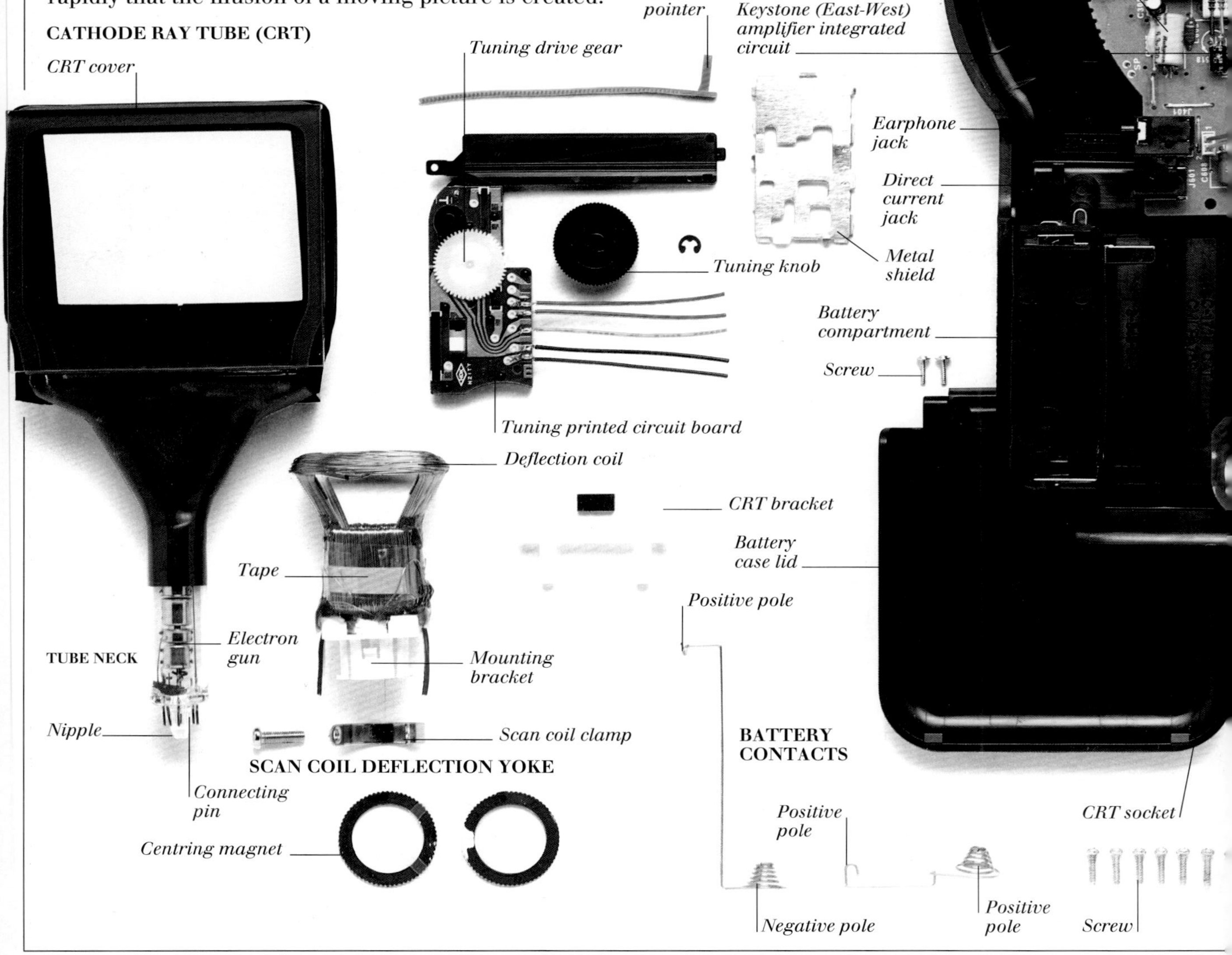

CRT socket

Screw

Positive pole

Negative pole

BATTERY CONTACTS

Positive pole

Speaker

Extra-high tension lead

Focus control

Intermediate frequency coil

Choke

Coil

Glue

Horizontal frequency adjustment

Capacitor

Volume control knob

Power switch

Power knob

Fly-back transformer

Filter ornament

Filter

Plastic cap

SONY

PRINTED CIRCUIT BOARD

Plastic sheath

Antenna holder

Window

Front cabinet

Ornamental strip

Watchman

Chair

A TRADITIONALLY MADE DINING CHAIR, such as the Regency-style carver shown here, is held together, not by nails or bolts, but by snugly fitting joints, screws, dowels, and glue. Its curved arms and top splats, as well as its tapering legs, are cut from seasoned – that is, dried – mahogany. Mortice slots in the back legs receive the tenon tongues of the top and bottom splats; angled grooves at the top of the back legs, called rebates, take the curved arm rail. Though the various joints are so tight-fitting that they could produce a solid frame on their own, screws and glue are used to give the joints added strength. The comfortable, upholstered seatpad shown here consists of a patterned cover, calico lining, and foam stuffing that has been treated for fire safety; it is supported by webbing stretched across a wooden frame.

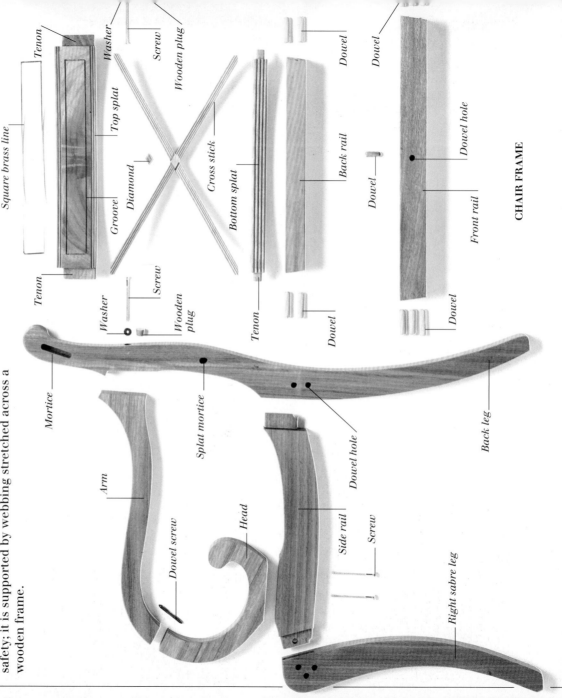

Top splat

Arm

Head

Seatpad

Left sabre leg

Front rail

Back leg

Cross stick

Bottom splat

Tenon

Square brass line

Tenon

Groove

Top splat

Diamond

Cross stick

Bottom splat

Tenon

Washer

Screw

Wooden plug

Washer

Screw

Wooden plug

Dowel

Dowel

Back rail

Dowel

Dowel

Dowel

Dowel hole

Front rail

CHAIR FRAME

Mortice

Splat mortice

Dowel hole

Back leg

Arm

Dowel screw

Head

Side rail

Screw

Right sabre leg

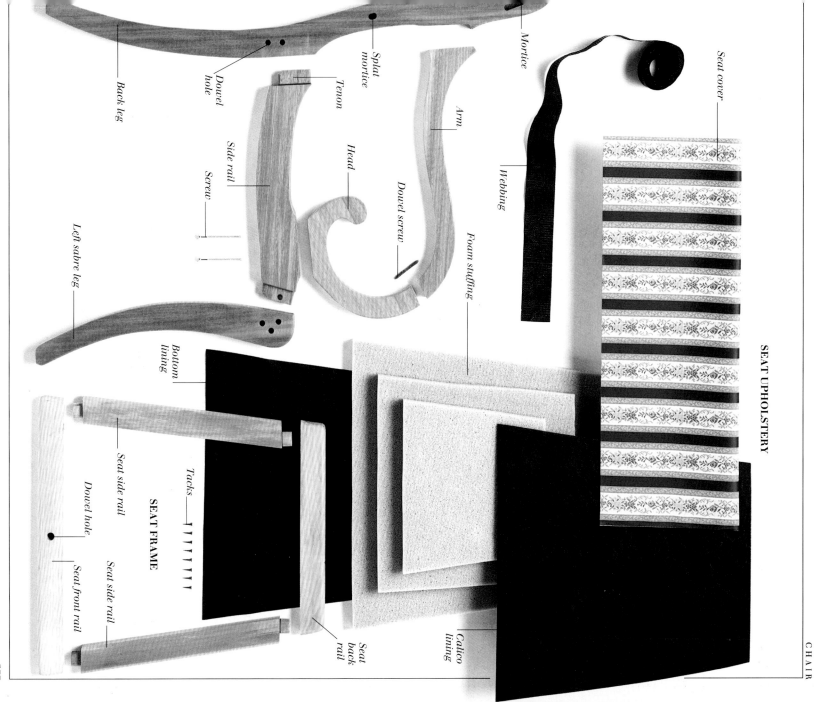

Back leg

Dowel hole

Splat mortice

Tenon

Mortice

Seat cover

Side rail

Head

Arm

Screw

Webbing

Left sabre leg

Dowel screw

Foam stuffing

SEAT UPHOLSTERY

Bottom lining

Tacks

Seat side rail

SEAT FRAME

Dowel hole

Seat side rail

Seat back rail

Calico lining

Seat front rail

Toaster

MOST ELECTRIC TOASTERS NOT ONLY GRILL slices of bread, they also pop them up when ready. While the slices rest on a spring-loaded rack, electric heating elements toast the bread. At the same time, a bimetallic strip heats and expands. One of the two metals in this strip expands more quickly than the other, causing the strip to curve. As it bends, it completes an electrical circuit and activates an electromagnet. The magnet attracts a catch, releasing the spring that holds the rack down in the toaster. The elements switch off, and the toasted slices pop up.

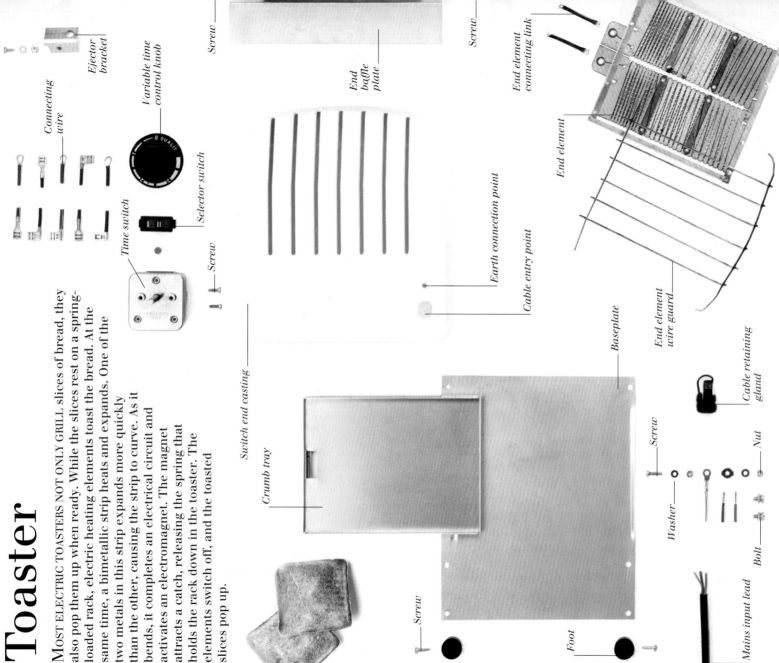

Ejector bracket

Connecting wire

Variable time control knob

Selector switch

Time switch

Screw

Screw

Screw

End baffle plate

End element connecting link

End element

Earth connection point

Cable entry point

Baseplate

End element wire guard

Cable retaining gland

Switch end casting

Crumb tray

Screw

Washer

Nut

Bolt

Screw

Foot

Mains input lead

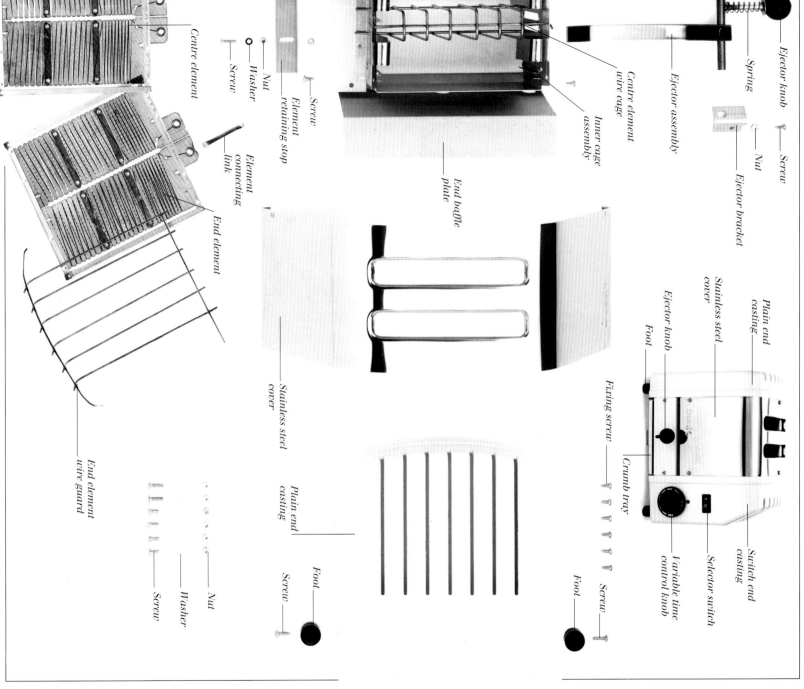

Centre element

Screw
Nut
Washer
Screw

Element
retaining stop

Element
connecting
link

End element

End element
wire guard

Screw
Washer
Nut

Centre element
assembly

Inner cage
assembly

End baffle
plate

Stainless steel
cover

Plain end
casting

Foot
Screw

Ejector knob
Spring
Ejector assembly
Nut
Screw
Ejector bracket

Plain end
casting

Stainless steel
cover

Ejector knob

Foot

Fixing screw

Crumb tray

Variable time
control knob

Selector switch

Switch end
casting

Screw

Foot

Lawnmower

THE SHARP BLADES OF A LAWNMOWER – whether driven by electrical, petrol, or human power – shave grass close to the ground. The petrol-powered type shown here has a small engine that is electrically ignited by a battery and spark plug. This engine rotates a horizontal blade at the base of the lawnmower that slices the grass against a fixed blade. A grass bag at the back of the machine collects the cuttings. As the engine rotates the blades, it also turns the rear wheels, moving the lawnmower forwards. Gears ensure that the horizontal blade spins faster than the wheels so that all of the grass is cut neatly before the lawnmower moves on.

Rear tyre

Wheel cover

Upper gear case

GEAR CASE ASSEMBLY

Half pulley

Drive-shaft

Door

Rear wheel

Spring

Oil dipstick

Oil fill tube

Screw

Wheel bolt

Blower shroud

Fuel tank

Screw

Cap

Screw

ENGINE AND RECOIL ASSEMBLY

Flywheel

Recoil case

Starter cup

Bolt

Screw

Muffler cover

Air filter

Air filter cover

Belt guard

Chain drive-belt

Door seal

Screw

Blade cover

Engine pulley

Shoulder screw

Front wheel

Housing

Throttle guard

Height adjuster

Muffler

Screw

Front tyre

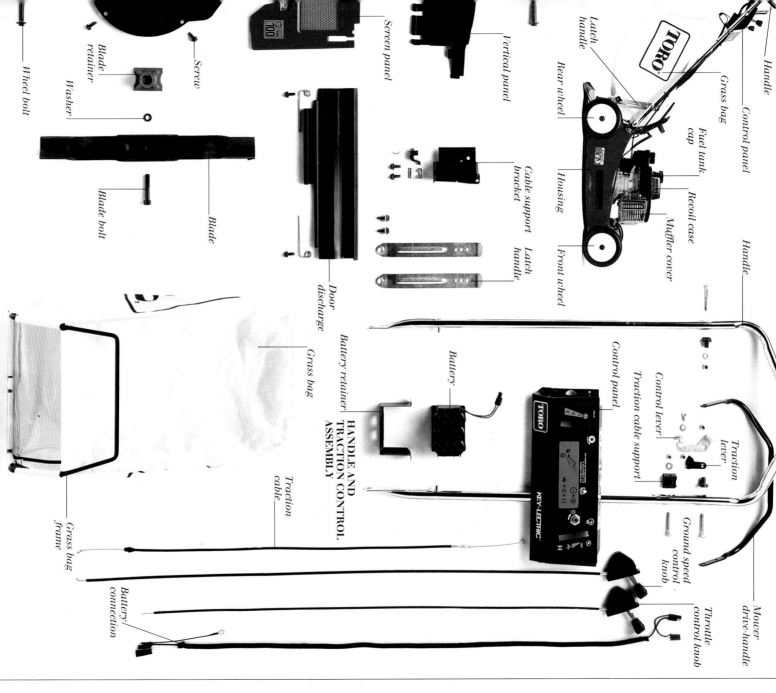

Wheel bolt

Blade retainer

Washer

Screw

Blade bolt

Blade

Screen panel

Vertical panel

Cable support bracket

Door discharge

Latch handle

Rear wheel

Housing

Latch handle

Grass bag

Fuel tank cap

Front wheel

Recoil case

Muffler cover

Handle

Control panel

Handle

Mower drive-handle

Throttle control knob

Ground speed control knob

Traction lever

Control lever

Traction cable support

Control panel

Battery retainer

Battery

HANDLE AND TRACTION CONTROL ASSEMBLY

Grass bag

Traction cable

Grass bag frame

Battery connection

Saddle

THE FIRST HORSE RIDERS HAD NO SADDLES; they sat bareback, clinging to the animal's mane. Next came a simple cloth saddle. The leather saddle, which was invented about 2,000 years ago by the warriors of the Asian steppes, revolutionized horse riding. On this saddle, horsemen could gallop towards the enemy, fire arrows in all directions, and stay on their horses. Modern saddles are of two main types. The Western saddle is a heavy, working saddle used mainly by ranch hands in the United States. It has a metal horn at the front for securing a lasso and a high cantle at the back to keep the rider on the horse. The English saddle is a much lighter affair. Designed for sport, it allows the horse to gallop fast. Its drawback is that it provides less stability; to stay on the horse, the rider must grip the animal with the knees.

ENGLISH SADDLE

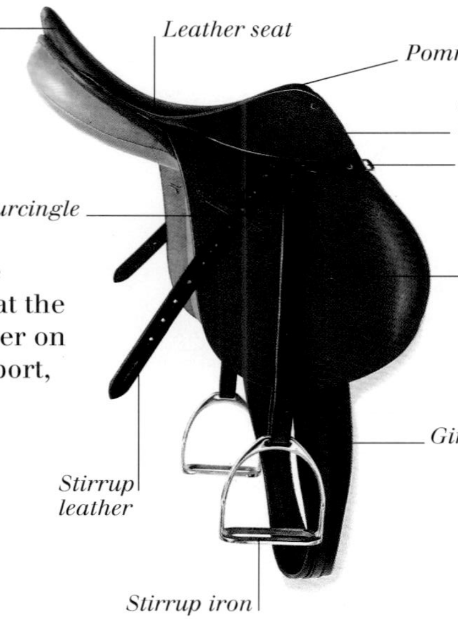

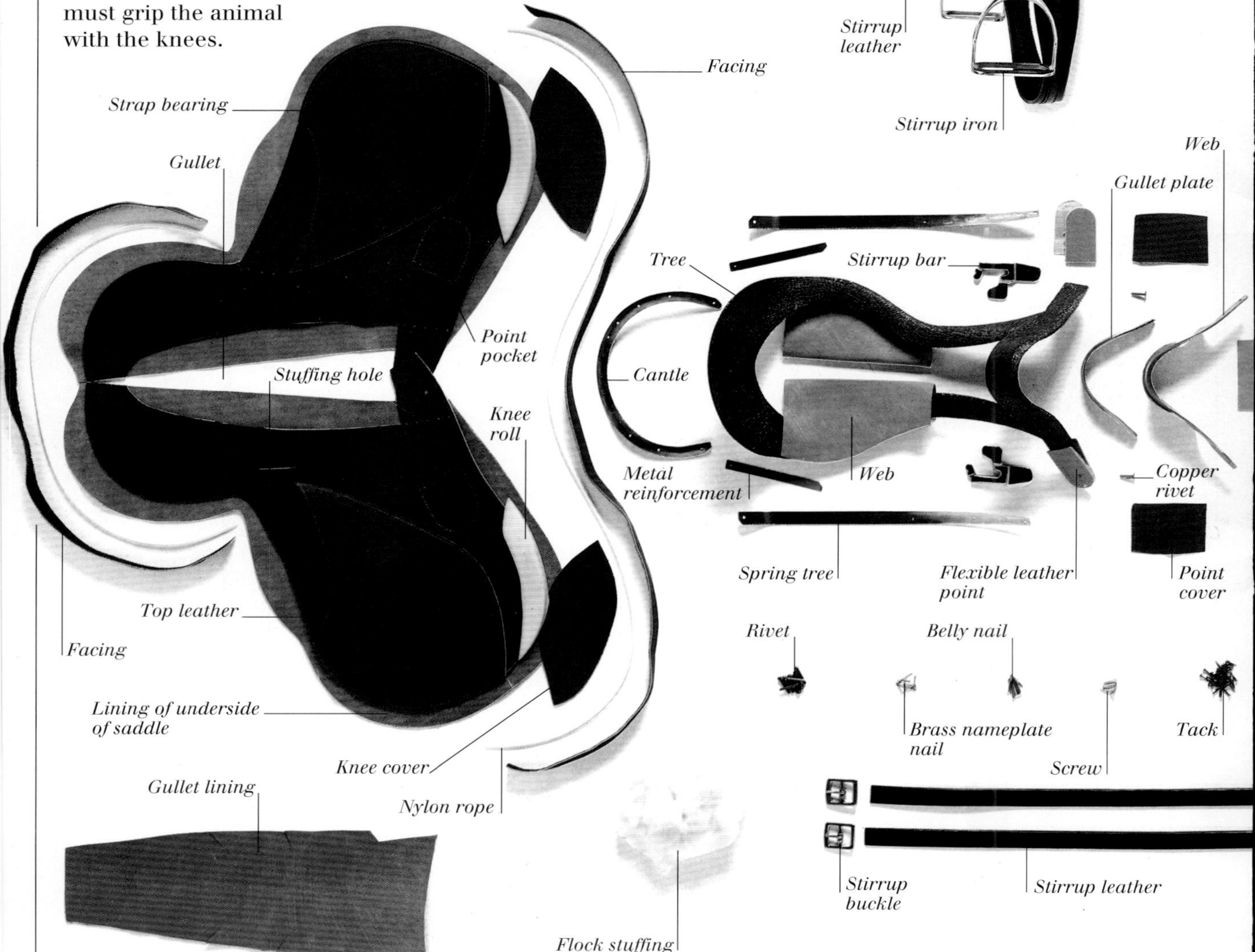

Sloped head
Pommel
Dee
Block flap
Girth
Leather seat
Cantle
Surcingle
Stirrup iron
Stirrup leather

Web
Gullet plate
Copper rivet
Point cover
Tack
Stirrup leather
Flexible leather point
Belly nail
Brass nameplate nail
Screw
Stirrup bar
Web
Spring tree
Rivet
Stirrup buckle
Tree
Cantle
Metal reinforcement

Facing
Point pocket
Knee roll
Nylon rope
Strap bearing
Gullet
Stuffing hole
Knee cover
Top leather
Facing
Lining of underside of saddle
Gullet lining
Flock stuffing

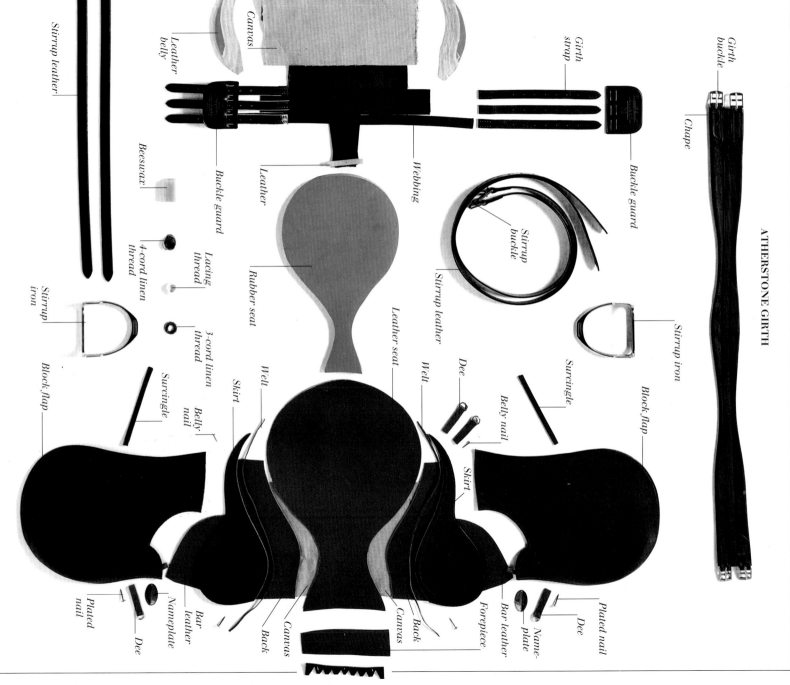

Stirrup leather

Canvas

Leather belly

Beeswax

Buckle guard

Leather

4-cord linen thread

Lacing thread

Rubber seat

3-cord linen thread

Stirrup iron

Block flap

Surcingle

Belly nail

Skirt

Welt

Leather seat

Welt

Dee

Surcingle

Stirrup leather

Stirrup buckle

Girth strap

Webbing

Buckle guard

Block flap

Stirrup iron

Girth buckle

Chape

Plated nail

Dee

Nameplate

Bar leather

Back

Canvas

Canvas

Back

Forepiece

Bar leather

Name-plate

Dee

Plated nail

Skirt

CD-ROM

A CD-ROM IS A TYPE OF COMPACT DISC (CD) that can be used to produce images on a computer screen. ROM stands for Read Only Memory, which means that the digitally recorded data registered in pits on the surface of the disc is fixed and cannot be altered or replaced. The CD is loaded into the CD-ROM player, where the data on the spinning disc is read by a laser. CD-ROMs are different from vinyl records in that they are not read along a spiral groove, from outer circumference to inner edge: instead each image or piece of information has a co-ordinate on the disc, which is located by the laser. Information picked up by the laser is relayed to the computer, where it is translated into the text and images that appear on screen. The information is relayed through a SCSI (Small Computer System Interface), which processes the electronic impulses between the disc drive and the computer system. The user can move around the program by clicking on different parts of the screen with a mouse (a hand-held tool with a clicking button whose movement on its pad is mimicked by an icon on the screen). The image in the viewing area (see opposite) can be changed by clicking on the active scrolling button: this moves a rectangular panel down the scrolling figure in the navigational panel. Clicking on active text will provide a new screen with more information, either in the form of text and diagrams, or as narrated animated sequences.

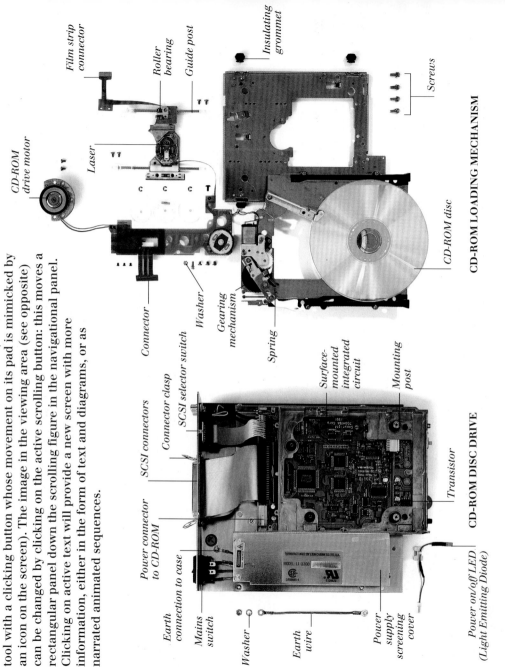

CD-ROM drive

CD loading tray

Caddy cover flap

Push button

Front bezel

CD-ROM CASING

CD-ROM drive motor

Laser

Film strip connector

Roller bearing

Guide post

Insulating grommet

Screws

CD-ROM LOADING MECHANISM

CD-ROM disc

Connector

Washer

Gearing mechanism

Spring

Surface-mounted integrated circuit

Mounting post

SCSI selector switch

Connector clasp

SCSI connectors

Power connector to CD-ROM

Earth connection to case

Mains switch

Washer

Earth wire

Power supply screening cover

Power on/off LED (Light Emitting Diode)

Transistor

CD-ROM DISC DRIVE

CONTENTS PAGE

The Ultimate Human Body

BODY MACHINE

BODY ORGANS

BODY SYSTEMS

ZOOMING INTO MULTI-LAYERED INFORMATION

INITIAL SCREEN UNDER
BODY ORGANS MENU

HEAD
YOUR HEAD contains your brain. Most of your sensory organs are which is protected by the strong, interlocking bones of your skull. your eyes, ears, mouth, and nose.

Hair, skull and scalp

Eye

Nose

Brain

Mouth and lip

Ear

CLICKING ON "EYES" LABEL
PRODUCES MORE INFORMATION

EYES
THESE DELICATE ORGANS injury to your eyelids, thin folds bony sockets of fat protected within of skin that close rapidly. Each eye is moved by six muscles which outside they are protected from are attached around the eyeball.

Skin

Blood vessels

Bone

Around the eye

Inside the eye

EACH LABEL PRODUCES A
FURTHER SCREEN

INSIDE THE EYE
THE EYE is a hollow sphere filled to form an image on the retina. with air-like fluids that help Here, millions of cells that enable you keep the eye in shape. Light rays to detect light and colours. The cells entering the eye through the pupil send messages to the brain, which are focused by the cornea and lens then makes sense of what you see.

Conjunctiva (Thin, clear layer covering cornea)

Vein

Cornea

Lens

Iris

Vitreous humour (Clear jelly that fills the space behind the lens)

Optic nerve

Retina

THE FINAL IMAGE SHOWS
MICROSCOPIC DETAIL

LENS
THE LENS of your eye is on the objects that are near and those far through the centre of your eyeball. front surface of your eyeball. It is transparent and light passes away, the lens must change its to be focused onto the shape. The many fibres around the back of your eye. To focus on both lens allow this by pulling against the outer rim of the lens.

Filters

Lens

Navigational panel

Navigational figures

Options button

Help button

Index button

Back button

Active scrolling button

Scrolling figure

Pronunciation button on/off

Picon (pictorial icon)

FIND OUT MORE

BODY MACHINE

BODY MACHINE   BODY ORGANS   BODY SYSTEMS

Viewing area

ABOUT THE BODY MACHINE

BODY MACHINE

What are you made of?

How do reflex actions work?

How do you swallow?

Why do you blink?

Why do you chew your food?

How do you hear?

What happens when you sleep?

How often does your heart beat?

How do your joints move?

Active text

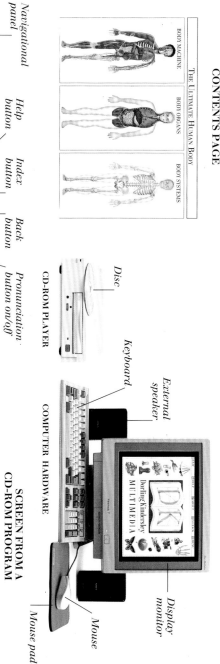

Disc

CD-ROM PLAYER

External speaker

Keyboard

COMPUTER HARDWARE

*SCREEN FROM A
CD-ROM PROGRAM*

Dorling Kindersley
MULTIMEDIA

Mouse pad

Mouse

Display monitor

Books

THOUGH THE PROCESS OF BOOKBINDING today is usually mechanized, some books are still bound by hand. The pages of a book are printed on large sheets of paper called sections, or signatures. When folded, sections usually make 8, 16, or 32 pages. To assemble a hand-bound hardback book, the binder first places the folded sections in the correct order within the endpapers. Next, he or she sews the sections together along the spine edge using strong thread and then pastes them with glue for extra strength. After trimming the pages, the binder puts the book in a press and hammers the spine to round it. The binder then glues one or more linings to the spine. The cover, or case, comes last. To make this, the bookbinder sticks cover boards to the endpapers, front and back, and then covers them with cloth or leather.

LEATHER-BOUND BOOK

Leather cover

Gold embossing

Tail

Ribbon

Joint

Fore-edge

Rib

Spine

HALF-BOUND BOOK

Corner piece

Marbled paper

Tail

Spine

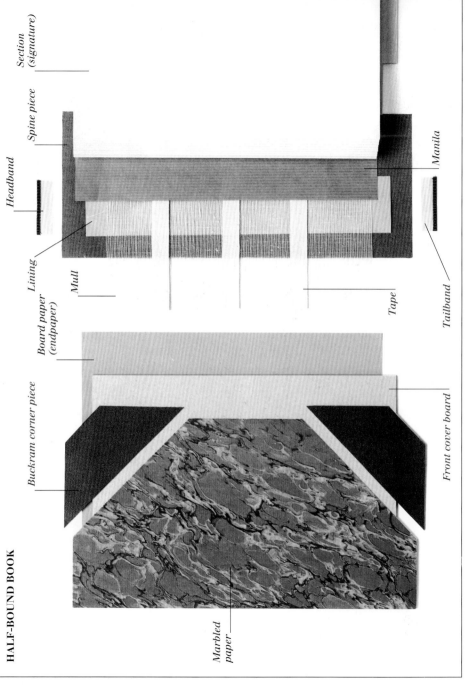

Section (signature)

Spine piece

Headband

Manila

Lining

Mull

Board paper (endpaper)

Tape

Tailband

Buckram corner piece

Front cover board

HALF-BOUND BOOK

Marbled paper

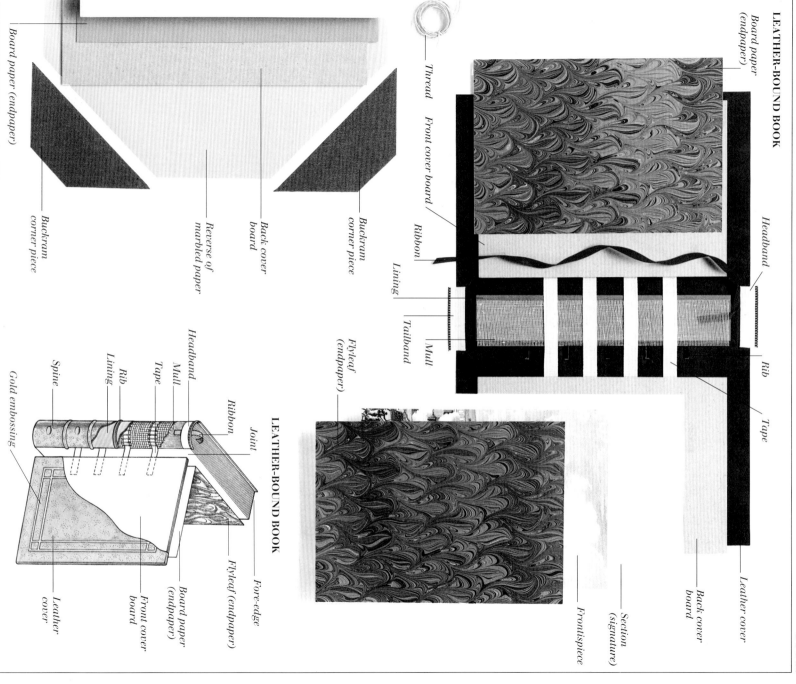

Board paper
(endpaper)

Thread

Front cover board

Headband

Ribbon

Rib

Lining

Tailband

Mull

Tape

Flyleaf
(endpaper)

Leather cover

Back cover
board

Section
(signature)

Frontispiece

Board paper (endpaper)

Buckram
corner piece

Reverse of
marbled paper

Back cover
board

Buckram
corner piece

Headband

Mull

Lining

Tape

Rib

Ribbon

Joint

Spine

Gold embossing

Leather
cover

Board paper
(endpaper)

Front cover
board

Flyleaf (endpaper)

Fore-edge

Camera

A CAMERA IS AN INSTRUMENT for recording images on photographic film. It consists of a light-tight box with a shutter, a lens containing a diaphragm, and a viewing system. When the shutter is released, the film is exposed to light from the subject that is being photographed. Adjusting the shutter speed alters the time for which the film is exposed to light. The diaphragm, by altering the aperture of the lens, controls the intensity of light entering the camera. The total amount of light entering the camera is called the exposure. The lens focuses the light on to the film. When there is insufficient light to produce an adequate image, a flashgun may be used to give extra light.

FRONT VIEW OF CAMERA

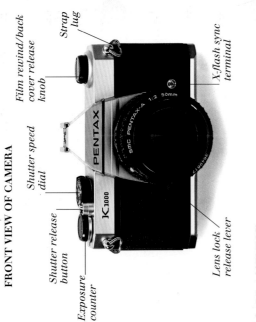

Film rewind/back cover release knob

Strap lug

X-flash sync terminal

Shutter speed dial

Shutter release button

Exposure counter

Lens lock release lever

FRONT BOARD ASSEMBLY

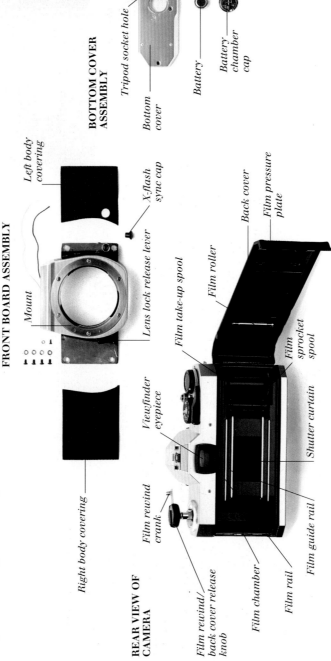

Left body covering

X-flash sync cap

Mount

Lens lock release lever

REAR VIEW OF CAMERA

Right body covering

Film rewind crank

Film rewind/ back cover release knob

Film chamber

Film rail

Viewfinder eyepiece

Film guide rail

Film take-up spool

Film roller

Back cover

Film pressure plate

Film sprocket spool

Shutter curtain

BOTTOM COVER ASSEMBLY

Tripod socket hole

Bottom cover

Battery

Battery chamber cap

LENS BARREL ASSEMBLY

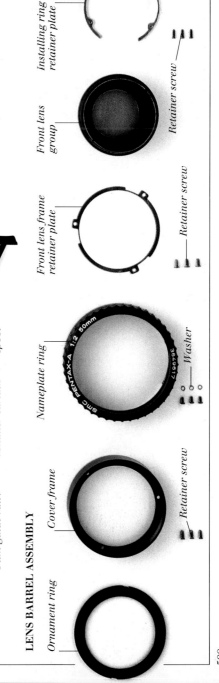

Installing ring retainer plate

Retainer screw

Front lens group

Front lens frame retainer plate

Retainer screw

Nameplate ring

Washer

Retainer screw

Cover frame

Retainer screw

Ornament ring

TOP COVER ASSEMBLY

Counter dial cover

Counter dial

Window

Retainer screw

Exposure counter dial

Washer

Counter dial housing

Wind lever install spring

Strap lug

Hole for film rewind button

Retainer screw

MAIN BODY

Viewfinder eyepiece

Prism retainer spring

Prism retainer plate

Film wind lever

Wind lever collar

Prism retainer plate

Pentaprism

Depth-of-field guide

Focusing ring

Aperture auto-lock button

Shutter release button

Top cover

Shutter speed dial knob

Shutter dial knob spring

Speed dial knob

Film rewind crank

Film rewind/back cover release knob

Film rewind crank

Hot shoe

X-contact

Shutter speed index

Shutter speed indicator

Film speed indicator

Main barrel assembly

Distance scale (focal length scale)

Aperture/distance index

Lens alignment node

Lens lock release lever

Shutter release button

X-contact

Hot shoe

Cover frame

Retainer screw

Film speed indicator

Shutter speed dial

Retainer screw

Rewind shaft

Rewind shaft collar

Film rewind crank

TOP VIEW OF CAMERA

ft m
∞ 10 15 3 8 26 1.5
A⁻ 22 16 11 8 5.6 4 2.82

Cocked indicator

Film wind lever

Shutter speed dial

Exposure counter

Supporter ring retainer plate

Supporter ring

Diaphragm blade

Opening and closing plate

Installing ring

Rear lens group

589

C A M E R A

Appendix: useful data

UNITS OF MEASUREMENT

Length

Metric unit	Equivalent
1 centimetre (cm)	10 millimetres (mm)
1 metre (m)	100 centimetres
1 kilometre (km)	1,000 metres

Imperial unit	Equivalent
1 foot (ft)	12 inches (in)
1 yard (yd)	3 feet
1 rod (rd)	5.5 yards
1 mile (mi)	1,760 yards

Area

Metric unit	Equivalent
1 square centimetre (cm²)	100 square millimetres (mm²)
1 square metre (m²)	10,000 square centimetres
1 hectare	10,000 square metres
1 square kilometre (km²)	1,000,000 square metres

Imperial unit	Equivalent
1 square foot (ft²)	144 square inches (in²)
1 square yard (yd²)	9 square feet
1 acre	4,840 square yards
1 square mile	640 acres

Volume

Metric unit	Equivalent
1 cubic centimetre (cc)	1 millilitre (ml)
1 litre (l)	1,000 millilitres (ml)
1 cubic metre (m³)	1,000 litres

Imperial unit	Equivalent
1 cubic foot	1,728 cubic inches
1 cubic yard	27 cubic feet

Mass

Metric unit	Equivalent
1 kilogram (kg)	1,000 grams (g)
1 tonne (t)	1,000 kilograms

Imperial unit	Equivalent
1 dram (dr)	27.344 grains (gr)
1 ounce (oz)	16 drams
1 pound (lb)	16 ounces
1 hundredweight (cwt) (long)	112 pounds
1 hundredweight (cwt) (short)	100 pounds
1 ton (long)	2,240 pounds
1 ton (short)	2,000 pounds

Capacity (liquid and dry measures)

Metric unit	Equivalent
1 centilitre (cl)	10 millilitres (ml)
1 decilitre (dl)	10 centilitres
1 litre (l)	10 decilitres
1 decalitre (dal)	10 litres
1 hectolitre (hl)	10 decalitres
1 kilolitre (kl)	10 hectolitres

Imperial unit	Equivalent
1 fluidram (fl dr)	60 minims (min)
1 fluid ounce (fl oz)	8 fluidrams
1 gill (gi)	5 fluid ounces
1 pint (pt)	4 gills
1 quart (qt)	2 pints
1 gallon (gal)	4 quarts
1 peck (pk)	2 gallons
1 bushel (bu)	4 pecks

TEMPERATURE SCALES

To convert from Celsius (C) to Fahrenheit (F): F = (C × 9 ÷ 5) + 32
To convert from Fahrenheit to Celsius: C = (F - 32) × 5 ÷ 9
To convert from Celsius to Kelvin (K): K = C + 273
To convert from Kelvin to Celsius: C = K - 273

Celsius	-20	-10	0	10	20	30	40	50	60	70	80	90	100
Fahrenheit	-4	14	32	50	68	86	104	122	140	158	176	194	212
Kelvin	253	263	273	283	293	303	313	323	333	343	353	363	373

AREAS AND VOLUMES

CIRCLE

Radius r
Diameter d = 2 x r
Circumference = 2 x π x r
Area = π x r²
(π = 3.1416)

TRIANGLE

Sides a, b, c
Height h
Perimeter = a + b + c
Area = ½ x b x h

RECTANGLE

Sides a, b
Perimeter = 2 x (a + b)
Area = a x b

CYLINDER

Radius r
Height h
Surface area = 2 x π x r x h (excluding ends)
Volume = π x r² x h

CONE

Radius r
Height h
Side l
Surface area = π x r x l (excluding base)
Volume = ⅓ x π x r² x l

RECTANGULAR BLOCK

Sides a, b, c
Surface area = 2 x (a x b + b x c + a x c)
Volume = a x b x c

METRIC - IMPERIAL CONVERSIONS

To convert	Into	Multiply by
Length		
Centimetres	inches	0.3937
Metres	feet	3.2810
Kilometres	miles	0.6214
Metres	yards	1.0940
Mass		
Grams	ounces	0.0352
Kilograms	pounds	2.2050
Tonnes	long tons	0.9843
Tonnes	short tons	1.1025
Area		
Square centimetres	square inches	0.1550
Square metres	square feet	10.7600
Hectares	acres	2.4710
Square kilometres	square miles	0.3861
Square metres	square yards	1.1960
Volume		
Cubic centimetres	cubic inches	0.0610
Cubic metres	cubic feet	35.3100
Capacity		
Litres	pints	1.7600
Litres	gallons	0.2200

IMPERIAL - METRIC CONVERSIONS

To convert	Into	Multiply by
Length		
Inches	centimetres	2.5400
Feet	metres	0.3048
Miles	kilometres	1.6090
Yards	metres	0.9144
Mass		
Ounces	grams	28.3500
Pounds	kilograms	0.4536
Long tons	tonnes	1.0160
Short tons	tonnes	0.9070
Area		
Square inches	square centimetres	6.4520
Square feet	square metres	0.0929
Acres	hectares	0.4047
Square miles	square kilometres	2.5900
Square yards	square metres	0.8361
Volume		
Cubic inches	cubic centimetres	16.3900
Cubic feet	cubic metres	0.0283
Capacity		
Pints	litres	0.5683
Gallons	litres	4.5460

NUMBER SYSTEMS

Roman	Arabic
I	1
II	2
III	3
IV	4
V	5
VI	6
VII	7
VIII	8
IX	9
X	10
XI	11
XII	12
XIII	13
XIV	14
XV	15
XX	20
XXI	21
XXX	30
XL	40
L	50
LX	60
LXX	70
LXXX	80
XC	90
C	100
CI	101
CC	200
CCC	300
CD	400
D	500
DC	600
DCC	700
DCCC	800
CM	900
M	1,000
MM	2,000

PHYSICS SYMBOLS

Symbol	Meaning
α	alpha particle
β	beta ray
γ	gamma ray; photon
ϵ	electromotive force
η	efficiency; viscosity
λ	wavelength
μ	micro-; permeability
ν	frequency; neutrino
ρ	density; resistivity
σ	conductivity
c	velocity of light
e	electronic charge

MATHEMATICS SYMBOLS

Symbol	Meaning
+	plus
−	minus
±	plus or minus
×	multiplied by
÷	divided by
=	equals
>	is greater than
<	is less than
≥	is greater than or equal to
≤	is less than or equal to
%	per cent
√	root
π	pi (3.1416)
°	degree
∞	infinity
≈	is approximately equal to
∠	angle
∥	parallel to

CHEMISTRY SYMBOLS

Symbol	Meaning
+	plus; together with
−	single bond
•	single bond; single unpaired electron; two separate parts or compounds regarded as loosely joined
=	double bond
≡	triple bond
R	group
X	halogen atom
Z	atomic number

BIOLOGY SYMBOLS

Symbol	Meaning
○	female individual (used in inheritance charts)
□	male individual (used in inheritance charts)
♀	female
♂	male
×	crossed with; hybrid
+	wild type
F_1	offspring of the first generation
F_2	offspring of the second generation

POWERS OF TEN USED WITH SCIENTIFIC UNITS

Factor	Name	Prefix	Symbol
10^{18}	quintillion	exa-	E
10^{15}	quadrillion	peta-	P
10^{12}	trillion	tera-	T
10^{9}	billion	giga-	G
10^{6}	million	mega-	M
10^{3}	thousand	kilo-	k
10^{2}	hundred	hecto-	h
10^{1}	ten	deca-	da
10^{-1}	one tenth	deci-	d
10^{-2}	one hundredth	centi-	c
10^{-3}	one thousandth	milli-	m
10^{-6}	one millionth	micro-	μ
10^{-9}	one billionth	nano-	n
10^{-12}	one trillionth	pico-	p
10^{-15}	one quadrillionth	femto-	f
10^{-18}	one quintillionth	atto-	a

NOTE: The American system of numeration for denominations above one million is used in this book. In this system, each of the denominations above one billion (1,000 millions) is 1,000 times the preceding one.

Index

Nineteenth-century building 492-493
Renaissance building 474-475
Shoe 568
Archaeopteryx 57, 84, 85
Arched brace 473
Arched doorway 474, 475
Arched facade 493
Archegoniophore 118
Archegonium
Fern 121
Liverwort 118
Moss 119
Scots pine 122
Archery 548-549
Archery screen 377
Archimedes 40
Architrave
Ancient Egyptian temple 458-459
Ancient Greek temple 461
Ancient Roman building 463, 465
Baroque church 479-481
French temple 485
Gothic building 473
Neoclassical building 478, 482-483
Renaissance building 476-477
Archivolt
Baroque church 479, 481
French temple 485
Gothic church 471
Medieval building 467-468
Renaissance building 477
Arch of aorta 253
Arch of Titus 463
Arch-plate 493
Archway 493
Medieval church 469
Moulding 485
Arctic Circle
Satellite map 265
Surface currents 297
Arctic Ocean 265
Arcturus 18, 21
Hertzsprung-Russell diagram 23
Area measurements 590
Areola 160
Areole 156
Arête 286-287
Argentina 331
Argon
Atmospheric composition 301
Mars' atmosphere 43
Mercury's atmosphere 35
Periodic table 311
Venus' atmosphere 37
Argyre Planitia 43
Ariel 48
Aries 19, 20
Aril
Lychee fruit 148
Yew seed 123
A ring 46-47
Aristarchus 40
Aristillus 40
Aristoteles 40
Arkab Prior 21
Arkansas hone-stone 452
Arm
74-gun ship 380
Calligraphy characters 445
Chair 576
Gorilla 203
Human 210

Lion 194
Roman anchor 372
Starfish 174
Volkswagen Beetle 341
Armature
Power drill motor 566
Sculpture 452, 454-455
Armature spindle 566
Arm bud 260
Arm coupling 573
Armed sports 556-557
Armour
Battleship 394
Gun turret 396
Ironclad 393
Armoured dinosaurs 92
Armoured seat back 409
Armpit 211, 234
Armpit bight 388
Arm rail 576
Armrest 329, 407
Arms of Brazil 394
Armstand dive 558-559
Arrector pili muscle 235
Arricio 434
Arrow head 109
Arse 382
Arsenic 311
Arsia Mons 43
Arsinoitherium 57, 75, 104-105
Art deco style 495
Twentieth-century building 494, 495
Artemon 372
Arterial system
Brain 252
Kidney 256
Arteriole 252
Artery
Abdominal 173
Alveolar 247
Anterior tibial 253
Axillary 253
Basilar 252
Brachial 253
Central retinal 240
Common carotid 215, 251, 253
Common iliac 215, 253, 257
Coronary 250-251, 253
Digital 231, 253
Dorsal metatarsal 253
Epibranchial 179
External iliac 215, 225, 253
Femoral 225, 253
Gastric 253
Hepatic 248, 252-253
Interlobular 256
Internal carotid 243, 252
Internal iliac 215, 253
Lateral plantar 253
Orbital 179
Peroneal 253
Popliteal 253
Posterior cerebral 252
Posterior tibial 253
Pulmonary 182, 251, 253, 254-255
Pulp 247
Radial 231, 253
Renal 256-257
Splenic 253
Sternal 173
Subclavian 215, 251, 253
Superior mesenteric 253, 256
Superior thyroid 244
Testicular 257
Ulnar 251, 253
Umbilical 260
Vertebral 223, 252
Artesian water 292

Arthropoda 168, 170, 172, 278
Articular capsule 252
Articular cavity
Hip joint 225
Metatarsophalangeal joint 252
Artificial elements 310
Artificial fly 562-563
Artificial light 319
Artificial lure 563
Artillery loop 389
Artillery wheel 334
Artiodactyla 104, 198-199
Artist's easel 437
Artist's signature 437, 445
Artist's stamp 445
Art nouveau style 495
Arundinaria nitida 151
ARV Super 2 light aircraft 424-425
Arzachel 40
Ascender 445
Ascending aorta 251
Ascending colon 249
Ascraeus Mons 43
Asexual reproduction 154
Ash
Mountain building 62
Rock cycle 266
Volcano 272-273
Ash chute 395
Ash-cinder volcano 272
Ash eruptions 272
Ash head 540
Ashlar 464, 486
Asia
Cretaceous period 72-73
Earth's physical features 264-265
Himalaya formation 62-63
Hominids 108
Jurassic period 70
Middle Ordovician period 64
Quaternary period 76-77
Tertiary period 74-75
Triassic period 68
Asian buildings 490-491
Asian elephant 200-201
Asparagus setaceous 64
Ass 198
Association football 524-525
Astatine 311
Asterias rubens 175
Asterina gibbosa 175
Asteroids 52-53
Solar System 30
Asteroxylon 78-79
Asthenosphere 58-59
Astragal
Church of the Sorbonne 486
Ship's shield 395
Astragalus 183
Astrolabe 376, 377
Astronavigation dome 408
Asymmetric ridge 283
Atacama Desert 264
Atalanta Planitia 36
Atherstone girth 583
Athletics 542-543
Atlantic Ocean 264-265
Quaternary period 77
Tertiary period 75
Triassic period 68
Atlas
Baroque building 482
Horse 199
Human 222
Moon 40
Atlas mountains
Earth's external features 39
Artesian water 292

Quaternary period 77
Satellite map 265
Atmosphere
Earth 38-39, 64, **300-301**
Jupiter 45
Mars 43
Mercury 34-35
Neptune 51
Pluto 51
Saturn 47
Uranus 49
Venus 37
Water cycle 288
Atoll 298-299
Atoll development 299
Atomic mass 309, 310
Atomic number 310
Atomic weight 310
Atoms 306, **308-509**
Chemical properties 310
Chemical reactions 312
Periodic table 310
Atrial diastole 250
Atrial systole 251
Atrium
Hong Kong and Shanghai Bank 498
Human 215, 250-251
Sponge 166
Attached column
Ancient Roman building 465
Baroque church 480
Gothic building 473
Medieval building 468-469
Neoclassical building 479
Attachment-bracket 424
Attachment lug 404
Attachment plate 424
Attack line 554
Attack radar 420
Attic
Baroque church 480-481
Cathedral dome 487
Neoclassical building 478, 483
Attic vase 372
Attraction 316-317
"A" turret 394
Auda 491
Auditorium 479
Auditory canal 242
Auditory meatus
Chimpanzee 202
Seal 204
Auger 374
Augusta National Golf course 546
Aureole 471
Auricle 242
Auricular surface 223
Auriga 18, 21
Aurora 38, 301
Australasia 264-265
Australia
Cretaceous period 72-73
Jurassic period 70
Late Carboniferous period 66
Middle Ordovician period 64
Quaternary period 76-77
Railway track gauge 331
Satellite map 265
Tertiary period 74-75
Triassic period 68
Australian Desert 265
Australian rules football 524, **528-529**
Australopithecus 77, 108
Lower jaw 107
Tertiary period 74
Autofeather unit 419

Autogiro 422
Automatic cylinder lubricator 342
Automatic direction-finding aerial 425
Automatic door 328-329
Automatic Train Protection (ATP) 330
Automobile freight car 327
Autopilot 412
Autumn wood xylem 134
Auxiliary air intake 420-421
Auxiliary generator 327
Auxiliary power unit 417
Auxiliary power unit inlet 415
Aves 188
Avimimus 87
Avogadro 41
Avro triplane IV 402-403
Avro Tutor biplane 402-403
Away swing bowler 338
Awning 499
Axe 109, 374
Axial gland 175
Axial tilt
Earth 38
Jupiter 44
Mars 42
Mercury 34
Moon 40
Neptune 50
Pluto 51
Saturn 46
Uranus 48
Venus 36
Axilla 211
Axillary artery 253
Axillary bud 134
Dicotyledon stem 127
Durmast oak 131
Leaf scars 154
Axillary vein 253
Axinite 270
Axis
Azolla sp. 158
Horse 199
Human 222
Seed 152-153
Pine cone 122
Axis of rotation
Jupiter 44
Mars 42
Mercury 34
Moon 40
Neptune 50
Pluto 51
Pulsar 28
Saturn 46
Uranus 48
Venus 36
Axle
Avro triplane 402-403
Blackburn monoplane 400
Bus 333
Curtiss biplane 399
Honda VF750 365
Lockheed Electra airliner 407
LVG CVI fighter 405
Steam locomotive 324
Axle bolt 425
Axon 239
Aythya fuligula 188
Azimuthal map projection 265
Azo yellow 442
Azurite 306

B

B-17G Flying Fortress bomber 408
Baboon 202
Bach 35
Back
Block and tackle 383
Elephant 200
Horse 198
Human 210
Lion 195
Saddle 583
Back-board 532
Back bone 222
Back box 571
Back check 514
Back cover 588
Back cover board
Half-bound book 587
Leather-bound book 587
Background radiation 10
Back judge 526
Back leg 576-577
Back line 535
Back plate 571
Back pocket 528
Back rail 576
Backrest
ARV light aircraft 425
Lockheed Electra passenger seat 407
Backs
Handball 535
Hockey 540
Soccer 524
Volleyball 534
Back sight 549
Backstay 378, 379, 380
Backstay stool 381
Back strap 560, 561
Backstroke 558-559
Backward defensive stroke 538
Backward dive 558
Backwash 294
Back zones 534
Bacteria 56
Bactrian camel 199
Baculum 144
Badger 194
Badminton **544-545**
BAe-146 jetliner components 412-415
Baffin Island 264
Baffle 341
Baffle plate 347
Bage, C. 492
Baggage compartment door 423
Bagneux Church 468-469
Bahada 282
Bail 538
Bail arm 562
Bailey 466
Bailly 467
Baird's beaked whale 205
Bait fishing 562
Balaenoptera musculus 205
Balance 232
Balance and muscle coordination 237
Balance weight
Jaguar V12 engine 345
Mid West rotary engine 411
Balancing drilling
Mid West rotary engine 411
Wankel rotary engine 547
Balanophyllia regia 167
Balata surface 546

605

608

Ovate leaf
  Ice-plant 129
  Live-for-ever 129
  Strawberry 128
Ovda Regio 36, 37
Overarm pass 535
Overhand knot 388
Overhand serve 534
Overhead camshaft
  engine 368
Overhead pass 532
Overhead valve engine
  (OHV) 367, 369
Over-reach boot 555
Overs 538
Oversailing fascia 477,
  482, 486
Overthrust fold 61
Overturned fold 61
Oviduct
  Barnacle 173
  Brachiosaurus 90
  Butterfly 169
  Crayfish 173
  Dogfish 179
  Lizard 185
  Spider 170
  Tortoise 187
Ovolo 486
Ovolo moulding
  Cathedral dome 487
  Gothic church 472
  Neoclassical building
    480
Ovotestis 177
Ovules 140-143
  Bishop pine 124
  Dehiscent fruit 151
  Fertilization 146
  Pine 122
  Scots pine 122
  Smooth cypress 123
  Yew 123
Ovuliferous scales
  Bishop pine 124
  Pine 122
  Scots pine 122
  Smooth cypress 123
  Yew 123
Ovum
  Ancient Roman building
    462
  Fertilization 146-147
  Scots pine 122
Oxalis sp. 157
Oxbow lake 293
  River features 290
  River's stages 289
"Ox-eye" window
  Baroque church 479, 481
  Cathedral dome 487
Oxides 268
Oxygen
  Atmospheric
    composition 301
  Early micro-organisms
    78
  Earth's composition 39
  Earth's crust 58
  Earth's formation 38, 64
  Helix Nebula 17
  Mars' atmosphere 43
  Mercury's atmosphere
    35
  Periodic table 311
  Photosynthesis 138
  Seed germination 152
  Structure of red
    supergiant 26
  Respiration 255
Oxygenated blood 255
Oxygen bottle 408
Oxygen group 311
Oyashio current 297
Oyster fungus 114

Oysters 176
Ozone 64
Ozone layer 300

P

Pachycephalosaurus 69,
  83, 100
Pachypteris sp. 68
Pachyrhinosaurus 103
Pacific coastline 295
Pacific Ocean 264-265, 272
Pacific plate 59
Pacing races 554
Pacing sulky 554-555
Pacinian corpuscle 234-
  235
Pack-ice 296
Packing tissue
  Dicotyledon leaf 126
  Fern rachis 121
  Golden barrel cactus 156
  Haworthia truncata 157
  Horsetail stem 120
  Leaf succulents 157
  Lithops bromfieldii 157
  Monocotyledon leaf 126
  Roots 132-133
  Stem 134-135
  Stem succulents 156
  String of hearts 157
  Water lily leaf 159
Padded coaming
  Avro biplane 403
  BE 2B bomber 404
Paddle
  Eurypterid fossil 79
  Kayak 560
Paddlesteamer
  19th century 390-391
  Iron 392-393
Paddle wheels 390-591,
  392
Padmakosa 489
Page 586
Pagoda 490
Pahoehoe 272
Painted Desert 277
Painting knives 436, 442
Painting tools 442
Pair-cast cylinder 343
Paired cylinder 342
Palace of Westminster
  492-493
Palaeocene epoch
  Fossil record 279
  Geological timescale 57
Palaeontology 278
Palaeozoic era
  Fossil record 279
  Geological time 56
Palais de Fontainebleau
  476
Palais de Versailles 482
Palatine Chapel,
  Aix-le-Chapelle 484
Palatine tonsil 212, 244-
  245
Palatoglossal arch 244
Palazzo Stanga 482
Palazzo Strozzi 474-475
Pale calcite 26
Pale feldspar 26
Palette 143, 436
Palette knife 436
Paling 466, 477
Palisade mesophyll 126,
  159
Palladium 311
Pallet 570
Palm
  Danforth anchor 386
  Hand 211
  Roman anchor 372

Sailmaker's 384
  Tertiary plant 74
Palmar arch 253
Palmaris longus tendon
  231
Palmar vein 253
Palmate leaves 130, 136
Palmate venation 129
Palmette 460-461, 479-480
Palmoxylon 74
Pamirs 265
Pampas 264
Panavia Tornado GR1A
  420-421
Pancreas
  Bird 189
  Bony fish 181
  Chimpanzee 202
  Dogfish 179
  Domestic cat 195
  Frog 182
  Human 215, 249
  Rabbit 196
  Tortoise 187
Pandas 194
Panduriform leaves 136
Pane 494
Panel 485
  Asian building 491
  Baroque church 479-481
  Cathedral dome 487
  Gothic building 473
  Islamic building 488
  Medieval building 466,
    469
  Modern building 496-498
  Neoclassical building
    478-479
  Nineteenth-century
    building 493
  Renaissance building
    475
  Twentieth-century
    building 494
Pangaea 66, 68-69, 70
Panniers 360, 361, 362
Panoplosaurus 94
Panicle 131
Pantheon 462-463
Paris Metro 328
Pantile 464, 482
Pantograph 328, 330
Pan troglodytes 202
Paper
  Acrylic paint 442
  Books 586
  Calligraphy 444, 445
  Pastels 440
  Printing processes 446,
    447
  Watercolours 438
Paper stumps 440
Papilla
  Flower 140
  Hair 235
  Renal 256
  Tongue 244
Papillary muscle 251
Pappus 142
Papyriform column 459
Parabellum machine-gun
  405
Parabolic dune 283
Paraboloid roof 496, 499
Parachute seed dispersal
  150
Paradise palm 126
Paragaster 166
Parallel dunes 283
Parallel river drainage 288
Parallel shaft 382
Parallel venation 126
Parana River 264
Parapet
  Ancient Roman building
    465

Asian building 491
  Baroque church 481
  Dome 486
  Gothic church 470-472
  Islamic tomb 489
  Medieval building 467
  Neoclassical building
    478, 485
  Nineteenth-century
    building 493
  Twentieth-century
    building 494
Parapet rail 483
Paraphysis 117, 119
Parasaurolophus 98-99
Parasitic anemone 166
Parasitic cone 272-273
Parasitic plants **162-165**
Parasitic volcano 275
Paraxeiresia 373
Parcelling 388
Parchment
  Gilding 432
  Imitation 445
Pareiasaur 81
Parenchyma
  Dicotyledon leaf 126
  Dryland plants 156-157
  Fern rachis 121
  Golden barrel cactus 156
  Horsetail stem 120
  Monocotyledon leaf 126
  Pine stem 125
  Roots 132
  Stems 134-135
  Water lily leaf 159
Parent plant 154
Parietal bone
  Bony fish 181
  Chimpanzee 202
  Human 220-221
Parietal fenestra 102
Parietal lobe 236-237
Parieto-occipital sulcus
  236-237
Parietosquamosal frill
  102-103
Pariipteris 66
Paroccipital process
  Iguanodon 96
  Plateosaurus 88
Parrel
  Dhow 376
  Longboat 380
  Sailing warship 377
  Viking karv 375
Parrel beads 384
Parrel tackle 376
Parthenon 461
Partial solar eclipse 32
Partial veil 115
Particle attraction 307
Particle properties 318
Passiflora caerulea 130
Passing brace 473
Passion flower 130
Pastels **440-441**
Pastern 198-199, 554
Pasteur 41
Patagonia 264
Patella
  Domestic cat 195
  Elephant 201
  Hare 197
  Horse 199
  Human 219
  Platypus 206
  Rhesus monkey 202
  Scorpion 170
  Spider 171
Patellar surface 225
Patera
  Neoclassical building
    480

Renaissance building
  476
Paved floor 492
Pavilion 489, 495
Paving slab 499
Pavlova 37
Pavlovia 278
Pavo 20
Pavonis Mons 43
Paw 195
Pawl 380
Pawl slot 387
Paxton, J. 492-493
Pazzi Chapel 475
Pea
  Dry fruit 150
  Danforth anchor 386
Peach 131, 148
Peacock 20
Peak halyard 380
Peat 280
Peccaries 198
Pecopteris 66
Pectineus muscle 225-
  226
Pectoral fin
  Bony fish 180-181
  Lamprey 178
Pectoral fin ray 181
Pectoralis major muscle
  226
Pedal board 514
Pedal cluster 340
Pedal-damper bar
  mechanism 516
Pedal disc 167
Pedal-driven bicycle 358
Pedal gland 177
Pedalia 372
Pedals
  Bass drum 518
  Bicycle 320, 358-359
  Eddy Merckx racing
    bicycle 360
  Harp 511
  Hi-hat cymbal 518
  Piano 514
  Rossin Italian time-trial
    bicycle 361
Pedal stop 514
Pedestal
  Ancient Roman building
    462
  Baroque church 480-481
  Dome 484, 486-487
  French temple 485
  Harp 511
  Neoclassical building
    479
  Renaissance building
    476
Pedice 168
Pedicel
  Brassavola nodosa 162
  Clematis 131
  Dicotyledon flower 127
  Dry fruit 150-151
  Fertilization 146-147
  Florists' chrysanthemum
    129
  Flowers 140-141, 143
  Fruit development 146-
    147
  Oxalis sp. 157
  Pitcher plant 113
  Rose 131
  Rowan 131
  Russian vine 131
  Succulent fruit 148-149
  Sycamore 131
  Vegetative reproduction
    154
  Water lily 159
Pedicle of vertebra 223
Pedicle valve 278

Pediment
  Ancient Greek building
    460
  Ancient Roman building
    462-463
  Baroque church 480-481
  Neo-Baroque building
    493
  Neoclassical building
    478
  Renaissance building
    476
Pedipalp 170-171
Peduncle 140, 142-143
  Aechmea miniata 162
  Brassavola nodosa 162
  Everlasting pea 129
  Florists' chrysanthemum
    129
  Indehiscent fruit 150
  Peach 131
  Peruvian lily 129
  Rowan 131
  Russian vine 131
  Succulent fruit 148-149
  Toadflax 129
  Vegetative reproduction
    154
  Wind-pollinated plant
    144
Peephole 412, 414
Pegasus 19, 20
Pegasus Quasar
  microlight 426-427
Pegasus XL SE microlight
  427
Peg-box 510-511
Pegmatite 26
Peg of vertebra 222
Pelagic clay 299
Pelecypoda 176
Peloneustes philarcus 71
Pelota 540
Pelvetia canaliculata 116
Pelvic fin
  Bony fish 180-181
  Dogfish 179
Pelvis
  Bird 189
  Bony fish 181
  Dinosaur 81
  Domestic cat 195
  Elephant 201
  Hare 197
  Horse 199
  Human 256, 258, 259
  Kangaroo 206
  Lizard 184
  Platypus 206
  Rhesus monkey 202
  Seal 204
  Turtle 187
Penalty area 524
Penalty box 524
Penalty kick 530
Penalty spot 529, 540
Pencils 430
Pencil sharpener 430
Pencil slate sea urchin 175
Pendentive 479, 484, 488
Pendulum 570
Penguins 188
Penis
  Barnacle 173
  Dolphin 205
  Human 211, 259
  Snail 177
Pennant number 397
Pennsylvanian period 56
Penny washer 383
Pens 430
Penstock 514
Pentaprism 589
Pentaradiate symmetry
  174

Acknowledgments

Dorling Kindersley would like to thank (in order of sections):

The Universe
(consultant editors – Sue Becklake, Gevorkyan Tatyana Alekseyevna):
John Becklake; the Memorial Museum of Cosmonautics, Moscow; The Cosmos Pavilion, Moscow; The United States Space and Rocket Centre, Alabama; Broadhurst, Clarkson and Fuller Ltd; Susannah Massey

Prehistoric Earth
(consultant editors – William Lindsay, Martyn Bramwell, Dr Ralph E. Molnar, David Lambert):
Dr Monty Reid, Andrew Neuman, and the staff of the Royal Tyrrell Museum of Palaeontology, Drumheller, Alberta; Dr Angela Milner and the staff of the Department of Palaeontology, the Natural History Museum, London; Professor W. Ziegler and the staff, in particular Michael Loderstaedt, of the Naturmuseum Senckenburg, Frankfurt; Dr Alexander Liebau, Axel Hunghrebüller, Reiner Schoch, and the staff of the Institut und Museum für Geologie und Paläontologie der Universität, Tübingen; Rupert Wild of the Institut für Paläontologie, Staatliches Museum für Naturkunde, Stuttgart; Dr Scheiber of the Stadtmuseum, Nördlingen; Professor Dr Dietrich Herm of Staatssammlung für Paläontologie und Historische Geologie, München; Dr Michael Keith-Lucas of the Department of Botany, University of Reading; Richard Walker; American Museum of Natural History, New York

Plants
(consultant editor – Richard Walker):
Diana Miller; Lawrie Springate; Karen Sidwell; Chris Thody; Michelle End; Susan Barnes and Chris Jones of the EMU Unit of the Natural History Museum, London; Jenny Evans of Kew Gardens, London; Kate Biggs of the Royal Horticultural Society Gardens, Wisley, Surrey; Spike Walker of Microworld Services; Neil Fletcher; John Bryant of Bedgebury Pinetum, Kent; Dean Franklin

Animals
(consultant editor – Richard Walker):
David Manning's Animal Ark; Intellectual Animals; Howletts Zoo, Canterbury; John Dunlop; Alexander O'Donnell; Sue Evans of the Royal Veterinary College, London; Dr Geoff Potts and Fred Frettsome of the Marine Biological Association of the United Kingdom, Plymouth; Jeremy Adams of the Booth Museum of Natural History, Brighton; Derek Telling of the Department of Anatomy, University of Bristol; the Natural History Museum, London; Andy Highfield of the Tortoise Trust; Brian Harris of the Aquarium, London Zoo; the Invertebrate Department, London Zoo; Dr Harold McClure of the Yerkes Regional Primate Research Center, Emory University, Atlanta, Georgia; Nielson Lausen of the Harvard Medical School, New England Regional Primates Research Centre, Southborough, Massachusetts; Dr Paul Hopwood of the Department of Veterinary Anatomy, University of Sydney; Dean Franklin

The Human Body
(consultant editors – Dr Frances Williams, Dr Fiona Payne, Richard Cummins FRCS):
Derek Edwards and Dr Martin Collins, British School of Osteopathy; Dr M.C.E. Hutchinson of the Department of Anatomy, United Medical and Dental Schools of Guy's and St Thomas' Hospitals, London. Models – Barry O'Rorke (Bodyline Agency) and Pauline Swaine (MOT Model Agency)

Geology, Geography, and Meteorology
(consultant editor – Martyn Bramwell):
Dr John Nudds of the Manchester Museum, Manchester; Dr Alan Wooley and Dr Andrew Clark of the Natural History Museum, London; Graham Bartlett of the National Meteorological Library and Archive, Bracknell; Tony Drake of BP Exploration, Uxbridge; Jane Davies of the Royal Society of Chemistry, Cambridge; Dr Tony Waltham of Nottingham Trent University, Nottingham; staff of the Smithsonian Institute, Washington; staff of the United States Geological Survey, Washington; staff of the National Geographic Society, Washington; staff of Edward Lawrence Associates (Export Ltd), Midhurst; John Farndon; David Lambert

Rail and Road
Rail **(consultant editor – John Coiley)**
Michael Ashworth of the London Transport Museum

Road **(consultant editors – David Burgess-Wise, Hugo Wilson)**
The National Motor Museum, Beaulieu; Alf Newell of Renault UK Ltd; David Suter of Cheltenham Cutaway Exhibits Ltd; Francesca Riccini of the Science Museum, London. Signore Amadelli of the Museo dell' Automobile Carlo Biscaretti di Ruffia; Paul Bolton of the Mazda MCL Group; Duncan Bradford of Reg Mills Wire Wheels; John and Leslie Brewster of Autocavan; David Burgess-Wise; Trevor Cass of Garrett Turbo Service; John Corbett of The Patrick Collection; Gary Crumpler of Williams Grand Prix Engineering Ltd; Mollie Easterbrooke and Duncan Gough of Overland Ltd; Arthur Fairley of the Vauxhall Motor Company; Paul Foulkes-Halbard of Filching Manor Motor Museum; Frank Gilbert of I. Wilkinson and Son Ltd; Paolo Gratton of Gratton Museum; Colvin Gunn of Gunn and Son; Judy Hogg of Ecurie Bertelli; Milton Holman of Dream Cars; Ian Matthews of IMAT Electronics; Eric Neal of Jaguar Cars Ltd; Paul Niblett, Keith Davidson, Mark Reumel, and David Woolf of Michelin Tyre plc; Doug Nye; Kevin O'Keefe of O'Keefe Cars; Roger Smith; Jim Stirling of Ironbridge Gorge Museum, Staffordshire; Jon Taylor; Doug Thompson; Martyn Watkins of Ford Motor Company Ltd; John Cattermole, Customer Services Manager at London Northern Buses; F. W. Evans Cycles Ltd; Trek UK Ltd (Bicycle); Sam Grimmer

Physics and Chemistry
(consultant editor – Jack Challoner)

Sea and Air
Sea **(consultant editors – Geoff Hales and Harvey B. Loomis):**
David Spence, Gillian Hutchinson, David Topliss, Simon Stephens, Robert Baldwin, Jonathan Betts, all of the National Maritime Museum, London; Ian Friel; Simon Turnage of Captain O.M. Watts of London Ltd; Davey and Company Ltd, Great Dunmow; Avon Inflatables Ltd, Llanelli; Musto Ltd, Benfleet; Peter Martin of Spencer Rigging Ltd, Southampton; Peter Rowson of Ratseys Sailmakers, Southampton; Swiftech Ltd, Wallingford; Colin Scattergood of the Barrow Boat Company Ltd, Colchester; Professor J.S. Morrison of the Trireme Trust, Cambridge; The Cutty Sark Maritime Trust; Adrian Daniels of Kelvin Hughes Marine Instruments, London; Arthur Credland of Hull City Council Museums and Art Galleries; The Hull Maritime Society; Gerald Clark; Peter Fitzgerald of the Science Museum, London; Alec Michael of HMB Subwork Ltd, Great Yarmouth, and Ray Ward of the OSEL Group, Great Yarmouth; Richard Bird of UWI, Weybridge; Walker Marine Instruments, Birmingham; The International Sailing Craft Association; The Exeter Maritime Museum; Jane Wilson of the Trinity Lighthouse Company, London; The Imperial War Museum Collections; Thorn Security Ltd; Michael Bach

Air **(consultant editor – Bill Gunston):**
Aeromega Helicopters, Stapleford; Aero Shopping, London; Avionics Mobile Services Ltd, Watford; Roy Barber and John Chapman of the RAF Museum, Hendon; Mitch Barnes Aviation, London; Mike Beach; British Caledonian Flight Training Ltd; Fred Coates of Helitech (Luton) Ltd; Michael Cuttell and CSE Aviation Ltd, Oxford; Dowty Aerospace Landing Gear, Gloucester; Guy Hartcup of the Airship Association; Anthony Hooley, Chris Walsh, and David Cord of British Aerospace Regional Aircraft Ltd; Ken Huntley of Mid-West Aero Engines Ltd; Imperial War Museum, Duxford; The London Gliding Club, Dunstable; Musée des Ballons, Calvados; Noel Penny Turbines Ltd; Andy Pavey of Aviation Scotland Ltd; Tony Pavey of Thermal Aircraft Developments, London; the Commanding Officer and personnel of RAF St Athan; the Commanding Officer and personnel of RAF Wittering; The Science Museum, London; Ross Sharp of the Science Museum, Wroughton; The Shuttleworth Collection; Skysport Engineering; Mike Smith; Solar Wings Ltd, Marlborough; Julian Temple of Brooklands Museum Trust Ltd; Kelvin Wilson of Flying Start

Architecture
(consultant editor – Alexandra Kennedy):
Stephen Cutler for advice and text; Gavin Morgan of the Museum of London, London; Chris Zeuner of the Weald and Downland Museum, Singleton, Sussex; Alan Hills and James Putnam of the British Museum, London; Dr Simon Penn and Michael Thomas of the Avoncroft Museum of Buildings, Bromsgrove,

Worcestershire; Christina Scull of Sir John Soane's Museum, London; Paul Kennedy and John Williamson of the London Door Company, London; Lou Davis of The Original Box Sash Window Company, Windsor; Goddard and Gibbs Studios Ltd, London, for access to stained glass windows; The Royal Courts of Justice, Strand, London; Charles Brooking and Peter Dalton for access to the doors and windows in the Charles Brooking Collection, University of Greenwich, Dartford, Kent; Clare O'Brien of the Shakespeare Globe Trust, Shakespeare's Globe Museum, Bear Gardens, Southwark, London; Ken Teague of the Horniman Museum, London; Canon Haliburton, Mike Payton, Ken Stones, and Anthony Webb of St Paul's Cathedral, London; Roy Spring of Salisbury Cathedral; Reverend Gillean Craig of the Church of St George in the East, London; the Science Museum, London; Dr Neil Bingham; Lin Kennedy of Historic Royal Palaces; Katy Harris of Sir Norman Foster and Partners; Production Design, Thames Television plc, London, for supplying models; Dominique Reynier of Le Centre Georges Pompidou, Paris; Denis Roche of Le Musée National des Monuments Français, Paris; Franck Gioria and students of Les Compagnons du Devoir, Paris, for access to construction models; Frank Folliot of Le Musée Carnavalet, Paris; Dr Martina Harms of Hessische Landesmuseums, Darmstadt; Jefferson Chapman of the University of Tennessee, Knoxville, for access to the model of the Hypostyle Hall, Temple of Amon-Re; staff of the Palazzo Strozzi, Florence; staff of the Sydney Opera House, Sydney; staff of the Empire State Building, New York; Nick Jackson; Ann Terrell

The Visual Arts
(consultant editor – Pip Seymour):
Rosemary Simmons; Michael Taylor of Paupers Press, London; Tessa Hunkin and Emma Biggs of Mosaic Workshop, London; John Tiranti, Jonathan Lyons of Alec Tiranti Ltd, London; Chris Hough; Dr Ashok Roy; Satwinder Sehmi of Alphabet Soup, London; Phillip Poole of Cornelissens, London; George Weil and Sons Ltd, London; The National Gallery, London; Chris Webster of the Tate Gallery, London; China Art Cultural Centre, London; London Graphic Centre, London; A.P. Fitzpatrick, London; Flowers Graphics, London; Intaglio Printmaker, London; Falkiner Papers, London; Edgar Udny and Co, London; John Green

Music
(consultant editor – Susan Sturrock):
Boosey and Hawkes Music Publishers Ltd, London, for permission to reproduce extract from The Prodigal Son by Arthur Sullivan; The Bass and Drum Cellar, London; Empire Drums and Percussion, London; Argents (part of World of Music), London; Bill Lewington Ltd, London; Frobenius organ at Kingston Parish Church, Surrey; Yamaha-Kemble Music (UK) Ltd, Tilbrook, Milton Keynes; Yamaha Atelier, London; Akai (UK) Ltd, Hounslow, Middlesex; Casio Electronics Co. Ltd, London; Roland (UK) Ltd, Fleet, Hampshire; Richard Schulman

Sports
The Sports Council Information Centre, London; The British Olympic Games Committee; Brian Crennell of Black's Leisure Group (First Sport); Lillywhites of Piccadilly, London; Mitre Sports International Ltd, Huddersfield; David Bloomfield of the Football Association; Denver Athletics Ltd, Norfolk; Greg Everest and Keith Birley of the British League of Australian Rules Football; Peter McNally of the Gaelic Athletic Association; Rex King of the Rugby Football Union, Twickenham; Neil Tunnicliffe of the Rugby Football League, Leeds; Wayne Patterson of the Basketball Hall of Fame, Springfield, Connecticut; Brian Coleman of the English Basketball Association; All American Imports, Northampton; George Bulman of the English Volleyball Association; Julie Longdon of Mizuno Mallory (UK) Ltd; Juliet Stanford of the All-England Netball Association; Jeff Rowland of the British Handball Association; Cally Melin of Adidas UK Ltd; Patrick Donnely of the Baseball Hall of Fame, Cooperstown, New York; Ian Lepage and Stephen Barlow of the Hockey Association, Milton Keynes; Alison Taylor and Anita Mason of the All England Women's Lacrosse Association, Birmingham; David Shuttleworth of the English Lacrosse Union; Les Barnett and Jock Bentley of the British Athletic Federation Ltd, Birmingham; Mike Gilks of the Badminton Association of England; Gurinder Purewall for advice on archery; Chris McCartney of the US Archery Association; Geoff Doe of the National Smallbore Rifle Association, Bisley, Surrey, for information and reference material on shooting; Fagan Sports Goods Distributors, Surrey; Konrad Bartelski for advice on skiing; The British Ski Federation, Edinburgh; Mike Barnett of Snow and Rock of London; Sally Spurway of Mast-Co. Ltd, Reading; Sarah Morgan for advice on equestrian sports; Steve Brown and the New York Racing Association Inc, New York; Danrho of London; Alan Skipp and James Chambers of the Amateur Fencing Association, London; Carla Richards of the US Fencing Association; Hamilton Bland and John Dryer of the Amateur Swimming Association, Loughborough; Cotswold Camping Ltd, London; Tim Spalton of Glyn Locke (Racing Shells) Ltd, Chalgrove; Terry Friel of the US Rowing Association; House of Hardy; Leeda Fishing Tackle

Everyday Things
City Clocks (Clocks); Christopher Cullen of Babber Electronics; Sony UK Ltd (Mini-television); Black and Decker Ltd (Drills); British Footwear Manufacturing Federation; Grenson Shoes Ltd (Shoes); The Folio Society; R S Bookbinders (Books); Pentax UK Ltd (Camera); F E Murdin of the Decorative Lighting Association; Habitat (Lamp); Chingford Reproductions Ltd (Chair); Dualit Ltd (Toaster); J B Dove; Toro Wheelhorse UK Ltd (Lawnmower); WandH Gidden Ltd (Saddle)

PHOTOGRAPHY:
M. Alexander; Peter Anderson; Charles Brooks; Jane Burton; Peter Chadwick; Simon Clay; John Coiley; Andy Crawford; Geoff Dann; Philip Dowell; John Downs; Mike Dunning; Torla Evans; David Exton; Robert and Anthony Fretwell of Fretwell Photography Ltd.; Philip Gatward; Anna Hodgson; Gary Kevin; J. Heseltine; Cyril Laubscher; John Lepine; Lynton Gardiner (American Museum of Natural History, New York); Steve Gorton; Michelangelo Gratton; Judith Harrington; Peter Hayman; Anna Hodgson; Colin Keates; Gary Kevin; Dave King; Bob Langrish; Brian D.Morgan; Nick Nicholls; Nick Parfitt; Tim Parmenter and Colin Keates (Natural History Museum, London); Tim Ridley; Dave Rudkin; Philippe Sebert; James Stevenson; Clive Streeter; Harry Taylor; Matthew Ward; Jerry Young

PHOTOGRAPHIC ASSISTANCE:
Kevin Zak; Gary Ombler

ILLUSTRATORS:
Julian Baum; Rick Blakeley; Kuo Kang Chen; Karen Cochrane; Simone End; Ian Fleming; Roy Flooks; Mark Franklin; David Gardner; Will Giles; Mick Gillah; David Hopkins; Selwyn Hutchinson; Mei Lim; Linden Artists; Nick Loates; Chris Lyon; Kathleen McDougall; Coral Mula; Sandra Pond; Dave Pugh; Colin Rose; Graham Rosewarne; John Temperton; John Woodcock; Chris Woolmer

MODEL ,AKERS:
Roby Braun; David Donkin; Morrison Frederick; Gordon Models; John Holmes; Graham High and Jeremy Hunt of Centaur Studios; Richard Kemp; Kelvin Thatcher; Paul Wilkinson

ADDITIONAL DESIGN ASSISTANCE:
Stefan Morris; Ulysses Santos; Suchada Smith

ADDITIONAL EDITORIAL ASSISTANCE:
Helen Castle; Colette Connolly; Camela Decaire; Nick Harris; Andrea Horth; Stewart McEwen; Damien Moore; Melanie Tham

INDEX: Kay Wright

Picture credits:

Action Plus 530tc; Anglo Australian Telescope Board 11cl, 11cra, 11cbl, 12tr, 12bc, 13tl, 13bl, 14tl, 16b, 17tc, 17bl, 22tl/D.Malin 16tl, 26tr, 27tl; Austin Brown and the Aviation Picture Library 426tl; Baptistery, Florence/Alison Harris 453r; Biophoto Associates 217ca, 217cra, 228cbc, 228cbc 230tr; Paul Brierley 311bra; British Aerospace/Anthony Hooley 412tl, 415tl; British Aerospace (Commercial Aircraft) Ltd 416tl; By prmission of the British Library 432tl, 445bl; British Museum 459tl, 459tr, 460tr, 460tc, 460tb, 489b; BP Exploration 299; Duncan Brown 25tl; Frank Lloyd Wright, American, 1867-1959, Model of Midway Gardens, 1914, executed by Richard Tickner, mixed media, 1987, 41.9 x 81.3 x 76.2, 1989.48. view 1. Photography courtesy of the Art Intitute of Chicago 495t; J.A. Coiley 331cr; Bruce Coleman Ltd/Andy Price 272tl; Courtesy of the Board of Trustees of the Victoria and Albert Museum, London 454-455b; European Passenger Services 329tl; ESA /PLV 11bl; French Railways 329c; Geoscience Features 311cla; Robert Harding Picture Library 62tl; Michael Holford /British Museum 372bl, Michael Holford 374tr; Hutchison Picture Library 60cl; The Image Bank/Edward Bower 306tr; Jet Propulsion Laboratory 11cbr; 30bc; 31bc; 31bcr; 38tl; 42crb; 44cb; 44cbr; 44bc; 44br; 46tl; 46cr; 46cb; 46bc; 46br; 50tl; 50cra; 50cl; 50c; 50cr; 50br; KeyMed Ltd 248bl, 249bl, 249bcl; Department of Prints and Drawings, Uffizi, Florence/Philip Gatward 431tc/Uffizi, Florence/Philip Gatward 433tl; Dr D.N. Landon (Institute of Neurology) 228bl,br; Life Science Images/Ron Boardman 244bl, 244br; The Lund Observatory 15bc; Brian Morrison 329tl, 329tr; © The Henry Moore Foundation 455tr; Musée d'Orsay, Paris/Philippe Sebert 437tc, 441tc;

Musée du Louvre, Paris/Philippe Sebert 453tl, 453l, 453br; NASA/AUI 13tr; NASA/JPL 11 cbr, 11br, 30tl, 30bl, 30br, 30bc, 31bc, 31bcr, 31bl, 34cr, 38tl, 40tl, 40cr, 42cr, 44tl, 44cb, 44cbr, 44bc, 44br, 44cr, 46crb, 46tl, 46cr, 46cb, 46bc, 46br, 48tl, 48cra, 48bca, 48bc, 48br, 50tl, 50bc, 50bc, 50cbr, 50br, 50cr, 52cr; National Maritime Museum 373br, 392-393b; National Medical Slide Bank 217cr; Nature Photographers/Paul Sterry 286tl; Newage International 317bl; Oxford Scientific Films/Breck P. Kent 166tl; Planet Earth 274tr; Quadrant 326tr; Margaret Robinson 332tl; Giotto The Expulsion of the Merchants from the Temple Scala 435tc, 435bl, 435br; Science Photo Library 10bl, 13tr, 28tr, 214bcr, 214bl, 236tr/Michael Abbey 225tc/Agema Infrared Systems 318tl/AGFA 220tl/Biophoto Associates: 217crb/Dr Jeremy Burgess/Science Photo Library 132tr; Dr Jeremy Burgess 255bcl/CNRI 214tl, 214cl, 214c, 214cr, 214bl, 214clb, 214crb, 214blc, 214br, 217cb, 235bcr, 238tl, 249bcr, 253tr, 253cra, 256tl; Science Photo library /Earth Satellite Corporation 288cl, 293br/Dr Brian Eyden 228cbr/Professor C. Ferlaud 245bl/Vaughan Fleming 311tl/Simon Fraser/U.S. Dept.of Energy 214bcl, 266tl/Eric Grave 217br/Hale Observatories 52br/Max Planck Institute for Radio Astronomy 15tl/Jan Hinsch 225tc/Jodrell Bank 11 tr, 13c / Manfred Kage 217c, 235br, 237br/Dr William C. Keel 13br/Keith Kent 316tl/Russ Lappa 310bra/Astrid & Hans-Freider Michler 217tr/Dennis Milon 52bl/NASA 11cla, 12tl, 15tr, 30c, 31br, 32tl, 35tl, 36tl, 36cl, 36cr, 36bc, 42br, 42tr, 44tl 52tl, 291tr, 300tl/National Optical Astro Observatory 52tr/NIBSC 253crb/Novosti Press Agency 42bc/Omikron 244bc/David Parker 63bl, 304-305, 308br/Philippe Plailly 308tl, Roussel-UCLAF/CNRI 217tc/Rev Ronald Royer 52cr/Royal Observatory, Edinburgh/D Malin

11tl, 11cr,12c, 16cl, 16cr, 17br/David Scharf 235bl/Dr Kaus Schiller 248bl, 248bcr, 248br/Secchi-Lecaque/Roussel-UCLAF/CNRI 253br/H. Sochurek 214cb/Stammers/Thompson 230tl/Sheila Terry 234tl/US Department of Energy 310bc/U.S Geological Survey/Science Photo Library 8-9, 30bcr, 42tl, 42bl/Tom Van Sant/Geosphere Project, Santa Monica/Science Photo Library 273tr, 281tr, 296tr, 297tl/Dr Christopher B. Williams/(Saint Marks Hospital)249br; Oxford Scientific Films/Animals Animals/Breck P. Kent 167tl; Pratt & Whitney Canada 418-419b, 419t; Science Museum 306bl,306bcl. 306 bcr, 324t, 326-327b, 330tr, 331ct, 331 cb; Sporting Pictures 524tl, 544cr; Tony Stone Worldwide 280tl; David Bomberg St Pauls and River 1945/Dinora Davies-Rees/Tate Gallery 431bc; David Hockney A Bigger Splash 1967/ © David Hockney/Tate Gallery 443tc; J.M.W. Turner The Burning of the Houses of Parliament Tate Gallery 439tc; Vision 26tr, 27c; Jerry Young 306tl; Dr Robert Youngson 241cr; Zefa 217bc/Janicek 276tl/H. Sochurek 210tl, 250tl, 254tl,/G. Steenmans 292tl

Jacket:
Indianapolis Motor Speedway Foundation front cover bc; NASA background to 2001 on spine, front cover, front inside flap

(t=top, b=bottom, a=above, l-left, r=right, c=centre)

Every effort has been made to trace the copyright holders. Dorling Kindersley apologises for any unintentional omissions and would be pleased, in any such cases, to add an acknowledgment in future editions.

Some pages in this book previously appeared in the *Visual Dictionary* series published by Dorling Kindersley. Contributors to this series include:

Project Art Editors:
Duncan Brown, Ross George, Nicola Liddiard, Andrew Nash, Clare Shedden, Bryn Walls

Designers:
Lesley Betts, Paul Calver, Simone End, Ellen Woodward

Additional design assistance:
Sandra Archer, Christina Betts, Alexandra Brown, Nick Jackson, Susan Knight

Project Editors:
Fiona Courtney-Thompson, Paul Docherty, Tim Fraser, Stephanie Jackson, Mary Lindsay

Editorial Assistant:
Emily Hill

Additional editorial assistance:
Susan Bosanko, Edward Bunting, Candace Burch, Deirdre Clark, Jeanette Cossar, Danièle Guitton, Jacqui Hand, David Harding, Nicholas Jackson, Edwina Johnson, David Lambert, Gail Lawther, David Learmount, Paul Jackson, Christine Murdock, Bob Ogden, Cathy Rubinstein, Louise Tucker, Dr Robert Youngson

Picture Researchers:
Vere Dodds, Danièle Guitton, Anna Lord, Catherine O'Rourke, Christine Rista, Sandra Schneider, Vanessa Smith, Clive Webster

Series Editor:
Martyn Page

Series Art Editor:
Paul Wilkinson

Managing Art Editors
Philip Gilderdale, Steve Knowlden

Art Director
Chez Picthall

Managing Editor
Ruth Midgley

Production:
Jayne Simpson